STAGE BY STAGE

THE BIRTH OF THEATRE

By the same author

NOVELS

The Volcano God

The Zoltans: A Trilogy

The Dark Shore

The Evening Heron

Dreams of Youth

Easter Island

Searching

SHORT STORIES

The Devious Ways

The Beholder

The Snow

Three Exotic Tales

A Man of Taste

The Young Greek and the Creole

The Spymaster

The Young Artists

FANTASY

The Merry Communist

PLAYS

Prince Hamlet

Mario's Well

Black Velvet

Simon Simon

Three Off-Broadway Plays

Three Poetic Plays

CRITICISM

Myths of Creation

The Art of Reading the Novel

Preface to Otto Rank's *The Myth of the Birth of the Hero and Other Essays*

Preface to Kimi Gengo's *To One Who Mourns at the Death of the Emperor*

Some Notes on Tragedy

Preface to Joseph Conrad's *Lord Jim*

POETRY

Private Speech

Philip Freund

STAGE BY STAGE

THE BIRTH OF THEATRE

PETER OWEN
London and Chester Springs

PETER OWEN PUBLISHERS
73 Kenway Road, London SW5 0RE

Peter Owen books are distributed in the USA by
Dufour Editions Inc., Chester Springs, PA 19425-0007

First published in Great Britain 2003 by
Peter Owen Publishers

ISBN 0 7206 1170 9

A catalogue record for this book is available from the British Library

Printed and bound in Croatia by
Zrinski SA

for William Hobgood
A truly loyal friend

CONTENTS

ILLUSTRATIONS

Between pages 256 and 257

Roman mask, with staring eyes and gaping mouth, from the later Hellenistic and Roman period, first to second century AD (© British Museum, London)

Hellenistic mask of a young woman from New Comedy, first century BC to first century AD (© British Museum, London)

Terracotta figure from Myrina, Lemnos, showing a *pornoboskos* or pimp. He is a New Comedy character with a distinctive corkscrew beard and elaborate headgear, second century BC (© British Museum, London)

An Etruscan figure from Canino, Italy, showing an actor wearing the mask of a flatterer, second century BC (© British Museum, London)

Small sculpture showing a miscreant slave on an altar, one of the stock situations of New Comedy, first to second century BC (© British Museum, London)

Two Greek statuettes from Myrina showing two strolling actors with comedy masks, first century BC (Musée du Louvre, Paris, © AKG)

Terracotta wine *krater* from Apulia, southern Italy, depicting a scene from a phylax play, *c.* 350 BC. (© British Museum, London)

Terracotta wine *krater* depicting a parody of the story of Cheiron and the Centaur, 380 BC (© British Museum, London)

Roman mosaic from Pompeii showing seven actors behind the stage. It is thought to represent a satyr chorus rehearsing; first century AD (Museum of Archaeology, Naples, © AKG)

Roman wall painting from Pompeii depicting a theatre scene, first century AD (Naples, Museum of Archaeology, © AKG)

Roman mosaic from the Villa of Cicero at Pompeii showing street musicians, first century AD (Museum of Archaeology, Naples, © AKG

Roman wall painting from Herculaneum of a theatre scene; copy from the first century AD of a Greek original from the fourth century BC (Museum of Archaeology, Naples, © AKG)

Roman mosaic showing a writer of tragedy and an actor of comedy, third century AD (Archaeological Museum, Sousse, Tunisia, © AKG)

Aeschylus, 525–456 BC (Museum of the Capitol, Rome, © C.M. Dixon)

Sophocles, 496–406 BC (Lateran Museum, Rome)

Euripides, 484–407 BC (Istanbul Archaeological Museum, © AKG)

Aristophanes, *c.* 448–380 BC (Offices Museum, Naples)

Between pages 512 and 513

Theatre of Nations Festival, Seoul-Kyonggi, Korea, 1997 (© Ellen Stewart Private Collection, La MaMa Theater Archive)

Katharine Hepburn as Hecuba and Irene Papas as Helen in a film version of *The Trojan Women* directed by Michael Cacoyannis, 1972 (© Michael Cacoyannis)

Two actors at a woman's window from an unidentified play depicted on a wine *krater*, southern Italy, 350–340 BC (© British Museum, London)

Buster Keaton and Zero Mostel in the film *A Funny Thing Happened on the Way to the Forum*, 1966

Greek vase depicting a chorus dance with Hephaestus and his blacksmith's hammer, Dionysus and the Muse of Comedy with *thyrsi* and Marsyas with double pipe (undated) (Musée du Louvre, Paris)

Choral dance from archaic times on a very early Attic vase

The chorus of Maenads from Sir Peter Hall's production of *The Bacchae* at Epidaurus, 2002 (photo Sir Peter Hall)

The Archarians by Aristophanes presented at Epidaurus, directed by K. Arvanitakis and designed by George Souglides, 2000 (photo George Souglides)

The chorus from *The Greeks*, directed by John Barton for the Royal Shakespeare Company, 1980 (© Reg Wilson Collection, Shakespeare Centre, Stratford)

Sir Laurence Olivier among the chorus in the 1945 London production of *Oedipus Rex* (© John Vickers)

The chorus from *The Trojan Women* directed by Andrei Serban and originally presented at La MaMa Theater, New York, 1974 (© Ellen Stewart Private Collection, La MaMa Theater Archive)

The chorus of Old Men from *The Orestia* by Aeschylus, directed by Sir Peter Hall at the National Theatre, London, 1981 (© Zoë Dominic)

The principals and chorus in the *Electra* section from *Fragments of a Greek Trilogy*, directed by Andrei Serban and originally presented at La MaMa Theater, New York, in 1974 (photo Perry Yung, © Ellen Stewart Private Collection, La MaMa Theater Archive)

Euripides' *Alcestis* directed by Robert Wilson and presented by the American Repertory Theater, Boston, 1986 (© Richard Feldman)

Alcestis directed by Robert Wilson, 1986 (© Richard Feldman)

Greek Attic vase painting depicting a scene from Aeschylus' *Persians*: the ghost of Darius appears to Atossa (Vatican Museum, Rome)

Douglas Campbell as Oedipus surrounded by members of the chorus of *Oedipus Rex*. Production directed by Tyrone Guthrie, Stratford, Ontario, 1955 (photo Donald McKague, © Stratford Festival Archives)

PREFACE

Another book on the Classic period. Yes. But I dare to believe that my entry differs in some aspects from all others covering this far-off yet not remote epoch, the seminal one. To begin, my intention is to single out certain enduring, ever-repetitive dramatic themes to which, from generation to generation, playwrights have been compelled to return, engaging in individual explorations, arriving at ever-fresh variations, some slight, some profound. What causes this is that the Classic scripts yield the essential plots and archetypal characters that work best on stage, providing an inexhaustible fund of ideas for tragedies by Aeschylus, Sophocles and Euripides, as well as those by Shakespeare, Racine, Strindberg, Arthur Miller; and also – in another genre – for lively farces and satires by Aristophanes, Menander, Plautus, Terence, and after them Hans Sachs, Lope de Vega, Molière, Grillparzer, Noel Coward. In other words, theatre feeds on itself. The earliest story devices are still effective; they are the "tricks of the trade", necessarily learned during every dramatist's apprenticeship. The characters, as eternal as human nature itself – accompanying the age-old devices – are part of a readily available framework and infrastructure at hand for every serious professional theatre craftsman; a knowledge of them is required. In the kit, so to speak, are his traditional tools. With them, for two millennia, dramatists and players have offered their talents to earn the applause of audiences who attend to share in an outsized experience.

The characters in the best Classic plays are archetypal and immortal because they are taken from life. We recognize them at once. Skip centuries – we still identify them. Hamlets and Don Juans are still among us, on stage and off. Electra is the unhappy, frustrated girl next door. Again and again, playwrights have reincarnated woeful Phaedra, frustrated in marriage, wracked by illegitimate lust, finding a better copy of her husband in his son – or surrogate son. Though in different dress, she reappears behind our footlights as Abbie in Eugene O'Neill's *Desire Under the Elms* and Amy in Sidney Howard's *They Knew What They Wanted.*

Beyond fixing on the recurrent themes, plots, characters, as well as tried-and-true bits of stagecraft, I have tried to place them in their historical context, the *Zeitgeist* of each, the oft-changing societal influences that also formed them, since not all of our persona is shaped by inner drives but also reflects environmental forces that from period to period undergo irresistible alterations – "no man is an island". We are composed in good part by where and when we are, circumstances beyond our control that are never static or durable for long, our world always in daunting flux, our culture in evolution, simultaneously the same and different, advancing and retreating, then advancing once more, only to fall back again.

So many changes mean that revivals of our Classic plays, some written twenty-five hundred years ago, and subsequently delved into and boldly adapted to suit new times, offer perplexing challenges to directors and players in ever later eras. How shall a nineteenth- or twentieth-century company present *Oedipus at Colonus*? What lines or actions need to be replaced or elucidated? Should a playwright conceive another, more topical treatment of the same material? A long train of responsible modern dramatists have taken this risk. Their new versions borrow some facets of the Classic works that exist in perpetuity while adding and taking away other sides of them, to render the story more immediate and relevant. A Medea brooding in London's East End, a Pseudolus capering on Broadway, might call for considerable transformation.

I thought that examining all this would be of genuine interest to theatre-lovers – and especially to thoughtful students and workers in the profession – and have sought in this survey to trace latter-day handlings of the Classic tragedies and farces, how they have been restaged in the intervening centuries, and chiefly in our own period. If my emphasis is on the most recent decades, it is because twenty-five hundred years is too great a span to be condensed in much detail in a single book, and so much more information concerning those productions is accessible to us, and perhaps more comprehensible.

I do not claim to have been the first to perceive the incredible long lives of these Classic characters. The most celebrated revenant, probably, is the *miles glorioso*, the braggart soldier, dating from Etruscan days at least and reintroduced in scores of Renaissance farces, and finally epitomized in the revelling, bumptious person of Falstaff. But the inevitability of encountering these stage figures again and again has not been investigated with as broad a scope as here.

Also, I have not limited my catalogue of revivals and free adaptations of Classic plays to the many that have occurred in London, New York and Continental European capitals. There has been a production of Sophocles' *Antigone* by the Inuit of Alaska, which doubtless called for more than a bit of reinterpretation. And there have been other fresh treatments of the great European playwrights in Asia and Africa.

Further, I have looked to psychologists and philosophers to account for what emotional promptings and subconscious compulsions draw writers and spectators originally and for ever to these repeated dramatic themes and familiar figures.

I would like to explain that this book came about by chance. The editor of my *Myths of Creation* invited me to luncheon and asked me to provide him with another study like it. I replied that I lacked time, because I had just agreed to give some lectures on theatre history at the university where I was teaching. "Excellent," he said, "just convert your notes into a book for us." To me that sounded an easy, congenial task, and I readily assented. It was stipulated that I should deliver a volume of approximately 650 pages, and shortly afterwards I signed a publishing contract.

Starting to work, however, I soon felt a history of that length was too schematic. I wanted to include more playwrights, tell more about their scripts and how they were staged, the pervasive characteristics of their eras: what, in particular, did their audiences demand of them? A history of the world's theatre in 650 pages would be too superficial. My usual feeling had been that a book that is too condensed is more difficult to read and absorb than one that is more leisurely and more roundedly informative. I preferred to expand my imagination by entering into the realms already richly detailed.

Needless to say, the publisher was not pleased with my decision to enlarge my commitment, nor with the long wait that ensued. Eventually, the editor went elsewhere, as his kind habitually does, and I repurchased my contract.

Left on my own, I proceeded at a very deliberate pace. My concept of the book grew larger and larger. I began to use the word "stage" in its broadest sense to embrace not only the authors of farces, comedies and the noblest tragedies, but also composers, librettists and choreographers of operas, operettas, musical comedies, ballet and the mutation called "modern dance". All these are included in what is thought of as "theatre". Nor should such a history omit the names of great actors and singers, mimes, puppeteers and circus performers, along with directors and scene designers, costumers and important theorists and critics, innovative impresarios – Jacques Copeau, Max Reinhardt, Vsevelod Meyerhold, Orson Welles.

The sheer number of stages and actors establishes, indeed, that the dramatic impulse is universally manifested; theatrical activity of one kind or another has been a constant for ages, even in the most barren areas of the world. Man has an inherent need and drive to mirror, imitate and rearrange the thronging reality encircling and pressing in on him; he seeks to explain, probe, heighten, mock, castigate and celebrate human behaviour, while entertaining himself and his fellows by doing so. He has a similar impulse to fantasize, to sing and dance, and incessantly to poeticize language, all to enlarge and embellish his own life. Theatre is also a means by which he has paid homage to the gods; he has tried to ward off malign fate by learning about himself and others, and it is also an effective vehicle for moral preachment, perhaps a teaching by vivid illustration. The drama is a vital aspect of our culture, an outlet for personal and collective deep feelings, some of them unconscious or unformed. It is not as marginal or frivolous as it is sometimes described by those not fully acquainted with it. I believe that justifies the time that I and a steadfast reader might devote to learning more about it.

Granting myself a dispensation from a publisher's deadline, I wrote and wrote, lectured and lectured, enriched my notes. Scouring publishers' lists and library index cards, I collected hundreds of theatre histories, biographies, anthologies and various reference books for support. On my holidays I travelled to over ninety countries: Russia, Bulgaria, Greece – the airy heights of Delphi – Israel, Egypt, Tunisia, Ethiopia, South Africa, together with China, Korea, Japan, Thailand, Cambodia, Ceylon (Sri Lanka), Burma (Myanmar), Chile, Peru, Venezuela, Mexico. Wherever possible, I took in operas, dance recitals – moonlit puppet shows in Bali and dramatized rituals – whatever were the native forms of elevated worship or vulgar entertainment. I made it a habit to read at least one play a day (a good many in translation), so that the total was somewhere in the thousands. Soliciting facts, in New York, Moscow, Cape Town I interviewed producers and playwrights; some in person, some by telephone, some by correspondence – the Hungarian and Polish cultural attachés in Washington and a Florentine archivist were very helpful. My manuscript grew and grew, covering thousands of pages. All this research was enjoyable, fascinating. I was so engrossed in it that I gave no thought to the problem of publication. At the end of thirty years, my task was finished. But this was only a first draft, quite rough. The prose needed correction and polishing. In the thirty years that had unfolded, a torrent of new books filled with facts and critiques relevant to my early chapters had come on the market; I wanted to add or insert specific *aperçus* from them. Contemporary authors had written more plays or had died or won prizes, so there was minor updating to be done concerning them.

I began a second draft, crowded with fresh details, and my manuscript doubled and even tripled in length, becoming quite unwieldy. And I still had heaps of notes to incorporate. All too soon I realized that the calendar had altered for me, too: I no longer had enough time left to accomplish my omnivorous project. Nor could it be a feasible publication; it would be too expensive.

Accordingly, and reluctantly, I must content myself with excerpting from my first and partial second drafts several shorter and separate studies, wholly self-contained, of which *Stage by Stage* is my first offering. I am working on others, with two more under way, the next to treat with the Oriental stage, and after it a volume dealing with Medieval and Renaissance theatres in Western Europe.

A preface is where the author acknowledges his debt to others and offers apologies for his work's inevitable shortcomings.

I boast of having laboured alone, but of course I have had invaluable help, drawing exhaustively on a horde of predecessors. No bibliography at the tail end of this text would repay them adequately. Above all I owe much to distinguished historical surveys by Allardyce Nicholl, Sheldon Cheney, Edward Quinn, John Gassner, Arthur Hobson Quinn, George Freedley, John A. Reeves, Kenneth McGowan, William Melnitz, Vera Mowry Roberts, Barnard Hewitt, Margot Berthold and others, and I have rifled through all the encyclopaedias of the drama – especially those issued by the Oxford University Press, McGraw-Hill, the *Encyclopaedia Brittanica* and other standard sources – *Groves'*, Walter Rigdon's *Who's Who of the American Theatre*, an indispensable compendium of data about stage people; James Vinson's *Contemporary Dramatists*, and similar guides by Myron Matlaw, Toby Cole – her *Playwrights on Playwriting* – Bernard Sobel and John Russell Taylor – his *Penguin Dictionary of the Theatre*. I have availed myself of *The Dance Encyclopedia*, edited by Anatole Chujoy and P. W. Manchester; and Ferdinando Reyna's *A Concise History of Ballet*; along with various trenchant writings by Lincoln Kirstein on that subject, such as his *Blast at Ballet*; and articles by Edwin Denby and the prolific Cyril William Beaumont. Of assistance in tracing the rise of opera have been Alfred Einstein's *A Short History of Music*, Sir Jack Westrup's *An Introduction to Musical History*, Richard Anthony Leonard's felicitous *The Stream of Music*, Henry Edward Krehbiel's *A Book of Operas*; the immense reference volume – of Italian origin – put together by many contributors and published in English as *The Simon & Schuster Book of the Opera*; and collaborative efforts like *Opera, A History* by Christopher Headington, Roy Westbrook and Terry Barfoot; *How Opera Grew*, by Ethel Peyser and Marion Bauer; *The World of Opera*, by Wallace Brockway and Herbert Weinstock;. and, as mentioned before, stacks of biographies of playwrights and composers, actors and directors, and other kinds of performers.

Let me add that I am grateful to James Robert Carson for helping me obtain the illustrations for this book and to James Ryan and Antonia Owen for their editorial assistance. Who but Mr Ryan would have questioned my authority on correct spelling in Medieval French?

Magazines devoted to theatre and opera have been most helpful, and especially newspapers, among them the *New York Times*, *New York Herald-Tribune*, *New York Post*, *New York Daily News*,

Wall Street Journal, New York Observer, The Times of London, the *Daily Telegraph*, the *Guardian*, the *Financial Times*, and weeklies such as *Time, Newsweek, New Yorker, America, New York*, and the niche monthlies *Opera News, Dance, Tulane Drama Review, Cue.* The most utilized is the *New York Times*, not only because it has been delivered to my doorstep every morning but also because it is the most assiduous in covering the American scene and often foreign stages, too; no other daily has a staff of dance critics as large and remarkably knowledgeable, for example, and it has had a succession of drama reviewers who, for the most part, have been perceptive and even eminent. Indeed, two have been honoured during their lifetime by having Broadway theatres named after them. In recent years, however, I have been limited in the range and variety of daily reviews on which I could depend; once numerous, their ranks have been reduced by the gradual consolidation and disappearance of newspapers published in New York and other capital cities. Some have been supplanted by television "critics" whose hurried commentaries tend to be too brief and glancing to have much permanent worth.

Where at all possible, I have used excerpts from reviews, the morning-after reports on a play or opera or ballet that has just opened or been brought back, so that I could impart a sense of immediacy: how was the work received and judged by its first audience? Or by spectators a decade or generation later? That fixes the play or musical work in its true context. I also want my reader to enjoy the illusion of having actually been present, sharing the tumult that greeted Hugo's *Hernani* or Stravinsky's and Nijinsky's *Rite of Spring* or Odets' *Waiting for Lefty*. In the same way, would we not like to know what diverse members of Sophocles' public thought of his offerings, or the visceral reaction of Shakespeare's rowdy hearers, those standing in the pit – not merely the views of courtiers and members of the literati, who have left us scattered comments, but the opinions of the ordinary ticket-buyer and workaday critic? Also exposed here and opened to measure is the quality of writing about past and contemporary playwrights and their works in the twentieth century. (Obviously, much of my research about this is applicable to later chapters than those to be found in *Stage by Stage*.)

For a "world history of theatre" to be all-inclusive and unquestionably authentic it would be best, even mandatory, that its author have fluency in three or four hundred different languages. I had little hope of mastering, let us say, Portuguese, Cantonese, Magyar, Arabic – so I have had to borrow from books by scholars native to each country or well acquainted with its culture, and especially its politics and dramatic literature. To them, time and again, I owe the plot summaries of the plays that fill these and subsequent pages, the stage-works that I have not seen or cannot read for myself. Some of these many thousands of scripts are in print and have been translated into English, but by far the majority have not been; for them I must rely on secondary sources.

Some further explanations: titles of scripts are very difficult to render in another language if they consist of plays on words, or idioms somewhat too elusive, or are topical references no longer meaningful, or allusions simply too local. In such instances I lacked the courage to venture an English equivalent. Similarly, all too often the names of characters have variant spellings in foreign plays depending on who is the translator, and this has been a besetting problem. Whenever this occurs, I beg tolerance.

I do not voice my own judgement of all these dramatists and their works: I lack the arrogance that requires. Who is wise and knowing enough to offer a personal evaluation of 3,000 years of dramatic and musical literature? Or to appraise the ingenuity and interpretive talent of every famed choreographer and dancer? That is also why I have excerpted the opinions of so many contemporary and subsequent critics of their accomplishments. Also, I delight in reading thoughtful reviews that are at odds with one another, exposing the often baffling diversity of taste among people who see the same piece of art.

As a result, much here is paraphrase, which I concede is an oblique form of theft. But it is unavoidable, since an extended use of direct quotation is not permissible; indeed, there are legal limits to how much one may brazenly appropriate from others. Yet an historical survey, by its very nature, must be paraphrastic unless its factual content is reinvented, as it probably should not be. This is especially the problem with a work as lengthy and detailed as mine. I would prefer to borrow straightforwardly and openly, and have done so wherever I deemed it possible. Often I have felt that facts and views have been better expressed by someone else than I could rephrase them and have done him the favour of letting him be heard in his exact words. In addition, my sources are faithfully credited parenthetically in the text, chapter by chapter. But I have eschewed the usual footnotes, so beloved by my fellow academics but which here would consist of a prodigious number and clutter up the page. They would add substantially, even prohibitively, to the expense of printing. Anyhow, I have always found footnotes to be distracting and unsightly, and frequently intimidating to the lay reader, and I am heartened by a comment of Judge Abner Mikva: "If God had intended us to use footnotes, He would have put our eyes in vertically instead of horizontally." A sage decision from the bench!

As I have mentioned earlier, I have not appended a complete bibliography of the many books I have consulted – it would run for many pages and be of scant use. It would also add greatly to the printing cost. *Stage by Stage* is not intended for perusal by other drama historians, of whom there are at most a handful, but for theatre people and the general reader who shares my interest in the always colourful story of the multifaceted performing arts. My fellow academics can easily find the same source-material where I did – in library catalogues.

Though I have been conditioned by my own academic background to research with great care, to verify all facts meticulously with an almost religious zeal, I cannot convince myself that my book is wholly free of errors. The text is studded with dates; determining the correct ones has often caused me much trouble. Frequently, those found in the sources are at odds, and I was not sure which to choose. Again, the date cited for a play might be that of its composition, or of its publication, or of its initial staging, which might have preceded or followed its first appearance in print. I could not always be certain which was which. Sometimes I give two or all three, but in my view the date of staging is the most relevant, as almost invariably a script might not be wholly faithful to the playwright's summary conviction as to how the action and dialogue should go. Having seen it "on its feet", he has changed his mind about many details.

Again, the birth dates of authors are not always readily discovered. A great many are misted by time and lost, far too remote and obscure. A few writers have found it expedient to misrepresent their age. A group of women playwrights, reluctant to reveal their years, have withheld their "vital statistics" from biographical directories. A newspaper obituary might say that an author was "sixty" but not give the year of his birth. If he died in 1960, he might have been born in 1900, but possibly in late 1899 or early 1901, depending on the month. In such instances I might yield to an impulse and make a guess, for the possible error could not be more than a mere few days or weeks. Except for a subscriber to astrology, the mistake would not be of any importance.

Proper names in the plays discussed by the throng of commentators here may have varied spellings; for example: Herakles, Hercules; Elektra, Electra. In quoting, I have respected the usage preferred by each author; some Anglicize, some do not. Granted, the result is a seeming inconsistency, but not one for which I bear responsibility, since I hesitated at violating the variant – for whatever reason – each writer had chosen.

My hope is that the publisher or my literary executor will select a successor (or successors) who can make use of the voluminous added detail I have been collecting and arranging, my huge trove of notes, and who perhaps will contribute a good amount of his own research and insights to round out my overly ambitious project. His similar delving will richly reward him.

In sum, when I ask myself why I spent so many years at this very long and demanding task, the answer comes easily. I have loved theatre all my life, and I have been curious about the magical forms it has taken in all past epochs and elsewhere on distant stages today.

Finally I am eager to acknowledge Robert Heiser's unstinting help in readying this lengthy manuscript for an impatient press.

1

MAGIC: CHANT AND DANCE

Drama originated, in large part, along with man's belief in the spirit. Sigmund Freud conjectures that prehistoric man, gazing into the quiet waters of a pool or eddying brook, saw the face of a stranger staring back at him: it was always the same stranger. When he walked in sunlight or moonlight, an insubstantial figure, a shadow, followed or preceded him. Was it not the same stranger who revealed himself on the surface of the reflecting waters? An insubstantial being was attached to him that he came to consider his "soul", a spirit inhabiting his body, an *alter ego.*

When he dreamed at night, often with frightening clarity there returned the ghostly images of those whom he had once known who were dead: his father, brothers, friends – or, it might be, the foe he had once killed in battle. Each of them, too, had harboured a personal spirit. Obviously the almost invisible self that had dwelt in the dead person was immortal, lived on after his physical disintegration, and even came back to haunt his slayer.

To early man, living – as Carl Jung suggests – in a world in which it was difficult to distinguish between what was real or unreal, tangible or phantasmal, the whole natural realm surrounding him seemed invested with friendly or menacing spirits: he animated the world, peopled it with supernatural forces; he imagined nymphs in the waters, dryads in trees, demons in the hostile, slashing wind and rain, the fearful thunder and lightning that suddenly set fires in the forest and sent tall pines crashing. The evil forces threatened him always: primitive man, with good reason in the dangerous and shadowed, tangled forest, was near-paranoid.

In his borning mind there evolved a unique resource. He became convinced that he could control the menacing forces around him by imitating them: throughout all the earliest religions, as Sir James Frazer demonstrates in his *The Golden Bough*, flows primitive man's reliance on the power of imitative magic. In ritualistic chants and dances, he portrayed those evil beings whose threat he hoped to counteract: sucking in his cheeks and shouting fiercely as though he were the blustering gale, or leaping abruptly upward like the hot-rock-splitting demon who hid in the fiery volcano, or whirling about and whistling like the fierce and frigid spirit of hail and sleet. Before going off to combat against marauders of another tribe, he simulated the battle and "slew" his foe, having persuaded himself that by such dramatic gestures he ensured his victory. He put on the skins of the species of animals he planned to hunt, and fell "dead" when struck by imaginary clubs, stone axes or spears loosed or wielded by his fellow-huntsmen; or he dropped into bough-covered pits as though he were the beast that he had cunningly sought to trap. His chants included onomatopoeic echoes of the dying creature's bleats or cries. Setting out on the chase, he would first enact a pantomime in which he ran and dodged as swiftly as the antelope whose likeness he also scratched – with surprising skill – for magical purposes of control on the walls of his caves. After doing that, he was encouraged that he could successfully overtake his elusive prey.

Frazer and other anthropologists have collected thousands of such instances of imitative magic. If primitive man wished the sun to rise, he built a fire in the murky light before full dawn; or he ceremoniously sprinkled water on the long-parched earth to invoke rain. To heighten the accuracy of his mimicry, he might also wear masks – of light wood, leather or stiffened cloth – designed by the tribal artist; now, more than ever, the hunter or warrior was like the demon of wind, or fires, or storm, or resembled the bounding wild creature who would be pursued and slain. Many of these masks were grotesque, terrifying, and some display a true aesthetic instinct that has elicited the envy and admiration of modern artists like Picasso and Modigliani. And the masks, whether realistic or shrewdly conventional, might add mystery and solemnity to the ceremony; they might be elaborately adorned with shells, feathers, beads, precious stones and ores, so that they were veritable works of painted or stained sculpture. Sound effects and other "properties" were added.

Hunting and impending warfare were only two events celebrated in this fashion; there were other major rituals that became highly anticipated social occasions, prompted by the changing seasons and the observance of significant natural phenomena. These ceremonies, ever more sacred, were presided over by the shaman – medicine man, voodoo man or witch-doctor – of the tribe or clan. Frequently, the shaman was the chief performer as well as the producer, director and choreographer. Eventually every step and gesture in the enactment was ordained, hedged by taboos, the "staging" jealously supervised by these playwrights-priests-stage-managers, who alone knew how to conduct it and whose self-interest was happily served thereby.

Perhaps early man's strange faith in the efficacy of imitative magic sprang from his personal success in advancing himself by copying his elders and others. Aristotle suggests this, when he writes: "It is clear that the origin of [dramatic] poetry was due to two causes, each of them part of human nature. Imitation is natural to man from childhood, one of his advantages over the lower animals being this, that he is the most imitative creature in the world, and learns at first by imitation. And it is also natural for all to delight in works of imitation." Imitation, then, would seem to partake of magic by being a source of both pleasure and successful action.

Further enhancement of enjoyment in imitation arises, as Friedrich Schiller propounds, from man's inherent love of play. Indeed, it is significant that a drama is called a "play", and those participating in it "players". A considerable element of childish love of make-believe has always been present in man's theatre from its beginning in "staged" events around the campfire to their performance today in the glow of klieg lights and footlights.

In his dances, too, early man gave expression to his innate sense of rhythm, stronger in him then but a compulsion that may still overwhelm his so-called civilized descendants today, especially the young. To the beat of crude drums and shaking gourds, growing faster and louder to the accompaniment of his shrill cries, he freed his wild, pent-up energy and raw emotion. It was inevitable that he did so by rhythmic movement, for he still had no other adequate means of voicing his inchoate feelings, superstitious fears, vague, irrational hopes. He also acknowledged, by his foot-stamping and leaps and muscular contortions, his awareness of the rhythm that subliminally pulses through all the natural scene from darkness to daily light on to falling darkness and moonrise again. He was aware, too, of rhythm in the round of the seasons from winter to spring, and from burgeoning summer and multicoloured autumn to cruel, bleak winter again; as well as from eager young life to the diminishment of vitality leading to death; next, overlapping the death of the aged, to squalling new life again. So the world's rhythm was in him, too, as much as in the orderly succession of far-off planets and drifting constellations overhead, the swaying trees, the rippling waves of sunlit grass on the veldt, and pounding surf on the glaring beach.

Nor were all ritualistic occasions devoted merely to imitative magic. Some had a proprietary impulse: their purpose was not to command the forces of nature, but to appease them. A sense of sin and guilt in the tribal community was exorcized by abasement and sacrificial offerings, which might include the killing of human or semi-divine (kingly) scapegoats. Coupled with this was another belief, totemism, aboriginal man's well-founded feeling that he was closely akin to the animal world: hundreds of tribes – the Inuit in the far north, clans in jungles along the Orinoco and on hot, breezy isles in the South Seas, and in the tangled rainforests of Central Africa – had creation myths that attributed their origin to sodomy between the first man or woman (or the lone survivor of a world-catastrophe, a volcanic fire-rain or a vast forest-fire or deluge) and an animal conveniently at hand, a beaver, a wolf, an emu or a snake, or it might even be a mollusc. Others held sacred a beast (or even fish, fruit or nut) that was the tribe's principal source of sustenance. Though it was necessary for survival to kill the totem animal, a symbolic ceremony of contrition and apology was observed at a fixed time each year.

A great deal is known about such pantomimes and dances, for they are performed even today by peoples in many regions of the earth: War Dances of the spectrally tall, thin Watusi in Africa and the ferocious Naga in north-east India, Rain Dances of the Navahos and Zunis in the arid American Southwest, Monkey Dances of the Balinese.

Some rites were a form of history: legends of the tribe were recounted, or the fabulous deeds of culture heroes (archetypal figures, such as the founder of the race, the tribe's "fire-thief", "dragon-slayer" or saviour) retold in chants and danced pantomime; or a warrior or huntsman boastfully recounted, with dramatic embellishments, his own past exploits. Since writing was largely undeveloped, history had to be oral, and accompanied by illustrative gestures for fuller communication, for brute man's vocabulary, too, was still limited.

With time came the gradual "enskyment" of the culture heroes: slowly but steadily they acquired, through repeated tellings of their legendary deeds, attributes that were supernal. They were next supposed to have been supernaturally conceived and to have descended to earth from the high heavens to which they subsequently returned. They were regarded as semi-divine, then divine, as beings to be worshipped.

Later, as early man became less nomadic and at least to a minor degree more sophisticated, his other deities too – the personification of natural forces – grew more anthropomorphic, less fearsome and more fanciful: for the Greeks there were those charming nymphs and slim dryads, and a host of flagrantly amorous gods on Olympus, whose scandalous doings provided material for bright fables. But totemistic traces remained in the Greek pantheon, and even more so in the Egyptian. Many of the Greek deities were half-divine, half-animal: Pan was part goat, Dionysus could assume the shape of a boar, the lecherous Zeus became a bull. At will the frisky and all-too-human and sometimes bloodthirsty Greek gods metamorphosed back into animal forms. For Egyptians, Osiris is a bull, Isis a hawk, Sekhmet a cat or lioness. This motif will continue in the drama, diminishing yet never entirely vanishing, a magical element that lingers long.

Further, primitive man celebrated rites of passage or initiation, when the young males reached puberty and were tested by circumcision and other physical and psychological ordeals to determine their courage and nervous strength. Are they ready to assume the responsibilities of manhood, morally worthy to share the clan's religious secrets?

As the huntsmen and wandering tribes came out of the thick woods and turned ever more to tilling the earth and building hut-villages, fertility rites assumed primacy for them: the procession of seasonal changes, the solstices, were marked with beseeching awe; festivals honouring the gods of vegetation and reproduction became the most important of all occasions. Especially spring, the hopeful time of sowing, of planting seed, was the chief ceremony, with similar harvest rites almost as significant. In the myths of a great number of primitive peoples in the four quarters of the globe a tale of almost identical pattern or motif is related: it is of a fertility god who is mutilated and dies, only to be miraculously reborn through the intervention of his father or mother, who are top divinities in the heavenly hierarchy. Such myths are found everywhere, in Japan, China, India, Samoa, Mexico, Africa. Anthropologists interpret them as allegories of the rhythmic seasonal changes that govern the natural world and man: the torture and mutilation refer to autumn, when trees are stripped bare of falling leaves and the boughs are broken by equinoctial storms, while all foliage dies; the god's death is an allusion to the white sleep of winter; the resurrection describes spring, the fecund season, when vegetation comes back to make green again the stark earth. But as the myth grows in complexity, the fertility god is also a divine scapegoat for whom the totem animal may be, through metamorphosis, an emblem or token or pragmatic substitute. In many versions his death is self-sacrificial, and the world and mankind are created out of his body parts and blood. Everywhere, then, spring is hailed joyously in his impregnating person – even orgiastically, with phallic pantomimes, songs and dances, though preceded by rites of mourning for the suffering and death of the year-god, whose assured reincarnation is welcomed.

In the western hemisphere the most highly developed cultures – Aztec and Inca – are believed to have staged such festivals with many theatrical elements, and even to have used poetic scripts. Such plays, both serious and comic, were acted at court by elderly and young noblemen; they celebrated notable historical incidents, the biographies of kings or – in the lighter works – domestic and lesser daily events; others had religious content and were closely supervised by priests, who coached the performers.

In the Near East, in the even then crowded lands around the Mediterranean, myths of saviour-and-fertility gods – vegetation gods – were especially popular, and particularly so in cults in Egypt, Persia, Babylonia, Syria, Phrygia and Greece. In Egypt the vegetation god was Osiris; in Persia, Yima (and, later, Gaya Maretan); in Sumeria, Marduk; in Syria and Phoenicia, Adonis (also known by his Semitic title of Lord, or Tammuz); in Phrygia, Attis; and, most important to us, in Greece the vegetation god was Dionysus. Though not the only theme of early drama, it is soon the chief one.

Four thousand years ago in Egypt, as inscribed by I-kher-nefert on a Twelfth Dynasty stele in a German museum, annual religious pageants commemorating the death and rebirth of Osiris were held at Abydos and other places. Osiris, begotten by Earth – Nut or Nuit – and Ksy – Geb or Sibu – was married to his hawk-sister, Isis. His jealous rival was his brother Set – Seth – god of Death. (Egyptian deities undergo many name-changes.) Osiris was the corn-god, the tree-spirit and, ultimately, god of the Underworld, patron of fertility; he is often depicted as having huge genitalia and three phalluses. His birth occurred on 25 December, the winter solstice, the day the sun is born. The envious Set persuaded him to lie in a coffin, then shut the lid and fastened it and hurled the box into the Nile. Though bearing his child Horus, Isis, after a long, difficult search, recovered the corpse, but Set got it away from her and dismembered it, dispersing it in fourteen different pieces. Again, Isis hunted for her lost husband–brother, discovered the scattered parts, reassembled them, and with air stirred by her hawk-wings re-endowed the dead god with breath and life.

In the pageant at Abydos, and, it is assumed, in similar ones at Heliopolis and Busiris, this myth was re-enacted at imposing eighteen-day ceremonies that began with ritual ploughing and sowing. The passion play of the suffering, murder, transfiguration and reappearance of the fertility god was performed by hundreds, perhaps thousands, who constituted the cast, taking assigned roles in the procession of many episodes. Descriptions of these rites are provided by Vera Roberts (*On Stage*), who draws on E. A. Wallis Budge's *Osiris and the Egyptian Resurrection*; Margot Berthold (*A History of World Theatre*), whose bibliography lists several German texts with lengthy titles by E. Brunner-Traut, J. Horovitz, K. Sethe and W. V. Soden; John Gassner (*Masters of the Drama*), who also cites Budge; and Oscar G. Brockett (*History of the Theatre*), who credits James H. Breasted's *The Development of Religion and Theatre in Ancient Egypt* as a source. According to these four, if we compile details offered by each, a feature of the pageant was an elaborate "sacred boat", propelled and guarded by a swarm of priests, attendants and devout followers. Several times the foes of Osiris attacked the boat but were driven off in mock battles so realistically portrayed that, legend has it, some of the actors sank with bloody hurts, even losing their lives. At sacramental moments, human sacrifices occurred. For three days a search was made for the far-flung limbs and members of the god, who was then entombed.

Mourning followed; chants of lament. At the pageant's conclusion all participants marched a mile and a half in files to and from the new Shrine of Osiris, ordered built by King Usertsen III, where at last the radiant image of the risen god was shown to the jubilant multitude. As Gassner tells it: "To promote the magical purpose of the rite even further the Egyptians made figures of the god and buried corn with him, so that the sprouting of the seed which symbolized his resurrection might promote the growth of the crops."

The scale and scope of these pageants, with their scenery and properties such as the sacred boat, argue a degree of supervision and planning that goes far beyond the ritualistic imitative magic of primitive man: this is now a form of theatre, of staged spectacle, though the ties to magic and religion are omnipresent. I-kher-nefert, a high official in the government of Sesostris III, in the Twelfth Dynasty (between 1887 and 1849 BC), is identified as having been appointed by his Pharaoh to take charge of the pageant at Abydos, and he acted a leading role in it. He is thus a "professional", dedicating his talents to theatrical effects, and his account is first-hand, though how to interpret it is not always clear, which has led to scholarly disputes.

A strongly stressed factor here, also implicit in the primitive ceremonies, is that of "conflict", which is to be the basic requirement of drama in all ages, in all places. Whether it is the conflict of man with natural forces, or with his human foes, or even a symbolic duel between divinities as in the passion play of Osiris, the element of combat, struggle, is at the very heart of every plot. Furthermore, there were individualized roles: Osiris, Wepwawet, Ap-uat and others are characterized and impersonated. It is possible that the Pharaoh himself had the part of the cherished Osiris, and most likely that priests were among the other leading actors. The eighteen-day duration of the passion play certainly implies that some kind of story was used. I-kher-nefert relates: "I organized the departure of Wepwawet as he goes to the rescue of his father." Berthold adds: "It seems clear, therefore, that the god Wepwawet, in the form of a jackal, opened the ceremonies. Immediately after the figure of Wepwawet 'there appeared the god Osiris, in full majesty, and after him, his ennead – the nine gods of his entourage. Wepwawet was in front clearing the way for him . . .' In triumph Osiris travels along in his ship, the Neshmet bark, escorted by the participants in the mystery ceremonies. They are his comrades-in-arms to fight against his enemy Seth." Later, I-kher-nefert proudly reports in detail on his share of the action: "I repulsed those who had rebelled against the bark Neshmet and struck down the enemies of Osiris."

Brockett dates the rites to 2500 BC, and they were regularly observed until about 550 BC, hence they continued for a span of 2,000 years, which is still five centuries before anything comparable in

Greece. However, Brockett also quotes several Egyptologists who claim that this spectacular pageant was never truly a "passion play" re-enacting the martyrdom and return of the beloved god, but instead was meant to honour a succession of dead pharaohs, each represented in turn by the beloved god, so that essentially it resembled a "royal funeral". In any event, Abydos was where the head of Osiris was said to be buried, which was why thousands of pilgrims journeyed there each year. It is not certain, either, that all the episodes in the tragic story were enacted there: possibly some scenes were performed at different times in other cities that honoured the popular god, such as Busiris, Heliopolis, Saïs and Letopolis.

Besides the stele of I-kher-nefert, pictographic inscriptions on the walls of temples are a vivid source of information about Egyptian beliefs and religious practices. The forms of dance are portrayed and can be studied. The mural writings in temples and tombs, in addition to what is contained in papyri, suggest what might have been the content – the plot and dialogue – of episodes in the Abydos festivals as well as other sorts of religious–theatrical presentations. The hieroglyphic material on walls comprises what are called the Pyramid Texts, which have also provoked much scholarly controversy. But from them has come a large body of knowledge, however variously it has been interpreted.

The accession to the throne was also marked by an elaborate festival that included a kind of theatre, the Coronation Plays. One such is the Memphite Drama, dated to about 3100 BC, in the First Dynasty; here the divine protagonist is Ptah, a manifestation of the triune supreme deity. Another known piece commemorates the inauguration of Senroset I about 2000 BC, in the Middle Kingdom. If a pharaoh reigned as long as three decades, the anniversary jubilee recognizing his good luck in having survived took the shape of a *Heb Sed*, a reconstruction of events during his lengthy tenure.

A direct outgrowth of earlier shaman rituals were the Medicinal Dramas in which priests, to establish their ability to effect miraculous cures, solemnly re-enacted the legend of how Isis had saved her child, the falcon Horus (the sun god) from an almost fatal scorpion's sting. This called for magical phrases and herbal applications. The Pyramid Texts offered prayerful instructions (or "stage directions") for the resurrection of the dead, those whose wrapped mummies were locally entombed; a vast number of such texts, perhaps as many as 4,000, are believed to have existed. Once again, they are thought to have derived from invocations at the rites that anticipated the fructifying return of spring.

The Greek historian Herodotus, who visited Egypt (fifth century BC), offers an account of fanatical ritual combat that he saw at Papremis in ceremonies honouring divinities, Ptah and Horus; as many as 1,000 men, armed with clubs, guarded the entrance and assaulted a host of intruders to protect the image of their god as it was borne into his temple. "There is a fierce struggle, in which heads get broken, and not a few, I believe, die of their wounds. The Egyptians, however, denied that there were any deaths." A relief on a wall at Kheriuf depicts just such a riotous scene.

The Egyptians had no playhouses: probably the "acting" consisted mostly of eloquent recitations and incantations, chanted or sung with or without musical accompaniment – rattle and sistrum – and there were troupes of dancing girls – princesses – at court or in the temples, attendant on sacrificial or funeral rites. If impersonating a god – the falcon Horus, the jackal Wepwawet – the actor might wear an animal head mask. Once set, the traditions were inflexible; the full power of drama never evolved. Several millennia later, in the twelfth century AD, a special genre of shadow play made its appearance, borrowed from the Orient and devoted to exploiting folk legends and historical tales.

In Syria, women ceremoniously mourned for Tammuz, also a cherished vegetation god, who died each year and in spring was resurrected from his dwelling in the netherworld, where his wife Ishtar, a fertility goddess, faithfully went to search for him. Images of the god were thrown into Mesopotamian rivers, strewn with uprooted flowers earlier planted and adoringly tended in his honour. Tammuz was the god, too, of life-giving waters.

In Athens, much later, the myth of Tammuz – now better known as Adonis (a Semitic term for "Lord"), a beautiful mortal, but perhaps like Osiris a personification of the sun – was told in a different version: the handsome but luckless boy was beloved of both Aphrodite, goddess of Life, and Persephone, queen of Death and the Underworld. Ares, also called Mars, was jealous and resentful of Aphrodite's infatuation with this youthful rival. The angry war-god, disguised as a wild boar, fatally gored the hapless boy; from his blood, spilled upon the ground, sprang up the anemone. Zeus, ruler of Olympus, intervened between the quarrelling goddesses and decreed that Adonis, still designated a vegetation god, should spend half of each year in daylight, fondled by Aphrodite, and the remaining half in Hades, embraced by Persephone in her shadowed realm.

Elsewhere in Asia Minor, especially in Phoenicia and Cyprus, the ceremony of mourning for his death was called the Adonia, and his loss bewailed by distraught women with naked breasts and wildly flowing locks; soon after, his resurrection was ecstatically and orgiastically acclaimed.

In Babylonia and Alexandria, the marriage and couching of Adonis and Aphrodite were re-enacted with carven images, dramatic tableaux, accompanied by narrative hymns and offerings of ripe fruits, flowers and baked sweets, all symbols of fecundity. This theme of the "sacred marriage" between a god and a human, an advance from the story of Osiris, is incorporated in many Near Eastern ritual observances. It is depicted in a magnificent mosaic, well preserved and attributed to 2700 BC, on which the rulers of Ur and Isin lay claim to divine kingship because they are descended from the mating of that unequal pair.

There are suggestions of secular dramas at a later date in the Sumerian empire. A dialogue called "Hammurabi's Conversation with a Woman" portrays the great king, author of the *Codex Hammurabi*, cleverly outwitted by a woman of whom he is enamoured. It is believed to have been a court play enacted after his death or elsewhere in a palace of a rival ruler. Other examples of secular works have been discovered, among them – listed by Berthold – *Master and Slave*, an Akkadian dialogue much like the mime plays, Atellan farces and comedies of Plautus, which arise centuries afterwards in Rome, and the Commedia dell'Arte of the Renaissance. A servant, deft at punning, mocks the good advice given him by his master.

German scholars discern a marked theatrical character in the Sumerian "divine disputations", seven of which have been found. Berthold says of them: "They all were composed during the period when the image of the Sumerian gods became humanized, not so much in their outward appearance as in their supposed emotions. This criterion is crucial in a civilization: it is the fork in the road where the way to the theatre branches off. For the drama develops from the conflict symbolized in the concept of gods transposed into human psychology."

Often evident in these "divine disputations" is the humour of insult, each of the participants praising himself and derogating his or her companion. Ashnan, the grain-goddess, argues with Lahar, the sheep-god, over which is more helpful to humankind. In another debate, the virtues of Mesopotamia's fierce summer are pitted against those of the Babylonian winter as to which provides a much milder climate. In a third colloquy, the god Enki quarrels with Ninmah, the Mother-goddess; he descends to the underworld and then returns, conforming to a very familiar design. Inanna, a fertility-goddess, is banished to the underworld from which she may return only if she can find someone to take her place. She chooses the royal shepherd Dumuzi, her lover, as her substitute. He becomes Prince of the World of Shadows. Here is repeated the theme of the "sacred marriage", the mating of god and human.

In Babylon, during the rule of Nebuchadnezzar, its inhabitants marked the New Year and paid tribute to Marduk, the city's god, with a twelve-day sacrificial ceremony. At its climax came a huge procession, described by Berthold, who in turn draws on the German scholar Harmat Schmökel: "There was Marduk's colorful retinue, followed by the much-honored cult images from the country's great temples, symbolizing 'a visit of the gods,' and in their train the long file of priests and the faithful. At predetermined points on the red-and-white-paved processional way to the New Year's festival house, the column was halted for recitations of the epic of creation and for pantomime performances. This great ceremonial spectacle honored the gods and the sovereign, and it amazed and thrilled the populace. 'It was theatre in the setting and garb of religious cult and demonstrates that the ancient Mesopotamians had, at least, a sense of dramatic poetry . . .'"

Similar festivals for other divinities were held during the third and second millennia BC in the cities of Ur, Uruk and Nippur; there were like observances at Mari, Umma and Legash. Supposedly fabled Persepolis, the Persian city of splendid tombs and palaces, was established chiefly as the site of the elaborately bedecked New Year's pageant.

The organization of these extravagant, procreative rituals in the Near East, as in Egypt, was a further move towards theatre as it is now known. The recurrent motifs of the stricken, risen god and the sacred marriage gradually infiltrated and infused Greek culture, inspiring like ceremonies there. From these, and especially from the Dionysian festivals, Western drama descends.

2

A REALM OF DIONYSUS

The mystery cult of Dionysus, "horned child" of the promiscuous and incestuous Zeus by his daughter, the earth-goddess Persephone, was based on a myth of the son being ruthlessly pursued by the murderously jealous Titans, the rivals of Zeus. Seeking to rescue him, Zeus has his son metamorphosed into a goat, then a bull (totem and fertility symbols); but such ruses failed. Incited by Zeus's offended wife Hera and overtaking the young god, the relentless Titans cruelly dismembered him; they boiled the torn pieces of his wracked body. His Olympian father swallowed his son's bloody heart, then promptly begat him again through the mortal Semele (herself destined to be an earth-goddess). The virile young god was resurrected, a miraculous event hailed every spring with chants and vigorous dances by his devotees in mystic ceremonies.

Woven of many complex strands – the "sacred marriage" reappears here – the myth has many sources and gradually spread in many versions. Obviously, much is borrowed from the legends of Osiris, Adonis and Mithra. But in all the story's forms Dionysus is a procreative and vegetation god; in one variant, he himself begets the lecherous Priapus by Aphrodite. In these many versions Dionysus is appropriately described as the bull-god, the goat-god; also as Bromius; in Thrace, he is Sbazius, and elsewhere he is called Zagreus or Bacchus, patron of the ripe grape, the wine-god. In hysterical rites, his initiates symbolically drank his blood (wine of new vintage) and partook of his flesh (slivers of roasted goat) in a drunken frenzy during which they believed themselves possessed by the spirit of the god (their intoxicated state being described as one of "enthusiasm", from "*entheos*", (or "the god within"). In this moment of "at-one-ment", or communion, the god's divinity was briefly theirs, an attainment that drove them beside themselves. In Crete, says Frazer, the worshippers bared their teeth, tore to pieces a live bull and raced off insanely through woods.

At the beginning of the cult's festival in Athens, perhaps in the interest of economy, a goat rather than a bull was sacrificed. A statue of Dionysus was placed to overlook a ceremony that was loud with music and hazy with swirling incense. In another reminiscence of totemism, the celebrants garbed themselves in goatskins; their hoarse chants mimicked the beast's piteous, expiring bleats. Subsequently, their choric laments came to be referred to as *tragoidia*, "goat songs". The ritual precincts were sacred: no impieties were allowed there. All traditions were rigidly observed. The rites clearly combined elements of totemism, imitative magic and gestures of propitiation: by offering an animal sacrifice and giving loud, urgent expression of their desire to repent, and by cajoling and flattering the god, his initiates sought to ward off the ills – punishment, suffering and death – that were dramatically enacted. The reborn Dionysus was a divine scapegoat who by his hideous ordeal would purge the cultists, freeing them of the evils with which they were plagued.

Scholars conjecture that at some of the earliest Dionysian rites, as at those for Osiris, there might also have been human sacrifices, knifed at the altar and eaten by the intoxicated, half-mad Bacchic devotees, whose irrationality knew no limit. (Much later, Euripides in *The Bacchae* gives us a frightening picture of the women's crazed excesses during their revels and dances on the forested mountain slopes.) The cult of Dionysus, at first considered alien and barbaric, because Asian, soon grew highly popular in Greece. As Friedrich Nietzsche (in his *The Birth of Tragedy*) has pointed out, the cult gave vent to another side of the Greeks' human nature, their emotionalism and propensity to anarchic impulse, that was the opposite of the "Apollonian serenity" preached by the later Periclean sages and poets, a sense of unwavering dignity represented by balanced and reserved examples of Hellenic sculpture and painting, and by noble monuments like the Parthenon.

The eminent classicist Gilbert Murray, along with others, believes that Grecian tragedy evolved from this pantomimic retelling of the horrible death of Dionysus, the year-demon, as a major segment of his followers' solemn mourning for him. The pantomime was performed in a dithyramb, a "leaping-dance", but to it were steadily added narrative songs, so that the dithyrambs became predominantly choral, guided by the cult's priests who grew more professionally adept at theatrical arts, and eagerly anticipated by much of the populace. (Though Aristotle, in his *Poetics*, states that tragedy evolved from the dithyramb, Sir Arthur Pickard-Cambridge – alluded to in John Ferguson's *A Companion to Greek Tragedy* – contradicts that assumption. To most scholars, however, the evidence is weighty enough to establish that the dithyramb was a very decisive influence, if not the only one. This question, and plenty of others, have long been a subject of academic debate.)

In Athens, in response to demand, there were such festivals year-round. The citizens, especially the cult members, found many occasions for holidays. In particular, a crown of ivy and a goat were a fitting prize to the poet who composed the best hymns to Dionysus. More and more details of the god's story were incorporated, enlarging the dramatic content of the pantomime and dances. Predominantly, though, these were rites of spring; coming at the end of March and beginning of April, they marked a new season of bright Mediterranean sunlight, of quickened blood and aroused erotic impulses, joyfully welcomed after months of chill winds and grey, rainy skies. A second Dionysian festival, the Lenaea, was held in January and early February, but the spring observance, the Great Dionysia, or the Dionysian Eleutherius as it was called, remained the principal event.

When it was apparent that the Dionysian revels were a fixed and possibly disruptive feature of the Athenian calendar, prompting a large outpouring of tipsy, begarlanded participants, the more sober religious and civic leaders of the city-state, concerned to subdue them, gradually took steps to change the tumultuous rites into stately processions and more orderly episodes. They were transferred into sedate and official occasions, graced with Apollonian dignity and grave beauty. An *archon* was appointed to preside over the ceremony, and the city council established strict rules to control and guide it. Its phallic aspect, the orgiastic element, was separated from the tragic to become what is now identified as comedy, a largely independent art form. This is thought to have begun in the seventh century BC.

(Studies of the origins of Greek drama are numerous. For this chapter suggestions have been drawn from Nietzsche's important essay and writings by Gilbert Murray and John Ferguson as well as histories and studies by Sheldon Cheney, Allardyce Nicholl, John Gassner, Gilbert Highet, O. G. Brockett, Will and Ariel Durant, and not least by the imperious Lane Cooper.)

The earliest Dionysian rites are believed to have been held in an indentation on the northern slope of the Acropolis, in an improvised, tamped-down dancing-ring with a few rude wooden seats in a semicircle. Mostly the spectators sat on the hollowed, bare, or in spots grassy, hillside. Some archaeologists assert that the archaic Greek theatre, including the one at Athens, was more likely a quadrangle, but this is a detail of no great moment. All the existing ruins of the theatres date from later periods; modern ideas about them are largely derived from those. In the sixth century BC, by order of the tyrant Pisistratus, who was desirous of retaining the popular favour that had put him in power, a new Theatre of Dionysus accommodating 15,000 was built on the southern flank of the hill overlooking the city. It was very near the grove of olive trees sacred to the god and the handsome new Temple of Dionysus Eleutherius, adjacent to a smaller one that had long housed his image. One reason for replacing the original structure by an open-air stone amphitheatre was that during a performance of a play by Pratinas the wooden benches collapsed, injuring many in the crowded audience. The fanlike tiers climbed towards the gleaming, colonnaded Parthenon, the *orchestra* – or playing-ring – having as its natural backdrop distant, sunlit Mount Hymettus and the glistening, blue Aegean. In the playing-ring was an altar – *thymele* – for incense and sacrifices, a pedestal for the statue of the deity, and close by a few marble seats or thrones for the priests of Dionysus; all other seats were without backs, and being of stone were hard; consequently, many spectators, lacking physical fortitude, brought cushions with them for the day-long performances.

The formal Great or City Dionysia, at the height of its career, lasted five or six days. All shops were closed, all official business and the courts suspended. In their best dress, the citizens of Athens – old and young, the rich brightly garbed and riding in their chariots, the poor more modestly on foot – formed the long, brilliant procession that bore the image of Dionysus from Eleutherae and set it up on the pedestal in the *orchestra* so that the god himself could see all the activities staged in his honour. Some in the procession carried vessels of oil for libations at the altar, wine-jars, or led the noisy animals destined to be sacrificed. Later the god's image was returned to the temple in a parade of equal grandeur, but this time by eerie, flickering torchlight. (At one period the god is said to have been personified by a young man.) Besides two or three days of feasts and athletic games, the ceremonies comprised poetry recitations and concerts that by now had become contests between choric and dancing groups from towns throughout the province of Attica. For the most part, the singers and dancers were amateurs. Each of the ten *demes* (or tribes) of the region named a wealthy, prominent citizen to serve as *choregus*, which meant that in return for the accolade he must foot the costs of production: that is, of rehearsing the performers and musicians of the particular chorus of which he had been chosen the patron or "angel". The amount he spent often determined the outcome, victory or defeat in the contest, and some of the stagings were very extravagant: they were "status symbols". Five hundred singers participated, a group of fifty from each *deme*, and each chorus had a leader whose role was constantly enlarged, giving him the most to sing and mime, until his part was comparable to that of a soloist in an oratorio.

Brockett says that a Dorian Greek poet, Arion (*c.* 625–585 BC), is reputed to have been the first to compose dithyrambs on specific heroic subjects and even to title them. He lived not in Athens but Corinth, and the natives of that city later asserted that tragedy was a Dorian invention, a claim which Brockett rejects, though he grants that certain elements of the dithyramb – "lyric poetry, choral singing and dancing, and mythological subject" – were greatly strengthened there.

In 535 BC the benign, canny Pisistratus ordained a play competition that would occupy three full days of the festival. Scripts for these full-fledged dramatic enactments, submitted by ambitious poets, were screened by the *archon*, who, rumour had it, sometimes accepted bribes that influenced his choice. There was an age limit: the author had to be at least twenty years old. The poets often composed the music for their expanded dithyrambs, too, and directed their own works, and personally painted the scenery. The first three prizes were grants of money – a sleek goat and an ivy wreath no longer sufficed. The tyrant's aim was not only to divert the citizenry with a new, rising form of entertainment, but also to encourage plays on themes drawn not only from the legend of Dionysus but also from the Homeric epics. Beyond this, they celebrated events in Athens's military history, to instil in the citizenry stronger feelings of patriotism, while downgrading the parts played by certain aristocratic families who might compete for the power the tyrant concentrated in his own hands.

The initial winner of the dramatic competition established by Pisistratus in the same year or the next – 535 or 534 BC – was Thespis of Icaria, a singer and director, now turned playwright. Legend has it that Thespis, his face covered with white lead to heighten his resemblance to the god's cadaver, leaped upon the altar and addressed his speeches to the chorus and its leader, thus becoming the first solo actor, their response providing the first dialogue. Other versions have him singing his lines from a table or small platform hitherto used for sacrifices. By his gesture he established the *orchestra* as a stage, a site for acting, rather than a mere dancing-ring, in this huge theatre. (The term for this area comes from "*theatron*", a "place for seeing", and precedes that for the smaller Roman enclosed and roofed "*auditorium*", a place for hearing.) Very likely Arion and some of his fellow Dorian poets had employed some dialogue in their dithyrambs, but what Thespis was offering was a work with a far more extensive use of speech and fairly well-developed plot. Solon, famed for his wisdom, accused him of being a "fabulous liar", in tribute to his story-telling ability. Thespis is also credited with taking his troupe on a ship-shaped wagon and performing in other cities, thus going on the earliest known road tour.

As depicted on vase paintings, Dionysus had originally come to the Greek mainland on such a ship, together "with his flute-playing satyrs". The wagons, or ship-floats, also conveyed the high priest in the splendid procession to the Great Dionysia. Some authorities doubt the story of the touring wagon, but these inspired advances in performing – and others – have resulted in the hardy, resolute race of actors being for ever dubbed "Thespians".

For the convenience of new poets (or "makers") like the ambitious Thespis, the *orchestra* was floored with stone, and a roofed building – the *skene* – to house the actors was erected at a peripheral point, the apex of the broken semi-circle, where the action could be clearly viewed by the huge throng of spectators. At first a wooden hut, the *skene* was in time enlarged, becoming an elaborate two-storey stone structure, its façade boasting a row of columns to serve as the drama's setting, its steps, entrance and pediment suggesting a palace or the portico of a temple. At either end, wings – the *paraskenia* – enclosed the playing-space. When the actors had to change costumes or were "off-stage", they conveniently retired into the *skene*. Sometimes the central door of the three to the *skene* – it was dubbed the "royal" one – was thrown open to expose a tableau, such as the sprawled, blood-smeared bodies of Agamemnon and Cassandra, or the pitiful slaughtered children of the betrayed Medea. Through this door, too, which finally swung ominously shut to hide them, the adulterous Clytemnestra and her lover Aegisthus took their last exit in Aeschylus' sombre drama. Minor characters, or the second actor, entered or left by the side doors. In front of the *skene* was a slightly raised area, the *proskenion*, where the actors performed, while, as before, the chorus occupied the *orchestra*.

Yet another purpose was fulfilled by the *skene*: mounted on its roof, hooks and pulleys raised and lowered the gods who might have roles in the story, intervening miraculously. The gods, like Medea in her dragon-drawn chariot, made their entrances and departures on almost invisible ropes, sometimes rapidly, a theatrical device that stage craftsmen have never relinquished. In later times the Roman term for these cranes and pulleys, *deus ex machina* – the "machinery of the gods" – came to denote a clumsy plot contrivance whereby the characters are extricated from their dilemma by chance or coincidence, a last-minute external happening, disappointing the audience which has looked for a more logical resolution.

The crane was by no means the only stage device available to the Greek dramatist. Sometimes use was made of a low, semi-circular, wheeled platform on which were piled the bodies of the slain. The cart – *ekkyklema* or *eccylema* – would be rolled forward, so that the gory heap was fully observed by all in the theatre who, because of the wide sight-lines, might not otherwise be able to see the tableau recessed too deeply beyond the flung-open doors. Trap doors were introduced to allow the rising up of ghosts and apparitions. Painted scenes – *pinakes* – of limited size were attached to *periaktoi*, triangular prisms that revolved, so that they could present three or four backgrounds successively or alternately. Some had a narrow ledge at the base on which an actor portraying a god could stand, hidden from the audience; then suddenly, as the prism swung about, he made an appearance with a startling clap of thunder. Pollux, in his ancient treatise on the Greek stage (second century AD), also refers to a lightning-machine, which may have been a prism with three sides painted deep black, and across them a jagged lightning-flash inscribed in white or gold. Brass jars, into which stones were poured and rattled, created thunder. Entranceways for the chorus were at two ends of the *skene* and were designated *parodoi*.

The natural background, however, the shining water, the distant, hazy mountains, the sunny sky, provided the playwrights with an even more effective scene to which they frequently alluded and which they shrewdly exploited. In Aeschylus' *Agamemnon*, for example, Clytemnestra exclaims:

> There is the sea – its caverns who shall drain?
> Breeding of many a purple-fish the stain
> Surpassing silver . . .
> [Translation: Gilbert Murray]

At that, a single wide gesture of the performer's arm indicated the blue expanse of ocean that stretched in view of the spectators. Euripides, in *Iphigenia in Aulis*, is supposed to have achieved a stunning impression by opening his play at the hour just before dawn, which was the time at which the performance itself started each day. He has Agamemnon ask:

> What star is that, sailing there?

To which his old attendant replies:

> Sirius, in his middle height near the seven Pleiades riding.

Soon afterwards, as the last shadows of night lifted and the first cold glow streaked the heavens, with gleams of gold just tipping the clouds, we are further told:

> That silver light
> Shows the approach of morn, the harbinger
> Of the sun's fiery steeds.

Allardyce Nicoll says admiringly, "What an effect this synchronization of dramatic setting and actual physical phenomena must have had!" But one imagines that the playwright also ran considerable risk if he was that dependent on the weather. It was a chance taken again by Aeschylus in his *The Eumenides* and Sophocles in his *Antigone*, both of which begin with poetically evoked dawn-settings.

Similar theatres, inevitably varying in some details, were built throughout Greece, in Sicily, and elsewhere around the Mediterranean, and the ruins of many still stand. As will be noted further on, some are still utilized for modern productions of operas and other spectacles.

The chorus, borrowed and absorbed from the dithyrambs, is a distinctive feature of Greek tragedy, especially at its height in the fifth century BC, the great literary epoch of concern here. But the history of the rise of drama was also marked by the chorus's inexorable decline. Steadily it was given a more important share of the action, as is seen in the works of Aeschylus and Sophocles, while simultaneously it was cut in size and its musical declamation shortened. The process was one by which the time allotted to choric dancing and chants was more and more compressed, while the actors – first only one, then two, and then three – were singled out and granted increased opportunities for dialogue. Practical considerations most probably contributed to this. Fifty dancers were expensive to train and costume, and unwieldy to handle and integrate, as playwrights sought ever more compact and unified plots. Accordingly, the chorus was conveniently split up into four groups of twelve members with a leader for each, and each group was assigned to one of the various short plays, also four in number, on a programme. Even these smaller segments were eventually reduced in size, though Sophocles on one occasion employs as many as fifteen choristers. At a much later stage, in the third and second centuries BC, the tragic chorus vanished altogether. In comedy, where the chorus came late, its role was also gradually diminished but persisted much longer.

Both Aeschylus and Sophocles gave the chorus a part in the dramatic action, involving the leader (*coryphaeus*) prominently in verbal exchanges with the actors. Mostly this was Sophocles' innovation, with Aeschylus late in his career emulating his more skilful, younger rival. But Aeschylus from the first has his chorus comment intimately and relevantly on the turbulent happenings in the story.

The plays were operatic; the choruses, in their intervals of dancing and chanting, and particularly at high moments, were accompanied by music: flutes or pipes, tambourines, drums, plucked strings, lyres (*kitharas*) and other instruments. Most often the flute (*otobos*) was used alone; its effect, Ferguson suggests, was "staccato, percussive, rhythmical". About the kinds of music used there is still much argument among scholars. Arion is credited by Solon with having been responsible for various forms of appropriate music for dramatic emphasis. Customarily, the playwright was also a music composer.

The chorus was soon employed to accomplish several major aims. For one, it could be a helpful expositional device. Though the plays were largely based on Homeric legends and historical events, with which members of the audience ought to be familiar, the mass of people were hardly that well informed. Even today a drama taken from a classic source or a historical incident would face spectators who possess only a hazy grasp of the facts. This problem was overcome by having the chorus relate the circumstances leading up to the current plight of the characters. They did this in snatches, as nearly as possible at just the right moment, making a valuable contribution to the hearers' comprehension of the events. The chorus's rhapsodic and expositional interruption was also a device for denoting the passing of time, since the drama had no intermission. In *Agamemnon*, for instance, between the time that Troy falls and the over-proud warrior king arrives back in Argos, several months elapse; this is glossed over by scenes between his impatient queen, Clytemnestra, awaiting him at home, and the hostile chorus, and by other passages in which the members of the chorus, representing Argive citizens, discuss among themselves what is now taking place or impending. Properly handled, this device is equivalent to a modern film "cut-away", where by shifting abruptly from the conflict erupting at a high moment in the play to another subject, suspense is raised – the tantalized spectators having to wait until the chorus's chant is ended for the action to resume, the next episode in the struggle to get under way. This "cut-away" or choric interlude is also a means for "lowering the temperature", reducing the tragic tension at moments when it might become too severe for an audience to sustain.

The chorus might also be the author's mouthpiece. Very often it moralizes on his behalf, obliquely expressing his philosophical and ethical views. Aeschylus, for one, is fond of preaching to the audience, passing judgement on the incidents and characters through the medium of the chorus. But the chorus might also be the voice of the townspeople, the common folk, defining communal values by which the anarchic struggles and outrageous ambitions of the persons in the drama are assayed: thus it is a jury, serving to universalize the theme of the play, giving it a larger significance, presenting it as judged by most of the citizens of Argos or Thebes, or even by the rest of Greece, or possibly a large share of mankind. Much of the immense dignity and towering size of Greek tragedy derives from the heightening role of the chorus, through which approving or disapproving humanity utters its solemn judgement.

Besides this, the chorus creates a suitable atmosphere: if dire acts are about to take place – the dangerous slaying of Agamemnon, the piteous murder of the innocent Cassandra, the horrifying death of Clytemnestra at the hands of her vengeful children, Orestes and Elektra – the chorus prepares a properly ominous mood by its sombre chants, its forebodings, its oft-repeated but unheeded warnings. What is more, the choric passages provide the author with opportunities to display his lyrical gifts. The superb poetic quality of fifth-century Greek tragedy is often a cause for astonishment. But poetry recitals were a component of the Great Dionysia; at first chanted, they were later presented without music so that the words might be more clearly heard. Much earlier the Homeric epics had achieved remarkably high flights of narrative writing. Melic poetry – poetry set to music – had long been a common feature of Greek literature; even historical surveys and philosophical arguments were frequently written in verse. Each of the greatest tragic authors, Aeschylus, Sophocles, Euripides, has an individual poetic style, and so – and this is more unexpected – has Aristophanes, the leading writer of ribald comedy. In the works of Euripides, particularly, are lyric passages of rare beauty that often seem to have been inserted for no other purpose than to bring on the chorus, and to let the author exhibit his remarkable facility with words and the lasting freshness of his imagery.

Lest the words of the songs be slurred or unintelligible, and to avoid monotony, the chorus adopted several means of delivery. Sometimes it chanted in unison; but at other times it alternated the lines antiphonally, the leader reciting one line, the group replying to him with one voice, much like a pastor and his congregation engaged in responsive reading in today's churches; or, again, each line might be spoken separately and successively by a different individual member of the chorus. All three methods might be used to good effect in the same play. The chorus also reacted with gestures to deeds perpetrated by the actors: at a violent act, such as Medea's frightful slaying of her children, or Oedipus' merciless self-blinding, the choristers might recoil as one, turning away their eyes or swerving their whole bodies from the hideous sight; or it might hold up arms in supplication or exaltation.

The group's dances similarly underlined, lent strong emphasis to the emotions of the protagonist and antagonist in the drama. The exact nature of the dances can only be guessed at from scattered vase paintings and temple bas-reliefs, which unfortunately are static. Experts suggest that the choristers took small hops, in a more or less fixed position, much like the up-and-down movements or jigs of nineteenth-century Hasidic worshippers. This was done in Laurence Olivier's revival of *Oedipus* (1946). In other modern reconstructions of the plays, directors have staged the dances quite differently: some employ broad choreographic patterns in which the chorus circles or sweeps around the focal characters, narrowing the distance or retreating, or perhaps describing a figure of eight or a cross like an "x", or spreading out in larger and looser arcs. But anyone attending a contemporary production of a Greek classic must testify that the chorus's dance movements considerably reinforce and heighten dramatic impact at crucial moments in the story.

Philip W. Harsh in *A Handbook of Classical Drama* gathers the experts' speculation about the dancing and other group movements:

> The members of the chorus had each a definite position in the *orchestra*: the terms defining these were borrowed from military strategy, and one movement was a marching movement in rectangular formation. Choral lyric is patterned in a *strophe* followed by an *antistrophe* in identical rhythm (though not, in view of the pitch accent of Greek, with identical melody). In view of the explicit statement of a scholiast on Euripides' *Hecabe* (647 BC), we may take it as certain, despite the skepticism of some scholars, that during the strophe the chorus moved round the circular *orchestra* to the right, during the antistrophe to the left, and during the *epode* stood still. We know from Hesychius of lines on the floor of the *orchestra*, like our chalk marks, to guide position and movement. There is a puzzling account of dance in Plutarch, written in his study centuries after the event. He identifies *phora*, movement and step, *schema*, pose and gesture, and *deixis*, interpretation. We have some miscellaneous evidence about these. We know for example of movement such as "walking past the four," perhaps with five rows of three dancers moving so that those from the front now pass to the back or vice versa, and the "double dance" no doubt with two half-choruses facing and matching one another. We know of gestures such as "the flat hand," a slapping movement to indicate joy, sorrow or anger, and "the snub-nosed hand," tensed and bent away and used in many different connotations. We know of dancing with staffs, which I have seen used with great power in *Oedipus at Colonus* at Bradfield School. We know of the energetic "fire-tongs" with leaps involving the quick crossing of the feet just as a modern ballet dancer does; of the miming of ball games, of acrobatic dances; of spectacular splits; of rhythms associated with rowing and (almost certainly) with flying; we know of dances of joy and sorrow, victory and defeat; we know of processional dances, usually in the anapaestic rhythm (i.e., 4/4 time). *The Bacchants* is in many ways unique; *ionicus a minore* (dddd) predominates in many passages. The dances were wild and authentically Bacchic, miming the joys of the chase; the tambourine was used in accompaniment; and there was a superb solo dance for Agave.

(Staffs were carried by the chorus in the Olivier presentation of *Oedipus.*)

The chorus stayed mostly in the *orchestra*, a bit removed from the *proskenion*, the slightly higher platform on which the actors held forth. Some playwrights sought to find a logical reason, within the plot framework, for the group's presence; thus in Aeschylus' *Agamemnon* and Sophocles' *Oedipus* the choristers comprise the townspeople of Argos and Thebes; in Euripides' *The Bacchae* they are first the maenads who have followed Dionysus from Asia, and later the women of the town who are joining their queen in the Bacchic revels. But many poets offer no excuse for the presence and participation of the chorus: it was simply a convention of Greek tragedy and required no other pretext.

Like so much else in the festival, the form of choric passages obeys strict canons, though many playwrights might alter what was traditional if a sharper dramatic effect is achieved. First comes the *parados,* the entrance song of the chorus as with stately pace it marches into view of the spectators. Sometimes the *parados* is preceded by a prologue (*prologos*) spoken by a lone actor, such as the watchman in Aeschylus' *Agamemnon,* or else expository dialogue like that between Sophocles' Antigone and her sister Ismene, outlining the situation at the play's opening, or reminding the audience of a substantial share of the myth to be treated by the drama. The main choral interludes (*stasimons*) are made up of the *strophe* (question) and the *antistrophe* (response), and then the conclusion or *epode.* The last song and section of the play, with the chorus departing and the drama winding up, is called the *exodos.* Originally, as noted above, the *strophe* and *antistrophe* refer to the chorus's turning to the left, then to the right, as it recites the stanzas of each *stasimon* or ode in sustained alternation; later, the *strophe* often suggests a moral problem posed and next answered in the *antistrophe.* The verse is unrhymed (though often misleadingly rhymed in some English translations of the plays), but it has an intricate metrical structure: the lines might be dactylic, anapaestic, iambic, trochaic, spondaic and of varied lengths; or in lyrical portions use more rare (to us) and subtle measures such as the cretic, paeon, bacchiac, dochmiac, Aeolic, Ionic and still others; all these rhythms are ably matched to the emotion they seek to voice, slow to indicate melancholy, rapid to express anxiety or excitement. Most of the dialogue is in six-foot iambic lines, and so this cadence predominates. Modern translators have usually been unwilling – or unable – to cope with such involved shifts of rhythm; only readers familiar with archaic Greek can appreciate the true genius of the Dionysian poets in arranging the speeches and songs.

German classical scholars in the late nineteenth century argued about the ultimate function of the Greek chorus, its deeper role. In *The Birth of Tragedy* Nietzsche takes issue with August Wilhelm von Schlegel, poet and critic, who described the chorus as "the quintessence of the audience, the 'ideal spectator'". Nietzsche denies that the singing, dancing chorus is Apollonian, as he himself defines that term. For him, it is not true that "the democratic Athenians represented in the chorus the invariable moral law, always right in the face of passionate misdeeds and extravagances of kings". A more satisfactory explanation, in his view, is that of the Romantic dramatist and aesthetician Friedrich Schiller, for whom the chorus enhances the stylization of the plays, "a living wall which tragedy draws about itself in order to achieve insulation from the actual world, to preserve its ideal ground and its poetic freedom". An author, by means of the chorus, creates a realm of ritual and illusion rather than one that is a mere realistic copy of a dull daily world. Going further, Nietzsche believes the chorus's contribution is larger and more fundamental than that. It is the continuing medium through which the Dionysiac element, man's instinctive kinship with nature, finds expression. Nietzsche traces the chorus back to its wilder, dithyrambic origins, as a revel, a dance of leaping, goatskin-clad satyrs. "The cultured Greek felt himself absorbed into the satyr chorus, and in the next development of Greek tragedy, even state and society, and all that separated man from man, gave way for the onlooker before an overwhelming sense of unity which led back into the heart of nature." Along with this came "a metaphysical solace (with which, I wish to say at once, all true tragedy sends us away) that, in spite of the flux of phenomena, life is at bottom indestructibly joyful and powerful". The chorus of satyrs personifies the "forces of nature" that "dwell behind all civilization and remain unchanged in mankind through generation after generation, and despite historical progress. . .". With the happy earthiness of this chorus, "the profound Greek, so uniquely susceptible to the subtlest and deepest suffering, who had penetrated into the terrible destructive processes of both nature and history, consoled himself". The Greek spectator is thus "saved by art, and through art life reclaimed him". This very personal interpretation by Nietzsche of the chorus's effect on the audience is not supported by an examination of its tone and activity in all Greek plays, but does describe what is clearly manifested in not a few of them.

Tragic actors soon won popular favour, and some were singled out for their exceptional talent, highly paid and honoured. They were given the title of *hypokrites*, which at first connoted "answerer" – to the questions and challenges posed by the chorus – rather than "impersonator", the term's later meaning. After a while the actors had their own "guild" with members in all Attic towns, and were exempt from military duty; besides this, if they encountered blockades and battle-lines they were permitted safe passage through them. Travelling throughout Greece, they performed in minor cities and at dramatic festivals everywhere, especially at an important though lesser event called the Rural Dionysia held annually at the seaport of Piraeus. The players' moral repute was low, but that did not much harm them. In fact, to many it only made them seem more enviable. Ironically, their special status was owing to their link to religious rites.

Though acclaimed and well recompensed, the hardy tragic actors could not expect to have their faces widely recognized, because the make-up – white lead, purslane, red cinnabar – introduced by Thespis had given way to masks, an innovation also attributed to that first actor–playwright. The mask, of course, was derived from earlier magical practices, but in the vast Theatre of Dionysus it had other purposes. In an amphitheatre of such size, the actors' miens could not be clearly discerned by the huge assembly of spectators. The masks enlarged the performers' features, and were usually sculpted and painted to express a dominant emotion or character trait such as pride, anger, horror, grief; and also the approximate age of the person. Some alternation of this frozen face might be achieved by raising or lowering the head, or turning it to a fresh angle to present it in a different light. But then, too, the actor could change his mask, and did this frequently in various scenes of the play. Later, masks offered individual characteristics, and some had realistic details, like the blood-smeared one worn by the just blinded Oedipus.

Several other advantages accrued to the actor from his use of a mask: it enabled him to assume more than one role in the same play, which was necessary because there were only two, at most three, actors in any production. Three actors could take on as many as eleven or thirteen parts in a work, providing there were never more than three characters on stage at any one moment. By adding a mask, the performer could also portray a wide range of types, and also female roles – only men and boys were permitted to belong to the companies. The passionate Clytemnestra, vengeful Elektra, sweet but weak Ismene, lorn Iphigenia, fierce Antigone and Medea, wan Eurydice – all these heroines of Greek tragedy were enacted by strong-throated men. A brass megaphone was built into the gaping mouth-piece of the mask for added resonance: it amplified the performer's voice, so that he might be heard by the 15,000 or 17,000 onlookers who had eagerly gathered to behold and hearken to him. Acoustics in these outdoor theatres were natural and said to have been superb; even so, the megaphone was a help. The chorus, too, wore masks.

Pollux enumerates thirty types of masks for tragedy alone. Six depict categories of old men – some bald, some with scanty white locks and some with beards. Eight kinds of young men are also depicted: some pale, emaciated; some ruddy; some with beards, some clean-shaven. Some black-haired, some fair-locked. And there are a variety of messengers and slaves. The same diversity marks the false-faces for feminine roles.

Reliance on masks for facial expression placed a greater burden on the actor to lend verisimilitude to his role by the rich and skilful use of his voice, and by effective gesture. His body movements were somewhat hampered by his heavy, padded costume, which consisted of a *chiton*, a free-flowing robe that hung from the neck to the ankles, with sleeves that covered the arms to the wrist (unlike the sleeveless garments worn by Athenians in daily life). Girdled just below the breast, its unusual lines increased the impression that the actor was of exceptional height. The *chiton* was ornately designed and of bright hues, the patterns formal, geometric, but in places figured with symbolic animal shapes. Over this robe and the right shoulder might be flung a long cloak, or else a short mantle might adorn the left shoulder. These were gorgeously coloured, and their tones could indicate the fate or emotional state of the character: dark or dim shades signified that his destiny would be sorrow and lamentation. A queen's costume, of elaborate materials, would be predominantly of royal purple. Kings also wore a short, heavily quilted jacket (*kolpoma*) to inflate their burly regal size. Realistic details might be added: for a king, a crown; for a hobbling old man, a walking stick; for Medea, a barbaric princess, excessive jewellery.

Not only the padding and lines of his costume gave the tragic hero an aspect of abnormal sturdiness and height: he wore boots – *cothurni* – with thick, wooden soles, also painted a symbolic hue; these literally "elevated" him, and the degree to which they added to his stature accorded with his rank in the drama: that is, a king would have the most heavily raised boots, so as to make him – and his retinue, his military leaders, and a priest like Tiresias – taller than any mere subject. Lesser characters were commensurately shorter, and the soles of the chorus were scarcely thickened at all, resembling sandals; for dancing, the choristers might be barefoot.

A further effect of heroic height was achieved by a lofty head-dress (*onkos*), which extended above the wood-and-cork or linen mask. In consequence, the actor in a leading role might seem seven and a half feet tall, hence a striking figure, "god-like", awesome, so richly caparisoned. In the immense theatre he was that much more easily seen by the multitude of spectators. A story, dismissed by Vera Roberts as probably apocryphal, tells of an audience in Spain taking flight in panic when a visiting troupe of Greek tragedians suddenly came on stage. These were surely no humans! The members of the chorus would be uniformly dressed as to colour and design. The hue of their garments might also be chosen to match the mood of the drama, bright or dark.

In the fifth century BC the exaggeration achieved by the actors through their dress was not as great as it was to be in later periods, when the quality of playwriting was in decline and the importance of acting waxed higher; until finally, as in any decadent theatrical era, crowds came more to see the competitive acting than to pay respectful heed to the scripts. The names of some of the performers have been preserved, including that of Polus who was paid as much as the equivalent of $1,200 for two days' appearances. Among other "stars" was Callipedes, who was so vain and boastful that he earned a rebuke from King Agesilaus. Seeking praise for his ability to "sing like a nightingale", he evoked this response from the ruler: "I have heard the bird itself." Some of the playwrights themselves were actors, as was Aeschylus. Greatly admired was Nicostratus, along with Neoptolemus, Aristodemus, Phrynichus and Athenodorus, according to historical record, though alas nothing remains of their art. Of the highly recompensed Polus another story is told, that he summoned up the appropriate emotion when portraying Electra mourning over the remains of her dead brother by clasping an urn filled with the ashes of his very own son. Some actors linked their careers with those of particular dramatists: Mynniscus and Cleander regularly appeared in the plays of Aeschylus, Tlepolemus and Cleidimides in those of Sophocles. In a later period, roles were assigned by lot, a rather hit-and-miss procedure that must have made the author–director's task most difficult. Among actors, then as in all times since, much jealousy, backbiting and rampant vanity were reported to be prevalent.

A special facet of Greek theatre is the important role of the Messenger. His is a major assignment, always, in a tragic drama, for usually he brings news vitally affecting the fortunes of the hero. Very often he describes a catastrophe not easily shown on stage and hence said to have occurred out of sight of the audience. In Sophocles' *Oedipus* the Shepherd (substituting for the role of the "Messenger") comes with word of the death of Corinth's king. In Aeschylus' *Agamemnon* the Messenger provides a vivid word-picture of Troy's fall and the arduous homeward journey of the victors. In Euripides' *The Bacchae* a shaken Messenger relates the fatal revels during which Pentheus is slain by his deluded mother. Some of the finest speeches in a tragedy are given to the Messenger; such passages are the equivalent of arias in a nineteenth-century Italian opera. Reliance on this device was necessary because, as noted above, most kinds of physical violence – even between individuals – could not be portrayed on stage. It was not only shipwrecks and the sacking of cities that could not be visibly enacted. Clad in bulky costumes and standing on their elevated soles, the players could not move about agilely enough to enact killings and combats; besides, if one of the actors had to emulate a corpse throughout an episode, he could not retire to the *skene* to change his mask and, returning, double in another role. If the murdered victim were seen only in a tableau, perhaps trundled forward on a cart, the actor could be replaced by a supernumerary. Though there were never – or perhaps rarely – more than three actors, and twelve or fifteen in the chorus, "supers" – mutes – were often used to swell the cast at a spectacular moment, as when Agamemnon returns in arrogant triumph from Troy at the head of his soldiers, or when the household guards of Clytemnestra and the followers of the tricked, slain king confront one another with drawn swords. The absence of overt physical violence on stage led to the later, mistaken belief that Greek tragedy was primarily static and characterized by a "classical reserve". Any reading of the plays will correct that idea: the stories are filled with bloody incidents, which for pragmatic reasons do not take place on stage but are instead graphically detailed by the Messenger, his having been a poetically eloquent eye-witness.

Spectators learned to accept many conventions. For instance, there were three doors to the *skene*, one on either side of the "royal" door that presumably was an entrance to the palace or temple. If the actor took his leave by the one at the right, the spectator knew that it led to a lesser temple or mean dwelling somewhere in the city near by; if the actor chose the door at the left, he was supposedly going to fields and countryside. (Later the *skene* had five doors.) If the actor wore a hat, it denoted that he was a traveller. Audiences had to catch such cues.

Aspirants for professional acting parts had to undergo considerable training. By Sophocles' time some specialized in particular roles for which they might be physically equipped. The *protagonist*, or chief player, needed a strong tenor voice. (One of the reasons that women were excluded from acting was that their voices were too weak to carry in the vast amphitheatres.) The main supporting roles went to the *deuteragonist* who had to be a baritone; he might be Creon, opposed to Antigone. The third role was that of the *tritagonist*, a bass, who would be a king, a herald or the like. The younger members of the troupe worked their way up through the ranks. Various rules about working conditions were set by the guild – those enrolled in it called themselves the Artists of Dionysus – with other guidelines laid down by the Amphictyonic Council. The actors had a priestly aura because the festival was linked to the cult of Dionysus. That accounted for their being spared having to do military service. As said before, to be an actor carried much prestige. The *protagonist* was apt to be the head of the company; he might be a contractor, paying the actors in accordance with their status, overseeing most details so that everything met the demands set by the guild, and assigning roles.

It has already been remarked that the audience was mixed. Assuredly, some of the spectators were sophisticated and cultured at this time, the fifth century BC, the apogee of Hellenic civilization. But most in the vast throng were unruly and boisterous, unlettered, hard to please. At first the performances were free; later, tickets were sold; and finally – after 420 BC – the city-state granted two *obols* to all who could not afford the entrance price. The tickets took the form of discs: lead for entrance, ivory for reserved seats. The rich also sent their servants long in advance to find and hold good places. Since the plays began at dawn and lasted seven or eight hours, people brought food. Aristotle suggests that the success of a work might be determined by how much was consumed by hungry spectators during its unfolding. Sitting on hard stone benches, they might grow inattentive, restless, eat more.

Any actor who failed to commend himself would be pelted with olive pits, orange skins, dates, figs or other fruit rinds. Catcalling and jeers provided interruptions. Bad plays were drowned out by howls and cut off abruptly. On occasion, when the crowd was provoked by an offensive or impious script, serious rioting broke out. Aeschines was nearly stoned to death by the hostile mob in one such outburst. Aeschylus, too, was thought guilty of having betrayed some of the secrets of the Eleusinian mysteries and put in peril of his life. The first version of Euripides' *Hippolytus* also provoked a tumult, and he was forced to revise it. Actors often hired claques to counter the derision by their support and extra-loud applause.

Rehearsals and other preparations were kept secret, but sometimes excerpts from the plays were given in advance to arouse public interest. These *proagons* were staged at a spot adjacent to the theatre itself.

Ten judges of the play contest were selected by lot on the first morning of the drama festival. A long list of names was compiled and submitted by the august Council. At the end of the competition each judge put down his first, second and third choice on a tablet and dropped it into an urn. From this vessel the *archon* withdrew only five tablets. The prizes were awarded by a count of these; the other five tablets, never scrutinized, were destroyed. This double safeguard was supposed to ensure a fair decision, since there was no way of knowing beforehand just who would be the judges or which five would have their votes counted. Even so, bribes were said to be paid; besides which, the over-cautious judges were often swayed by the crowd's applause. No less a person than Plato objected that the literary quality of the drama was being "debased" by this hearkening to popular approval. Again, the amount of money spent on a production by the *choragus* might influence the judges and the spectators, too, as might the skill and grace of the more talented actors. Some plays of true merit failed at first, because they were staged ineptly or handicapped by a stingy budget. Yet the need to please the crowd was a prod to the poets: faced by a demanding, restive audience, plays had to be stirring, filled with action, sincerely moving or entertaining, a legitimate criterion for any kind of theatre.

Originality was of scant importance; there were hardly any fresh plots, though Agathon is said to have attempted to compose one. Most repetitively, the stories continued to be taken from the myths and the revered tales of Homer, or they were based on recent historical events, as were Phynichus' *Fall of Miletus* and Aeschylus' *The Persians.* For the cultivated ticket-buyer, suspense did not arise from what would happen next. The real interest was in *how* the playwright would treat a theme that was already over-familiar. For those spectators, an offsetting excitement came from knowing that a disaster impended – Clytemnestra would slay her unfaithful husband, Oedipus would learn the terrible secret of his birth, the hapless Iphigenia would perish – and watching the shrewd means by which the dramatist built towards that blood-chilling climax. Anticipation counted more than suspense. Poets were allowed considerable licence to change familiar basic details in the story for dramatic effect: characters might be interpreted from a radically different angle, and a new personal moral judgement – the author's – might be offered. The flute music, too, might vary. (The flute player was often seated in the centre of the *orchestra*, atop the table that served as an altar. Among the sponsors, there was sharp competition to hire the best master of that musical instrument.) Certain mythical themes were favourites, and author after author tried his hand at novel versions of those plots.

The plays, having liturgical overtones and staged in sacred precincts in the presence of the priests of Dionysus, had great inherent dignity. This was maintained by the emphasis upon tradition applied not only to the ever more conventional style of the performances but also to the poet's respectful and intellectual handling of his subject and caution about the moral values he enunciated. That was true until a comparatively late date, and changed only with the advent of Euripides, a bold but calumniated iconoclast.

The depth and seriousness of the plays also derive from the Greeks' earlier magical ceremonies having been an outgrowth of tomb-rites, the worship of the dead, akin to ideas found in the Pyramid Texts of the Egyptians. Bringing back the spirits of the departed, early man imaginatively denied the awful finality of death. This is a subliminal element in the tragedies. John Gassner observes: "The drama still overcomes the prime dread when man, ennobled by his passionate struggle and his fortitude, survives in a spiritual sense." By paying tribute to dead heroes, the poet confers enduring life on them. The plays celebrate not only the shining, terrible story of Dionysus, who held forth the promise of resurrection, eternal rebirth, but also the legends of semi-mythical figures (the culture heroes) who had gradually become the god's surrogate. Their deeds and destinies, too, achieved immortality through poetry, and again through dramatic enactment. Such heroes, who to a degree become semi-divine, were the fire thief Prometheus, the storied Agamemnon, Orestes, Oedipus, Creon, even the hapless Hippolytus. If at first the dazzling Dionysus was the sole figure about whom the plays were constructed, he eventually vanished as the protagonist. In only one very late play of Euripides, *The Bacchae*, has Dionysus a principal role. But of more than 397 listed Greek tragedies (of perhaps more than 2,000 given throughout the history of the festival), not more than thirty-two are extant, so it is possible that the god was presented in a host of other works no longer accessible. What it is essential to note, however, is that the Greek tragic hero is larger than life; he is, as has been said, "godlike": he always has kingly stature. The Greeks anthropomorphized their deities, so the line between human and the divine is seldom clear; mortals like Adonis and Heracles became gods. An ordained transference slowly took place: the suffering and fall of the often superhuman tragic hero paralleled the story of the tormented god who died and was reborn, and who was also a divine scapegoat, by his self-sacrificial gesture (such as that of Oedipus) lifting guilt or even a pestilence from the feuding, murderous family clan or tainted city.

As the dramas, or new passion plays, evolved in this Greek theatre, the hero is shown bringing down punishment – *nemesis* – on himself by an insolent deed or flaw in his otherwise noble nature. The tragic flaw (*hamartia*) is usually overweening pride (*hubris*) that arouses the ire of the gods, who jealously and mercilessly strike him. His fall is the greater because of his high rank and hitherto fame and good fortune. Agamemnon is renowned as a conqueror, but in the flush of victory has grown far too arrogant and vain. Oedipus is clever and resolute, but also reckless and over-confident. Hippolytus is prissy and frigid. Pentheus, self-righteous, is prurient. Above all, the authors of the tragedies preach the virtue of moderation (*aidos*). In his moment of utmost triumph, swelling with egotism as he returns home, Agamemnon warns himself, though he does not heed his own good advice:

> Aye, and not to fall
> Suddenly blind is of all gifts the best
> God giveth . . .
> [Translation: Gilbert Murray]

Throughout ensuing theatrical history, this is to continue as the formula for "tragedy": a man of high attainments is brought low by a crack, an excessive trait, in his nature; he is betrayed by his inordinate lust, greed, ambition, boastfulness, stupid or blind obstinacy. In the swiftly moving play, one such quality in him is externalized or exampled by his perpetrating some flagrant act of folly. So the Greeks gave lasting form to a kind of serious drama which by its grandeur becomes a touchstone for all other moral or philosophical theatre, in any country or age, that is to follow. All subsequent "tragedy", even that of Shakespeare and Goethe, is for ever to be measured against the Greeks' achievement.

At the drama contests, three rather lengthy one-act plays were presented each morning by one of the trio of authors who had passed the *archon*'s careful screening. Scores of other scripts by as many would-be dramatists had been submitted for his approval, but rejected. Sometimes, especially at first, each author's plays constituted a trilogy, but in later days they were apt to be on quite diverse themes.

The afternoons were dedicated to works of a lighter sort, by the same three writers, satyr plays, comedies, to which the cruder, fun-loving part of the audience looked forward.

More or less, the tragedies were crafted on a fixed model. After the prologue and *parodos* came further and fuller exposition, then the *agon* – the confrontation between protagonist and antagonist – which led, by an abrupt reversal of fortune for the hero, to incidents of "suffering", then the dénouement, and the final passage or *exodos.* In the unfolding of the story there would also be fateful recognition scenes or discoveries: the true identity of someone revealed, as the long-exiled Orestes cautiously makes himself known to his sister Elektra; or Oedipus learns that he is Laius' son; or Agave realizes to her horror that the young man she had decapitated in her drunken, Bacchic frenzy is her own child. Or the discovery might be of a different sort: Clytemnestra exposes to the elders of Argos her long-pent, hidden hatred for her royal husband. Ultimately and more subtly, the discovery might be the recognition by the hero of the moral error or character flaw in him that has been responsible for his ruin: that is, he attains "enlightenment". Roughly, this pattern divided the story into five sections, or episodes, traditionally separated by four choral odes, though the chorus sometimes interrupted more than four times. All this flowed on without pause, for there were no intermissions, but these carefully spaced breaks laid the groundwork for what are later to be called "acts". Apart from the regular intervention of the chorus, the progression of the story was rapid, from introduction and preliminary exposition, to a fuller and more helpful explanation of the background, and next to a conflict or heated debate, to a climax and catastrophe, and to a final fall of tension, a closing lament, a moral judgement, or a prayer and benediction. In the hands of Sophocles, classical dramatic structure along these lines reached such perfection that it has never since been matched.

3

THE GREAT TRAGEDIES

The earliest of the major Greek tragic poets, Aeschylus, was born in 525 BC, only ten years after the victory by Thespis at the first drama contest inaugurated by the shrewd Pisistratus. The overlapping indicates how quickly Greek tragedy rose to its remarkable maturity. From its true beginnings to its height is a span of little more than a half century. During that time a host of playwrights sprang up and most of them seem to have been truly prolific at composition. From scattered references by their contemporaries their names are known and in some instances the titles and subjects of their plays, but all the scripts have vanished. Some of these poets have already been mentioned. Among them is Arion, who boldly but futilely sought to create original stories and wholly "fictional" characters in contrast to mythical and Homeric figures, who somewhat amusingly were deemed "actual". Arion was responsible, as has already been said, for transforming the wild dithyrambic chorus into a more disciplined body devoted to coherent mimetic presentation. He also introduced the *strophe* and *antistrophe.* So admired were his lyric gifts that legends soon clustered about him, too. On a sea journey, according to one story, sailors threatened to rob and stab him. To elude them, he dove into the water; a dolphin, hearing his last song, swam up from the waves to carry him safely ashore on its scaly back.

Choerilus produced no fewer than 160 plays, all now disappeared. Pratinas, most ironically, is best remembered because it was while a work of his was being staged that the wooden stands collapsed, necessitating their replacement by the new Theatre of Dionysus.

Phrynichus, as has been noted, was the author of *The Fall of Miletus*, which brought on him the ire of officials and spectators alike. So bitter were the recollections and shame aroused by this script that he was fined 1,000 drachmas, while an edict was issued against any other play on that topic, an unwelcome reminder of how the Athenians' neglect was to blame for the loss of that city colony. More popular was his *The Women of Phoenicia,* dealing with the theme of Salamis, the crucial battle in which the Greeks had dispersed and wrecked a flotilla of Persian ships, and therefore for the citizens a happier memory. A pupil of Thespis, Phrynichus was the first to ask permission to don female masks and to offer feminine characters. By this device, he further developed the role of the "answerer" who could now appear alternately in a male or female role, with changes of costume and mask behind the *skene*, encouraging the advance from simple declamation to a degree of physical stage action.

The first extant scripts are those of Aeschylus, seven from the lengthy list of those he is believed to have turned out, of which the titles of seventy-nine are known or at least attributed to him. Some accounts place his total output at ninety plays. Why his were saved, and just these seven, inspires conjecture. The temptation is to suppose that he, along with his great rivals Sophocles and Euripides, was so superior to the several hundred other playwrights of that half-century that only their compositions have survived. Are these the best scripts by the operation of Gresham's law in reverse? The driving out the bad! Who can be certain? It is highly probable that scores of fine dramas by this trio and their predecessors, contemporaries and successors are gone by ill luck. Until the advent of Aeschylus the rule was that a play could not be staged more than once; it was allowed only a single performance. After Aeschylus' death, however, the Council permitted the revival of his works: they were so admired, and the demand to see them again was so strong. This argues that his primacy was early recognized.

In time, plays produced at the City Dionysia were also taken on tour to other cities of Greece. Of interest is how these ancient works survived after the subjugation of Athens. The invading Romans prized them highly, and collected them, especially the scripts of Euripides that were already preserved on sturdy, long-lasting papyri. In Byzantium, the Eastern Roman capital, cloistered monks also gathered and affectionately recopied them. When the city was sacked by successive waves of Saracens and Turks, the monks fled Byzantium to find haven in Italy and took along the precious papyri. Slowly the plays became known to Renaissance scholars; even more gradually newer copies were carried northwards, dispersed about the Continent, particularly Germany, until they reached England, not becoming familiar to classicists there much before the eighteenth century. They were preceded in London and the universities by the derivative works of Roman playwrights, Plautus, Terence, Seneca. As a consequence the less accomplished Roman drama exerted a far greater influence on the Elizabethan theatre than did the still unknown Athenian masterpieces.

As the number of readers acquainted with Greek diminished, English translations of the plays appeared. The idiom in which the translations were couched changed considerably in every cultural era and continues to do so. Eighteenth-century versions of the plays, some still in use by students, now sound ridiculously stilted: they are rhymed, have an over-regular meter, and employ "thee" and "thou" and word inversions that were acceptable, even deemed mandatory, in pre-Wordsworthian days.

In the late nineteenth century Gilbert Murray attempted fresh translations; his ambitious task encompassed all thirty-seven extant fifth century BC scripts. He carried out this project in a Romantic vein, using a rapid flowing cadence, sometimes inverting the word order and adding rhymes throughout, and even inserting lush adjectives, in the exuberant manner of Swinburne, the style very *fin de siècle*, belonging to his period. In addition to being an esteemed scholar, Murray possessed lyric gifts of not inconsiderable merit. His versions had an enthusiastic welcome, many persons proclaiming that the true verbal splendour of the ancient dramas was opened to them at last. These translations helped to restore the plays to the stage – mostly at colleges, but more prominently at Harley Granville Barker's Royal Court Theatre in London.

(Gilbert Murray has attained immortality in other ways: a friend of George Bernard Shaw, he is the acknowledged model of Adolphus Cusins, the young, bright, articulate professor of Greek in Shaw's *Major Barbara*. Further, in the second act of that comedy, a character quotes lines from Murray's just published translation of Euripides' *The Bacchae*. In a grateful prefatory note Shaw describes Murray's version as having "come into our dramatic literature with all the impulsive power of an original work". In later years the energetic Murray dedicated much of his life to organizing groups seeking to establish world peace. He helped to draft the covenant of the utopian League of Nations.)

A few decades later, in the 1920s, even before the long-lived Murray completed his demanding task, the poet and critic T.S. Eliot faulted the popularly acclaimed translations. Eliot charged them with being unfaithful to the tone and style of the originals, especially in the instance of Aeschylus' plays, where Murray not only effectively rhymes the speeches but frequently over-decorates them. The poetry of Aeschylus is sparse, austere, masculine, which the Murray rendition is not. Eliot's point is valid. The accuracy of Murray's interpretation of what the lines mean cannot be seriously questioned, however, and he is remarkably insightful.

Inspired by Eliot's attack, which reflects the anti-Romantic spirit of a newer age, a flock of other twentieth-century poets and scholars brought out versions of the Greek tragedies that are more prosaic, even flat, yet claiming to be more authentic; that is, more literal. In particular, a good number of English translations of Aeschylus' *Agamemnon* and Sophocles' *Oedipus* have been issued. Readers, therefore, may select from many and choose those most pleasing to themselves. Let them take care, though: a "modern" translation might give no idea of the force and beauty of the language, the prodigal richness of image and metaphor.

Students and other spectators who have the good fortune to see the plays staged in Greece – several are put on every summer, primarily for foreign visitors – will hear them spoken in modern Greek, not the archaic speech of the originals, which most contemporary Athenians would not fully understand.

Certain periods in history are transcendent. Among them is the Periclean, during which the four great Athenian playwrights – Aeschylus, Sophocles, Euripides and the master of comedy, Aristophanes – knew one another. This concurrence, the emergence at one time of four supremely talented writers, is approximated again throughout the lengthy chronicle of the drama: in Spain, Germany, England, France, Scandinavia, Ireland, the United States. A golden age of artistic creativity occurs, a dazzling explosion of accomplishment, though not always simultaneously in every medium, painting, sculpture, music, poetry, drama.

Why such epochs appear has puzzled historians. Some point to this period in Greece, the fifth century BC, having coincided with the democratic rule that began with Pisistratus' election to office and ended about the time, some decades later, when democracy became corrupt and decadent and tyranny resumed. In such a society, with intellectual freedom prevailing, the arts have their best chance to flourish. Other historians argue that military triumphs that filled the city with pride, a spirit of confidence and buoyancy, led to its outpouring of great art. The bright age of playwriting in Athens came to a close with the city's later defeats at the century's end. But history offers many examples to the contrary, where the best art sprang up after dire military reverses, as in Germany following the First World War and in stricken, impoverished Italy after the Second. Still others assert an important factor in stimulating artists is climate, and that dark, rainy periods which oppress the spirit and induce brooding call forth work that is more searching and profound. Those holding this belief attempt to prove their theory by a study of weather records of past eras, and where the data do not exist they offer their own projections, though not always convincingly. Oswald Spenger had a novel suggestion, that heightened sunspot activity, which fills the atmosphere with an excess of cosmic rays, is what evoked abnormal artistic production.

Finally, it has been propounded that what counts above all is competition: a man of genius appears, and his example is a prod and challenge to his rivals, as Shakespeare and Goethe were in their effulgent span of days and Aeschylus in his.

Scion of an aristocratic family, Aeschylus was born in Eleusis; his having been resident there accounts for his intimate knowledge of the Eleusinian mysteries, the ritual of which doubtless impressed him deeply, though he was later accused of inadvertently betraying some aspect of them in one of his dramas. When he was twenty-six years old he had his first play accepted by the *archon* for the Great Dionysia. At least, it was submitted then; there is a measure of uncertainty about all the details of his life, and various sources provide contradictory items. In 490 BC, in his thirty-fifth year, he was in the army alongside his two brothers, helping to disperse the Persian horde at Marathon. (The law exempting actors from military service had not yet been proclaimed; he took up arms at various times until he was sixty.) His personal heroism on that occasion spread his fame. A painting to commemorate his martial deeds as well as those of one of his brothers was installed at the theatre. In 480 BC he was again in battle at Artemisium and then Salamis, and the following year at Plataea. By profession both a priest and an actor – dramatists often had that status – he had won his first dramatic prize in 484 BC, at the age of forty-one, between his bouts of soldiering, and was awarded it assuredly eleven times more, though L.R. Lind puts the number of his prizes at more than fifty. Adventurous, he undertook two journeys to Syracuse, in far-off Sicily – and, indeed, died there on his second visit, in 456 BC, in his sixty-ninth year. Playwrights tend to live long; perhaps it is not that the occupation is healthful, but rather that it takes a person of hardy constitution and vigorous drive to persist in this phase of the theatrical trade.

He is described as having been an eccentric young man. Some people deemed him mad, or at least as having the fits of frenzy or irrational possession that Plato attributes to poets. Legend says that his inspiration to be a playwright first came to him while he was in a grape arbour in a mystic trance, during which Dionysus appeared to him and commanded him to compose tragedies for the festival. He was deeply immersed from early youth in the Eleusinian mysteries, and the rhapsodic quality in his work may have been influenced by their ecstatic ritual and strain of Orientalism. Was he merely emotional, instinctive, in his authorship, and was he something of a hallucinated, automatic writer? Sophocles said of him: "He did what he ought to do, but did it without knowing." Less kindly gossip had it that he wrote best while imbibing deeply of the wine-cup. The Greeks, whose humour was always malicious, also spread the story that his death in Syracuse, where he was long favoured and much honoured at the court of Hieron, happened when an eagle, mistaking his bald pate for a rock and wishing to crack a tortoise shell on it, dropped its clutched prey and broke the old man's skull. Yet despite all this mockery he was deeply revered in Athens, and when he died a monument was dedicated to him; and, as has been said, his plays, in response to public clamour, were the first to be allowed revivals, inaugurating the theatre's permanent repertory.

His work is always on a grand, almost epic scale. He chooses large subjects – "slices of Homer" is the phrase frequently used for them – but he leaves his scenes somewhat rough-hewn, without the polish characteristic of Sophocles: his episodes do not have the subtle jointure, the smooth transitions, that his successors will contrive. His verse is rich in striking metaphor and imagery, his dialogue frequently has power and sharpness, but sometimes a crudity which prompts one classical scholar to complain that "He wields the pen as one more familiar with the spear; the warrior of Marathon does fierce battle with particles and phrases." But his audience was less knowledgeable, less critical, than those Sophocles and Euripides will have to please a few years later. Aptly, Gilbert Murray compares his first, rude work to that of an archaic sculptor whose *Kouroi* "stand with limbs stiff and countenance smiling and stony". It is claimed that he directed his own plays and acted in them. Overcoming any initial shortcomings, his mastery grew steadily. Even in old age, he learned from his younger rivals.

Of his scores of lost works, little more than the names are known. Some lines and fragments have been found here and there; some comments by his contemporaries afford other inklings. Knowledge of the myths on which he based his dramas allow guesses as to what might have been his subject-matter, if not his handling of it. Among his vanished scripts are the *Lycurgean* trilogy, concerning Dionysus and a king of Thrace who like Pentheus of Thebes scorns the god and rouses his ire; and a script recounting a similar fate, death, befalling Orpheus, also at the hands of maddened Bacchants; another about Hector and Achilles at the fall of Troy; and also *The Women of Etna*, set in Sicily, which was Aeschylus' second home; *The Thracian Women*, which concerned itself with the Homeric hero Ajax; and *Weighing of the Souls*, purportedly a piece laden with "cosmic speculation".

His dominant traits are simplicity of spirit, joined – as might be expected – with patriotic fervour, a strong strain of religiosity and moral seriousness. His temperament is markedly conservative, though he is identified in the history of theatre as a vital innovator. He is credited with introducing the second actor, a move from which has grown drama as we know it today, for it freed the action of total dependence on the chorus, making possible the development of more elaborate plots and more fully delineated characters. Dialogue could now be endlessly expanded. His work, naturally, is closer in form to the ancient dithyrambs than is that of his successors: he assigns a far larger share of lines to the chorus. In his first existing play, *The Suppliant Women*, the chorus predominates, and this is mostly true of *The Persians*, too. Both, then, deserve to be judged in that respect as "primitive".

The Suppliant Women, generally thought to be the oldest Athenian play now available – Harsh dates *The Persians* as earlier – tells of the fifty daughters of Danaus, King of Egypt, who are besought in marriage – impiously, because incestuously – by fifty cousins, the sons of Danaus' menacing brother Aegyptus. Taking flight, these harried virgins and their father reach Argos, where they ask asylum from

Pelasgus, its king. He hesitates to consent lest his act give offence to the more powerful Egyptians and plunge his city into war with them. The Danaids claim descent from the Argive princess Io and therefore are more definitely entitled to shelter. Desperate, the young women vow to defile the temple by hanging themselves at the altar. Furthermore, by refusing traditional hospitality Pelasgus will displease the gods. "I see and shudder," he declares. "There is no issue free from disaster."

But the elders of Argos unanimously vote to grant haven to the hapless young women: a democratic procedure! Just then, the sails of the pursuing suitors are beheld. A Herald has been sent by the Egyptians; with his followers, he brutally attempts to force the maidens to board the waiting ship. Instead, the jubilant chorus of girls turns towards the city, where Pelasgus will now afford them protection behind its high, fortified walls. Raising their voices joyfully and gratefully, they march from the *orchestra* safe and unwed. Their father, Danaus, deplores the "unholy love" the Egyptians had proposed.

Some scholars find the play more rewarding for what it reveals of the theatre's past than for what it foretells of the future: that is, it is still chiefly choral, the best example of what the dithyrambs were like. Though Aeschylus employs two actors, he treats one of them awkwardly. Danaus is inexpertly drawn. Yet it is believed that *The Suppliant Women* is the first work of the usual trilogy given at the festival, and this is only a fragment, with partial characterizations and many themes left dangling, incomplete. In the missing scripts, thought to be *The Men of Egypt* and *The Daughters of Danaus* – this final piece winning a first prize, either in 466 or 463 BC, but possibly composed much earlier – war between Argos and Egypt ensues, Pelasgus is slain and succeeded by Danaus, who ultimately is compelled to let his daughters marry their relentless cousins. His instructions are that on the marriage night they shall kill their unwanted new husbands. One bride, Hypermnestra, spares her mate, Lynceus, having fallen in love with him. For her disobedience, she ought to be punished most severely, but Aphrodite pardons her. Harsh suggests that here, as elsewhere, Aeschylus is involved with the nagging issue of "individual responsibility in a world where the divine voices sound conflicting".

Scholars have difficulty visualizing the staging. In addition to the principals, the action calls for the fifty daughters, the fifty suitors and a troupe of handmaidens for the Danaids bodyguards. How large was the cast? By this date the size of the chorus had been reduced; consequently it may be assumed that there were a host of supernumeraries, or that Aeschylus' prestige had risen to where he had permission to hire a far larger chorus than was now the rule. (A late twentieth-century version of the work is described further on.)

The play has a political background that is unstated. A military alliance between Athens and Argos was negotiated, and similar ties to Egypt were proposed, in an effort to divert that country from joining forces with Persia, the perpetual foe of Athens. The Athenian audience, which was sophisticated and deeply interested in such affairs, would have heard echoes of these diplomatic moves in the script. It may have been tact in choosing the right moment that delayed production of the play for thirty years, when presumably it was still relevant.

Since the leading characters are Egyptian, Aeschylus, who has an innate flair for spectacle, could make the most of the exotic costuming and masks, as well as opportunities for pageantry, the suppliants waving boughs and dancing before the altar, singing, with music of unusually intricate rhythm. Apparently for this play the *orchestra* was ringed with statues of the gods to whom the fearful young women pray for rescue, or else the Olympian images line the *skene*'s façade. The rising action is matched to an oncoming storm that is roiling the sea, tossing the ships at anchor nearby, threatening the approaching barque bearing the Herald.

The Suppliant Women displays many other qualities of the author: his tendency to educate and moralize, his "almost Hebraic intensity of religious feeling" and his poetic control, especially in choral writing, where his skill at mating the subtlest meaning and ephemeral mood to the right rhythm is repeatedly evident. All this is shown by his facility in giving voice to the despair of the maidens in odes of "startled, wild, uncouth language". Most significant, too, as H.D.F. Kitto says, is that even this early Aeschylus sounds his basic philosophical theme: a good, decent man is made to suffer for no reason that he can understand. The wisdom of the gods is inscrutable. "Through no Aristotelian flaw of character, through no deficiency of sense, intellect or morality, has the King (of Argos) fallen suddenly into this awful dilemma. A disharmony in the make-up of things, and a perfectly innocent man is broken. Here in the earliest of Greek tragedies is found one of the most purely tragic situations; the Flaw in the universe, which the philosophers will have none of, is plain enough to Aeschylus."

The chorus declares:

> What Zeus craves is not easily traced out.
> It is a flame in the dark,
> but the way of it is murky to the sight
> of men, mere mortals. . . .
> Cross are the ways
> and dark the forest openings of his thought.
> None can see through it.

Other themes, much used by Aeschylus later, are the struggle for dominance between male (in a "patriarchal" society) and female (in a "matriarchal" society); the opposition between Greek ways and Oriental (barbarian) customs; and the still Utopian value of lawful democracy as against wilful autocracy. In particular, these will recur in *The Persians* and the *Oresteia.*

It is the poetry that impresses most. To instance just a few lines (finely translated by Richard Lattimore), here is Danaus describing the approach of the Argive king:

> I see dust, the silent messenger of armament,
> but there's no silence in the axles that are turning
> in the wheels. I see the army, the sloped shields
> and shaken spears, the horses and curved chariots.

It is magnificent how, in a few words, the tread of a whole army is suggested, though on stage is beheld only one chariot, perhaps, and a small band of supernumeraries. Similarly, the unseen Egyptian ship is conjured up in vivid word-pictures:

> . . . I see
> their craft, for it is well in sight, no detail lost.
> I recognize the trim of the sail, the side bulwarks,
> the prow with eyes tracing ahead the vessel's course
> the steering oar rigged at the stem, by which she handles
> only too well, or so the ship's enemies think.
> Her seamen are seen plainly too, their swarthy limbs
> conspicuous in contrast to the white attire.

The Danaids have an exotic cast of features betokening their violent natures:

> O stranger maidens, it is hard for me to believe
> you when you say that you are born of Argive blood.
> For you are more like ladies of Africa
> from the show of you, not like the women of our land.
> Then too, the Cyprian look that's carved in female forms

> by male artificers is your look. They say, again,
> that nomad women, much as you are, sit astride
> their saddled camels and ride them as if they were horses.
> These live in the country next the Ethiopians.

An exquisite passage offers a metaphorical reference to the cowering maidens and birds of prey, who are likened to the rapacious Egyptians swooping down on their victims:

> If there stands near one who can read the cries of the birds,
> some native who hears our outcry
> will think he hears the cry of Tereus' wife
> Metis the queen, the pitiful
> nightingale, the hawk-driven
> who from the green and the brown leaves ever debarred
> mourns for her lost country
> combined with grief for the murder of Itys, her son.

(The poet is very fond of allusions to hunted birds and particularly to the nightingale.)

Another aspect of the play, and one also encountered in later scripts, is Aeschylus' abiding fascination with geography: Pelasgus recites a roll of place-names, much as will Clytemnestra in *Agamemnon.*

The Suppliant Women is imperfect, but the impress of genius is clearly discernible. This is equally true of *The Persians* (472 BC), widely believed to have been his next surviving script, though the date and placing have occasioned some argument, as has already been remarked. Possibly fifteen to twenty years had elapsed since what might be his last preserved text, the interim filled for him with service in the army and the writing of many now unavailable entries in the annual contest. The subject, the sea battle at Salamis, was very recent history, the play appearing a mere eight years after the actual event. His *choregus* for its presentation at the festival was none other than the perceptive Pericles, who had not yet ascended to power. Even so, it was bold of Aeschylus to undertake the venture, in as much as Phrynicus had gained great success with *The Women of Phoenicia* only four years earlier. Indeed, Aeschylus openly borrows some phrases from the earlier piece. Doubtless he drew far more inspiration from his personal participation in the famous battle, having been a spearman aboard one of

Themistocles' ships, together with the lingering pride he shared with his fellow Athenians in his city's triumph over its hated, aggressive enemy.

The play, as did Phryincus', occurs not in Greece but in Susa, at the palace of the Persian monarch; several reasons have been suggested for this. One is that Aeschylus would have been forbidden by the *archon* to show and name living Athenians in a solemn work at the festival, and another was his need of a scene remote in place, if not in time, since he was writing – as Greek artistic tradition dictated – a conventionalized, poetic drama. But even more, the play could only be a tragedy if it exposed the shattered emotions of the Persians, the defeated, rather than the Greeks, the exultant victors.

The sea battle itself, of course, could not be staged: it could only be reported by a messenger, who consequently has the leading role. In his first-hand account, Aeschylus proves how well he could portray the horrible sights and sounds of warfare:

> Our own ships fouled on our own ships with brazen
> beaks, and sheared the ranged oars all down the side,
> while the Greek galleys, taking every advantage,
> circled, enclosed, slammed, and the hulls of our ships
> rolled over, you could no longer see the water
> so crammed it was with ships' wreckage and men killed.
> The rocks of the shore and spines of reefs were clotted with dead
> bodies, and every ship of our barbarian host
> still afloat sought to row away in orderless flight.
> But our men! They speared them, mauled them with the stumps of oars
> and offbreak of the wreckage like a haul of fish
> or school of tunny, and the mingled noise of groans
> and high screams was everywhere on the open bay
> until night darkened and the eye of day withdrew.
> [Translation: Richard Lattimore]

Savage and true! Aeschylus never glorifies war or advocates launching one.

Oriental colour is lent to *The Persians* by its setting and characters, the rich barbaric costumes and masks. The actors wore turbans for heightened verisimilitude. As with *The Suppliant Women*, the work is largely choral. It has little action. The dowager queen and nobles of the Persian court are waiting to hear the outcome of the fateful conflict. First they tell how strikingly accoutred are their armies, and then pray to their gods for a great victory. A real advance over *The Suppliant Women* is the rounded characterization of the dowager queen, Atossa, whose son Xerxes is away at the head of the Persian forces. When the messenger brings news of the catastrophe at sea, he lists those killed, never answering her unspoken question, until the anguished queen, overcoming her regal pride, asks, 'Who has *not* fallen?' Atossa then learns that her son has been spared, though his supposedly invincible fleet has been routed and destroyed.

An unusual scene is that in which the ghost of Darius, Xerxes' father and far more sovereign predecessor on the Eastern throne, responds to incantations and rises from his tomb to prophesy further dire humiliations for his degenerate son and decadent Persian satrapy. He even predicts in detail the subsequent encounter at Plataea, where the Persian army is to be wholly annihilated. This ingenious contrivance allows Aeschylus to describe that subsequent battle (in which, one recalls, he also fought), though Plataea occurred some years after the date at which *The Persians* is set. This incident of the return of Darius in the play brings to mind again the theory that tragedy had in it reminiscences of the tomb-rites and ancestor-worship of primitive Greeks.

Aeschylus, in this work, takes considerable poetic licence with historical fact: he compresses the time element, making the battle of Salamis more singular and crucial than it was in reality, by omitting references to other crises and turning points in the very long campaign: not quite so much hung on the outcome of this one encounter. He also falsifies no little the true characters of Darius and Xerxes, portraying one wiser and braver, the other more weak and craven, than they were.

The play lacks the often observed unity of place: each of the three main episodes at Susa has a different setting. What is justifiably admired is the author's ability, as in *The Suppliant Women* and later works, to endow his play with a wide scope, an almost epic breadth, by inference alone. The choral passages unfold relevant details of what has happened before the current action, or what is happening elsewhere at the moment, or what is going to ensue. Aeschylus has this gift for filling in, with the help of an eloquent and always well-informed chorus, the former incidents and causes leading to present events, and then again – through the chorus, or an oracle, or a prophetic vision such as that of the ghostly Darius – revealing what is to follow. From this, as well as from the blunt and simple yet intense nature of the passions voiced by his larger-than-life characters, comes the illusion of size his tragedies consistently create.

Once more he uses his story to illustrate a profound moral lesson. In *The Persians*, apparently, he hoped to show how the *hubris* of Xerxes led to his downfall: ambitious and vain without warrant, he has dared not only to assault the Athenians – an autocrat hurling hordes against a democratic people – but has also outraged their gods. Aeschylus' purpose is not merely to boast of a recent, stirring Greek victory; he also intends to create a religious drama. The Persian invaders have despoiled the statues of Greek divinities, desecrated their altars and burned their temples. For such acts the "barbarians", and especially Xerxes, are to be punished by divine fiat. Such is the warning spoken by the omniscient Darius, risen from his marble-capped grave:

> Into the third generation the piled dunes of the dead
> voiceless shall indicate before the eyes of men
> that one who is born mortal should not think too high.
> For lawless violence comes to flower and bears a crop
> of ruin, and the reaping of it is full of tears.

Indeed, the gods themselves strongly intervene, enlisting the sword-wielding Greeks as their weapon to smite the impious Xerxes.

Overall, *The Persians* is not Aeschylus at his best. It is too slow-moving, lacks clear focus, has little theatrical impact. But it too is believed to have been part of a trilogy, the second panel, preceded by *Phineus*, of which little is known, except that it revolves about a seer who is blinded by Zeus for revealing the god's plans, and depicts the slaying of the Harpies by Boreas' sons. *The Persians* was followed, it is likely, by *Glaucus of Potnias*, the content of which is the subject of even vaguer and more confused speculation. John Ferguson comments: "We can see how a [first] play might be detached from its sequence and stand on its own. But the middle play depends upon its context; if you detach the props from both sides it must surely fall." He adds: "Yet we are told that Aeschylus assented to the performance of *The Persians*, detached from its trilogy, in Sicily."

In Ferguson's view: "*The Persians* is not a play as plays have generally been understood. Nothing happens. . . . Xerxes arrives, though his arrival changes nothing. This is a play of situation. Most tragedies lead up to and away from a moment of pathos. Here, pathos is inherent throughout, and we as audience and the participants on the stage pass through foreboding, confirmation, explication, and emotional response."

The pathos is conveyed in dark-hued poetry. In Ferguson's translation, a prophecy of doom is enunciated by the chorus in the prologue:

So from the land of Persia
the flower of manhood is departed,
and the whole land of Asia which nursed them
grieves with unbearable longing,
parents and wives count the days
and tremble at the long-drawn time.

Certain key words are repeated – "departed", "fallen", "much-golden" – like leitmotifs, and Ferguson wonders if similar and matching repetition occurred in the accompanying music. The "much-golden" is used in references to the Persians, their ostentatious wealth, their ornaments of dress; even their weapons are gilded, in contrast to the naked steel of the Greeks' swords. Such display of gold is effeminate to Greek eyes. In battle, too, the Persians shoot arrows, the Greeks hurl deadly spears.

Not only is unity of space violated, but also unity of time. The disappointed Xerxes returns from Salamis after a passage of only a few lines chanted by the chorus. A similar compression of time, a hasty elapse, is found again when Agamemnon returns to his domain from Troy. It is a stage device that works surprisingly well, winning a ready acceptance from the spectators. Aeschylus early discovered how to accomplish it.

What is remarkable is the empathy that Aeschylus has for the grieving Persians, the compassion with which they are drawn by this former soldier, who time and again at mortal risk fought against them. All those at the court in Susa, save only Xerxes, have dignity and courage; especially Atossa and Darius, who are noble, imposing figures. Most details of the battle are authentic, and the poet lends further convincing colour by his accurate use of Persian names and a sprinkling of idioms.

Ferguson's summary is apt: "*The Persians* is not a great play, but we can see a great dramatist behind it in the depth with which he treats his theme, and not least in language, spectacle, and dramatic effect."

In 466 BC Sophocles took the first prize away from Aeschylus, who won again the following year with *The Seven Against Thebes*, the third play in a trilogy, the missing parts of which are *Laius* and *Oedipus*. After the exposure of Oedipus' unwitting sin and his expulsion from Thebes, it was decided that the kingship should alternate between his sons, Eteocles and Polynices, brothers sharply jealous of each other. Polynices kept to his vow, abdicating after a year; Eteocles, once enthroned, refused to relinquish his rule. A fierce quarrel resulted; Polynices fled the city, sought his exiled, blind father, asked help. Oedipus, enraged, cursed both of his heirs and prophesied they would die by the sword.

Polynices formed an alliance with Adrastus, King of Argos, by marriage to a daughter of the royal house. Then, with an army headed by himself and six champions renowned for wielding axes and other sharp-edged weapons, he returned and laid siege to Thebes, he himself and each of his chief supporters attacking one of its seven gates.

Here the play begins; it is concerned solely with Eteocles. His hated brother Polynices, encamped outside the city, never appears. The second actor's role is a Spy, who reports to Eteocles all preparations in the enemy's quarters. The chorus serves as a band of Theban young women panic-stricken, hysterical at the prospect of the rapine and slaughter that might follow a sack of Thebes.

With heroic dignity, Eteocles methodically gets ready to repel the impending assault. As he learns the identity of each of the seven challengers, and to which opening in the walls each has been assigned, he chooses suitable defenders from among the best Theban warriors, matching them man to man in view of their individual qualities. At the seventh gate he himself must make a stand, having no one else on whom he can fully rely. Only at the last moment does he discover that he will oppose the traitorous Polynices, heading the foe's contingent there. The chorus begs him to refrain: the spectacle of brother against brother is intolerable. In an outburst of long-pent fury, the hitherto calm and rational Eteocles pours forth his resentment against Polynices. The bloody duel occurs off-stage; the Messenger brings word that Oedipus' dark prophecy has been fulfilled: the brothers have slain each other. Having refused to divide the kingship, they have reached a different settlement (in words Englished by John Stuart Blackie):

> They strove for land, and did demand
> An equal share.
> In the ground deep, deep, where now they sleep,
> There's land to spare.

Despite unfavourable odds, the remaining six Theban defenders are victorious: clearly the gods side with them against a defector who has brought strangers to punish his native city. The challengers have been too proud and boastful. At last, the siege is lifted.

Antigone and Ismene, sisters of the dead young men, come to mourn for them, and Antigone vows to bury the rebellious Polynices, though the Theban senate has issued an edict against his interment. The introduction of a new conflict at the tag end of the play is deemed spurious, however, possibly added by some other hand, seeking to dovetail this tragedy into Sophocles' much admired

Antigone. It is an artistic blemish because it suggests a fresh and unresolved problem at the final moment.

Though the *hubris* of the unseen Polynices is clear – he has violated his blood loyalty to Thebes and his benighted family – some commentators feel Eteocles is wholly blameless and his death illustrates once again Aeschylus' feeling about "the senseless shape of things". Like Pelasgus in *The Suppliant Women,* Eteocles is an innocent victim of malign fate, above all in being forced to oppose and kill his own brother. But perhaps this exculpation of Eteocles overlooks his original fault in refusing to share the crown with his brother after having pledged to do so.

Another theme enunciated by Aeschylus in *The Persians,* and found again in the *Oresteia,* is that of inherited guilt. Both Laius and Oedipus gravely sin – Laius, a sodomist, has been cursed by Pelops for a dastardly act – and his house is horribly stained: Eteocles and Polynices are the last of their line, the family taint having descended on them. Aeschylus does not imply that the warring brothers, born of incest between Oedipus and Jocasta, are without fault: they have inherited the worst qualities of their reckless sire and lecherous grandsire. Theirs is, by heredity, a psychological predisposition to violence and unrestrained ambition, and in action a lack of morality. Like his father, too, Eteocles is both clear-sighted yet apt to be blinded by anger.

Much praised is the excellent balance between Eteocles' role and that of the chorus, the apportionment of the lines. Yet many commentators pronounce the play dull and static in places. With the antagonist always off-stage, it lacks visible conflict. Similarly absent are verbal exchanges and psychological interplay between the hostile brothers. What is said to have helped at the original performance was the "superlative verve and skill" of the dancing by Telestes, presumably the chorus leader.

A much kinder appraisal of the play comes from H.D.F. Kitto who deems it a perfect example of what he calls "Old Tragedy", that is, tragedy composed for only one or two actors, and more lyrical than dramatic in essence. In this work the role of the second actor, the Spy, is wholly subsidiary. He does no more than supply information needed by Eteocles. Lyrical tragedy is exactly the right form for a single actor given to thinking aloud, agonizing to himself, with the chorus as sympathetic echo or foil. The hero is presented alone with his fate and ever more engulfed by it: from this grows tension as his character is revealed and tested in a "terrific crescendo". Kitto suggests that up to this point Aeschylus had not introduced the third actor, because he had no need for him, though much later he did borrow his presence from Sophocles when the requirements of his work changed. So far his dominant subject was man's relation to God: for a religious writer such as Aeschylus, one actor was enough, and lyrical tragedy – the tragedy of character – was the most suitable vehicle.

John Ferguson also expresses special appreciation of this drama:

> *Seven Against Thebes* is a play of unexpected power. It does not show us Aeschylus at his very greatest; for that we have to wait for *Agamemnon* and *Prometheus*. The restriction on the actors, both in number and treatment, causes a certain stiffness. Yet within the medium, it is masterly. The title, whether Aeschylus' or not, tells us something about the play. . . . The main characters do not appear. They are brought to our imagination partly by sounds off-stage, partly by the scout who acts as a go-between, partly by the hysteria of the chorus, partly by the solid, ominously silent departure of the six champions, partly by Eteocles. The chorus is magnificently handled, with a combination of musical lyricism and dramatic realism found in no other play. Eteocles too is realistic; perhaps for the first time we feel we are encountering a full human being on the Attic stage. But at the last the theme of this play, considered in isolation from the rest of the trilogy, is war, and it is the dramatist's success in evoking the emotions of the beleaguered city, whether in terror or reasoned defiance, that arouses our fear and our pity.

Analysing the poetry, Ferguson finds that Aeschylus inserts a principal image that serves as a motif throughout: it is of the sea and ships, to which allusions are made incessantly. The writing has great vividness, summoning up noises of war. For each woman, in her panic, "The clang of hoofs on the soil of my country rings in my ears. The sound draws near, it takes wings, it crashes down with the irresistible thunder of a mountain-torrent." Again: "Do you hear the clang of shields? Do you not hear it?" And again: "I shudder at the clang. It is the sound of a host of spears." And: "I hear the rattle of chariots circling the city." And: "The wheels are weighted, the axles groaning. Artemis, have mercy! The very air is mad with the shimmer of spears." And: "A shower of stones on top the battlements! Apollo, have mercy! The thrumming of bronze-bound shields at our gates!" All the gods are frenziedly beseeched, one by one. The clamour of war, the nerve-tightening fear it induces, are chillingly, viscerally captured and conveyed. The sea image returns:

> A surge of crested soldiers is seething
> round our city, whipped up by the winds of war.
> [Translation: John Ferguson]

Along with a patriotic fervour, a condemnation of the havoc of war resonates throughout the work. To borrow from Ferguson's English version once more:

When a city falls, many
disasters ensue.
There is conflagration, the whole
city is stained with smoke.
The god of war breathes fury,
slays the masses, defiles holiness.
There is tumult in the town, the network
of towers rises against it.
One man faces another
and falls by the spear.
Cries stream with blood
from breast-fed babies,
fresh-nursed cries resound.
Pillage and pursuit, blood-sisters are there,
one plunderer passes another,
plunderless plead with plunderless,
willing to have a partner,
longing for the like or more.
What comes of it all?

Could that succinct description be surpassed? Has it ever been?

Near the end, the bodies of the slain brothers are ceremoniously wheeled in, and the nautical metaphors are introduced once more.

Now, friends, row down the wind
of your tears, beating hands on your head,
with a stroke which speeds past the river of Death
the sacred ship with black sails, the ship of grief
which Apollo may not board, nor the sun lighten,
to the unseen shore which awaits us all.

The date of *Prometheus Bound* is uncertain, some authorities placing it between *The Seven Against*

Thebes and *The Oresteia*, others putting it later, for the reason that a third actor appears briefly in the prologue. Ferguson guesses that it was written in 457 or 456 BC, during Aeschylus' last stay in Sicily, since the text contains a description of an eruption by Mount Etna and yields other more nebulous clues, some of them semantic – "traces of Orphic language" – and references to a Sicilian physician, founder of an academy of medicine on the island. If Ferguson's guess is valid, the *Prometheus* would be Aeschylus' last surviving work. Beyond doubt, though, it falls into the same category of Old Tragedy to which Kitto consigned *The Seven*: it centres on the figure of the chained Titan and is largely a monologue or tirade by this agonized culture-hero who on behalf of mankind has dared to defy Zeus, King of Olympus. Equally unclear is whether *Prometheus* is the first or second panel of a trilogy.

In any event, *Prometheus Bound* differs substantially from Aeschylus' other known scripts: it is a religious allegory with no human characters, only personified natural forces such as Power, Violence and a galaxy of minor gods comprised of Hephaestus, Oceanus and Hermes. As in *The Seven*, the hero is pitted against an unseen antagonist: here, Zeus. Of importance here is not what happens, but what the hero feels, endures, learns. "Revelation, not action, is the source of its dramatic tension."

According to the myth, which exists in various forms, Prometheus has abetted Zeus in a struggle to overthrow his father Cronos, King of the Gods, so that Zeus himself might own the Olympian throne. In possession of supreme power, Zeus has proved cruelly despotic: "New-made kings are evil." Prometheus, the creator of man, fashions him of clay. The tyrannical Zeus wishes to destroy mankind and shape a new race to replace it; Prometheus protects the still frail and stupid creatures he has brought to life. He infuses them with hope and intelligence to help them survive and prosper, and teaches them tool-making and the arts. Finally he steals fire from heaven for them. Enraged, Zeus orders Power, Violence and Hephaestus – the last of these, god of the forge – to bind the rebellious Titan to a jutting rock in the Caucasian Mountains, in a spot of endless, lonely silence at the end of the world, with scorching sun and heat. Hephaestus reluctantly assists in this task. Here the cosmic drama opens.

After a short time the three captors leave; the fettered Prometheus is left solitary, in brooding, angry silence. Even in this far-out, rocky isolation he is not alone for long: the Oceanids, a chorus of the daughters of Oceanus, soar towards him – they are perhaps lowered by the cranes – and offer consolation, and then stay to hear the writhing Prometheus' groans and furious charges of crimes by the heavenly monarch who has taken such bitter vengeance against him. (One must keep in mind that in the Greek conception of divinity, Zeus is ruler of the universe, but even so his power is limited: he may torture the insubordinate Titan but not wholly destroy him, for Prometheus too is immortal, and

Zeus could be deposed, just as he has overthrown Cronos, who in turn mercilessly usurped sway over Olympus from the grasp of his own father Uranus.)

The chorus pauses in its tearful hymns of comfort. Oceanus flies in astride a winged monster, a four-legged griffin, to counsel Prometheus' submission to the dictates of Zeus, advice that is rejected by the cruelly crucified Titan. This episode briefly alters the mood, for Oceanus, a craven and politic trimmer, is a semi-comic figure. He departs, frustrated in his mission, and somewhat fearful at being seen near the dangerous subversive. The Oceanids renew their lament for Prometheus. Next enters Io, doomed to journey endlessly about the world and to be incessantly pursued by gadflies. Once beloved of Zeus, she too has been made to suffer, transformed into an endlessly tormented heifer by Hera, Zeus' jealous wife. (Cataloguing Homerically the past and future wandering of Io, Aeschylus once more displays his fondness for geographical descriptions, both factual and fabulous.)

Prometheus, who unknown to Zeus has a gift of prophecy – his name means "foresight" – assures Io that after further ordeals he and she will once again be free. Destiny is on their side: inexorable Necessity. He foresees a union between the King of Heaven and Thetis whereby a son will be begotten, who will murderously succeed his father, the adulterer. Later, a descendant of Io – Herakles – will be Prometheus' saviour.

When Io leaves, Hermes appears: Prometheus' boast of having a secret vital to Zeus brings the gods' swift messenger to demand that the pinioned Titan divulge it. Otherwise his tortures will grow steadily worse: when a quake splits the crags of this promontory he will be swallowed by the earth, only to rise into the light again, where a sharp-beaked vulture or eagle will endlessly feast on his liver. The Titan, still obdurate, shouts his defiance. At the play's close, the threatened cataclysm is starting: The chorus flees in terror, and Prometheus begins to sink out of sight, to Tartarus, crying:

> . . . the earth is convulsed.
> Out of the deep the roaring of thunder
> rolls past, and flickering fire of the lightning
> flashes out, and the whirlwinds
> roll up the dust, and the blasts of all storms
> leap at each other, declaring
> a war of the winds,
> and the air and the sea are confounded.
> These, most clearly, are strokes from Zeus

coming upon me to cause me fear.
O my glorious mother, O Heaven
with circle of light that is common to everyone
you see me and see this injustice.
[Translation: Rex Warner]

(Prometheus is the son of Themis, goddess of Earth – hence his talent with clay – and also of Right and Law.)

This bold Titan, clenching his fists, shouting against all threats and pains visited on him by Heaven, is a figure cherished by later poets: he is likened to the Old Testament Job, to Milton's Lucifer, to Goethe's Faust – indeed, he was much admired by Goethe, and also by Shelley, who in emulation composed a verse-drama *Prometheus Unbound* (the title, also, of a succeeding but lost play in Aeschylus' trilogy). He was a model used by Byron, the wild-spirited Romantic. Prometheus, fire-thief, an enskyed culture hero starkly portrayed in this powerful passion play, is the archetype of all great rebels and divine scapegoats, all martyred and self-sacrificial lovers of mankind. Also, all the repeated themes abounding in Aeschylus' other works are read into this tragic allegory: it is another affirmation of the need to oppose tyranny in whatever form it takes, even if it be the despotism of a malign god.

Considering Aeschylus' reputation for religious orthodoxy, this interpretation of the play is startling. But some consider it a gross misconception of what this earnest Greek poet was attempting to say. He was called "god-intoxicated". True, the play is an early, ambitious, daring effort to probe into the problem of the existence of suffering, evil and injustice in a god-ruled universe. One familiar answer has been that God and His workings are inscrutable, beyond human grasp; hence He must be obeyed. To defy Him blindly, as this Titan has done, is folly, *hubris.*

Prometheus Bound is only part of a trilogy; it is recorded that at the end of the third play Prometheus and Zeus are reconciled. In attaining this rapprochement, Zeus relents no little and grows more kindly, while Prometheus has been taught by terrible experience that he must accept limits, "accomplish his purpose within the nature of things". Knowledge may bring suffering, and the ability to read the future may well be a curse, not a blessing, as is shown again in the figure of Cassandra, the unhappy seer in this poet's *Agamemnon.*

What is most interesting and significant here is Aeschylus' apparent idea of an "evolving" God, a deity who changes and learns to love mankind, even as Promethean man learns to love Him in turn. A very modern theological approach!

If *Prometheus Bound* is static on the stage, its subject is highly dramatic, as is the intensity of its poetic lines. Even though the trilogy's conclusion might have mollified most of the city's priests, it must have taken courage for Aeschylus to have composed Prometheus' vehement tirades against the supreme God and to have his actor utter them while facing a huge, often riotous audience at a sacred festival. But there are no reports of disturbances provoked by those passages: perhaps this play, despite its seeming heresy, contained truths so close to home for those spectators that collectively they heard it in compulsive quiet.

The image most often repeated in the dialogue is that of "healing". The Promethean tragic flaws are pride and intransigence. An intellectual rebel, he has not rightly interpreted Zeus' intention, which might have been to create an even higher race of human beings, more nearly perfect than those slapped together from lowly clay.

Two years before his death, Aeschylus brought forth *The Oresteia*, a trilogy derived from Homer's grim account of the ill-fated offspring of Atreus, King of Argos. This great work is preserved intact; the most famous part is the first play, *Agamemnon*. Some speak of this trilogy as the highest achievement in the history of drama; at the very least, it must be acknowledged as a work of marvellous power and meaning. It has continued to haunt the imaginations of a hundred generations.

A close study of *Agamemnon* reveals certain fundamentals of drama, and of Greek tragedy in particular. Since the play is almost 2,500 years old it is in a form that seems alien to the modern theatregoer. Furthermore, it is based on several complicated legends not fully familiar to the average playgoer or reader; it is filled with allusions that often call for scholarly explication and – yes – footnotes, though here there are none.

The complex mythological background also serves to clarify many other Greek dramas based on the same melodramatic Homeric theme, including several scripts by Sophocles and Euripides: Atreus and his brother, Thyestes, are descendants of Tantalus of Phrygia and his son Pelops, both crime-stained; this tradition of violence continues in the family. Atreus and Thyestes, in turn, kill their stepbrother. Later they themselves become fierce foes, when Thyestes seduces Atreus' wife (some versions say their own sister, Aerope, and others say a handsome youth beloved of the bisexual Atreus). In a deed of incredible vengeance, Atreus slays several of his brother's young children, dismembers them, has their thin bones and tender flesh cooked in a stew, invites the hated Thyestes to dinner, and serves him the parts of his children. A surviving son, Aegisthus, a child of incest – his mother is Thyestes' daughter – has sworn to even the score with his murderous uncle Atreus and all of his line. The details of this hideous story were known to those Athenians acquainted with Homer's epic who could tell others in the audience why the House of Atreus was blood-smeared and cursed.

The famed warrior kings, Menelaus and Agamemnon, are sons of Atreus. Both lay suit to the beauteous Helen. When Menelaus finally wins her, he extracts a vow of aid from his rivals if ever anyone should take Helen away from him.

Paris, good-looking son of Priam of Troy, is asked by three goddesses to judge which is the most fair. Aphrodite, goddess of love, succeeds in bribing him, promising him possession of the world's most beautiful woman. Paris visits the palace of Menelaus, furtively woos Helen and prevails upon her to run away with him to Troy.

Enraged, Menelaus calls upon her former suitors to keep their pledge and join in reducing Troy and recapturing his wife. Meanwhile, his brother Agamemnon has wed Clytemnestra, sister of Helen; they have three children: Elektra, Iphigenia and Orestes. Heeding his brother's summons, Agamemnon joins forces with him and is voted leader of the assembled Greek army, an honour he coveted and in which he much glories.

At Aulis, *en route*, the huge Greek fleet is becalmed. No wind comes, or storms arise; the flotilla cannot sail. The encamped troops grow restive; many talk of abandoning the expedition. Seeking advice from Calchas, an oracle, the brother–kings are told that Agamemnon must sacrifice his daughter Iphigenia to the offended goddess Artemis. He hesitates: he knows that his queen, Clytemnestra, will never assent to the death of her child, for any reason whatsoever. He sends back to Argos a misleading message that he plans a marriage between Iphigenia and the great hero Achilles. Proudly, Clytemnestra comes with the girl, expecting to participate in an elaborate celebration. Instead, arriving at Aulis, she learns how cruelly she and the girl have been tricked by the wily, ruthless Agamemnon. The virgin Iphigenia is seized and slain in sacrificial rites before the awed gaze of the entire army.

With dark and burning hatred in her heart, Clytemnestra goes back to Argos and rules there during the long absence of her husband. Aegisthus, the angry cousin of Agamemnon, becomes her lover and plots with her to kill the Argive king when and if he comes home from the war, which drags on for ten costly years. During this time, Elektra – the other daughter of Agamemnon, and perhaps overly attached to him – has proved troublesome and as punishment is married off to a peasant. The boy–prince, Orestes, has fled from Aegisthus to safety in far-off exile with his tutor.

Aeschylus begins his trilogy at this point. On the parapet of a watchtower in Argos stands a lonely old sentry who gazes at the still dark sky and the far reaches of the just dawning sea. In a beautiful evocation of the scene, the brightening water and the waning constellations, the watchman deplores his solitary task. In lyrical rhyme worthy of Swinburne, in Murray's translation, he grumbles:

This waste of year-long I have prayed
God for some respite, watching elbow-stayed,
As sleuth-hounds watch, above the Atreidae's hall,
Till well I know yon midnight festival
Of swarming stars, and them that lonely go,
Bearers to man of Summer and of snow,
Great lords and shining, throned in heavenly fire.

He is waiting, as he has for weary months and years, for word from Troy of that far city's ultimate fall and the war's ending. He represents Aeschylus' full-scale use, for the first time, of the third actor, who will also play the all-important messenger. He not only sets the mood, but also stands for the ordinary man who hates war and military duties, as opposed to such glory-seekers as the king. As Kitto points out, however, Aeschylus, in contrast to Sophocles, never uses the third actor to complicate the action or alter the plot.

Some scholars read the watchman's role differently, suggesting that he is not a simple, neutral onlooker but instead a spy keeping track of what is happening locally and about to report to whomever pays for his services.

Suddenly a remote glimmer of light increases to a blaze of fire, a beacon's light. The guard reports to the palace, and torches are lit there. A triumph-cry is heard from within, and Queen Clytemnestra and her train of attendants hurry forth and kneel before the altar. At the same time the chorus enters, a group of Argive elders, and the full dawn breaks. Why is the queen praying and offering incense and sacrifices to the gods? they ask. She does not reply, but hastens back into the royal dwelling to complete preparations for her hated husband's return.

The chorus, bewildered, recounts the tragic history of the House of Atreus, and especially of the death of the innocent Iphigenia. They tell how Calchas, the oracle, decreed it, and how Agamemnon, to satisfy his ambition, yielded to the revolting demand. The story is unfolded impressionistically, not in a straightforward narrative; it shuttles back and forth in time, touching on highlights, like the memory-focus process itself; Aeschylus does not assume that the audience has full knowledge of the ugly legend.

And winds, winds blew from Strymon River,
Unharboured, starving, winds of waste endeavour,
Man-blinding, pitiless to cord and bulwarks,

And the waste of days was made long, more long,
Till the flower of Argos was aghast and withered;
Then through the storm rose the War-seer's song,
And told of medicine that should tame the tempest,
But bow the Princes to a direr wrong.
Then "Artemis," he whispered, he named the name;
And the brother Kings they shook in the hearts of them,
And smote on the earth their staves, and the tears came.

But the King, the elder, hath found voice and spoken:
A heavy doom, sure, if God's will were broken:
But to slay my own child, who my house delighteth,
Is that not heavy? That her blood should flow
On her father's hand, hard beside an altar?
My path is sorrow whereso'er I go.
Shall Agamemnon fail his ships and people,
And the hosts of Hellas melt as melts the snow?
They cry, they thirst, for a death that shall break the spell,
For a Virgin's blood.

Yet faced with this harsh dilemma, Agamemnon yields to his ingrained ambition:

To the yoke of Must-be he bowed him slowly,
And a strange wind within his bosom tossed,
A wind of dark thought, unclean, unholy;
And he rose up, daring to the uttermost,
For men are boldened by a Blindness, straying
Toward base desire, which brings grief hereafter,
Yea, and itself is grief;
So this man hardened to his own child's slaying,
As help to avenge him for a woman's laughter
And bring his ships relief!

Next, the chorus offers a superbly clear picture of the tremulous Iphigenia's last moments:

> Her "Father, Father," her sad cry that lingered,
> Her virgin heart's breath they held all as naught,
> Those bronze-clad witnesses and battle-hungered;
> And there they prayed, and when the prayer was wrought
> He charged the young men to uplift and bind her,
> As ye lift a wild kid, high above the altar,
> Fierce-huddling forward, fallen, clinging sore
> To the robe that wrapt her; yea, bids them hinder
> The sweet mouth's utterance, the cries that falter,
>   – His curse for evermore! –
>
> With violence and a curb's voiceless wrath,
> Her stole of saffron then to the ground she threw,
> And her eye with an arrow of pity found its path
> To each man's heart that slew:
> A face in a picture, striving amazedly;
> The little maid who danced at her father's board,
> The innocent voice man's love came never nigh,
> Who joined to his her little paean-cry
> When the third cup was poured.

(The saffron stole is a symbol of her chastity. The paean cry, at the third cup, is an allusion to a domestic sacred ritual.)

With foreboding, the chorus continues to relate the fateful past incident and moralize, expressing a grim hope: "Only may good from all this evil flower . . ."

Clytemnestra and her train of attendants re-enter from the palace. She is in a state of high excitement. Once more the elders question her, asking the reason for her preparations. She tells them: "the Greeks have taken Troy". They are incredulous. How can she know this, their leader demands. She repeats, with strong certainty, "Ilion is ours."

Aeschylus had learned by now that a drama gains power by exploiting two kinds of conflict. One is the basic opposition of individual temperaments, values or goals that so often divide human beings. The other and lesser kind, because it is on the surface, though it still fulfils an important role in building theatrical impact, is the vocal contradiction required by effective dialogue on stage. So now the chorus chides the queen for having invented or unwittingly imagined her news. Says the leader of the chorus, deprecatingly: "Such joy comes knocking at the gate of tears." By this he means that Clytemnestra has been anxious to hear such news and hence has too readily fancied it.

She is offended by their scepticism and parries it. "Aye," she grants, guilefully, "'tis a faithful heart that eye declares."

Greek audiences liked irony, and for them there was much that was ironical in Clytemnestra's declaration of her love for her loathed, faithless husband.

Again, the leader of the chorus insists on knowing what proof she has of the fall of distant Troy. He still believes that her news is merely wish-fulfilment. Clytemnestra is adamant. Her word is true, "unless a god hath lied". The leader asks: "Some dream-shape came to thee in speaking guise?" Clytemnestra greets this question with scorn: "Who deemeth me a dupe of drowsing eyes?" The leader: "Some word within that hovereth without wings?" Clytemnestra: "Am I a child to hearken to such things?" Leader: "Troy fallen – But how long? When fell she, say?" The queen replies: "The very night that fathered this new day."

This exchange is evidence of Aeschylus' rare craft and theatrical instinct. Finally, the leader, still sceptical that the queen could have the word from Troy so quickly, asks: "And who of heralds with such fury came?"

The message has reached the queen by a series of fire-signals. This passage, or aria, is a magnificent Homeric catalogue, compact of striking imagery, and again revelatory of Aeschylus' liking of such lists, a fondness he shared with much of his audience; people in that still narrow world were fascinated by geography, by place-names; in addition, the Greeks were bold voyagers and traders, explorers.

Clytemnestra recounts (sings):

> A Fire-god, from Mount Ida scattering flame
> Whence starting, beacon after beacon burst
> Told Hermes' Lemnian Rock, whose answering sign
> Was caught by towering Athos, the divine,
> With pines immense – yea, fishes of the night

Swam skyward, drunken with that leaping light,
Which swelled like some strange sun, 'til dim and far
Makistos' watchmen marked a glimmering star.

She describes how the signals were sent from peak to peak:

A far light beyond the Eurîpus tells
That word hath reached Massapion's sentinels.
They beaconed back, then onward with a high
Heap of dead heather flaming to the sky.
And onward still . . .
Across the Asôpus like a beaming moon
The great word leapt, and on Kitheiron's height
Uproused a new relay of racing light.
. . . Out over Lake Gorgopis then it floats,
To Aigiplanctos, waking the wild goats,
Crying for "Fire, more Fire!" and the fire was reared,
Stintless and high, a stormy streaming beard,
That waved in flame beyond the promontory
Rock-ridged, that watches the Saronian sea,
Kindling the night.

The message is always intact:

. . . To the Atreidae's roof it came,
A light true-fathered of Idaean flame.
Torch-bearer after torchbearer, behold
The tale thereof in stations manifold,
Each one by each made perfect ere it passed,
And Victory in the first as in the last.

In all, this aria consists of thirty-seven lines of superlative poetry of which these few are excerpts.

Here, throughout, the translation is Murray's.

Clytemnestra offers her generous prayer that the victorious Greeks will spare "Ilion's conquered shrines"; the conquerors should be free of offence against the gods of any people, even a hostile one.

She returns to her palace. The chorus, in a chant, summons up a vision of her sister, Helen, the beauteous queen whose dereliction has brought on all this long misery and destruction. Also of Menelaus, whom she has betrayed:

> She hath left among her people a noise of shield and sword,
> A tramp of men armed where the long ships are moored;
> She hath ta'en in her goings Desolation as a dower;
> She hath stept, stept quickly, through the great gated Tower,
>   And the thing that could not be, it hath been!
> And the Seers they saw visions, and they spoke of a strange ill:
>   "A Palace, a Palace; and a great King thereof:
>   A bed, a bed empty, that was once pressed in love:
> And thou, thou, what art thou? Let us be, thou so still,
>   Beyond wrath, beyond beseeching, to the lips reft of thee!"
>   For she whom he desireth is beyond the deep sea,
>   And a ghost in his castle shall be queen.

Even now, the elders are unconvinced that Clytemnestra's report might not be exaggerated and misleading, mere hearsay and rumour.

> The fire of good tidings it hath sped the city through,
> But who knows if a god mocketh? Or who knows if all be true?
>
> 'Twere the fashion of a child,
> Or a brain dream-beguiled,
> To be kindled by the first
> Torch's message as it burst,
> And thereafter, as it dies, to die too.

Too lightly opened are a woman's ears
Her fence downtrod by many trespassers,
    And quickly crossed; but quickly lost
The burden of a woman's hopes or fears.

A lapse of time ensues. As has been said, not all Greek plays observed the strict twenty-four-hour span of action recommended later by Aristotle. Finally a herald arrives, his garments stained and torn. He falls to the ground, kisses the soil of his native Argos, then gratefully salutes the surrounding altars. A veteran of the wars, he is given a lengthy passage of superb description of the experiences and feelings of a soldier who is now home from battle. For him, the struggle is past and "all is victory". His summary:

And, for our life in those long years, there were
Doubtless some grievous days, and some were fair.
Who but a god goes woundless all his way?

One of the remarkable aspects of his speech is how modern – or timeless – it is. He gives in harrowing detail a picture of the long campaign.

Oh, could I tell the sick toil of the day,
The evil nights, scant decks ill-blanketed;
The rage and cursing when our daily bread
Came not! And then on land 'twas worse than all.
Our quarters close beneath the enemy's wall;

And rain – and from the ground the river dew –
Wet, always wet! Into our clothes it grew,
Plague-like, and bred foul beasts in every hair,
Would I could tell how ghastly midwinter
Stole down from Ida till the birds dropped dead!

But why remember how dire it was? His mood becomes one of stoic resignation.

Why think of it? They are past and in the grave,
All those long troubles. For I think the slain
Care little if they sleep or rise again;
And we, the living, wherefore should we ache
With counting all our lost ones, till we wake
The old malignant fortunes? If Good-bye
Comes from their side. Why, let them go, say I.
Surely for us who live, good doth prevail
Unchallenged, with no wavering of the scale.

He is set to forget, rejoicing that he for one survived.

Restlessly, Clytemnestra comes back. It has been suggested that her partly unmotivated exits and entrances serve to externalize her inner tension and indecision: she is too tense and cannot possibly stand still or silent. Her comings and goings at irregular intervals also create a sense of time passing; though the action unfolds on stage continuously, it actually contains several widely spaced incidents and major events.

Earlier the elders taunted her for being a woman and dismissed her announcement of Troy's ruin. She reminds them of the doubt with which they had heard her:

Long since I lifted up my voice in joy,
When the first messenger from flaming Troy
Spake through the dark of sack and overthrow.
And mockers chid me: "Because beacons show
On the hills, must Troy be fallen; Quickly born
Are women's hopes!" Aye, many did me scorn;
Yet gave I sacrifice; and by my word
Through all the city our woman's cry was heard,
Lifted in blessing round the seats of God,
And slumbrous incense o'er the altars glowed
In fragrance.

No matter. Agamemnon himself will soon be here. He will tell what happened. She eagerly awaits him:

What dearer dawn on woman's eyes can flame
Than this, which casteth wide her gate to acclaim
The husband whom God leadeth safe from war? –
Go, bear my lord this prayer: That fast and far
He haste him to this town which loves his name;
And in his castle may he find the same
Wife that he left, a watchdog of the hall,
True to one voice and fierce to others all;
A body and soul unchanged, no seal of his
Broke in the waiting years. – No thought of ease
Nor joy from other men hath touched my soul,
Nor shall touch, until bronze be dyed like wool.

Again she retreats into the palace.

The elders know all too well that Clytemnestra is not speaking the truth. The Greek audiences, delighting in irony, took great pleasure in misleading speeches like hers, in which words have a double meaning, especially any spectators familiar with the legend who knew that she is in fact plotting Agamemnon's murder.

Herald and chorus again hold the stage. More of the background of the story is sketched in, including a further account of the Greek army's exceedingly rough voyage back from Troy. The herald, in a particularly strong passage, describes a dreadful storm encountered by the home-bound galleys:

Two enemies, most ancient, Fire and Sea,
A sudden friendship swore, and roved their plight
By war on poor sailors through that night
Of misery, when the horror of the wave
Towered over us, and winds from Strymon drave
Hull against hull, till good ships, by the horn
Of the mad whirlwind gored and overborne,
One here, one there, 'mid rain and blinding spray,
Like sheep by a devil herded, passed away.
And when the blessed Sun upraised his head

> He saw the Aegean waste a-foam with dead,
> Dead men, dead ships, and spars disasterful!

A masterful poetic image, but it is more: an illustration of the vengeful wrath of God, which broods over the protagonist and antagonist of this tremendous drama.

The elders resume their moralizing. Men have said that good fortune awakens the envy of the gods:

> Ever of great bliss is born
> A tear unstaunched and heart broken.

This accords with the Greek belief that high fortune precedes a catastrophic reversal. A legend tells of a Greek ruler who refused a military alliance with the tyrant of a neighbouring city-state, only because the latter had been far too lucky: surely he was destined to meet disaster. Aeschylus, through the chorus, offers a different view:

> But I hold my thought alone. . . .
> 'Tis the deed that is unholy shall have issue, child on child,
> Sin on sin, like his begetters; and they shall be as they were.
> But the man who walketh straight, and the house thereof, tho' Fate
> Exalt him, the children shall be fair.

This echoes the Biblical injunction that the sins of the fathers are visited upon the sons until the third generation. The wicked have ample cause to fear, says Aeschylus, but not those who enjoy good fortune yet are virtuous: the gods will spare a blameless man, however lofty his rank and prolonged his run of luck. The chorus enlarges on this theme, asserting that virtue in one who is humble grants more honour than would ill-gotten riches and noble station:

> Justice shineth in a house low-wrought
>   With smooth-stained wall,
> And honoureth him who filleth his own lot;
> But the unclean hand upon the golden stair
> With eyes averse she flieth, seeking where

Things innocent art; and, recking not the power
Of wealth by man misgloried, guideth all
To her own destined hour.

(Kitto believes that Aeschylus was a great choreographer, and that the changing rhythms of these passages indicate what must have been the dancers' movements – and the music that prompted them – and that the same low iambic metre and possibly the same body movements and hand gestures, together with the matching music, accompanied and emphasized visually and pantomimicly the fateful *hubris* of the characters. Today this is called sign language and body language. Kitto traces indications of such dramatic patterns of physical movement throughout the play.)

After this lengthy but powerful build-up to his entrance, at last Agamemnon and his troops appear in a resplendent procession: the Argive king in his high, gilded chariot, and behind him the captive Trojan princess Cassandra, Priam's daughter, in another chariot; and behind them ranks of soldiers, slaves and huge piles of booty, a lavish display of barbaric arms, shields and the Argive lion or white horse embossed on some of them, all flashing in the sunlight. Aeschylus excels at such spectacular effects. The newcomers are hailed in song by the populace of their native city, and finally by the leader of the chorus, who cannot resist lamenting the king's long absence from Argos and chiding him for it, but closes his remarks with a veiled, well-meant warning:

But on this new day,
From the deep of my thought and in love, I say
"Sweet is a grief well ended";
And in time's flow Thou wilt learn and know
The true from the false,
Of them that were left to guard the walls
Of thine empty Hall unfriended.

The proud Agamemnon accepts the leader's praise as his due. Aglow, exultant, he does not seem to recall the terrible price of his victory: the temples despoiled, the vast suffering, the many lives lost, his own young daughter sacrificed. Yet in this drama, as elsewhere, it would seem that the flaw in the Aeschylean tragic hero is not altogether the cause of his downfall; he is equally the victim of an Evil Fate which has predestined his misfortune. He is a son of the vicious, bloodstained Atreus.

At the end of his reply, he takes note of the indirect warning in the leader's greeting:

Lo, to the Gods I make Thanksgivings,
But for thy words: I marked them, and I mind
Their meaning, and my voice shall be behind
Thine. For not many men, the proverb saith,
Can love a friend whom fortune prospereth
Unenvying; and about the envious brain
Cold poison clings, and doubles all the pain
Life brings him. His own woundings he must nurse,
And feels another's gladness like a curse.
  Well can I speak. I know the mirrored glass
Called friendship, and the shadow shapes that pass
And feign them a King's friends.

Clytemnestra and her retinue of women appear on the steps of the palace. Her greeting is sharp of utterance, tinged with reproach; though she professes eagerness – and longing – for his long-delayed return. She is inwardly in turmoil, for she does not know what are Agamemnon's intentions towards her; she herself is possibly in great peril, as, most certainly, is he.

  I will no longer hold it shame
To lay my passion before men's eyes.
There comes a time to a woman when fear dies
Forever. None hath taught me. None could tell,
Save me, the weight of years intolerable
I lived while this man lay at Ilion.
That any woman thus should sit alone
In a half-empty house, with no man near,
Makes her half-blind with dread! And in her ear
Always some voice of wrath; now messengers
Of evil, now not so; then others worse,
Crying calamity against mine and me.

Always the stories of his misfortune had reached her:

> Oh, had he half the wounds that variously
> Came rumoured home, his flesh must be a net
> All holes from heel to crown! And if he met
> As many deaths as I met tales thereon,
> Is he some monstrous thing, some Geryon
> Three-souled, that will not die, till o'er his head,
> Three robes of earth be piled, to hold him dead?
> Aye, many a time my heart broke, and the noose
> Of death had got me; but they cut me loose.
> It was those voices always in mine ear.

This beautifully vivid speech, shrewdly shaped by feminine psychology, and boasting imagery that helps to paint the overall dark, gory mood of the drama, conveys the tension mounting in this fiercely emotional woman.

She explains that their son, Orestes, has gone into safe exile because the city has been rebellious. The audience knows that she is lying, that Orestes has fled because his father's cousin Aegisthus, who is also his mother's lover, threatened him.

Though transparent to the spectators, her attempts at guile succeed for the moment. She protests that she no longer bears a grudge against her husband. She has wished only for his return unscathed.

> But for me,
> The old stormy rivers of my grief are dead
> Now at the spring: not one tear left unshed.
> Mine eyes are sick with vigil, endlessly
> Weeping, the beacon-piles that watched for thee
> For ever answerless. And did I dream,
> A gnat's thin whirr would start me, like a scream
> Of battle, and show thee by terrors swept,
> Crowding, too many for the time I slept.

From all which stress delivered and free-souled,
I greet my lord: O watchdog of the fold. . . .
These be my words to greet him home again,
No god shall grudge them. Surely I and thou
Have suffered in time past enough! And now
Dismount, O head with love and glory crowned,
From this high car; yet plant not on bare ground
Thy foot, great King, the foot that trampled Troy.

One of the great moments of the play is reached. The queen's bond-maidens have spread a tapestry from Agamemnon's high chariot to the portal of the palace. Most translations describe this silken rug as "purple", but Gilbert Murray suggests that it should be "crimson" – literally, a "red carpet", a silken stream that is appropriately and symbolically blood-coloured.

Clytemnestra's intention is that the king shall tread this to the fate that awaits him in the royal dwelling-place. But Agamemnon merely stares down at it. After a pause, he replies to her:

Daughter of Leda, watcher of my fold,
In sooth thy welcome, grave and amply told,
Fitteth mine absent years. Though it had been
Seemlier, methinks, some other, not my Queen,
Had spoke these honours. For the rest, I say
Seek not to make me soft in woman's way;
Cry not thy praise to me wide-mouthed, nor fling
Thy body down, as to some barbarous king.

That the bond-maidens have prostrated themselves before him is a daringly excessive act of deference, for such gestures of submission were ordinarily paid only to semi-divine Asian monarchs, hated and despised by the freedom-loving Greeks.

Nor yet with broidered hangings strew my path
To wake the unseen ire. 'Tis God that hath
Such worship; and for mortal man to press

Rude feet upon this broidered loveliness . . .
I vow there is danger in it. Let my road
Be honoured, surely; but as man, not god.
Rugs for the feet and yon broidered pall . . .
The names ring diverse! . . . Aye, and not to fall
Suddenly blind is of all gifts the best
God giveth, for I reckon no man blest
Ere to the utmost goal his race be run.
So be it; and if, as this day I have done,
I shall do always, then I fear no ill.

For a Greek mortal to accept the honours that should be paid only to the gods would be a grave fault, a dangerous one.

But the Queen, wishing to lead him into a vital error, cleverly tempts him, appealing to his self-conceit and over-strong pride, the tragic flaws in his character that will draw him on to *hubris*.

Clytemnestra: Tell me but this, nowise against thy will.
Agamemnon: My will, be sure, shall falter not nor fade.
Clytemnestra: Was this a vow in some great peril made?
Agamemnon: Enough! I have spoke my purpose, fixed and plain.
Clytemnestra: Were Priam the Conqueror . . . Think, would he refrain?
Agamemnon: Oh, stores of broideries would be trampled then!
Clytemnestra: Lord, care not for the cavillings of men!
Agamemnon: The murmur of a people hath strange weight.
Clytemnestra: Who feareth envy, feareth to be great.
Agamemnon: 'Tis graceless when a woman strives to lead.
Clytemnestra: When a great conqueror yields, 'tis grace indeed.
Agamemnon: So in this war thou must my conqueror be?
Clytemnestra: Yield! With good will to yield is victory!

At this moment of incandescent drama, the dialogue between these two strong persons at cross-purposes, each line epigrammatically turned, topping the preceding one, represents a conflict not of mere surface contradiction, as when Clytemnestra was mocked by the elders or later chided them in turn for their disbelief; instead, it lays bare the basic opposition between protagonist and antagonist from which springs this always taxing play. Clytemnestra, sometimes called "a woman with a man's heart", is sharper, more quick-witted than her king.

Agamemnon does yield, as secretly he has wished to do from the first, for his vanity is overwhelming. He accepts the adulation offered him, consenting to walk not only on the rich tapestry but also in Oriental pomp and arrogance between the ranks of the prostrate attendants:

> Well, if I needs must. . . . Be it as thou has said!

He adds:

> Quick! Loose me these bound slaves on which I tread,
> And while I walk yon wonders of the sea
> God grant no eye of wrath be cast on me
> From afar!

The reference to the "wonders of the sea" is to the fish-blood used to dye the handsome rug (and which most likely would be red rather than purple). "The eye of wrath", of course, is an allusion to God in Olympus. Agamemnon equivocates further, as his shoes are unlaced and removed from his feet, so that he will not spoil the scarlet carpet:

> For even now it likes me not
> To waste mine house, thus marring underfoot
> The pride thereof, and wondrous broideries
> Brought in far seas with silver. But of these
> Enough.

Now, before entering the palace, he points to Cassandra in the second chariot:

> And mark, I charge thee, this princess
> Of Ilion: tend her with all gentleness.

God's eye doth see, and loveth from afar,
The merciful conqueror. For no slave of war
Is slave by his own will. She is the prize
And chosen flower of Ilion's treasuries,
Set by the soldiers' gift to follow me.

In this speech, of course, he is as deceitful in accounting for Cassandra's presence as has been his queen, in her own way, towards him. But he is also foolish: he can hardly hope to hoodwink Clytemnestra this easily. His behaviour is beset by self-blindness and self-indulgence. He forgives himself, or explains away, his every fault and wrongdoing, and expects others to look upon him as tolerantly, which they are hardly apt to do.

He dismounts from his splendid chariot as the assembled throng raises a cry of triumph. Clytemnestra boastfully proclaims, in what is essentially another superlative aria, an inventory of the palace's lavish appointments:

There is the sea – its caverns who shall drain?
Breeding of many a purple-fish the stain
Surpassing silver, ever fresh renewed,
For robes of kings. And we, by right indued,
Possess our fill thereof. Thy house, O King,
Knoweth no stint, nor lack of anything.

Her gesture is towards the actual blue Aegean that provided a natural background for the Dionysia.

What trampling of rich raiment, had the cry
So sounded in the domes of prophecy,
Would I have vowed these years, as price to pay
For this dear life in peril far away!
Where the root is, the leafage cometh soon
To clothe an house, and spread its leafy boon
Against the burning star; and, thou being come
Thou, on the midmost hearthstone of thy home,

Oh, warmth in Winter leapeth to thy sign.
And when God's Summer melteth into wine
The green grape, on that house shall coolness fall
Where the true man, the master, walks his hall.

Though the argument has seemed trivial, it is symbolically momentous. By now Agamemnon has passed into the palace, and looking upward his murderous queen beseeches:

Zeus, Zeus! True Master, let my prayers be true!
And, oh, forget not that thou art willed to do!

She follows the king, and their retinues trail after them. Cassandra is left alone with the elders.

This Trojan princess is one of the most poignantly drawn figures in all dramatic literature. The chorus recites the legendary background of this hapless girl: beloved by Apollo, she had attempted to out-trick the god, who then avenged himself by endowing her with the gift of prophecy and decreeing that none should ever heed or believe her warnings. Her alarms about the dire fate of her native city had been given no credence by her father, Priam, nor had they been hearkened to by her heroic brothers. So now, in her chariot, the captive Cassandra cowers in fear, clearly foreseeing her own imminent death from a blade wielded by Agamemnon's jealous queen.

A mood of rising terror and doom, dim but growing foreboding, is created by the chanting chorus: Cassandra's visions, at first inexplicable to the elders, have a gruesome intensity that is contagious. At times the old men misread her half-choked utterances, thinking that she refers to past deeds of horror in the House of Atreus – the slaughter of Thyestes' children – rather than murderous acts shortly to occur. Several times Clytemnestra reappears at the palace portal and impatiently summons Cassandra to come within, but the frightened girl, obdurately silent at the command, refuses. Clytemnestra argues with her. "I speak thy name, Cassandra; seeing the Gods – why chafe at them? – have placed thee here." She promises to give the luckless captive "what'ere is due", implying that she will be kind to her, but of course meaning to kill her. Cassandra trembles, almost paralysed with dread and unable to respond.

The leader of the elders recognizes her state:

Oh, doom is all around thee like a net . . .

CLYTEMNESTRA: Methinks, unless this wandering maid is one
Voiced like a swallow-bird, with tongue unknown
And barbarous, she can read my plain intent.
I use but words, and ask for her consent.
LEADER [*to Cassandra*]: Ah, come! 'Tis best, as the world lies today.
Leave this high-throned chariot and obey!

The queen's impatience grows. She is anxious to be within the palace to observe Agamemnon's doings.

CLYTEMNESTRA: How long must I stand dallying at the Gate?
Even now the beasts to Hestia consecrate
Wait by the midmost fire, since there is wrought
This high fulfilment which no man thought.
. . . If dead to sense, thou will not understand.
[*To the Leader of the Chorus*] Thou show her, not with speech but with brute hand!
LEADER: The strange maid needs a rare interpreter.
She is trembling like a wild beast in a snare.
CLYTEMNESTRA: 'Fore God, she is mad, and heareth but her own
Folly! A slave, her city all o'erthrown,
She needs must chafe her bridle, till this fret
Be foamed away in blood and bitter sweat.
I waste no more speech, thus to be defied.

She hastens back into the palace. Compassionately, the leader of the elders turns to the still voiceless Cassandra:

I pity thee so sore, no wrath nor pride
Is in me. – Come, dismount! Bend to the stroke
Fate lays on thee, and learn to feel thy yoke.

Cassandra, moaning to herself, is possessed.

Otototoi . . . Dreams. Dreams.
Apollo. O Apollo!

The second elder asks:

Why sob'st thou for Apollo? It is writ,
He loveth not grief nor lendeth ear to it.
CASSANDRA: Otototoi . . . Dreams. Dreams.
Apollo. O Apollo!
LEADER: Still to that god she makes her sobbing cry
Who hath no place where men are sad, or die.
CASSANDRA: Apollo, Apollo! Light of the Ways of Men!
Mine enemy!
Has lighted me to darkness yet again?
SECOND ELDER: How? Will she prophesy about her own
Sorrows? That power abides when all is gone.
CASSANDRA: Apollo, Apollo! Light of all that is!
Mine enemy!
Where hast thou led me? . . . Ha! What house is this?

In her vision, she recognizes it:

This is the house that God hateth.
There be many things that know its secret; sore
And evil things; murders and strangling death.
'Tis here they slaughter men. . . . A splashing floor.

This is a weird, uncanny scene, to some it is one of the strangest and most stirring ever written.

SECOND ELDER: Keen-scented the strange maid seemeth, like a hound
For blood. – And what she seeks can sure be found!

Again, he supposes that she is talking of the past killings, not of those shortly to come.

> CASSANDRA: The witnesses – I follow where they lead.
> The crying . . . of little children . . . near the gate:
> Crying for wounds that bleed
> And the smell of the baked meats their father ate.

By the "witnesses" is meant the Furies, the Eumenides or Eryinnyes, terrible bird-like creatures who pursue the guilty. Born of drops of blood shed on Earth by Cronus when he was mutilated by his divine son, they had serpents twined in their hair, were winged and had bleeding eyes.

> SECOND ELDER: Word of thy mystic power had reached our ear
> Long since. Howbeit we need not prophets here.

He is saying again, mistakenly, that what she speaks of is history, not prophecy. But she, in her trance, contradicts him:

> CASSANDRA: Ah, ah! What would they? A new dreadful thing.
> A great great sin plots in the house this day;
> Too strong for the faithful, beyond medicining . . .
> And help stands far away.

As she continues, the prophetess foretells the whole dreadful action – which the audience is never to see for itself – enlarging the suspense, while darkening and deepening the ominous, cold mood. Her vision, vague at first, grows progressively more definite, moving from past to present and to future events. Much is made of references to the net Clytemnestra will cast over Agamemnon; elsewhere it is compared to "the net" Zeus had earlier thrown over Troy.

Cassandra calls out to the invisible queen:

> O Woman, thou! The lord who lay with thee!
> Wilt lave with water, and then . . . How speak the end?
> It comes so quick. A hand . . . another hand . . .

That reach, reach gropingly . . .
Ah, ah! What is it? There, it is coming clear.
A net . . . some net of Hell.
Nay, she that lies with him . . . is she the snare?
And half of his blood upon it. It holds well . . .
O Crowd of ravening Voices, be glad, yea, shout
And cry for the stoning, cry for the casting out!

Again, still disjointedly:

Ah, look! Look! Keep his mate from the Wild Bull!
A tangle of raiment, see;
A black horn, and a blow, and he falleth, full
In the marble amid the water. I counsel, ye.
I speak plain. . . . Blood in the bath and treachery!

This is an exact description of Agememnon's ghastly end as it shortly occurs. The leader, bewildered and troubled, tries to dismiss the prediction as a trick:

What spring of good hath seercraft ever made
Up from the dark to flow?
'Tis but a weaving of words, a craft of woe
To make mankind afraid.

Cassandra now sees even more fully her own imminent death and bewails her undeserved fate:

Poor woman! Poor dead woman! . . . Yea, it is I.
Poured out like water among them. Weep for me. . . .
Ah! What is this place? Why must I come with them . . .
To die, only to die?
LEADER: Thou art borne on the breath of God, thou spirit wild
For thine own weird to wail,

Like to that winged voice, that heart so sore
Which crying always, hungereth to cry more,
"Itylus, Itylus," till it sing her child
  Back to the nightingale.

He is alluding to the legend of Philomela, who to spite her husband Têreus slew their little son and was herself transformed into a nightingale to mourn him for ever.

CASSANDRA: Oh, happy Singing Bird, so sweet, so clear!
  Soft wings for her God made,
  And an easy passing, without pain or tear . . .
  For me, 'twill be torn flesh and rending blade.

The doomed girl recalls her past and the luckless events set in motion by her amorous brother that have indirectly brought her as a captive to Argos:

Alas for the kiss, the kiss of Paris, his people's bane!
Alas for Scamander Water, the water my fathers drank!
Long, long ago I played about thy bank
  And was cherished and grew strong;
Now by a River of Wailing, by shores of Pain,
  Soon shall I make my song.

Says the leader:

It stabs within me like a serpent's tooth,
The bitter thrilling music of her pain. . . .

Cassandra, recovering from her prophetic trance, slowly regains clear senses. The chorus asks how she came to be endowed with this fatal gift. She confesses that she had once lied to Apollo and has ever since been punished for it. She pauses, at one moment: "Time was, I held it shame hereof to speak."

The elder tells her: "Ah, shame is for the mighty, not the weak."

The stabbing pains of prescience visit her again, a vision of the slaughtered children of Thyestes returning and being vividly depicted.

For modern taste the scene is too long and repetitive, but the Greek audience had come to spend a whole day at the festival, not a mere two hours. So, again and again, Cassandra spells out her hideous forecast of the slaying of Agamemnon by his obsessively vengeful queen. Despite the repetition, or partly because of it, the confrontation grows ever more powerful:

> I warn ye, vengeance broodeth still,
> A lion's rage, which goes not forth to kill
> But lurketh in his lair, watching the high
> Hall of my war-gone master. . . . Master? Aye;
> Mine, mine! The yoke is nailed about my neck. . . .
> Oh, lord of ships and trampler on the wreck
> Of Ilion, knows he not this she-wolf's tongue,
> Which licks and fawns, and laughs with ear up-sprung,
> To bite in the end like a secret death? – and can
> The woman? Slay a strong and armèd man?
> What fangèd reptile like to her doth creep?
> Some serpent amphisbene, some Skylla deep
> Housed in the rock, where sailors shriek and die.
> Mother of Hell blood-raging, which doth cry
> On her own flesh war, war without alloy . . .
> God! And she shouted in his face her joy,
> Like men in battle when the foe doth break.
> And feigns thanksgiving for his safety's sake!
> What if no man believe me? 'Tis all one.
> The thing which must be shall be; aye, and soon
> Thou too shalt sorrow for these things, and here
> Standing confess me all too true a seer.

She predicts more overtly: "Man, thou shalt look on Agamemnon dead." And, again, her own end:

God, she will kill me! Like to them that brew
Poison, I see her mingle for me too
A separate vial in her wrath, and swear
Whetting her blade for him, that I must share
His death . . . because, because he dragged me here!

Coming to herself, as her oracular trance, a fit of possession, wears off, she angrily rips off her veils, throws them on the ground, tramples them; breaks the staff she has carried, which identifies her as a seer.

She foresees Orestes' ultimate return and triumph, begs that she be remembered, too, and her needless murder avenged. She prays that her death will be quick, merciful.

Leader: O full of sorrows, full of wisdom great,
Woman, thy speech is a long anguish; yet
Knowing thy doom, why walkst thou with clear eyes,
Like some god-blinded beast, to sacrifice?
Cassandra: There is no escape, friend; only vain delay.
Leader: Is not the later still the sweeter day?
Cassandra: The day is come. Small profit now to fly.
Leader: Through all thy griefs, Woman, thy heart is high.
Cassandra: Alas! None that is happy hears that praise.

With rising courage and dignity she moves toward the palace, then recoils shuddering: "Ah, faugh! Faugh!"

Leader: What turns thee in that blind
Horror? Unless some loathing of the mind . . .
Cassandra: Death drifting from the doors, and blood like rain!
Leader: 'Tis but the dumb beasts at the altar slain.
Cassandra: And vapours from a charnel-house . . . See there!
Leader: 'Tis Tyrian incense clouding in the air.
Cassandra [recovering again]: So be it! – I will go in yonder room

To weep mine own and Agamemnon's doom.
May death be all! Strangers, I am no bird
That pipeth trembling at a thicket stirred
By the empty wind. Bear witness on that day
When woman for this woman's life shall pay,
And man for man ill-mated low shall lie:
I ask this boon, as being about to die.

LEADER: Alas, I pity thee thy mystic fate!

CASSANDRA: One word, one dirge-song would I utter yet
O'er mine own corpse. To this last shining Sun
I pray, when the Avenger's work is done
His enemies may remember this thing too,
This little thing, the woman slave they slew!
O world of men, farewell! A painted show
Is all thy glory; and when life is low
The touch of a wet sponge out-blotteth all.
Oh, sadder this than any proud man's fall!

At long last, Cassandra goes into the palace where she will perish.

Suddenly Agamemnon's cry for help is heard from within. The chorus, in ensemble, has been moralizing on the uncertainty of man's good fortune. Hearing the desperate cry, they are immediately thrown into panic and confusion. Shall they respond? Stand still? Flee? While they argue – their fright and indecision strikingly modern and eternally human – the ferocious deed in the palace is consummated. The great doors, flung open, reveal the tableau of Clytemnestra, bloody axe in hand, bent over the sprawled bodies of the king and his luckless concubine.

Highly over-wrought, the bloodstained queen addresses the appalled, outraged crowd of elders. Her wild, passionate outburst is more than an exposure of her true feelings, long hidden, and more than an attempt at self-justification: she must hold this hostile group of men at bay until Aegisthus arrives with help. She proclaims multiple reasons for her horrible act, the drama reaches a new, higher climax.

Oh, lies enough and more have I this day
Spoken, which I shame not to unsay.

How should a woman work, to the utter end,
Hate on a damnèd hater, feigned a friend;
How pile perdition round him, hunter-wise,
Too high for overleaping, save by lies?
To me this hour was dreamed of long ago:
A thing of ancient hate. 'Twas very slow
In coming, but it came. And here I stand
Even where I struck, with all the deed I planned
Done!

She depicts the killing in ghastly detail:

'Twas so wrought – what boots it to deny? –
The man could neither guard himself nor fly.
An endless plenteousness of robe, I flung
All around him, and struck twice; and with two cries
His limbs turned water and broke; and as he lies
I cast my third stroke in, a prayer well-sped
To Zeus of Hell, who guardeth safe his dead!
So there he gasped his life out as he lay;
And, gasping, the blood spouted. . . . Like dark spray
That splashed, it came, a salt and deathly dew;
Sweet, sweet as God's dear rain-drops ever blew
O'er a parched field, the day the buds are born.

The queen orders the aroused elders to disperse, but they refuse to accept her command.

LEADER: We are astonished at thy speech. To fling,
Wild mouthed! such vaunt over thy murdered King!
CLYTEMNESTRA: Would'st fright me, like a witless woman? Lo,
This bosom shakes not. . . .
Curse me as ye will, or bless,

'Tis all one. . . . This is Agamemnon: this
My husband, dead by my right hand, a blow
Struck by a righteous craftsman.

The elders revile her: she replies in kind. So strongly is she drawn, this prototype of Lady Macbeth, that despite her cruelty and murderous guile she is a strangely sympathetic figure, dynamic and resourceful. She defies the threatening crowd of men:

Aye, now, for me, thou hast thy words of fate;
Exile from Argos and the people's hate
For ever! Against him no word was cried
When, recking not, as 'twere a beast that died
With flocks abounding over his wide domain,
He slew his child, my love, my flower of pain . . .
Great God, as magic for the winds of Thrace!

She demands:

Why was he not man-hunted from his place,
To purge the blood that stained him? . . . When the deed
Is mine, oh, then thou art a judge indeed!
But threat thy fill. I am ready, and I stand
Content; if thy hand beateth down my hand,
Thou rulest. If aught else be God's decree,
Thy lesson shall be learned, though late it be.

She accuses Agamemnon of promiscuous infidelity and voices her contempt for the now dead Cassandra:

What should I fear, when fallen here I hold
This foe, this scorner of his wife, this toy
And fool of each Chryseids under Troy;

And there withal his soothsayer and slave,
His chanting bed-fellow, his leman brave,
Who rubbed the galleys' benches at his side.
But, oh, they had their guerdon as they died!
For he lies thus, and she, the wild swan's way,
Hath trod her last long weeping roundelay,
And lies, his lover, ravisht o'er the main
For his bed's comfort and my deep disdain.

A new climax is attained: Aegisthus and his armed forces arrive and confront the furious townspeople. Each group aims spears against the other: the visual opposition is another stroke of great theatricality. Aegisthus defends his role in the plot: vengeance is due him for his dead brothers; he asserts – because of his kinship to Atreus – his right to the throne. The crowd hurls insults at him and taunts him for having allowed a woman to do his work, the bloody slaying.

In turn, Aegisthus threatens to be a harsh master if they resist him. He says that because he is too well known he could not appear openly in Argos while Agamemnon lived; hence he had to depend on the queen's resolute help. A clash of arms is about to take place, but Clytemnestra suddenly intervenes. She has been standing in exhausted silence, but now she begs for peace. Her blood lust is spent; her boiling passion has subsided. She begs them:

Nay, peace, O best-belovèd! Peace! And let us work no evil more.
Surely the reaping of the past is a full harvest, and not good,
And wounds enough are everywhere. – Let us not stain ourselves with blood.
Ye reverend Elders, go your ways, to your own dwelling everyone,
Ere things be wrought for which men suffer – What we did must needs be done.
And if of all these strifes we now may have no more, oh, I will kneel
And praise God, bruisèd though we be beneath the Daemon's heavy heel.
This is the word a woman speaks, to hear if any man will deign.

Murray suggests that she has actually been half mad, "possessed by the Daemon of the House", when she committed her crime; now the Daemon has left her.

The crowd is still not cowed. Aegisthus again threatens them:

I will be a hand of wrath to fall on thee in after days.

LEADER: Not so, if God in after days shall guide Orestes home again!

AEGISTHUS: I know how men in exile feed on dreams . . . and know such food is vain.

LEADER: Go forth and wax fat! Defile the right for this thy little hour.

AEGISTHUS: I spare thee now. Know well for all this folly thou shalt feel my power.

LEADER: Aye, vaunt thy greatness, as a bird beside his mate doth vaunt and swell.

CLYTEMNESTRA: Vain hounds are baying round thee; oh, forget them! Thou and I shall dwell

As Kings in this great House. We two at last will order all things well.

The sullen adversaries separate, leaving Aegisthus' spearmen on guard, as he and Clytemnestra enter the palace, and the great doors swing shut.

Two thousand five hundred years old, this amazing play contains all the elements of truly good theatre: conflict between visible and interesting antagonists, for high stakes; serious moral issues; rounded characters of great dynamism and relative complexity.

Stage figures are seldom as complicated psychologically as those presented in books, for a staged performance limits the nuances of personality that the novelist and short story writer may attempt. Here the rapidity at which dialogue must progress, and the emphasis on physical action, preclude more than the slightest subtlety, nor does a mass audience sense it or appreciate it. Besides, the language is stylized, with mystical overtones; austere yet remarkably vivid, charged with effective imagery; epigrammatic, and at high moments surging with a wide range of emotions to superb poetry. Moreover, *Agamemnon* offers splendid "roles"; it provides fine opportunities for the actor to display the utmost virtuosity. Aeschylus offers dazzling spectacle: the entrance of the blazoning chariots and victorious soldiers with their flashing shields and helmets and their rich loot; the spreading of the crimson carpet and gestures of sacrifice, amidst the curling smoke from burning incense and meats on the altars. Everywhere are evidences of Aeschylus' flair for the theatrical: the lonely watchman scanning the stars from his lofty perch; the "unmotivated" entrances of Clytemnestra, to stress her excitement and wilfulness; the skilful build-up of Agamemnon's long-delayed arrival; Clytemnestra's attempt to trick both Agamemnon and Cassandra, when the audience is well aware of what she is up to – this "sharing of secrets" with an audience is a lastingly successful device in the hands of a sophisticated theatre craftsman. Then, after the fateful debate between the king and queen, follows the eerie scene of Cassandra's chilling visions, breaking her own long silence, and her tragic submission; and after, the revelation of the gory murders; the abrupt reversal of Clytemnestra's character, the indecision and debate among the horrified and partly intimidated crowd. Their reaction provokes new tension and agitation, further engendered by Clytemnestra's openly bared defiance of these hostile townspeople; and at the last moment, when suspense can be sustained no more, the incursion of Aegisthus and his men, the final opposition, pointing of spears and exchange of threats, and the ultimate triumph of Clytemnestra and her malicious ally.

It is suggested that Aeschylus had another intent in writing this drama: he was propagandizing for the end of primitive justice through blood feuds in favour of resort to law courts which had just been established in Athens. He is saying that if a wrong is too harshly and impulsively punished, it only begets a new wrong, which in turn incites yet another act of retribution, forging an endless chain of crimes. What more horrible lesson of the folly of feuding, of recklessly taking justice into one's own hands, than this story of Atreus' bloodstained family? It should be noted that the third play of the *Oresteia* ends with a trial at which the young avenger is judged by the gods and absolved of the slaying of his mother. The trilogy has been called "an eloquent plea for a new religion of forgiveness".

Aeschylus, the moralist, may well have had some such secondary purpose. (F.L. Lucas, in *Greek Tragedy and Comedy*, expresses his rather surprising opinion that Aeschylus is not a serious thinker, though he holds that *Agamemnon* is the "finest of all ancient drama".) Murray and others believe its message to be that man should learn by suffering, as God Himself has learned: the old gods, the old laws, are barbarous. A new conception of them is needed and at hand. "If we accept the view that all art to some extent, and Greek tragedy in a very special degree, moves in its course of development from Religion to Entertainment, from a Service to a Performance," says Murray, "the *Agamemnon* seems to stand at a critical point, where the balance of the two elements is near perfection. . . . It is not, like Aeschylus' *Suppliant Women*, a statue half hewn out of the rock. It is a real play." Yet, as Murray further argues, it is something more than a play. "Its atmosphere is not quite of this world." In its size and intensity, it attains sublimity. It is also, in the purest sense of the phrase, a "criticism of life".

H.D.F. Kitto remarks that even the messenger and the guard are humanized figures, speaking of their own emotions, their fear, weariness, relief, not merely imparting needed background information. A new level of realism is the important consequence.

In sum, Lucas matches Murray and Kitto and a host of other critics in his admiration for Aeschylus' accomplishment, but he cites one defect in the work: the title character, Agamemnon, is sketchily drawn. He appears only briefly and is allotted less than two hundred lines. He betrays no noble side to his nature; Lucas feels that Agamemnon might better have been shown as "rash indeed and proud, yet brave and royal and human". It is hard to see how any such redeeming qualities could be attributed to a "hero" who assents to the sacrifice of his young daughter and boastfully returns home with a concubine. In accordance with tradition, the play bears Agamemnon's name because he is the one whose fate is irrevocably determined; actually, the principal roles are those of Clytemnestra and Cassandra, who are given considerably more to say and do. An Agamemnon characterized differently would have yielded an altogether different play; surely Aeschylus is entitled to his own interpretation of these mythological figures.

Even so, Lucas finds much else to praise:

> [The play] is brilliantly heightened by symbolism and suspense. And the dramatic conflict here becomes vivid as never before. . . . Clytemnestra lives and moves in our minds as no earlier figure on the stage had ever done. She has already some of the intricacy and mystery of life – hysterical strength of passion in crisis, nervous reaction after it, and a mixture of motives that leaves us wondering – how far was she really moved by revenge for Iphigeneia, how far by guilty love for Aegisthus? (Presumably we are meant to feel that anger for Iphigeneia began the estrangement, adultery followed, jealousy of Chryseis and Cassandra added their sting; now, with her husband's return, Clytemnestra must strike or perish.) . . . Then there is the music and muscle of the verse, both dialogue and lyric. Perhaps the greatest speech in all Greek drama is that insidious welcome of Clytemnestra to her hated husband, as passionate in its wild imagery as the oriental Isaiah. Indeed the whole scene strangely recalls another masterpiece of Biblical style – the harlot wife of Proverbs. . . . Nor did Aeschylus ever equal these choruses, with their visions of Iphigeneia and of Helen – of the innocent life sacrificed to the cold malignancy of the State and, on the other hand, to a single frivolous soul. Never did he muse so magnificently as here – on the mystery of the world, "Zeus, who'er He be"; on the futile horror of war; on the captive victim, who is yet nobler in her clear vision than the blind victor who crushes her; on the forsaken husband, watched intolerably by the cold marble eyes of the statues in his empty hall.

Lucas concludes: "This tragedy was, I think, never to be outdone on the European stage till, two thousand years later, another king murdered through a wife's adultery, and destined to be avenged by his son, stalked spectral along the battlements of Elsinore."

(As Lucas and others have remarked, if the plot of *Hamlet* is reduced to a bare outline, the many likenesses to details in the *Oresteia* are revealed. After a long absence, a young Danish prince returns to his native land and discovers that his father has been killed by the queen and her lover, a close kinsman. The prince's claim to the throne has been ignored. Filial duty and communal pressure call for an act of retaliation on his part, however reluctant he is to undertake the part, since it means that he must inflict mortal punishment on his own mother. He hesitates, the moral burden at times unsettling his mind. Striking similarities, yet Shakespeare had no known access to Aeschylus.)

The second part of the *Oresteia, The Choephori* (or *The Libation Pourers*), will not be analysed here at as much length, for it is far less often read today, and seldom acted. In it is told the even more terrible story of the vengeance taken on Aegisthus and Clytemnestra by her children, Electra and Orestes. Seven years have passed; Electra has remained in Argos suffering many humiliations. She awaits the return of her exiled brother, who has found refuge at the court of King Strophius of Phocis. There he has formed a close friendship with Pylades, the king's son.

At last the two young men do make their way back to Argos, their purpose to recapture the kingship rightly Orestes', though long since forcibly usurped by his mother's lover. Secretly reaching his home city, Orestes goes first to his father's tomb and lays there a lock of his hair, a token of his grief; absent from Argos at the time of his father's violent death and not daring to go back, he had not been able to mourn at Agamemnon's burial-place. A cry is heard; Electra and a chorus of serving women, appearing from the palace, also make their way to the tomb. They bear offerings and bitter lamentations as they have done ceaselessly since the dread event, the unavenged death of the murdered king. They come at the order of Clytemnestra who has been visited by a nightmare in which the slain dead threaten her. Discovering the lock of hair on the grave, and identifying it as resembling Orestes', Electra speaks longingly of her brother. She speculates that he has sent it as a tribute. The chorus breaks in:

> Why then, this news is greater cause for tears,
> If in this land he never shall set foot.

Hidden in shadows, the young men overhear this. Next, Electra beholds a footprint and deems it familiar, and her brother steps forth from his concealment to acknowledge his presence. Can this really be her almost unknown brother? Finally convinced of his return, she is overjoyed. She immediately urges him to repay their mother in kind and also kill the now despotic Aegisthus, strengthening the youth's already half-formed intent. Orestes claims that Apollo has also commanded him to carry out the perilous deed. (This translation is by Dudley Fitts.)

> Loud and long
> His prophetess predicted chilly blasts

Of pestilence to turn the heart's blood cold,
If I should fail to seek those murderers out
And put them to the death my father died,
Their lives for his. . . .
Or else the penalty, he said, would fall
On my own soul –

Every form of physical ill will be visited upon him – "ulcers with ravenous jaws to eat the flesh . . . hoary hairs out of them . . . the fierce assault of the Furies, sprung out of a father's blood" – if he disobeys the god's fierce dictate. He recites his many motives for quick and vigorous action: the god's command, his own grief at the loss of his father, his desire to regain the kingship of which he has been wrongly deprived, a wish to free his brave countrymen from the grip of Aegisthus' overbearing rule.

Disguised as merchants from Phocis, the two young men knock at the palace doors and request hospitality. Clytemnestra appears, grants it. She speaks of the bad dreams that have troubled her, especially one in which she has seen herself giving birth to a snake; suckling it at her breast, she had been wounded by its fangs, her blood flowing along with the maternal milk. Orestes, who has already learned of this dream from Electra, interprets it as another sign that he is ordained by the gods to slay his mother. Now, meeting these supposed strangers from the town where her son has been dwelling in exile, Clytemnestra hears that Orestes is dead; they ask if his remains shall be returned to Argos for burial. The queen, while protesting a mother's grief, cannot hide her true joy at the news. She hastens to apprise Aegisthus of it, and the greater safety it promises them.

Hearing from his former nurse even more about his mother's heartlessness, Orestes' purpose hardens. With the help of the nurse, he contrives to have the sceptical and cautious Aegisthus greet him in the palace unguarded and strikes him down. Next he kills his startled mother, who first calls for a warrior's axe to defend herself, then pleads for mercy, which momentarily causes him to hesitate.

I mean to kill you by his side.
While he lived, you preferred him to my father;
So sleep in death beside him.

Clytemnestra's last words are:

> My pleas are vain – warm tears on a cold tomb. . . .
> Ah me, I bore a serpent, not a son.

Both bloody deeds take place out of sight, within the palace. In a very long speech over the bodies of the fallen pair, Orestes says:

> I weep for all things done and suffered here,
> For the whole race, and weep for my own fate,
> Marked with the stains of this sad victory.

The chorus adds:

> No man upon earth shall be brought to the end
> Of his days unwounded by sorrow.
> Distress is for some
> Here present, for others abides yet.

This is a repetition of the message clearly stated in the *Agamemnon*: none shall go through life unscathed.

Almost at once Orestes experiences revulsion at his matricidal act:

> – I know now what
> My end will be – my wits are out of hand,
> Like horses that with victory in sight
> Stampede out of the course, and in my heart
> As fear strikes up her tune, the dance begins –

Though the chorus praises him for his courage, his deliverance of the city from tyranny and his cleansing it of the infection of a most foul crime, he only perceives the Furies approaching and closing in on him.

> Ah!

What are those women? See them, Gorgon-like,
All clad in sable and entwined with coils
Of writhing snakes. Oh away, away!

The chorus assures him these are but fancies, but he screams:

To me they are no fancies – only too clear –
Can you not see them? – hounds of a mother's curse! . . .
O Lord, Apollo, see how thick they come,
And from their eyes are dripping gouts of blood!

He flees Argos, going once more into exile, this time an outcast by his own volition. The chorus chants in bewilderment at the deeper meaning of all these violent events, as the second play ends.

The Libation Bearers is short, direct, perhaps too linear, lacking the more accomplished craftsmanship and subtler psychology with which Sophocles and Euripides are to treat the same horrible story. By reversals of fortune, frequent shifts of supremacy from protagonist to antagonist and back again, suspense can be intensified: little of this occurs in this drama. Nor are there crucial shifts of mood; Orestes is critically beset by doubts only after he has committed the vengeful slayings. Yet more than adequate suspense is created for the spectators by the knowledge that a son is about to kill his mother, the most unspeakable of acts. Aeschylus may have felt that Orestes' driving single-mindedness of purpose, his overall lack of doubts, is required to steel him for his formidable task. Besides, he is obeying a god's injunction. As the middle script of a trilogy, *The Libation Bearers* serves mostly as a bridge to the ensuing *Eumenides*: the larger moral issues are to be debated there, and therefore are not anticipated or diluted here, though it is obvious throughout that Orestes is not absolutely convinced of the rightness of his objective; now and then he drops hints of latent questions, partially repressed hesitations. In this piece, however, the overt emphasis is on dramatic action, how the long-awaited vengeance is finally accomplished.

Some differentiation is seen between the motivations of Electra and Orestes, the impulses of a once loving but bitterly mistreated daughter and a wrathful, ambitious, thoroughly manly son. The chorus is almost monotonous in its incessant cry for elemental justice, the *lex talionis* for ever prodding Orestes to reply to the murder of his father with the death of the slayers, an eye for an eye, a tooth for a tooth.

The choral passages are not often digressive, as in the *Agamemnon*; for the most part they keep strictly to the task of pushing forward the matter at hand: this would seem to show the influence of his younger rivals on Aeschylus. Another innovation is that it is Orestes, rather than the chorus, who in effect brings the play to its close, pouring forth his inner thoughts and feelings in a very long aria, though the chorus is given the last few summarizing lines.

Of note, the nurse's role is not like that of the messenger in earlier works: she has a small but active and necessary part in the plot, helping to trick Aegisthus and bring about his downfall. Here Aeschylus is using the third actor in a way wholly new to him; again, in doing this, he was probably beholden to Sophocles. With dramatic genius, however, he makes the nurse a sharp foil to Clytemnestra: her genuine sorrow at Orestes' supposed death is in edged contrast to the unnatural joy of Clytemnestra, his mother, when told her son is no more. By this contrast, not only is the queen's hard-heartedness more clearly illustrated, but her murder justified or, at least, made somewhat more acceptable to what might otherwise be a shocked audience.

Eumenides (*The Furies*) rounds out the *Oresteia.* In flight from the winged creatures, pursued by them everywhere, the exhausted Orestes beseeches refuge in Apollo's own temple at Delphi, that bright-aired mountainous shrine, seat of the oracle, navel of the world. These "Spirits" are symbolic externalizations of the youth's by now overwhelming sense of guilt and frightful remorse. Apollo promises Orestes succour, but they are visited by the reproachful ghost of Clytemnestra who complains of harsh treatment in the other world. She summons up loathsome, supernatural figures to hound Orestes even more. When Apollo seeks to drive them off, they accuse him of not respecting divine laws and violating their ancient rights. Apollo himself has been much at fault in ordering Orestes to slay his mother. This conflict becomes the core of the drama, with Orestes a victim and pawn in the Olympian struggle.

The Furies shriek:

> This is the doing of the younger Gods,
> Who transgress the powers appointed them.

And, again, they accuse Apollo:

> Thou art not an abettor in this work;
> Thou art the doer, on thee lies the whole guilt.

In turn, Apollo argues that Clytemnestra deserved her punishment as a treacherous wife:

> What of the woman then who slew her man?

The chorus replies:

> That is not death by kin and common blood.

The sin of matricide is more heinous than adultery or a wife's murder of her husband.

The Furies refuse to abandon their pursuit of Orestes. Guided by Hermes, he is sent by Apollo on a year-long journey to the temple of Athena, goddess of Wisdom, whose impartial judgement is sought.

The tormented youth pleads that he has been "taught in the school of suffering" and been purified – through Apollo's intervention – of his gory taint. In the "hearing" that follows, before the goddess and citizens of Athens, the case is cleverly argued by both sides. The Furies, as prosecutors, claim that "justice" will cease to prevail if exceptions to the age-old laws, especially those involving patricide and matricide, are granted. Orestes replies that he did only what Apollo decreed.

Apollo appears before the "court", accepting responsibility for the young man's act. He claims to have been led by principles laid down by Zeus, his own father, who looked upon the killing of a parent as the worst offence of all.

The chorus reminds Apollo that Zeus had rebelled and put his own father, Kronos, in chains. The sun-god answers that such an act still falls short of murder. Besides, the tie to the father is stronger:

> The mother is not parent of the child,
> Only the nurse of what she has conceived.
> The parent is the father, who commits
> His seed to her, a stranger, to be held
> With God's help in safekeeping.
> [Translation: Dudley Fitts]

Therefore Clytemnestra's crime was far worse than that of Orestes and merited the dire retribution heaped upon her. Apollo tells Athena, for having sprung full-born from her father's brow, she owes her respect and affection to Zeus over all others.

The vote of the human judges is a tie; as a consequence, Athena has the right to decide the outcome and elects to absolve Orestes, because she – who had no mother – sets a higher value on a father's claim for allegiance.

In an eloquent address to her Athenians, the goddess ordains the permanent establishment of a tribunal to settle future disputes: this is, of course, further propaganda by Aeschylus on behalf of the Council of the Areopagus, to which in this play he symbolically lends a divine sanction. (At this time, the leader Ephialtes had deprived the Council of some of its former powers.) Henceforth, by decree of Athena, the city's patron deity, blood revenge shall be replaced by dispassionate judgement, bringing all family feuds to an end.

The Furies, angered even more by their defeat, threaten to plague the city, but Athena finally appeases them with soft words and concessions and wins their assent to her verdict. The trilogy ends with a procession and hymns in praise of Athena and bright promises for the blest city under a new rule of law.

The Furies allows Aeschylus full scope for his love of spectacle. The drama festival still retained many elements of the earlier masquerade and danced pageant, and references have already been made to Aeschylus' choreographic gifts. He is also said to have been the most daring of costumers and to have created his own stage designs. Legend has it that so realistic and horrifying was the make-up of the Furies that pregnant women in the audience suffered miscarriages at beholding them, the hostile figures writhing, snorting fire from their gaping nostrils; children shrieked in terror. In all his plays, an aspect is his fondness for fantastic characters: in *Prometheus*, for example, the horned Io, Zeus' former lover who has been changed into a heifer; and, in the same work, Oceanus who rides astride a bounding, winged horse. Ghosts abound, too: Darius, in *The Persians*; the dreadful, risen spirit of Clytemnestra in *The Furies*. To the inventive Aeschylus is attributed the padded shoe, the *cothurnus*, that lent the tragic actor added height; and the use of painted masques so much more expressive than the blank linen employed by earlier dramatists. He also conceived many mechanical devices in addition to those previously available on stage.

This last play is almost Sophoclean in form, showing that even in old age Aeschylus was alert and adaptable, not to be outstripped by his younger competitors. The spectator is plunged much earlier into the action; in this respect, the drama differs greatly from the *Agamemnon*, with its long, slow build-up. The chorus is used throughout not to narrate or rhapsodize, but as a strong antagonist, a collective actor participating at every turn of the story. Conflict flares throughout, and once more a dark mood is conjured up with an unwaveringly assured poetic instinct, from the opening moments when the priestess of Delphi, beholding the sleeping, black-garbed, blood-covered Furies in the sanctuary, shrinks from them in horror and takes flight from the sacred precincts.

On the other hand, in this work there is little in the way of character drawing: most of the figures are abstractions, personifying moral attitudes, which has largely tended to be true in other Aeschylean dramatic compositions. His plays have frequently been described not as tragedies of character but tragic explorations of moral and religious ideas, and his treatment of them is usually – though certainly not always – stylized, unrealistic, which is appropriate to their allegorical nature. The dramatic situation itself, the moral choice facing the daunted hero, is the playwright's dominant concern; as allegories, his works do not tell a story so much as test ethical ideas, religious concepts. The ultimate decision does not depend greatly, if at all, upon the temperament or personality of the hero. Indeed, in most of the Aeschylean plays the heroes are blameless, victims of fate; their dilemma does not arise from a character defect. In some instances they are made to pay for errors committed long before by their fathers.

In all this allegorizing and moral probing, Aeschylus reveals himself as deeply troubled and questioning. A great and immensely influential radical in art, his spirit is otherwise conservative, which was his political inclination. Yet in religion many of his beliefs are heretical: his faith is hardly the conventional one of his day. In *Prometheus* he suggests that the Godhead is evolving, changing. Zeus is glimpsed as gradually becoming more kindly, forgiving. Man learns through suffering – a constant Aeschylean theme – and when the sinner acknowledges and expiates his offence he is absolved, as occurs with Prometheus and Orestes. The plays also indicate that Aeschylus' thought is advancing towards monotheism, though he never fully reaches it. His temperament is depicted as half Oriental, and half Hellenic, rationalistic.

Like most conservatives and puritans, who distrust human nature, Aeschylus believes in original sin: God – the Unseen Wrath – seeks out and punishes human transgressions, and no less the sins of the fathers for which, cruelly, the sons must pay. But how else could one account for the otherwise inexplicable sufferings of the innocent? Also present in the works of Aeschylus is what J.J. Bachofen was to discern as a struggle between a patriarchal and matriarchal structure of society in ancient Greece: it is a very obvious theme in *The Furies.* As attested by Athena's climactic speech, Aeschylus is fully on the side of man-dominated culture, the superior claims of the father. Evidences of this struggle between the sexes will be seen in dramas by other authors of this period.

Scarcely any of the prescriptions afterwards laid down by Aristotle for tragic drama apply to

Aeschylus' extant plays. Indeed, Aristotle barely mentions him in the magisterial *Poetics*, though he had to be quite familiar with his prize-winning contributions. But if Aeschylus stresses ideas, which Aristotle held to be only a subordinate aim of a dramatist, for the most part he integrates them effectively into the plots, having them almost indivisible from one another.

Twenty-five hundred years ago this strange poet enlarged and refined the spiritual content and purpose of theatre, raising ever higher its ritualistic dignity. He infused his dramas with intellectual challenges and human passions, transmuting what had begun as a primitive ceremony of chanting and masked dancers into moving and sophisticated dramatic enactments, using theatre as a vehicle for asking on mankind's behalf the eternal cosmic questions: the very nature of God, the often elusive distinctions between good and evil, right and wrong, that have for ever tantalized beleaguered men and women.

The *Oresteia* also provided one of the major dramatic themes of world theatre. Various treatments of this gripping story were written not only by the great Greek playwrights, but also by an endless line of later authors. As pointed out, strong strands of it are found in *Hamlet.*

The eighteenth-century Italian verse-dramatist, Vittorio Amadeo Alfieri (1749–1803) included an *Agamennone* among his efforts at revisions of classical tragedies in the manner of French plays of that period.

Among twentieth-century writers who have attempted significant new interpretations are Gerhart Hauptmann (*Die Atriden-Tetralogie*: *Iphigenie in Delphi, Iphigenie in Aulis, Agamemnon's Death, Elektra*); Hugo von Hofmannsthal (*Elektra*, a play later adapted as a libretto for Richard Strauss's opera); Eugene O'Neill (*Mourning Becomes Electra*); Jean Giraudoux (*Electra*); Robinson Jeffers (*Tower Beyond Tragedy*); Jean-Paul Sartre's *The Flies*; Robert Turney (*Daughters of Atreus*); Jack Richardson (*The Prodigal*), a list that is not complete. O'Neill's version has been used as the text for an opera by Marvin David Levy. A dance drama, *Clytemnestra*, choreographed and initially enacted by Martha Graham, has stayed in her company's repertoire.

By all accounts, Sophocles (497/6–406 BC) was one of the most fortunate persons ever born. He was handsome, so much so that as a youth he was chosen to lead the near-nude striplings of Athens in the procession after the great victory of Salamis. His physical beauty may have been partly responsible for his bisexuality (his voice was high, and he sometimes essayed feminine roles in his plays). But he married, had several children – legitimate and illegitimate – and in old age was notably fond of courtesans, while he had a flirtatious eye open for good-looking boys. Apparently he never lost his own good looks: a possibly idealized or wrongly identified statue of him in the Vatican Museum shows him still an impressive figure. (It is known that his likeness in bronze by Lycurgus adorned the theatre in Athens as early as the fourth century BC, and Benoulli has compiled a guide to forty-three marble busts purporting to be of the poet, one of them a herm bearing his features in the British Museum, and in the painted Colonnade in Athens there was also a representation of him engaged with his lyre.) Such artworks and memorials testify to the lofty regard in which he was held by his fellow-citizens and their descendants.

According to William Nickerson Bates, in his short examen *Sophocles*, a fair amount of what is known about the poet's life is taken from an anonymous thirteenth-century manuscript found in Paris and yielding a biographical sketch and the surviving plays. It is not without demonstrable factual errors but is based on data from much earlier writers of the third and second centuries BC, including Hieronymous of Rhodes, a peripatetic philosopher; Satyrus, who followed the same wandering profession; Carystius of Pergamum, as well as others whose dates are less certain: Neanthes of Cyzius; Lobon of Argos, who quotes the inscription on Sophocles' tomb; Istrus of Callatis, a music historian; and Aristoxenus of Tarentum. Two other sources from a later period are the Byzantine scholar Aristophanes (not linked to the far earlier and immortal Greek concoctor of bawdy farces) and Suidas, author of a valuable *Lexicon*. Fragments of papyri and carved legends on monuments have contributed additional cherished small items of information.

Born in Colonus, a town near Athens, Sophocles had a wealthy father, Sophillus, who owned a sword-making factory where – it is hypothesized – slaves were the workers. When Athens's battles impoverished others, his father – an armourer – prospered. The son had a good education, winning prizes in wrestling and music; in the latter art his teacher was Lampros. The comely young man's way through life was made even easier after he developed a close friendship with Pericles, the enlightened and benign tyrant of Athens, and his personal popularity accrued to him not only for his early disclosed accomplishments but also for his congeniality, his gentle nature, his unceasing wit and charm. Among his companions, besides Pericles, were his rivals Aeschylus, Euripides and the eminent sculptor Phidias, as well as the brilliant, gossipy historians Thucydides and Herodotus, from whose writings he sometimes borrowed. The acidulous Aristophanes spoke kindly of him, which he was not apt to do about anyone else. Sophocles even chose exactly the best period in which to live, the dazzling Periclean Age, after the rigours and dangers of the Persian invasions, which he was spared, and just before the decline and fall of Athens, which occurred a few months after his equally well-timed death.

By virtue of his excellent connections, spontaneous sociability and popularity, he was handed many cynosures: at one time he served as head of a board of ten officials who monitored the collection of tribute monies paid to Athens by other cities that had become its colonies. He was even named a general during the Samian War, though he was not to win fame as either a financier or a military leader. He had a religious turn of mind, held priestly rank – as did Aeschylus – and sometimes officiated at sacred rites. As he grew older, his opinion was sought on many affairs, about some of which he admitted to having little competence.

Throughout his years, he had vigorous health; one of his physical skills, besides wrestling, was as a juggler. In startling contrast to this, he performed publicly on the harp, and was a composer as well. His other talents were manifold and diverse: at first he took roles in his own plays, sang in them and very effectively directed them; however, because of his high voice, which did not carry well, he eventually gave up acting.

Like Aeschylus, he was an ingenious designer of stage devices, and the introduction of the *periaktoi*, the revolving painted prisms, is credited to him. His plays were constantly acclaimed. He was far more applauded than either Aeschylus or Euripides and was especially successful at comedy, the light, amusing playlets that rounded out the serious trilogies. He won first prize for tragedy at the Great Dionysia over and over and was never ranked less than second in any contest. His victories in the festival competitions are variously set at eighteen to twenty-four, depending on the source and possibly on whether his successes at the Lenaea are included. Among those opposed to him on some occasions were Euphorion, a son of Aeschylus, and Sophocles' own son, Iophon, both of whom followed their fathers' vocation. In one instance Euphorion came in first.

Sophocles' first triumph, which was at the expense of the titanic and more seasoned Aeschylus, was in 468 BC, when the new arrival was twenty-eight: he was thirty years younger than the Athenians' favourite playwright. His offering was a tetralogy of which one work was his *Triptolemus*. Plutarch relates that the reaction among the spectators was divided and heated. To avoid trouble, the *archon* refrained from choosing the judges by lot in the customary way; instead he waited until a group of ten generals moved forward to perform traditional libations and then abruptly named them the jurors. They were considered to be of such unassailable repute that their decision would not be questioned as having been corruptly influenced or for any other reason partial. They selected Sophocles.

His long chain of successes and his extensive output would suggest that he was superficial (in fact, the name "Sophocles" connotes "Entertainer"), but on the contrary he was a profound artist. He had high poetic gifts, together with an unbelievably fine sense of form and structure: he is probably the best dramatic craftsman who has ever written for the stage. He was an acute psychologist, and like

Aeschylus a bold and major innovator. Beginning with works in the manner of his older rival, he gradually perfected a shape of play that is all his own. As already remarked, he added the third actor, a breakthrough that revolutionized the theatre, for now the author could broaden the scope of his plots, lengthening their enacted portion and allowing more physical conflict, while shortening and diminishing the importance of the static chorus. He also ended the practice of writing trilogies with linked stories, replacing them with more compact yet lengthy one-act plays, each plot self-contained and emotionally resolved. The separate works no longer had open and dangling ends and less exposition was required in them, for it was no longer necessary to sketch in what had preceded or to prepare for a sequel. A faster pace and strengthened coherence results. He excised digressive material. Though he sometimes increased the size of the chorus from twelve to fifteen, he gave it far fewer lines to chant. At this period the Sophists had sharpened their methods of debate and had a growing circle of interested auditors in Athens; some of this skill of give-and-take, of Socratic verbal parry and thrust, undoubtedly served as a model to Sophocles and other playwrights of his generation in honing and heightening dialogue. In his scripts, actors now engaged in more verbal exchanges and carried the chief burden, in beautifully contrived plots; in sum, Sophocles developed – if he did not originate – the tragedy of character, of individual psychology and personal destiny, again in contrast to the Aeschylean tragedy of fate, which is more concerned with the cosmic and universal. This is partly because Sophocles is said to have had in mind, far more clearly than Aeschylus, the specific resources of the theatre of his day.

He paid close heed to details of staging, insisting on having his actors and choristers shod in white shoes, with members of the chorus also carrying curved staffs with which they could gesture emphatically.

He lived to be ninety or ninety-one; some hazard that he attained ninety-five. His death is attributed to various causes, some of them as bizarre as the tale of the demise of Aeschylus: he is said to have choked while swallowing an unripe grape, to have collapsed from over-stress while publicly reciting passages from his *Antigone*, or to have become over-elated at having won first prize with that script; whichever way it happened, his end seems to have been sudden and short, so he was spared prolonged suffering. Phrynichus wrote, eulogistically, in his comedy *Muses*: "Happy Sophocles, who died after a long life, fortunate, clever, who composed many beautiful tragedies and died happily without having experienced any evil." A fine obituary, indeed!

Perhaps one of the most remarkable things about this amazingly lucky man, however, is that in his plays his philosophical outlook is blood-chillingly pessimistic. In his *Oedipus* the chorus says: "Not to be born is, past all prizing best. . . ." The next best thing, the chant continues, would be for a man to die the very moment after his birth. And elsewhere:

> Call no man fortunate that is not dead.
> The dead are free from pain.
> [Translation: Gilbert Murray]

What can account for this bleak attitude, in a man of such happy temperament and life-long easy circumstances? It is simply that Sophocles did not let his own good fortune blind him to the misery and sufferings of others. He also sensed his own vulnerability. He realized, as he put it, that "Human life, even in its utmost splendour and struggle, hangs on the edge of an abyss." For this reason, Matthew Arnold said of him, in a phrase that has become attached to almost every mention of Sophocles, that he was one "who saw life steady, and he saw it whole". His vision was, truly, realistic and well rounded. He overcame the artistic handicap of being too good-looking, of having events always favour him. He had what the Spanish philosopher Miguel de Unamuno has called "the tragic sense of life", another phrase often conjured up by references to the unflinchingly honest author of *Oedipus* and *Antigone.* Despite his serenity, his was a constant awareness of how laden is man's burden, how fragile his joy. In this, he was – as Edith Hamilton has perfectly described him – "the quintessential Greek".

The exact number of Sophocles' plays is not known, the estimate being somewhere between 112 and 132; he was astonishingly prolific for such a busy man, though of course many of these works consisted of just one act, and at least seventeen may be spurious. Only seven of his complete authentic scripts remain. Titles and fragments of most of the lost works, sometimes a mere few lines, or haply enough of them to reconstruct a scenario, have been preserved – some on crumbling papyri, from beneath Egyptian sands. (They have been compiled by William Nickerson Bates in an excellent handbook. In it are clues to the subjects of at least a hundred of the missing plays, a task made simpler by their being largely based on episodes in Homer's graphic account of Troy's fall and what followed that disaster. Other epic poems and legends also provided him with copious material.)

Earliest of the remaining Sophoclean tragedies is generally conceded to be *Ajax*, probably composed at some point between 450 and 440 BC, when the poet was nearly fifty. This means that for scholars a full grasp of his earlier poetic style and skills of stagecraft is beyond reach. It is believed that for a time he wrote in the grand manner of Aeschylus and handled his themes similarly, while gradually developing his own verbal idiom and feeling for structure. *Ajax* is seen as transitional in his progress, retaining some aspects of the Aeschylean formula but with touches that are novel and distinctly his own. Embodying what has come to be labelled as the Sophoclean "tragedy of fate", it tells how Ajax, one of the mightiest Greek warriors at the siege of Troy, is driven mad by jealousy and shame. Offended by Odysseus, in a quarrel over an award of the armour retrieved by both from the corpse of Achilles, he vows to slay all he fancies have slighted him, not only the chosen Odysseus but even the campaign's leaders, Agamemnon and Menelaus, both shown as mean-spirited. To thwart him, Athena, to whom he has been rude, spurning her help and thus committing *hubris*, distorts his vision. Because of that, he runs amok, wielding his sword furiously, but slaughters only a flock of sheep that he mistakes for armed soldiers. Recovering his senses, overcome by mortification, an object of laughter and ridicule, he commits suicide. He stabs himself with a sword once belonging to his Trojan foe, the famed Hector, now his own after an exchange of gifts between the two fierce champions.

In typical Sophoclean fashion, the play begins at a late point in the story, after the hypersensitive Ajax, bawling aloud his wrath, has already destroyed the hapless sheep meant to be provender for unfed troops. What interests the author most is Ajax's state of mind as he rouses from brief madness and hastens towards self-destruction. The climax is attained early, however, and the second half of the script is taken up by a prolonged dispute between Ajax's half-brother Teucer and the generous, forgiving Odysseus, on the one side, and other less lenient Greek leaders about the proper burial of the self-slain hero. This proves to be an anti-climax, a fault found in other lesser works of Sophocles, along with occasional lapses of poetic taste, metrical ones. Offsetting these are a well-drawn portrait of the vain, self-absorbed Ajax, together with excellent delineation of a modest, discreet Odysseus and a sympathetic Tecmessa, Ajax's self-effacing slave wife who, despite the indifference he has displayed towards her, serves him and his memory tenderly, always faithfully. Odysseus, compassionate and rational, seems to be Sophocles' mouthpiece and consequently is as important in the drama as Ajax. Speaking with calm reason, he very well incorporates the qualities that Sophocles had intended when he said – as reported by Aristotle – that he portrayed men "as they ought to be", that is, large-souled, even-tempered, well-meaning. It is those who are ill-tempered, vain, egotistic, selfish, like the otherwise heroic Ajax, who plunge heedless into ruin.

Sophocles' sympathy for the harsh lot of women slaves is expressed in his kindly drawing of Tecmessa, a view much in advance of his times, and there is delicacy of feeling in the scenes between Ajax and Tecmessa and their little son, Eurysaces, who has a non-speaking part. The child's presence does much to humanize the work.

The chorus represents the crew who have sailed under Ajax's command and are unswervingly loyal to him, having steadfastly admired him. After his suicide, they yearn to return home.

The play is everywhere steeped in pessimism and despair, a conviction of the transitoriness of life, the vexing flux of fate.

> Immeasurable Time in his long course displays
> all things from darkness and then buries them again.

And Odysseus: "I see all of us mortals are nothing but shadows and insubstantial smoke."

Here one finds Sophocles making good use, for suspense, of an oracle, Calchas, who warns Ajax that he must survive Athena's curse during this day or lose his life. Later, the dramatist will similarly employ an oracle to heighten a mood or prepare the spectator for improbable events, notably in his *Oedipus.*

Since Ajax was a great hero to the Athenians, indeed a cult figure to some, the subject of the tragedy had to be treated carefully. The theme was chosen by numerous other contestants, among them Aeschylus. It is hardly as attractive to modern theatregoers and is seldom staged or studied today. In medieval times, however, Bates reports, *Ajax* was among the most liked and widely read of Sophocles' scripts and many copies of it were circulated; some of the manuscripts have been preserved. It is also recorded that the title role brought fame to the actor Timotheus of Zacynthus who excelled in the suicide scene. Much argued is whether Ajax kills himself in full view of the audience, in violation of classical tradition, or if the stabbing took place off-stage, which is not clear in the text.

The play has a political overtone: it is explicitly anti-war. Descriptions of the horrors and wastefulness of battle are truly stark.

Highly effective are Ajax's frequent and quick shifts of mood as he contemplates imminent death, his intention wavering, inspiring matching changes of emotion in Tecmessa and his sailors, who want him to live; he voices fear, shame, despair, anger, contrition, resolve.

Plutarch states that Sophocles is "uneven", and Lattimore concurs in this judgement, but then remarks that if, because of its structural defects, *Ajax* is not a good play, it is at the same time, by virtue of the power of its poetry, a great one. The verse is replete with alliteration, clever and subtle nuances in the use of words which prompt multiple connotations – as well as significant ambiguities – and above all irony, of which Sophocles is a master. Images of light and darkness, and symbolic allusions to Hector's sword – "a gift from my most hated friend" – and the prevalence of disease are repeatedly evoked.

In his summary, Ferguson offers this opinion: "*Ajax* is not at the last a great play, but Ajax is a great role for a great actor."

Sophocles' comparatively minor play, *The Trachiniae* (*The Women of Trachis*) is tentatively ascribed to 420 or 412 BC and relates the sensational story of Deianeira, Heracles' wife. Learning that her husband has a concubine, Iole, she is overwhelmed by jealousy. She sends him a poisoned robe, which causes him to die in agony. This deed is no little reminiscent of one in Euripides' later offering *Medea*, except that the outcome of Deianeira's centaur gift is unintentional: Nessus, a centaur, has told her that the robe would enable her to regain Heracles' love. The centaur, perishing from a blow struck by the Greek hero, has avenged himself. When a messenger brings news of her husband's physical torment, the remorseful Deianeira kills herself. Heracles, dying, is brought in on a litter. He upbraids her memory, until he discovers that her purposes were pure and she was maliciously deceived. After that he shows no interest in himself and his own fate.

Like Ajax, Heracles is completely self-centred. He admits to the fault of infidelity, gives the young Iole to his son, Hyllus, and decrees that his body be cremated. Indeed, he would like to be cast into the flames while he is still alive, but his son dissuades him from insisting on any such horrible end. The chief reason for his wish that Hyllus wed Iole is his inability to stand the thought of anyone else than his son sleeping with a woman whom he himself possessed. Vanity and self-centredness scarcely go further. Yet, Sophocles may be saying, it is this very ruthless selfishness, this self-concern and self-belief, that has made Heracles a great man, a cult hero. Men rise to heights because of their faults as well as their virtues.

In this work Sophocles concentrates on a study of jealousy and the longing that the middle-aged feel for vanishing youth and love, while possessed by a hopeless desire to recapture them. Arguably that is the play's sole dimension: it shows how a great and supposedly invulnerable man is brought low by a weak, distraught woman and a mean, cunning enemy. Yet it might also be said that it is an instance of a good method in art, whereby the universal is revealed in the particular.

Critics disagree as to whether *The Trachiniae* rises above melodrama to attain tragedy. When Sophocles wrote the play, during a time of experiment and transition or very late in life when his powers were declining, is another point of speculation. Some experts even deny that *The Trachiniae* is his, a claim resembling the attempt of Shakespearean scholars to delete the Bard's less successful pieces from his canon. Yet this script by Sophocles has admirers, among them Ezra Pound, who translated it, with a prefatory note saying: "[It] presents the highest peak of Greek sensibility registered in any of the plays that have come down to us, and is, at the same time, nearest the original form of the

God-Dance." Less of an iconoclast than Pound, who was always ready to speak for the opposition, H.D.F. Kitto comments on the many indubitable merits of *The Trachiniae*: "Where, even in the work of Sophocles, shall we find a more moving tragedy than that of this desolate wife who, at what is for her the supreme crisis, tries to win back her husband's love, but destroys him instead?" The much-hearkened-to literary pundit Samuel Johnson termed the drama "puzzling". Earlier, in Roman times, Cicero thought so highly of Heracles' extended, boastful recital of his fabulous accomplishments and misfortunes that he translated most of it into Latin.

Ferguson is convinced that the play is Sophocles' and joins the many other critics who see in it the influence of the innovative Euripides: the use of a lengthy prologue for exposition, the overall looseness of structure – the story breaks into two parts, the first half given over to the sorrowing Deianeira, the second to the stricken Heracles; man and wife are never seen together, which offers the possibility that the same actor, masked, would take both roles. (Euripides himself wrote a tragedy on this subject but many years later.) As is his habit, Ferguson traces the poet's use of recurrent imagery: the allusions to animals, which are appropriate symbols, since Deianeira, before she was won by Heracles, was wooed by the river god, Achelous, who approached her in the shape of a bull, a snake, "a man like a bull", and Nessus, the centaur, half man, half horse. All these were driven off by Heracles, whose nature also proves to be bestial, monstrous – he has sacked and razed the town of Oechalia, only to seize, rape and carry off the virginal Iole, keeping her captive. The image of "disease" is connected not only to Heracles' intense physical suffering, but also to his mental state and his propensity to be briefly obsessed by "love", passionate infatuation, desire "wild like a beast" which impelled him to possess Deianeira and Iole and, earlier, other women, regardless of the cost.

Two prophecies, instinct with irony, are another Sophoclean feature. Heracles' prediction, which he has inscribed on a tablet, and which governs much of Deianeira's actions, is that fifteen months from the day of his departure, a date now at hand, will mark either his death or the start of a quiet, happy life for him. Besides, it has been said that Heracles is invulnerable; he might not be slain by any living foe. Instead, he is killed by a dead creature, one he himself has ferociously dispatched.

Sophocles has a fondness for unpleasant subjects: Ajax goes pathetically insane, Heracles dies in physical agony, Oedipus staggers blindly after gouging out his eyes, all in full gaze of the spectators. This obsession with pain is exampled again in the *Philoctetes*, but here the sustained impact of the hero's dreadful suffering is balanced – in the view of many commentators – by the idyllic setting of the story and the nobility of Neoptolemus, Achilles' son, who is given the leading part. The indications are that this play was written when the author was eighty-six or eighty-seven years old, and supposedly it reflects the serenity he attained in his closing years. Yet it is difficult to accept this drama as "idyllic" or "serene" when its ulcerated hero is for ever groaning and howling because of unbearable hurts. In the legend borrowed by Sophocles, Philoctetes enlists for the expedition against Troy. *En route* the Greek flotilla tarries at Chryse, where Philoctetes steps on a serpent and is bitten in the heel. It is a punishment imposed by the irate goddess Hera, whom he has offended. The wound festers, will not heal, and emits a loathsome stench; Philoctetes disturbs the air with his cries. His companions find his moaning too onerous; they transfer him, asleep, ashore on Lemnos and heartlessly sail off without him. His ulcer lingers, suppurating, sparing him not a moment of relief. Living in a cave, as ten years pass, the solitary Philoctetes barely sustains himself by hunting. He is fortunate, however, in having a magic bow, once the gift of Apollo to Heracles, which the dying Heracles in turn presented to Philoctetes as a reward for setting a torch to his funeral pyre. The arrows shot by this bow are fleet and sure, missing no target.

The Trojan War drags on. Helenus, a prophet, is captured and reveals that the war can only be ended by a battle in which the Greek forces are led by Philoctetes and his supernatural bow, along with the valiant, guileless son of Achilles, Neoptolemus. The difficulty is that by now Philoctetes hates the Greek leaders, the Atreiad brothers Agamemnon and Menelaus, and no less Odysseus, who had contrived to desert him on the island. How can they recover the bow? Odysseus, ever cynical and cunning, portrayed here quite differently from in *Ajax*, concocts a plan: the attractive Neoptolemus will be sent to Lemnos and with Odysseus' secret help will persuade the sick hero to alter his hostile attitude, or at least relinquish the sacred weapon. In this endeavour the ingenuous youth is successful: his dead father and Philoctetes had been fast friends as well as companions-in-arms. In a moment of distress Philoctetes entrusts the magic bow to Neoptolemus, who immediately makes off with it. Though briefly exultant, Neoptolemus cannot abide having played this cruel trick. His conscience is sensitive. The youth's kindness and natural honesty led John Gassner to describe him as "one of the most likable young men in the world of the theatre". Others have found this rather strong praise; to them he sounds at times over-naïve and less than bright. But left on the island, and weaponless, Philoctetes would soon starve to death. Neoptolemus defies Odysseus, who charges him with disloyalty. After the youth returns the bow to the anguished, bitter Philoctetes, the sick warrior still refuses to join the Greek foray. His only wish is to sail to his own country and eventually avenge himself on Odysseus and the brother kings. At the last moment a demigod, Heracles, becomes visible in an epiphany and commands Philoctetes to serve the Greek cause against the obdurate Trojans. This accomplished, the castaway's excruciating wound will be cured. The play ends on a happy note, though most certainly a contrived one, a pure example of *deus ex machina.*

Philoctetes won first prize at the festival of 409 BC. Other Greek tragic poets had earlier chosen the same unpleasant subject, including Aeschylus and Euripides, as well as Achaeus, the elder Philocles, Antiphon and Thedectes. It was obviously suited to Athenian taste.

The chorus consists of sailors from Neoptolemus' ship. They voice compassion for the marooned, afflicted man; they also conspire with Neoptolemus, as they have been rehearsed to do.

The script is well constructed, with clever twists of plot, as Neoptolemus seeks to deceive Philoctetes, then relents. It is unusual, in that it has an all-male cast. The characters are of a piece throughout with Philoctetes adamant, Neoptolemus wavering, his assigned task ungrateful. Philoctetes suffers not only from his disgusting wound, but also from the gnawing thought of how unjustly he has been treated by the leaders of the campaign for which he had volunteered and where he could have won glory by a display of courage and the helpful effects of his wonderful weapon. He remains strong, in spite of his unceasing pain, determined to survive and ultimately exact retribution. Only the intervention of a god can change his long-nurtured resolve. Neoptolemus is thoroughly human, essentially good, though sometimes tempted and misled by his elders. Odysseus is a glib time-server. The introduction of the *deus ex machina* at the end is probably due to Euripides' influence; such effects were spectacular, the figure of a god atop the *skene,* here a giant warrior in a lion-skin and bearing a club. Audiences looked forward to them; such climaxes were highly effective. Sophocles obliged his spectators and resorted to a resplendent one.

Philoctetes is drenched in Sophocles' pessimism and disenchantment. Thus Neoptolemus declares, only too sagely, "In war the best, not the worst are killed," and Odysseus, in seeking to persuade the young man, makes a shrewd case for expediency and chicanery, insisting that the end justifies the means, and any lie or other form of deceit is excusable if it yields success.

> Yes, I too, when young, was slow of speech and quick of hand,
> But now, experience has taught me
> Words, not deeds, rule over men in everything.
> [Translation: Kathleen Freeman]

And, again, in defence of lying:

> When one stands to gain, scruples are out of place.

He promises the hesitant Neoptolemus a "double reward". The young man asks what it is, and Odysseus replies that he will win the title of being "*clever* as well as *brave*". At this point, his loyalties split, Neoptolemus exclaims: "Right! I will do it – and goodbye to honour!"

The play is small in scope, having few philosophical overtones. Possibly it had an oblique reference to events in contemporary Athens of which the always politically minded spectators were very aware: the character and plight of Philoctetes might have been likened to that of Alcibiades, who was accused of impious behaviour and exiled. He too had proved almost invincible in battle, resembling Philoctetes with his magic bow, and though many Athenians detested him, the citizens badly wanted his bold generalship and help in their war against Sparta and looked for his return.

Once more Sophocles makes use of an oracle, for the play is driven by Hellenus' prophecy that Philoctetes and Neoptolemus are needed to storm and overthrow Troy. Though the chorus has a reduced role, it is tightly woven into the action at every step, to sharpen each scene and propel the plot. It may have been from the younger Euripides that the aged Sophocles borrowed the courage to dress his hero in soiled, smelly rags, a bit of realism but a deviation from the traditional garb of a tragic character, especially of a high-born protagonist. Even in his most advanced years, Sophocles was open to artistic change and ready to learn from others, not least from contestants belonging to the next generation.

The literary merit of the dialogue and choruses have been variously appraised. Ferguson describes some passages as having "an eloquent lyricism", but several other critics dismiss the poetry as less than Sophocles' best. The verbal exchanges between the three principals are clear, often terse and edged with conflict, and Neoptolemus, though purportedly unworldly, shows at moments a gift for equivocation and doubletalk that demonstrates the author's skill at such responses. Besides, there is much Sophoclean irony in the half-truths addressed by Neoptolemus to Philoctetes.

Ferguson perceives here a universal subject that is not fully enough developed. "Sophocles continually writes in terms of a divine cosmos and man's disharmony, part wilful, part ignorance. For Philoctetes the wound symbolizes the disharmony, the bow the promise that harmony may be restored. *Philoctetes* is to be seen alongside *Oedipus at Colonus* in having as its theme this restoration of harmony." But, as measured by Ferguson, "the divine dimension is absent".

Interestingly, the scripts of Aeschylus and Euripides based on the same plot have vanished, but scholars have recourse to the ancient text of a lecture by Dion (or Dio) Chrysotom describing how the three treatments differed. Sophocles effected many changes in the story: among others, he had the chorus made up of sailors from Neoptolemus' ship rather than native Lemnians, as they are in Aeschylus' version, and no longer has Odysseus the chief agent in recovering the bow and winning Philoctetes' allegiance, but instead has the young man, Achilles' son, responsible for the successful effort. If the sailors are Lemnians, it follows that Philoctetes is not desolately alone on the barren island. Euripides lends importance to another character, Diomedes, who assists Odysseus in his ruses.

Sophocles wrote a sequel, *Philoctetes at Troy*, the date lost. Seven fragments of it have been found but tell little of its content, which presumably dealt with the hero's fabulous deeds at the destruction of Troy after his ulcer is cured.

The overwrought descendants of the House of Atreus appealed to Sophocles as exceedingly dramatic subjects, as they did to his two great contemporaries. His *Electra*, of uncertain date, parallels the action of Aeschylus' *The Libation Bearers*, as well as that of Euripides' play, recounting how Orestes and his obsessed sister murder both Clytemnestra and Aegisthus. Some scholars believe the Euripides' work, also titled *Electra*, had already been produced, and that Sophocles, shocked by it, wrote his own version to rectify several of the younger writer's high-handed deviations in the story line. The point is debatable, however, some holding that the Euripidean effort came later. That all three versions of the legend staged by these master playwrights are preserved enables modern critics to compare them, a fascinating exercise.

Sophocles' *Electra* departs from Aeschylus', principally, in emphasizing not the implicit moral issues but instead offering an almost Freudian study of Agamemnon's neurotic daughter. Indeed, the central person of the play, as the title indicates, is Electra, not Orestes, who dominates Aeschylus' script. The part of Aegisthus is enlarged, and the dynastic struggle brought far more to the fore; Orestes is chiefly goaded not by a wish for revenge but by his desire to regain the sceptre rightly his.

The plot here is much more deftly handled than in *The Libation Bearers* (though some assert not as well as in Euripides' treatment); and of course it exists as an independent work, not part of a trilogy. Some think its manipulation is superior even to that of *Oedipus*. The action begins with Orestes' return in secret to Argos. He is accompanied not only by his friend Pylades, who throughout keeps silent, but also by an old servant, Paedagogus (the Tutor), who had rescued the boy and fled abroad with him and now serves as a guide to the city with which Orestes is no longer familiar, having been away since early childhood. The site is in front of the royal palace as before.

The initial exposition is brief and the plot gets under way very quickly. Orestes, already resolved upon the death of his mother and her paramour, the usurper, instructs Paedagogus to concoct a report of his untimely death in exile. He is quite prepared to spread any number of lies, explaining: "To my thinking, no word is base when spoken with profit," which is an echo of Odysseus' argument in *Philoctetes.* Cries are heard from within the palace: the voice of Electra, lamenting her father's slaying and her own harsh circumstances. Orestes delays meeting her, withdrawing to pay tribute at his father's grave. The scene is next taken over by Electra and a chorus of her maidens. Unlike in *The Libation Bearers,* where she is seen for only half the play, in this version she is on stage at length, almost always prevailing over it. Her plight is vividly expressed, the humiliations she must bear, the hostility of her mother and stepfather. Nor will she be silent about her intense feelings:

> I shall cry out my sorrow for all the world to hear.

When the chorus points out that she provokes much of her distress by her open antagonism to Clytemnestra and Aegisthus, she justifies herself passionately. Her motivations are strong and clearly articulated. The chorus counsels her that her grief is borne to an irrational excess; it will not bring back Agamemnon:

> . . . from the all-receptive lake
> of Death you shall not raise him,
> groan and pray as you will.
> If past the bounds of sense you dwell in grief
> that is cureless, with sorrow unending,
> you will only destroy yourself,
> in a matter where the evil knows no deliverance.
> Why do you seek it?
> [Translation: David Grene]

Very early the spectators are presented with the psychological question of Electra's exacerbating sorrow and her absolute rejection of any consolation. Before this play ends, Sophocles gives a thorough and convincing analysis of her disturbed emotions. She first says:

> Simple indeed is the one
> that forgets parents pitifully dead.
> Suited rather to my heart

the bird of mourning
that "Itys, Itys" ever does lament,
the bird of crazy sorrow.

And later her complaints grow keener, better argued. The chorus tells her:

Not alone to you, my child
this burden of grief has come.
You exceed in your feeling far
those of your kin and blood.

The allusion is to Orestes and to Chysothemis, a younger sister, whose mourning has more rational bounds. But Electra cannot be persuaded to emulate her. Even so, the chorus advises the tempestuous young woman to conceal her unquenchable anger towards her mother and the king:

Take heed you do not speak too far.
Do you not see from
acts of yours you suffer as you do?
To destruction self-inflicted
you fall so shamefully.
Superfluity of misfortune,
breeding wars in your sullen soul
evermore.

This is a constant motif in Sophocles, recurring in *Oedipus*, too, that a man, though at the mercy of Fate, can by his own psychological flaws worsen his condition. The chorus entreats Electra "not to breed sorrow from sorrow". But she insists:

What is the natural measure of my sorrow?
Come, how when the dead are in question,
can it be honorable to forget?
In what human being is this instinctive?

Ever more obvious by now is the strain of masochism that Sophocles discerns in the intransigent character of this young woman.

Again Electra pours forth in several wonderful speeches (arias) her complaints against the queen and her malign paramour:

> What sort of days do you imagine
> I spend, watching Aegisthus sitting
> in my father's self-same robes, watching
> at the hearth where he killed him pouring libations?
> Watching the ultimate act of insult,
> my father's murderer in my father's bed
> with my wretched mother – if mother I should call her,
> this woman that sleeps with him.

With more indictments, to conclude:

> In such a state, my friends, one cannot
> be moderate and restrained nor pious either.
> Evil is all around me, evil
> is what I am compelled to practice.

Chrysothemis, Electra's sister, appears. (She is not included in either Aeschylus' or Euripides' versions.) Sophocles liked, as in his *Antigone*, to use contrasting figures such as these, foils for each other, sisters of very different natures. Though resentful of Aegisthus, Chrysothemis has accommodated herself to the status quo at court, prepared to compromise in order to survive, to avoid needless suffering.

When Electra exhorts her, she replies:

> Will you never learn, in all this time
> not to give way to your empty anger?

She admits to being sickened at what she sees and must endure:

> But under pain of punishment, I think,
> I must make my voyage with lowered sails,
> that I may seem to do something and then prove
> ineffectual. But justice, justice
> is not on my side but yours. If I am
> to live and not as a prisoner, I must
> in all things listen to my lords.

Electra upbraids her sister for her inaction. She explains that her own public grief is not in vain; it embarrasses and hurts the ruling pair. Chrysothemis has heard whispers of further strictures to be put on Electra, actual imprisonment, and begs her to desist. In answer, Electra's masochistic impulses, her craving for martyrdom, her loathing of the world around her, are even more fully revealed, so that Sophocles' portrait becomes rounder and deeper. Even the prospect of incarceration, shut away from the light of the sun, is welcome to her.

> That I may get away from you all, as far as I can.

At Clytemnestra's bidding, Chrysothemis is bringing sacrifices to Agamemnon's tomb, to help the queen dispel her "night terrors". Electra persuades Chrysothemis against carrying out her mother's errand; instead, the two of them, Agamemnon's daughters, should place locks of their own hair on the grave. The sympathetic Chrysothemis agrees to this token gesture. Later it becomes clear that this is a clever "plant" by Sophocles for a surprising twist in the skilfully handled plot.

Clytemnestra comes from the palace. Her mind is beclouded by a nightmarish warning that Orestes will kill her. Frightened, and with strange logic, she is on her way to Apollo's shrine to offer propitiatory sacrifices. Even now, beset with supernatural fears, she is dynamic, strong-willed, sharp of tongue. Mother and daughter start to quarrel at once and exchange insults, threats, recriminations, in an episode of high theatricality. The dialogue shows Sophocles at his best, the speeches pithy and marked by cruel ripostes. The older woman and the younger are actually very much alike – both are fierce, with a streak of malice. Clytemnestra restates her reasons for having slain the arrogant Agamemnon – the conscienceless death of their daughter Iphigenia – but Electra challenges her to explain away her marriage to his enemy, the despotic Aegisthus. The young woman also offers an excuse for Agamemnon's sacrifice of his child; in her mind she has absolved him of responsibility for that earlier crime.

As Clytemnestra further rebukes her for her indiscipline, Electra shouts back: "Ugly deeds are taught by ugly deeds." At a significant juncture, Paedagogus arrives. He serves in this instance as the traditional messenger and brings a long if fabricated report of Orestes' death by accident in a chariot race at Delphi. (It was apparently rare in a Greek play for a messenger ever to bring a happy account.) At this dark information Clytemnestra is overjoyed, though she acknowledges that her emotion is unnatural, most unmaternal.

> But now, with this one day I am freed from fear
> of her and him. She was the greater evil;
> she lived with me, constantly draining
> the very blood of life – now perhaps I'll have peace
> from her threats. The light of day will come again.

Left to herself, Electra is plunged into gloom and wailing.

Chrysothemis returns from her visit to the grave, excited. She tells Electra that she has wonderful news: Orestes is back in Argos. She intimates – or seems to – that she has seen him. Electra's hopes are raised, only to be cruelly disappointed when Chrysothemis explains: she has found a lock of hair on their father's tomb that could be Orestes'. Electra tells her that it cannot be so – word has come of Orestes' death in a chariot mishap. Two very apt theatrical "reversals" are effected here by Sophocles, his predilection to inject moments of hope just before moments of profound dejection, thereby adding ironic notes.

If Orestes is dead, Electra herself is ready to exact retribution, though she pleads with Chrysothemis for help. The younger girl, prudent, refuses. Throughout the play the conflict is unceasing, between mother and daughter, sister and sister, and with the chorus and Electra nearly always at odds. Displeased with Chrysothemis' refusal, Electra again vows to undertake her task alone.

Disguised, Orestes returns, bearing in an urn – supposedly – his own ashes. Step by step, testing her, he discloses his identity, in a "recognition scene" that Aristotle later faulted as being too prolonged, especially in contrast to the one by Euripides, which Aristotle deemed just the right length. When Orestes finally names himself, she is beside herself with relief and joy, after having been shaken with grief at the thought of his death. Her display of semi-maternal emotion and tenderness for him, her hopelessly lost but now recovered younger brother and ally, causes her to seem much more human than before, a more dimensional character.

Paedagogus rejoins them, goading them to act at once. "Delay is ruinous. It is high time to have done with our task." The build-up of suspense, which now comes in a rush, is achieved with superb economy of means. While Electra beseeches aid before the statue of Apollo, Orestes hurries into the palace and slays Clytemnestra, whose voice is heard:

> My son, my son,
> pity your mother!

And again:

> Oh! I am struck!

Electra, insatiable, cries out to her brother:

> If you have strength – again!

The dreadful deed done, Orestes rushes out and conceals himself, awaiting the hated but now feeble Aegisthus, who, having learned with glee of his stepson's factitious death at Delphi, is eager to have it confirmed by the queen. Seeing a mantled corpse, he is told by Electra that it is Orestes, but when the gloating usurper lifts the shroud he discovers Clytemnestra's bloody body instead. The speeches are replete with overtones and undertones once again, the sort of double speech at which Sophocles excels. Unarmed, Aegisthus instantly realizes that he is trapped. Accepting the imminence of his own death, he goes as ordered into the palace, pursued by the remorseless Orestes. The chorus proclaims:

> O race of Atreus, how many sufferings
> were yours before you came at last so hardly
> to freedom, perfected by this day's deed.

Here the play ends, abruptly.

Throughout, doubt is never cast on the rightness of the vengeance exacted by Agamemnon's offspring, and Aegisthus' heartless and repulsive behaviour argues that his death is only too well deserved; while by now the edge has been taken off any natural shock at Orestes' act, and at Electra's fierce, almost psychotic jubilation at the destruction of her mother. Sophocles has arranged this very well, so that the audience is more ready to accept the horrible resolution of the drama without condemning the troubled and courageous young perpetrators.

Sophocles' dramaturgic skill is as clearly demonstrated in this work as in any other script of his. The rhythmic pulse set by its verse is stunningly varied. The characters deftly avoid repeating information already given. The action opens in *medias res* – in the middle of the story – and the exposition, the background necessary for understanding the plot, is neatly distributed as the narrative swiftly unfolds. The spectator is told at an appropriate moment how Clytemnestra slew her husband, how the child Orestes was spirited out of reach of Aegisthus' dynastic ambitions, and the tense state of affairs at the Argive court since then. The chorus has little to do, much less than in *Philoctetes*, but does counsel Electra during her lengthy monologues, serving as a sympathetic listener and sounding-board for her morbid, brooding plaints. Often remarked is that the play begins with a morning scene – the fresh light and bird calls are alluded to – yet it quickly gathers a darksome, ominous atmosphere.

Is this work really a tragedy or, like the *Philoctetes*, a highly charged, intensely poetic melodrama? Critics have asked the question. *Electra*, by Sophocles, barely pauses to weigh the profound moral issues its subject insists should be considered. The hero is not beset by the Furies after his matricidal deed. He voices no doubts or sense of guilt. That side of the play – and of the characters – is missing. In that respect the people in it are flat, shallow, agents of action, ruled only by tempestuous emotion, as are those who take part in melodrama.

The poetry, unlike that of Aeschylus, never rises to lyrical splendour; rather, its language is epigrammatic and sparse, its imagery very exact in its application. Of note, the style is deliberately archaic, helping to place the time of the drama in remote antiquity, making its primitively violent events and blood-feud more plausible.

Some scholars seek to read religious meanings into this apparently straightforward theatrical work. Many references in it to Apollo, the god's seeming intervention at moments – as when Clytemnestra, after her apparently divinely inspired warning in a dream, beseeches his aid, and a moment later Paedagogus comes with the false news of Orestes' death – strike those commentators as possibly significant. But the critics have not satisfactorily resolved the ambiguities here. Does Apollo command, or even approve, the act of matricide? Is he abetting it, or attempting to thwart it? Is natural law at work, the simple principle of retribution? An unnatural deed provokes an unnatural response? Euripides speaks more clearly on this issue. What may have been Sophocles' intention is too hard to discern; the scholars in their debates about it descend to etymology, the precise meaning of certain words in ancient Greek. Such arguments are too fine-drawn, too subtle, to be summed up here, which is not to say that they lack merit.

It is chiefly for his so-called "Theban Plays", however, that Sophocles is most admired. These three, all dealing with aspects of the legend of Oedipus, ruler of Thebes, were not composed as a trilogy and probably were not written in chronological order: it is believed that *Antigone* (442 BC) was produced before *Oedipus*, for which no sure date is available, and it is known that many more years elapsed before Sophocles added the *Oedipus at Colonus* (405 BC) to the haphazard trilogy; nevertheless, the three are now often read as a deliberately conceived unit, telling a somewhat continuous story.

Of the three, *Oedipus* is the most famous, perhaps along with *Hamlet* the best-known and most applauded play in all dramatic literature, a work of archetypal stature. It is one of the supreme artistic achievements of the world. (The proper Greek title of the script ought to be *Oedipus Tyrannus*, but it is more frequently called *Oedipus Rex*, as it was known to the Romans in the Latin version, and now in English as *Oedipus the King*; possibly this is because "tyrant" has become a pejorative term, which it was not in Athens then.)

The story of Oedipus has profound adumbrations. This is what has happened before the play opens. The gods have laid a curse on King Laius of Thebes for having introduced an "unnatural vice" into Hellas. On three occasions an oracle has warned that Laius and his wife, Queen Jocasta, will beget a son destined to kill his father and marry his mother. Accordingly, Laius shuns his wife's bed, but Jocasta, young, amorous, gets him drunk and entices him into her arms. In time a male child is born. Frightened, heartless, Laius has the three-day-old infant's foot pierced by a spike (hence later his name "Oedipus", the "swollen-footed" or "club-footed") and orders him exposed to die on a hillside beyond the walled city. A humane shepherd, finding the baby and rescuing it, gives it for adoption to the childless King Polybus and Queen Merope of Corinth, whose heir the "lucky" infant becomes. Years elapse. At a banquet, a drunken guest tells the royal young man that he is not truly the son of the rulers of Corinth. Oedipus seeks out the Delphic oracle, who – as the voice of Apollo – had prophesied that he would be responsible for the death of his father and then enjoy a sexual union with his mother. The horrified youth, still mistakenly believing Polybus and Dorian Merope to be his parents, flees from them, lest the prediction come true. He travels a winding, mountainous highway to Thebes. At a narrow crossing of roads his progress is blocked by the chariot and retinue of a cursing, arrogant old man who refuses to move to the edge and let him pass. Oedipus himself is hot-tempered, imperious; he quarrels with the irascible old man, and in a rage lashes out and slays him. He does not realize that by ill chance he has encountered King Laius – father and son have the same contentious temperaments. Continuing his fateful journey, his access to the city is blocked by the Sphinx, a maiden monster with the face of a woman, the wings of a bird and the hindquarters of a lion, who offers glory to whoever answers her riddle, or death to whoever fails. Oedipus, bold of mind, recklessly self-confident, accepts the challenge. The Sphinx asks: "What is it that walks on four legs in the morning, two in the afternoon, and three at evening?" Oedipus, with little hesitation, responds: "Man. As a child, he crawls on all fours; in adulthood, he strides on two legs; as an old man, he leans on a staff." Hearing this, the nettled Sphinx quickly perishes. At long last, the way to the beleaguered city is cleared for travellers. The grateful citizens offer Oedipus the kingship of Thebes. He marries the newly widowed queen, Jocasta, as custom ordains, and mounts the throne, unaware that the dark, horrible prophecy has been fulfilled. Oedipus reigns wisely and well for two decades, having two daughters and two sons by Jocasta. He is respected and feared.

This epochal legend is fathomlessly old: gold seals discovered in a rock tomb close by Thisbe in Boeotia and dating from about 1500 BC show two scenes from it, Oedipus confronting his father and, later, sword in hand approaching the Sphinx. Three epic poems of great antiquity, the *Oedipodeia*, the *Cypria* and the *Thebais*, from all of which some fragments are preserved, relate the tale at length, and elements of it are found in the *Iliad* and the *Odyssey* of Homer. Aeschylus wrote a tetralogy on the subject that is lost but was doubtless known to Sophocles. Euripides also chose it, as did a host of minor dramatists. Sophocles added some surprising turns that complicate the plot, such as Oedipus' link to the royal house of Corinth. He also omits Apollo's command to Laius, through the oracle at Delphi, not to have offspring.

Interestingly, *Oedipus* did not win first prize at the festival; the honour went to an offering by the poet Philocles, tentatively identified as a nephew of Aeschylus and the author of no fewer than a hundred tragedies, all of which have vanished. However, *Oedipus* was presented along with two other dramas and a satyr play by Sophocles, a group which collectively may not have merited the highest favour, despite the surpassing accomplishment of one piece, *Oedipus*. Whether this award is another instance of contemporary popular judgement having been sadly in error, or whether Philocles' lost works were actually better than Sophocles', is a tantalizing question like so many others never to be resolved.

Things gradually worsen in Thebes; it is visited by a pestilence. At this point, Sophocles' play begins: the proud Oedipus comes from his palace to learn why the populace, especially the very young and very old (the chorus), are gathered here raising their heartful prayers and lamentations. At their head is an aged priest. They have white bands about their locks and bear olive branches entwined with strips of wool; approaching the altar, they place the branches on the steps, in a symbolic gesture of supplication, a desperate plea for relief. They beg Oedipus, as the wisest among them, to deliver them from the plague: crops are withering, women and cattle have become sterile. Thebes is being laid waste. Oedipus had rid them of the Sphinx; he must rescue them again. He shares their bafflement and distress and has already sent his brother-in-law, Creon, to Delphi to consult the oracle. He has also ordered the aged, blind seer Tiresias brought to him.

Creon arrives first and brings good tidings, having heard from the oracle the cause of the plague. Thebes is beset, its men dying, its women barren, because the murder of Oedipus' predecessor, King Laius, has not yet been solved or avenged. The city must be purged of the killer, a source of pollution.

Oedipus rashly promises to seek out the culprit and drastically punish him. His eyes shall be gouged out. As Thebes' king he himself will undertake this, because Laius has left no heir to enact retribution, and because a similar fate might befall him – Oedipus – and he would not want to have his slaying go without retribution.

. . . So I must act as if he were my father.

Only one witness to the encounter is still living. Oedipus commands that this man, too, be summoned for rigorous questioning, which leads to a chain of great confrontations of ever rising theatrical impact, the speeches growing shorter, at times almost staccato, the rhythm of the action accelerating in like measure, to the climax of Oedipus' self-discovery. This crucial exchange calls for a considerable variety of vocabulary and accents, each character being articulate in his own personal manner, and the chorus at times lyrical, at other moments prosaic, as the situation requires. By giving each character an individualized speech-pattern, and having each behave predictably, Sophocles presents a sharply drawn assembly of participants, each secondary figure dominated by a single trait, as effective theatre usually needs to have them be, without any loss of believability and humanity.

The reluctant, blind Tiresias is led in by a boy. (Legend has it that Tiresias lost his sight by deciding a quarrel between Zeus and Hera in a way that displeased the jealous Queen of Olympus.) When Oedipus insists that the old man reveal what he knows about the death of Laius, Tiresias evades answering, rightly fearing this king's easily stirred wrath. Oedipus' temper is hotter and shorter than ever: he threatens the aged seer, if he does not reply. Finally, Tiresias, while faltering and clumsy in movement, speaks with direct pointedness: none else than Oedipus himself is responsible for the city's plight. At this, Oedipus, further enraged, accuses Tiresias of plotting with Creon to overthrow him, so that Creon, Jocasta's brother, may succeed to the throne. Tiresias denies the charge: "Creon is not your trouble; you yourself are."

Oedipus cruelly taunts the old man for his blindness. The aged seer replies: "You have eyes, but see not," and adds, "This day shall be your birth and your destruction." He predicts that the one to blame for polluting Thebes will be found all too soon and punished:

> He shall be blind who sees, shall be a beggar
> Who now is rich, shall make his way abroad
> Feeling the ground before him with a staff.
> He shall be revealed at once as a brother
> And father to his own children, husband and son
> To his mother, his father's kin and murderer.
> [Translation: Albert Cook]

The tremulous old man is taken away.

Creon, hearing of Oedipus' anger at him, returns and fiercely refutes the accusations hurled against him. This new face-to-face encounter reaches an even higher pitch than the one between Oedipus and the blind Tiresias. Oedipus, deeply suspicious, will not listen to Creon's defence.

Jocasta appears, having overheard the quarrel between her husband and brother, and tries to halt it. Creon asserts that he has but repeated the words of the Delphic oracle, the mouthpiece of Apollo. To quiet Oedipus' growing fear, Jocasta relates how once before a prophet foretold a dire fate, the death of Laius by the hand of his own son, a prediction that had not come to pass. At first Oedipus is reassured, but as Jocasta continues her account, detailing how Laius had instead been killed by "robbers" at a turn in the road in Phocis, and cites the exact day, Oedipus grows worried. Belatedly, he asks for a physical description of Laius, and is told that except for white hair the dead man much resembled Oedipus himself. How many were in the king's retinue, Oedipus demands. "Five," Jocasta recalls.

Oedipus, ever more apprehensive, agonizingly awaits the sole survivor of the incident, who – he learns – had left service at the Theban court shortly after Oedipus ascended to the throne. At his own request, the man had become a shepherd once again. Now Oedipus confesses to Jocasta that he had slain an old man, together with his small train of followers, who fitted the description of Laius, in just such circumstances as Jocasta has stated. His one hope is that the survivor will confirm that a band of "robbers", not a lone man, caused Laius' death.

Jocasta argues that the shepherd had certainly not lied, for he had no reason to do so; and also that *her* son could not be responsible for the crime since that unwanted child was long since dead.

Jocasta goes to Apollo's nearby shrine briefly to pray for succour. At a crucial moment a messenger rushes in. He has come from Corinth and seeks Oedipus. Bearer of "good news", he hopes to be generously rewarded by the Theban king. Polybus of Corinth has died; the people of that city wish Oedipus to succeed him.

To Oedipus this means that he need no longer fear the vision of the oracle, since he has had no part in his "father's" demise. His spirits, and those of Jocasta, are instantly uplifted. Jocasta again declares that Apollo's oracle has spoken falsely. Oedipus searches his mind: has even his absence from Corinth caused King Polybus' death? The messenger reassures him: Polybus, aged, has succumbed to natural causes. But what of the possibility that Oedipus might still cohabit with his mother, for Queen Dorian Merope is alive. Says Jocasta, at this:

> Be not afraid of marriage with your mother.
> Already many men in their dreams
> Have shared their mother's bed. But he who counts
> This dream as nothing, easiest bears his life.

Sophocles here anticipates Freud by centuries.

Eager to win favour, the messenger hastens to put Oedipus' fears further at rest by revealing an important secret. Oedipus is not the child of Polybus and Dorian Merope: he was found on the slope of Mount Cithaeron, outside Thebes, by a shepherd who gave the exposed child to none other than the messenger himself (formerly a shepherd), who in turn passed the helpless baby to the Corinthian royal pair. He can still identify Oedipus by his pierced foot, and by the name he bears due to his deformity. This tremendous "recognition scene", in which in rapid succession joy is turned to catastrophe, hope to despair, illusion to truth, is considered one of the greatest ever written. It was for Aristotle, later, a model of how, in supreme plot-making, a major recognition scene should lead to the hero's enlightenment along with a significant and even fatal reversal of fortunes.

Oedipus insists that he must speak to the shepherd who found the child, who is also – he learns – the one survivor of the lethal contest on the road to Thebes. Jocasta urges him to desist:

> Don't, by the gods, investigate this more
> If you care for your own life. I am sick enough.

But Oedipus cannot stop his now relentless quest for the truth; his dynamic nature will not let him do so.

> It could not be that when I have got such clues,
> I should not shed clear light upon my birth.

Fearful, Jocasta retreats into the palace. Oedipus supposes that her emotional disturbance arises from her concern lest he, her mate, be proved to have been of lowly birth, while she is of royal blood.

All too soon, Oedipus has his overwhelming answer as to who he is. The first shepherd is brought in. Like Tiresias, the old man does not wish to speak, and for the same reasons. When Oedipus threatens him with torture, the shepherd's tongue is loosened. At first he equivocates, but then tells the full truth. Out of pity, he had spared the child that Laius and Jocasta had ordered him to abandon and let perish on the hillside. Unable to bear this knowledge, Oedipus utters a cry, turns away and rushes into his palace.

The chorus offers dirgeful chants. Then comes a second messenger with word that Jocasta is dead; she has hanged herself. Oedipus, discovering her body, has cut her down and placed her on the marble floor. Then:

> He tore the golden brooch pins from her clothes,
> And raised them up, and struck his own eyeballs,
> Shouting such words as these: "No more shall you
> Behold the evils I have suffered and done.
> Be dark from now on, since you saw before
> What you should not, and knew not what you should."

The doors of the palace open. Self-blinded, blood pouring from his pierced eyeballs, Oedipus staggers from the royal dwelling-place. He pronounces his self-exile: he will leave Thebes, and begs only for someone to guide him.

The unforgiving Creon, assuming the kingship, speaks coldly to Oedipus; he will ask advice from Apollo as to how the heedless, guilty Oedipus shall be treated henceforth.

Oedipus begs that Jocasta be granted proper burial, and that he himself, a poor blind wanderer, be allowed to depart. Dependent now on a stick to tap his way, he illustrates all too well the final phase of his description of "man" once given in answer to the Sphinx's riddle. He has also fulfilled the harsh prophecy flung back by Tiresias in response to his cruel taunts, confident at the moment of his high prosperity. In another symbolic touch, he who had once had the sockets of his ankles pierced at his father's command now has the sockets of his eyes similarly pierced – with pins from his mother's brooch.

Oedipus asks that his little daughters be brought to him; hands trembling, he caresses them, bids them a piteous goodbye. He calls them his sisters, rather than his daughters, and foresees their future hardships as the offspring of incest: none will marry them. He commits them to Creon's care. He expresses regret that he did not die as a child on the mountainside, as his parents had decreed for him.

The chorus, appalled at this last spectacle, warns that until dead no man can be counted lucky or happy or without the prospect of enduring pain.

The universal impact of this tragedy is attributed to several clear aspects of it, and perhaps to some not so clear but instead peripheral and subliminal. In recent decades Sigmund Freud has helped to bring it to the attention of a wider audience by attaching the name "Oedipus" to a neurosis – a complex – that arises from a son's unconscious sexual fixation on his mother and consequent jealousy and hatred of his father, whom he wishes to supersede, which prompts in him several kinds of inhibitive or compulsive behaviour. Freudian psychoanalysts point to the ancient legend on which the play is based as an example of a repressed wish to which primitive man often gave expression in personal dreams and collective mythology, as Sophocles has Jocasta intimate in a line cited above. Later scholars and psychologists, however, take issue with this – among them J.M. Bachofen, Otto Rank and Erich Fromm – remarking that though there are parallels to the Sophoclean drama, the motivations of the Oedipus portrayed in it are not Freudian at all: he is hardly jealous of his father, for he does not know Laius to be his progenitor; he does not desire to possess his "mother" sexually, for he is unaware of who she really is; he marries her solely because as the consort of its queen he will have a more legitimate claim to the Theban throne. Both the man killed on the road and the newly widowed queen had been total strangers to him, and he does not learn their identity until long after his deed, so that none of the elements of the Freudian interpretation fit.

A quite different explanation for the play's stature and "popularity" – an appeal which is surely paradoxical, because the subject is so unpleasant – is its aesthetic perfection. Of the plot it has been said – and endlessly quoted – that it resembles the Parthenon in the rightness of its construction: no part of it is out of place, each fits exactly, and the whole has an excelling consistency and harmony. Not a speech or episode can be removed, or transposed, without a vital alteration of the entire design. The plot has unassailable logic, inevitability. It unfolds with unfailing suspense and exploits every sound dramatic device. Its superlative form has a hypnotic effect on an audience. Aristotle, in his *Poetics*, a bible of the craft of playmaking, has no fewer than eleven allusions to it and singles it out as the model, the criterion, of the well-made play, and for that reason a script to be studied in detail and emulated by other writers.

Oedipus is also a metaphysical detective story – again resembling such later masterworks as *Hamlet* and *Crime and Punishment*. Who is the murderer? Who is morally guilty, the source of the plague? What is the deeper truth? The search is inward as well as external: "Who and what am I?" Oedipus asks himself. The plot is an extraordinarily fine "objective correlative" of that spiritual and psychological query. And, in modern terms, it embodies "the search for the father", a theme fashionable in recent literature.

An infinity of other meanings can be read into the play. Though it has perfect form, it is composed of wild coincidences and melodramatic elements. Walter Kerr comments that these far-fetched "improbabilities", like those in Shakespeare's *Lear*, are readily acceptable by an audience because they correspond to what man knows of the true chaos and anarchy of life under its ordered, rational surface. Indeed, it is worthwhile to recall here Eric Bentley's observation that melodrama only confirms man's inherent paranoia, his conviction that malign forces are aligned against him, and the excesses of melodrama are not in reality excesses at all, but factual pictures of what happens to us during a lifetime. The evil fate that waylays Oedipus might be considered on one plane to be exaggerated and symbolic, yet on another plane to be realistic, because mischance, the most unexpected and harmful twists of events, dog all of us. The misfortunes that befall Oedipus, the tragic hero, are heightened and exceptional, but no one can say that they are impossible.

Kitto contends that what Sophocles affirms in this play, as in his *Electra*, is that certain natural forces in life and the universe must be maintained in balance, and the violent deviations, the anarchic imbalances, set in motion by such dynamic agents as Clytemnestra and the rash, headstrong Oedipus only invoke counter-forces that restore the fixed natural order once more. What follows an unnatural act is not predetermined by the gods, except in so far as it is a "natural consequence" of the outrageous deed that has for a time upset the rational and perhaps divine order of things. Linked to this belief is one put forward elsewhere, that perfection in a work of art such as the *Oedipus* implies a similar world-order which governs man's destiny.

Nikolai Berdyayev interprets *Oedipus* as a "passion play", comparable to such stories as the drama of Job in the Old Testament and of Jesus of Nazareth in the New Testament. In it we hear a protest elicited by the sufferings inflicted on man, who is the "unjust sufferer", that is, the man who suffers unjustly, without due cause. Essentially, it is a presentation of the problem of the existence of Evil in a universe ruled by a kind God.

Other grapplings with this cosmic theme in Job and the story of Calvary embody the Hebraic and Christian answers to the question raised here by Sophocles. The explanation given by the Hebrew prophet is that man is too small and his mind too limited for him to understand the wishes and intentions of an Almighty Jehovah, an omnipotent and angry Deity; and the Christian reply is a transcendental and salvationary one: suffering in this world has little significance, for what really counts is what happens in the next world, for which a man must daily prepare himself by prayer and a steadfastly virtuous life.

The Greek answer, as Berdyayev sees it, is that propounded by Sophocles in his Theban Trilogy: "the tragic truce with fate". Man accepts the inevitability of pain and death, and does so with stoic dignity and nobility. This is better displayed in Sophocles' *Oedipus at Colonus*, the sequel to *Oedipus*, but it is clearly implied here by the courage with which the unflinching, self-punishing Oedipus accepts the dire outcome of his harassed, frantic search.

Jocasta warns Oedipus to drop his questioning. Some critics think that the hero's *hubris* is an excessive intellectual curiosity. Like modern man, especially like a contemporary atomic scientist, he does not know when to halt his search: he probes too insistently, until at last he learns more than he can cope with; he has opened Pandora's box. Like Dr Faustus and Hamlet, he should have let well enough alone. Oedipus might be compared to those high-minded physicists who split the atom and ever since have had to live with the knowledge of having burdened mankind with the daily spectre of an imminent holocaust. Better for Oedipus had he stopped his pursuit of truth at an expedient moment. One aspect of the play is a picture of man's vain ambition to know too much, his foolish belief that he can know the truth about anything, even about himself. Should he possess the gift of reading the unknown, and should he seek to rival the gods in his risky quest for omniscience?

Is the play "deterministic", as has often been said? Does it declare that man is the helpless victim of the gods, of fate? But the oracle only *predicts* what will happen to Laius, Jocasta and Oedipus: the persons of the drama make the tragic events come about, each through a flaw in his or her moral character. Each – Laius, his unhappy queen, his luckless son – has committed an offence. Laius is notoriously immoral and cruel; Jocasta seduces him and is responsible for his having an unwanted son; Oedipus is vain, suspicious, easily excited. He is patronizing and a braggart. In almost his first speech he alludes to himself as "world-renowned and glorious, whom all men call great". Is this not one facet of his *hubris*, his overweening pride? When Tiresias warns him not to ask dangerous questions, he replies with a boastful reference to his having solved the riddle of the Sphinx: "You mock me for that which made me great." Greek audiences may have wondered why, after his having heard the prophecy at Delphi, a bare twelve miles behind him, he allowed himself to quarrel with and kill a man old enough to be his father, and then marry a woman whose age would easily permit her to be his mother. His faults are psychological: they, rather than the gods, have determined his fate. The Delphic oracle has merely foretold what lies in store for him, since he persists on a headlong, self-willed course of action. That is his nature. He is, as the poet W.H. Auden puts it, punished for having mental fissures and excrescences in his psyche.

Similarly, his self-punishment goes far beyond what his deed merits. "What madness overcame you?" cries the chorus, on beholding his hasty blinding. He has again acted irrationally, excessively, if all too consistently. "What daimon drove you on?" His own daimon: his over-confident, aggressive, unrestrained, even uncontrollable personality. He does not demonstrate the intelligence he claims to have. The play is a "tragedy of character".

Yet another way of looking at Oedipus is to behold him as the "unjust judge". This is another favourite Sophoclean theme. Oedipus condemns the unknown culprit out of hand, knowing nothing about him or the circumstances. In doing so, he unwittingly pronounces sentence on himself, who is the offender but in many respects innocent and entitled to at least a measure of mercy. Should not an "unjust judge", an intemperate and reckless arbiter of other men's lives and fortunes, be punished in this way? He is treated as harshly as he treats others. Does he not deserve this severe retribution? To Creon, in *Antigone*, the same fate is meted out.

Oedipus' self-condemnation, which is unintended, is strikingly ironic. As has been noted, the Greeks delighted in such irony. This play abounds in brilliant instances of it: the neat inversion of Oedipus' being the seeing man who is "blind", by contrast to Tiresias, the blind man who can "see". Oedipus rails at Tiresias and jeers at the old man's affliction, then himself is blinded, setting out on a journey "dragging his dreadful foot". These inverted overtones appear earlier and again when Oedipus proclaims: "In doing right by Laius I protect myself, for whoever slew Laius might turn a hand against me." He must avenge Laius, who had no son to do it. Ironic, too, is his ultimately embodying the very answer – a three-legged old man – to the riddle the solving of which has brought him eminence and high prosperity; and it is ironic that the shepherd who discovered the infant Oedipus, and thought to do a kind deed, perpetrated instead a most unfortunate one, which he must bitterly regret.

Sophocles stresses also the irony of Oedipus' passing unfair judgement on Creon, only to have the situation quickly reversed, with Creon placed where he issues commensurately harsh judgement of the fallen Oedipus. Jocasta assures Oedipus that the "death" of her child proved once and for all that oracles are not to be heeded – she laughs at the pretensions of oracles, which was still somewhat heretical in Sophocles' day – but does not realize how unhappily accurate has been the grim prophecy.

The background of the story echoes with irony: Oedipus flees from Corinth after learning of the forecast, to prevent its coming true, thereby only helping to hasten its fulfilment. Most of this tragic irony is apparent to the audience because it shares with the playwright a secret as yet withheld from the hero, a device that is one of the most effective in drama. Throughout the work, too, moments of sudden hope precede those of profoundest despair, another dramaturgical trick that Sophocles practises far better than any other writer in literary history.

Francis Fergusson emphasizes Oedipus' image as that of, once again, the "divine scapegoat", providing the play with an anthropological dimension. The city is blighted by pestilence, its crops withered in the nearby parched fields, its herds and women sterile. The king, fulfilling an immemorial role as sacrificial victim, must die to purge his community of sin, in this instance his own. Samuel Selden holds a similar view: "Throughout the play of *Oedipus* the issue is not the king's happiness but the state's health." Fergusson sees the Dionysiac theatre as having been for the Greeks "a sacred combat of which they were spectators but also participants in a sense". And: "When one considers the ritual form of the whole play, it becomes evident that it presents the tragic but perennial, even normal, quest of the whole City for its well-being. In this larger action, Oedipus is only the protagonist, the first and most important champion." A historical fact, not cited by Fergusson, is that a plague had raged through Athens at a date possibly only slightly preceding the play's production, so that the subject of collective suffering and its causes might have had a special relevance for Sophocles, and strong topicality for the first audience, though this is conjectural.

Fergusson evades any clear explanation of why Oedipus' unwitting individual act should have contaminated not only himself but all others involved in the story, and why those others must be made to feel pain along with him, except that there are echoes here of the tragic drama's origin in festivals that celebrated the "withering which Winter brings, and calls, in the same way, for struggle, dismemberment, death" before renewal (as in *Oedipus at Colonus*). Ultimately, Fergusson thinks, the play is ambiguous; it is a mysterious work, and modern attempts to reduce it to a firm and clear statement of this or that are artistic and critical errors.

Others reply that this goes contrary to the clear-headedness that marks Sophocles' work, his sure, deft craftsmanship, the lucidity of his poetry, the rational bent of his temperament. If nothing else, Sophocles seems always to urge that his people should conduct themselves calmly, logically. Is it not less than likely that he would offer a deliberately vague or obscure play? He was not inclined like Aeschylus to the mystical. The god so frequently referred to in his works is Apollo, not Dionysus, whose cult was mindless. But this is not to suppose that he was unaware of the inexplicability of the cosmos and the bewildering purposes of forces throbbing and pulsing through it.

Another mythical motif that recurs here, as through much of drama in every age, is that of "the changeling". Richard Lattimore, like Otto Rank and J.K. Newberry before him, discerns here the eternally fascinating "story-pattern of the lost one found". The persistence of this plot-premise in many forms of drama for thousands of years must be examined. "The child is noble, the child is unwanted and put away and usually thought dead." Or perhaps it has been kidnapped, lost, or left alone and impoverished when its parents are killed. Belatedly its true identity is discovered, as happens with Oedipus, and its royal rank is revealed. In *The Myth of the Birth of the Hero*, Otto Rank elaborates from a psychoanalytical point of view on probable deeper significances of this enduring motif. This will be looked at further in a discussion of the origins of comedy, a genre in which the "changeling theme" is even more prominent.

J.K. Newberry, in *The Rainbow Bridge*, suggests that Oedipus and his similarly ill-fated daughter Antigone were once deities who became humanized, and their story is once more a telling of the death and mutilation of fertility symbols. In such dramas the son nearly always marries his mother: an instance is Tammuz. But speculation does not end there. Immanuel Velikovsky, in his *Oedipus and Akhnaton*, seeks to trace the legend's source and the figure of Oedipus far back to an Egyptian Pharaoh and his troubled family ruling in a dimmer span of history. The mythological elements brought together in the creation of the half-female Sphinx and its trivial riddle are rich and have been extensively studied.

Oedipus might also be a political allegory, with many other topical references besides the one to the plague that had lately ravaged Athens. This is proposed by Bernard Knox in a substantially documented work in which he posits that Oedipus is meant to represent Athens: phase by phase, his traits are those of the city-state itself, as depicted in Pericles' Funeral Oration, a collective portrait of its citizenry. The doubt cast upon prophecy, voiced by Jocasta, echoes a burning debate in Athens at that time. Richard Lattimore sees Oedipus as typical of the always wary and suspicious tyrant, the sometimes ruthless ruler unsure of his power, though still possessing rare qualities of patriotism and at moments compassion. What playwright has ever been untouched by topical influences and his own cultural context? Says Knox: "Both the virtues and faults of Oedipus are those of Athenian democracy. . . . The audience which watched Oedipus in the theatre of Dionysus was watching itself."

Another topical side of the drama is perceived by John Ferguson, whose *A Companion to Greek Tragedy* has been frequently quoted here (and who is not to be mistaken for the eminent critic, the late Francis Fergusson – a sibilant double "s" – author of *The Idea of a Theatre*, a truly seminal book and another much valued source). Throughout the play, which he scans line by line as is his habit, Ferguson finds evidences of Sophocles' use of "scientific language", incorporated into images and metaphors and reflecting the playwright's interest in and adaptation of what Athenians of the Periclean era were calling the New Learning, a result of contemporary advances in knowledge by Protagoras, Parmenides, Zeno and Gorgias. In the dialogue and choric passages are found repeated allusions to mathematics and medicine – questions are asked on how to cure the sickness of the state, how to free it of the plague and purge Oedipus and Jocasta of an inward moral pollution. Also, a strange significance is accorded numbers that mysteriously seem to recur and somehow govern or attach themselves to events, especially 3 and 5 – Oedipus, when stricken and aged by his self-discovery, is reduced to walking with a stick on "three legs"; the confrontation with Laius occurred at a juncture of three roads; the rule in Thebes is shared by three, Oedipus, Jocasta and Creon; there were five persons in Laius' party; and so on. Sophocles also indulges in plays on Oedipus' name, using phrases like "wandering with a miserable foot", uttering "a fierce-footed curse", proclaiming "high-footed laws". In a further chain of metaphors, Oedipus is likened to a hunter – tracking the murderer, he himself is later to be hunted – and to a helmsman and a ploughman.

Though conceded to be a towering work, *Oedipus* has detractors, among whom is the much respected Cambridge University classicist F.L. Lucas. In the preface to his translation of the script he sets forth his reservations concerning it.

> This is often thought the greatest of Greek dramas. It is rather, for me, the most astonishing – a masterpiece of pure "theatre". Its characters are not very attractive, its theme repulsive, its plot incredible; yet, after two thousand years, it still grips. The psychoanalysts, of course, have their explanation, and that may help. But dramatic success would be simple if it sufficed to write plays about incest. There have

> been plenty. But Walpole's *Mysterious Mother*, for example, is stone dead: *Oedipus lives.* Why?
>
> It rests on a primitive legend of popular fatalism. What would a decent man least like, and be least likely, to do? To kill his father and marry his mother. Well, answers this story, if it is fated, he will do it, struggle how he may.

Lucas then recounts a similar parable, of the merchant of Baghdad who vainly tried to avoid his appointment with Death awaiting him in Samarra.

> To flee your fate is to rush to find it.
>
> Handling a story far less neat, the skill of Sophocles lies precisely in bewitching his audience to overlook its flaws. What would have been the *rational* course for Oedipus? If he had absolute faith in oracles, he could only resign himself; what must be, must. If his faith was less absolute, the safest remedy was immediate suicide; if that was too drastic, he could resolve at all costs never to murder or marry; if he found those pleasures indispensable, he could at least resolve never to murder or marry anyone who could conceivably be even ten years older than himself. What, instead, does this wise man do? Only ten miles from the fatal oracle which has just warned him, out of momentary pique he kills an unknown old gentleman (to say nothing of three servants) in a futile bicker about being jostled off the track. Then, having broken the heart of the Sphinx by reading her riddle, he allows the grateful Thebans to marry him to an equally unknown lady of unknown age. Doubtless Jocasta may have looked younger than she was; but we are further asked to believe that Oedipus lived happily with her for a dozen years or more, without a word said of his past life, or of hers, or her late husband's death.
>
> Granted, all this falls, as Aristotle says, "outside the play".

(Lucas refers here to Aristotle's rule, in the *Poetics*, that an implausible action is less likely to trouble the spectator if it has occurred in the past, before the story starts; or offstage, so that it is only reported and not seen.)

> But even when the play has begun, this clever reader of Sphinx's riddles fails to see the obvious clues that are there (even after his wife has seen them), and sees fantastic conspiracies that are *not* there. We are further asked to accept a holy prophet who comes to Oedipus to lock the frightful truth in deepest silence, but is provoked by a most unholy irritability to bellow it in public. We are asked to accept holy gods that doom a man unborn to parricide and incest; then leave him to beget four innocent chil-

dren; then kill off guiltless multitudes with a plague, merely to bring about the revelation of this guilt they have imposed upon their victim.

How many competent dramatists would dare undertake such a plot? And what a dramatic hypnotist that, in spite of all, could bring it to success?

For Sophocles has not here, like Shakespeare sometimes, redeemed a fantastic plot by the human warmth of his characters. Jocasta, indeed, is moving; and the two herdsmen are vividly, though slightly, drawn. But Creon seems only a worthy stick; Tiresias, a cantankerous dervish; the chorus, the usual band of melodious admonishers; Oedipus himself (though some critics have admired him), a somewhat self-complacent, self-blinded, wildly suspicious and choleric person. His sneer at Jocasta (when she begs him to seek no further), that no doubt she is snobbishly afraid his birth will not prove sufficiently noble, though doubtless meant to heighten the impression of blind pride before its fall, seems itself needlessly ignoble. And when the truth breaks, he rouses in many of us less pity than repulsion by a frenzy that pursues Jocasta sword in hand (as if incest would be improved by matricide), then futilely digs out his own eyes. This last may, indeed, be truer to life than rationalists suppose – modern psychology has recorded a neurotic who destroyed his own eyes with pieces of glass because he could no longer bear his own criminal impulses and wished to blot out a world grown intolerable. But perhaps a more illuminating parallel is the frenzy of Philoctetes when, robbed of his bow, he shouts for an axe so that he can hew off his own limbs rather than accompany his hated countrymen to Troy. The "gentle" Sophocles certainly chose to create characters who are anything but gentle.

As for critics who discover profundities of thought in this tragedy, they have not much to show but the final moral that no man should be called happy until safely dead. One doubts if a play could live long on this fossil chestnut. It might have been another matter if Sophocles had led up to the conclusion of universal forgiveness of all human sins and frailties because, in the words Fitzgerald chose for his own epitaph, "It is He that hath made us, and not we ourselves." But not till a generation later, in the far more thoughtful *Oedipus at Colonus*, did Sophocles stress the fundamental innocence of his hero, and strikingly turn this figure of outcast pollution into a guardian genius of the kindly land that sheltered him.

And yet it moves. How? Not by its ideas, not by its characters, not by plausibility of plot. But its great scenes grip. The first quality of drama is to be dramatic. And this quality the play has, supremely – thanks to the brilliance with which its action, cunningly delayed, yet never too much slowed, deviating now one way, now another, closes at last inevitably on its victim. In their suspense the audience are fascinated as if they watched some wanderer on a mountain blindly circling nearer and nearer to the precipice. He need not be a very attractive character – enough that he is a man. And to what is, in

> fact, the first detective play, the first "thriller" in European literature, Sophocles has added his gift of style, his gift of tragic irony. *Oedipus the King* does not appear to me the highest kind of drama. Its influence value seems slight. One feels that Plato must have as much disapproved its emotionalism as Aristotle admired its skill. But its pleasure-value has lasted. If it is not a play of the most admirable kind, of its kind it is an admirable play.

In a similar vein, though in a manner less wry, John Ferguson faults much of Sophocles' treatment of the plot.

> It is, of course, a mighty play. Aristotle valued it highly for its structure. The *peripeteia*, by which action designed to one end leads to its diametrical opposite, is peculiarly impressive. In the first place, is a double *peripeteia*; one in the background, where Oedipus in turning away from Corinth toward Thebes flees headlong into the jaws of the very destiny he is trying to avoid; one in the foreground, where the Corinthian messenger, who comes with news of glory and security for Oedipus, brings degradation and disaster. Second, this second *peripeteia* coincides with the truth about Oedipus and his identity, a coincidence that Aristotle regards as endowed with special power. Third, the scene itself has been well analyzed by Jebb. The thread of evidence from the reported statement of the herdsman to the place of the murder seems to show that Oedipus killed Laius, being presumably unrelated to him. The thread of evidence from Corinth shows that Oedipus is not the son of Polybus and Merope and relieves him of the fear of parricide and incest. In this scene the weaving together of the two threads shows that Laius' killer committed parricide and incest.
>
> There are other structural points. In the central episodes the truth is revealed in reverse order – first the suspicion that Oedipus killed Laius, then Jocasta's account of exposing the child, and eventually the identification of its birth. In this way the play operates on a double time scale, the events on stage and the revelation of the past. The irony, perhaps more intense here than in any other play ever written and at times almost too intense, is part of the structural strength: so are the cross-rhythms we have noted in the third episode. . . .
>
> Modern critics tend to add the extraordinary skill of Sophocles' portrait of Oedipus. To Aristotle Oedipus is an excellent subject for tragedy, because he is pre-eminently great and glorious without being pre-eminently just and virtuous, and because he falls through a fault but not a criminal fault. The modern critic admires Sophocles' instinctive psychology: whether or not we should take Oedipus as representative of the Oedipus complex, he is a study in repression. So, it is suggested, we should

interpret his failure to see the truth, his temper, his projection of blame onto Creon, and his behavior, which is wrong but realistically portrayed. Again we are aware of the poet's increased mastery; there is something of both Antigone and the earlier Creon in Oedipus, but the touch is more certain and the portrait more persuasive.

Yet for all its merits *King Oedipus* has three grievous defects. The first is its intrusive improbabilities. Aristotle tries to suggest that they lie outside the plot. Even so it is hard to swallow Oedipus' ignorance of the story of Laius; hard to credit that Oedipus and Jocasta had never compared oracles; hard to think that with those oracles before him Oedipus would ever allow himself to marry a woman twenty years his senior; hard to suppose that the evidence of the pinned feet had never come out. But the improbabilities do not all lie outside the plot. Even if we allow Oedipus' extraordinary obtuseness to be a matter of repression, we have still the implausible coincidence that the messenger from Corinth and the survivor from the battle of the crossroads should be the very two herdsmen who alone could identify Oedipus. The second defect is the inevitability of Oedipus' destiny. It was this that Freud saw: "The *Oedipus Rex* is a tragedy of fate: its tragic effect depends on the conflict between all the all-powerful will of the gods and the vain efforts of human beings threatened with disaster; resignation to the divine will and the perception of one's own impotence is the lesson which the deeply moved spectator is supposed to learn from tragedy." Freud explains the play's continuing appeal because Oedipus' fate might have been our own, "because the oracle laid upon us before our birth the fate which rested on him." Knox made a gallant attempt to rescue the play from the curse of inevitability. The play, he maintains, is not about Oedipus' murder of Laius and marriage with Jocasta, but about his discovery that he has done these things, and that is not inevitable. But we cannot think that the tragedy lies not in the acts of offense but in the fact that Oedipus found out. Dramatically we cannot in this way separate act from discovery. The play starts with the pollution caused by the act. The inevitability of Oedipus' destiny does detract from the power of the play.

The third defect is the brutal description of Oedipus' self-blinding, followed by his appearance with a new, eyeless, blood-smeared mask for a scene of lamentation. Aristotle claims that the play excites pity and fear by what is heard rather than seen. But this is not true. As Oedipus appears at the end, the chorus cries, "Disaster fearful for men to see." This scene abandons the traditional reticence and reserve of Greek art. It is close to Grand Guignol. . . .

The power remains. Waldeck wrote well: "There is no meaning in the *Oedipus Tyrannus.* There is merely the terror of coincidence, and then, at the end of it all, our impression of man's power to suffer, and of his greatness because of this power." Yet even that is not the full truth. In another age of

> New Learning, Thomas Fuller wrote, "Who hath sailed about the world of his own heart, sounded each creek, surveyed each corner, but that there still remains much *terra incognito* of himself?" . . . Oedipus is indeed, in words that Seneca used in another context, *notus nimis omnibus, ignotis sibi*, "too well known to the whole world, unknown to himself." For the riddle of the Sphinx, as De Quincy saw, is answered in the life of her destroyer – the weak infancy, the strong independent manhood, the blind man's stick. There is meaning in the play; it is meaning that we in yet another age of New Learning do well to take to heart; it is most simply in words that were themselves associated with Delphi – "Know yourself."

Richard Lattimore, too, dwells on improbabilities in the plot, listing still others. If Thebes was terrorized by the Sphinx that obstructed the city's highway, why did not Tiresias, the all-knowing, answer the riddle and destroy the monster? Why did he, the holy man, permit the townspeople and their cattle to die in a plague, when he knew how it could readily be lifted? He had only to speak out. What accounted for the long silence of the shepherd who had escaped from the fatal encounter at the crossroads? Surely he recognized Oedipus as the slayer. Lattimore suggests that the rapid pace of the unfolding action gives the spectator no time to raise such questions. It is irrational for Oedipus to blind himself, says Lattimore, but the act is committed in a moment of frenzy, in which "reasoning of any kind is too reasonable". Afterwards, when the fit of wildness ebbs, in the final pathetic scene, "Oedipus is himself again, reasoning, and justifying." The blinding also reduces Oedipus to near helplessness, "within moments turned into an old man", fulfilling the portrait in the Sphinx's riddle. "In this sense," Lattimore adds, "but I think in this sense only, Oedipus is Everyman." A further observation: "Oedipus is the tragedy tyrant driven by his plot, but he is more, a unique individual and, somehow, a great man, who drives himself."

A more recent study, Frederick Ault's *Sophocles' Oedipus: Evidence and Self-Conviction*, offers a fresh slant, arguing that Oedipus is mistaken in thinking himself guilty of killing his father and marrying his mother. He does not ask the right questions and wrongfully accepts the blame. He misuses "language as the weapon". The spectator shares Oedipus' costly error in believing that his responsibility for the crime has actually been proved.

Another bothersome detail: what has delayed the outbreak of the plague? Laius is long dead, at least five years – Oedipus has fathered four children after killing him. Why has this blight descended on the blameless citizens of Thebes only now?

What can really be known of the intentions of an author who wrote over two thousand years ago, in a vastly different age? Sophocles might well have had purposes – personal, artistic – of which later generations of readers and spectators have no intimation. Another relevant question is how conscious of every aspect of his work is any poet or playwright. George Bernard Shaw, defending himself after elucidating the intellectual content of Richard Wagner's *Ring* – an explanation at variance with Wagner's own specific description of what he was doing – appeals to what he calls "the unconscious wisdom" of artists. They may state clearly what they meant to accomplish, but such claims are comparable to Henry VIII's ingenious guess about the circulation of his blood, before Harvey's scientific discovery of it. Whether Shaw would have admitted that the same lack of full awareness was true of him in his own work is an interesting speculation.

The psychologist Carl Jung has formulated a concept of the artist as the unconscious vehicle of the prevalent ideas or attitudes of his times; or else the very contrary is true of him: he is a "corrective force" in society, holding opposite views to those dominating a cultural epoch, righting the balance. In a Classical age, some rebel poets and painters are Romantics; in a rational era, some are escapists and mystics; a measure of dissidence is needed to maintain the health of any period. Such delineations of the artistic personality are debatable but beyond doubt have elements of truth. To some extent, Sophocles' *Oedipus* will always remain impenetrable to after generations, even though he might not have meant it to be "mysterious" or "ambiguous".

Certain great works of art, like *Oedipus*, *Hamlet* and *Faust*, contain symbols that are inexhaustible. Each new generation discerns fresh and relevant significance in them, as has the twentieth century in this great play. It has, too, like the *Agamemnon*, acquired an increased size and grandeur from its immense age, while defying its antiquity. The painter Delacroix, speaking of cathedrals, said that they gained an added beauty for him when he thought of all the tears shed and hopeful prayers whispered in them. In the same way, for over two millennia of readers and spectators, some of the drama's primal excitement and emotional purgation has been evoked and its impact abetted.

Walter Pater, in his essay on the *Mona Lisa*, compares it to the grain of sand in the oyster shell that becomes a lustrous pearl by accretion, the cumulative response of all those who have gazed at it with wonder down the years. Marcel Proust relates how, as a child, he was taken to see Racine's *Phèdre*. Seated in the audience of the venerable Comédie-Française, he conjured up what it must have been like to have been here on the first night two centuries earlier when *Phèdre* was first presented, and then reviewed in his fancy all the great actresses who had since essayed the part. Much the same might be the state of mind of the present-day spectator when approaching this limitless Sophoclean story, which is so crowded with philosophical and psychological stimulation.

The subject of Oedipus has attracted many other treatments, no less than thirteen by ancient Greek dramatists, among them four lost scripts by Aeschylus and Euripides. The Roman statesman, philosopher and playwright, Lucius Annaeus Seneca, composed an even more gory version in the first century AD, probably intending that it be read rather than performed.

In 1550, Hans Sachs included *Die unglückhafige Königin Jokasta* among his voluminous works. The Neoclassical Age brought forth two Oedipus dramas in French, one by Pierre Corneille (1659), followed in the next century by a drama from the versatile Voltaire (1718); these were matched in English with a collaborative blank verse effort by the poet John Dryden and the actor Nathaniel Lee. More recent ventures have been the Austrian poet Hugo von Hofmannsthal's *Oedipus and the Sphinx* (1905), which had its première in Berlin, and his *King Oedipus* (1907). André Gide, a Nobel Prize winner, published his *Oedipe* in 1931 and had it staged at the Avignon Festival in 1949. A Spanish variant of the classic drama is by Benito Perez Galdós. Perhaps the best known and widely produced adaptation of the plot is Jean Cocteau's *The Infernal Machine* (1934), which deals mostly with Oedipus' confrontation with the enigmatic Sphinx. Igor Stravinsky based a much-sung cantata on the Oedipus story, using a French text also by Cocteau but translated into medieval Latin; it is meant to be enacted with only huge puppets visible, but in practice robed singers usually substitute in full view on stage. The famed Martha Graham has choreographed a dance work, *Jocasta*, which examines a different aspect of the play. The story also serves as a libretto for several operas dating from the Neoclassical eighteenth century; to them should be added George Enesco's *Oedipe* (1934) and Wolfgang Rihm's one-act *Oedipus* (1990). Many of these works will be discussed in fuller detail on later pages.

The most notable English translations of Sophocles' original scripts, *Oedipus Rex* and *Oedipus at Colonus*, are by William Butler Yeats, the Irish poet – also a Nobel Prize winner – who in 1928 undertook the task for the Abbey Theatre in Dublin with which he was closely associated. He renders the dialogue in a style that is comparatively simple, at times austere. Actors find it helpful and effective, fitting the tongue; but in his *Oedipus Rex* Yeats omits certain choric passages in which a foundling abandoned on a mountainside is looked on as protected by "divine wild spirits of the place" and akin to them and wild natural forces and possibly even to be the child of a wandering, heedless god, "Pan, Apollo, Hermes, or Dionysus". The excision of this theme offends Lattimore, who writes in his *The Poetry of Greek Tragedy*: "*Oedipus* is acted today, often professionally, and more frequently, I believe, than any other Greek play. It is commonly given in what almost passes as an authorized version – that of Yeats – which has cut down or cut out those daemonic passages we have been considering. It is good theatre, and it is truly dramatic, but it is no longer haunted." A dimension, a hint of the mystical and supernatural, is missing.

There are numerous other English translations, by Gilbert Murray, R.C. Jebb, Sir John Sheppard, Thomas Howard Banks, Clarence W. Mendell, F.L. Lucas, Kenneth Cavander, Albert Cook, Dudley Fitts and Robert Fitzgerald, Anthony Sloan, Stephen Berg and Diskin Clay, John Lewin, Paul Roche, Don Taylor, to name a bare few of recent date. Some are in prose, some rhymed.

Oedipus at Colonus, written close to the end of Sophocles' long life, has scholars wary of fixing its exact date. According to most accounts, it was staged after the poet's death, the production under the supervision of his son or else of his grandson, the latter named Sophocles the Younger. Though the last created work making up the Theban Trilogy, it is nevertheless story-wise a sequel to *Oedipus the King* and is most often read and studied as such; and, for that reason, an examination of it is placed here, rather than later, where it belongs if the three plays were to be put in the order of their composition.

Banished into perpetual exile, Oedipus has undergone many hardships and ultimately reached a rocky, thickly wooded grotto – "overgrown with laurel bushes and a wild vine"– on the outskirts of Athens. He is companioned only by his elder daughter, the faithful and devoted Antigone. Sick and old, in tattered garments, he asks her where they are. His fierce temper seems to have greatly abated. He has learned to bear his altered lot, for:

> Three masters – pain, time, and the royalty in the blood
> Have taught me patience.
> [Translation: E.F. Watling]

Antigone hears the voices of nightingales and sees a city in the distance. She identifies their resting-place as "a kind of sacred precinct". This is Colonus, and they are told by a passing countryman that the ground is indeed holy, the dwelling-place of the Eumenides. Oedipus tells his daughter that he has had the promise of Apollo that he is to end his days in just such a holy place as this, ruled by Unseen Powers and All-seeing Kindly Ones. He prays that he has at last reached the conclusion of his difficult, tormented wanderings. The signs of his end are to be earthquake, thunder and lightning.

The chorus (countrymen of Colonus) appear; they wish to rout the intruder from this sacred ground. Oedipus is led to a rock seat where he is no longer an impious trespasser. When the countrymen discover who he is, the slayer of his father, they are appalled and revile him, ordering him to leave. They fear that he will corrupt their homeland, as he once polluted Thebes. Antigone vainly begs for their pity. Oedipus demands that Theseus, King of Athens, be brought here to him, so that he may ask for the city's traditional hospitality, an altogether proper request.

Unexpectedly – it seems almost a miracle – Antigone's sister, Ismene, is seen approaching on horseback. She brings ill-tidings from Thebes: Oedipus' two sons, Polynices and Eteocles – who have done nothing to assist their father – are quarrelling over which is to occupy the throne of Thebes, where their uncle Creon still rules as regent. His sons, of course, are also his half-brothers. The elder, Polynices, has been driven out. He has formed an alliance with Argos, marrying a princess there, the daughter of King Adrastus, while preparing to return with alien forces and besiege the town. (This is the subject of Aeschylus' *Seven Against Thebes.*) Ismene says that the citizens of Thebes wish Oedipus to return, to live out his days close by, and after his death be buried near the city's walls, though he may never be able to re-enter it or even touch its soil. A new Delphic prophecy has warned that only their former king, Oedipus, is able to protect the people of Thebes.

Oedipus refuses this bid. He will not return while his banishment is still enforced. He knows that his sons want his help in their struggle, but he resents their selfish neglect of him. He explains that though he blinded himself and voluntarily sought exile, he later realized "how much my wrath had overleaped itself to punish me too heavily for my sins". He had been outcast against his will. His sons had never intervened on his behalf. He feels that neither is fit to reign in Thebes.

The chorus advises him to make an offering, a libation of pure water and honey, with his face turned towards the dawn, to the spirits of the holy grotto. Ismene performs this hallowed rite for him. King Theseus comes, grants asylum to Oedipus, and vows to thwart any attempt by his sons to carry him back to Thebes for their own purposes.

In an ode, the chorus sings of the beauty of Colonus (which is still famed as Sophocles' birthplace):

> Here in our white Colonus, stranger guest,
> Of all earth's lovely lands the loveliest,
> Fine horses breed, and leaf-enfolded vales
> Are thronged with sweetly-singing nightingales,
> Screened in deep arbours, ivy, dark as wine,
> And tangled bowers of berry-clustered vine;
> To whose dark avenues and windless courts

The Grape-god and his nursing-nymphs resorts.
Here, chosen crown of goddesses, the fair
Narcissus blooms, bathing his lustrous hair
In dews of morning; gold crocus gleams
Along Cephisus' slow meandering streams,
Whose fountains never fail; day after day
His limpid waters wander on their way
To fill with ripeness of abundant birth
The swelling bosom of our buxom earth . . .

This is Sophocles paying lyric tribute to his native region. But it also contributes, better than any scene-painting might, the setting for this momentous and apocalyptic close of the heroic Oedipus' life.

Next to visit Oedipus is his brother-in-law Creon, who had ordered him from Thebes. Joyfully and rightly, Oedipus at first thinks his banishment has been lifted, but he quickly detects a political motive hidden beneath Creon's sweet-sounding bid for his return, and angrily rejects it. The two old men quarrel bitterly, the devious Creon revealing that Ismene has been seized; she is to be taken back to Thebes, with the same fate ahead for Antigone. He commands his guards to take hold of the elder sister. The helpless Oedipus appeals to the chorus (the countrymen) for support, and they demand Antigone's release, but she is roughly carried off. The chorus still opposes Creon, who orders that Oedipus be kidnapped as well. Hearing the outcries, King Theseus and his attendants rush in and confront Creon's men. The Athenian ruler berates Creon for his insolence and for violating local laws, as well as for breaking in on the shelter duly accorded the aged Oedipus.

Oedipus now articulately claims to have been innocent, a victim; he feels wholly guiltless in spite of the dreadful acts he once committed; they were preordained and quite unwitting on his part.

Theseus tells his men to intercept those making off with the two young women. Creon, lacking sufficient forces, yields his captives and sullenly departs, while the chorus imagines what might have been a violent confrontation and battle between Thebans and Athenians. Oedipus eloquently praises Theseus and his followers: "Nowhere else but here have I found justice, godliness and truth." Throughout the play, Athens is flattered and exalted by the author, which doubtless pleased many in his audience. In fact, it is apparently Sophocles' notion to have Oedipus die and be buried near Athens, rather than in Thebes, as in the original legend.

Yet another suppliant comes to Oedipus: his son, Polynices. At first the father will not hear him, describing the young man as "my worst enemy"; but Theseus and Antigone prevail upon the old man to let the tearful and seemingly repentant Polynices approach and plead his cause. Oedipus sits in adamantine silence, and it is soon apparent that Polynices, like Creon, has a selfish motive: he wants Oedipus to back his claim to the Theban throne. In a flash of his former temper, his father tongue-lashes him, blaming him for all his misfortunes. He denies Polynices the right to call himself his son, curses him and predicts death in battle for both Eteocles and him. He says that all the two young men will possess of Thebes is enough ground for their graves. Cringing, Polynices departs, after asking Antigone to promise him a proper burial if in fact he should perish during the attack on Thebes. Thunder resounds. Oedipus reads it as a sign that his own end is near. He asks that Theseus be sent for. Blessing his daughters, and Theseus and Athens, and vowing to watch over the hospitable city for all time, providing his burial place be kept secret by Theseus and successively one of the king's heirs for ever, Oedipus goes off to die while the storm rages, meteors streaking in the sky. The chorus sings of these great wonders and asks for divine mercy for all.

After a long pause, a messenger returns with an account of Oedipus' death: first he bathed, then prepared himself; a voice was heard telling him not to delay further. Soon afterwards he had simply vanished.

> In what manner Oedipus passed from this earth, no one can tell. Only Theseus knows. . . . Maybe a guiding spirit from the gods took him, or the earth's foundations gently opened and received him with no pain. Certain it is that he was taken without grief or agony – a passing more wonderful than that of any other man.

He has been a Lear-like figure, and his end reminds one not a little of the death of Moses as described in the Old Testament.

Weeping, Antigone and Ismene beg that they be allowed to return to Thebes, and Theseus says, "It shall be done."

Pessimism runs through the play, and though it is often facilely spoken of as a "serene" work, it has a full measure of melancholy, as befits its subject. Says the chorus:

> Show me the man who asks an over-abundant share
> Of life, in love with more, and ill content

With less, and I will show you one in love
With foolishness:
In the accumulation of many years
Pain is in plenty, and joy not anywhere
When life is over-spent.
And at last there is the same release
When Death appears
Unheralded by music, dance, or song,
To give us peace.
Say what you will, the greatest boon is not to be;
But, life begun, soonest to end is best,
And to that bourne from which our way began
Swiftly return.
The simple playtime of our youth behind,
What woe is absent, what fierce agony?
Strife, and the bloody test
Of battle, envy and hatred – and at length
Unloved, unkind,
Unfriended age, worst ill of all, and last,
Consumes our strength.

Again, Oedipus has lamented:

Time, Time, my friend,
Makes havoc everywhere; he is invincible.
Only the gods have ageless and deathless life;
All else must perish. The sap of earth dries up,
Flesh dies, and while faith withers falsehood blooms.
The spirit is not constant from friend to friend,
Joy turns to sorrow, and turns again to joy,
Between Athens and Thebes the sky is fair; but Time
Has many and many a night and day to run

On his uncounted course; in one of these
Some little rift will come, and the sword's point
Will make short work of this day's harmony.

(The last five lines of this passage might also be taken as a topical reference to troubles then rising between Athens and Thebes, which had allied itself with hostile Sparta.) But it is true that Oedipus has learned resignation, complete self-acceptance, that he now feels himself mostly blameless for the misfortunes that have beset him, and that he goes to his last rest with calm, no final complaint or hesitance, and even with moments of exaltation. Symbolically, at this ultimate point, he who is blind leads the others to the appointed place.

Much that is autobiographical has been discerned in this play. It is not only appropriate to a man near ninety who himself was approaching death, but in the denunciation of the ungrateful and disloyal Polynices there is thought to be a strong echo of a quarrel which had recently occurred between Sophocles and his son Iophon, who was jealous of favours shown by the aged playwright to one of his illegitimate offspring. Iophon sought to have his father declared "incompetent", but Sophocles is said to have appeared in court and refuted the charge of senility by a public recitation of passages from *Oedipus at Colonus,* on which he was then engaged. All who heard his recital agreed that the poetry was magnificent, that Sophocles had never written with more dramatic vitality and grandeur: his stylus was more firmly held than ever.

The structure of the play is looser, more fluid, than is true of *Electra* or *Oedipus the King,* but the form seems well suited to the subject, the mood, the pace of a slow, shuffling old man, moving towards his mortal close. A criticism often made is that the work is "static", but actually the incidents are richly and ingeniously varied, with the successive arrival of the stranger, the chorus, Ismene, Creon, Theseus and Polynices providing ever fresh interest and conflict: this is accomplished very skilfully. Oedipus is shown in many aspects: weary and defeated; proud, with hope resurgent; a tender, loving father to his daughters; fearful and bereaved when he thinks he has lost them; and with terrible temper aroused as he rebukes his son. Finally, he is possessed by an attitude that is uplifted and mystical. The portrait is truly rounded, remarkably impressive. Increasingly defiant, this Oedipus recovers his heroic stature, and far more than in *Oedipus the King* he is the tragic protagonist, noble in profile, awesome and a figure to be revered.

Bachofen, applying his theory that the Greek dramas echo a cultural struggle between patriarchy and matriarchy, points to the final incident here, Oedipus' disappearance into the bowels of the earth and his reception by the Earth-goddess as a further illustration of that profound clash. Oedipus, who killed his father, is now a representative of the matriarchal cult or principle. Jocasta's transgression, as a mother, is that she consents to the killing of their child to save her husband. "It is she who by committing this crime starts the chain of events which eventually leads to her own, her husband's, and her son's destruction," writes Erich Fromm, in similar vein. When Oedipus gives his answer to the Sphinx, "Man", he is affirming the primacy of man – humanity – reflecting the values prevalent in a matriarchal world, in contrast to those in a patriarchal culture in which law and the absolutist state and a hierarchal order supersede the rights of the individual.

Once more, John Ferguson scans the imagery for repetitive motifs and finds them alluding to blindness and sight, including "insight" and self-knowledge. Since the tremulous Oedipus is without vision, his groping dependence on mere touch and sound lends poignancy to his reduced state. In as much as the scene around him must be described to him in detail by the hovering Antigone and others, ample opportunity is given Sophocles to insert graphic poetry, which he richly provides. Other recurring motifs have to do with "wandering" or "journeying" – an old man seeking his way, ending his life's arduous travels – and to "learning" and "teaching"; he imparts the sad wisdom he has acquired, declaring that such wisdom can only be gained through living and suffering. As Ferguson observes, Oedipus has to an extent assumed the role of Tiresias in this subsequent drama.

As far as is known, Sophocles is the only Greek playwright to have chosen the subject of what befell the stricken Oedipus after his abrupt expulsion from Thebes; it is easy to grasp what drew him to write it, and it is the longest, by 250 lines, of his surviving scripts. Ferguson sees a trace of Euripides' influence in Sophocles having Oedipus dressed in tatters, instead of the traditional formal garb worn by tragic actors; it was Euripides who introduced the use of such realistic attire. Though it is not clear, Sophocles may have added a fourth actor to his cast, unless two players alternate as Theseus, and the same device might have been employed in representing Ismene. That the actors wore masks made that deception possible.

Bates admires the drama as a vehicle for a great performer, and Ferguson argues that the aged Oedipus is not truly a self-portrait of the amiable, congenial playwright, "any more than Prospero is a self-portrait of Shakespeare", but it is "a projection of elements he knew to be in himself below the surface". He adds: "This is in many ways a finer play than *Oedipus the King*; certainly it has fewer faults. Of course it is drama of a different kind; it is properly less taut, there is less room for irony, less evocation of *Schadenfreude*. As the work of a man all but ninety, it is probably without parallel. The flexibility that is still open to learn from others is astonishing. . . . The play is immensely exciting; it is tender and moving; it is also in the most sacred sense mysterious."

Oedipus at Colonus is not staged as often as the other scripts in the trilogy. The Anglo-American poet T.S. Eliot borrowed the story's outline and updated it in his *The Elder Statesman* (1958). Far earlier, it inspired an opera *Oedipe à Colone* (Versailles, 1786) by Antonio Sacchini, much in the manner of Gluck. Quite a strange development is an adaptation of the Sophoclean tragedy as an Afro-American music-drama, retitled *Gospel at Colonus* and set in a black Pentecostal church. Produced and directed by Lee Breuer, a leading figure in New York's avant-garde theatre, and embellished with a "glorious" score by Bob Telson, it was tried out in workshops beginning in 1979, first put on formally at the Brooklyn Academy of Music (1983), thereafter toured intermittently with stops that included the Houston Grand Opera, the Arena Stage in Washington, DC and the Tyrone Guthrie Theater in Minneapolis, as well as broadcast on public television (1985); next, it was brought back to New York and Broadway with considerable success (1988).

From the pulpit the pastor initially announces: "I take as my text this evening *The Book of Oedipus*," as though he is referring to an Apocryphal book in the Christian Scriptures. What follows is, word for word, the text of Sophocles' play as translated into English by Robert Fitzgerald.

Breuer, quoted in *Playbill*, explains: "It's not a gospel show, but gospel music is used as an inspiration for re-creating a classic Greek experience, and I believe it's the correct metaphor for our time." Both Breuer and Telson, a Harvard-trained musician, are white, and accordingly were somewhat intimidated at undertaking a work in an idiom that was not native to them. But Telson, though Jewish, speaks of finding "in those joyous and unbridled services 'a depth of sincerity and passion' unlike anything he had encountered anywhere else". Breuer told *Playbill*'s interviewer: "Not only did the structure of the service – from anthem to sermon – remarkably reflect the form of the Greek play, but also [he] recognized in the exuberant singing and dancing of gospel the 'great ecstatic experience' that could provide both catharsis and counterpoint for the deeply tragic story."

Only three performers in the cast of sixty-four were professional entertainers; the others were recruited from gospel singing groups. The pastor was represented by the distinguished player Morgan Freeman (an Academy Award winner for his film work); the role of Oedipus was assumed by Clarence Fountain, who is actually blind, and who was backed by his own singing group, the Five Blind Boys of Alabama, who formed a sort of mini-chorus, alternatively given Oedipus' lines. Other choirs participating included the Institutional Radio Choir of Brooklyn, J.J. Farley and the Original Soul Stirrers, and the J.D. Steele Singers. From time to time they were joined by enthusiastic audiences, who interspersed "Hallelujah!" and other exuberant responses. The organist was Butch Heyward, a member of the Institutional Church of God in Christ in Brooklyn; he was initially reluctant to take part, but was urged by friends, "Go. God is opening doors for you." He explained: "So we just walked on through."

Many of the singers were equally hesitant about participating in a secular drama based on a pagan Greek script. As Breuer tells it, "Depth of faith is critical to gospel. There have been many examples of gospel singers who have been unable to summon their fiery talent outside the church." He stressed to his cast that essentially the story was Christian: "An old man is redeemed through suffering." They were convinced when Morgan Freeman delivered the sermon, "the Speech of the Messenger. . . . It was all about the everlasting virtue of life, the love of God, the love of a Father for his children. At that moment, they understood two things: one, that they could've heard that sermon in church. And two, it was delivered by someone called The Messenger, and that's what they called Martin Luther King." In the cast finally assembled, five members were ordained Pentecostal ministers.

For the delivery of the pastor's sermon, Breuer borrowed from Martin Luther King's highly declamatory style of speech, which was both emphatically repetitive and percussive, with a hypnotic beat, generically African. This "heightened" language swayed the listener, with an effect that was quite visceral.

In another interview, on this occasion with Wendy Smith for the *New York Times*, Breuer expanded on some of his other original goals: "I've always been interested in a narrative or lyric style of theater, pre-Ibsen, where as much importance was given to the story element as to the dramatic." He underscored the narrative element in Sophocles, "the odes and narrative poems which are interspersed with dramatic scenes". His cast had no trouble accepting this form of theatre, because "the church is a narrative experience, too: you have a Bible story – for example, the story of Job – which is the narration, and then you extrapolate and moralize on it. *Oedipus at Colonus* also provides a compelling story. It is the climax of the tragic Greek hero's spiritual journey from parricide and incest to the temple at Colonus where he finds redemption through suffering." Breuer pointed out that the Rev. Earl Miller, who portrayed Theseus in the work, had said that "the entirety of black preaching is based on story-telling". That was why Breuer had sought singers and members of the church community and no more than a handful of professional actors. His instruction to the cast in rehearsal was "Do it like you do in church." That proved to be the right direction.

"What I found was the Pentecostal, Afro-American church, which is part of the American language, gives you a living experience of catharsis in the world today. I wasn't trying to say anything about gospel, because I don't want to presume that I know anything about it. I was trying to say something about classical theater. Gospel was a metaphor, gospel was an inspiration, gospel was the living repository of an emotion and a spirituality that had become academic and archeological in our theater."

His decision to have six singers enact the role of Oedipus was prompted by his study of Kabuki, the classic Japanese theatre. In Kabuki, "sometimes parts of the story are choral works and characters are abstracted into choral entities. So I had this idea that each character could have a narration with its own chorus. . . . Then the outer circle is a great chorus that narrates the entire work."

Breuer had spent a year in Greece. "It was hard for me to walk around those theaters with the altar in the center of the stage and not know that they were basically churches. . . . So I began trying to find a language for this feeling. I think all theater is finding the right translation for your audience, and I wanted to translate Greek tragedy into an American language for American viewers. I wanted to show them: This is the cathartic experience, this is what Aristotle was talking about, this is what Greek tragedy is, this is what our entire Western dramatic culture is based on. You begin to understand catharsis by experiencing it."

When the play reached Broadway, Jack Kroll wrote of it in *Newsweek*: "This is one of the most marvelous shows of the decade, based on one of the most inspired ideas of any time. Director Lee Breuer has taken Sophocles' great tragedy and turned it into a blend of gospel concert, dramatized super-sermon and general jamboree. . . . Talk about a Greek chorus! *Colonus* is a triumph of reconciliation, bringing together black and white, pagan and Christian, ancient and modern in a sunburst of joy that seems to touch the secret heart of civilization itself."

Edwin Wilson, in the *Wall Street Journal*, greeted the work as "one of the most exhilarating and original theater pieces to appear in some time. . . . *Oedipus at Colonus* is Sophocles' valedictory – the final statement of one of the world's great writers. Mr Breuer and Mr Telson recognized it is not so much a traditional drama as an elegiac message on the end of life. As such, they felt it could be conceived of in terms of a black church service of the kind found in Baptist or Pentecostal faiths. They were right; the transformation works amazingly well. From early on, black preachers incorporated the cadences of the Old Testament in their sermons, and singers made the stories of the Bible the subject of their spirituals. In its own way, Sophocles' play has a strong affinity with Old Testament language and lore. Therefore, when the minister in *The Gospel at Colonus* begins the evening by intoning, 'I take my text from the book of Oedipus,' we feel at home right away. . . .

"The piece is part drama, part oratorio, part religious service; Mr Breuer has blended the elements into a consistent whole. He has also used devices of the avant-garde theater to good effect. Several characters are represented at times by singers and at other times by the minister or another performer.

There is no confusion, only dimension added to the characters."

Wilson was especially stirred by the music, Telson's "infectious, original score, a rare purity of tone in the voices of the soloists, and joyous close harmony by the gospel groups. My feelings were also confirmed by a sequence toward the end when two singers representing Antigone and her sister Ismene sang without microphones. The sound was glorious."

For the *New York Times*, Mel Gussow had this to say: "An unlikely but inspired marriage of Sophocles and gospel songs, *The Gospel at Colonus* opened Thursday at the Brooklyn Academy of Music as part of the academy's Next Wave of experimental music, theater and dance events. The work is on the crest of that wave, inundating the audience with jubilant music and soulful testimony about the power of redemption.

"As a risk-taking theatrical conceptualist, Mr Breuer has sometimes been charged with distorting classics. In this case, he remains faithful, though not subservient, to his source, and gives immediacy to Greek tragedy. . . . It is surprising how organically *Oedipus* can fit within the framework of a gospel musical, the cadenced lyricism of Sophocles merging with Mr Telson's rhapsodic rhythms.

"Individually and in unison, this is a heavenly choir, a feeling that is enriched by the stage setting designed by Alison Yerxa – a celestial cyclorama of sky-flying seraphs. The band is split in two, with half in a pit on stage, half high in a perch."

At moments, for Gussow, the singers reached towards ecstasy. And yet, "For all the moments of exaltation, the show never forgets to be playful. When Oedipus' traitorous son Polynices arrives to patch things up with his father figure, he addresses the audience. 'I'll tell you why I came,' and he does. During the self-serving monologue, Sam Butler plays a low-down guitar in the pit band, and then looks up and wins a laugh with the comment, 'He's so slick!'"

Previously, Breuer had worked on a small scale "with unlimited inventiveness", but Gussow noted that *Gospel at Colonus* was mounted on a grand scale, "almost the equal of a Robert Wilson opera epic.

"After Oedipus' death comes an apotheosis. Swaying multitudes of gospel singers, led by the clarion voice of Joyce Taylor, exhort 'Lift Him Up,' and the stage threatens to lift off from its moorings, joining the show in an evangelical musical flight."

An even more astonishing demonstration of the timelessness and eternal relevance of Sophocles' writings is provided by *Antigone*, which – as earlier stated – was the first of the Theban Plays to be composed and produced (arguably in 441 BC), though it is now usual to regard it as the final work of the great trilogy, since the events in it occur after Oedipus' death. It is said to have been Sophocles' thirty-second entry in the annual festival and to have been so popular that it had many revivals in the next century. Legend has it that a re-staging of it won a first prize, which so excited the aged Sophocles that he died of a heart attack. By another account, the crowd was so impressed by the play's first performance that Sophocles was appointed to be a general for the oncoming campaign against Samos. In modern times *Antigone* has been enacted as often as *Oedipus the King*, and perhaps even more frequently.

The plot is not found in Homer, and most likely is wholly Sophocles' invention, though this is not yet certain. Aeschylus' *The Seven Against Thebes* covers some of the same ground, but Antigone's role in it is less conspicuous, and her quarrel with Creon not a focal element. The final lines of *The Seven Against Thebes*, which seem to foreshadow the conflict in *Antigone*, are believed to be spurious, a later addition by quite another hand, not Aeschylus'.

At the opening of Sophocles' drama, the struggle for the Theban throne has already ended. The rivals, the brothers Polynices and Eteocles, have slain each other; the sceptre is firmly grasped by Creon, their maternal uncle. After the civil strife, he desperately seeks to restore order. Having sided with Eteocles, as rightful heir, he decrees that his nephew shall be buried as a hero with solemn rites: the body of the rebellious Polynices is to be left uninterred, to rot in the sun and feed the carrion birds. This is outrageous, wholly contrary to Greek religious custom. Their father's grim prophecy, in *Oedipus at Colonus*, has been fulfilled.

Antigone and Ismene have returned to Thebes. The new ruler's edict shocks Antigone, who dislikes Creon and harbours a strong blood obligation to her errant brothers. Her feeling is that they should be treated equally in death; the proper rituals should be observed for both. She is determined to see this happen and urges Ismene to join her in the endeavour. Though sympathetic to her sister's vow, Ismene is afraid of the consequences. Once more, after Sophocles' fashion, the characters of the two young women are profoundly contrasted. Says Ismene, when Antigone voices her defiance of their uncle:

> Your heart burns! Mine is frozen at the thought.
> [Translation: E.F. Watling]

Ismene is inherently prudent, guided by common sense. Antigone is like Oedipus, impulsive, obstinate, aggressive. The chorus describes her: "the violent daughter of a violent father". Since Ismene will not assist her, Antigone resolves – like Electra, when refused help by Chrysotomis in Sophocles' earlier play – to perform the forbidden deed of burial alone. Ismene urges her to be cautious and furtive. "Do not breathe a word. I'll not betray our secret."

Antigone retorts: "Publish it to all the world! Else I shall hate you more." Hers is an almost inhuman boldness and resourcefulness. Indeed, like Electra, she seems to welcome martyrdom.

Ismene retreats to the palace. Antigone withdraws to perform her grisly task, interment of a corpse whose stench is already offensive to the guards standing watch on the now deserted field of battle.

Creon enters, fierce, blustering. He informs the chorus (the Elders of Thebes) of his ruling: not only shall the remains of the "traitor" Polynices be desecrated by being denied a grave, but anyone disobeying the royal order shall be severely punished.

The play moves swiftly. A bumbling, comic sentry reports, in great trepidation, that someone has already buried Polynices and left no trace. Creon suspects a plot among surviving dissidents in the city to continue the rebellion and overthrow him. Upbraiding the guard, he threatens him with death unless the culprit is discovered quickly.

Scarcely a choral chant later (though it is a notable lyric passage), the frightened guard is back with "wonderful" news: the sentries have dug up Polynices, as Creon has commanded them to do. The person who previously buried him has since then returned, openly attempted to cover the corpse again, cupping up the earth with her bare hands. As depicted by the craven guard:

> She admitted it,
> I'm glad to say – though sorry too, in a way.
> It's good to save your own skin, but a pity
> To have to see another get into trouble,
> Whom you've no grudge against. However, I can't say
> I ever valued anyone else's life
> More than my own, and that's the honest truth.

Here Sophocles presents another effective contrast, the soldier – a man – who is fearful of his life, and a girl who is willing to sacrifice herself merely to honour her dead brother. Creon learns that the guilty one is his own niece, and the captive princess Antigone is led in by other guards.

Astounded and disbelieving, Creon is furious at the unrepentant Antigone. An intense exchange of charges follows between the two hotheaded members of the same family. Had she heard of his edict? "Yes," she replies. And had she dared to contravene it, he asks. She shouts back:

Yes,
That order did not come from God. Justice
That dwells with the gods below knows no such law.
I did not think your edicts strong enough
To overrule the unwritten, unalterable laws
Of God and heaven, you being only a man.
They are not of yesterday or today, but everlasting.

Antigone declares that Creon hates her. Creon asserts that she is like the dead Polynices in defying his authority and that she is now aiding his hidden foes in Thebes.

Ismene, dragged in, is accused of a part in the "conspiracy", and condemned to death, though Antigone avows her sister is innocent. By now, however, Ismene is ready to share Antigone's fate.

The young women are led away. Antigone is to be walled up in a dark cave and left with bare sustenance. On second thought, Creon absolves Ismene.

The chorus: "For mortals greatly to live is greatly to suffer."

Antigone has been betrothed to Haemon, Creon's son, who deeply loves her. Now the young man comes to plead mercy for her. At first he speaks respectfully, almost with humility, but warning his father – as had Antigone – that his dictate is highly unpopular with the Thebans. Creon berates his son for disloyalty. The chorus lends the weight of its voice to Haemon's; the king cries out:

Indeed! Am I to take lessons at my time of life
From a fellow of his age?

Haemon insists:

No lesson you need be ashamed of.
It isn't a question of age, but of right and wrong.

He again tells his father that the people of Thebes take Antigone's side. A significant passage ensues:

CREON: The people of Thebes! Since when do I take my
orders from the people of Thebes?

> Haemon: Isn't that a rather childish thing to say?
>
> Creon: No. I am king, and responsible only to myself.
>
> Haemon: A one-man state? What sort of state is that?
>
> Creon: Why, does not every state belong to its ruler?
>
> Haemon: You'd be an excellent king – on a desert island.

It is impossible not to believe that these lines had a strong topical reference to Athenian politics, the constant struggle in the city against anyone seeking to wield power despotically.

His father denies the son's passionate entreaty, swearing they shall never see each other again. Antigone returns to learn her fate. The chorus commiserates with her, yet adds: "You are the victim of your own self-will." Stubborn to the end, Antigone is taken away to an isolated, rocky cell.

Another pleader comes on her behalf, the blind seer, Tiresias, who had foretold the catastrophe that overwhelmed her father. But as had Oedipus before him, Creon refuses to heed the blind man, lashing at him as a false prophet with a political motivation – "I say all prophets seek their own advantage." In turn, Tiresias heaps terrible curses on the king and predicts a dreadful outcome for this day.

After the aged man departs, Creon is revealed to be deeply shaken. He asks the elders (the chorus) for help and enlightenment, and now hearkens to their solemn advice. He consents to free Antigone. Somewhat relieved by this change of heart, he decides that he himself will go to release her.

The chorus sings a hymn to Dionysus, whose mother, Semele, was a daughter of Cadmus, founder of the city. Sophocles is obviously signalling a time-lapse.

Suddenly a messenger breaks in with horrible news. On his way to Antigone's place of imprisonment, Creon halted to oversee the ritual burial of Polynices. Meanwhile, Haemon had reached the cave enclosing Antigone; forcing himself in, it was only to find her dead, a linen rope, woven of her skirt, knotted in a noose about her throat. She has ended her life in the same manner as had her mother, Jocasta. At the sight, the distraught Haemon seized a sword and thrust at his approaching father, missing him; then he fatally stabbed himself with the weapon.

Creon returns, bearing in his arms his son's body. He is greeted with word of another dark denouement. His wife, Queen Eurydice, learning of her son's suicide, has also driven a blade into her heart. Creon has lost the two people he loves best. He begs for death: "Let me not see another day."

The chorus concludes:

Ask nothing.
What is to be, no mortal can escape.

And:

Of happiness the crown
And chiefest part
Is wisdom, and to hold
The gods in awe.
This is the law
That, seeing the stricken heart
Of pride brought down
We learn when we are old.

The play is an instance of the drawn-out, ever-recurrent conflict between "church and state", when the forces of religion and subjective emotion are pitted against naked political power; a dissenting individual, with an uneasy and sensitive conscience, confronts a hard-headed ruler who is guided by pragmatic considerations and reacts in a manner that he considers reasonable if ruthless. *Antigone* is the first known "social drama" or "problem play". The heroine responds to instinct and obeys its blinding dictates; while Creon, having to maintain his authority during a perilous pause in civil anarchy, senses a need to be firm, even harsh. His obligation is to impose peace on a city not yet recovered from fratricidal struggle.

On neither side of the conflict is the issue as simple as that, however. Creon is strong enough to assume his odious responsibilities, convinced that he proceeds in the best interests of the state. A middle ground, given voice by Haemon, is that the response should be tempered by mercy, that one-man rule should make way for governance by councils, and with an ear given to the whisperings and wishes of the people; Haemon is urging a more democratic regime. Since he is the most sympathetic and reasonable person in the drama, he is probably speaking on Sophocles' behalf.

The nineteenth-century German philosopher and aesthetician, G.W.F. Hegel, saw *Antigone* as concerned primarily with the moral dilemma of how far dissent can be allowed to go. Hegel, with an absolutist bent, felt that Creon is chiefly in the right in his stand against the rebellious girl, though far from blameless. To Hegel, *Antigone* more clearly defines the tragic hero than does *Oedipus the King*:

Creon has excellent traits but is undone by a tendency to fanaticism; a single quality in his personality is emphasized above all others, so that his character is out of balance, lacks harmony; this imbalance hurtles him towards destruction. Both Creon and Antigone are fanatical; they share the same fatal flaw.

Many lines in the play are consonant with Bachhofen's interpretation of Greek tragedies as reflecting a conflict between patriarchal and matriarchal cults in early societies. Several times Creon shouts his angry refusal to let a woman dominate him. "Better be beaten, if need be, by a man, than let a woman get the better of us." Again, "We'll have no women's law here while I live." Antigone is the defender of "the family" and its traditional pieties, a matriarchal role.

Like Oedipus, Creon has been an "unjust judge", pronouncing his edict and meting out drastic punishment before he is fully possessed of the whole story. He threatens the innocent guard with death, when first hearing that Polynices has had a ritual burial. (This might consist of no more than scattering dust on the body.) He assumes that both Antigone and Tiresias have the worst motives, rather than benign if – from his point of view – "misguided" ones. He is also suspicious and almost as harsh towards the harmless Ismene. "Poetic justice" claims him. He is punished as severely as are his victims. Sophocles was much involved with this theme.

Once more an oracle has a prominent role. Sophocles, who was known for his piety, suggests here that priests have a special knowledge. The fateful prophecies delivered here, like the ones in *Oedipus the King* and *Oedipus at Colonus*, bear strange weight. Oedipus, Jocasta and Creon belittle the oracles and depreciate their motives – the seers are mercenary, or have been bribed by the ruler's political foes – but all three doubters come to bad ends, the forecasts proving harshly true. Again, the prophecies do *not* make the tragic events come to pass: the soothsayers merely foresee them. Very possibly Sophocles himself was sceptical of Delphic pronouncements as, centuries later, was Christopher Marlowe of witchcraft, and merely exploits them as a helpful theatrical device. Aristotle remarks that if dire events are foretold in a play, they are made to seem more plausible and even inevitable as a consequence – however far-fetched they might otherwise be – and more portentous. An audience, easily impressed, is persuaded that there is a divine design of some sort in what might otherwise be deemed simple coincidence or incredible mischance.

Antigone is far more than a "social drama". It is also a confrontation, a family quarrel, between two persons with dynamic wills; both antagonists are sharply depicted. For this reason, that its people have vitality and do not exist only to illustrate a concept or prove an idea, the work attains a success rare in the realm of the "problem play".

In recent years Antigone has been looked on as a very sympathetic figure. John Gassner describes her as "one of the most appealing characters in literature" and adds that Sophocles has endowed her "with the morning beauty of Shakespeare's Juliet", though he does admit that she is also "strident and single-willed", hence not quite a romantic heroine. To Hegel she is far less than perfect; he cites the contemptuous, even abusive tone with which she speaks, in contrast to the hesitant if sensible and well-meaning Ismene. She is self-righteous, impatient, rude. She does not allow her uncle to save face at a troubled moment when he is seeking to establish his authority. Openly defying him, she issues her challenge first through Ismene – telling her to publish it to all the world – and then within plain hearing of the chorus of elders, who, though they both like and pity her, cannot bring themselves to condone her effrontery. She is opinionated, will not retreat or compromise. Creon complains to the elders: "How can I be deemed to rule the state, if I cannot govern my own family?" But she will not give way. It does not satisfy her that, having made the traditional gesture of respect towards her dead brother, she need not fault herself if she has not succeeded in the attempt, since her means are limited. She returns obsessively to the place where he lies. In all this, and in her ready acceptance of her own death, she exhibits something more than courage; there is also – as with Sophocles' Electra, whom Antigone greatly resembles – a masochistic strain. She clasps the martyr's role. At the end she quails from her dreadful entombment, yet one might feel that she welcomes it as well. A heroine? Yes, indeed, when one thinks how bold, decisive and defiant she is.

She could also be viewed as one of those young women – like Joan of Arc – who change the world, and who become legends and are honoured by subsequent generations. Yet it is quite different to have such a self-appointed martyr in one's own family and to encounter her daily. One can feel sorry for Creon, who must prevail against a girl as obdurate as this shrill daughter of Oedipus.

Since Polynices is dead before the play opens, the spectator does not know whether he truly deserves Antigone's sacrifice. (In *Oedipus at Colonus*, written decades later, he is shown as cunning, selfish, treasonable. He has mistreated his father, the aged, dying exile who curses him and predicts an inglorious end for him.) Antigone's sophistical argument that she owes a greater duty to a brother than to a husband or lover, since with both parents dead she could never have another brother, is scarcely to be taken seriously; it seems to display some of the irrationality of her adamant stance against her uncle. Her statement to Creon that she was "born to love not to hate" is hardly demonstrated here (though it is to be amply proved in *Oedipus at Colonus*, where she serves her blind father compassionately and selflessly). She is full of fury against Creon from the start, speaks almost venomously to her sister, and never once alludes tenderly to Haemon, the heir to the Theban throne who adores her so much that he kills himself at her loss. The "morning beauty of Juliet" is surely not to be seen here. Yet by her very obstinacy and fiery conviction she serves splendidly as a foil to the strong-minded Creon. For that purpose, if she is not sentimentalized in the actress's portrayal, she is most effectively realized by Sophocles.

Actually, Creon has the leading part in the play. Indeed, Antigone is gone from the stage long before the climax is reached; the final scenes are Creon's alone. Throughout, he has far more speeches; his role is half again as long as hers. She is not even mentioned in the closing lines, and only the corpse of Haemon is exhibited by his sorrowing father. It is Creon whose character develops and changes and whose suffering is most fully displayed; the final agony is reserved for him. Antigone's role is simple and obsessive; she creates the dilemma that he must solve. Her inflexibility makes her somewhat uninteresting after the conflict unfolds for a time. Since she will not change or yield, he alone might. Will he? That becomes the crux of the play. Sophocles skilfully portrays in Creon a certain type of ruler, benignly responsible yet despotic, who is tainted by power. As the familiar saying goes, "Power corrupts, and absolute power corrupts absolutely." In his own eyes, Creon has become "indispensable". He is vain, as stubborn and rude as she is. Like Oedipus before him, he is shrewd and suspicious. Any act of his is justified, if it sustains him in command, because he alone can rule Thebes wisely. So, for him, the end now justifies any means that he might employ. The terrible consequences of his *hubris*, his self-corrupting pride, are brutally externalized.

Haemon is clear-headed, responsible, generous in spirit; he is very different from his father and his beloved. He gives voice to, and embodies in his personality, the middle way – calm speech, a show of respect, logic – that Sophocles advocates in his extant tragedies. Haemon is caught in the midst of the struggle, loses his reason and dies – overwhelmed not only by Antigone's suicide, but also by his aborted murderous attack on his father. Interestingly, in his pleas to Creon, Haemon vents no personal emotion: he does not speak of his love for Antigone, which one assumes must be intense if he is ready to kill his father, and then himself, because of her. The lovers are never shown together on stage and there are no romantic speeches exchanged between them. But Athenian spectators did not yet favour scenes of that sort.

Creon's wife, Queen Eurydice, is barely heard. Bates remarks that hers is a "short but striking" part. She speaks but nine lines, listens intently to the report of the messenger and then departs without a word. This silent exit of the queen must have been very effective in the theatre. "No speech which she could have uttered could have produced the same effect as this tragic silence. One could not find a better example of the dramatic skill of Sophocles. The device is one that he used elsewhere."

Bates has equal praise for the character of the nervous guard. "He is a man of the lower class, upon whom has been laid an unpleasant and dangerous duty which he cannot avoid. . . . He is worried and tries to conceal his anxiety by treating the matter lightly. He thinks he can best save his own skin by playing the buffoon. All this is natural. . . . Sophocles was particularly happy in depicting such characters."

In Bates's opinion *Antigone* does not afford a major actor an opportunity to show his full virtuosity. "The *Antigone* was not written with such an end in view. The play is good proof that a tragedy may be great without providing a role for a great actor. At the same time it is evident that the *Antigone* might be effectively presented even with actors of moderate ability, and no doubt that often happened."

The structure of the drama is exemplary. It is compact. Once again, as Sophocles is inclined to shape his scripts, the action unfolds quickly, with a crisis already at hand and the exposition being brought in later as needed. In the very first scene the whole event is rehearsed – verbally – and from a personal, feminine slant: the two sisters confiding in each other. Sophocles inserts, too, a high moment of hope and reversal – when Creon, impressed by Tiresias and the advice of the elders' warning, relents and countermands Antigone's sentence – only to have that relief and rise of spirits followed almost immediately by a second reversal and the chilling catastrophe. The dialogue is spare, strong, some of the lines whip-lashing, and the play contains two of the most admired odes in Sophocles' canon. One is the paean to Love (Eros) which follows the encounter between Haemon and Creon. The young man has not spoken of his heart's deep feeling for the doomed girl, but the chorus tells of it indirectly by asking in a song:

> Where is the equal of Love?
> Where is the battle he cannot win,
> The power he cannot outmatch?
> In the farthest corners of earth, in the midst of the sea,
> He is there; he is here
> In the bloom of a fair face
> Lying in wait;
> And the grip of his madness
> Spares not god or man,
> Marring the righteous man,
> Driving his soul into mazes of sin

And strife, dividing a house
For the light that burns in the eyes of a bride of desire
Is a fire that consumes.
At the side of the great gods
Aphrodite immortal
Works her will upon all.
[Translation: E.F. Watling]

The other, the most acclaimed of all poetic passages by Sophocles, is the ode in praise of human daring and accomplishment. It has no seeming relevance to anything that precedes or follows it in the text of the play, but none the less is welcome because of its literary quality and affirmative note, rare in Greek tragedy, and especially in the work of this author:

Wonders are many of earth, and the greatest of these
Is man, who rides the ocean and takes his way
Through the deeps, through wind-swept valleys of perilous seas
    That surge and sway.

He is master of ageless Earth, to his own will bending,
The immortal mother of gods by the sweat of his brow,
As year succeeds to year, with toil unending
    Of mule and plough.

He is lord of all things living; birds of the air,
Beasts of the field, all creatures of sea and land
He taketh, cunning to capture and ensnare
    With sleight of hand;

Hunting the Savage beast from the upland rocks,
Taming the mountain monarch in his lair,
Teaching the wild horse and roaming ox
    His yoke to bear.

> The use of language, the wind-swift motion of brain
> He learnt; found out the laws of living together
> In cities, building him shelter against the rain
> And wintry weather.
>
> There is nothing beyond his power. His subtlety
> Meeteth all chance, all danger conquereth.
> For every ill he had found its remedy,
> Save only death.

And so on. This, from the most pessimistic of dramatists, is uplifting. (Comparing a half-dozen English translations of these two poems, a reader unacquainted with Greek finds very different renditions: but though the language is at variance, their content is fairly consistent.)

John Ferguson pores over the metaphors strewn throughout the dialogue and choric interludes and discovers that here the imagery most frequently is of animals: Creon treats people like animals, he speaks of Ismene as a viper; the elders observe that Polynices descended on Thebes like an eagle, but now he himself has become a prey for birds; the messenger tells how Haemon rushed at his father "with the eyes of an animal". Creon brings out what is bestial in those about him. Of equal importance are metaphors that allude to storm, darkness and light, scattered through many passages and indicative of the "stormy" atmosphere, the emotional turbulence, prevailing in this unhappy royal family.

Ferguson makes several unusual points about the plot. One is that Antigone has not been guilty of the crime of Polynices' initial burial.

> Why did Antigone, having achieved the burial safely, attempt it again? The question has dogged interpreters of the play. For by the ritual burial, the immutable laws of heaven have been satisfied, and the uncovering of the body does not undo the burial. Antigone is not merely protecting the body from animals at the second burial, she is fulfilling the ritual, with libations. The explanation is simple. Antigone did not perform the first burial, could not have performed it, did not know it had been performed and never admits to performing it. Creon proclaimed his ban on burial during the night and set a watch. When Antigone and Ismene meet it is daybreak, and the burial has already been performed. But Antigone has not been near the body. The deed she plans with Ismene is the one she performs under cover of the noontide dust storm, as the bronze bowl for the libations also proves. When the guards charge her with

> both acts, she does not admit them; what the guard says is that she does not deny the charges; the wording is careful and explicit. The sentry says that there are no tracks around the body, no animal tracks, and *a fortiori* no human tracks. In fact no human was responsible, and the chorus gives the right answer when they attribute it to the gods. So we have the colossal irony of Creon swearing by Zeus that the perpetrator shall be punished, when the perpetrator is Zeus. The gods can look after their own.

Is this, in fact, what Sophocles intended? Ferguson's reading of it is quite unique. Or is the explanation that, like Homer, Sophocles sometimes nods?

As Ferguson sees it, Sophocles' message in the drama is that both sides are wrong. "This was the audience's view, and it was Sophocles' view. . . . Creon's refusal to be ruled by a woman is natural, and it is his tragedy that Antigone's view of the situation is the true one. Wilamowitz said perceptively, 'The people approve of what she did, but they do not approve of the fact that *she* did it.' The gods condemn the refusal of burial, but in making the burial their own concern condemn Antigone's disobedience. To the Athenians, Antigone has *hubris*, and however good her case she cannot be justified. That is what the play is about, and why it is called *Antigone*. It is in Antigone not Creon that the curse on the house of Labdacus is fulfilled."

For Ferguson, the script loses stature as it nears its end. "[It] is marvelous up to the Bacchus ode, but then it falls away. . . . The Eurydice episode is a sad aberration. She enters, speaks nine lines, hears the messenger, goes out and commits suicide. We cannot feel this as a tragedy, and as a means to Creon's downfall it creaks at the joints and puts the play off balance." This critic also finds fault with Creon's delay in freeing Antigone, which results from his first halting on the way to bury Polynices, which causes him to arrive too late at the cave. Why does he do this? "Plainly because of his psychological make-up. He has held out against the burial; when his resistance is broken down the burial is all important, and he carries it out with needless elaboration. The refusal of burial has caused the pollution; it must be undone. The state still comes first. Of course, this makes for splendid melodrama – the arrival just too late. But it *is* melodrama, and will not stand up to reflection. And here, as with the dragging in of Eurydice, Sophocles has been diverted from Antigone to Creon."

To L.R. Lind the work has quite different facets and meanings. "Criticism of Sophocles' *Antigone* has since Hegel made much of the opposition between the rightful demands of the family versus those of the state, which led to the formulation of an abstract conflict between 'divine' way, upheld by Antigone, and man-made law, represented by Creon." A useful dichotomy, which can lead to a discussion of the play, says Lind, but surely not the only way to understand it. "The well-worn *hamartia* of

Aristotle – the theory of the tragic flaw of character in a person which brings about his downfall, likewise does not take us far." That is because, to Lind, Antigone is prompted by only the noblest of motives.

> She is certainly not deliberately seeking martyrdom nor does she act through mere stubbornness or ignorance of the consequences. Hers is a supreme, completely voluntary courage which chooses the right and makes no compromise with reality; in fact, for her the true reality consists simply in the execution of her duty according to ancient Greek conventions: the burial of her brother.
>
> Yet she does not self-consciously emphasize her religious duty: that theme is gradually subordinated to a more generalized and wholly feminine resistance to Creon which may be more reasonably interpreted in terms of an unavoidable clash between two strong personalities, both bent upon doing what, to each, seems right. Antigone has made her free choice within the framework of a situation which if left undisturbed would have become intolerable in its implications of personal dishonor.
>
> Creon's arbitrary decree, though not without precedent or parallel in Greek tragedy, is on the other hand defended by him with desperate and sophistical arguments until his defense collapses completely into contrition and remorse. . . . Creon's *hubris* – his fatal excess of behavior – lay in his unwillingness to yield to Antigone before it was too late, in his failure to see the sinister development of events and to withdraw with honor from a position which in the end became impossible for him to maintain. He himself states to the chorus the moral of his action: "It is hard to do – to retreat from a firm stand – but I yield, I will obey you. We must not wage a vain war with fate." Antigone, though her action leads to death, has at least the comfort of having acted in a cause commended by all the Greek views of decent behavior toward gods and men. Creon's tragedy is further deepened by the overtones of political dissatisfaction with his government that is voiced by the people; he has mistaken firmness for harsh intolerance, a steadfast stand for hatred, since one cannot avoid the conclusion that much of his behavior is determined by his personal feeling against Polynices and not by governmental policy alone. Antigone is to some extent the symbol of national resistance to a tyrant, a name and a figure dreaded and feared by the historic Greeks.
>
> . . . It is clear that Sophocles is praising the virtues of compassion, moderation, and sympathy in this profound analysis of human suffering, which he can neither justify nor explain. Kitto says that is "the very core of Sophocles' philosophy, that virtue alone cannot assure happiness nor wickedness alone explain disaster." Further, there is certainly the curse on the house of Laius to reckon with. . . . Even the innocent must suffer under this curse, Ismene and Haemon as well as Antigone; for Creon the retribution brought upon himself by the wrong he has done the dead is clearly a dominant theme in the play.

These are all part of the lesson that *Antigone* teaches. Yet they are vague ideas indeed compared to the simple, unmistakable words of Antigone herself when she tells why she must bury her brother and thus bring ruin upon herself.

Here Lind quotes Antigone's rationale for her risky act, that she has a higher duty to Polynices than to any other person, since she can never have another brother. He does not agree with A. Jacob, R.C. Jebb and other Sophoclean scholars who regard the speech as most likely spurious, not the poet's own, and who point out that in it she does not even mention Haemon, "her fiancé, the pallid Romeo of this Greek drama. . . . Yet nothing in the play is better authenticated and more in keeping with the actual Greek feeling in such a crisis. Romance had a different meaning to the Greeks than it has for us. The fact is, Antigone is perfectly logical and correct in this statement."

The structure of the play is flawed, in Lind's opinion, because Antigone disappears from it a mere two-thirds of the way through. "Her subsequent actions are reported by others and the focus of emotion turns irresistibly to Creon. We watch in fascinated horror as he stumbles from one blunder to another. . . . Despite the play's title it is hard to believe that Creon's fate was not at least equally significant to Sophocles.

"A tragic and intolerable situation – willfully and stubbornly brought to pass by two powerful and inflexible personalities – all other characters are foils for these two – set against the dark history of a luckless family makes this play one of Sophocles' greatest."

F.L. Lucas, in a brief and acidulous foreword to *Antigone* in his *Greek Tragedy and Comedy*, casts a different if somewhat idiosyncratic light on the script.

This play would be admirably clear – if only it had not been explained. . . . Harder to be simpler. No question that Creon was wrong – a man not ill-meaning, but intoxicated with his new authority. A Greek audience would soon place him, merely by the way he speaks. "This fellow," they would say, "talks like a *tyrant*" (a species of animal only too familiar to them, as to us, alike from literature and life). Tiresias, the voice of Heaven, condemns Creon as forcibly as Nathan condemned David. By that, even the wavering chorus are convinced. Creon himself is convinced – too late, for now the judgment falls. Who indeed would not be convinced?

Not Hegel. For him, as already mentioned, life was divided against itself by constant conflicts harmonized in higher and higher syntheses. Thus Antigone and Creon are both partly right, partly wrong; they clash; they suffer; but justice is done and there is no place for pity. Such is the true essence of tragedy. And since *Antigone* so nearly fitted his formula, it became for Hegel the grandest work of ancient or modern times. Sophocles might have been gratified by the praise; he would have been stupefied by the interpretation. Some, indeed, may feel that, with his Prussian state-worship, Hegel was himself a good deal too like Creon – except that no character of Sophocles could express himself in a style so execrable.

But ingenuity did not end with Hegel. More modern critics have explained that Antigone says nothing of her love for Haemon, because she was really in love with her dead brother Polynices. A little Freud is a dangerous thing. There is still time for other critics to discover that Antigone was also (in *Oedipus at Colonus*) in love with her father; and Electra, no doubt, with her brother Orestes. One would have thought Greek tragedy already contained more than enough incest (a tedious theme, I think), without importing more. Nor is it clear why a dramatist who elsewhere treats the subject with brutal frankness would here veil it in innuendo too obscure for any audience. The question is not: "Was Antigone in love with her brother?" (outside fiction she does not exist), but: "Did Sophocles mean his hearers to think so?" If so, he failed; and if he was so bad at conveying his meaning, it hardly matters what he meant.

Then there is the theory that Polynices was buried the first time, not by Antigone, but by Ismene. But life is too brief for brooding on mares' nests.

The play keeps a special appeal because its central problem is still so deep and wide. It may be said, indeed, that we read too much into it – that Sophocles was merely depicting a simple clash between the laws of God and the laws of Man, not foreshadowing Hitler and Stalin. Yet we need not be too afraid of anachronism in seeing Antigone as an immortal type. Her "unwritten" laws may often change; they may not be eternal, as she dreamed; but where is their home? In the individual conscience. *That* endures. And again it rises, again and again, the cold power of the State, whether single despot or compact majority, claiming as Caesar's the things that are God's. In the Sparta of Sophocles' time, next to the meeting-place of the magistrates was reared, with grim purpose, the Temple of Fear. That too the ages have not destroyed. Today it casts its gloomy shadow far across the earth. The challenge met by Antigone was essentially the same for Socrates, for Joan of Arc, for Charlotte Corday, and for our world today – the conflict of the Many and the One.

Dramatically, I think, the play weakens towards the close; it flags without Antigone; as Ajax without its hero. . . . The cursing of Tiresias, and the descriptions of Antigone's death and Haemon's despair, are indeed vivid, but less vivid; there is, as usual, too much lamenting; and it is hard to be much moved by Queen Eurydice's death – she was never really alive.

But though not Sophocles' most perfect play, it contains perhaps his greatest speech – Antigone's burning vindication of the unwritten laws. And she remains, it may be, his most immortal character – hard, at times, and headstrong, like Cordelia, but heroic as few heroines have been – "stern Daughter

> of the Voice of God." If the story is true that the Athenians made Sophocles a general for having written this work, it may not have been very prudent of them (though generals had many duties *not* military); but it does great credit to their hearts.

Whether or not *Antigone* won a prize at the Festival is not recorded, but as has been noted it was popular and often repeated. Euripides' play with the same title is among those lost; it is believed that he elected to give his version a happy ending. Six fragments remain of a script on the subject by the Roman playwright Lucius Accius (or Attius, 170–*c.* 90 BC). The French "Humanist" Robert Garnier (1545–90), renowned in his day, ventured an *Antigone* (1580). Another French adaptation by Jean de Rotrou (1609–50), put on in 1638, preceded *Le Thébaïde* (1664) by Jean Racine (1639–99), which was a failure when staged at the Palais Royal. An Italian treatment by V.A. Alfieri (1749–1803), which was brought out in 1783, was influenced by these Neoclassical models. Comparatively recent is *Antigone* (1917) in German by the then youthful Walter Hasenclever (1890–1940), a protégé of Max Reinhardt, who produced it, transforming the ancient story into an anti-war parable; it proved to be a "proclamation of human rights" of acknowledged power; in English, the work is called *The Death of Antigone.* A much later German handling of the theme is by Berthold Brecht (1898–1956). In French, by Jean Cocteau (1889–1963), there is *Antigone* (1922). Emperor Frederick William IV of Prussia in 1841 commissioned Felix Mendelssohn (1809–47) to compose incidental music for a German translation of Sophocles' *Antigone.* Further indication of German interest in the problem involved in the story is the opera by Carl Orff (1895–1982), *Antigonae* (1949), with a libretto based on a translation by the poet Friedrich Hölderin (1770–1843), who also dedicated his talents to rendering *Oedipus the King* into that tongue.

During the Second World War, while the Nazis occupied Paris, Jean Anouilh (1910–87) found it difficult to choose a subject for a play that would pass a vigilant German military censorship. In Sophocles' classic work Anouilh saw the possibility of a drama that, outwardly unexceptionable, yet applied to the situation of the French Resistance fighters. His *Antigone* (1943), granted permission by the hoodwinked Nazis for staging in Paris, is an only slightly altered version of the original tragedy. Performed in modern dress (Creon is attired in a tuxedo), it has added touches of humour and romantic interest – Haemon and Antigone are given scenes together. The Germans apparently remained unsuspecting, though it was clear to alert Parisian audiences that Creon was to be recognized as the Nazi governor of the city and Antigone as a secret member of the Maquis. Perhaps it got by the authorities because it was not always clear just where Anouilh's sympathies were: he makes Creon a considerably more reasonable antagonist. Later, when the playwright was asked on whose side he was, he evaded a direct reply, saying: "On both sides."

An instant success in Paris, it became a favourite in many other countries after the war, and is still acted very frequently, especially in regional theatres and by innumerable college groups. If anything, it has supplanted the original work; though it closely adheres to Sophocles' treatment of its theme, it has the advantage of being shorn of mythological allusions, and therefore of being wholly intelligible. With those minor changes, this ancient play has become a very topical work, implying that the Antigones of this world are still very much with us. She is one of drama's archetypal figures. (Some further studies of most of these works will be made elsewhere.)

Sophocles' tragedies have not lost their appeal to readers. In 1991 the largest English and American publisher of paperback books reported that its current edition of *Three Theban Plays*, translated by Robert Fagels, was the best-selling title on its list.

It is told that when Sophocles died his funeral procession was blocked by Spartan forces besieging Athens until the god Dionysus himself appeared to Lysander, the Spartan leader, and won from him a safe-conduct for the mourners, who then crossed the battle-lines and bore the playwright's body to the family's ancestral tomb in Deceleia. Poets composed graceful epitaphs for him, and for a long time Athenians paid him divine honours, bringing sacrifices to his sepulchre.

Euripides' rank among the major Athenian dramatists is perpetually disputed. Some deem him superior to Aeschylus and Sophocles; this opinion was especially held during the Neo-romantic period, the nineteenth century, since by temperament Euripides was romantic, a rebel spirit. Each age values an artist in accordance with its own special outlook: in art there is no fixed hierarchy of accomplishment. The very trait that brought Euripides the highest esteem a score of centuries after his death, his liberal bent, caused him to be widely unpopular among his contemporaries.

He was born on the island of Salamis, possibly the year of the great battle there. He was fifteen years younger than Sophocles. His aristocratic – or at least well-to-do – parents were refugees from Phyla, an Attic town that had been invaded by the Medes. Later, Aristophanes and other satirists sought to belittle his lineage, suggesting that his mother was a greengrocer's daughter and had peddled fruit and vegetables in the marketplace; but this claim gets little scholarly credence. In his youth, encouraged by his father, he showed skill at athletics, a preoccupation of which he quickly wearied; afterwards in his *Autoclys* he declared: "Of all the ten thousand plagues of Hellas there is none worse than the breed of athletes." He was often possessed by such peculiarly jaundiced moods. Among his other diverse talents were an ability to paint and to compose scores in a radical style to accompany his stage works. He was the mentor of Timotheus, whose music was so advanced that it offended the tradition-minded. Euripides also did frequent stints as a soldier but hardly enjoyed them.

His early education was unusually complete: in boyhood he took part in ceremonial worship as a cup-bearer and torch-bearer in festivities honouring Apollo at shrines in his parents' native Phyla, a town noted for its small but handsome temples and its orthodoxy. Like many rebels against formal religion, he was brought up in a milieu of exceeding piety, and at first accepted the priests' tenets without question. But his mind was inherently sceptical, despite his romantic bent, and this attitude was sharpened by his later education: he became a disciple of the bold scientist and rationalist Anaxagoras, attended the lectures of Prodicus, and developed a friendship – or at least an acquaintance – with the "secular saint" Socrates, whose growing influence on him was profound. Rumour even had it – such stories were maliciously inspired by his enemies – that Euripides' plays were secretly revised for him and greatly improved by Socrates. What is better attested, however, is that the much younger philosopher, who usually shunned theatre, never missed a performance of a work by Euripides, even travelling on foot to productions of them at Piraeus, the nearby seaport. Another of the youthful writer's masters, and afterwards a frequent visitor at his house, was the almost equally acclaimed philosopher Protagoras, an agnostic in religion, whose relativistic, humanistic credo was summed up in the oft-cited phrase, "Man is the measure of all things." As all this shows, Euripides belonged to the so-called "Enlightenment", or liberal Sophist movement. He lived at the very height of the Periclean era, when Athens blazed with great art – sculpture, painting, architecture, music – and keen intellectuality.

His aesthetic sense was acute, and he is a lyric poet of the utmost sensibility, his phrases often rising to rhapsodic heights. A rationalist like his many friends and teachers, he embraced and was inspired by the new scientific spirit, a Socratic questioning of all established values and beliefs. In a martial period, when Athens foolishly and self-destructively launched itself on unrewarding imperialistic ventures, he was an outspoken pacifist, to a rash extent that even exasperated his wife. (Ironically, his parents had named him Euripides in tribute to a battle engagement by the Greek fleet in the strait called Euripus off the coast of Euboea.) He was a dissenter in many aspects of Greek culture. He felt that much of the mythology that furnished the subject-matter of the plays was brutal, that it glorified legendary behaviour that was shameful; he also insisted that the religion of the common man was encrusted with childish superstition, barbaric and primitive, unworthy of a sophisticated and educated race. He disapproved of the inferior rights and place allotted in Hellenic society to women and slaves. He was a reformer, looked upon with suspicion by the priesthood, as well as by political conservatives, who kept up an unceasing fusillade of calumny against him.

His position was increasingly dangerous, and he had to proceed cautiously. He learned to equivocate deftly, seeming to say one thing when on second thought it grew apparent to a hearer that he meant the opposite. So he had two different kinds of listeners, those who thought he was paying pious tribute to the gods, and those who read into his lines a subtle contempt for the Olympian arbiters of man's destiny. He especially rejected polytheism and had scorn for oracles, categorizing them as dishonest. A professional soothsayer was one who "speaks few truths and many lies". Efforts to read the future by consulting the entrails of birds were nonsensical. Religion and oracles sanctioned far too much violence, rapine and sacrifice. He suggested that the conduct of the Homeric heroes was quite as scandalous as that of the cruel, callous and immoral gods whom they too closely imitated. His opinions evoked outcries of rage and shock.

The comic playwright Aristophanes was one of Euripides' most determined foes; his raucous revues often contained passages parodying lines in Euripides' tragedies. The argument was *ad hominem*: the Greeks, when feuding, did not believe in fair play. To degrade and make fun of him, Euripides' opponents called him a woman-hater and an easily deceived husband, both of which claims were pure libels.

In time, Athens's military fortunes waned; the city's foraging armies were defeated, and soon in the frustrated city a hunt for likely scapegoats was on. All "Leftists", most of them Euripides' associates, were assailed for having spread traitorous ideas that had corrupted and weakened Athens's ability and will to fight its external enemies. Aroused by demagogues, a purge began, with popular fury against "intellectuals". Pericles, the tolerant ruler, was impeached. Anaxagoras was banished; Protagoras was no longer able to preach his "atheism". Socrates was brought to trial for having misled Athenian youth through probing and irreverent argument. Charges of sacrilege, heresy and dishonesty were lodged against Euripides, too, but he was freed because it could not be clearly adduced that the iconoclastic, "unpatriotic" or "impious" opinions spoken by his characters were in actuality his own, a dodge that has exculpated many a playwright through the centuries since then.

Acquitted, Euripides still thought it was wise to accept voluntary exile, not only for his safety but perhaps also as a protest against Athens's mad, jingoistic course. His artistic reputation was such that he was promptly granted haven at the court of King Archelaus of Macedon.

After a mere eighteen months there he died. He was a venerable seventy or more (406/407 BC?). The cause of his death is uncertain. Rumours spread by hostile priests attributed his demise to a grisly mishap: while he strolled in the moonlight, the king's savage watch-dogs had set upon him and torn him to pieces; but the story is most likely mere wish fulfilment on the part of his angry detractors, a myth forged to point a moral, that the "defamer" of the gods had been appropriately repaid by them.

Aeschylus and Sophocles had dared to pose religious questions, but were still "true believers". Euripides' scepticism was not always nuanced: "If gods do evil, then they are not gods." In the opening lines of his *Melanippe* (of which no full script remains), he wrote, echoing Protagoras,

> O Zeus, if there be a Zeus,
> For I know of him only by report –

His plays frequently provoked riots at the Great Dionysia, and he won first prize only five times, one victory occurring after his death. On occasion, elsewhere, he was even more perilously outspoken:

> Do some say that there be gods above?
> There are not, no, there are not. Let no fool,
> Led by the old false fable, deceive you.
> Look at the facts themselves, yielding my words
> No undue credence.

Further, in *Melanippe*, is this bold statement:

> The gods . . . whom mortals deem so wise,
> Are nothing clearer than some winged dream;
> And all their ways, like man's ways, but a stream
> Of turmoil. He who cares to suffer least,
> Not blind as fools are blinded by a priest,
> Goes straight . . . to what death, those who know him know.

Nor did he believe that virtue was its own reward, or that the gods exact a toll of those guilty of misconduct:

> . . . I say that kings

Kill, rob, break oaths, lay cities waste by fraud,
And doing thus are happier than those
Who live calm, pious lives day after day.

Still, he covered his tracks most of the time, his always suspenseful plays also attracting spectators by their impassioned lyricism, the beauty of his music and his trick of not resolving the metaphysical questions he raised, so that his personal views were not fully exposed, while they provoked interesting ideas. Again, his characters were speaking, not Euripides himself, or at least that was his ready argument in defence. Frequently, his prologues and epilogues, in which gods appear and declaim, seem to be artistic blemishes. But these deities, uttering conventional pieties, are used to veil what is really in the body of the play. They are false beginnings and endings, "disclaimers", comparable to the prefatory note a modern novelist inserts for legal reasons in his book to the effect that none of his characters are copied from real persons. Take away the prologues and epilogues and you are apt to have the true Euripidean drama.

Forced to compromise, he found that he could use the Homeric wars to suggest parallels to what was now happening in Athens, the mistakes that were so draining and costly. This resort to an implied historical likeness between past and recent or present events, but not an outright statement that they are akin, has proved to be a handy stratagem of use to dissident playwrights ever since, especially to those working under very oppressive regimes. They have appropriated it time and again since Euripides' day. It protects the author. If there is a perceptible similarity, the responsibility for seeing it passes to the spectator, whose response to it he may keep to himself. One immediately recognizes this as the device employed by Anouilh when adapting *Antigone.*

Learning of Euripides' death in a foreign land, and suddenly realizing his eminence, the somewhat chastened leaders of Athens requested that King Archelaus return the dramatist's body, but that monarch refused to part with the corpse; and finally the Athenians agreed to put up a cenotaph to memorialize the city's great son.

He began his career as a dramatist at twenty-five, and during the next fifty years wrote between seventy-five and ninety-five scripts. His first, now lost, was *The Daughters of Pelias* (455 BC), only a year after the death of Aeschylus. From all reports, it anticipated the themes of some of his later pieces, the *Medea* and *The Bacchae.* In it, Medea, a foreign sorceress, seeks to punish the ageing King Pelias for having cheated her husband of an inheritance. She persuades his daughters that if they slay him he can be brought back to life and rejuvenated by her spells. Through the play shines the ancient rite of *sparagmos*, the mutilation or rending apart of the scapegoat, be it king or totem beast, that is a source of the Dionysia and hence Western theatre. Jason is repulsed by the terrible vengeance plotted by his barbaric Cretan wife, the Minotaur's sister. He rejects her; she has lost him by the very excessiveness of her love. One sees here a first instance of Euripides' insight into abnormal psychology, especially in the realm of sexuality. The play won only third prize.

Another aspect of the playwright's gift is shown in two other early works, *The Cyclops* and *Rhesus* (though not all scholars concede that Euripides wrote *Rhesus*). *The Cyclops* is a satyr play and will be described later. *Rhesus* is a very minor piece, romantic and somewhat Oriental in colour; it dramatizes Book Ten of the *Iliad.* The action takes place in the Trojan camp during the prolonged siege; the leading characters are Hector, Paris and Aeneas, as well as a simple soldier, and most prominently Rhesus, a Thracian king, the son of the River Strymon and the Muse of the Mountains. Rhesus has come with a band of spearmen to help the Trojans. Hector feels that this pledged assistance is too late, when the invaders have been routed and the end of the struggle is in sight. Rhesus has been delayed by a Scythian attack on the northern borders of Thrace; it had to be thrown back. He promises to annihilate the Greeks once and for all. In a wolf-skin, and crawling on all fours, Dolon is sent to spy on the Hellenic camp. He is killed by Odysseus and Diomede, who slip through the Trojan lines, intending to surprise and slay Hector or some other hero at rest and unawares. Hector is not in his tent. Guided by the goddess Athena, the pair stab the sleeping Rhesus instead and narrowly make their escape in the dark. Confusion ensues; Hector castigates the captain of the guard for neglect, but the Thracians accuse Hector himself of having plotted their king's death. In an epiphany, the Muse of the Mountains appears to mourn her son and assigns guilt for the act to Odysseus and the ungrateful Athena. At the close, an angry Hector makes ready to lead a daylight attack on the Greeks.

An adventure story, *Rhesus* is suspenseful in good part, and at the end ascends to poetic heights. Some scholars deem it partially or wholly the work of a later hand, and it has been submitted to many tests, even word-counts, but with no clear indication of its authorship. Stylistically it sounds Euripidean, but there are some infelicitous passages. Murray suggested that it might be a very early work by the poet, whose genius is manifest in it at times, and that it was altered here and there by actors and producers years after his death.

A touch that does seem to be Euripides' is the compassionate and beautiful moment when the Muse weeps for her son, while the Trojan soldiers quietly listen: Euripides, the pacifist and humanitarian, perhaps made a first public appearance here.

In 438 BC he composed another romance, *Alcmaeon at Psophis* (a lost work), and *Alcestis*, preceded by *The Women of Crete* and *Telephus* (this pair also lost). The hero of *Alcmaeon at Psophis*, like Orestes, is guilty of matricide, having killed Eriphyle, his mother, for which he is punished by the Furies. He marries twice: to regain a marvellous necklace he has given his first wife, Alphesiboea, he resorts to trickery, succeeds at it, and is able to present the ornament to Callirrhoe, his second spouse. Finally he is slain by Phegeus, the father of Alphesiboea. About *The Women of Crete* little is known: apparently it dealt with the philandering Aerope, the wife of Atreus, who falls in love with a commoner. She is sentenced to death by drowning, but is spared by a sailor, another man of lowly birth. Euripides furnished her with some remarkable love lyrics and portrayed her frustrations quite sympathetically, which aroused a measure of scandal. *Telephus* is remembered because in it Euripides dressed a character in beggar's rags, which established his claim as an innovator: it was a parting from tradition that was emulated by Sophocles, though initially it evoked objections. The story is of the King of Mysia, Telephus, who is wounded by Greeks on a scouting expedition, while they are preparing for their Trojan campaign. Only the spear itself that pierced him can heal him. Disguised as a beggar, he goes to Argos where the Greek fleet is gathered. He explains his need to find the right spear. Odysseus sees through the disguise, and Telephus is forced to seize the infant Orestes as a hostage to protect himself.

Alcestis seems to have been the fourth and only surviving offering in this tetralogy. This script baffles scholars, who greatly prefer to classify stage pieces as tragedies, melodramas, comedies or farces, since it does not clearly fit in any one such category. They compromise by referring to it as a "tragicomedy", a genre which Euripides may be said to have created.

For this story he drew on a lost poem by Hesiod and possibly an earlier play by Phrynichus, of which only a few words remain. King Admetus of Pherae in Thessaly is fatally ill. He is visited by Apollo, who tells him that he can recover only if someone else consents to die in his stead. No kin or friend is ready to take over Admetus' death sentence. He even beseeches his parents that one of them, being aged, should make the sacrifice; but the old couple, still loving life, deny his desperate plea. Finally, out of her deep love for the stricken Admetus, his wife, Alcestis, offers herself to Death. In the underworld, however, the goddess Persephone, a daughter of Pelias, takes pity on the remarkably faithful, altruistic young woman and miraculously restores her to life.

Euripides changes the story somewhat: Heracles has come to visit Admetus, finds the house in gloom, belatedly learns of Alcestis' generous deed, and that she is near her last breath. The mighty hero, after too much wine, vows to wrestle with Death for the departed woman and bring her back to her husband. He is successful in this amazing feat, which is one of his famed superhuman "seven labours".

Death is portrayed as "The Destroyer", not "The Healer", an ugly figure dressed in black, sword in hand. Apollo has won Admetus' reprieve by tricking the Fates: as punishment for an offence against his father, Zeus, the bright god has lived in King Admetus' palace as a slave, and Admetus has shown himself to be both very hospitable and devout, so that the imprisonment has been unexpectedly pleasant. But now, as the god of light, Apollo must leave, because he cannot encounter the god of darkness. The two deities meet briefly, however; they exchange angry words.

Alcestis is depicted tenderly, even sentimentally (Euripides has that persistent fault); she is given lines of lyrical quality. Admetus, on the other hand, is a coward, a fool. Heracles, clad in a lion-skin, a club in his grasp, is a vulgar, tipsy braggart and practical joker. The play varies in tone from pathos to farce, incongruous shifts of mood which – as has been said – have baffled the critics. But Euripides may have done this for a special purpose, to make fun of the ridiculous old legend, boldly to portray the gods in an absurd light. Both Apollo and Death talk like poltroons. At times the play seems almost a parody. To fit the conventions of the Greek theatre, Alcestis must spend her final moments *before* the palace, not on her couch within it. The chorus of elders, anticipating the sorrowful entrance of the king and his dying spouse, ask themselves how they shall respond to such a lachrymose tableau:

> At the sight of such woes
> Shall we cut our throats?
> Shall we slip a dangling noose around our necks?
> [Translation: Richard Aldington]

Admetus, after extravagantly bewailing the "loss" of his wife, and vowing never to remarry, and to have her marble likeness carved, can hardly wait to bed another woman; and Heracles, having at the very tombside rescued Alcestis from Death's horrible grasp, plays a cruel trick on his "bereaved" friend: he brings Alcestis back with her face shrouded, and offers her to Admetus as a woman he has won as a prize in a contest. Only at the end, in an amusing "recognition" scene, does the king learn her true identity. Earlier, Admetus and his father, Pheres, have exchanged insults at the funeral, each taunting the other for his unmanly fear of death. The father, cynically, replies to his son's reproaches: "I indeed begot you . . . but I am not bound to die for you." Even for the old, life is sweet.

The play's ending is ambiguous: Alcestis keeps silent, leading some critics to suggest that Euripides, the rationalist, means to imply that she had never expired but was merely in a coma and still is; while others contend that Heracles has brought back a corpse, which accounts for his "prize" being speechless throughout the final scene, and that the "wife" Admetus carries to his bed is only a cadaver. A grisly joke, if so. But it may be that the playwright is merely evading, by Alcestis' silence, exceedingly difficult questions about what life is like in the after-world; and also sustaining interest by using the time-old theatrical device of "mistaken identity", a trick which allows Alcestis, always suspicious of Admetus' protestations, to hear again his vows of fidelity to her memory, and to discover how hollow they are. (Another possible reason for the silence might have been that the same actor had the roles of Heracles and Alcestis, and in the final scene Alcestis was played by a wordless masked supernumerary.)

By downgrading Admetus, Euripides was lessening the stature of a conventionally admired king of antiquity, and at the same time suggesting that a mere woman, whose place in Greek society was far inferior, was capable of infinitely greater courage.

Since the play was among the four by Euripides given at the Great Dionysia, as if it were a satyr play, it seems clear that he himself took it lightly.

Indeed, much of the tetralogy was experimental. In the *Telephus*, which preceded *Alcestis* in the programme, Euripides' showing a beggar dressed in rags was a touch of unprecedented realism, offending spectators who thought that the ceremonial function of the theatre required stylized, richer costuming. It is said that such superficial realism was a first and not insignificant step towards a deeper social and psychological realism in Greek tragedy, a movement in all aspects of which Euripides was foremost, a leader. On the same programme, too, the *Women of Crete* provided another startling theme: a princess infatuated with a man of lowly strain, and ultimately saved from death by a kindly sailor, who defies the commands given to him by his hard-hearted betters. Obviously, his innate character is superior to theirs. Euripides is to make this implicit statement often; it was part of his propaganda against the Athenians' harsh treatment of slaves. Moreover, he does not condemn the Cretan princess for her indiscretion in loving a man whose blood is not royal. Failing to find fault with her, he might even be said to have approved of her unconventional behaviour. In all four plays he represents interesting portraits of women, the unvirtuous Aerope, the amorous Alphesiboea, the resourceful Clytemnestra – whose part in this piece is to assist Telephus – and the gentle Alcestis. The class system in Athens is also viewed satirically in another way. In Ferguson's words, "Apollo is a caricatured aristocrat, Death a caricatured democrat." Admetus is bourgeois, bluntly prosaic and unimaginative.

Some critics hazard that in *Alcestis* Euripides was trying to enlarge upon and alter the form and content of the satyr play, giving it more substance and adding more poetry and a few serious notes to its ribald buffoonery and whimsy. If this is so, the play might be seen as a transitional work to what is later to be called Middle Comedy, which in turns leads to New Comedy.

The major phase of Euripides' work begins in 431 BC, when the playwright, nearing his fiftieth year, entered the drama contest with his still popular *Medea.* In many respects it is one of the most realistic theatre works ever written, though its ending reverts to the *deus ex machina* of which he was over-fond. A play of terrifying power, it is a challenging vehicle for an actress (in fifth-century Greece, an actor) of profound emotional strength and projection. Medea, the magician–princess of Colchis, has sacrificed everything – even the lives of her father, King Aietes, and brother, Apsyrtus – for the sake of the Greek sea-adventurer Jason, aiding him and his Argonauts in their theft of the fabled Golden Fleece. The pair sail off together and continue on the ship's wanderings. Jason, ungrateful, grows weary of her, though her powers of witchery are of inestimable value to him. By law they have not been able to marry since she is a foreigner. The Argonauts' vessel reaches Corinth, where Jason perceives a chance to inherit the throne if he weds Glauce, the king's daughter. This means he must rid himself of the intensely demanding Medea. King Creon of Corinth obligingly exiles her, so that Jason and the chosen Glauce can be joined. Jason plans to keep the two children he has had by the barbarous Medea. When Medea learns of his treacherous intentions she calls upon her magical arts to take a hideous revenge. At first she pretends to accept the situation, sends a gift of richly embroidered robes to her rival, as she has done before, when disposing of Jason's enemy, his uncle King Pelias of Iolcus. Glauce, happily donning one of the beautiful robes, is set afire and burned to death, and her father King Creon – trying vainly to beat out the flames and rescue her – also perishes in the inextinguishable blaze. To complete the punishment of Jason, Medea murders the two children and lets him see their bloody corpses, their young throats cut.

Climbing into a winged chariot, she piles the children's bodies atop it and escapes by riding off into the sky, a stage-effect that of course was accomplished at the Great Dionysia by the employment of cranes and pulleys.

What distinguishes the *Medea* is its unsparing portrait of a jealous and humiliated woman. One German critic has said of it, "Here we see the feminine soul as no Greek dramatist ever exposed it before." In her rage at life, her cries of torment at her fate, her fury at her betrayer, the foreign Medea is a stirring figure and has often been likened to Aeschylus' Clytemnestra and Shakespeare's Lady Macbeth, though she is far more vocal than they ever are, if only because the focus is always on her. Jason, too, is well drawn: calculating, hardened by ceaseless ambition, an adventurer who has lost the romantic and sexual ardour of youth, he is now interested in furthering his fortunes heedless of the cost to others. Medea is no longer useful to him, and like many middle-aged men who have outgrown their first love he is ready to cast her off. Though Medea is fierce, she holds the spectator's sympathy almost to the last moment: her plight is one with which anyone can identify, and only her final deeds – the frenzied murders – make her abhorrent and alien.

In this drama, too, Euripides offers another strong tract for the rights of foreigners and women, both of whom had inferior status in Hellas. (Even Pericles fell foul of the narrow, harsh ruling that marriage to an outsider, a "barbarian", was illegal.) The play was so daring and controversial that it took last place in the annual contest, though it has long since triumphed in the world's theatre.

In it, too, Euripides was choosing fresher subject-matter, turning to a legend less well known and less often worked over. The plot had not been utilized by either Aeschylus or Sophocles. (A charge was made that Euripides plagiarized an earlier play by Neophron, about whom little is now known, except that he was an experimenter, but scholars who analyse the language, style and meter of fragments of the supposed predecessor insist that it belongs to the fourth century BC, hence after Euripides' time. But it is possible that he was influenced by certain structural innovations in other scripts by Neophron, though not in the *Medea*.) In any event, Euripides changed many elements of the legend that supplied his material.

In *Medea* his poetry is both passionate and sensuous, and nowhere more eloquent than in Medea's oft-quoted plaint about the sorry lot of women, destined to be subordinate always to their designated masters. A woman is the unhappiest creature born. To marry, she must have a large dowry. She must learn the strange customs of a new home or court where she goes to live, and she must divine her husband's every whim and even unexpressed wish. Her husband also becomes a "tyrant over our body – an evil yet more bitter". Yet even if the husband is wicked or cruel, a divorce will make a woman infamous. If a man is not happy with her, he can simply go abroad, find his physical pleasure elsewhere, "while we to him alone must look for comfort".

> But we, say they, have a safe sheltered life
> at home, while they are risking theirs at war.

Is it a man who bears the greatest pain and danger?

> Sooner would I three times
> Stand in the shielded ranks, than bear one child.

Euripides, a feminist, states the case with characteristic insight and compassion.

The fault found with *Medea* is its contrived ending, her escape by magical means. Medea has superhuman powers; could she not prevail over the errant Jason earlier, and without exacting the dreadful toll of her own children? Aristotle is among those who object that too much suffering is needlessly caused here.

One justification for the startling ending is that Euripides is simply following the legend. Another is that no other resolution is feasible: having committed these frightful acts, where can she go? The Corinthian king has banished her to Athens, but would a woman who had murdered Creon, Glauce and her own children be welcomed there? Nor could she return to Iolcus, where the death of the usurper King Pelias was on her bloodstained hands. Not to her native Colchis, where she had been responsible for the killing of her own father and brother. Only a supernatural conclusion is acceptable, and Euripides, a keen dramatist, grasped that. It also lifts the moral of the play to a cosmic plane: the gods, who rule the world, have made Medea what she is, and at last they intervene to rescue her.

Euripides does handle his chorus, the women of Corinth, somewhat awkwardly; they participate in the action to a degree, but stand by idly while Medea slaughters her babes, an inconsistency which it is hard to reconcile. Perhaps this shift of attitude occurs too suddenly. At the dire moment the chorus sings of the advantages of childlessness, as if to lend warrant to the distraught mother's insane deed.

Also asked is whether *Medea* is tragedy or only superlative melodrama. By Aristotelian criteria Medea is not a tragic heroine, for she fits few of the demands outlined in the *Poetics*. But the same could be said of almost all extant Greek dramas; they do not actually conform to Aristotle's ideal prescription. On stage *Medea* yields a stirring experience, one from which the spectator does not quickly recover. One explanation for this: "She is tragic in that her passions are stronger than her reason. A woman of her nature is bound to cause suffering to all around her, and surely to herself." The play is not simply melodrama, because the irrationally motivated Medea is truthfully drawn, and the purpose of the play is not the mere arousal of theatrical excitement, but something far more. It illustrates that an excess of passion, of rage, is destructive to all, another oft-repeated Euripidean theme.

With this new Euripidean psychological realism, the larger simplicities of Aeschylus and Sophocles are gone. "Euripides shows men as they are," Sophocles said, not wholly approvingly. Medea is an extraordinarily strong role, yet she lacks the blunt, gripping obsessiveness of a Clytemnestra or Electra, a single-mindedness which endows them with even greater impact on stage. The multiplicity of motives of Euripides' characters causes them to be somewhat opaque, ambiguous, hence – people can never be fully understood – more lifelike, but at moments less dramatic. This is especially true when their unconscious impulses are hinted at or finally exposed, and their psychology is strikingly modern. But, again, much of this is at the expense of theatrical force. In her frenzy and irrationality, Medea is a far from clear figure; her character is beclouded by her complexity, with the result that she is not always as dynamic as she might be, unlike the single-minded, vengeful Clytemnestra and Electra. Euripides tends to over-subtilize her and dilutes his portraits and dramas further by a regrettable habit of digressing, philosophizing, often at inappropriate moments. He views his people with both sentimentality and detachment, a mixed approach, one that seems paradoxical, though on stage it is usually natural-seeming enough since his characters retain a pulsing life. The lesson he unwittingly teaches other playwrights, however, is that subtlety and complexity are anti-theatrical and, as a generality, audiences have little patience with inner cerebral debates.

In stressing Medea's foreignness, the liberal-spirited Euripides was taking up yet another deeply felt cause. Greeks, and especially Athenians, looked upon aliens with disdain – as has been noted, their contemptuous term for them was "barbarians", from *"barbaros"*, an allusion to the crude manner in which many of them spoke – or "barked" – Greek. Many exclusionary laws were passed, among them one in Athens stipulating that descent from both an Athenian father and mother was required of anyone who hoped to hold citizenship (450 BC). Euripides was protesting against the harshness of this edict. Very different, Medea asserts, was her treatment of "foreigners" – Jason and his Argonauts – when they had been in her native land.

Much praised is the portrait of Jason, who is described by one critic, Gilbert Norwood, as "a compound of brilliant manner, stupidity and cynicism". Once a heedless adventurer, he has outlived his daring and foraging and now yearns for comfort and security. His attempt to regain the throne of Iolcus, rightfully his, has failed. The citizens of that city, appalled by the cruel death of his uncle King Pelias by the machinations of Medea, have forced the guilty pair to flee, which has brought them to Corinth. Now Jason sees how he might become heir to Creon's domain by marriage to the princess Glauce (who is never seen in the play). He is, as Ferguson says, "the complete egotist", totally self-centred. Though he has lived with Medea for years, he is so conspicuously lacking in empathy that he scarcely knows her; and to get rid of her he is even willing to relinquish his children to her. The role is so unsympathetic that it demands much of the actor's resources to convince an audience that he is an adequate foil to an emotionally unrestrained Medea; but his seeming legal status as a husband and actual father empowers him and helps to shape him as a strong enough antagonist, since by local custom the final word is always his.

Realism tinges the sketches of the nurse and tutor, both of whom have homely personal quirks that make them quite human. King Creon is weak, though by self-deception he often believes himself to be strong. Thoroughly conventional in his thinking, he lets his kindly impulses overrule his practical intelligence, so that he does not act effectively when the need is for him to do so. He fears Medea because of her reputation as the wielder of dangerous witchcraft. The troubled, prattling Aegeus, who has a pivotal scene with Medea when she beseeches his support, is no less well drawn. To be noted is that all these parts, including the roles of Medea and Jason, were probably taken by only two actors who rapidly changed costumes and masks.

Just before the ending, Medea wavers between mother-love and infusing fury, her crippling infatuation with Jason and deep outrage at his ingratitude. Here there is a series of magnificent arias, screams from her stricken victims, a final scene between her and the collapsing Jason, and her soaring, spectacular departure in the golden sun-chariot, signalling a divine intervention.

If Euripides was the first to choose this powerful subject, he is hardly the last; his example has led a lengthy series of dramatists, composers and choreographers to embrace it. The new versions have been wrought in many different languages and dispersed venues, proof of its broad and enduring capacity to stir drama-goers. In first-century Rome, Seneca offered his version. The great French poet-playwright Pierre Corneille (1604–84), at the advent of the Baroque Age, chose it for his first tragedy, *Médée* (1635). An Austrian, Franz Grillparzer (1791–1872), in his *Medea* (1821), which is the third part of an ambitious trilogy on the Golden Fleece, concentrates on "the perils of love and sexuality". The three plays explore the earlier relationship between Medea and Jason. Replete with full-throated emotions – hurt love, burning hate, jealousy, rejection and humiliation – the Medea theme has been an obvious choice for operas. Marc-Antoine Charpentier (*c.* 1650–1704) based his *Médée* (1693) on a play by Thomas Corneille (1625–1709), younger brother of Pierre and author of many works now mostly forgotten, though often quite successful in his day. The opera, revived in Paris in 1984, was rapturously hailed as a long-neglected masterpiece. Luigi Cherubini (1760–1842), self-described as "Italian-born and French by adoption", wrote his best work, a *Médée* (1797), which had its première in Paris. Its libretto is by François-Benoit Hoffman. A work of great force, it had fewer productions than it merited because of the exacting nature of the lead singing role. After Paris, it was staged in Berlin (1800), Frankfurt-am-Main (1855) and London at Drury Lane (1865). Cherubini himself was so demanding and short-tempered that during his lifetime many impresarios were hesitant to deal with him. In Italian, in a translation by Carlo Zangarini, his work finally reached La Scala, Milan (1909). A triumphant revival at the Florentine Maggio Musicale (1953), with Maria Callas assuming the title role, brought Cherubini's opera firmly into the modern repertoire worldwide with stagings in Dallas, San Francisco and New York City; in the last of these cities it was initially done in concert form, and the Medea was Eileen Farrell, hardly as gifted an actress as the intense, dynamic Callas but possessor of a soprano voice "of enormous range and volume". She appeared in the role many times elsewhere.

Cherubini's *Medea* was the inspiration, frankly acknowledged, of *Medea in Corinto* (Naples, 1813) by Johannes Simon (or Giovanni Simone) Mayr (1763–1845), a Bavarian who studied and worked in Italy, mostly in Bergamo, and was later a teacher of Donizetti. By commission, he wrote this piece in "the French manner", which meant that *secco* recitative was replaced by declamatory recitative with continuous orchestral accompaniment, perhaps the first Italian opera in this form, that is, one having no unmusical speech passages, alternating with arias and sung lines. Of admirable quality, this opera has been recorded. His younger contemporary, Gioacchino Rossini wrote, "If the composers of our day were to study the operas of Mayr, who is always dramatic . . . and ever melodic, they would find all that they are looking for." In his time, Mayr seemed destined for immortality, but somehow that did not happen.

Another German composer, Georg Benda (1722–95), *Kapellmeister* at Gotha for nearly three decades, composed a *Medea* (1775) that is still frequently heard in his native country; he is credited with having invented the "melodrama", in which there is no singing but only speech combined with instrumental support, an innovation that interested Mozart, who adopted some elements of it, as too did Carl Maria von Weber.

Twentieth-century handlings of the legend have been a German Expressionist play *Medea*, written by Hanns Henry Jahn to protest the great slaughter in the First World War, a presentation described by John Gassner as "sanguinary"; and, in France, a one-act opera, *Médée* (1940), by Darius Milhaud (1892–1976), with a libretto by Madeleine Milhaud, a piece commissioned by the French government, its first effort to encourage native composers – unfortunately, a month later Paris was occupied by Nazi troops; however, two more performances were allowed by the authorities, and by then Milhaud was away and safely in America, where he was to stay for many years. A major dance piece by Martha Graham, *Cave of the Heart*, centres on Medea. (Of these derivative works, more will be written later.)

In his *Medea* Euripides has the chorus acknowledge the dread power of sexual lust:

When Love with inordinate might
Invades the heart, he bringeth not

Virtue nor goodly renown:
Yet if with a temperate ardour
Cypris comes, no God hath a charm that excels hers.
Aim not, O great Queen, an invincible shaft in deadly passion
Steeped, nor draw thy golden bow against me.

The next extant play, *Hippolytus* (428 BC), is even more directly concerned with the overwhelming force of sexual desire, and is indeed the most Freudian of Greek dramas. Simultaneously realistic and symbolic, it introduces yet another theme into world theatre that is to be repeated for ever. It springs from the legend of Phaedra, a Cretan princess. Daughter of Minos and sister of the Minotaur, and a prize of war, she is married to Theseus, King of Athens and Trozen. He is old enough to be her father, but still vigorous and virile. From an earlier liaison with Hippolyta (in some versions, Antiope), he has a handsome, illegitimate son, Hippolytus, who much resembles his father, except for being, unhappily, conceited and priggish. Returning from a hunt, the youth pays homage to Artemis, goddess of chastity; he deliberately slights Aphrodite, cruel goddess of love. He declares: "No god who hath night homage pleases me." To chastise him drastically, Aphrodite casts a spell on his stepmother, who conceives an irresistible infatuation for him, easy to do because the youth is nearer in age to her than is her absent husband. Physically he is an idealized form of his father.

Sickening with desire for the young man, she confides her passion to her elderly servant-companion. She languishes, feverish almost to the verge of death, starving herself. Her ascetic stepson is heedless of her strange malady until her nurse (who is a surprising prototype of the bawdy nurse in Shakespeare's *Romeo and Juliet*) interferes "to save her lady's life", and urges her to yield to the grasp of her desire. The nurse first proposes to offset the malady with a magic philtre, for which a fragment of Hippolytus' garment is needed. Phaedra desperately consents, though she rejects the nurse's suggestion that she should have an affair with the young man, since only that will quiet her longing. "You speak evil well – go not beyond this much."

The older woman argues that even the gods indulge in adultery, and cites several legendary instances. "Yet they stay on in heaven . . ."

Why should Phaedra seek to be morally superior to the gods themselves? The young woman's resolve is shaken.

The nurse reveals Phaedra's obsession to Hippolytus. He is outraged, feeling defiled by the idea. In a famed speech he delivers a diatribe not only against his "depraved" stepmother but all womankind:

O God, why have you sent this counterfeit,
this vileness, Woman, to inhabit the world?
. . . Bringing this pest into our homes,
we first lay out our fortune, like a corpse;
This proves how great an evil a wife is:
her father, who begot and brought her up,
banishes her and pays a dowry too,
to get rid of the monster. And the man
who takes the noxious growth into his house
is glad to cover up with handsome jewels
so miserable an idol, and improve
its shape with draperies as best he can –

A whole catalogue of woman's failings:

I loathe a clever woman. In my house
let there not be one more intelligent
than women should be. Aphrodite breeds
a lot more mischief in the clever ones,
who stop at nothing, but the helpless kind
have too few brains to make fools of themselves.
[Translation: Donald Sutherland]

Shamed by her servant's brazen indiscretion, Phaedra determines to kill herself, though Hippolytus has promised to tell no one of the indecent proposal. But glowering, scorned, she is equally determined to punish her stepson for the contempt he has expressed for her. She hangs herself, leaving behind a note in which she accuses him of having tried to rape her.

Theseus returns, finds his wife a suicide, is grief-stricken. He is also bewildered about the reason for her act. But when Phaedra's accusatory note is discovered, his anger against his son erupts: he invokes a curse, a deed of vengeance, one of three promised him earlier by Poseidon, to bring about Hippolytus' death.

The startled young man, learning of Phaedra's suicide, comes to offer condolences but quickly has to defend himself. Intemperate, Theseus will not listen to him. Yet another "unjust judge", he pronounces his verdict before having possession of all the facts. The frigid youth, asserting his innocence, extols his own moral excellence, his prolonged chastity. His father, unpersuaded, protests: "You kill me with your sanctimony." Hippolytus replies:

> You see that sun? this earth? They have not beheld
> any man born more virtuous than I.

He lists all the proofs of his past good conduct. He claims that he has, in his own words, "a virgin soul".

Banished from Trozen, Hippolytus is soon the victim of his father's curse: he is in his chariot, racing along the seashore, when an apparition rises from the waves and frightens the horses. In a resultant mishap, as described by a messenger, the chariot overturns and the youth is badly mangled.

His broken, bleeding body is brought back to his father, who is appalled. After the boy's departure the voice of Artemis, the goddess worshipped by Hippolytus, has spoken to Theseus, affirming the youth's guiltlessness. Heartbroken, self-reproachful, the king receives the bloody form of his son. The youth dies in his father's arms. Artemis promises Hippolytus a semi-divine role in the hereafter, to be a patron deity of virgin girls.

The final lines of the play are replete with criticisms of the gods, and especially of the cruel Cyprian love-deity:

> . . . for Aphrodite willed these things to be
> to glut her anger.

To Hippolytus, Artemis says:

> Poor friend! . . .
> Nobility of mind has ruined you.

And again:

> Unscrupulous Aphrodite worked this out.

When Theseus laments:

> The gods drove my mind astray,

Hippolytus moans:

> Alas!
> If mankind's curses could but reach the gods!

Artemis vows to take revenge by harming a mortal dear to Aphrodite, and so it is made to seem that men are hapless victims of the callous Olympians and their petty jealousies and quarrels. It does not matter to Aphrodite that, whatever Hippolytus' offence, poor Phaedra is largely faultless. Similarly, Poseidon aids in the destruction of Hippolytus for a crime that he did not commit. Should human beings worship such gods?

Clearly, Hippolytus has been guilty of excess, his virtue approaching the fanatical. He has been arrogant on that note: that is his *hubris*; his is an overweening pride. But he also says: "Men may well do wrong when the gods determine what they do."

The tragedy is concentrated on Hippolytus, for Phaedra vanishes midway from the action, leaving the ill-fated youth and his father to hold the stage thereafter. In the many later versions of the story, by a host of other writers, it is Phaedra who is given the leading part.

The scene between Hippolytus and the nurse, in which she suggests the amorous encounter, occurs off-stage. In an earlier version by Euripides called *Hippolytus Veiled*, Phaedra herself had avowed her love to her stepson, as well as personally resorted to philtres to win his affection, but this was far too indecorous and aggressive for audiences to tolerate and caused disturbances at performances. Euripides revised the work (an almost unprecedented move), and it was only after he did so and let time elapse that he offered the play again under a slightly altered title and won first prize. Even so, he was deemed to have portrayed the shameless, foreign woman much too kindly. He added other changes in the new draft: originally the setting was Athens not Trozen; Phaedra was far more wanton, even nymphomaniacal; Hippolytus was accorded a formal trial, at which he was confronted with false evidence trumped up by Phaedra; pursuant to his banishment, the truth was belatedly revealed, an exposure that led to Phaedra's suicide. After the failure of Euripides' first version, Sophocles embraced the subject and had success with it; whereupon Euripides returned to the story, which had obviously captured him, and matched his rival. Sophocles' script has not survived.

Euripides' picture of Phaedra is quite compassionate. She feels that, like her mother and sister Ariadne, her destiny is to be destroyed by love, and one reason for killing herself is that she does not want to share their ill-fame. Her pride, too, is excessive, yet it is clear that though she rejects the suggestions of the nurse she almost passively agrees to them, for she actually wishes to accede to them. In the same way, her fasting has been a way of getting Hippolytus' notice. She is without appetite, but also punishing herself, and partly doing it to win his sympathy, and all this complex motivation for behaviour attests to Euripides' sharp and very modern psychological insight.

Theseus is punished not only for being unjust towards his son, but for all his past iniquities, especially his mistreatment of Hippolyta, the boy's mother. His character, and his ambivalent feelings towards his son, contribute to the tragedy. He has never really approved of the prim, morally superior, overly intellectual youth. Theseus' sins are visited upon his son, as those of Phaedra's mother (who fell in love with a bull and begot with him the monstrous Minotaur) seem to descend on the unlucky daughters, Ariadne and Phaedra, both of whom – like their mother – let the power of a mad infatuation overcome them.

Hippolytus has been particularly welcomed by those whose interpretation of literature is Freudian or Jungian, for the young protagonist is an interesting study of sexual frigidity. Euripides suggests that the boy's anti-feminism is somehow linked to his illegitimacy, as though he blames his mother for it, though in truth she had suffered harshly at the hands of his savage father. Hippolytus makes frequent references to his not being legitimate, and in his tirade against women laments that the world could not be peopled by some means other than a physical act between the sexes. His animus towards Phaedra is strengthened by her having legitimate children whose claim to succeed to Theseus' throne is more likely to be acknowledged than his, a bastard son. A sexual act brought him into the world with this stigma, and he unconsciously resents it. Sex disgusts him, and Phaedra, who has superseded his mother, is by that fact – and her role as his father's new bedmate – a source of repulsion to him. His mother, as an Amazon, had a similar distaste for sex and was a devotee or perhaps even a priestess of Artemis' cult, so that his inclination towards frigidity is inherent. The Amazons, to appear less feminine, had one breast amputated. Artemis is also a mother-image to him, and his allegiance to her and resultant emotional coldness is somewhat Oedipal. He identifies the chaste goddess with his mother, his memory of whom he both shrinks from and is drawn to, and this confusion makes him unable to touch any other woman by an erotic impulse. Theseus also implies that his son is a member of the Orphic cult – which held that the body was vile and the flesh should be subjugated – and describes him as maladjusted, neurotic, self-centred and narcissistic, having few friends because he is unable to participate in normal human relationships. Hippolytus has no pity for Phaedra; he is almost sadistic in rejecting her.

The play is obviously an allegory, a religious satire, a philosophical tract: the characters are both very real and yet representative of certain abstract ideas. (The name "Hippolytus" means "slain by horses".) The major struggle is between Aphrodite and Artemis, who stands not only for chastity but altogether for the self-disciplined, inviolate self that allows little or no contact with others. Yet, to Euripides' considerable credit, he has not written a mere morality play. The characters are plausible and exceedingly palpable. As H.E. Barnes has said, "The story is so humanly probable that divine intervention is gratuitous." The tragedy has a universal sweep that lifts it high, making it a compelling theatre-piece for centuries. This is partly a result of the verse, which is often magical, overflowing with the passion that it simultaneously celebrates and decries.

The chief blame is placed on the Cyprian goddess. Euripides is saying that sexual desire, like the other irrational forces in man, cannot be wholly controlled and far too often unseat his reason. Therefore man must come to terms with his true nature. "Mortals who flee Aphrodite too much suffer a malady no less than who too much pursue her."

Though she is the goddess of chastity, Artemis is also depicted rather unflatteringly. Among her other shortcomings, she is too finicky to witness her disciple's very last moments: the death of a virtuous youth distresses her too much. After a lyrical aria, she irresponsibly takes wing, leaving him to expire without her final comfort.

If Aphrodite and Artemis are portrayed so satirically, how is the spectator expected to believe that they are still able to work such havoc on luckless human beings? Euripides apparently implies that the harm is real, but that the conception of the gods current in his day was febrile, primitive. Certain irresistible drives caused whirlwinds in the world, and in the breasts and hearts of people, that were cosmic or elemental in nature, and these could be personified in such deities as these might be but unhappily were not; such forces should be represented by more sophisticated and abstract symbols.

Critics find the construction of the play marred by a clumsily expository prologue, in which Aphrodite offers a summary in advance of all that is to happen, a device that diminishes the suspense. Besides this, and dictated by the offended response of the Athenian audience, the crucial meeting between the nurse and Hippolytus occurs off-stage, which deprives the work of what might have been its most dramatic scene. The plot also loses some appeal by the early disappearance of Phaedra, the most poignant and interesting character. But again, Euripides was forced to keep her off because of the hostility the encounter provoked, so this loss was unavoidable. Taking all this into account, the prologue does give the work a unity it might otherwise lack: the play does not fall into two halves as it proceeds, since an overall plan of it is given from the very beginning. The prologue, with its synopsis of the action, serves as a framework in which one can immediately see the people in the right perspective, as victims not only of their own flaws but of a fate imposed on them by inexplicable, cold-hearted deities.

Euripides made no significant changes from the myth on which he based his work: the story itself is often compared to that in the Old Testament of Joseph and Potiphar's wife, and a similar Egyptian tale, *The Two Brothers.* Some scholars, and particularly anthropologists, including Sir James Frazer, Jane Harrison and Gilbert Murray, see it rooted in the concept of the resurrected year-god. As has already been mentioned, some versions of the myth tell how, by the intervention of Artemis and Asclepius, Hippolytus is brought back to life to fulfil his role as a minor deity. But a happy ending of that sort, if incorporated visually in the play, would have blunted a tragic effect, and Euripides wisely eschewed it.

Historically, the mythical Hippolytus enjoyed a semi-divine status, especially in Trozen, with shrines in sacred wooded groves (he was a consecrated huntsman) from which, most appropriately, horses were excluded. Virgins, on the last night before their marriage, brought locks of their hair as offerings, as foretold by Artemis in Euripides' dramas. Elaborate scientific and pseudo-scientific explanations of the myth have occupied recent scholars for many decades and are a fascinating study in themselves: they suggest that Hippolytus was in reality a sun-god; or that he might have been a priest of the cult of Artemis and that such priests originally gelded themselves in her service but later merely took a vow of steadfast chastity as a symbolic "emasculation". The myth was doubtless humanized long before Euripides heard it, and his adaptation in turn did much to further the inevitable process of translating the legends of the gods into stories that dealt with men and women but still kept an inherent universality.

Scanning the verse with his usual attention to the most minute detail, Ferguson discerns that Euripides elaborates on three principal motifs in his imagery: the sea (from which a dripping Aphrodite first arose) – in Ferguson's words, "The foam of the sea is the foam that surrounds the semen, the *aphro* of Aphrodite" – with frequent evocations of watery phenomena throughout, linked to the ocean, rivers, violent storms over the waves, verbally enforcing the characters' emotional turbulence. Ferguson puts it: "The sea represents the illimitable subconscious powers of human nature." And horses: not only is Hippolytus, the huntsman, devoted to them, but he perishes when, suddenly alarmed, they rear up and overturn his speeding chariot, mangling him. This can be read to symbolize the sexual force, which this "virgin athlete" has reined in and sought to control, only to have it turn on him, to his destruction, at a moment of psychological crisis. Finally, there are frequent references to birds, exquisitely phrased, as Phaedra yearns to escape from her dilemma, to rise above it, free of it: to be able to take flight from herself, from the nearness of Hippolytus, from her claustrophobia in the House of Theseus.

Ferguson adds other shrewd insights into Hippolytus' long-hidden conflict: "Deep down he is not chaste but frightened of sex." He also remarks on the paradox that Euripides has embedded in the drama: the uninhibited nurse is the wiser person, urging Hippolytus to view Phaedra charitably, because human beings are not perfect. "The immoral Nurse is right; the moral Hippolytus is wrong." Discussing Aphrodite's opening speech, with its heavy burden of exposition, deplored by most critics, Ferguson says: "Euripides likes a prologue that sets the scene; if we are to know all, a divinity must tell us, and Aphrodite does; Euripides abjures the more obvious forms of surprise." Of the demanding goddess of love, most castigated here but praised in a hymn by the chorus, Ferguson writes: "In a sense it is Aphrodite's play, and we see her in this song not as destructive but as the eternal ruler of youth."

Astringent as always, F.L. Lucas comments very briefly in a note preceding his translation of the play:

> Here, as in *Medea*, but far more finely, Euripides has studied a divided soul. And Phaedra's conflict is still real to us – the struggle of duty and honour against devouring desire. Indeed, with this play, the Goddess of Love, who opens it, begins also that long reign of hers in the theatre, which has grown at times too tyrannous.
>
> . . . Euripides might well have called his play after his heroine. He has drawn better characters; but never a character better. The Nurse, too, lives with coarse but devoted vitality that yet does not clash too crudely, as Euripides' realist characters sometimes do, with the play's romance. Unfortunately, Phaedra does not find any adequate counterpart in the noble prig Hippolytus; still less in the irritable old Theseus. Therefore the play languishes after her death, till it revives for a moment as Artemis bids farewell to the dying Hippolytus.
>
> Apart from this, it is one of Euripides' best plots. The issue is still living; and Phaedra's revenge from beyond the grave, though horrible, is not unconvincing. And whereas the prologues of Euripides are often as dry as half-animated theatre programmes, and his epiloguing deities often too like pantomime magicians, here the Aphrodite of the opening and the Artemis of the close, balanced as

harmoniously as sculptured figures at the ends of a temple-pediment, stand for eternal realities – the two sides of Nature; the lush Nature that cares for fecundity, not for chastity; and the colder Nature of the lonely hills and "winds austere and pure". If both are amoral, that too is true. No Greek play expresses better the Greek sense of the importance of measure, balance and restraint. With too little passion, life becomes a kind of death; with too much, it can become Hell.

Further, if Euripides was never a saner thinker, he was never a finer poet than here in some of the lyrics – the romantic longings of his tortured Phaedra, or the flight of his chorus from the nightmare before them in dreams of the legendary past, of the legendary ends of the earth.

. . . It is typical too that *Hippolytus*, as we have it, is a second attempt. Ages ago "Longinus" (first century AD) noted that Euripides was a laborious, not an effortless, genius; like a lion needing to lash itself with its tail. I doubt if Euripides was much like a lion: but it remains true that, where Aeschylus gives a sense of intuitive inspiration and Sophocles of happy balance between creation and self-criticism, Euripides, like our own age, seems to suffer often from a critical excess that cramps spontaneity and leads alternately to repression and to exaggeration. But, if he needed a hammer, he hammered well. Had only *Hippolytus* and *The Bacchae* survived, we should not know his versatility; his influence would have been far less; but he would hardly have seemed a smaller poet – very possibly a greater.

This delicate yet sensational plot has yielded many subsequent treatments over the more than 2,000 years since Euripides explored it. The great Roman poet Virgil appropriated it. Besides Sophocles', some of the best-known handlings of the premise are found in Seneca's *Phaedra*; in three French tragedies, *Hippolytus* (1573) by Robert Garnier, *Phèdre* (1677) by Jean Racine, and a competing and different interpretation by Nicolas Pradon (also 1677); in *Don Carlos* (1784) by Johann Christoph von Schiller (1759–1805), which is about a Spanish prince in love with his young stepmother who earlier had been affianced to him; in *The Passion Flower* (1913), by the Nobel-prize-winning Jacinte Benavente (1866–1954), who inverts the situation – a young stepfather is enamoured of his stepdaughter; in the Italian *Fedra* (1909) by Gabriele d'Annunzio (1863–1938), whose sexually avid heroine is slain when a ray of moonlight is aimed at her by the goddess Diana, yet another protector of the ever-chaste Hippolytus. Three leading American playwrights have also exploited the theatrically rich subject: Eugene O'Neill (1888–1953) transfers the conflict to a nineteenth-century New England farm in his *Desire Under the Elms* (1924) and views it very seriously; the same year it was handled quite lightly, as folk-comedy, by Sidney Howard (1891–1939), in *They Knew What They Wanted* (1925); Howard won a Pulitzer Prize with it, snatching it away from O'Neill – he has a vagrant, treated like a "son" by an Italian vineyard-owner in California, steal the affections of the old man's newly arrived mail-order bride. Robinson Jeffers, in his long poem *Cawdor* and verse-play *The Cretan Woman* (1954), investigated the subject twice.

Johannes Simon Mayr's opera, *Fedra* (Milan, 1820), with libretto by Luigi Romanelli, closely approximates Racine's play, though it ends with the heroine taking poison and then most decorously expiring off-stage. More recently, the Italian composer Ildebrando Pizzetti (1880–1968) fashioned another opera, *Fedra* (Milan, 1915). A modern-dance work, *Phaedra* (1962), is among the many realizations of classical myths by the choreographer Martha Graham. The exuberant Sidney Howard script, *They Knew What They Wanted*, was subsequently adapted as a Broadway musical comedy, *The Most Happy Fella* (1956), with score and book by Frank Loesser (1910–69); highly lucrative – even more so than the play – it has been accorded numerous revivals, among them inclusion in the semi-classical repertory of the New York City Opera Company. (In various places hereafter, most of these will be covered more fully.) Films and novels have also come to grips with the theme.

In the decade after *Hippolytus*, Euripides wrote several dramas prompted by the ongoing hostilities between Athens and its arch-foe Sparta. Their chronological order is still conjectural, though many attempts to date them have been made by scholars. One method is to trace the playwright's changing personal mood and the public's contrasting attitude towards the exhausting war. His reaction fluctuated from patriotic fervour – once more he took up a spear to fight for the city he loved, and to which he frequently paid lustrous tribute in his odes – to growing disgust at the endless, costly strife. At first he felt it exigent that Athens win, for it was democratic. Sparta was despotically governed. His native city was cultured and prized art; in Sparta the spirit was militaristic and anti-intellectual. But he was stricken by the inhumanity of the struggle. As his pacificism mounted and was openly displayed, he was ever more the target of the imperialists and the war-minded who deemed his opinions traitorous.

The Homeric epics provided allegorical material for these intrinsically topical plays. Of the four in which his support of Athens's martial effort shines most clearly, the first may have been *Andromache*, perhaps written a year after *Hippolytus*, or some time between 430 BC and 424 BC. In this work an ugly portrait of Menelaus, the relentless Spartan king, was doubtless inspired by contemporary events. Summed up by one critic as a "hard and brilliant tragedy", it emphasizes the ruthlessness, treachery, arrogance and stupidity of the Spartans. Lacking unity – it has been aptly described as three plays in one – it is indisputably powerful.

Daughter of Priam, King of Troy, the hapless Andromache, sorrowful widow of the renowned hero Hector, is taken captive and reduced to slavery at the court of Thessaly, in Phthia. She becomes the possession and unwilling bedmate of Neoptolemus, son of Achilles – no longer living – and grandson of the aged Peleus. She has borne Neoptolemus a son. Hermione, daughter of Menelaus, is Neoptolemus' wife; she is childless and resents Andromache's having given him a long-desired heir. When Neoptolemus undertakes a pilgrimage to Apollo's temple at Delphi to make amends to the god, Andromache is at Hermione's mercy. Menelaus comes to visit his daughter and brutally takes up her cause. He seizes the child and threatens to have it killed unless Andromache quits the sanctuary, a shrine to Thetis, to which she has fled from Hermione's accusation that she has practised evil magic. She fears for her life and sends messages, pleas for rescue, to the child's great-grandfather, old Peleus. At first these bring no response, but at a crucial moment Peleus arrives and, with the authority given him by his age, drives away the bullying Menelaus. Hermione is in panic. Word is brought of the slaying of Neoptolemus at Delphi, a crime ordered by Orestes, son of Agamemnon, and thus the nephew of Menelaus. Before the outbreak of the Trojan War, the Spartan ruler had promised Hermione to her cousin Orestes, but while Menelaus was off on the Trojan campaign she had instead been married to Neoptolemus; now, having disposed of his rival by trickery and murder, Orestes has come to reclaim the bride pledged to him. He takes her away. Peleus weeps at the loss of his grandson, whose body is carried on stage. (Before now, Neoptolemus has made no appearance in the play.) The treacherously slain warrior is to be buried at Delphi, as a lasting reproach to Orestes and his evil agents. An epiphany occurs: the sea-goddess Thetis, wife of Peleus and mother of Achilles, is lowered by crane. She advises Peleus to grieve less, since death and sorrow are the inevitable lot of all mankind. Andromache is to go to Molassia to wed Hector's brother: her child will be the founder of a royal line there, and Peleus and the Trojan dynasty will be granted immortality as a consequence.

Sophocles is believed to have written a play called *Hermione* that delved into the same legend; if so, it is lost. Andromache is said not to have been a character in it: here she has been added by Euripides, who makes her the focal figure in his drama. So far as is known, *Andromache* was not put on in Athens but, instead, in another Greek city, though where is not determined.

Generally, the work is viewed as propaganda, a "political tract", designed to show how Sparta's philosophy of "might makes right" brings in its train only rapine, suffering, ruin to its hapless victims. Once more the principal figure is a foreign woman, much put upon, bravely resistant, superior to most of those about her. The characterizations are simplified: Andromache, reduced to being a concubine, is noble, innately wise, ever-sorrowing at the death of her husband, the Trojan prince Hector, and ready to die to spare her child or else to die with him. Her rival, the pampered, jealous Hermione, is base; and not only Menelaus but all the Spartans are wholly evil. What is quite unconvincing is that Menelaus, who has led the assembled Greek armies to the conquest of Troy, is here a boastful coward and poltroon, easily chased off by the verbal assaults of old Peleus, himself a near-senile, nattering fraud. Orestes, elsewhere a hero, is unexpectedly a deep villain, a sinister plotter, heedless of all moral restraints. The poetry is at times mediocre, not Euripides at his best, and at places the chorus is weakly used.

Even so, the play ranks amongst Euripides' more respected works because of its theatrical effectiveness, especially his skill at evoking pathos from scenes delineating Andromache's harassing plight. She is imbued with tenderness at high moments, and with force and clarity of mind as she parries Hermione's threats in sharply dramatic verbal exchanges. As a stage piece, *Andromache* has a lasting vigour.

The text is filled with knocks at Apollo and his Delphic oracle. When Neoptolemus' mutilated body is carried in on a litter, the messenger states pointedly:

> This is the way the god who gives his sacred word
> To others, who is judge of all of what is right,
> Has paid Achilles' son who offered to atone.
> He has remembered, like a man who bears a grudge,
> An ancient quarrel. How can Apollo then be wise?
> [Translation: L.R. Lind]

Ferguson praises the felicitous concision of the fifty-line prologue, as Euripides has composed it. "This type of monologue establishing the plot is admittedly artificial, but, given the convention, it could hardly be better done, and the ancient argument comments on its clarity and construction." To Ferguson, the appearance of Peleus "in the nick of time" is a bit too melodramatic. Euripides' observation – given to Peleus – on the glory unfairly bestowed on generals is worthy of notice:

> The command sit proudly in office, and think big,
> put airs over the commons; they are nothing.
> The commons are a thousand times their betters in mind;
> they lack the will to power and the crookedness to get there.
> [Translation: John Fergus]

A populist sentiment, for certain, but Ferguson considers this political side of the tragedy to be only a secondary aspect of it.

> *Andromache* is not in the first flight of Euripides' plays. . . . But it is good theatre. In structure it is a diptych, and this has hampered its interpretation. Euripides is feeling toward the form he is to use with such brilliant success in *Heracles*. The play is not an anti-Spartan tract. There are anti-Spartan passages, but they are incidental, not central, like the attacks on Apollo and Delphi; it is a mistake to treat Orestes as a Spartan. What Euripides does is to spotlight Spartan wickedness in the first part, and gradually to spread the light till it falls on all the Greeks.

The play, as Ferguson perceives it, is about wisdom, self-knowledge. Only two people in the tragedy possess it, Peleus and Andromache. Though Peleus took part in an earlier sacking of Troy, he has since gained wisdom with age that brings him to renounce the folly of violence. In summary, Ferguson says: "But Peleus has only learned wisdom, Andromache possesses it, and that is why this is her play. Euripides is tearing down our conventional judgments, and he uses this gracious, courageous woman to do so." In Andromache is "a warmth of love" that endows her with wisdom. "Peleus has to work this out through suffering. Only Andromache's importunacy leads Peleus to change what needs to be changed: only Thetis brings him to accept what cannot be changed. Andromache has this wisdom from the first, though she too has to exercise it through suffering. She is the norm to which Peleus aspires. That is why she, a foreigner, is brought back in Thetis' speech to found a line of Greek kings. For not merely Spartan treachery and brutality, but the violence of the whole of Greece denies this wisdom."

Euripides' tragedy was to inspire Racine's much cherished drama, *Andromaque* (1667), which F.L. Lucas deems a greatly improved handling of the subject, with more stress on psychology than mythology and a better picture of "the primitive fierceness of human passions, even beneath the silks and satins of Versailles". The theme has also begotten an opera, *Andromaca* (Naples, 1742) by Leonardo Leo (1694–1744), who was later *maestro di cappella* at the Neapolitan court. A notoriously slow worker – it was once necessary for the king to post a guard outside the museum's door to ensure he would deliver a composition on time – he was nevertheless fertile enough to turn out over fifty operas. At points in his *Andromaca*, some critics say, the action and music "match the dramatic power of Euripides and Racine in their treatment of the story, and this *opera seria* may be among the finer achievements in the genre". It has certainly not been heard in recent years.

The second of the war-related plays, *The Children of Heracles* (preserved in a somewhat fragmented state, possibly with scenes missing) tells how the Athenians championed the cause of the hero's orphaned children by martial action against Argos. It flatters Athens by depicting it as humanitarian, quick to seek and obtain justice for those in need of such assistance. Though the play's date is unrecorded, several topical references in the dialogue suggest that it was staged in or near 429 or 428 BC.

Most classical scholars hold it in poor esteem, for a work by the great Euripides. For instance, Schlegel dismisses it as "very paltry", and cites its weak ending. Lucas has no kind words for it: "A rather thin patriotic play", and Gassner waves it off as "a not very striking play". G.M.A. Grube, in his *The Drama of Euripides*, is quite reserved in his appraisal of it. Yet, as nearly always, some contradictory opinions about it have been issued. G. Zuntz, in *The Political Plays of Euripides*, speaks very highly of its structure, summing it up as "a gem of concentrated presentation", and Ferguson feels that it has been generally misunderstood. "The false evaluations arise from a failure to relate Euripides' thought to the play's political context, and a consequent too-ready acceptance of the play as a glorification of Athens." He is convinced that, contrary to most readings, the playwright is not praising but condemning his city for its espousal of war as a remedy for people's ills.

Though Euripides draws on a myth once again, he alters it in so many details that his plot may be said to be almost wholly original. After Heracles' death his children take flight from persecution by Eurystheus, the King of Tiryns, at whose bidding their father had performed his fabled twelve labours. They are accompanied by Heracles' friend, Iolaus, an old man who has become their protector. The group reaches the Temple of Zeus at Marathon, where they ask sanctuary. Adorned with the garlands of suppliants, the boys remain at the altar throughout the drama, mute observers of the action. Also with them is Alcmene, mother of the dead hero, but at first she is inside, out of sight, with a cluster of girls. Some of the older boys, led by Hyllus, have gone to search for haven somewhere else.

A herald, sent by Eurystheus, arrives and demands that the children be surrendered to him. His manner is rough, intimidating. Euripides seems to be showing how Athens is descending from an ordered, disciplined society to a state of increasing anarchy, a result of the ever-pressing Peloponnesian War. Iolaus' cries for help bring on a chorus of local elders who ask what is wrong. They question the herald, who impatiently asks to speak to King Demophon, when he appears at the right moment. In the king's eyes the herald's behaviour is savage and unacceptable. To the threat of war on Athens, if it does not yield the fugitives, the noble ruler, son of Theseus who a generation earlier granted shelter to Oedipus, sets forth his arguments against the herald's claims and states his readiness to fight on the children's behalf. The chorus agrees: "This land always tries to help the helpless, when right is on their side." While Iolaus prays at an altar, Demophon departs to consult the oracles and rally his soldiers.

Disappointed and disheartened, Demophon returns with horrible news. The seers have told him that Persephone demands the sacrifice of a virgin, a condition that puts him in a fearful dilemma. Though he is its ruler, Athens is a democracy. He cannot arbitrarily ask his people to provide a girl for the dread rite. Iolaus tried to impart this information to the children, but his voice breaks as he is overcome with emotion. The door to the temple opens slightly; a girl glances out, attracted by the noise. Iolaus offers to give himself up to Eurystheus, but Demophon declares that would a useless gesture. The girl watching from the temple's portal, Macaria (whose name means "blessed"), is Heracles' eldest daughter; she asks questions and grasps the problem. Without hesitation she offers herself as the sacrifice, whereby – in Lucas's tart comment – she joins "Euripides' army of maiden-martyrs", and also takes her place in his roster of foreign women graced with inherent nobility.

Her death is not in vain: a battle ensues, and the Athenians rout Eurystheus' forces. Hyllus has gathered an army to augment the city's troops. Peleus dons armour and joins the struggle. During the fray Hyllus challenges Eurystheus to single combat, which is refused. Instead, the cowardly tyrant flees, chased and overtaken by a miraculously rejuvenated Iolaus, over whom two stars appear in the heavens – epiphanies of Heracles and his wife Hebe, goddess of youth. Eurystheus, a prisoner, is led back; he is confronted by Alcmene, the mother of Heracles, who has already promised freedom to the slave-attendant who brought word of the victory. She submits the captive to a vicious tongue-lashing. (In the myth, Eurystheus is slain by Hyllus, who has him decapitated, after which Alcmene scratches out the glazed eyes. Euripides saw fit to soften that detail of the story.) In this final scene Alcmene threatens to kill her son's foe; the chorus of elders tries to prevent her. After some wrangling she succeeds, countering the chorus's objections: but first Eurystheus bids farewell with remarkable dignity, asserting that he does not fear to die. Alcmene is implacable, crying out that his body shall be thrown to the dogs. Hardly the resolution of a tragedy ending on an exalted note, nor one evoking an emotional or spiritual "catharsis"!

Macaria is poignantly appealing, and her voluntary sacrifice is a high and moving point of the play; Euripides excels at portraying such young women, virtuous, compassionate, altruistic. Demophon is decent and generous, and Iolaus has similar traits.

Paradoxical is the portrayal of Eurystheus. Before his long-delayed entrance he is said to be hateful, monstrous, sadistic. Yet when he finally appears he is the very opposite: soft-spoken, gentle, composed; and though described as craven, he accepts his death with rare bravery. This raises some questions about Euripides' true intention in *The Children of Heracles*. Is not the play, with its comic touches and moments of extravagant fantasy, really mock-heroic?

Iolaus, kindly and well intentioned, a defender of the oppressed, is a Polonius-like old man overgiven to moral platitudinizing. His bones are so creaky that he can barely support the armour he puts on – with arthritic difficulty – before setting out for battle; he is a Don Quixote, ultimately a figment of fantasy. Equally fantastic is his rejuvenation in the heat of the fray, and the astral guidance overhead provided him by the shining images of Heracles and Hebe. Why does Euripides resort to fantasy here, unless his purpose is satiric? He might not be glorifying the warlike Athenians but obliquely ridiculing them. This is a strange play, with many ambiguities. Is the playwright implying that, by rumour or design, Athenians exaggerate the extent of evil in the nature and behaviour of their enemies? Do they not delude themselves that they are morally superior to everybody else, creating pretexts and justifications for their predatory excursions? Do Athenians lay boastful claims to great feats-at-arms, while in reality there are too many instances during campaigns of their leaders' ineptitude? And do they, with flattering self-deception, assure themselves that some gods are especially fond of them and may be relied on for protection? Perhaps Euripides is saying this, or again maybe he is not.

In the third "patriotic" play, *The Suppliant Women* (*c.* 421 BC), Theseus, King of Athens, receives a delegation of Argive women who beseech him to intervene and obtain the burial of their warrior husbands and sons, fallen during the siege of Thebes. Accompanying them is the elderly King Adrastus. (This story has the same background as that of Aeschylus' *Seven Against Thebes* and Sophocles' *Antigone.*) Most eloquent and persuasive is Aethra, Theseus' mother, who joins her voice to the chorus of pleaders. The youthful Athenian ruler is somewhat self-important and moralistic, fond of lecturing people, even grey-locked King Adrastus, who urges him to take up arms against the Thebans on behalf of the bereaved women and retorts that he has come for help not sermons. Similarly, when a herald from King Creon arrives, Theseus engages him in a debate about the comparative merits of democracy and autocracy. The Thebans scornfully reject the Athenians' petition until Theseus leads a successful campaign against them and brings back the ashes of the fallen Argives, who are at last accorded elaborate funeral rites, which provide opportunities for theatrically effective spectacle; they are the chief feature of this play. Indeed, some of them are so demanding that scholars are uncertain as to how they could have been staged.

The script abounds with seeming inconsistencies. Theseus, who is pious – verging on the superstitious – and an advocate of settling disputes by peaceful negotiations, finally takes up arms and resolves the quarrel with Thebes by means of war. Adrastus, who has been asking for martial support, veers over to deploring the savagery of the battlefield and its human toll. In the view of some commentators Euripides is saying that most wars are bad, but a few are just. Both Adrastus, the defeated, grovelling Argive leader, and the rude envoy from Creon, the Theban tyrant, are unwise men of power who bring disaster upon their people. Theseus fights only because he has to, and for very limited objectives. He is prudent, enlightened. What is more, he depends on the consent of those he governs, for in Athens the poor have as much voice as the rich and strong, a civic right that earns the contempt of the Theban spokesman. (Possibly Theseus is meant to represent the fiery, intelligent Alcibiades, whom Euripides admired for a time, though before long he became disillusioned with him.)

Euripides sees and presents both sides of every question. In the exchange between Theseus and the herald the faults of democracy are set forth:

> Here in the game of policy thou yieldest
> To Thebes the first advantage. For my country
> *Does* "bow to a single master" – not a mob!
> *We* have no windy demagogues that puff
> With flatteries our State this way and that,
> Each to his own advantage – honeyed talkers,
> Today delightful, fatal in the end;
> That they evade the penalties of failure
> By further calumnies of other men,
> How should a multitude that cannot weight
> The speeches that it hears, direct a city?
> Ripe counsel is a surer, safer guide
> Than a people's rash decisions. Can poor peasants,
> Even though they be not boors, find leisure
> From all their labours, for the common weal?
> And what a plague for all a country's noblest,
> When some mean fellow, that climbed up from nothing,
> Rises to fame by a tongue that dupes the crowd!

Theseus responds:

> Nothing so deadly to a state as despots
> For first of all it means there are no laws
> Common to all – but one, that wields the law
> In his own hands, is master. So right dies.
> But where the law stands written, rich and weak
> Alike have justice – poor men can accuse
> The prosperous, charge for charge; and humble folk
> With right upon their side, defeat the mighty,
> For *this* is Liberty – when the herald cries:
> "Who has good counsel for the common weal,
> Now let him speak." Then he that wills to speak,
> Has honour he that wills not, holds his peace.
> What rule more than this?
> And where the people governs, it takes pleasure
> To see the city rich in growing youth;
> But despots dread it – so they kill the best
> And wisest (as they judge), to keep their power,
> How should a country grow to greatness thus,
> When some hand plucks and docks what's young and stirring,
> Like the tall ears in some spring field of corn?
> [Translation: F.L. Lucas]

Here is Euripides at his most didactic and discursive, a tendency often present in his work and considered by most critics to be a major fault in a dramatist, though the ideas do have a startling relevance for many modern spectators.

In *The Suppliant Women* Euripides is certainly more than a mere "patriotic poet", lending his pen to Athens's war-fervour, hoping to sustain morale among the citizens: the script of the drama is too pessimistic in tone for that. A disenchantment with warfare is all too apparent. Euripides himself had been in battle and, dismayed by its horrors, gives the following lines to his characters:

If Death were visible in the casting of the vote,
Greece would not be destroying herself by her war-lust.

And again:

You cities, who could remedy your troubles by reasoning,
prefer to settle matters by slaughter.

And still again:

Life is a short thing; we should pass through it easily
with as little trouble as we can.
[Translation: H.D.F. Kitto]

Once more, by his growing pacificism, he is skirting danger. He also makes the point that the claims of all humanity, larger by far than those of Athens's alone, must be met. Theseus exemplifies this when, after triumphing over the Thebans, he refuses to enter their city and thus prevents a new massacre. The tragic cost of war is also illustrated by the plight of the children left orphans by the intrinsically senseless struggle. In the funeral rites, they carry the ashes of their fathers. At the end there is only a vision of the foolish war continuing for ever, as the sons of the fallen Argives pledge themselves to take vengeance.

The many religious notes adumbrated throughout are mostly references to Demeter, the mother goddess, to whom the suppliants pray and for whom they sing and dance, for in her is the power of fertility. The scene is Eleuis, the sanctuary of that deity, and her statue and altar stand to one side, and an altar to Kore on the other, before the Building of the Mysteries (*Telesterion*). At the end, though, it is Athena who dominates, who here is bloodthirsty, quite the opposite of Demeter, who is a sort of *"mater dolorosa"*.

Aethra is the outstanding figure. She knows how to handle men and bend them to her will, and accordingly is seen controlling her compliant son Theseus.

Many echoes of Aeschylus and *Seven Against Thebes* are heard. At times Euripides offers what he feels to be more "correct" interpretations of particular speeches and acts in the earlier drama, and elsewhere he even parodies a few Aeschylean passages, as well as Pericles' classic funeral oration.

Very popular for several centuries in the ancient world – in Rome as well as Greece – *The Suppliant Women* is hardly known today except to scholars; there have been few if any stagings of it in recent years. Yet as spectacle, visible or poetically reported, it has hardly any equals among the extant Greek tragedies. Theseus presides over the burning of the unburied bodies of the Argive warriors; Evadne, the young widow of Capaneous, dances atop a rock, then leaps into the flames of his pyre to be with him again, her ashes to be mingled with his. She is dressed in festal garb, much like a surviving wife being sacrificed in an Indian *suttee.* The chorus shrinks back in horror, while her father Iphis is overcome. It is an unforgettable moment, a stroke of sensational, visceral theatre, for which Euripides has a sure instinct.

Among critics there is a divergence of opinion about the play's structure: the majority deem it loose, with the Evadne scene very poorly integrated. Gilbert Norwood, in his *Essays in Euripidean Tragedy*, calls the script a "hodge-podge" and conjectures that some parts might have been added by a later hand. But Ferguson argues otherwise: "We see men and women in the grip of a war situation, cold or hot, and this said, the play, so far from sprawling, as some have suggested, is tightly knit." About its overall merit there is a similar division, ranging from Van Hook's ranking it as Euripides' worst venture, to F.L. Lucas's judgement of it – "A piece with much spectacle, some ideas, but little genuine drama" – to Del Grande's rather surprising tribute to it as among the poet's finest work.

(An added comment: Evadne's plunge, from a high rock on stage, is steep and perilous, an athletic feat requiring exceptional agility to be smoothly performed by a masked actor in long, fluttering garments.)

Euripides' fourth play during this troubled decade is *Heracles*, its date surmised to be anywhere between 424 and 414 BC. Its varied qualities have earned it adjectives such as "beautiful" (Gassner), "rather frigid" (Lucas), "puzzling" (Ferguson), and others similarly disparate. The great hero is of uncertain parentage: lustful Zeus had stolen into the bed of the mortal Alcmene in the absence of her husband Amphytrion. Which of the two is the father of Heracles, also known as Hercules, now the mightiest of warriors? Hera, the Queen of Olympus, jealous wife of Zeus, has never ceased persecuting Alcmene's son. He has been busy performing his fabulous labours; at this point he has descended in the Underworld to bring back Cerberus, the three-headed hound, and thereby cleanse the earth of violence. While he is away on this well-intentioned task, his family – wife, Megara, and three children – are in Thebes. Along with them is Amphytrion, now aged and impotent, an exile from Argos, whose ruler Eurystheus has agreed to permit the old man's return if Heracles successfully performs his errand. In the interim Lycus, the tyrant of Thebes, persecutes the family, who are near death from starvation and thirst and have taken refuge before an altar dedicated to Zeus. Lycus threatens to kill them. Fortunately Heracles, clad in a lion-skin, reappears at just the right moment. With Amphytrion's contrivance, Lycus is lured into a cave where he is slain by Heracles, who awaits him there.

Hera is infuriated by this turn of affairs. She sends two minor deities – Iris, the Rainbow; and Madness, the Gorgon of Night, wearing a horrifying mask, snakes in her hair, a long black robe – in a car that is lowered by a crane. They carry out Hera's instructions, which are to overcome Heracles' senses. He is seized by a spell of insanity, changed into a bull, and – off-stage – kills Megara and the children. When he recovers and learns what he has done, his despair is limitless. He blames himself for the hideous deed, though Amphytrion vainly seeks to console him, insisting the fault is the implacable Hera's.

Heracles, contaminated by the dread act, must withdraw from human society, never to be touched again by the hand of anyone. He speaks of suicide. His restoration to reason and health occurs when Theseus, King of Athens, comes to renew a bond of friendship forged much earlier when Heracles had rescued the benign Athenian from Hades. Theseus, with calming words, and in spite of the proscription, puts his arm about Heracles' shoulders; the "magic touch" is truly healing. He gives way to tears. Given new strength, the hero is persuaded to renew his efforts to benefit humanity, ridding the world of the allegorical monsters besetting it. Theseus leads him back to Athens for purification.

Though Ferguson thinks the extended opening of the play is "powerful", many other commentators object that it is feeble and flat, lacking dramatic action. But the climactic scene of Heracles' bout with insanity is one of the strongest Euripides ever wrote, and deeply moving is the hero's discovery that during his psychotic episode he has killed his cherished wife and children. As demonstrated in *Medea*, and later again in *Electra*, the portrayal of abnormal states of mind fascinated Euripides; as a romantic artist he did very well at it; and he excelled as well in providing macabre *frissons*, Grand Guignol effects. The children are the prey of the animalistic blood-lust aroused in Heracles, while Madness, adorned with her headdress of reptiles, swirls furiously about him in her chariot to the wild, joyless sound of shrill flutes; a gale sweeps the stage and an earthquake seems to rock the altar and palace. Then, after an abrupt silence, a messenger brings word of the slaughter. Earlier, another striking passage has Megara and her children, the intended victims of the evil Lycus, appear in their grave-clothes, providing a grisly thrill that the spectators would not quickly forget. But some of the final moments of the play reach sublimity, and there is much beautiful lyricism throughout the writing.

Though the play has the usual supernatural apparatus, its tone is rationalistic. The suggestion is strong that Hera's goading of Heracles to madness is symbolic only, and that his dementia arises from his own prolonged inner tensions. One of the questions much discussed is whether Heracles' "labours" on behalf of mankind are real or only illusory. In the same sceptical spirit, the hero is allowed to doubt his reputed godly origin. He elects to name Amphytrion as the father he prefers over the heedless Zeus, possibly his divine begetter.

The play is "patriotic" in its kindly depiction of Theseus and its fulsome tributes to the Athenians, the friends and helpers of all good people, the zealous foes of the unjust. A much less favourable image is created of the Thebans, who were allies of the Spartans. The role of Amphytrion is especially prominent. He is rueful, ever complaining at how age has weakened him. Some commentators hold that Euripides, who was nearing sixty, identified with the unhappy Amphytrion, a feeling that inspires the chorus to chant:

> Ah Youth, still loved delight:
>   Old age upon me lies
> Heavy as Etna's height;
> It bows my head, and the light
>   Darkens before my eyes.
>
> What profit, though I lorded
>   O'er all the East as king:
> Or golden treasures hoarded? –
>   Youth is a fairer thing.
> In the house of wealth still Youth is best
>
> And lovely is Youth to the neediest.
> But Age I hate.
> [Translation: F.L. Lucas]

And so on, for twenty-nine more lines, in a notable ode.

The celebration of friendship as a healing force is a signal point made by the script. Significant, too, is Heracles' choice of Amphytrion, a put-upon mortal, rather than Zeus, a deity, as the one he desires to acknowledge as his father. The chorus sings: "If only the gods had understanding, had wisdom as men know wisdom." The Olympians are depicted as too often cruel and mischievous; Euripides, the sceptical humanist, is once more subtly inserting his negative view of them.

The shape of the work has been faulted for breaking at the middle, the two parts seeming utterly disparate. But this is a structure that Euripides used in several of his plays of this period. Some think the action has a new kind of linkage, less overt and restrictive than the neat, well-organized plotting that was practised to perfection by Sophocles and later advocated by Aristotle in his *Poetics*. Is Euripides careless or inept in this respect, or is he experimenting with a different, looser handling of his material, in which a unity is achieved by a consistency of mood, the dominance of certain characters whose adventures and development bind together a variety of incidents? And is dramatic unity achieved by the tone adopted by the author, and by his unique, very personal way of looking at people and events? Is he demanding more freedom to tell his story as he deems best? Unity is also abetted by recurrent images in the poetry – leitmotifs, so to speak – as Aeschylus and Sophocles knew very well.

With *Hecuba* (probably 425 or 424 BC, or even as late as 422), Euripides' anger at the frustrated expedition against Sparta, which by now had lasted about six years, is ever more sharp and explicit. (In Greek the play is *Hecate*, but as with *Oedipus Rex* the Latinized title has long become widely familiar.) When first staged at the Festival it had scant success, for reasons easy to grasp. In the aftermath of the fall of Troy the Greek victors are depicted as base and cruel towards their captives, the pathetic aged Trojan queen and her children; and, in her desperate efforts to protect or avenge them, even she is reduced to savagery. All, Greeks and Trojans alike, are the victims of war.

The play enjoyed widespread popularity in the Middle Ages and Early Renaissance, especially in Byzantium, where the lecturers prescribed it for study in schools. Dante makes a reference to it, in lines descriptive of Hecuba's dolorous fate, and Erasmus, the greatest scholar of his age, devoted himself to translating it into Latin. Stiblinus rated it Euripides' topmost work. Shakespeare knew of the luckless queen; she is an unhappy character in the play that Hamlet has performed by travelling actors at the castle.

With Troy under siege, King Priam and his wife, Hecuba, send their youngest child to the court of Thrace to be cared for by its ruler, Polymestor. They provide the boy, Polydorus, with a hoard of gold to ensure his future. Unbeknownst to them, the evil Polymestor kills the boy in order to steal his treasure.

Hecuba has an unusual opening: the prologue is spoken by the boy's ghost, who recounts what has befallen him. He explains that details of his murder have been revealed to his mother in nightmarish dreams.

The scene of the play is a shore near the ruins of Troy, where Hecuba and her train of maidens are being held captive by the Greeks, who have not yet taken to their ships. The proud queen has been reduced to slavery, as have been her attendants who now comprise the melancholy chorus. Hecuba's other sons have lost their lives in the siege, and her daughter and daughter-in-law are in bondage. Only one child is still with her, the young virgin Polyxena. Odysseus, cold-hearted and crafty, visits Hecuba with dire news. An oracle has proclaimed that the Greek army cannot leave until Polyxena is offered as a sacrifice at the grave of Achilles to appease his restless spirit. The leader of the Greeks, Agamemnon, has chosen Priam's daughter Cassandra as his concubine, and Hecuba appeals to him to spare the innocent Polyxena, volunteering to die in her place or else together with her. In this play Agamemnon is portrayed as evasive, weak and irresolute. The girl Polyxena is quite ready to yield her life. She is delicately sketched, described by one critic as an "existentialist" heroine: her preference is for immediate death rather than years of servitude and misery: "My eyes are free. I freely renounce the light of day." Hecuba refuses to part with her: "I'll cling to her like ivy to an oak tree." Her mother's plea is futile: the Trojan princess is led away.

After a choral interlude, a Greek herald brings word of how bravely Polyxena had accepted her untimely fate. Even the Greek soldiers had been stirred by her show of courage. Hecuba, told that she can prepare the girl's body for burial, sends her attendants to the nearby seashore for saltwater with which to wash the corpse. They return bearing a small figure wrapped in a cloak, which Hecuba supposes is her daughter. Uncovering it, she discovers instead the remains of her son Polydorus, drowned and borne ashore by the waves. Hecuba shrieks her shock and sorrow, recognizing that her horrible dreams were true. Quickly her pain and grief turn to hatred, an overwhelming desire for vengeance that quite transforms her, changing her into a Medea-like creature. She instantly shapes a plot, sending a messenger to the Thracian court, bidding Polymestor to come at once on an urgent matter, bringing his children with him, to hear a new proposal.

Unaware that Hecuba knows of the boy's murder, Polymestor and his sons and bodyguards come to the seaside camp. He assures her that Polydorus and the gold are safe. He is the total hypocrite. Playing on his greed, Hecuba entices him into her tent by promising him more gold that she claims to have concealed there. He must leave his guards outside, but his children may accompany him. There is a brief song by the chorus, then hideous screams are heard. Exultant, Hecuba rushes from the tent: she has exacted retribution, putting out Polymestor's eyes and butchering his children.

Howling, and crawling on all fours, the blind man follows her from the shrouded scene of carnage.

Agamemnon, learning of Polymestor's crime, refuses him succour. The Thracian, cursing, prophesies that Agamemnon will die at the hand of Clytemnestra, and Cassandra, too. In return, Agamemnon orders the Thracian gagged and next abandoned on a desert island. Hecuba leaves, finally to inter her children, her maidens depart to begin their long slavery, and the Greeks board their ships for home.

But first Hecuba must face a trial for her sanguine deed. Polymestor defends himself, asserting that the boy Polydorus would have grown to be a foe of the Greeks. Hecuba now has Agamemnon on her side. After she tells of Polymestor's deceptiveness and avidity, it is decided that her fierce act of vengeance was quite justified. As always, Euripides is especially gifted at crafting such debates, those addressing moral issues.

The more or less constant traits of a Euripidean drama are in evidence again in his *Hecuba*: a foreign woman, beset, married, even tortured, but fiendishly resourceful, retaliates in a murderous fashion: Medea, Phaedra, Hecuba. Children, helpless and doomed, face a plight certain to evoke a wet-eyed response from spectators. Criticism, ever less veiled, is aimed at the war-lustful rulers of the city, and there are barbs – ever more sharp – at a lingering, primitive religious superstition; the gods are displayed as hardly kind to human beings. The stories, incidents chosen from myths and Homer, are egregiously gory, so crowded with acts of bestiality, needless mutilation and rampant killings that they prefigure the similar bloodthirstiness of the far later Senecan and Jacobean theatres. (It must be recognized that the Periclean epoch was civilized but had its savage side, much as had Rome in the age of Nero and Caligula, and Europe in the seventeenth and twentieth centuries.)

The play, again, is slackly organized, episodic, a diptych, hinged midway, the action of its first half building to the discovery of Polydorus' body, and afterwards concentrating on Hecuba's remarkably changed nature. As ever, Euripides creates vital characterizations, though by now his cast is largely familiar. Hecuba, as has been said, varies only slightly from Medea. Of her exemplary youngest daughter, who goes unflinchingly to her death, Lucas remarks astringently: "Polyxena is a noble character. But Euripides repeats this theme too often. One begins to suspect that he is out to draw tears; and virgins should not be used as onions."

One who was not awed by Euripides' heart-wringing tragedies was Aristophanes, who parodied some lines from *Hecuba* in his buoyantly farcical *The Clouds*.

The poet turns from the subject of war and its fearful toll to adopt the subject in a lighter and more ironic vein, in his *Ion* (*c.* 420 BC), a play that bedevils those scholars who like to categorize Euripides' works. Again, it might be called a tragicomedy – its tone is often tongue-in-cheek. Euripides, at sixty, had just been released from his last tour of military duty. He was still imbued with patriotism, but he harboured not only anti-war feelings but heightened heretical views. Now he struck out even more brazenly at the popular concept of the gods in his time.

One morning, in dawn-light near Delphi, Creusa, daughter of King Eurechtheus of Athens, was plucking flowers in a dewy field when she was seized and ravished by lecherous Apollo. Later she secretly bore the god's child and abandoned it to perish in a cave, after having wrapped it in a shawl that she herself had woven and embroidered, and left it with a gold chain in a basket. (These are the traditional tokens that along with birthmarks are later to identify "changelings" in most plays in the genre.) Apollo, with inconsistent benignity watching over his offspring, had the boy discovered and brought up by his priests, to become a servant in the temple at Delphi. This exposition is delivered by Hermes, the winged messenger, in a prologue that strangely contains several inexplicable contradictions and errors. At the play's opening the boy is an attractive teenager, pious, naïve, warm-hearted, dedicated with the ardour of a St Francis of Assisi to his task of keeping clean the shrine; he sings prayerfully and talks to the darting birds, though he also has to shoot arrows to drive them away from that lovely spot. He has no knowledge of his semi-divine origin.

In the intervening years Creusa has been married to Xuthus; he knows nothing of her rape by Apollo; the pair are childless, and Xuthus desperately wants a son. Their thwarted wish brings them on a pilgrimage to Delphi. Xuthus stops *en route* to consult a lesser oracle; Creusa arrives alone and encounters the nameless youth, to whom she is instantly drawn. The conscience-stricken Creusa intends to ask Apollo what befell their lost son: did the exposed infant survive, or was it attacked by wild beasts? Pretending that she is speaking on behalf of a "friend" of whom Apollo took advantage, she beseeches this handsome, friendly youth to be her intermediary with the god. He is shocked and replies that it would be folly to question a divine being about such a self-incriminating matter, and especially in these sacred precincts consecrated to him. He is more than a bit taken aback: could the Apollo whom he adores be guilty of such misconduct? Looking heavenward, he implores:

Helios,
answer me;
say
you are blameless;

could you take
a mere child
and betray her?
Could you betray her
and leave
your own child
to die?

No,
no,
no,
you are our Lord,
our virtue –

You punish
man's evil;
you could not
(it were unjust)
break laws
made for mortals.
[Translation: Hilda Doolittle, *aka* HD]

Creus goes off. The youth continues sweeping the steps of the temple's portal with a myrtle branch. At the shrine, Xuthus has been told by the lesser oracle that the first person he beholds after leaving the temple will be his "son", who will continue the royal line. That proves to be the devout temple servant, of course, whom Xuthus hails rapturously, promptly naming him Ion (which means "Coming"). He embraces and kisses him, but is rebuffed by the chaste, innocent youth, who interprets the hug as a homosexual advance – a mistake that must have amused the Athenian audience. Xuthus promptly explains himself, but Ion has natural doubts. How could he be this Athenian stranger's son? He questions Xuthus closely, obtaining an admission that quite some time previously – just the right number of years – Xuthus had paid another visit to Delphi and, drunken, had enjoyed an affair with a maenad, a frenzied priestess of Bacchus: a consequence of that intoxication is Ion, their illegitimate child. Ion accepts this seemingly logical explanation, but now longs to meet his unknown mother. The father and son depart for Athens, after warning the chorus of Creusa's attendants to say nothing of what has been learned.

Indiscreet, the chorus does not heed this admonition; the attendants tell Creusa that her husband and his newly found bastard son have gone to the city, where at a feast the youth is designated a prince and heir. The news is bitterly painful to the barren Creusa: her husband has been unfaithful to her and has fathered a child by another woman. Hatred for both of them seizes her, especially after an old retainer suggests that Xuthus has merely concocted the tale of the oracle's revelation. The aged man, on whose advice Creusa frequently relies, proposes that she should kill Xuthus and Ion. At this moment, Creusa, angry and jealous, has a great solo in which she indicts Apollo for his cruel and shameless treatment of her. He had let *their* child be torn to pieces by hawks or vultures. The old retainer adds his voice to her sacrilegious denunciation of the god. Creusa finally decides to spare Xuthus' life, as in other respects he has always been good to her. What she cannot bear is the thought that the heartless Apollo, and not some other god, has allotted her husband this boy. The young interloper must die, even though when first encountering him she had been unaccountably attracted to him. She feels "betrayed by God and man alike". She gives the old man a vial of poison, of ancestral and divine origin, and sends him to participate in the feast being held in Athens to celebrate Ion's introduction there.

After a choric chant, marking time, a messenger arrives to report that at the festive rites Ion was about to drink from the tainted goblet when a slave uttered a word of ill omen, causing the youth to spill the potion. He courteously asked for a fresh one. But a bird, dipping its beak in the splashed wine, dropped dead, exposing the plot. The old man, being seized, soon confessed Creusa's part, and the Delphic priests immediately condemned her to be hurled to her death on rocks below a high cliff on Mount Parnassus for having attempted to kill a servant of Apollo, one who had laboured in the god's own temple. Creusa, who has come to the shrine to beseech the gift of birth from the bright god, is instead to have death from him.

As her pursuers approach, she takes refuge at Apollo's altar. Ion arrives and fiercely upbraids her, not yet suspecting that she is his mother. Pythia, the high priestess, intervenes and orders Ion to withdraw and return with his father to Athens. She gives him the basket-cradle in which he was found as a child and bids him to search the whole world for the long-sought woman who bore him. On seeing the basket and shawl, Creusa utters a cry and rushes forward. Before he unfolds the cloth, she describes the embroidery on it and demands that it be given back to her. This leads to a joyful "recognition" scene, and mother and son are reunited. Ion, having discovered his true identity, wishes to inform Xuthus, but Creusa persuades him that the secret must be kept. What still bothers the puzzled Ion is that his adored Apollo, now acknowledged to be his father, has indulged in some outright lies. Athena, the goddess sister of Apollo, is lowered by a crane; she has been sent by the embarrassed god to set all to rights, though obviously things have not gone at all as he intended or predicted. In a last look into the future, there is promise that Ion is to be the founder of the race of Ionians.

The play was received as forthrightly "blasphemous", but Euripides' iconoclastic criticism of the Delphic oracles was permissible because at that moment Delphi was an ally of hostile Sparta. The plot is beautifully developed, neat at every point, and everything moves quickly, at a pace required of a stage-work. Euripides was a top-flight dramaturgist when he bothered to be. *Ion* is a tragicomedy, not only because it ends happily but because in it Euripides deftly ridicules Apollo: what a scoundrel he is, at every turn; while his chief disciple, the wide-eyed Ion, is at best a simpleton, not unlike Voltaire's ingenuous Candide. Yet Euripides also shows that he can portray the freshness and idealism of youth almost lovingly, as earlier with Polyxena. By contrast, Xuthus is gruff, complacent, blunt of speech, yet kindly, an extrovert. The dialogue is lucid, laced with irony throughout. In addition to Creusa's major aria, there are choruses of sonorous poetry. Her attendants have never before been at mountainous Delphi and engage in extensive sightseeing, which lets the playwright offer precise descriptions of the site, its magnificent vistas and clear, cold air, in passages that resemble a travel brochure.

One school of thought has it that Apollo is not Ion's father – Xuthus is, after all. In the half-light of dawn the fainting, hysterical adolescent Creusa, grappling with a clumsy, burly figure, only imagined – or preferred to imagine – that she had been violated by a god, when in fact it was a plain mortal, the drunken Xuthus, who possessed her. This would carry Euripides' blasphemy even further; he might be hinting, for the benefit of the more sophisticated segment of his audience, that Apollo did not exist. Or that the simple Ion, a devout believer, was at best only Apollo's "spiritual child".

Not only the "changeling" theme – to be explored, as has been said, at greater length in a later chapter – but also the perennial and closely linked motif of "the search for the father" which historically begins in myth are involved here, as they are in *Oedipus*, *Heracles* and many other plays; it is surmised by some scholars that *Ion* was presented together with *Heracles* at the Festival, along with the lost *Alope*, which concerned a child of Poseidon, the three comprising the usual group of works by the same author, and in this instance each treating with a question as to whether a leading character has a valid claim to divine paternity, the answer tending to be somewhat elusive and ambiguous.

One reason Ion is anxious to discover who his mother might be, and especially after his adoption by Xuthus, is that he does not want to be looked upon as a "foreigner" in Athens; Xuthus, though wed to Creusa, is an outsider, a ruler only through his tie to her. A law recently passed denied many privileges to the foreign-born, so here Euripides is adding a topical allusion, a political overtone, as he regularly did. Ion fears that unless he can establish that he is an Athenian by birth, on the maternal side at least, he will face enmity in the city. Euripides' advocacy of women's rights echoes again in speeches by Creusa, who rails against the double standard of morality by which men can take their sexual pleasure whenever and wherever they desire, but women are bound to be rigidly virtuous.

The atmosphere throughout is luminous. Less serious and ambitious than some of Euripides' other works, *Ion* is none the less a tidy little masterpiece, truly elegant. It is a *jeu d'esprit*, entirely artificial, but also quite delightful, the satirist in Euripides at his most pointed and assured. This is high comedy, and yet like other works in that genre it has its serious and tragic moments. Unfortunately its premise is so esoteric, so special and unfamiliar, so distanced and difficult for modern audiences to appreciate, that *Ion* is not likely to be revived today. Euripides is immortal, but not all his outpourings are destined to be.

Having demonstrated that he could write a "well-made" play, the poet–dramatist gave vent to his full animus against war in a mighty but almost plotless work, *The Trojan Women* (415 BC), a script that *has* gained in stature and impact through the ages. It was part of a tetralogy that garnered second prize. The other components of the offering were *Alexander*, *Palamedes* and *Sisyphus*, the last a satyr piece; the three tragedies were linked by being drawn from Homer's narrative and other stories about the fall of Troy. Only *The Trojan Women* remains. The tetralogy appeared shortly after Athens had overrun and razed Melos, and just before a new expedition was to leave for Sicily to add Syracuse to its dominion. The unprovoked massacre at Melos, a neutral city, and the brutal designs on Syracuse by the unappeased militarists, now ascendant in Athens, had shocked the Athenian intelligentsia for whom Euripides was one of the remaining spokesmen. *The Trojan Women* was his passionate protest, combining deeply felt emotion and poetic fervour. *Palamedes* described the undoing of an idealist, possibly modelled on the exiled Protagoras, or the soon-to-be martyred Socrates, falsely accused of treason; and *Alexander* dealt with the early years of Paris, himself a "changeling" and bearer of a curse from birth, the son of Priam and Hecuba and seducer of Helen. It is likely that the formlessness of *The Trojan Women* is attributable in some degree to its now being truncated from the other two linked dramas that originally preceded it.

Troy lies in ashes, the rich, gleaming, impregnable city a fiery ruin: the remorseless Greeks have slaughtered its champions and heroes. King Priam's widow, the white-haired Hecuba, has been enslaved together with her women. Her daughter Cassandra, prescient of her own death at the hands of a jealous Argive queen, is to be Agamemnon's concubine. The younger daughter, Polynexa, will be sacrificed at the grave of Achilles. A daughter-in-law, Andromache, is selected as the prize of Neoptolemus and must live in anguish with memories of her beloved Hector, Priam's and Hecuba's great son. Hecuba herself is to belong to cunning Odysseus. Only the fickle, faithless Helen, stolen from Menelaus by Paris (Alexander), is to be spared, eventually returned to her husband's embrace, though her willing elopement had brought on the long siege and the high-walled city's disastrous fall.

The Trojan Women might be considered the first "collective drama", concerned not with an individual hero or focal protagonist but a group of persons. The Greeks are depicted with scorn, as thoroughly expedient and base, wholly without compassion.

The expositional prologue is spoken by Poseidon, the patron deity of now immolated Troy, who laments its smoking, smouldering destruction and takes rueful leave of it. He is confronted by Athena, who indignantly charges her Greeks with savagery for which they shall soon be punished. Together she and Poseidon, the sea-god, vow that the expeditionary force will be shipwrecked and scattered on its homebound voyage. The allegory, meant as a warning and a rebuke, is clear from the beginning: the Athenian fleet was gathering in preparation for an imperialistic raid on Sicily, where a like fate might very well await them. The situation at Troy parallels closely that of pillaged Melos.

Hecuba, clad in grey, is prone on the ash-strewn ground; she lifts herself to survey the city's shattered landscape. She must face her harsh new life. Her song is sorrowful, as are the odes of the chorus that accompany her throughout much of the action. Troy's queen, she is now sovereign over nothing.

Her former attendants gather about her; their repeated question is what now will happen to them as they go into slavery. Talthybius, a Greek sergeant, brings the edicts of his army's leaders. He does not as yet inform Hecuba of Polynexa's death, but starts by telling her that Cassandra has been assigned to Agamemnon, even though she is a seer and a priestess of Apollo, sworn to retain her virginity. Neoptolemus, who claims Andromache, is the son of Achilles, the killer of Hector. Hecuba prepares to bid farewell to the unfortunate young women most dear to her.

Wild Cassandra is brought in by soldiers; she is attired in her priestess's robe, with garlands and emblems, and bears a bridal torch, and sways and dances as might a bride, though certainly marriage is not her prospect – instead, as she already foresees, death is. Verbal images of fire recur throughout the play, enhanced by a background of smoke and small flames.

Andromache comes in a chariot that is laden with heaps of loot, the Greeks' spoils of war, of which she is a part. Her child, Astyanax, is on her lap. Talthybius announces that the little boy is to die; the

Greeks fear that otherwise he will grow up to take revenge for the slaying of his father Hector and the degradation of his mother Andromache. The child is to be hurled from the city's walls on a high cliff on to the sharp rocks below. Hecuba and Andromache are shocked and for a time speechless with horror at this hideous decree. Even gruff Talthybius is appalled and hesitant at having to carry out this task. Hecuba and the chorus are given deeply moving songs of loss and lamentation. Gilbert Murray has written: "This scene, with the parting between Andromache and the child which follows, seems to me the most absolutely heart-rending in all the tragic literature of the world. After rising from it one understands Aristotle's judgment of Euripides as 'the most tragic of the poets'." Snatched from his mother's frantic clutch, the boy is carried off by Talthybius and the armed guards.

Menelaus appears, vowing to kill Helen, who is not too daunted by his threats. The other Trojan women are in tatters, but she is still richly arrayed, flaunting her voluptuous beauty. Hecuba urges Menelaus to dispatch his immoral wife, the cause of Troy's misery, but he is weakened by seeing her again and, still dazzled, is obviously fast losing his resolve. He postpones her execution, ordering her to be dragged out by the hair. Helen argues that she is quite blameless, herself a "victim" of Aphrodite, who had irresponsibly promised her to Paris. The goddess of love, not she, is at fault. Hecuba calls for her death, depicting her as shallow and selfish, but Helen's words and unmatched charms clearly beguile her aggrieved husband too strongly. Their relationship is not immediately settled, but a future reconciliation is subtly prefigured as they depart. In this debate Hecuba is revealed as not old and exhausted, but still filled with anger and hate, capable of a lust for vengeance. To Helen's plea of innocence, because Aphrodite has prevailed over them, Hecuba retorts:

> . . . All wild things that in mortality
> Have being, are Aphrodite; and the name
> She bears in heaven is born and writ of them.
> [Translation: Gilbert Murray]

This might seem to be Euripides' true religious belief: that "love" is a cosmic force inhabiting all forms of life, a concept that is poorly represented in the over-simple, popular image of the Cyprian goddess.

The crushed body of little Astyanax is borne in and handed over to his stricken mother, whose grief is beyond measure, as is Hecuba's. His little form is readied for burial; Andromache has him laid on his father Hector's huge shield.

The victorious Greeks prepare to embark on their long ships. The last of their gestures is to set ablaze what is left of the devastated citadel. Into the darkness, through smoke fitfully lit by the renewed fires, Hecuba and her driven women take their pathetic departure.

The script is episodic, disjointed, excessively static, yet it achieves a remarkable and moving unity of mood, and looks forward to modern works such as Maeterlinck's *Interior* and Synge's *Riders to the Sea* in its simple yet exalting lyricism and sombre atmosphere, which is one of desolation and hopelessness. More than a topical play, it is a drama of universal applicability, wherever the grotesque horrors of war are imposed upon suffering humanity. Even the gods are displeased by the wanton butchery of the Greeks and the despoliation of sacred shrines, and predict dire retribution that shall haunt and befall the homebound raiders. Gilbert Murray wrote further of *The Trojan Women*: "Far from a perfect play, it is scarcely even a good play. It is an intense study of one great situation, with little plot, little construction, little or no relief for variety. The only movement is a gradual extinguishing of all the familiar lights of human life, with, perhaps, at the end, a suggestion that in the utterness of night, when all fears of a possible worse thing are passed, there is in some sense peace and even glory." Yet the work is drenched in unflinching pessimism, for extinction overcomes all, and at the end the women vanish into darkness. Hecuba has told Andromache:

> Death cannot be what Life is, Child; the cup
> Of Death is empty, and Life hath always hope.
> [Translation: Gilbert Murray]

But the spectator already knows that Hecuba's own death is imminent; she will not survive the sea-voyage. Significant, too, has been the scene between Menelaus and Helen, which is not only highly theatrical but at the same time disappointingly ironic, for in it Euripides implies that evil often triumphs while pure goodness and innocence fail.

Both Poseidon (at the end of the prologue) and Hecuba (near the close of the tragedy) issue warnings:

> Blind is the man who sacks cities
> with temples and tombs, shrines of those whose work is done.
> He brings desolation, himself so soon to die.
> [Translation: John Ferguson]

And again:

> The man is blind who thinks he's well established
> With solid satisfaction. Fortune's a dervish,
> Leaping now one way now another.
> No one controls his own happiness.

Near to the time he brought forth *The Trojan Women*, Euripides devoted himself to composing an *Electra* (416 or perhaps 413 BC), the story handled effectively but quite differently by his elders Aeschylus and Sophocles. In academe there is lively conjecture – as has been stated – about whether Euripides' version shortly preceded or came after Sophocles', and close scrutiny to determine which playwright sought to "correct" the other's interpretation. Euripides offers a more "modern" and "rational" plot, its details altogether more plausible, the whole an example of his higher realism. His changes in the story are bold. The action occurs not in the conventional setting of the broad, marble steps of the Argive palace but instead outside a peasant's lowly hut, near the city's border. Aegisthus and Clytemnestra have chosen a base-born husband for the recalcitrant Electra. (Her name means "unmarried".) Perhaps their thought is that marriage will tame her, or else they wish to punish and demean her; however, the peasant is portrayed as the noblest person in the play. In fact, he is the only admirable one. The returning Orestes recognizes the lowly man's true virtues, though it is obviously Euripides speaking through him:

> Alas, we look for good on earth and cannot recognize it when met, since all our human heritage runs mongrel. At times I have seen descendants of the noblest family grow worthless though the cowards had courageous sons; inside the souls of wealthy men bleak famine lives while minds of stature struggle trapped in starving bodies.
>
> How then can man distinguish man, what test can he use? the test of wealth? the pauper owns one thing, the sickness of his condition, a compelling teacher of evil; by nerve in war? yet how, when a spear is cast across his face, will stand to witness his companion's courage? We can only toss our judgments random on the wind.
>
> This fellow here is no great man among the Argives, not dignified by family in the eyes of the world – he is a face in the crowd, and yet we choose him champion. Can you not come to understand, you empty-minded, opinion-stuffed people, a man is judged by grace among his fellows, manners are

> nobility's touchstone? Such men of manners can control our cities best, and homes, but the well-born sportsman, long on muscle, short on brains, is only good for a statue in the park, not even sterner in the shocks of war than weaker men, for courage is the gift of character.
> [Translation: Emily Townsend Vermule]

This excerpt from an even longer speech is typical of Euripides' tendency to digress, in a didactic vein, and hardly fits Orestes' character, but does illustrate the radical cast of the playwright's thought, his commonsensical, populist attitude. To praise a mere slave in this fashion was daring, indeed. The husband, possibly because he fears Orestes' return, has not attempted to consummate his marriage to the royal princess; consequently Euripides presents a young woman who is not only virginal but also sexually repressed. Her morbidity, however, has yet another origin: a fixation on her dead father, a fiercely jealous hatred of the mother whom she deems wanton.

In Euripides' version, Electra has no sister. Orestes does not accept the risk of appearing at court under a false name, but instead lurks cautiously out of sight after his arrival in Argos. He finally gathers the courage to introduce himself to his sister as a close friend of Orestes, to learn for certain her feelings for him. Aristotle acclaimed this "recognition scene" as better than that by Sophocles, which is prolonged too far; here, says the Greek critic, it is just the right length. Some discern in it, too, a parody of the one in Aeschylus' *The Libation Bearers*. The meeting occurs not at the palace, in the city's heart, but near the frontier, where it is more credible that Orestes would venture.

Orestes is not an ambitious extrovert, as depicted by Sophocles, but nervous, weak, hesitant; he commits matricide largely at Electra's goading. He is the tool of her almost psychotic obsession. Aegisthus is not seen. A messenger reports how, as Aegisthus, unguarded, was supervising preparations in a field to sacrifice a bull, Orestes approached him, feigned to be a stranger and was hospitably welcomed. In a moment, Orestes bared his weapon and killed his astonished, courteous host when his back was turned. He fell to the ground screaming, his spine split open. Nothing related about Aegisthus encourages the spectator to feel that he deserved to be murdered. Orestes' behaviour is hardly heroic.

Clytemnestra is not the tigerish queen who browbeats men in Aeschylus' *Agamemnon*, nor the still hateful mother created by Sophocles. She is rueful, openly regretting her past deeds, acknowledging her crucial mistakes. She has come to the hut out of kindness; Electra has lured her with a false report of having borne a male child and bids her mother to visit the infant. When she arrives, Clytemnestra explains persuasively enough the reasons for her anger at Agamemnon, who not only sanctioned the sacrifice of the innocent Iphigeneia but brazenly returned to Argos with Cassandra as his concubine.

> . . . and introduced her to our bed. So there we were,
> two brides being stabled in a single stall.

Clytemnestra's slaying is therefore the more repugnant, and it becomes even more so because it is the final event of the play, rather than an earlier one, as in Sophocles' script. Where Sophocles seeks by restraint to lessen its horror, Euripides strongly enlarges upon its every aspect.

In a decidedly repulsive scene, Electra gloats over the corpse of Aegisthus, the butchered interloper. Ironically, Electra entices her mother into the hut by a trick like that once used by Clytemnestra to entice Agamemnon into the palace where he was slain. In the hut is hidden Orestes with his bloody sword. The audience is told that when the weak-willed Orestes hesitated, covering his eyes with his cloak, Electra thrust her hand upon his to drive in the blade. Clytemnestra's death-cry is heard.

Two shining figures appear above the cottage: Castor and Polydeuces, brothers of Clytemnestra and Helen. They bring about the resolution of the story: Electra is to wed Pylades, her brother's friend; Orestes is to flee Argos, tracked by the unremitting Furies, until he finally stands trial at Athens, is acquitted and granted respite and years of peace in Arcadia. They also reveal that Helen was actually never at Troy: Zeus had sent a phantom there who simply resembled her: his purpose was to make serious mischief. Orestes and Electra tearfully embrace and depart on their separate ways after "a great sobbing sigh" that is echoed by the gods:

> Ah! That cry is fearful
> even for gods to hear.
> I and the powers of heaven
> feel pity for men's troubles.
> [Translation: John Ferguson]

Electra, morbid, neurotic, dominates this gory melodrama. Her hair is habitually dishevelled, her clothes disarrayed; it is all too clear that unconsciously she enjoys her abasement, her humiliation; she revels in unhappiness, beating her breast, bewailing her lot, crying for vengeance, even – with mockery – bowing before her loathed mother. Euripides the romantic, the psychologist, ventures deeply into a study of abnormality, an exercise that detracts from the universality of his play but heightens its theatricality. In the intensity of her emotion, Electra is like his Medea and Phaedra. No character in this work is of tragic stature; they are creatures of the stage, real but not profoundly moving, because they are too special. But they are also unforgettable, because drawn so starkly. Euripides excels in portraying women who, violently stirred, driven to an extreme, become almost monomaniacal.

Yet he aimed at more than melodrama. He was again condemning "divine" Apollo "who was no god of light in ordering this". As has been noted, Euripides was able to express himself with some impunity because the Delphic oracle had sided with Sparta and was out of favour with Athenians. Orestes, obeying the god's injunction, cries: "Apollo, your holy word was brute and ignorant." In the epiphany at the end of the drama, Castor and Polydeuces pass a further adverse judgement on the deity and his sponsoring of a "primitive morality", the blood feud, the barbaric law of an eye for an eye, a tooth for a tooth, that has haunted and wrecked this degenerating royal line. "He knows the truth but oracles were lies." And the last time we see them Electra and Orestes are conscience-stricken, overcome by the terrible act they have just committed, a deed Orestes has already described as prompted by a "polluted demon . . . in the shape of god". Striking, above all, is Orestes' description of the dying Clytemnestra:

> You saw her agony, how she threw aside her dress,
> how she was showing her breast there in the midst of death?
> My god, how she bent to earth
> the legs which I was born through?
> And her hair – I touched it –

The chorus (women friends of Electra) is allotted some decorative passages but is not integral to the action. More and more, as Euripides moved towards naturalism, he was inhibited from making important use of the chorus, though no one wrote more beautiful poetry for it, however barely relevant it might sometimes be. On occasion he invents a pretext for the awkward presence of the group in what should be a private scene. Much of the clumsiness in the structure of his plays is due to the boldness of his experimentation.

Seen against the background of Athens at war, Euripides' repudiation of violence as a mode for settling human affairs can be construed as a pacifist chord sounded once again and, to those who perceived and heard it, a powerful one. He also remains a consistent defender of women: a protest against the low value the Greeks placed on them is articulated by Clytemnestra who, alluding to the sacrificial death of her youngest daughter, asks: "If Menelaus had been abducted would I have had to kill Orestes to save my sister's husband?" Iphigeneia, a mere girl, was not held dear enough, hardly of equal worth to a son.

The poetry is of the highest order. Here is Ferguson's translation of Electra's opening words, as she enters from the hut, a jar atop her matted tresses:

> Black night, nurse to the golden stars,
> in your blackness I bear this bucket on my head,
> and fetch water from the river,
> not driven to this by any compulsion,
> but exposing Aegisthus' brutality to the gods.
> I pour out my grief to the open sky, to my father.
> That damned daughter of Tyndareus, my mother
> has banished me from home, to oblige her husband.
> She's borne Aegisthus other children
> and treats Orestes and me as bastards in our own home.

Straightforward, dramatic, graphic.

Euripides implies subtly that much of Electra's self-degradation is public role-playing, to win sympathy: she drops the part at times, reverting to the speech and inherent manner of a princess, a nuance of characterization that displays the poet's insight and shrewdness.

In the nineteenth century this *Electra* was not greatly admired; indeed, Ferguson quotes F.A. Paley who assailed it as "skimble-skamble stuff, whose only merit is that it is easy Greek and eminently suitable for schoolboys"; while A.W. von Schlegel regarded it as "perhaps of all Euripides' plays the very vilest". On its behalf, however, G.M.A. Grube stated: "In its own genre this is undoubtedly Euripides' masterpiece." Gilbert Murray found it "a close-knit, powerful, well-constructed play". Among twentieth-century commentators, Lucas has this opinion:

> Aeschylus had treated the matricide of Clytemnestra as a religious moralist, Sophocles as a pure dramatist; Euripides comes to it with the just indignation of a critical humanist. It is a monstrous crime; the poetry that idealizes it is monstrous; the religion that could instigate it is monstrous also. *Écrasez l'in-*

> *fâme*. . . . Electra herself is a realistic study of a young woman poisoned by loneliness, childlessness, and obsession with vendetta. She might have shone in a Resistance movement; she might have made a fanatical young Communist; she presents a vivid picture of the way a narrow personality, not without heroism, can feel herself called to save the world, and lose its soul in the process. It is as if an Antigone, by some hateful perversion, has grown too like Creon. . . . Good rationalist propaganda; but not pleasant drama. Its motto might be Lucetius' – "To so much misery can Religion lead."

He does not rank it among Euripides' best works.

Ferguson offers this evaluation:

> The late Twentieth Century, with its own mood of "sickness" and its own violence and revolt against violence, is better able to understand it. Clearly it is written by a master of the theatre. It makes its point with rare pungency. Its greatest strength lies in the characterization. Electra is a brilliant pathological study, fascinated and repelled by sex, with her masochism and sadism, her fixation on her father and hatred of her mother, her obsessive hopes and fears, her dominating personality. And alongside her, Orestes, a weak and cowardly poltroon, marked by fatal irresolution. Between the two there is a kind of Medea–Jason situation; she is powerful, he is empty. In all there is only one decent character, the peasant "the only gentleman present" (says T. England ironically), a breath of sanity in a world of explosive and destructive madness. For behind all the dramatic skill of Euripides lies the strength of moral indignation. There is a better way than violence. Peasants like Electra's husband appear in the theatre of Aristophanes, and they too are a breath of sanity in a world of explosive and destructive madness. . . . The solution of *Electra* is no solution. Euripides does not believe in gods who will intervene to save the ships. But man, if he will heed, may still save himself – and others.

Curiously – if the report is true – Euripides and *Electra* did save Athens. Only a decade later (404 BC) the city fell to Sparta and its allies, whose soldiers prepared to raze it and impose slavery on its citizens. By chance, the leaders of the occupying forces heard a man of Phocis absent-mindedly raising his voice in a choral passage from the play, about the heroine's deep despair at her homelessness and desolation. Moved to pity, the Spartan victors chose to spare the city and its people.

A failure at the Festival, *Iphigeneia in Tauris* (between 414 and 409 BC) was Euripides' attempt to have a tragicomedy replace a requisite satyr play. It is a variation of the Homeric story of Iphigeneia. Though Agamemnon heartlessly consented to his young daughter's being sacrificed at Aulis, to propitiate an offended Artemis, at the very last instant the goddess relented. Secretly a deer – or hind – was substituted for the girl, who was miraculously wafted to Tauris, where she unwillingly became a high priestess in a temple devoted to the worship of Artemis. At this shrine, on the northern shore of the Black Sea, a wilderness in the Crimea, all foreigners were slain on the altar, with Iphigeneia reluctantly presiding over the rites, her role being to consecrate the victims.

Her brother Orestes and his friend Pylades come in disguise to Tauris, intending to steal the statue of Artemis from the temple and carry it to Athens, a better location: this is to fulfil a task set by Apollo to help Orestes expiate the slaying of Clytemnestra. The recovery of the statue will end their pursuit by the relentless Furies. The obstacles, however, daunt Orestes: the statue is well guarded, almost inaccessible.

In a nightmare, Iphigeneia is warned of the death of the brother she has scarcely known (he has been in exile while she was growing up). She is mourning him when a herdsman brings word: some Greek strangers have been captured. This has happened because Orestes, in a fit resembling madness, inflicted by the Furies, has battled imaginary foes, waving his sword and betraying his hiding-place.

The captives are to serve as sacrifices to Artemis, according to the barbarous local custom; and Iphigeneia is more prepared than usual to conduct the hideous ceremony:

> For since Orestes is no more alive,
> Now, where my heart was, there is only stone.
> Strangers who come today, no matter who,
> Will find in me a woman beyond tears,
>   Unhappiness, O friends, can harden us
> Toward other sorrow harsher than our own.
> [Translation: Witter Bynner]

In an unusually ingenious "recognition scene" that follows shortly, she discovers who the prisoners are, while they learn her surprising identity. Much of this is the consequence of a scheme shaped by Iphigeneia to free one of them to bear a letter to Orestes, after she is told that these young Greeks are from her native Argos, and that in fact her brother is still living. Pylades, chosen to deliver the message, simply hands it to Orestes in the presence of the astonished Iphigeneia. Before this, in an interesting episode, Orestes and Pylades dispute which of them shall die and which one shall escape with Iphigeneia's aid. Like Damon and Pythias, each chooses as a matter of friendship and honour to have the other let go, though he himself must perish; they are remarkably unselfish.

With the facts better known, the three plan to make off with the sacred statue and leave behind the hostile shore. Iphigeneia takes charge. A true daughter of the capable Clytemnestra, and a true sister of the domineering Electra, she lies deviously to Thoas, King of Tauris, about the need to dip and lave the image of Artemis in sea water for purification – it has been polluted by being near a matricide. The Taurian king is taken in by this ruse, and the remaining action – at an ever more rapid pace – is crowded with clever intrigue and suspenseful strategies, as the three narrowly make their escape, conveying the statue to Athens. At the end, Euripides resorts to the *deus ex machina*, an epiphany of the divine Athena who extends her protection to the fugitives.

The play contains several very sharp criticisms of the gods. Iphigeneia can scarcely credit the wickedness of the chaste deity she serves:

> And what does Artemis ask of me here?
> . . . She so delicate
> In all these ways will yet demand the blood
> Of human beings on her altar-stone!
> It cannot be. . . . It is not true.
> . . . O Artemis,
> These people, being murderers themselves,
> Are charging Thee with their own wickedness.
> No! I will not believe it of a God!
> [Translation: Witter Bynner]

And, again, Orestes decries the significance of dreams and the pretensions of oracles, as well as the sagacity of the Heavenly Ones themselves:

> Dreams, lies, lies, dreams – nothing but emptiness!
> Even the Gods, with all Their name for wisdom,
> Have only dreams and lies and lose Their course,
> Blinded, confused, and ignorant as we.
> The wisest men follow their own direction
> And listen to no prophet guiding them.

None but fools believe in oracles,
Forsaking their own judgment. Those who know,
Know that such men can only come to grief.
[Translation: Witter Bynner]

He speaks even more bitterly, in Job-like accents, of Apollo:

. . . When treacherous Phoebus through his oracle
First lied to me, then tricked me, luring me far
From home, lest watchful eyes in Hellas see
That Gods as well as men break promises,
I trusted Him, with all my faith and will,
Even at his command, killing my mother,
And in return He has forsaken me.
[Translation: Witter Bynner]

True, at the very end the prophecies are borne out, but only by the intervention of another deity, and this seems to be merely a device by which Euripides covers his bold impiety, again much as a modern author prefixes a novel with a statement that if any of his characters bear a close resemblance to living persons, it was not his intent but simply a coincidence, a ploy which deceives only the most unsophisticated.

The plot is partly original and very nicely contrived, the spectator's attention held fast, and the chorus (of captive temple maidens) given odes of rare lyric beauty, with delicate imagery and an appropriately light rhythm. Throughout, the tone is romantic, and this is one reason, together with its happy ending, for the work being categorized as a tragicomedy. No tragic climaxes arise, no principal figure dies, and no moral enlightenment is attained or suggested.

The character of Iphigeneia is somewhat complex: she is divided by her love and hatred of the Greeks who have so mistreated her. The sketch of Orestes is mostly lacking in depth: elsewhere he is portrayed by Euripides as emotionally sore-beset, tormented inwardly as well as outwardly; here, he is only courageous, loyal, as befits the hero of a rousing melodrama, a thriller, which is all that *Iphigeneia in Tauris* pretends to be.

Euripides demonstrates once again that he has more than professional skill in dramaturgy when he chooses to exercise it. He is superb at stirring up and then sustaining excitement on stage and introducing sudden reversals. The play also has poignant moments that catch the loneliness and nostalgia of exiles, as voiced not only by Iphigeneia but also by the chorus of Greek temple maidens far from home, much against their will: they infuse the work with the poetic impulse that always flows from Euripides when inspired. At the close, they too are freed by the intervention of Athena. The "barbaric" Taurian setting doubtless gave Euripides an opportunity to compose and insert exotic music and dancing.

What of the frequent criticism that Iphigeneia lies and is treacherous, betraying the hospitality of the trusting King Thoas? She has an obligation, in Greek eyes, to those who have given her haven from her murderous fellow-countrymen who had sought her as a sacrifice. But the lives of her brother Orestes and his friend Pylades are in jeopardy, and her obligation to respond to family ties is far stronger, superseding her debt to the easily beguiled Thoas.

The play is about people with whom an audience readily identifies and whose fears and hopes are quickly shared. Here are no Medea or Electra whose qualities are either superhuman or pathologically excessive.

Euripides liked to turn to light works of this sort, ironic and mocking; he had begun early with *Alcestis* and now goes further in that direction, mingling comedy, sentimentality, melodramatic adventure and fantasy. Lucas remarks: "Here Euripides allows himself, like Aristophanes in *The Birds*, like Shakespeare in *The Tempest*, to relax into a happier mood of romanticism. Far away on the shores of the Crimea it was perhaps possible to forget for a moment the darkening horizons of war at home. Escape is one of the gifts of poetry – not a fault, as puritans have pretended, unless it is abused. It can serve like that gift of anodyne 'nepenthe', which Helen in her beauty brought to Telemachus." Alluding to Iphigeneia's trickery, her final deception of Thoas, Lucas adds: "This lively episode has shocked some critical persons by its duplicity. . . . But I own that I cannot breathe at such moral altitudes." His summary: "An unusually exciting plot; and some good characters – the melancholy, bitter Iphigeneia; the loyal Pylades; the neurotic but resolute Orestes, who mistakes cattle and dogs for Furies. But, not unamusingly, Euripides the rationalist intrudes himself even here. Orestes' Furies are imaginary; Iphigeneia's dream is false, or at least deceiving; and she cannot resist a little higher criticism at the expense of gods who are supposed to like human sacrifices. But those Voltairean touches are not enough to injure what remains, though not a great play, a very pleasing one."

In eighteenth-century France much use was made of the dramatic elements of *Iphigeneia in*

Tauris, one instance being a version by Claude Guymon de la Touche (1757), which had frequent performances at the Comédie Française, benefiting from the period's vogue for tragedies on ancient subjects. In 1779 Germany's supreme poet, Johann Wolfgang von Goethe (1749–1832), chose to explore the story's depths in a prose drama bearing the same title. Later, after his lengthy sojourn in Italy, he transformed his work into a verse play of considerable profundity, treating seriously the moral issues confronting the characters (1787), an aspect slighted by Euripides.

Euripides' play has also inspired a string of operatic interpretations, among them *Ifigenia in Tauride* (1768) by Baldassare Galuppi (1706–85), which had its première in St Petersburg, where the composer was on leave from his post as *maestro di cappella* at St Mark's in Venice. He had been invited by Catherine the Great to mount a number of Italian works, including his own. Galuppi, a pupil of Lotti, was highly regarded for his light, satiric pieces, several of them set to librettos by Carlo Goldoni. Modern critics find his music rather thin, over-laden with prolonged recitatives.

Another *Ifigenia in Tauride* (1763) by an Italian, Tommaso Traetta (1727–79), bowed in Vienna. Widely travelled, the composer had studied in Naples and laboured at the Bourbon court in Parma, before moving on to Mannheim, Vienna, St Petersburg and London. He was much influenced by Rameau and even more definitely by Gluck, who personally conducted Traetta's *Ifigenia* in Florence (1767). This score is still praised.

A musical adaptation of the play was turned out by Gian Francesco Majo (1732–70) and had its first performance at Mannheim (1764). Majo added to his list of operas based on Greek dramas one that he extracted from Sophocles' *Antigone*, variously titled by the composer *Antigono* (Venice, 1767), *Antigona* (Rome, 1768) and later for English and French audiences *Antigone*. He impressed the young Mozart, who may have borrowed several of Majo's technical devices, especially his flexibility in handling ensembles and choruses.

The attraction of Greek material, and especially of Euripides' *Iphigeneia in Taurus*, is curiously illustrated by a competition in France between the great innovator Christoph Willibald Gluck (1714–87) and one of his leading rivals, Niccolo Piccini (1728–1800), each of whom brought out, a mere two years apart, a work exploiting the same story. Both composers had large and contentious clusters of admirers, including persons of high intellectual and social stature, the opposed groups loudly proclaiming their favourite to be the superior musician. Gluck was of German stock, though born in Bohemia, and Piccini was from Naples, but the setting of their contest was Paris. The two were friends, despite the noisy argument, and Gluck had not sought the open clash. An English musicologist and observer, Dr Charles Burney, declared Piccini to be "among the most fertile, spirited and original of composers . . . having a vigour, variety, and especially a new grace, a brilliant and animated style". The director of the opera house gave Gluck a straightforward adaptation of Euripides' drama, to which he adhered rather closely. Piccini took numerous liberties with Euripides' plot. The contemporary and historical verdicts are that Gluck won hands down, his entry recognized as a lasting masterpiece. The first staging of Piccini's belated work was considerably handicapped, too, by the unfortunate circumstance that the prima donna was obviously tipsy, which prompted the witty lady herself, Sophie Arnould, to remark: "This is not *Iphigénie en Tauride*. It is *Iphigénie en Champagne*."

To this decade in Euripides' career belongs his *Andromeda* (412 BC), lost and known only by a few fragments: they are lines of impressive beauty. A fantasy, it is about a heroine who is chained to a bluff over the sparkling blue ocean, from the depths of which a sea-monster will rise to claim her, except that most opportunely Perseus comes hurtling from the sky to rescue her. A love story, it won great popularity, and it is told that young men fervently quoted phrases from it for centuries afterwards. Famed speeches from it began, "O Love, high monarch over gods and men . . ." and "O holy Night, how long is the path of thy chariot!"

In the same year (412 BC), *Helen* has Euripides venturing further in the romantic, tragicomic vein he had worked in *Ion* and *Iphigeneia in Tauris*. The premise of the play much resembles that of *Iphigeneia*: Helen was not in Troy at all, but in Egypt the whole time. The Trojan Helen was only a "breathing phantom", whereas the real Helen had been carried off by Hermes. All this was the doing of the ever-interfering Hera, to circumvent Aphrodite. This variant of the legend was not of Euripides' making but dates back to a poem by one Stesichorus (*c.* 610–550 BC), who was supposedly blinded by an angry Helen, now a goddess, for having accused her of infidelity; he recanted by writing another poem exculpating her, whereupon his sight was restored along with Helen's reputation. (It should be kept in mind that Helen, sister of Clytemnestra, was the offspring of Leda and Zeus, hence had an inherent claim to divinity; she was worshipped in Sparta and elsewhere.)

According to Euripides, her behaviour in Egypt has been exemplary; she has guarded her virtue, hopefully waiting for Menelaus to find and reclaim her. The idea probably appealed to the poet because it suggested – ironically – that the Trojan War had been for nothing, only to recover a wraith. The gods had willed the long struggle merely to reduce the population, which was growing too fast. Euripides adds a villainous Egyptian pharaoh, Theokylmenus, who wishes to marry the irresistible Helen, though she steadfastly rejects him. Theokylmenus, the son of Proteus, orders the killing of all Greeks who land on his coast. After Troy's fall, Menelaus and the phantom Helen sail for home but are shipwrecked on the Egyptian shore. To avoid the wicked pharaoh, the real Helen has taken sanctuary in his father's tomb, dwelling there near the palace gates. Enter Menelaus in wet, ragged clothes – he has hidden the phantom Helen in a cave, while he looks about. Though seventeen years have passed since they last met, he encounters and recognizes his lost wife almost at once: her beauty is as ripe as ever. She also knows him as readily. The "recognition scene" has its comic as well as its serious facets; for a time Menelaus fears that he has *two* wives and is puzzled by it. The play is in this mixed mood throughout, which has baffled many critics of it, who describe it as "entertaining but elusive", asserting that it is to be enjoyed rather than analysed.

Having also survived the shipwreck, one of Menelaus' soldiers appears, bringing word that the other Helen has vanished from the cave, strangely dissolving into upborne vapour. Ah, those conniving gods!

The distressed couple vow to commit suicide together if they cannot get away. To make their escape they win the silence of Theonoe, a priestess, the pharaoh's clairvoyant sister, a saintly character. Outsmarting Theokylmenus, much as Iphigeneia had Thoas, Helen begs and obtains a ship from him, explaining that Menelaus has drowned and she is bound to enact a ritual at sea in his memory, after which she will at last marry the Egyptian. The Greek pair sail off, while the unwary Theokylmenus joyfully prepares to wed Helen when she returns, which of course she never will. Wrathful at having lost her, he threatens to kill his guilty sister and sets off in pursuit of the wily fugitives, but is halted in both attempts by Castor and Polydeuces, "the starry twins", in another epiphany – this pair, bright sky-dwellers, are Helen's dead brothers, transformed into minor immortals.

Only a year before the play was staged at the Festival, imperialistic Athenian forces in Sicily had met a disastrous setback, and now the allies of Sparta were gathering, assembling a large fleet with Persian assistance, to prepare further resistance and counter-attack. Euripides, offering a work in which the Trojan War was depicted as pointless, serving an illusion, may well have been making a comment on Athens's policy and situation, an anti-militaristic statement, a plea for peace.

To be noted, too, is that once more he puts forth a play in which the women, Helen and Theonoe, are more intelligent and resourceful than the men. Theonoe, besides, is morally superior to them all.

Here the Greeks do not conduct themselves well; they lie and cheat; and, while escaping, they needlessly slaughter the Egyptian sailors, with even Helen encouraging the carnage.

As he liked to do, Euripides gives his story a colourful foreign setting, opportunities for pageantry and exotic spectacle. But as one has come to expect, he is digressively preachy at moments, decrying the frenzied pursuit of riches, placing a high value on the search for "justice". The lines contain many slaps at oracles; why had Calchas, the seer, not revealed that the true Helen was never in Troy? The gods are again denounced as petty and spiteful. The slaves excel their masters in virtue and intelligence. Menelaus and Helen have scant dimension, save when Helen piteously complains at being everywhere reviled and blamed for having caused the war, though she is quite innocent. Everything is phantasmal, based on rumour or a false account of events – a Pirandellian touch.

The work is playful, a compound of the comic, the earnest and the ironic. It is hard to discern in what spirit Euripides wrote it. Certainly he is deadly serious in this passage (translated by Richard Lattimore):

> Mindless, all of you, who in the strength of spears
> and the tearing edge win your valors
> by war, thus stupidly trying
> to halt the grief of the world.
> For if bloody debate shall settle
> the issue, never again
> shall hate be gone out of the cities of men.
> By hate they won the chambers of Priam's city;
> they could have solved by reason and words
> the quarrel, Helen, for you.
> Now these are given to the Death God below.
> On the walls the flame, as of Zeus, lightened and fell.
> And you, Helen, on your sorrow bear
> more hardships still, and more matter for grieving.

A.W. Verrall aptly compares *Helen* to *A Midsummer Night's Dream* or something topsy-turvy by Gilbert and Sullivan, and hints that Euripides was in fact making fun of his own work, by stressing humorous parallels in the plot and action to his *Andromache, Hippolytus* and *Iphigeneia in Tauris*, his reliance on a formula. Verrall argues further that *Helen* was probably not written for public performance but for private recitation – and that it was also intended, in imitation of Stresichorus, as a recantation: by making Helen so insipidly good the dramatist was paying a tentative tribute to womankind, whom he had often been accused of libelling by offering characters like the murderous Medea and obsessed Electra. It was Euripides' own kind of apology, wry, sly and delicate.

Another critic, Gilbert Norwood, has called the piece Shavian because of its oft-shifting tone, but the witty Irishman from Dublin was scarcely capable of the exquisite poetry that adorns this light work, which not only contributes to establishing tragicomedy as a legitimate genre, but also prefigures what before long is to be known as New Comedy.

The play soon evoked a burlesque take-off by Aristophanes, *Thesmophoriazusae*, put on a year after *Helen*'s staging at the Great Dionysia.

Euripides' good humour, if it was that, soon vanished. His next offering, *The Phoenician Women* (410/409 BC), is the longest of extant Greek tragedies; it reverts to the story of Thebes besieged by Oedipus' son, Polyneices, and his foreign allies, determined to dethrone his brother, Eteocles, a situation used by Aeschylus in *Seven Against Thebes* and as background by Sophocles in *Antigone*. Crammed with incidents – overstuffed, some commentators say – *The Phoenician Women* has eleven principal characters and gives the impression of being three or more plays in one, so crowded is it with plots and sub-plots: added to this, much of it is harrowing. Oddly, Euripides presents both Oedipus, blind and a prisoner, and his wife Jocasta as still alive and in Thebes when the dynastic struggle erupts between their angry sons. Creon and Antigone have roles, too, and at the play's end she is vowing to defy her uncle and bury the corpse of Polyneices after the battle. During a truce Jocasta tries to reconcile her sons, but to no avail, though the meeting is marked by an eloquent passage in which the over-ambitious Eteocles spells out his compulsive desire to rule others:

> I, were it in my power, would break my way
> Far as earth's verge, where rise the suns and stars,
> Or deep beneath it, could I only win
> That greatest of all gods, high Sovereignty. . . .
> Therefore come sword, come fire!
> Harness my chargers, with chariots fill the plains!
> Never will I resign my royal throne!
> For if man *must* do wrong, then it were best
> Do wrong for Sovereignty.
> [Translation: F.L. Lucas]

Legend has it that Julius Caesar often cited these lines.

Jocasta kills herself over the bodies of her mutually slain sons in "a meadow of wild lotus" where the two young men have fallen outside one of the city's seven gates.

Creon's younger son, Menoeceus, a mere stripling, is sacrificed – a willing suicide – to ensure the triumph of Thebes over its besiegers, in fulfilment of a prophecy by an irate Tiresias. Euripides' fondness for having children go nobly to their death to serve a cause, a sure device for conjuring tears from spectators, is on display yet again.

As soon as word comes of the mutual killing of Polyneices and Eteocles, Creon, who has been Eteocles' mentor, moves with craft to secure the succession for himself. He banishes Oedipus, asserting falsely that Tiresias' prophecy has decreed that he should do so. Stricken by his many losses, the bereaved, blind Oedipus and his loyal daughter are expelled, beginning their arduous journey by wandering off to the sacred heights of Mount Kithairon, "where only the Wild White Women of Dionysus dance their mystic dances", far from human crime and bestiality. The drama closes without the usual epiphany.

Euripides motivates Antigone's zeal to bury Polyneices more firmly than does Sophocles. Her brother is almost a stranger to her, but when from a palace window she first glimpses the young man in his splendid armour her fancy is captured by him. Later, his dying plea is that he be ceremoniously interred in his native ground. Eteocles has asked Creon to forbid that honour to a traitor.

An outstanding scene is the debate between Polyneices and Eteocles in the presence of Jocasta, and an eloquent passage is Euripides' description of the animal designs emblazoned on the great shields of the seven legendary champions who defend the city's gates.

The play is about a curse and blood feud reinvented from generation to generation, much like the endless wars on which Athens itself was embarked. In recounting the grim history of the House of Laius, as the chorus does, and as it is enacted by the current participants, a catalogue of human transgressions unfolds, incest, rape, patricide, fratricide, envy, deceit.

The work was part of a trilogy, which – with a satyr play added – must have imposed on the spectators at the Festival a very long session. Euripides was awarded the second prize for it. The titles and subjects of the other offerings in the group are believed known, though not for certain, and all abound with deeds of excessive violence. Most scholars agree that the text of this play has been tampered with by actors in later times, with extra lines or scenes awkwardly interpolated, though the changes are probably minor ones.

For a long period, up to and through the Byzantine epoch, *The Phoenician Women* was highly regarded and popular. Many of the epigrammatic lines were widely familiar and quoted, especially in Rome.

Martin Mueller, in his esoteric *Children of Oedipus*, traces the play's further career.

A funeral ceremony for a dead hunter in Kankalaba, Burkina Faso, in which an antelope and a warthog are ritually hunted. This ritual is traditionally accompanied by music.

Dancers with feather ornaments in Bamako, Mali.

A Greek vase depicting actors dressed as birds dancing to the accompaniment of a flute player; 510–490 BC.

Painting from the inside of a Greek bowl showing Maenad with snakes in her hair, *thyrsus* staff and leopard in her hands; *c.* 490 BC.

A wine *krater* depicting a Dionysian scene; fourth century BC.

The character of Dionysus, played by Greg Hicks, in *The Bacchae* at Epidaurus. This production, originally presented at the National Theatre in London, was directed by Sir Peter Hall and designed by Alison Chitty, 2002.

The Theatre of Dionysus in Athens. Performances in honour of Dionysus originally took place on another site, but in 498 BC they moved to this location at the foot of the Acropolis. The remains that can be seen today are mostly from the Hellenistic period.

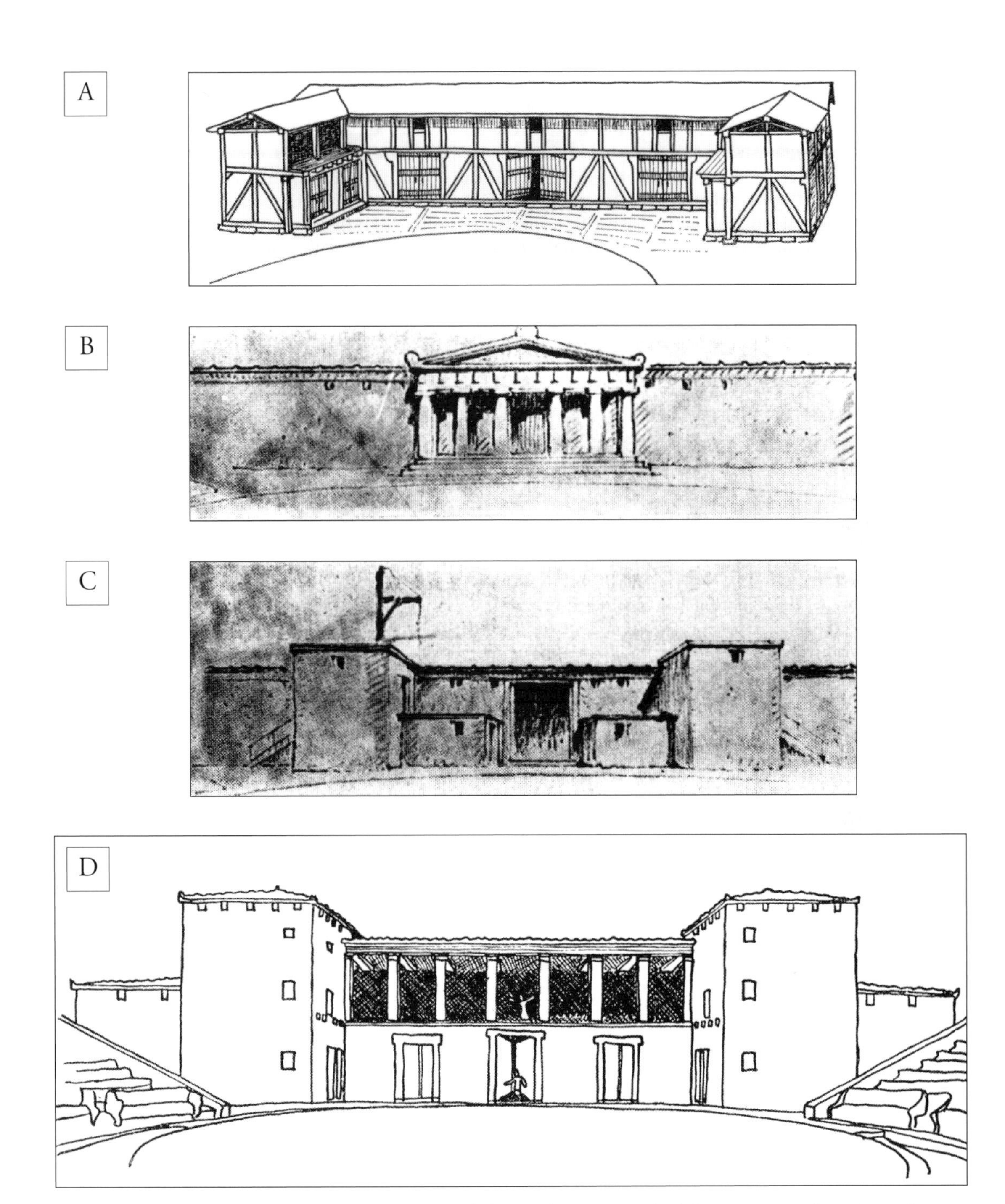

Reconstructions of the *skene* from some of the earliest periods. The top two drawings show theatres from the fifth century BC (A and B), with A depicting the Theatre of Eretria, Euboea, and the others the Theatre of Dionysus, Athens; D shows speculative later development of the previous constructions of the Theatre of Dionysus.

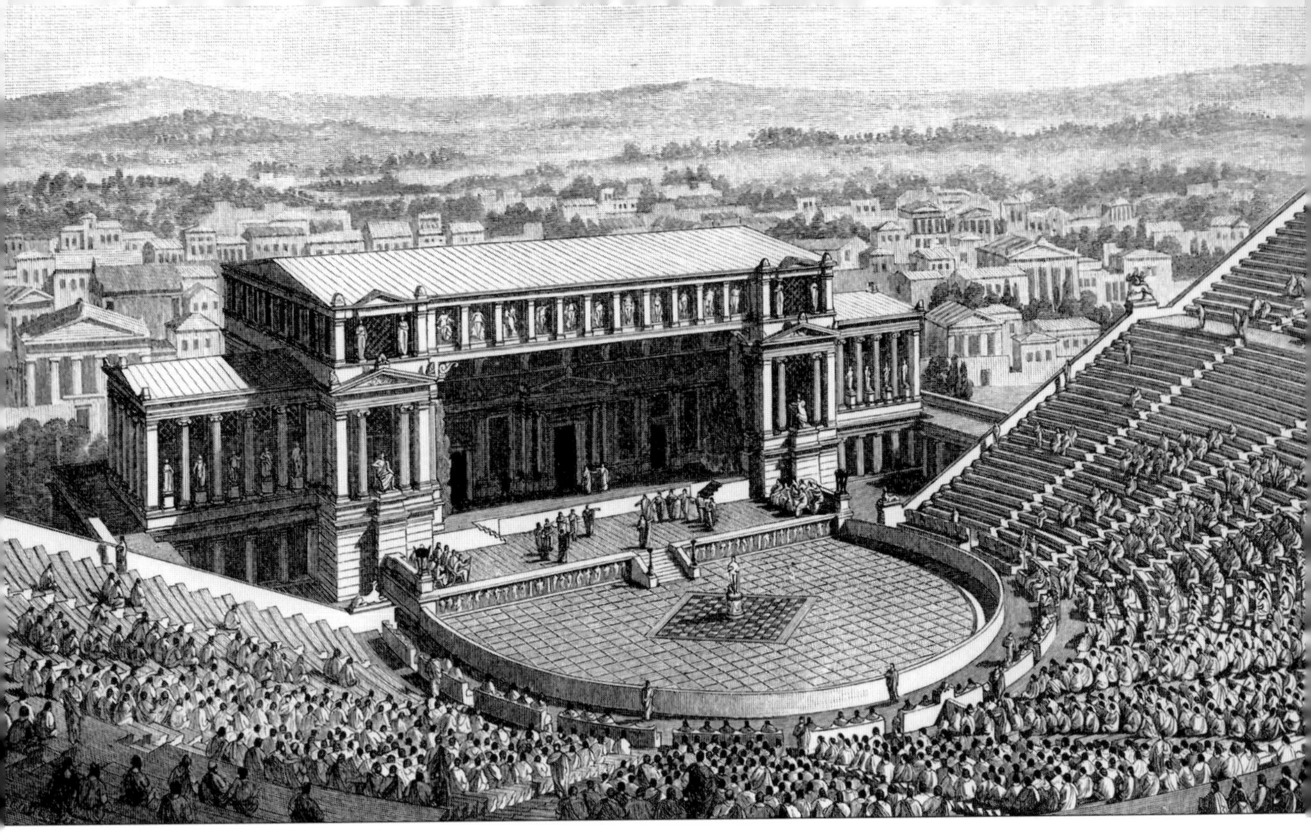

A nineteenth-century reconstruction of the Theatre of Dionysus, Athens; woodcut by G. Rehlender, *c.* 1895.

The Theatre of Epidaurus. This was built at the end of the fourth century BC when Epidaurus was an important place of healing, with a temple dedicated to Asclepius.

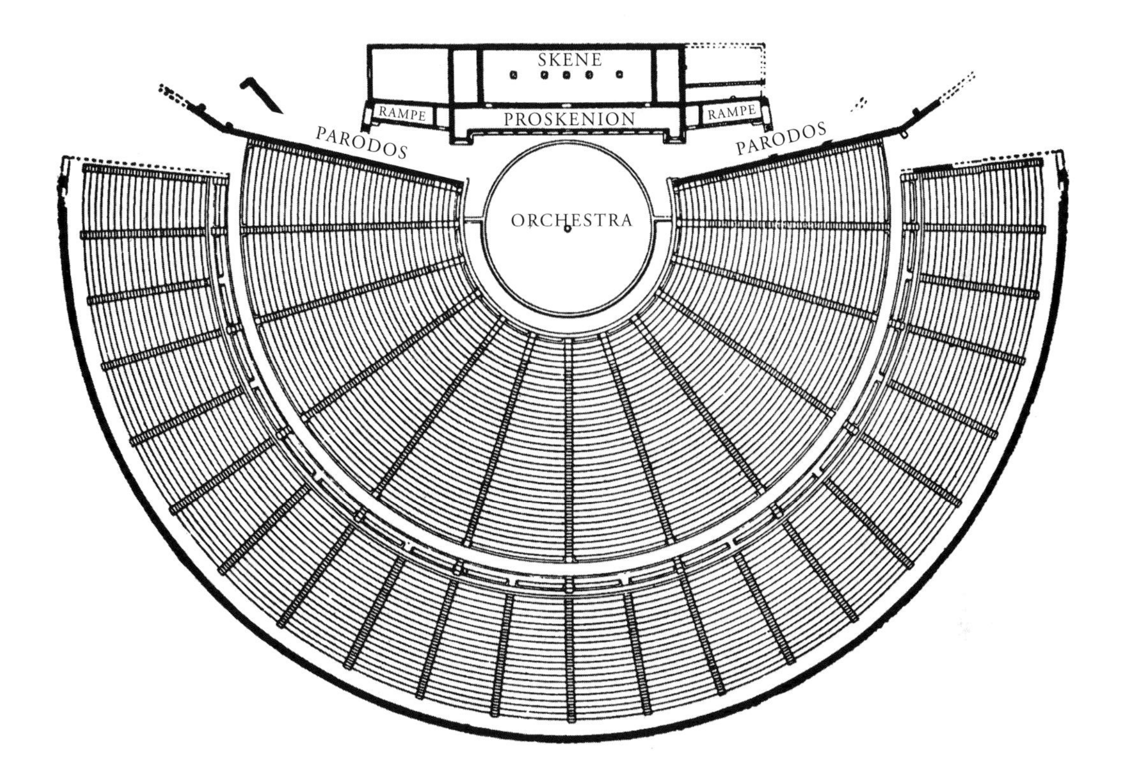

Plan of Epidaurus. The theatre could seat around fourteen thousand people; it had a raised stage reached by ramps and a circular orchestra.

The curtain call for the opera *Medea* by Cherubini, starring Maria Callas, performed at Epidaurus, 1961.

The theatre at Delphi, built in 160 BC, which could seat five thousand people.

The theatre at Petra, Jordan, built in the first century BC by the Nabateans and later extended by the Romans; it could seat eight thousand people.

The Roman theatre at Orange, France, built in the first century BC.

The Roman theatre at Palmyra, Syria, built in the second century AD.

A small Greek terracotta figurine depicting an actor with a tambourine and mask; *c.* 370–350 BC.

Tragic mask, Greece; fourth to fifth century BC.

Terracotta mask with grizzled beard and wreath around the head; 300–275 BC.

Hellenistic mask showing a young man from New Comedy;
first century BC to first century AD.

Roman mask, with staring eyes and gaping mouth, dating from the later Hellenistic and Roman period; first to second century AD.

Hellenistic mask of a young woman from New Comedy;
first century BC to first century AD.

Terracotta figure from Myrina, Lemnos, showing a *pornoboskos* or pimp. He is a New Comedy character with a distinctive corkscrew beard and elaborate headgear. His head is heavily garlanded with a floral wreath worn over fruit and ivy leaves which cascade down over his shoulder; second century BC.

An Etruscan figure from Canino, Italy, showing an actor wearing the mask of a flatterer; second century BC.

A miscreant slave on the altar was one of the stock situations of New Comedy. Note the actor's mouth visible through the mask; first to second century BC.

Facing page: Two Greek statuettes from Myrina showing strolling actors with comedy masks; first century BC.

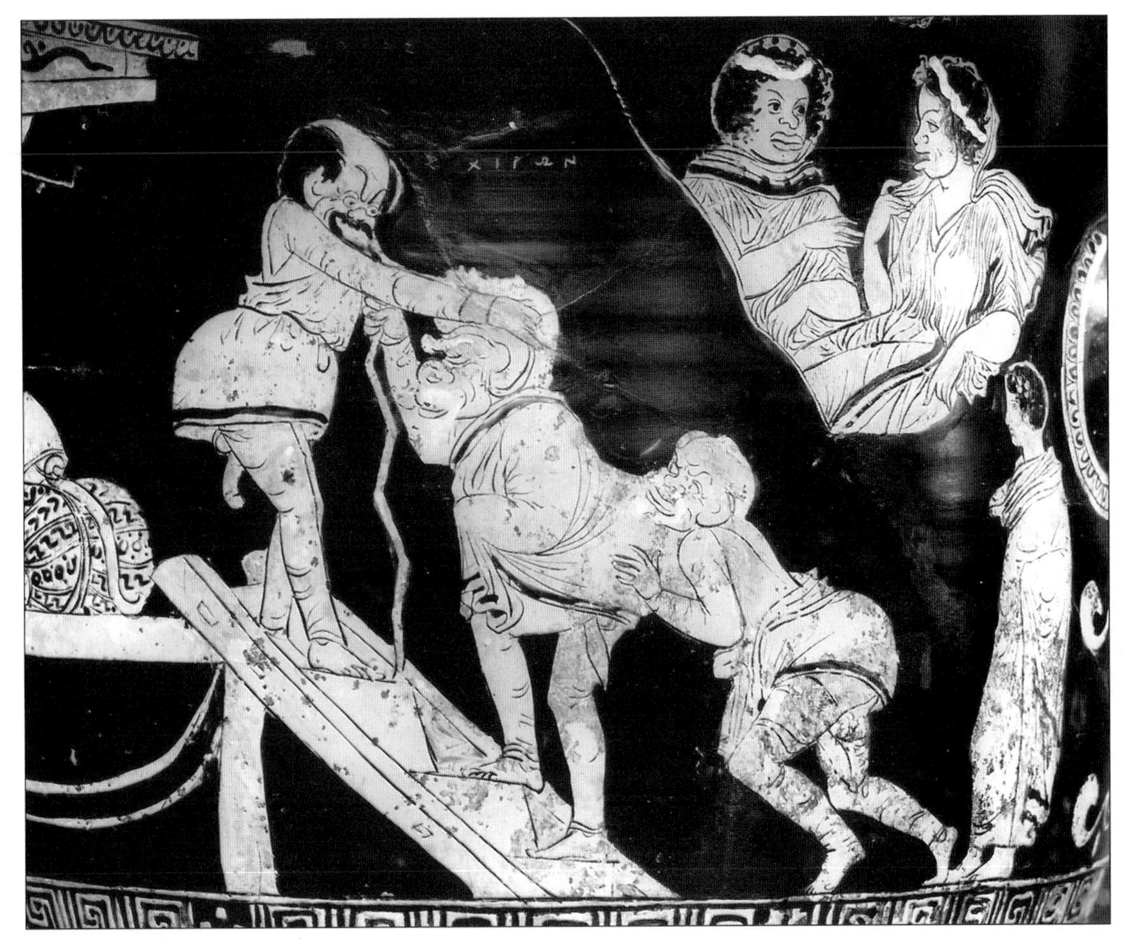

Terracotta wine *krater* depicting a parody of the story of Cheiron and the Centaur. Achilles is on the right and two elderly nymphs are at the top. The stage represents a sanctuary, and two actors masked as servants are pushing Cheiron towards it; *c.* 380 BC.

Terracotta wine *krater* from Apulia, southern Italy, depicting a scene from a phylax play. Armed phylax actors fight a duel in front of Hera, who sits on her throne. The warriors are Daidalos and Enyalios; *c.* 350 BC.

Roman mosaic from Pompeii, showing seven actors behind the stage. It is thought to represent a satyr chorus rehearsing; first century AD.

Roman wall painting from Pompeii depicting a theatre scene; first century AD.

Roman mosaic from the Villa of Cicero at Pompeii showing street musicians; first century AD.

Roman wall painting from Herculaneum of a theatre scene. This is a first century AD copy from a fourth century BC Greek original.

Roman mosaic showing a writer of tragedy and an actor of comedy; third century AD.

Aeschylus (525–456 BC); this sculpture is a Roman copy of a Greek original.

Euripides (484–407 BC); stone relief from Smyrna depicting Euripides with a mask of Heracles between the *skene* and Dionysus; first century AD.

Sophocles (496–406 BC); this sculpture is a Roman copy of a Greek original.

Aristophanes (*c.* 448–380 BC); this sculpture is a Roman copy of a Greek original.

> Since the nineteenth century, critics have generally despised *The Phoenician Women* because its indiscriminate piling up of horrors appears to them a first sign of the decline of Attic tragedy into melodrama and sensationalist rhetoric that characterizes the history of the genre in later antiquity. Sixteenth-century critics, however, thought very differently. Far from despising the work for its loose structure and crudely quantitative conception of tragic suffering, they admired it for precisely the same reasons that later brought it into disrepute. "It is highly tragic and full of vehement passions," Stiblinus commented in a preface to it, and Hugo Grotius, in his translation of the play, singled it out as "the masterpiece of Euripides, and indeed of Greek tragedy as a whole".

In Neoclassical France, in the seventeenth century, *The Phoenician Women* provided crucial plot-suggestions and characters to thriving playwrights, in particular to Jean Routou, whose *Antigone* – previously mentioned – borrows incidents from it, as well as from Sophocles' play. On the other hand, in the early eighteenth century a preface by a Jesuit priest, P. Brumoy, to his anthology *Le Théâtre des Grecs* (1730), deplores the lack of unity as well as the profusion of sub-plots in Euripides' script, which – as someone has said – seems to be held together by agglutination. Aristotle's precepts were now being viewed by the scholarly as mandatory, absolutes, the only acceptable guidelines.

Mueller shows how, in the early nineteenth century, Friedrich Schiller combined elements of *Oedipus* and *The Phoenician Women* in his *Die Braut von Messina* (*The Bride of Messina*, Weimar, 1803), which deals with fratricide in a different setting – Sicily – and later time. Schiller sought to restore and modernize Greek tragedy. He was particularly attracted by the classic form of *Oedipus*. His rhymed verse-drama, which has a chorus, tells of the Duke of Messina who fathers a girl. He is warned in a dream, interpreted by an Arab, that she will bring ruin to his two sons; accordingly, he orders her killed. His wife intervenes and has the child secluded in a convent; there she grows up unaware of her noble origin. Allowed to attend the Duke's funeral, she sees one of his sons, Don Caesar, and falls in love with him. Enmity between the two brothers has already involved Messina in civil war. Like Jocasta, their widowed mother Isabella seeks a reconciliation. For a time this is accomplished, for both young men have sickened of the struggle. On a hunt, Don Manuel comes across a beautiful young woman, Beatrice, still sheltered in the convent. Fearing she is in danger, he rashly abducts her; he has no intimation of her true identity. Don Caesar returns from a mysterious errand, beholds Beatrice and is smitten by her charm; he soon claims her for his bride (hence the play's title). Neither brother has grasped that she is their sister. This sets the stage for the fratricide that ensues, after hints are given, and suspicions grow, provoking many reversals of hope and despair. Don Caesar fatally stabs his brother, then in expiation kills himself, fulfilling the curse that has long hung over the family. The tragedy, with its additional suggestions of incest, contains almost as many horrors as the Sophoclean and Euripidean scripts from which it candidly derives, though in many aspects it is quite reductive.

Later critics of *The Phoenician Women* have dissented greatly in ranking it. Gilbert Murray took it as "a large experiment", and H.D.F. Kitto hailed it as "a dramatic pageant", having a different intention from the conventional Greek tragedy, and in those terms achieving its end very artfully. F.L. Lucas is exasperated by it, describing it as the work "of a tired and depressed old man, stumbling on mechanically. . . . Incorporating too much, it bursts. . . . Episode tumbles over episode, in alternations of pathos and bathos. . . . Some will feel at the end of it as if they never wished to hear of Thebes again. Swinburne grew childishly ribald at the expense of poor Mrs Browning and her 'Euripides the human, with his *droppings* of warm tears'. Certainly 'droppings' seems an understatement. But such rivers of them as flow here yield nothing electrifying. One sickens of being as systematically harrowed as if one were a field."

John Ferguson assays it somewhat as did Kitto: "The play has obvious theatrical merits, as the Byzantine commentators well knew. It is, apart from anything else, a magnificent pageant of Theban mythology, spectacular and rich in characters, though it is surely a counsel of despair to see this as its prime purpose and main merit. Besides this, it contains powerful epigrammatic rhetoric." Ferguson suspects that one of the Theban brothers resembles the playwright himself. "Something of Euripides' self shines through Polyneices, a patriot even in his disaffection; the poet went abroad with his eyes open, knowing that a stranger in a foreign court must learn to keep his mouth shut and suffer fools with apparent gladness (a line which cost Mamercus Scaurus his life to quote under Tiberius), and he put these into the picture of the exile." And: "Polyneices speaks calmly. His position is paradoxical; he comes in wisdom and unwisdom and it echoes his father's paradox, who 'sees darkness'." Of the ending, Ferguson writes,

> Here is no *deus ex machina* to bring the thing to a spuriously happy conclusion. The contrast with *Orestes*, whether or not that play belongs to the same sequence, is marked and obvious. For we have seen spurious religion decreeing crime; we have seen a curse indeed, but that curse renewed from generation to generation by a free choice; we have seen the curse finding its outlet in fratricidal war, such as was still raging in the Greek world; we have seen the spirit of violence turning men into beasts, wisdom degenerating into cleverness, light that brightens yet consumes as fire, and all the ambiguity of our human condition; and at the last we see Antigone poised at a choice between escorting her father

> to his place of rest, and acts (like the threatened murder of Haemon) which, springing from a warm and sympathetic nature and a hatred of injustice, nonetheless renew the cycle of violence. . . . It was this choice Euripides laid before his people.

In many ways *Orestes* (408 BC) is a sequel to *Electra*. The action occurs six days after the slaying of Clytemnestra. He is ill, fevered, at times delirious, and being watched over by his sister with perverted affection. He might be described as deranged, aghast at the crime against his mother. He is in rags, unwashed, foaming at the mouth. Electra herself is unnerved. The populace of Argos has imprisoned the pair in the royal palace to await a trial by the Assembly. The penalty is likely to be stoning to death.

Menelaus, their uncle, has entered the city and is their only hope, though their expectations are unrealistic. He is a cowardly opportunist plotting to succeed to the throne, now that his nephew and niece have murdered the queen and her foreign consort. It does not deter him that the citizens are hostile to him, with justification blaming him for the Trojan War. He is accompanied by Helen, who is again depicted – as in *Hecuba* – as heartless and shallow, a fit mate to her primping, petulant husband. She has been smuggled in at night, concealed by darkness, lest the Argives see her; they blame her for the loss of their husbands and sons. The couple's young daughter, Hermione, is with them.

Menelaus pleads logically enough that he cannot rescue the prisoners, his kinfolk: an outsider, he dare not interfere in Argos; besides, he has not brought enough spearmen. Orestes upbraids his uncle fiercely, bringing their hidden enmity into the open. Yet another fiery scene ensues between Orestes and his grandfather, Tyndareus – father of Clytemnestra – who advocates the rule of law and insists with bitter reproaches that the young man should not have resorted to murder to avenge Agamemnon.

Pylades, faithful companion of Orestes, breaks into the palace and declares that he shares the prisoners' guilt, having abetted the crime. The two young men are about eighteen or nineteen; their excessive friendship is romantic. At the Assembly the condemned argue their case unsuccessfully; the sentence is death. They are granted a single day in which to take their own lives, if they so elect.

Electra begs Orestes to kill her. He refuses; he feels bloodstained enough. Yet shortly, Pylades – who controls the mad Orestes – concocts a wild scheme to slay Helen as a reprisal against Menelaus, though perhaps they might be doing him a favour. Electra has an even more fiendish idea: they will kidnap Hermione, the cousin whom she hates, and hold her hostage, a knife at her throat, to bargain for their freedom.

The crazy, melodramatic plan is carried out. Helen eludes them, with divine help, but the innocent Hermione is seized; Menelaus and his men, rushing to the palace, find it impenetrable. Orestes is on the roof, shrieking insanely, hurling insults, threatening to slash Hermione's veins. Menelaus seeks to make terms with his nephew, but finally is so overcome by anger that he orders an assault on the formidable palace, to which Orestes and his unstable companions set fire.

At this blazing moment Apollo appears over the fiery rooftop and halts the imbroglio; he has already rescued Helen, when her Phrygian guard was scattered, and has transformed her, actually the daughter of Zeus, into a minor deity, "Queen of the eternal sea", the goddess of sailors in distress. Setting other matters to rights, he decrees that Orestes – restored to his senses – shall marry Hermione, while Electra is to be given in marriage to Pylades. The strange story ends happily, if at first glance somewhat incongruously.

Here Euripides has boldly updated the legend, so that it exemplifies the moral values and customs not of antiquity, Homer's epoch and later, but of his own day. He treats the by now familiar tale as though it were, for him and his audience, a contemporary event and seeks to make every turn in the plot, except for the ending, quite plausible. Orestes barely excuses himself with the plea that he was acting as Apollo bade him. Instead, his behaviour simply matches his irrationality. Euripides has modernized the drama's psychology. Orestes' madness largely accounts for his actions as well as the folly of those around him – his insanity is communicated to them – and the playwright's fascination with and insight into abnormal states of mind have never been better manifested. (True, the Furies are responsible for his derangement, but are they not a perfect symbol for whatever pathological disturbance has caused a human mind to go wildly astray?) Gilbert Murray was convinced that the astonishing theophany that closes the drama is best understood as Orestes' self-induced vision and then his emergence from a hypnotic trance possibly associated with his anguished and turbulent mental disorder. He awakes from it, with Hermione in his arms, as might a partially rigid sleepwalker from a horrible dream. Menelaus, too, has been mesmerized by the "god". Seen thus, the ending is surprisingly logical.

In one scene Orestes mistakes Helen for the ghost of his mother, a natural error since Clytemnestra and Helen were sisters, and both were famed for their beauty. Orestes' futile defence of his pursuit of a vendetta, his attempt to justify his deed of matricide and its repudiation by Tyndareus give the play a social dimension. Euripides, like Aeschylus, preaches against the perpetuation of feuds, in which people ignoring the Athenian courts take the law into their own hands, one act of violence only inviting a reprisal, and so on endlessly.

Orestes has been faulted as "uneven", but two foremost classical scholars have emphatic praise for it. To A.W. Verrall it is "one of the triumphs of the stage, and may still be described as supreme of its kind. A tragedy in the strict sense it hardly is or could be. But for excitement, for play of emotion, for progression and climax of horror, achieved by natural means and without strain upon the realities of life, it has few rivals in the repertory of the world. The chief instrument of effect is the fury, the insanity, of despair. Villains of some sort, and fools of the worst sort, the assassins of Clytemnestra must be. But for this very reason they are hideously dangerous to themselves and to others, moral explosives of enormous force and instability." He terms *Orestes* not a tragedy but "a highly spiritual sort of melodrama".

H.D.F. Kitto observes: "The *Orestes* is an outstanding illustration of the freedom and strength of the Greek genius. Almost at one bound we have passed from a drama which is at least called statuesque to drama whose imaginative tumult rivals anything on the romantic stage; yet this is done with the minimum of interference with the traditional forms and with a firmness of control hardly surpassed by Sophocles himself.

"The play contains topical allusions and Shavian touches, having moments of humor and fantasy. There is a verbal swipe at Cleophon, an Athenian demagogue. Orestes and Pylades are portraits – caricatures might be a better word – of youthful members of the upper class who had leftist political inclinations at that time, favoring democracy providing the movement had acceptable leaders. When *Orestes* was staged, the return of the imperialist Alcibiades was believed imminent." Euripides held him and his war-minded party in the lowest regard. "He had betrayed his country once. A play suggesting a young man who had committed one crime will commit others of the same sort may well appear a warning." Ferguson continues: "There is rejection alike of Left-wing demagogy and Right-wing conspiracy. But above all there is explicit reference to an implicit concern with the war."

With its spectacular climax and its at times penetrating study of wild, uncontrolled young radicals, *Orestes* was greatly popular for centuries in the ancient world, and it is said that more lines were quoted from it than from all the works of Aeschylus and Sophocles together. Unforgettable is the scene in which the House of Atreus finally vanishes in bright tongues of fire: it reminds modern spectators of Wagner's climax of his *Ring*, the *Götterdämmerung*.

Ferguson's interpretation of the play's resolution differs from Gilbert Murray's:

> The ending is ludicrous – intentionally. Humanly speaking, Helen is dead, and since Menelaus cannot possibly touch the decision of the Assembly, Hermione's throat will be cut, and the palace will go up

> in flames, forming a pyre for the three warped adolescents on the roof. If *Orestes* is really pro-satyric and belongs in the same cycle as *The Phoenician Women*, the juxtaposition of realism and unrealism makes the point still more effectively. As Arrowsmith puts it, "If the experience of the play is a real one, what remains after Apollo leaves is not the taste of a happy ending, but the image of total disaster: the burning palace, the dead girl, the screaming mob, and degenerate heirs dying in the arson of their own hatred." The logic of violence is such that not even a god can halt it.

Quoting further from William Arrowsmith:

> The political climate of the play itself graphically represents the state of affairs in Athens, and presumptuous or not, I am tempted to see in the play Euripides' prophetic image of the final destruction of Athens and Hellas, or that Hellas to which a civilized man could still give his full commitment. It is a simple and common symbolism: the great old house, cursed by a long history of fratricidal blood and war, brought down in destruction by its degenerate heirs. The final tableau is the direct prophecy of disaster, complete, awful, and inevitable, while Apollo intervenes only as an impossible wish, a futile hope, or a simple change of scene from a vision that cannot be brooked, or seen for long because it is the direct vision of despair, the hopeless future.

As usual, Euripides – through Orestes – condemns Apollo for having ordered the fearful crime. Also, it need hardly be said, the play is a fountain of beautiful poetry.

Euripides, by now in his late seventies, was more than ever in disfavour in Athens. His long series of plays attacking the war, his relentless defamation of the mythical and legendary heroes of Hellas, his overt religious heresy, made him ever more offensive to the ruling conservatives. He was their natural target, along with other prominent members of the city's cognoscenti. Athens was smarting from military defeats; the people and their leaders were seeking to fix the blame: had not these critics of the city's imperialistic policies weakened its resolve to fight? As described earlier, he was brought up on charges, among them an accusation of financial fraud, but acquitted. At the trial certain lines from *Hippolytus* were read aloud to prove that he advocated lying. Scandalmongers were anxious to blacken his name, belittle him. They spread stories of his personal misfortunes: had not his second wife been unfaithful? He decided to go abroad. Old, weary, disenchanted, he went first (408–407 BC) to Magnesia, in Asia Minor, where he was not unknown, and next to Macedonia at the court of King Archelaus, who welcomed him.

The country was wild, ruggedly mountainous, half-barbaric, yet a better haven, for many other intellectual refugees from Athens had already gathered there, most of them his friends: Timotheus of Ion, the accomplished and inventive musician whose mentor he had been, and whom, supposedly, he had once saved from suicide; a rival playwright, Agathon, another bold innovator; Thucydides, the immortal historian, along with the much acclaimed painter, Zeuxis. In this brilliant company he was in the right climate again.

Meanwhile, in Athens, the libels about him were still loudly voiced. The grave faults of characters in his plays were attributed to him, his enemies asserting that his writings were largely autobiographical, which largely they are not.

In exile, in his twilight years, Euripides began to work again, like an ageing Bernard Shaw, and wrote two more of his extant plays. (A third, *Alcaeon*, is lost.) Of the two surviving, one, *Iphigeneia in Aulis*, he left somewhat unfinished; it is believed that it was completed for production by someone else, perhaps his son Euripides the Younger, also a dramatist and considerably talented. In any event, the son staged it in 406 BC, soon after his father's death.

Again Euripides returns to the Trojan War, to the crucial incident at Aulis where Artemis demands the sacrifice of Iphigeneia, the virgin daughter of Agamemnon and Clytemnestra, as the price of propitious weather, allowing the Greek fleet to set sail against Priam's citadel. All to recover the kidnapped Helen . . . In effect, Euripides turned out a broad cycle of plays fully encompassing the Homeric story, but he did not compose them in sequence or connect them, any more than had Sophocles with his Theban Plays; and even more than Sophocles he reshapes the legend, while portraying the characters inconsistently from drama to drama. Here, for example, Menelaus is less fatuous than in *Helen*, less villainous than in *Orestes*. If the separate works were arranged in the chronological order of the events they depict, the resulting epic would not make complete sense.

It is dawn at Aulis – mention has been made before that the first lines might have been uttered at the Great Dionysia even as the sun rose, dimming the already waning stars. (Two openings of the play are indicated, one a traditional prologue spoken by Agamemnon, to provide the background of the story, the other an initial colloquy between the Argive leader and an old slave – it is not clear which of them Euripides intended to use in his final draft.) Troubled by Calchas' prophecy that he must offer the life of his young daughter, Agamemnon has sent a message to her mother, telling his queen to bring the girl, whom he will give in marriage to Achilles. But second thoughts, doubts, have already overtaken him: consequently he has sent off a second message, rescinding his instructions. Menelaus, suspecting that Agamemnon might waver, is keeping watch on him. He intercepts the old slave, the secret messenger, and snatches the letter from him. When Agamemnon learns of this, a fierce quarrel divides the "brother kings". Each accuses the other of folly and over-ambition, Agamemnon of being untruthful, treacherous, a crafty opportunist yet irresolute; Menelaus of being selfish, cruel, uxorious. They are interrupted by word of the arrival of Clytemnestra, together with her shy, lovely daughter Iphigeneia and her son Orestes, now only a little boy. Agamemnon, indeed a weakling, breaks into tears at the news. Menelaus relents at the sight and urges him to spare his daughter; however, it is now too late. The impatient Greek soldiers, long delayed, have also heard that Clytemnestra and Iphigeneia are in the camp and full-throatedly cry for the sacrifice. The kings, their leaders, feel helpless to oppose the troops' demand.

Achilles discovers the ruse that has been perpetrated on the mother and girl. He is wrathful that his name has been used and vows to save the attractive young Iphigeneia. He considers himself dishonoured by the trick; but in the face of the soldiers' threats to stone him he backs away, lacking followers to resist them. Agamemnon, glory-loving, is also reluctant to yield his headship of the stranded Greek force whose ships are becalmed by Artemis' dictate. As Achilles says:

> Our dignity
> Still rules our lives, and still we serve the mob.
> [Translation: F.M. Stawell]

The two kings also fear the cunning Odysseus, who might swerve the army's loyalty from them.

Clytemnestra, at first delighted at the prospect of her daughter's marriage to the great hero, then appalled, infuriated at the deception practised on her, assails Agamemnon, pleading passionately, frantically with him, pitting her strong will against his, but wholly in vain. She is majestic and tragic in a futile defence of her child.

Iphigeneia, overwhelmed by affection for her father, happy to be with him and to wed the mighty Achilles, is next frightened and horrified at her imminent fate – she begs for her life. Suddenly she is converted to an acceptance of the sacrifice. She cannot permit Achilles' strength to be lost to the Greek cause only for her sake. She, a mere girl, can help her father's soldiers attain a victory. Achilles vows to stand by her side at the sacrificial stone, to lend his moral support if she quails under the knife at the last moment.

Clytemnestra bids goodbye to her beloved child. The chorus, of awestruck women from Chalkis, a nearby town, intone a cry of triumph. Exalted, Iphigeneia goes almost willingly to her death, idealistically bearing the role chosen for her by the gods and her bloodthirsty fellow-countrymen.

In a superimposed ending, possibly added – as has been suggested before – by Euripides' son, Artemis relents and spares the brave, selfless girl, substituting a doe on the altar and magically transporting Iphigeneia to the far land of the Tauri. Clytemnestra, recovering from a fainting spell, refuses to believe in the miracle. It is implied that she is already thinking of vengeance. But most modern commentators feel that Euripides' truncated close, which shows the girl mystically uplifted and acquiescent, is a far stronger climax to this drama, which by turns has episodes that are tender, poignant, exciting, harsh, ironic, and at high moments is infused with an other-worldly spirit.

John Gassner maintains that Euripides was condemning in this play not only the cruelty of war, but also the ugliness of the mob-spirit, whose victim he himself had but recently been in Athens. Martin Mueller takes the same view:

> *Iphigeneia in Aulis* belongs to the group of late Euripidean plays in which the crisis of values experienced in the latter half of the Peloponnesian War is projected into the legendary past. Specifically, the play deals with the disintegration of political leadership and its replacement by mob violence. The ultimate pressure on Agamemnon is neither the will of the gods nor his allegiance to the Greek cause, but the fear of reprisal from a rebellious army. The leader capitulates before the angry zeal of his own troops, their naked barbarism. Talk of the "will of the gods" and "a patriotic cause" are mere pretexts for the desire of these armed men to loot, rape and slaughter. Achilles' own Myrmidons are among the very first to reject his command. He, too, is powerless. Euripides' play draws its energy from its trenchant critique of this lawless world. The most effective scenes may appear to be the private scenes in which the emotions of father, mother, and daughter find a touching expression. But the pathos, especially of the scenes between father and daughter, derives precisely from their being misplaced in the play's primary context, a corrupt political world in which the values of elementary human bonds cannot flourish.

Euripides does not vary his formula. Once more the claims to greatness of the legendary warrior-heroes are caustically scaled down; they are shown as mere careerists, disingenuous schemers. Achilles is self-important, overly concerned with preserving his public image, something of a sham, self-deceived, a poseur. Though he respects Iphigeneia for her courage, pities her and vows to rescue her – which he does not – and grants that she is beautiful, he has no intention of marrying her or anyone else. Too many women desire him, as it is.

Several sides of Agamemnon are revealed: he is not without feelings but stricken with grief at yielding his daughter, who is apparently his favourite. At her arrival, when she greets him joyously, the lines are laden with irony: she innocently misinterprets his every speech; his words are heavy with guilt, hidden by *double entendres.* Simultaneously, he is weak and has even more pity for himself, his dread obligation, his inability to control events. Almost desperately he tries to justify his decision with arguments that sway Iphigeneia, though not Clytemnestra. More than possession of Helen is at stake in the war; the honour and reputation of Hellas and its "culture" must be saved. Also, there is the matter of family pride, his and Menelaus', rulers of Argos and Sparta, the chosen heads of this massive expedition. At all cost, they must prevail. Of his feckless ambition, with which Menelaus charges him, he says little. In sum, he is not a monster but well intentioned, yet behaves monstrously out of inadequacy, his purposes endlessly shifting.

Menelaus, the betrayed husband, is still lusting for his fabulous bedmate; he must redeem his personal honour and also that of Sparta's royal house and is quite without scruple. Of the men in the play, only the old slave is truly virtuous – another recurrent Euripidean motif.

The gods – the inappeasable Artemis, whom Agamemnon had once involuntarily crossed – are as hard-hearted and bloodthirsty as the human beings over whom they callously preside. Calchas, the oracle who calls for the sacrifice of Iphigeneia, "is base, ambitious, like every prophet born. . . . They do no good: they are never any use."

Mueller is illuminating:

> In Euripides' play Iphigeneia makes her decision at a moment when the entire Trojan enterprise threatens to collapse in anarchy. She has only one protector, Achilles, but even he is powerless against the fury of the mob. If she relies on his help for her safety, she will save neither him nor herself, and the Greek cause may be ruined. This situation of imminent chaos is the consequence of the intrigues and machinations that precede it, and it is also the disclosure of their moral reality. In order to understand the open and forthright manner of Iphigeneia's decision, one must recognize how every step that has brought her to her impasse has been beset by falsehood. She was lured to the camp through the false promise of marriage – a contrast between promise and reality which is structurally identical with the contrast between Electra's pretended childbirth and her plan to kill Clytemnestra in the Euripidean *Electra.* In both cases the flagrant abuse of one of the great life-giving occasions of human existence points to the despicable nature of the intrigue. Falsehood is equally present in Agamemnon's futile effort to save Iphigeneia. When his intrigue fails, he refuses to save her openly, but his fear of army reprisals

> is not morally sanctioned by the fact that it is only too well founded. This army and its leaders are responsible for each other's actions and deserve one another. Iphigeneia not only saves the Greek camp from the threat of moral anarchy on this particular occasion; more important, her deed sets an example for future action and demonstrates moral values that have been conspicuously absent. At the same time, the play leaves little hope that the example will in fact be followed. This is the source of the despairing pathos of the play.

A clone of the many other self-sacrificing virgins of both sexes depicted by Euripides, characters always certain to evoke the maximum flow of teardrops, Iphigeneia is yet vital and irresistibly appealing. Her very childishness makes plausible the ease with which she is persuaded that the gift of her life will help to assure the victory of Greece over its Trojan enemies. And, besides, is not the existence of one man worth that of ten thousand women? Her declaration to that effect will startle a spectator today. She is also sure that the Greeks are immeasurably superior to the barbarians whom they are about to overrun and destroy. Euripides doubtless looked on such ideas as nonsense, but they represented a large segment of the popular thinking of Athenians of his time. By putting those idiotic beliefs in the mouth of a child who is lured by them to go to her death with scant protest, he is most likely indicating his burning contempt for them.

Here, too, a brave woman – even a young girl – is more admirable than all others. Clytemnestra, joining her, is for once on the right side, savagely defending her cherished child. At this stage of the story the queen is young and almost as beautiful as her sister Helen. In her confrontation with Agamemnon she pours forth – as does he – the mutual resentments stored up in their troubled marriage. The French critic Simone Weil remarks that Euripides shows here the extent to which he was a sensitive and shrewd observer of men and women and their intimate relationships. Some of this may have been autobiographical, if his own second marriage was as difficult as gossip had it. Very touching is Iphigeneia's plea to her mother not to hate Agamemnon.

The chorus has a minor role yet is given "glorious" poetry, very simple and natural, in a style that anticipates Menander and New Comedy. Gilbert Murray stresses that the play is an advance – or, at very least, a marked change – over traditional fifth-century tragedy. It is less static, less stately, a bold transitional work towards a different concept of serious theatre. He considers it a very estimable script, though not Euripides at his true best. Kitto dismisses it as "thoroughly second-rate", a tired work, yet not without merits or interest for its place in theatre history. He assumes that the ageing Euripides left it unfinished because he recognized all too well its many shortcomings, which are basic in the plot and the illogic of much of its action. But Murray considers the plot quite admirable, and Gassner rates the drama "powerful for the searching quality of the characterization, which is full of light and shade". And Gassner also approves of it as a "stinging attack" on many of the human social evils that still offended Euripides.

John Ferguson hails the script's "sheer theatricality" and points to the inspired succession of reversals between hope and utter distress that ably sustain suspense, not easy in a work essentially linear. Lucas weighs in: "The play lacks the depth of *The Bacchae*; but the old poet had produced few plots so dramatic in the modern sense, few characters more natural. It does not give the modern reader much idea of Greek drama at its best; but it is one of the easiest Greek dramas for a modern to enjoy."

Gilbert Norwood says that the play is about "five ordinary characters under the strain of extraordinary circumstances". Each of the adults, Agamemnon, Menelaus, Clytemnestra and Achilles, has weaknesses and faults, and Iphigeneia is an innocent child rushing to make an immature judgement as to how she should act, yet purely motivated. "Here is human nature – you – the one constant in human affairs. Look at the compromising self-centred mess we make of human nature. If only we could keep the child's view." Is that, as Norwood suggests, Euripides' statement in this unfinished testament?

In the late Middle Ages *Iphigeneia in Aulis* was translated by Erasmus, who perceived in it a resemblance to the Biblical story of the sacrifice of Isaac. The most subtle and distinguished later use of the legendary incident at Aulis is found in the verse drama, *Iphigénie* (1674), by Racine, written as a vehicle for the actress La Champmeslé, who had captured the French poet's affections.

Several operas are indebted to the play, beginning with *Ifigenia in Aulide* (1713) by the then youthful Domenico Scarlatti (1685–1757), with a libretto by Carlo Sigismondo Capece which followed Euripides' text quite closely; however, the score is lost. Towards the end of the century two more works with identical titles appeared, the first by Gluck in 1774, the libretto supplied by F.L.G. Lebland du Roullet (1716–86), based on Racine's drama, and staged at the Paris Opéra under the auspices of Princess Marie-Antoinette, who had been the composer's voice pupil. It was considered a landmark, "a perfect blend of words and music", a forerunner of a new opera genre, embodying Gluck's theories of what the form should be. In 1788 Luigi Cherubini (1760–1842) brought out his musical interpretation of the tragedy, with an Italian libretto by Ferdinando Moretti (d. 1807) that draws on both Euripides and Racine. In this, the ending is significantly changed: Iphigeneia, exhausted by her ill fortune, commits suicide.

In 1968 a notable revival of the play in New York at the Circle-in-the-Square, with the famed Greek performer Irene Papas as Clytemnestra, was an unexpected success, achieving a long run. It reflected the *Zeitgeist*, which was anti-war. It seemed to have references to the unpopular American campaign in Vietnam. In the *New York Times* Clive Barnes wrote:

> The strength of Euripides is his humanity – he always saw the man beneath the crown and would inveigh at the immortality of wilful gods and an errant fate. It is this humanity and spirit that is so heartbreakingly caught in this most moving production. . . . Here is great theater and an adornment to the New York stage.
>
> . . . The play undoubtedly has one of the most pathetic and touching themes in Greek tragedy. And because of its very human motivation, despite the crucial command of an oracle, there are no shafts from the gods to deflect interest from a situation that is not without its contemporary significance. For one of the things *Iphigeneia in Aulis* is about – or rather, now seems to be about – is a person's duty toward a nation pursuing a war he feels to be worthless.
>
> . . . Using an impressively fluent and yet understatedly poetic English version by Minos Volanakis, Michael Cacoyannis had directed this Euripides with a forceful feel for its contemporary relevance. At first the directions seems uncertain – wavering between a ritualistic view of tragedy, to an extent unavoidable in the Greek classic theater, and the naturalistic approach to which the play lends itself.
>
> It is in keeping with Mr Cacoyannis's view of the play (a view that the ancient Greeks themselves might have found sentimental) that he rejects the play's disputed happy ending. He prefers to finish with Iphigeneia's being led to sacrifice, and Clytemnestra, caught in a spotlight that is tantamount to a cinematic close-up, in a ashen-blaze of grief.
>
> The cast is exceptionally strong. That fine Greek actress Irene Papas is a Clytemnestra of the most noble passion, with a wine-dark voice that rolls like distant thunder, bold eyes, and a cry of anguish that echoes in the soul. She plays Clytemnestra as a wife and mother more than a tragedy queen, and not once would one forget that here was a woman giving up her child. As she stood, hopelessly aghast, while Iphigeneia calmly argued all the fine reasons why she should go to her death like a girl embracing a lover, this Clytemnestra, still yet tortured, wrenched the heart with her electric impassivity.
>
> Jenny Leigh was almost as impressive as Iphigeneia, superbly expressing first the girl's swift surge of youth, then her fear of boundless death, and finally the resignation that comes to her by choosing death as if it were by her own will.
>
> . . . The staging looked beautifully convincing, and with a simple setting and well-designed costumes, all by Michael Annals, it had a great deal of atmosphere, which was helped by Marvin David Levy's sombrely, lambently elegiac music.

It was considered remarkable that a play by an author nearly eighty could have such a vital impact 2,400 years after it was written.

His physical decline had not lessened this poet's ardour. Like the *Oresteia* of Aeschylus and the *Oedipus at Colonus* of Sophocles, products of both dramatists' old age, Euripides' own last effort, *The Bacchae* (406 BC), composed in his final months as he approached death, is astonishingly fresh and vibrant, saliently original in form and theme. Also, it is hard to reconcile it with most of what Euripides had written before, a fact leading to a considerable body of critical literature by later interpreters. It is often called enigmatic, for it is both iconoclastic and traditional, nor is it fully possible to discern Euripides' intention in it.

Once more the scene is Thebes, but in antiquity, for Cadmus, the city's legendary founder, is still alive though doddering. (Valuable contributions to explaining the seminal myth and its relation to the play have been made by R.P. Winninton-Ingram in his book *Euripides and Dionysus*; by Gilbert Norwood in his essay "*The Bacchae* and Its Riddle"; and by Gilbert Murray, A.W. Verrall, Philip Vellacott, Richard Lattimore, F.L. Lucas and H.D.F. Kitto, to mention only a few others who have published studies of the play. One of the most interesting of these is Verrall's; his approach is "rationalistic", viewing *The Bacchae* as a sceptical examen by Euripides of "mass-hallucination".) It was in Thebes that Semele, daughter of Cadmus, had given birth to Dionysus, fathered by Zeus in a lightning flash that also killed her. Her still smouldering dwelling and tomb were left in ruins, at the instigation of Hera, the jealous mate of Zeus.

Dionysus, quiet and smiling, accompanied by his Bacchantes, a dancing, chanting chorus of Lydian women, comes in homage to his mother's grave. He, the god of fertility, has already caused green vines to grow over it. He also intends to win over his native Thebes to his worship. The city is now being ruled by his cousin, King Pentheus, who, together with the women of his royal family, and especially his mother Queen Agave, have imposed a censorious and rigid moral rule. They are disdainful of Eastern mystical cults, and especially the orgiastic rites of Dionysus, now spreading from Asia and infusing Pentheus' realm. Pentheus also denies that Semele was impregnated by Zeus, and spreads scandalous stories about her. The strong sensual unrest amid his people alarms him. To counter it, the prim, ascetic king has ordered all followers of Dionysus (Bacchus) imprisoned in the royal stables, and when he learns that a stranger from Asia Minor and a troupe of "wild women" have entered Thebes he commands that they be seized, confronts and rebukes the god (who is in human form) and has him and all his followers shut away. Seeing the god as a mere mortal – in effect, blindly denying his divinity – Pentheus accuses him of being a charlatan, a deceitful evangelist inciting disorder and lasciviousness.

Miraculously, by some phenomenon the exact nature of which has prompted much debate among scholars but perhaps would be an earth tremor, the prison structure topples, freeing Dionysus. The palace burns and a flame leaps up on Semele's tomb. Dionysus retaliates against Pentheus by instilling the women of Thebes, including Queen Agave, with licentious impulses: they desert the city, after the fashion of Bacchantes, to revel uninhibitedly on the forested mountainside of Kithaeron, there performing the secret rites of the god. He exerts a hypnotic influence over the priggish, dogmatic, insecure young king, who, at the god's prompting, puts on women's attire so that he can go into the mountains to spy on the Maenads' mysterious practices. The women, discovering the "peeping Tom" in the high branches of a tree, tear him to pieces and, bearing his mutilated body, return in triumph to Thebes, his mother – transported, in a fit of possession – holding high her son's severed, hairy head, which she mistakenly believes to be that of a lion. When she recovers her senses and realizes what has actually occurred, her maternal grief breaks her. Pentheus is also mourned by his grandfather, Cadmus, and by the aged, blind prophet Tiresias, both of whom had warned the young man to be more lenient towards the revellers. They themselves had joined the Bacchic dances, even though – with thyrsi (wands) in hand and vine-leaves in their hair and garbed in fawn-skins – they had unhesitatingly taken the risk of appearing ridiculous. The old men had shrewdly acknowledged the potent force of this god, who brings to man either joy or self-destruction. In accepting his gift they were renewing their youth inwardly, however foolish others might deem them.

Clearly an allegory, the play is derived from a legend which had also served Aeschylus in his lost script *Pentheus*, of which some fragments remain, enough to indicate Euripides' borrowing from it, as well as hints from earlier poets who explored the subject. It is also similar to the popular myth of Lycurgus of Thrace, who was punished for having denied the godhood of Dionysus. Some commentators suggest that Euripides might be making amends in this final work for his many previous attacks on the gods, for he preaches in it the wisdom and futility of trying to oppose their power. But others see the poet as ending his career with an even more vigorous protest against them, since the Dionysus portrayed here is vain, cruel and remorseless, inflicting a terrible vengeance on Pentheus and his hapless mother. He is a radiant figure, but also effeminate – indeed, Pentheus has taunted him for a display of those qualities, which paradoxically accompany his innate bestiality and savagery.

What makes the work particularly interesting is that it is one of only two Greek dramas extant in which Dionysus appears as a character, not wholly through a surrogate – a tragic hero, an Oedipus, an Eteocles – and also because, as Gilbert Murray points out, in form it embodies fully the original shape of the Greek passion play: the story of the mutilation and death of a scapegoat is re-enacted, the hero's suffering described. "There is Lamentation mixed with mad Rejoicing. The scattered body is recovered. . . . The whole scheme of the play is given by the ancient ritual. . . . There was never a great play so steeped in tradition as *The Bacchae*."

The victim here, though, is not Dionysus himself, but Pentheus, who is not divine, who even denies the godhead; so the direct application of the ritual is hardly accomplished, though Murray and others argue that the young king must be seen as another aspect of Dionysus. Into him the god had "entered" – the play is certainly a presentation of "enthusiasm" in the original sense – and finally the sacrificial victim takes, in the befuddled minds of the frenzied, intoxicated mob, an animal shape; he becomes a sacred totem, to be hunted and eaten, so that the worshippers can share his virtues and superior physical traits: now, a mountain lion. (The women revellers often seized upon a wild goat and tore it to pieces, which they ate.) At the moment of Pentheus' possession, when the bestial god takes control of him, inciting him to spy upon the women, the young king's willpower and self-discipline collapse, leading him to assent to the dangerous venture. However, this might be an over-complex interpretation, not easy to clarify, and to some not wholly convincing.

Whatever Euripides' basic purpose, *The Bacchae* is a remarkable study of religious fanaticism, as well as of the impact of a new religion – this cult, or any other – that sets itself in opposition to older, more traditional creeds; and also a picture of mass frenzy, which again might be equated to the war-madness that Euripides had observed and been made the victim of in Athens. It might also be a comment on how it feels to become a "scapegoat", as had befallen him at the hands of the Athenian "hawks" who had sought to excuse their military defeats by passing along the blame to "traitors" among the city's liberal intellectuals and artists. It is, no less, a graphic instance of the "flight from reason" that follows upon war-weariness or any prolonged period of social strain: the desire to return to the simplicities and joys of the natural life, with a physical closeness to healing and purgative primitiveness, in pungent pine forests: to regain there the pleasures of the body, in dance, sexual contact or unleashed violence, or all three – and then, after exhaustion, to seek respite in states of mysticism and quietism. No less is it a celebration of group intoxication, collective irrationality. The same phenomenon has been remarked in our century in such outbreaks as the Nazi movement with its reversion to racism and embrace of pagan mythology; or in the rise of a philosophy based on guidance by the "wisdom of the blood" advocated in the novels of D.H. Lawrence and urgently accepted by his disciples; or in the gentler but noisier surge of youthful Hippies in the sixties to "drop out" from a too materialistic society: people were to learn, to their surprise, that even the Hippies, the "flower-children", could in a trice turn surpassingly violent and blindly destructive. Vellacott terms the play a warning against all forms of mass hysteria.

Like *Hippolytus* and *Electra*, the play offers an almost Freudian picture of sexual repression; but Pentheus differs from Hippolytus, in particular, because he is not actually frigid but instead prurient. He is naggingly curious about sex, not – like Hippolytus – largely unaware of it. He is quick to accuse the Stranger of effeminacy, yet himself is readily seduced to undertake transvestism; and his unhealthy fear of sexuality is shown to be bound up with voyeuristic desires, which the flagrant revels arouse and bring out. *The Bacchae* is amazingly modern in its psychology, again testimony to Euripides' sharp perception of human behaviour and its disguised motives. Pentheus is extraordinarily complex. He is not the usual tragic hero, because he is unstable, highly suggestible and decidedly neurotic. He is also intelligent, and takes seriously the kingly role passed on to him by his grandfather Cadmus, and his responsibilities to the state; but he is also over-sober, narrow-minded and unimaginative. (His name means "grief-stricken".)

Part of Pentheus' failure, his *hubris*, is that he is an "unjust judge", intolerantly, high-handedly meting out punishment without adequately understanding what is afoot; as a result he, the hunter, is soon the hunted and doomed. Similarly he, so respectable, who rebukes the two old men for their foolish, undignified "masquerade" in fawn-skin, is before long even more ridiculously attired, self-deprived of his masculinity. Possibly he has sipped from a cup with Dionysus; he is drunk; the god – the wine – has entered into him and taken total possession of him.

Disaster is visited almost as harshly upon the shifty, sophisticated Cadmus, who has only belatedly recognized the divinity of his grandson, Dionysus. He and his wife are ordered into exile, where they are to undergo a change into the shape of serpents. His daughter, Agave, is also punished for her initial disbelief; she has unwittingly slain her son; now she too is sent into solitary banishment, her person for ever polluted and abhorrent. When Cadmus cries out, "Gods should not be like men, keeping anger forever," the relentless Dionysus replies: "Zeus my father ordained this from the beginning." The gods are pitiless: no other interpretation of this is possible. Is not Zeus also an "unjust judge"? Is that God's *hubris*?

The play moves with an incisive rush to its horrible climax, never allowing the spectator to relax his interest. Kitto, who has a strong affinity to classic form, deems *The Bacchae* the best constructed of Euripidean tragedies, saying that it has the highest degree of organic unity; it is free throughout of the usual philosophical digressions. The ageing dramatist returned to earlier models, such as *Medea* and *Hippolytus*, but if anything surpassed them in a fine revelation of his theatrical craftsmanship. The dialogue is shot through with irony, strange, terse and sardonic rejoinders; also present are frequent reversals, surprising yet deeply logical, arising from convincing psychological compulsions and drives.

Nowhere else has Euripides, too often careless in his handling of the chorus, used it so well, making it an active and even necessary participant in the story. Indeed, the work is not named *Pentheus* but instead *The Bacchae*, perhaps singling out the Asian group of spirited women as having primacy.

Much of the play's text is ambiguous, allowing for widely different interpretations. Though it is a tragedy, its protagonist – Pentheus – is not heroic. Young, obstinate, perplexed and untested, he is unsure of himself as a ruler and hastily resorts to force to impose his dictates. He has poor judgement. Repressing feelings in himself, he is repressive of others who evidence the same emotions and sensual desires. He vainly and futilely tries to use force against the god. Vellacott observes that Pentheus himself is a Dionysiac by nature. "His half-consciousness of this, his fear of what he is, produces his crude puritanism."

Glenn L. Loney writes:

> Pentheus is punished for his lack of moderation. When Dionysus finally reaches him, he is able to transform this young ruler's cold reason into feminine coquettishness. From being masculinely hard, tough, unyielding, he finds himself going just as far in the opposite direction, becoming silly, soft, pliant, even weak. What this implies is not anything so trite as that Pentheus was a latent homosexual. Instead, it is an example showing what happens when one lives by extremes. Just as reason and passion are matched opposites which may be kept in balance by moderation, so also are the masculine and feminine qualities in a human being.

Loney emphasizes that Euripides is saying that moderation rather than abstinence is the key.

> A man cannot deny or hide parts of what he is. He must come to terms with the All of his being. To "Know Thyself," one must do more than search the caverns of the mind; one must know the darker corridors of the heart as well. Dionysian desire, passion, and lust are as much part of us as reason. When they are forgotten, ignored, or suppressed, a reservoir of unfulfilled longing builds up which may burst the dam of self-control in ways quite shocking even to their seemingly helpless servant.

Yet, as Pentheus recognizes, the civilized state must also preserve order; there cannot be a complete abandonment of decorum. To borrow from Vellacott once more: "The tragedy of Pentheus is not that he tried to do what was wrong; but that he was the wrong man to do it – he was, in fact, precisely the unbalanced, excitable type of person who most easily falls victim to the allurements of Dionysiac indulgence."

In the play, as Lattimore remarks, "The divine mystery combines with and actually grows out of heroic legend. The supernatural and the natural are so combined as to make one course." Other miracles, besides the opportune earth tremor and fiery destruction of the palace, are "seen as though they were sense perceptions". One such astonishing feat is described by a herdsman, an onlooker, who tells how Pentheus was placed in his high perch, from which to spy on the carousing women:

> And now I saw the stranger do a marvellous thing.
> Grasping the topmost skyward tip of a tall fir
> he bent, bent, bent it down to the dark ground,
> and curved it, like a bow, or as a cartwheel is inscribed
> by compasses that mark its outer running edge.
> So with his hands the stranger bent this mountain tree
> down to the earth, a thing no mortal man could do,
> then, seating Pentheus on the top of the fir boughs
> let it go backward and upright between his hands,
> but gently, taking care not to shake him off, and now
> the tall fir tree stuck up straight into the tall sky
> holding my master seated on its back.
> [Translation: Richard Lattimore]

But does Euripides ask us to believe that such things as these actually happened? John Ferguson thinks not; instead, we are supposed to assume that Pentheus and the others are possessed by illusions, until they can no longer discern the real from the imagined – that is the hypnotic effect the god has on them, or also has the intoxicating wine, the essence of Dionysus. Ferguson points out that supposedly the earthquake has been accompanied by flames that engulf and raze the palace, but thereafter Pentheus never once makes mention of its loss – he does not ever lament its disappearance. And afterwards there are several references to his entering and coming from it. Nor does anyone else comment on the havoc brought by the blaze. Or was it only the royal stables that vanished? Ferguson proposes, "The simple fact is that Euripides has deliberately created an ambiguous miracle. Even the apparently explicit statement that Bacchus broke his house down to the ground may carry a spiritual and symbolic meaning. That Dionysus has the power to create hypnotic illusion in Pentheus is already clear, and becomes clearer in the scene that follows; and his power to create mass hysteria is unquestioned. But the whole point of the play is that illusion is a form of reality. When Pentheus sees Dionysus as a wild animal, he *is*, for Pentheus, a wild animal. When the Maenads see Pentheus as their prey, he is their prey."

The revels of the Maenads are not always orgiastic. The Dionysiac cult was one of a plight with nature. On the slope of Mount Kithaeron the possessed women relax, chaste, most drowsing, a few gently communing with wild creatures or plaiting flowers – a serene, pleasing picture; much in accord with the romantic view of what should be man's relation to his still unspoiled world. As Euripides has the herdsman depict it:

> Just when the sun's rays first beamed out to warm the earth,
> I was pasturing my cattle and working up towards the high ground;
> when I saw three groups of women who had been dancing together.
> The leader of one group was Autonoe; your mother Agave was at the
> head of the second, and Ino of the third, stretched out and
> quiet. Some rested on beds of pine-needles, some had pillows of
> oak-leaves; they lay just as they had thrown themselves on the
> ground, – but with modesty in their posture; they were not drunk
> with wine, as you told us, or with music of flutes; nor was there
> any love-making there in the loveliness of the woods.
> (Translation: Vellacott)

The herdsmen gather, argue and decide to attack the women, capture them and bring them back to Pentheus. Agave, alerted by the lowing of the cattle, springs up, arousing her companions. The women, each using her thyrsus as a spear, beat off the attackers, who flee, fearing they will be torn to pieces. But the cattle become the Maenads' prey, rent limb from limb, the flesh stripped and swallowed – as if it were the god who was being eaten, as indeed it might be. (This very long aria is one of the most beautiful, vivid and powerful in all of Euripides' consistently eloquent tragedies.) The pastoral scene and Elysian mood suddenly veer from utter tranquillity to the very contrary, an outburst of savage fury and destruction. What is displayed is the opposite sides of nature, the soothing and kindly and the abruptly bestial. Among his other forms, Dionysus is the bull god. The women consume the fragments of the cattle they have slain – eating the deity, the sacred totem.

Dionysus warns Pentheus: "You are godless; it makes you blind." As in the famed scene between Oedipus and Tiresias, the sightless prophet – here politic, a trimmer, saying only what it is advantageous to say – has sensed and seen in Dionysus and his wild cult what the sharp-eyed Pentheus has failed to mark, a rebellion against reason, a surging force that cannot be denied, one that in the body of the state propels anarchy and a "mass surrender to the supernatural". One theory has it that history shows alternately prolonged periods in which order reigns, and then sudden breakdowns of discipline in which irrationality and violence take over, scattering all social norms. Some observers believe that Greece had reached such a point, after years of well-organized rule by Pericles and his successors, and after a generation of exhausting war, and that Euripides perceived and reflected the threatening public change in his play. For many decades the Greeks had made progress towards creating a "civilization", finding a better way to lead their personal lives and to govern themselves democratically, by assemblies, debates, courts and voting; but the apparent results were military defeats, humiliations and corruption, and now there was an impulse to throw off bothersome restraints and resort to riotous behaviour and other physical outbursts, a turning away from the intellectually and ethically guided life to an existence dominated by freely expressed emotion, through an embrace of cults such as the Dionysian, going to uninhibited extremes. Lucas puts it: "It is not hard to be critical, to undermine beliefs, to start men asking questions. But to make them find sane answers – that is less easy. Men think they think; but their thought is largely the shuttlecock of passion, desire, or fear. Who can master Dionysus? Besides, may it not be that life is too terrible, except for the strongest nerves, to face without intoxication?"

Much is made of the influence on Euripides of his having moved to Macedonia and settled in its lofty altitudes and pure air. He was given a new perspective in this setting, and perhaps its towering, craggy environment inspired the "mountain freshness" of his poetry, the magnificence of the imagery that floods this play, incredibly youthful and responsive for a man of advanced years. The chief feature of *The Bacchae*, this "mystery play", is its unceasing lyricism, its leaping Ionic rhythms, its blood-stirring verse. "As a piece of language," declared Lord Macaulay, "it is hardly equalled in the world." He found it "a most glorious play. It is often very obscure, and I am not sure that I understand its general scope. . . . And whether it was intended to encourage or to discourage fanaticism, the picture of fanatical excitement which it exhibits has never been rivalled." Similar is Gilbert Norwood's appraisal: "Intoxicatingly beautiful, coldly sordid, at one moment baffling the brain, at the next thrilling us with the mystic charm of wood and hillside, this drama stands unique among Euripides' works." It is also suggested that in Macedonia the aged playwright saw the cult of Dionysus still being celebrated with primitive fervour by mountain-roving bands of excited women: he could sense the full force of this ecstatic and mystical new faith, with its appeal to the innate energies of mankind, which elude the attempt to control human conduct by mere sober thought. Always conscious of man's elemental, latent desires, symbolically represented by his gods, Euripides here pays fearful tribute to them. It is hardly true, as Murray would have it, that the play is "a heartful glorification of Dionysus". It is with rueful awe, even a shudder, that the poet depicts the cruelty and sinister inconsistency of this force that rules the universe, its offering to many unpredictable moments of Edenic respite and tender healing that may be rapidly transformed into ferocious hostility.

Kitto singles out as a special accomplishment how Euripides projects his tragic theme entirely into the action. "There is real symbolism, not a diagram." The opposing points of view are not embodied in abstract characters but in vital persons, in a situation brought to a sharp focus.

The theatrical trappings so dear to Euripides are present in abundance: the foreign scene, the exotic music, to which the dancers in fantastic costumes – fawn-skins, with leaf-twined wands – whirl and lope headlong; as well as the spectacular earthquake and fire, and the return of the Maenads with their gory trophy.

The Bacchae brought Euripides' astonishing career to a close, his spirit still unreconciled to cosmic dictates as he had experienced them. In Vellacott's words: "We cannot expect the universe to be on our side, or even to be impartial."

As death drew near, the poet summoned up his remaining strength in one last effort and left as his testament to the beauty and difficulty of life this great play with its mystical overtones, its profound ambiguities and its clear but still defiant statement. The world is a place of much loveliness and a host of natural wonders, but no benign purpose can be discerned in it, and wise but foolish man, his reason inadequate, is the victim of Heaven, which works to undo him through the weakness of his flesh and the irrational elements in his psyche. He must control himself, as best he can, by the exercise of his reason, yet never wholly deny the bestial and ecstatic forces that conjoin in him. If he is rational, he must also permit himself to be irrational. By an excess in either direction he may well bring ruin on himself.

What most impresses about Euripides is his courage, his versatility, the wide scope of his work – he attempted almost every variety of tragedy, melodrama and tragicomedy as well as farce. His compassion was deep, his understanding of people was astute, his intelligence elevated in every sense of the word, his instinct for theatrical effect was cunning and inspired, and his gift for romantic poetry was unexcelled even by the great rivals who surrounded him.

The Bacchae was staged posthumously by his son (405 BC) in Athens and also in northern Greece. Following Euripides' death, indeed, interest in much of his work grew immensely; acclaim for his plays exceeded that given to those of Aeschylus and Sophocles, for the spirit infusing his dramas fitted the new Hellenistic taste: his scepticism, urbanity and realism, even the homely touches he inserted, were much to the liking of later audiences. Paradoxically, his sentimentality and his predilection for evoking pathos were of a piece with the feeling expressed by such sculptural works of the times as the writhing group *Laocoön* with its exaggerated gestures and movement, showing how melodramatic was the tone and craft of art produced in the subsequent epoch, how far behind were left the statuesque calm and heroic dignity of Periclean Greece, how decadent – in the sense of being endlessly imitative – was the tragic drama that followed.

Heinrich von Kleist (1777–1811) chose *The Bacchae* as the model for his verse-play *Penthesilea* (1808). The details of the plot and the characters differ greatly from the Greek work, but the theme – the ambivalence of Dionysus and the irresistible power of the erotic drive – is taken from Euripides, as Kleist openly acknowledged. The story revolves about the uncontrollable and destructive love of the Queen of the Amazons for her avowed enemy Achilles.

A one-act opera, *Die Bassariden* (1966), by Hans Werner Henze (1926–), with libretto by W.H. Auden and Chester Kallman, brought Euripides to the modern stage with a largely dissonant score. Pentheus is shown as obsessed by religion and fearful of sex. This interpretation was put on in several European capitals and finally staged in the United States by the Santa Fe Opera Company (1968). A more unusual operatic version, *The Manson Family* (1990) by John Moran, was heard at the Lincoln Center in New York City; it updates the original script by superimposing on it an actual character, the Californian mass-murderer Charles Manson, who – a charismatic, Dionysiac cult figure – led a group of susceptible young women on a rampage of killings, numbering among their victims a Hollywood film actress, Sharon Tate, and her unborn child. At the time of the staging, Manson and his followers were still serving life terms in prison.

Among many English translations of the play is one by the Nigerian dramatist Wole Soyinka (1934–), a Nobel Prize winner. The work was presented at the Old Vic (London, 1973) and at the Minor Latham Playhouse (Columbia University, New York City, 1987), directed by Paul Berman, with music by Raphael Crystal.

At the Great Dionysia it became customary to revive an old play to start the programme before the new works were introduced. A few names of later playwrights are remembered, by way of contest records and contemporary theatre historians, the two poets most often mentioned being Agathon, to whom there has been an earlier allusion, and Philocles, whose entry took the first prize from Sophocles' *Oedipus.* As also noted, the three major dramatists had sons who inherited a share of their sires' talent: Euphorion, a scion of Aeschylus; Iophon, an heir of Sophocles; and Euripides the Younger (sometimes described as a nephew). Only fragments of their works have been come upon.

For at least eight or nine centuries the plays were pored over and enacted throughout the Greco-Roman world; during much of this time, acting and scene design, as always in a period of the theatre's decline and degeneracy, became more prominent than the plays themselves, a phenomenon already observed. Guilds of actors kept busy and gained prestige and privileges; individual players won fame and fervent followings, and directors rose in importance. In the third century BC Alexandria in Egypt flourished as a centre of dramatic activity. Ptolemy II, a cultured ruler, collected a huge library of Greek papyri, the most renowned in the Classic world. In AD 641 the port city was besieged and conquered by Imar ibn al-As, who ordered the library destroyed by fire, possibly at the urging of Caliph Omar, who was convinced that only the Koran deserved to be kept and read, a report deemed by some historians to be apocryphal. Earlier, Christians too are said to have been overtly hostile to the library's large assemblage of "pagan" tomes and took steps to disperse and negate them. By most accounts, the complete works of Aeschylus and Sophocles were stored there, but only a handful of the texts escaped the flames or other means of dissolution. As has also been noted, more than a half millennium later the Greek dramas were still intensely admired, studied and evaluated in Byzantium, the capital of the Eastern Roman Empire and a city by then mostly Greek-speaking. Here the full canons of Sophocles and Euripides were carefully preserved, but they were largely ruined or lost when Byzantium was sacked and looted (AD 1203), not by Vandals or Goths, but by Crusaders, chiefly Venetians fiercely at odds with the rulers of the Eastern dominion. Whatever scripts were rescued here were borne to safety in South Italy by monks who had treasured and devotedly and meticulously copied and recopied them, along with other literary works.

Looking back: in Rome, and elsewhere in its far-flung realm, new versions of the Greek themes used by the Periclean masters were composed and staged until Hadrian's reign, in the second century AD, and productions continued in Athens until at least the fifth century AD.

The physical theatre steadily evolved. The orchestra, or dancing-space, was narrower, and the platform was elevated, making use of the roofs of one-storey buildings flanking it. The *skene,* heightened to two storeys and enlarged, was ornamented still more to serve as a decorative background. The area saved by reducing the platform was partly allotted to the auditorium, and partly to the larger *skene.*

Effects accomplished by stage machinery received even more attention. The chorus, as has been said, gradually disappeared.

By the fourth century BC the Greek theatre utilized at least 350 professional singer–dancers who assumed both tragic and comic roles, most of them as part of the ever-diminishing chorus; the recruitment of amateur players was lessened. The names of some of the leading actors still resound, and some have already been mentioned here: to repeat them and add others, they were Polus, Theodorus, Thettalus, Neoptolemus, Athenocorus, Aristodemus. They toured everywhere. About 350 BC a new requirement called for each of the three leading actors at the Festival to appear in at least one work by each of the three competing playwrights, to ensure that each poet had access to the very best histrionic talent. Inspired acting or its lack was not allowed to blind the judges to the intrinsic merits or defects of the scripts apart from the performer's contribution.

During the reign of Alexander the Great, who assumed the throne in 336 BC, at the advent of the Hellenistic Age, theatre was encouraged and sponsored throughout his wide realm and was no longer confined to the two Dionysian holidays. Many of the established conventions of tragedy were abandoned. On one occasion Alexander celebrated a military victory by bringing together as many as 3,000 performers from the scattered regions over which he presided.

If this later period is not esteemed by subsequent generations for the output of its playwrights, it did yield one extraordinary achievement, the essay on "Tragedy" in a longer treatise, the *Poetics*, by the most influential of all Greek philosophers, Aristotle (384–322 BC). Born in Stageirus, a minor Greek settlement in Thrace, he was the son of a court physician in service to Amytas II of Macedonia (393–369 BC). His father gave the youth lessons in anatomy, before sending him to Athens where for perhaps two decades he was a pupil of Plato, the greatest of teachers, whom he reluctantly admired, though he was usually in disagreement with him, eventually dedicating himself to refuting many Platonic doctrines. Plato had quickly recognized the young man's earnestness and brilliance. After his mentor's death Aristotle attached himself to the court of Hermeias, a former slave who had also been enrolled at Plato's Academy and had since made himself the virtual dictator of Atarneus and Assus, in a region of upper Asia Minor. The now middle-aged savant married Hermeias' daughter. Shortly, Hermeias was assassinated, a deed promoted by the Persians, who believed him to be planning an alliance with Macedonia to cross their borders. Aristotle and his wife, Pythias, fled to Lesbos. With his scientific bent, he spent his days there gathering data on the island's natural history. In 343 BC he was invited by King Philip of Macedonia to undertake the education of his son, Alexander, unruly at thirteen. Aristotle carried out this task for four years. He was given an additional assignment of restoring

Stageirus, his birthplace, which had been ravaged and laid waste during a military campaign. He drew up for it a code of laws which greatly satisfied its citizens.

In 334 BC he returned to Athens and with funds provided by his former student Alexander established a Lyceum, where he lectured on rhetoric, ethics and philosophy and a host of other topics. He accumulated an extensive library, cultivated a zoological garden and founded a museum of natural history. Guided by him, his pupils spread out to collect knowledge of every sort, facts applying to history, botany, social customs, biology, sports, animal habits. With this encyclopaedic bank of information he had material for his numerous treatises on an astonishingly wide variety of subjects. Much of his thinking is still deemed remarkably sound, though some of his ideas have been outdated by new scientific experimentation over the very long passage of time.

In the *Poetics*, his analysis of dramaturgical principles is as might be expected, based on his direct observation of theatrical performances, and results in what is essentially a valuable handbook for playwrights on how to construct effective stage works, as well as offering standards by which an audience might judge them. The essay is disjointed, incomplete and repetitive: scholars conjecture that the *Poetics* might have been a somewhat rambling lecture, and the text now accessible merely notes taken and saved by an attentive student. Furthermore, it is likely that Aristotle's comments are inspired by the drama of his own day (*c.* 330 BC), about seventy years after the Periclean Age, rather than by the tragedies of the three masters best known today, for many of his strictures do not apply to the works still extant. He barely refers to Aeschylus, mentions Euripides only a few times, but as has been remarked does cite Sophocles in eleven instances, and with high praise. His favourite – overwhelmingly – is *Oedipus.* It is one of the only two plays now available that can be said to answer the requirements for tragedy as Aristotle conceived them to be. Yet his precepts – or rather, suggestions – have a universal validity, which explains the enormous persuasion they have exerted on theatre since his significant and insightful formulation of them.

The *Poetics* is especially interesting, too, because it offers Aristotle's beliefs, written much closer to the event, about the origins of Greek tragedy and comedy, both of which he connects to man's imitative instinct, a source to humankind of both pleasure and instruction; and, in particular, he traces the rise of tragedy from the "dithyrambs" at the Dionysia.

(Some scholars have recently questioned the long-held theory that Greek tragedy arose from religious ritual, suggesting instead that it descends in largest part from Homer's *Iliad*; but it seems hazardous to contradict one of Aristotle's acute intelligence who expressed his view 2,400 years earlier, in an age of fresher recollection.)

Aristotle's definition of a tragedy calls for it to be "an imitation of an action that is serious and also as having magnitude, complete in itself; in language with pleasurable accessories . . . with incidents arousing pity and fear, wherewith to accomplish its catharsis of such emotions" (Translation: Ingram Bywater). By "magnitude" it is supposed that he implies not only a work of suitable length, but also a theme of some importance: a tragedy does not treat with a trivial subject. It may be brief, but the longer a work is, the more impressive it is. The language should also have elevation, be lyrical, enhanced by poetic imagery – and by "pleasurable accessories", a reference to flute music and rhythmic choric dancing. He includes spectacle among the legitimate elements of a tragic drama, but relegates it to a lower aesthetic level, a contribution from the scene-designer and costumer rather than the poet.

A dramatic work must have unity, especially of action, and – if possible – of time and place as well, the best limit being "the revolution of the sun" or twenty-four hours, though the working out of the plot need not always be confined to that short time-span. Later interpretations of the *Poetics* as having laid down an absolute restriction as to that are in error: they had their origin in Roman commentaries. The plot must revolve around a single crucial incident in the life of one person. He stresses this over and over. Only what is positively necessary for the unfolding of the story should be included; all else should be omitted. Unity does not follow from the events described having befallen one person; that alone does not make them an integrated whole. Such episodic works are to be avoided. The story must be built up of causally linked components, each occurrence leading logically and, if possible, inevitably to the next, and the plot must appear to have a beginning, a middle and an end. The primacy of plot over all the other elements of a stage work is repeatedly emphasized. Characterization, though of consequence, is secondary. Many plays that have exciting plots but only thin characterizations and banal speeches are successful, for they capture and hold the audience's interest; but plays that rely on subtle portrayals, fine poetic dialogue or intelligent discourse, but lack a strong, suspenseful story-line, fail quickly. Young, unskilful writers often do well at character-drawing and polished dialogue but cannot master the art of plot-making, which is far more difficult. "The first essential, the life and soul, so to speak, of tragedy, is Plot." Characters are created to carry out the plot, rather than the reverse.

Plots must be plausible. If the story contains marvellous premises or surprises, which is desirable, the implausibilities or sudden and unexpected turns of events should occur off-stage, or should precede the opening of the drama, as is done in Sophocles' *Oedipus* and Euripides' *Iphigeneia in Tauris.* The audience, merely hearing of far-fetched or miraculous happenings, will accept them more readily than if they are visually presented. The coincidences whereby Oedipus killed his father and married his mother have already taken place before the play begins; similarly, by divine intervention Iphigeneia has been wafted from Aulis to Tauris before the drama's start. In the same way, strange happenings should be prepared by portents, such as signs and prophecies, so that they appear to be fulfilling some supernatural design.

A good plot should be "complex", rather than simple: it should contain "recognition scenes", or sudden discoveries, which in turn lead to powerful reversals of fortune, again as illustrated in Oedipus' learning of his true identity, and Electra's coming to realize, joyously, that the stranger who has approached her is Orestes, her long-lost brother. Various ways to handle such "recognition scenes", by resorting to the exposure of scars, finding of tokens, experiencing memory-jogs and using logical deduction, are set forth in detail, and Aristotle's perception here reveals how shrewd and practical is his instinct for dramatic craftsmanship. He ranks the baring of scars as the least estimable device – it is too easy – and, as might be expected of one of his mind, reliance on logical deduction the most artistic means.

Simply because a bizarre incident has actually happened here or there does not assure that the same exceptional event will be credible in a play. Therefore the "probable" is more desirable than the sometimes astonishing "factual". "The story should never be made up of improbable incidents; there should be nothing of the sort in it." In treating historical events and personages, too, a high degree of poetic licence is to be permitted the dramatist. His aim is not to write history, but to shape an exciting play.

The tragic hero should be a man not all good, nor yet all bad or vicious, but rather an "indeterminate kind of personage, a man not pre-eminently virtuous and just, whose misfortune, however, is brought upon him not by vice and depravity but by some error of judgement". Disaster is occasioned by the tragic flow – *hamartia* – in an otherwise good man, or at least one well intentioned, the flaw most often being his *hubris*, an excess of pride that is offensive to the gods. (At this point, Aristotle adds, with a bias permissible in one of his epoch, "Such goodness is possible in every sort of person, even in a woman or a slave, though the one is perhaps an inferior, and the other a wholly worthless being.") The hero should perhaps be somewhat idealized: "As Tragedy is an imitation of persons better than the average, we in our way should follow the example of good portrait painters, who reproduce the distinctive features of a man, and at the same time, without losing the likeness, make him handsomer than he is." Aristotle also prescribes that the persons of a play should behave consistently, in accordance with their characters; or, if they have the trait of inconsistency, they should be consistently inconsistent. Their actions should be appropriate to their station in life, and to their sex, and always be plausible.

According to Aristotle, the best conflict is one between members of the same family, for these arouse the most powerful audience response. "When the tragic deed is within the family – when murder or the like is done or meditated by a son on father, by a mother on son, or a son on mother – these are the situations the poet should seek after." Previous and subsequent centuries of playwriting have confirmed that, whether it be found in Aeschylus' *Oresteia*, Shakespeare's *Hamlet*, Webster's *Duchess of Malfi*, Schiller's *Don Carlos* or O'Neill's *Mourning Becomes Electra*, the murderous strife that erupts within a family is most apt to grip and stir spectators, because of the blood-tie that intimately binds the antagonists and resists ever being loosened.

Least clear to recent commentators is exactly what Aristotle meant by the "tragic *katharsis*", the experience of some – but not all – playgoers who feel uplifted and even exalted after having imaginatively shared the character's disastrous fate; the self-blinding of Oedipus, the dismemberment of Hippolytus, a victim of injustice. Literally thousands of pages have been written by critics in an attempt to explain how, by arousing the emotions of pity and fear in the spectator, witnessing a catastrophic dramatic event brings about a complete and satisfying purge of such feelings. Some think this simply follows from emotional exhaustion: the spectator, having vicariously suffered with the tortured hero, is at play's end drained, "all passion spent", like the better state of a woman who has "enjoyed a good cry". The purge is physical, nervous. Others contend that what the cringing, horrified spectator feels, when the last line is spoken, is psychological relief, a realization that a similar misfortune has been spared him, that it has happened to someone else, a fictitious hero, no one of flesh and blood. Collingwood puts it this way: "In *katharsis* the emotions are 'earthed' by being discharged into a make-believe situation." The play serves as a lightning rod. Furthermore, the example of the tragic hero who meets disaster with courage and dignity is an inspiration: man at his best is shown to be not craven, but noble, defiant, and hence he achieves "victory in defeat". His is what has been called by Ernst "the smiling heartburst" that evokes admiration and transmits an impulse to emulation in the onlooker.

Gilbert Murray offers still another explanation, pointing out that the plays took place in a religious context, and suggesting that the *katharsis* corresponds to an early ritual *katharsis* ("a purification of the community and poisons of the past year, the old contagion of sin and death, which was the function of the festival and mystery play of the dismembered bull-god, Dionysus". A parallel to this is to be found today in the Jewish Yom Kippur, the annual holy day on which congregants fast to purge themselves symbolically of faults committed during the past year. But many other explications of Aristotle's somewhat mystical concept of *katharsis* have been propounded, and perhaps none is complete or altogether conclusive.

Much more is contained in the *Poetics*, such as the proper meter to be used by poets in composing their dialogue and choruses. It is by far the most perceptive work ever written about dramaturgy, and playwrights ever since have studied it closely. It has wielded authority for over 2,000 years, having special weight throughout the eighteenth century, the Neoclassical Age and the early nineteenth century, and again at that century's end and the beginning of the twentieth, discernible in the formal structure of works of writers as varied as those of Henrik Ibsen, August Strindberg, George Bernard Shaw, Tennessee Williams and Eugene Ionesco, some of whom at times overtly flouted Aristotle's principles yet ultimately accepted them.

4

GREEK TRAGEDY THROUGH THE CENTURIES

The creeping advance of the Renaissance northwards from Italy brought the Athenian tragedies to France, Germany and England quite belatedly. For a long time Latin was familiar mostly to a small circle of lay intellectuals in the newly founded colleges and to the clergy, and Greek to far fewer, which limited any general public acquaintance with the plays. Among the earliest and most illustrious North European translators was the great Dutch scholiast Erasmus (1466?–1536), who took on two of Euripides' offerings. He was particularly interested in *Iphigeneia in Aulis* because of its resemblance to the Biblical account of Isaac's readiness to sacrifice the life of his child in submission to God's demand, followed by the supernatural intervention that stayed the father's hand. Erasmus was dismayed at the difficulty that beset him in interpreting the by now corrupt Greek texts.

One of the problems besetting Renaissance scholars and clergy in accepting the plays was how to reconcile fifth-century BC Greek values with the Christian beliefs and ethics that had long since superseded them. The best way to revitalize these remarkable literary works was to change them in accordance with latter-day tastes and governing philosophical concepts. Fifteenth-century Europe was very different from Pericles' day. Besides, Roman drama – Seneca's heritage – stood between the remote Golden Age of Greece and this new era; it distorted the picture of what classical drama had truly been like. Senecan melodrama was far better known, perhaps in some measure because it was more recent and Latin was far more current. Along with Seneca's legacy, the Latin comedies of Plautus and Terence outpaced the Greek works in travelling north, providing structural models, plot ideas and stereotypical characters to the Spanish, French and – in England – Elizabethan and Jacobean playwrights.

As Mueller shows in *Children of Oedipus*, the themes of Sophocles, Euripides and Seneca took on fresh life in France and England of the sixteenth and seventeenth centuries – even on into the eighteenth. Early in both countries, and somewhat later in Germany, playwrights discovered and plundered the mythology and original plot-inventions that had served the ancient tragic poets. They did this by adopting a variety of forms, ranging from faithful translation to boldly free adaptation, avoiding clear or oblique imitations by changing the place, altering the characters' traits and behaviour, updating or even "modernizing" the story so as to make it more topical in one way or another. (A passing note: Aeschylus was drawn upon the least, possibly because he wrote in the older form of Greek, harder to decipher.) In a great many instances, elements of two or more Periclean plays were combined, or Senecan touches added, to bring forth a "new" tragedy.

In Italy itself, where copies of the Periclean scripts were cloistered, the Humanist movement, dedicated to the recovery of almost forgotten classical learning and literature, caught fire among playwrights when the Venetian printer Aldus used his press to make accessible all the seven extant works of Sophocles (1502), followed a year later by publication of the full body of Euripides' surviving plays, and then in 1518 by those of Aeschylus. Here was a feast of exciting poetic subject-matter for a series of current Italian writers who unhappily were, as Gassner phrases it succinctly, "journeymen rather than masters of their trade". It must be said that they left nothing of lasting worth.

Nevertheless, a "landmark" borrowing from the Athenians was *Sofonisba (*1515), by Ciro (Giangiorgio or Giovanni) Trissino. Possessed of much erudition, Trissino had written an *Arte Poetica*, paying tribute to the ideas of Aristotle, as well as to others propounded later by Horace, the Latin poet and critic. Trissino's purpose in *Sofonisba*, often described as the first European tragedy to be modelled consciously on Greek tragedy, was to elevate the undistinguished playwriting of his day; accordingly, he carefully gives his drama a shape conforming to that of works seen at the Dionysia. He also chooses to use blank verse rather than the classical prosody then in vogue. But his play is about an incident in the Punic Wars: the daughter of a Carthaginian general is forcibly separated from her master, an East Numidian prince. Seized by the King of Western Numidia and carried off to Rome, she drinks a fatal cup of poison sent to her by her husband. Trissino's chief inspiration is Virgil and the *Aeneid*, not Greek mythology or Homer's animated and vigorous epics, and his *Sofonisba*, though dignified and well intentioned, is woefully static. He lacks a true feel for theatre. Yet he was widely emulated by other Italian writers.

His fellow Humanist and friend, Giovanni Rucellai (1475–1525), fashioned his *Rosamunda* to take a form like that of Sophocles' *Antigone*, but making use of local history it concerns the fate of characters at the mercy of a tyrant during the Lombard invasion of northern Italy, and it too is exceedingly static. Still, as has been said, plots based on more recent events and occurring in nearer places had more appeal to contemporary audiences. Rucellai did venture an *Orestes* derived from Euripides' *Iphigeneia in Tauris.*

A third Italian Humanist, Lodovico Dolce (1508–68), went directly to Euripides' *The Phoenician Women* for the subject of his *Giocasta*, in which the sons of Oedipus are rivals and ultimately engage in mortal combat. Lodovici Martelli, a Florentine, composed *Tullia* (1533), which owes a debt to Sophocles' *Electra*; it concludes with an epiphany, the semi-divine Romulus arriving most expediently to resolve the characters' dilemma.

The recurrent Greek themes, incest and outrageous family mayhem, were reintroduced by Giovanni Battista ("Cinthio") Giraldi, professor of philosophy and rhetoric in Ferrara, whose *Orbecche* (1541) has a pile of moral horrors and slayings that far exceeds those in the House of Atreus. Among the victims are children, a father, a husband and a grandfather. At the climax the unhappy Princess Orbecche herself commits suicide. This wild farrago, like so many other pieces of the period, was far more Senecan than Greek. Its initial performance was given in Giraldi's own home. The spectators were grasped by it so strongly that a host of imitations quickly ensued. In this work, and others that came later, Giraldi observed the unities of time, place and action: the façade of a palace is the background, and messengers bring word of off-stage happenings. He published an essay, *Discorso delle commedie e delle tragedie* (1543), quoting from Aristotle and offering an interpretation of *katharsis* that anticipates the theories of the French classicists and, in Germany, that of G.E. Lessing. One of Giraldi's prose tales, *Moro di Venezia*, is the source of Shakespeare's *Othello*, so his influence is not inconsiderable.

Incest is also a theme in *Canace* (1542), a tragedy owing much to *Orbecche*; its author, Sperone Speroni, also a professor of philosophy and rhetoric in Padua, became the focus of a fierce and long-lasting controversy in the academies of the day after the script appeared in print, the question being debated having to do with artistic concepts, an argument that continued even after Speroni's death.

This group of Renaissance playwrights, called Humanist because the promptings of its members were secular, had intentions quite different from those working in the serious medieval theatre, dedicated to serving the Church and enforcing its teachings. Though the plays are filled with egregious bloody deeds and bloated emotions, and for the most part are now tedious to read, being of interest only to literary specialists and theatre antiquarians, the fascination with Greek subject-matter did lead more inventive and gifted spirits to create the forms of opera and pastoral drama, an accomplishment of true significance. (This period will be revisited in Chapter 6, covering Greek comedy.)

The French Humanist playwrights have already been mentioned. At court, a centre of theatre activity, there was much curiosity about the *tragédie à l'antique*, while the poets who made up the Pléiade, the circle headed by Pierre de Ronsard, developed an enthusiasm for reconstituting a drama like that of the Athenians. Another initiative was an edict in 1548 against any further performances of mystery plays, the most conspicuous component of the medieval religious pageants. Etienne Jodelle, a youthful member of the circle, not only translated Sophocles' *Antigone*, but also delved into *Plutarch* and wrote *Cleopatra Captive* (1552), the first of the Neoclassical tragedies there. He observed Aristotle's prescribed unities, and had a single setting – before a palace, and beside it a tomb for Anthony – that contained the action. He was twenty and himself essayed the role of Cleopatra. His fellow members of the Pléiade were so pleased with his efforts that they ceremoniously brought him a goat, traditionally ivy-garlanded, a pagan gesture that evoked protests and charges of scandalous impiety. He was also responsible for a *Medea* and a *Didon se sacrifiant*, a subject drawn from Virgil. (Throughout the sixteenth century the sad fate of love-lorn Dido was a favourite theme of playwrights in Italy, France and England, as was the exotic and heroic legend of Cleopatra, the beauteous and seductive Egyptian.)

After Jodelle came Mellin de Saint-Gelais, a court librarian, who translated Trissino's *Sofonisba*, eschewing the verse for prose and obtaining from Henri II a gala production at the royal Château de Blois (1556). In "sumptuous costumes", the king's own daughters had roles, and among the spectators was the Scottish princess Mary Stuart, shortly to wed the Dauphin.

The sixteenth century soon saw a growing profusion of other Humanist poet–playwrights; they held the stage through the seventeenth, a period which they gradually shared with the Baroque and Neoclassical; they included the richly gifted brothers Pierre and Thomas Corneille, along with Jean Racine, Jacques Pradon, Paul Scarron and lesser rivals. Going into the eighteenth century, the theatrical picture was increasingly dominated by the taste of Louis IV's dictatorial minister Cardinal Richelieu, who decreed that only Neoclassical works were acceptable to him, and who made Aristotle's precepts sacrosanct. This Neoclassicism flourished in the prodigious output of the philosopher–satirist–tragedian Voltaire (1694–1778), who wrote fifty-three plays. This was also the era of earnest writers such as H.B. de Roqueleyne Longpierre (1659–1731) and J. de LaGrange-Chance (1677–1758). Noteworthy is Prosper Jolyot Crebillion (1674–1762), author of the horrific *Atreus and Thyestes* (1707), in which the father quaffs a flagon of his children's blood, a melodrama followed shortly by an *Electre* (1708) which gives Aegisthus a son and daughter who lamentably are infatuated with Orestes and Electra, further complicating the legendary plot.

A number of the prominent Humanists have been identified on previous pages, together with the titles of their translations, adaptations or other compounded and updated versions of the Greek and Senecan tragedies. Others most respected among them are Jean de la Taille (1533–1608), Jacques

Grévin (1539–70), Robert Garnier (1544–90), Pierre Matthieu (1553–1621) and Jean de Routrou (1609–50). The best known of them will be reported on more lengthily where appropriate elsewhere; for that the reader should find the index helpful.

Throughout these years – and even centuries – a number of Humanist and Baroque playwrights wrote erudite essays embracing the aesthetic "laws" of Aristotle and Horace; the three unities were to be rigidly obeyed. An early composer of such a treatise in France was Lazare de Baïf (*c.* 1496–1547), a scholar and diplomat; he translated Euripides' *Electra* (1537) and *Hecuba* (1544?); his essay, *Définition de la tragédie* was published in 1537. His son, Jean-Antoine de Baïf, emulating his distinguished parent, translated Sophocles' *Antigone* and a Plautine comedy. (It might be remarked here that most of these playwrights had professions by which they earned a livelihood greater than what accrued from their labours with quill-pens at their desks in quiet seclusion. Grévin was a physician and Garnier a magistrate.) From Matthieu, a lawyer and historian, emanated a *Clytemnestre* (published 1589); from J.V. Vivien de Chateaubrun a *Philoctète,* in which the wounded hero shares his island exile with a daughter of whom Neoptolemus becomes passionately enamoured; from Jean Galbert de Campistron (1656–1723) an *Andronic* (1685) that inverts the story of *Phaedra* by having a son overwhelmed by illicit love for his young stepmother; from Claude Guymond de La Touche, an *Iphigeneia in Tauris* (1757) in which he follows the practice of Voltaire and simplifies the plot, restoring its original clear outline.

In Germany, the then Humanist movement coincided with the Reformation, and its advocates were largely adherents to the spreading Protestantism. Neoclassical precepts and ideals were spelled out for scholars and teachers in a treatise by Julius Caesar Scaliger (1494–1558), where Aristotle's guidance was fully accepted with only a few added personal suggestions.

Martin Luther's friend, the educator Philipp Melancthon (1497–1560), rendered Euripides' *Hecuba* into Latin (1525); similarly, Joseph Scaliger, a contemporary teacher, accomplished the same task with Sophocles' *Ajax.* Recasting a work from one ancient language to another might strike a modern reader as an oddly motivated enterprise, but Latin was more generally studied and publicly far more familiar. An innovator, Melancthon founded a private academy in which his pupils staged not only the Euripidean work but also plays by Seneca and Plautus that spared him the labour of translation to Latin but to which he added explanatory prologues in German.

For the most part, Protestant-sponsored schools were where the rediscovered classical scripts were staged, with students assuming roles, though most of their offerings were on religious and not remote pagan subjects. Another noted headmaster, in Strasburg, Sturm, introduced mandatory recitations of the plays in his rhetoric courses; in time these were no longer delivered in Latin but instead in the vernacular, with townsfolk invited as spectators. A novel feature was the visual enactment of incidents that the Greek dramatists had merely reported by the indispensable messenger. In addition to hearing how Ajax was slain by Agamemnon, the spectator could witness a performance of the violent deed. The messenger's description was kept as well. Indeed, those speeches were so prized that in some instances a new one was inserted if the Greek poet had not provided one or if it was missing. An instance of this occurs in Scaliger's version of *Ajax*.

Over the next several decades the Germans borrowed very liberally from the French Humanist and Baroque dramatists but with results of little distinction; until Goethe, hitherto a Romantic poet, went to Italy and underwent a conversion to Neoclassicism, a psychological change that produced in Weimar scripts of major merit such as his *Iphigeneis in Tauris* and Schiller's *Bride of Messina*, neither of which is a near adaptation of the tragedies of Euripides and Sophocles, though both are haunted by the plots and themes of the fifth-century BC dramas. To this category, too, belongs *Medea* (1821), a segment of *The Golden Fleece* trilogy by Franz Grillparzer (1791–1872).

Throughout the nineteenth century there was great interest among German philosophers and historians in antiquity and the art and literature of the Hellenes, as evidenced by an outpouring of books on them; it began with Lessing and culminated in Nietzsche's *Birth of Tragedy*, along with speculations and minute philological analyses by other scholars prompting controversy that, while overly pedantic, acrimonious and narrow in scope, often shed light and established new ways of looking at the plays of the three Athenian poets: how the scripts were staged, how the lines should be declaimed, the exact meter prescribed, the possible connotation of certain words and phrases.

The Dutch jurist Hugo Grotius (1583–1645), writing about the laws of war and peace during his exile in France, took on the added tasks of dramatic criticism and translation of the Greek tragedies.

In Italy, Alfieri (1749–1803) contrived his versions of *Agamemnon* and *Oreste* – as noted before – and faithfully observed the three unities in all his stage work, but his spirit was Romantic, his plays fiery pleas for his country's freedom.

England's exuberant Ben Jonson (1572/73–1637), largely self-educated but far better versed in Latin and Greek than his friend Shakespeare, was able to quote from Aristotle and Horace – though not always accurately – and sprinkle his frequently rough dialogue with classical allusions, which he did with delight. A forerunner of Classical Humanism in his own world, that of London's theatre, he vowed fidelity to the Aristotelian concepts of formal structure, language and the three unities, but used Roman rather than Greek characters and stories in his serious plays, and though he borrowed

New Comedy stereotypes to people his farces he gave them contemporary dress. Neoclassicism was not firmly installed in England until some later poets, John Dryden, Nathaniel Lee and James Thomson in the late seventeenth century, endorsed it and made it the fixed theatre mode. The work of this period has also been dubbed Pseudo-classic. As already listed, Dryden and Lee in tandem wrote an *Oedipus* (1679) in which the ghost of Laius appears and reveals his son's unwitting guilt. To modern taste, the heroic dramas of Dryden and Lee are dull and bombastic, and Lee's melodramatic effects often preposterous, but in his day Dryden was England's pre-eminent poet, and Lee, though mentally ill – Allardyce Nicoll unkindly dubs him "the Bedlamite" – had lucid intervals and won loud and surprisingly long-lasting applause for his fustian offerings. He was an actor and knew how to stir spectators. Dryden's initial aim, when writing for the stage, was to fashion rhymed dialogue. Eventually he reverted to blank verse, an example from *Oedipus* being this speech in which the metaphysical, Job-like question repetitively asked is "Why, you Gods, was virtue made to suffer?" The answer is attempted in Act V:

The Gods are just. –
But how can Finite measure Infinite?
Reason! alas, it does not know it self!
Yet Man, vain Man, would with this short-lin'd Plummet,
Fathom the vast Abysse of Heav'nly justice.
What ever is, is in its Causes just;
Since all things are by Fate. But pur-blind Man
Sees but a part o' the Chain; the nearest links;
His eyes not carrying to that equal Beam
That poizes all above.

A twentieth-century actor would have difficulty with that speech, and his audience would be even more perplexed in seeking to comprehend it. Dryden did far better in his comedies, and his *All for Love*, a revision of Shakespeare's *Antony and Cleopatra*, is admirable and remains viable.

The *Agamemnon* (1738) of James Thomson, though it did not win much attention, absolves Clytemnestra of directly instigating her husband's murder; the blame for that is placed on Aegisthus, who does not expose his plan to her until as late as Act IV. Until then the queen is almost persuaded by Agamemnon that the sacrifice of Iphigeneia was necessary to save the state. Clytemnestra is about to warn Agamemnon of his danger, but jealousy and anger aroused by beholding Cassandra deter her after Aegisthus instils in her the idea that the Trojan princess is the conqueror's mistress. Agamemnon is delineated as generous and kind, a view also held by Electra, who envies her sister Iphigeneia's chance to be a glorious martyr. Many other changes were made by Thomson, who adds new characters to the cast, one of them Melisander, a replacement for Pylades in the role of wise counsellor to Orestes, whom he rescues after Agamemnon's slaying. In another play, *Edward and Eleanore* (published 1739), Thomson transposes Euripides' *Alcestis* to the Near East during the Crusades and gives the story a happy resolution.

Greek subject-matter, but certainly not classical form or supposed restraint, is found in *The Tragedy of Orestes* (*c.* 1616) by Thomas Goffe, which drips Senecan gore and exhibits Orestes and Pylades taking fiendish pleasure while piling every sort of cruelty on Aegisthus and Clytemnestra, whose infant is killed before their eyes, its blood squirted into their faces and also handed to them in a cup. Eventually Orestes, Pylades and Electra, having accomplished their familial murders, are punished and end their own lives. Here Neoclassical drama regresses to the genre of Elizabethan revenge tragedy. The play was performed by students at Christ Church, Oxford.

5

MASKED AND UNMASKED

During Victoria's long reign, when manners were sedate, the Greek dramas were read but very seldom staged. Indeed, the Lord Chamberlain, official censor, denied a licence for production to an English version of Sophocles' *Oedipus* because it touched on incest. Nineteenth-century English intellectuals were enthusiastic about the world of the ancient Hellenes, which they largely glorified. They looked back at Pericles' age as a sunlit epoch that celebrated the exploits of handsome, muscular athletes and abounded with revered sages – Socrates, Plato, Aristotle – in cities graced with noble temples and superb sculpture. Of that, they had first-hand knowledge, the cracked Elgin marbles having been carried off from a hill in Athens and enshrined in a London museum. What is more, Athens was governed democratically. And, of course, the Victorians had an easy familiarity with the Homeric epics and heroic body of myths. The accepted image of life in the fifth century BC was now largely a convenient and congenial invention, especially cherished by aesthetes, even by such sophisticates as Walter Pater and Oscar Wilde. Only a few paid close heed to the darker notes sounded by the tragic dramatists, though most university graduates had probably studied them in the original Greek, since mastery of that language and Latin was required by all students of literature.

It was in the late 1880s, when Granville-Barker put on Gilbert Murray's treatments of Euripides' *Hippolytus* and *The Trojan Women*, and then *Electra*, and after a considerable lapse of time *Iphigeneia in Tauris* and Sophocles' *Oedipus*, that the beauty and power of the enacted plays were realized. George Bernard Shaw's voice was not the only one to shout praise. Allardyce Nicoll says of them, "The texts by Murray (though a later world would be ungrateful to them, scorning the Swinburnian rhythms) did much more for Greek drama in English than any other translations have achieved. Ivor Brown was only reasonable when he said fifty years on, remembering Murray with affection, 'If Greek plays are acted now in English, the version chosen may be some bare-bones prosaic stuff which convinces you that, whatever Greek tragedy may have been intellectually, it had no pulse of poetry, no leap of metre, no warmth of phrase.'"

In Germany and Austria a similar service was performed by the tireless showman Max Reinhardt with productions of Sophocles' *Oedipus* (1910) and Aeschylus' *Oresteia* (1911) in Munich, Berlin and Vienna.

Much earlier, at Covent Garden, Londoners had seen the German production of *Antigone* for which Mendelssohn had composed incidental music. It inspired James Robinson Planché (1796–1880), a versatile creator of the English extravaganza, to produce *The Golden Fleece* (1845), a burlesque version of Euripides' *Medea*, for the aptly named Olympic Theatre, which he operated. He designed it to be given "after the Greek manner", which called for a chorus and a raised stage. The chorus consisted solely of Charles Matthews Jr, a comedian like his well-known father and an author in his own right. The lead, Medea, was taken by Madame (Lucia) Vestris, a lady of high profile in London's theatre history, who was usually paired in farces with Matthews, her husband, and who often headed her own company and had herself managed the Olympic for a time. As described by Michael Booth, in *Prefaces to English Nineteenth-century Theatre*, the plot was "generally that of Euripides, with the omission of a tragic ending. Instead, Medea and her two children fly off, to the finale of *Post Horn Galop*, in a chariot drawn by two dragons. . . . Matthews introduced the play to the audience, sang explanatory songs *solus* and a duet with Medea, called on Jason to save his children, and led off the finale – a thoroughly ingenious and wittily conceived role, and one of Matthews' most famous parts." Planché wrote a number of other lively parodies of Greek themes, among them *Olympic Revels* and *Olympic Devils*, the latter dealing with the legend of Orpheus and his Eurydice.

A bit later in Paris, the German-born composer Jacques Offenbach (1819–80) and his acridly witty librettists Ludovic Halévy (1834–1908) and Henri Meilhac (1831–97) discovered that humour could be extracted from the Greek legends, resulting in two of their many frolicsome operettas, *Orphée aux enfers* (1858) and *La Belle Hélène* (1867); both works are still frequently revived. But these operettas did not as directly parody or burlesque the Athenian tragedies as had Planché in his raid on Euripides' *Medea*. Instead, as sharply edged satires they owed rather more to Aristophanes.

In Athens, theatre almost vanished during the centuries of Byzantine and Turkish domination. In 1834 there was not a single playhouse or acting company in the city where the solemn Dionysia had once been celebrated, but the following year the Théatron Scontzópulos was opened, occupied by its own troupe but mostly by ensembles from France and Italy. The number of such venues soon multiplied. In 1888 a municipal theatre was established and offered opera with native singers; only in 1930 was Etonikon, a national theatre, founded, its first two directors Photos Politis and Dimitrios Rondiris.

A significant event was the arrival of young Crete-born Alexis Minotis (Alexander Minotakis, 1900–91), who in 1925 finished his compulsory military stint and began an apprenticeship with a commercial troupe in Athens and then, together with the actress Katina Paxinou (1900–1973), joined the new Greek National Theatre, which they eventually headed. The pair were married a dozen years after their first meeting (1940). They and their company dedicated themselves to reviving the classics, not only the fifth-century BC Greeks, but also Shakespeare, Ibsen, Strindberg and Pirandello alongside O'Neill, Lorca, Brecht and Beckett. These plays were taken on tour throughout the nation, but outside the country too, as far as the United States, and the troupe gained international prestige.

The couple's lives were replete with hazard and adventure. During the Second World War Minotis was twice captured by the German invaders but escaped, made his way to Cairo, and next to Los Angeles, where he was reunited with his wife, who had earlier taken refuge in London. She had spent eighteen hours adrift after the ship on which she voyaged was torpedoed and went down. In California he eked out a living playing small roles in English-language films, while she was more fortunate and was given major character parts, particularly as Pilar in *Farewell to Arms* and Christine Mannon in *Mourning Becomes Electra.* The pictures were great successes, which added to her renown. As Pilar she won an Academy Award. On the stage she had already been acclaimed for her Clytemnestra (1932), Anna Christie (1932), Mrs Alving (1934), Electra (1936), Hedda Gabler (1942) and Jocasta (1952). She herself translated the O'Neill into Greek.

In 1950, after an eight-year absence, the pair returned to Athens and restored the National Theatre; they continued to stage the revered tragedies as well as experimental new works. Through their efforts the plays of Aeschylus and his contemporaries were revivified and well represented in their homeland.

Athens and elsewhere in Greece provide sites where the fifth-century dramas can be seen in what might be considered ideal circumstances, by taking advantage of the still extant, scattered open-air theatres which, though partly ruined, have the grandeur of their lasting natural settings and miraculously serve their original purpose. The two most prominent locations are at Epidaurus and Herodes Atticus, both near the Parthenon on its hill-crest. Other remnants of ancient Greek theatres similarly utilized are at Ephesus, in the mountains at Delphi and on the island of Rhodes, where spectators have commanding views that stretch far beyond and below the playing-ring. Such performances have proved to be lucrative tourist attractions, drawing thousands. The plays are given in modern Greek, not as originally written. Even so, the actors bear an added burden, since a good part of the audience is foreign and cannot understand what is being said, despite many of them being reasonably acquainted with the story's outline.

Minotis essayed *Oedipus* in London (1939), during an engagement in which he took the title role of *Hamlet* using Greek. (His English was described as "resonant, only slightly accented". A critic called his interpretation "stirring and fresh".) At various times he undertook other Shakespearean characters: Henry V, Richard III, Shylock. As he aged, he became strongly associated by his public with the protagonist of *Oedipus at Colonus*, which he and the company presented at the City Center in New York (1976). Mel Gussow, in his review in the *New York Times,* found the unfamiliar language a considerable obstacle. "There is a timelessness about the play, and about the production. The staging by Alexis Minotis, and his performance, are filled with authority and authenticity. Actually, there is a stately, almost a monumental, quality to the production that does not make it easy to watch. In *Oedipus at Colonus* words are the actions. It is a passionate, but not always a dramatic play, an obvious reason why the work is rarely performed. In this production we do miss the language." Though headsets with an English translation were available, Gussow did not find them adequate. He suggested:

> The best advice is to ignore the commentary and watch the stage. As Oedipus says about himself, "Ears are his eyes." Seeing this production, our eyes become our ears.
>
> We see a stage set for a graveyard. The chorus, composed as if sitting for a frieze, is stone against stone. Oedipus is leonine and chalky white, weighted by his beard, his trials and his woes. He rests on a rock and stares, as the obviously anguished Antigone tries to be comforting. Seeing her sister, Ismene, in the distance, she is a vision of joy. Oedipus scarcely registers a reaction, but embraces both daughters.
>
> In Mr Minotis's performance, there is a quiet, sustaining power. This is, after all, Oedipus reaching the end of his agony. Seldom does the actor raise his voice, but we feel the intensity of his scorn as Creon tries to convince him to return to Thebes and as his own ungracious son attempts, with great guile, to ally themselves together as homeless outcasts. This Oedipus is above flattery but not yet beyond misery.

> . . . He waits. He endures. Finally thunder and lightning strike, and we feel his final leap to attention as he hears his symbolic call to death. Gracefully, he exits. "This is the end of tears," says the chorus. "No more lament." The play itself is a lament, a threnody for a lost king.

On the occasion of this visit to New York – the company had been there once before, shortly after the Second World War, in 1952 – he was interviewed by Nicholas Gage for the *New York Times.* The son of a fabric manufacturer, and one of ten children, Minotis related, he had seen his first play when he was twelve and was taken to a performance by a touring company. He immediately decided that he would be an actor. "My family thought that going into the theater was like going into prostitution, but the theater saved my life. I had a tendency toward self-destruction, but theater was a kind of religion, like going into a monastery on Mount Athos."

He had first met Katina Paxinou when she came backstage after a performance to see a friend who was a member of the troupe. "She never took an acting lesson in her life, but she had a voice, so mature! She was full of poetry. After her, nobody can play Electra." Their marriage, a dozen years later, took place because they foresaw that the war's outbreak might part them, a wise perception. "She was going to London to play in *Hedda Gabler*, and I was to go there soon after to play Shylock. Before that, we had not had time to marry; we worked day and night in the theater." After the Battle of Dunkirk, when the British forces retreated from the Continent, the pair were without contact with each other for two years. Minotis reached Cairo by way of Izmir, Turkey, and made his way to the United States when the exiled King of Greece, George II, provided him with a visa as a royal courier.

Minotis paid tribute to Photos Politis, the first director of the National Theatre, under whom he had served part of his apprenticeship. "He told us that theatrical art is to express the human soul. Theater is not to please the audience, but to make them understand, to elevate them."

His first job in Hollywood, he smilingly told Gage, was as the butler in Alfred Hitchcock's *Notorious.* "I found myself standing in a line with six hundred other European actors who had accents. As you came up to the table, you were asked your name, nationality, height and last film credit. When I replied I was Greek and had never made a film, they were disgusted and waved me on. Hitchcock was standing nearby and said: 'Greeks are good actors. I saw a first-class production of *Hamlet* in London once, by a Greek company.' Turning to me he asked, 'Did you ever see that production?' 'Yes,' I said. 'I was in it.' 'What part did you play?' 'Hamlet.'

"'Stop!' Hitchcock shouted to the casting directors. 'Give this guy some gravy!' And after that for eleven weeks he had one thousand dollars a week sent to me, whether I worked or not."

In Rome he became friendly with the Nobel-Prize-winning novelist William Faulkner, who was writing a film script, *The Land of the Pharaohs*, and had seen Minotis in New York as Oedipus. Faulkner insisted that the Greek actor be signed to portray the High Priest in the picture, because "I was the only actor alive who knew how to wear a tunic."

In New York a bond was also formed with Eugene O'Neill. One night, though Carlotta Monterey, the playwright's wife, sought to discourage it, Minotis visited their apartment and read for them the first act of *A Long Day's Journey into Night.* Subsequently, Minotis and Paxinou translated the work into Greek and produced it in Athens, with Paxinou as the morphine-addicted Mary Tyrone.

When interviewed by Gage, the actor was seventy. He said, "I have lived too long, but I have lived a conscious life, that is the important thing." His wife had died three years earlier, and he felt lost, having no children, being alone. He threw himself into his work to a degree that was by his own account "fanatic". During the years of the rule of Greece by a military junta, beginning in 1967, Minotis and Paxinou had refused to perform, and Paxinou died just as the repressive junta began to lose power (1973).

Of his role in *Oedipus at Colonus*, Minotis revealed to Gage his conviction that the work was autobiographical. "I am not playing only Oedipus; I am playing Sophocles. I have spent seventy years preparing to play *Oedipus at Colonus.*" For him, the tragedy has as much meaning as it had borne 2,400 years before. "Oedipus' fate is symbolically the fate of every human being. While man may be helpless in controlling what happens to him, within himself he can choose to live honestly and to die with dignity. Oedipus blinded himself so that he could open the eyes of his soul to the truth. Today, men are most interested not in how to live a good life but in how to make a good living; no one thinks about dying. But living is one thing; how to make a death is another. *Oedipus at Colonus* has a happy ending, because Oedipus accepts death on his own terms. He pursued the truth no matter where it led him and endured nobly the suffering it brought him." Minotis lived two decades after this, dying at ninety.

Some members of the National Theatre of Greece returned to America in 1984, invited to participate in the cultural side of the Olympic Games held in Los Angeles; they brought with them a production of *Oedipus Rex* that had been staged two years earlier at the Epidaurus Festival. The director was Minos Volanakis, the Oedipus was Nikos Kourkoulos, the Jocasta was Katerina Helmi; they were accompanied by other players and a chorus of thirty-two. After the Los Angeles engagement the company stopped for performances in Detroit, Montreal, Boston, Washington, DC, Chicago,

Toronto, Ottawa and New York City, where it occupied the Vivian Beaumont Theater in Lincoln Center. Once again a *New York Times* critic questioned whether a play "so highly rhetorical" was the best choice to send to a country where Greek was not widely comprehended. Richard F. Shepard found compensations:

> Cause for gratitude arises not only from the exportation of a play that is one of the constant beacons in mankind's often blurred study of itself but also from a staging that has the sight and feel of an authentic work in its native habitat. Sitting in the Beaumont's amphitheater seats, the sense of being in the audience at an ancient amphitheater is created by the impressively spare and tilted stage. The players are clad in robes and masks that contribute a diversity and color sorely needed in this merciless, hard story.
>
> Minos Volanakis, the director, has virtually choreographed the chorus, reversing its traditional static stance so that it now acts as a conduit for the story not only in words but also in theatrical exercises that have its members standing, kneeling, snaking about the set, sometimes doffing their austere robes to show that the chorus, too, is composed of mere men.
>
> Despite its visual attraction, language, in this case, creates a formidable barrier between audience and performance.

Shepard observed that many of those in attendance represented the elite of New York's Greek community and could grasp Volanakis' translation into his modern native speech, but not even they could understand all of it, especially

> the subtle use of terms common in Greek Christian liturgy inserted into a script about pagan gods. But for those who didn't, the house was simply too dimly lit – aptly for this stark tragedy – for one to follow the synopses that tell of each scene in the one-act play during its one-hundred-minute course.
>
> *Oedipus Rex* is a tragedy told in words, not in events onstage. . . . Here is fate so cruel it even makes the pure at heart demonstrably guilty. It's hard enough to get this across in one's own language and virtually impossible to do when spoken in another tongue. Nikos Kourkoulos, in the title role, is a powerful and handsome performer with a strong delivery, but one suspects that there are cultural differences in how this role would be interpreted in English-speaking theater – perhaps with more modulations of voice, allowing for introspective lows and the manly assertive highs.
>
> Although some may be interested in seeing imaginative stagecraft from a country where theater was born, others, less venturesome and curious, may find *Oedipus Rex* something of a chore. That is

> what prompts the wish that this talented ensemble might have brought us something that might better vault the barriers of vocabulary by appealing more to the eye than to the ear, to the heart than to the brain.

Another acting group, the Greek Tragedy Theatre, founded and directed by Dimitrios Rondiris, came from Athens to the New York City Center. The company offered Sophocles' *Electra* and afterwards Euripides' *Medea* (1961) for separate two-week engagements. Irene Pappas, a noted actress, was Clytemnestra in the *Electra*; both productions were given in Greek, with earphones allowing a simultaneous translation.

In Athens various schools of thought evolved as to the right approach to staging the hallowed works. Ianthee Vassiliades, in a special article in the *New York Times* (1980), told of the debates among Greek directors, actors and teachers about whether current productions should preserve something approximating their original form or should be made more relevant to twentieth-century audiences. Those who favoured drastically updating the plays came to be known as the "renegades", while those opposing them were designated the "classicists". One problem, of course, was that no one could propound with certainty how the plays actually had been mounted. In the late 1970s a typical "renegade", Ioannis Tsarouchis, a recognized painter, put on a highly political version of Euripides' *The Trojan Women* in which the male members of the cast wore tuxedos and bathrobes and recited their lines in a Greek dialect similar to that of refugees from Asia Minor. Quite different was a venture by Lino Karzia who, a few years earlier, presented several of the tragedies with the actors masked, wearing the high wooden boots, huge gloves and thick shoulder pads that endowed their bodies "supernatural proportions", an effect reinforced by their stylized gestures and exaggerated vocal delivery. Most directors of both camps adopted stark settings and sombre costuming, and their carefully rehearsed choruses adhered to close unison when chanting choral passages.

The "renegades" argued that the classic theatre was losing its appeal and nearing extinction. "It impresses but does not move," Vassiliades wrote, quoting Constantine Livadeas, an actor and head of a section of a Greek television channel devoted to drama. "It depicts a different reality." Again, among the "classicists", Michael Cacoyannis, a film and stage director of international reputation, maintained: "The authors transcended their century and their Greekness. Though the playwrights were summarizing their world, they stretch to cover this world. There is not one human issue that has not been covered by Aeschylus, Euripides and Sophocles, the three greatest playwrights of all time." Yet he was on the side of those who felt the plays must be freshly conceived to have the utmost significance to contemporary spectators. "Any attempt to reproduce the style of ancient times is betrayal. But the worst disservice one could do the author is to force the play into a superficial modernization which keeps the audience interpreting symbols and inevitably localizing the play."

Pelos Kataselis, heading a private drama school in Athens, contended that in an age of anti-heroes, such as the late twentieth century, this ancient drama more than ever met an urgent psychological need. "It illustrates the beautiful throughout time. It is a vital necessity."

Alex Minotis, tending towards orthodoxy, went even further in asserting that the characters in the tragedies were best portrayed by Greek actors, that it was their natural birthright, latent in their genes; a view to which not all subscribed, especially those who might have beheld Olivier as Oedipus.

In spite of all this debate, Vassiliades reported, vast audiences flocked to the open-air theatres at Epidaurus and elsewhere. In addition to tourists, the crowds were filled with working-class Greeks. In the colder seasons the companies toured to other cities, isolated villages and abroad, often assisted by subsidies and under government sponsorship.

A difficulty was recruiting young performers for the classic plays. As explained by Vassiliades:

> The physical demands are exhausting and the rewards not enough to win aspiring actors away from television and modern theater. An actor in ancient theaters had to be heard by fifteen thousand people, and that still requires strong lungs, excellent articulation, a tenor's voice. "He who plays ancient drama is an athlete, not an actor," declares Thanos Kotsopoulos. Kakia Panagiotou, who has starred in the classics in Greece and abroad, finds it a demanding but rewarding experience. "It is a katharsis of the soul, a huge effort, for everything must be grandiose, everyone must be a hero," she says. But younger performers no longer are willing to undergo the years of apprenticeship such projection requires. "Playing in the chorus is necessary training before moving on to leading roles," says Antigone Glykofridis, an Oceanide in the National Theatre's production of *Prometheus Bound.* "But there are few leading roles, and it is hard to move beyond the chorus."
>
> "You need everything in the chorus," complains Beatrice Deliyianni, another member of the troupe. "You need to have a good voice, to dance well, to act well. Everyone gives all they've got in the chorus, but this is overlooked within the total performance." For young players, the result has been growing disenchantment. To them, not only is the work too rigorous, the rhetoric too artificial, but the chances of gaining fame too slight. Even Nora Katselis, the daughter of Pelos and Aleka Katselis,

> prominent exponents of the classical theater, quit taking roles in it. Speaking of his wife, Aleka, one of Greece's most respected tragic actresses, Pelos Kaletis, her personal coach, attributed her success to her long years of preparation. "Aleka had been playing Medea for four years in a row when I finally told her, 'You are at last feeling the role the way you should. Medea's words must come straight from the womb.'"

Vassiliades voiced his concern that "while the ancient Attic drama is likely to survive any battle over how it should be staged, and to continue moving modern audiences regardless of nationalities, the diminishing numbers of young Greeks willing to dedicate themselves to it regardless of the physical and financial toll it exacted, will deal it a severe blow".

Revivals of Greek tragedies have hardly been limited to Athens. During the second half of the twentieth century stagings of these plays have grown in number throughout Western Europe, North America, even the Orient. In many instances the controversies heard in Greece about the right style of presentation of the plays have been loudly echoed. Here a director sought to be as faithful as possible to the original tradition of staging, and there another updated the plays to a moderate extent – perhaps employing a much smaller chorus to keep down costs, or eschewing masks that modern actors wore with discomfort – and everywhere not a few productions have been idiosyncratic and bizarre.

Author by author, a partial list might begin with Aeschylus' *Prometheus Bound,* exploring a cosmic theme of universal concern, but stocked with odd mythological figures and projecting symbols with extraordinarily obscure clues, hardly an easy experience for modern audiences, and a most daunting task for twentieth-century performers. After seeing a production of this allegorical tragedy at Yale University headed by a professional cast that included the noted English actress Irene Worth, who had enjoyed a long, varied career, the drama critic of the *New York Times,* Walter Kerr, commented:

> It really isn't possible, is it, to play Io in Aeschylus' *Prometheus Bound*? Io, as the *Oxford Companion to Classical Literature* has it, "is a mortal whom Zeus has loved and Hera's jealousy has turned into a heifer. She is doomed to lone wanderings pursued by a gadfly, and haunted by the ghost of the myriad-eyed Argos." Try that on for size. Io is a speech, not a person, a mythological remnant with which we have lost sensitive contact. Miss Worth, eyes glazed but beginning quietly, moved downstage, made her rav-

ishing by Zeus harrowingly, terrifyingly intimate, went on to detail her subsequent torments with such tactile intensity that we found ourselves flinching from each threatened sting. The performance was a mystery in the old sense: a source of awe, of wonder.

But the wonder could be explained. Miss Worth was able to play Io – to make her stripped flesh real flesh, and that without loss of iconographic stature – because she had played so many other challenging roles before now. She had climbed, step by step, test by test, to a mountaintop of her own, where she could turn in any direction and rearrange the emotional weather to suit her needs. An actress's resources may at last come to seem infinite, but that is because she has transformed herself so often that she has simply lost count. What is left is reflex, result of a thousand and one inventive nights.

This Yale production (1967) was directed by the protean Jonathan Miller and, in addition to Irene Worth, had the acting services of Kenneth Haig, also an English star. The translation and adaptation were by the American poet Robert Lowell. His rendering was hardly faithful. In his book *Subsequent Performances*, Miller recalls:

Lowell's version of Aeschylus' *Prometheus Bound* is twice as long as the original, and it is difficult to tell whether it counts as a translation or not. When Lowell wrote his version, he visualized it in the classical setting referred to in the original text. But when I came to stage it, I superimposed yet another level of translation by setting it in a seventeenth-century limbo. Lowell was pleased to discover that his own work, not to mention that of Aeschylus, contained more than either he or his Greek antecedent had knowingly put into it. So what can one make of the claim that the author's intention is the only reliable criterion by which the validity of interpretation is to be judged? . . .

I was immediately struck with the enormous difficulty of staging the play. The idea of an actor tethered to a rock in the middle of the Caucasus is not a very promising start to a theatrical evening, and although this might sound a sweeping generalization it is invariably true that nature looks atrocious on stage. This problem made me think about changing the play's setting, despite the fact that Lowell's stage directions described the mountaintop as Aeschylus had intended. Here is an example of interpretation that might have been seen as typical of the modern director's cavalier attitude towards the author's intention and a trick he would never perpetrate with the author in attendance. But the opposite happened when I discussed this with Lowell. He saw that it would be awkward in practice and, with his enthusiastic collaboration, we came up with an alternative setting.

I looked for a metaphorical counterpart that would suggest some sort of constraint and imprisonment but allow this complicated historical dialogue to take place without the embarrassment of a nasty piece of nineteenth-century naturalism. The Greeks themselves would not have staged the play literally so I did not feel that we were violating a theatrically "authentic" staging. I searched for a way of boxing the work that would allow the production to make references to antiquity, but in some sort of dramatic parenthesis. Having read Frances Yates's *Art of Memory,* I had some ideas about memory theatres and realized that it might be possible to set the play, not in the place where it is said to occur, but in some sort of theatrical limbo that could refer to the rock without representing it. Working with the designer Michael Annals, we set the play in a late Renaissance limbo in the world of the seventeenth century, and on the edges of the Thirty Years War. This meant that we could start by suggesting that an atrocious and terrible execution or torture had just taken place from which a prisoner is brought in accompanied by Force and Power, so named in the text but not necessarily represented as such on stage. By putting the play inside a vast Renaissance courtyard, with walls reaching up into the flies and down into the basement, we used a mnemonic device whose architecture referred to antiquity without requiring a slavish representation of it. In the niches of this great theatre, as Frances Yates suggests, we placed shattered statues, images reminiscent of the characters in the play. The audience could then see Prometheus and Io, with her horns, so that they were put in mind of the myth itself while what they saw enacted on the stage was not the myth but a mnemonic of it. In the same way that Lowell's interpretation of Aeschylus was an imitation, a mnemonic of the original work, so the staging served to place the play inside an ironic framework which released it from a literal production.

The actor playing Prometheus was on a tiny pedestal poised in the middle of the pit and surrounded by the shattered architecture of the courtyard. As we had excavated and removed the stage to extend the towering walls below ground level there was only a narrow catwalk leading to the platform from the back of the theatre. The staging evoked a feeling that some great unknown disaster might occur; it was as if a war had been waged out of sight but nearby. From the beginning to the end of the play Prometheus could not move off the rock but was free to move around the tiny rostrum. This suggested his imprisonment without him having to lie back for two and a half hours in a position that Lowell had provided.

While it would have been unwise to conclude from the enthusiasm with which Lowell accepted this radical interpretation of his work that Shakespeare would have agreed to comparable ideas from his director, it does demonstrate the unfinished nature of the script in relation to a performance which takes shape under the eye and protection of the author. I suspect that playwrights fall into two distinct categories with regard to the interpretability of their work. There are writers, like Lowell, who are more explicitly poetic and for whom the possibility of undisclosed meanings is part and parcel of their

> philosophy of art; and a second group with a much more intolerant attitude to interpretation who believe, perhaps with good reason, that they are in the best possible position to know everything about the meaning and intention of their work.

It would seem that Miller's treatment of *Prometheus Bound* would require a rather knowledgeable audience – but this staging took place at Yale, where one supposes that the significance of the Baroque dress, the shattered statues and the mnemonics were readily grasped.

Miller quotes from a critic, E.D. Hirsch, who opposed his view that a director should have full licence to alter a text and setting, a practice that would lead to a "chaos of interpretations – a veritable slum of alternative ideas about what the work in general means", to which Miller replies: "I think he [Hirsch] is over-optimistic about the extent to which any artist knows what he means, certainly the extent to which a complex and interesting artist knows what he means." He grants that a director too may exceed limits in making changes such as his. "There *must* be a notion of a constraint – and this is introduced by the language, and by the notion of genre. If the genre within which the playwright is working is not recognized as a constraint it is possible to misidentify the play and to start to stage it in ways that denature the work."

As shall be seen, Miller then went on to make a career of staging plays and operas and changing their settings and periods, an approach which has often invited critical dissent and popular controversy. (One question he does not answer is whether a director, any more than an author, always knows just what he is doing.)

A highly eccentric version of the legend, seeking to make it scarifyingly topical, was *The Prometheus Project*, presented Off-Broadway in New York by the experimentalist Richard Schechner (1985). The title echoes the "Manhattan Project", the code name for the secret effort during the Second World War to manufacture a lethal atomic weapon. As summarized by Walter Goodman in the *New York Times*, Schechner's two focal figures were the archetypal sufferers:

> Prometheus who spent thirty or 30,000 years having his liver pecked at by a vulture because he had stolen fire from heaven, and Io, who was changed into a cow by the lustful Zeus and wandered the world tormented by the stings of a gadfly. In Mr Schechner's work, Prometheus becomes the unwitting contributor of the atom bomb to mankind, and Io becomes the prototype of the sexually abused woman. That, at least, is what I gather is intended in these "four movements and coda," since Mr Schechner is not a teller of tales, but an evoker of moods.

The first and most striking movement relies heavily on slides adapted from Renzo Kinoshita's book about Hiroshima, *Pica Don.* They begin with the town's families awakening to a pleasant day, birds flying and flowers growing, and conclude with a blast. For perhaps a quarter of an hour, to the accompaniment of a piercing sound, the ten people onstage go about various small tasks, in slow motion, as though trying to take up lives destroyed by the bomb. The evening's busiest performer, Becke Wilenski, moves continuously in circles, arms outstretched, face distorted to a silent scream. The cellist Mollie Glazer plays Bach, and the choreography by Terry Beck compels concentration. The movement is concluded with a passage from a Bach oratorio, sung by the accomplished Miss Wilenski: "Hear ye, Israel. O hast thou heeded my commandments?"

All this is watched by a motionless figure in a leather coat. His expression is pained. Given the title, he must be Prometheus, suffering at the sight of what he has wrought in bringing fire to mankind.

Mr Schechner's strengths come through here, especially his ability to pack emotion into simple, repetitive actions, to deliver a message through movement. He is less effective when using words, as demonstrated by an odd interlude in which a voice criticizes the slides, in Japanese, for being inaccurate; these remarks are simultaneously translated by two other overlapping voices. The episode is out of sync in more ways than one.

The second movement features Annie Sprinkle, described in a press release as "one of America's foremost and innovative porno movie stars," doing a burlesque turn, *Nurse Sprinkle's Sex Education Turn.* Clothed in an extremely snug nurse's outfit, which soon disappears altogether, Miss Sprinkle gives a most explicit lecture in her teeny voice, to the accompaniment of rude noises from four dirty old men in raincoats who constitute her onstage audience. A film is shown of her performing a fairly typical X-rated movie sequence under the direction of a tough-sounding man. Now and then the performers stop the action to stare accusingly at the audience, as if to say, "Aren't you ashamed, watching such stuff?" Well, Miss Sprinkle, who abounds in everything but subtlety, is easy to watch, and anybody who wanted to walk out on her would have to cross the stage.

The theme of this passage, exploitation of women, is presented more emphatically in the third movement, when Miss Sprinkle puts on the heifer's head of Io, and is joined by a group of virginally garbed women, who pass the next several minutes running back and forth across the stage. The sweep of this chorus, with its slightly changing patterns, builds up cumulative force, reminding us of poor Io's endless running, and the women's gestures of pain recall the Hiroshima sequence. Two of the runners break away from the group, to tell, panting, of sexual assaults by men.

The final movement finds a naked Prometheus being bound up in a tiresomely elaborate manner by two men and a woman. This time the repetitive movements have no impact; you want the tiers-up to stop fooling around and get on with the job. Finally, they do finish; an interpreter tells us how Prometheus was tortured, and Io returns for a sort of reconciliation in which large phrases are tossed about, on the order of "We are only temporary manifestations." They are joined by the rest of the cast, and we learn, "It is the nursery of life itself that is being poisoned." When the words start, the proceedings go slack.

Now, one does not wish to appear unappreciative or literal-minded or, may the Muses forbid, Philistine, but there are difficulties of meaning in *The Prometheus Project.* Mr Schechner is making connections between Hiroshima and pornography, between pornography and rape, between rape and political torture, between torture and Hiroshima. More than that, the equal attention given to the various movements and the way one echoes another suggest that sexual abuse weighs as heavily on his scales of horror as the dropping of the atom bomb. Despite the stage effects, the connections remain dubious, and the notion of any sort of equivalence gives a perversely trendy feeling to an often engrossing experiment.

A far leap from Aeschylus, who in his day was no less daring a breaker of moulds.

Jan Kott, a Polish observer of theatre who had considerable influence on directors in Western Europe and the United States, put forth a fresh analysis of Greek tragedy and *Prometheus Bound* with which Schechner may have been acquainted. In *The Eating of the Gods* (1975, English translation), Kott asserts that "bloody deeds" are what the classic Greek dramas are about. Sophocles' seven extant plays include six suicides and one other try at self-destruction. Heracles experiences agony from the poisoned shirt clinging to his back and strives to tear it off. Ajax, made mad by the vicious edict of Athena, goes about killing dogs and slashing throats of bulls; he is deluded into seeing them as his stalking human foes. But the most significant figure is Prometheus, "the supreme sufferer". After the Second World War any reading of the Greek tragedies must be affected by the hideous legacy of that convulsion, its landscape of concentration camps with their smoking ovens fuelled by the corpses of people. Prometheus is a heroic champion of mankind against human and divine tyranny; he has taken on the responsibility of being "mediator and saviour". As such, he is the great desperate rebel, who if successful might himself become a new omnipotent despot; failing, he is reduced to being a scapegoat. The titanic struggle calls for bloodletting, a cumulative excess of cruelty.

The uncompromising confrontation involves a kind of psychological cannibalism, a ceremony or ritual in which one antagonist – a son opposed to a father, a rebel defying a tyrant – seeks to "devour" his persecutor, to share his natural attributes, to assimilate his strength. After the climactic moment there comes a flash of illumination, a clarifying light or healing epiphany, a new view of the world, a restoration of a simulation of order after horrible chaos. "If mediation does not, never did, and never will exist," Kott says in summary, "if cruelty is the rule of the universe, one can confirm it even with one's own agony." That is man's lot, the inexorable tormenting condition of his mortality. Kott points to Samuel Beckett's *Happy Days*, in which a paralysed man, Willie, gazes yearningly at a half-buried woman, the fatuously prattling Winnie, as the modern equivalent of Aeschylus' probing of the Prometheus myth, his election of it to represent a cosmic maleficence. Yet Kott's conclusion is not fully nihilistic. "Prometheus' greatness is his revolt without hope" – a paraphrase of a dictum by Albert Camus, the Absurdist.

Carl Orff's opera *Prometheus* (1968) has Aeschylus' play as the basis for its libretto but takes many liberties with it: the words used are ancient Greek, the directions are in Latin, the musical indications in Italian, and the scene is changed from a towering, isolated rock in Scythia to a steaming jungle. Even more iconoclastic is the orchestration: "no violins, huge phalanxes of wind instruments, four banjos, and no fewer than forty-two percussion pieces – not including the four pianos, whose keyboards were smashed by forearms and whose strings were struck with cymbals and strummed with fingernails". The score – "simple, severe and static" – carried farther than ever before Orff's conviction that "music should be set to words, not the other way around", and approached his goal of arriving at "a skeletal idiom of powerfully primitive, repetitive sounds".

Except for Prometheus and Io, the singers were partly obscured by grotesque masks and headdresses and declaimed their lines in incantatory drones; while the orchestra "rolled along in seemingly endless *ostinato* figures or erupted with brash punctuations". An unsigned reviewer for *Time* magazine, present at the work's première in Stuttgart, described its reception: "After two uninterrupted hours, some members of the audience may have welcomed the concluding thunderbolt from Zeus that plunged Prometheus into the netherworld; yet most cheered and stomped for twenty minutes when Orff appeared for curtain calls. The notices were more divided. Hans Stuckenschmidt, Germany's leading music critic, wrote that 'the performance counts among the best that one can see and hear today in European theaters.' But *Der Spiegel* scoffed that the opera sounded like a 'prehistoric equinoctial celebration of a voodoo ritual.'"

Rather scanty have been revivals of Aeschylus' *The Persians* outside Greece, possibly because its exotic setting is remote and the historical event it portrays is too little known by twentieth-century spectators, or else because it is an essentially static work, a threnody more than a drama. In 1970 the play was mounted in New York at St George's Church. A reviewer, again in *Time*, had this response:

> Men do not seek tragedy, but it lies in wait for them when they least expect it. They pursue fame, fortune and glory. They strive to found dynasties, subdue the earth, fathom the depths of the sea and the limits of space. In an instant of high-arching pride as men vault to these ambitious goals, fate fells them, and they return to the dust from which they came. The ancient Greek tragedies are cautionary tales of how men incur the wrath of the gods by trying to be gods.
>
> These plays are timeless precisely because man is changeless. After more than two thousand years, the dramas of Aeschylus, Sophocles and Euripides are the most scrupulously exact and eloquently moving accounts that man possesses of the nature of his destiny. Aeschylus' *The Persians* is one of the earliest of these tragedies. Set before the tomb of Darius the Great shortly after the Battle of Salamis, in which the Persians were crushingly defeated by the Athenians, the play is a spoken song of lamentations for the cruelly spent valor of Persia's princes and the fall of a mighty empire.
>
> Aeschylus had fought at Salamis, as he had at Marathon where his brother was killed, and he knew war. While the play is intrinsically undramatic, it is a remarkable achievement, humanly speaking, in that a victor aches with the torment of the defeated, recounts the terrible battle deaths of the slain, shows their widows and mothers keening in desolate, inconsolable grief. It is a kind of reverse *Henry V*, as if Shakespeare had set his play in France after the Battle of Agincourt, put his words in the mouths of the tiny remnants of once-proud French survivors, and evoked the pain in a French mother's heart.
>
> The church setting makes *The Persians* seem like a hushed memorial service for the dead of all wars. Despite an occasional stilted phrase, the John Lewin translation is fluent, vivid and clear. The cast performs with tender gravity, and Jacqueline Brookes, in particular, brings affecting dignity to the role of King Xerxes' mother, as does J.A. Preston as the bearer of unbearable news. Underscoring the dialogue like a chorus of tears is the samur music of composer Nasser Rastegar-Nejad. If someone commissioned a great poet-playwright to write a drama for Moratorium Day, this would be it.

A presentation of *The Persians* at the Schauspielhaus in Düsseldorf (1987) chose costumes and other visual symbols to turn it into a "lamentation of German guilt for World War II".

Using much the same formula, the decidedly eccentric American director Peter Sellars offered a partly updated text by Robert Auletta to stage a *Persians* set against the very recent Gulf War – the violent and catastrophic rollback from Kuwait of invading Iraq. In Sellars's version the defeated, bereaved

Iraqis lament their deep losses. The play, after its début at the Salzburg Festival (1993), was scheduled to be seen at the Edinburgh Festival, the Los Angeles Festival, and in Paris and Berlin. John Rockwell, of the *New York Times*, wrote from Salzburg: "At times this stage production's Saddam-like harangues grew monochromatic. Still, a full audience applauded the fine acting by a cultural potpourri of a cast."

Of the *Oresteia* there have been innumerable productions, some of the individual plays comprising the trilogy, some of the three in combination, in a variety of styles, and not without surprising mutations. Early in the century the prodigious, tireless German showman Max Reinhardt displayed to Berlin audiences his idea of how the Aeschylean work should be done. He put it on at his colossal Zirkus Schumann, where could be seated more than 3,500, and later 5,000 after he had it expanded and renamed the Grosses Schauspielhaus. When an opportunity afforded, Reinhardt liked staging on a monumental scale. In post-Second World War Paris the Barrault-Renaud Company, organized by the famed acting husband-and-wife couple, added an *Oresteia* to their repertoire (1955), with a French translation by André Obey, an author best known for his *faux-naïf* scriptural play *Noah*.

Dancer and choreographer Martha Graham, one of the first proponents of the modern anti-balletic idiom, delved into mythology and the Greek tragedies for her *Clytemnestra* (1958), conceived as a "ritual drama". As described by Anna Kisselgoff in the *New York Times*:

> The story of the *Oresteia*, transposed to a nearly wordless pageant, takes on a full ceremonial cast in Miss Graham's treatment. How it is told, and how it will affect us is all that matters.
>
> The telling, it happens, is anything but straightforward. Miss Graham's masterpiece uses cinematic techniques of flashback and her own narrative devices in which one person plays several characters or one character is depicted by more than one person.
>
> Essentially, she tells her story three times. The first act, if seemingly the most confusing, is also the most interesting. The action, or rather vision, is a projection of Clytemnestra's mind. This is typical Graham. A towering figure, in a moment of crisis, looks back upon the crucial events of her life. Through the heroine's jumbled sensibilities, events begin to take shape. Helen of Troy is seduced by Paris . . .
>
> By the time we have sorted out the characters in the first act, Miss Graham is ready to tell her story in relatively linear terms in the next two acts. Even so, the beauty of her chronology is that it is never pat, there is always time for an eruption from those wonderful grotesque Furies, hurtling their distorted bodies through the air.
>
> Years before Lawrence Durrell wrote *The Alexandria Quartet*, Miss Graham made ambiguity of

motives a major theme. Seeing this grand piece of theater again, one marveled at how she provides many answers and yet none. Does Clytemnestra, in this version, kill Agamemnon because he kills her daughter? Or is it because he mistreats her?

Every possibility was made clear on this occasion by an unusually strong cast that individualized each character. Yuriko Kimura, as Clytemnestra, suffered visibly when Iphigeneia suffered. And yet she could be as strong as she was soft, dueling with Terese Capucilli's astoundingly forceful Electra, and mocking in her parody of Donlin Foreman's pompous Agamemnon.

The wide range of Miss Kimura's performance, expressed both in movement and face, was at its most distilled in what could be called her pure-dance solos. Every downhead turn was done with amazingly slow completeness and every slide down to the knees had a compelling urgency.

Mr Foreman gave us a fine fool – manly and stupid – and Jeanne Ruddy's Cassandra, not as desperate in her crazed solos as expected, had an out-of-the-corner-of-the-eye intensity that worked. . . . A major performance came from Jean-Louis Morin, who made Aegisthus properly effete and yet malicious – all his gestures were clear.

Peter Sharling handled the difficult role of Orestes with great finesse, his stiff frame collapsing into broken cowardliness. . . .

On this occasion, John Ostendorf and Johanna Albrecht, as the spine-chilling singers, were in the pit rather than onstage for technical reasons. Halim El-Dabh's fragmented oriental and insistent modern melodies, conducted by Stanley Sussman, resonated with real power.

The Graham company revived *Clytemnestra* "superlatively" in 1984. The first act of the work was brought back again in 1988 with a largely new cast. Jack Anderson was at hand for the *New York Times* and caught other interpretations and nuances: "Peggy Lyman in the title role was a proud, haughty queen. Then intoxicated by wine and lust, her coarseness suggested she was behaving in a manner far below her noble station. Pascal Rioult was loutish as her lover . . . and Ms Dakin was a seductive Helen of Troy. Particularly compelling performances were offered by Ms Capucilli – who as Electra expressed her resentment in sudden, impatient spasms of movement – and Maxine Sherman, who as the prophetic Cassandra tried to remain still, then burst into gestural frenzies. As the Watchman, Mr Rooks made his solo a collection of beautiful poses and falls, but without conveying that the man he portrayed was literally watching and waiting, searching for a signal that would reveal the Trojan war had ended and King Agamemnon was coming home." Anderson felt that some of the dancers lacked fire. He objected, too, that the work was not offered in full. "It is unwise to present only one act of the evening-long *Clytemnestra*, a dance in which much of the power is derived through the way its epic proportions make it resemble a nightmare from which no one can awake."

Sir Tyrone Guthrie was an outstanding English producer and director. He was knighted in 1961 for his accomplishments in all aspects of staging classical drama, opera, musical comedy and farce. He was invited to leading theatres throughout the world, but most prominently in his own country, Canada and the United States, and was a co-founder of the Minnesota Theater Company, a distinguished regional group in Minneapolis-St Paul, the Twin Cities. Five years after receiving his title he undertook an *Oresteia* (1966) there. The production was repeated locally in 1968, then brought to New York for a limited engagement. Welcomed as a novelty, some of it evoked much comment, mostly favourable, but some of it disagreeable, as in an unsigned notice in *Time* magazine:

> Beware of Tyrone Guthrie bearing Greek gifts. The pity and terror of tragedy are alien to his impish nature. He has an irresistible urge to inject modernity into a classic through props, stage tricks and character stunts rather than to extract what is timelessly significant in the play. He is more like a Master of Ceremonies introducing variety acts than a director exploring drama. All of these traits mar his direction of the Minnesota Theater Company's' *The House of Atreus*. The production is ambitious in intent but puny in passion, execution and depth. *The House of Atreus* is an adaptation by John Lewin of Aeschylus' trilogy, the *Oresteia*.

A synopsis is inserted, and then this critical judgement is added:

> The cast wears somber masks as they did in the original Greek production, and for a while this adds a dimension of hieratic awe to the play, but soon the lack of human expressions reduces the effect to a kind of puppet show. The women's roles are played by men, also a custom with the ancients. At the outset this is forceful and a trifle unsettling. Yet eventually the lack of sexual differentiation erases the fact that this is a bitter domestic tragedy.
>
> The language transpositions from the Greek lack eloquence, spareness or precision, and the contemporary colloquialisms jar the ear. Lines like "You mean you intend to kill your mother?" produce wildly inappropriate laughter from an audience saturated with Freud. The prevailing style of the evening is that of neo-Shakespearean swashbuckling and the barely adequate cast seems to relish all opportunities for bombast and comic clowning. The chorus resembles the witches from *Macbeth* multiplied. The murders might as well have been performed by Richard III. Elizabethan Greeks are a nov-

> elty all right, but they reduce the play to historical pageantry, horseplay and melodrama when it ought to be blindingly focused on man's ineluctable rendezvous with fate.

But many spectators found the production fascinating. The audience was small, made up mostly of students and faculty members from New York's many colleges and universities.

In 1966, too, the civic leaders of Ypsilanti, Michigan, a place hitherto best known for being in the heart of a celery-growing region, and at that time having a population of 27,000, decided to found a Greek theatre, a project consonant with the city's name being of Greek origin. A persuasive factor was that the affluent suburbs of Detroit were not a great distance away, and the huge University of Michigan at Ann Arbor was a mere ten-mile drive, so that a sizeable audience for a cultural event might well be attracted. In addition, a local school, Eastern Michigan University, could also contribute a goodly number of spectators as well as its baseball field, which was converted into an amphitheatre for the open-air festival. Alexis Solomos, of the Greek National Theatre, was appointed director. He gathered a cast that was fully professional and even eminent, consisting of Judith Anderson, Ruby Dee, Donald Davis and Jacqueline Brookes. (Miss Dee was one of America's foremost black actresses.) The opening offering was the *Oresteia*. Robert Kotlowitz, who attended, reviewed the play for *Harper's Magazine*:

> Of confidence the company's director, Alexis Solomos, has plenty. He has stood up to the massive demands of the trilogy without giving quarter in any direction.
>
> Everything is big, if not monumental: stage, sets, sound amplification and the performances he has pulled from a wholly imported cast. . . . For once, Miss Anderson, whose personality onstage has always tended to dominate ordinary mortals, has been kept to life size as Clytemnestra; while she is everywhere equal to the role, her passion never exceeds her colleagues'. The Anderson voice is neither beautiful nor particularly powerful, but it speaks clearly and with a certain grandeur: two perfect tools for transmitting Thracian hypocrisy and lust.
>
> In Jacqueline Brookes, the company has one of the few actresses in America with any experience in playing Greek tragedy. Young, tall, strong, vivid, she intones her lines as a slave with authentic grief, giving a grim, unrelenting but never monotonous performance. As Orestes, John Michael King speaks in rich, lush tones, but he seems emotionally hesitant, a little afraid of passion. Donald Davis makes a stately Agamemnon, so weary when he gets back from the Trojan Wars that he can barely hold his head up, while Karen Ludwig is both vulnerable and aggressive as Electra.

One revelation of the production is Ruby Dee, who acts on the very edge of convulsion as Cassandra. When she is frustrated she simply lies down on the floor and thrashes around in agony: no halfway measures here. Miss Dee is clearly ripe for any part she would set her mind to. Both Shaw's and Shakespeare's Cleopatra, for example, could use her talent, which is made up of equal parts of vigor, suppleness, conviction, unusual stamina, and a winning, beautiful smile.

The other revelation is the chorus, perfectly trained by Mr Solomos and the choreographer Helen McGehee. They enter for the first time as I am told they do at Epidaurus, pounding their walking staves in unison on the floor of the stage. Then they form shifting patterns in front of the audience and begin to tell the story of the House of Atreus, to bemoan the dead at Troy, belittle the mind and face of Helen, to preach, moralize, worry aloud. In and out of the action they wander, rejected by Clytemnestra, warned by Cassandra, welcomed by Agamemnon. The action of the play moves on their feet and they set its style.

The Richard Lattimore translation is both grave and graceful, dense with human sympathy, and fully suggestive of the play's pain and compassion. The *Oresteia* is agonizingly long; it goes on at eight in Ypsilanti and is finished well after eleven, a nearly four-hour attempt to enlarge our paltry emotions and reach our intelligence. The palace that Eldon Elder has designed stands wide and tall (stretching, I would guess, from first to third base). When the watchman of the House of Atreus appears on the top of its walls, he stands literally on the top of a real wall, silhouetted against the twilight sky. That is the clue to this *Oresteia.* It is big and real, without concessions to naturalism.

An American playwright, David Rabe, delved into the *Oresteia* theme in his *The Orphan* (1973), given at New York's Off-Broadway Public Theater. He had won his reputation with two works dealing with the experience of American soldiers in the Vietnam War, *The Basic Training of Pavlo Hummel* and *Sticks and Stones*, the latter piece so provocative that the CBS television network refused to broadcast it. *The Orphan* treats with that war only obliquely, but Rabe sought, in the words of T.E. Kalem in *Time* magazine, "to relate it to the problem of evil throughout human existence". Further, Kalem remarked:

Often as silly and awkward as it is ambitious, the play nonetheless bears the mark of a dramatist who dares and cares.

The bulk of the play is a retelling of the *Oresteia* legend, and it makes for some restive or torpid listening depending on the playgoer's mood. The basic story line is intact. . . .

Rabe has drastically minimized Electra's role, but he provides two Clytemnestras, possibly to differentiate the mother's grief from the lust and vengefulness of the mistress (Rae Allen).

The strained pseudopoetic rhetoric and portentous declamatory style remind one of Maxwell Anderson scaling his molehills of dramatic verse. An intermittent side-bar monologue features an innocuous-looking Manson family girl casually relating the horrors of the Sharon Tate murders with a lubriciously contented purr. Together with the repeated cue name of My Lai and references to the slaughter of the innocents, of whom Iphigeneia is the first, Rabe's intent is clear to the point of didactic overkill – to make the curse and crimes of the House of Atreus appear to be the inevitable pattern of all human behavior.

To the Greeks, the *Oresteia* was an exemplary tale of moral downfall designed to evoke pity and terror. Rabe's tone is pejorative, like that of a prosecuting attorney who is pressing playgoers to confess that men are bloody-minded beasts. There is no court of appeal in *The Orphan.* God is dead, absolute power has produced absolute corruption and society is a cracked veneer of hypocrisy.

With such a grim, bleak view, relentlessly abetted by Jeff Bleckner's stolidly reverential direction, there is little room for such diversionary tactics as entertainment or such revisionist behavior as love and the spontaneous response of one human being to another. Only one actor seems to escape the arid dogmatism of the evening – Marcia Jean Kurtz as Clytemnestra the mother. When she pleads for her daughter's life, she reveals a tenacity and a tenderness that banish all curses and shame all crimes.

(The allusion to the Manson family and the shocking, senseless Sharon Tate murders has already been explained. My Lai was a Vietnamese village, the scene of an atrocity committed by American soldiers that subsequently brought on an outcry and courts-martial.)

Two evenings were required for a staging of the *Oresteia* at Vienna's renowned Burgtheater (1976), as conceived by Luca Ronconi, an Italian guest-director. Ronconi (b. 1913), who had been trained at Rome's Accademia Nazionale d'Arte Drammatica, and then been a member of Vittorio Gassman's acting company, had eventually taken up directing, winning attention with his own adaptation of Thomas Middleton's seventeenth-century tragedy *The Changling* (1966) and then with imaginative revivals of other classic dramas, among them Shakespeare's *Measure for Measure* (1967) and *Richard III* (1968), quickly followed by Giordano Bruno's Humanist comedy *Candelaio* (also 1968), in association with the Teatro Stabile of Turin. He had great success with a dramatization of Ludovico Ariosto's sixteenth-century epic poem *Orlando Furioso,* bringing new life to the tradition of fantastic Italian folk spectacle and making good use of a "freely structured space", which is to say distributing his performers on fifty wheeled wagons arranged in a circle around a plaza, with the audience moving about and choosing which episodes to watch, as did throngs in the Middle Ages. The offering had its première in Spoleto in and before a church, and was later seen in Belgrade, Milan, Paris, Edinburgh (in an ice rink) and New York (in a "bubble theater"). In 1971 his *XX* had the spectators placed in separate rooms, from which the enclosing walls were gradually removed. At first, each group saw upsetting events and heard disturbing voices and noises from elsewhere. When all the walls were taken away, the audience was told to disperse, because a *coup d'état* had just occurred. Ronconi explained that he was trying to show how dictatorships were prepared, with too few innocent persons unaware of what was happening until a crucial moment arrived. These excellent credits had brought him to Vienna and established him as the Burgtheater's specialist at putting on ancient Greek plays. His *Oresteia* was preceded by his interpretations of Euripides' *The Bacchae* and Aristophanes' *The Birds.*

A *New York Times* correspondent sent this account of the six-hour *Oresteia*: "[It] begins with splendid sights that dwarf its actors – an illustrated history of the Trojan War, abstract copper figures representing the old gods, Clytemnestra making her first appearance through a slit in a white curtain that nearly fills the stage, Agamemnon and Cassandra entering on a moving sidewalk, the red carpet on which Agamemnon is to go to his death descending from above like the stroke of fate that it symbolizes. In the second play, human figures take over: Electra and Orestes, dressed shabbily in modern costumes (like the hapless chorus of the first play) take a merely human vengeance on Agamemnon's murderers without excessive help from the designer. The last play shows a weary old Orestes in a tattered black overcoat finding his savior in an impersonal, machinelike, silverclad Athena, accompanied by a herd of silverclad robots who are the Athenian citizens. Why do Athena and the Athenians look like Buck Rogers in the twenty-fifth century? First, because Ronconi cannot resist a terrific stage picture and, second, to emphasize Aeschylus' theme, the triumph of an impersonal, orderly justice over the rule of passion and vengeance. This is the dispassionate future, as seen by Aeschylus, Ronconi, and Buck Rogers." (Buck Rogers was a character in a popular science-fiction comic-strip.)

A young Romanian director, Andrei Serban, making a new career in New York, was in charge of an *Agamemnon* (1977) mounted at the Vivian Beaumont Theater, a constituent part of Lincoln Center in New York. The work was an offering there of Joseph Papp's New York Shakespeare Festival which often produced plays by writers other than the Bard. Ellen Stewart, the energetic head of Off-Broadway's La MaMa, a boldly avant-garde acting group, had seen a sample of Serban's work at a festival of student theatre in Zagreb, Yugoslavia (1966) and urged him to come to America, an invitation that he accepted three years later. A chance encounter with a youthful composer, Elizabeth Swados, from Buffalo, New York, in the lobby of La MaMa – some accounts say in the basement – led to an artistic collaboration of exceeding importance to both. Productions of three Euripidean tragedies (1974) – his staging, abetted by her more than incidental music – startled New York's critics and public alike. With his *Agamemnon*, the collaborators were enabled to move uptown, to the outer precincts of Broadway; Serban had already shifted his efforts there under Papp's sponsorship, doing a version of Chekhov's *The Cherry Orchard*, also with incidental music by Swados. A feature of the Serban–Swados method was the mixed intelligibility of the text, the dialogue being a combination of modern Greek and English – translation by Edith Hamilton. A cast of twenty-nine populated their *Agamemnon*. The chorus variously sang, chanted and intoned in an ever-changing pattern marked by Swados: as described by the critic Margaret Croyden, "a few of the men shrieked ominously like vultures; a cluster of women wailed their woe in sobbing vowels. Other members of the chorus spoke sometimes in verse, sometimes in song, sometimes in syncopated rhythms. Strange elongated 'oos,' 'grs,' and 'trs,' soft sliding 'shys,' and trigger-like consonants reverberated to produce a combination of sounds from another time and another world – the mythic world of the primordial Greeks." In Swados's words, the play had not been set to music but "sound structured".

This *Agamemnon* was enacted on the Beaumont's vast open stage – it has a depth of 120 feet – on which the designer, Douglas Schmidt, erected a stark set, exposing the bare brick walls at the rear. Huge palace doors stood in the centre, and moveable benches allowed some spectators to share the triangular acting area, which was flanked by ramps that led to a pit below. At moments, simulations of massive rock formations were slid in from the rear to suggest, among other purposes, Troy's horrible devastation. His search, and that of Swados, Serban said, was to find means of projecting "emotional and mythic power". (More details of the Serban–Swados collaboration on producing the Greek tragedies will be found on ensuing pages.)

A one-act opera, *The Cry of Clytemnestra* (1980) by John Eaton, with libretto by Patrick Creagh, has had a number of hearings, among them two performances during the Summerfare Arts Festival, a then annual event at the State University of New York at Purchase (1982). Bernard Holland, of the *New York Times*, journeyed there.

> Mr Eaton's often-vivid dramatic piece stayed close to its Greek setting, but he and his librettist also added overtones of twentieth-century feminism. This is the ancient legend told from Clytemnestra's vantage point, and in this retelling, she is both aggrieved and grieving. Mr Eaton's opera serves, in fact, as an apologia for her murderous behavior, and we are made to share her unhappiness in excruciating depth.

> Such updatings of ancient histories often have a way of weakening the messages of both past and present, but so inventive was Mr Eaton's music and so swift, uncluttered and simple was Gerald Freedman's staging that there was in the end, very little preachiness here, except perhaps in the less musically interesting quarrelings between Clytemnestra and her daughter Electra.
>
> . . . The opera is mainly a vehicle for its Clytemnestra, Nelda Nelson, and her strong soprano was admirable for its ability to sing fortissimo over long periods and to utter fierce wails of anguish. Phyllis Hunter struggled with Mr Eaton's high tessitura, but her early aria, an exercise in bel canto style bent gently and imaginatively out of harmonic focus by the composer, had a great deal of charm.

Holland commended the singing of Timothy Nobel, the Agamemnon, whose voice has "power and forcefulness", but was less impressed by the tenor Colenton Freeman as Aegisthus; the critique included praise for Edith Diggory, the Cassandra, but offered a less kindly judgement of Joan Patenaude-Yarnell and Glenn Siebert as Electra and Orestes, though the cast as a whole was rated strong.

> The sets and lighting by Lawrence Casey and Tom Sturge were effective and simple, with sail-like and woven panels defining the action. Mr Casey's costumes, in the case of Clytemnestra and Cassandra at least, featured cleavage almost to the waist.
>
> Mr Eaton's music was often arresting, especially in its blending of traditional orchestral devices, percussion effects and synthesized sound. The electronically echoed phrases of Agamemnon's and Cassandra's singing and the eerie accompaniments to Cassandra's prophecies were particularly interesting.

The orchestra, however, had difficulty coping with it, the string playing tending to sag.

> Mr Eaton has a good ear for instruments and an almost uncanny way of emulating voice colors with instrumental sound. The soft high tones of Iphigeneia, for example, were answered beautifully by mirror images of sound from the pit.
>
> If Mr Eaton's music suffered at all, it was from a surfeit of its virtues. The evening was so unremitting in its dark agonies and stentorian emphasis, so incessant in its catalogue of injury and injustice, that one longed for an ironic countersubject or two to lighten the burden. There is, however, strong music here, and music that commands our attention.

In London, spectators saw *The Greeks* (1980), contrived by John Barton, who compressed ten classic tragedies – seven by Euripides, one by Sophocles, one by Aeschylus (*Agamemnon*) and one derived from Homer – into an on-flowing nine-hour work, arranged in three trilogies, staged over three consecutive nights at the Aldwych Theatre. Sandra Salman, in a dispatch to the *New York Times*, described it as probably the most ambitious and provocative London theatrical undertaking of the past decade. "Barton (1928–) had begun his career as a director while still a student at Cambridge, with a production of *Macbeth* (1949), when he was barely twenty-one. Continuing his work there, and becoming a Fellow of King's College (1954–60), he mounted scripts for the Marlowe Society, leading to a controversial offering of *Dr Faustus*, which he heavily edited and rewrote, his habitual practise when approaching revivals of the classics. In 1963, he adapted and edited a three-play cycle of Shakespearean dramas that he brought together under the title of *The War of the Roses*, directed by Sir Peter Hall, whom Barton assisted; it was a major success." In reshaping the plays, he inserted no fewer than 1,000 lines of his own, boldly defying the long-held precept that one may freely cut a Shakespearean text but not add to it. The next year, he was appointed Associate Director of the Royal Shakespeare Company, where he participated in putting on a lengthy series of the Bard's comedies and tragedies.

"Appropriately Olympian in scale," as Sandra Salman phrased it, *The Greeks* was made up of *Iphigeneia in Aulis*, *Achilles*, *Andromache*, *The Trojan Women* (*Achilles* an original work by Barton, drawn directly from Homer's *Iliad*), and then *Hecuba*, *Agamemnon*, *Electra* (the last of these by Sophocles, the other two by Euripides), and finally *Helen*, *Orestes* and *Iphigeneia in Tauris* (all by Euripides). Each trilogy had a title that identified its prime content: *The War*, *The Murders*, *The Gods*; each had a subtitle, *Sin*, *Punishment* and *Retribution*, with the whole serving to relate the history of the bloodstained House of Atreus and the Trojan War. The translation was by Kenneth Cavander, who shared credit for the adaptation.

The acting company aggregated twenty-four, requiring a high payroll for a modern theatre and believed to be one reason the presentation, a hit in London, was not transferred to Broadway. Most of the actors were assigned at least two parts. The leading roles were taken by Janet Suzman and Billie Whitelaw, with Ms Suzman appearing as both Clytemnestra and Helen, most suitably, since the myth has them twin sisters. But she also acted as a member of the chorus. Ms Whitelaw was by turns Andromache, Athena, Artemis and a chorus member. To Jon Shrapnel was given the very opposed characters of Agamemnon and the god Apollo, while Tony Church was alternately Menelaus and the wily Odysseus. Day-long rehearsals, held six days a week, were carried on for nearly four months, with different scenes being worked on in scattered studios on separate floors. As far as possible, actors attended frequent run-throughs of all ten plays to gain a sense of the cycle as a whole and how their roles fitted into it. With cast members playing multiple parts, the intricate scheduling of rehearsals proved a truly daunting task. It was likened to a jigsaw puzzle.

Conversing with Ms Salman, Barton laid out some of his purposes, the substance of which she forwarded to the *New York Times.*

> Filled with violence, love, suffering, frivolity, irrationality and reason, the stories, in Mr Barton's view, are among the most exciting and moving in our culture. However, the Greek plays have been mistreated by translators and directors in "overly earnest, inflated productions" and misunderstood by audiences who have forgotten the ancient myths. His solution was to present the story in its entirety by borrowing from an assortment of playwrights as well as creating a new play based on Homer's *Iliad.*
>
> While the basic plots and characters have been preserved intact, some of the most minor subplots have been dropped, some characters have been shifted from one play to another, and a few of the more obscure characters have been combined or eliminated altogether. The long passages of purple rhetoric favored in most translations have been pared down, and members of the chorus – which, in every play, consists entirely of women – speak individually rather than in mournful unison.

The idea for *The Greeks* had been incubating in him for a decade and a half, after he conducted a studio experiment at Stratford using abridged Greek plays and Platonic dialogues. Subsequently he delayed for two years after learning that the National Theatre was planning a production of the *Oresteia*; then it was indefinitely postponed.

> There was no complete cycle dealing with the Trojan war and the House of Agamemnon, partly because the Greeks had never dared to rewrite Homer. "Then I realized that there was sufficient information, provided one could take the heretical step of mixing up playwrights."
>
> . . . Working from translations, he reduced the high-flown rhetoric favored by Victorian classicists to the "terse, laconic style" that he and Mr Cavander believe is more faithful to the original Greek.
>
> . . .
>
> "Greek dialogue is almost devoid of metaphor or imagery. The overall effect is very architectural, almost punchy." An example from one of the plays is the stark statement, "My name is Helen," which is spoken by Miss Suzman. "There's nothing between the lines, no psychological subtext," he noted.

"The verbal ambiguities are lacking, so the actor has to bring out the mysteries." To accommodate the entire cycle, the Aldwych stage has been turned into a tilted, concave disk, with the look of sun-baked mud, on which actors sit or kneel. Lighting and minimal scenery – a few olive trees, tents, a shrine – indicate place and season. Taverna-style music comes from bouzoukis, flute, trumpets and guitar. Because the style was rich in inversions and opposites, said Mr Barton, music was composed "on a Wagnerian *leitmotif* principle. There are seven basic motifs, each with an opposite. I wouldn't normally be as schematic as that, but it's in the plays."

He had spent more than a year on the script, selecting, writing and rewriting the Greek originals. In all, he had prepared six drafts before the start of rehearsals. Weaving the plays together as a unit, he sought to keep as much as possible of the authentic texts.

The final *Electra*, for example, was based on Sophocles, but borrows from Aeschylus and Euripides. Aeschylus' *Agamemnon*, as the most famous of the plays, was the least altered, except for the wholesale sex change of the chorus to women – "for consistency," said Mr Barton. "We also made the chorus more simple and natural than usual, to make them seem more integral to the play."

The feminization of the chorus – its members mature during the cycle from giddy young girls, doting on Achilles, to sad old women – resulted in a cast of sixteen women and eight men, and a marked emphasis on women. "Feminism is implicit in the material," Mr Barton said. "The men treat women shabbily in lots of ways." "All the crucial moral questions are given to women" in the plays, said Mr Cavander, pointing out that the men are motivated mainly by "moral cowardice or political calculation or sheer blind passion."

Also inherent in the material, according to Mr Barton, are contradictions and inconsistencies. While these become more glaring when the plays are run together, they have not been smoothed over. "I love the contradictions," Mr Barton said. "Apollo is the god of reason and unreason. Clytemnestra turns from the loving wife into the husband-killer. The contradictions give the cycle a certain coherence of tone."

In his other directions, too, Mr Barton maintained, he has kept to the spirit if not the letter of the ancient Greeks. The first two parts of the trilogy, filled with almost unimaginable atrocities, are also leavened with occasional humor. Helen, whose face launched those thousand ships, whistles her cuckolded husband, Menelaus, to her side. Achilles is visited by his sea-nymph mother, a scatterbrained spirit who brings him his armor as if it were a hot meal.

> In the last part, Mr Barton gives full vent to Euripides' black humor, mixing horror and absurdity. Helen, draped in a bath towel and sunbathing on a sarcophagus, is revealed to have lived out the war years in Egypt, in innocence and boredom, while the gods sent her "double" to Troy. Orestes and Electra, sentenced to death for their mother's murder, try to save their necks by seizing Helen's daughter as hostage – an act of terrorism for which Mr Barton equips them with blue jeans, machine guns and cans of kerosene. Apollo intervenes, rescuing the girl – who soon reappears in a cocktail dress – and whisking Helen up to Olympus in a confusion of strobe lights and disco dancing. "There is good and bad in all you have done," a gilded Apollo fatuously tells the crowd. "That's the way the world is."
>
> "Some people will be horrified," said Mr Barton, "but I don't think we've twisted the spirit of the plays. I hate the clichés of updating the classics. Helen doesn't wear sunglasses. But she can anoint herself with modern suntan lotion because the Greeks anointed themselves with oil. It's like a fairy tale, moving back and forth in time."

"Enter Orestes, in Blue Jeans, with Machine Gun," was the heading over Ms Salman's article in the *New York Times.*

Scholars might have been surprised by Cavander's remark that the Greek playwrights used scant imagery, similes or metaphors. However, most of the theatre critics approved of Barton's accomplishment. A reviewer for the *The Times* declared: "The story, addressed to a public coming fresh to the legends, is spellbinding." A writer in the *Financial Times* agreed enthusiastically: "Mr Barton has achieved the astonishing coup of suggesting what it must have been like to sit with an audience in Athens." The *Guardian*'s critic had some doubts: "To achieve a consecutive narrative, Barton has to yoke together works of uneven quality." He noted "a descent from the peak of great drama" – attained in *Iphigeneia in Aulis* – "to the plateau of good dramatization" reached in the *Achilles* from Barton's hand.

"Olympus on the Thames" was T.E. Kalem's review in *Time* magazine:

> Barton has made the classic treasures of Western drama accessible to modern playgoers by using straightforward, idiomatic English and concentrating on the endlessly probing light of the Greek mind as the essence of our civilized heritage.
>
> We are in a misty dawn of antiquity when we first see the chorus of high-spirited young women on the stage of the Aldwych. They are prompting one another on the ancient myth, the way children count on their fingers. It sets the conversational tone of this dramatic cycle and evokes a time when

people felt themselves to be not only the prey and pawns of the gods but their intimates as well.

. . . All Greek tragedies move through pitch points of passion, moments when men look into the abyss of self-revelation. In Euripides' *Iphigeneia in Aulis,* which begins this cycle, there are three pitch points. The first comes as Agamemnon reasons with his daughter about the need for her death. Shrapnel sensitively conveys the deep inner anguish of a man torn between duty to his country and love for his child. As Clytemnestra, Suzman moves through a parabola of feelings, marking her again as one of the finest actresses on the English-speaking stage. And as Buxton reaches the heartbreaking conclusion that the one life she has to give for Hellas is the noblest life to have lived, she radiates a great and unforgettable purity of spirit.

The final scene in this segment is a visual stunner. The rising wind whips the garment about Clytemnestra's knees. Alone, burnt-eyed, she raises an arm as she watches the Greek fleet under full sail, a Botticelli Venus transformed into a *mater dolorosa.*

For chronological reasons, Barton had to supply the second play in *The War* himself. He has culled it from Homer and called it *Achilles.* Considering the audacity of the work, the result is exemplary. Achilles is played with sullen vanity by Gwilym, and as his mother Thetis, Annie Lambert manages to suggest both a divine sea nymph and a contemporary cocktail-party hostess who, when asked about her mating with a mortal, Peleus, remembers the moment as "brief, hot and sandy."

[Kalem takes note of the] three basic speech patterns of Greek tragedy. Hecuba embarks on a lamentation that might be called the first language of the Middle East, stretching around the Mediterranean crescent from the Wailing Wall of Jerusalem to the melancholy, snakelike flutes of the Casbah. The second mode is anathema, the curse absolute. The third is the speech of self-absolution. Protagonists in Greek plays never blame themselves for their actions. Either the gods made them do it, or their enemies are culpable, or they are the victims of *tyche*: luck or blind chance.

As Hecuba plays the blame game, Helen, "the whore of Troy," is responsible for everything. Helen (Suzman) appears, as haughty as an international star. She seems to regard the Trojan War as her biggest hit ever. Menelaus is ready to butcher her for adultery, but he is so afraid of Helen's siren sway that he does not look at her. Silkily, she makes her excuse. She was in the power of Aphrodite – her will was not her own. Menelaus' meat-cleaver hand drops. Helen sashays away, whistling in sultry triumph.

The true pitch point of *Trojan Women* involves Hector's widow, Andromache (Billie Whitelaw) and her toddler son. Odysseus has convinced the Greeks that if the child grows to manhood, he may lead Troy in another war. . . . He must be torn from his mother's skirts and dashed to death from the city's topless towers. One of the most wrenching scenes in all of Greek tragedy is shatteringly performed by Whitelaw when her little boy is taken and returned as a tiny corpse in the shell of Hector's shield.

This is the gory part of the epic: blood lust and revenge couched in the name of justice. Polymestor (Oliver Ford Davies) is an erstwhile friend of Troy to whom King Priam and Queen Hecuba sent their youngest son, Polydorus, for safekeeping – along with a stock of gold. But in Greek tragedy, today's friend is tomorrow's fiend.

As soon as he knew that Troy had fallen, Polymestor murdered the boy and took the gold. Unknown to him, the sea-rotted corpse has drifted to shore and is dumped before Hecuba's gaze. She is past weeping now. She wants the gift of death, surcease from all sorrow. But she has a priority: vengeance. Before the final curtain, Polymestor lurches forward on all fours, his eyes' sockets craters of streaming blood. He utters the primal howl that punctuates these plays. It is the moment when all reason has toppled and the dogs of fate rend man with total indifference.

Agamemnon returns to his palace, triumphant.

He is the happiest of men, or so he thinks. The chorus of crones, clad in ominous black, knows better. . . . All too soon the cries of horror sound as if from some echo chamber in Hell. The fates are inexorable: the bodies of Agamemnon and Cassandra are eventually hurled onto the stage like the carcasses of animals, and Clytemnestra emerges spattered with blood.

Electra completes this portion of the cycle. It begins as a long threnody by Electra (Lynn Dearth). Stoking a cauldron of hatred toward her mother Clytemnestra, Dearth is a cauldron herself.

Electra's brother Orestes (Gwilym) comes home as a stranger. After the famed "recognition" scene, Electra embraces him with incestuous ardor. Modern audiences can easily comprehend Freud's comment that he had merely systematized what the Greek poets had known all along: the slaying of the parent remains a ritual whose power to chill has lost nothing in two thousand five hundred years.

To Kalem, the third part of the cycle was almost anticlimactic, "partly because of the caliber of the plays and partly because of the treatment". He found *Helen* scarcely more than an amusing cartoon skit. He did not particularly like the sudden introduction of anachronisms.

In *The Gods* plays, Barton accelerates the tempo of the tragedies and elides parts of the stories, after somewhat reducing their gravity. Moreover, pro-feminist sentiments are catered to by rendering certain lines as if in oral italics. That is surely an error, since the women in Greek tragedy are the strongest feminine figures in all of dramatic literature.

Any enterprise of this magnitude must have flaws, but in this case the virtues formidably outweigh them. While the Greeks had no word for sin, this is indeed a grand parable of sin, grace and redemption, which very nearly produces *katharsis* in the classic sense. With the aid of towering performances and stark sets, plus the ensemble work of the Royal Shakespeare troupe, John Barton has elucidated the meaning of the Greek texts, evoking the ideals that animated them. A special citation should be awarded to Nick Bicât for his inestimably evocative music. Taverna-like, elegiac, militant, his melodies evoke the epoch when Attica was vernal and bore something more than gnarled olive trees.

To Barton must belong the final honors. He has brought us the Greeks' greatest gifts and restored the original titans of drama to our petty stages. May Zeus smile on him.

The Greeks eventually came to America, first to the Williamstown Theater Festival (1981), in the university town of Williamstown, Massachusetts, which each summer welcomed a highly professional acting group long presided over by Nikos Psacharopoulos. Charles Michener, in *Newsweek*, declared that the production was the zenith of the company's then twenty-seven years' history. "Everyone knows that Greek tragedies are good for you; this production makes them exhilarating." Psacharopoulos had shortened the offering by three hours, so that it could be enacted on two evenings of three hours each.

The purpose of *The Greeks* is simple – to tell the most powerful of the Greek stories, the fall of the House of Atreus, in chronological order. Led swiftly but with absolute clarity through the dizzying events, the audience can settle into an intimacy with the real stuff of these eternal works – their brilliant, deluded, irrepressible quarrels about what it is to be human.

"Who is to *blame*?" With this opening question, *The Greeks* cuts to the quick of the matter with the heightened laconicism that distinguishes the Cavander and Barton adaptation. As the endless "blames" are acted out . . . we miss that spiraling intensity of the original tragedies. Also lost, as horror outdoes horror, is an ultimate sense of *katharsis.*

But the gain is enormous. History becomes palpable as it swirls through John Conklin's marvelous set, a golden-gray universe centered on the fateful openings and closings of the great door to Agamemnon's house. Euripides in all his goading irascibility dominates, but we get a splendid anthology of Greek poetry in all its colors.

Michener had praise for the cast, which had been allowed only three and a half weeks of rehearsal time. "Lacking the opportunity to create sustained characters, most of the actors work in primary colors." Outstanding were Christopher Reeve as Achilles, Jan White as a formidable Clytemnestra, Carrie Nye as Helen and Maria Tucci as a "beautifully sorrowing" Andromache. "Best of all is the Agamemnon of Donald Moffat, who catches a different facet of this ungodly father figure in each of his five plays, and who delivers the most haunting human aria of the cycle in his speech in *Iphigeneia in Aulis*: 'Listen to the sea./ Once we come to know it/ We Greeks are never the same.'"

Robert L. King, for the *New York Times*, spoke to the actors and the translator about the motivations of the two productions, the problems encountered and how they were solved. As perceived by King, Barton's staging was "imbued with a distinctive personal vision that gave it a firm, if critically controversial, authority". By comparison, Psacharopoulos "faced obstacles serious enough to make production here [Williamstown] commercially risky and artistically daunting". King continued:

> Mr Barton wanted both to tell the story of the House of Atreus and to dramatize its pertinence for our time. . . . According to Mr Cavander, Mr Barton's idea was to dramatize a progressive degeneracy in society – as Greece moved away from the heroic ideal, he said, it became "more materialistic, more violence prone, like our own." To project this view, Mr Barton costumed his performers in fairly traditional garb for the first two parts, *The War* and *The Murders*, but in the final segment, *The Gods*, Helen wore a towel as she applied suntan lotion while lolling on a sarcophagus. In the most challenging display of relevance, Orestes and Electra, clad in jeans, kidnapped Helen's daughter with the help of machine guns and cans of kerosene, in a scene that led one critic to complain of an "anachronistic" reminder of Patty Hearst. Mr Barton extended the basic conceit by having Apollo's departure to Olympus accompanied by strobe lights and a disco beat.

(The Patty Hearst alluded to was an heiress of a very rich, prominent American family who was kidnapped by radical terrorists, imprisoned for months and converted to their cause, finally joining them in robbing banks as a gesture of protest against capitalism. Her captors, besieged, ultimately met a fiery death.)

King learned:

> A native of Greece, Mr Psacharopoulos was stimulated by the RSC production, but his enthusiasm was tempered by two objections. It "concentrated too much on the legend," he says, "rather than on the

emotional life of the material," and its "gadgets" were distracting. "All the laughs in the Helen scene were over the suntan lotion," he adds. "I couldn't hear the words."

To realize his vision of the emotional force of *The Greeks*, Mr Psacharopoulos had to clear several practical hurdles. The first was to reduce the work from nine hours to six, and from three plays to two, retitled *The Curse* and *The Blest.*

Mr Cavander was eager to reduce his own "original text" because he likes "to make the story move." He sees the new version as a distinct improvement. "We have gained speed," he explains. "In England, by spreading the story over three nights and by putting in all the details, I'm sure a certain sense of the overall arch of it was lost." Mr Cavander maintains that although he sacrificed "a lot of interesting color, none of the principal thrusts of the story have been lost by cutting it down to two evenings."

Even so, the new version called for ten scene changes and costumes for a cast of sixty. Much of the work was done by apprentices who paid to study at the theatre during the summer. The cast received Equity rates. A voice coach, Marjorie Phillips, and a choreographer, Randolyn Zinn, were borrowed from the Guthrie Theater in Minneapolis at a basic fee. Some of the extra costs of this large-scale venture were met by private contributors.

"Limited by practicality to one set, John Conklin designed 'three main areas' on the stage: 'a big carved stone entrance' that is 'always connected with a power' either temporal or divine; 'an altar representing human use of the gods,' and 'a big ramp out into the house to draw the audience in, so that the play comes out through the proscenium.'"

Many of the actors were strangers to one another.

Sitting on the steps of the theater during a break, the esteemed performer Edward Herrmann (Apollo) was asked if such a large, diverse group could achieve harmony in only a few weeks of rehearsal. His reply was couched in praise for Mr Psacharopoulos. "Nikos is a remarkable fellow," he said. "He has this group of astonishing people up here. They are all very successful in their own right, but everybody likes to come up here and play. It's like going back to the source. We all come up here to work for nothing, to put on a play. There's a very special atmosphere, an astonishing lack of ego and problems. Harmonious? Yes."

Later that same day, Mr Moffat was asked whether only an established company like the Royal Shakespeare could meet the challenges of *The Greeks* without a discordant clash of acting style. "In my experience," he said, "the ensemble is a myth. It can happen in a Broadway show in three weeks' rehearsal, or a company can be together for four years and it doesn't happen. Style and ensemble are things you notice after the fact. We don't set out to create an ensemble."

Mr Moffat attributes much of the success of the present company to Mr Psacharopoulos: "There are many extraordinary performances in these plays, and we have all come from different places. But there is a unity of purpose, largely due to Nikos and his approach.

"The 'cunning' method," Mr Moffat explained, "breaks up the plays, rehearsing as you would shoot a movie script, out of sequence with a piece here and a piece there, so you never get a sense of the whole." Unlike John Barton who encouraged his actors to attend rehearsals of the cycle plays in which they did not appear, Mr Psacharopoulos withheld completed scripts from his cast so that they would be surprised by a sense of wholeness at the run-through. In a surprising contrast, the Royal Shakespeare Company rehearsed *The Greeks* some fourteen weeks, about four times as long as Williamstown; Mr Psacharopoulos, nonetheless, devoted twelve hours daily to rehearsals to make up some of the difference.

Paradoxically, some time was saved by expanding the cast from twenty-four to sixty. With little doubling and no principals in the chorus, preparations in distinct areas could go forward at the same time.

. . . The actors who shuttled through tightly timed rehearsals did not ignore the pertinence of *The Greeks* for our time; even as he insists on the emotional core of Greek drama, Mr Psacharopoulos also takes the larger view. He observes, for example, that as in Troy, "war starts from silly incidents so many times. That is why the material is so immediate, because our society keeps making reaffirmations of strength."

"Ideally," in Mr Cavander's view, "as the two evenings go on, it should become progressively more uncomfortable to accept the givens of the original story, and one should begin to question more and more, as the characters do, the rightness of what they are being forced to go through. Finally, it ends, I think, on a statement that one cannot trust the gods. One has to be entirely human. One has to take responsibility for one's own life."

Shortly afterwards (1981), *The Greeks* was offered by the Hartford Stage Company, in Hartford, Connecticut. A critique of this performance was written by Mel Gussow, also for the *New York Times*. The work was distilled to seven hours and given as a trilogy. Gussow saw it at "a special one-day marathon, beginning at noon and ending after eleven at night, with lunch and dinner breaks for actors as well as theatergoers".

At Hartford only Euripides' *Andromache* was omitted from the Royal Shakespeare version. Gussow commented:

> While one is aware of omissions and distortions in reducing the works to manageable playing proportions – and also the shortcomings of some of the Hartford performances – there is no denying the ambitiousness of the event.
>
> *The Greeks* compensates in clarity for what it loses in density. One major criticism of the cycle is that it is simply not long enough. It is a chronological collage. . . . Each play is introduced and linked to the others, with the text of each pared to an average of forty-five minutes. Naturally the result is something of a hybrid of styles. There is, however, a dramatic arc to the trilogy . . . sweeping from the sacrifice of *Iphigeneia in Aulis* all the way to the restitution of *Iphigeneia in Tauris.* By the end, we have lived through several explosive decades of Greek history and have observed a complex emotional canvas. Major figures such as Agamemnon, Menelaus and Clytemnestra are studied in depth at various junctures. Clytemnestra, for example, is seen not only as the monster of *Electra* but also as the deceived mother of *Iphigeneia* and the humiliated wife of *Agamemnon.*
>
> Although theatergoers are invited to see individual sections of the cycle, for the greatest effectiveness, it is advisable to see all three in sequence. The cycle makes us aware of motifs, refrains of regret and humanizing contradictions of character – the waste of youth, the sufferings of women, the shifts of guilt to the gods.

At an intermission, Gussow overheard two women in the audience complaining that up to that point their emotions had not been stirred deeply enough.

> They should have waited until the end of the long evening, and the reuniting of Iphigeneia and Orestes. We first saw the two of them almost eleven hours earlier, Iphigeneia as a sacrifice to the gods and Orestes as an infant in the arms of Clytemnestra. Embracing, the two siblings bond together in a tearful and purgative proclamation of hope and conciliation.
>
> The cycle takes us from the siege of Troy through the horrors of the house of Atreus, telescoping the action so that events tumble after one another in a kind of domino effect. Everything affects something else; nothing happens in isolation.
>
> On one level, this is the liveliest and the most lucid performance of Greek tragedy one has seen, although some poetry has been sacrificed. The language has been colloquialized, sometimes too much

so, which adds to the briskness of the performance and also the work's adaptability to an American company.

Wisely, the co-directors – Mark Lamos and Mary B. Robinson – have individualized the speakers in the chorus. Nothing is intoned. The chorus is entirely composed of women, emphasizing the fact that we are seeing ancient Greece from the female point of view. It is the women who are brave, self-sacrificing and godlike and the men who are deceitful, hypocritical and cowardly. The chorus becomes a unified voice protesting male domination.

John Conklin, the set designer, has backed the broad open stage with a long stonelike wall that serves as the gates of Troy, a sea bulwark, and an entrance to a palace. Through artful lighting – by Pat Collins – the scene changes its complexion.

Stage pictures add immeasurably to the impact of the event: the captive Trojan women huddled behind barbed wire awaiting slavery; the chorus lurking in deep shade outside Agamemnon's house like watchful figures from a Kazantzakis novel: a bright white beam of light leaping out of an open door and impaling an act of matricide.

There are twenty-seven actors in the Hartford cast, many of them doubling in roles, an admixture of experienced professionals and neophytes. The trilogy stretches, and, in some instance, strains, the actors.

Gussow lists the players, none of whom had the renown of those who had the lead roles in the London and Williamstown offerings. He chose for the most commendation Kevin Conray "as a furious Orestes", Mary Layne as "the two faces of Iphigeneia (saintly in Aulis, demonic in Tauris)", Jean Smart "lending a womanliness to her portrayals of Clytemnestra and Helen". Electra, as interpreted by Jennifer Harmon, was "an overwrought vixen". He adds:

The inspiration of the cast is Margaret Phillips. Deceptively slight of stature, this powerful and mature actress, too rarely seen on the stage, enrobes Hecuba with her velvet voice and assertive presence. She becomes the heart and conscience of *The Greeks*, and when she is not Hecuba she blends in as one of the chorus.

With his Hartford productions of *Undiscovered Country*, *Cymbeline* and *Kean*, Mr Lamos demonstrated his dauntlessness and his ability to realize drama on a grand scale. *The Greeks* is a challenging adventure – for theatergoers as well as the Hartford Stage Company.

By 1981, only a year after *The Greeks*, the National Theatre was ready with Peter Hall's long-delayed *The Oresteia.* At last, at hand on the banks of the Thames was the newly inaugurated Olivier auditorium which afforded a space "not dissimilar to the one Aeschylus actually used when the trilogy won him the annual Dionysian playwriting competition in March, 458 BC".

This adaptation was by Tony Harrison, who viewed the drama from a different perspective:

> The victory of father-right over mother-right is the social pendulum of this trilogy. To have women play women in our production would have seemed as if we in the twentieth century were smugly assuming that the sex war was over and that the oppressions of the patriarchal code exist only in past centuries. The maleness of the piece is like a vacuum-sealed container keeping this ancient issue fresh.

The London critic Benedict Nightingale took his place among the eager spectators: "The production Mr Hall has just unveiled is a major project for him and, judging by the journalistic interest it has generated in England, a matter of some importance to theatre audiences, too. Would it work? *Could* it work, given the presence of an all-male cast wearing full-length masks throughout, not to mention the forbidding subject-matter of the three plays themselves?" After a rather detailed synopsis of them, Nightingale concluded with a sharp summary of *The Furies* in which the guilt-ridden Orestes, charged with matricide, faces a court

> in a murder trial whose implications are weighty enough to attract some very senior legal talent. The Furies prosecute, Apollo defends, and the goddess Athena presides over a jury of freeborn citizens whose six–six split vote ensures Orestes' acquittal.
>
> Thus the divinely sanctioned democracy of Athens plays its part in solving the Oresteian knot, a matter of obvious satisfaction to Aeschylus but possibly of less moment to us nowadays. Could we really take more than an academic interest in a two-thousand-five-hundred-year-old saga rawly describing the feuds of men and gods and piously celebrating the moral and political supremacy of an antique city?
>
> As it turned out, the answers to these questions were various. Mr Hall's production, played in front of steel walls as vast, brooding and inflexible as the fate they presumably symbolize, is often stunning to look at.
>
> When the red-robed, black-haired, shiny-faced Clytemnestra looms like some implacable Egyptian priestess over the corpse of the husband she has just stabbed to death; when Orestes and Electra, frail, pale figures kneeling hand in hand, implore their father's ghost to rise from the grave, accompanied by the increasingly urgent cries of a grey, baleful chorus of Trojan slaves; when the avenging

Furies, wearing their coven uniform of black tatters, white faces and stringy orange hair, weave and swirl and sway across the stage, menacing the mesmerized Orestes: at such times one feels ready for ten hours of Aeschylus, instead of the five-and-a-half the trilogy actually runs.

Harrison Birtwistle's music, its plunks, bangs and sudden, alarming shrieks adding greatly to the tension and atmosphere, proves an unequivocal success; Jocelyn Herbert's masks, a more equivocal one. At their not-infrequent best they are marvellously expressive and also strangely ambiguous. They even seem to alter according to the mood of the speaker, so that at one moment the Furies' faces seem to be boggling with disbelief, the next seething with vindictiveness.

But not all the fifteen-man cast succeed in projecting their voices and emotions strongly enough through their masks, and only one, the unidentified actor playing Orestes, has evolved a body-language sufficiently eloquent to compensate for his loss of face.

It would be a pity if Mr Hall followed the advice some London critics have already given him, and abandoned masks altogether, since they rivet the eye and also serve to remind us that the characters are elemental, not psychological beings. But the masks themselves could be more resonant, the physical movement more inventive, and, perhaps, the company itself more female. Why conform to the Equity rules of Aeschylus' day, and cast men as women, when we disregard Elizabethan practice and don't ask boys to play Juliet, Portia and Cleopatra? [Pictures of the masks show them to be far weaker than those used earlier by Tyrone Guthrie.]

Actually, the most oppressive mask, the one that acts as a barrier between us and Aeschylus, turns out to be Tony Harrison's translation. It is vigorous, vivid, highly alliterative, a daring mix of colloquialisms ("blab", "made mincemeat of") and fake-primitive compound nouns ("godstones", "skyflames", "god-grudge", "gravedirge").

The result, sounding like a collaboration between the author of *Beowulf* and some street-café poetaster in jeans, hardly explains why Sophocles and Aristophanes both thought Aeschylus' style remarkable for its weight and majesty. Worse, it proves distracting, attention-grabbing, less a clear channel to Aeschylus himself than the verbal equivalent of an unusually spirited river-regatta.

Moreover, it contains at least one serious omission – the opening chorus's famous testimony to the mystery of Zeus, who helps man "learn wisdom through suffering", a phrase which itself encapsulates Aeschylus' theme – and it gives unnatural and sometimes specious emphasis to the trilogy's concern with matters sexual and cosmosexual. Daughters become "she-children", sisters "she-kin", gods and goddesses "he-gods" and "she-gods". *Eune morsimos*, meaning "marriage ordained by fate", is "bed-bound sanctified by the she-gods of lifelot". And so the translation goes on, its aim presumably being to draw attention to the sexism implicit and explicit in the play.

True, the patriarchal gods imported into Greece by Indo-European invaders around two thousand BC had displaced or absorbed the old, indigenous goddesses by Aeschylus' time. True, this reflected social change. True, women in fifth-century Athens had hardly more rights than slaves. True, the female sex is spoken of slightingly by several of Aeschylus' male characters.

But it's surely wrong to see the trilogy too exclusively as concerning a turning-point in the great sexual struggle. It is, after all, also about other and more welcome examples of human evolution: spiritual, moral, social, political, judicial.

The Oresteia shows man struggling from chaos to civilization. It describes the breakdown of the old, private system of correcting wrongs and the discovery of a new, public means of ensuring that right prevails. It involves the attempt to reconcile law with justice, mercy with fear, reason with instinct, the claims of the divine with those of the human. In other words, it concerns tensions still with us, has dated more in externals than in essence, and was well worth reviving as Peter Hall believed. And that, of course, is unfortunate as well as fortunate. Brave and imaginative as his production undoubtedly is, it hardly has the size, scope and force *The Oresteia* demands.

John Barber had the following to say in the *Daily Telegraph*:

Again and again one is startled and enthralled. As when skyscraper-high doors open to reveal the corpses of Cassandra and Agememnon, his arm raised, frozen in rigor mortis. Or when Orestes first enters, supremely graceful, looking like a Japanese prince. . . . Or when the Furies surround and absorb Orestes, as in the slime of a spider's web. Or the wonderful conclusion, when the actors make us all stand, and parade through us, ritualistically, while a living torch flame symbolises the coming of enlightenment.

In 1982 the National Theatre's company was invited to perform *The Oresteia* in the amphitheatre at Epidaurus, the first time a non-Greek production of a Hellenic classic had ever appeared there. The next year (1983) the work was taped before a National Theatre audience, and this version was belatedly broadcast in the United States (1986). John J. O'Connor, television critic of the *New York Times*, took objection to the late hour chosen for the showing, from 10 p.m. to 12.30 a.m., and to the presentation being in two segments done on consecutive nights, the break resulting in a loss of firm continuity. "Any new version of *The Oresteia* is bound to set off scholarly and artistic sparks," O'Connor remarked. "Authenticity is largely a matter of conjecture. Interpretation is distorted by personal biases.

Sir Peter makes the most of the story's more sensational ingredients – cannibalism, murder, corruption – while stressing that, as he has put it in his published *Diaries*, there is a 'sexual basis to the whole thing.'" Sketching the story, O'Connor sums it up:

> Pursued by the vengeful Furies, Orestes stands trial and is found not guilty, essentially on the male-based argument that a man's life is more important than a woman's. Meanwhile, the ramifications are reaching to the very foundations of society and public morals. Good contends endlessly with evil. In the final synthesis, powerfully realized, the Furies become the Kindly Ones. A measure of justice is achieved in the affairs of gods and men.
>
> Mr Harrison's translation aims to capture the "clunkiness" of the original by Aeschylus, and at times it may be a bit too successful. He employs numerous compound words. Some are subtly precise. Instead of using god and goddess, for instance, which might imply a sense of diminution for the female, Mr Harrison reverts to He-god and She-god. Occasionally, however, his compounds grate, most notably in the frequent use of the term "grudge," as in blood-grudge, and so forth. But, by and large, Mr Harrison has devised a text that is indeed, in Mr Hall's words, living, dramatic and actable.
>
> The all-male cast uses masks, giving the production the highly stylized, ritualistic appearance of all primitive drama. Speaking directly to the audience, never to each other, the actors use body movement and gesture to indicate who is declaiming at any particular time. The masks, credited to Jenny West, are extraordinary, their frozen features lending themselves to different emotional messages as the scenes evolve and change. In rehearsal improvisations, the actors were instructed to "go with" the masks, molding their voices and movements to them. Many of the resulting images are stunning. Greg Hicks's interpretation of Orestes is particularly outstanding.
>
> The bulk of Mr Birtwistle's score is used to provide a percussive beat or "pulse" for the text. The performers are rigorously kept from giving their readings a naturalistic tone. For television, Toby Wallis, the editor, has frequently coordinated the on-screen images with the pulse, changing the picture in time with the beat. It is one way of bringing movement to sketches of the production that are relatively static visually.
>
> Under the most inspired circumstances, *The Oresteia* is demanding theater. As Sir Peter once observed, it is not about playing characters, it is about saying something important. Tackling the work today, in a world seemingly addicted to entertainments, clearly requires courage. This production has the added virtues of being intelligently conceived and brilliantly performed. The opportunity to see it shouldn't be missed by anyone serious about the theater.

Intimations of Hall's lengthy preparation for his staging of the work are found in the *Diaries* to which O'Connor refers. The plan began to gestate in Hall's thoughts as early as 1975, when he noted: "How wonderful it will be to do Greek plays in the Olivier. I think I know how." Again, he wrote: "This is the most exciting project that I have ever contemplated." At another time, hearing of Barton's interest in the subject, he pondered a collaboration. In 1978 he recorded: "I read *The Oresteia* yet again – twice – and thought and thought and thought. I now feel it might be arbitrary and boring to do it with all men, partly because I was irritated on Friday by the company's anxiously progressive questions about whether it was right for men to play women? Of course it is. But there is an element of doubt in my mind. The play's political progress from matriarchy through patriarchy to democracy is something so violently sexual that we've got to make that work." The *Diaries* testify to numerous meetings and discussions with Harrison, translator, and Birtwistle, composer of the incidental music.

On one occasion, Hall travelled to Bradfield College to see a student production of *Agamemnon* (1976).

> Their Greek theatre is made out of a chalk pit. The evening was very illuminating – and showed up a lot of problems. The chorus didn't work, partly because the music was *conclusive*. Aeschylus is entirely ambiguous and contradictory all the time. To sing resolved cadences with great affirmative climaxes is absolutely foreign to him, and fragments the drama into little scraps. A lesson could be learned from Monteverdi here – always starting the next phrase on the resolving chord of the previous one.
>
> I thought all the boys at Bradfield learned Greek – which was one reason they did Greek plays. Not a bit of it. Only one member of the cast was a Greek scholar; five of them had done Greek O-level. But the majority, including Clytemnestra, had learned the text by heart in the language lab and then recited it. They knew what it meant, but they didn't know Greek. So here we were watching a play in a language which neither the actors nor the audience understood. Yet the emotion communicated.
>
> I was struck by the nineteenth-century tradition of the classics where Aeschylus, Euripides and Sophocles are thought of as good public school types and members of the Church of England. Next to me sat a bishop gravely following his Greek text, while the story of cannibalism, murder and corruption was enacted before us. To the Renaissance the classics were subversive – almost revolutionary. But to the English public school they were pillars of conformity.
>
> Tony Harrison and Harry Birtwistle were also there, learning lessons. When we come to do *The*

Oresteia we must condense – they didn't, not enough; have masks – they didn't; and the chorus must *use* their bodies – they didn't.

Some jottings concerning the rehearsals:

This was my big day. After all those years, I started *The Oresteia.* We talked to the actors – Harry Birtwistle, Tony Harrison and I – about methods of work, not about the Greeks or Greek dramas. Then we went through the play. Three main factors – the use of masks, the use of percussion, and the whole text being spoken by the actors to the audience, not to each other – were understood from the start. The cast were reading through simple cardboard masks, some of them wearing glasses on top of their masks.

. . . I asked the actors to sit in a tight little circle with this thought: They were the chorus of old men who had to go out and face a public meeting and explain the sacrifice of Iphigeneia. How were they going to tell what happened? Was it treason, was it necessary? Was it a crime which would brand the family for the rest of time, or was it an heroic act to start an heroic war? So they sat around and pondered and made the chorus live, each fragment taken by a single voice, qualifying, arguing, contradicting. We then tried to turn that private anxiety into a public demonstration. But it became generalised. . . .

An exciting day on *The Oresteia,* working nearly all the time on masks. A lot of the actors were very shaken by the problems. But I feel now that I know absolutely how I want the project to be, to look, to sound. I've rarely been so certain in my life. But I also know, having seen this Everest in very hard contours, that it's going to take me virtually the rest of the year to get it up.

. . . Another good day on *The Oresteia.* In the afternoon we read thirteen different versions of the *Iphigeneia* chorus. These were by Milton, Swinburne, Pope, various Romantic poets, Macneice, and the intellectuals of the Thirties. All were totally unspeakable and undramatic. It is incredible to believe they came from the same original. They also had no consistent texture; the vocabulary was drawn from a ragbag of "poetics". Tony Harrison's version emerged the clear victor. It is living, dramatic, and actable. . . .

Strange feeling at *Oresteia* rehearsals working on the mask techniques that Michel Saint-Denis taught me in the early Sixties at Stratford. Michel learnt them from Copeau, and taught them to George Devine who passed them on to John Blatchley and Bill Gaskill, and Bill in turn passed them on to Peter Gill and Keith Johnstone. Some of my actors are therefore full of the same training that

> Michel gave me, and it has changed very little. Why? Because it is based on something that works in human terms. Where did Copeau get it from? The mimes of the nineteenth century perhaps. It's believed to go all the way back to the *Commedia.* No one will ever know. The theatre does not chronicle itself well.
>
> These are the techniques we are following. Treat your mask with respect. Go with it. Do not talk with it in your own voice. Hide its straps, its elastic. Believe in it. Study it first in your hand, then put it on without looking in the mirror, then look at yourself quickly in the mirror. Become what you see, it is no longer yourself, be the person the image suggests. This person is always in the early stages very childish, anarchic, frequently vulgar. But slowly, as with us over the last week, the masks grow up. Actors begin to search in their new faces for what is wise, what is balanced, sophisticated, intelligent. So some of them are today able to talk fragments of Tony Harrison's text with a certain degree of strength. It has of course been learnt beforehand. So it's not read. If you read in a mask you are a man reading a script, not an actor glancing at his text.

From the actress Yvonne Mitchell, whom he visited when she was dying, Hall learned that when Saint-Denis was teaching at the London Theatre Studio his students always chose "the old and grotesque masks . . . never the young and beautiful".

A footnote in the *Diaries* reveals that, when planning to put on the trilogy at Epidaurus, Hall proposed a daylight staging, opening the performance at 6 a.m., but the organizers of the festival dissuaded him from doing so.

A very different means of exposing Aeschylus' characters was that of the performance artist Lynn Swanson, who was abetted by masks and puppets in presenting a trilogy of what she described as "mordant updates of mythological heroines" comprising, entirely in her own person, "Agamemnon, Iphigeneia, Achilles and even the Trojan Horse". This was part of the Poetry Project at St Mark's Church in New York City; her series culminated in 1985.

In New York, again, in 1985, the Off-Broadway City Stage Company (CSC) added *The Oresteia* to its repertory. The small but unintimidated troupe had previously undertaken Sophocles' *Theban Trilogy* and Ibsen's *Peer Gynt,* equally formidable ventures. The presentation was in two parts, the first consisting of *Agamemnon,* the second of *The Libation Bearers* and *The Furies,* closely interwoven and here retitled *Electra/Orestes.* Each section was introduced by a short prologue borrowed from Euripides' *Iphigeneia in Aulis,* serving as expository bridges. The translation used was by Robert Fagles, to whom the linked works represented "our rite of passage from savagery to civilization". Mel Gussow, of the *New York Times*, deemed the translation "felicitous as well as idiomatic, the most impressive aspect of the production".

> As always, the CSC is adventurous. . . . While one is grateful for the attempt at Aeschylus, and there are several individual performances of merit, the result is a cycle of inconclusively blended ingredients.
>
> . . . *The Agamemnon* begins the epic on a doleful note. Admittedly, this is not a play of action. The work's singular dramatic event, Clytemnestra's slaying of her husband, Agamemnon, and his captive, Cassandra, occurs off stage. But even by that measure the performance is static.
>
> So much of the success depends on the actress playing Clytemnestra. Karen Sunde, who is the CSC's most experienced performer, takes a mannered approach, standing stately and rolling her eyes as if to transfix dissenters into submission. She turns out to be a ubiquitous presence, even into ghosthood in the third play. Once he removes his Darth Vader helmet, Tom Spiller is a fairly forceful Agamemnon, as is the Cassandra of Essene R., although she has a tendency to be elocutionary. The chorus, taking its masks on and off, is dirge-like.
>
> The performance markedly improves with the more overtly dramatic *Electra*, chiefly because Ginger Grace assumes center stage in the title role. She plays Electra with a feline ferocity, and Sheridan Crist is a stalwart Orestes.
>
> Christopher Martin's intention as director and designer is to make *The Oresteia* relevant to a contemporary audience, and in that regard the result is inconsistent. In pursuit of that goal, he prefaces the trilogy with photographic projections of men in battle and offers interludes of music (by Bob Jewett and Jack Maeby) that underline the drama with a quivery beat that might be a warmup to a war of the Jedi.
>
> Not until the third part, *Orestes*, does the director reveal his interpretation. Enter Apollo, Charles H. Patterson in reflecting sunshades and white fatigues, looking like a mercenary soldier on the prowl (not exactly one's image of Apollo) and followed by an actress on roller skates – the only one in the production.
>
> Amy Warner's Athena, also in battle white and later in ball gown, is no less incongruous, but she strikes an oddly provocative note of willful superiority. In an artful lighting effect, shafts of light shoot to the stage and stand like columns, effectively serving as the temple at Delphi. The production itself could be considered intriguing in its unevenness.

(The "Darth Vader helmet" and the "Jedi" are, once again, references to science-fiction characters whose garb was often likened by designers to that worn by Athenians in the Periclean Age. The actress

"Essene R." apparently chose to have her name listed in that shortened form.)

A mere year later *The Furies* – under just that title – had a showing in an unusual space, the huge Gothic crypt of the Cathedral of St John the Divine (Episcopal) in New York. It focused on the first two plays only. For this enterprise two troupes joined forces, the Talking Band of the United States and the Roy Hart Theater from France. In attendance was John Rockwell, a music critic of the *New York Times*.

> Both groups have done excellent work here in the past, and *Furies* has its moments. But ultimately it fails to find a sufficiently fresh or compelling style to justify yet another production of these archetypal tales of the House of Atreus.
>
> The evening lasts 105 minutes, broken only by a brief pause between the first two parts of *The Oresteia* in the Robert Lowell translation. The style employed mixes straight acting, a sort of *Sprechgesang* chant and, here and there, background music and sounds provided by actors playing saxophones or creating sound effects or wordless song.
>
> The trouble is that these fracturings of conventional theatricality don't go far enough, and the actual articulation of the text is neither convincingly achieved in traditional terms nor coherently altered in some new direction. Something more radical, along the lines of the Roy Hart production of *Pagliacci* seen last season at Café La MaMa, would have been welcome.
>
> The best work comes from Richard Armstrong of the Roy Hart company, who offers a Ludlamesque Clytemnestra, campy but poignant; he also achieves the most interesting extensions of speech in the direction of song, and his lapses into French are somehow nicely eerie. Complementing him is Tina Shepard of the Talking Band as Electra, strong, calm understatement in a cast given mostly to ranting.
>
> The crypt itself is an interesting space in which to play, its ancient mysteries contradicted by insulated heating ducts. It is also afflicted by an odd odor. Paul Zimet of the Talking Band directed *Furies*, with Mr Armstrong as associate director, and Jun Maeda contributed the Peter Brookish dirt-floor setting. Beverly Emmons did the simple but effective lighting, and others in the cast are Jack Wetherall as Orestes, Jonathan Hart as Cassandra, William Badget as Agamemnon, Daniel Prieto as Aegisthus and Ellen Maddow, Harry Mann, Rosemary Quinn and Rossignol.

("Ludlamesque": that is, in the manner of Charles Ludlam, a founder and star of the Theater of the Ridiculous, who interpreted famed heroines of classic drama in "drag" for broadly humorous effect.)

The translation used here had been published by Robert Lowell, an American Pulitzer Prize-winning poet and dramatist. Reviewing it in the Literary Supplement of the *New York Times*, David Grene, an academic classicist, editor and colleague of Richard Lattimore, had compared it to William Butler Yeats's version of Sophocles' *Theban Plays*. His critique was headed "Aeschylus Diminished".

> In both cases a poet made the new plays from existing English translations rather than from the Greek, cutting here, adapting there, though both Lowell and Yeats undoubtedly reached beyond the translations to something in the original that the translator had seen but not sufficiently appreciated. Such things are certainly to be found by a poet, as distinct from a scholar, especially when the new translator is as gifted and sensitive as these two men were.
>
> Versions such as Lowell's and Yeats's have a definite aim, which is not necessarily simply to convey the sense of the original author's words – though I think neither Yeats nor Lowell would have lightly disregarded what they felt to be Aeschylus' true meaning. Yeats wanted an acting version for the Abbey stage, Lowell something of the same, yet a little qualified. "Richard Lattimore's (translation) has had my admiration for years; it is so elaborately exact," he noted in a preface to this volume. "I have aimed at something else: to trim, to cut, and be direct enough to satisfy my own mind and at a first hearing the simple ears of a theater audience."
>
> Such a definite purpose as this – as distinct from actual translations – has some advantages. It may be said, right off, that Lowell's version of the *Oresteia* makes a splendid play. In some places he has done this by means of stage directions partly implied in the Aeschylus text; in others, he has relied on his own imaginative invention. When Orestes reveals the bodies of Clytemnestra and Aegisthus and turns to the audience, saying
>
> "You that hear these ills
> see this machine, my wretched father's fetters
> bonds of his hands and yoking at his feet"
>
> (my own literal translation), the effect is immensely enhanced by Lowell's previous comment: "Pylades holds up the noosed and weighted robe that Agamemnon was killed in. Somehow the sight of the robe seems to madden Orestes." The controversial passages in the *Choephoroi* in which Orestes leaves the signs on the grave – the hair offering, the print of the shoe, the fragment of swaddling clothes – which Euripides was to deride for its archaism within fifty years of the production of the *Oresteia*, has been rewritten by Lowell:

> "these locks of my hair, this blood-knot
> of red feather dipped in blood"

and later:

> "Do you see this hunter killing the wolf
> and his bitch on this piece of tapestry?
> You wove it with your own hands, and sent it
> to me in my exile."

Lowell's shortening and tightening have gotten rid of much that cannot be rendered for a modern audience or perhaps even for the general reader today, who knows nothing of the Greek language or theater. Lowell's breaking up of the chorus in the *Agamemnon* into various voices chanting different stanzas pays off in directness and comprehension. In the *Choephoroi*, in the long dirge at Agamemnon's grave, the gradual indistinctness in tone, moving from direct address to ritual invocation, makes effective much that is nearly impossible to convey with emotional value in a more literal translation.

Lowell's is a beautiful play, with very few of what can be called downright blemishes. What is it then, if anything, that we miss in his version? In the first place, the density of the original poem. Lowell presumably wanted to avoid this when he spoke of writing for a live audience. No one really knows how much the Athenians understood of this extraordinarily rich poetry at first hearing. Aristophanes in *The Frogs* intimated that even a contemporary Greek audience might have failed to comprehend a great deal.

There is no doubt that Aeschylus' style is in the highest degree daring and innovative in vocabulary, grammar and construction. These are in harmony with the apparent vividness of poetic imagination and linguistic power. Consider the following passage: "Your word does not lighten me," says the chorus (*Agamemnon* 1120), "but to my heart the blood drops run back saffron-dyed, as the life sinks and the lights sink with it for those fallen by the spear." This literal rendering conveys the difficulties. The poet is combining a metaphor from sunset with the double sense of light and eye, and the physical action of the blood that for some reason of his own he sees as turning yellow rather than red. Lowell cuts this passage out altogether. Mr Lattimore tries to render it into poetry that I cannot but think has a false note:

"And to the heart trickles the pale drop
timed to our sunset and the mortal radiance."

The temptation to a modern translator in such a matter is either to cut or to substitute a kind of poetry that is more acceptable. But Aeschylus was like that, and perhaps we ought to settle for the strangeness and roughness of a literal rendering. There was a creative poet there whose images and metaphors were his own and no one else's, and if we brood over them even in their bare bones we may learn more about poetry than by trying to make them over in our own terms.

Nor do I think that Lowell's terseness and directness help in the greatest of all tasks of the Aeschylean translator: to capture the complex structure of this huge trilogy. The combination of the Trojan War and the matricide, the conflict of the old and new gods (that is, the new male gods and the old female gods), and the resettlement of the old gods in a new function in Athenian society haunt and permeate the three plays, in recurrent images and phrases, in tones and half-tones. Lowell has managed each phrase sharply and well. But somehow his very directness goes against the spirit of the thing. It is more than probable that the *Oresteia* cannot be rendered into a tongue other than Greek in a way that satisfies the needs of the poetry. There is no ground for depreciating Lowell; he did what he set out to do and did it well. But his translation fails to convey much of what is greatest in the Aeschylean trilogy.

In Baltimore, Maryland, at the Theater of Nations festival, also in 1986, a feature was Tadashi Suzuki's *Clytemnestra*, derived from *The Oresteia.* Arthur Holmberg, of Harvard University and serving as North American editor of the *World Encyclopedia of Contemporary Theatre*, sent the *New York Times* this brief exegesis: "[It] shows how every boy must kill his primary identification with his mother to become a man. . . . Another major thematic concern that surfaces in productions at the festival is the fear of war in general and nuclear holocaust in particular. Mr Suzuki resituates *The Trojan Women*, generally acknowledged to be the greatest antiwar play ever written, in the atomic rubble of a gutted city. An old woman stumbles into a graveyard and relives the horrors of war. The ceremony of death and destruction is witnessed by three giant figures in black, who watch impassively as mankind systematically destroys itself."

Nor had this many productions of the trilogy within such a short span of years exhausted American interest in the *Oresteia.* At New York University, students in the drama department of the Tisch School of the Arts had the courage to mount yet another interpretation of the three plays. The cycle was presented in two parts split over two consecutive evenings, after which it was repeated in the same order (1989). The programme was directed by Bevya Rosten, with music by Vincent Katz. The following year, *Clytemnestra* (1990), "a theater, dance and video production", assembled by Jeffrey Fiske, was enacted at Montclair State College in nearby New Jersey.

French critics and playgoers responded strongly to *Les Atrides* (*The House of Atreus*, 1991) as conceived by Ariana Mnouchkine's avant-garde Théâtre du Soleil and staged in the Cartoucherie (cartridge factory), a cluster of former munitions-manufacturing sheds adapted for use by her troupe and located in Vincennes, on the eastern outskirts of Paris. To reach it, spectators rode the Métro to its last stop and then took a shuttle bus.

The *New York Times* received a lengthy appraisal of this offering from Michael Ratcliffe, literary editor and former theatre critic of the *Observer* of London, who recounted:

> The Théâtre du Soleil has pioneered a vision of epic narrative theater and applied it to the life of Molière, the French Revolution, three plays by Shakespeare, the torments of contemporary Cambodia and the partition of India in 1947.
>
> In all of these Miss Mnouchkine's theatrical vision combined a tragic sense of corrupting power with spectacular live music, athletic tirelessness and sumptuous visual display. At the same time, she is the consummate magpie and synthesist, drawing music, costume, movement and acting styles from Europe, Africa, China, India. Like Peter Brook, her near-contemporary and fellow director in the same city, Miss Mnouchkine (pronounced Mu-NOSH-kin) has created a true theater of the world, informed by the elements of human behavior common to all mankind.
>
> And the world comes to Vincennes. Unlike Mr Brook, Miss Mnouchkine, now in her sixties, seldom tours. Where he aims for the essence of simplicity, she observes the wicked ways of men with a striking yet disciplined flamboyance. The achievement is peculiarly French, for theater in France is the most hospitably cosmopolitan on earth – inspired by curiosity and enthusiasm for the beauty of ideas beyond Europe. When the tide of empire receded in France, it left behind a legacy of dazzlement and sophistication. The Théâtre du Soleil is part of that. Post-imperial indifference is a phenomenon of London, not Paris.
>
> Born in 1964, the Théâtre du Soleil has long since transcended mere fashion, creating few imitators and no school. Its popularity in France is undimmed, and Parisian audiences are now perched on the edge of their seats for the rhetorical dance-play toward which more than two and a half decades of vivid story-telling have led – *Les Atrides*, comprising the *Oresteia* trilogy of Aeschylus, preceded by Euripides' *Iphigeneia in Aulis.*

Three of the plays – *Iphigeneia, Agamemnon* and *The Libation* – are in repertory; *The Eumenides* – the last play of the *Oresteia* – will complete the cycle, probably next spring. You will be fortunate if you ever see a more exhilarating production of the first great tragedies in European drama.

Les Atrides has recently ended its first sellout season at the Cartoucherie. . . . [It] is scheduled to be performed throughout 1992. French epic theater projects enjoy a long life. [Plans to bring it to New York, where the Théâtre du Soleil had never appeared, were eagerly discussed but then had to be reconsidered in view of budgetary problems.]

Miss Mnouchkine's understanding of history is timeless and her sense of place universal; artificial frontiers melt as easily as those between gender and race. The Greek plays themselves precede many such simplifying distinctions – concepts like "Europe" and "Asia" make little sense in a cosmos stretching from Sicily to the Indus – and they belong to a sexually ambivalent world. The mostly male chorus in *Les Atrides*, brilliantly led by a woman (Catherine Schaub), plays dizzy young girls in the first play, bitter old men in the second and grieving slave women in the third.

The audience is permitted to watch the actors putting on their make-up before the show. Then:

A slow, Kabuki-like crescendo of thunderous drumming compels the chattering to stop at the start of each play. The grandly pig-tailed Jean-Jacques Lemêtre, whose sexy, sweet-sharp score accompanies the action throughout, commands a battery of more than 140 instruments. He has been with Miss Mnouchkine as composer and musical director for ten years. The samurai of European musical theater, he moves with virtuoso speed and silence among clarinet, accordion, tiny violin and double bass, from raps recalling Bartok and Grappelli to percussive gaiety and sinuous Ottoman despair.

Miss Mnouchkine's actors rarely just sneak onto the stage; they arrive with a stride and a flourish, frequently at a run. Urgency brings them to this place, and it is theirs to command. Nothing in *Les Atrides* distracts us from their skills or from the flying, sculptural impact of Nathalie Thomas's dramatically cut clothes. There are no changing panoramas, no fancy furniture, building or props.

Guy-Claude François, the designer, sets the cycle in a bare, dusty yard enclosed by a low, chipped concrete wall. It is a kind of corral in which some sort of violence has already taken place: stock-car racing, perhaps, or the breaking-in of wild horses and young bulls; but more likely, to judge from the stains on the walls, mass-execution of enemies without trial. The newsreel-banality of evil is here.

This mean and ominous place stands, in the first play, for the port of Aulis on the eastern coast of Greece. King Agamemnon's restless army is so becalmed there, on its way to fight in Troy, that the

> desperate King has promised to sacrifice his daughter Iphigeneia in return for a stiff wind across the sea. In the plays of the *Oresteia*, the enclosure stands for Agamemnon's own city of Argos.

Here Ratcliffe encapsulates the whole story in two sentences, saying, parenthetically, "That's all the plot you need to know." He goes on:

> But it could easily be the shabby main square of any poor village between Corfu and Afghanistan at any time. And it is the perfect, uncluttered setting for a great dance of life and death.
>
> *Les Atrides* is from first to last a dramatic dance-play. Even the curtain calls are danced. If you cannot hoof it in this weightless and archaic world, you cannot express, or defend, yourself in any way. The troubled Agamemnon, for example (Simon Abkarian), shuffles precariously to the floor like an old camel unsure of his ground to ponder what awful choice to make next; the condemned Iphigeneia (Nirupama Nityanandan) seizes the chorus with desperate ecstasy, urging them to welcome the patriotism of her sacrifice.
>
> In *The Libation Bearers*, the adolescent Orestes (Mr Abkarian again) cannot dance at all. Both literally and figuratively, he has to learn the steps of survival on his first bloody day back home, and after the off-stage slaughter of his mother and her lover, he stamps tight, furious little booted steps of joy into the hard earth. These dance rites of manhood are short-lived.
>
> Miss Schaub leads most of the choruses with a feverish urgency, letting out little yelps of pleasure and cries of distress. Time and again, the impression is given that the dance must be kept going at all costs, or the city, the court and the civilization will collapse. The line between terror and exaltation remains a fine one throughout.
>
> Five actors share most of the roles, large and small, but despite the outstandingly gifted Mr Abkarian, the cycle is dominated by the watching, dancing chorus of twelve (sometimes thirteen), who play no part in the action but animate it throughout by the vivacity and violence of their reactions. As any chorus should, they guide the responses of the real innocent spectators, ourselves: We are so stunned by their declamation and dancing that we are tempted to surrender our innocence and join in.
>
> This is a company of athletic dancing actors, not of dancers who can act. They worked with a dance instructor, began with traditional Greek dancing and improvised from there on. Euripides' young maidens of Aulis bump, grind, simper and sway like chorus girls as they gossip about legendary weddings and Greek heroes, mime the noonday airlessness of Troy and rise from the ground as one.
>
> Miss Mnouchkine's old men of Argos, impotent for service in war, mutter and bleat like sheep;

> their preferred dance is the literally staggering dervish-whirl with which they celebrate the fall of Troy, but after ten years most of them are no longer up to it and totter breathless to the ground. They look splendid in scarlet, but their splendor is powerless and absurd.
>
> Blink – at the start of the third play, *The Libation Bearers* – and the chorus, mourning Agamemnon, seems to have burst from the walls, stiff forearms thumping their breasts and battering the air above their heads to ward off invisible harm. In seconds they fill the stage with an orgy of professional grief in burgundy and black, teaching Electra how to mourn, cocking their ears like dogs at every whispered mention of Orestes' forbidden name. We see him before they do, in fact, at the very start of the play, when the young prince peers like a curious farmyard animal over a gate at the back – revenge never arrived more sweetly or comically than this.

Ratcliffe digresses briefly to pay tribute to the unusual gifts of the thirty-year-old Abkarian, a player of Armenian descent:

> He is tall, witty and commanding, with a curved nose like the beak of a heraldic bird on either side of which dark eyes bide their time or gleam with the menace of a preemptive strike.
>
> His energy is phenomenal and he moves from role to role with the relish and generosity of a great actor (which he could well become): a preposterous Achilles, an ominous messenger from Troy, a formidable leader of the Argos old boys, a goofy nurse. His Agamemnon is a tragic knave, imposing but foolish, racked with the grief of a man caught in a net of impossible choices; only a small, thin smile occasionally cracks the enameled white face to reveal the anguish beneath. His Orestes is raw before the pitiless world.
>
> The feminist Mnouchkine has always been more interested in, and much better at, the redeeming womanliness of men than the enforced masculinity of women, and, in rejecting Clytemnestra, the bloodthirsty drag queen of convention, she presents instead an elegant, exhausted wife-mother (Juliana Carneiro da Cunha), the justice of whose cause is never in doubt. But this ducks the evidence of Clytemnestra's ruthlessness and Miss da Cunha's performance is the single element in the great enterprise that remains unresolved.
>
> I said the chorus plays *almost* no part in the action, because at the end of *The Libation Bearers* they are, to their horror, compelled to help Electra and the servants remove the bodies of Clytemnestra and her lover. When the ground grips the mattress on which they lie, it has to be pulled, shoved and dragged by all hands available off stage as Mr Lemêtre's instruments thunder a final cannonade and

the dogs of retribution begin to bark. It would be hard to imagine a more panicky and undignified scramble to remove the evidence of bloodletting from the general gaze, nor a more thrilling cliffhanger for the fourth and final play to come.

Aided by a substantial government subsidy, the company did take its costly production on tour: it attracted throngs in Babelsberg (East Germany) where it made use of an old movie studio. In the south of France, an outdoor engagement was beset by summer storms. Having selected a site alongside a river in Toulouse, the troupe had its performance washed out when floodgates gave way: all the expensive costumes were soaked. By the next morning, however, the overflowing river had subsided, the skies cleared and the sun – for whose healing rays the company was named – dried out the sodden wardrobe, allowing the actors to carry on with their dedicated task.

The more formidable obstacle raised by the cost of a transatlantic tour was overcome when the Florence Gould Foundation in America and various French government agencies, as well as banks and other corporations doing business in the United States, offered further support. (An earlier crossing had taken the troupe to Los Angeles for the 1984 Olympic Arts Festival to present a Shakespeare work in French.) Now the company visited Montreal for three weeks, assured of a largely French-speaking audience, and Los Angeles again, and then New York for eleven days as part of the annual New Wave programme sponsored by the progressive-minded Brooklyn Academy of Music (1992).

This second North American appearance was preceded by a flurry of feature articles on Greek and French theatre, besides interviews with the highly articulate Mnouchkine. In the *New York Times* she was described by John Rockwell, a music critic, as "A cheerful woman with a handsome face, a winning grin and Brillo-like gray hair, given to baggy yet comfortable stylish clothes. She combines the images of fierce theatrical moralist, bubbling happy child, nurturing mother and forbidding French intellectual."

Born in Paris in 1939, she was the child of Russian expatriates. Her initial link to theatre was forged at Oxford. "'I went there to study psychology. But I joined the Oxford University Drama Society, and one day I said, 'Of course, this is what I want to do.'"

During a year's journey to Asia in the early 1960s she had observed and absorbed Oriental dramatic approaches and techniques; this led to her founding the Théâtre du Soleil (1964). Subsequently, she returned to the Far East for additional studies, attempting an osmosis of its dramatic principles, then adapting them in personal ways as each new project was undertaken by her group.

The company's title came from the spirit of idealism that animated it. Mnouchkine explained to

Rockwell: "At the time theatres were named for their directors, but I could not imagine calling it Le Théâtre Ariane Mnouchkine. We were looking for light, heat, beauty, strength, fertility."

Following Stanislavsky's model, the troupe is organized as a commune, on an egalitarian premise, with no designated stars, though some players are outstanding and most frequently assigned leading roles. Rockwell: "From the first, it was a visionary enterprise, a band of Leftist romantics convinced that they could change the world. And though the personnel has turned over completely, the vision remains consistent." Mnouchkine summarized: "Théâtre du Soleil is the dream of working, being happy and searching for beauty and for goodness. It's trying to live for higher purposes, not for richness. It's very simple, really."

Casts are multi-ethnic, as is also true of Peter Brook's experimental company, a contemporary and rival group in Paris. The most prominent actors, Simon Abkarian, Juliana Carneiro da Cunha, Nirupama Nityanandan and Brontis Jodorowsky, are of different races and widely varied backgrounds. Abkarian, who represents Agamemnon, Achilles, Orestes and Orestes' nurse, a chorus leader and a messenger, is a French-born Armenian, who was raised in Lebanon and then became a long-time resident of Southern California where he worked as a cabaret dancer. The Clytemnestra and Athena is the Brazilian Juliana Carneiro da Cunha, trained as a ballet dancer in Maurice Bejart's school. Nirupama Nityanandan, seen as Cassandra, Iphigeneia and a chorus leader, is from Madras, where for twenty years she studied to be a Bharata Natyan dancer, a mistress of controlled, subtle gestures. Jodorowsky, from Mexico, had a Chilean father and French mother: he takes a broad range of secondary roles in *Les Atrides*. A similar mix of racial strains and cultural outlooks prevails throughout the troupe.

Originally the actors were pledged to remain with the company lifelong, but this proved to be impractical. The average stay is six or seven years, so the general complexion of the troupe is consistently youthful. Salaries are low. All income is distributed to the actors, who number about twenty-six, and to the backstage workers and administrators, the roster adding up to about sixty, the total sometimes changing. Usually Mnouchkine rejects contributions from corporations; the financial support gathered for the North American journey was an exception to a rule that reflects her disdain for possible materialistic influences.

At intervals, ten-day workshops for outsiders are held; these are not considered to be auditions, but very often new members are recruited from those taking part in the preliminary exercises.

Members of the company do not share living quarters but have separate apartments, possibly together with non-participants.

According to Rockwell, "Artistic decisions are described as simple deductions from unassailable 'evidence'; that doubling parts may make dramatic sense is dismissed as coincidence. 'What I call theatrical evidence just emerges,' Miss Mnouchkine said. 'It's not discussed. We discuss when something goes wrong, when for two or three days we are stuck. When the work is going, we don't discuss, we work.'" Yet the final decision is hers. As one of her players sees it, she is like a Zen master. "She directs not by adding things but by taking things away, down to the more and more simple, the more essential."

In Rockwell's paraphrase: "Dismissive of most acting today, with its uninflected imitation of life, Miss Mnouchkine prefers a broadly emotive style that recalls what we know of early Western theatre and that still exists in the non-Western world. Not for her, despite her own academic background, the psychological identification of the typical modern Western actor. 'We flee daily life,' she said in an interview in *The Drama Review.* 'We do not talk of psychology but rather of the characters' souls. The theatre is not supposed to represent psychology but passions.'"

This conviction has led her to employ masks (or masklike make-up) "to liberate acting from pale realism. In *Les Atrides,* the masks and make-up become simpler as the plays approach modernity. Yet, Miss Mnouchkine says, the mask is always there – 'the mask of character.' She categorically rejects the idea that she has poached on exotic cultures. 'What we do derives completely from the action of the characters. Iphigeneia is not using the real steps and *mudras* of India, which would mean nothing to us. She's just showing her feelings. She's not using the codes; she's using what is inward.'"

The largest of the three warehouses occupied by the company is used as the theatre; it seats 1,200 spectators on sharply raked benches. The performing area is a huge open square – no curtain, wings, flies or alterable scenery. Away from Vincennes, this bare setting is always replicated. . . . Mnouchkine insists on that.

Music in coordination with the speeches and physical action is incessant and emphasized. It is supplied by Jean-Jacques Lemêtre, a member of the troupe for fourteen years. His role, as described by Rockwell: "When actors are speaking, he leaps among the battery of exotic instruments, a megalomaniacally inflated one-man band, though for the chorus dances he falls back on recorded ensemble music. He says his music is so intimately wedded to speech rhythms that having other musicians accompany him would be nearly impossible, and a live dance ensemble would be too expensive."

An unsigned brochure issued by the Brooklyn Academy of Music depicts him vividly: "A large man with a pigtail, Lemêtre looks as if he had just returned from a desert pilgrimage with a horde of rare finds. He works on an extraordinary collection of two hundred instruments – aside from percussions there are violins, basses, clarinets, flutes and original inventions – and moves from one to the other, taking a swipe at a drum on the way. He composes by first improvising on the action during rehearsal; from this splintered sound, he creates an Oriental mosaic. Each of the main protagonists – Agamemnon and Orestes, Clytemnestra and Electra – has his or her own theme song."

In contrast to the bare setting, the costumes – by Nathalie Thomas, Marie Hélène Bouvet and Catherine Schaub – were opulent and theatrically striking. The brochure tells us: "They are unisex – tunics, pantaloons and braided belts out of the Arabian Nights. Beards are woolly, Nebuchadnezzar-style; gold jewellery gleams on black and white, red and gold brocades. White face make-up dramatizes the pathos of dark, elongated eyes." And Rockwell reported: "Faces covered with chalk-white make-up, like masks; headpieces, and costumes with full skirts, vests and glittering ornaments that are an ingenious hybrid of the ethnic cultures stretching from Southern Italy through the Middle East to Southern India."

Much noted has been Mnouchkine's powerful handling of the chorus, here headed by Catherine Schaub. According to Rockwell: "[It] changes from fiercely joyful women in *Iphigeneia* to soldiers overcome by the horror of war in *Agamemnon*, to black-clad, vulturelike harridans in *The Libation Bearers*. In *The Eumenides* they become terrifying mythic beasts, no longer dancing but growling and snarling, led by three harpies straight from a Brechtian proletarian netherworld and standing as eternal threats to human benevolence." The opening scene is one in which a double door at the distant rear "swings open and in they surge – fifteen red-clad women (though some are really men) stamping and swaying with a gleeful joy that is very close to barbaric fury".

Comparing Mnouchkine's troupe to that of Peter Brook, Rockwell found "its stylistic fusion more diverse and organic, its enunciation of the French language more elegant and its dance and music closer to Pina Bausch and other European choreographers".

A dynamic force, Schaub, the multi-faceted chorus leader, is trained in the arts of Kathakali, the sacred dance of India, so the choreography is not wholly Central European nor even predominantly so. The brochure explains:

> The movement that begins as innocent folk dance can turn majestic, mystic, seductive, or propelled by dire events, become a barbaric war dance. Heedless of their elaborate headdresses, the chorus leaps over walls, moving in for the kill, keening like lost souls on their way to Hades, turning antique tragedy into something that goes on in front of our eyes. . . . Abkarian does an unforgettable solo as the tortured Agamemnon: a mysterious, confidential side step, as if cringing from the heat of the day, the horror in store.

> The exits and entrances have a Kabuki flourish; the chorus dances with the abandon of Greek islanders. They crouch on the wall and peer down, predicting the worst under a billowing blue island sky. They herald the bad news – hot as this morning's tabloids – that vengeful wife! those ungrateful children! Stories we have not been able to shake off since the birth of Greek theatre twenty-five hundred years ago.

Though sparse, the setting is mood-creating:

> A low wall runs around the stage, marking off city limits; it is a combat zone, a *corrida*. The stone has a rust patina – blood has been spilled here. This hollowed-out pit is the matrix for all family and civil strife – the war between the sexes, between gods, a duel under Apollo's sun. Gates rise; messengers of doom hurtle through; slain bodies are rushed on right through the audience, wrapped in blood-soaked sheets.
>
> . . . Out of infanticide and matricide, vengeful wives and jealous children, Mnouchkine has made a musical tragedy. Every step of this savage ceremony has been choreographed for actors who move at breakneck speed and practically sing their text; they also inhabit several parts, from king to messenger, from prophetess to the lowest of the low – the Furies' rabid watch dogs.

Though *Iphigeneia in Aulis* is by Euripides and not part of Aeschylus' *Oresteia*, written fifteen years earlier, Mnouchkine chose to include it and place it first as a clarifying prologue. "I wanted people to understand Clytemnestra's tragedy, to feel for her. The Atreus family was hounded by destiny, but they made bad choices. Why does a father sacrifice his daughter for war and glory? Why can't a mother forgive?"

In Brooklyn, the Academy's huge stage was not large enough to accommodate the production; instead, the company was presented at the specially refitted Park Slope Armory, in size equivalent to two football fields. (Similarly, the Montreal engagement had utilized a sports stadium. One critic remarked that such a vast setting was appropriate; in ancient Athens, the theatre of Dionysus held audiences of 14,000.) In both Montreal and Brooklyn the troupe played to sold-out houses.

Brooklyn's spectators could rely on hired earphones and a simultaneous English translation by William M. Hoffman, from French versions by Jean and Moytte Bollack (*Iphigeneia in Aulis*), by Mnouchkine herself (*Agamemnon* and *The Libation Bearers*) and by Hélène Cixous (*The Eumenides*).

Of the Paris staging, a critic in the monthly *New Criterion* exclaimed that the company had put on "the most exciting and innovative theatrical experience on earth". New York's reviewers were hardly as fully persuaded that Mnouchkine's treatment of the great Greek tragedies was that superlative, though they were decidedly impressed. William A. Henry III wrote in the magazine *Time*:

> In Anglo-American theater, the most important creative artist is normally the playwright or an actor. On Continental stages, from Munich to Moscow, it is almost always the director, who becomes as much of an *auteur* as in film. Even classic texts serve as mere points of departure.
>
> Of the Western World's foremost *auteurs*, none is more distinctive and idiosyncratic – or less culturally bonded to the West – than Ariane Mnouchkine of France. Her troupe's arrival in the US this week may be, paradoxically, the most prestigious theatrical event of the year and the least influential. It is sure to inspire admirers but probably cannot inspire imitators. Mnouchkine's work is spellbinding, in part for its eerie beauty, unrestrained energy and power, but also because its Asian-influenced anti-realism is so remote from anything American – or, for that matter, French.
>
> Mnouchkine calls herself populist but is scholarly enough to borrow from a dozen classical cultures, ranging from British to Balinese. She heatedly denies being avant-garde but despises realism as "the end of theater" and shrugs off as "limiting and uninteresting" questions about the inner life or psychology of her characters. She delights in interrupting a tense narrative with choral dance and music staged in a highly personal mélange of styles, mostly from Asia, which she considers "the true home of acting." Having argued a few years ago that no Westerner could understand Shakespeare because no one (except, of course, Mnouchkine and her disciples) could attain the requisite intellectual distance, she now insists that the only way to comprehend Greek drama, the wellspring of Western culture, is to see it through the prism of her favorite form and principal influence, the Kathakali dance drama of Southern India.
>
> She makes her case in *Les Atrides*, a nine-hour cycle of four productions. . . . Two years in the making – including eight months of rehearsal – the shows just completed a three-week run in a Montreal hockey arena. Mnouchkine refuses to perform in a conventional theater. In New York, sponsors had to remove 375 military vehicles from a Brooklyn armory.
>
> To mount the plays, Mnouchkine, fifty-three, "studied the Greek language for the first time in my life." But she rejected the use of classical masks, because they "conceal rather than reveal" character, and chose instead Asian-style face painting. Although she adopted the Greek idea of a singing and dancing chorus, she pragmatically trimmed it from a classical fifty people to about fifteen and substituted Indian sound and movement.

The overall result is weird, thrilling and distinctly modern. In this interpretation of a myth of multigenerational male grief and retaliation, the central figure is a woman. Clytemnestra's just grievances seem as evident to the audience as they are invisible to the gods and men around her. Bereft of a child killed to propitiate war gods, then abandoned by the husband who slew their daughter, she turns murderous avenger. But she is killed by her own son, and her plea for retribution is deflected by the heavens. At every turn she is a victim of politics, deemed more important than matters of the heart. Brazilian actress Juliana Carneiro da Cunha takes the audience on a rich emotional journey. In a *tour de force*, she doubles as Clytemnestra's divine nemesis, Athena.

During the nine hours, long stretches are languorous. For those unfamiliar with Kathakali, the dances can look a lot alike. Still, when the chorus is in full cry, stomping and whirling, an onlooker may have the sense of seeing Greek tragedies as they appeared in their origin in daylong religious festivals. The final play, *The Eumenides*, depicts nothing less than the birth of modern society: the supplanting of clan vengeance by the rule of law. Mnouchkine burdens the elegantly simple poetry with clunky symbolism, costuming the chorus, a sort of jury, as apes. Though the final words are uplifting, the last image is of these emblems of the atavistic, scuttling across the stage. It is a daring, haunting – and characteristically excessive – gesture.

For Jack Kroll, in *Newsweek*, what was entertainment for fifth-century Athenians was still no less so,

at least in the thrilling version of Aeschylus' trilogy created by Mnouchkine and her gifted performers. . . . It is, simply and overwhelmingly, our story, the story of the human race in its attempt to shake off the endless cycle of violence and replace it with the rule of law.

The ancient Greeks would have laughed at our debates over violence in the arts. Their theater was awash in blood. The myth of the house of Atreus is an epic sideshow – infanticide, regicide, matricide, patricide, every kind of -cide, plus cannibalism and assorted horrors.

Kroll gives a synopsis of the plot, then:

Such are the bare and bloody bones of these complex and potent dramas. Mnouchkine's staging brings to life that old saw, "total theater." Drama, music, dance, brilliant costumes and make-up, but above all, energy galvanize the huge stage space. Mnouchkine does wonders with the chorus, who constitute from play to play a microcosm of the body politic, swarming like acrobats over the high walls that flank the stage, leaping down again to reform in a battalion of blazing color.

Kroll metes out high praise for the actors, especially Catherine Schaub, the chief *coryphaeus* (chorus leader), who

is astonishing as she moves from powerful speech to eloquent song to sensual, ecstatic, shoulder-shaking dancing. Schaub alone is total theater.

Mnouchkine has boldly grafted an Oriental performing style – mainly the precise, ritualized gestures and masklike make-up of the Kathakali theater – onto this bedrock of Western theater. In a time of burgeoning ethnic enmity, the stage becomes a synthesis of East and West. This feeling reaches a climax in the final play, *The Eumenides*, when Athena imposes a new harmony on the family whose internecine war is a symbol of all human conflicts; Mnouchkine turns the three chief Furies into bag ladies, dressed in tattered duds and sneakers, and costumes their chorus as hellish dogs, snarling, growling, cowering and cavorting. It's an unforgettable image. These Furies want blood, but Athena cajoles them into accepting a new identity – Eumenides, the "kindly ones" who take their place in a new civic order of democracy and justice. As the cycle ends, the dogs, fearful and confused, slowly rise on their hind legs. Animal bloodlust has become human understanding.

The Greek plays are profoundly political and spiritual. That's the theatrical ideal of Mnouchkine, fifty-three, a handsome woman of passionate intellect. For her these twenty-five-hundred-year-old works have a sharp relevance to today's social traumas. "As artists our mission is to warn – to yell, to shout and to celebrate any small victory," she says. "What's happening in Eastern Europe is terrible. These Greek plays train the intelligence and the senses. They're full of demons, and today a big demon has been defeated, but all the small ones have been let loose." *Les Atrides* evokes, identifies and dispels those demons.

(Mnouchkine's citing of Eastern Europe was prompted by the concurrent dissolution of two Communist states there – the Soviet Union and Yugoslavia – followed by prolonged civil strife and "ethnic cleansing".)

Frank Rich, in the *New York Times*, was downright unfriendly. The source of his annoyance:

Ariane Mnouchkine, the Parisian director, may or may not be one of the world's greatest theater artists, but who can doubt that even by France's high standards in the field she is a champion control freak?

Those attending *Les Atrides*, the four-play, ten-hour cycle of Greek tragedies with which Ms Mnouchkine and her company are making their New York début, will quickly learn that there are strict rules to be obeyed.

Late-comers are not admitted to the Park Slope Armory, where *Les Atrides* is being presented to audiences on punishing bleacher seats under the auspices of the Brooklyn Academy of Music. There are no intermissions. There are no reserved seats, a form of democracy that prompts some ticket-holders to line up hours before curtain-time and that leads to picturesque shoving matches, some of them involving celebrities, once everyone gets indoors. During the on-site meal breaks that separate the matinée and evening plays during a weekend marathon, those who finish eating early find attendants blocking the passageway from the picnic tables (dimly lighted, also per Ms Mnouchkine's orders) to the performance space.

"Didn't you hear? You're all part of the human sacrifice," said an usher to complaining patrons eager to escape captivity for a post-lunch, pre-*Eumenides* stroll. Not so many people laughed as you might think.

Given this militaristic atmosphere – which even extends to the director's choice of venue, whether an armory in Brooklyn or a former munitions factory outside Paris – it is easy to imagine the chilling authenticity she will bring to one of her pet projects for the future, a piece on Vichy France. But Ms Mnouchkine's relentlessly tight leash on her theatrical realm, which in *Les Atrides* sometimes creates an onstage airlessness to match that in the auditorium, can also produce remarkable results.

This is certainly the case with *The Libation Bearers*, the middle play in the Aeschylus' trilogy about the House of Atreus but the third play of Ms Mnouchkine's quartet, in which Euripides' *Iphigeneia in Aulis* is a prelude. For contemporary sensibilities, *The Libation Bearers* may be the most action-packed drama of the lot: As Orestes returns from exile to avenge the murder of his father, Agamemnon, he is propelled into a reunion with his sister, a grueling act of matricide and finally a mad escape from the Furies. Yet in the Théâtre du Soleil rendition, the storytelling is neither modern nor archaic in the presumed manner of the fifth century BC but timeless. Ms Mnouchkine fulfills her idea of a cosmopolitan, ritualistic theater that is beyond language, plot or any kind of realism and that instead digs deeply into the primordial passions, many of them ugly, that seem the eternal, inescapable legacy of the human race.

The director accomplishes this feat with the multicultural devices that typify the entire cycle. The playing area is a vast wooden corral, a neutral space reminiscent of the sandboxes used by that other Parisian theatrical visionary, Peter Brook. The performers appear in opulent ceremonial costumes of vaguely Asian provenance. The stagehands are Kabuki-ish while the chorus's choreography emulates the Kathakali dance dramas of Southern India. The musical accompaniment, composed by Jean-Jacques Lemêtre and generally played by him in a rustic bandstand containing more than 140 exotic instruments, careers from eclectic Eastern folk improvisations to Kabuki percussion to recorded Indian music to what might be a hyperventilating Bernard Herrmann film score for Alfred Hitchcock. The acting, fiery and grand and never inward, is classical French (even if the actors themselves are not).

From the moment Orestes (Simon Abkarian) arrives at Agamemnon's tomb, *The Libation Bearers* exerts a subterranean, not easily articulated pull on a viewer's psyche. Some of this is a matter of ominous mood, whether created by the buzzing of Mr Lemêtre's strings or the cold blue lighting that shrouds Orestes' return. There are also arresting tableaux, including the tall, windblown altar that reveals the sleeping Clytemnestra on what will be her death bed. And there is the high-throttle confrontation between mother and son, as Clytemnestra runs but cannot hide from Orestes, whose monomaniacal pursuit of his prey turns the wooden arena into a bullring.

But the most extraordinary *coup de théâtre* in *The Libation Bearers* – and, for that matter, in *Les Atrides* – arrives after the blood is spilled: as the lights dim to black and the barking of approaching dogs rises to a terrifying pitch, individual attempts to remove the bloodied mattress bearing the mutilated corpses of Clytemnestra and her lover, Aegisthus, come to nothing. Finally the entire chorus must advance to do the macabre deed, and the apocalyptic spectacle leaves the anxious audience in dread of an unchanging world in which blood inexorably begets blood and evil forces are never tamed.

So upsetting is *The Libation Bearers* that the cycle's concluding play, *The Eumenides*, has a tough time evoking a persuasive vision of justice, peace and reconciliation in its savage wake. Though Ms Mnouchkine makes the most of her leaping chorus of Furies – snarling, mutated hellhounds, part canine, part simian and reminiscent of the furious apes in Stanley Kubrick's *2001* – her staging becomes flat once the theater's first courtroom drama begins. When handed lengthy passages of discourse, the director tends to settle for static recitation of the text. Whether heard in French or through earphones in William M. Hoffmann's able English rendering, the talk is numbing, not just in the debates of *The Eumenides* but also in the expository first hour of *Agamemnon.*

The text throughout is somewhat idiosyncratic, seemingly to further the feminist viewpoint that is the undisguised and at times fascinating ideological agenda of *Les Atrides.* By opening her cycle with the Euripides play in which Clytemnestra must sacrifice her daughter Iphigeneia (a touching Nirupama Nityanandan) to the dubiously greater good of her husband's war machine, Ms Mnouchkine makes her principal heroine a far more sympathetic (and dominant) figure in the Aeschylus trilogy to come. The director further stacks the deck by imprisoning most of the male characters behind masklike make-up while giving the women more literal and figurative freedom of expression. By the time *The Eumenides* arrives, this slant is more sentimental than provocative; Athena is presented as a syrupy *guru* (embodied by Miss da Cunha, the previously mesmerizing Clytemnestra), and the Brechtian bag ladies who lead the Furies are transformed into beaming automatons of saintly matriarchy.

Ms Mnouchkine's artistic ideology shapes *Les Atrides* more than her politics does, however. And the extraordinary payoff of her perfectionism, her lengthy rehearsal period and her cultural cross-breeding can be found in all four plays. The dancing of the androgynous chorus, led and co-choreographed by the amazing Catherine Schaub (who also co-designed the costumes), has a fervor, precision and ethereal lightness that cannot be matched by many dance companies, let alone theatrical troupes. Fierce dramatic images, often achieved with means as simple as the rushing forward of a platform or the tearing of a curtain, abound. The five principal actors, each playing multiple roles, may engage in old-fashioned histrionics, but they do so with a commitment and brilliant intensity that flirts with greatness in the case of Mr Abkarian's portraits of Agamemnon, Achilles and a finally feral Orestes.

What the director's controlling esthetic forbids, by definition, is unruliness, emotional or otherwise, that does not fit the precise meter of her neo-classicism. While early arrivals to *Les Atrides* are encouraged to watch the actors put on their make-up in an open but roped-off dressing-room area behind the bleachers, the spectators soon discover that even this ostensible backstage space is rigorously designed. The rungs under too are color-coordinated with the costume accessories hanging above, and every object is as neatly displayed as the goods in a department store window.

Are these impeccably sober, silent actors freely warming up in their own domain, or are they merely executing another one of Ms Mnouchkine's meticulous illusions within the confines of a public cage? Either way, it is a beautiful, strangely antiseptic and poignant sight that, like much of *Les Atrides*, creates an elegant, hermetically sealed world of pure theater that is securely and safely cordoned off from the spontaneity of life.

A somewhat different response was elicited from Patrick J. Smith, editor of *Opera News*, hitherto a stranger to stagings of the Athenian tragedies:

The four works which I saw in two days, were given in a deliberately hieratic, ceremonial style influenced by Indian and Japanese theater – a style, moreover, surrounded by music (composed and played primarily by an extraordinary one-man band named Jean-Jacques Lemêtre).

In my first extended contact with classic Greek theater, I was impressed by the works, especially the inventive genius of Mnouchkine and her solutions to the vexing problem of the Greek chorus. Here she had the text declaimed by only one of them, with the remainder dancing, so that their expressivity was demonstrated in movement rather than words.

In one of the intermissions, the president and executive producer of BAM, Harvey Lichtenstein, asked me: "Is this opera?" "Of course," I answered, for if Lemêtre's music was supportive, the amalgam of music, movement and declaimed text are closer to opera than to the kinds of theater that are seen in our playhouses.

More than once I was reminded how close these Greek dramas are to the Wagner operas, especially the *Ring* cycle. Wagner knew his classics and understood the overarching aura of destiny and fate so well expressed by Aeschylus in the trilogy. Indeed, I would say that only Wagner and Berlioz (in *Les Troyens*) were able to capture that intensity in their operas – Gluck wrote several on similar subjects but never managed that tone, and other great opera composers, such as Verdi, were uninterested in that type of expression.

The style of speaking, also, presumably modeled on French declamatory practice, is closer to operatic singing than to current modes of speech in the American theater. The enunciation of the French text (translated from the original) by actor Brontis Jodorowsky was as precisely elegant and forceful as that of Luciano Pavarotti, opera's champion enunciator.

I will now become parochial: I have been saying that opera is the greatest theatrical art form, in that it encompasses the others and goes beyond them. These Greek "operas" only reinforce my conviction; moreover, their stature as works and as a specific theatrical production makes me see for the first time what Bertolt Brecht meant when he called most plays "culinary theater." Those entertain the body: these refresh the soul.

Although the company remains true to its Utopian ideals from the Sixties, the Utopia seems now to be expressed in religious terms – the theater as a sacred space and art as an avenue to the divine. "That is all very personal, very intimate," Miss Mnouchkine said: "We never go on stage thoughtlessly, without saluting it, some little sign, just putting a hand on the stage. For some it's religious, for others superstitious, for others just a habit. Our actors never step on the stage without realizing that it relates to spirit and the progress of the mind."

In that practice the troupe is emulating some groups in the Far East where Mnouchkine studied and travelled and where shrines on or adjacent to the platform allow the performers to pay due devotion to the deities that preside over theatre activities.

On a more mundane level, exampling the Théâtre du Soleil's egalitarianism, Mnouchkine is often glimpsed during intermissions as she collects and carries away scattered dirty dishes.

A rather odd variation on the *Oresteia* is Thomas Berger's novel, *Orrie's Story* (1990). Berger adheres almost mechanically to the plots of the Greek plays, bringing them up to the present day. Here Orrie is the erstwhile Orestes, now a weak-willed college student; Aegisthus is a mysteriously wealthy businessman commonly known as E.G.; Agamemnon is the ill-fated Augie Mencken, who claims to have been off to the wars, though in fact he has been busy elsewhere courting Cassie (Cassandra); and Clytemnestra appears as Esther, an avaricious shrew who murders her husband in his bath in order to profit from his Army insurance. Orestes' companion, Pylades, is Paul Leeds; Anthony Pollo, a defence attorney, stands in for Apollo at a trial presided over by Judge Thea Palliser (Pallas Athena). A critic in the *Wall Street Journal* suggests that, rather than perusing this book, "its action dictated in large part not by the temperaments of the characters but by the need to parallel Aeschylus", time would be better spent reading Eugene O'Neill's *Mourning Becomes Electra.*

In Minneapolis the Tyrone Guthrie Theater (by now renamed in honour of its first director) emulated the many experimenters in London, Paris and New York by compiling yet another trilogy, an evening devoted predominantly to Clytemnestra's ill fortunes, a work devised by Garland Wright, who also staged it (1992). David Richards, representing the *New York Times,* flew westward to inspect what the theatre had accomplished.

> Picking among the splendid ruins of what has survived of the dispersed fragments of ancient Greek dramas, Wright has pieced together a forceful version of the queen's saga. . . .
>
> He's repaired to Euripides' *Iphigeneia in Aulis* for the first half of his two-part endeavor. . . . The second part is made up of Aeschylus' *Agamemnon*; the shortest, it runs a scant fifty-seven minutes; *Iphigeneia* is the longest at ninety minutes. Mr Wright wants no distractions, no digressions. This is to be primarily a story of women – Clytemnestra (Isabell Monk) and the three daughters, Iphigeneia, Electra and Chrysothemis, who figure in her destruction.
>
> You can easily accuse the venturesome director of taking liberties. He is, after all, using three sets of blueprints to build one edifice. What makes Sophocles different from Euripides, and Euripides unlike Aeschylus, is being conveniently downplayed. Even more, there is a strong ideological bent to

the productions that says as much about late twentieth-century civilization as it does about values in fifth-century BC Greece. Still, the edifice is a grand one, and its lean and elegant spaces house some stunning displays of fury.

The gods do not come off well, but that's to be expected. They've always taken particular delight in maneuvering helpless mortals into impossible situations and then watching them wriggle. The revelation of what you could call the Clytemnestra trilogy, although Mr Wright doesn't, is how badly the men fare. They're patronizing, arrogant, cowardly, headstrong and, for all their ringing appeals to might and right, amazingly ineffectual.

What's more, they're definitely the supporting players. Their recklessness may help determine the course of the drama, but within the drama, the positions of theatrical prominence are occupied by women, who must deal with the messy consequences of male barbarism and ego. The feminist overtones are unavoidable. Clytemnestra may be a queen, a mother, a lover and a murderer. At the Guthrie, she is, above all, a woman who refused to be victimized.

The choral interludes are kept to a minimum, and when the members of the chorus speak, they tend to do so as individuals, straggling voices in the crowd. The enormity of the drama eludes them. For the most part, they watch from the sidelines with the dazed brow and fretful eye of the "humbly born." Susan Hilferty's masks give them that hollow, dumbfounded look you often find on the pedestrians scurrying across German Expressionist canvases.

Singing and dancing, although integral parts of Greek tragedy, are similarly limited. Instead, it falls to the composer Michael Sommers, who is tucked away in the gridwork high above the stage, to punctuate the action with music of his own creation. He's concocted an eerie assortment of noises – twangs, thumps, rumbles and microphone squawks – none of which augur well for the characters. The pleasantest sound, I suppose, is the light shimmer of wind chimes, but even that has an ironic edge, since wind – or the lack of it – is at the root of Clytemnestra's agonies.

When we first meet her in Euripides' play, she is a proud, doting mother, summoned by her husband, Agamemnon, to the seacoast town of Aulis. . . . Accepting the inevitable, Iphigeneia persuades herself that by dying she will contribute to the eventual defeat of Troy, Greece will remain free and "my name will be blessed." Kristin Flanders undergoes impressive transformations in the role – from the giggling bride-to-be, filled with flirtatious delight; to the wan rag doll, stunned by destiny; to the sacrificial victim, flush with religious ecstasy and trembling with new-found purpose.

Ms Monk, an imposing actress with a grave, almost subterranean voice, is no less mutable. But Clytemnestra's transformation is essentially a regression to a more primitive self – the noble queen, supplanted by the pleading mother, who gives way to the raging beast defending her offspring. Her futile efforts leave her spent and prostrate. Then as the winds begin to stir, indicating that Artemis has been appeased, Ms Monk lets loose with a protracted 'Noooooo' that rises from her bowels and rips savagely through the air. She is not only protesting a daughter's death but a universe that seems without a moral center.

Indeed, even as Iphigeneia is discovering a faith, Clytemnestra is losing hers. The woman who appears ten years later in *Agamemnon* and eight years after that in *Electra* will no longer believe in the gods. You can already see it at the end of *Iphigeneia.* Agamemnon has just announced a miracle: as the knife was about to strike Iphigeneia, the body vanished from the altar. In its place appeared a bleeding deer. "Your daughter has been taken to heaven," he reports joyously. But the look on Ms Monk's face, a look of dull, implacable anger, suggests otherwise. What a strange story, it says. What possible consolation can I take from it?

In *Agamemnon,* Clytemnestra has acquired a lover, Aegisthus, and her rage has long since congealed into a cold, unquestioning resolve: they will murder Agamemnon on his return from Troy. To the herald, announcing that the triumphant warrior's chariot approaches, she exults: "For ten years I have waited . . . ," then pauses ambiguously. You fully expect her to conclude "for this moment" or "for my revenge." But she lowers her eyes and adds "faithfully," instead – a loyal wife, if only for duplicity's sake.

It's not certain that Agamemnon (Stephen Pelinski) would notice her deceit anyway. His command to the chorus, "Rejoice, old men, you are ruled by a king again," pretty much defines him and his suffocating *amour-propre.* In a rare moment of luxuriousness in the mostly spare and sober staging, Mr Wright has a covey of handmaidens lay down a path of blood-red silk squares to the palace door. They flutter to the ground, making a carpet of deceptive delicacy, considering the brutality that waits at the other end. Agamemnon has no qualms about crushing it under foot. Overhead, drums and cymbals erupt in mad tumult.

It's a chilling moment, partly because the king goes so dumbly to his death. But just as chilling, in its fashion, is Clytemnestra's subsequent reference to the killing as a "harvest," as if murder were in the natural order of things. Once she was numb with grief. Now she is merely numb.

In *Electra,* she has also grown old and stiff of joint and come to resemble an aging witch who has mislaid her magic and can no longer stave off mortality. Accordingly, the focus shifts to her children – the dutiful Chrysothemis (Ms Flanders again, making a surprisingly strong case for a basically passive character); the wild Electra (Jacqueline Kim), who lives only to see her mother slaughtered; and the wily Orestes (Paul Eckstein), who will return secretly from exile and eventually do the horrible deed.

Ms Kim, a slight actress whose size belies her powers, gives the galvanizing performance here. It looks like Method madness, at first. The wracking sobs and the convulsive rage, seemingly anchored in a deeply personal sense of injury, threaten to go over the top. The more you watch, however, the more hypnotic her delivery. Psychological realism turns into something close to mystical possession. At one point Electra is tricked into thinking that Orestes is dead and that his remains lie in the urn at her feet. Reaching into it, Ms Kim scoops up a handful of ashes, then smears them greedily over her tear-stained face. Her lamentations are close to tribal keening. She could be putting on a gray funeral mask.

Such ferocity is in direct contrast to Douglas Stein's set design, which has the cool formality of a Japanese garden. A cyclorama of pale blue curtains marks the back of the Guthrie's thrust stage, which has been divided by a large black ring into an outer and inner circle. Small stones – talismans, perhaps – have been placed with ritualistic care around the ring. This could be holy ground. Or was. It is obviously an arena for incantations and supplications.

At the same time, there is an emptiness to the set, suggesting that the divinities have long since fled and left mankind to its foolish devices. Cassandra, captured in the Trojan War and brought back in shackles to Greece, takes one look about and concludes sorrowfully, "God hates this place."

I was reminded of the absurdist *King Lear* that the English director Peter Brook staged several decades ago in a blasted Beckettian landscape, and wondered at times if Mr Wright wasn't propounding an absurdist Greek tragedy. Men and women are not the playthings of the gods here. They evoke the gods simply to justify the havoc of their lives.

That's why the productions seem so representative of our own times. Our leaders, too, refer endlessly to a national mythology, which is supposed to inform our collective destiny. In its name, ideals are advanced and sacrifices exacted. And yet that mythology may be no more than a smokescreen masking arrantly self-interested deeds.

Is something in the air? Next month, the French Director Ariane Mnouchkine brings her widely acclaimed production of *Les Atrides* to the Park Slope Armory in Brooklyn. Going the Guthrie one better, it is a four-play cycle. . . . We'll have to wait and see exactly where that arc lands us, although Miss Mnouchkine has a similar skepticism toward the proud and her own disenchantment with the powerful.

In the interim, the final word belongs to Clytemnestra speaking at the Guthrie from beyond the grave. The blood feud has played through another round. Ms Monk's shrouded body has been laid out in the inner ring for all to behold. Then her rustling voice comes up, like a dry wind, urging women everywhere to awake, for they serve no good asleep.

"Arise, you furies, you women," the voice implores, "and kill my shame – kill my shame – shame." This time, the cry for vengeance sounds suspiciously like a call to sisterhood.

An American adaptation of the work was observed in an academic setting by Donald Lyons (1994) of the *Wall Street Journal*:

The American Repertory Theater in Cambridge, Mass., is staging the greatest of all plays not written by Shakespeare: the *Oresteia* of Aeschylus. I saw the first play, the *Agamemnon*, on a recent Saturday afternoon and can report that some of the feral action and wild language and cosmic grappling of Aeschylus do make it to the stage of the Loeb Drama Center. Director François Rochaix creates an excitement, a *frisson* of fear and menace, through much of the play's uninterrupted 105 minutes. The spare white palace of King Agamemnon, in Robert Dahlstrom's design, works well. The play's chorus of Argive elders, which has a lot of back story to tell, is at once grotesquely garrulous and profoundly wise. Well-handled by Mr Rochaix, who moves them about with energy and clarity, the elders are creatively garbed in black; the decorum of their attire varies from episcopal sobriety to Groucho tux.

Some of the acting in the secondary roles is good: Natacha Roi makes a touching Cassandra, despite the arbitrary handicap of having to utter most of her lines in Greek, a fashionable gimmick doubtless intended to underline the foreignness, the Otherness, of the Trojan princess, but without warrant in Aeschylus, where she speaks the same Greek as everybody else. Will LeBow, got up to resemble the last of the Mohicans, gives an angry fierceness to the role of Clytemnestra's lover/accomplice Aegisthus, who usually comes off as a whiny weakling.

But the principals are wanting: Charles Levin rolls on in a tank as a fat and foolish Agamemnon, a Rodney Dangerfield getting no respect in Greece. It's a standing temptation for lazy directors to turn this character into a buffoon and in the process to send up a military icon of the day. The only loss is Aeschylus' character, who is a tragically complex figure and not a macho cartoon.

Randy Danson plays Clytemnestra as a fidgety, giggly manic-depressive; we miss the solemn, sinister majesty of a hungry lioness. Her two décolleté cocktail gowns – one white for gloating, one red for blood – do not add subtlety.

The gravest misconception is that of adapter Robert Auletta (he's previously adapted Aeschylus and Sophocles for Peter Sellars – uh oh). Mr Auletta hungers for timeliness and relevance, and tinny colloquialisms begin to fall like acid rain: Helen is "as beautiful as any movie star." Clytemnestra complains that she is treated like an "overwrought virgin preparing for her senior prom;" "body bags" come

> in from Asia; Agamemnon talks of "photo opportunities." It's not, after all, as if Mr Auletta commands the innovative linguistic vigor of a Marlowe or a Robert Lowell; he just writes dumb graffiti on the palace wall. Contemptuous distrust of the audience's ability to take Aeschylus straight is elitist. People are smarter than you think, Mr Auletta. Maybe there ought to be a Court of Public Translation where impertinent adapters could be tried.

Among the lost works of Aeschylus is a tetralogy (470 BC) of which only fragments remain of the first play. A Romanian director, Silviu Purcarete, pieced it together, endowing it with a French title, *Les Danaïdes* (*The Suppliants*), and then proceeded to oversee its staging. It relates the harrowing flight of fifty Egyptian virgins left defenceless, torn from their native land and compelled to beg sanctuary from the ruler of Argos. Purcarete mounted this drama on a broad scale, rivalling Peter Brook's bold handling of the sacred Indian epic *Mahabharata* and Ariane Mnouchkine's similarly dynamic *Les Atrides.* He signed up a company of 120 actors and musicians and utilized a series of outdoor venues. The production was seen in short succession in Bucharest, Vienna, Amsterdam, Avignon, Dublin, Paris, Rome, Glasgow and Birmingham (UK), most often as part of local theatre festivals.

It was sampled in New York City (1997), performed in French, interpreted by English supertitles. Its stay was limited. In the *New York Times* Ben Brantley's enthusiasm was muted.

> If you prefer your cosmic spectacle more on the somber than the sunny side, then *Les Danaïdes,* Silviu Purcarete's reconstruction of an Aeschylean tetralogy, may be the ticket for you. In this visually artful if thematically clunky staging of the ancient Greek tragedy, which opened on Tuesday (with a cast that staggeringly numbers more than 100) as part of Lincoln Center Festival '97, the deities who control earthly destinies just won't give a mortal an even break.
>
> Played by six sibilant-voiced actors (Mariana Buruiana, Micaela Caracas, Mihai Dinvale, Jean-Jacques Dulon, Victor Rebengiuc and Alexandru Repan), the Olympians are a glacial, contemptuous and sepulchral-looking lot, clad in white dinner jackets and Yohji Yamamoto-style layers of fabric. (Wouldn't you just know that the gods would be chicer-than-thou?)
>
> As Aeschylus' tale of ethnic and sexual conflict unfolds, with a prototypical war between men and women ending in unspeakable carnage, the members of the immortal sextet gather over what look like illuminated laboratory sinks and play idly with models of buildings and boats. They speak periodically of the cruelty of human fate, occasionally groan orgasmically and, toward the play's end, waltz merrily through a field of corpses.

They are also given to rhythmic, disturbingly prurient wheezes. That's the laughter of the gods and not a hopeful sound. It is first heard in the production's opening scene, after the actors stare with glittering eyes at the audience, which is assembled on tiers of folding chairs in Damrosch Park and rasp out a single word: "Europa."

That's the only directly topical allusion that Mr Purcarete allows in his work. But it's more than enough to establish that this ambitious director has more on his mind than Greek mythology.

If his interpretation of the material is even bleaker than that of Aeschylus, whom certainly no one considers a laugh riot, Mr Purcarete has come by his despair honestly, having lived through the Kafkaesque brutality of the Ceaucescu dictatorship and the political chaos that followed it.

Accordingly, he finds in this archetype of Greek tragedy, long believed to be the first major work of its kind, natural metaphors for the clash of national identities that continues to plague Eastern Europe. What his play firmly implies is that bloodshed breeds only bloodshed in an eternal cycle from which survival is the best that can be expected.

That's only part of the original Aeschylean equation, in which savage devastation is worked through to a more civilized, humane order: The moments of philosophical calm, and the emotional complexity that register in a reading of *The Suppliants,* are not to be found here. When the gods comment that suffering breeds enlightenment, it is in a vicious, sarcastic tone that is far from consoling.

This single-minded pessimism makes the production a one-note affair, even as Mr Purcarete's ingenious stagecraft assumes an impressive myriad of forms. In the flight of the fifty daughters (played, yes, by a chorus of fifty actresses) of Danaos (the bare-breasted but bearded Coca Bloos) from the barbaric cousins (fifty strapping actors) who wish to wed them, there is oddly little to engage one's feelings directly. Fear and pity, the classic elements of *katharsis,* are all but eliminated for an angry but oddly sterile sense of the merciless patterns of history.

What's most noteworthy here is Mr Purcarete's extraordinary manipulation of his choruses, especially the women. Wearing the remarkably protean costumes of Stefania Cenean (also the designer of the gaping black hole of a set), the daughters of Danaos, who seek sanctuary in the state of Argos, appear first as a flock of faceless women in blue robes, clutching suitcases.

Usually bathed in a glowing blue (the impeccable lighting is by Mr Purcarete and Vadim Levinschi), they fluidly assume an assortment of geometric configurations while alternately wailing, praying and giving off birdlike sounds of dismay. They are conducted like an orchestra by their hermaphroditic father. Ms Bloos makes a vividly creepy entrance emerging limb by limb from a white trunk.

The suitcases, in what becomes a canny symbol for the life of those forced into nomadic exile, are used to create fortress walls, altars and lookout towers. And in the evening's most visually startling moment, a wall of suitcases is broken through by the herd of the sons of Egyptos, who have followed their cousins to Argos, and the chaste blue light dissolves into a hot, angry ember.

The use of the male chorus members is largely less successful. They often seem like a rowdy band of fraternity boys out on a panty raid. But the climactic scene of women's revenge on the men, in which their nightgowns become white tents illuminated by lanterns, is stunning.

There is, by the way, one politician in *Les Danaïdes.* That's Pelasgos (Mr Rebengiuc), the king of Argos, who promises to defend the beleaguered women. But since he's a grizzled, cough-racked old thing on crutches, he's not a very reassuring presence. Anyway, it turns out he's Apollo in disguise. It's an index of Mr Purcarete's cynicism that the gods are equated with a decadent head of state.

In 1999, not long after the death of Ted Hughes, England's poet laureate, a single volume was brought out containing his translation of the three plays that add up to the *Oresteia.* It met with considerable carping from academic critics. For one, Garry Wills in the *New York Times* found Hughes's renditions tending to prolixity where Aeschylus is terse and pointed. Wills cites four lines of the original dialogue that Hughes allowed himself to enlarge to twenty-three. (It must be said that as language *per se,* quite for its own sake, Hughes's additions are highly vivid and effective.) Nor is the exact sense of words in the speeches always exactly conveyed. In Hughes's defence, however, it might be argued that university professors, most likely to be given such books to review, are seldom willing to acknowledge an adaptor's imperative need to strip the most revered classic of a plethora of mythological allusions unfamiliar to impatient modern spectators. The adaptor must also find spontaneous-sounding equivalents of archaic Greek phrases and idioms, often no easy task. The true test is not whether the translation is minutely authentic but whether it can be effectively spoken and acted by today's and tomorrow's players, and whether the play will firmly hold the audience's interest throughout, which beyond question requires that lines and action be readily understood with plays moving at a rapid pace. Aeschylus, Sophocles and Euripides – practical theatre-workers – are known to have altered their scripts and even changed their endings to meet spectators' demands.

Early in 2000, New York's Pearl Theater Company offered its concept of all the three plays of the *Oresteia* in one night, alternating in repertory with William Congreve's *The Way of the World.* In the *New York Times* D.J. Bruckner was moved to exclaim: "Given the stature of the trilogy in the history of Western drama, this is somewhat like listing Wagner's *Ring* cycle as a one-day presentation in an opera repertory. The *Oresteia* is, of course, shorter than that. And, fortunately, ambition is not the only virtue to applaud in this rare undertaking." He conceded, "The story certainly has a grand sweep," and went on to give a synopsis of it; dwelling particularly on the third play,

> called *The Furies* in the translation used here but more commonly known as *The Eumenides* (*Kind Spirits*). Here the god Apollo clears Orestes of guilt for murder but Orestes is pursued by the Furies, traditional hellhounds of vengeance, to the temple of Athena in Athens where his case is presented to the citizens.
>
> When they divide evenly on the vote to convict or acquit, Athena breaks the tie in his favor. She persuades the Furies to abandon vengeance forever and to occupy a cave under Athens as benign demigods who join the Athenians in bringing disputes over moral conduct under a rule of justice that can be understood by, and participated in, by all humanity.
>
> Some of his rivals later in the fifth century BC ridiculed Aeschylus for his lofty language and Olympian views, but the trilogy is one of Greece's finest intellectual heritages. Most of the roles are types rather than individuals, but the breaking of the relentless and often religiously dictated arch of family vengeance is enthrallingly dramatic. And along the way Aeschylus, a veteran of the battles of Marathon and Salamis, which saved Greece from Persian tyranny, has some fun teasing his civilian audience about pompous war heroes (Agamemnon) and about baffling military technologies like communications over unimaginable distances by hilltop beacons.
>
> And he does create three magnificent characters: the implacable Clytemnestra; Orestes' old nurse, who has inspired stage imitators for twenty-five hundred years; and the chorus of Athenians in the last play, who make up a single, unforgettably eloquent character.
>
> The playwright's taste for spectacle, music and dance was notorious; performance of the three plays surely took a day. Under Shepard Sobel's direction, the Pearl's apparently tireless cast gets through them all in three hours. The meters of the Greek text let one hear the rhythm of the ancient dances, and some viewers might wish there were more spectacle here. But even in this very prosy translation the compression of the action turns the battle of ideas into gripping combat, and in the first and third plays the suppleness and variety of voices in the Greek chorus is something the audience can easily feel; they speak for us and occasionally we want to cheer them on, especially during the verbal duels between Clytemnestra and the chorus in *Agamemnon.*
>
> Unaccountably, the chorus in this version of *The Libation Bearers* is so shrill, and so inept in a brief effort to sing a few lines, that it drains some force from the play. And a few effects seem very ill-advised: the garment used to trap Agamemnon is a net that might snare a rhinoceros in full gallop, so huge that not even this vain king could have been tricked into its meshes. And it is a mistake to make the Furies a trio

> of oddballs resembling the Sand People in *Star Wars.* To the popular Greek imagination there was nothing fuzzy about these fierce pests; their transformation at the end must have seemed like a vision of salvation.
>
> Those and a few other grumbles aside, this production is a revelation. When Clytemnestra stands over her dead husband declaring "what we did had to be done," and Orestes then straddles her body saying he feels like a charioteer whose horse is so out of control that "I do not know how it will end," the terror of madness seizes the audience and Aeschylus' appeal to reason is sublime.

Celia Wren, managing editor of *American Theater* magazine, interviewed the pair responsible for the Pearl production. Her article came out in the *New York Times.* Shepard Sobel, the director, told her that for more than fifteen years the company had cherished the idea of embracing the venerable trilogy: it was a goal for which they had been preparing themselves, "knowing it was the top of the mountain in many ways". At last they felt ready; for them the moment was at hand. He was convinced – Wren's paraphrase – that he was "subconsciously responding to recent world crises". In his own words, "The last few years have seen what seems to be an explosion of barbarian impulses. Race wars and ethnic wars, and the most horrid kind of violence – neighbors against each other in the Balkans, in the Bronx, all over the place." The *Oresteia,* in which a repetitive reign of violence is abruptly halted, had a moral to impart; staging it could be a "public service". If it were done well enough, and enough spectators were drawn to it, it could contribute in however small measure to bringing an end to the harsh mind-set too prevalent in the current world scene.

For the translator, Peter Meineck, too, the plays "resonated with the *Zeitgeist*", the current climate of ideas, and he saw an outlook shared alike by fifth-century BC Aeschylus and late twentieth-century mankind. "New York now is the Athens that was." (Apart from serving as translator, Meineck was associated with the Aquila Theatre Company as its producing artistic director.) He warned, though, that the "topicality" of the trilogy should not be over-emphasized or its impact diminished by appending too many nice, erudite footnotes to its ancient text: it is, above all, a vital, "gripping horror story", an aspect which should be chillingly realized in its enactment.

Struck by beholding many *Oresteias* suddenly appearing almost simultaneously on stages around the country and abroad, Celia Wren took a census of them and included it in her article. The Clarence Brown Company in Knoxville, Tennessee (site of the University of Tennessee) had just created *The Millennium Project* – "group developed" – a "variation" on the Greek story; after a local showing, it was to be a feature at a festival in Bratislava, Slovakia. A month later the Sledgehammer Theater in San Diego, California, mounted the première of Kelly Stuart's *Furious Blood,* retelling the grim, sturdy drama from a "savagely comic" feminist point of view. After the lapse of a month, the Here Arts Center in New York City sponsored Aaron Mack Schloff's *Agamemnon vs. Liberace*, the title implying a very odd juxtaposition. Unfortunately, nothing about the content of this work could be learned other than that it was "a wacky gay sendup".

The Millennium Project, like Kelly Stuart's *Furious Blood* – and representing the input of graduate students at the university – stressed Aeschylus' supposed anti-feminist bias. In his scripts men are always in conflict with women: Agamemnon lets Iphigeneia be sacrificed to enhance his own prospects, Clytemnestra avenges his unpardonable betrayal, Orestes slays his mother, the feminine Furies overtake Orestes – the struggle between the sexes is endless, until Athena intervenes, rebuking Apollo and rescuing Clytemnestra's vengeful son who murders her for justifiably raising a knife against his father. "Male power" triumphs; the plays are viewed as being about the eternal feud raging between patriarchy and matriarchy, an interpretation suggested earlier by Bachofen. Clytemnestra is portrayed more deeply and sympathetically, with Aeschylus' characterization of her dismissed as an effort to "demonize the feminine". The script's final draft bears Amy Russell's name as adaptor, and Henry Baranowski is credited as director.

Furious Blood includes episodes omitted by Aeschylus depicting the cruel death of the hapless Iphigeneia, thus strengthening Clytemnestra's motivation for tricking her husband and stabbing him, as he had tricked her and killed her beloved child. The implacably hostile Electra is reduced to being a "shrill shrew", which also tilts the audience's sympathies towards her distraught mother. At the conclusion, Apollo appeals to the spectators: do they not prefer the "glamorous Athena" to the hideous Furies? The language is often blunt and vulgar – and modern – and the humour exceedingly broad.

Another trendy motif is introduced: defence of the environment. The threat of a plague that will devastate Greece is uttered by the Furies in phrases that sound as though they might be referring to acid rain. Ms Russell concurred that she and the students felt that the *Oresteia* could be a vehicle for oblique commentary on "science, technology, the heedless destruction of the natural world, the apocalyptic flavor of the times".

The Ted Hughes version of Aeschylus' *Oresteia* was quickly put to use by the Royal National Theatre in London for a production that was taken to the DuMaurier Stage Festival in Toronto (2000), after which the company embarked on an international tour with it. The staging was guided by Katie Mitchell, who permitted many anachronisms of speech and attire: the characters were in late twentieth-century dress. There was a deliberate attempt to link the situation in the trilogy to the contemporary civil strife in the Balkans following the break-up of Yugoslavia. Agamemnon wore the uniform of a

Bosnian warlord. Ms Mitchell explained: "We decided we'd try to find the simplest modern equivalent to every moment in the play, so that someone who knew nothing about Greek drama or the story could understand at once what was gong on." She felt that such updating was necessary when spectators found themselves in a world plunged into turmoil. "A lot of us feel morally thrown and don't know how to find our bearings morally and politically. To some extent the production was working that through."

Some reviewers were none too kind; they deemed the modern touches "distracting" and "gimmicky", and objected that the company's resources were quite inadequate for an offering of such scope. Mitchell acknowledged the shortcomings and pleaded that the trilogy was a taxing undertaking. To her, too, the *Oresteia* was "an extraordinary, impossible mountain".

It has been argued rationally that updating plays implies that the translator and director believe that the educated spectator lacks the knowledge and imagination to place himself transiently back in a past world, for two hours accepting its values, and learning what life was like in a previous era, which might help towards a better understanding of the now. "Updating" could be taken as implicitly insulting to an audience. Do not the "updaters" underestimate the intelligence of their spectators? Besides, how often would an unwary and unsophisticated ticket-buyer hasten to a box-office to purchase admission to a play called the *Oresteia*? Play-going is expensive. Usually, people who go to the theatre have read critiques or heard by word of mouth what sort of entertainment awaits them and choose what they already like.

In San Francisco, in a theatre significantly named Exit Left, Mark Jackson directed a comedy, *Messenger No. 1*, that also borrowed a scenario from the *Oresteia* but preached a different message, one far less optimistic than others read into the script. Is Aeschylus helping to bring about a new world in which the rule of law will lead to the peaceful attainment of equality and fairness? Not so. Jackson protested to Celia Wren: "If the trial-by-jury system was designed to replace blood-based justice, why hasn't violence decreased?" He asserted that the justice system is for ever flawed because it was created by members of the upper class. Wren reports, "His comedy explores the frustrations that beset Argos's working-class messengers while spoiled aristocrats like Orestes reap the benefits of democracy."

As the twentieth century rounded to a close, Aeschylus received more homage in New York City during Poetry Week (2000). Robert Lowell's *Prometheus Bound* was publicly performed at the Unterberg Poetry Center – this was only for a single evening, but major talents were involved. Once again the acclaimed English actress Irene Worth had the daunting role of Io, Zeus' gadfly-infested, beloved heifer; and Jonathan Miller was the director. In all, three Greek verse plays were put on at one-week intervals, as local events to herald National Poetry Month.

A new century was at hand. The Denver Center for the Performing Arts announced plans to stage an *Oresteia* during its next season (2001), testimony that yet other groups – even far-Western regional ones – felt obliged to acknowledge the trilogy's greatness and the players' confidence in their ability to do it justice.

Overwhelmingly, comparatively recent stagings of Sophocles' tragedies have consisted of the *Theban Plays*, either the whole trilogy or its separate components, especially *Oedipus Rex* and *Antigone.* After a considerable absence from their view, Londoners had an opportunity to rediscover the *Oedipus*, performed in a French translation by Jules Lacroix, when the Comédie Française visited in 1893. It was an item in the troupe's lengthy list of offerings that did not draw crowds or even much critical attention. But William Archer, drama reviewer and playwright, early champion of Henrik Ibsen and George Bernard Shaw, was there. He has left his impressions of the occasion.

> If I had been obliged to select one play from the repertory of the Comédie Française, and to see it only, I should without a moment's hesitation have chosen *Oedipe Roi.* And I should have chosen rightly. The immediate pleasure of seeing the great tragedy roll majestically along was as keen as it was rare; and the reflections excited by the performance were so innumerable that I want to write a book about it instead of a paragraph. There is no play in the world so brimming with historical, technical, and ethical interest. A complete analysis and criticism of it – involving, of course, a comparison and contrast between it and the masterpieces of the modern stage – might be to the Drama what Lessing's *Laokoön* is to the plastic arts. Nay, it ought to be a great deal more, for it would practically amount to a history of the evolution of dramatic forms. Ah! what a book I see in my mind's eye! – a very miracle of acumen and erudition!

He expressed his regret that the book must be unwritten,

> – known and appreciated by myself alone. For the general public, of course, *Oedipus Tyrannus* cannot have the absorbing interest it has, or ought to have, for specialists, so that I was not surprised to see a comparatively, though not an exceedingly, meagre house. But I should at least have expected all the specialists – to wit, the dramatic critics – to be at their posts on so rare an occasion as the production in London of a tragedy of Sophocles. They may have been present – from where I sat I could see but

a small portion of the house – but if so, their raptures must have struck most of them speechless, for I searched the morning papers in vain for a notice of the event. Several of them contained careful appreciations of a play named *Fireworks*; but of the *Oedipus Tyrannus* never a word! Perhaps the original Greek sings so sweetly in the ears of the critics, that they shrink from listening to the worthy Jules Lacroix's alexandrines; but, in that case, I beg to assure them, they neglected an opportunity. However familiar we may be with it in the study, there is always something to be learnt from seeing a play on the stage; and Sophocles in French is much nearer the real thing than Sophocles in Greek, as recited from time to time at the universities. All the rule-of-thumb scansion in the world can never restore to us the true rhythmic movement of the iambic line, any more than the untrained voice of a callow undergraduate, bow-wowing his lines with all the vowels transmuted into English, can reproduce the splendid resonance of tone which rang through the vast theatres of Athens and Syracuse. Now in the French performance we at least have rhythm and melody, though not *the* rhythm and melody, and we have certainly all the sonority that is necessary or desirable in our smaller and roofed-in theatres. Moreover, we have the solemn dignity of carriage which belongs to the drama of gods and heroes. The actors do not, indeed, wear the cothurnus, but their performance is "cothurnate" none the less. In a word, we have as near an approach as is conceivable, under modern conditions, to the tragedy of the ancients; and I should have thought that, as a mere item of news, that would be at least as interesting, even to the man in the street, as – well, as *Fireworks*. But no, "the oracles are dumb"; and, to tell the truth, this silence of theirs seems to me eloquent.

Yes! it is an experience, which I, for my part, would not willingly miss, to listen to a drama twenty-three centuries old, and to thrill with the same sense of tragic irony, to feel one's heart-strings gripped with the same pity and terror which moved the Athenian populace in the Theatre of Dionysus, at the other end of history. For it is an intensely moving story this of the downfall of King Oedipus. The man who can criticise the plot as Corneille and Voltaire did (so I read in Jules Lemaître) must be strangely lacking in historic sense. Lemaître himself seems to me to treat it rather too much as if it were a play of Sardou's. To be sure, Oedipus ought, if he had been strictly reasonable, to have baffled the oracle by refraining from killing any gentleman, and from marrying any lady, whom he did not know to be younger than himself. But an oracle is not to be trifled with in that way. The very awe of the thing resides in the feeling that the powers who predict know how to accomplish their prediction, even by blinding the reason of their victims. That would not be a good plea for Sardou, but it was perfectly good for Sophocles and his audience; and the whole fun of the thing, if I may phrase it so, is to put ourselves in the place of the Athenians. Then, again, Monsieur Lemaître confesses that Oedipus's great "pathos-scene" (technically so called) at the end of the play bored him "horribly"; and adds that, if everyone were sincere, everyone would say the same thing. Such an assertion, of course, silences all argument; I can only affirm, with all the sincerity of which I am capable, that the scene moved me very deeply. "The sin is in the will, not in the material act," says Monsieur Lemaître. Why, certainly; we say so, we think so, and some of us, now-a-days, have even succeeded (more or less) in *feeling* so as well. But if that truth has even now entered but imperfectly into the world's consciousness, how much further was the world of BC 440 from any effective realization of it! And how much further still the primitive Hellenes, among whom the folk-tale of Oedipus took its rise! No doubt Sophocles, as Monsieur Lemaître states, realised the truth as we do; but is it a dramatist's business always to make his characters act by the light of pure reason? The question is not whether Oedipus *ought* to have "taken on" as he did about the little accident of his manslaughter and marriage, but whether he *would* have done so. Monsieur Lemaître must surely be aware that, even in this rationalistic, Herbert-Spencerian age, thousands of men are worrying themselves in strait-waistcoats or Salvation jerseys, if not into their coffins, over "sins" for which they are no more morally responsible than was Oedipus for his parricide and incest. And shall we refuse him and them our pity? That would be Pharisaic rationalism with a vengeance.

Mounet Sully's declamation, or rather intonation, of his verses seemed to me absolutely what the play and part demanded. His habit of marking both the caesura and the end of the line by a sort of prolonged roar on the vowel of the last syllable is, as a rule, apt to become monotonous; but I don't think it is possible, in antique tragedy, to emphasize too much the rhythm of the lines. His appearance was superb, and his intense earnestness gave the whole thing an air of living reality, so that we never for a moment felt the performance to be a mere academic revival of a curiosity of literature. It was a hundred times real, as vital, as *Par le Glaive* or *Henri III et sa Cour*. Paul Monnet made a magnificent Tiresias, and Albert Lambert *fils* was excellent as the old shepherd. Madame Lerou's Jocaste, too, seemed to me profoundly and memorably tragic. Her last exit is a piece of incomparable stagecraft on the part of the despised Sophocles – despised of the morning press. If there is anything more impressive and even appalling in drama, I should like to hear of it. The appearance of Oedipus in the last scene, with his empty eye-sockets yet streaming blood, was undeniably hideous; but for my part I am never so much "*mis dedans*", as Sarcey phrases it, in the theatre, as to forget that red paint is, after all, red paint. My experience last Thursday night, rather to my own surprise, was a curious proof of this. In real life I am horribly sensitive to anything wrong with the eye of another person. I will go a mile out of my way to avoid seeing a bleared eye, and the merest glimpse of inflamed lids or a bloodshot eye will make

> my own eyes smart and water. Consequently, I rather expected that the gory orbits of Oedipus would cause me sensible discomfort; but no! I felt none whatever. . . . My nerves were unmoved.

In 1910 Max Reinhardt presented a massive production of *Oedipus Rex*, embellished with a huge cast, at the Concert Hall in Munich; then at the Zirkus Schumann in Berlin; next, at the Zirkus Busch in Vienna (1911); and, finally, at London's Covent Garden (1912), where his star was John Martin Harvey. He did another *Oedipus Rex* in 1920 at his Grosses Schauspielhaus.

Quite excited was the popular reception of an *Oedipus* about three decades later, with Londoners flocking to see the Old Vic's staging (1945) of the tragedy, featuring Olivier's heart-rending portrait of the self-blinding protagonist. His animal cry of realization and horror when he discovered the nature of his unwitting deed echoes in the memories of those who heard him. (In his memoirs he reveals how the cry, that chilled and shrivelled the hearer, had been painstakingly tested and rehearsed – he was strictly a "technical" actor – guided by a recollection of the piteous howl of a small creature trapped and freezing in the snow.) Against an austere set, the chorus, all its members white-bearded and garbed in black, contributed a sober touch. The direction was by Michel Saint-Denis, the translation by William Butler Yeats, the costumes by Marie-Helene Daste, the scene design by John Piper, the lighting by John Sullivan. Tiresias was played by Ralph Richardson, Jocasta by Sybil Thorndike (and later by Ena Burrill), Creon by Harry Andrews. In a dazzling exhibition of versatility, Olivier had the *Oedipus*, a short work, coupled on the same programme with Richard Sheridan's satirical eighteenth-century farce *The Critic*, in which he was Mr Puff, an "unctuous and skittering" reviewer. When the Old Vic production reached the Century Theater in New York (1946), the *New York Times*'s Brooks Atkinson remarked:

> *Oedipus* and *The Critic* are somewhat farther apart than the poles, and it obviously would take better than genius to think of putting them together. The Old Vic must have that, and from the searing tragedy and the light burlesque they have brought an excellent evening to the local theater. It is repertory showing what it can do, and it also is Laurence Olivier showing himself as an exceptionally fine actor. Changes of style do not dismay him; he masters alike both tragedy and bubbling froth.
>
> As Oedipus, he is the dark figure of doom. At the beginning his playing is low-pitched, conversational. When Oedipus hears the prophecy that he is to kill his father and then marry his mother, there is unbelieving uncertainty, a groping for anything away from the truth. At the end, when Oedipus knows the prophecy has been fulfilled in all its horror, Mr Olivier rises to the highest tragic play-

ing. The character is thought out and grows, and the actor speaks the poetry and underscores the inevitable sweeping forward of the events. . . . Olivier has offered a model.

Atkinson found the other parts well taken.

Michel Saint-Denis has staged the production simply, with a chanting chorus and suitable and somber music by Anthony Hopkins. The scenery, also, is simple – two towering columns with a step and platform between. The Old Vic's emphasis again is right – on the play and those who play it.

A few years later Olivier directed his wife Vivien Leigh in *Antigone* (1949). She was famed for her roles in films, but her desire to surpass the acclaim earned by Olivier in *Oedipus* was insatiable. Her emotional balance was fragile, and her identification with the distraught Antigone was so strong that she came close to a nervous breakdown.

The Olivier *Oedipus* proved how effective as a stage-vehicle a revival of Greek tragedy could be, and how it might appeal to modern spectators. But apparently it set an intimidating standard that other actors were not eager to challenge.

One who did so was James Mason, whose films had won him a broad following. Talented and intelligent, aristocratic in appearance, he was somewhat detached in manner. Richard Collier, in his *Make-Believe: The Magic of International Theatre*, recounts: "After a death scene that reduced even the stage hands to silent awe, he called abruptly to an electrician: 'That fifth light on Number Two batten needs bringing up if I'm to be shown to full advantage.'"

Mason's Oedipus was on view in Canada during the second season of the Stratford Festival (1954), directed by Tyrone Guthrie, who had helped to establish the enterprise there – the stage had been designed to his specific instructions, in collaboration with Tanya Moisewitsch. Guthrie had already put on his version of the tragedy in Israel and Helsinki; the mounting at Stratford was deemed to be his final and "definite interpretation" of it. As he was to do later with the *Oresteia* at Minneapolis, he resorted to all the traditional artefacts of ancient Greek theatre.

A local critic sent a report to the *New York Times* describing the play as the Festival's most impressive offering:

Guthrie, the British director who is the strongest contributor to Stratford's achievement, has devised a production here that fuses the ancient forms of Greek theater into stunning new abstractions.

. . . This Oedipus Rex breaks through the heavily wreathing, choking smoke of incense, brought by the dark suppliants of Thebes, to tower above them as a golden king-symbol, crowned, masked and towering on the *cothurnus*, or platforms, that ancient Greeks used to enlarge their principal performers.

In answer to the pleas of his people, whom he once rescued from the terrible Sphinx, this great one faces in turn the other figures of the tragedy.

First, there is the eyeless prophet, Tiresias, stumbling and falling in movement but direct and pointed in accusation. Oedipus himself, he insists, is the man who has now brought his country to new disaster.

Creon, brother to the Queen, on whom Oedipus turns as the instigator of the blind man's accusations, is a proud monolith of bronze, towering to equal height as the King himself. When Queen Jocasta comes to keep the peace between them, she is equally heroic, silver-masked and forceful.

Driven on to uncover the secret of his parentage . . . the golden Oedipus confronts them in turn and after them the two shepherds, gnarled roots of men, who finally give him the unwanted key to the truth.

And all around him, moving in sculptural masses, encircle the chorus, fearing, dreading and supporting him in his fateful plunge.

. . . Then a messenger appears on the darkening stage that Jocasta and her son-husband have left as their shame has been forced upon them. His shattering description of the scene within the palace is followed by the reappearance of Oedipus, darkly shrouded in his self-inflicted blindness. There follows the strangely twisted scene between the blinded outcast and his daughters and then Oedipus descends from the platform for the first time, going down through the audience to exile.

While responding fully to Guthrie's creation, we are faced with one major weakness. Unfortunately the weakness is at the heart and core of the play – within the figure of King Oedipus himself.

James Mason plays the great role with moments of deep emotional feeling, but his whole performance is scaled down below that of the heroic figure that he achieves physically. Impressive, almost godlike in appearance, he does not suggest the high pride that comes before the tragic fall. Later he stirs pity in his recounting of the moment when he killed the man who is now revealed as his father, but greater heights remain unscaled.

Eleanor Stuart does achieve what her partner does not. Her Jocasta is both a woman and a symbol of a woman, strong, protecting and scornful of augury. Her cry as she withdraws from the stage lingers in the mind as did that cry that once burst from an earlier Oedipus.

The other Canadian actors supporting Mr Mason fill out their unaccustomed acting shells with remarkable ease. Robert Goodier as the brazen Creon and Douglas Rain as the messenger are the most

> forceful contributors, while the remarkable English actor Douglas Campbell reinstates his claim as a superb comedian by drawing a legitimate, if unsuspected, laugh from his role as the man from Corinth. And the men of the chorus sustain and urge forward the drama while serving faithfully the schemes of voice and movement Dr Guthrie has set down for them in this extraordinary piece of ritual theater.

In sum, this Canadian writer thought Stratford's *Oedipus Rex* "a production of magnificent form and intention", lacking greatness in only one detail, but still a notable accomplishment of modern theatre.

Wearing a deeply carved mask, and heavily robed, Mason may have been at a disadvantage in expression and illustratory gestures, and to some degree vocally hampered. The masks covered the face fully, as did those Guthrie was to use in Minneapolis. Olivier was bare-faced, and in other traditional stagings of Greek dramas most actors have been encumbered only with half-masks, permitting them to project their lines without sounding muffled.

In France, beginning in the 1930s, the fashion was to write variations on the classic Greek themes, sometimes updating them, and sometimes ringing *outré* changes on them. Instances of this are André Gide's *Oedipe* (1931), subsequently produced by Jean Vilar at Avignon (1949), and Jean Cocteau's *The Infernal Machine* (1934), the latter frequently revived. Cocteau is also the librettist of Igor Stravinsky's "brief but monumental" opera-oratorio, *Oedipus Rex* (1926–7), which is in medieval church Latin, except that the narrator's part is to be sung in whatever is the language of the audience. In this task, Cocteau adheres fairly closely to Sophocles' text.

In New York the series of dance-dramas by Martha Graham probing Greek mythology, which had its inception about this time, included her *Night Journey* (1947). It begins when Jocasta first grasps the hideous truth of her incestuous physical love for her son. Tormented, her mind flooded with images of acts now too horrible to evoke in memory, she recognizes that only her death can absolve her. Initially, Graham herself had the role of the queen, Erick Hawkins that of Oedipus, Mark Ryder that of Tiresias. The piece has remained in the Graham Company's repertoire, with a number of cast changes, such as Bertram Ross dancing as Oedipus; Stuart Hodes and, next, Paul Taylor taking over the part of the blind seer. Among the other distinguished artists who collaborated on *Night Journey* are the composer William Schuman who provided the score, and the sculptor Isamu Noguchi the setting and costumes.

When the piece was seen anew (1992) – soon after Graham's death – Anna Kisselgoff reappraised its achievement in the *New York Times*, declaring that it not only has some of the greatest choreography she ever produced but also serves as a model of artistic collaboration.

At the work's first performance of the season on Friday night at the City Center, Christine Dakin's Jocasta relived the tragedy of her unwitting incestuous marriage to her son amid Isamu Noguchi's spare and ever-striking decor. Noguchi's famous sculptural bed, fashioned out of male and female sexual symbols, was as resonant with meaning as his series of exquisitely ornamented pedestals, serving both as ruins and as stepping stones for Oedipus as he makes the entrance that a frantic women's chorus tries to prevent.

William Schuman's atmospheric score finally attains a true and hair-raising power when that chorus, here led with spell-binding vigor by Denise Vale, executes the ensemble choreography that holds a special place in the entire Graham repertory.

Anguished, unable to prevent the unpreventable, the seven women are the essence of desperate energy, clawed furies rebounding from the floor to the score's insistent beat or digging deeper into that floor like human corkscrews. Here is the Graham idiom at its most percussive and virtuosic. Every breath in every body contraction is made kinetically apparent, and the ensuing release serves to carry the dramatic momentum forward.

Ms Dakin's Jocasta and Donlin Foreman's Oedipus, seemingly swept along by the wave of flashback that makes up the narrative, pulled out all the right stops. Ms Dakin, now projecting more fiercely than in the past, admirably embodied the relevant emotions. Her solos were portraits distilled in movement.

The choreography's crucial double image is the embrace in which Jocasta, crosslegged on Oedipus's thighs, caresses her partner as if he were a baby. Thus wife-mother embraces her husband-son. Like Ms Dakin, Mr Foreman emphasized the Graham idiom's shape and angular fluency. The passion of their dancing was deeply felt. The strong cast was completed by Pascal Rioult as Tiresias, the blind seer who reveals the couple's incest by dramatically cutting through the symbolic cord that binds them. This moment was gripping and here Mr Rioult too gave a committed performance.

At the season's second presentation of *Night Journey*, now with several cast changes, Jennifer Dunning of the *New York Times* was somewhat disappointed, her response being that the new dancers failed to give the piece

the Graham feel of something etched in flesh and stone. Given the challenging task of playing alluring lover to a son, Terese Capucilli made Jocasta's chill, lethal figure scrambling to her destiny on fast-moving little feet yet an imposing figure of stillness. Kenneth Topping was a handsome youth who claimed his lover boldly, with just the right appropriative swing of a leg over her reclining body. But he was almost lyrically light in his portrayal.

There was little sense of warmth from either and so it was hard, with the exception of two moments, to imagine the two as lovers. Those exceptions were a high arabesque promenade for Mr Topping that communicated youthful ardor and a clinging embrace in which Jocasta and Oedipus almost tremble in each other's arms.

Peter London was a fine, monumental Tiresias, towering implacably over the proceedings. Next time, however, it would be nice to see that staff of his thud more portentously against the floor in Tiresias's final walk.

The National Theatre of Budapest added an *Oedipus Rex* to its repertoire (1962). Endre Marton, the director, dispensed with masks; his actors wore white robes with ornate stripes along the arms from shoulder to cuff, and the chorus had stylized, tightly curled white headdresses, banded in black, and matching white beards, also stylized, in the Assyrian fashion, above black tunics, a sombre contrast. The setting provided similar contrasts, making much use of stark highlights and ominous shadows. The translation into Magyar was by Nihaly Babits.

An Italian *Oedipus Rex* (1967), a motion picture written and directed by Pier Paolo Pasolini, based on Sophocles' tragedy and combined with elements of the *Oedipus at Colonus*, transplants the stories to Mussolini's era, but with flashbacks to the original dramas. Here, from the *New York Times*, is Vincent Canby's summary of the film, which was given a much belated showing in that city several decades later.

Through the window on the second floor of a middle-class house, in a room dimly lit by electricity, a woman gives birth to a son. In a quick succession of brief scenes, we see how the baby, as it grows up to be able to totter around on its own, earns the jealousy of his handsome father, a member of Mussolini's militia, while his beautiful mother is torn between love for husband and child. On a night of national celebration, the small boy gets out of bed and makes his way to the window where he watches the fireworks that both enthrall and frighten him.

Cut, suddenly, from this scene, which the Freudians might call primal, to some prehistoric past and an arid, barren landscape. A man, in rags, carries an infant. He stops, puts the baby on the ground, raises his sword, but cannot bring himself to skewer it. Instead, he leaves the child to the forces of nature.

It's within this curious, very personal frame that Pier Paolo Pasolini sets his free, sometimes inscrutable but always handsome adaptation of Sophocles' plays.

Canby felt that the picture contains somewhat more Pasolini than it does Sophocles.

Even though all never becomes clear in it, [it] remains a fascinating film, one that demonstrates the late, controversial Italian director's gifts as one of the most original and perverse film poets of his generation. It's not always necessary to understand Pasolini to be riveted by what he does.

. . . By far the most effective portions of this *Oedipus* are those modern, semi-autobiographical sequences by which Pasolini frames the myth of the prince who, in innocence, murders his father, marries his mother and, when he learns the terrible truth, gouges out his eyes and goes into a wandering exile.

These sequences, which form the principal part of the film and were shot in Morocco, are pictorially arresting but so chilly they seem dead. As I'm sure Pasolini intended, they are pageant-like, having the manner less of drama than of ritual that must be played out according to prescribed rules.

Silvano Mangano, who also plays the mother in the opening sequence, is a passionate, stunning-looking Jocasta. However, as Oedipus, Franco Citti looks so contemporary that one must assume a point is being made. He has the rough good looks of a boxer, but the performance is so stolid that when the camera comes in for a tight close-up of his eyes – as it frequently does – one sees only a pair of disembodied eyes. There's no awareness of a mind behind them.

The excellent supporting cast includes Alida Valli, as Oedipus's adoptive mother; the Living Theatre's Julian Beck as Tiresias . . . and Pasolini himself as high priest.

As he did in his *Medea*, Pasolini shows us a lot of action that the original playwright only talks about. Though *Oedipus at Colonus* is credited as one of the sources, there's nothing of it in the film, unless it has been used to suggest the closing sequence set in contemporary Bologna, the point of which completely escapes me.

It's also difficult to understand how Pasolini connects the contemporary frame with *Oedipus the King*, which, toward the end, includes the great if enigmatic speech, "There, now all is clear, willed, not imposed by destiny." Pasolini publicly acknowledged his initial hatred of his own father, but in this film the father is seen as a viciously antagonistic, possessive man who hates his son from birth. The gods have nothing to do with it, nor, for that matter, for the son's attachment for his mother.

> ... Giuseppe Ruzzolini's photography is very good, both in evoking the contemporary world and the legendary past, where even the costumes seem to be alive. People wear bits and pieces of bushes and trees. They decorate themselves with metal ornaments that appear to have been put on right out of the ground, as if the jewelry still belonged to the primeval landscape over which this ancient society has yet to gain dominion.

The earliest of at least four English-language versions of *Oedipus Rex* broadcast in the latter half of the century had in its title role the Canadian-born Christopher Plummer, a young player – only twenty-seven – rapidly ascending to international stature. The script relied on the Dudley Fitts–Robert Fitzgerald translation, condensed by the drama critic Walter Kerr. An unidentified reviewer in *Time* magazine observed:

> Plummer was a kingly king – handsome in bearing, condescending in modesty, impetuous in anger, regal even in his sudden descent to the living death decreed for the man who slew his father, lay with his mother and could no more than any other mortal "make the gods do more than the gods will." Through television, perhaps millions were able for the first time to see and hear the people of Thebes bid farewell to their fallen, blinded king with Sophocles' final lament:
>
> "Let every man in mankind's frailty,
> Consider his last day, and let none
> Presume on his good fortune until he find
> Life, at his death, a memory without pain."

Robert Goodier, who had been with James Mason in the Guthrie production at Stratford, repeated his excellent portrayal of Creon.

A novel rendering of the tragedy was that given by the Roundabout Theater in New York (1970); the Oedipus was a black actor, Gordon Heath, and the place was removed to a presidential palace on a Caribbean island, the time in the 1930s. This fresh conception came from "Anthony Sloan", actually the director Gene Feist. Clive Barnes, for the *New York Times*, had doubts about the unusual approach.

> The myth of Oedipus is as complex as the psychiatrists would have us believe. The new version by

Anthony Sloan is described in the program as "a free adaptation of the ancient myth." But in this freedom it allows itself I wonder if it has not lost some quality of the myth in the retelling.

. . . It is traditionally the French who love to transpose legends and update miracles. Surely the heart of what has been transplanted must be kept beating – here I feel the patient has died in the operating theater.

Mr Sloan has very properly noticed that Oedipus is a man who in fulfilling his destiny is passing through a ritual of passage, and the author has decided to concentrate on the ritual itself, which he compares to the ritual of a bullfight.

The bullfight metaphor is an apt one, for even though the result of a bullfight is never quite predetermined, so the matched rituals of tragedy and *corrida* are not quite parallel, and the final outcome is not too seriously in doubt. But where Mr Sloan really goes wrong is in changing the nature of Oedipus's plight.

Oedipus is a tragic figure in the classic sense because he is forced forward by his own spirit to a state of self-discovery. He uncovers himself, strips his heart and mind naked to disclose his sins. He does not know that his wife Jocasta is also his mother. Neither does Jocasta know this – they are both creatures of mousetrap destiny. But in Mr Sloan's realization of the theme not only does Jocasta know of the sin, but so also does Oedipus.

The Jocasta, played by Elizabeth Owens, is white. Barnes continues:

Here Oedipus's position – and the author's – is that a fact is not the truth until that fact has been brought into the open. It is an interesting, even persuasive concept – but it is not a tragic theme. So we feel a little ironic compassion for this Oedipus, but the situation lacks the dimension of tragedy.

The play might have had more life of its own had the writing been more expressive. As it was, it seems caught uneasily between conversational simplicity and a deliberately heightened utterance that might be thought the voice of tragedy. Yet the author did not appear adept in either style – like a man who is more bilingual than comprehensible.

As with much of Off-Off-Broadway the quality of the acting varied a lot. The occasion was notable for marking the return to a New York stage of that very fine Black actor, Gordon Heath, after more than two decades. A man born to play the prince, Mr Heath has an instinctive nobility and moves and talks with all the natural authority of a classic hero. The rest of the cast was less powerful by half.

Thomas McCann had a certain evil exultance as Haemon, there was a flaunting beauty to Charlotte Forbes's Antigone, and Elizabeth Owens did moderately well in conveying the painful ambiguity of this Jocasta. Gene Feist's staging effectively conveyed a sense of decay and ritual – especially in the mock bullfight ritual – and used the theater-in-the-round adroitly.

A reviewer for *Time* magazine, still anonymous, offered this assessment:

Greek tragedy used to be inaccessible to the American temperament. In a play like *Oedipus*, for example, it was felt that the punishment of the hero was horrifyingly in excess of his crime, and that too much of the action rested with the will of the gods and too little within the control of the man. In the past decade, public events have brought home to Americans a growing awareness that fate may not be in one's hands but at one's throat. The dirge-like destiny of the Kennedys, the war in Vietnam, racial turmoil, urban carnage, the generational vendetta and the growth of drug addiction have moved an entire nation toward at least the beginnings of a tragic sense of life.

What this means in terms of the theater is that US stages are likely to carry a far higher traffic of classic Greek tragedies than they ever have before. Some of these will be presented unmodified in fresh and colloquial translations. Others, like the new Off-Off-Broadway Roundabout Theater production of *Oedipus,* will alter the text in order to link it more closely to contemporary minds, sensibilities and responses. It is important to note that the playwright, Anthony Sloan, a pseudonym adopted by the Roundabout's artistic director, Gene Feist, has not tampered with the basic myth. Oedipus has murdered his father, married his mother, sired an incestuous brood, and his eyes are gouged out. What Sloan has done, albeit with lesser esthetic power and wit, is what Anouilh and Giraudoux have done with the Greek myths.

. . . His emphasis is on death, ritual and the family. The family is presented as a verbal killing ground where people prepare for real death. The ritual of death itself is a *coup de théâtre*, a mock bullfight complete with toreador costumes in which the killers and the killed are all humans. The conceit works in that both Greek tragedy and the bullfight derive their heightened drama from an imminent awareness of death.

In Sophocles' *Oedipus the King*, Oedipus and Jocasta's daughters, Antigone and Ismene, are very young and silent. Sloan, however, has drawn on all versions of the Oedipus myth, and in his play the daughters are teenagers or older, both articulate judges of their parents. Antigone is a haughty spitfire, Ismene a dutiful but skeptical daughter. Unlike Sophocles, Sloan includes the incestuous pair's son

Polynices and implies a homosexual relationship with Jocasta's nephew Haemon. A very up-to-date household, indeed. When Oedipus is bent on throttling Haemon at one point, Jocasta begs him to stop, calling out "Oedipus, I am your mother – obey me!" The irony, and the insight, of Sloan's version of the myth is that Oedipus has deeply known it all along, known that the skeleton in every man's closet is himself. So has Jocasta known it. So have the children. This is not, therefore, a discovery of the self but an unveiling of the rottenness of the self. Sloan seems to be saying that this is the way the world runs from day to day, with people living out lies, guarding their "images" and losing their souls, until the inadvertent truth, like murder, outs.

Oedipus depends on the title actor. Gordon Heath, who last played on the US stage twenty-two years ago, has the regal carriage and authority of a king, the torn heart of a father, the muted passion of a husband and lover who finds himself a son. Since he is black, he is, like his ancient predecessor, "a stranger in Thebes." But he knows that black is the color of all men's fates. After he is blinded, a weeping Jocasta asks, "What words do you have for me, Oedipus?" His answer strikes the purest vein of authentic Greek terror, the knowledge that never to have been born at all would be the only destiny. Oedipus, the sightless seer, says:

> "You will live, Jocasta.
> This is my sentence upon all of you.
> You will live."

Heath had won notice and success earlier when given the lead in *Deep Are the Roots* (1945) by Arnaud d'Usseau and James Gow. In that topical drama he was a young lieutenant, a hero, who returns from the Second World War to an unchanged, racially segregated Deep South where he meets frustration when seeking to marry a white girl he loves. The play thrived for fourteen months on Broadway, and another six months in London's West End. Finding life in Paris more congenial than at home – "a free air and a free people" – Heath settled there, the proprietor of a nightclub that prospered for thirty years. He also acted in Paris and London, speaking French as well as English, and directed the Studio Theatre of Paris, a company that offered English-dialogue productions. His biography, *Deep Are the Roots: Memoirs of a Black Expatriate*, appeared shortly after his death (1991) at seventy-two. In 1977 he had returned briefly to New York to play Hamm in Samuel Beckett's *Endgame*, again at the Roundabout.

Another noted Afro-American player who essayed *Oedipus Rex* was James Earl Jones, who participated in a staging at the Episcopal Cathedral of St John the Divine in New York City (1975). This was a workshop performance restricted to three weekends. Opposite him was Jacqueline Brookes as Jocasta. The translation was by John Lewin, and it focused – in Jones's words – not "on the damnation of being incestuous but on the betrayal of Oedipus by his parents" who had readily agreed to the infant's abandonment and death from exposure and starvation. "The Oedipal thing is almost secondary. I wish Freud had known that." He told an interviewer that while in college he had served as a one-man chorus in an *Oedipus Rex* put on by students. Of great physical stature, with an unusually deep, strong voice, the stalwart Jones had also played King Lear.

The next Oedipus to confront the New York critics was Robert Stattel in Christopher Martin's offering of the *Theban Plays* (1980–81) at his long-established Off-Broadway Classic Stage Company. The separate tragedies making up the trilogy rotated in repertory, with Stattel assigned the lead role in the first two. On some occasions, such as New Year's Eve, the trilogy was presented intact, given the title *The Oedipus Cycle*, with the audience viewing *Oedipus Rex* in the afternoon, taking time to leave the theatre for an early dinner, then returning at six for the *Oedipus at Colonus* and, after a forty-five minute intermission, *Antigone.*

Interviewed by Eleanor Blau of the *New York Times*, who observed that none of the cast wore sandals, Martin explained he had his actors attired in "'timeless costumes, at once classical and modern, so that the actors look like what we know as people, not characters out of a period play.' Thus the men had long coats rather like suit jackets, over ordinary trousers and shoes."

The set for *Antigone* was unusual: "The actors are covered with dust and the main source of light is fluorescent. 'It is cold, stark, dehumanized,' Mr Martin said. 'There's a very modern feeling to it.'" He had also avoided any translation that forced the work to sound like Tennyson or the King James Bible. Instead he chose a version by the English poet Paul Roche, who "'understands the beauty of the ancient Greek language, which lies in alliteration, rhythm and the juxtaposition of sounds, not lyrics and rhyme.'"

The *New York Times*'s critic, Mel Gussow, welcomed Martin's

> monumental effort . . . On the basis of the first of these tragedies, it is evident that, at the CSC, artistry has caught up with ambition. *Oedipus Rex*, staged by the company's artistic director, proceeds swiftly and inexorably to its terrifying conclusion, and in Robert Stattel, the company has an experienced classic actor capable of heroic stature.
>
> As Oedipus, Mr Stattel moves from haughty concern for a dying city to a determined quest for

truth even at the expense of self-incrimination. The actor stalks fate with the unswervable intensity of an attorney prosecuting a puzzling crime. He stresses the character's arrogance, an arrogance that is in excess of his ability to command.

Tracing the path of the prophecy, he is undeflected by any serious thought that he himself might be guilty. Dismissing a dumbstruck Jocasta, persisting in his demonic search, he proclaims, "Storm, then, burst away!" and the actor's voice resounds as if from a sepulcher. He is, of course, about to descend to his doom. When he is finally confronted with the truth – that he has slain his natural father and married his mother – he greets it as if he were a suicide walking into the tide. The pride that has led him to insult hesitant messengers – why are they afraid to offer him information? – sends him rushing to his destiny.

Taking a cue from his perceptive translator, Paul Roche, Mr Martin, as director, does not overplay the magisterial aspect of the drama. Nor does he allow Oedipus to be less than kingly. Instead, using Mr Roche's lyrical adaptation, he charts an appropriate middle course. This is a lucid, straightforward production easily accessible to young audiences.

Terry A. Bennett's setting is a checkerboard of large opaque squares, a brightly lit terrace with silvered boughs resting on low platforms. There is an absence of panoply. The austerity of the costumes and the stage design is matched by the immediacy of the performance.

John MacKay, as the leader of the chorus, manages to be conversational while projecting an air of authority, and Eric Tavaris's Creon is a faithful man of subdued strength. Mr Martin and Karen Sunde as Tiresias and Jocasta are among the production's other assets. There are, however, a few weaknesses in the casting.

Harnessing the ninety-minute performance is the figure of Mr Stattel. Even when he is offstage, we are conscious of his presence, and when he is on stage he is impassioned in his rage and in his merciless sense of guilt. Blinded, cursing the injury he has inflicted on his family, Mr Stattel's king embraces his children as if to shelter them from the overwhelming tragedy. It is, of course, too late; Oedipus is a man "preserved from death precisely for disaster."

Trying to assess the reasons for the CSC's growth, one must acknowledge the improvement in direction and design, and the ability of the company to attract actors of reputation, as exemplified by Mr Stattel. Previously a stalwart actor with a number of major companies, including the Repertory Theater of Lincoln Center and the American Shakespeare Festival at Stratford, Connecticut, he has created a new and significant career at CSC, playing some of the most challenging roles in dramatic literature. His residency with this Off-Broadway troupe replenishes the actor and rewards theatergoers."

In the same spring season (1981) an *Oedipus the King* sponsored by the determinedly avant-garde Brooklyn Academy of Music (BAM) had a sharply hostile reception, one critic transferring the adjectives "fatally flawed" from the drama's tragic hero to the production itself. This interpretation was an undertaking by a comparatively new troupe, only in its second year, organized by the Academy itself. The translation, recently published (1978), was a collaborative effort by Steven Berg and Diskin Clay. This revised text was duly and thoroughly examined by Bernard Knox in the *New York Times Book Review*, who granted that the problems facing a translator are

> numerous and formidable, especially formidable when the poet is Sophocles. His dramatic style, pitched midway between the opulence of Aeschylean imagery and the comparative sobriety of Euripidean rhetoric, can conjure out of highly formal language the illusion of passionate, unpremeditated speech; it can also invest a simple statement with reverberating ironies as well as a characteristic grave music. In addition, the tragic genre itself presents sobering challenges. The spoken sections of the play are encased in lines which are metrically as inexorably regular as the Alexandrines of Racine (by comparison Shakespeare is a maverick), and extended passages of dramatic dialogue consist of line-for-line exchanges. And the sections which were sung (some of them, the choral odes, were also danced) are framed in rhythmic structures of an intricate exactness which is completely alien to English verse.
>
> . . . Steven Berg is ambitious; his dialogue, though direct and forceful, is pitched in a high poetic key. And there are passages where he succeeds brilliantly. In the counter-speeches of Oedipus and Tiresias, for example, he manages to transpose into speakable and memorable English both the fierce eloquence of Oedipus's accusation and the demonic authority of the blind prophet's reply. But Mr Berg has the defects of his qualities. Even in this scene there are a few self-indulgent touches: a superfluous image at the end of Tiresias' speech ("an ember of pain. Ashes"), a three-line expansion of the hint of desolation conveyed to the Greek audience by the one word *Kithairon* (some explanation was justified, but not three lines). Elsewhere and often Mr Berg allows himself much more license: "I am afraid, afraid/ Apollo's prediction will come true, all of it,/ as God's sunlight grows brighter on a man's face at dawn/ when he's in bed, still sleeping/ and reaches into his eyes and wakes him." The Sophoclean original runs: "Yes, afraid that Apollo will turn out to be correct." This interpolation is all the more distressing because it interrupts a swift sequence of dramatic revelations which in the original is couched in the cut and thrust of single-line dialogue.
>
> In his approach to this problem, the strict regularity of the iambic speeches, Mr Berg renounces any attempt to reproduce the form of the original; he uses an elastic line: his, in fact, runs the gamut

from one syllable to twenty. This freedom of maneuver removes the temptation to pad out the line, a temptation to which earlier translations often succumbed in their efforts to reproduce, line for line, those series of rapid question and answer which sometimes strike the modern ear as faintly comic. (Housman's brilliant parody of the results was enough to put an end to the practice: *Alcmaeon*: "A shepherd's questioned mouth informed me that –" *Chorus*: "What? For I know not yet what you will say." *Alcmaeon*: "Nor will you ever if you interrupt.") Our translator sacrifices formal balance for dramatic economy and cuts to the bone where he thinks he sees fat. . . . Creon leads up to his defense against Oedipus's charges with a series of rhetorical questions to which the answer, as both men know, is Yes. "Are you married to my sister?" asks Creon, and Oedipus answers with a line which would not be unfairly represented by: "A negative answer to your inquiry is out of the question." Mr Berg translates: "I married Jocasta." If these exchanges had been written by Euripides it is likely that there would have been cause for surgery, but Sophocles is a subtle operator and should be approached with caution. . . . The periphrases of Oedipus's reply reflect a sarcastic impatience with Creon's pettifogging courtroom techniques.

It is, however, in the translation of the allusive, lyrical odes that the poet comes into his kingdom; here the more literal the rendering the less effective it is likely to be. Paradoxically enough, Mr Berg, who is so generous with his own contributions in the dialogue, here shows restraint; except for some overemphasis and undue expansions in the climactic ode which comes after the revelation scene, he has written moving poetry which re-creates much of the power and beauty of the original. Occasionally, in fact, it comes close to perfection, as in the lines on the plague: "and lives one after another split the air/ birds taking off/ wingrush hungrier than fire/ souls leaping away they fly/ to the shore/ of the cold god of evening/ west." The principles which underlie these lyric translations are explained in the preliminary notes, which contain a valuable discussion of the nature of Greek choral poetry and the aim of the translations: "to reproduce in English, which has no tradition for this kind of song, the essential gaps and ambiguities of Greek choral song by a kind of Broken Poetry."

This excerpt is included to suggest the obstacles besetting any translator who must at one and the same time seek to placate academic critics – Bernard Knox is professor of Greek at Harvard University – together with practical-minded stage directors and, not least, the actors who must cope with the lines. Knox paid tribute to Berg for his risky experiments. "It is the fate of such innovators to rise high above the norm when successful and fall just as far below it when they fail. Mr Berg is no exception." He also had praise for Diskin Clay for adding his "valuable notes on the plays, many of which will command the attention of his professional colleagues", and for having written "a perceptive and innovative introduction. This lucid but profound exploration of the Sophoclean tragic vision is the distillation of his long study of the text, and an authoritative critical statement, an arresting reassessment of an acclaimed masterpiece."

This new translation, whatever its merits, apparently did not serve the Brooklyn Academy players well. In *New York* magazine the often abrasive John Simon exclaimed:

> The BAM Theater Company production of *Oedipus the King* does not fill us with terror, only with pity. Though most of the acting and all the directing is terrible, the result, when not laughable, is simply pitiful. On the credit side, Ming Cho Lee has designed a splendid set. A square, parapeted courtyard made of genuine seeming boulders has a graceful altar down front. It yields, backward, to a walk with one or two steps in it, leading to a low, wide wall. In it is a square portal, with two more square portals beyond and beyond: An interplay of rectangles in powerful perspective suggests austere vastitudes grasping at infinity. While the stage remains empty, we believe in this *Oedipus.*
>
> But presently there is a Priest who, thanks in part to Jenifer von Mayrhauser's uncharacteristically bad costuming, looks, acts, and sounds like a witch doctor. Then comes a chorus of four, quite unable to suggest the anguished citizenry of Thebes. There is the chorus leader (Gerry Bamman), who looks like a storefront philosopher moth-eatenly enacting a Biblical patriarch. There is a character from a Japanese woodcut (Gedde Watanabe), with rote, unfelt movements and of impenetrable speech. There is a squatting figure (Laura Esterman) that looks like a shrunken *fellah* (could this be the Egyptian Thebes?) and utters an occasional croaking sound. And there is a Black woman with a dazed look that once or twice turns into a glazed half-smile. When the Priest was joined by the Black Oedipus (Joe Morton), I wondered whether this wasn't perhaps *King Solomon's Mines.*
>
> There is no sense to Emily Mann's staging. Characters either declaim stiltedly or rattle along with street-wise naturalism, often shuttling between the two modes. The chorus members do not interrelate as a chorus, but as mother and son, brother and sister, or such – except when each sits in his corner, nodding or shaking his head. Sometimes, like a multiple echo, they mutter the last few syllables of someone's just finished speech. The actors tend to bellow or whisper, neither of which is intelligible. At times, Bill Vanaver's puling music drowns out the words. Arden Fingerhut's mercilessly cold, uniform lighting (no doubt the director's idea) flattens out whatever the acting doesn't.

A Homeric catalogue of faults ensues; no need to itemize them all in this history.

There are a few tolerable performances. Richard Jamieson, though unclear when he raises his voice, is a sturdy Creon. Jerome Dempsey, even if gotten up like a drunken Silenus, is a credible Corinthian Messenger. Randle Mell, when he doesn't wax inaudible, is a perfectly acceptable Second Messenger (here called "Servant"). Of the others, Joe Morton, the Oedipus, is the best. Though his walk, bearing, and speech are far from kingly, and although he is frequently adrift between attempts at poetry and settling for everyday prose, he has a good voice with an enunciation that does not falter even at *fortissimo.*

. . . But the worst, the rock-bottom worst, is Gerry Bamman's chorus leader. Lines are delivered in a colorless monotone that either lapses into a whine or enlivens things with an absurdly wrong emphasis ("I'll say the next *best* thing . . ."). When Bamman raises his voice, the singsong is even nastier and takes leave of all meaning. His movements and posture are those of a contemporary vulgarian, and he cannot even clench his fists with the dignity of conviction. Worst is his would-be-profound look, which comes out midway between the lobotomized and the cretinous. And he gets to butcher virtually *all* of the chorus's lines; could this be because he is the director's husband? . . .

The translation, by Stephen Berg and Diskin Clay, is smooth, literate and actable, but takes unwarranted liberties. No wonder: it is part of the series of translations presided over by William Arrowsmith, one of the new breed of classicists who do not interpret, only self-servingly reinterpret. We get unpleasant near-anachronisms such as "rational" and "such idiocy!" And we get interpolations such as the chorus leader's saying to Oedipus, "You are the abyss," followed by "We are the abyss." And the famous last line is trivialized into "Unless on your last day you can look back and say, 'I lived, I didn't suffer.' "

There are difficulties with producing Greek drama today that seem to me well-nigh insurmountable. Aside from growing evidence that Sophoclean poetry cannot be satisfactorily Englished, there is ample proof that the stagecraft of Greek tragedy does not translate into modern stage practice. A present-day *Oedipus* always looks like a piece of stodgy antiquarianizing or slick modernization, neither of which works.

Yet even if the project must fail, it can do so honorably, and is worth undertaking from time to time. Not, however, if the director is going to opt for vulgar flashinesses. What does Miss Mann do when Oedipus expresses the resolve never to behold the light again? The word "light" is detached from the context, uttered as a cry of horror, echoed by several other characters, and used as a signal for all to prostrate themselves as if struck by lightning. Tragedy does not need this kind of trowel. But this production does raise one interesting question: Why are half the characters (not necessarily the mighty ones) shod, and the other half (not necessarily the lowly ones) barefoot?

A *New York Times* reviewer was more polite but hardly more approving. The Brooklyn Academy had put on an *Oedipus* too hurriedly, as was

> painfully evident – since the present company was first pulled together just two seasons ago. Given the training of our actors and the experience of our directors – training and experience confined largely to theatrical realism – there's virtually no way to establish a repertory company in a few months flat. You can announce that you're going to do it; and you can select the most flexible players from those willing to join you. But those who *are* willing will most likely come unequipped to handle Shakespeare and Ibsen and Sophocles in a rush. Artistic director David Jones's group at BAM has had a few able, reasonably adaptable players this season and last (this season fewer than last). But for the most part Mr Jones has had to make do, and making do is never good enough when the schedule is ambitious. Appealing as most of his younger players are, most were green when the first curtain went up (on Shakespeare) and considering how little time is left for training during the many urgencies of playing repertory, most are green still.
>
> As this *Oedipus* reminds us. Gerry Bamman, for instance, has been able to handle standard realism well. Here, as the exceedingly dispirited leader of the chorus, his inflections remain so realistically pitched that you half expect him to beg a cigarette of the next Theban he meets. Michael Gross, his Tiresias done up in a beard that rather suggests John Barrymore as the younger Svengali, clearly does not know how to shape a long speech so that it will climb to a climax without losing variety. Richard Jamieson's Creon is harsh, rasping; an unhappy blur is made of that splendid speech in which this particular political man declares himself content to have "the privilege of power without its cares."
>
> The new translation of the play by Stephen Berg and Diskin Clay seems slanted toward a conversational quality that may be meant to help naturalistic actors over old poetic hurdles (occasional lines as prosy as "What can I do for you?" turn up). But the problem is not really to adapt the muscular, musical verse to limited actors. Surely we must do it the other way around.

The auspices of the Brooklyn Academy of Music lent much prestige and authority to the venture and raised high expectations. But the lesson seems to have been that to stage Greek tragedy requires a very experienced and well-rehearsed ensemble of actors. To be remarked, too, is the number of black players chosen to be Oedipus, to some spectators an incongruity and without precedent. In one instance a reviewer justified the casting because Oedipus was seemingly a "stranger" in Thebes. But to others that made no sense. Laius and Jocasta are white: would they have a black child? The selection of black leads surrounded by mostly white casts reflected an effort at this particular moment in Broadway's history to provide more opportunities for black members of Equity, especially in leading roles, though sometimes this was at the expense of plausibility. The classics were good vehicles for this. Shakespearean productions were similarly peopled with black courtiers who were conspicuously in attendance on English kings. As an institution, Actors Equity consistently sought to be in the forefront of political and social liberal movements.

Two years after having been exposed to Robert Hall's production of the *Oresteia* in English, audiences at the Athens Festival were given an *Oedipus Rex* in German, classically performed by a company from that country (1985).

American theatre-lovers who had an abiding interest in the Athenian tragedies but who had been somewhat frustrated by the visits of Minotis and Volkankis offering *Oedipus* in – to them – an unintelligible modern Greek, had two more chances to experience first that play and then the full trilogy when they were broadcast on television in English. From London, on film, came a vivid interpretation of the ill-fated ruler of Thebes by Keith Michell. Australian-born, Michell was a long-time member of the Old Vic (and, before that, of the Young Vic), had essayed a wide range of Shakespearean roles at Stratford and been artistic director of the Chichester Festival where this *Oedipus* was initially staged (1973–4). Highly versatile, he also played in musical comedy and appeared in a television series as Henry VIII and a host of other parts, varying from Abelard, the monastic lover of the nun Heloise, to a shrewd, dapper ex-convict turned insurance-claim investigator. The showing of this Oedipus, quite unfairly, was not accorded much attention.

The complete *Theban Plays*, which followed in 1988, also got little notice, though the cast was a remarkably strong one, comprising Michael Pennington as Oedipus, Claire Bloom as Jocasta, John Gielgud (now Sir John) as Tiresias, John Shrapnel as Creon and Cyril Cusack as a Theban citizen. The aged king in *Oedipus at Colonus* was portrayed by Anthony (also now Sir Anthony) Quayle, and the title role in *Antigone* was assigned to Juliet Stevenson. All of these were major players, most of them of international stature; even so, the three plays were broadcast in New York City on Sunday afternoons, not on prime time (though elsewhere on Friday nights), in sequence, one play on each of the three Sunday matinées. The translation was by the director, Don Taylor. The host and commentator was Michael York, a well-known film actor. The project was a collaboration between the BBC, the South Carolina Educational Television Network and Films for the Humanities Incorporated. The producer, Louis Marks, declared that what was sought was an effect of "timelessness". He elaborated: "The whole thrust of the thing is to show these plays as fresh today as they were over two thousand years ago. We wanted to get beyond the preconceived idea of people in Greek plays wearing long bathrobes and moaning incessantly." Taylor's translation made use of "a modern idiom, but is absolutely accurate", said Marks in a telephone interview with Eleanor Blau of the *New York Times.* The set, by David Myerscough-Jones was a "spare, misty arena outside the gates to the king's palace". Costumes, by June Hudson, were a mixed lot from several historical periods: "elegant Empire gowns for Jocasta, barrister robes for the chorus – Victorian cutaways, with black cloaks – a white silk suit for Oedipus, a kind of World War I uniform for Creon", all meant to look "indeterminate". At first glamorous in his tailored white attire, "the ideal hero", Oedipus is later reduced to appearing in rougher clothes as his faults are discovered.

In his review, John J. O'Connor, television critic of the *New York Times*, wrote: "The concept works. *Oedipus the King*, unfolding like some eternal mystery, is powerful. Its characters are archetypes embedded in our psyches, filling us with wonder even as we shudder. And the cast is about as good as you'll get nowadays." But not all critics and viewers shared O'Connor's ready acceptance of these radical stylistic choices.

What was called a "dance opera", epically scaled by Ellen Stewart, *Mythos Oedipus* (1988), written and directed by her and based on Sophocles' play with "added material", was staged first in Greece and shortly thereafter in New York at her La MaMa ETC, an Off-Off-Broadway drama centre fervently dedicated to avant-garde theatrical experiments. An unusually large number of artists worked in tandem with Ellen Stewart on this offering: it had a score by Elizabeth Swados, Sheila Dabney, Genji Ito, David Sawyer and Michael Sirotta; the musical direction was by Dabney and Sirotta; the choreography by Min Tanaka, Manhong Kang, Maureen Fleming Odo and the ensemble; the design by Jun Maeda; the costume design by Eiko Yamaguchi; and the masks by Gretchen Green. The aim was to create "an exalted vision of the triumph of suffering over fate and to compel an audience to approach the well-known story with a fresh imagination". This "dance opera" was repeated the next year and coupled with another piece, *Dionysus Filius Dei* (1989), a wordless work except for a minimal vocal score by Elizabeth Swados. Added to the previous cast was the twenty-two member Great Jones Repertory Company. For this, the choreography was by Stewart and participants of her group; the set design was by David Adams, Mark Tambella, Watoku Ueno and Stewart herself; the costumes by Sally J. Lester; the masks by Stephen Loebel; and the Greek translation of the vocal parts by Eleni Petratos. Many of these persons also had acting roles; John Kelly was Dionysus.

Of this double programme D.J.R. Bruckner observed in the *New York Times* under the heading "Dancing Divinities":

> What eludes the eye often escapes comprehension and baffles the emotions. . . . The god Dionysus is especially seductive to actors and playwrights since, historically, theater in the West either developed out of the Dionysian cult or grew up alongside it. But the many stories about and reference to this often terrifying god that are scattered through ancient literature are not widely known now, and in *Dionysus Filius Dei* they are not explained or given a dramatic structure at all; in one long sequence we are taken on a tour of Dionysus' progress through eight kingdoms as he drives people to orgies of lust and madness, but we are given no hint about how his bloody adventures inspired a powerful sinister religion or how they lead to his apotheosis at the end.
>
> There are some spectacular scenes in this piece; the appropriately barbaric music is haunting; and at times the sensuous energy of the dancing suggests the frightening and orgiastic power the ancients said Dionysian ceremonies had.
>
> But there is entirely too much mystery here. This version of the legends omits the most dramatic story of the god: eventually Apollo, the god of reason, accepted Dionysus into his own temple and from this union rose the tension underlying much of Western art and philosophy. Miss Stewart's play has some emotional power – none of the ancient Dionysus myths is innocent, after all – but the hero here is Dionysus before he was drawn into the Apollonian circle of light, and at the end he remains only what he was at the beginning: a shadowy alien.

The cruellest aspects of the ancient story are exploited in *Oedipus*, a one-act opera by Wolfgang Rihm, its libretto drawn from Sophocles by the composer, a work that had its American debut in an open-air performance by the Santa Fe Opera company (1991) in Arizona. To the *New York Times* its rain-soaked senior music critic sent this report:

> Tragedy has become a lost word in modern usage. A child dies of illness. A mother is hit by a car. These are calamities, senseless. Tragedies inspire awe. They deal with superior people who are in the end humbled by forces greater than they, and make audiences ponder the mysterious contradiction of free will upon which a preordained fate has been superimposed.
>
> In Wolfgang Rihm's *Oedipus*, life is hell – literally. Its collection of grotesque oppressors and humiliated victims walk over a stage that glows red like oversized coals. Played here Wednesday on a wet desert night, this eighty-minute exercise in unpleasantness – drawn from the Sophocles play and from German commentaries on it – turns tragedy into derangement, malice and pornographic violence.

Mr Rihm's uninterrupted exposition begins with Oedipus's confrontation with the Sphinx, played in concert by four women. The rest is a collage of solemn flashback, private lamentation and personal injury. The Shepherd is tortured with a chainsaw. Jocasta hangs herself and dangles for our edification. Two streams of blood spurt when Oedipus blinds himself. At the end Creon drives him away in mad fits of sadism.

What are the Germans up to? Where is the confident megalomania of Wagner, the stern sureties of Brahms? George Grosz and Kurt Weill at least saw the funny side of their subjects. Thomas Mann's severe eye was accompanied by a reverence for civilization.

This *Oedipus* – like Henze's *We Come to the River* heard here in 1984, like the update of Gluck's *Orfeo* brought to the Brooklyn Academy of Music last season, like so much of the art and writing from this part of the world – harbors, on the other hand, a humorless disgust for all things alive. There is little tragedy in the relentless assault on the dignity of man; indeed on its end of the emotional spectrum. Mr Rihm's horrors are as absurd as the sweet excesses of Walt Disney's *Bambi*, and for the same reasons.

The Santa Fe Opera produces these horrors with considerable aplomb. Mr Rihm, moreover, is a composer with resources. His angular music uses layers of wind choirs, acid percussion and barren timpani strokes to establish his moods. He makes hollow amplification into a legitimate sonority, like a mute applied to brass instruments.

Much is spoken or chanted antiphonally from loudspeakers on either side of the audience. In this format Carol Borah Palca's English translation comes through. From the stage, few words are understandable.

Bruno Schwengi's sets and costumes observe the trend toward merging periods into a jumbled and timeless universality. His men are shaved bald. Women are hags, Craig Miller's lighting is cruel brilliance and shadow.

The vocal lines move along hard, flat surfaces. Emily Golden's Jocasta is particularly strong. Rodney Gilfry and David Rampy attack the roles of Oedipus and Creon aggressively. Tiresias is William Dooley. George Manahan's musicians may have been distracted by the wetness of this exposed theater on Wednesday, but handled difficult music sufficiently.

Apart from the North American tour by Minotis in *Oedipus at Colonus* (1976) and the run of the Breuer–Telson adaptation of Sophocles' valedictory work as an African-American oratorio, *The Gospel at Colonus* (1988), this work had few revivals during these years, except when it was included as the middle panel of the *Theban Plays*. Much the same was true of the *Antigone*; it capped the trilogy wherever that was given, but there were comparatively few stagings of it as an independent play. But there was another reason for this: almost everywhere, theatre groups found Anouilh's updated version (1944) more relevant and appealing, especially in the immediate post-Second World War period. As has been noted, the Anouilh adaptation had world-wide popularity, especially on college campuses – with the simplicity of its setting and costumes it was admirably suited to stagings there and commended itself as being "modern" while having a classical theme that won it approval in academe; indeed, a perfect fit.

Another topicalized version of *Antigone* is that with a Marxist bias by Bertolt Brecht, which had its début in Kur, Switzerland (1948). Its basis is Hölderlin's almost word-for-word German translation of Sophocles' script; however, Brecht takes great freedom with Hölderlin's rendering of the play's brittle dialogue. Hölderlin himself subtly alters Antigone's attitude towards her governing deities. Whereas Sophocles has her declare, concerning her resolve to defy Creon and bury her slain brother, "It is not Zeus who laid this duty on me," Hölderlin has her state, "my Zeus did not forbid my doing it". Brecht omits the religious aspect of Sophocles' drama altogether. The conflict of values is presented wholly in human terms, as an opposition of political forces.

As summarized by Pierre Biner in *The Living Theatre*, a history of the experimental New York troupe headed by Julian Beck and his wife Judith Malina,

> Eteocles is a "good soldier" who fights for Thebes, without concern for matters beyond that. Polynices is a deserter who refused to fight in a war that seemed unjust to him; he flees upon seeing Eteocles' body trampled upon by the warriors' horses. Creon has been ruling for some time, and the war is being waged for possession of the iron mines of Argos. It is an economic war; he who has iron, has arms. In his prologue to the play, Brecht depicts another Antigone, another Ismene, in Berlin, 1945, finding their brother dangling from a butcher's hook in the street. . . . [The dread Nazi SS has punished him for desertion.] In the author's mind the prologue could be replaced by something else: slide projection, etc.
>
> Brecht leaves Eurydice out of his version, but unlike Sophocles, he appends the story of Megaros, Creon's second son, and makes him die in battle. Antigone is neither a heroine nor a revolutionary in Brecht's adaptation; what she does is just, but she does it too late. She ought to have opened her eyes sooner, as others ought to have opened theirs. She buries Polynices, because Creon's law is human law, therefore it may be broken by humans. Brecht's *Antigone* is the tragedy of "too late". The chorus is

turned into the elders of Thebes by Brecht; they accept Creon's deeds by their silence. Towards the end, when they can no longer ignore the catastrophe Creon has brought upon them, they abandon him. But it is too late by then, for the catastrophe is their own extermination.

The essential element in Brecht's version is the transposition of the divine aspect into a political one. This does not mean, however, that all irrational residues have been filtered out. The gods may have vanished, but Antigone's consecrated devotion has been preserved, along with the very obscured myths related by the author, the mystery of which was liked by Brecht, who seems to have made up some myths of his own, like "the brothers of Lachmyia" (verse 547), which are totally unknown in Greek or world mythology.

Thirteen years later, while on a side trip to Athens during the Living Theatre's first European tour (1961), Beck and Malina came upon a copy of Brecht's play; the book contained the text, the author's stage directions and photographs of the Swiss staging. They were attracted to it at once, since it celebrated "civil disobedience", their fervent cause.

With great care, Judith Malina translated its free verse into English. The script was revised several times before rehearsals began. Only a few cuts and changes were made, save that the prologue was reduced to pantomime with sound effects.

Biner recounts:

> During Brecht's rehearsals for the première of the play in Kur, the actors who were put at his disposal, except for the great Helen Weigel, had only the slightest experience with the technique of "distancing" that Brecht invented. Accordingly, he devised a sort of connective text for the rehearsals; an actor announced what was happening and thereby was prevented from counting on the element of surprise in interpreting his role; the "distancing" defused the action in advance and emphasized the mythological, archaic, and historical aspects of the characters.
>
> The Living Theatre distributed this text among a number of actors who recited it in the language of the audience, in the clearest and most didactic manner they could achieve.

Their stage was bare; the lighting was concentrated on wherever the action was occurring: Thebes (the stage); Argos (the apron and/or the auditorium). The whole cast, of more than twenty, was always on stage or in the auditorium as the action required. The actors wore everyday attire: "mostly undershirts, blue jeans, gym shoes or no shoes at all". Antigone was dressed in a sleeveless black shirt and black slacks, which helped to conceal that she was pregnant. After the birth of her child she continued to use the same costume. There was no curtain, and no props.

> When a seat for Tiresias was called for, an actor would lie down on his back, raise his backside, and provide a prop for the seer. Creon, opposite, rested on a throne formed by the Elders. When a battering ram had to be raised against Argos, two actors would lift a third with flexed muscles above their heads, and move him in the manner of a steam hammer. Antigone walked on the back of a crouched actor – a slave – it is said that she, too, "has eaten bread baked in humble ovens", thereby acquiescing in the iniquity of Thebes' social structure.
>
> The sound effects were constant and varied, produced entirely by the actors' voices and bodies. An actor punctuated the rhythm of a dance of Bacchus for three-quarters of an hour by clacking his tongue and slapping his palm against his thigh. At times, the sounds were imitative: wind, waves, the subdued breaths of sleep; at times analogical: Hindu or Gregorian chants. One might say, with Judith Malina, that the production was "staged with total sound".

As conceived by Brecht, many events in the play were not shown but merely reported: the battles, the slaying of the brothers, the interment of Eteocles and death of Polynices, Antigone's reburial of the corpse. Malina's evocation of the mythical sources of her inspiration were also only recited. As done by the Living Theatre, all these were mimed, even the most obscure choral passages.

> The actors turned themselves into pliable plastic. They descended into the auditorium three times. In these incursions, they pantomimed the fatal battle between the brothers, and then raised a choric chant about man's propensity for evil, while lifting their arms in curves as if to embrace the audience, and lastly they emitted a rambling, hollow sound from time to time, upon the death of Megaros, who had been in the audience throughout, as if to indicate that the events unfolding on the stage were but the visible surface of a deeper, permanent struggle in Thebes. . . .
>
> The verses Brecht assigns to the Elders were divided between them and the People. (The Elders were made into Creon's docile instruments. He had castrated them on stage.) Among the inhabitants of the city, there were certain citizens clever enough to become senators, without ceasing to remain members of the citizenry, in order to sustain a tyrant. Tyrants exist only in the complicity of the people, or their elected representatives, and by citizens who choose to abrogate their rights at a given moment. Creon has prevailed only by virtue of being propped up in this manner; he is but a gear, turn-

ing only because other gears are turning. This is why he was so often placed in the centre of a diffuse group of Thebans when he spoke his lines; he is a creature of many heads, a many-limbed dragon, a brittle creature who falls down more than once in the course of the play.

It would be too simple to point a finger at the guilty. The evasion of responsibility, the dissolution of a character, of an individual among the masses, is a complicity. This is also why the Bacchic celebrations of the Thebans were not interpreted as simple *joie de vivre* but – more significantly – as something communicated, controlled from a distance by Creon, the way he controlled the soldiers' movements at the beginning of the play, making them into the arms and legs of a Creon by a masturbatory caress. The people are "absent". The events in Thebes and Antigone's disobedience alarm him, but he chooses not to think further about them.

The Living Theatre declined to accuse the "most guilty" – Creon, in this case – or to spread the guilt so as to cover everyone equally; instead, it suggested various degrees of guilt. No one is blameless; if Thebes is the way it is, the fault lies neither entirely with Creon – because then the spectator would identify with the innocents, that is, everyone else – nor entirely with the Thebans. A Creon must exist in order to profit from the situation; it is easy to become a Creon.

To talk about collective responsibility is inexact. The Living Theatre dramatized precisely the responsibility of each individual, which is a different matter altogether.

While the audience was entering and seating itself, the actors advanced one by one, facing the spectators. The lights were on, both on stage and in the auditorium. The actors grouped and regrouped; their expressions were fixed and hard, all more or less alike. The intent was to have the spectators feel disquieted. There was a threatening atmosphere, a hostile environment. Eventually, the actors crouched, hid their heads in their arms and began to wail. Creon's warriors descended on Argos. The battle ended, a long silence ensued. Malina recited the first lines of Antigone's story. Ismene joined her. At the play's close, with Thebes prostrate, the devices of the initial scene were repeated: The Argives (the audience), having defeated the Thebans, made ready to exterminate them. The actors formed a line at the stage's edge. At the final words intoned by the chorus, as the applause rose, the actors cowered, terrified by their imminent destruction at the hands of the Argives. These victims were forcing the departing spectators to dwell upon the nightmarish fate of the Thebans and the meaning of "art". The members of the company retreated in terror to the rear of the stage, where they huddled petrified by fright. "What have we done?" they asked, and vanished in darkness.

Creon was portrayed as gaining his ends by violence and flattery, at times proving himself an effective military commander, at other moments talking drivel, which the inattentive masses take for wisdom. His people, not perceiving how his "good fellow" behaviour masks his ruthlessness, were otherwise almost totally preoccupied with their own petty concerns. Theirs was a "mental deformity", an overwhelming self-absorption with their own well-being. An exception was Antigone, whose thoughts are whole-heartedly dedicated to the sacred. She is inspired by the legends of ancient heroes who by sacrifice attained a holy death. As Biner puts it: "She lets herself be intoxicated by this arrogant pride, but soon seizes hold of herself – a determined little girl who does not want to be indebted for her own death to anyone or anything, except herself. She is anarchistic and she encourages anarchy; her fault is that she is too late."

There have been too many delays; the time for recovery is exhausted. Biner quotes André Bonnard, who in *La Civilisation grecque* says, "The existence of Antigone is what constitutes the promise and exigency of a new society, remade by the measure of man's freedom."

The Living Theatre turned to many sources for its physical imagery, for the most part from archaic sculpture and painting, especially that displayed on vases and friezes, including Egyptian bas-reliefs. But they went even further afield, borrowing iconic effects from Roman columns – here "composed of three dead bodies", suggesting that such commemorations of "triumphs" were built of the slain who had given their lives to protest war, as had Polynices, Antigone and Haemon – and even from carved North American Indian totem poles. Antigone, having knelt to scrape up the dust, carried it in her mouth to the place where she sprinkled it over her brother's corpse. "Each gesture of spreading it is accompanied by a mournful intake of breath ('haaa . . .'), because the life of the body communicates itself to the dead matter. Antigone's gesture is a representation of Polynices' resurrection in the form of a revolutionary impulse: She gives 'life' to Polynices by rebelling, as she gives 'life' to the dust she deposits in her mouth."

Brecht retained certain ambiguous details from Sophocles,

> such as the guard's terrified report that Polynices' body had been buried, although no footprints, wheel-marks, or signs of tools could be found, that it had been done by someone neither human nor animal. Who could have committed the act? The Living Theatre found the solution in a phantom – Antigone's phantom, her "double". During his report, the guard raises Antigone by the waist, she places her feet upon his, and in this position he walks her to Polynices' body. Her eyes are widened, her mouth forms an O. She enacts a series of mysterious gestures over the body, thereby illustrating the guard's secret thought: A phantom has done it. Then she exclaims, "Stop that," aimed at Creon, who does not like

> nonsense, and runs off emitting the sound – "rrrrr . . ." – of a little girl committing a prank. As she runs off she touches the trembling Thebans as a child would touch the poles of a fence, rattling them as she scoots by. The spell is broken.

Brecht's script does not call for Polynices' body to be in evidence, but the Living Theatre had an actor lying rigid in full sight for two hours. Malina described him as "the magnetic pole" of the play, the proof of Creon's injustice and errors, the cause of Antigone's and her lover Haemon's defiance. It is also a warning of the death that impends for Thebes. "Carried by Haemon and Antigone, Polynices 'lives', because he said 'No' to death, because his revolt generated the revolt of others. The Living Theatre is proclaiming the primacy of life, for between Creon and Polynices the dead one is not the one who lost his life."

Much of the symbolism and significance of the production was imparted to Biner by Julian Beck and Judith Malina through interviews. *Antigone* remained in the Living Theatre's repertory. (A fuller explanation of Brecht's theories and practices, and the eventful history of the Living Theatre, requires more space than is available here.)

Budapest was treated to two *Antigones* in a single decade, the first put on at the Deryne Theatre (1962) where it was staged by Laszlo Kertesz, with a translation into Magyar by Gergely Csiky. The tragic heroine was duly young, even girlish, blonde, touchingly earnest; her powerful antagonist, Creon, surly, black-bearded, his expression lowering. The second offering, using a new translation by Imre Trencsény-Waldapfel, was mounted by György Várady at the Cave Theatre Fertörákos (1971). Here the dark-robed chorus was reduced in numbers to a mere five, with unusually full white beards and moustaches, and the director relied on lighting – deep shadows often surrounded the characters – for dramatic effect. Antigone was dressed in virginal white, her threatening uncle in a black garment with white piping and a black headband, so that the visual confrontation was clearly externalized as one between darkness and light.

Quite conventional was the *Antigone* presented by the Lincoln Center Repertory Company and directed by John Hirsch in New York City (1971). The senior drama critic of the *New York Times*, Stanley Kauffmann, had this thoughtful assessment of it:

> The *Antigone* of Sophocles was Hegel's ideal of tragedy, and I'm not about to quarrel with him, although I expect to go to my grave without deciding whether *Antigone* or *Oedipus Rex* is the best play ever written. *Antigone* is the great work about choice (the conscious), *Oedipus* the great work about fate (the

unconscious). Hegel esteemed the former because *Antigone*, which was 440 years old when Christ was born, epitomized for him the human condition as he saw it around him. He saw that the conflict between men is not between good and evil (how many men are consciously evil?) but between opposing visions of good. People behave according to what they take to be truth, not according to what they take to be falsehood, but each man's view of truth is necessarily partial. And each man takes his partial truth for the whole. Hence our disasters.

Creon, though hot-tempered, is a king obeying tradition, law, and the duties of kingship, rigorously free of favoritism to his family. Antigone obeys the obligation of sacred family ties at the expense of law and continuity and peace. Their conflict kills Antigone and Creon's son, affianced to Antigone, and Creon's wife, and it ruins Creon; yet which side was (in Hegel's terms) without spiritual value? The issue here is the burial of a dead rebel, but it is prototypical of virtually every divisive issue in human affairs. If Creon had wavered, it would have been corruption to him; if Antigone had wavered, it would have been corruption to her. The play ends with Creon desolate and repentant, seeing that the truth he thought whole was only partial. But if he had spared Antigone and condoned her law-breaking, she might well in time have come to see that her own truth was limited.

The chief conceptual defect of John Hirsch's production is that it takes sides from the beginning, thus subverting Hegel (let alone Sophocles!). Creon is fierce, Antigone is fine, and that is more or less that. A heroine and a heavy are created, in post-classic sentimental vein.

There are some other flagrant faults. Although Charles Cioffi speaks well as the chorus leader, most of the chorus members are dreadful and are badly managed by Hirsch. The choruses become a posing, patched-up bundle of interludes, nothing choric at all about them in speech or movement, quite unlike the choruses staged by Michael Cocoyannis and Alexis Solomos elsewhere.

The setting is a huge frieze by Douglas W. Schmidt with gigantic figures that have pieces missing from them. Does Schmidt think that the Greeks *erected* ruins?

But there are assets. The translation by Dudley Fitts and Robert Fitzgerald is springy and live, immediate yet not vernacular. The music by Lukas Foss sounds Greek. Almost nothing is known of ancient Greek music, so if it sounds Greek, it's Greek. The costumes by Jane Greenwood have good, thick, sculptural feeling.

As Antigone, Martha Henry shows intensity and intelligence. Her face is notably undistinguished, but her voice pounds with some force. (Tandy Cronyn, the Ismene, has an excellent theater face but an undeveloped voice.) Henry has little fire or commanding stature, but in a modestly competent, resident-theater way, she gives a credible, clear performance.

> Many have said that Philip Bosco overdoes Creon, that he starts too high. Academically, that's true. But the part has apparently been designed by the director as a villain of sorts, and Bosco is fulfilling the design. The really astonishing thing about his performance is that, though he does start high, he doesn't run down; he can sustain it. I can't think of many other American actors who have Bosco's vocal range and stamina, or his feeling for style. Here is an actor who can be a king without silly pomp, who knows how to carry in his dead son's body and lament over it. Bosco lacks certain refinements of artistic intelligence, particularly in realistic drama; his performance in *An Enemy of the People* this year was almost monotone. But he is one of the few Americans really at home in classic and romantic drama. (What a curse!)

A decade elapsed, and then New York had an *Antigone* at Joseph Papp's Shakespeare Festival (1982), which despite its name consistently put on plays by authors of all periods, from antiquity to the present. The direction was entrusted to Joseph Chaikin, who had gained a reputation for earnest and original work. The producer, Joseph Papp, who presided over a large complex of theatres devoted to experimental ventures – some accepted as inspiring and substantial, others viewed as incomprehensibly eccentric – explicated in a *New York Times* interview that *Antigone* "is certainly a political play. A play about the abuse of power and resistance to abuse of power. That's the literal part. But even more important, it deals with things that have to do with fate. It has a chorus that comments on what's right and what's wrong. So, in a certain sense, this is an abstract play in the finest meaning of the word. I feel good about it." What impressed him most was that *Antigone* was both abstract and literal at the same time. "I don't go out of my way to find abstract plays. I don't plan things this way. I don't even know I'm doing abstract plays until I've done four or five of them and see they're the same. . . . The basic line of this theater hasn't changed, you know. This theater has always had a social character. I give it that character because I'm a social character."

Frank Rich, who had now become the new senior drama critic of the *New York Times*, did not concur with Papp's and Chaikin's perception of what message Sophocles' tragedy should stress, nor how it should be put on.

> As staged by Joseph Chaikin at the Public Theater's Martinson Hall, *Antigone* is a classic, all right – a classic howler. The laughs begin as the lights go down, when we hear a strangled offstage scream that sounds like an outtake from a grade-Z horror movie. The climax comes roughly seventy minutes later when the wizened old chorus leader surveys the wreckage of the house of Oedipus and asks, in

a Mel Blanc accent, "*Whoever* thought it would come to *this*?"

Whoever, indeed? One hates to laugh at the expense of Mr Chaikin who can create such imaginative theater pieces out of contemporary texts. But what in the gods' names was he thinking of this time? According to a program note, he views Sophocles' play as "a political tragedy", but even a reductivist reading of *Antigone* isn't served by this cavalcade of poor acting, banal language (courtesy of a new translation by John Chioles) and directorial hijinks.

The silliness knows few bounds. Hearing that Antigone is going to defy Creon, Ismene reacts with much eye-rolling and a petulant, teen-age sing-song – as if Antigone had just announced her intention to cut her bangs, not risk her life. When the messenger tells Creon of Eurydice's demise, the announcement "Your wife is dead" is made with the offhand diffidence of a department-store clerk refusing to accept a personal check. This doesn't prevent the king, played with nonpareil hamminess by the often reliable F. Murray Abraham, from dropping to the ground in a drooling tantrum befitting a child who has just stubbed his toe. By then you, too, may be on the floor.

Speaking of drooling, there is also Priscilla Smith – a female Tiresias who quite literally spits out her prophecies. She appears with a young boy who signs her lines – and never mind that the prophet is blind, not deaf. The attempts at mime don't end there. Let there be a reference to the ripping of clothes, and the cast will tear at its breasts. Upon telling us that "Creon began to run," a messenger breaks into a paroxysm of jogging that, thanks to his heavy boots, reduces the rest of his speech to a Theban clog dance.

As you can see, Mr Chioles's translation is flat at best – and at worst a cornucopia of clichés (Creon: "Whatever I touch comes crashing down") and tortured English ("Antigone was caught openly in the act of defying the law"). Lest we miss Sophocles' nascent feminism, Mr Chioles usually uses the word "person" as a substitute for "woman" (but not for "man"). The poetry, among other aspects of the text, has vanished – which is just as well. The singing chorus of elders fractionalizes and garbles its group recitations, all the while swaying about like the doddering witches' coven in *Rosemary's Baby.*

Mr Chaikin's idea of heightening the "political" content of the drama is to have his cast accent the relevant buzz words, most especially "power." Yet the play isn't just an unequivocal struggle between a saintly individual and an evil state; Antigone and her uncle are both trapped in a somewhat ambiguous moral universe. To heighten the tragedy, the director also emphasizes the more emotive words ("anguish," "sorrow," "grief") – usually with guttural gasps and shrill cries that sound less like primal screams than strangled catcalls.

The intention often seems to be a rip off Peter Brook, to which end Sally Jacobs has contributed

> a gray expanse of a set and Richard Peaslee some wan bird music. But the actors don't have the technique required to do the stylized tricks and, in any case, Mr Chaikin has ladled his borrowed conceits onto the play arbitrarily and externally. His more acrobatic staging notions – Creon relentlessly circles the Guard, Tom-and-Jerry fashion – are so clumsily executed that they add unintentional visual slapstick to the aural gags. We also get a blast of electronic buzzing, no doubt piped in from Richard Foreman's *Three Acts of Recognition* at the neighboring Anspacher.
>
> Though Mr Abraham may be the most unprepossessing ruler ever to tempt the fates, his Creon is at least consistent: he swallows words when he's shrieking and he swallows words when he deigns to speak like a human being. At all times, he's an expert handwaver. Among the rest of the cast is the talented Lisa Banes, who might be a decent Antigone if given a chance, and, in the chorus, no less than Ronnie Gilbert of the Weavers. Even their serious efforts can't impede what is surely the most perversely jolly romp through theatrical antiquity since last Fall's Elizabethan-disco musical *Marlowe.*

(Mel Blanc was a film comic, best known for doing voice-overs for animated cartoons. The Weavers were a popular singing group. Murray Abraham went on to considerable esteem as an actor, receiving an Academy award for his portrayal of Salieri in the film version of *Amadeus.* The Tom-and-Jerry reference is to an animated cartoon series. The adjacent Anspacher Theatre was part of the complex of auditoriums managed by Joseph Papp, and the *Three Acts of Recognition* occupying it was by a contemporary German playwright, Botho Strauss, with direction by Richard Foreman.)

Only two years passed before Sophocles' play was on the stage of the La MaMa ETC once again, but this time in a most remarkable guise, for now it was the *Yup'ik Antigone* (1984), adapted by 33-year-old David Hunsaker, a kayak maker, musician and writer from Juneau, Alaska. He had noticed a marked affinity between the themes and rhythms of Inuit (Eskimo) legends and classic Greek tragedies. He was inspired to retain many features of the Antigone story, especially its strong motifs of revenge and defiance, while replacing many other aspects of it with local references. This done, he assembled a company of four players, all of them residing in Toksook Bay, a tiny Bering Sea village of 450 on an island off the Alaskan west coast. Of the four players, only one had ever been off the island, and that one only to Bethel, a mainland town of 3,500 people. Hunsaker chose Toksook Bay because its inhabitants still performed their ancient dances and passed on their native legends. "We wanted a place where the culture was still very much alive, not a place where there were just a few elders who remembered a few old songs," he told a *New York Times* correspondent. Hunsaker himself was not an Inuit. For the traditional Greek chorus he substituted Inuit dancers and chanters in fur-trimmed parkas who were cued by throbbing sealskin drums. The names of Greek deities were changed to those of Inuit gods. Hunsaker's intention was to have the players speak English, but the elders of Toksook Bay overruled him, requiring that the play be in Yup'ik, one of the two native tongues used in Alaska. For comprehension by spectators, a storyteller synopsized the ensuing action at the start of each scene. Having won sponsorship and a grant of $46,000 from an oil company, the Atlantic Richfield Foundation, an enterprise in the region, and enthusiastic approval from the elders of Toksook Bay after his agreement to use Yup'ik, Hunsaker organized his project. As reported to the *New York Times*:

> The native women made the costumes, fashioning stage parkas out of canvas and attaching fox pelts as ruffs. They beaded hats and sewed sealskin into *mukluks*, or Eskimo boots. The village men translated an English version of *Antigone* into Yup'ik. Men and women debated which songs and legends should be used and taught the cast of young people those they did not know.
>
> On audition night, everyone in town showed up. Mr Hunsaker chose two high school students, a seal trapper, and a recent university graduate with a degree in sociology as his players. The four shared all the roles in the play. A third high school student was signed on as stage manager.
>
> The Eskimo cast has no trouble understanding the heart of the drama – Antigone's determination to see her fallen brother properly buried despite an edict from the King that he be left to be eaten by dogs. "There are some tragic Yup'ik stories, legendary stories, that were told about the revenges and the terrible things that happened among the old villages," said Theresa John, a 27-year-old member of the cast.

The troupe toured to four Alaskan cities, then accepted an invitation to appear at the Biennial Theatre of Nations Festival in Nancy, France, and then had its booking at La MaMa; the travel was facilitated by an added grant from the Atlantic Richfield Foundation of $80,000. Worried about the food that they might encounter, the cast brought with them a quantity of dried seal meat and a jar of seal oil.

Jennifer Dunning, a dance critic of the *New York Times*, attended the first of twelve performances at La MaMa.

> *Yup'ik Antigone* may be one of the most powerful and challenging of the many adaptations in which Sophocles' drama has been presented. Though it is not without a problem or two, it combines Greek legend with Eskimo myth and ritual for theater of simple grandeur.

The bare-boned acting and story-telling evoke the long, cold nights, violent seas and ice floes, and danger of life ashore in Toksook Bay, the small island fishing village that is the home of the production's four actors. The rituals and myths of Toksook Bay prove to be surprisingly similar to the Greek legend from which Sophocles drew his play.

Yup'ik Antigone unfolds in a handsome set designed by Bill C. Ray. Rearing tusks, painted with hieratic hunting figures, suggest a portal to the spirit world. Hanging on wires across the stage are traditional masks created by Patrick Fisher, themselves worth a trip to the theater. They are plucked unceremoniously and worn as the plot demands. Creon, King of Thebes, carries a harpoon, and the characters are dressed in parkas, fur-trimmed and beaded hats and boots.

The scene is set by taped narrative and poetry written by David Hunsaker, who developed the production. Spoken in English, the words juxtapose nicely colloquial narrative with haunting poetry that offers mood-setting Eskimo myth. The poetry is spoken affectingly by Martina Woods.

Look up at the sky, she murmurs hoarsely, and see the green lights made by the snowshoes of Raven, the god who created the whole world but then left man alone in this dangerous and unclaimed place. "The most submissive dogs learn to love the harness best," Creon thunders at Antigone, ordering her death after she buries her warrior brother against Creon's wishes.

The ninety-minute production unfolds in smooth-flowing segments. Each advance of the plot is preceded by changed song and subtly ritualistic dance, in which the actors accompany themselves on drums, with additional accompaniment from two Toksook Bay elders who sit at the side of the stage and watch the proceedings.

It was the village elders who insisted on the actors speaking the language of the Yup'ik Eskimo. Its sound, together with the actors' stark, pure playing style, is off-putting at first. Though the heroine's name has a fine spitting ring to it – *"antikonigh"* is how it sounds – the speech sounds relatively uninflected to ears accustomed to the vivid modulations of New York English. But patience is rewarded by the play's slow but steady build to a stunning ritual climax.

The Eskimo actors play many roles but are seldom recognizable from character to character. Darlene Sipary's Antigone is a strong young woman; her Aanaq (Eurydice) suggests that the Toksook Bay high school student has impressive dramatic presence. Paul C. Moses, the young trapper who plays Creon, makes a stern, forbidding tyrant. James Asuluk, another village student, stands out as a sullen, stunned young Haemon, Antigone's fiancé and Creon's son, as a coarse and zany sentry, and as a shaman Angalkuq (Tiresias) of great dignity. Theresa John, a sociologist, is compelling as Antigone's troubled, sympathetic sister.

This entry was further testimony of the diverse ways in which Sophocles' tragedy could be interpreted, the richness and depth of its plot and characters.

In London, also in 1984, the National Theatre offered an *Antigone*, with Jane Lapotaire as Oedipus' heroic, self-righteous daughter. Peter Sproule was the Creon. John Burgess and Peter Gill were the co-directors. B.A. Young, in the *Financial Times*, said Lapotaire and Sproule "could not have been better". Michael Billington, in the *Guardian*, asserted that the production was "gripping and urgent"; and Jane Edwardes, in *Time Out*, pronounced it "crisp and compelling". In general, Gill was admired as a brilliant director, his work usually outstanding for precision and clarity.

The first film treatment of *Antigone* was in Greek (*c.* 1961), the producer Sperie Perakos, and the director and scenarist George Tzavellas. The title role was taken by Irene Papas, Creon by Manos Katrakis, and most of the supporting actors were recruited from the various national theatres. The Greek Ministry of Education contributed its resources "virtually without limit", regarding *Antigone* as a cultural treasure. Exploiting the "lucidity, flexibility, motion and size" attainable on film, an element of spectacle was added, Tzavellas believing that "the Greek theatre's conceptual and structural purity, its soaring poetry, deeply human protagonists and monumental settings" were ideally suited to the new medium. It was also his conviction that "the time was ripe for bringing to vivid life on the screen the stupendous characterizations and the piercing insights into the human condition that are the hallmarks of classic Greek drama". He was resolved, however, not to be seduced by the opportunities for spectacle. His screenplay sought to "conserve the authentic text and structure of the original masterpiece and concentrate on making lucid and glowingly alive the magnificent poetry and profound humanity" of the author. In sum, Tzavellas described his goal as "entertainment in its highest form".

A decision was reached to film *Antigone* in its "historic setting as a drama taking place at the moment it was being viewed on the screen". To recreate pre-classical Thebes and the correct dress and manner of its citizens, the producers relied on ancient documents, drawings, archaic sculptures and artefacts provided by a range of government agencies. Scholars were consulted as to the most nearly precise meaning of the Sophoclean dialogue and possible nuances of the dramatic situations. For the battle scenes during the city's siege, more than 600 soldiers and 150 horses of the Royal Guard and the Army were assigned by the appropriate Ministries, with King Paul's own white steed lent as a mount for Katrakis in his role as King Creon. Much of the location shooting took place on the outskirts of Athens, particularly on a field that was said to retain the exact terrain and flora of pre-classical times. Tzavellas arranged camera angles so as not to include the Acropolis, which had not existed until long after the period of the play and was not in Thebes. One alteration of *Antigone's* original form was the handling of the chorus; much less of the story needed to be described verbally, since it could simply be shown, and while the movements of the chorus can be and often are an effective stage device they are hardly cinematic. Other means had to be evolved to carry out the chorus's usual narrative and poetic contributions.

On film, too, is *Antigone/Rites for the Dead* (1990), a work featuring the dancer and choreographer Amy Greenfield, who also directed, wrote, edited and produced it. In colour, eighty-five minutes long, it has Bertram Ross, a former Graham dancer, as both Oedipus and Creon. In her review, Jennifer Dunning of the *New York Times* found him to be a gifted actor who lent his two roles a good deal of authority and was possessed of a strong voice and a firm classical delivery. Dunning also had praise for the musical score by Glenn Branca, which she thought "highly effective until it settles into soprano whinnying toward the end". But she felt that Miss Greenfield's perspective of the drama was too limited.

> [It] opens with Antigone leading her blind father, Oedipus, into enforced exile through a green forest that brings the two to a majestic waterfall. It ends with the death of her uncle Creon, who stumbles into an equally majestic landscape of rocky cliffs after witnessing the death of Haemon, his son and Antigone's lover. Everything about the film is majestic, in fact, and that is one of its greatest problems.
>
> Ms Greenfield's strong-faced Antigone is obdurate and high-minded from the start. She has no chance to grow or change, as Janet Eilber's Ismene does so persuasively. Imaginatively, Ms Greenfield chose the Empire State Plaza in Albany to suggest the Greek city of Thebes. But its vast, white-marbled vistas are too much of a piece with the cliffs and desert where the action takes place. And the camera is unrelievedly rhetorical, too, rocking convulsively at times and zooming in, again and again, on wet, bloody or dirt-streaked flesh grappling with flesh in battle or embrace.
>
> The script and costuming are strangely casual, for no apparent artistic reason. "Of course," Antigone answers matter-of-factly when Creon tells her she must die. Many of the costumes look like dancers' studio and street clothes, and Haemon's fashionable ponytail is jarring.

A group calling itself the Irondale Ensemble Project was responsible for still another strange transformation of this great tragedy – it was staged at the Off-Off-Broadway House of Candles in New York City (1992). For the *New York Times*, Stephen Holden prepared a critique:

What could possibly connect Sophocles' *Antigone* with the art of clowning? That question is explored in considerable depth by the Irondale Ensemble Project in its iconoclastic production of the Greek drama. . . . It is also elaborated in program notes that quote from Bertolt Brecht and Joseph Campbell. Brecht praises a show he saw in which a clown banged his head, sawed off the swollen bump and ate it, as wittier than anything in the entire contemporary theater. Campbell, musing on the appeal of clowns, suggests that children see in them reflections of a primal innocence.

These ideas are rather hazily integrated into the Irondale Project's interpretation of the play, in which Creon is a circus ringmaster and Antigone a stubborn woman-child in clown whiteface. In the company's tiny performing space on the Lower East Side, several of the performers enter by descending from ropes. The seven-member Walter Thompson Orchestra plays a dissonant score that juxtaposes circusy marches with a galumphing arrangement of *The Man on the Flying Trapeze.*

The production varies in tone between a clown show with slangy interpolations and a fairly straightforward reading of pieces of the play. Terry Greiss's Creon veers between a twinkly, avuncular ringmaster and a megalomaniacal despot. As these metamorphoses take place, *Antigone* suggests, among other things, an allegory of public life in an age when politics have become show business. The charming, faintly seedy ringmaster who welcomes the audience is the public face of power, while the vengeful monarch who against reason and decency demands the death of a disobedient subject is the behind-the-scenes reality. The Greek chorus does song-and-dance routines, and seems as fickle and susceptible to manipulation as the American populace in its responses to George Bush.

An attempted *coup de théâtre* near the end of the play turns tragedy into farce. Creon chases Antigone around the stage brandishing a knife that turns out to be a rubber stage prop. After attacking her with other fake weapons, he settles for landing a custard pie in her face.

But if that's end of the show, it's not the end of the story. Thebes becomes a plague-ridden hell piled with corpses.

The production's basic clown metaphor seems forced. But once it has been asserted, the other parallels between ancient and contemporary times fall into place.

Once more London had a look at the Theban Plays, this time as embodied by the Royal Shakespeare Company and housed in its new home, the ultra-modern Barbican Centre (1992), a complex of theatres, concert halls and cinemas. The Sophocles tragedies were presented in an auditorium designated as The Pit, and the offering was titled *The Oedipus Tragedies. Oedipus* was given in the late afternoon, at 4.30; performances resumed at 7.30, after a supper intermission, and a second intermission of twenty-five minutes preceded the third work. During the previews the order of the plays alternated, so that each drama served as a starter in turn, allowing the spectator to take in the trilogy less arduously, a single play at a time.

The chorus, masked, was conventionally attired in white. The *Guardian*'s critic found the production to be "Greek tragedy at its most compelling . . . music, movement and speech are deftly integrated . . . the RSC firing on all cylinders". The direction was in the hands of Adrian Noble; the fresh translation of the text was by Timberlake Wertenbaker; the set designer preferred to be identified by a lone name, Ultz.

Of Sophocles' other plays, *Electra* has most often been before the public as an opera, translated into German and fashioned into a libretto by the Austrian poet Hugo von Hofmannsthal, with music by Richard Strauss; it had its début in Dresden (1909) and is in the repertory of companies throughout Europe and North America. Hardly a popular favourite, since its score is so harsh and its story so bleak, it none the less holds the boards because it is a work of high quality and great power. Otherwise, Sophocles' script has had to compete with other handlings of the identical legend by Aeschylus and Euripides; of the three, the Aeschylean version has the advantage of being an indispensable part of the *Oresteia.*

Electra, Agamemnon's vengeful daughter, stalked her prey on Hungarian stages twice during the 1960s. In 1966 the Katona Theatre, Kecskemet, enacted the gory legend of matricide, translated by Gabor Devecseri into Magyar from Sophocles' script. The work was directed by Béla Udvaros, who garbed the protagonists and antagonists in an appropriately austere black. The players were barefaced. Perhaps inspired by this production, the essayist László Gyurkó fashioned an arresting new version of the story, *Electra My Love* (1968), which enjoyed a long life at the National Theatre in Budapest, where it was done under the guidance of Béla Both and remained in the repertory for a good many years. Gyurkó saw in the legend a way to enunciate his own philosophy of historical processes. As summarized by Miklós Almási in *The Hungarian Theatre Today*, Electra alone is heroically consistent, holding implacably to her principles. Even though Orestes is supposed to be lost, she remains obsessively loyal to her resolve.

> Perhaps that faith helps Orestes to return. He comes back, makes his reckoning with Aegisthus; it has been enough that one person at least has believed in the likelihood of his reappearance. He considers his revenge to be complete; only Electra asks that no mercy be shown to the town where everyone has been in league with the usurper. Orestes, however, subscribes to belief in the educating power of historic possibility, and is convinced that men will know what to do with freedom. He will not give in to

his sister, his love, even when she is prepared to carry their argument to the breaking point. Electra must perish so that Orestes can realize his humanist aims. She fails tragically, but her name is nevertheless, or perhaps just because of that, placed on the temple wall, honouring her memory, proclaiming her an angel of loyalty, piteously a dead woman.

So strong and long-lasting was the impression made by *Electra My Love* that eventually the author was given a workshop of his own, the 25th Theatre, dedicated to politically oriented stage pieces. He revised his script to conform with suggestions put forward in the course of discussions with critics and audience members, as the play continued to provoke excited public debate. His aim was to stimulate the rethinking of history and long-held values. The spectator could become a participant in shaping the text.

Already cited, the Serban–Swados treatment of *Electra*, which was first presented in Bordeaux (1973) and then at Sainte-Chapelle in Paris, before Ellen Stewart brought it to La MaMa in New York (1974), demonstrated that it could deeply stir and sharply disturb an audience. Given as the final play on an evening's program called *Fragments of a Trilogy* – the other parts being Euripides' *Medea* and *The Trojan Women* – it exemplified new techniques in staging Greek drama, a few facets of which have been previously described. In the *New York Times* Clive Barnes began his review in this manner:

> Most of the time I write about plays, good, bad, or indifferent. Once in a while I write about the theater. It always sends shivers down the back of my typewriter. . . .
>
> The Romanian-born Mr Serban is one of the most interesting and innovative directors around anywhere in the world. He, and his vitally important musical collaborator, Elizabeth Swados, state in the program that they "have both participated in the work of Peter Brook's International Center of Theater Research, with which they feel connected in their explorations." It is a statement that is, all at once, modest, accurate and misleading. Miss Swados is Mr Brook's composer, and Mr Serban has also intervened in Mr Brook's experiments with time, place and life. Yet this trilogy, which has been brewing for more than two years, belongs entirely to them. It is a personal extension of Mr Brook's work into the layers of the theatrical unconscious.
>
> All three plays are surprisingly different in approach. And all are verbally impossible to understand. This is a non-verbal theater of aural communication. Mr Serban uses language like music. His actors talk ancient Greek, Latin, a touch of this and a touch of that, and guttural dirty. A linguist couldn't understand it, but, like anyone else, a linguist would just know what they are acting.
>
> The immediacy of Mr Serban's theater fare transcends the narrative notion of knowing what

happens in any literary sense. Mr Serban makes you feel such basic emotions as love, suffering, anguish, disgust and fear, at a level not so far removed from reality. Of course, they are in essence totally removed – no theatrical experience can duplicate, for example, the raw thrust of real pain – but that particular removal has the tincture of poetic honesty to it. Mr Serban's theater helps you to know what you think.

The plays – all rightly described as "fragments of a trilogy" – are oddly different in texture. They are all music pieces in a sense – for Miss Swados's lambently twanging music provides the cave for the performance. It is a dramatic world very much structured to its sound environment.

. . . *Electra* is a ritual of fulfillment complete with a live snake and live dove. Mr Serban is nothing, if not strong on symbolism.

This musical-dramatic trilogy is beautiful, and dedicatedly acted by its cast who make it not only touching but also credible. You have to wander through these Greek myths, remembering this and forgetting that. Put the mind on hold. Nothing, deliberately, is as explicit as fine words. Everything depends on the theatrical act, which may not be understood in any conventional literary sense, but comes upon you as a familiar of life.

The next year (1975) Mel Gussow – also of the *New York Times* – was at La MaMa to welcome a partial revival of the programme which kept the same title, *Fragments of a Trilogy*, but had now shed *Medea*.

Following a triumphant tour of Europe and the Mideast, Andrei Serban has returned to the United States with his astonishing versions of Greek classics. . . . This Romanian-born director's daringly experimental work is clearly in a class with that of Peter Brook and Jerzy Grotowski. It is nothing less than a reinvention of theater.

Euripides and Sophocles speak to us in our language (in translation) about an ancient time and timeless themes. Mr Serban's heretical response to these towering classics has been to banish words. His plays are performed in ancient Greek (and also in Latin and other unrecognizable languages), in throaty and guttural raspings that have no relevance to speech as we know it today.

What is lost is a certain specificity of character (we are not always sure who is speaking to whom), psychological shadings, and lyricism. But what is gained is immense. Mr Serban's plays are excavations deep into the human heart. In place of words are the emotions the words represent: pity, terror, anger, anguish, guilt, revenge.

Nonverbal theater has never seemed so searingly evocative. The plays communicate directly with cries, whispers, silences, looks and images.

. . . These visions would be powerful even if removed from us by a proscenium stage or in a film. Mr Serban's innovation is to turn the entire theater into a stage and to involve the action with the audience.

. . . Following a long intermission, the actors return to play *Electra.* Again we are seated – two long peninsulas of people divided by the distilled essence of *Electra.* The characters introduce themselves, their names the only words we recognize in the evening.

Electra is even more deeply symbolic and personal than *The Trojan Women.* A live dove and a live snake represent polarities. There is a draped, roving spirit of the dead Agamemnon, as well as a blind Oedipus. Axes are raised for murder. In contrast to the opening epic, this is an intimate, impacted cry of agony. The acting, particularly by Priscilla Smith as Electra, is almost unbearably intense.

At the end, with Clytemnestra and Aegisthus dead and Agamemnon revenged, the chorus surrounds Electra and rings clarion notes on individual bells – a peal of rebirth and renewal.

On opening night, Ellen Stewart, the guiding mother of La MaMa, joined the chorus with her own bell (which she customarily rings before performances). The moment was a celebration, the evening a fulfillment of Miss Stewart's monumental efforts in sustaining and expanding theater. A collaboration across countries, spanning the barrier of language, *Fragments of a Trilogy* is pure and phenomenal.

A dozen years later (1987), *Fragments of a Greek Trilogy* was brought back to La MaMa, with several members of the first cast along with new players. Once more, Mel Gussow, of the *New York Times*, greeted it with rapture and awe. To him, it was

primal theater . . . a mesmerizing evocation of pity, terror, guilt and retribution . . . its urgency and originality intact. The *Medea,* given in a basement room approached by walking through corridors-as-catacombs, was sparsely lighted by candles and done "as a kind of black mass." . . . The emotion carries the words, as Medea, knife raised, re-enacts the curse she has sworn against her husband. The narrow room becomes a wind tunnel with the drama reverberating against the walls, leading to the final moment when Medea reveals the dead bodies of the children, placing the evidence of her revenge in the hands of the horrified Jason.

The Trojan Women takes place throughout the large expanse of the Annex. Led by actors, theatergoers move through the environment as the action explodes – on rolling carts, on promontories, and, at

> either end of the theater, on elevated stages. In Mr Serban's most terrifying image, Helen is caged like a cornered beast, stripped and brutalized. The orgiastic nightmare is counterbalanced by moments of plangent lyricism, as, at the conclusion, the women of Troy are linked by ropes and sent into exile.
>
> Subtitled an "epic opera," this is the most musical of the three pieces; the wailing is orchestrated into melody. Here, as elsewhere, Miss Swados's score is inextricable from the visual and dramatic elements, accompanying the action as a kind of pulse.
>
> . . . *Electra* unfolds as the most direct and accessible of the fragments. On a long open stage, the characters introduce themselves, clicking off their names; there is no question about their individual identities or their motivations. The dramatization takes place under bright lights – in stark contrast to the blackness of *Medea.*

Priscilla Smith was once more the "impassioned" Electra, while also alternating in the role of Medea with Karen Evans-Kandel, who had a "fierce intensity". Gussow remarked that the "entire cast, children as well as adults, has been deeply indoctrinated in the Serban method, which manages to bridge two thousand years and approximate the archetypal. *Fragments of a Greek Trilogy*, the latest in a series of twenty-fifth-anniversary events at La MaMa, makes so much other current theatre seem insignificant in comparison."

The American poet Ezra Pound was an arrogant, erudite and influential figure; for a time he had been an associate of William Butler Yeats and a mentor of the youthful T.S. Eliot, and had come to be regarded an important leader of the avant-garde. During the Second World War he was living in Italy and, having strong right-wing prejudices, broadcast pro-Fascist propaganda. After the Allied victory he was arrested and found guilty of treason. Out of respect for his literary renown, he was pronounced criminally insane and confined not in a common prison but in St Elizabeth's asylum in Washington, DC; his friends and admirers continuously agitated for his release. While there, in the late 1940s, he worked on *Pisan Cantos* and translated Sophocles' *Electra*, collaborating with a classics scholar, Rudd Fleming. Three decades after he regained his freedom and returned to Italy, his unpublished and unproduced version of the play – it was titled *Elektra* – was finally enacted Off-Off-Broadway in New York by the CSC Theater, of which Carey Perloff was now the artistic director (1987).

Pound was an advocate of translating the Greek tragedies into English by a resort to colloquialisms, so that the verbal exchanges would sound like modern speech. In his *New York Times* review Mel Gussow betrayed his uneasy awareness of this bold and irreverent use of language.

The Pound *Elektra*, filled with vernacular and anachronisms, is not likely to replace existing translations, and it lacks the urgency, for example, of Andrei Serban's interpretation (in *Fragments of a Greek Trilogy*). It is both idiosyncratic and prosaic. However, it has a fascination as a minor work by a major poet, and as Ms Pamela Reed and her fellow cast members demonstrate, it is extremely actable.

In her production, Ms Perloff has approached the play as if it were a midcentury American approximation of *Marat/Sade*. Behind locked gates in a prisonlike mental home, Elektra leads us into the tragedy of the House of Atreus. The two-woman chorus could pass for prison matrons. Klytemnestra (Nancy Marchand), with a Rastafarian hair style and slit skirt, seems to have succumbed to her own kind of insanity, and the swaggering Orestes (Joe Morton) may remind one of the hero of *One Flew Over the Cuckoo's Nest*, arriving cowboy-style, to put the house in order.

Studiously reaching for informality, Pound deconstructs the dialogue from the sublime to the Ridiculous. The characters annoyingly drop their g's (as in "Now, you're talkin'") and speak like movie tough guys. Elektra is irritated by all the "yammering" and Klytemnestra by the "yattering." The daughter calls the mother "Old Big Talk," and, in a moment of anguish, the chorus cries, "God, where the hell are you, Zeus?"

When Orestes reveals his true identity to Elektra, instead of saying the customary, "Look at this signet ring that was your father's, and know if I speak true," Mr Morton looks his sister right in the eye and says, bluntly, "Here's Dad's ring." To say the least, that does not have the ring of Sophocles. One allows for the possibility that the adaptation is unfinished, that, in some of his dialogue, Pound wrote the poet's equivalent of "dummy lyrics," presumably to be replaced at a future date by something more graceful. Part of this *Elektra* is, however, intentionally amusing, as exemplified by the tutor (William Duff-Griffin) who is steeped in an Irish brogue.

In any case, the adaptation cuts to the plot and, through all the alterations in language, the character relationships and basic emotions are undimmed. Most of the actors seem capable of handling a more authentic adaptation. This is especially true in the case of Ms Reed, who conveys both aspects of Elektra's madness – her mania and her angry cry for vengeance. As she tells her brother of her plight, she is a figure of utter abandonment. Her eyes mist over, as she says in disbelief about Klytemnestra, "They say she is my mother."

Despite the character's slanginess, Mr Morton is a very credible Orestes and Ms Marchand convincingly accentuates the sensual side of Klytemnestra. Among the other supporting actors are Mr Duff-Griffin, Lola Pashalinski and Isabell Monk as the chorus and Veronica Cartwright as Elektra's surviving sister.

In the program, it is suggested that Pound identified with Elektra as a postwar prisoner unfairly confined and waiting to be rescued. If so – and the parallel is certainly questionable on political grounds – the poet did not let it interfere with his desire to retell a timeless story in modernist fashion.

Surveying the London theatre (1989), Jack Kroll of *Newsweek* took in a current mounting of a Greek classic:

> For sheer womanpower nothing beats Fiona Shaw as Sophocles' Electra. Staged by the star young woman director of the Royal Shakespeare Company, Deborah Warner, this *Electra* is as clean and simple as a ritual knife in the heart. Warner accepts the ancient Greeks' moral violence as a primal fact of human history, and Fiona Shaw embodies that furious purity with blood-curdling energy and the athleticism of a hit woman of the gods. Wearing only a tattered black tunic, she embarks on her vengeful quest against her mother, Clytemnestra (Natasha Parry), and her stepfather, Aegisthus (Gordon Case), who had murdered Agamemnon, father of Electra and her brother Orestes (Piers Ibbotson). In a Peter Brook-type set – a pit, a trickling stream that runs with blood, a huge door that vibrates with the blows of murder – Warner focuses the tragedy's matricide and regicide, making it a cideshow of thunderous impact. With her cropped hair, her falcon face, Shaw looks like a cross between Virginia Woolf and Samuel Beckett. With the power and poetry to be the next Glenda Jackson, Shaw is an arresting figure in a brilliant array of women who are moving to the center of the British stage.

(A rare word, "cide" – here it means "killer", as in "matricide" and "regicide".)

The Strauss–von Hofmannsthal opera version of Sophocles' play underwent a further transformation in a German production by Günter Krämer (1990) that was recreated by Uwe Hergenroder for the Spoleto Festival USA in Charleston, North Carolina (1992). Edward Rothstein wrote in the *New York Times*:

> There were two distinct ways to experience Strauss's *Elektra* on Friday night at the Gaillard Municipal Auditorium here.
>
> The first was to attend to the provocations of its European director Günter Krämer . . . This would have meant trying to figure out the meaning of the staging and sets: why the mythic courtyard of Agamemnon's house is supplanted here by a bare white stage lighted up like a hospital room with a scrim consisting of Venetian blinds; or why Elektra, the daughter of the murdered king, is dressed in a white running outfit; or why her mother the murderer is wrestled into a wheelchair and drugged by

attendants who look like black-suited prison camp guards, or why Elektra's sister, Chrysothemis dances about the stage like a confused teen-ager. . . .

But there was a great relief toward the opera's end when black sliding panels sealed off the set, as if in honor of Orestes' arrival; full attention could then be given to the singing. For the Elektra was the forty-three-year-old Deborah Polaski, the accomplished American dramatic soprano who in 1988 suddenly pulled out of a developing operatic career for reasons that have their own operatic character.

By her own account, God came to her in a hotel room in San Francisco, after she had sung Brünnhilde at Bayreuth, telling her to abandon her singing. After a year of silence, she felt able to return to opera without slighting what she calls her "spiritual consciousness." Engagements came through in Europe, including Bayreuth, where her career had been the strongest. . . . And here in Charleston, she brought her Elektra to life.

It is a role that for all its nearly Godless fury, Ms Polaski seemed to know intimately. She gave her voice a warm clarity, almost erotic in introspective moments; her middle range seems unusually flexible. Elektra's opening paean to her dead father was delivered with only her face visible through closed blinds; nostalgic anxiety was entirely evoked through the voice. Her welcome of Orestes was even more sensuously nuanced. When Elektra triumphantly mocks her mother, Ms Polaski created mounting intensity, less through increasing volume than through changing her voice's timbre, giving it more bite. Occasionally, when hitting high notes, she tended to harshness and a shade of sharpness as well, but this was an impressive performance.

It was all the more unusual because of the type of character the director created with Ms Polaski. Hers was not a frenzied, near-mad Elektra; until the end, she was instead the calmest one onstage, the most controlled, the most manipulative. Even at the most strenuous vocal moments, Ms Polaski kept her body relaxed and poised. There was little posturing in either the vocal or the physical sense.

The insight into character was notable in other performances as well. Helga Dernesch, as Clytemnestra, respected the limitations of her voice, now in the mezzo range, giving her lines a potent intensity through crisp articulation, singing as heightened speech. The directors had her appear as a sort of a rich decadent society lady ripe for the Betty Ford clinic for recovering alcoholics.

Katerina Ikonomu tended to be more vocally stringy and strained as Chrysothemis, though she had the difficult task of creating a character that instead of being the most conventional (as in the score) was the most crazed. Knut Skram's Orestes was virile, if a bit unexpressive; Manfred Jung as a tuxedo-dressed Aegisthus had to bear the indignity of being carried on the bare backs of six shuffling men. Spiros Argiris conducted the festival orchestra with fervent energy.

Ultimately, of course, the production itself could not be ignored. Even the opera's conclusion was radically altered: Orestes retreats into madness after killing his mother, holding her hand and rocking back and forth while Elektra retrieves the buried axe (here a meat cleaver) to slaughter herself.

But there was a shocking plausibility to those changes. The main problems were those with the attempts at conceptual drama. Elektra and her siblings were casually dressed; their elders were formal, wealthy, decadent. It was impossible to tell the difference between sanity and insanity. (Everybody has a turn behind the institutional blinds.) Along with symbolic oddities (Chrysothemis drawing a chalk *graffito* heart with Orestes' name) and textual oddities (a white-suited Elektra is described as unkempt and filthy), all this created a near-parody of German avant-garde taste. The production was rescued from itself by its respect for character and by the singers' respect for their roles. That was the way this production (which may also be seen on Tuesday and Friday) was finally experienced by its audience; the performances earned the cheers.

One would think that the play most unlikely to have many revivals in the twentieth century would be *Ajax*, in which Sophocles' hero is seized by madness; slays animals while he is under the delusion that they are his foes; then, after returning to his senses and ashamed, falls on his sword and dies. But this story, with its heap of gory details, attracted the youthful, wilfully eccentric Peter Sellars during his very brief reign as artistic director of the Kennedy Center in Washington, DC (1986). Regarded by some as a genius, and by others as a sort of *idiot savant* of the theatre, Sellars displayed his originality and singular flair for odd effects by having the adaptor, Robert Auletta, bring the work up to the present day, locating it in the precincts of the Pentagon, the US Army's vast headquarters, and casting a deaf actor, Howie Seago, in the name role, having him "speak" in sign language, his words translated by one or another momentarily on-the-scene supporting player.

Sylviane Gold, representing the *New York Times*, sent this description of what she called "Peter Sellars's reckless, impassioned staging" of the tragedy. At the opening,

> Mr Sellars, of course, dispenses with a curtain, and the stage is so dark that the lights can hardly be said to go up at all. But when the play starts, we do see a man seated at a desk with his back to the audience. He is shuffling papers. He shuffles, and shuffles, and shuffles; and even when he finally starts talking to the disembodied voice that interrupts him, he never turns to face or even half-face the audience. Mr Sellars traffics in about-face theater.

Yet, she found that even at its worst, Sellars's staging could astonish, creating a number of "inspired surprises . . . even several moments of transcendent, overwhelming beauty".

. . . As rewritten by Mr Auletta, Ajax is now an American general after a hard-won American victory in a drawn-out, Latin American war. Athena struts around in a slinky silver evening gown; the chorus of Ajax's faithful troops wears battle fatigues; and Ajax's wife, Tecmessa, is the daughter of a defeated South American dictator.

Mr Auletta has followed Sophocles' story line with great fidelity, so he's given himself a great many problems. He can't, for instance, account in any contemporary way for Athena's magical powers, so he doesn't try. She seems out of place among the uniformed personnel. And when Mr Auletta does try for a modern analogue for ancient Greek belief, substituting burial at Arlington for the all-important Greek burial rite, it hardly seems equivalent.

But the difficulties in Mr Auletta's adaptation dwindle to insignificance beside the flamboyant directorial innovations of Mr Sellars. At one point, Mr Seago, an actor of truly heroic build, is sealed in a man-sized aquarium tank, ankle-deep in sloshing blood. Furiously signing as he squeezes the blood from an organic-looking mass in his hand, Mr Seago is manhood gone murderously berserk, terrifying and terrifyingly awesome. The production reaches classic heights again when the chorus, having seen the deranged, blood-soaked general, keens a blue lamentation of heartbreaking intensity.

Such epiphanies – and that is what they are – make up for Mr Sellars's less happy inventions, which include a messenger with the tackiest white wings I've ever seen on a stage; some real confusions of action and word; and an unremittingly banal Tecmessa. About-face theater marches on.

In *Newsweek* Jack Kroll was more sympathetic:

The ancient Greek theater is the lost paradise of popular culture, a theater that was spoken, danced and sung, whose language ranged from sublimity to profanity, that scared its audience with blood and thunder and lifted them with religious exaltation. The daring Peter Sellars outdares himself recapturing much of that mix in his audacious production of *Ajax* at the Kennedy Center . . . Sellars and playwright Robert Auletta update Sophocles' tragedy from the Trojan War to the near future, after an American victory in Latin America. As in Sophocles, this version relates the consequences of Ajax's enraged assault upon his fellow generals who have slighted him. Instead he slaughters the Army's cattle, which the goddess Athena has deluded him into believing are the generals.

> Sophocles' depiction of the deranged pride that can destroy a hero is transmuted with startling power by Auletta and Sellars. The action takes place in front of the Pentagon: this becomes a potent theatrical metaphor that fuses two cultures into a timeless immediacy. Ajax's slave-consort Tecmessa has become his Vietnamese wife, played with fierce sorrow by Lauren Tom. And the chorus of Greek sailors has become a chorus of fatigue-clad GI's, led by the Robeson-voiced Ben Halley. But Sellars's most inspired move is to cast Howie Seago, an actor from the National Theatre of the Deaf, as Ajax. Seago creates a devastating, frightening, moving portrait of a shattered spirit. Not since Olivier's Oedipus has an actor come so close to the primal power of Greek tragedy.

Sellars's cast included not only a deaf actor but also whites, blacks and Asians. Interviewed by Arthur Holmberg, he explained his use of Afro-American music. He had built the choral odes on "spirituals, Mississippi moans and chain-gang chants. 'I needed music to make the chorus more lyrical. Black music is the bedrock of popular American music. Since it expresses deep sorrow, it created the right emotional context for the play.'" He added: "I return to the Greeks because it was a civic-minded theater that discussed unflinchingly serious public issues. Sophocles was not anti-military. He himself was a general. But he asks hard questions like, 'Given a military engine, how can one contain it within moral limits? At what point does justified self-defense become a lust for power?'"

Shortly after the play's run, a box-office disaster, Sellars took a year's leave of absence, from which he announced that he would return. "Absolutely." As generally assumed, however, he did not, going elsewhere to direct a modern opera. Roger L. Stevens, chairman of the American National Theater Academy, which provided some of the funds for Kennedy Center projects, was asked about the audience reaction to Sellars's tenure. "We certainly didn't do much business. You need two things in the theater, people on the stage and people in the seats. He had some ideas that just didn't work out." Irvin Molotsky and Warren Weaver, Jr, in their jointly written column, remarked that having a deaf actor in the title role of *Ajax* was "apparently too far out for Washington audiences, which stayed away".

Sophocles' *The Women of Trachis* at the Residenz-theatre in Munich (1987) portrayed the results of male brutality, both psychological and physical. A web of lies by Herakles, Lichas and Nessus entraps Deianira, the hero's wife. In one climactic episode the chorus of women ferociously turn on a soldier intent on raping them; they emasculate him. The play's message is that the unequal sharing of power between the sexes leads to an inability to feel love.

Strange pastiches continued to appear. Directed by Michael Silk, an eleven-member troupe of student actors in the Department of Classics at King's College in London put on a *Herakles*, a new verse drama contrived of portions of scripts by Sophocles, Euripides and Aristophanes. Half of the dialogue was in English, the other half in ancient Greek, as were all the songs. This hybrid work was brought to New York (1983) and presented at the Horace Mann Theater of Columbia University.

Philoctetes, with which Sophocles won a prize in his extreme old age – perhaps near ninety – is yet another painful story with diminished appeal to modern spectators. It did have a production in Brussels, however (1994).

Among the plays of Euripides, *Medea* has been consistently popular, perhaps more so than any other of his works. The mid-twentieth-century rediscovery of Luigi Cherubini's operatic version, *Médée* (1797), partly contributed to this; it was reintroduced at the Florentine Maggio Musicale (1953) as a vehicle for the remarkable Greek-American singing actress Maria Callas, and two years later in New York by the American Opera Society where the role was given to Eileen Farrell, far from famed as a dramatic interpreter but possessed of a soprano voice of "enormous range and volume". Both performers were equal to this "grand fiendish part", as a much earlier observer described it. Word spread of the great success of Callas and Farrell, and both artists toured separately with the work; it was greeted as a long-neglected masterpiece (it had, however, been kept alive in Germany); Cherubini's *Médée* abruptly entered repertoires worldwide, though often offered in concert performances rather than fully staged.

In 1984, in France, the Opéra de Lyons reached back further and put on an "exciting two-day double bill" – John Rockwell, in the *New York Times* – which included Marc-Antoine Charpentier's lyric tragedy, *Médée* (1982), by Gavin Bryars, an avant-garde British composer, in collaboration with Robert Wilson, the experimental stage director, designer and playwright. The Charpentier was being revived after three hundred years and revealed a "wonderful score", in an authentic French Baroque style. Later in the same season Opéra de Lyons also scheduled Cherubini's interpretation of the tragedy.

The five-act Charpentier work, based on Thomas Corneille's libretto, lasted four hours, and Wilson's eccentric if sometimes striking handling of it elicited whistles and jeers from a restive audience, but John Rockwell, a critic with a marked affinity to the avant-garde, found it "riveting". The Bryars–Wilson piece, also four hours in length, was based on Euripides' text, somewhat altered and adapted. It was sung in modern Greek, with a scattering of English and French phrases and a number of contemporary allusions. For both operas, the handsome period Greek costuming was by Franca Squarciapino. Rockwell's response to the new work was neither approving nor hostile; he felt that the score was somewhat conventional, lacking individuality and conviction, the vocal writing rather "faceless". Yet he acknowledged that it had moments of appeal for him. The dual programme was next moved from Lyons to Paris for a brief run at the Théâtre des Champs Elysées.

The attraction of *Medea* as a play (without music) possibly lies in its being built around a challenging role, one tempting to a major actress with a strong constitution, and its having a story of a woman who sacrifices greatly to help her husband or lover, and then is flouted and abandoned by him when he turns to a younger rival, a situation which seems to arouse latent fears in feminine spectators, while ambitious men are able to identify with the moral plight of Jason.

Richard Collier relates that in 1941, during the Second World War, Lewis Casson (later Sir Lewis) and his wife Dame Sybil Thorndyke toured Wales with a repertory of classic plays, including Shaw's *Candida* and Euripides' *Medea.* A large portion of their audience was made up of miners whose tastes surprised the actors; the miners dismissed *Candida* as "frivolous and insubstantial" and much preferred the *Medea.* "This is the play for us," one told Dame Sybil; "it kindles a fire." Another said: "There's no light pastry about this. It's good solid meat." Collier recounts: "Villagers walked miles from one valley to another to see the play again, and given this heady acclaim, Sybil was minded to exercise restraint. 'I mustn't wail too loud,' she remarked, as Medea prepared to mourn her children offstage. 'They can't see me, and they'll think it's an air-raid siren.'"

The much-gifted American poet Robinson Jeffers lived on the California coast, in a then isolated stone tower built with his own hands. From it, as he wrote, he could gaze out at the smooth or tossing Pacific. A friend and neighbour was the Australian-born actress Judith Anderson, who had been hailed for her Lady Macbeth in Maurice Evans's haunting production of Shakespeare's drama, and as the Queen in Gielgud's unforgettable *Hamlet,* as well as other stage leads in works such as O'Neill's *Strange Interlude* and *Mourning Becomes Electra,* Zoe Akin's *The Old Maid,* Chekhov's *The Three Sisters* (and later in films, especially as the sinister Mrs Danvers in *Rebecca*). For her, Jeffers now freely translated Euripides' text, and his adaptation was brought to the National Theater on Broadway (1947) with an exceptionally strong cast, the Jason being Gielgud – who also directed – and the role of the nurse taken by the hearty, robust Florence Reed.

Brooks Atkinson, the *New York Times*'s long-time senior drama critic, was there.

> If Medea does not entirely understand every aspect of her whirling character, she would do well to consult Judith Anderson. For Miss Anderson understands the character more thoroughly than Medea, Euripides or the scholars, and it would be useless now for anyone else to attempt the part. Using the new text by Robinson Jeffers, she set a landmark in the theater at the National last evening, where she

gave a burning performance in a savage part. Mr Jeffers's "free adaptation," as it is called, spares the supernatural bogeymen of the classical Greek drama and gets on briskly with the terrifying story of a woman obsessed with revenge. His verse is modern; his words are sharp and vivid, and his text does not worship gods that are dead.

Since Miss Anderson is a modern, the Jeffers text suits her perfectly and releases a torrent of acting incomparable for passion and scope. Miss Anderson's Medea is mad with the fury of a woman of rare stature. She is barbaric by inheritance, but she has heroic strength and vibrant perceptions. Animal-like in her physical reactions, she plots the doom of her enemies with the intelligence of a priestess of black magic – at once obscene and inspired. Between those two poles she fills the evening with fire, horror, rage and character. Although Miss Anderson has left some memorable marks on great women in the theater, Medea has summoned all her powers as an actress. Now everyone realizes that she has been destined for Medea from the start.

The general performance and the production are all of a piece. As the nurse, Florence Reed is giving an eminent performance that conveys the weariness and apprehensions of a devoted servant who does not quarrel with fate. John Gielgud's Jason is a lucid, solemn egotist well expressed in terms of the theater. As Creon, Albert Hecht has the commanding voice and the imperiousness of a working monarch. The chorus of women, which has been refreshingly arranged in Mr Gielgud's unhackneyed direction, is well acted. . . . The parts of the two young sons are disarmingly represented in the guileless acting of Gene Lee and Peter Moss. Hugh Franklin as Aegeus and Don McHenry as the tutor give agreeable performances, innocent of the stuffiness peculiar to most classical productions.

Ben Edwards' setting of the doorway to a Greek house is no more than pedestrian designing, although Peggy Clark has lighted it dramatically, and Castillo has dressed the characters well without the conventional theatrical effects – the lightning and the surf especially, for, unlike the acting, they derive from the old-fashioned theater of rant and ham.

Out of respect for Miss Anderson's magnificent acting in this incarnadined drama, they ought to be locked up in the lumber room. For she has freed Medea from all the old traditions as if the character had just been created. Perhaps that is exactly what has happened. Perhaps Medea was never fully created until Miss Anderson breathed immortal fire into it last evening.

Most critics were in agreement that Medea was Judith Anderson's most intense achievement. A few felt that she began at too high a pitch and from there was unable to rise to a greater height as the tragedy gathered and progressed, so that to compensate she was ultimately forced to shriek.

Three and a half decades later, *Medea* was revived (1982), with another well-regarded Australian-born actress, Zoe Caldwell, in the title part. (Miss Caldwell's husband, Robert Whitehead, was once more the producer. He also served as director. The adapter Jeffers was no longer alive.) On this occasion Judith Anderson – now eighty-four and long since retired – announced her willingness to accept the secondary role of the nurse. This proved to be a *coup de théâtre*, the reappearance of the legendary Miss Anderson garnering a great deal of public attention, which was decidedly helpful, though Zoe Caldwell had a solid reputation of her own. Mitchell Ryan was Jason, and Paul Sparer was Creon.

In *Time* magazine T.E. Kalem had strong reservations about the presentation.

> Zoe Caldwell has received a Tony nomination for her performance in *Medea*, and in this paltry season, no one would begrudge her that. Yet the accolade outshines the achievement. Caldwell's interpretation of the role is singular and peculiarly self-indulgent. With all the formidable artistry of her craft, the actress fashions a character of insatiable sensuality. If this production had a subtitle, it could be *By Lust Possessed.* Caldwell's gestures are endlessly provocative. Her hands urgently stroke her upper thighs: when she slips to the floor, she writhes orgiastically. True, she has been driven half-mad since her royal lover Jason cast her off in favor of King Creon's daughter. But she seems to miss past days of glory less than past nights in Jason's bed. Caldwell's most moving and Euripidean moments come when she cradles and fondles the two young sons she has borne Jason, then steels herself to kill them in a monstrous act of revenge against their father. From moment to moment she is wretchedly torn between maternal love and a scorned woman's hate.
>
> Magnificently true to the spirit of Euripides is Judith Anderson – as well she should be. She acted the title role in the adaptation's memorable 1947 première. At eighty-four, Anderson plays Medea's redoubtable old nurse and reaches a peak with the oncoming slaughter of the innocents, vainly attempting to thwart the horror with chilling words of prophecy.
>
> Director Robert Whitehead, who produced *Medea* in 1947, has not fired up other key actors. Paul Sparer's Creon is more like a pompous chairman of the board than a Corinthinan king, and Ryan's Jason is a callow marital climber rather than the hero who brought home the Golden Fleece. The Grecian temple designed by Ben Edwards has a brooding, darksome majesty. A pity so much of this production lacks it.

Similarly negative was Jack Kroll in *Newsweek.*

> After twenty-five hundred years Euripides' *Medea* remains the ultimate statement of women's rights. Even with all of today's news stories of mothers murdering their children, it's not easy to come to

terms with the most devastating infanticide in cultural history. But we must face the fact that Euripides saw Medea as some kind of hero and even, finally, as a godlike figure. The greatness of this astounding play comes in our terrifying realization that Medea's act is the unthinkable extremity of a just cause. We must feel the profound injury to Medea in her betrayal by Jason, who has abandoned her for the young daughter of Creon, King of Corinth. This isn't *Shoot the Moon*, Athenian style; Jason's betrayal of a brilliant, proud and noble wife who has steeped herself in blood to help make him a hero is a violation of the deepest human covenants, a covenant embodied by the children they both love. Euripides creates an apocalyptic emotional logic that drives Medea out of the realm of "rational" motivation into a state beyond reason. All the creative force that expressed itself as a loving wife and mother becomes the destructive force of a woman betrayed not only by a man but by the society that supports him.

To make this transcendent barbarism work in our "enlightened" age requires the theatrical magic of a potent actress. Zoe Caldwell is a potent actress; her Medea is a *tour de force* of absolute control of voice and gesture. But she has chosen to play the role in an outmoded *art nouveau* style; she slithers like Theda Bara, preens and poses like Gloria Swanson as Norma Desmond. It's a staggering feat of seamless virtuosity, but the emotional and psychological associations of this style have long since been devalued; they simply don't project any real dramatic truth anymore. We need a new choreography that will make us accept the inevitability of Medea's transformation from a fiercely loving to a savagely hating creature. And the weakness of the surrounding production (directorial credit to Robert Whitehead) doesn't help, except for the presence of eighty-four-year-old Judith Anderson, for whom this powerful adaptation by Robinson Jeffers was written. Dame Judith now plays the Nurse with an eloquent simplicity that's beautiful to behold.

Another dissenter – his accustomed stance – was the implacable John Simon of *New York* magazine.

There is in *Medea*, as in most Greek drama, a debate between the human and the divine. By removing this *agon* for the benefit of intelligent but not learned audiences – and to suit his own misotheist and misanthropic needs – Jeffers, whose dramatic poetry does not attain redemptive dimensions, did indeed reduce the play to a secularized and primitive horror story. But even the prosody of the play is crude compared to the worst of his poems, in which he would not have stooped to the clumsy coarseness of "me driven by the hairy snouts from the quadruped marriage bed," the dated inversion of "Your sword your want?", the frantic overuse of an epithet such as "dark" (in quick succession, "dark with anger," "dark wisdom," "dark rumors"), and such repeated facile triads as "Ah, rotten, rotten, rotten," "All dead, all dead, all dead," "Wretched, wretched, wretched I am," and the like.

It may be that great acting could over-leap such obstacles, but there are only two decent performances here: those of Pauline Flanagan as the First Woman of Corinth and Giulia Pagano as the Third. (The Second, played by Harriet Nichols, is unsatisfactory in every respect.) Because the scenery is sparse and not of high quality, Zoe Caldwell, as Medea, feels obliged to chew up the play instead. She has a fine voice and elocution, with which, however, she impersonates an operatic diva gone suddenly tone deaf, or, more precisely, a theremin in the hands of a palsied player. Unearthly wailings, caterwaulings, tremolos, base rolls, shrilling, and stage whispers jostle one another for little or no reason, and hardly a line is free of manic rubato that stretches, now a vowel, now a consonant, to the length of a polysyllable. Worst of all is the reading of Jeffers's already heavy-handed ironies to milk laughs from the not learned but intelligent groundlings, with the tone of Shirley Temple trying to sound like Thelma Ritter.

Miss Caldwell has movements to rival her delivery. Jealous rage drives her to the body language of a punk-rocker. Plotting revenge is done to quasi-dance steps like those of someone trying to extricate herself from a tub of molasses. Frequent sensuous caressings of the loins look like an ambidextrous person's attempts to rub simultaneously two spots out of her dress. When this Medea listens to the account of Creon's and Creusa's deaths, she runs through an anthology of recumbent and semi-recumbent orgasms from those of lower animals to those of human beings, all in slow motion. Several trunkfuls of mannerisms are used up without achieving a single believable moment.

Judith Anderson, who created the original Medea of 1947 (scarcely better, though less offensively), now plays the Nurse as a prim, supercilious librarian with little energy, fading audibility, and some difficulty with her lines. Mitchell Ryan's Jason sounds and performs like a New Jersey policeman undertaking a costume part for a PAL benefit; Paul Sparer's Creon is all bluster and croaks, like someone trapped in a cracker barrel resonating away. As Aegeus (whose name is mispronounced all around), Peter Brandon turns an impotent old king into a brain-damaged young lout.

Ben Edwards's set falls painfully between stylization and realism and looks obtusely like a set; Jane Greenwood's costumes alleviate their obviousness with touches of the ludicrous; Martin Aronstein's lighting is conventional except for some rather beady stars. David Amram's music is mostly archaizing *bouzouki* when it doesn't sound like a piano being tuned or a car revving up. Robert Whitehead, the distinguished producer, makes a directorial début scant in imagination but exemplary in uxoriousness,

> allowing his leading lady and wife to get away with considerably more than the prescribed amount of murder. His attention to detail does not even extend to getting the cast to pronounce *Delphi* correctly; I thought at first they were consulting Leonard Melfi.

(John Simon was not the New York theatre's favourite critic.)

But a host of other reviewers heaped praise on the actress though not always on the entire offering. Among them was Frank Rich, of the *New York Times.*

> Euripides has a strong ally in Zoe Caldwell, who brought her special flame to the otherwise routine revival of *Medea* that opened last night at the Cort. Possibly the most modern of Greek dramatists, Euripides demands an intense psychological realism from actors – and that is what Miss Caldwell has bestowed on her marathon role. This actress makes us believe in the warped logic by which Medea murders her two sons to wreak vengeance on Jason, the ambitious husband who has betrayed her for a Greek princess. And because she does, we are, by evening's end, brought right into the thunderclap of Euripides' tragedy.
>
> As befits a barbaric sorceress lost in exile, Miss Caldwell is set off from the rest of the company by her swarthy complexion: her eyes are dark horizontal slashes that summon up an exotic East. There is seething physicality to her every gesture; mercurial and sinuous. She is indeed, as Robinson Jeffers's adaptation has it, a mixture of "serpent and wolf." Yet she is a woman, too. Though Miss Caldwell has many opportunities to chew up the scenery, she usually resists them by shading her portrayal with carefully considered nuances. This at times almost Hedda-like Medea makes the lineage from Euripides to Ibsen abundantly clear.
>
> One of Miss Caldwell's trump cards is wit. Her Medea gets genuine laughs when she sarcastically extols the virtues of "civilized" Greece and her "kind" Jason – neither of whom have treated her with anything like civility nor kindness. The heroine's sexuality is also turned up full throttle. When Miss Caldwell suddenly kisses Jason (Mitchell Ryan) in the midst of their debate, we see the hot-blooded lust that once made her sacrifice all for him – just as we later see the inverse of that passion in her orgasmic cries of hate and murder. And underneath the frenzy, there is a helplessness as well. Quietly asking how she has been "pulled down to the hell of vile thoughts," Miss Caldwell becomes a blank; she's so adrift from reason that the answer is really lost forever.
>
> From there, it's only a small leap to the unthinkable. In the crucial scene with the sadly childless Aegeus, Miss Caldwell's sly smiles show us the idea of child murder taking root in Medea's crazed mind. When, at last, the crime is at hand, the actress fully dramatizes the struggle between her hunger for

> revenge and her love for her sons. One moment she is drawing the boys to her breasts in full maternal affection; then she is taking them behind closed doors to spill their blood. There is a relentless sweep to the extreme transition. Like the gods, we can understand, if not pardon, the primal impulse that drives her to the ultimate act of annihilation.
>
> Well paced and often brilliantly calculated as this performance is, it isn't quite perfect. In the early scenes, Miss Caldwell's body language – the tremulous fingers, the shaking thighs, the slithering to the floor – can be stylized to the point of mannerism. Her voice, happily, never follows suit. It is a superb, supple instrument – husky, yet feminine and full of longing. When she partakes of her "bottomless cup" of hate, she heaves with a primordial ooze that threatens to make the earth open up before us.

This critic, too, found fault with Robert Whitehead's direction, looking upon it as too "by-the-book" and "musty" and cutting too much ground from under the star. The return of Dame Judith, now as the nurse, "gives the *Medea* the valuable resonance of theatrical tradition. While her delivery of the early speeches sounds a bit too patrician and occasionally matter-of-fact, she builds steadily. Her climactic attempts to thwart the heroine's mayhem – a chorus of 'no's' that sends her off her tree-branch cane and up Medea's steps – are harrowing."

Rich singled out the Chorus Leader and the Third Speaker, Pauline Flanagan and Giulia Pagano, for commendation. "The rest of the acting is bland or bombastic. . . . While Mr Ryan's Jason is fine in his final collapse – when he caves in to his nihilistic awareness that it no longer matters 'who lives and who dies' – he's far too plodding a dissembler along the way. Because his overtly callow rationality is no match at all for Miss Caldwell's savage force, the play's central argument is left unengaged."

The costumes, too, offended Rich – they were "attic Attic". He applauded Ben Edwards's "majestic set, reportedly a reworking of the one he did in 1947 . . . lighted with an eerie glow of foreboding by Martin Aronstein, and with music to match by David Amram. Otherwise, Mr Whitehead's staging is frieze-like in its rigidity, and awkward in its deployment of the chorus. True, *Medea* is a very hard play to stage, but that doesn't mean one must approach it as if it were a boulder to be pushed up a cliff. But once Mr Whitehead does get to the peak, in the last fifteen minutes, the payoff is considerable. At that point, Miss Caldwell's volcanic eruption at last sets fire to this *Medea*, and even the dead wood around her must burn hellishly in her wake."

Walter Kerr, one of Rich's predecessors, was still contributing his perceptive commentary on Sundays in the *New York Times*'s Art and Leisure section. He coupled his opinions of the *Medea* and Athol Fugard's *Master Harold and the Boys*, which had also opened during the past week.

Euripides' *Medea*, which has just returned to Broadway in Robinson Jeffers's adaptation and with the superlative Zoe Caldwell in its central role, was written in 431 BC. Athol Fugard's play, now at the Lyceum in its impeccable Yale Repertory Theater production, was given its world première last year. Say it was written yesterday. And then note that in the 2,412 years that have elapsed between the two turbulent dramatic statements, we seem not to have advanced an inch in coping with culture clashes, racial clashes, and the love-hate relationships they breed and breed and breed.

Different as the two plays are, they share a curious common ground. To take most obvious instances first, each play makes a violent climactic moment out of the terrible tug and pull that a divided psyche – divided between fierce attraction and fierce rejection, between lust and loathing, between friendship and fear – can create.

Miss Caldwell, say, has spent a considerable time and a torrent of venom damning the Jason who has lured her away from her own "barbaric" land and then betrayed her by marrying another. When Jason, in the person of a muscular and persuasive Mitchell Ryan, descends the worn stone steps of Medea's Corinthian palace, there are sharp, savage words between them. As Miss Caldwell advances and retreats like a tethered animal, lashing her lover with scorn for having made her "abominable" in her own sight, we sense her claws growing sharper. The claws flash into view. With a breakaway cry, as though lunging out of a forest, Miss Caldwell hurls herself half way across the stage at the man she must punish, fingernails aimed at his eyes. Reaching him, without transition she is wrapped in his arms as he is locked in her kiss.

The ferocity hasn't changed; only its purpose is altered. The heat of hate and the heat of amorous passion have become one unrestrained force. The startling union will be sundered, quickly. In a moment Miss Caldwell will be a broken creature, turning once meaningful syllables into sung pain. But for a single flashing instant the double truth has been evident. Hatred *cannot* subside because love has not.

. . . *Medea* is so highly charged with very personal passion that we tend to overlook the social background on which it is fought. Medea's rage with the unfaithful Jason is doubled because he has stolen her from her native land, left her rootless. But Jason is proud of having done so: he has freed her of "Oriental superstition" and introduced her to the glorious rational light of Greece. For Greece's Apollonian glories this Medea displays a hearty contempt. Mention to Miss Caldwell a prophecy brought from Delphi and the curl of her lip is as dismissive as the cackling laughter that begins deep in her throat. And when she settles herself to a deceptively domestic grouping – handsomely arranged by director Robert Whitehead – it is to mock the image she created. Spreading out before her the golden cloak that will become a gift to Jason's new bride and that will promptly burn that bride alive, Miss

Caldwell slyly purrs that "There is nothing like this in the world – at least in the Western world." The clash of the intuitive and the rational, the magical and the mundane, the "barbaric" and the "civilized" is always there to be drawn on. And Euripides, when he wrote the play, did not find the alien Medea or her "dark wisdom" in any way unfavored by the gods. The gods sent a chariot from the heavens to rescue her.

Indeed, Miss Caldwell may be at her very best in a tempestuous evocation of the exile's plight, homeless, unwelcome on any shore, "held a little lower than a scavenger dog, kicked, scorned and slaved." My one reservation about the actress's performance has to do with the itchiness of her curbed sensuality. Her hands are incessantly busy, stroking her thighs, curving toward her breasts, beginning to reach toward objects beyond her. We believe, readily, in her unabashed sensuality.

But because the sexuality is now inhibited, defeated, eternally unsatisfied, this Medea tends to rein in sharply each extended gesture. Miss Caldwell herself is extraordinarily graceful, physically free. But by cutting off a thrust of the wrist or the first step of a stride in mid-flight, turning each new movement in on itself, the actress sometimes produces a curious effect that is both busy and inhibited at the same time. We are grateful for those moments when her unfettered impulses take over and she sweeps past us full circle or raises a bared arm in the sustained authority that is her birthright.

If the evening boasts one speech that is more mesmerizing than any other it comes from Judith Anderson. Miss Anderson was, of course, Mr Jeffers's original Medea; having in effect invited Miss Caldwell to succeed her, she is content to appear in the supporting role of the Nurse. What she does with the passage in which she must remember and report the flaming torch that Jason's intended bride becomes is scarcely to be believed.

She does not begin, as almost any lesser player would have done, in a transparent state of shock at what she has seen. She was present when it happened. But she was present for *all* of it, not just for its terrifying ending but for its gay and playful beginnings. And now, if she is to remember it at all or account for it truly, she must go back to its beginnings, back to the way the world was before flame exploded in its face. She has been traumatized by the event and can only reconstruct it by reliving it, listening again to girlish laughter as Creon's daughter tiptoes to a mirror to admire herself in her new-found finery. Miss Anderson takes us through it frieze by frieze, split-second by split-second, feeling only the emotion of the picture now passing her mind's eye, holding back the horror until it can no longer be evaded. The effect is to make the horror all the more real and all the more intense when it does come; it is an extraordinarily imaginative reading of the passage.

And so, as so often happens, the very end of the season has given the season much of its weight.

In the phalanx of those on the side of Robert Whitehead's new production was Clive Barnes, formerly of the *New York Times* but now on the *New York Post*. "A *Medea* to be remembered! It certainly brings distinction to Broadway, and in Miss Caldwell's mighty and supremely variegated performance you have the inestimable joy of seeing a magnificent actress . . . Miss Caldwell, with her dusky, aquiline beauty, is a haunted, haunting figure . . . a sight to watch". He had equal praise for Judith Anderson's nurse. In *Newsday* Allan Wallach wrote: "With her distinguished predecessor on hand it is fitting that Zoe Caldwell is a commanding Medea in her own right." He was impressed by Whitehead's staging, Ben Edwards's set, Jane Greenwood's costumes and Martin Aronstein's lighting. "Fine visual effects." For United Press International Glenne Currie summed up: "An extraordinary, blazing hypnotic performance by Zoe Caldwell as Medea which will rank in theatrical history alongside that of Dame Judith Anderson's thirty-five years ago. Dame Judith, now playing the Nurse, will break your heart." William A. Raidy, of the *Newhouse Newspapers*, viewed the presentation in much the same vein. "All around, the occasion is an auspicious and joyful one for the American theater. Zoe Caldwell is unforgettable. . . . *Medea* has come back to life with passion and unmistakable artistry."

The radio and television reviewers declared the evening to be "staggering". "An unprecedented turn of events in our theater." "One of the major acting events of the season . . . The cries of agony reverberate in Zoe Caldwell's scorching performance." "Brilliant! Go see the work of Zoe Caldwell and the young Euripides." "A very powerful *Medea*."

In an interview before the play opened, Zoe Caldwell revealed that as an apprentice actress in Australia she had been cast in a small part in the chorus of *Medea* when Judith Anderson had taken it there on tour. She had been given no chance to know the star. "I do have very strong recollections of her performance then. The rest of us were no good. Unfortunately, we had an English director who liked neither Judith, Euripides or the play, so he tried to make us speak it as though it was Shakespeare, which didn't work. We were all awful, except there in the middle was Judith and she was stunning."

The idea to revive the play with Whitehead as producer and Caldwell as Medea was Miss Anderson's; her goal was to raise money for the Jeffers Foundation, which was seeking to restore Tor House and transform it into a museum honouring the poet. She sent for Whitehead, with whom she had quarrelled during the original production and to whom she had not spoken since then. He was reluctant to obey her summons, in view of their stormy relationship, but she had persuaded him to undertake the task. It was also on her initiative that she had assumed the secondary role as the nurse. Her suggestion had been to have the work presented openly, locally, but instead the ensemble was tried out by invitation at the University of Tennessee and then at the Kennedy Center in Washington, DC, before arriving at Broadway, with Fran and Barry Weissler as additional producers.

Zoe Caldwell had been nervous, after reading the critical notices of Anderson in the earlier staging; she felt that the role belonged to the elder actress for ever. Also, the prospect of doing it with Anderson performing in the same scene was disquieting. "I was afraid she'd be saying 'Psssst! Not like *that*!' all the time. But it was not like that at all. I said to her at the outset, 'My Medea, darling, is going to be different from yours, because your heritage is Scottish and mine is French, and although we're both Australians our lives have been very different, too.'" (Miss Anderson, in turn, admits she had moments, at first, watching Zoe and thinking, "I can do it better.") But all went smoothly during the rehearsals. "Judith's marvelous to work with . . . I'm sure the old production never had this real-life relationship between Medea and the Nurse. It helps the play enormously." In acting the episodes with the boys, Caldwell thought of her own two sons of approximately the same age.

Of Jeffers, Miss Anderson recalled that they had consulted frequently on his adaptation, since he had no theatre experience. "I don't mean I worked on it with him, but we talked a great deal about it. I'd say, 'I want another beat there, and a bit more strength there,' or whatever, and he'd always say, 'You know best, Judith, you know best.' He was a scholar who spoke Greek when he was eight years old – a great mind and a great human being."

A year later, the production was broadcast on public television (1983). John Corry, in the *New York Times*, pointed out how it differed from the stage version.

> Zoe Caldwell took a risk when she did *Medea* on Broadway last season. She played her character with a full-throated, full-blooded womanliness, filling the stage with a heated physicality. A proscenium arch is one thing, however, and a television screen is another, and what fills one can simply overflow the other. On the television production which will be seen tonight, it is obvious that care has been taken so that this didn't happen. The production is a triumph of nuance.
>
> It is not that Miss Caldwell is giving us less on television; her Medea is as full of fury and bitterness as her Medea on stage. The stage production, however, was almost completely Miss Caldwell's. Her performance absorbed everything about her. Even standing still and silent, which the role did not require her to do very often, Miss Caldwell was a magnetic field. She was inescapable.
>
> The camera changes focus. Other things swim into view. Judith Anderson's nurse, for one, is more imposing on television, more full of presence. Miss Anderson looks, she listens, she scarcely seems to be acting at all. When the nurse tells Medea that she has seen Creon and his daughter burning alive,

> the flesh falling from their bones, Miss Anderson speaks quietly, but is certain that even as she speaks she sees the flames. The camera, forcing us to look squarely at Miss Anderson, Miss Caldwell huddled against her, narrows our vision. We see with a different mind's eye.
>
> . . . On stage, Miss Caldwell showed a scorned sexuality, trusting the audience would find in the portrayal of a woman renounced the insane logic driving her to the final horror. On the television screen, there is less sexuality; there is more grief. Medea is still a wild, Asian princess, but now there is a childlike quality there, too. Huddled against the nurse, she is plaintive. Pleading with Creon, she is almost pathetic, more a supplicant than a sorceress, more broken than betrayed. The camera closes in on the shadings. Miss Caldwell is deepening what already was a memorable performance.
>
> There is one unwelcome surprise in the production. . . . We are reminded that Mr Jeffers was a poet before he was a dramatist. Language is heard more clearly on television than in a theater, and some of Mr Jeffers's language, heavy with imagery, suggests that it was written more to be read than to be spoken.
>
> Meanwhile, Mark Cullingham's direction for television is responsible for much of the production's success, although in one instance Mr Cullingham would have been better advised to have stayed with Robert Whitehead's direction for the stage. On stage, the women of Corinth carried the bloodied bodies of the children out of Medea's temple. It was a stunning moment, emphasizing the human tragedy. On television, we see only a picture of the bodies lying on the floor. It was without emotional context, too flat an image. Forgive Mr Cullingham for this. It is still a splendid production.

In the decades between the first offering of Jeffers's adaptation and its revival with Caldwell and Anderson, other interpretations of the tragedy reached New York. As already noted, the diva Maria Callas (1923–71) was renowned as much for her dynamic and intense acting as for her singing. In 1969 she appeared in a non-musical film of the play produced by Franco Rossellini and directed by the noted Pier Paolo Pasolini.

Andrei Serban's stage version, with music by Elizabeth Swados, which was later included as part of their *Fragments of a Greek Tragedy*, scored a success that afforded it several revivals shortly thereafter. Serban, using Euripides' text mostly, interspersed passages and incidents from Seneca's derivative *Medea*, high-handedly mixing the ancient languages. The pair's unusual method of presentation has been largely described on earlier pages. *Medea* was the first work on which Serban and Swados joined their fresh talents after their initial encounter at La MaMa (1972), where the play was produced later that same year. Clive Barnes, still with the *New York Times*, was greatly struck with the staging and performances.

Theater as mystery and ritual – the theater as a nonverbal experience of tragedy – this is what Andrei Serban's cryptic reworking of *Medea* is all about. It is a potent theatrical event, and it offers deep insights into the nature of the dramatic experience.

. . . The production takes as its starting point a question. The question posed by Peter Brook is: "What is the relation between verbal and non-verbal theater? What happens when gesture and sound turn into word? What is the exact place of the word in theatrical expression? As vibration? Concept? Music? Is any evidence buried in the sound structure of certain ancient languages?" Well, perhaps there is more than one question there, but the answer is at least postulated by this strange and fascinating *Medea.*

. . . I have no ancient Greek whatsoever, and my Latin is now so rusty it is virtually in a state of irredeemable corrosion. Once in a while a phrase would float into my literal mind – but most of the text used is Greek rather than Latin, and I was never once conscious of listening to words. Only sounds I heard, sounds that added to the total impact of a theater ritual.

We know the story. Jason, Medea and Creusa, the classic sexual triangle. Passion and revenge, love and death – these are themes that run through the theater as essential commonplaces. A production such as this *Medea* seeks to shake the ordinary into the realm of the extraordinary. It tries to review by ritual what has been lost by acceptance.

The entire production has an authority and integrity that open doors to the possible theaters of the future. A woman betrayed by hate and destroyed by action is on the rack of her history. Verbal comments are meaningless compared with the physical realization, the simple spectacle, of her despair.

There are times when not to understand, or rather not to understand completely, is more important, more instant, more significant than the total comprehension of a situation. Ambiguity and mist are both qualities that can enhance life into art, or at least that perception of life we call art. *Medea* is a strange, yet enriching experience.

An hour or so in a basement – watching people tear their hearts out in musical, unknown languages – this in itself, with the chaste candlelight and soft voices, is a pristine experience.

The performances were fine – with Priscilla Smith's intense Medea, and Jamil Zakki's long-suffering Jason being outstanding. This was a theatrical occasion of great interest. Mr Serban is a most persuasive director. But more important, he is also a very honest director. He has it in him to make a contribution to the theater.

In a later *New York Times* article (1974) Julius Novick remarked:

For *Medea*, the most tightly focused and obsessive of the three plays, the principal actors rage at each other from two platforms, with the chorus and the spectators seated in between. . . . Serban's direction is finely tempered and balanced. He knows the use of contrast: the impact that one candle can make in a huge, dark room. (The lighting by Laura Rambaldi – an orchestration of spotlights, torches, candles – makes a tremendous contribution throughout the trilogy.) The most amazing of the performers is Priscilla Smith, who plays Medea and Electra – but the whole company is amazing. They give and give and give, but they never wallow in their own emotions as actors in avant garde productions so often do; their discipline is beautiful.

After leaving the *New York Times* Stanley Kauffmann was with the *New Republic*, where he wrote:

For sheer visceral excitement, the high point of the 1971–1972 season was a stretch of ten minutes or so in the middle of a forty-minute production of *Medea* at La MaMa Theater Club. Everything I had heard about this production prejudiced me against it. It was in Euripides' Greek, with some choruses in Seneca's Latin; only a small audience was allowed, and they went through an extended ritual of admission. It sounded like stale Off-Off-Broadwayfaring.

The first moments confirmed prejudice. We were ushered into the ground-floor theater of La MaMa, where I thought we were to see the play. Then, after about fifty people had arrived, we were conducted downstairs, past actors in costume holding candles and reciting lines in Greek or Latin, along a cinder-block corridor to the basement. Here we were seated on facing benches against the long sides of the rectangular room, with members of the chorus interspersed among us. At each of the narrow ends of the rectangle were some steps and a simple doorway. The ceiling was covered with billowing burlap. I was ready to leave.

Very soon I was rooted. The director, Andrei Serban, was moving to a single, strong idea: that the core of *Medea* is primal stuff, that comprehension of each utterance – when the play is known and the motions are elemental – is no more necessary here than in great opera. In both arts, cognition of language may even be an impediment to full release. All that we need, in giant drama, is the impassioned sound of words whose general meaning we know. Details of verbiage can sometimes weigh us down.

One need not take this approach as a fiat for all classic productions in order to see how it worked in this instance. During the minutes when Jason and Medea faced each other at opposite ends of that small room, storming full-throatedly at each other in a completely foreign language, I felt the blood of this ancient drama quicken as I have rarely felt it in productions of large plays.

Serban prepared for these moments with intelligent patterns of movement; with Elizabeth Swados's music-and-sounds, to create a barbaric aural atmosphere; with careful dynamics of the chorus; and, chiefly, by his work with his principals, Priscilla Smith and Jamil Zakki. Smith looks more like Smith College than Colchis, but she and Zakki transcended themselves. Their bodies were completely invested in what they were doing, their voices were two full, round columns battering at each other.

All the cast, even the children, were caught in Serban's intensity, and made a seamless fabric of conviction. I keep thinking even now of the children's dangling legs as, after being slaughtered, they were handed down through a gap in the burlap ceiling to their horror-struck father below.

Serban is a Romanian, a student and associate of Peter Brook, and is now director-in-residence at La MaMa. Productions there don't "run"; they appear, disappear, and often reappear. *Medea* has since gone touring in Europe and may be back. Serban will presumably be back and must be watched. The stuntishness in him is much less than his main thrust: quintessential guts and revelation.

In the very same season a fully intelligible *Medea* was sponsored by the well-established Off-Broadway Circle in the Square (1973), which invited Minos Volanakis to adapt and direct the drama, and Irene Papas to portray its troubled heroine. T.E. Kalem, in *Time* magazine, viewed the play as one of "vitriolic passion" with demands that the lead actress fully met.

The first thing to note about *Medea* is that it is an un-Greek tragedy in Aristotelian terms. Though Medea fell in love with Jason through the agency of the goddesses Hera and Aphrodite, the deities are conspicuously absent from the play as instruments of inevitability. The heroine does not fall through a fatal flaw, or die, and the *katharsis* of pity and terror is largely missing. Medea wreaks havoc on herself and those around her by fulfilling her own nature, that of being a creature of unbridled emotions. To Euripides and his Greek audience, the tragedy was probably regarded as that of all humankind whenever passion overcomes reason.

In his fluent adaptation, director Minos Volanakis has taken another tack. He views *Medea* as a social tragedy in which the heroine is victimized as a racial alien and violated as a woman simply because she is a woman. Greece's Irene Papas, who has often played aggrieved and grieving women (*Electra, Iphigeneia in Aulis*) brings to the role a controlled intensity, an innate intelligence, and an implacably stubborn anger. To humanize the part, however, is to make it somewhat less awesome in its sweeping horror. The paradox remains that the Greek playwrights gave us a gallery of women who bewail their

> powerlessness while these very same women are as flintily, dauntingly formidable as any of their sex ever seen on or off a stage.

In *Newsday* Allen Wallach declared: "Irene Papas gives a bravura performance that is profoundly right. A barbarous, believable Medea!" To accompany her "searing" interpretation, Volanakis had provided a production of overall strength.

Douglas Watts, in the *Daily News*, was of a like opinion: "The production is stunning. One is filled with admiration for the imaginative staging and the handsome design." Volanakis's adaptation was "free and colloquial". William Glover, for the Associated Press, concurred: "True theatrical power. A vibrant production." In the same spirit, Jack Gaver reported for United Press International: "A taut and engrossing production. The staging is spectacular."

In the *New York Times* Clive Barnes commented:

> *Medea* is a difficult play if only because its story never seems quite as inevitable as in most Greek tragedies. And also the antagonist, Medea, is far more important than the protagonist, Jason. What are we to make of a wronged woman who wreaks so terrible a revenge on her faithless husband? She kills his second wife and then, deliberately, kills her own two sons, leaving Jason barren on his native soil.
>
> Minos Volanakis, who has adapted and staged this version, sees Medea as a tragic heroine. He sees a certain contemporaneity in the play – not only in realizing Medea's place as a member of a depressed Greek Minority, women, but also in using the ultimate in violence to achieve her freedom.
>
> This, then, is a more sympathetic Medea than most. She goes through the play with an implacable – or almost implacable – resolve. She is determined to have her rights at any cost, to herself, to Jason, even to her children. She will not be dishonored in an alien land.
>
> It is perhaps in keeping with Mr Volanakis's concept of a modern *Medea* that his translation has little of the "classic utterance" common to most English translations of Greek tragedy. He deliberately courts the familiar and the conversational. At times, this works with some vigor, but at other times it sounds a little idiosyncratic and unnecessarily jazzy. It is a difficult course to steer between the unnaturally heroic and regrettably bathetic, and Mr Volanakis's steering here is not always impeccable.
>
> The difficulties are increased by the elaborate staging, which runs at marked variance to the attempted vernacular of so much of the language. Most of the actors wear masks – Medea and the messenger are exceptions – placing them on a seemingly different plane of reality from the rest. The purpose of the masks is hard to discern.

There is a certain dramatic effectiveness to Jason's taking his mask off when faced with the full wrath of Medea's revenge, but elsewhere all the masks seem like a ritual in what is meant – I presume – to be a rather more naturalistic reading of the play than is customary.

Certainly, Miss Papas as Medea is naturalistic. But her encounter with the puppet-strutting Creon becomes as much an encounter of styles as anything else. At least Mr Volanakis does manage to keep Medea in the play's eye; and also, by stressing her humanity, he does much to make her sympathetic.

Miss Papas is a very fine, controlled Medea. Her fires are subterranean, and she smolders with a carefully dampened passion. At times, the very evenness of her intensity becomes monotonous – there is a constant fierceness here. But that is part of her playing – her unrelenting determination and unwavering desire for justice are the key to her interpretation.

If Medea is made more sympathetic, perhaps by the same token, Jason must become less so. John P. Ryan's Jason is a male chauvinist pig of the most unattractive variety. Even at the end he hardly wins sympathy for the tragedy that has engulfed him – which is presumably the director's intention, but it is an intention that makes hard going for the actor.

Al Freeman as the messenger, who tells of Jason's new wife, and as her father, the King, is exceptionally good. He speaks the lines with a sense of shock but also with a sense of retribution.

All in all, this is a *Medea*, with its elaborately contrived settings by Robert Mitchell, of interest. And Miss Papas is splendid.

A collateral treatment is *A Dream of Passion* (1973), a film written, produced and directed by Jules Dassin, an American living in Athens and married to the highly esteemed Greek actress Melina Mercouri (daughter of a statesman and herself later to head her country's Ministry of Culture). For fifteen years Dassin, well known in the cinema field, had aspired to make a film based on the legend of Medea. He attended a trial in Italy of a woman who had killed her children when her husband abandoned her for a rival. "She sat there grieving for her children and at the same time not repenting for what she did. She felt she was right to do it." Yet Dassin was balked in his attempt to shape the film – he told Nicholas Gage, of the *New York Times* – because he was unable to reconcile compassion for the woman and deep repulsion at her dreadful act. At very long last, having watched his wife perform in the Euripidean *Medea*, he found the key to his film and turned out a draft of the screenplay in a bare few days. He had also been inspired by reading about an American woman, residing in Greece, who had murdered her children and, like Medea, was an expatriate. In the resultant film a present-day actress – Mercouri – is preparing to enact Medea but cannot fully comprehend or enter into the character. She learns of an American woman convicted of the crime of slaying her children after her husband has betrayed her. To evoke public notice for the oncoming film, the actress gets permission to visit the imprisoned woman, finds herself drawn to her. A close relationship evolves between them, and the actress acquires new psychological and emotional insight into the tragic heroine she is to impersonate.

Making use of the score that Samuel Barber had composed three decades earlier for Martha Graham's dance drama *Cave of the Heart* (1946), Michael Smuin choreographed his own interpretation of the legend (1977) for the San Francisco Ballet, of which he was the artistic director. After a lapse of fifteen years his *Medea* was revived by the Dance Theater of Harlem (1992), staged by two members of the all-black company, Robert Sund and Evelyn Cisneros. Other choreographers had similarly availed themselves of Barber's music. Jack Anderson gave the *New York Times*'s readers this summary:

> Mr Smuin's ballet is a shocker. His Medea is a proud, fierce woman who is appalled to discover that her husband, Jason, is in love with Creusa. When the sons of Medea and Jason fail to persuade their father of his folly, they and Medea conspire to kill Creusa. And when Jason continues to mourn his mistress's death, Medea murders the two young men.
>
> Unlike some theatrical treatments of the myth, this one conceives the sons not as innocent little children, but as sophisticated youths who have a good idea of what adultery means and what sex is all about. One startling image follows another. Jason and Medea dance a passionate *pas de deux*. Later, there is an acrobatically erotic duet for Jason and Creusa. The sons, bent on vengeance, trap Creusa in some ropes with which Medea eventually strangles her. And although the murder of the sons occurs offstage, their corpses are revealed in a blood-soaked finale.
>
> The choreography is always flamboyant; at its worst, it is bombastic. But Mr Smuin knows how to stir up excitement, and the cast danced with remarkable conviction. Lisa Attles was a commanding Medea. Only a fool would cause her temper to flare. But because Donald Wilson was foolish as well as handsome as Jason, she soon became not his marital partner but his deadliest enemy. Tai Jimenez was both alluring and impetuous as Creusa, and, in the interpretations of Lawrence de Maeyer and Calvin Shawn Landers, the sons were sturdy lads.

Continuing after its creator's death, the Martha Graham Dance Company restored her *Cave of the Heart* to its repertory forty-seven years after the work's début. In the *New York Times* Anna Kisselgoff, a steadfast admirer of Graham's output, welcomed this dance-drama's return.

> [It] is the most flamboyant example of her preoccupation with the essence of emotion: what she called the "thing itself."
>
> Emotion, for Graham, is to be embodied in dance and not depicted. The primary passion in *Cave of the Heart* is jealousy. As Christian Dakin's forcefully pained performance made clear in this instance, Graham never wavered from the heart of the drama. Medea, a woman scorned, becomes the embodiment of hate and jealousy.
>
> The power of *Cave of the Heart* lies in its extreme theatrical concentration. Both Graham and Isamu Noguchi, who created the sculptural décor, turned to resonant symbols. Graham's Medea resembles a snake, spewing venom in the ferocious central solo. Her serpent dance zig-zags in space and slithers on the floor.
>
> One need not be familiar with the entire myth: that Jason has left Medea for the Princess of Corinth. We do not see Medea kill her children but after she has poisoned the Princess with a magic crown, she encases herself in Noguchi's magical golden bush, symbol of her final journey to the sun. Samuel Barber's score cuts to the work's melodramatic heart.
>
> Coming up from the ranks under Graham's supervision, Miss Dakin is now at her peak, her form and technique now at a point of greatness. She plunged headlong into the six arabesque-like turns known as "Cave turns" with expressive ease. Her Medea is, aptly, a study in distortion and more pained than crazed.
>
> Graham also made the secondary roles crucial to the action. Miki Orihara, a dancer with admirable individuality, gave a lively tone to the aggressive Princess. As she scampered up Jason's thigh, her relationship to him was instantly defined. Donlin Foreman was nicely pompous as one of Graham's brutes.
>
> Janet Elber missed some of the asymmetry in falls specific to the Graham technique (both feet were pointed whereas one should be turned in). But her one-woman chorus has an exceptionally vivid edge. Struggling fiercely with Medea to prevent the inevitable, she was later agitated and stricken: she caught the nuance of crucial dramatic detail.

The 1980s, for some reason, burgeoned with several even more exotic variations of the *Medea* theme. Such a one was a staged reading in New York at the Latino Playwrights Spring Festival of a new play by Pedro Santaliz, *The Interior Castle of Medea Camuñas* (*El Castillo Interior de Medea Camuñas*). The readings, in Spanish, were supervised by the author, who described his script as a "free adaptation" of Euripides' classic drama in "a Spanish sit-com style". The troupe participating in the festival was the twenty-year-old El Nueva Teatro Pobre de America Inc, alternating action in Puerto Rico and New York City. The first presentation took place at the Center for Puerto Rican Studies at Hunter College (1983), the second series at the Henry Street Settlement's Arts for Living Center (1984).

Quite as *outré* as the *Yup'ik Antigone* was the *Kabuki Medea* (1978), which originated in Tokyo, as a production of the Toho Company, a business corporation dominating stage and screen ventures there. Directed by Yukio Ninagawa and installed as a part of his group's repertory, the *Kabuki Medea* toured internationally, reaching New York in 1986, after which it travelled to Vancouver, where it was to appear at Expo '86. The New York engagement, week-long, was sponsored by Joseph Papp, who presented the play at his open-air Delacorte Theater in Central Park; it received financial subsidies and other assistance from the Agency for Cultural Affairs of Japan, as well as the Japan Foundation, and several export firms. As with most productions under the auspices of Papp's New York Shakespeare Festival at the Delacorte, the tickets were free.

Yukio Ninagawa, celebrated in Japan for his production of Western classical works as avant-garde spectacles, sought to fuse in them Japanese and Western elements, while developing his own expressive idiom. He had already staged *Oedipus, Hamlet, Macbeth* and the *Threepenny Opera* with this aim. He explained to Jennifer Dunning of the *New York Times*: "We're trying to arrive at something in between the styles of Japanese theater and European realism. We are hoping to absorb from Western culture and then create by criticizing and breaking down what we have in Japanese traditional theater. We are looking to fashion something totally new from the débris." (More about the career of Yukio Ninagawa and his troupe will be taken up later.)

The all-male company consisted of twenty-five. Mikijiro Hira, the Medea, was a disciple of Stanislavsky and had also attended the Actors Studio in New York. Co-founder of the Moscow Art Theatre, Stanislavsky and his Russian fellow-players had formulated the famous "Method" of preparing a role. Ninagawa had become convinced that Stanislavsky had exerted a bad influence on him and his actors, since the Method was not suited to age-old, stylized theatres like Noh and Kabuki, which had very distinctive techniques of their own. "We were all trying to imitate the West – the Actors Studio," Hira added. "And Mr Ninagawa shares that background. But what we did was to use that as a base to take off from. It was the first time I felt I was doing something on my own." Ninagawa stressed this: "If you are doing Chekhov, it will work. It won't for fixed traditional theater like ours. And when one is dealing with modern avant-garde theater it doesn't do the job. There is a fine line. A very delicate tension. I try to find that line."

In discussing his *Medea*, Hira emphasized that "the impediment of a heavy costume added much to his interpretation, for which he borrowed some movement from traditional Japanese acting techniques. 'The feeling in that costume is that I don't want to be crushed. I am feeling inwardly that I have got . . . to . . . make . . . it.'" He also drew on the sadness of a recent divorce, in which he lost custody of his children. " 'I use that as a kind of sense-memory.'" He did not attempt to speak in a woman's voice in the play, and at times strode in an unfeminine manner beneath his robes. Jennifer Dunning remarked: "Given the glittering stylized headdress and makeup, which includes fringes of delicate green-glass tears and exposed, gold-filigreed breasts, this is a creature beyond gender." (The multicoloured costume, more specifically described, weighed forty-four pounds and was made "in part from the backs of fifty antique-silk sashes".)

The *Kabuki Medea* is set "somewhere in time"; its locale is a Japanese temple. The chorus bore Japanese stringed instruments with which to accompany the action.

Mel Gussow, of the *New York Times*, braved stormy weather to witness the offering:

> The Toho Company production of *Medea* is an evening of primal theater, an interweaving of Eastern and Western performance techniques cohering in a cross-cultural version of a seminal work of Greek tragedy. Deeply influenced by Kabuki and Noh theater, the production acts to transform Euripides into a Japanese classic. As directed by Yukio Ninagawa, the work is related to the films that Akira Kurosawa has made from Shakespeare; it is true in spirit to the source and rich with its own demonic Oriental character.
>
> Playing in the title role, Mikijiro Hira is most decidedly the star of this all-male, highly stylized production. Through Mr Hira's performance, the Japanese version excavates to the heart of Euripides, powerfully restating this story of the blackest revenge. The play is performed in Japanese, without translation; though one misses the Euripidean poetry (in one of the various English translations), there is no difficulty in following the emotions of the eternal story.
>
> At its opening on Wednesday night at the Delacorte Theater in Central Park, the play had an elemental directness – in two senses of the word. Despite an almost steady rain, the play was performed in its entirety. The drizzle did not deter the Toho actors, but it certainly dampened their ornate costumes (and also the audience). One sidelight: the rain caused steam to emanate from Mr Hira's costume. He seemed surrounded by a vaporous cloud, an evocative, though accidental metaphor for a Medea on fire.
>
> Except for his deep masculine voice, Mr Hira is a totally convincing Medea, in emotional depth an equal to many English-speaking actresses who have played the role. The actor moves authoritatively

> through the play, an avenging angel repeatedly tortured by conscience but undiscouraged in the plunge toward Medea's maniacal act.
>
> The other actors, especially Hatsuo Yamaya's sympathetic Nurse and Masane Tsukayama's imperious Jason, also manage to master the cross-cultural techniques. There are several minor demurs in regard to the performance. Medea's children – twinned, white-costumed cherubs forever locking their arms – are given, in their vocalization, a falsely comic dimension. Whenever they are on stage, they chatter nonsensically to each other.
>
> The score is a collage of East and West, but the director might more effectively have held to Eastern music. By far the most plangent music is the surging sound of Japanese stringed instruments played in unison by the sixteen-man chorus. The music marches along with the chorus.
>
> The director handles the chorus with a sculptural and balletic poise. In small or large groups, wearing flaring costumes, they look like massed winged creatures, watching, horrified, as Medea acts out their darkest fears. When Medea speaks, the chorus remains motionless, as Mr Ninagawa artfully parallels dialogue and silence, movement and stasis.
>
> Visually the conception is striking, filling the New York Shakespeare Festival theater with the sweep of an epic imagination. The evening leads inexorably to its tragic conclusion, as Medea snatches a knife and, without a flinch, rushes offstage to end the lives of her children. As we watch, Medea ascends in a chariot, in a final *coup de théâtre*, moving higher and higher over the stage until she seems to be flying into the still-threatening sky.

(This feat was accomplished with help of an eighty-foot crane. In his interview with Jennifer Dunning, Hira expressed worry that, his voice already spent, his last lines might not be heard from that extreme height.)

Possibly having heard of the Tokyo *Kabuki Medea* – or it may have been a spontaneous inspiration – the Chicago-based Wisdom Bridge, a well-accredited experimental group, staged its own version of the Greek tragedy, similarly conceived and identically named (1985).

After its local run, this version was on display in Washington, DC, as part of a regional theatre festival held at the Kennedy Center (1986). Sylviane Gold, of the *Wall Street Journal*, saw it there and deemed it seriously wanting, suggesting that, if it had been a success in Chicago, that might have been because audiences in that city had little familiarity with Kabuki, Noh or Bunraku. Unfortunately for the Wisdom Bridge players, a touring company of Japan's greatest Kabuki performers were exhibiting works from their standard repertory in an adjacent theatre, which put the American actors at a marked disadvantage. "True, audience members got an opportunity to see a *tour-de-force* performance by Chicago's Barbara Robertson, and a chance to ponder on the surprisingly comfortable fit of Japanese clothing on classical myth. But they could hardly expect to be impressed by the marvels of Japanese theatrical ingenuity and technique, or not to notice the many crudenesses of performers not schooled in them for a lifetime."

Another Oriental interpretation, but this time in English, was put on by the Pan Asian Repertory Theater in New York (also in 1986). This company, its roster mostly filled by Chinese, Korean and Japanese actors, is a long-time feature of the city's theatre and is subsidized by various foundations and the National Endowment for the Arts. Alkis Papoutsis served as director of this play. (The Pan Asian's artistic-producing director was Tisa Chang.) Of the offering, D.J.R. Bruckner wrote in the *New York Times*:

> Someone leaving the Susan Bloch Theater after the Pan Asian Repertory's *Medea* was heard mentioning soap opera. That is not entirely unfair; many soaps are held together by bits purloined from classics. And *Medea*, the tale of a woman with unusual powers who plots a wild revenge after her husband, the most famous hero in the world, abandons her for a princess, might inspire years of torrid television afternoons.
>
> That is one of the reasons it is perilous to stage this play. But its power makes it seductive to actors and directors. When Ching Valdes-Aran as the heroine in the Pan Asian's version broods on revenge – in a soliloquy beginning "How shall I do it?" – and determines to murder her own children, she is truly terrifying. It is a fine moment that makes one envy her grip on spectators' emotions.
>
> There are not many such powerful episodes in this production. The English translation of Euripides' play is credited to Claire Bush and the director, Alkis Papoutsis. Very free adaptation is closer to the truth. Understandably, they wanted to trim the rhetoric of the original and emphasize action, and they are well advised not to try imitating the high-flown language of the Greek version, the grandeur of which is unmatched in other of Euripides' plays. But the liberties they have taken are too great.
>
> In some cases one is left wondering what some lines mean, and in others, where the translators reach for current colloquialisms, they do not always consider that their phrases come freighted with distracting associations, as when Medea says "all dogs are the same under the skin" or "a real hero does not abandon children" or "I have lost . . . my pearls of great price." The anachronistic intrusion in that last remark is merely annoying, but the overall use of slangy expressions is worse: it deprives Medea of her majesty and strangeness and thus guts the play of much of its capacity to produce terror and pity. Sometimes it produces the opposite: when Aegeus, having consulted the oracle, is asked by Medea what Apollo said, he replies, "The usual; he answered with a riddle." That is amusing, but this play can be shattered by a smile.

Even more unsettling is the tampering with the plot at the climax. No one expects a small company in a small theater to supply a dragon-drawn chariot for Medea to put her murdered children in and fly off her roof, denying pleas from Jason below to let him touch them. But when, in this version, she opens the house and lets Jason go in to see their bodies, his subsequent pleas to see and touch them are reduced to nonsense. And one wonders why they have cut out the few lines these children have in Euripides' play, cries for help heard as their mother kills them offstage. The omission of them here considerably weakens the play's ending.

Not all the action used to fill the spaces left by the stripping down of Euripides' speeches is appropriate. Dances given to the three women who rather ingeniously take the place of the chorus in this version are uniformly ungainly if not ludicrous, and Medea's dance with the poisoned veil and tiara she is about to send to Jason's new bride reminds one of harem girls in cheap films. During the episode in which she is pretending reconciliation with Jason, the two fall into a wrestling embrace and kiss of the same provenance. Finally, there is far too much screaming throughout. Such noise does not substitute for the waves of fear produced by the relentless, cadenced lines of the original play.

Even in such a version, however, Miss Valdez-Aran's performance is striking, occasionally almost overpowering. And Kati Kuroda as the Nurse is a haunting presence of suffering, a woman whose clarity of vision and understanding is unbearable since she is powerless to avert the tragedy she eloquently witnesses. One would like to see these two in a less hokey version.

This profusion of *Medeas* in such a short span of time was certain to tickle the fancy of Off-Broadway parodists. Charles Ludlam, founder and star of the Ridiculous Theater Company, was New York's deftest practitioner of that genre of humour. Before his premature death at forty-four he had dashed off a satirical sketch derived – most disrespectfully – from Euripides' tragedy, much as the raffish Aristophanes might have done twenty-four centuries earlier. This was in 1984 and he left it unproduced. Three years later (1987) Ludlam's quirky *Medea* was staged, with his successor, Everett Quinton, and another leading member of the troupe, Black-Eyed Susan (as she chose to call herself), alternating in the roles of Medea and the nurse. Like Ludlam, his close friend Quinton usually appeared in "drag". In the *New York Times* Frank Rich, who cherished the comic ensemble, had this to say:

Of all the memorial tributes the theater has bestowed on its fallen giants this year, perhaps the most painful to watch was the one given in July by the Ridiculous Theater for Charles Ludlam, who died last Spring. . . . The tribute was in part dedicated to demonstrating the continuity of the company Mr

Ludlam left behind, and to this end, Ridiculous troupers nobly performed scenes from past triumphs. But Mr Ludlam was not merely the igniting spirit, artistic director and playwright-in-residence of the Ridiculous – he was also its foremost performer. Instead of affirming the company's artistic survival, each of the memorial's haunted sketches seemed to accentuate the enormous size of the vacuum left by Mr Ludlam. One kept waiting for the star entrance that never came.

The effect of *Medea*, the Ridiculous company's first official post-Ludlam production, is much more salutary. Everett Quinton, the new artistic director, has gone quite intelligently and modestly about the task of getting started again in earnest. *Medea* is a Ludlam script – but, at fifty minutes, it is not fiendishly demanding, and, in its first production, it is unburdened by memories of a past rendition. The staging (by Lawrence Kornfeld), set (by Jack Kelly) and costumes (by Mr Quinton) are in the authentic Ridiculous style, right through to a *coup de théâtre* featuring Helius's chariot. Rather than pretend that a single performer might re-create the Ludlam presence, Mr Quinton and Black-Eyed Susan are taking turns as Medea and the Nurse.

Medea seems an appropriate play to do, not just because it bills itself, half-jokingly, as "a tragedy" – do we laugh or cry when Medea first cries out, "I want only to die"? – but because it is such a typical illustration of its author's unique brand of classicism. Mr Ludlam bends Euripides to his own idiosyncratic comic whims without ever really departing from the outline of the original. The Ridiculous *Medea* is a succinct deconstruction, not a broad parody, and its laughter derives less from mocking Greek tragedy than from ruthlessly and insightfully exposing its conventions. One is reminded all over again of how much Mr Ludlam's topsy-turvy modern theater was rooted in the centuries of theater that came before.

Though the laughter is far from continuous, *Medea* is at its best when rudely pointing up the continuity between Euripides and Hollywood dramatists of the 1930s and 1940s. The evening opens with the projection of a lightning bolt on a map of Corinth, and quickly gets down to cases. "You Greeks are idiots with your fatalism and your democracy," says Medea, who will soon greet Jason's betrayal with the exclamation "This is the pits." The production's chorus (led by the voluminous Katy Dierlam) is a trio of unwanted, loudmouthed extras, while Medea's sons are played by remarkably ambulatory plastic dolls. . . . The highfalutin poetry is boiled down to its essential clichés – "Hell hath no fury like a woman scorned!" – and the offstage gore, with its imagery of "molten flesh and innards and excrement," is a cue for gleeful B-movie sensationalism rather than wails of grief.

To see *Medea* in each of its casting configurations, which I did, is to learn, as the company must be learning, about both the abilities of the performers and the whole nature of the Ridiculous performance style. That Ms Susan is by far the funnier Medea may have little to do with the fact that she is a woman. (Indeed, a male Medea triumphed in the Toho Company's serious Japanese version of the play seen in Central Park last year.) What makes the role take off in Ms Susan's interpretation, as it does not in Mr Quinton's more matronly performance, is her gift for capturing, with her Mae West swagger and Barbara Stanwyck rage, the particular kind of woman that Mr Ludlam had in mind.

Yet Mr Quinton is hilarious as the nurse. Wearing a silver wig that makes him look unaccountably like Hume Cronyn in drag and constantly clucking in mock sorrow over Medea's latest tempting of the fates, he is an ideal second-banana to Ms Susan just as he was to Mr Ludlam. While the Ridiculous Theater Company's fate is impossible to predict, two evenings of its *Medea* do leave the promising feeling that its heirs are searching their own talents to find the founder's artistic legacy rather than enshrining what is irretrievable in the past. The mourning multitudes who left flowers in Sheridan Square last Spring owe Mr Quinton and his gallant company the committed, demanding audience that is essential for their rebirth this Fall.

A reincarnation of *Medea* of a quite different sort was accomplished by the Royal Spanish National Ballet the very next year (1988) on a visit to New York, when it was the final number in an evening of four dance-works. Anna Kisselgoff, in the *New York Times*, began her notice:

The Royal Spanish National Ballet does not have great dancers but proficient ones. No matter. The company's début Monday night at the Metropolitan Opera House was greeted with wave after wave of delirious applause.

There is obviously a huge hunger for Spanish dancing in the United States, and this company from Madrid, whose dominant style comes from the heel-stamping idiom associated with flamenco, offers further proof. It is not a classical ballet troupe as its name implies, although – with its principals, soloists, corps and orchestral accompaniment – it is organized very much along the lines of a ballet company.

Its best offering, in fact, resembles a ballet. This is a flamenco-style *Medea*, a dance-drama that takes up the entire second half of the program that is being presented through Saturday night. José Granero's skillful choreography and updated retelling set the familiar tale in a provincial Spanish town full of patriarchal machismo and raging feminine temperament. Merche Esmeralda, a guest artist who will alternate in the title role with Ana González, offers a shattering dramatic performance that is enhanced by the serpentine beauty of her fluid dancing.

The preceding items being presented were little to Ms Kisselgoff's liking. The performers, she felt, lacked individuality, elegance and concentration, though obviously the enthusiastic audience was of a different opinion. But she returned, in a more laudatory vein, to a summary of the major offering.

> In *Medea*, the company's dancers were miraculously transformed, losing their impersonality and carving themselves into full-blooded dramatic characters. Andrea d'Odorico has created a striking set, a façade of a ruined house with a central arch behind which a sky turns fiery red after Medea kills her children, leaving her Jason traumatized in the midst of what was a small-town wedding to the daughter of Creonte – here depicted as the village boss surrounded by rakish young toughs.
>
> Mr Granero's choreography to Manolo Sanlucar's score (libretto by Miguel Narros) gives the dancers a welcome dramatic handle. José Antonio comes into his own with his devastatingly passionate Jason. Juan Mata is a Creonte of great authority; Maribel Gallardo gives his daughter a patrician air. Victoria Eugenia gives the cameo role of Medea's nurse great depth. And when Miss Esmeralda's back-arching, seething Medea finally closes the huge doors of the house at the end, she does so after a performance of tragic dimension.

Included in the 1992 Edinburgh Festival was a Romanian production of *Medea*, as well as one of *Electra* using ancient Greek.

The inexhaustible fascination with this intense drama was evinced once more by yet another version of it a short time afterwards, strikingly directed by Jonathan Kent and starring Diana Rigg, an actress of growing artistic stature. Produced in north London by the small Almeida Theatre Company, together with the Liverpool Playhouse, the play enjoyed enough success to be moved to the West End, and from there to New York for what was projected to be a limited engagement and where it was received with almost equal acclaim. The English ensemble was transferred intact. Said Clive Barnes, in the *New York Post*, "Hell hath no fury like Diana Rigg. The supporting cast is superb – particularly Tim Oliver Woodward's nobly insensitive Jason and John Turner's arrogant Creon. This is a *coup de théâtre* that should not be missed – it has the sacred breath of renewal to it." Of a like mind was Howard Kissel in the *Daily News*: "A thrill ride. Jonathan Kent's direction moves the play like a juggernaut. The image which Kent, translator Alistair Elliot, and designers Peter J. Davison and Wayne Dowdeswell have created has a savage theatricality that is thrilling and contemporary. The supporting cast is strong, especially Donald Douglas as Aegeus and Dan Mullane as a messenger." Michael Sommers, of the *Newark Star-Ledger*, was remarkably moved and excited: "Diana Rigg is incandescent. Her white-hot fury as a woman scorned scorches Broadway with Promethean fire. You can't keep your eyes off this woman." In the *Christian Science Monitor*, Frank Scheck was happy to report: "Great theatre still exists. Beautifully acted and visually stunning. Unforgettable." Expressing his opinion of a play, for him the first time he had ever done so in print, the *New York Times* humorist Russell Baker turned serious to say: "We sit mesmerized, horrified, absolutely still, not a cough in the house for ninety astounding minutes as Euripides gives us a lesson in what theater is all about. Euripides on Broadway! New York, New York, you're a wonderful town." Michael Kuchwara, of Associated Press, was riveted as he watched Diana Rigg "prowling the stage like a caged tigress".

This surge of approval was largely augmented by the response of drama critics heard on radio and television broadcasts. Jess Cagle, of WCBS, declared the *Medea* to be "the most thrilling event on Broadway", a view shared by Joan Hamburg of WOR, who was convinced that "anyone interested in theater and drama must see this *Medea.* A staggering evening, truly extraordinary. I am haunted by Diana Rigg. She uses her brilliance to give us a performance of rage and intellect. See it." On WNBC, Pia Lindstrom was similarly impressed: "Diana Rigg snarls, she bites her words off with an intensity that is chilling, she is a monster of pain and anger. She is terrific: a Medea of cold intelligence and icy determination. . . . Don't let Euripides scare you – *Medea* is sizzling hot." And, to add one more, Roma Torre, of NY-1: "A performance that will go down as a classic in stage history. If you appreciate theater at its best, this is a can't miss. The Gods will be pleased."

Fuller commentaries were forthcoming from Edwin Wilson, of the *Wall Street Journal*, and the theatre reviewers in the large-circulation magazines. Wilson:

> Despite the fact that Greek tragedy is the fountainhead from which Western theater springs, it remains the most difficult form of drama to recreate in our own day. Greek plays employ a chorus for which we have no modern equivalent; they invariably contain long speeches describing events that take place offstage; and then there is all that raw emotion that can easily become too melodramatic. When, therefore, someone finds a way to transmit the power of a Greek play to a modern audience, it is a major accomplishment.
>
> Director Jonathan Kent's new production of Euripides' *Medea* not only achieves that goal, it is exciting theater on its own terms. *Medea* is one of the most awesome and frightening tragedies ever written. . . . In mounting it, Mr Kent made several key decisions, all of them inspired. The setting created by scene designer Peter J. Davison and lighting designer Wayne Dowdeswell is the corner of a courtyard: a three-story structure of huge, metal panels. They reverberate with a frightening, ear-splitting clang. The message is clear: Fearsome events are being hammered out within these walls.

Mr Kent uses the set to excellent effect. Traditionally the primal screams and first words of Medea are uttered offstage; she is heard but not seen. Here, Medea is revealed in a panel on an upper level, seated in a chair, her face turned from the audience as she speaks. In other words, her physical presence is felt from the beginning.

In the scene where Medea is agonizing over whether or not to carry through her infanticide, a harsh, triangular beam of light slashes across the stage, pinning her in a corner. At the climax of the play, after Medea has murdered her sons inside her palace, three enormous metal panels break loose, falling with a clangor that lifts spectators from their seats.

Mr Kent has also extracted maximum impact from his chorus, three ladies of Corinth (Judith Paris, Jane Loretta Lowe, and Nuala Willis) dressed in black Greek peasant outfits who chant and speak Jonathan Dove's score, sometimes in harmony, sometimes with a single voice. Their admonitions to Medea are counterpoint, relief, and agonizing prophecy of the black deeds to come. It is the most impressive use of a Greek chorus I can remember.

None of this would work, though, without a transcendent actress in the role of Medea, and here Mr Kent has triumphed with Diana Rigg. She has an incredible vocal range, moving from the rich deep resonance of a cello or viola, to the insistent peal of an oboe. One moment she unleashes fearsome cries and the next she colors a humorous exchange with deadly irony. Along with her vocal prowess is her presence and bearing. Always marked by dignity, intelligence and style, Ms Rigg moves like quicksilver from one emotion to another but always with an unmistakable resolve. Her Medea is not a mindless barbarian but rather someone who knows exactly what she is doing. She agonizes over her course of action, but once she has made her decision moves relentlessly toward her goal. This makes the outcome that much more awesome and appalling.

The new translation by Alistair Elliot is modern and accessible without being colloquial. An excellent cast performing with Ms Rigg has been imported from London. For eighty-five minutes without break, this is one of those rare experiences when a work of art from the past becomes a painful reminder of the fearful forces swirling around us today.

A single aspect of the presentation finally won over William A. Henry III, of *Time*:

One dazzling image can be enough to make an otherwise competent production unforgettable, and the *Medea* that has been imported from London to Broadway climaxes with an astonishing tableau. After wreaking the most comprehensive revenge that a scorned wife has ever devised – slaying her husband's

> royal fiancée and soon-to-be father-in-law, then slaughtering her sons so that her husband's bloodline will die with him – Medea sets sail for a new life. Most stagings leave her outside her home merely talking of departure. In director Jonathan Kent's version, a wall topples to reveal Diana Rigg apparently already at sea. Hunched during her period of rage and oppression, she stands proud as a ship's figurehead, clouds streaming past, golden light burnishing her. Then she turns and looks back, toward the scene of her unrepented misdeeds and, surely, toward an audience agape at the beauty and power of this finale.
>
> The rest is more ordinary. Rigg is wonderful in quiet moments but awkward in striving for the unchained melodrama that Zoe Caldwell achieved in a 1982 revival. The balance of the cast, also from London, is workmanlike, save for Nuala Willis, whose keening songs redeem the most archaic of theatrical ploys, the chorus. The set, a vast wall of rusted metal panels that bang like thunder and rumble away at key moments, is effective but excessive, a tacit confession of shaky faith in the play's words. That doubt is foolish. *Medea* is *the* greatest role ever written for a woman, fiercer than Lady Macbeth, more lovelorn than Phèdre. Despite Rigg's shortcomings as Euripides' virago, the role makes her the odds-on contender to join Caldwell and Judith Anderson, who played the part on Broadway in 1948, as winners of a Tony Award for Best Actress.

Marc Peyser, for *Newsweek*, took more wholehearted pleasure in Kent's reading of the play, finding its message timeless and universal. "Euripides' Medea may have been born in 431 BC, but she looks more modern every year." Her problem was what to do when the father of her children, the man she loves obsessively, abandons her, and how is she to make her way in a world increasingly hostile to her.

> The startling production that opened on Broadway last week, starring Diana Rigg, answers these questions with startling immediacy.
>
> In a year when the theater seems oddly preoccupied with crazed, jilted women (*Sunset Boulevard*, Stephen Sondheim's *Passion*), *Medea* is still irresistible. . . . The challenge of the play is to make Medea's barbarity believable, not just spectacle. It's not surprising that Rigg energizes the role with brainy aplomb. Her Medea stalks the stage like a linebacker in flowing crimson, barefoot and surprisingly asexual. When Zoe Caldwell brought the last *Medea* to Broadway in 1982, she juiced up the character's sexual energy, underscoring Medea's hotbloodedness. Rigg – using an accessible, if somewhat unpoetic translation by Alistair Elliot – zeroes in on Medea's mind. She hangs on every mention of her

> cleverness – "Come then, Medea. Use all your knowledge now. Move toward horror!" she exhorts herself in a mesmerizing voice – while turning the references to femininity and sex into throw-away jokes. It's not losing the man that infuriates her, but losing her pride and wasting her superior talents on such an unworthy object.
>
> Except for the gripping scene where she debates whether or not to murder her sons, Rigg's brain-powered Medea almost never dissolves into wails or rants. She doesn't have to. The dazzlingly lit set of acid-corroded walls is a physical manifestation of the play's scalding emotions – especially in the shattering final scene. The set and a black-cloaked, three-woman Greek chorus that sings in haunting fugues form a vibrant canvas on which Rigg paints a chilling portrait of controlled rage. Director Kent assaults all the senses simultaneously. . . . What outrageous good fortune.

As usual, two reviews appeared in the *New York Times*, one by David Richards (who had replaced Frank Rich as senior drama critic in the daily edition), as well as a second appraisal by Vincent Canby in the Sunday Arts and Leisure section. As viewed by Richards:

> Mountain climbers have Everest. Swimmers have the English Channel. Actresses have *Medea*.
>
> The title character of Euripides' tragedy is one of the huge, ravenous roles of dramatic literature. It will take everything a performer can give, then ask for more. Sheer talent is not enough. Courage and a certain recklessness are required to conquer it. A wild and exotic creature who knows potions that cure and poisons that kill, Medea is also a forsaken wife and tortured mother. She is one of us and not like us at all.
>
> In the London-born production that began a limited engagement last night at the Longacre Theater, Diana Rigg brings a blazing intelligence and an elegant ferocity to the part. In the course of the ninety-minute production, she grovels ignominiously at the feet of men. But by the end, she stands over them like the mighty figure-head of a ship about to sail for distant lands. For the actress, who has always managed to suggest impeccable breeding even when she is behaving abominably, the evening is a triumph.
>
> It can also be counted a considerable success for the director, Jonathan Kent, who has set the play in an abstract box that could be the courtyard of a grim prison. The three-story walls are made of rusting metal panels. Whenever someone pounds on them, they produce thunderous echoes. The doors shut with a clang. Peter J. Davison's austere design does more than convey a sense of Medea's exile in a foreign land – an incarceration, really – it is a potent image for an inhospitable universe, conceived by the gods for man's misery and pain.

Working closely, Mr Kent and Mr Davison have engineered a spectacular climax for a tragedy that consists primarily of a series of increasingly horrible revelations. . . . Atrocity follows atrocity. Then, vengeance taken, she locks herself behind the rusted walls.

The biggest jolt is still to come, however. "Unbar the doors," howls a grief-stricken Jason, desperate to see the corpses of his sons but unable to find a way in. Suddenly, as if shaken by an earthquake, the metal wall before him collapses, the panels crashing to the ground with a colossal din. There, high above, stands Medea in a blood-soaked gown: victorious, remorseless, inhuman. Jason's pleading exasperates her. The last word out of her mouth before the lights fade is "rubbish." She virtually spits it down at him.

The women of Corinth, who make up the chorus, are the sorts of Greek peasants who hover like crows on the fringes of *Zorba.* Their clothes are black and their faces are lined. Sometimes they sing their choral passages (Jonathan Dove has written the haunting musical line). Sometimes they speak them. But for all their woeful thoughts, they mostly communicate a fearful helplessness, before taking to wooden chairs on the sidelines. The play is Medea's. So is the agony.

Unlike Zoe Caldwell, who emphasized the sexuality of the character (and won a Tony Award for her efforts), Ms Rigg sees Medea as a woman of restless intellect. An original fervor informed Ms Caldwell's performance; she had a savage growl in her voice. A passionate sense of injustice propels Ms Rigg, whose voice never entirely loses its intrinsic musicality. Her hair is swept back into a tight braid, a style that sets off her grave and handsome features. Initially, only the aggressive jut of her chin and the smolder in her eyes give her away.

While some of Paul Brown's modernistic costumes – in particular, a greatcoat for the king that seems to be growing hair – are a bit wacky, the lighting by Wayne Dowdeswell and Rui Rita is almost brutal in its directness. At one point, a merciless shaft of light actually forces Medea into a corner, even as she is wrestling with her conscience and trying to steel herself to the awful deeds ahead. In what may be the best messenger role ever written, Dan Mullane, motionless in a fierce spotlight, describes ghastly offstage events with frozen horror. He could be responding to a police grilling.

The male characters in *Medea* don't come off well. But then they never have, and Alistair Elliot's stripped-for-action translation of the play further emphasizes Euripides' feminist sympathies. Either the men are smug and patronizing (like John Turner's Creon) or else they're smug and self-serving (like Mr Woodward's Jason). Although Aegeus (Donald Douglas) shows some understanding of Medea's plight and promises her asylum in Athens, he's got a prudent streak running down his back and makes it clear that she'll have to get there by herself.

None of them can hold their own against her on moral or dramatic grounds. And when Ms Rigg allows herself to indulge in some traditional feminine wiles, their defenses prove pathetically weak. "I am clever," she admits boldly to Creon, before realizing her error and backing down. The voice softens, and she adds, "but I am not *that* clever." The qualification is shrewd, self-protective. She's not ready for the kill yet.

Let men boast that they take all of life's risks while women sit safely at home. "I'd rather stand three times by my shield," she responds, "than once give birth." Ms Rigg, who always had a wry wit, does not forgo it here. In addition to the knife in the folds of her robe, irony is one of her weapons. Medea, a victim, is also a victimizer.

The contradictions are tantalizing. I'd want to see her if I were you.

Vincent Canby faulted the production for several reasons.

Let's face it: Medea, though grievously wronged by her husband, Jason, is not exactly your prototypical battered wife. She's the daughter of the king of Colchis, the granddaughter of the sun, a wife, a witch, a mother, a primeval terror in her own right. Medea is not a woman to be easily characterized. "I am adept at everything that's hidden," she boasts to the women of Corinth. She then goes on to commit atrocities that astonish even her. To play her mostly as a victim is to humble one of literature's most titanic creations.

Yet even if the initial concept of the production is wrong-headed, the Euripides' *Medea*, now in a limited engagement at the Longacre Theater, is efficient, polished and high-toned. It's also a theatrical event, marking the return of Diana Rigg, who plays the title role, her first appearance in New York since 1975 and her bewitching performance as Célimène in *The Misanthrope*. Further, this *Medea*, directed by Jonathan Kent, is fashionably contemporary in its theatrical effects and in Alistair Elliot's new translation. Mr Elliot does not veer eccentrically from other versions, but he makes more pronounced the feminism that is built into the Euripides text without, however, being its point.

If Medea fascinates, it is in part because she is the mistress of the black arts. They are her heritage in the barbaric land from which she fled to Greece with Jason, after helping him steal the Golden Fleece. Medea, who has been badly treated, can give as well as she gets. Before the dark events related by Euripides, she had already committed several ghastly murders, though always in the cause of Jason's career. It's not the murders she is regretting at the beginning of *Medea*. She is furious at the ingratitude of Jason who, having settled with her in Corinth, has abandoned her and their two small sons to marry the daughter of Creon, the king.

Friendless in a foreign city, what is a witch to do? Medea thrashes around her palace and moans for all the neighbors to hear. Her faithful old nurse and the women of Corinth wait outside, predicting dire consequences. Medea considers suicide but rejects it: "It's not the dying I dread but the thought of leaving my enemies alive and laughing at my corpse." When Creon learns that she has threatened his life and his daughter's, he gives her twenty-four hours to get out of town. This is more than enough time for Medea to wipe out the royal house of Corinth and to leave Jason without heirs: to prevent others from murdering her sons, she butchers them herself. Medea overcomes the most basic instinct governing human conduct; she puts herself beyond the comprehension of the minds of ordinary men.

Euripides acknowledges the disadvantaged status of women, but if he has any interest in changing that status it doesn't show in *Medea.* He's more concerned with the spectacle of passions so grand and terrible that, by resisting all rational analysis, they reveal some measure of the depth of the soul. It's not a concept easily understood in our world, where the Medeas live in the suburbs. They become infatuated with bouncers and autobody mechanics, do their bloody deeds in fits of momentary derangement (which they never remember), then sell their stories to television and become famous.

The gorgeous Ms Rigg is equipped with a big velvety voice and the gift to command it. She's a voluptuous Medea, but she's also a very civilized one. She looks as if she's come not from the edge of the known world, a place where they eat with their fingers, but from Belgravia. She wears the kind of classically cut gown (blood red in this case) that Mainbocher once designed for Lynn Fontanne, something so simple of line that it never goes out of style, so well stitched that it always hangs perfectly. Her skin is milky white, her auburn hair parted in the middle and gathered in a single braid at the back. Medea is described as a barbarian but comes on like the fashion plate of Corinth.

Things have somehow got back to front in this production. Jason taunts Medea with the idea that, without him, she would have lived out her life in the rude obscurity of Colchis. Yet it's Ms Rigg's elegant Medea who civilizes what appears to be the barbarian world of Corinth. At least that's how Greece is evoked in Peter J. Davison's severe, handsome, vaguely Expressionistic set. Representing the forecourt of Medea's palace, the set looks like an open-air dungeon, one plated in the bronze that gives the age its name. When a door closes, it sounds as if an entire tier of cells at Sing Sing were being locked up for the night.

The set seems to exist for its own theatrical effect. It makes stunning images possible. At a crucial moment in the play's supposedly cathartic climax, several bronze plates fall from the palace façade with an astounding clatter. Revealed inside is Medea with the bloodied corpses of her sons, the tableau framed by the ropes holding the bronze plates. The ropes look like marionette strings, possibly a reference to the interfering gods, though the gods have nothing to do with Medea's and Jason's domestic problems.

Ms Rigg speaks Mr Elliot's lines with consistent if studied intelligence. She roars, but she never loses her composure or knocks a hair out of place. The fire inside is always under control, something Ms Rigg's Medea seems to have learned in boarding school. This is in decided contrast to the way that Judith Anderson played the role in the 1940s. Anderson was more wild actress than wild woman but, when you watched her, you were never in any doubt that you were seeing an extremely raw ego in torment – I didn't see the 1982 production in which Anderson played the Nurse to Zoe Caldwell's Medea.

At the Longacre, whatever Euripides had in mind is bent into the shape of a well-spoken, great-lady star vehicle. Everybody else is at the star's command, the men especially. No matter what their status or the sense of the scene, they often stand in that stock-company feet-astride position that indicates orders are being awaited from their monarch. For all her wailing, this Medea is remote, chilly and awfully regal.

There are good moments in Mr Elliot's text, a number of which go to the chorus of the three women of Corinth, well played and sung. . . . Apollo, one of them notes early on, liked women "dumb and dancing/ And chose no woman poet to inspire." Banalities abound. In response to Medea's "O Love, how great a curse you are to mortals," Creon answers feebly, "Well, that depends on the circumstance." The high point of this *Medea* is not the end of the play but the first of its title character's two encounters with Jason. Medea pours out her scorn for a man who, it becomes apparent, is doubly loathed for not having been worthy of her love in the first place.

Though the production began at North London's sometimes adventurous Almeida Theatre (1992), it looks and sounds as if it had been tailored for mainstream audiences right from the start. The proper ingredients are all there: some new-found feminism, the strikingly memorable set and the sometimes gross contemporary locutions: "But," Medea says sarcastically to Jason during a fight, "in the much-used phrase, let's try to be friends." The audience laughs in appreciation and relief. Such lines divert the mind from the central, unknowable mystery of Medea herself.

An even more discordant voice was John Heilpern's in the *New York Observer*:

O, world! O, Anglophilia! And poor old Euripides, too. The acclaimed British import of *Medea* on Broadway, Diana Rigg giving, it's said, "the greatest acting performance of the decade," left me only astonished by its averageness and worse. I appear to be in a minority of one in saying this, but so be it. "Come then, Medea," as the lady says. "Use all your knowledge now. Move toward horror!"

While the high-minded custodians of our culture are moaning about the theme-park Disney-fication of Broadway with *Beauty and the Beast*, we ought to look at a few similarities with this *Medea*. It's a theme-park production for the masses, too (though one that makes audiences feel superior). It is a Beauty without the Beast, and in a murderous mood. I shall come to Ms Rigg shortly. At ninety minutes in length, it is "The Best Moments of *Medea*" – easily digestible, edited highlights of the epic drama for "the cultured" who make no effort. Its metallic set and theatrical effects are much talked about, *pace* Disney (though the sets are familiar). It has cute stage children: the two insufferably blond sons of Medea with invisible halos and white tunics who are made all the more adorable in case the audience fails to feel something when Mom knifes them to death.

Jonathan Kent's new production does not trust the audience for a second. It either tries to flatter us via generalized artiness – the wailing "poetic" peasant chorus in black with its foreboding "song-speech." (But can we really follow all that they are saying? And what are they doing, dancing a Hasidic dance?) Or the production, designed to make Euripides accessible, leaving absolutely nothing to chance (or to the imagination), hammers home the high drama – characters literally hammering on the metallic scenery, lest we miss the point, or the drama, or fall asleep.

Above all, this is a *Medea* simplified and vulgarized for the modern age as a fashionable feminist tract, a Euripides (*circa* 485–406 BC) with Lorena Bobbitt on his mind. *Medea* is somewhat bigger than that. It is like reducing *Lear* to a ninety-minute version whose message is Father Knows Best. *Medea* belongs to the savage, irrational underworld of dark myth, not *Inside Edition*. Euripides had his ironies about the cornered role of women, but he was no feminist. The notion that *Medea* is simply a melodrama about a tragic heroine betrayed by an unfaithful husband is a misreading of the play. If not, what are we to feel when Medea kills her children?

This is no semi-realistic bourgeois drama about a wronged woman's revenge. Medea is a serial killer, isn't she? She killed her brother without conscience and betrayed her own family to help her husband, Jason, steal the Golden Fleece. Her sister in spirit is Lady Macbeth. Is the marriage of Medea and Jason convincing? I wonder. The Macbeths are certainly a solid couple. We know couples like them. But Medea is a problem (and her marriage is imbalanced.) *She is not human*. The Devil knows where she came from. She is a witch casting spells, the Devil's disciple.

Medea actually has magic powers. When Jason abandons her to marry King Creon's daughter, she sends the happy bride a magic robe that burns her to death. Is this a feminist plea, or an expression of unearthly power and terror? The King is also murdered, after which Medea butchers her young children. Infanticide. She murders the living image of their father.

I couldn't sense the barbaric in Diana Rigg's performance. She seemed to me too human, too elegant in her blood-red robes, too modern. Perhaps in this popularized interpretation, she must play Medea as a victim. But she appears to be overplaying her, literally and alarmingly, as a Javanese puppet – as if manipulated by godly strings. Except when she is in repose, Ms Rigg's arms and hands and even her neck are never still, jerking and fluttering theatrically throughout. She is seen to be acting. But the real Medea is manipulated by no one, not even the gods. She should be the puppeteer, not the puppet.

Ms Rigg's center within Medea is intelligent, cold and composed within her vengeance. There is no mystery to her portrayal, no strangeness of terror. Her tone is more of bitter outrage, a Medea made pragmatic and rational. Of course she dominates and rips up the stage! She is too accomplished an actress not to do that, and this is a star vehicle. The "supporting" players are middling. Crucially, Tim Oliver Woodward's workmanlike Jason with his little ponytail lacks the tragic stature to convince us that Medea would marry him in the first place. She'd spit this Jason out for breakfast. And of course, Ms Rigg's voice has the fire and range associated with "great" British acting. It is easier than it sounds. But New Yorkers should not always prostrate themselves cravenly at the feet of the British and exclaim, as they invariably do, "Oh my. If only we could talk like that."

There are some in the cast who do not speak well. The Messenger, Dan Mullane, delivers the news of unspeakable events with the flat unmusical tone of a waiter reciting the dinner specials. Ms Rigg herself slips into the well-bred South Kensington accent at times, as if she's having a nervous breakdown in Harrods. What else can I complain about, not being an Anglophile? Among much, the line delivered by the grief-stricken Jason, "Unbar the doors," is not sufficient excuse for the set to collapse. Medea's line to Jason, "But in the age-old phrase, let's try to be friends" is typical of the production's clangingly inappropriate attempts to be witty and contemporary. And the brief House of Horrors sight of those poor adorable blond boys painted with stage blood and the sound of their tiny high-pitched screams shook us all to the marrow of our bones, no doubt. But the final image, or old-fashioned stagy tableau, of a statuesque Ms Rigg posing on high against clouds streaming by, takes the biscuit.

(Several topical allusions on these pages may soon need clarification. Sing Sing is a New York state penitentiary. The Disney Company, having enjoyed a great success with its cartoon version of the fairy-tale *Beauty and the Beast*, brought a live-actor adaptation of it to Broadway where it revelled in opulent but seemingly unnecessary stage effects. A young woman, Lorena Bobbitt, offended by her husband's inadequate love-making, had sexually mutilated him. *Father Knows Best* was a popular, very wholesome situation comedy series on television. *Inside Edition*, also a long-running television programme, featured the sensational aspects of current news events, such as murders and marital scandals, by interviewing the unhappy people involved in them.)

Before leaving London for the New York engagement, Diana Rigg replied to queries put to her by Matt Wolf on behalf of the *New York Times.* Was her daily personal life clouded by her prolonged immersion in the role of *Medea*? No, she replied. All that was readily left behind at the stage door. "It's dreary to carry any of that with you. Obviously, I've felt a lot of Medea's emotions but not quite to the same degree. I have nothing to work out; I have no rage. Performance is a matter of developing and enlarging, but it begins and ends with the text." Wolf asked: "Still, how do you enact the murder of a child, particularly when you are yourself a mother?" Her explanation: "The play will answer you; the text tells you. Its psychology is so pure that when Medea reaches that point, there are no alternatives, none. But, if a performer gets trapped into behavioral manifestations of a character, then you find yourself in a corner unable to get out; a balance must be achieved."

Wolf noted: "The playwright Tom Stoppard, for whom Ms Rigg had appeared in the premières of *Jumpers* and *Night and Day* in London in the Seventies, said the actress 'chimed' with his sense of 'the theatrical event as a technical problem, a pragmatic affair. Whatever else it has to be, it is also a mechanism. Diana Rigg has that, as well as a knowingness about the world, which gives her characterizations tremendous clarity and intelligence.'"

At about the same time, Marc-Antoine Charpentier's late-seventeenth-century Baroque opera *Médée* was revived once more (1993) in a production guided by the New York-born musicologist, conductor and harpsichordist William Christie (1944–). An acknowledged specialist in the musical styles of the period, Christie had become a professor in that subject at the Conservatoire National Superieur de Musique de Paris, the first American to hold tenure there. He also founded Les Arts Florissants, a period-instrument ensemble (1979), leading it in public and recorded concerts and seventeenth- and eighteenth-century stage-pieces, especially those and others by Lully, Charpentier's arch-rival at the court of Louis XIV, where so many jealous factions thrived.

This more ambitious *Médée* project was jointly financed by a virtual consortium of local governments and arts councils, plus a dozen-and-a-half foundations, commercial firms and private donors, in Europe and abroad, testimony to Christie's amazing skill as a fund-raiser. Serving as co-producers were the Théâtre de Caen, the Opéra du Rhin (Strasbourg) and Opéra Comique (Paris). After the elaborately mounted presentation played in the sponsoring cities and elsewhere in Europe, it was brought to the Brooklyn Academy of Music for four performances, widely anticipated to be the high-point of the season (1994). From there the piece returned to Europe to participate in Lisbon's Summer Festival.

By chance, the appearance of *Médée* at the Brooklyn Academy, across the East River from Manhattan, coincided with the limited run on Broadway of *Medea* with Diana Rigg, which afforded critics an opportunity to contrast the two very different dramatizations of the searing Greek tale. Euripides told his story in ninety minutes. Thomas Corneille's libretto stretched it to a full four hours, a length which an otherwise enraptured audience largely found wearisome, but which accorded to the demands of the Baroque age. The players wore seventeenth-century dress, which is how the work was originally performed for Louis XIV and his Dauphin, who welcomed Charpentier's version, though the general public did not; the King and the Dauphin eagerly came to several repeat performances of it, after which it had disappeared and was mostly forgotten.

Christie's search for total authenticity in the physical production was frustrated. He explained to Allan Kozinn, of the *New York Times*: "The few historical stagings I've seen have given me the impression that there is a lot more work to be done. The problem in the French repertory is that with very few exceptions, we have almost no information about how people behaved onstage. We don't know where the choirs were, how people came in and out. It was probably extremely static. What we're doing has nothing to do with historical re-creation whatsoever. You will see, for example, French court costumes. But there are also costumes, especially in the Underworld scenes, that are styled directly from late eighteenth-century Goya. It used historical elements. But it's a very eclectic, a very personal interpretation."

In Christie's phrase, the staging, conceived and directed by Jean-Marie Villégier, was "post-modern". A single set was used throughout, instead of the changing scenes indicated in the score: designed by Carlo Tommasi, it consisted of a high, domed hall with mythological figures painted on the ceiling, above brick walls, a gallery and a rough wooden floor. Bruno Boyer's lighting borrowed hues from the music and the volatile emotional states of the characters. The nobles' attire, rich and varied, had been sketched and fashioned by Patrice Cauchetier. The dancers were enlisted from the Compagnie Fêtes Galantes, a group established in 1993 by Béatrice Massin and dedicated to the exploration of Baroque choreography, though not intent on interpreting it too literally, but allowing some modern infusion.

Not only was the five-act *Médée* done without cuts, but it was preceded by an irrelevant prologue in which unctuously flattering allegorical tribute is paid to the victorious Sun King, Louis XIV, the patron of the opera. This was customary in works presented at the French court, especially when the country was at war. Villégier sought to integrate this prologue into the story by having Medea's infant sons appear in it. In a programme note he argues: "It is in the Prologue that I have decided that we should meet Medea's children, children who are promised to Death, who are introduced into this world through a baptism ceremony. We therefore find ourselves on one side in an environment of purity, innocence and luminosity before being plunged into the exact opposite in the third act which, like a kind of terrible echo of this naïve dream, becomes a nightmare, a devilish cult . . . madness." He states that in retaining the prologue he has been influenced "by the music and not the words. We are dealing here with music whose accents are often decidedly religious. It is music which celebrates a social order based on divine right, a hierarchical world, a world of ritual, a world which is at one and the same time rigid and reassuring." Like Christie, Villégier is an expert on the Baroque, having directed a long list of works in that distinctive style, both operas and plays.

The orchestra numbered about forty. "*Médée* is a *tragédie lyrique* . . . which means that you have a very strong libretto with lots and lots of text, and that it's as much a superb piece of theater as it is a superb piece of music," said Christie. He likened it to Lully's *Atys*, which he had also offered in New York in a similar staging two years earlier. "There are differences. The connoisseur is going to notice that there is much more music in *Médée*. The orchestra's participation is heavier and more sophisticated, partly because Charpentier is Charpentier. He liked orchestras, he liked orchestral color, he liked a texture that is meatier than you find in Lully. It's a big orchestra, but it is needed, because Charpentier was very specific, right down to the exotics, like the bass flute." The original manuscript is lost. Christie relied on a score printed in Paris by Christophe Ballard in 1694, a year after the opera's première.

H. Wiley Hitchcock, in an article in *Opera News* (May 1994), details the period instruments – a core of strings, plus recorders and flutes, reeds, harpsichord, trumpets and timpani – constituting this orchestra, an index too lengthy and technical to include here. The group of musicians at Louis XIV's court was twice or more the size of any like ensemble to be found accompanying opera in Italy at that time, a fact about which the denizens of Versailles were proud and boastful. The consequence was a greater sonority. "There was no orchestra richer, more diverse or powerful anywhere in Europe."

The infighting at court and elsewhere in elite circles between the partisans of Lully and Charpentier embodied a paradox. Lully, an Italian expatriate, sought to establish an autonomous French tradition, a pure one. Charpentier, French-born, had studied in Rome under Giacomo Carissimi and largely clung to Italianate conventions. The *tragédie lyrique*, with its light and airy vocalism, "gracefully ornamented in the style of the French *air de cour*", was Lully's innovation, as was the device of the *comédie-ballet* that he and Molière invented, with Lully providing the cheerful dance music. After the dramatist and the composer broke off their inspired collaboration, Lully was succeeded as Molière's collaborator by the young Charpentier, then still in his twenties; this relationship continued after Lully's death. Despite the controversies both creators' music provoked, however, as to which of the two was best, Charpentier's works contain much that was clearly influenced by Lully's example.

The Opéra in Paris was dominated by Lully's devotees. Charpentier wrote other operas, but the Paris Opéra's doors were shut to them; *Médée* was his only piece ever staged there. In a Lullist manifesto, by the critic Le Cerf de Viéville, *Médée* was dismissed as "wretched . . . an abomination", its music "harsh, dry and stiff in the extreme"; it had eight or ten performances, after which it was not heard again for 200 years. The singer who had the title role, Marthe Le Rochois, was praised in the monthly *Mercure Galant*, however, which said that she portrayed the vengeful heroine with "warmth, subtlety and intelligence", adding that "true connoisseurs found many admirable passages" in the text and score. Thirty years later, Sébastien de Brossard, a composer and musicologist, pored over the published script and wrote generously of *Médée* in these bold terms: "It is unquestionably the most expert and exquisite of all [the operas] that have been printed, at least since the death of Mr de Lully . . . although thanks to the cabals of the envious and ignorant it was not received by the public as well as it deserved." (Quoted by Hitchcock.)

To lengthen the story, Thomas Corneille begins the action much earlier than does Euripides or Seneca, or indeed his more elegant brother Pierre Corneille, who had also tried his hand at the grim drama. Euripides opens *in medias res*; Jason has already cast off Medea and married Creusa. Seneca has the marriage just taking place, and Pierre Corneille has the pair already wed but their union unconsummated. Thomas Corneille reverts to an earlier day, the arrival of the fugitives, Jason and Medea, in Corinth, where they desperately need a haven. Throughout, Jason is shown as weak and wavering, hardly the impetuous hero of the *Argonaut* who has stolen the precious Golden Fleece. Medea is exceedingly complex, proud but intensely jealous, unwilling to listen to ill-favoured news, seeking acceptance by others, fond mother, but when angered a heartless sorceress. There are awesome scenes of witchcraft and black magic, an episode in which Creon first goes mad, instead of dying expeditiously while trying to save Creusa from her poisonous fiery robe as Euripides has it. And there is a banquet, as well as courtly dance interludes.

The *New York Times*'s laudatory review, by Edward Rothstein, bore a stark headline: "A *Médée* That Turns Antiquity Into Life". The notice began:

When Médée calls upon the evil phantoms of the Underworld to serve her will in Marc-Antoine Charpentier's opera, when she slowly allows a magical cloak to release its poison and watches her romantic rival writhe in agony and when she declares that she has even murdered her own children in her desire to wreak revenge on her unfaithful husband, Charpentier doesn't raise his voice. He doesn't abandon the dance forms and gracious manners of French Baroque opera. The singing doesn't explode in Lucia-like extravagance. The remarkable expressions are contained, restrained; the sense comes through subtle shifts in texture, and through the clearly articulated French text, which is almost always set with one note for each syllable.

But by now, William Christie and his early-music group, Les Arts Florissants, have shown how large a universe of emotion lies compressed in this musical style, how a supple sense of pulse governs these declamations, how violence, jealousy and tenderness can be revealed in the ways in which lines are sung and text pronounced. And that is exactly what was accomplished in the much-awaited production of *Médée* that Mr Christie conducted at the Brooklyn Academy of Music on Thursday night, an antique language was turned into a living tongue, its every nuance brought to life.

That was clear in the orchestra's playing, but also in the impressive performance by Lorraine Hunt as Médée. Here, as part of a remarkable cast noteworthy less for the intrinsic quality of its voices than for its interpretive imagination and beauty of the phrasing, she stood out as both a character and an artist; her voice is not large, but it is used with great skill, giving each line sense as well as shape. In an opera filled with weak, duplicitous men, she became a fierce, unforgiving figure of considerable presence.

. . . Mr Villégier also responded very closely to Mr Christie's musical style: the characters dance and move and sing and carefully shape their expressions in ways we associate with the period in which the opera was first performed. We experience *Médée* as it might have seemed to the Sun King: as a drama about courtly manners and diplomacy undone by passion and madness.

The production sets up its own circumscribed world within which small details take on large significance. (Even the super-titles were intelligent.) Béatrice Massin's choreography creates a visual language that is the counterpart of Charpentier's musical one; extremes of emotion are expressed within a formal structure. I didn't agree with Mr Villégier's radical transformation of the Prologue to the opera. He deliberately ignored the words and created a baptism scene in a church. (The Prologue's references to love, constancy and victory have far more to do with the opera's themes than Mr Villégier noted.) There were longueurs during the course of the four and a half hours as well.

But Mr Christie's approach to this score was once again a revelation: he has widened the range of the work compared with his 1985 recording. Two casts will be alternating performances until Sunday. The cast I saw included Mark Padmore as Jason, Bernard Deletré as Creon, Agnès Melion as Créuse and Jean-Marc Salzman as Oronte. They had clearly been submersed in Mr Christie's musical universe, in which the text and the music can seem different aspects of a single expression. Now, with Mr Christie's vision of the French Baroque, our universe seems larger.

Rothstein's review was followed a few days later by this semi-light rumination from the *New York Times*'s senior music critic, Bernard Holland:

Theatergoers have been exiting Broadway's *Medea* with fear in their hearts. Men run home to wives and lovers determined to be nicer. Divorce and separation inspires dread. Women listen to Diana Rigg's rage and feel their feminist sentiments boil. Men look apprehensively over their shoulders and try to smile.

The same story was told last week in Brooklyn, where William Christie and Les Arts Florissants played Marc-Antoine Charpentier's *Médée* four times. On both sides of the East River, a woman kills her children, poisons the minds and bodies of her rivals and reduces an errant husband to jelly. So how is it that Broadway's update of Euripides can make our insides churn and Charpentier sends listeners away from the Brooklyn Academy of Music in a relative state of calm?

Broadway, to give one reason, goes to Euripides' stark original, while Charpentier preferred the elegance of Thomas Corneille. But maybe music, and especially the 300-year-old Baroque music, has something to do with it, too. Lorraine Hunt singing *Médée* has arranged horror into neat little rows of melody and harmony, therefore rescuing us from it. Miss Rigg reduces horror to an unbearable concentrate so superfactual that it scares us silly. It is about distance. The play crowds us physically; by association we fear for our own lives. The opera invites empathy and awe but safely from afar.

Most music, at least until recently, has tried hard to civilize the unpleasantnesses of life. It does not do away with pain but it makes pain orderly. Pain can develop a rhythm of its own, but pain first appears as disruption. Music puts it in its place, creates beginnings, middles and ends, whereas in life we fumble for the origins of our pain and can only guess at its outcome.

Life, indeed, is not an opera. In it, chords do not resolve, but modulate *ad absurdum.* The passing day does not respond to the guidelines of sonata form. No death rattle ends in plagal cadences. At one point, Charpentier's Jason espouses passion in neat, dancing triple time. We are touched by the beauty of it but are our libidos aroused?

Louis XIV of France, for whom *Médée* was written, used protocol and court ritual to keep his nobility occupied and thus at bay. *Médée* sublimates violence in much the same way. Its grammar of harmony and dance forms create elaborate rules of courtesy through which the rage of Medea is tempered. Broadway's *Medea* stabs us in the heart.

Perhaps the major miscalculation of the Brooklyn *Médée* was its heated acting style, a late nineteenth-century vociferousness set against sets, costumes, dances, instruments and performing style that were reserve itself. This staging evidently aims to make physically palpable what the other elements do not. It does not work.

For music is the master here. Médée, for all her supernatural powers, is its servant, too. Her magic spells and her consuming hatreds are subject to meter and rhythm. Even the spectacle of infanticide must bow to harmonic resolutions. The theater also abstracts Medea's acts of violence but only to make them more visceral. Médée is every inch the magician. Miss Rigg is not. Hers is the condensation of an anger accumulated and ignited by untold millions of women wronged.

Music may be losing this power to tame the effects of life. More and more, operas tell us that theater comes first and music waits in the wings ready to add a little color when needed. At the climactic moment of *Medea* on Broadway, a wall of metal panels collapses with a gigantic clatter. The effect is devastating, unnerving. In 1693, this would have been a sound effect, an interruption of music. In 1994, it becomes music, an operatic music for our time.

This new music has little life of its own. It exists to serve image and language. Indeed, the creators of this clattering wall feel no obligation to beguile, to comfort, to order or to civilize: they are clever manufacturers of ugliness and take pride in their work. Louis XIV would have had them arrested.

The Nuyorican Poets Café was the venue for the tragedy given a different slant. D.J. Bruckner wrote in the ubiquitous *New York Times* (1996):

Theater Double and its managing director, Dennis Moritz, are nothing if not brave. With *Jason and Medea* – written by Mr Moritz and performed by a cast of nineteen – they invite, even provoke, comparison with a play that twenty-four hundred years after it was written has few challengers for dramatic power. That Euripides remains the champion is no surprise; that this company's effort at the Nuyorican Poets Café (236 East Third Street, Lower East Side) has many effective moments is gratifying.

Those moments owe more to the director, Michael Leland, and this disciplined troupe than to the playwright. Mr Moritz introduces race as a factor in the Corinthians' fear of Medea, and he draws

> our attention so insistently to the history and character of Jason, of Creon and even of a couple of soldiers that in the end we are more mystified by Medea's tragedy than horrified by it.
>
> His language is not soul-stirring. Creon bets that Jason "can certainly keep my daughter in line"; Jason tells Medea he "will always have a warm spot" for her, and Medea, defying the Corinthians, can think of nothing more eloquent than: "Hate me, then! Just shut up!"
>
> But there are those moments: when Creon and his troops let us feel the threat Medea felt; when the Corinthian women reflect with sardonic humor on women's lives in the ancient world; above all, when the final slaughter is described in a choked scream. Then you think this company could do almost anything well, a reminder, perhaps, of Euripides.

In a history long and strange, the amazing count of *Medeas* and endlessly varied adaptations of it continued through the last three years of the twentieth century. Shortly in the wake of its success with Irene Papas in *Electra* (1997), the National Theatre of Greece returned to the City Center in New York with its *Medea* (1998), the company now led by Niketi Kontouri with Karyofyllia Karabeti as the savage avenger. In the *New York Times* Peter Marks's review was almost as cruel. He thought this offering was far inferior to the *Electra*, which had been "whirling, incantatory, so throbbingly alive you could hear its heartbeat. This time things have cooled off considerably." The new import was a severe version of the tragedy that put

> more stock in a display of style than the delivery of substance.
>
> The production replaces life's blood with ice water. Although it is performed in modern Greek with English supertitles, and is populated by characters from Corinth and Athens, the look and feel suggest an art film from Scandinavia. No doubt, on its second visit the troupe, led by the director Niketi Kontouri, wanted to show off other colors. But did so many of them have to be shades of white?
>
> Ms Kontouri's handiwork is admirably disciplined; there is not a hair out of place, not a stylized gesture wasted in a two-hour presentation that is closer in spirit to performance art or dance. The actors are technically accomplished yet impassive; they strike attitudes rather than express depth. The audience is deliberately prevented from feeling much toward the characters; and although the English translation is absolutely clear, the story has little power to penetrate, to shock. It all passes in a fitful pageant, beautiful despite the tale's ugliness.
>
> This *Medea*, in fact, featuring the exotic Karyofyllia Karabeti in the demanding title role, is never less than visually arresting. The twelve women of Corinth, wearing helmets of white fabric that give

them the appearance of mummified soldiers, strike dramatic poses as the lighting bisects them at odd angles. Other times, they make bird noises as they stretch long elastic bands around the keening Ms Karabeti, who wears a knit dress with a red train and a streak of makeup of identical color through her hair and down her forehead. The elastic bands are extensions of the ocher-colored backdrop, which divides into dozens of flexible, vertical strips, suspended and separable like the strings of a harp.

These interior-decorator touches are tasteful, but their function is far from clear in the story of a betrayed wife who horrifically takes revenge on her unfaithful husband by slaying their children. Among forty-four classical plays that survive, *Medea* is one of the starkest and most wildly emotive, a relentless descent to the slaughterhouse, and its central role is a magnet for powerhouse actresses: Diana Rigg and Zoe Caldwell are among the performers who've made a triumph of it in New York.

But Ms Kontouri seems uninterested in any dramatic buildup. Her ideas are cerebral, yes, and also intentionally uninvolving. That Medea's sons are disappointingly represented by a pair of life-size dolls (white, naturally) provides a sense of the emotional remove at which the director keeps us. And the play's staging is so formalized as to seem part of a legal proceeding.

For long stretches, characters walk out, plant themselves center stage and recite, a routine that reinforces a static tendency in the script. One advantage, though, is that the eye is freed to linger over the titles projected on the screen above the stage, because rarely does anything move below.

The striking Ms Karabeti, as angular and balletic as a flamenco dancer, is by far the most watchable aspect of this *Medea* (pronounced in Greek, by the way, as MEE-dee-ah). Her grace and beauty may not be apparent to her brutish lout of a husband, Jason (Lazaros Georgakopoulos), given to utterances like "It's natural for a woman to be angry when her husband is marrying again," but we know a domestic goddess when we see one. Ms Karabeti beats her breast, collapses artfully like a broken bird and stares angrily into the middle distance, announcing her defeat – while planning her macabre victory.

Still, unlike the devastating London-born *Electra* now running at the McCarter Theater in Princeton, NJ, *Medea* betrays no authentic sense of human toll. The actors talk until they stop, and we, in the end, aren't the wiser.

On the Pacific coast, John Fisher, a thirty-three-year-old aspirant for a doctorate at the University of California in Berkeley, was an appointed instructor in acting while preparing his dissertation on "the use of history in drama". He was diverted from his task by an ambitious, rather solemn student production of the *Oresteia* that inspired him to dash off a send-up of Aeschylus' epic trilogy

(1992) sung and danced to the tunes of Cole Porter. Given stage-life by his friends and fellow students, this sprightly venture proved a local hit, prompting Fisher to write eight more hopefully hilarious spoofs in the next five years, at the cost of completing his dissertation and getting his advanced degree any time soon. These parodies of classic plays and broad satiric sketches about major figures of the past – Cleopatra, Napoleon *et al* – so amused faculty, students and Berkeley residents that some of the offerings were moved from an acting workshop on the university campus to the 500-seat Stage Door, a commercial playhouse in San Francisco across the Bay, where they were taken up by a professional management, while they retained their amateur casts. As play followed play, the company clung together; David Littlejohn, in the *Wall Street Journal*, observed, "they dance together, make music together, sometimes live together, the tangible intensity of their youthful camaraderie providing much of the energy and fun of the shows. As characters, they retain their own names, and at least a portion of their offstage personalities."

John Fisher's signal hit had been *Medea, the Musical* (1992), which by the time of Littlejohn's dispatch to the *Journal* (1996) was still ongoing, no end indicated.

> The work depicts a not-very-good theater troupe trying to put on a confused, gay-feminist musical version of Euripides' drama, full of frantic singing and dancing and omnisexual romancing among the cast. Mr Fisher himself plays a hectoring, hard-to-please director named John, who keeps interrupting his own play.
>
> The music, when it is not simply "borrowed" from popular standards in the college-musical tradition, is written by Corey Schaffer, who has scored and played in many of Mr Fisher's works. Mr Schaffer also plays keyboards downstage right, and (like everyone else) has to put up with John's tantrums and fixations.
>
> First performed on the Berkeley campus in the Summer of 1994, *Medea, the Musical* transferred to a forty-seat basement South of Market Street in San Francisco the next year, with the help of funds raised at a cabaret benefit. There it won a handful of local "best play" awards and attracted the attention of a Bay Area entrepreneur, whose $75,000 investment in its downtown run has long since paid off. In mid-November, the cast began alternating on Tuesday nights with performances of Mr Fisher's ninth play, called *UC: A Farce*, in which he plays a graduate student at Berkeley (his actual day job) who keeps falling in love with difficult undergraduates. Sharp, high-spirited and ingeniously put together, *UC* carries the agonies of politically correct discourse to hysterical extremes, and ends up mocking its own hypersexed plot with a voluptuous but chaste orgy/striptease.

> . . . In March, with support from HBO, he will take *Medea* to the Aspen Comedy Festival in Colorado, in the hope of attracting attention outside the Bay Area. But wherever he goes, the author insists on taking the whole troupe with him. "I write for them," he says. "I don't know who else I'd use." Would he go to New York or Los Angeles? "I'd do it in a minute. I only write cheap-budget plays because I'm forced to. I'm not committed to poor theater."
>
> Not all the productions are low-cost. The *Camp Drag Disco Extravaganza*, a memorable, thirty-nine person spectacle, nearly broke the departmental bank in 1994. It was full of the jokey references to history, literature and dramatic theory one might expect from a PhD candidate in the use of history in theater, endowed with equal parts of learning, wit and an irrepressible camp sensibility. All of Mr Fisher's texts – like those of so many gay playwrights today – are truffled with knowing references to new and old movies, Broadway musicals, Top Forty songs and celebrity icons. Key signifiers in his subculture, they are valuable tokens in a seriocomic code. Opera is worked in as well; but then opera is just another form of pop music to many gay men.
>
> Two of Mr Fisher's earlier bittersweet, nonerotic comedies are built around tangled gay and lesbian romances in Berkeley and San Francisco, crafted specifically for and around his student actors. Mr Fisher includes female as well as male couples in his works, which helps preserve them from the cloying self-pity, the tiresomely clever bitchiness, and the crowing self-celebration that infect a number of recent gay plays. In *Medea*, in fact – by having the gay male lead fall in love with the straight actress playing Medea, thanks to a misdirected arrow from Eros's bow – Mr Fisher put in question the very notion of any fixed sexual identity. Halfway through the orgy scene in *UC* everyone is directed to change partners – and everyone does. All of these plays include enough high-kitsch music and spectacle – often intended as parody or commentary in itself – to keep up the entertainment and attention levels between icky romantic dialogues and islands of semiserious debate.
>
> In *Combat!*, Mr Fisher's most ambitious work so far, a dramatic three-and-one-half-hour spectacle is built around the treatment and experiences of gays and lesbians.

San Francisco offered a liberated, open moral climate at this time; it was a city to which homosexuals, learning they could live there openly without risk or fear, flocked from all regions, as for the same reasons others did to Greenwich Village on the East Coast. By now their numbers had become so large that they comprised a significant bloc of voters able to determine the outcome of local elections, providing them further protection from public disapproval and the possibility of harassment. This emancipated climate enabled Fisher to be frank about the erotic lifestyles he featured in his satires.

Some might look on slapstick parodies like Ludlam's and Fisher's as regrettable vulgarizations of cherished, noble works – despoliations of our cultural legacy. The humour is usually crass, sophomoric. But keep in mind the tradition of the satyr plays, the rowdy, often obscene after-pieces that Athenian contestants at the Dionysian Festival were obliged to append to each group of three tragedies, demanding that their authors mock the earnest stories they had cunningly fashioned, strenuously bidding for each spectator's tears. The satyr plays represented another facet of human nature; an opposite response to daunting events, agents for healing, they were another if very different abettor of *Katharsis*.

Off-Broadway, at the Douglas Fairbanks Theater, a programme of short works by the film-maker Neil LaBute, *Bash, Latterday Plays* (1999), each conceived as a monologue, caught the attention of critics who were taken aback by the playlets' sheer brutality. The author declared that he had chosen to use monologues in emulation of the ancient Greek dramatists who did not have horrific events occur onstage but let a selected character – most often a "messenger" – depict them verbally, perhaps chanting or singing. The second monologue in *Bash* was titled *Medea Redux* and had a present-day setting. A teenage girl, seduced by a male teacher, becomes pregnant. Abandoned by the man, her hideous retribution culminates in infanticide. Mormonism was also a strand in this shocking piece, LaBute having become a convert to that faith; it was a component here of his other two stinging short dramas.

With antic intent John Fisher titled his parody *Medea, the Musical*, but in a very different mood a clique of zealous and talented artists and technicians attempted to raid Euripides' play for its plot and put it on Broadway in the guise of a serious drama embellished with popular, commercially viable songs and dances. This *outré* enterprise was preceded by promotion on a scale seldom if ever aimed at sceptical New Yorkers. The *New York Times* ran a series of articles reporting week by week how each step in the mounting of the work was progressing, capped by interviews with its creators and cast members. Such unpaid publicity was of inestimable worth. Anticipation of the piece's unveiling was high, and the advance sale of tickets stimulated – and they were costly, as was the much-touted and very lavish production. Needless to say, the time of the story was updated – to the 1890s – the place to the bayous of Louisiana and a prison in Chicago, with Medea renamed Marie Christine and the role assigned to a promising young African-American actress, Audra McDonald. The Jason, played by Anthony Crivello – now Dante Keys – was white, so the themes of miscegenation and class distinctions were somewhat more highlighted.

The book and music were by Michael John LaChiusa, a newcomer who with this entry could boast of having two musical works running on Broadway in the same season; but until now he was somewhat looked down upon by the New York critics who considered his music weak and derivative and his choice of subject-matter eccentric. So there was a hurdle to surmount.

Of many minds about *Marie Christine*'s libretto and score, the reviewers were as one in declaring Audra McDonald surpassingly fine in the title role. For some, the question was whether *Medea* was really material for a Broadway musical. However, Ben Brantley, in the *New York Times*, did not dwell on that; his critique was headlined "The Promises of an Enchantress":

> The magic is real, all right, a force that brooks no denial, no resistance. Like most unearthly powers, it doesn't break down into easily defined elements. But when Audra McDonald sings her first notes as the Medea-like heroine of *Marie Christine*, Michael John LaChiusa's solemn, sometimes somnolent musical tragedy at Lincoln Center, there is clearly sorcery at work.
>
> That opening line of melody, pitched at the low end of Ms McDonald's wide register, is simple, as are the words it is teamed with: "My name is my mother's name." Yet the phrase shimmers with elemental energies just waiting to be unleashed, and the implicit potency hypnotizes. There is no doubting that this enchantress can make good on every threat and promise she utters. Underestimate her at your peril.
>
> *Marie Christine*, which opened last night at the Vivian Beaumont Theater at Lincoln Center under Graciela Daniele's direction, is a resounding confirmation of Ms McDonald's status as a vocal artist of singular skills and sensibility, the foremost interpreter of a new generation of composers that includes Jason Robert Brown, Ricky Ian Gordon, and Adam Guettel. Those who have felt that this twenty-nine-year-old performer, who has picked up a Tony for each of her three previous appearances on Broadway, was ready for a fall will not see her stumble here.
>
> The swirling, complex music of Mr LaChiusa (*First Lady Suite*, *Hello Again*), who wrote *Marie Christine* expressly for her, taps her oceanic potential in ways her performances in *Carousel*, *Master Class* and *Ragtime* only hinted at. Ms McDonald, in turn, is Mr LaChiusa's ideal translator, giving emotional precision and centeredness to an intricate score that refuses to settle into one steady stream of style or sentiment.
>
> Mr LaChiusa is working from the disparate clashing strands of American culture; Ms McDonald, whose command of musical dialects here ranges from the operatic to gospel, turns that paradox into something intensely personal, finding conflicting impulses in a single breath. Like Maria Callas, who famously sang Cherubini's *Médée*, she can convey overwhelming fierceness and fragility at the

same time. Neither Mr LaChiusa's music nor Ms McDonald's character can be confined by a simple equation.

Unfortunately Mr LaChiusa's libretto for *Marie Christine*, a tale of doomed love between an arrogant young sea captain (played by Anthony Crivello) and its racially mixed heroine in the late nineteenth-century New Orleans and Chicago, does not reflect this sense of the ineffable. There is often a baldly didactic quality to the show's book and lyrics as it considers the socially oppressive climate of its time, and a melodramatic clunkiness that evokes the language of B-movies about bad women. And even Ms McDonald's magic can't transform the tedium of much that surrounds her.

As a musical portrait of an individual, *Marie Christine* is stunning; as a compelling, complete production, it still feels oddly unfinished. Although the evening has a creditable leading man in Mr Crivello, only Ms McDonald gives the show the sharpness it demands. When she isn't singing, there's a diffusiveness to *Marie Christine* that pre-empts full emotional engagement.

Despite ravishing orchestrations by Jonathan Tunick, the score rarely achieves much momentum or intensity on its own, and its recurrent motifs don't haunt the imagination as they should. This is especially true in the grim second act, with its catalog of murders; this bizarrely deprives its heroine of the big soliloquy of an aria that is her due as well as her audience's.

Similarly, the stylish, shorthand choreography in which Ms Daniele specializes (also on display at the moment in *Ragtime*) only rarely seems more than a series of picturesque gestures. One tends to feel lost and lonely when Ms McDonald isn't onstage, and I found myself wishing that *Marie Christine* had been presented as a musical monologue. As it is, the handsome production that has been lavished on the show overburdens it.

That the evening has grand ambitions is evident from the moment you take your seat. Christopher Barreca's set, which creates the feeling of a classical amphitheater cast in shades of black and which has been brilliantly lighted by Jules Fisher and Peggy Eisenhauer, glowers imposingly. No doubt about it, as Mr LaChiusa's musical forebear Stephen Sondheim (whose influence is much felt here) might have put it, it's tragedy tonight at the Vivian Beaumont.

In a lovely departure from the traditional overture, before the house lights go down the orchestra begins to tune up, with different instruments sending their voices into the air. At the same time the ensemble, dressed in Toni-Leslie James's somber period costumes, files on the stage with seeming randomness.

An alphabet of sorts is established, the ingredients that will coalesce to tell a story. The nature of that story is made evident when the orchestra comes together in an ominous dissonant chord capped with the clash of cymbals. A group of women, writhing like figures in a scene from *The Snake Pit,* trace the perimeter of the stage's central circle.

Ms McDonald appears in silhouette, as she is interrogated by a trio of harpylike prisoners (Jennifer Leigh Warren, Andrea Frierson-Toney and Mary Bond Davis), who will act throughout the show as the heroine's personal Greek chorus, with a slight flavor of both the Andrews Sisters and the weird sisters of *Macbeth.* "Before the morning I will be a witness," they intone.

What follows is a tale not so distant from that of Medea according to Euripides, one of seduction, betrayal and horrific vengeance. Mr LaChiusa's variations on the classic archetype play nicely into his theories, set forth in recent interviews, of the eclectic nature of American culture and the musical theater best suited to interpret it.

Marie Christine l'Adrese (to be played by Sherry Boone at Wednesday and Saturday matinées) is herself a hybrid, the daughter of a rich French father and his mistress, a woman of color well versed in the ancient magic of Africa and Hispaniola, which her daughter has inherited.

This maternal legacy is given literal form by the spectral presences of Marie Christine's mother (the elegant Vivian Reed) and of a drummer (David Pleasant), who is seen through a scrim as he beats an insistent tattoo that keeps snaking its way into the score. The music is a subversive counterpoint of idioms that run up against and melt into one another, with a cumulative effect that is far less schematic than these descriptions might suggest.

Ms McDonald sustains her character's contradictions beautifully as we follow her courtship by the show's Jason figure, Dante Keyes (Mr Crivello), the self-serving young man from Chicago who stumbles upon Marie Christine in a park on Lake Pontchartrain.

A mélange of shyness and slyness, uncertain girlishness and overweening pride, European decorum and earth-shaking passion, Ms McDonald's Marie Christine conveys all these traits with quicksilver changes in vocal timber and facial nuance. She is a model of both extraordinary self-possession and self-destructiveness, and the battle waged between the two is heard in practically every phrase she sings.

Mr Crivello's Dante is less complicated, a handsome opportunist of cheap charm and sexual magnetism who never quite acquires the heroic stature needed to balance Ms McDonald's sorceress. He has several exquisite moments, particularly in the second-act number in which he sings a fable to his young sons by Marie Christine. That he occasionally brings to mind Robert Taylor's wooden Armand playing opposite Greta Garbo's transcendent Camille isn't inappropriate.

Marie Christine's passions, like those of immortal heroines ranging from Medea herself to Anna Karenina, are not meant to find a worthy object. How could they? It's the process of those passions working through their own internal course, one destined to end in annihilation, that fascinates.

That doesn't account, however, for Mr LaChiusa's forays into the scenes designed to evoke the social orders of Creole New Orleans and in the second act the back-room political world of Chicago. The attendant numbers, which range from a grand ball that ends in murder to the humiliation of Marie Christine by a squalid ward boss (Shawn Elliott) and his flunkies, have curiously little impact. Much of the second act, which like many Greek tragedies relies on accounts of horrible things happening off-stage, is a bit of a sleeping pill.

Nor have deeply gifted performers like Mary Testa, as a hard-bitten Chicago saloonkeeper, and Darius de Haas, as Marie Christine's foppish younger brother, found a way of meeting the taxing demands of Mr LaChiusa's music on their own terms. No one, in fact, feels like a fully fleshed character with the exception of Marie Christine.

But what an exception she is. If this production fails to make a persuasive case for Mr LaChiusa's ability to shape a complete, satisfying musical, it definitely points to new possibilities for defining character within the genre. Ms McDonald makes the most of those possibilities and then some. The commitment, conviction and full-strength talent she brings to the evening becomes its own argument for the endurance of the American musical.

Writing for a "niche" paper, the *Village Voice* – long-standing, appealing to Greenwich Village's semi-bohemian, avant-garde intellectuals – Michael Feingold consistently proved himself a perceptive and knowledgeable theatre critic. He was authoritative to readers who were apt to be very different from those of the *New York Times.*

What do women want, at the end of the millennium? In Michael John LaChiusa's *Marie Christine*, the apparent answer is that they want today's challenges a century early. A version of the Medea story set in eighteen-nineties' America, *Marie Christine* stays stubbornly stuck in its author-composer's own time, offering neither a way back to the savage myth nor a reflection of our nineties in the mirror of the nineteenth century's. Proficient, skilled, and imaginative, LaChiusa marshals an enormous panoply of approaches to tell his tale, but it doesn't hold together, even with the towering talent of Audra McDonald at its center, because the myth won't supply what he needs from it; his constantly shifting strategies only diffuse it further. At times this last Broadway musical of the twentieth century seems to contain every mode of music theater the century has tried, from the Stravinskyan fanfare that starts its prelude to the Schoenbergian (or maybe Boublil–Schoenbergian) chorale that sends the heroine to death in a blaze of glory. In between, the ghosts of Puccini and Gershwin, Britten and Copland, Kern and Sondheim and Weill and Poulenc come and go in the gloom. LaChiusa's never literal in his derivations; he just has an acute ear and a *fin de siècle* omnivore's taste.

He falls into his sounds-like ways, in part, because his dramatic structure offers him nothing strong with which to resist them. Euripides cleverly concentrated everything his audience needed to know about Medea in five episodes, demarcating the last terrifying day of her life in Greece. Deconstructing his inexact analogy till it sprawls all over the stage (easy on Christopher Barreca's appropriately unfocused set), LaChiusa begins at the end, flashes back to an approximate beginning point – and then flashes further back from there. Marie Christine's in a Chicago jail, telling her story to the other women prisoners; then she's a wealthy mixed-race Louisiana girl living with her brothers on the shores of Lake Pontchartrain; then she's a child learning vodun from her mother. The story can't take a step forward without taking two steps back, even after Marie Christine's eloped to Chicago, where the political ambitions of her white lover, Dante Keyes, bring on the traumatic climax. LaChiusa's breadth of source material is as strong as his technical range – "realized" folk songs and Caribbean chants, nineties piano-rag numbers burlesqued à la Bock and Harnick or teased with dissonances in the manner of Blitzstein or Jerome Moross. It seems he can do anything – except, apparently, ask himself why he does it.

Some of Medea's reasons, too, are mysteries, which is why Euripides's play retains its power to chill and transfix. But the women who surround her, her old Nurse and the Chorus, are always precise in their response to her actions. She's been brutally treated; no women, and few men, would fail to sympathize. But each scene of the tragedy offers her better alternatives than those she chooses, and the other women tell her so; looking for revenge on men and society, she victimizes those as powerless as herself: her own children and another woman. Far from a feminist, Medea's scary because she demonstrates that cruelty – the viciousness of the abuse victim turned abuser – isn't a male trait, but part of our common humanity: Push a woman too far and she'll act just like a man.

Putting the story in Jim Crow America, and mixing it up with a welter of competing issues – women's rights, civic corruption, class barriers, cultural imperialism – only blurs its conflicts. Medea's a foreign princess; Jason and Creon are worthy opponents of equal status. In contrast, Marie Christine, illegitimate offspring of a plantation owner and his slave, is a person of no legal standing in her native Louisiana; her lover, Dante, a prostitute's son, and the sleazy political boss who becomes his prospective father-in-law are if anything even lower on the social scale. This slippage in rank reduces the myth to a matter of politics: Not what tragic powers are inherent in women, but what rights they can justly claim becomes the point at issue – a point only peripheral to the myth. (Medea's offered a series of varyingly just settlements, none of which appeases her wrath; Marie Christine's never offered anything except "Do as you're told" and "Get out of town.") As a result, the violence in which the action's suffused always seems to be out of place in the story LaChiusa's telling. Medea escapes, unpunished, in a chariot drawn by dragons, a warning to us that violence, human and primordial, will be back; Marie Christine, unburdened of her story, has some vague kind of apotheosis about having loved "too much and more," presumably on her way to the gallows. And all because she couldn't own property in Louisiana or vote in Chicago.

Though LaChiusa's blurry conception is often conveyed in equally blurry lyrics, his music, with its constant restless invention, probably deserves a fairer hearing than it gets here. More than any new score I've heard recently, it wants unplugging: Scott Stauffer's smeary, dulling sound design should be done away with, and the piece moved into an opera company's repertoire, where we could relish LaChiusa's musicianly composing, and the niceties of Jonathan Tunick's delicate scoring. Most of Graciela Daniele's drifty, cluttered staging should be tossed out too, and its replacement supported by lighting that sculpts rather than flattens. And the piece should be sung no more than twice a week: Resourceful and centered even when the story isn't, vivid even with the blandest words, Audra McDonald dives into the title role and carries it as easily as if Brünnhilde and Boris Godunov together would be a mere day's work to her. But this can't go on forever; she's an artist, not a dray horse. If composers keep piling such demands on her, her simplest strategy will be to get out of the commercial racket and start her own opera company, where she can schedule an occasional rest for herself. She gets strong support from Darius de Haas as her wastrel brother, and from delicious Mary Testa, as the local dragon chariot. Anthony Crivello, as Dante, has vocal strength and sexy charm, but no more. And somebody might have told him that Chicagoans don't say "Chicah-go."

Fintan O'Toole, in the *Daily News*, was more favourably impressed. To him *Marie Christine* was "a sensation". His summary:

Michael John LaChiusa's brilliant reworking of the Medea myth manages at once to make it fresh and to retain its gut-wrenching compulsion. There is a fiercely uncompromising fusion of story and song. Everything about Graciela Daniele's fluid, elegant production is in harmony with this basic intention. Her choreography moves the cast with a stately formality appropriate to the ritual enactment of a tragic fate. Audra McDonald's voice wraps around the angular score with such mastery that her songs seem as natural as speech. She is regal. And Anthony Crivello creates a personality powerful enough to captivate this queen. *Marie Christine* will not easily be dislodged from the mind.

Some reviewers liked the rich and colourful décor. They hailed the work as "beautifully staged" and "a spectacle that should not be missed". A radio broadcaster (D. Richardson, WOR) predicted this visceral response by spectators: "The story and superb performances will keep you riveted until the final blackout. The end is shocking, to say the least. This is a serious musical made for the enjoyment of serious theatergoers."

That the subject was so serious prompted a debate as to what theatrical category *Marie Christine* truly belonged. The opinions evoked filled much space on the *New York Times*'s pages. Terry Teachout initiated the colloquy.

> The neon sign in front of the Vivian Beaumont Theater at Lincoln Center calls Michael John LaChiusa's *Marie Christine* "a new musical." So do all the posters. Whether or not Mr LaChiusa specifically requested that the show be advertised in this way, there can be little doubt that he approves, since he recently wrote an essay for *Arts & Leisure* in which he firmly stated that *Marie Christine* was a musical, not an opera.
>
> Now, Mr LaChiusa can call *Marie Christine* anything he wants: it's his show. But I have seen it twice, one time with Audra McDonald in the title role and the other with her alternate, Sherry Boone (whose first-rate performance, incidentally, disproved the widespread notion that *Marie Christine* is nothing without its star). On both occasions, I came away certain that it was an opera – and that the author's claims to the contrary were doing him a disservice.
>
> To be sure, neither genre is easy to define. Though *Tristan und Isolde* is definitely an opera and *Annie Get Your Gun* a musical, much of what comes in between is up for grabs. French opéra-comique and German Singspiel, for example, both have spoken dialogue and songlike arias. Oscar Hammerstein II rewrote the libretto of *Carmen*, the quintessential opéra-comique, and successfully brought it to Broadway as *Carmen Jones*; Mr LaChiusa himself sees *The Magic Flute*, a Singspiel generally regarded as among the highest and most profound expressions of the operatic ideal, as a "prototype" for the modern musical.
>
> But *Carmen* and *The Magic Flute*, different though they are from *Tristan*, also have something essential in common with it: they are *scores*, unified musico-dramatic structures whose separate parts serve a larger theatrical end. *Annie Get Your Gun*, by contrast, is a play with free-standing songs, nearly all of which can be sung on their own. And while the arias of Bizet and Mozart are fully as hum-

mable as Irving Berlin's songs, they aspire to a higher level of technical sophistication and emotional intensity.

What about *Marie Christine*? My guess is that about two-thirds of it is sung, and much of the spoken dialogue is accompanied by the orchestra. Of the thirty-five musical numbers, only one, *Way Back to Paradise*, is a self-contained song that ends with a clean break for applause. The harmonic language is often quite dissonant, at least by the prevailing standards of American popular music. And as if all that weren't enough to give the game away, *Marie Christine* is a tragedy without a trace of Hammersteinian uplift. (As Bugs Bunny says in *What's Opera, Doc?*, "What didja expect in an opera – a happy ending?")

Why, then, is Mr LaChiusa unwilling to call his creation by its right name? Because he doesn't want it to be an opera. In his essay, he claims that opera is "elitist" and unrepresentative of America's "mongrel culture." He goes so far as to define opera as "what Europeans used to write" (except, presumably, for Mozart). But he is tilting at a straw man. His main objection to the genre turns out to be that "the 'pure' sound that classically trained American singers strive for is essentially Eurocentric.

"It's blasphemy to even suggest it," he added, "but why can't opera singers combine vocal styles?" The answer, of course, is that many of the younger ones – Bryn Terfel, Anne Sofie von Otter, Sylvia McNair and Dawn Upshaw among them – have been doing it for years. Ms McDonald is a classically trained soprano whose method of vocal production is "Eurocentric," yet it doesn't stop her from singing Mr LaChiusa's bluesy melodies with thrilling conviction.

The key word here is "elitist." Mr LaChiusa, who admits to having had to pawn his piano after writing *Marie Christine*, clearly longs to be popular. Alas, he longs in vain. Broadway today is about *Beauty and the Beast* and *Footloose*, not complex scores that demand your full attention at all times. To call *Marie Christine* a musical is implicitly to claim that it has more in common with these simple-minded shows than *Carmen*. Not only is this untrue, it's bad marketing, the equivalent of a bait-and-switch scam. Labels are unfashionable these days, even politically incorrect, but sometimes they still matter. Had *Marie Christine* been billed as "a new opera" and produced by, say, Glimmerglass Opera, it would have drawn a different, more adventurous kind of audience, one better prepared to grapple with its challenging blend of pop-flavored rhythms and prickly harmonies.

Mr LaChiusa is not the only opera composer who insists that he's writing musicals. Stephen Sondheim continues to do the same thing, ignoring the increasingly obvious fact that his best work belongs in opera houses. Chicago's Lyric Opera recently announced that it would produce *Sweeny Todd* in 2002, with Bryn Terfel in the title role. I couldn't be happier; I think it's one of the finest operas composed

> by an American. So is Adam Guettel's *Floyd Collins*, a post-Sondheim show whose expressive ambitions place it far beyond the constricting ambit of the contemporary musical. And so is *Porgy and Bess*, a masterpiece that never truly came to life until opera companies embraced it.
>
> Is *Marie Christine* worthy of being produced alongside these works? I believe so – but we'll never know for sure until Michael John LaChiusa shakes off his morbid fear of being branded an elitist and allows it to be marketed as the excellent opera that it is.

Teachout was the music critic of *Commentary* and a contributor to other magazines. A reply to him came from Anthony Tommasini, on the staff of the *New York Times* and highly respected (and sometimes feared by singers) for his expert knowledge concerning vocal techniques, his reviews often acerbic.

> In the lobby of the Vivian Beaumont Theater during the intermission for *Marie Christine* people have been talking intently, wondering whether the work they are hearing is a musical or an opera. It's almost as if before they decide how good it is they have to figure out what it is.
>
> . . . What is the difference between a musical and an opera? There is no definitive answer. In recent weeks the question has been debated anew in these pages. It's always intriguing when a work blurs the boundaries between the two genres, as many operas and musicals do. But there is a difference, an important one, that is being forgotten by composers from each field who try to play it safe in some mushy middle zone.
>
> Obviously both genres involve the mixing of words and music. But in the musical, words hold the upper edge. The opposite is true of opera. If you accept that difference, then many further defining aspects of each genre – singing styles, orchestration, the role of spoken dialogue, the importance of melody, the appropriate degree of musical complexity – all follow logically.
>
> Some opera experts will howl in protest at the suggestion that words in opera are not every bit as important as words in musicals. Yes, it would have been inconceivable to Verdi and Wagner that audiences would not understand the languages of operas they were hearing: when their operas were performed in, say, Paris, they were translated into French. Yes, until the 1950s, when the conductor Herbert von Karajan began presenting Mozart's Italian operas in Austria in the original Italian, the works were always performed in the native tongue, German. And yes, the use of supertitles has drawn large new audiences to the opera house.
>
> Yet at times opera has also thrived with audiences who had scant idea of what the words meant.

Think of the German-born Handel's long run in London as a composer of hugely popular Italian operas for English-speaking audiences.

Like many American buffs, I grew up hearing opera on the radio and attending performances at the Met (seated in the stratosphere), while having little idea of what the operas were about. Later, when I found out what was going on in, say, *Rigoletto*, it was of course revelatory. But did it exponentially increase my love of the opera? Not really. And uncounted numbers of operas with lame librettos, like *Il Trovatore*, are beloved repertory staples. But imagine hearing the stylish current revival of Cole Porter's *Kiss Me, Kate* performed in Italian. Even Italian-speakers in the audience would find it odd, for every nuance of the music was crafted to lift and spin out those wonderful words. ("I would gladly give up coffee for Sanka/Even Sanka, Bianca, for you.")

Memorable melodies have been a hallmark of the musical. Still, the great Broadway tunesmiths knew that the primary function of melody was to service words. Many tricky tunes are memorable because clever words are bonded to them in our minds. Think of Porter's *Anything Goes.* ("In olden days a glimpse of stocking was/Looked on as something shocking but/Now God knows, anything goes.") How many Puccini fans who can easily hum the gorgeous melody of *Un bel di, vedremo* could recall even the next line of text?

The true achievement of the great musical lyricists is sometimes taken for granted. Consider this couplet from *Once in Love with Amy*, introduced by Ray Bolger in the 1948 show *Where's Charley?*, words and music by Frank Loesser: "Ever and ever fascinated by 'er/Sets your heart afire to stay." Two lines later the internal rhyme ("by 'er/afire") and the line rhyme ("to stay") are echoed with wistful beauty: "Ply her with bonbons, poetry and flowers,/Moon a million hours away."

Loesser, a poet of Broadway, came up with a supple, breezy tune to caress those words. You can get a clear sense of how important words were to these masters by listening to recordings of them singing their own songs. Loesser had no voice to speak of, but his affectionate, gently snappy rendition of *Once in Love with Amy* (accompanying himself on the piano) has never been topped. And Porter's historic recording of *Anything Goes* in his twangy voice is taken at a strikingly moderate tempo, so that all the words are clear.

Broadway cherished its great singers, like Ethel Merman, John Raitt and Barbara Cook. But countless singers with merely serviceable voices have also excelled there. Fred Astaire, with his teeny tenor, was an urbane stylist and a master of putting words across. In opera the voice reigns. Of course when a superb vocalist has the ability to make words come alive, this is true greatness in operatic singing. Still, fans have long thrilled to the work of many singers with poor diction, like Dame Joan

Sutherland, because their voices were so extraordinary that no one cared.

In defining the musical too much emphasis is accorded the genre's mix of spoken text and song. Many operas do this, too, notably *Carmen* and *Fidelio.* The inclusion of dialogue does not turn these operas into proto-musicals. Even *The Magic Flute,* which Mozart wrote for a people's theater, is thoroughly an opera, with complex ensembles, sublime arias and, in the duet of the two men in armor, an evocation of Baroque sacred music.

The great Broadway musicals, no matter the degree of spoken dialogue, have an overall musical shape that their creators rendered carefully. A musical cannot go too long without a song before the balance is thrown off. There are two famous scenes that are badly miscalculated in this regard. One is the long soliloquy by the cross-dressing dancer in *A Chorus Line,* a blatantly emotional speech that always elicits nervous applause. The other, in *Cabaret,* is Sally Bowles's confession to her sometime boyfriend about having had an abortion, which makes audiences squirm, not because of the subject matter. The problem is that both speeches stop the musicals in their tracks.

Marie Christine, Michael John LaChiusa's retelling of *Medea,* is neither an opera nor a musical. It's a clunky hybrid. In the *New Yorker* the critic John Lahr called it an "opsical," which could be defined, he wrote, as "an empty vessel that makes a big sound." In a *New York Times* essay published prior to the show's opening, Mr LaChuisa warned his musical-writing colleagues to trust the genre and not ape opera, which he considers somewhat elitist. In *Marie Christine* he does not seem to have followed his own advice.

There is a revealing pastiche number in Act I, when Dante promises to take Marie Christine to Chicago that is as close as the score gets to a jazzy Broadway song, and it's pretty good. The words are lame: "We're gonna go to Chicago/And we're gonna have fun./We're gonna live in a tower/Stretching up to the sun." The rhythmic swing is stiff; the tune is awkward. The self-trained Mr LaChiusa lacks a real melodic gift. You can't hear this song without wondering whether the real reason he has been working the middle ground is because he is no facile songwriter.

The difficulties of the score, especially the leaping, fussy vocal lines do not pay off. Rather than sound intricate, the music just seems bored. The contrapuntal ensemble writing in *Guys and Dolls,* by Loesser, is more sophisticated than anything Mr LaChiusa has done. And his word-setting is faulty. Even the remarkable Audra McDonald cannot project the lyrics with consistent clarity.

The pre-opening advertisements stated that the engagement was limited to six weeks. With previews, *Marie Christine* stayed for ten and a half weeks; hardly long enough to repay the costs of the elaborate staging. The production was subsidized by grants from the National Endowment for the Arts, the New York State Council on the Arts, the New York Department of Cultural Affairs and three cultural private foundations, an unusual array of support for a Broadway musical. LaChiusa and Graciela Daniele, the director and choreographer, had worked together developing it for three and a half years.

To the second season of Newark's newly inaugurated New Jersey Performing Arts Center, the Edafos Dance Theatre on tour from Greece (2000) added its own choreographic evocation of the compelling legend. In Dublin the famed Abbey Theatre scheduled a *Medea* (also in 2000) to be put on by the stage and film director Deborah Warner, with Fiona Shaw in the wrenching title role. The plan was to have the chorus, on alternate nights, speak either English or Gaelic, again carrying Euripides' poetry far from its author, a different word-music that would sound strange to him. For certain, in the world of drama *Medea* is a durable and omnipresent archetype.

Apparently convinced that New York had not had enough exposure to Euripides' masterly drama, the Off-Broadway Jean Cocteau Repertory Theater intruded on the season with its conception of *Medea* (2000), with a translation by Philip Vellacott. Or perhaps, by arriving so soon after the closing of *Marie Christine*, the company wished to remind ticket-buyers of the plot and characters of the original play, the authentic, unaltered stark tragedy with all its suspense and grandeur. Wilborn Hampton had this succinct appraisal for the ever-trusting readers of the *New York Times*:

> If ever a playwright was ahead of his time it was Euripides. While Aeschylus and Sophocles were winning prizes with tragedies full of philosophical jousting with Zeus and agonizing over the fates, Euripides was exploring what we would today call character development, and it is his concentration on the individual that makes his plays more accessible to present-day audiences.
>
> In *Medea*, which is being given a vibrant and lusty staging by Eve Adamson at the Jean Cocteau Repertory, Euripides takes a story that was old even when he wrote it in 430 BC – a husband leaving his wife for a younger woman – and examines the horrific extremes to which a scorned woman will go for revenge.
>
> It was Medea, after all, who helped Jason secure the Golden Fleece, who gave up her own promising career as a princess to marry him and bear his children, and now he is dumping her for the young daughter of King Creon. "Jason was my whole life," Medea explains. It's a familiar refrain, even in the twenty-first century.
>
> Ms Adamson, one of our most consistently excellent directors, focuses on the realism inherent in

Euripides' play and builds it into a chilling domestic melodrama with catastrophic results, a sort of *Fatal Attraction* for fifth-century BC Corinth. Moving the action around an empty bed in Robert Klingelhoefer's spare, surreal set, Ms Adamson emphasizes the motivational themes of passion and betrayal. Even the horror-movie elements in *Medea* (that flesh-eating dress, for example) are turned to a high theatrical effect that is underscored by Ellen Mandel's eerie original music.

In Elise Stone, one of the Cocteau's most consistently fine actors, Ms Adamson has an earthy Medea capable of bridging the centuries to turn the Greek tragedy into a contemporary one.

Fiery, sexy and sultry, Ms Stone commands the stage from her first entrance with her long black hair flowing like a Medusa and her dress slit up to her thighs. Ms Stone uses a remarkable vocal range in breathing life into a mythological character that is all too human: from a pleading and seductive tone in her manipulation of Creon and Aegeus she turns to hot-tempered fury in her confrontation with Jason, then finally expounds her murderous plans for revenge in an other-worldly voice that sounds like the demon in *The Exorcist.*

As Jason, Jolie Garrett delivers a credible performance of a man who is blind to anything but his own desire, and the Cocteau veterans Craig Smith and Harris Berlinsky offer fine turns as Creon and Aegeus, the kings respectively of Corinth and Athens. A three-woman chorus, which emerges from the audience to plead with Medea, deliver their warnings earnestly and in unison.

The only distractions among the cast are in one or two readings that fall into the monotonous declamatory style that some think is endemic to Greek tragedies. But Ms Adamson knows better, and she and Ms Stone turn this *Medea* into a very modern play.

Athenians were privileged to hear *Medea* in Russian performed by the avant-garde Theatre Taganka (1995) on tour from Moscow. This special event took place in Megaron concert hall; for those desiring to understand the dialogue in full, Greek subtitles were provided. The Russian translation was by the Nobel-prizewinning poet Joseph Brodsky, who in his later years accepted exile from his homeland – the Soviet Union – choosing to live and die in New York, where he was made exceptionally welcome.

To supplement the Taganka's offering, Cherubini's opera *Médée* was also given, presented by the Athens State Orchestra, with Grace Bumbry, the African-American soprano, as the wrathful and merciless agent of retribution.

Euripides' *Hippolytus*, with its eternally fecund plot, seems to have been largely replaced by Racine's *Phèdre*, in which the focal character is not a frigid young man, as in the Greek original, but instead his poignantly obsessed, distraught youthful stepmother. An exception is Martha Graham's approach to the thematic material in two dance works widely apart in time, *Phaedra* (1962) and *Phaedra's Dream* (1983). On one occasion the two pieces were performed during the same engagement, "nearly back to back" – as noted by Anna Kisselgoff in the *New York Times* – with Christine Dakin a "superb Phaedra in both versions and in a blazing *tour de force*, managing to give a very different interpretation in each work of the same character".

In Ms Kisselgoff's view, Graham's earlier *Phaedra* was the more substantial creation, the second effort

> long on concept and short on choreography. Nonetheless it has a special twist that has its roots in Greek drama.
>
> Here, in Miss Graham's reductionist outline, Hippolytus is made to spurn his stepmother because he is attracted by a male figure called the Stranger. Miss Graham is too astute to leave things at that. She has made the action part of a dream, and the dream itself is presented at first as a ritual drama with the characters offering Noh-like bows to the public.
>
> The character of the Stranger is never revealed. In true Graham style, he may be an inner aspect of Hippolytus, symbolizing a secret instinct. Or he may even be a fantasy father-figure, for at a key moment the son folds up on the Stranger's thighs just as Theseus did on the lap of Jocasta in Miss Graham's *Night Journey*. Oedipus, unaware that he is Jocasta's son, is also her lover in that scene.
>
> It is not too much to suggest Miss Graham expects her public to catch the choreographic allusion to her own work and that the incestuous image we think we see in *Phaedra's Dream* is actually there.
>
> Euripides, in his play *Hippolytus*, suggested that his hero was asexual, beholden to Artemis, goddess of chastity; he had, in fact, angered Aphrodite, goddess of love, for his "scorn of women."
>
> Miss Graham takes it from there in *Phaedra's Dream*. Hippolytus is seen caught up in a tug of war between Phaedra and the Stranger. Miss Dakin, "asleep" and writhing on her bed, foresees the drama to come, including Hippolytus's death. Isamu Noguchi's monumental décor includes a huge disk and a lintel fragment that the characters nearly use as weapons. There is one highly memorable moment when Miss Dakin sits in a split atop the wheel, a defiant angry spirit.
>
> The performance as a whole was marked by a remarkable tension and anger. Donlin Foreman's powerfully danced Stranger was the aggressor and Kenneth Topping's Hippolytus was not an unwilling player in this domestic triangle. Too often one overlooks what strength and support the male

partners commit to the Graham choreography. Both men were outstanding, and one won't forget Mr Foreman plunging into a back fall while Miss Dakin stands on his thighs.

The music – George Crumb's *Lux Aeterna* – was played on tape and tended merely to hang in the air. The dancers had to plow through the sound and Miss Dakin was the inexorable leader of the pack, fighting every instant for what her heroine desired.

In *Phaedra* on Friday night she showed, most impressively, a very different and lyric face as a woman torn by desire. Miss Graham has made this Phaedra a victim of the gods or goddesses. The all-new cast featured Mr Topping again, looking properly bewildered as this Hippolytus. Denise Vale's Aphrodite had a prom-queen tinge that was not out of place and Thea Nerissa Barnes, ambiguously turning a smile into a snarl, was a witty Artemis. Mr Foreman's Theseus was a nuanced drunken lout who was still a king. Kim Stroud as Pasiphae, Phaedra's mother, danced with provocative angular force. It was an exciting cast, brimming with apt theatricality.

The many forms this great and richly substantial play might take was strikingly illustrated by the appearance of *Hippolytos* in an English translation by Robert Bagg, from a Kannada adaptation by Raghunandana. This work was produced by the State Theatre of South India, Nataka Karnataka Rangayana, and co-produced by Evangelos Tsurdinis. Brought to La MaMa in New York City (1992), the presentation was jointly sponsored – and partly subsidized – by the Consulate General of Greece, the Alexander Onassis Center for Hellenic Studies, Cult Productions and Christopher G. Kiis, an impressive list of prestigious and generous patrons. The undertaking was a cosmopolitan one, the director, Vasilios Calitsis, Greek; the actors Indian; the incidental musical by B.V. Karanth and Philip Kovvantis, an intermingling of Greek and Indian idioms; the sets and costumes – by George Ziakas and Prema Karanth – representing the talents of artists of contrasting racial strains and very different cultural backgrounds.

D.J.R. Bruckner wrote in the *New York Times*:

One can argue about the direction given by Vasilios Calitsis to Euripides' *Hippolytos* . . . but the performance is spectacular and brings some real excitement to this most troubling and dramatically difficult of all the ancient Greek plays.

Instead of exploring the psychological labyrinth in the text, which tempts most directors, Mr Calitsis goes for the grand theatrical effect, and he achieves it. In fact, for all but the rarest viewer, exploration of the text will be impossible; this is a verse version in the Kannada language of South India

> mixed with some lines of the Greek original. For those who have forgotten the story, occasional projected supertitles remind one of what is going on.
>
> A formidable array of electronic and costume-making technology makes gods and choruses glow or flame up out of voids. A score by the Indian composer B.V. Karanth and Philip Kovvantis, based on both Greek and Indian dance music and played on traditional Indian instruments, gives the rhythmic speeches of the play an operatic quality. And the choreographed movements of the actors as well as of the chorus have the odd effect of heightening one's apprehension as the sense of doom in the play becomes almost palpable.
>
> Occasionally the special effects are distracting and the sound amplification annoying, and a couple of scenes are so stretched out they lose essential tension. But on the whole this is a powerful presentation of a mind-twisting drama about divine injustice, the incestuous desire of a woman for her stepson and her posthumous revenge on him for his chastity, and the suffering of a husband and father deranged by his wife's lies and the hidden purposes of angry gods.
>
> The members of this company – especially N. Mangala as Phaedra, K.R. Nandini as the nurse who, in trying to help Phaedra conquer her lust by confessing it, betrays her, and K.C. Raghunath as Hippolytos – make the characters and chorus grow larger than life as the gods involve them in dark Olympian struggles. Their characters are alien enough and elevated enough to be believable in such a situation, and yet close enough to be pitiable.

Similarly rare have been modern presentations of *Alcestis*, though the highly eccentric, innovative American director Robert Wilson essayed a staging of it for the American Repertory Theater in Cambridge, Massachusetts (1986), which, according to the critic Arthur Holmberg, marked a major shift in the young director's career.

> It is the first time he has grappled with a verbal text. Mr Wilson pared the chorus's long speeches down to repeated metaphors of silence and night. This strategy heightened the poetic tension and lent a haunting quality to Euripides' mystery play that takes place on the border between life and death – as if a disembodied voice were trying to reach us from the other side of the tomb (emblematically present in the form of a looming Cycladic idol).
>
> Through mime and stylized gestures, Mr Wilson turned the chorus into human hieroglyphs. Thanks to the pioneer work of Lillian Lawler (*The Dance of the Ancient Greek Theatre*) we know that mime as well as music, poetry and dance played major roles in the Greek chorus. Mr Wilson used choral

mime to create three ritual sequences: a celebration of fertility, the slaughter of a sacrificial lamb, a mourning procession. This flow of dreamlike images – disarticulated, enigmatic – seemed to seep up from a collective subconscious.

During rehearsals at the American Repertory Theater, Mr Wilson drilled the chorus over and over again to get the precision and control he wanted. "Hold your head down four more beats before you look up," he admonished in the ritual-sacrifice scene. "You're not a real peasant, that's not a real goat. Make those movements more stylized. Don't be a realist. Be a formalist. Once you get those movements down right, the text will fall into place."

On a break, Mr Wilson remarked that "Ezra Pound gave me an important clue about how to use the chorus. He said the fourth dimension is stillness and the power over wild beasts. The chorus must reach that power over wild beasts. And through the chorus the audience must hear silence and see the invisible. The chorus is the fourth dimension."

Further, Holmberg observed:

Wilson turns *Alcestis* into a meditation on the mortality of civilizations. He constructed his set from the broken artifacts of vanished cultures – a Corinthian column, a statue of an ancient Chinese soldier, the prow of a Viking ship. He replaced Euripides' final chorus of joy with a vision of the Apocalypse. Admetus wanders off alone in a lunar landscape. Red light floods the stage, and the industrial city in the back explodes. Laser beams sear through the mountain that crumbles into an avalanche. The audience leaves the theater with the sound of dry leaves scratching its ears.

"In *Alcestis, The Civil Wars* and *Einstein on the Beach,*" Mr Wilson said, "I was concerned with the biological instinct for destruction and self-destruction. It's a real possibility that we may blow ourselves up. The terror of war is its beauty. To shock people back to sanity," he added, smiling angelically, "you have to make the death drive as seductive as possible."

Mel Gussow, of the *New York Times*, having made the journey to Cambridge, was less persuaded of the production's artistic validity.

Acting as a theatrical conceptualist, Robert Wilson creates his own scenarios, sometimes in collaboration with others. Then, with himself as director and principal designer, he activates his vision, flooding a stage with iconographic imagery. In contrast to his previous work, *Alcestis* is the first instance of Mr Wilson's applying his talent to a classic dramatic text, in this case, Euripides' profound study of sacrifice and rebirth.

Though one might have hoped for the equivalent of Andrei Serban's environmental version of Euripides' *Trojan Women*, which made theatergoers witnesses at the fall of Troy, this is not the case. Intellectually, *Alcestis* falls far short of Euripides – emotionally, it does not move one to pity and terror (as did Mr Serban's *Trojan Women*), but visually, it has moments that are astonishing.

Candidly, Mr Wilson assumes authorship. This is *Robert Wilson's Alcestis*, "based on a play by Euripides," with a prologue by Heiner Müller (aptly entitled *Description of a Picture*) and an epilogue in the Kyogen manner, with music by Laurie Anderson.

Alcestis, Euripides' first extant play, deals with the conflict between chance and necessity, as represented by Alcestis's acceptance of her role as sacrificial victim in place of her condemned husband, Admetus. Mr Wilson's apparent intention is to move beyond Euripides and to transmogrify the play into a performance piece of broader geographic universality, one that encompasses Egyptology as well as Oriental arts.

The evening begins with eye-impelling sculptural imagery. One side of the stage is a sarcophagus within a giant sarcophagus, towering totemically, and next to it is the figure of Death, man-size but with huge moth-like wings. Behind a scrim we see Herakles brandishing a club and looking like a titanic cave man. Juxtaposed next to this fearsome tableau is the sleeping figure of Admetus (Paul Rudd), presumably dreaming what is to come.

On tape, Robert Brustein, the theater's artistic director, reads a litany by Mr Müller, which, at least on one hearing, is elliptical. That voice is joined by other overlapping voices – an undertow that seems to pull the images into existence. The effect, for the theatergoer, is like wandering in Admetus's mind.

The prologue flows organically into the main body of the evening, a ninety-minute fragmentation and rearrangement of Euripides' play, in the Dudley Fitts–Robert Fitzgerald translation, with the intrusion of words by others. Apollo, Admetus and Herakles remain fairly close to the original, but others diverge broadly. Admetus's servant becomes a loutish clown and Admetus's father has his head encased in a plastic box that looks like a small oxygen tent.

As in the prologue, it is the stage pictures – not words or characters – that fix our attention, the sudden placement of figures, some of them seemingly floating on air or apparently rising from unseen caverns. In the background is a craggy mountain that resembles depictions of Delphi.

Through the middle of the stage flows a river, which acts both as the Styx and as the equivalent of the Ganges. In one of the evening's most striking scenes, three women stand in the river and wash their long hair in choreographic unison. There is also, less interestingly, a soundscape – ticking clocks, bird calls and what sounds, unnerving, like a helicopter in flight.

The cast is large and it is difficult to differentiate between those who are acting and those who are standing in for scenery. Dominated by Death, played convincingly by Rodney Hudson, the evening moves, not quite inexorably, to Admetus's reunion with Alcestis, restored to life.

When the play reaches a point of sacrifice, it seems to swerve into another landscape. A goat-like figure is eviscerated and its "blood" is used to paint the characters; a laser beam shoots from the back of the theater and carves a hole in the mountain. At this moment, one unavoidably thinks of Steven Spielberg, wondering if the Temple of Apollo had not been somehow confused with the Temple of Doom.

But, to the end, Mr Wilson remains in earnest, trying, sometimes failing, to merge his vision with that of Euripides. Then, after an intermission, he changes tone with a brief epilogue, a Kyogen play, *The Birdcatcher in Hell.* The aim, as with the prologue, is to play upon Euripidean themes, in particular, the matter of rebirth. However, compared to what has preceded it, the epilogue is child's play, neither Japanese nor evocatively Wilsonian, and Miss Anderson's birdlike musical murmurings are minimal.

Though one certainly does not want to discourage Mr Wilson's involvement with classics, it must be said that his most visionary art has been with *The Life and Times of Joseph Stalin, Einstein on the Beach,* and other imagistic, historical theater of his own invention.

(The reference to Steven Spielberg is an allusion to the director–producer of wildly romantic adventure fantasies and science-fiction films.)

The Wilson production took part in the Festival d'Automne, Paris, later the same year (1986). And of course, Gluck's operatic version, *Alceste,* has kept the legend before various publics worldwide.

Also rarely produced is *Orestes,* but in 1968 the influential director and essayist Jan Kott, while a guest professor at the University of California in Berkeley, staged an updated transformation of the tragicomedy with student actors. Judy Stone sent this account to the *New York Times:*

Jan Kott sees a vision of doom for America today in the lines Euripides wrote some four hundred years BC: "Greece is in grief and in trouble. This is what I think – Greece some God has driven mad."

Kott, the Polish scholar who has been involved in all the war, revolution and anguish of his own times, has taken an ancient Greek tragedy and moved it to modern-day Washington, DC, to lay bare the madness and violence that he sees threatening America. His production in hippie dress of Euripides' neglected play *Orestes* has played for the last three weeks at the University of California.

The controversial reverberations may equal those created by his book, *Shakespeare Our Contemporary.*

As a backdrop for all the action, Kott uses a photographic blowup of the Capitol in Washington to take the place of Agamemnon's palace in Argos at the end of the Trojan War. It is six days after Orestes, egged on by his sister Electra, has killed their mother Clytemnestra and her lover to avenge her murder of Agamemnon, their father. The play is concerned with the efforts of Orestes and Electra to escape punishment. Without changing a line of Euripides, Kott makes the degeneration of a great Greek ruling house seem a mirror of our own.

Through a loudspeaker, an interracial chorus pleads with the Furies to release Orestes from his madness, mourns the blood drenching the shrine of Delphi, "holiest of holies and navel of the world," as silent scenes of the war in Vietnam and of antiwar demonstrations in Oakland, California flash across a screen.

Kott says he wanted to find a way to express his sense of the Greek drama and to stage a Greek play within the limitations of a college production, to discover a new use for the chorus where there was no amphitheater for it to move about. The use of some lines taped and amplified through the loudspeaker frees the chorus for movement and for mime – including a flashback to the murder of Agamemnon. Kott made only minor cuts in the text and added music ranging from John Cage to rock'n'roll and an anarchist anthem.

"My goal was to play two instruments at the same time – to save the Greek topics and relationships and the Greek meanings about Argos and the Trojan War and, at the same time, to find a relationship to modern times," Kott said. "I want to translate from one to another language, both theatrically and ideologically."

In Kott's staging, the victorious Menelaus, an opportunist and a coward, wears the khaki of a US general. In tropical suit and Panama hat, Tyndareus, father of Clytemnestra and Helen, becomes a Southern senator whose devotion to law and order is hollow and vindictive. Pylades, Orestes's pal, is a Hell's Angel on motorbike – tough, effeminate and loyal; Helen, a painted, petulant whore in black bra and panties, still shirking responsibility, still blaming the gods for singling her out for the seduction that caused the Trojan war. Orestes, in his hippie love beads, prepares to murder Helen and her daughter Hermione to escape the punishment for his first crime, while Electra screams: "Murder! Butcher! Kill the whore who killed so many brave young men, the wounded and the dead, those for whom we mourn."

Orestes and Electra, self-righteous but consumed with destructiveness, start to set Argos to the torch and tongues of flame – liquid projections – slowly stain the Capitol's façade. Then the *deus ex machina* Apollo, transformed into a headless Statue of Liberty, intervenes to halt the destruction. In a wild, ironic ending, the chorus waves streamers of black and red ribbons and bursts in the Italian revolutionary song *Bandiera Rossa* with its resounding "*Viva l'anarchia e la libertà*," while others march on stage to rock music, carrying placards that say: "Burn, Baby, Burn," "Apollo Kills," "We're All Murderers," "Get Out of Troy Now," and "Violence Against Violence."

The play, effectively acted by a student cast, was sold out prior to the start of its thirteen performances. The literal-minded who came looking for obvious parallels to today were confused about the points that Kott was trying to make; some felt that the symbolism was strained and pretentious. Those who expected an evening of "moving" Greek tragedy were disappointed. Others, like this reporter, were fascinated and disturbed by the subtle insights and ironies Euripides-Kott provoked about the themes of alienation, responsibility, law and order, violence, and the multiple levels of meaning each carries within itself.

Kott, who is now writing a book about Greek drama, *A Fool Against the Establishment*, is teaching drama at Berkeley this year while on leave from the University of Warsaw. He pointed out that something like the new wave of violence in American life existed in Greece during the Peloponnesian War between Athens and Sparta. The violence was reflected in Greek domestic life as well as in foreign policy. A year after Euripides wrote *Orestes* in 408 BC, he went into voluntary exile, disillusioned with Greece.

Sympathetic to Euripides' feeling about Greece, Kott said: "I see America driven mad in the same way. To foresee this moment when the old values are destroyed . . ." He paused, searching for the precise phrase, rubbing his right thumb and forefinger to strike the spark that would produce the right word. "I think of England; the time of the olde merrie England has ceased to exist. The olde merrie America stops existing too. In this period of transition, we have in reality violence against violence. We have riots against the police and, as in the play, right and wrong exist in the same act, confusing the same act. It seems to me that the irony of this play, the bitter taste, is what we are feeling now. This bitter taste of the war, this bitter taste of the demonstrations, this bitter taste of the riots. It is rather like the pessimists' forecast, this vision of destruction when people from both sides – the people of the establishment *and* the people against the establishment – become mad. This is the tragic dilemma of America. The violence is at the same time necessary . . . and pernicious.

"The tragedy of American civilization, the tragedy of the Negro, is that it is impossible to find a good solution. But the business of a play or a director," Kott added, smiling slightly, "is not to find solutions but to visualize this bitter taste, this great fear for the future. It seems to me that is done in the last dance of the production which begins happily – and then the music goes down and down and the actors dance like paralyzed puppets into a nightmare."

Kott has had nightmares of his own. No, not of his own, he would say, but of his generation, "that whole lost generation of the left in Europe." Born in Warsaw in 1914 into an assimilated middle-class Jewish family, he was raised as a Catholic and even thought for a time of becoming a monk. He got a master's degree in law in Warsaw and then a PhD in French literature in Paris. Before World War II, he was part of the Surrealist poets' circle and associated with the Progressive Catholic movement. During World War II, he fought with the Polish army and served in the Polish underground.

He didn't think the young would ever learn from those old stories, but he loved their new and universal taste for tolerance, for "each one doing his own thing." "History is a very good thing – for scholars," he said. "But every generation has to go through it themselves, just as every girl has to go through it even though love is full of despair and deception. We can say that at the end will be despair, but we have no choice. We have to go through it. I'm for the involvement even though I know very well the price of involvement is despair."

At the time Kott was at the university in Berkeley, its campus was a centre of turbulent protests against being conscripted to serve in the Far East. As soon as the draft ended, the demonstrations stopped. Kott's gloomy predictions were not fulfilled, at least not immediately.

In 1993 an enterprising group of players, somewhat defiantly calling themselves En Garde Arts, conceived a different kind of open-air Greek theatre. They staged a radically altered *Orestes* on the rusting, abandoned piers of the Penn Rail yards in New York City. Advance notices with pictures, in the *New York Times*, showed the setting to have as a background the "broad Hudson River, the serrated New Jersey skyline opposite, and the twisted spines of two large piers". Ann Hamburger, founder and producer of the non-profit company, defined its mission as "to challenge the notion of the traditional well-made play" and "to create a theater that is visually exciting". On previous sallies about the city the group had presented works in Central Park – Mac Wellman's *Bad Penny* (1989) – and in the meat-packing district – Reza Addoh's and Mira-Lani's *Father Was a Peculiar Man* (1990). Chosen indoor settings were the dilapidated Victory Theater on West 42nd Street for Mac Wellman's *Crowbar* (1990), and a room in the legendary but rather seedy Chelsea Hotel, scene of the notorious murder of Nancy Spungeon by her lover, the drug-frenzied punk rock singer Sid Vicious – Penny Arcade's *A Quiet Evening with Sid and Nancy* (1989). All these had garnered a good share of attention. "Commissioning playwrights, directors, composers and performance artists to fashion theater for specific sites has frequently brought En Garde critical praise," said the *New York Times*. "With existing architecture for a set, the history of the site is often evoked at the same time. And under a night sky or in an unexpected environment, old themes may seem new again and timeless."

The director of *Orestes* was Tina Landau; adjustments to the skeletonic "set" were accomplished by Kyle Chepulis; the lighting was manipulated by Brian Aldous; the costumes were by James Schuette; the musical score – original – was by John Gromada, who also handled the sound effects. The updated script was by Charles L. Mee, Jr.

D.J. Bruckner, on hand for the all-seeing *New York Times*, told how the evening went:

> At the end of the production, staged in front of a twisted steel relic of an old Hudson River pier, a *deus ex machina* pops up: Apollo, in this case Brendan Sexton, 3rd, a seventh-grader from Staten Island who, pounding his fist in a baseball mitt, decrees peace for a world nearly destroyed by maniacs.
>
> Mr Mee's dark vision of society – here America as collapsed Greece – is not brighter than in his other plays, but his humor is sharper. And the company, under Tina Landau's direction, makes this romp through the legends of the House of Atreus a refreshing experience.
>
> The Atreus family – each generation did in either its parents or its children – is prime meat for Mr Mee. Orestes, prodded by his sister, Electra, has just killed their mother, Clytemnestra, because she murdered their father, and the siblings are in a mental hospital whose inmates speak in snatches. Mr Mee borrows from many sources, including *Soap Opera Digest* and the serial killer John Wayne Gacy.
>
> Electra (Theresa McCarthy) schemes to rescue Orestes (Jefferson Mays) from a patricide trial with the help of their war-hero uncle, Menelaus (Jeffrey Sugarman), just back from the ashes of Troy with his wife, Helen (Jayne Amelia Larson). But Menelaus is a political trimmer and Helen is too busy with clothes and skin care to notice much else. Tyndareus (Frank Ralter), the father of Helen and Clytemnestra, arrives in a chauffeured town car to denounce all of them in a hilarious mock-Homeric sendup of current political hypocrisies.
>
> Threaded through all the dialogue are hallucinations of well-known murders and the bizarre psychological defenses presented by some killers. And there is some very witty use of musical commentary, most notably in a thundering operatic climax to a suicide pact, and in an ensemble rendition by nine nurses of a version of *Long Ago and Far Away*.
>
> Finally, Orestes' buddy Pylades (Steven Skyfell), a hoodlum in a blue silk suit, concocts a plan: Orestes kidnaps Helen's little daughter, Hermione, and holds her at knife point fifty feet up on the old

> pier girders while Pylades and Electra, in a column of smoke, taunt a pleading Menelaus. Then the cops pull a raid and Apollo appears with his magic solutions, a pastiche of face-saving endings tacked onto the lurid ancient tales by some Greek dramatists and poets.
>
> In response to this divine nonsense, one of the patients seizes the young god and dumps him into the river as the lights go out. It's not one of the great mythical streams of Greek saga, but Mr Mee's theme is us, now, and the Hudson serves well.

It would also seem that the work draws more on the spirit of Aristophanes than of Euripides.

Three years later (1996) Jeff Cohen somewhat re-adapted this script for the troupe and installed it Off-Broadway at the One Dream Theater. Ben Brantley, the *New York Times*'s senior drama critic, took its measure:

> Describing sensational murders in the ennobling terms of Greek tragedy is a favorite device of mass-media journalists, so it seems only fitting that Greek tragedy should return the compliment. In *Orestes: I Murdered My Mother*, tabloid television invades the world of Euripidean drama, and the medium seems remarkably at home.
>
> "Orestes, you killed your own mother, and frankly I'm a little afraid of you," says a talk-show hostess (Christine Cowin), apparently a graduate of the Barbara Walters school of interviewing, as she addresses the legendary matricide. "If you were me, what would you ask yourself?"
>
> The scene draws easy laughs. But for the show's director, Jeff Cohen, who also wrote this adaptation of the Euripides text, it is part of a more provocative point. In the age of *Oprah* and *Hard Copy*, television does indeed provide its own synthetic equivalents to ancient Attic tragedy, turning family horror stories into public forums and serving up fast-fix catharses.
>
> This *Orestes* can be glibly (if amusingly) satiric in addressing such parallels. (Peter Appel's impersonation of a Regis Philbin-like character is terrific.) But it sometimes strikes deeper chords. When a cosmetically perfect television reporter (nicely played by Kathryn Hahn) brings devastating news to a deranged Elektra (Corrina Lyons), it's a pungent reminder of the creepy, prurient ways in which today's journalists assume the roles of messengers as well as the classic chorus.
>
> The scene is the high point of an often forced-seeming production with many longueurs. Mr Cohen has a smart concept here. But he hasn't been able to integrate Euripides' original story and imagery in ways that convince or compel, despite a hard-working cast of youthful intensity. As so often happens with television, the commentators steal the show from their subjects.

(The various names cited were those of then popular on-the-air talk-show hosts.)

Unhappily, *The Trojan Women*, the most effective of Euripides' anti-war plays, has never lost its relevance. Consequently it has had comparatively frequent revivals. Not long after the end of the First World War English-born actress, director and producer, Margaret Webster (1905–72), daughter of the theatre celebrities Sir Ben Webster and Dame May Whitty, made her professional London stage début in the chorus of *Trojan Women* in support of Sybil Thorndyke, who was Hecuba (1924). In time Miss Webster became mainly active in the Broadway theatre, presenting Shakespearean works and contemporary plays of superior quality, and in 1941, during the Second World War, in London and later in New York, offered a *Trojan Women* in which she took a role, and in which her mother, Dame May, was the defiant, sorrowing queen. It had a limited engagement but made a deep impression.

Michael Cacoyannis, adapting Edith Hamilton's English translation, prepared a screen play and directed a film making use of it (1970). Previously his stage version of Euripides' tragedy had been seen in New York at Circle-in-the-Square, a leading Off-Broadway group (1963). The critical assessment then was that "without being terribly adventurous, it still captured the power of what is essentially more of a ritual than a narrative drama". One who especially admired the treatment, however, was Howard Taubman, at that time the *New York Times*'s senior play reviewer. Said Taubman:

> What if the world listened to the poets for a change? What if it had taken eternally to heart the searing words Euripides set down in *The Trojan Women* in 418 BC?
>
> The thought overwhelms the imagination. Let's think more modestly and let's propose that we pay attention to *The Trojan Women* here and now. For this great tragic canvas of Euripides is as pertinent as ever, and it can be studied in a large-voiced, passionate display, which opened last night at the Circle-in-the-Square.
>
> Michael Cacoyannis, the Greek director, has staged Euripides' masterwork with the boldness of a man who knows in his own bloodstream that this is drama meant not for the dusty archives but for any place and time where fear and cruelty are perils. He has not hesitated to let it roar and keen and sing out as it laments man's fury and hymns his power to endure.
>
> This production is in the mainstream of the style used for modern productions of the Greek classics in Greece – with a difference. Mr Cacoyannis has toughened the fiber of the approach, which on the basis of performances I saw in 1962 in the amphitheater of Herod Atticus under the brow of the Acropolis, has become arty and flaccid.

He uses his own choreographed movement for the chorus of Trojan women, and it is flexible and intense. He has obtained a score from Jean Prodomides that heightens the ominous mood, and he has let the chorus break into chanting in the odes that brood over the story's final section.

Mr Cacoyannis is not afraid to demand a wide vocal range from his actors. At first it is somewhat startling to hear a performer let out all the stops within his power, for our theater tends to be neat, precise and narrow in its bounds.

But these Trojan women are torn by wrenching griefs. They mourn the loss of everything they hold dear. And through them Euripides is indicting his own Greece, which could besiege, capture and sack a neutral island like Melos, murder its adult males and enslave its women and children.

While this production does not shy away from largeness of utterance, it also knows how to be heart-rending in restraint. Thus Mildred Dunnock as Hecuba, the gray queen, can denounce with a grim, towering rage, she can thunder at Menelaus and she can say farewell to her slain grandson, Astyanax, lying on his father's shield, with subdued tenderness.

Carrie Nye as the crazed Cassandra has full scope for her painful visions. Joyce Ebert as Andromache expresses her anguish at the loss of husband and country in great, wrenching cries and then, when she hears that her boy, Astyanax, will be flung from the tower, she says good-bye in hushed incantatory phrases that affirm the preciousness of life.

Jane White's Helen is crafty in her self-esteem and shrewd in her effort to save herself. Alan Mixon's Talthybius is dutiful, yet sympathetic. Robert Mandan's Menelaus hovers on the edge of renewed frailty. The women in the chorus speak and move well.

Mr Cacoyannis uses the long, rectangular playing space and a broad flight of steps leading to a platform with a white luminous screen as a background with a fluidity that is both natural and dramatic. The theater in which he staged *The Trojan Women* at Spoleto Festival last year surely had no such layout.

The translation, the late distinguished Edith Hamilton's, is direct and sinewy, all the better because it eschews floweriness. Mr Cacoyannis, like Miss Hamilton, treats Euripides as if a great dramatic poet of two millenniums ago were still worth attending. And curiously enough, he is.

The film, produced in Spain after a lapse of seven years, was a more ambitious effort. Cacoyannis gathered four of the world's best-known stage-and-screen actresses: Katharine Hepburn, as Hecuba; Vanessa Redgrave, as Andromache; Genevieve Bujold, as Cassandra; and Irene Papas, as Helen, the four drawn from the United States, England, Canada and Greece. The newspaper gossip columnists speculated at length on how these highly paid stars would get along together, but no rumours of friction emanated from the studio in Madrid during the shooting.

The film was a disappointment to Vincent Canby, cinema critic of the *New York Times*.

The Trojan Women . . . is the kind of film that a lot people will feel called upon to praise for the fact of its having been made at all. The argument is that there simply aren't that many people around who won't rest until they put Euripides on film, and, after all, any Euripides-on-film is better than none.

I'm not too sure, at least as long as there are printed texts available and those occasional theatrical productions, such as the one Cacoyannis himself staged at the Circle-in-the-Square. . . .

The film that Cacoyannis has made is not bad, but something that is somehow more offensive to anyone interested in the possibilities of motion pictures to enrich and excite the mind. This *Trojan Women* is high-class mediocre. Cacoyannis has slightly trimmed the Edith Hamilton translation (the gods have been excised from the text), and added at least one hilarious exchange of dialogue for continuity's purposes (Herald: "Tell Menelaus to come at once to the women's camp." Soldier: "What's up?" Herald: "They're after Helen's blood.")

What's most disheartening, however, is that he has chosen a banal style that falls midway between the literal realism of the film's exterior landscapes and the poetic realism of the play's language. This is a confusion, I might add, that is further compounded by a series of casting coups that look like the remains of thirty years of Miss Universe contests.

All of these women are good actresses, but their manners and methods are so different from one another that the effect of the drama, which should be that of one long, carefully orchestrated moan, is squeaky and Babel-like, as fragmented as the close-ups (mid-forehead to bridge-of-nose) with which Cacoyannis periodically studies the faces of his Spanish-looking chorus. . . .

Katharine Hepburn, flinty New Englander that she is, plays old, gray-headed Hecuba, not so much like the defeated Queen of Troy she is supposed to be, but more like an apple grower's widow who weeps a lot.

Hecuba is the center and the power of *The Trojan Women*. She is the mistress of the awful ceremonies that make up the drama, presiding helplessly but with almost pre-moral strength over the horrors the Greeks have committed on her family, Troy and the human race.

Miss Hepburn speaks most of her lines with small, elegant accents that have little to do with epic grief, and only in her final confrontation with Helen, the one who had brought the ruin down on them all, does her Hecuba suggest real depth and passion. Genevieve Bujold, the French-Canadian actress, is a more or less elfin Cassandra, which is not, however, the way I imagined her.

In their own, very different ways, Vanessa Redgrave, as Andromache, and Irene Papas, as Helen, are quite interesting. Miss Redgrave is very English, but she is also an actress of such classic beauty, and classical authority, that she commands attention. So does Miss Papas, an actress I haven't always admired, but here her dark, ageless, almost masculine beauty gives real dimension to the role of the woman who was once the most beautiful in the world, and may still be.

I suspect that Cacoyannis needs the limitations of the stage to give his work automatic discipline, to fix the focal point, which the film never finds.

On the stage, *The Trojan Women* takes place outside the Greek camp, with Troy in the background, but it is probably placed effectively against a minimum of scenery and props. In Cacoyannis's film, I never was sure where we were supposed to be, and since the picture opens in such dense clouds of smoke, I was genuinely surprised when, at the end, Troy is finally set afire. I'd assumed it'd already burnt down.

In spite of the fact that *The Trojan Women* is a kind of moving fresco, or frieze, which should be kept at a certain distance, Cacoyannis often uses his camera subjectively (most atrociously when it spirals to earth, as if it were the body of the boy, Astyanax, being hurled to his death from a cliff). The director, however, doesn't pursue any style long enough for it to become dominant. The result, like the accents of its leading ladies, is a confusion of compromises that tell you the plot, which is not important, but communicate hardly any of the exaltation, which is.

As a segment of the Serban–Swados *Fragments of a Greek Tragedy*, Euripides' drama at La MaMa had a strong impact (1974). Mel Gussow wrote in the *New York Times*:

The plays communicate directly with cries, whispers, silences, looks and images. The images are unforgettable: Helen stripped, shorn of her hair, smeared with offal and ravished; a child encaged like a captured beast on the way to slaughter; a suicide rolling in ritualistic slow motion down an incline, weaving her body in exquisite patterns like an angel tumbling from the heavens.

These visions would be powerful even if removed from us on a proscenium stage or in a film. Mr Serban's innovation is to turn the entire theater into a stage and to involve the action with the audience.

... As the actors charge among us, as Elizabeth Swados's music throbs in the background, we feel almost as if we are witnesses at the fall of Troy (and at Troy would we have understood the language?).

> The play becomes credible, and also symbolic and impressionistic. This is an interpretation, a variation on a classic theme, as if the director were choreographing or composing a piece of theater.
>
> Actually, *The Trojan Women* is designed as "an epic opera," and the composer is symbiotic with the director. Miss Swados's music is inextricable from the event. With its eerie pulsating rhythms, it seems to derive from the fall of Troy itself.
>
> Having witnessed the savaging of a people, for the second half of *The Trojan Women,* we sit on benches and watch the final devastation of a nation, the banishment of womankind as it is herded out of the arena.

In this production, Jane Lind was Hecuba; Valis Mickens, Cassandra; Priscilla Smith, Andromache; Joanne Peled, Helen.

Julius Novick, in another *New York Times* article, said of this *Trojan Women* that "it is the most musical and variegated" of the pieces in the trilogy. "Its scenes take place in various parts of the auditorium, and the audience moves to watch them. Cassandra dances with two flaming torches on a platform in a corner above the three-man, wind-and-percussion orchestra; Hector's wife and son are caged on the stage; Helen is savaged on a cart in the center of the room; the members of the chorus move through the crowd of spectators. Near the end, the actors guide the audience up into the side galleries, and the remaining action expands to occupy the whole auditorium."

Of the unintelligibility of the speeches, Novick comments: "A great deal is lost: the specificity of comprehensible language. But a great deal is gained as well. The high strangeness of the unfamiliar sounds makes us listen differently, and feel differently. The trilogy gets along so well without understandable words because a musical sensibility has been exercised on every moment of it. . . . Miss Swados has done more than compose a musical score for the productions. She has worked in close collaboration with Serban; presumably as a result, the actors who perform the trilogy have a great spectrum of sounds at their disposal – singing, chanting, keening, whispering, moaning, guttural shouting – all chosen for their expressive power."

Arthur Holmberg allows Serban to expand yet again on this use of non-verbal communication when presenting a classic play noted for its magnificent poetry. "In the beginning, words and magic were one. I wanted to spin a pattern of sounds with the power of a mantra. I paid strict attention to the sequencing of vowels and consonants. I wanted to drive the sounds of language into the audience's ear like a nail. I had to ask the actors to produce sounds they had never produced before, sounds that come not from the throat but from the whole body. And if one puts together the right sounds in the right order, a litany is created that reaches the depths of the subconscious. Western theatre lost this magic after the Greeks. It's been lying at the bottom of the sea for over two thousand years. We must keep searching for the key that will unlock their theatrical secrets."

A convert to Serban's argument, Holmberg affirms: "[He] has created a sensuous sound spectrum that explores not the meanings of words but their music. By riveting the audience's attention on the physicality of language – its pitch, volume and timbre – Mr Serban induces a trancelike state and reveals speech as a powerful orchestra capable of reaching the fringe of consciousness where words cannot go but meaning still exists."

Inspired by *Fragments of a Greek Trilogy* while it was on tour in Japan some years later, the Waseda Little Theatre undertook its own production of *The Trojan Women* which eventually was brought to New York and the Gershwin Theater at Brooklyn College (1979). Set initially in post-war modern Japan, the time was soon returned to an earlier Samurai epoch, the cast employing both Noh and Kabuki movement. At first this company had sought to emulate Western methods as much as possible, but Tadashi Suzuki, the director, was finally convinced of a need to go back to Japanese sources; this led him in the early 1970s to require that his actors study and absorb traditional Noh and Kabuki techniques before taking up contemporary works. The result, in the opinion of David Oyama in the *New York Times*, was a *Trojan Women* that was "shattering and unforgettable", with a truly memorable portrayal by the leading actress, Kayoko Shiraishi.

New York saw another *Trojan Women*, now in a choreographic adaptation, during an engagement by the Louisville Ballet, again at Brooklyn College (1985). This dance version had been created by Alun Jones, the company's director, five years earlier (1980). Jack Anderson, a *New York Times* critic, summed up its merits in this fashion:

> The ballet is clearly well intentioned. But even the best intentions could not save it if its choreography were inept. Fortunately, Mr Jones's work is usually interesting and at times eloquent.
>
> Mr Jones is greatly helped by a commissioned score by Karel Husa, who was also in the pit to conduct it. Rumbling and snarling with the drums and trumpets of battle and shivering and sighing with anguish, the music gave the choreography solid support and built to shattering climaxes.
>
> The ballet began strikingly when Helen Starr, Hecuba, the defeated queen, tottered to her feet and despairingly reached toward her head, as if to touch a crown that was no longer there. Here, and in other dramatic sequences, Miss Starr's gestures were meticulously timed.
>
> Among the most effective of the episodes were those for Hecuba and an ensemble of women, all

wearing long robes. They often danced linked together, pausing to assume architectural formations. Later, there was a chilling scene in which the women ran frantically, dodging warriors' spears. Still later, the way Miss Starr embraced a slain child while other women gathered around her was reminiscent of a Renaissance *Pietà*.

Mr Jones's treatment of the Greek soldiers was less convincing. The choreography for them emphasized repetitive strutting and, as if to hint at contemporary parallels to Euripides, some of the strutting recalled goose-stepping. Mr Jones's point was worth making, but he made it perhaps once too often. He should also have resisted the temptation to give Dale Brannon, as a Greek herald, a brief variation with virtuosic turns. Mr Brannon performed them well, but one could argue that they were out of keeping with the overall tone of the ballet.

Whereas Euripides could both present a dramatic situation and, through dialogue, comment upon it, Mr Jones occasionally seemed hampered by the lack of words. Thus it was not always clear what Diane Downes, as Cassandra the prophetess, was actually prophesying, and some of her despairing gestures were too similar to those of Rebecca Adderton, as Andromache.

Nevertheless, when Miss Downes's Cassandra thrashed as if struck by invisible whips, then stood perfectly still, as if petrified by her knowledge of the future, one knew that, for her, the gift of prophecy was a curse, not a blessing. And Mr Jones's choreography always conveyed a sense of the monstrousness of war and the desolation it brings.

Every scene of *The Trojan Women* may not have been equally effective. But the ballet is an honest effort, and Mr Jones deserves praise for choreographing it.

A *Trojan Women*, in a pared-down English translation by Richard Lattimore, was proffered Off-Broadway by the Pearl Theater troupe, directed by Shepard Sobel (1991). D.J.R. Bruckner, of the *New York Times*, assayed it.

The Trojan Women remains the most gut-wrenching antiwar play of all, able after twenty-four hundred years to arouse pity and terror, and plenty of both.

For his version at the Pearl Theater, Shepherd Sobel makes some deep cuts – principally in the chants of the chorus – and emphasizes the relentless grinding-down of the widowed and enslaved Trojan women. His production lasts ninety minutes and leaves one feeling hammered. People who know the original will miss some of the sweeping choral odes; their meaning is often murky, but they give the play a slow, majestic rhythm that heightens the terror.

> There are problems with Mr Sobel's direction. His vision of Cassandra (played by Laura Rathgeb) is really annoying. She acts like a kind of prancing Ophelia out of her wits, when in fact her dances and ravings should reveal possession by a dreadful god. And a few other actors have not been instructed that their characters are supremely dignified and their composed demeanor should make their fate more terrible.
>
> The key roles are the old queen, Hecuba; Hector's widow, Andromache; and Helen of Troy. Bella Jarrett is a wonderful Hecuba, a dangerous fury filled with contempt and sorrow, who knows how to make words caress, or lash and tear. Donnah Welby's Andromache embodies despair itself when the triumphant Greeks murder her young son to finish off the Trojan royal family. And Robin Leslie Brown has the right mixture of sensuality, fear and defiance to be a believable cause of war.
>
> Finally, a word should be said about Astyanax, the killed child. Ancient Greek commentaries give no clue about how this silent role was handled. In this case Carlo Alban is admirable, most admirable in death. It has been many years since I have seen an actor of any age play dead so convincingly for so long. It is a great relief to see him galvanized again during curtain calls.

Since *The Trojan Women* is comparatively simple and inexpensive to mount with regard to setting and costumes, offers fine roles and is academically respectable, it is given by undergraduate acting groups quite repetitively, and especially – the cast being predominantly female – at women's colleges. Euripides' message has great appeal to the young, who can recite the lines with fervour. Robert Hall, in his published *Diaries*, notes the appearance of his son Christopher and daughter Jenny in a student production at Cambridge University (1979).

Universal identification by audiences with the play is borne out by its having been produced not only for those speaking Japanese but also for those who use Yiddish. Carole Braverman's *The Yiddish Trojan Women* (seen in New York in 1996) is loosely derived from Euripides and led the essayist Margo Jefferson to expound on it at length from a feminist point of view in the *New York Times*:

> [It] has craft, it has passion, and it asks real questions about how we live: what we believe in, what we yearn for, what we'd kill or die for; what principles we want to live by and which ones we're willing to live with until something better comes along.
>
> Ms Braverman's play is scheduled to close on February 18 at the American Jewish Theater. I want it to relocate and reopen again soon. (It originated at the Women's Project and in revised form had a very successful run last year at the Cockpit Theatre in London.) It deserves to go on being seen.

It is not, as the title suggests, an adaptation of Euripides' tragedy. It takes the basic material of that play – the destruction of a nation and a culture through war; the fate of the women survivors – changes the countries and cultures in question, and looks long and hard at the choices the survivors make.

What happens to you, as one of Ms Braverman's women says, "when every taste is gone but the taste of ashes in your mouth?" How do you (how would any of us) survive: bravely, slyly, selfishly? What do you remember about how you survived? And how does what you try to forget mark you and your descendants? If you have established a new life in another country, what happens when you see war starting up there, "naked, brutal force" again, but in a new form, with the killers speaking different languages and wearing different national dress?

The world destroyed in *The Yiddish Trojan Women* was a village of Polish Jews; the war was a pogrom. When the play opens, the survivor, Devorah (played by Joanna Merlin) is a grandmother in Brooklyn who had outlived three husbands and is about to marry (and outlive) a fourth. She is also about to be overtaken by the power age has to make the past mean more than the present. You can no longer arrange and edit your memories; stray words or actions take you backward, not forward. When you look outside your Brooklyn window, you see the village of your childhood; when you look at your granddaughters, you see your dead relations; when you start to tell a story you love, you end up telling one you had tried to bury years ago.

As Devorah is driven further into her past against her will, those well-polished accounts of how charming and sought-after she was give way to scarier things: the image of her husband's brother whom she lusted for and of his high-minded sister whom she betrayed; the sight of the murderous Polish soldiers moving toward her village on horseback as she ate wild strawberries in a field nearby. Her two granddaughters and her grand-niece are puzzled, interested and sympathetic in the benignly patronizing way of the young. Mostly, they are obsessed with their own lives.

They are in their 30s, when the choices people make start to leave marks, and they are living in the early 1980s – the greedy, success-driven Reagan years. Brenda (Marilyn Pasekoff) is a stand-up comic who is determined that grit and savvy ruthlessness will ease her journey from the strip joints of New Jersey to the sleek studio environs of *The Tonight Show*. Her sister, Abby (Lori Wilner), is a labor organizer. The factory she has just unionized is about to move to Guatemala. There, the Government-imposed price of unionization is death, and it is a price supported by the Reagan Administration. Their cousin, Tess (Laura Esterman), "Miss Tenure-Puss," Brenda calls her, teaches mythology, "the stories that all people make up – to explain the mystery of things," as she puts it: to explain, to justify and to make bearable.

There is nothing sappy or decoratively sentimental about these sisters. All Abby and Brenda have in common is the accident of birth to the same parents. And Tess, who loves Abby for her courage and Brenda for her Chutzpah, will have to choose between them as surely as if she were choosing between feuding suitors or warring countries.

In the meantime, she is making her way through an affair with a young, sexy working-class guy named Luke who has no interest in mythology and no capacity for abstract thought. To my surprise, despite this set of stock characteristics, Luke becomes a real character too. Actually, as written, I found him a little too dumb; when he first appears, his lines have that "Will you folks out there in the audience get a load of this ignorant hunk?" sitcom tone, but they get more varied as the play goes on, and Hugh O'Gorman plays Luke with such forthrightness that you stop smirking and start listening.

It's not the tragedies of life that defeat you, it's the messes, said Dorothy Parker, a line that would not be worth repeating if her point weren't that most of us aren't much good at either. In this play, every woman gets her share of both. With its pogroms and private betrayals, Devorah's past seeps into the lives of her grandchildren. Each one finds herself caught between plain old selfish need (I want love, I want sex, I want money and fame); ethics (how far will I go to get what I want?); morality (if I believe in social and political justice, will I put myself on the line for them?), and history (what happens when my actions determine whether people live or die?).

The play's power is that it makes us live through every one of these choices intensely and intimately. "Our hearts are so small, so small, and even that gets broken," says Tess at the play's end.

In the next incarnation of *The Yiddish Trojan Women*, I hope to see subtler direction than Richard Sabellico was able to provide; more of the tonal shifts that convey the intimacies and antipathies of family life; and a tension that sustains itself between scenes instead of disappearing with each blackout only to be reestablished through passages of music.

Ms Esterman, Ms Pasekoff and Ms Wilner have a good sense of their characters but they can do more. (And Ms Esterman could do with fewer mannered shrugs and whimsical facial expressions.) Joanna Merlin originated the pivotal role of the grandmother, but I feel she is still grappling with it: with the Yiddish-inflected speech (it must flow from her as naturally as tough-girl Brooklynese flows from Brenda) and with Devorah's struggle to express her blocked memories. Ms Merlin falls into a kind of trance, but it grows monotonous when it needs to be hypnotic.

When the play slips on a piece of glib dialogue or a plot twist, it recovers and goes on gathering force. I went home and kept thinking: about history and politics and what it means to see them allied with (indivisible from) sex, career ambitions and chitchat; the books we like to read, the bad jokes we tell and all the everyday stuff that we vainly hope will contain the messes and ward off the tragedies.

Michael Cacoyannis staged another Euripidean tragedy, *Iphigeneia in Aulis*, at New York's Circle in the Square (1970) and then, seven years later (1977), brought out a film version of the play. As before, too, the *New York Times*'s senior theatre and motion picture critics were sharply at variance as to the degree of his success in these two somewhat different ventures. Irene Papas, a Cacoyannis favourite, appeared in both offerings, but now as Clytemnestra.

About the staged work, Clive Barnes, a dance reviewer who had replaced Taubman, had this to say:

> The strength of Euripides is his humanity – he always saw the man beneath the crown and would inveigh at the immorality of wilful gods and an errant fate. It is this humanity and spirit that is so heart-breakingly caught in a most moving production of *Iphigeneia in Aulis*, which last night opened at the Circle in the Square. Here is great theater and an adornment to the New York stage.
>
> Although Euripides' sole authorship of *Iphigeneia in Aulis* is often questioned, the usual ending being particularly suspect, the play undoubtedly has one of the most pathetic and touching themes in Greek tragedy. And because of its very human motivation, despite a crucial command of an oracle, there are no shafts from the gods to deflect interest from a situation that is not without its contemporary significance. For one of the things *Iphigeneia in Aulis* is about – or, rather, now seems to be about – is the person's duty toward a nation pursuing a war he feels to be worthless.
>
> The worthless war is the battle to retrieve Helen from Troy. Is it a war over a whore? Euripides at times suggests it is. Or is it rather a war to protect Greece from the barbarians? As his heroine goes with glory to her death, Euripides also suggests that it is not even that. Against this background of waiting armies, a strange domestic tragedy is played out.

Barnes synopsizes aspects of the plot, including the seer's warning.

> What follows is the agony of four people: Agamemnon, his daughter, his wife Clytemnestra, and Achilles, the young hero used as a bait to bring Iphigeneia to Aulis. It is the agony of people faced with a directive from the gods that they know to be unjust.
>
> Using an impressively fluent and understandably poetic English version by Minos Volanakis, Michael Cacoyannis had directed this Euripides with a forceful feel for its contemporary relevance. At

first the direction seems uncertain – wavering between a ritualistic view of tragedy, to an extent unavoidable in the Greek classic theater, and the naturalistic approach to which the play lends itself.

As a result, the heroes occasionally lurch around the stage like stylized giants, while the chorus is treated with an almost idiomatic freedom. Yet as the tragedy approaches its climax, such inequalities fade away, and Mr Cacoyannis presses toward the end with his actors pouring out their lines with a noble simplicity.

It is in keeping with Mr Cacoyannis's view of the play (a view that the ancient Greeks themselves might have found sentimental) that he rejects the play's disputed happy ending. He prefers to finish with Iphigeneia's being led to sacrifice and Clytemnestra, caught in a spotlight that is tantamount to a cinematic close-up, in an ashen-blaze of grief.

The cast is exceptionally strong. That fine Greek actress Irene Papas is a Clytemnestra of the most noble passion, with a wine-dark voice that rolls like distant thunder, bold eyes, and a cry of anguish that echoes in the soul. She plays Clytemnestra as a wife and mother more than a tragedy queen, and not once could one forget that here was a woman giving up her child. As she stood, hopelessly aghast, while Iphigeneia calmly argued all the fine reasons why she should go to her death like a girl embracing a lover, this Clytemnestra, still tortured, wrenched the heart with her electric impassivity. Jenny Lee was almost as impressive as Iphigeneia, superbly expressing first the girl's swift surge of youth, then her fear of boundless death, and finally the resignation that comes to her by choosing death as if it were by her own will.

The men perhaps get the worst of it, but they also provide performances of solid merit. Mitchell Ryan's Agamemnon, part politician, part hero, part father, provided a subtly judged performance of a man of patchy conscience who wants to do the right thing but hasn't truly got the moral equipment to know what the right thing is.

Against such a detailed portrayal, Christopher Walken's heroically spoken and finely ardent Achilles and Alan Mixon's not-all-villainous Menelaus lost something in the comparison, just as their roles had already lost something in the playwright's original insight. The chorus was led with sharp intensity by Erin Martin.

The staging looked beautifully convincing, and with a simple setting and well-designed costumes, all by Michael Annals, it had a great deal of atmosphere, which was also helped by Marvin David Levy's somberly, lambently elegiac music.

The film adaptation of *Iphigeneia in Aulis* fell under the eye of the *New York Times*'s Vincent Canby, who once again took exception to much of what the director had done. The screenplay was by Cacoyannis, and the dialogue was in Greek abetted by English subtitles. Canby's comments are acidulous:

> Because Euripides (480–406 BC) was Greek and Michael Cacoyannis (1922–) is Greek, there is a tendency to applaud Mr Cacoyannis's thoroughly ponderous attempts to make the ancient Euripidean tragedies comprehensible to contemporary audiences. We are asked to believe that the playwright and the film maker share some sort of deep cultural bond, as if they'd been in the same class at Athens High. Good old Mike and Rip – the Mutt and Jeff of the Acropolis.
>
> The bond may well be there, but it isn't apparent in the films Cacoyannis has made to date – *Electra* (1962), *The Trojan Women* (1970), which was a big-budget production with an international cast that spoke various kinds of English, and now *Iphigeneia*, a Greek-language version of the last Euripides tragedy, *Iphigeneia in Aulis*.
>
> Like *The Trojan Women*, *Iphigeneia in Aulis* is a bitter reflection on the war that Athens had been waging against Sparta since 431 BC, and that Athens would lose in 404 BC with the complete destruction of her defenses. When it was written in 407 BC, *Iphigeneia* was a topical play in which the playwright substituted Troy for Sparta. Even though Euripides was then in exile, he wasn't foolish enough to believe that such an attack on state policy would get very far if staged frontally.
>
> *Iphigeneia* is not a conventional tragedy. There are no easily recognized heroes in the way Euripides dramatized the story of the Trojan War. . . . There's not a truly noble person in the entire play, not even the doomed Iphigeneia who, though she goes bravely to her death, goes as a deluded child for all the wrong reasons.

Canby argues that Clytemnestra is outraged "not because she cares about her daughter that much but because she fears how much she will suffer the loss of a daughter". Here is where Cacoyannis errs, in his opinion:

> Euripides' method in *Iphigeneia* is oblique – nobody ever means everything that is said. This undercurrent of furious irony is something that is completely lost in Mr Cacoyannis's *Iphigeneia*, whose characters have been so simplified as to become tragic stereotypes. It's not that the text has been tampered with but the manner in which it's played and set.
>
> Irene Papas, with her magnificent profile intact and her eyebrows in full bloom, plays Clytemnestra as if she were Mother Earth and not the complicated, selfish, conniving bitch she should be.

> Miss Papas's Clytemnestra asks for sympathy, as does the Agamemnon of Costa Kazakos, though he also manages to convince us of the contradictory desires that have been his undoing. Iphigeneia is played by Tatiana Papamoskou, a tall, skinny, doe-eyed twelve-year-old who looks as if she might grow up to be a terrific Dior model, which has nothing to do with ancient Greece or Euripides.
>
> In *Iphigeneia*, as in *The Trojan Women*, Mr Cacoyannis employs all sorts of comparatively snappy film techniques – the hand-held camera, the zoom lens, and the subjective camera by which we look out through the eyes of the character – to make us believe that we are there. It never works and can't work. We're not meant to get inside these characters, but to stand aside and observe the spectacle as a single, headlong ritual.
>
> Mr Cacoyannis's fondness for photographing these densely packed, poetic melodramas in scenic, real-life landscapes distracts from the text and demolishes the actors, whose grandly theatrical mannerisms look silly in sets as big as all outdoors. People in the film tend to run in a half-crouch, the way a stage actor runs when he wants to indicate a spring even though he's covering no more than ten feet of stage space.
>
> The film is not without its own paradox: The best thing in it is all wrong. This is a pre-credit sequence in which we are shown the state and condition of the Greek forces in Aulis as they await orders to sail to Troy. We see their boredom as they lie about the beaches, their ships idle, their rations low, their anger accumulating. The sequence has a lazy, eerie kind of beauty, but it should be the preface for a big, overblown historical pageant like *The Fall of the Roman Empire*, not *Iphigeneia*, which has no need for anything more than its action and the extraordinary text.

Whether Canby's deprecatory reaction is justified can only be judged by one who has seen the film. Some might consider his reading of Euripides' intentions quite personal.

The long-active Jean Cocteau Repertory, Off-Broadway at the Bouwerie Lane Theater, proved itself competent enough to attempt its own *Iphigeneia at Aulis* (1994). It was directed by Eve Adamson, who also did the lighting. Assisting her was Steven F. Graver, who was responsible for costuming the actors; and John Brown, who designed the workable set. An unsigned critique in the *New York Times* was highly favourable:

> In Eve Adamson's realization of *Iphigeneia at Aulis* by Euripides the stage is filled not with epic figures but with real people struggling for life and reason in a world they abhor but cannot escape. That is exactly what the playwright intended, and this production is swift, relentless and deeply disturbing classical drama, despite two serious casting problems.

The company's choice of a new translation by W.S. Merwin and George E. Dimock, Jr, is fortunate; these men have avoided the perpetual temptation to use Baroque meters and language to give a hint of Euripides' rich Greek. Their straightforward rhythms and vocabulary are very friendly to actors' mouths and our ears, and their version captures the spirit of the play: a commanding, passionate dignity. (Occasionally one wishes the cast had been given more help in pronouncing Greek names, especially the chorus.)

. . . Craig Smith is a fine Agamemnon: a good but weak man, a great commander enervated by fear. And John Lenartz as Achilles is equally apt: all muscle and muddle, a young man inspired by and entangled in heroic ideals he will never be mature enough to fully assimilate.

Unfortunately, the female characters are not so sharp. Adrienne D. Williams's Clytemnestra is appropriately shocked and frightened, a victim, in the first half of the play, but in the last half she mutes far too much the vengeful rage that should make this woman a demon of terror. Monique Vukovic also has difficulties with Iphigeneia. Iphigeneia is scarcely yet a teenager, and the power of the character springs from her vaulting into the comprehension of a wise adult once she knows her fate. Miss Vukovic starts as an adult and stays that way.

That said, this is a wonderfully satisfying production of a great drama that usually frustrates the efforts of modern companies. This performance makes the play's intellectual power dramatically forceful and it embodies the superb compassion of the playwright that reaches out over twenty-four hundred years and holds the audience in its grip from the first word to the last.

A director staging *The Bacchae* for modern spectators is beset with major difficulties. How is the actor who is Pentheus to treat the scene where he dons women's attire without evoking laughter that is incongruous in a tragedy, a shift of mood that riskily invades the spell? What of Agave's mad dance when she holds aloft her son's gory head, while under the pitiful delusion of having slain a lion? (And whenever have there been lions in the mountains of Greece?) Yet *The Bacchae* drew a surprising number of twentieth-century productions, some of which are enumerated here. What has been proved is that some audiences, adequately learned and sophisticated, truly appreciate and relate to this drama – or fable – that is laden with mythology and steeped in symbolism. And, again, its psychology is strikingly contemporary, Freudian, and even post-Freudian, in its portrayal of prurience and repressed sexual desires, and the force of drunken, orgiastic – Dionysian – impulses in even the most outwardly rational and civilized of humankind.

The Polish composer Karol Szymanowski, electing to write an opera that dealt with eroticism,

Menander (*c.* 342–291 BC); this sculpture is a Roman copy of a Greek original.

Tilla Durieux as Queen Jocasta in a production of *Oedipus Rex* directed by Max Reinhardt at the Deutsches Theater in Berlin, *c.* 1910.

Laurence Olivier as Oedipus, London, 1945.

Irene Worth and John Gielgud in Seneca's *Oedipus*, directed by Peter Brook, National Theatre, London, 1968.

Alexis Minotis in *Oedipus at Colonus*, New York, 1976.

Judith Anderson as Medea in a production directed by John Gielgud, New York, 1947.

An Italian vase painting depicting Medea murdering one of her sons; fourth century BC.

Stone relief depicting Phaedra and her stepson Hippolytus; third century AD.

Katina Paxinou as Jocasta in *Oedipus Rex*, London, 1952.

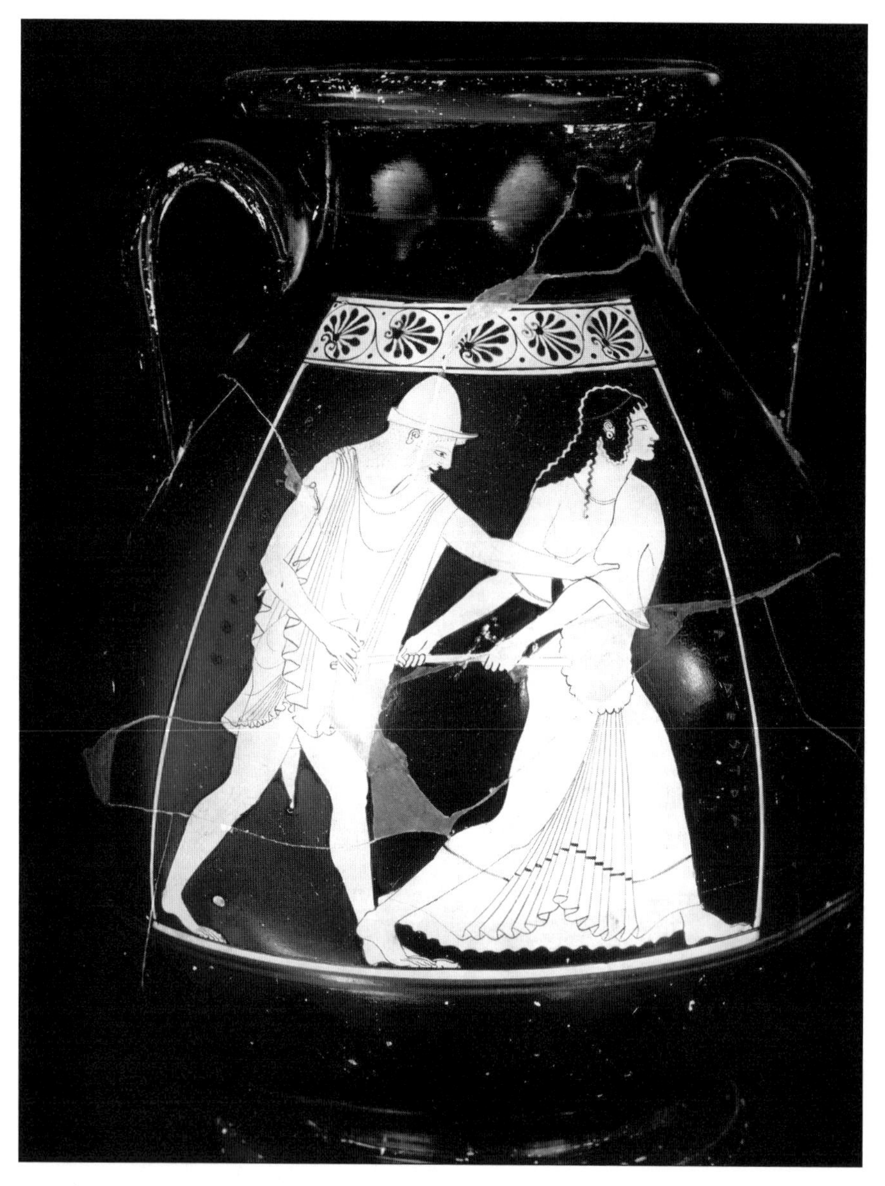

Greek vase painting depicting Clytemnestra trying to help her lover but hindered by Thaltybios, a follower of Agamemnon; fifth century BC.

The première of Richard Strauss's *Electra*, directed by Leo Blech, Berlin, 1909, with Marie Gotze as Clytemnestra and Thalia Plaichinger as Electra.

Marble relief from Herculaneum showing Orestes in Delphi climbing over a sleeping Erinys, with a statue of Apollo in front of him; first century BC.

Martha Graham and Paul Taylor in her ballet *Clytemnestra*, New York, 1958.

Roman wall painting from Pompeii depicting Medea and her children; first century AD.

Priscilla Smith as Medea in *Fragments of a Greek Trilogy*, directed by Andrei Serban, La MaMa Theater, New York, 1974.

Bronze relief from Olympia showing Orestes killing his mother and the flight of Aegisthus; *c.* 570 BC.

Zoë Wanamaker as Electra and Andrew Howard as Orestes at the Chichester Theatre, Sussex, in a production directed by David Leveaux, 1997.

The funeral of Astyanax, son of Andromache, in Andrei Serban's production of *The Trojan Women*, Theatre of Nations Festival, Seoul-Kyonggi, Korea, 1997.

Katharine Hepburn as Hecuba and Irene Papas as Helen in a film version of *The Trojan Women* directed by Michael Cacoyannis, 1972.

Two actors at a woman's window from an unidentified play depicted on a wine *krater*, southern Italy; 350–340 BC.

Buster Keaton and Zero Mostel in the film *A Funny Thing Happened on the Way to the Forum*, 1966.

FT-4
13

Greek vase depicting a chorus dance, with Hephaestus and his blacksmith's hammer, Dionysus and Muse of Comedy with *thyrsi* and Marsyas with double pipe (undated).

Choral dance from archaic times on a very early Attic vase.

The chorus of Maenads from Sir Peter Hall's production of *The Bacchae* at Epidaurus, 2002.

The Archarians by Arisophanes presented at Epidaurus, directed by K. Arvanitakis and designed by George Souglides, 2000.

The chorus from *The Greeks*, directed by John Barton for the Royal Shakespeare Company, 1980.

Sir Laurence Olivier among the chorus in the 1945 London production of *Oedipus Rex.*

The chorus from *The Trojan Women*, directed by Andrei Serban and originally presented at La MaMa Theater, New York, 1974.

The chorus of Old Men from *The Orestia* by Aeschylus, directed by Sir Peter Hall at the National Theatre, London, 1981.

The principals and chorus in the *Electra* section from *Fragments of a Greek Trilogy*, directed by Andrei Serban and originally presented at La MaMa Theater, New York, in 1974. The most recent revival was in 1997.

Euripides' *Alcestis*, directed by Robert Wilson and presented by the American Repertory Theater, Boston, 1986.

Alcestis, directed by Robert Wilson, 1986.

Greek Attic vase painting depicting a scene from Aeschylus' *Persians*; the ghost of Darius appears to Atossa.

Douglas Campbell as Oedipus surrounded by members of the chorus of *Oedipus Rex*. Production directed by Tyrone Guthrie and designed by Tanya Moiseiwitsch, Stratford, Ontario, 1955.

searched for an appropriate story. This led to *King Roger* (1926), for which he wrote the score, collaborating with his cousin Jaroslaw Iwaszkiewicz on the libretto, which they acknowledged was borrowed from an anonymous twelfth-century poem, but which obviously derives even more from Euripides' tragic play. Szymanowski devoted six years to his work until it was readied for its première in Warsaw.

A Christian king – a historical figure, Roger II of Sicily – is in a Byzantine church that is filled with Gregorian chants; suddenly he is confronted by an Arab scholar who warns of the appearance in the kingdom of a mysterious, handsome young shepherd preaching heretical religious ideas. The king's subjects wish him to condemn the stranger, who is wandering the countryside.

Again suddenly, the young man, seemingly a shepherd, enters the church and appears before the king, who is entranced by his charm. The queen – Roxanne – pleads that he be spared. Accordingly, the king invites the stranger to visit the palace that evening.

At the court, King Roger is further attracted by the handsome stranger's exotic singing and dancing, until the fervent shepherd asserts that he has been sent by God, a claim that the king deems horribly blasphemous. Despite the queen's renewed intervention, the young man is cast into chains by the guards and led off to prison. But the fetters do not hold him, and laughing he leads his converts – Roxanne among them – away to the nearby hills. Roger throws aside his crown and follows them. The shepherd, of course, is Dionysus in disguise, come from India.

In Act Three, at the ruins of a Greek temple, Roxanne greets her husband and explains the elements of the faith espoused by the stranger, who "exists in every living thing as a life force". The shepherd now reveals himself in his true form, Dionysus himself. Unlike the hapless Pentheus, who is savagely destroyed by his denial of ecstatic sexuality, Roger, now transformed into a pilgrim, opens his mind to this new religion.

Led by the pagan god, the Bacchantes engage in frenzied dancing, during the height of which Roxanne disappears. In the light of dawn, Roger watches the slow emanation of a new day, having been given a transcendent insight by the previous night's mystical experience. A Polish critic interprets the opera's message to be that "only through physical love can the mysteries of divine love be approached or creative work accomplished", a glorification of sexuality as "life-affirming", a thesis much like that of D.H. Lawrence, who similarly deemed the dogmatic Jewish–Christian insistence on preserving chastity as no less than a self-torturing perversion.

The score shows the influence of Wagner (*Parsifal*); Szymanowski had earlier been an admirer of Strauss (*Salome*), who is sometimes echoed; Szymanowski had been abroad and had absorbed many other musical idioms, including the Greek and Arab–Persian, elements of which are present here, the sum being remarkably harmonious and opulently and seductively atmospheric, and *sui generis*, largely his own.

A German commentator, H.H. Stuckenschmidt, has pronounced *King Roger* to be "Poland's most important musical work". It has an enduring place in the repertoires of that nation's opera troupes, and has scattered productions on foreign stages as well, though understandably performances in its original language are very rare beyond Poland's borders.

The decades in the second half of the twentieth century witnessed odd variations of *The Bacchae.* During this period the Italian director Luca Ronconi, who had become established in Vienna as the Burgtheater's specialist in the Greek classics, put on the play there with innovative touches. In the United States two "off-beat" explorations of the tragedy's moral content reached the stage in 1968 and 1969. The first of these, appropriately retitled *Dionysus in 69* – it was actually done the preceding year – was conceived by Richard Schechner and exposed at the Off-Off-Broadway La MaMa in New York, where Walter Kerr, the usually dispassionate drama critic of the *New York Times*, took an edged objection to it. His reasons for doing so:

> My problem is that I am not divine. You're divine, as all the freest new plays are telling us, only when you do what you want to do. And somehow or other I never get to do what I want to do in those playhouses – and now garages – where the actors are having a hell of a time doing what *they* want to do.
>
> In many of these playhouses – and now garages – the actors are very eager to have me join them. Take *Dionysus in 69*, which is currently letting people into its downtown garage, Thursdays through Sundays only, one at a time. (If you come with a date, one or the other of you has to go first, with that white door closing ominously on the back of whoever is bravest. Problem: Do you, as a gentleman, defer to your date, abandoning her to the living jungle of flesh that is already writhing inside and leaving her with no one of her very own to cling to? Or do you, intrepid explorer, precede her to tick off what ever booby traps there are, allowing her to stand on the slowly darkening street alone, wondering if she'll ever see you again? But this is a conventional hangup, of which we must have no more.)
>
> The actors in *Dionysus in 69*, which the ardently revolutionary Richard Schechner (of the *Drama Review*, which is sometimes fun in an excitable way) has put together out of old bits and pieces of Euripides' *The Bacchae*, first of all want me to sit where they are writhing. They are all over the place, on the floor, on ladders, on raw wooden platforms. They don't offer to move over, since they are very busy intoning hypnotic phrases like "Let the dance begin" and "Is Frank taking tickets?", so I look

around for an open spot that is not occupied by a woman's purse or a dancer's foot. I make a light step (I am fairly agile in some ways) to a not entirely occupied platform, just above an attractive blonde girl in a split jacket who is rolling her shoulders as though they were the well-oiled wheels of a locomotive engine, and I congratulate myself on at last being where the action is. Of course I can't be everywhere, not being divine, but on my pleasantly exposed perch I'm in it, with it, of it. I dangle my legs devilishly.

I'm not to get a free ride for long, though. Pretty soon the actors want me to dance. (Not just me, you understand; I didn't get any sort of preferential treatment; *everybody* is invited to get in there.) The Dionysian revels have begun. The boys have stripped to less than loincloths. The boys have undulated on the floor while the girls marched astride them, bare feet planted between buttocks. The god Dionysus has appeared to his worshippers (all so like Euripides) to snap finger cymbals and lift his skinny legs in rhythm beneath bushy hair, eyeglasses, and seedy mustache (not exactly like Euripides). The beat gets faster, some of the girls go topless, the garage spins, customers are cooed at: "Will you dance with me?"

I do not dance divinely. When it comes to dancing, I'm an up-tight person. (My wife refused to dance with me for twenty-five years, having tried once.) In theory, to be sure, this makes me just the man to be hauled onto that floor. Obviously I need a break-through. But I am something of a realist and I am not wholly convinced that darting into the melee is going to make a dancer of me; I think I am going to look pretty silly and maybe louse things up. This would be especially unbecoming in a reviewer, who would thereafter have to apportion himself a share of the blame. It just so happens that this isn't the particular breakthrough I want, and if this sort of group therapy is going to do any real good it's got to get at the actual trouble areas. Neither did I want to rush out and snatch one of the girls, if that's what you're thinking. I had got a pretty good look at some of the topless types by this time, and had reconsidered: There are girls and there are girls, and not all are equal. Or am I being too bold?

I didn't want to dance. I wanted to smoke. The evening is several hours long, there is no intermission (intermissions are bad for orgies, as I suppose the Greeks knew), and I had a profound conviction that I would find my favorite brand of cigarettes soothing. Aha. None of that. This is free theater, but not that free. It says plainly on the program, "No Smoking/No Cameras." I didn't care about the cameras, having forgotten to bring one, but it did seem strange to me that the theater of benevolent abandon should be so surly with those "Nos." Do they want me really wound up? No doubt it's all because of the Fire Department, and you can't fight everything.

But there's another problem. Even more than I wanted to smoke, I wanted to think. I happen to admire Euripides' *The Bacchae* very much. I think it's one of the greatest plays ever written. I also understood, perfectly clearly, that *The Bacchae* was not to be presented as such but was to be tampered with at will in an effort to see how relevant it might be to the contemporary urge toward ecstasy and the contemporary urge toward violence. (In the original, the god Dionysus gives his followers great joy and great pain; that is simply what a god does.) I was curious, eager for illumination, not at all put off by the mauling of a text. *The Bacchae* will still be there when we're all through roughing it up.

Here I was really stuck. I wasn't distracted from thinking by the flesh, freckles, pimples, grunting, cavorting, or the clap-hands clamor for "Wine!" I was kept from valuable meditation – I hoped it would be valuable – by the performers', and Mr Schechner's, careful determination that I get no hard information to work with. The suppression is deliberate. Speech is slurred, or underprojected, or blotted out by group cries; probably half the evening is unintelligible by design. When speech is intelligible, it is likely to be voided by a visual image. Pentheus, the puritanical young ruler who would like to put an end to revelry, announced himself disturbed by reports of excesses in the community. He makes his announcement the moment after he himself has come slithering through the sea of undulating flesh. Either his concern is meaningless or his memory extremely bad. The only possible conclusion one can see for the play, after Dionysus has streaked his own followers with rivers of blood, is an implication that the very openness and abandon we have been encouraged to share all evening long are an openness and abandon that must invariably end in violence. Can this be what the producers have in mind, or have we pressed our own minds too far?

There is a point to the emphasis on the physical, the refusal to let our minds do all the work. Our theatergoing has been mainly headwork for quite a long while now, conventional headwork, dusty headwork; there has been very little kinetic response, engagement at the gut, in it. What greater engagement at the gut might be like is persuasively indicated by one prolonged passage downtown. Pentheus wishes to silence the orgiastic impulse that has broken out all about him (and all about us, in far corners and over our shoulders). He tries to silence it physically, darting in and out among the mingled actors and spectators, clapping his hands over the mouths of the Dionysiacs who are beginning to whisper ecstasy again. He cannot go fast enough. For every whisper hushed there are three to break out elsewhere. The clatter creeps up on him, washes over him, drives him to another kind (the same kind?) of frenzy. Though here there is no direct contact between performer and spectator – he is not putting his hand over *our* mouths – we are surrounded by mounting sound in just the way he is. The effect comes off: We feel, as a physical presence, a rising pressure that cannot be stopped, and we share the pressure with the man who is trying to stop it.

There are other such interim successes, notably a wild flight in which Pentheus hurls himself, at breakneck speed, from platform to platform over our heads. His fear and his fury come quite close to us. Just enough of these provocations come by to keep you attentive, and not bored. And just enough come by to let you know that something kinetic is missing from our more routine experiences.

Still, the big question hovers. What is the best way to total empathy? Through actual hand-to-hand contact, shoulders brushed against the actor, direct muscular participation – with the mind lulled to sleep? Or is it best sought – as Euripides sought and did find it – in the awful penetration of words?

As things stand, the full contact does not work, has no cumulative possibilities short of rape, no staying power. We are intrigued but not truly involved. Those spectators who do join the dance dance feebly and are plainly glad to retire: one who submitted himself, at evening's end, to be pawed by a covey of Dionysiacs, simply submitted himself, returned nothing.

It is only the actors who are liberated in this sort of meeting, and there is something arrogant, condescending, and self-indulgent about that. Clearly they enjoy the unleashing of their own inhibitions. During an impromptu aside on opening night, an actress was asked by another performer how she felt about dancing on the night of Senator Kennedy's death. She thought intensely for a moment, then answered "I have to. It's my statement."

But it is *her* statement, not ours. She and her colleagues are in control of the master plan. They are free to do what they wish to do. We are only free to do what they wish us to do or invite us to do. That is not engagement. It is surrender.

I am still up tight.

In *Stages*, Emory Lewis, who reviewed for the magazine *Cue*, recalled the production more kindly.

In June of 1968, Richard Schechner, the editor of *The Drama Review* and briefly a student with Jerzy Grotowski, put his own environmental theories into practice in an old garage in an off-beat New York location. His engrossing, irritating, and sometimes successful *Dionysus in 69* started with Euripides' text, but then added and subtracted at will, inserting contemporary jargon and topical references. The audience, deprived of seats, was dispersed all over the garage. The action was everywhere. The actors (the boys reduced to jockstraps and the girls to abbreviated tunics) writhed along the floor in sexual embraces. Often they attempted to involve the audience in dances and other stage actions.

It is easy to laugh off these happenings as cultist activities of collegians, but that would be a spectacularly obtuse interpretation. The young are fervently searching for new forms, and they are profoundly discontented with the old proscenium theater.

But such experimentation has remained fun and games for a very small group of imaginative young people in New York City. It has not remotely touched most American citizens. And so the young have embarked on another adventure, the search for an ever-larger and more representative theater audience.

Schechner and *The Drama Review* were associated with New York University, which sponsored the magazine, prominent for its advocacy of avant-garde theatre. The following year (1969) a showing of *The Bacchae* took place in New Haven, site of Yale University; the production was supervised by André Gregory, also noted as one of the day's most iconoclastic directors. Julius Novick, a freelance critic, was in New Haven on behalf of the *New York Times*. He began:

Every age, I suppose, searches among the classics for those works which seem most particularly to mirror its own nature; and our age has found *The Bacchae*. This late tragedy of Euripides has never been so widely ignored as, say, *Ion*, or the *Helen*, or the *Rhesus*, but until recently it had not been widely read, and it had almost never been produced. The play is complex and ambiguous, but its story is essentially simple. The god Dionysus is opposed by Pentheus, the young king of Thebes; in revenge, Dionysus causes Pentheus to be torn apart by a band of crazed women led by Pentheus's own mother.

A strange and horrible tale; but *The Bacchae* is important to us because Dionysus, especially as Euripides here depicts him, is for better or worse the god of our times: the god of intoxication, of frenzy, of release-your-inhibitions and blow-your-mind, the god of freak-out, the god who makes you dance "until the mind splits open and the world falls in, and Dionysus is glad." Dionysus is glad a lot these days. We had better learn as much about him as we can; our survival may depend on it.

And so, more and more, *The Bacchae* is being talked about, and written about, and included in anthologies, and produced on the stage. It has been seen in student productions at Harvard and at Yale; it was done professionally in Boston last Fall; two major repertory companies were tempted by it, but dropped plans to produce it this season because of the tremendous difficulties it entails. *Dionysus in 69*, one of most important achievements of the experimental theater, is a free modern version of *The Bacchae* that employs improvisation, gymnastics, nudity, and audience participation to emphasize the terrible power of the Dionysiac impulse.

And now the professional Repertory Theater of the Yale School of Drama has mounted a production of *The Bacchae*, in a supple yet forceful translation by Kenneth Cavander. Its director is André Gregory, that stormy petrel of the resident theaters, whose work in the past has amply demonstrated his concern with violence, frenzy, and unconventional sex. His *Bacchae* is brilliantly theatrical in a very modern style (squirming and writhing actors, loudspeakers and flashing lights), but often the theatricality seems to exist for its own sake, and not for the sake of the play.

Santo Loquasto's fascinating set, for instance, is very different from the traditional Greek-tragedy palace-front. Mr Loquasto has located the play as if in a huge, shiny sheet-metal tube; under the lurid, evocative lighting that Suellen Childs has designed, it looks like some kind of mad psychedelic boiler-room. The floor is curved, so that the actors can slide and roll on it; there are platforms and pipes and poles for jumping and climbing; it is a wonderfully usable playing area. But this metallic limbo seems to exist almost without a context; there is little sense of its relationship to the city of Thebes, which has been so transformed by the advent of Dionysus, or to the hills where the Bacchae dance out their frenzy of worship and where Pentheus is destroyed.

Similarly, the chorus of worshippers of Dionysus, trained by Stanley Rosenberg of the La MaMa Plexus Workshop, is authoritative in its weirdness. It seems as if Dionysus has brought with him a strange group of itinerant lunatics, men and women both, romping obsessively in an eclectic style that seems largely based on the movements of children, with a strong admixture of acrobatics, and some Oriental stuff as well. They are interesting to watch, but some important things are missing from them: joy, connection with the fertility of nature, the sense that the service of Dionysus confers some benefits on his followers. Furthermore, their antics often take a somewhat unfortunate precedence over the words of Euripides' choral odes.

The Bacchae makes enormous demands upon its principal actors, and these demands are in the main well met at Yale. Pentheus is conceived in this production as a curt, black-booted dictator; David Spielberg's performance is neither particularly searching nor particularly vivid, but it is always competent. Mr Spielberg even manages to make plausible the difficult scene in which, maddened by Dionysus, he appears in woman's dress, ready to spy on the mysterious Bacchic rites. Mildred Dunnock plays Pentheus's mother, Agave, who returns from her revels on the mountain only to discover that the trophy of the hunt she carries so proudly is the head of her own son. Miss Dunnock exults with a crazy little smile, her vaunting pride undercut by a vague sense that something is wrong; her innate delicacy makes it touchingly clear that this is a gentle nature wrought up by the god to a totally uncharacteristic savagery.

But the dominant figure in this production is Alvin Epstein as Dionysus. Like the chorus, he neglects the easy joyousness that is part of what Dionysus represents, but he gives us a full measure of sensuality, strangeness, mystery, threat, and overwhelming authority, in a role that could easily make a lesser actor look foolish. At the end of the play, he stands on a platform high above the unfortunate mortals whose lives he has ravaged, rolling his knees and hips with cold, ironic sexuality, while his voice gives grim judgments over the loud-speaker system, and a live snake twists in his hands. There are not many actors who could upstage a live snake, but Mr Epstein does it; the snake becomes only a part of the horrible triumph of Dionysus. At this moment, and at certain others during the evening, the production's abundant theatricality ceases to be a distraction, and becomes a vehicle for the formidable power of Euripides' play; these moments justify this revival.

In 1973 Walter Kerr was in London and with sharp anticipation attended a staging of *The Bacchae* that launched the National Theatre's new season. He found the production to be a reductive one, and the heading over his critique of it the *New York Times* was: "Will We Ever See *the Bacchae* as Euripides Wrote It?" As he put it:

> I am about ready to give up on *The Bacchae.* Euripides' blasphemy-haunted but unblinking play in which the god Dionysus compels men to recognize his orgiastic presence within themselves – whether they wish to admit to anything so irrational or not – is, I would say, among world drama's ten or twelve uncontested masterpieces. Having been chilled and finally overpowered by it in the reading, I've been waiting half my life to hear and feel its harrowing rhythms on stage. I now conclude I'm not going to. I'm not going to because nobody is ever going to do Euripides' *The Bacchae.* Everyone who attempts it, whether as director or adapter, winds up doing his own play, a much narrower proposition.
>
> When, in New York, Richard Schechner made *Dionysus in 69* of it, he used it as an apologia for the counterculture, reducing its vast spiritual energies to the awkwardness of group-grope and finding no explanation at all for the unspeakable savagery of its conclusion. Now, for the opening bill of the British National Theatre's season, Wole Soyinka has come at it with another sort of special pleading in mind.
>
> Mr Soyinka is a Nigerian poet-playwright very much concerned with the immediate social and political needs of his own culture, and, attempting to serve these while paying lip-service to Euripides, he has imagined Dionysus as a champion of the internal proletariat, a god who has come to free urbanized, industrialized slaves.

This "freeing" is taken most literally. It is not a matter of that ecstatic release of the psyche that the god of wine has always offered man in return for total abandon, for a kind of drunken surrender to divinity. The freedom that is offered, rather, is a freedom from physical chains, chains that clank noisily and insistently as loinclothed members of the male chorus are led down a narrow runway from the bank of the Old Vic auditorium, prodded by helmeted guards and sent scurrying up a grillwork bank that rather resembles an old-fashioned typesetter's font, there to hug their knees and arch their backs in impatient despair.

There are not many lines in the text, which Mr Soyinka has freely reworked from the Gilbert Murray and William Arrowsmith translations, to support the slave-master-redeemer theme. A black and bearded choral leader can stomp his feet and cry in irony, "We are slaves and have no souls." Another can lament, "We are also waiting," intimating that the god is essentially a god of deliverance. At the very end, once Dionysus, no deliverer at all, has made a very bloody end of the ruler who challenged his godhood, a bystander, still in chains, can sigh, "I am a slave, nothing more, yet I mourn the fate of this man."

But that's about it. To help reinforce the unsatisfactory superimposition, director Roland Joffé has struck metal against metal everywhere, set the chorus to keening, murmuring, whispering whenever protest can possibly be suggested, locked up Dionysus himself in a great cage once the ruler Pentheus has decided to prove him no deity. Dionysus, looking very much like a Saint Sebastian before the arrows have been unloosed, is spread-eagled upside down – torso stripped, snakelike black curls trailing the ground – before he is hoisted into the bridgework trestles of the heavens. Wherever we can see manacles and thongs and griddles that men might be fried upon, we do.

But it is all irrelevant to the play that ought to be going forward, failing to establish Mr Soyinka's envisioned "twinhood" between Dionysus and the Yoruba god Ogun – who also happens to be a god of metals and of war – at the same time that it effectively distracts us from the Euripidean progression that is still there, half-buried, as burdened by chains as the slaves are. If we fight to keep ourselves alert, and to catch lines on the wing that are being cavalierly dismissed, we can almost hear it.

What is Euripides' progression? Structurally, it is composed of two movements, answering two questions. The first is the need of Dionysus – come as a man among men, swarthy, coolly arrogant, no doubt a libertine – to prove himself divine. To a rational man like Pentheus the prospect is unthinkable. Gods do not encourage wine-crazed cults, do not send obsessed women to lose themselves in mindless revelry on the hillsides, do not shatter the barriers so neatly imposed by age, sex and social role. Though Pentheus's own mother is at present tasting of the Dionysian delights, all religious sanction must be denied them. Divinity does not defy mind.

To show that Dionysus is merely mortal, Pentheus mocks him, shears his curls – the overtones of blasphemy should be horrifying here, but Mr Joffé's staging lets the scene seem a minor squabble – and imprisons him. The prison promptly comes tumbling down. A series of miracles follows, not the least of which is Dionysus's so bewitching Pentheus that Pentheus is persuaded to spy upon the hillside orgy. He is caught there and his own mother, blinded by ecstasy, tears him limb from limb, bringing back his mangled head as evidence of the day's glory. Not until she is released from her god-induced trance, returned to her rational self, will she know what she holds in her hands.

The play has moved to its second, ultimate question. What is a god, what is divinity? Dionysus exists. He has given men all of the good things of the earth. The good things of the earth – most symbolically wine – enable man to transcend himself, to go out of himself. There is indeed an exultation beyond reason. But if, beyond reason, there is ecstasy, there is also something dark, blind, ready for blood. If the one is a divine impulse, so is the other. And they are simultaneous, inextricable one from the other.

Is a god, then, good or bad, beneficent or malevolent, adorable or terrifying? He is none of these things, not in the either-or, pick-and-choose terms. He is the awful absolute. He is simply what *is*, make of him what we will. In fact, he is not to be "made something of," he can only be known and accepted. In the play's great climax – though the text has not come down to us quite complete – Dionysus justifies nothing, asks nothing. "I am neither cruel nor kind," he says, as his devotees stand bathed in blood. "I am, and cannot be denied."

It is the greatness of Euripides' play that he has been willing to look on the wholeness of the god, to press the concept of divinity beyond any borders we can fathom ("I can no longer understand the ways of God, I may blaspheme," an old man murmurs), to carry his dramatic search as far as the searching mind *can* carry it and to let his finding stand there, blazing, untouchable, irreproachable, appalling. The one thing he has not done is to trim his divinity to a tidy little purpose, whether sociological or political, reducing the godhead to a kind of mother's helper for the day. He has opened the play as wide as wide allows, wishing nothing away, staring directly into the sun. But that is the quality I have never seen on a stage, and suppose I never will.

The company performing the play at the National Theatre is surprisingly lackluster. There are two fine passages of narration, recitals of events we haven't seen which must be permitted to speak for themselves, without visual tinkering: David Bradley does one, Gawn Grainger the other. Both have a knack for turning words into eyes. Martin Shaw, as Dionysus, would do – most handsomely – for a painting of the role; his voice, however, hasn't the resonance to tame Pentheus. John Shrapnel is a

Pentheus who seems to have been costumed for a turn with the Flying Wallendas, though he gets through the role straightforwardly enough.

But Julian Curry's blind, skeleton-bald Tiresias is curiously music-hall without getting any laughs in return, and Paul Curran's elderly Cadmus on his way to join the dancing women bears an unfortunate resemblance to a grass-skirted Paul Ford taking off for the South Seas. Constance Cummings is adequate, though no more than that, as Pentheus's maddened mother; it is characteristic of the production that she should be robbed of her final revealing scream by choral voices, flattening the climax we expect.

It's odd, by the way, and I'm not sure enough has been made of it, that the devotees of Dionysus, god of wine and indeed of mysticism, should have been mainly women. It is so in the play, and it seems to have been so historically. Does that mean that the next *Bacchae* we see will prove Dionysus the founder of Women's Lib? No doubt. Let us be ready.

Sponsored by the University of Pennsylvania, an American première of Soyinka's adaptation was put on by the Interact Theater Company in Philadelphia (January–February, 1992). Two months later this led to a student production of Euripides' original play, staged by the school's Theater Arts Department in an outdoor amphitheatre (April 1992). In the brief interim – that is, March – the Philomathean Society, which claims to be the USA's oldest continuing collegiate literary group, held a mock trial of the semi-divine Dionysus, weighing the morality of his harsh behaviour. Next, during the ensuing summer, the university's academic orientation programme sent copies of Euripides' tragedy to all 2,200 applicants who had been accepted as freshmen; they were to read it before their arrival at the campus. In discussions before the term's start, they would be asked how relevant the play might be to the issues they themselves would soon face, questions dealing with religious beliefs, alcoholism and attitudes towards sexual conduct. The associate dean of the College of Arts and Sciences, Norman Adler, explained: "*The Bacchae* shows how classical culture is as contemporary as a Spike Lee movie," a reference to the African-American film producer whose highly controversial works exploring racial prejudice had gained much attention. (A large number of University of Pennsylvania students were drawn from the Black community.) Before autumn classes began, all undergraduates participated in the discussions; they were separated into small groups, each guided by a faculty member. The students' responses showed them to be greatly interested in the meetings. Some asserted that Soyinka's adaptation enabled them to grasp more clearly the play's ties to contemporary problems. A typical remark: "With the original Euripides version, I thought it was really trying to stretch things.

Soyinka's version is a lot different. It is awfully applicable. Soyinka's version does a lot more with anger and gender roles and race." Faculty members who took part – many of them from non-literary disciplines – also acknowledged having derived enjoyment and enlightenment from this experiment in "mutual learning", which the university resolved to repeat with other classic works of art and literature.

In 1975, the thirty-first year of the play festival at Epidaurus, Steven V. Roberts of the *New York Times* marked the event by interviewing several leading figures in Athens's theatre world. In particular, he sought their views on what had been Euripides' message in *The Bacchae*, which had been among the works staged there. Alexis Minotis was of the opinion that the main theme of that play, as of many classic scripts, is the pre-eminence of divine will. "It looks odd to us, because long ago we established man in the place of god. Maybe the attraction of these plays comes from some kind of longing for the unknown." The critic and author, Babis Klaras, believed Euripides meant his last drama to be an attack on tyranny, because the despotic Pentheus tries to place himself over the gods, a violation of natural law. The play and film director Michael Cacoyannis saw the Bacchae typifying the liberated spirits who, then as now, break social conventions and elect to live each day as it comes.

A clearer exposition of Cacoyannis's reading of *The Bacchae* was afforded to New York audiences when he offered it at the Circle in the Square (1980), three years after he had staged it in Paris at the Comédie Française (1977). He used his own English translation. The *New York Times* sent Richard F. Shepard to interview him. Said Cacoyannis: "This play is very avant-garde. There is not a subject it does not touch, from politics to sex. Even drugs, where he speaks of Dionysus and 'juices in the plants.' . . . Euripides dazzles me, not only in the writing, but in the execution. He wrote this play in exile, either as his last or next to last work, at the age of eighty. He was a revolutionary who didn't believe in the gods that everybody worshipped, but he believed in the gods we create in ourselves, in our nature. The Greek religion was the least mystical of religions, twelve people sitting on top of a mountain and arguing with one another, no guilt or remorse."

Shepard described Cacoyannis as now fifty, tense and articulate. He spoke flawless English, having been sent in his late teens from his native Cyprus for higher education in Great Britain, after which he had lived there for many years before eventually settling again in Greece. "I did the translation of *The Bacchae* only five weeks before rehearsals started, in desperation, when I realized other translations did not work theatrically. I'm very faithful to Euripides. I worked from original texts in old Greek. We studied old Greek in school and hated it, but later I appreciated it. If you are the director and have been an actor, you try to translate the words for the mouths of actors. Often, literary translations are not effective onstage, although Edith Hamilton's translation of *The Trojan Women* was superb both theatrically and literarily." (He had translated Shakespeare's *Antony and Cleopatra* into Greek for a production in Athens in which Irene Papas starred, and had carried out a similar task – with the help of a Russian collaborator – in fashioning a Greek version of Chekhov's *The Cherry Orchard.*) "But I love English. It's better than modern Greek. I have more trouble translating Shakespeare into modern Greek than I have translating Euripides into English. French is a terrible language to translate into. French is a musical language and English is an architectural language. I prefer to build in an architectural language."

He alluded to problems he had experienced in choosing players for his offering of *The Bacchae* at the Comédie Française: "I had to cast the French women as the Asian girls who accompany Dionysus to Athens, and it didn't work. At Circle in the Square, I have taken Black, Japanese and South American women as the chorus of Bacchae. I have given them the speech and body language to emphasize that they have come from outside the Greek culture, from the heart of Asia. I think it was the Himalayas that Euripides had in mind, the Himalayas as the place we believe to be free in nature, just as the youthful rebels of the Sixties believed a few years ago. This is no novelty on my part, this casting. Even if all the actresses were white, I would have had to make them Oriental."

Irene Papas, who was to be Agave, was interviewed by Joan Gage of the *New York Times*. She, too, believed the ancient drama was "appropriate for our time – it deals with religion, drugs, violence, terrorism". She regretted that modern productions of the Greek classics needed to be comparatively austere, "performed in browns and blacks", to hold down costs, and that they were often acted in a "stilted, artificial" style that Periclean spectators would hardly have recognized. They were accustomed to extravaganzas. "I believe that in the time of Aeschylus and Euripides the tragedies were great big spectacles with bright colors, elaborate scenery, costumes studded with jewels, masks, dancing and special effects. In *Prometheus Bound*, they say, forty women came out of the sky to meet him. How did they manage that? When Aeschylus' plays were presented, the many dancers and their movements were described as being like a tempest. The Furies were so frightening, that when they came on stage pregnant women in the audience suffered miscarriages. When I saw *Hair*, a dramatic musical, I imagined something like that with verses of Aeschylus. Bringing the tragedies close to the people, as an emotive thing, that's what's important, and that's what film does best. Art must affect the emotions, not the intellect."

Speaking further, she told Joan Gage: "The Greek tragedies never fail to reach people. They fail only because of failures of the translation or the actors." She was certain that Cacoyannis's rendering of the script was "beautiful, very direct and poetic and different. The American actors when they read it, said, 'Now we can understand the play. We can act it.'"

She agreed that *The Bacchae* was particularly complex and difficult. "It may be the best tragedy ever written. It reveals all the shades of the human psyche. It concerns what people do with what they know and what they don't know – why we're here and why we die. The audience takes pieces of it – each person will take the piece that applies to them."

All her roles in the classic Greek dramas were physically exhausting. "Because I am playing a human soul in its extreme capacity, not someone sitting around on stage making conversation." Agave's part, above all, contained extraordinary demands. "The character is not like Electra, who is logical – a character based on cause and result. I am playing the victim of the punishment of the gods. When she is crazy and still thinks she is holding a lion's head, Agave makes a very feminist speech: 'Here is the quarry we, your women, hunted down. Yes, we . . . with our own bare arms, our hands, our delicate fingers. What are they worth, your manly boasts? Where is the pride in power that relies on hideous tools for war?' she says to Cadmus, her father, 'You have sired the bravest daughter in the world. From now on, no more weaving at the loom, no little chores for me. I'm meant for greater things.'"

Papas's dream was to "play Electra in one of those ancient theaters, and to establish an international experimental theater of Greek tragedy. I'd encourage people from all countries to come and to experiment with the tragedies in their own languages, instead of being bound by a false respect for the text."

The Bacchae is among the most violent of all the Greek tragedies, but the grisliest deeds occur off-stage, with only the bloody head of Pentheus ever on display. Papas dismissed the notion that this avoidance of visible slaughter was dictated by a preference for "classical restraint". Instead, "What bothered the Greeks were the ideas behind the murder and not the gory thing that you see."

Papas, who has filled the roles of so many beset heroines, is the child of two teachers of Greek. She and her three sisters had been brought up on the verses of the ancient dramatists. "My father always used to say, 'Everything written nowadays is just one phrase of Euripides stretched to fill five volumes.' And he's right. The Greek tragedies were so condensed that modern drama, by comparison, is like diluted milk."

Clive Barnes, in the *New York Post*, hailed this offering of "Euripides' greatest play. This is an imaginative and illuminating rendering of a mysterious play that is nervily relevant to today's madness. The architecture of the play is the most exquisite and unexpected art. Michael Cacoyannis has directed with his sure sense of ritual. Christopher Rich and John Noah Hertzler are excellent. Philip Bosco and Irene Papas give totally memorable performances. Here is magnificence."

Of the same opinion was Douglas Watt, in the *Daily News*: "*The Bacchae* is startlingly modern. Philip Bosco is impressive. Irene Papas, lovely and heartrending, took the audience in the palm of her hand and wrapped up the evening for us. Her harshly musical voice, her beauty and her command move us as Euripides, master that he was, intended."

Peter Wynne, in *The Record* (of nearby Bergen, New Jersey), proclaimed the evening to have afforded "the most lucid and enjoyable version of this difficult play anywhere, anytime". Mary Campbell of Associated Press declared that for her this had been "an important, wonderful theater event! Irene Papas's performance is a *tour de force*."

At the same time, some qualifications were expressed by major critics, among them Jack Kroll of *Newsweek*.

> Euripides' *The Bacchae* is a stupendous, searing play. But like most productions of Greek tragedy, Michael Cacoyannis's staging at Circle in the Square can't really break through the centuries-old crust to the white-hot life beneath. Directors have gone to great length to solve this problem. In America, Peter Arnott used marionettes instead of actors. In Italy, Luca Ronconi had one actress, the brilliant Marisa Fabbri, speak the entire play as the audience moved through a series of rooms and spaces. In Germany, Klaus Michael Grüber used nudity, horses, glass walls and one hundred thousand watts of neon lights. Cacoyannis plays it straight, which is the most perilous method of all, and while the results are better than might be expected, the gulf remains – linguistic, psychological, spiritual, cultural – between twentieth-century New York and fifth-century Athens.
>
> Written when Euripides was in his seventies, *The Bacchae* ought to be closer to us than any of the great Greek tragic plays, with its theme of repressive moral law versus sexual excess, a theme that was spontaneously acted out in America in the countercultural explosion of the Sixties. Euripides takes no sides in this eternal debate between two poles of human desire and conduct, though he is clearly drawn to the god Dionysus as against King Pentheus of Thebes. Another theme that resonates with our time is the tension between the sexes: Pentheus is angry at the Dionysiac cult because it draws the women "from their looms," and the scene in which the disguised god gets the King to admit his voyeuristic fascination with the Dionysiac rites, and dresses him in women's clothing, still has power to shock.
>
> Cacoyannis is a distinguished interpreter of ancient Greek theater throughout the world. His translation of *The Bacchae* is lucid and fluent, with only a few jarring locutions like "Now hear this"

and "complete, of course, with full orgiastic trappings." His staging is supple and sensible, and he gets clarity and dynamic variety from his performers – Christopher Rich as Dionysus: John Noah Hertzler as Pentheus; Tom Klunis and Philip Bosco as the two old men, Tiresias and Cadmus, and Richard Kuss and Paul Perri as messengers who deliver the two overwhelming descriptions of the Bacchae, the Dionysiac women whose ecstatic rites escalate to murderous violence. As Agave, Pentheus's mother, who dismembers her son under the Dionysiac trance, Irene Papas carries her great beauty and authority and yet fails to stir us to pity and terror.

The key to this play is, of course, the chorus of women, the Bacchae, and this is the production's strong point – nine women of great beauty, insidious grace and poetic address. And yet the whole thing remained distant instead of immediate and overwhelming. But an hour later the closed-circuit telecast of the Muhammad Ali–Larry Holmes fight became true contemporary Greek tragedy, with Ali like Oedipus reeling to disaster from the tragic sin of *hubris*, overweening pride, while the chorus of spectators howled vainly against fate. You could almost see Euripides taking notes in his seat.

Frank Rich was even more disapproving. In his *New York Times* review he wrote:

For all the grueling excitement of its tragic plot, *The Bacchae* is a play about men's souls, not murder; about choice, not fate. When Dionysus, that cruel but joyous god of nature, arrives in Thebes, its citizens must wrestle with a central and timeless issue of human behavior. How much can we allow our rational selves to surrender to our natural, hedonistic hungers?

Euripides doesn't resolve the question any more firmly than R.D. Laing, but he dramatizes all the possible answers. In *The Bacchae* there are those who give themselves up entirely to the Dionysian revels, those who resist and those who try to have it both ways. As we watch these characters struggle between the irreconcilable extremes of emotional order and chaos, the playwright dramatizes an extraordinary psychological spectrum. The mythological framework of the drama may seem distant these days, but the dilemmas of its people have not aged a whit in twenty-four hundred years.

Michael Cacoyannis's production of *The Bacchae*, which opened last night at the Circle in the Square, is the play's first major revival since the 1960s, when Dionysus was understandably all the rage. It does not serve Euripides well. Indeed, if anything, Mr Cacoyannis's bland literal-minded reading of *The Bacchae* seems to go out of its way to turn a living classic into an inaccessible museum piece.

The lines are all there, in a new, reasonably colloquial translation by the director, and so is the story. But this is a production that offers little beyond conventional spectacle – in a theater space ill-designed for it – as if that were the sum of Euripides' art. It's a *Bacchae* without subtlety or characterization, without sexual passion and without tears.

The problems begin early, when we discover that both of the principal characters, Dionysus and Pentheus, are inadequately cast. It is from these two figures, who are also cousins, that the drama's dialectic is meant to spring.

Dionysus is supposed to be a magnetic, if scary, god, a sinuous Pied Piper of natural instinct. Christopher Rich, who plays the role, has the proper androgynous looks, but he lacks presence and vocal range. With his mechanical arm gestures and sly smiles, he is insouciant and smirky, not sensuous and mysterious. As his antagonist, the self-righteous young ruler who tries to banish the Bacchants from his kingdom, John Noah Hertzler is a shrill, petty tyrant and no more.

The weightlessness of these performances wreaks havoc on the play's best scenes. One of Euripides' cleverest theatrical ideas is that Dionysus and Pentheus eventually mirror each other to the extent that the drama's central issue can be seen in a tantalizingly ambiguous light. Pentheus becomes so fascinated by the Bacchants that he forsakes his rectitude and dresses as a woman to spy on them: the free-spirited Dionysus ultimately outdoes even Pentheus as an autocrat. That's all lost here.

When we arrive at Dionysus's crucial final moments, Mr Rich simply doesn't have the authority of a god who can banish mortals to the ends of the earth. Because Mr Hertzler plays Pentheus as a one-note prig, we can never believe that he would momentarily embrace ambisexuality and eavesdrop on orgies. Indeed, when he disguises himself in golden locks, it's a piece of farcical business out of *Charlie's Aunt* rather than a frightening or titillating portrait of psychosexual panic.

Mr Hertzler's performance also has the indirect effect of sabotaging Irene Papas, who plays Pentheus's mother, Agave. When Agave, a Dionysian convert, appears in the play's final section, she learns to her unfathomable horror that her excesses of orgiastic frenzy have led her to murder her own son.

The play's chorus does not fill in the passions that the rest of the production lacks. Mr Cacoyannis's multiracial crew of Bacchants chant Euripides' pantheistic choral odes with admirable clarity, but their Oriental gestures and bouts of eye-rolling are too stylized to communicate orgasmic abandon. We can accept these women only as mouthpieces for their leader's faith, not as practitioners of the entire production. Mr Cacoyannis has created a remote storybook *Bacchae* about how Dionysus consolidated his power in Thebes. Euripides' play tells instead of how that strange dark god struggles for power within ourselves.

Miss Papas does show off her considerable technique: her eyes gape in sorrow, her mournful moans rise to a piercing cry. And yet her tragedy doesn't seem real to us. It may be because the preceding ninety minutes have long since anesthetized our capacity to respond. But it may also be that this production's Pentheus is so hollow that we are almost glad he's been killed. Philip Bosco fares better in the role of Agave's wiser father, Cadmus. When he reaches out to Miss Papas with both empathy and terror ("I see her now! A sight to make the eyes bleed!"), this wonderful actor convinces us that there's at least one complete character on stage.

Also in the *New York Times*, in his scheduled Sunday article, Walter Kerr examined the play again, from a rather different perspective:

Oh, the traps that Euripides laid for unwary actors and directors when, toward the end of his life, he put together the burst of magnificence called *The Bacchae*. As a playwright, Euripides had always been craftily unpredictable: to help wrap up one quite moving and rather domestic dilemma, he had tossed in a wrestling match between a man and a god, with the chagrined god getting the worst of it (*Alcestis*). As a thinker, Euripides had always been counted a skeptic, one with relatively little use for gods of any kind.

In *The Bacchae*, he did a sudden, stunning, apparent about-face, treating the gods with a respect that did not leave room for humor where *they* were concerned; he also ended his play offering Dionysus such a glorious epiphany, and showing him ablaze with so much terrifying power, that a man could be forgiven for supposing the playwright a death-bed convert, or something like.

Over the years, some scholars have in fact regarded this curious but (on paper) utterly riveting play as the final testament of a true believer. Certainly the young god Dionysus, who has introduced men to the exhilarating release of wine and whose own blood is said to "burst from the grapes," is given the last word, the last shattering assertion of authority over disbelieving mortals. The action of the piece leaves no doubt as to who is in command. Yet, other scholars have clung to the notion that the piece is possibly a satyr play, one more sly dart at the whole mythological "foolishness" of Olympus. What kind of play can be one or the other, either or both? Or even more than these antithetical notions? *The Bacchae* has also been regarded, as William Arrowsmith has pointed out in his translation (not in use in the new production of the play at Circle in the Square), as a dramatization of the contest between reason and the irrational; aristocratic skepticism and popular piety; civilized order and the eruptive forces of nature. A heady brew, for sure.

And every one of these possible attitudes is reflected somewhere in the elusive, challenging, deeply disturbing work. No one understanding is ever pursued to the exclusion of its opposite. Room is left everywhere, there is always something more to be said, the relationship between man and the godhead is far more complex than any aphorism can suggest. In some frightening and unexpected way, the whole world of human-divine interplay is condensed into a very odd narrative, in fits and starts, in whispers and violent anathemas. We are at the religious, as well as the dramatic, frontiers, and any ill-advised step may take us over the brink. Euripides has demanded a very great deal of anyone daring to reproduce his vision.

It's precisely because the dare is so great and production so rare – an ungimmicked production is virtually unheard of – that we are bound to go to Michael Cacoyannis's new mounting at Circle in the Square with some kind of hope stirring along our spines. We know better than to expect perfection, an accounting of all that the play intimates. But Mr Cacoyannis, using his own new translation, is on more intimate terms with classic Greek drama than most contemporary stage directors. He has, in point of fact, already had more success with it than most, specifically in the admirable *Trojan Women* and the interesting *Iphigeneia in Aulis* he staged earlier for the same production company. A man, it would seem, capable of coping, even with a play about miracles.

But any miracles at the Circle in the Square are simply reported events in the narrative. Mr Cacoyannis hasn't been able to bring off the big one itself, hasn't succeeded in getting anywhere near the work's ultimate, ugly, harrowing yet haloed thrust. Of the various snares he has stepped into, the most damaging, I think, is Euripides's known fondness for irreverent humor.

Humor is there in the play, early on and then later in mid-flight. The question is: how much stress can be placed on it if it is to be kept as counterpoint to the evening's old blasphemies and a final terrible vengeance? The lights haven't been up all that long before two venerable, and just possibly senile, ancients pause as they make their way through Thebes to debate the question of whether the new-come Dionysus is or is not of divine origin. Dionysus has lately returned from the Orient, bringing a band of female devotees with him (he regards the Orient as "more civilized" than Greece for having accepted his creed first). He claims that Zeus himself has fathered him on Semele, though there are doubters in the community who hint that he is the product of a more mundane liaison. What are these gabbling elders, "ordinary" men respectful of traditional religion, to believe – the skeptical rumors, or the vast claims of the young man? It so happens that one of the debating cronies, Cadmus, is the lad's grandfather – and so might very well be skeptical.

He *is* skeptical, but not quite openly. As Philip Bosco plays him, he's been around quite long enough to know better than to make decisions too hastily or too firmly. He's an amusingly pragmatic fellow, really, ready to dig his elbow into his good friend's ribs and ask a wry question: "Even if the god is not a god – why say it?" A discreet silence will keep their bread buttered both ways, and maybe their wine bags full. Besides, Mr Bosco thinks it would be rather an honor to have a god in the family.

This is a grace-note, a shrewd dramatist's observation about one sort of human behavior, something to be tossed into the scales to help balance out the too-eager gullibility of others. Not all translators make it so explicitly self-serving or so specifically comic, as director Cacoyannis has. And the fact that the lines are read by the company's most persuasive performer may have something to do with the effect it has on us.

The effect it has, alas, is to set the tone for *everything* that follows; instead of being frightened or moved as the ruler of Thebes, Pentheus, takes Dionysus prisoner and is later torn limb from limb by his own mother as punishment, we are going to continue being casually amused. Somehow no space has been left in which to give the self-proclaimed god a degree of credence. Our attitude is intensified in a sequence in which Pentheus must dress himself as a woman.

The motivation for this sequence is utterly serious, alive with danger. Though the unbelieving Pentheus, enraged by the orgiastic rites in which his mother and the growing Dionysiac cult are engaged, claps the "god" into a cell, Dionysus readily and miraculously frees himself. He thereupon tempts Pentheus, who is as curious as other human beings. Would he like to spy upon the reveling female band? He would have to disguise himself as one of them, of course, in order to escape detection and death. Pentheus is willing, and does make an appearance suitably costumed.

Once again the mood turns swiftly, unambiguously comic. Pentheus, under the sexual spell of his tempter, begins primping, fussing about the hemline of his gown, worrying that his girdle has slipped. In the current production, not much open laughter is earned by the renewed accent; but it is very likely fatal.

For an attitude of mild amusement has long since spilled over onto the stances of Dionysus and the infuriated pacing of Pentheus. Neither of the performers – Christopher Rich as Dionysus, John Noah Hertzler as Pentheus – is up to the demands of this extraordinarily difficult play. Mr Hertzler is a one-dimensional ranter who cannot make us feel the blasphemy of his crude threat to shear away the god's curled locks. And Mr Rich is scarcely more than an insinuating posture, unable to persuade us of the somber seriousness in his claim that "My hair is holy, I wear it long for God."

Yet unless we can somehow credit the crime Pentheus has committed – feel a prickling of the skin as a god is vilified and then violated – we are certainly not going to accept, or become involved in, the awful punishment that is meted out for it. Irene Papas appears as Pentheus's mother, still enthralled to her god and his wine as she comes down from the hills carrying the severed head of her son. Since we are taking the entire occasion lightly, there is no way in which her evenly spaced, meticulously enunciated laments can distress us.

Neither can Mr Rich take us to the daemonic heart of the play as he reappears, in his bronzed glory and wearing a two-horned mask, to assert his rectitude. Miss Papas moans that she has done wrong, and is ready to confess it; but "You are merciless!" becomes her despairing accusation. As Mr Rich points out that mercy can never be *demanded* of a god, declaring bluntly and brutally that it is in the nature of a god to exert power and nothing else, we are meant to be filled with a kind of awe. A kind that recognizes the truth of what this god has said – that men may be responsible to the gods, but that the gods are not in turn responsible to men. Gods are plainly and simply *power*, and they are unapproachable. Euripides's play ends as a body-blow.

But these things – and they are the weight, the substance of the play's daring, open-eyed, wide-ranging speculation – are unable to assert themselves in a production that refuses, from the beginning, to dig beneath Euripides' occasionally wry surfaces. I'm afraid we must learn to beware small jests: given too much freedom, they can help do in a masterpiece.

Edwin Wilson, in the *Wall Street Journal*, similarly faulted the casting.

Even more than most Greek tragedies, Euripides' powerful play is difficult to stage. . . . Mr Cacoyannis's production suffers from several problems. Christopher Rich as Dionysus and John Noah Hertzler as Pentheus, for example, both lack the authority their parts require. The chorus – the Bacchae of the title – are supposed to be frenzied and obsessed, but they confine the frenzy to a series of studied screams and hula-like movements of the hips.

Only Irene Papas as the mother and Philip Bosco as her father convey the full force of the tragedy, but their scene comes in the final thirty minutes after the tragic effect has already been undercut.

Filled with exquisite lyric poetry and unforced occasions for dancing, as well as characters engendered by intense feelings, *The Bacchae*, now "discovered", was quickly recognized by twentieth-century composers as a surpassing subject for an opera, albeit a daunting one. In the *New Yorker* magazine (1991) Andrew Porter broadly scanned and evaluated a list of those who sought to master the story in that challenging genre:

Of all Greek plays, *The Bacchae* calls most insistently for music, even if only in the choruses:

> Come and adore
> Dionysus with dance and song and a thunder of drums!
> Let the god of joy in your shouts of joy be glorified,
> as into the shrilling of Phrygian cries and calls there comes
> the holy melodious flute, whose playful and holy sounds
> wander with us to the mountains, the mountains, an air so sweet
> the Bacchant stirs, like a filly at graze with a dam, her fleet
> limbs, and giddily skips and bounds!

I quote the first chorus from the translation by Donald Sutherland. In a glittering, confident essay that accompanies it he writes: "The chorus of *The Bacchae* motivates naturally a full debauch of Oriental modes, in various veins of religious ecstasy, lament, imprecation, longing, joy of revenge, and so on. Though the music is lost, one can trace the movements of its expression pretty well by the words, the way the topics go, governed mainly by musical considerations and not consecutive logic. Not that the text is simply libretto or 'book', but is partly that, and I think a certain prejudice toward musicality and musical procedures governs much more than the choruses."

Many composers have written incidental music for the play. (Wole Soyinka, in his politicized version, prescribes the kind of music he wants for that chorus: "extracting the emotional color and temperature of a European pop scene without degenerating into that tawdry commercial manipulation of teenage mindlessness.") There have also been *Bacchae* operas. Three have appeared recently on CD: Szymanowski's *King Roger* (1926), on Koch Swan; Harry Partch's *Revelation in the Courthouse Park* (1961), on Tomato; and Hans Werner Henze's *The Bassarids* (1966), on Koch Swan. Last year, Egon Wellesz's *Die Bakchantinnen* (1931) was revived in Bielefeld. Last month, Daniel Börtz's *Backanterna* had its first performance, at the Swedish Royal Opera. John Buller's *Bakxai* is due at the English Opera in May.

Buller's piece, we are told, sets the original Greek, and Börtz's libretto is Euripides in Swedish translation. In the other *Bacchae* operas, the play has been refashioned for the lyric stage. *King Roger*, with its glamorous, exhilarating score and elevated settings – Palermo Cathedral aglint with golden mosaics; Roger's palace, where Moorish exuberance and Norman austerity mingle; the ruined, romantic splendor of the theater at Syracuse – moves farthest from the original. Its hero, a nobler Pentheus, is not destroyed: sore tempted by the alluring Shepherd, deserted by wife and courtiers, who have followed the siren call, Roger remains faithful at the last to Apollo. (Buffalo is producing *King Roger* in April, and the Michigan Opera Theater is producing it in May.)

W.H. Auden and Chester Kallman, the librettists of *The Bassarids*, in an essay at the time of the première gave their reasons for the changes they made to Euripides – the "reasons, partly musical, partly dramatic, it would have been impossible to use *The Bacchae* exactly as written." A composer wants to be provided with good solo parts for, if possible, three male and three female singers, "while in *The Bacchae* there are only two important solo roles, Pentheus and Dionysus; and the only woman who makes an individual appearance, Agave, does so for the first time only when the play is already almost over." (In Euripides' day, the same actor would have played both Pentheus and Agave.) Moreover, in the play the chorus of women, singing and dancing, has the most important role of all: "In our times it is simply a given that singers cannot dance and dancers cannot sing. And so, when an opera is supposed to be a dramatic work for the stage and not a static oratorio, the chorus must be introduced very sparingly."

Auden and Kallman bring on Agave in their first scene, and to Euripides' cast they add her sister Autonoe, a soprano, and the nurse Beroe, a mezzo. Wellesz's *Bakchantinnen* adds a first-act scene for Agave, his prima donna (a dramatic soprano), and has roles for her sisters Ino and Panthea (two more sopranos). Partch's *Revelation in the Courthouse Park* intercuts Euripides with episodes in which Dionysus is the rock star Dion, the bacchantes are his groupies, and Agave is Mom, Dion-besotted, who has the first as well as the final word. Thus the *convenienze* – the operatic conventions, which include a nice balance of male and female voices – are observed. But there is merit in Euripides' dramaturgy. Commentary on *The Bacchae* has been concerned mainly with the Pentheus-Dionysus conflict and too little with Agave. In the theater – at live performances of *The Bacchae* and of the *Bacchae* operas – she becomes the tragic protagonist and the star, theatrically, emotionally, intellectually. Although she enters late, Euripides prepares the entrance early by putting words from her mouth into the narrations of the Herdsman and the Messenger, and we await her. She enters in wild triumph, holding aloft the head of the son whom in Bacchic madness she has dismembered. The scenes of her awakening, in solemn *stichomythia* with Cadmus, and of her quiet recomposition of Pentheus' limbs – lines missing in the play, but moving however they are reconstituted – are great theater. Her defiance of her cruel, divine nephew and her final lines affirm human dignity and decency in the face of gods' – fate's, the world's – malignant decrees:

> Let me fly far
> and find a place
> where stained Cithairon keeps not me in sight,

where I can see neither Cithairon's height
nor of the thyrsus any trace.
Let other Bacchae keep that holy rite!

The women of the chorus respond as if scales had fallen from their eyes.

I dwell on Agave because so many commentators underrate her role in the dramatic pattern: the victim of Dionysus, she then breaks free of him; speaks as King Roger might speak; speaks (I think) for Euripides as he wrote his last play, in Macedon, far from war-rent and now unworthy Athens. (In 405 BC, his indictment of Dionysus was performed in Athens' Theatre of Dionysus.) But no more than the *Ring* can *The Bacchae* be held to a single interpretation: each translation, each adaptation sheds its own lights. Sutherland writes of a "drama turning mainly on the confrontation of serious rational man by an irrational, brutal, and playfully malicious divine power." William Arrowsmith, in an introduction to his translation, rehearses the old view (the play as Euripides' deathbed conversion to the mysteries of Dionysus, after his lifetime of open hostility toward the Olympians) and the "even absurder" view that followed ("casting Dionysus as a devil and Pentheus as a noble martyr to human enlightenment"), and he proposes a study in *sophia*: a "wisdom" that includes self-knowledge, knowledge of others, and the ability (which Pentheus lacks and, I would add, Agave gains) to deal with crisis and catastrophe.

There is comedy in *The Bacchae* as the two old men, Tiresias and Cadmus, decide to join the rout and get with it – cruel comedy when one remembers who they are. (It is as if the Pope and George Bush, courting acclaim, were to join in an earnest public display of break dancing.) There is comedy crueller still – tragicomedy, at which one does not laugh – in the scene where Pentheus, stern ruler of his people, minces in drag toward his doom, bothering about the set of his curls and his uneven hemline; and in the (narrated) scene where, still in his pretty dress, he is toppled from a pine tree and protests in vain to the maddened murderous Agave that he's her son. (She, assisted by his aunts, tears him to bits, and they play ball with the pieces.) There is lyrical beauty in the landscape evocations of the chorus – an opening out to the wide world beyond Thebes and its immediate concerns. There is scenic spectacle in the earthquake, the crashing of Pentheus's palace, the final epiphany. The play, while formally, tautly contained within the unities, seems explosive. Arrowsmith says: "*The Bacchae* is finally a mysterious, almost a haunted, work, stalked by divinity and that daemonic power of necessity which for Euripides is the careless source of man's tragic destiny and moral dignity. Elusive, complex and compelling, the play constantly recedes before one's grasp, advancing, not retreating, steadily into deeper chaos and larger order, coming finally to rest only god knows where."

Dionysus is a liberator in Soyinka's version, which is subtitled *A Communion Rite* and mingles African and Attic myth. In an introduction Soyinka writes, "Dionysiac cults found suddenly fertile soil in Greece after centuries of near-complete domination by state-controlled Mysteries because of peasant movements in the wake of urban expansion." Worship of Dionysus "released the pent-up frustrated energy of all the downtrodden," and "in challenging the state Mysteries he became the champion of the masses against monopolistic repressions of the 'Olympian' priesthood, mercantile princes and other nobility." At the close, not blood but fountains of wine jet forth from Pentheus's head. The close of *The Bassarids*, on the other hand, is not joyful but ambivalent: fire blazes up and then sinks to reveal a blackened scene suggesting a return to barbaric superstition; but suddenly vines spring forth luxuriantly. In this opera, differing views of the god coexist. The poets considered Nazism a Dionysiac manifestation, and the god "a heartless monster, before whom we rightly tremble, but whom it is impossible to admire." The composer saw in Dionysus a savior: "The basic conflict in *The Bassarids* is between social repression and sexual liberation: the liberation of the individual. It shows people as individuals breaking out of a social context, as a road to freedom, as the intoxicating liberation of people who suddenly discover themselves, who release the Dionysus within themselves."

The Bassarids – the richest, the least simplified, of the *Bacchae* operas – lives in its score: a one-act, four-movement "dramatic symphony" in which the music of Pentheus is assailed by, and finally succumbs to, that of Dionysus.

Börtz's *Backanterna* is musically less ambitious – a different kind of piece from *The Bassarids*, whose librettists did not allow respect for Euripides "to interfere with the making of a new piece in a new medium." Börtz, who was born in 1943, is a prolific composer, with nine symphonies, several concertos, and much chamber music in his catalog; *Backanterna* is his first opera. It has been directed by Ingmar Bergman – his first opera since *The Rake's Progress* (apart from the television *Magic Flute*). The fourteen performances are sold out. (The Stockholm Opera, an 1898 horseshoe, where Jussi Björling, Nicolai Gedda, Birgit Nilsson, Elisabeth Soderström were nurtured, holds eleven hundred people; large enough for Wagner, small enough for Mozart, it allows a closer, more direct adventure than three-thousand-seat houses can offer.) Two earlier endeavors by Bergman to stage *The Bacchae* were frustrated: forty years ago, when money ran short, and seven years ago, when he fell ill. Börtz's collaboration with Bergman began in 1987, and the opera was finished two years ago. His score is music for the play – music quick to capture and enhance its volatile emotions, something more than incidental music, but something less than an opera for which the composer has first responsibility for the drama. Indeed, a good deal of the text is spoken, not sung. There are two acts, lasting about ninety and fifty minutes; the break comes as Pentheus sets out for Cithaeron.

Male-voice domination is avoided by casting a mezzo-soprano as Dionysus. Pentheus comments scornfully on the youth's long tresses and girlish complexion, and most translators and adapters add a stage direction describing his androgynous beauty. (Soyinka is the exception: "a being of calm rugged strength, of a rugged beauty, not of effeminate prettiness.") But Bergman presents us, disconcertingly, with a Dionysus who is all woman: a strapping female athlete in a black leotard, broad-belted, fondling her favorite girls, seducing her cousin as much by erotic physical contact as by her words. His Pentheus, a high baritone, is a tall, angry young tyrant, extravagantly violent in demeanor, and similarly dressed. (But while her long, straight blonde hair straggles free, his is tied back in a fashionable little bun.) There are touches of caricature, of comic-strip directness, in the staging. Tiresias and Cadmus enter as a pair of tippling clowns; Tiresias, who has been both man and woman, is a wide-ranging mezzo (the score prescribes "soprano/alto"), and Cadmus is a bass.

The bacchantes are an ensemble of thirteen solo voices, soprano, mezzo, and alto; a fourteenth bacchante is a mute dancer. The program book provides a biography and character sketch for each of them. Disciples who have left homes in Bactria, Media, Phrygia, Scythia, Thrace, Thessaly, Boeotia, the Peloponnese to follow Dionysus, they now have only Greek letters as names. In the first act, they wear colorful ethnic costumes; in the second, blood-streaked white smocks. The music Börtz has written for them is varied in movement and texture, with shifting metres, shifting emotions, antistrophe, refrain, and epode. Sometimes it is exciting, sometimes beautiful. The final chorus (Euripides' deliberately flat, dry "Gods manifest themselves in many ways. . . . Things unexpected happen") is a bare unison chant, and the last line ("as happened here") is spoken by Omega.

The bacchantes dominate this *Bacchae.* The writing for Dionysus and Pentheus is largely declamatory, often vehement, in extremes of register. . . . There are a few lyrical episodes, some periods of chanted recitation, and much speech – straight, or with just the rhythms indicated, or with pitch contours suggested in *Sprechgesang* notation. The work begins with rushing upward scales (a recurrent gesture of the score), each note sustained so that dense clusters accumulate. Dionysus' tirade, announcing his vengeance on Thebes, is cried through jagged intervals, alternating with *Sprechgesang* and chant, and closing with tender lyricism as he summons his bacchantes. The scene in which the god "hypnotizes" Pentheus – one of the four scenes that Auden and Kallman thought "excellent material for an opera" – is spoken over soft, dense string chords, gongs, and sliding wind notes. The two extended solos are spoken passages; the narrative of the Herdsman (it lasts about seven and a half minutes) and that

> of the Messenger (nearly twelve minutes), which are delivered freely – in high rhetorical style, with dramatic pauses and elaborate inflections – by actors from the Dramaten, the Royal Theatre company. Soft bell and gong strokes underpin the first; piano notes, harp, and gongs sound quietly during the second. At last, with Agave's entrance, music comes more sustainedly to the fore. . . . Her farewell is sung in long, lyrical lines almost unaccompanied, wound with an English-horn phrase and punctuated by a stuttering solo-cello figure.

Much of Andrew Porter's technical analysis of the score has necessarily been omitted here. He had kind words for the cast:

> Sylvia Lindenstrand was a strong, untiring Dionysus, with a lovely timbre in the lyrical episodes. Peter Mattei, a twenty-six-year-old baritone, made what the Opera's house magazine (citing his statistics: height six-feet-five, weight two hundred pounds, shoe size 14) called a "*katapulstart i opera-karriären,*" as a Pentheus with a powerful, focussed voice and a powerful stage presence. Anita Soldh was a moving Agave. Berit Lindholm, her Wagner soprano still keen and true, was an authoritative Alpha, the chorus leader. . . . The setting, by Lennart Mörk (who designed Bergman's Dramaten production of *Peer Gynt*), is a gray perspective box – "Pentheus's garage" the local nickname – in which the bacchantes spread a carpet and hang colored cloths. Bergman's staging is "old-style modern" – along lines that Wieland Wagner and Peter Brook have explored – spare, and precise. The bacchantes, ever present, sit around in carefully composed groups, listening to the principals; advance in carefully devised formations to sing the choruses; and also enact some Graham-type choreography, by Donya Feuer.
>
> The novel element in the *Bacchae* is the sense of women old and young who, like the twelve disciples, have forsaken all to follow a charismatic leader; but it needed the program note, with the brief biographies, to make this fully apparent. In another note the composer wrote of his fascination with Dionysus' Janus aspect, tender toward his followers, cruel to the Thebans: "Dionysus is a figure of light, a Christ who brings gladness." (Sutherland in his essay also ventures a Christ-Dionysus parallel.) But there is a startling addition to Euripides toward the end, after Agave's protest that Dionysus has treated Cadmus's house in tyrannous fashion and the god's retort that *he* was badly treated by the Thebans, in not being honored. (Some editions ascribe his lines to Cadmus.) In the Bergman-Börtz version, Dionysus descends from the *theologeion*, the god-walk, screams the lines at Agave, and, loutlike, hits her repeatedly, to five slashing chords, until she falls to the ground. Perhaps the final moral of *Backanterna* is that Dionysus is a brute.

Quite unique, and likely to stay so, is Partch's *Revelation in the Courthouse Park* (1961), which made its bow at the University of Illinois (Champaign-Urbana) and had a second staged presentation during the 1980s in the Great Hall of the University of Arts in Philadelphia – a performance which, as stated, was recorded – and again, later in the decade, at Alice Tully Hall in New York City (1989), fifteen years after the composer's death. Harry Partch (1901–74) was born in California, a son of Christian missionaries who proselytized for a time in China, but lost their zeal and returned to settle in isolated regions of the American Southwest, the dry states of Arizona and New Mexico. Brought up in a family that took an interest in music, he shared an artistic bent with a brother, Virgil, who was to win notice as a deft, amusing cartoonist.

Though aspiring to be a professional musician, Harry Partch was largely self-taught and his was the independence of an autodidact. He turned out conventional compositions until he was thirty, then abruptly destroyed his manuscripts and set off in a very personal direction. He took to vagabonding, moving randomly around the country, but then travelled to England where he accepted some formal schooling that later enabled him to obtain teaching appointments.

His brother's cartoons were praised for their originality, and that quality was also inherent in all of Harry Partch's new musical offerings. As a preface to the enactment of the opera at Alice Tully Hall, Bernard Holland remarked in the *New York Times*:

> Harry Partch lived either before his appointed time or else two thousand years too late. In his solitary art, music served a larger experience, one in which seeing, feeling and hearing joined together and erased the line between the sensual and the intellectual. Partch believed that the music around him thought too much, or at least thought to the exclusion of the rest of the body. Music, as he put it, "was afraid of, and suppressed, anything that happened below the neck."
>
> Anyone who wants literal proof that this twentieth-century iconoclast worshipped at the temple of Dionysus need only go to see his *Revelation in the Courthouse Park* tomorrow evening or Sunday afternoon.
>
> It is a theater piece that finds connexions between Euripides' play *The Bacchae* and the quasi-sexual hysteria of rock musicians and their followers. Scenes from past and present are juxtaposed; Dionysus is metamorphosed into the fictional Dion, a modern pop idol. The music plays Partch's exotic (and exotically tuned) instruments of wood, string and glass against the unequivocating assertiveness of a high school brass band.
>
> *Revelation* was conceived to be acted out in front of a Midwestern public building. . . . Both

architectural settings (at the University of Illinois and the University of the Arts) provided a visual pun on Greek Revival in a way the Tully Hall performances probably cannot.

The special difficulty of reviving and preserving the work arises because Partch's score is to be played on musical instruments that he himself invented and of which, for the most part, only single examples now exist. They belong to Danlee Mitchell, a Partch disciple, who has dedicated himself to keeping pure and alive his mentor's values. Mitchell has conducted the performances, which has also required that he personally instruct the singers and instrumentalists – forty of whom, for the Alice Tully Hall engagement, were drawn from the adjacent Juilliard School.

Bernard Holland (the *New York Times*'s senior music critic) explained that Mitchell's task was not easy.

> Partch's 43-tone scale (compared to the 12 tones to the octave) gives the mallet-percussion not only more notes to play, but also a layout irrelevant to the up-and-down design of the traditional keyboard. Jeffrey Milarsky is playing the Diamond Marimba, whose mounting and narrowing rows of keys resemble somewhat the steps of a Mayan temple. Mr Milarsky, who is fascinated by the quiet timbral subtleties of his newfound instrument, must nevertheless learn passagework that runs not across the keys, but diagonally up and down them. Partch's actual keyboard instruments are complicated by multiple stops for every key in the old black-and-white configuration.
>
> Partch invented and built devices like the Marimba Eroica, the Chromelodeon, Boo and the Spoils of War. They are deeply influenced by the music of Southeast Asia and may be taken as an answer to what Partch considered to be the bankruptcy of Western pitch relationships and the instruments devised to express them.
>
> Partch's instruments were meant to be not only heard but seen. The presence of musicians on stage is specified by the composer, and they are as fascinating to look at as to listen to. Some marimba-like instruments are grotesquely swollen, like mutants from a science-fiction movie, and require two players standing on a bench. The rhythms are highly complex, with different systems of movement operating at once.

In his discussion with Holland, Mitchell likened *Revelation* to a Broadway musical. "It is one of his least complex works technically." According to Mitchell, Partch said his music was a "physical projection"; he believed that "the West yearned for some physical, mystical and cathartic experience. He thought of himself as reviving ancient Dionysian practises and also as a harbinger for things to come in the nineteen-seventies and eighties."

Holland concluded:

> Mitchell says that "Partchniks" still work to uphold the composer's legacy, but in talking to him, one has the impression of a man presiding over a phenomenon that – like the celibate Shaker religion – bears the seeds of its own extinction. Mitchell guards and preserves Partch's instruments in San Diego and brings them out for performances like the one in New York. Without them, Partch's music simply does not work.
>
> Yet there is little indication that a Partch school will develop his ideas and copy his instruments. Indeed, Harry Partch may in the end be less a harbinger than a noble dead end. What will happen when Mitchell's devotional energies and curatorial efforts have been expended is disturbing to contemplate. Better go and see *Revelation in the Courthouse Park* while you can.

When Hans Werner Henze's *The Bassarids* was given in a concert version at Carnegie Hall in New York City (1990) by the Cleveland Symphony Orchestra, led by Christoph von Dohanyi, the conductor told Jamie James, a freelance scholar assigned by the *New York Times*, "I'm not so fond of operas in concert, you know. I've done so much opera in the opera house that I usually miss the theater. But *The Bassarids* is one piece that has not been performed often, and some of the music is very important music of our century." It was being heard in New York for the first time.

Jamie James remarked:

> No one is more familiar with this score than Mr Dohanyi, who led the world première of *The Bassarids* at the Salzberg Festival in 1966. The conductor's relationship with Henze began in 1965, when the composer asked him to lead the first performance of his opera *The Young Lord* in Berlin. Mr Dohanyi supported Henze's works when he had the top administrative posts at the Frankfurt and Hamburg opera houses.
>
> For Mr Dohanyi, the fascinating aspect of *The Bassarids* is its symphonic structure. "Here he has attempted something really special, which has not been tried so many times before, to combine the symphony and the opera."
>
> Like the composer, Mr Dohanyi believes that *The Bassarids* is just coming into its own: "At the time of the opera's première, Henze was considered to be a very difficult composer, but now he is much

closer to our time. The audience of today is somehow reacting to the music of its own era much more naturally than it reacts to the music of the last century."

In a trans-Atlantic telephone discussion with James, Henze too chose to stress the same unusual aspect of his offering. "Auden wanted an *opera seria*, with arias and all that, but I wrote a symphony." Though the piece has a libretto and singers, it is divided into four movements as are works in traditional symphonic form. James gave his own view:

> Mr Henze's comment points up his reputation as a composer who has always followed his own path and for whom the principal unifying theme in his output is its unpredictability. And yet almost anyone's short list of major living opera composers would include his name. Despite this and despite the relative accessibility of his music and the fact that many of his best works are set to English texts, his operas are only rarely performed in the United States.
>
> *The Bassarids*, like Richard Strauss's *Elektra* and Igor Stravinsky's *Oedipus Rex*, is one of the most imaginative and ambitious treatments of classical drama in twentieth-century opera.
>
> The story, closely following Euripides, tells how Pentheus, king of Thebes, is punished for denying the divinity of Dionysus. . . . In the finale, Dionysus is revealed to be a petty, jealous god; having exacted vengeance, he tells the Theban bassarids, "Down slaves, kneel and adore," and goes off on his jaunty way.
>
> The two opposing themes of the opera – the demands of society, epitomized by Pentheus, and those of the inner self, the creativity and sexual energy represented by Dionysus – are carefully distinguished in Henze's score.
>
> "When I wrote the guitar music for Dionysus," Henze said from London, "I was thinking of what Gloucester says in the prologue to *Richard III*: 'In a lady's chamber, to the lascivious pleasing of a lute.' The Dionysus in music is always in Sicilian dance rhythm, and Pentheus's music is in a marchlike time." From his own experience, he could appreciate the duality of human nature. "I had a strict evangelical Protestant education. I grew up with the fear of God, the love of punctuality, precision, hard labor and bad food. So I do know both sides." At the work's end, the diatonic sound world of Pentheus crashes to a halt with his death, and the chromatic music of Dionysus prevails.

He had written the opera in a mood of "ecstatic pessimism".

The editor of *Opera News*, Patrick J. Smith, began a column on *The Bassarids* this way:

When one thinks of living composers who have created a body of operatic work that even faintly rivals not so much Verdi, Puccini and Wagner but Donizetti, Gounod and Massenet, the list is very short. It is short in part because few people have the opportunity to hear the operas enough times either to make considered judgments, or to become used to them in a context of *Manons* and *Lucias.*

Certainly the German composer Hans Werner Henze belongs on any list, and certainly his continued neglect by the major opera houses of the world is another shameful example of their programming practices. I had heard his opera *The Bassarids* in Santa Fe, when it was done there in 1967, and at that time and subsequently did not rate it as highly as several of his other operas (notably *The Young Lord*). The concert performance of the work in Carnegie Hall on October 27 by the Cleveland Orchestra, chorus and soloists, conducted by Christoph von Dohanyi, proved me wrong; it is a masterpiece, certainly ranking among his finest works, and one which deserved greater exposure.

It would be hard, however, to improve on this performance. Dohanyi, who conducted the première in Salzburg, is an ideal interpreter, and his forces were excellent. In this two-hour work, derived by W.H. Auden and Chester Kallman from *The Bacchae*, the chorus serves as a binding element, as in the Euripidean original. The Cleveland Orchestra Chorus (Gareth Morell, director) made certain the chorus remained at the center of the grisly events, singing with force, accuracy and delicacy.

The story of King Pentheus's sacrifice – torn to pieces by his mother and his aunt – for defying the god Dionysus puts the opera in the tradition of one-act cumulative blockbusters like *Elektra.* If this work is a follower, however, it differs in that, though the cumulative power is similar, Henze provides a lot more lyricism and textural orchestral variety. Auden/Kallman's portrait of the repellent but everywhere controlling god Dionysus is the glory of the work; rarely has such a figure been seen on an opera stage – far more overweening, complex and chilling than such stage villains as the various Mephistos and even Boito's Iago. Kenneth Riegel was magnificent in a role that lies perfectly for his voice: in addition, he seemed in very good vocal estate. Vernon Hartman, as the beleaguered king, was equally persuasive.

One missed the added element of staging, which would have intensified the proceedings, but the ovations heard at the end – for the performance and for the composer – were heartily deserved.

Omitted from Andrew Porter's otherwise full list of musical interpretations of *The Bacchae* is one by Stephen J. Albert (1941–92), a Pulitzer-prize-winning American composer. Late in his career as an experimentalist, Albert gradually turned to a "neo-Romantic use of tonality and instrumental color" to create a musical setting for the tragedy (1970); his score is for "solo voices and an eclectic band that includes electric guitars and saxophones".

Off-Off-Broadway, in 1985, at the Alvina Krause Theater, Neal Weaver directed *The Bacchae* performed by a semi-professional cast, headed by Tim Hart, Rick Giolito and Dorothy Stinnette. The showing was not covered by reviewers from the larger New York dailies.

As he had done earlier with *Medea* in Tokyo, Tadashi Suzuki assembled another somewhat unique interpretation of a Greek play, *Dionysus*, based on *The Bacchae* (*c.* 1991), again combining traditional Noh and Kabuki techniques with elements of the modern and the abstract that marked his own style, one depending much on gesture and movement and little on words. He was delighted with an invitation to stage the work at the Juilliard Theater in New York, convinced that it was highly relevant, "because the United States is a multi-racial society with a strong consciousness about issues of group identity versus the rights of the individual". He referred to two then current crises, the turmoil in the collapsing Soviet Union and the toll taken by the Gulf War, and perceived them to be situations in which, as in Euripides' drama, "a lot of energy is extended to the establishment of group identities with resulting friction. . . . It's common in today's world to have people who are politically neutral get caught up and hurt by these struggles. My production takes the point of view of the character Agave, who is victimized by all the religious fervor." He thought the play would give insight into such societal and personal dilemmas.

Yet another exotic presentation of the play – assuredly – was that which occurred in China in 1996. Sheila Melvin, a writer based in Beijing, transmitted her impressions of it to the *New York Times*:

> Even as differences over Taiwan recently strained political relations between the US and China, cultural relations took a step forward with the staging of the largest US-China theater co-production to date.
>
> This was Euripides' *Bacchae*, a joint venture between the New York Greek Drama Company and the China National Beijing-Opera Theater. Though Greek tragedy is not normal theater fare here, *Bacchae* was performed before full houses and enthusiastically received by audiences and critics alike.
>
> Standing in the spotlight of a darkened stage, the robed and masked Dionysus gazed out at the audience and related his determination to avenge his mother's death and to be accepted by his human family as a god. As his voice faded, a drum began to throb. With fiercely measured grace, Dionysus lifted his left leg higher and higher, until it stretched above his head.
>
> "I am a god!" he cried.

The drum grew louder, the audience burst into applause, and Dionysus spun around, his leg still raised impossibly high.

When he exited the stage, the chorus of his followers poured onto it. The musicians, seated on stage with traditional Chinese instruments, began playing an ancient Greek-style composition and the chorus began to dance. Cloaked in robes of muted saffron, the chorus of men dressed as women sang their love for Dionysus, underscoring it as they hit the stage with *mao*, wooden spears used in Peking opera.

This cross-cultural *Bacchae* was successful because, of course, of the universality of the Euripides play, but it owed much as well to the ingenious and sensitive collaboration of the producer, Peter Steadman, the director, Shi-zheng Chen, and the performers and administrators of the China Beijing-Opera Theater.

As artistic director of the New York Greek Drama Company, Mr Steadman is dedicated to producing ancient Greek drama by using research into its original performance to create innovative contemporary productions. In ancient Greece, drama consisted of poetry, music and song. This tradition lives on in China, notably in Chinese opera. Greek actors performed with their faces masked; now preserved with masklike face makeup. In ancient Greece, male actors played multiple parts and assumed both male and female roles, just as they do in Chinese opera.

Mr Chen, who is also an opera tenor and a choreographer, got his start performing "model operas" as a child in the most tumultuous days of the Cultural Revolution. He was also in China in the heady early nineteen-eighties when theater was able to free itself from politics and again produce art for art's sake. Subsequently, he emigrated to America and has watched from New York as the loss of government funding and the impact of television and karaoke have seriously damaged the theater world of China. Determined to contribute to the revitalization of theater here, he has returned regularly to direct productions.

The China National Beijing-Opera Theater, which comes directly under the Ministry of Culture, is China's most prestigious Peking-opera company. However, it has more than five hundred performers and little money. Put in business terms, the company is much like a state-owned enterprise that has not been permitted to lay off its workers or significantly alter its product line but is not given enough money to produce any goods to sell. Like many enterprises, it is caught in the middle of China's incomplete reforms. Without enough money to launch major new productions, it essentially ends up paying many of its performers not to perform. On an administrative level, the theater was thus delighted to do a co-production because it needs the money, and because it wants to learn how to produce new "products." Its performers, who competed eagerly for the roles in *Bacchae*, were delighted because they are highly skilled actors, acrobats, singers and musicians who want to use their talents.

Mr Chen selected a cast of fifteen performers who excel at Peking opera, but who were willing to move beyond its rigid forms. The three principals – Zhou Long, Jiang Qihu and Kong Xinyuan – played all eight main roles, male and female. In choreographing their movements, and those of the chorus, Mr Chen says that he drew not just on his knowledge of Greek theater and Peking opera, but also on his experiences watching the ritual, shamanistic performances of the Miao, one of China's ethnic minorities. He also integrated traditional Chinese storytelling styles into the drama, to great effect. When Mr Kong, playing the Herdsman, tore off his mask, clacked together two tassel-trimmed cow bones in a steady beat and launched into a description of the Maenads' orgies in a peasant storytelling style, the audience roared with laughter.

Spoken parts in this production were in modern, colloquial Chinese, but the singing was in ancient Greek, which the performers spent weeks learning to pronounce under Mr Steadman's tutelage. (According to Mr Steadman, they memorized the lyrics by finding Chinese characters whose pronunciation roughly corresponds to the ancient Greek sounds and penciling these in on the score.) Further adding to the difficulty, the singing in Peking opera is normally performed as solos, not in choruses.

Music for the production was composed by Eve Beglarian, a New York-based composer. She drew on her own and Mr Steadman's research into ancient Greek theater and music to create a modern composition based on ancient Greek scales. Because these scales differ greatly from those of Peking opera, which does not have half notes, the musicians and performers found the music quite hard to learn.

Extra holes had to be bored in the *suona*, or Chinese clarinet, so that half notes could be played on it. An extra-strong *dizi*, or Chinese flute, had to be made because the high range of the Greek scales actually cracked the ordinary instrument. The drummer used special mallets to produce a softer, rounder sound.

Masks for the production were the work of Huang Haiwei, an artist and stage designer who spent two years studying *commedia dell'arte* mask making in France. He first carved wooden models, based on his own sketches, and then used these models to craft the leather masks that effectively – sometimes stunningly – provided the facial features and expressions for each character. The robes that swathed the performers were made of wool and embroidered in patterns both Chinese and Greek by elderly Beijing ladies who sew for Peking opera.

This production of *Bacchae* was largely funded by a grant made by the National Endowment for

> the Humanities to the New York Greek Drama Company. (The NEH's primary interest in supporting the production was for a video of the cross-cultural production, which will be used as a teaching tool in US universities.) Several years in the making, the production marked the first time that the China Beijing-Opera Theater cooperated with the West, and the first time the New York Greek Drama Company worked overseas. Many happy Beijing theatergoers hope it will not be the last.

The respected foreign director Liviu Ciulei was invited to interpret *The Bacchae* anew by the alert Guthrie Theater of Minneapolis in 1987.

Again, in New York, Dennis O'Connor sought to do the play solely in terms of dance, with all the participants in modern dress, and the *mise en scène* a night-long loft party, the drunken celebrants "gyrating to pop records" (1994). Jack Anderson, in the *New York Times*, found the result "surprisingly feeble". As he beheld it,

> Christopher Batenhorst, who played Pentheus, was required to do little more than sit, crouch and stand with total rigidity. The most striking choreographic sequences were for Linda Sastradipradja, Rebecca Wortman, Philip Adams and Mr O'Connor, as the Bacchae, the followers of Dionysus. . . .
>
> Allison Brown, who portrayed Pentheus's mother, moved with a frosty elegance, which thawed when she joined the revelers. Nancy Turano, Reba Perez, Joseph Lennon and Paul Sutherland made brief appearances as other mythological figures. The choreographic debauch never grew wild enough. Inexplicably, Mr O'Connor missed the opportunity to duplicate Euripides's terrifying climax in which Pentheus is torn apart in frenzy by his own mother. Instead, Mr O'Connor's *Bacchae* fizzled out in a depiction of hangovers.
>
> Euripides's play still forces theatergoers to think about divine and demonic possession. In contrast, Mr O'Connor's dance seems only a sermon against alcohol.

As a contribution to National Poetry Month (2000), the Manhattan branch of the Poetry Society staged a series of one-night offerings of the classic dramas, the second of them *The Bacchae*, adapted by C.K. Williams.

So, despite the difficulties inherent in its enactment, Euripides' tragic *outré* fable is endlessly revived.

In the last decade of the century a Greek director, Yannis Houvardas, reached back to an earlier work of Euripides, *Iphigeneia in Tauris*, and gave Off-Off-Broadway audiences a quite new look at the play (1992). D.J.R. Bruckner, of the *New York Times*, found this bold use of the text extraordinarily rewarding.

> The adaptation of Euripides' *Iphigeneia in Tauris* directed by Yannis Houvardas at La MaMa is so revisionary and idiosyncratic it makes Mr Houvardas a co-author, and a formidable one. Mr Houvardas, a leading director in Athens, severely trims the ancient play and turns it inside out to dramatize his own intriguing ideas about cultural confrontation.
>
> A brilliant white set suggests a mental-hospital ward where not one but eight Iphigeneias (this device works surprisingly well; no chorus is needed since the heroine is one all by herself) try in dreams to recover their past, some of it terrifying, before the doors open and the fiery volcanic world crashes in on them. The Greek and American cast, accompanied by mesmeric music composed and played by Genji Ito, speaks in a kind of chant (occasionally in Euripides' Greek if not often in his meters) that makes the performance, appropriately, a ritual.
>
> The original play is the bloodiest and most problematical in the Greek canon, its premise and conclusion equally unbelievable. But it has drama's first great letter scene, which is also a dramatic recognition scene, and a breathtaking escape sequence on a tempestuous sea.
>
> Mr Houvardas drains away much of the gore, but he keeps Euripides' Iphigeneia mostly intact: having escaped death at her father's hands as a blood sacrifice, she rules over a blood-sacrifice temple in a Scythian kingdom where she is accidentally found by her brother, Orestes, whom she is duty-bound to kill but with whom she escapes. He also retains the notoriously awkward *deus ex machina*, Athena, who finally intervenes to resolve the impossible plot. Here she is simply spectacular, a wondrous if weird delight. But as he pursues his exploration of personal pain in cultural conflict, he loses some of the astonishment of the letter scene and most of the excitement of the great escape.
>
> Nonetheless, for those who know the play – and it is a good idea to read it again beforehand since this director has chopped off chunks of contextual narrative – Mr Houvardas and his cast have created a resonating piece of theater that is a moving and profound meditation not only on Euripides' play but also on drama itself.

Self-isolated in a castle on the craggy Italian Riviera while the Nazis ravaged Europe, Germany's ageing, most renowned playwright, Nobel-prize-winner Gerhard Hauptmann, devoted himself to composing the *Atrides-Tetralogy* (1940–44), his last work, its four plays of varied length: *Iphigénie in Aulis, Agamemnon's Tod [Death], Elektra, Iphigénie in Delphi.* His choice of subject was consistent with his shift from Naturalism to Symbolism. Like Goethe, who in the eighteenth century had visited Italy and seized on the dire classic myth of the House of Atreus, essentially "modernizing" it, to express deep personal moral convictions, Hauptmann too makes many changes in the ancient story, bringing out his feeling that – in the words of Ralph Fiedler – the Atreus legend offers "an eternal valid characterization of the final consequence of human diabolicalness and the rejection of reason". Of the effectiveness of the *Tetralogy* as drama, little is known outside of Germany.

During the 1990s the summer theatre in Williamstown, Massachusetts combined Euripides' two plays under the title *The Iphigeneia Cycle* as they had done a few years before. There is no evidence that Euripides intended the two scripts to be linked in this fashion. Indeed, it is believed that the *Aulis* was left unfinished and only produced after his death, with the ending provided by a less deft hand and the rightness of the resolution disputed. Chronologically, the action in Aulis unfolds two decades before that in Tauris. By casting more youthful actors, the director can narrow the time-gap. But obstacles remain. The Iphigeneia in Aulis is an idealistic, courageous, tremulous adolescent who impulsively offers her life to further the Greek cause. In Tauris she is a priestess of Artemis who, to save her skin, oversees barbaric rites in which the throats of innocent captives are cut to appease the Scythian deity. Nor, to effect an escape, does she hesitate at being deceitful. The Williamstown troupe is noted for recruiting well-known Broadway players, but if the same actress portrays both roles she must be greatly resourceful. If two actresses are given the contrasting parts, they must bear at least some physical resemblance.

The Iphigeneia was twenty-three-year-old Anne Dudek, a recent graduate of Northwestern University, who told an interviewer that she was enamoured of the role because in it were contrasting innate traits of surrender and defiance. She yields to her father's selfish bid that she give her life to help the Greeks in the war against Troy – actually its trivial aim is merely to retrieve the perfidious Helen for the bed of his brother Menelaus. Later she is disillusioned and fiercely resentful. Somewhat cryptically, Miss Dudek elaborated: "The core of the first play is this intense longing for life, which dictates all the decisions she makes. By the end, she's this incredibly hardened, saddened character. But I think the anger comes out of a hope."

The director was JoAnne Akalaitis, who had been chosen by Joseph Papp as his successor as head of New York's thriving Public Theater. Her reign there had been brief, less than two years, her approach to the plays she produced in that span displeasing the critics and too many of Public's patrons, who denounced her as too "cerebral", "radical" and "idiosyncratic". Her ex-husband and onetime collaborator Philip Glass, the avant-garde minimalist composer, defended her, saying: "She is a truly original thinker, and that's very threatening to some people. When you bring real energy, skill and intuition to the work and you are unwilling to compromise, people get very angry." (Quoted by Nancy Hass in the *New York Times.*) Glass remained her "unabashed fan". Her attackers – again cited by Hass – asserted that she was a "bloodless modernist who disrespects Shakespeare, debases the Greeks and shamelessly distorts Jean Genet and Tennessee Williams". A harsh indictment, indeed! In detail: "The symbolist gestures she favors – sometimes her actors move in a kind of slow-motion Kabuki style or fall to the ground as if pulled by a demonic force – have been celebrated as inspired and decried as gimmicky. Her advocates say her penchant for updating classic works make them see the works anew; critics complain that she has a narrow academic vision and that her changes are gratuitous and distracting."

Her modern-dress *Iphigeneia Cycle* did not really go to those extremes; it was comparatively straightforward. She had first staged it at the Court Theater, a troupe founded by Jack Willis and in residence at the University of Chicago. Subsequently, her version was also brought to New York by the Off-Broadway Theater for a New Audience at the American Place Theater (1999). Anne Dudek was the Iphigeneia in New York, too.

Ms Akalaitis told Nancy Hass that she was the child of a working-class Lithuanian family and was brought up in Cicero, Illinois, a deteriorated suburb of Chicago. After earning a degree in philosophy from the outstanding University of Chicago, she was steadily engaged with experimental theatre. Among early influences on her were the theories of Jerzy Grotowski, with whom she worked for a short time, and the writings of Oliver Sacks, the neurologist who has made an intense study of "the other-worldly movements of encephalitis patients". Before and after her stay at the Public Theater, she was hired to direct groups in major regional and university theatres throughout the country and in Europe – Germany, Italy, France – among them the Hartford Stage, Bard College, the Actors Theater of Louisville, the Juilliard School, the Lincoln Center Theater and the Guthrie Theater, there and elsewhere championing the plays of Genet, Kroetz, Beckett, Jane Bowles and other startling and sometimes baffling new dramatists. Her own influence has been considerable, a number of her students having later established experimental theatres too – for one, the truly respected Wooster Group – or have achieved prominence as performers in Hollywood films and in Broadway offerings. In addition to her many other accomplishments, she was a co-founder of the theatre collective Mabou Mines, another important and enduring Off-Broadway enterprise. She has written plays of her own and taken a hand at adapting the classic scripts that she has staged.

That the *Iphigeneia Cycle* was of special significance to her is suggested by her revelation in another interview that its material was draining for her to direct. "It's very hard for me to rehearse these plays, because I actually cry all the time." So it would seem that her approach in her stagings is not wholly "cerebral" and that Euripides is still eternal and the irresistible "tear-jerker".

A decided oddity on the scene was Ellen McLaughlin's *Iphigeneia and Other Daughters* (1995), overseen by David Esbjornson for the long-active Off-Broadway Classic Stage Company on 13th Street in the East Village; Ben Brantley went down there to see it:

> You probably don't remember Chrysothemis. Unlike her relatives in *Iphigeneia and Other Daughters*, Ellen McLaughlin's revisionist take on the House of Atreus, she has had no famous plays, operas, ballets or complexes named for her. But at least, according to Sophocles, she was part of the most famous and bloodiest family of Greek legend. She was a good girl: she didn't kill anyone, and no one ever paid much attention to her.
>
> In this self-conscious meditation of a play . . . Ms McLaughlin lets Chrysothemis (Deborah Hedwall) have her say about "this pallid little female life we run out together." Women are not, she observes with dull resignation, "part of history." Forever on the edge of the greater drama, and largely unaware of its significance, she is the Rosencrantz and Guildenstern of a monumental story.
>
> An entire Stoppard-esque exercise probably could have been woven out of Chrysothemis' point of view, but Ms McLaughlin has cast her net much wider. As she sees it, this drab, dutiful daughter is but the most extreme example of the women who waited during the Trojan War, deprived of active identities in a world shaped by men.
>
> The dominant motif of the play is, accordingly, invisibility. "Look at me!" yells the defiant Electra (Sheila Tousey), who later observes, "I used to be someone: I was someone's sister; first I was someone's daughter. But that was a long time ago." Iphigeneia (Susan Heimbinder) describes her presence in the military camp of her father, Agamemnon: "I am not here; I am just some spell that is cast."
>
> Only proud Clytemnestra (Kathleen Chalfant), the husband-killing matriarch, insists, quite rightly, "I have always been at the center of the drama." But as Iphigeneia later says of her mother, "No woman can afford to be that interesting." Getting the point?
>
> A feminist take on Agamemnon's women, as they were portrayed by Aeschylus, Sophocles and Euripides, isn't exactly new. It has been implicit in everything from Ariane Mnouchkine's epic *Les Atrides* to the Clytemnestra-dominated trilogy at the Guthrie Theater in Minneapolis directed by Garland Wright in 1992. Certainly the archetypes in the original plays are rich and ripe enough for this kind of consideration. The question is how badly it needs to be stated.

Ms McLaughlin, who is probably best known as the angel in *Angels in America*, has bravely ventured into territory that has been taken on by half the major Western poets and explored in plays by everyone from Racine to Ezra Pound. She has a definite poetic flair, and there are flickers of a grave, inspired eloquence here. But she doesn't bring a lot that's new to the table.

The evening, which has been divided into three short plays and also features Seth Gilliam as Orestes, has been given the sort of elegant production one associates with the Classic Stage under Mr Esbjornson's reign as artistic director. There is a stark Attic setting by Narelle Sissons, costumes evoking the era of World War I by Susan Hilferty, and otherworldly music by Gina Leishman. Actors appear to be suspended on walls and freeze into ominous tableaux.

But *Iphigeneia* is a work that might fare better as a simple staged reading. Ms McLaughlin hasn't created characters as much as comments on characters. The language switches between abstract lyricism and the flip, distancing anachronisms so much in vogue now. (Clytemnestra asks Orestes if he would like some Jell-O or Ritz Crackers.) This isn't the most actor-friendly material, though the cast members, by and large, acquit themselves gracefully, particularly the formidable Ms Chalfant (who was also in *Angels*) and Ms Heimbinder.

In the play's first segment, inspired by Euripides's *Iphigeneia in Aulis*, Ms McLaughlin achieves a lovely, sustained imagery in which thematic intent comes through in descriptive detail, as it should. "Everything has become too important here," says Iphigeneia of the events leading up to her fabled sacrifice, "like something stared at for too long, until it could be anything."

Often, though, the playwright overworks her polemical alphabet to spell things out. Half the joy of theater is inference. *Iphigenia and Other Daughters* does most of the thinking for you.

About this time, several of the Greek dramas were filmed in England, including *Iphigeneia in Aulis*. In general, *Iphigeneia in Tauris* is more likely to be elected for production because it is more compact and suspenseful. Both plays have intellectually disappointing endings, dependent on *deus ex machina*, the seemingly wilful intervention of Artemis (Diana), a device to which Euripides resorts too often. Such miraculous solutions of dilemmas reductively categorize the plays as tragicomedies, the lesser genre that Euripides is credited with inventing.

The Iphigeneia legend has been best kept alive, however, by Christopher Willibald Gluck's two noble operas based on Euripides' handling of her harrowing strange tale. Again, *Iphigeneia in Tauris* is the better work, considered to be Gluck's masterpiece, and in consequence is the one more frequently staged. In 1993 it was put on at Covent Garden as a feature of the English Bach Festival, directed by Alain Germain and conducted by Marc Minkowski; it was the first presentation ever in England of the piece in period dress. Rodney Milnes wrote in *The Times*: The performance was profoundly stirring. . . . Is there a greater opera than *Iphigénie*? Not that I know of, and if the English Bach Festival were giving six performances instead of one, I'd go to them all." Equally enthralled was Stephen Johnson of the *Independent*: "Visually this new *Iphigénie* was almost uninterruptedly delightful and there was the added pleasure of feeling spectacle and music working in a kind of stylistic symbiosis. . . . The numerous ballet scenes with their sumptuously plumed soldiers, white robed priestesses and elegant furies were a treat for eyes and ears."

The restoration of a long-neglected work of high merit undertaken by a prestigious group such as the English Bach Festival at Covent Garden quickly attracts the notice of enterprising régisseurs elsewhere, often worldwide, inspiring numerous other revivals of it. This happened, and *Tauris* became a favourite musical offering as the twentieth century wound down. It was successful, despite Gluck's operas having a reputation for being beautifully melodious but slow and even static, a fault not easily tolerated by modern hearers.

Among the first to follow the English Bach Festival's lead was the Manhattan School of Music with an unevenly sung interpretation that was mildly applauded by Edward Rothstein in the *New York Times*:

> The matters at stake in many operas are not only what happens to the characters, but also what happens to the nature of opera itself; esthetic battles have accompanied staged ones. One of the masters of both forms of conflict was Christopher Willibald Gluck, whose 1779 opera *Iphigénie en Tauride* was performed on Wednesday night at the Manhattan School of Music. This production, directed by James Robinson, also yearns to take a role in contemporary debates about operatic presentation, though it does so with far less coherence than did Gluck.
>
> Gluck's impact on the evolution of opera was immense, and he made the issues clear from the very beginning of this elegantly dramatic work. He was opposed to the Italian style in which florid display of a singer's abilities could become an ornament to mythic tales. He wished, in his words, to "restrict music to its true office of serving poetry by means of expression."
>
> The entire first scene of *Iphigénie* is so tightly knit that it is experienced not as a series of recitatives and arias, but as a sentimental symphony with words. Even in the first pages of the work, in which a gracious, measured minuet gives way to an orchestral storm, we are meant to feel order overturned, the rational grace of the Enlightenment under attack; its rule will not be restored until the opera's close

(this tension may have made it attractive to Richard Strauss, who created his own version of the Gluck opera).

On this occasion, the conflict was well served in the supple singing of Pamela Moore in the title role. . . .

Miss Moore, one of Cynthia Hoffmann's graduate students at the Manhattan School, showed striking vocal and dramatic gifts; *O malheureuse Iphigénie*, the work's most famous aria, was simply sung, without the heart-on-sleeve emphasis it sometimes inspires. Ms Moore's phrasing could arch beautifully without strain and gracefully taper off in skillful appoggiaturas; her upper register had a slight tangy quaver that never went out of control. This was handsome, intelligent singing by a young artist who bears watching.

The tension between reason and disorder was also given surprisingly eloquent voice in the student orchestra led by Paulette Haupt. Ms Haupt treated the Scythian sections with an edgy energy, aided by Gluck's scoring for percussion; she was attentive to the subtle nuances of the score: the shifts in harmony between sections, or the startling way in which the chorus of priestesses joins suddenly in Iphigénie's lament.

The rest of the cast – primarily Marc Heimbigner as Thoas, David Timpane as Oreste, Jorge Garza as Pylade and Beth Clayton as Diane – were much more modestly effective, with some voices lacking much communicative power, others tending toward puffy pulsing. But it was in Mr Robinson's staging of the opera (sung in French with English supertitles) that Gluck's own battles became undone; its problem was not in representing the ordered beauty of the Enlightenment, heard in Iphigénie's aspirations, but in portraying the threats to it in Scythian society.

The sets by Anita Steward were meant to have a classical simplicity: simple gray walls representing the various scenes, and doorways through which the statue of the Goddess could be seen. They were marred by the rather obvious idea of having blood smears increasingly taking over the rear wall.

Similarly, Anna Oliver's costumes for Iphigénie and the Priestesses were effectively simple, but she clothed Thoas, the Scythian King, in a cloak of black velvet with electric yellow lining. Made up with a Kabuki-style face and a mane of black hair streaked with gray, he looked as if he had just stepped out of *The Rocky Horror Show*.

The Scythian ballet (choreographed by Francis Patrelle) called for the dancers, seemingly in black leather vests and black tights, to strut about in variety-show fashion. In fact, the Scythians in general were so campy in their outfits and behavior that they nearly undid the poised drama embodied in the music. The Furies were dressed in bras, grass skirts and African-style masks, for reasons best left unexplored.

> The result is a fractured production in which Mr Robinson seemed to yearn for the prerogatives accorded the contemporary opera director without trusting his more subtle instincts. Gluck, whose esthetic simplicity and directness were meant to replace "all those abuses against which good sense and reason have long cried out in vain," would probably have been dismayed. But he also would have applauded the production's successes, which make this too rarely staged work worth seeing.

Of particular interest, though, was a scholarly essay by Camille Naish included with the programme notes. As do other historians, she emphasizes that both Goethe and Gluck were "inspired" – literally – by the fresh, bracing air of the dawning Enlightenment, the oncoming Age of Reason. In shedding extravagant details, the show-offy frills and roulades that had been added to the performers' delivery, Gluck was seeking a return to relevance and simplicity, to plain-speaking in music. Everything had to be subordinated to the direct telling of the opera's story, a "purification", a revolution indeed, and one much opposed by the old guard. In Gluck's later works the characters are ruled not only by passions; once again there was an imposition of order, self-control, or at least a rational attempt to attain it, which was not always wholly possible. The work is to be a thoroughly integrated one: Naish writes of *Tauris*:

> The strength of this compact and energetic book resides in its fidelity to the intensely concentrated irony: the dire forebodings packed into the first half of the opera are all realized and resolved in the second. The storm which precipitates the drama corresponds to psychological turmoil in Iphigénie, who dreams that her father has been murdered by her mother, Clytemnestre; worse, Clytemnestre hands her a dagger and Iphigénie finds herself sacrificing her brother Oreste. This prefigures the moment in Act II when Oreste, tormented by the Furies, sees Iphigénie entering his prison, a younger image of the mother he has killed – a detail apparently insisted on by Gluck – and a subconscious substitution which Freud himself might have approved of. The phantasms of brother and sister become real in Acts III and IV when Oreste succeeds in replacing Pylade as the sacrificial victim; Pylade promptly returns to kill Thoas, who thereby meets the very fate he has tried so obsessively to avoid. The death sought by Oreste triggers the final peripeteia of recognition, for in evoking the death he believes Iphigénie to have met in Aulis, Oreste identifies himself as her own brother. Atonement then becomes expiation; Iphigénie's reluctance to perform the sacrificial office is justified by recognition and sanctified by Diane. For the ship driven by the storm to Tauris carries a heavy metaphorical cargo indeed: the curse upon the House of Atreus, the whole murderous drama of the house of Agamemnon,

from the initial sacrifice of Iphigénie to Clytemnestre's murder of her husband to Oreste's matricidal vengeance, now finally resolved. Just as Artemis-Diane intervened in *Iphigénie en Aulide* to save the heroine from Calchas's sacrificial altar and clear the way for marriage to Achilles, the goddess reappears at the conclusion of *Iphigénie en Tauride* – surely a luminous projection of a higher human consciousness – halting the battle between Scythians and Greeks and thus ending the ongoing cycle of bloodshed and revenge.

Six weeks before Gluck's second Iphigenie opera was first performed in Paris, Goethe's *Iphigenie auf Tauris* was given at a small court in Thuringen. Gluck was not influenced by this event and indeed, the two works are different in tone. Thoas, for example, is no longer a barbarian but an enlightened ruler, merciful, magnanimous, humane. The theme of the foreigner is present, but with a different emphasis: Iphigénie is painfully aware of her exile. Yet both artists view Greek myth in eighteenth-century terms: Goethe, through the ideals of classical humanism; Gluck, through the traditions of French and Italian opera he was in the process of reforming. It would scarcely prove surprising if twentieth-century interpreters view Gluck's revised operatic classicism through contemporary preoccupations. The Scythians' bloodcurdling xenophobia inevitably raises the dread specter of ethnic purging: we shudder and think of Belsen, of Bosnia.

In an opera deliberately devoid of sugary amorous intrigue we tend to seek hints of latent romance: the extravagant contest in devotion between Pylade and Oreste – to say nothing of the psychology of an Oreste haunted by visions of women threatening him with knives – may well suggest a fond warrior couple in the manner of Achilles and Patroclus, whereas an eighteenth-century audience would more probably have seen this truly as an heroic contest of friendship in the precious, declamatory French style.

Five years later, after preparing its offering at Glimmerglass in upstate New York, the New York City Opera Company brought its *Tauris* to the vast stage at Lincoln Center. (The two troupes were linked by having the same general manager, Paul Kellogg, who often arranged to have them share ventures.) Of course this was a much more substantial production, and it had a roster of superb young singers who had already achieved recognition in America and Europe. Despite these virtuous aspects, it prompted shock and controversy because it shifted its focus from Iphigeneia to her scantily clad brother Orestes and his half-nude close friend Pylades, the two young men competing intensely, each insisting that he should be the human sacrifice and that his companion's life should be spared. This picked up on Naish's comment that modern viewers might liken the bond between the two to "a fond warrior couple in the manner of Achilles and Patroclus". Now the implication was of an overt homoerotic relationship, an idea that had probably never occurred to Gluck and his librettist, the young Parisian poet Nicolas-François Guillard.

The conductor at the New York State Opera was Jane Glover, as previously cited a specialist in music of the period. The stage director was Paula Williams. In the programme notes Cori Ellison gives 1779 as the year of the work's première, which occurred at the Paris Opéra, where it was immediately recognized as Gluck's "crowning achievement". The story was a magnet to composers of the century; at very least a half-dozen other men chose to set it to music, among them Campra, Handel, Traetta, Galuppi, Jomelli and Piccinni, with Gluck the clear winner; part of this was due to the excellence of Guillard's libretto, the best ever provided to Gluck. It, in turn, was adapted from a play by Guymond de la Touche (1757), whose direct source was Euripides. Ellison comments: "If *Iphigénie* holds its own onstage as well as in the history books, it is because Gluck made epic myth and everyday human emotion meet on the same universal plane. In this case, the ageless myth is that of familial sacrifice (in the lineage of Isaac, Jesus, Idamante, to name a few) and the salvatory figure is a goddess, Diana. And the everyday human emotion is love, in many guises: the somewhat ambiguous love of Oreste and his companion Pylade, the filial love of Oreste and Iphigénie, the love of the priestesses for their leader Iphigénie, the love of the Greek captives for their Scythian captors, and, of course, the implicit love of Iphigénie and Oreste for their slain father – the love that unleashed the whole momentous chain of events. (But there's no conventional romantic love, mind you.)"

Ellison also points out that at moments Gluck's score seems at odds with the meaning of the words that are being sung. This may be intended to add a tincture of irony, in this story in which the characters resort to so much deceitful behaviour. It could also be that Gluck was perhaps the first composer to use music to probe the subconscious.

In the 1980s and 1990s the stages of London and New York looked crowded with yet more treatments of *Electra*, *Oedipus* and *Antigone*, some mostly conventional and some again exceedingly odd, as if their directors felt compelled to cast a glaring new light on these revered ancient works, discovering wholly fresh slants and meanings in them, perhaps bringing out a hitherto unsuspected relevance, making them surprisingly topical, lending them a twentieth-century importance. Certainly each successive production has to differ in some significant way from the one just preceding it. That imposes a striking demand, a risky challenge. But what director does not have a large ego? To be entrusted with guiding the revival of a Greek tragedy is *per se* an honour, and to undertake the gamble on one's own initiative is a bold statement of self-confidence, and additionally, whatever the impetus, here is an opportunity to become an *auteur*, as in films, to gain more credit and attention than the author or even the actors. With new plays in the USA, Dramatist Guild rules forbid making even slight changes in lines or plot without the consent of the playwright – often not readily granted and just as often precipitating unnerving confrontations – but with a classic script, the author long vanished and the language archaic and in places incomprehensible, the director has an utterly free hand. What a temptation!

Electra beckons. It is short, direct, and soon builds with unremitting tension. Its subject is certain to horrify an audience; the murder of a mother and her lover is not soon forgotten. An actress portraying Electra must be truly outstanding, having reserves of emotional and physical strength, capable of projecting sorrow, anger, hurt, grinding frustration, incitement; a virtuosic range and display of gifts. It is a signal role to which many aspire, as they do to Shakespeare's grim Lady Macbeth and many-aspected Cleopatra, Ibsen's Hedda Gabbler and haunted Mrs Alving; to succeed in it is to have a chance of attaining a lasting and lofty stature in the profession. Yet she need not be either beautiful or young. In fact, the play has *two* rewarding characters; Clytemnestra is also a commanding role, calling for a mature interpreter. And both women dominate the males throughout.

As with the Iphigeneia legend, the image of Agamemnon's brooding, vindictive, trodden eldest daughter was always in the forefront of theatregoers' awareness after it was exploited in a notable opera by the composer Richard Strauss (1864–1949) and his librettist Hugo von Hofmannsthal (1874–1929) which rapidly became and continued to be almost a staple for performance in many of the world's capital cities. An esteemed Austrian poet and dramatist – an idealist, a neo-Romantic and Symbolist – Hofmannsthal had published a German adaptation of Sophocles' account of the crime (1903); it was the first of a series of translations by him of the immortal Greek tragedies, his list also comprising *Oedipus and the Sphinx* (1905), *Oedipus the King* (1907), *Alcestis* (1909) and considerably later *The Egyptian Helen* (1928). In 1906 Hofmannsthal's *Elektra* came to the notice of Strauss, who was looking for a new subject and asked the poet to work with him on the shocking tale. The composer had a fondness for themes that might be deemed scandalous, even sensational – his *Salome*, utilizing Oscar Wilde's daringly erotic text which afforded glimpses of bisexuality, was taken off the Metropolitan's stage as offensive to its staid, wealthy subscribers. Hofmannsthal's *Elektra* was "pseudo primitive and torrid" – Gassner's phrase. This was just to Strauss's liking. Composer and librettist worked together for three years on this first collaboration.

(The correspondence between the pair during this period and later has been published and offers fascinating data and insights into how two major artists fashioned their remarkable music dramas, among them the brilliant *Der Rosenkavalier*.)

Elektra caused just the furore Strauss had in mind. A great composer surely, he also had a shrewd and mercenary side and knew how best to market his eternally valuable wares. The opera was soon produced throughout Europe and in the United States; it was praised and denounced by music critics and moralists, and consequently the public flocked to it. In France, Claude Debussy thought it "contrived and cold-blooded". (The two composers did not admire each other's work; on one occasion they met at a luncheon, where Strauss hardly discussed music, instead chiefly voicing his concern about collecting some overdue French royalties.) Sir Thomas Beecham conducted the opera at Covent Garden (1910). Ernest Newman, the dean of local critics – he has a lasting international reputation for erudition and sound judgement – viewed the offering as "abominably ugly"; whereupon Bernard Shaw, who for a spell was earning his keep as a music critic, jumped to the new piece's defence. Newman, who looked on Strauss as "undoubtedly the greatest living musician", ruefully saw *Elektra* as a "huge volcano spluttering forth a vast amount of dirt and muck, through which every now and then, when the fuming ceases and a breath of clear air blows away the smoke, we see the grand and strong original outlines of the mountain". This was Shaw's rejoinder: "There are moments when our feeling is so deep and our ecstasy so exalted that the primeval monsters from whom we are evolved wake within us and are under the strange tormented cries of their ancient struggles with the Life Force. All this is in *Elektra* . . . not even Beethoven in his last great Mass comprehended so much." He also compared Strauss's achievement to Wagner's in the *Ring*: "Not even in the third scene of *Das Rheingold*, or in the Klingsor scenes in *Parsifal*, is there such an atmosphere of malignant and cancerous evil as we get here. And that the power with which it is done is not the power of evil itself, but of the passion that detests and must and finally can destroy that evil, is what makes us rejoice in its horror." With characteristic Shavian arrogance, he declared that *Elektra* was to be treasured by "those of us who are neither deaf nor blind nor anti-Straussian critics (which is the same thing)".

In New York a reviewer for the *Sun* complained of Strauss's use of counterpoint, in which two or more melodies failed to harmonize with one another, as well as of the insertion of melodies that "spit and scratch and claw at each other, like enraged panthers". In the same vein the *Post* advised its readers that if they desired to "witness something that looks as its orchestral score sounds, let them, next Summer, poke into an ant hill and watch the black insects darting, angry and bewildered, biting and clawing, in a thousand directions at once". For its day the score of *Elektra* was "advanced", and even now is somewhat unique.

Over the years the Metropolitan was one of the many major houses that intermittently scheduled revivals of *Elektra.* When this occurred in 1992, John Simon, drama critic of *New York* magazine, contributed an article to *Opera News* in which he looked back at the reception given to Hofmannsthal's play before he transformed it into a libretto and had Strauss's tumultuous music added to it. The première had taken place at the Burgtheater, a monumental royal edifice ordered by the Hapsburgs in 1776 – the family was still reigning in 1904. The piece hardly opened to acclaim, though Hofmannsthal's distinguished fellow playwright, Arthur Schnitzler, sent him a note of congratulations. But to most of Vienna's arbiters of taste the work was too barbaric.

In France a quite unsympathetic notice came from the neo-classicist poet Henri de Regnier, quoted by Simon: "The Elektra of M. Hugo von Hofmannsthal, covered with sordid rags, lean and hungry like a she-wolf, howling and frantic, clawing the ground with her fingernails, fills the palace of Argos with her lamentations and romantic fury, for she is romantic, the Elektra of M. von Hofmannsthal, especially so by virtue of the words the poet has lent her, because in the structure of his drama he did not wander far afield from the givens of antiquity. . . . The play's novelty, then, is not in the events but in the hatred – frenzied, atrocious, savage, superhuman – that burns in the heart of the heroine, which she expresses with a singular force and eloquence, with a lyrical ferocity of words and images that makes of this Greek woman the maenad of dark discourse."

Simon's own analysis of *Elektra* as play and libretto leads him to the looming figure of Sigmund Freud, who was Hofmannsthal's contemporary in intellectually feverish Vienna. He perceives the opera's structure as comparable to that of a symphony, embodying four movements or confrontations between the principal characters. These head-on melodramatic meetings reveal the basic drives of the participants: Elektra's obsessive love for her slain father, Klytemnestra's hatred for the nightmarish fear of her son and daughter, Elektra's desperate need of her sister Chrysothemis' aid in exacting retribution from their fiendish mother, Elektra's joy in finding the long-lost Orest, who is not dead as rumoured. All the emotions aroused by these confrontations are extraordinarily complex.

> It has been noticed with shudders by some squeamish observers how passionate, even sexual, Elektra becomes about her sister. Yet, Hofmannsthal knew his Freud, and had just been reading Breuer and Freud on hysteria. That is the operative thing about Elektra, and not so much – if at all – incest and lesbianism.
>
> For Elektra is really a hysterical virgin. Hence her quasi-incestuous fixation on her murdered father, the incestuous feeling evolving from a hysterical virgin's need for a nonthreatening, protective

male figure, and also for the one man with whom sex might be safe. A love that, the father having been killed, becomes a passion for vengeance as a surrogate for sex. But Chrysothemis, more fragile and unaggressive, refuses. What we get is a lyrically impassioned rejection or unrequited love sequence, the *pathétique* movement.

Next, the nearest thing to a romantic love scene, the Elektra-Orest duet, the Siegmund and Sieglinde movement of the symphony. These ecstatically reunited siblings cannot live for love; they must suffer or even die for revenge or justice. Yet this brief movement of respite in their lives is a near fulfillment. It is the place where Strauss exacted the most significant revisions of the play text from Hofmannsthal:

"I need a great moment of repose after Elektra's first shout: 'Orest!' I shall fit in a delicately vibrant orchestral interlude while Elektra gazes upon Orest, now safely restored to her. I can make her repeat the stammered words: 'Orest, Orest, Orest!' several times . . . Couldn't you insert here a few beautiful verses until (as Orest is about to embrace her gently) I switch over to the somber mood? . . . I must have material here to work at will toward a climax. Eight, sixteen, twenty lines, as many as you can, and all in the same ecstatic mood, *immer sich steigernd* [rising to a climax]."

And the splendidly flexible lyricist-librettist obliged handsomely.

In Simon's view, the sustained collaboration succeeded because Hofmannsthal was "a better writer than anyone else who ever stooped, as it were, to the somewhat secondary role of librettist, with the possible exception of Auden and Boito". Again: "What makes this *Elektra* worthy as well as unique is the poetry, the sumptuously lyrical language that ennobles abjection, bloody revenge, horror. Far from being what T.S. Eliot deplored as 'dissociation of sensibility,' this is terror tamed by lyricism, misery transmuted into poetry. This is what grabbed Strauss." (John Gassner alludes to Hofmannsthal as "the finest poet in German since Goethe".)

At the end, her brother's sanguinary mission consummated, the tense Elektra finds emotional and nervous relief in a wild dance, so exhausting and extreme that she drops dead. Simon sees this conclusion as inevitable: "There follows the fourth movement, a kind of grotesque Mahlerian scherzo . . . in which Elektra, with sarcastic humility, ushers her stepfather into the palace of death. It would be a strange way to end a tragic symphony, with a scherzo, so there must be that epilogue or coda, Elektra's dance of triumph and death: the orgasm this young woman, condemned by a cruel trick of fate to chastity and deprivation, must find in a solitary dance of exultation and self-immolation."

After he had engaged for a time in translating and adapting Greek tragedies, Hofmannsthal delved into medieval theatre, bringing forth a version of *Everyman* that is staged every year at the widely attended Salzburg Festival, of which he and Max Reinhardt were co-founders. Unfortunately his career was cut short; grief-stricken, getting ready for the funeral of a son who had committed suicide, he himself suffered a fatal heart attack; he was fifty-five. (Much of this material on Strauss–Hofmannsthal is borrowed from the article by John Simon and a chapter in *Opera, A History* by Headington, Westbrook and Barfoot.)

Apart from the opera, a sharp reminder of Sophocles' tragedy was the return of Andrei Serban's handling of it (1987), a component of his earlier success *Fragments of a Greek Trilogy* at La MaMa. On this second hearing it elicited new approval from Arthur Holmberg in the *New York Times* for its "savage power" and strange emphasis on the "physicality of language", a large share of its dialogue being deliberately unintelligible, the actors relying for communication mostly on gesture and elemental sound.

For a visit to New York (1991) the Vienna Philharmonic arranged an unusual offering. John Rockwell, in the *New York Times*, was somewhat confounded by it, as too – it seems – was the audience. Here let Mr Rockwell explain:

> Carnegie Hall's dual presentation yesterday afternoon of *Elektra* the play by Hugo von Hofmannsthal and *Elektra* the opera by Richard Strauss was a grand occasion, perhaps too grand for the opera.
>
> But it was certainly a glamorous highlight of the hall's centennial season and a rousing culmination of the Vienna Philharmonic's American tour. And if details of the event seemed miscalculated, it still proved both a promising programming innovation and an opportunity to hear some absolutely glorious orchestral playing.
>
> Originally, the Vienna orchestra's visit was to have ended with a simple concert performance of Strauss's opera, conducted by Claudio Abbado – insofar as any performance of this overwrought, thunderously loud Expressionist outburst can be simple.
>
> Then Mr Abbado decided that he couldn't accord proper time and energy to *Elektra* and he turned over the baton to Lorin Maazel. This was a nice gesture, since Mr Maazel is not only an American, but also a predecessor of Mr Abbado as artistic director of the Vienna State Opera. As it happens, Mr Maazel is also a far more vividly theatrical conductor.
>
> It was Mr Maazel's idea to precede the opera performance with a dramatic reading of Hofmannsthal's words, an idea Carnegie Hall then realized. This allowed those who bothered to attend the

reading (about one-third of capacity) to gain insights into what attracted Strauss to Hofmannsthal and what Strauss brought to the poet's words – and, in general, how opera and theater differ as art forms (for one thing, length: the text took 45 minutes, the opera 108 minutes).

In addition to the big-time opera cast already engaged, Carnegie Hall hired a promising group of actors and built a striking-looking setting for the opera singers, with fluted columns and lecterns, looming above the orchestra like a ship's prow.

It is here, however, that one must begin to voice reservations. The hall provided copies of the libretto, but absolutely no history of the evolution of play into opera. It also kept the house lights dark throughout, so that no one could follow the text.

Hofmannsthal's play was based on Sophocles' version of the murderous Oresteia saga, the most overtly psychological of the Classical plays on this theme. Hofmannsthal shaped his drama under the influence of the birth of psychiatry in his native Vienna, in particular Breuer and Freud's *Studies in Hysteria.* The result, faithful to Sophocles yet seething with repressed irrationality, received its première from Max Reinhardt's Berlin company in 1903.

Strauss, searching for a follow-up to his *Salome,* basically set the play verbatim but with inevitable excisions and, in a few cases (above all, Elektra's recognition of Orest), some new lines.

Carnegie Hall should have performed Hofmannsthal's play as he wrote it in 1903. Instead, what one heard was a translation by G.M. Holland and K. Chalmers, accurate but unpoetic, of the opera libretto commissioned by the Decca Record Company of England. Insultingly, it was even labeled as a "script" in the program. Hofmannsthal's words do seem to cry out for music, but this comparison stacked the deck against his claims as a playwright.

The reading itself was honorably done, directed by Arvin Brown with Colleen Dewhurst as a tellingly hushed Elektra, consumed by a hatred she manages to hold in check until the murderous conclusion. Gloria Foster, Maria Tucci and Len Cariou were convincing as Klytemnestra, Chrysothemis and Aegisth, respectively, although John Rubinstein seemed too boyish as Orest. (Both cast listings were a hash of English and German.) Microphone balances were uneven, with Miss Dewhurst sometimes barely audible and some of the servants, deafening.

There are two famous anecdotes about Strauss at *Elektra* rehearsals. For the 1909 Dresden première, he is said to have shouted to Ernst von Schuch, the conductor: "Louder, louder, I can still hear the singers!" Later, his advice was to play the score softly, "like Mendelssohn's fairy music."

Mr Maazel chose to follow Strauss's first advice. As an occasion for awesomely rich orchestral playing rising to a climax halfway between the finale to Beethoven's *Seventh Symphony* and Wagner's *Love*

Death, this was an *Elektra* to remember. As a statement of Strauss's intentions, however, let alone Hofmannsthal's, it fell short.

Eva Marton, in the title role, has a fervent New York following. But she is the kind of wooden actress who, when asked to portray a beaten and starved hysteric, dresses in full prima-donna finery. And the setting made dramatic involvement difficult: Elektra was asked to interact with people standing behind her.

As a singer, Miss Marton was sometimes excitingly loud, as in her curse of her sister or her recognition of her brother. But she actually sings better quieter, when she can spin out controlled legato; yesterday, her blasts sounded both blowzy and dramatically unspecific.

The rest of the cast matched her, for better and for worse. There have been far more affecting Chrysothemises than Elizabeth Connell, but she did soar above Mr Maazel's mighty orchestral torrents. Klytemnestra has been a vehicle for some of the great aging mezzo-sopranos of the century. Mignon Dunn cannot claim greatness, but she pitched in vigorously in this dangerously campy part. Franz Grundheber made a solid, sonorous Orest, and the ageless James King was a properly fatuous Aegisth.

But in the end, good intentions and subsidiary achievements aside, it was the sound of the Vienna Philharmonic, whipped to an orgiastic frenzy by Mr Maazel, which defined the afternoon. For lovers of voluptuous sonority, that was probably enough.

The Vienna Philharmonic was followed by the Chicago Symphony who occupied Carnegie Hall (1995) with a semi-staged presentation of *Elektra* led by Daniel Barenboim. The senior music critic of the *New York Times*, Bernard Holland, was not altogether happy to be in attendance. He complained:

To Sophocles' clean, classic, cause-and-effect original, the Strauss-Hofmannsthal collaboration has added psychosis enough to satisfy the most eager central European appetite. Yet . . . on Thursday, a lot of the viciousness had to arrive by way of implication, or else from memories of past stage productions. And we are not *Elektra* starved. The piece appears regularly at the Metropolitan Opera; the Lyric Opera staged it for Chicago audiences just a few years ago.

In this concert setting, stage pictures were erased or reduced to bare sketches. A catwalk to the rear of the orchestra spanned the stage; players wore evening dress; gestures were at a minimum. In the opera house, Strauss moves the horrifying murders offstage, using sound and a glimpse or two to make them that much more dreadful. Mr Barenboim conveys the horror by pointing us toward his orchestra, where, indeed, he made us look for everything else on Thursday.

> Deborah Polaski as Elektra sang powerfully, albeit with a sanity and civility that no amount of implication made up for. Alessandra Marc flooded the role of Chrysothemis with beautiful soprano sound. Ute Priew and Falk Struckmann worked well as Clytemnestra and Orestes.

Holland acknowledged the proficiency of all in the cast, the orchestra, the conductor, but he hinted that New York – or, at least, the critics – were becoming sated with *Elektras.*

Commercial theatres usually consider putting on a revival only after a substantial lapse of time – a decade or two, or a longer interval. That assures finding a good many new ticket-buyers who might be curious about a classic or well-spoken-of work not familiar to them. Few people choose to go to plays they have already seen – ticket prices are too high, especially for the young. But now, almost treading on the heels of the Vienna Philharmonic's and Chicago Symphony's semi-stagings – in fact, only a bare year after the Chicago's offering – the National Theatre of Greece swept into the City Center (1996) for a ten-day engagement all given to Sophocles' original *Elektra.* (The name again with a "k".) The *New York Times* was called upon to provide a reviewer once more, in this instance from its Drama Department; the assignment was taken by Ben Brantley, the new senior critic (despite his youthful years). His observations:

> Grief walks in circles in this hypnotic interpretation. . . . The emotion, like the tragedy's anger-shrouded heroine, traces an orbit of despair that seems as fixed, in its way, as the figures on Keats's urn.
>
> In the title role, Lydia Koniordou moves in a repetitive, fluid path that corresponds to the oval of sand that dominates the stage at City Center, where the production (the company's first in New York in two decades) runs through Sunday. The play may end with the redressing of the past wrongs that have enslaved and embittered Elektra. But one leaves the theater with the sense that the chain of dark memories and lamentations can never really be broken.
>
> More than any of the great plays of the classical Greek theater, *Elektra* is an anatomy of a single emotion. While it addresses the cycle of murder and retribution in the bloody House of Atreus covered by Aeschylus' and Euripides' versions of the same tale, its focus is far less on the horrific events of a legend than the way they have shaped one mind.
>
> Much of the tragedy, accordingly, is a sustained, if diversely inflected, keen, like that of a woman at a wailing wall. The story of the unholy murder of Elektra's father, Agamemnon, by his wife, Clytemnestra, and her lover, Aegisthus, is told again and again. Elektra insists on it. "Can it be hon-

orable to forget the dead?" she asks, in response to the admonitions of the chorus, which observes, quite justly, that this woman knows nothing of moderation.

Elektra has been a favorite vehicle for actresses of strapping bravery and ambition, most notably Katina Paxinou. . . . It is risky territory.

In uncertain hands, Elektra can seem like the kvetch of all times, tempting audiences to sympathize with the character's mother and sister and the chorus, who keep telling her what amounts to "Enough of the complaining already, honey." The challenge is in universalizing her monomania while holding on to her unique psychological strength.

Fortunately, mourning does indeed become this Elektra. Ms Koniordou, who is also the show's director (in association with Dimitris Economou), has found a transfixing vitality in the part that speaks to everyone who believes that only remembrance can keep the dead alive.

Her life may have "gone by without hope," as she says, since the murder of her father in her childhood, but this is not a woman who has been stunted by grief. Indeed, she has feasted on it.

As Elektra alternates between contemplation of revenge and her own desired death, the commanding, large-boned Ms Koniordou, all feverish eyes and knifelike gestures, seems only to grow in a perverse, superhuman willfulness. (Portraying her mother, Aspasia Papathanasiou seems to have shriveled inversely from fear and bitterness.)

Ms Koniordou's performance and the production itself, although spoken in modern Greek, have a purely physical eloquence in which a harrowing ferocity of spirit is contained in ritualized movements. (On the other hand, the translated supertitles are bizarrely, even comically, clunky; you would definitely do well to read the play before seeing it.)

The sense of a circle, again, is crucial. As Elektra quarrels with her more practical, gentle-spirited sister, Chrysothemis (Tania Papadopoulou), and her tyrannical, conflicted mother, the women orbit each other in a slow, stately dance, maintaining an isolating distance.

The hems of their shawls and dresses (the striking, simple set and costumes are by Dionysis Fotopoulos) trace corresponding arcs in the sand. And when the pattern is broken, with the characters lunging into a fierce embrace or stranglehold, it is viscerally shocking.

The seventeen-woman chorus, meticulously choreographed by Apostolia Papadamaki, reinforces the same spiritual geometry, breaking and regrouping into curved or angled lines that suggest both awed timidity and the cohesiveness of a social order. There is mellifluous harmony and, at moments, confused dissonance in their collective voice. Before Elektra's imposing sorrow, they can reprove, recoil or console. They cannot, finally, assimilate it.

> Takis Farazis's music, a primal, haunted blend of percussion and woodwinds, and the sung lamentations all feed into the sense of a world in which mourning and the hope of revenge have become in themselves a religion. Deliverance finally arrives, in the form of Elektra's long-exiled brother, Orestes (Miltos Dimoulis), and the rhythms speed up accordingly as the play gallops toward a blood-soaked denouement.
>
> Actually, once the real action takes over in *Electra*, the production loses its grip. This is partly because the men – who also include Stefanos Kyriakidis as Aegisthus and Alexandras Mylonas as Orestes's mentor – don't really have characters to play. But one also suspects that Sophocles' greater interest was in the psychology of a woman who made a cult of her suffering.
>
> This Elektra achieves her apotheosis not with the play's end, but when she is earlier told (falsely) that her brother has been killed. "Now all I hold is nothingness," says Elektra, her sculptural face gone hollow, and the circle of anguish in which she has been trapped seems frozen into eternity.

For the modern Greek dialogue, the players availed themselves of a fresh translation by Yothos Heimonas, a contemporary poet. At City Center, English subtitles were added. The production had its première a few months earlier outdoors in the ancient multi-tiered theatre at Epidaurus.

Miss Koniordou, the actress–director, was interviewed by Dinitia Smith of the *New York Times*'s staff. After studying the classics at the University of Athens, she had continued at the National Theatre's School of Drama, where she earned a second degree. A major influence on her was Jerzy Grotowski, the Polish director and theorist, founder of the innovative Theatre of the Poor. Now, at forty-two, she held positions as artistic director of the Municipal Theatre of Volos and co-director of its musical theatre. For eight years she had thoroughly researched the "traditional forms" of Greek tragedy. She is one of the rare Greek actresses ever to have taken on the three different portrayals of Electra by Aeschylus, Sophocles and Euripides. In Aeschylus' *The Libation Bearers* she is pious, acting only at the gods' behest; in Euripides' play she is neurotic, spoiled, unwilling to listen to common sense or reason. As Miss Koniordou depicts her now, she is a heroic figure. "Sophocles tends to develop the characters and show them from many angles. His Electra is reluctant to become a mother-killer. She feels her weakness much more than she does in Aeschylus or Euripides. In Sophocles, her role is much closer to mourning than revenge."

As Miss Koniordou perceived the shape of the ancient tragedies, they were "very austere and condensed, which leads us into very modern forms. I deeply believe these are very modern pieces of theatre."

This production of *Electra*, as described by Dinitia Smith, was "almost Kabuki-like, set to the accompaniment of wind instruments and percussion". The scenic investure was minimal, almost abstract, in keeping with the style prevalent in the time of Pericles.

Smith relates: "At center stage is an urn for Electra's sacrifices to the gods. Most of the costumes are black and unbleached cotton, with touches of red to suggest the bloody doings of the Atreus family." Though belonging to no particular period, the style of the attire was traditionally Hellenic.

With Yorgos Heimonas's adaptation, the performance runs about an hour and forty minutes. Remarking on that, Miss Koniordou said: "These plays do not last long. They're so intense the audience can't absorb more. They create their own climate. When you sit outside in the amphitheatre at Epidaurus, you don't even feel the breeze in the air or hear the night birds sing."

The actress–director conceives of Electra as a woman who does not want to forget. "If she forgets what's happened, she will lose her humanity. We all face these dilemmas, whether to turn our head aside and forget terrible things." Yet she is a passive figure. It is Orestes whom she instigates to do the killing, which occurs out of her sight. All she knows of it is what he tells her. Hers is a "collective guilt".

The National Theatre of Greece's invasion of New York did not put a halt to the arrival of other anguished Electras. A staging of Sophocles' drama had been a huge success in London (1997) and rather shortly it was brought to the McCarter Theater in Princeton, New Jersey (site of Princeton University). The New York critics, having heard of the players' acclaim in England, hastened to Princeton to inspect the offering; their response was overwhelming, whereupon producers, too, descended on nearby Princeton. They were similarly impressed. Negotiations quickly ensued – it was necessary to obtain the consent of Actors Equity if an English cast was to be used – and financial terms had to be settled. This was happily accomplished, and *Electra* opened on Broadway (1998). It was most unusual fare to have aroused the zeal of producers in the commercial theatre, even though they are aware that every venture there is a gamble – but some are more risky than others. Broadway theatre rents are high, and advertising in the *New York Times*, *Post* and *Daily News*, as well as on broadcasts, is intimidatingly costly.

This adaptation of Sophocles' script was by Frank McGuinness, Irish as his name suggests; much was cut from the original – the effect was of a drama that had been drastically trimmed down. It had first been seen at the Chichester Festival (1997) before it was transferred to the Donmar Warehouse in London. The director was David Leveaux; other works guided by him had been on view earlier in New York. For the McCarter mounting several American actors had been selected for supporting roles, probably in part to meet an Actors Equity requirement. As reconstituted, the cast was deemed to be stronger than the one in London.

Zoë Wanamaker, who had the taxing title role, was the daughter of a well-established American actor, Sam Wanamaker; he had chosen to live and work in England where he had led the long, successful campaign to build a meticulously faithful copy of the Globe Theatre that had once housed Shakespeare's plays; unluckily, he died before the structure was completed. His prolonged efforts to bring it about were memorialized there. Born in America, his daughter was taken to London at the age of three. Growing up and entering her father's profession, she enjoyed a well-rounded career that led her to be in farces, comedies and dramas. She was also seen on Broadway in plays imported from Britain, twice winning Tony nominations. But she was not looked upon by the public as an actress of unusual stature. By now she was forty-nine. Though attractive in many ways, she was not conventionally beautiful, having a snub nose and a mouth that curved upwards at the corners, giving her what seemed to be a perpetual smile, a sometimes disconcerting Puckish aspect. Her facial features were so distinctive that she was widely recognized off-stage after her frequent television appearances, and this had begun to limit her opportunities. Theatregoers tended to identify her as Zoë Wanamaker, not the character she sought to portray. As she herself put it, for her to be Sophocles' Electra was "the role of a lifetime".

Opposite her as Clytemnestra was Claire Bloom, of quite mature age, whose lengthy résumé of intelligent and persuasive characterizations on film and television, and less often on stage, had earned her an assured and enviable reputation in both England and America. She bore herself with dignity and had aristocratic good looks. To play against her in a highly emotional duel was a hazard for the lesser-ranked Wanamaker. Even so, it was not known for certain if Claire Bloom could project the intensity that Clytemnestra was supposed to display.

Both actresses proved themselves up to the mark and far exceeded it, inspiring the veteran Clive Barnes, British-born, to write in the *Post*: "Zoë Wanamaker is magnificent! This is the most ferocious, most driven, most terrifyingly inevitable performance I have ever witnessed since Laurence Olivier played Oedipus more than fifty years ago. Wanamaker must now be regarded as the greatest British classic actress of her generation! David Leveaux has staged *Electra* with all the tension of a thriller!" And David Kaufman, in the *Daily News*, was equally shaken: "Zoë Wanamaker is electrifying in Frank McGuinness's sleek adaptation of *Electra*. She delivers what will be celebrated as one of this season's most memorable performances – and remain a landmark for many years to come." The adjective "mesmerizing" was applied to Wanamaker's interpretation by Linda Winer of *Newsday*. In *Variety*

Charles Isherwood proclaimed: "Electra is triumphant! Claire Bloom is spellbinding and magnificent!" Michael Sommers, of the Newhouse Newspapers, had experienced an evening at the Barrymore Theater which for him was "haunting, relentless, compelling and powerful!" No less moved was Michael Kuchwara, of Associated Press, who found the performance "devastating and blood-chilling! *Electra* has the power to make an audience shiver and gasp!"

The august – and comprehensive – *New York Times* printed three critiques of the play. The first, decidedly laudatory, covered the staging at Princeton. The opening at the Barrymore Theater, in Broadway's bustling precincts, was assayed by Peter Marks in the next morning's edition. The Arts and Leisure section of the over-extended Sunday issue contained another discussion of the play by Vincent Canby; this accorded with the *New York Times*'s policy of having more than one viewer's assessment of theatre ventures, since diminishing competition and the *Times*'s near-monopoly in reaching the city's middle- and upper-class readers gave its drama department too much influence – a play could live or die simply by what one *Times* reviewer thought of it. (The paper reached a host of out-of-town subscribers as well.) Additionally, Wanamaker was interviewed by Dinitia Smith, and other cast members too by Toby Zinman and Matt Wolf.

Marks was hardly restrained in his awe and enthusiasm.

> Leave it to a playwright who has been dead for 2,400 years to jolt Broadway out of its dramatic doldrums. Sophocles' *Electra* opened at the Barrymore Theater last night in a magnificent new production that represents soul-satisfying drama at its most passionately, intensely alive.
>
> In the director David Leveaux's startling staging, the play is both a timeless family tragedy and a lurid tabloid crime story. The foul deeds of *Electra* may have been recorded nearly two and a half millenniums ago, but in this masterly modern-dress version, they are as raw as the lead item off the police blotter. The portrait of a family convulsed by violence and betrayal is so potent and harrowing, it leaves you dazed and weirdly giddy. A daughter plots murder, a mother is butchered, a son is up to his elbows in blood. And you couldn't be more delighted.
>
> With the astounding Anglo-American actress Zoë Wanamaker in the title role, giving the proverbial performance of her career, this *Electra* is the most significant restaging of a classic on Broadway since a revisionist *A Doll's House* with Janet McTeer twenty months ago. It's a provocative evening that not only reacquaints you with the direct, unprocessed power of Greek drama but also provides a depth of pleasure you associate more frequently these days with great movies; you're swept along by the narrative, majestic in its directness and simplicity. If there is any justice in the theater

world, every playgoer with a hankering for drama with some flesh on it – no doubt about it, this is theater for meat-eaters – will place an order for this full-course meal, served in ninety gripping minutes.

Thanks to a sleek and hypnotic text by Frank McGuinness, who also wrote the *Doll's House* adaptation, and urgent, authoritative performances by a flawless ensemble that also includes Claire Bloom, Pat Carroll, Michael Cumpsty, Stephen Spinella, Daniel Oreskes and Marin Hinkle, Mr Leveaux's *Electra* is a family fight for any and every time and place. Designed by Johan Engels to exist in some fantastic limbo between the classical and contemporary worlds – the set encompasses both fragments of Greek columns and broken pieces of modern furniture – the production erases the 2,400-year gap in the blink of a blackout. Everything Sophocles' antique characters feel, from Electra's inflammatory grief to Clytemnestra's frozen ire, can stir as well, it seems, in latter-day hearts, even if today we shrink from expressing our darker impulses so boldly.

Something quite wonderful happens when ancient words are conveyed with such brio. A Broadway audience is galvanized. How strange, and cathartic, it can be to listen as characters vent their lusts and fears and rages without any hint of self-consciousness. Greek drama doesn't go in much for small talk; while the characters in modern drama live in a universe of subtext, shading the meaning of everything they say, Sophocles' figures have a refreshing lack of regard for obfuscation. "I want you to taste the bitterness of death" is how Orestes, superbly played by Mr Cumpsty, greets Aegisthus (the equally fine Daniel Oreskes), moments before slaughtering him.

Mr Leveaux's production was unveiled last year at the Donmar Warehouse in London and won Ms Wanamaker an Olivier Award. . . . After a brief run this fall at the McCarter Theater with its new American supporting cast, it arrived at the Barrymore for an eight-week run. Along the way, Mr Leveaux . . . has refined the climaxes sharper, improving the lighting effects and, it seems, helping the actors take bigger risks in coloring in the more schematic aspects of their characters' relationships. Electra's feelings for Orestes, for instance, are no more ambiguous. Upon his return from exile, she gives her brother a lingering kiss on the mouth. Seeing him again is a passionate relief for her; she gains strength in the revival of her homicidal hopes.

From its earliest incarnation, the power center of this production has been Ms Wanamaker and her shattering Electra, roaming Mr Leveaux's physically as well as psychically wrecked world in her murdered father's oversize coat. Her eyes puffy, her scalp dotted with red patches, as if she had been tearing her hair out in clumps, she is a figure of pitiless resolve, unable to purge her obliterating sorrow over the murder of her father. . . .

"Pain, pain, pain, pain," Ms Wanamaker declaims, the word shriveling in her throat like a dry cough, until it practically chokes her. The actress is endlessly inventive, but never strident or showy. In spite of her tragic countenance, it's a lyrical performance; the music in her raspy, octave-climbing speaking voice never stops. Neither does her agitation. Electra has lost everything in the loss of her father: power, position, control over her destiny – she is under a kind of house arrest – and her powerlessness is expressed in a restless pacing of the stage. This space offers no comfort, no consolation.

Such a forceful actress needs aggressive sparring partners, and in the terrifyingly grand Ms Bloom, she meets her match. Looking ravishing in a scarlet gown and voluminous red shawl, Ms Bloom's Clytemnestra is vainly, haughtily feminine. This woman dresses to kill. In her fiery exchanges with Ms Wanamaker, you get a vivid picture of a noblewoman enmeshed in her own desperate struggle to maintain her power. The portrayal unmasks Clytemnestra's maternal side as well; Ms Bloom has a splendidly manipulative moment in reminding Electra that it was Agamemnon's sacrifice of their daughter Iphigeneia that prompted her own murderous revenge.

The counterbalance to Ms Wanamaker's tumultuous encounters with Ms Bloom occurs in the more tender scenes with Ms Hinkle, playing her flexible sister, Chrysothemis. The impressive Ms Hinkle continues to grow in the role. Her stature is dictated by her softness. The actress has a delicate touch but stands her ground with Ms Wanamaker; her pleas for conciliation have the ring of sisterly concern as much as self-preservation. No less substantial is Mr Cumpsty's Greek statue of an Orestes. He embodies the heroic without ever seeming a stick figure. His reunion with Electra, masterminded by Stephen Spinella in his touching portrayal of Orestes's servant, is now the production's emotional centerpiece.

The performances work all the way down the line. Ms Carroll, in peasant garb, has found her footing as the play's navigator, Chorus of Mycenae, intelligently asserting herself as the conscience of the piece, choosing moments to egg Electra on or to advise a more cautious tack. Mr Oreskes, arriving late in the play and dressed in white linen, like a California businessman, lets us feel Aegisthus' sense of kingly prerogative at the precise moment that he realizes his life is about to end.

As befits the best of Greek tragedy, there's nothing frivolous in this production, and nothing overwrought. The brutal economy of the work comes to a stunning resolution in the play's perfect closing line enunciated by Ms Carroll. "The deed," she declares, "is done." A final moment, with the triumphant Ms Wanamaker poised on a damaged table. Over her face, she places a Greek mask. Lights out.

Somewhat less excited was Canby, yet he was deeply moved by what he had watched on the stage the night before. He had read the play, but before now not seen it performed.

Theatergoers who admired Diana Rigg's grand, actressy, haute-couture appearance in the Euripides *Medea*, which came to Broadway from London in 1994, are in for a shock when they see the *Electra* now at the Ethel Barrymore Theater. This production also has its quota of high-fashion, post-modern effects, but neither these, nor the occasional tin-eared line, can get in the way of the primal intensity of the Sophocles text. Played without an intermission, *Electra* runs only a little more than ninety minutes, while leaping the centuries with the speed of light-years.

Though you may come out of the theater quibbling about various aspects of the production (as I did), you may also be surprised to find that it haunts your consciousness for days afterward. Not just the fine, stern, unfancified performances by Zoë Wanamaker and Claire Bloom but the play itself. No matter that it is 2,400 years old or that its concerns seem arcane in our world. *Electra* remains an eerily fundamental theatrically dynamic work.

In Electra, daughter of the hero and king, Agamemnon, who was murdered by her mother, Clytemnestra, and her mother's lover, Aegisthus, we have a primitive, starkly realized Hamlet figure, one who has been stripped of all doubts and is committed to revenge. Also like Hamlet, Electra has become a trial to her family. Though years have passed since Agamemnon's murder, Electra continues to mourn him noisily and to harangue anyone who will listen with tales of the lovers' treachery. There is a curse on the House of Atreus.

No wonder Electra is not allowed off the premises of the family compound. She is a rabid, foul-tempered public spectacle: a tiny, eccentric wretch, hobbling around in her father's old British Army greatcoat, which dwarfs her and drags on the ground. The hair she hasn't yet pulled out of her head in paroxysms of grief stands up in lunatic tufts. . . .

Electra is a strong, aggressive woman, impatiently awaiting the return of her brother, Orestes, whom she sent away for safekeeping on the day of the murder. He was then a small boy. On this day, which is the time of the play, the now grown Orestes at last comes home. The rest of the tragedy can be played out as it must, the gods appeased and the cycle of violence ended.

Or so audiences in Athens (circa 418 BC–410 BC) were told by the Chorus at the end. Contemporary audiences don't have that reassurance. We have two choices: We can accept the play as we understand the Athenians saw it, which keeps the events at a polite distance; or we can see it in our own terms – violence breeding violence that breeds more violence, with no end of it in sight, all set in the interior landscape explored by Freud.

The gods are dead but, for us, the good doctor from Vienna marches on. For the time being, anyway.

Sophocles' *Electra* . . . seems to be a much more vital, more profoundly disturbing work than any of the *Medea* versions I have seen. . . .

Medea is much less complex in dramatic structure, being virtually one long monologue audited by the Chorus, the Nurse and others, and interrupted by the brief appearances of Jason, the husband, and Creon, the king. No wonder actresses love to play the role: there is scarcely anybody to upstage them. The actual dramatic confrontations are kept to a minimum. It is a great show of conflicted nobility and sacrifice: the woman pays, and dearly.

Euripides is considered to have brought a degree of humanity to Greek drama lacking in the work of Sophocles, his contemporary. Yet the *Electra* of Sophocles appears to be a far more theatrical work.

Consider Electra's confrontation with her mother when Clytemnestra, cool and in complete control of herself, points out the perfectly reasonable motive for the murder of Agamemnon. Weak man that he was, she says, he had sacrificed Iphigeneia, her daughter, and Electra's sister, to insure fair winds to Troy. She could never forgive him for that. Why didn't Menelaus, Agamemnon's brother and the husband of the purloined Helen, sacrifice one of his children?

Nonsense, Electra says in effect. The gods demanded the sacrifice after Agamemnon shot a deer while hunting in a sacred grove. Then she backtracks a bit. Even if the story about the deer is not true, Iphigeneia's sacrifice, which made possible the successful Trojan campaign, was hardly worth the backstairs murder planned and executed by Clytemnestra and her lover.

The two women are equals in furious family combat, as well as in the performances by Zoë Wanamaker as Electra and Claire Bloom as her mother.

The exiled brother, long away, finally returns. The despairing Electra, after being told that he is dead, finds that he is alive.

Their reunion is sweet but necessarily brief; Orestes, attended by his faithful old servant (Stephen Spinella) and a friend Pylades (Ivan Stamenov), must dispatch Clytemnestra before the return of Aegisthus (Daniel Oreskes). When Orestes emerges from the house, having killed their mother, Electra in her joy licks his blood-splattered arm. Expiation of this kind is intoxicating. The murder of Aegisthus is something of an anti-climax.

Canby liked most of the cast but considered the Orestes physically awkward and too young in view of the twenty years he has been far off, dispossessed of his rights. McGuinness's adaptation impressed Canby as "mostly clean and efficient", but to be faulted for occasional grating anachronisms in the dialogue. To get used to Johan Engels's stripped-down set took Canby a while, but ultimately it worked well, as did the sundry modern costumes.

After meeting with the actress, Dinitia Smith described her as "tiny with an upturned nose, glinty eyes". She was light of step and given to darting gestures. On stage, with a coat that was too big for her, she looked "like an adult whose soul has somehow been arrested in childhood. Because she can neither avenge the murder of her father, Agamemnon, nor forgive her mother, Clytemnestra, Electra remains suspended between childhood and womanhood. 'I'm a childless woman who is melting away,' Electra says." To Miss Smith, Wanamaker encapsulated her conception of the role. "She's a meteoric soul. She's a terrorist." Yet there were many other sides to the character drawn by Sophocles and re-created by this player. Smith notes that the actress made her initial entrance "like a fist", intoning her opening speech: "Divine light, sweet air, again hear my pain," a lyrical invocation, exposing a divided spirit.

Patches of Wanamaker's head were shaved and reddened to look as though handfuls of her hair had been pulled by the bloody roots during her paroxysms of obsessive grief and fury. "I want her to look horrible, like hell." She wears a coat that is too large for her – a perpetual reminder, a worn Army garment that was her father's – to emphasize her degradation, but also to serve as a visual symbol of their embracing attachment to each other, as if his arms were still about her. This also imparted a stark contrast to the attire of the imperious Clytemnestra, "Claire Bloom in a filmy, low-necked dress – Her mother who's abused her. She hates her, but she's her mother."

Since Electra is essentially a passive figure as "events swirl about her, the actress portraying her must transform suffering into action", not easy to do. "I think the deepest gesture in her is not violence but love. The most important question is not why she must avenge her father's death but what makes the grief so unbearable in the first place." Yet what caused Agamemnon to be so dear to her, and to remain so, is never made clear, since he does not appear in the play. The explanation of this crippling bond must be implied.

As for the play, Wanamaker said, "I knew America would love it." She claimed not to be surprised by its success in New York. Asked about the Laurence Olivier award given to her in London for her dynamic yet artfully shaded portrayal of Electra, she replied that it was "the accumulation of twenty-five years of training . . . during which she had played alongside more great actresses – Jane Lapotaire, Judi Dench – than any other actor on the British stage".

Before she metamorphosed into a troubled member of the House of Atreus, Wanamaker had not been interested in the Greek tragedies; she had seen them performed by masked players and had been "shut off" from them, made to feel "intellectually inferior". Quite the opposite had been Claire Bloom's response to the plays; from age fourteen or fifteen, in drama school, she had always been profoundly involved by their conflicts. This was her fourth participation in a Periclean classic. But until now she had been frustrated by stilted translations, a flaw that McGuinness had overcome for her. "This one carries you," she said to Toby Zinman. "It has a sculptural, rocklike, elemental feeling." Wanamaker paid much the same tribute to the revised text, when questioned by Zinman. "This to me was a new day. Frank's adaptation is pared down to its very wishbone; it's clean as a whistle, it's English that I can understand – sometimes slightly crass, sometimes slightly raw, sometimes strange to the ear, but it is accessible to me." During rehearsals, she had behaved much as had JoAnne Akalaitis while readying *The Iphigeneia Cycle*: to her surprise, she could not stop weeping. "I didn't realize there was so much in me, so much grief." This inner turbulence had continued while she was onstage. Her parents had been always in her thoughts; her performance was a "love poem" to them. Her father was in "exile" in England; he had gone there because he had been blacklisted during the McCarthy furore for his political activities in America. She thought that Electra spoke for all children whose parents suffered "through war or painful death of some kind".

In her conversation with Zinman, Claire Bloom, who had endured several unhappy marriages – as candidly set forth in her recently published memoir, *Leaving the Doll's House* – referred wryly to her characterization of Clytemnestra. "She powerfully takes her life and fate into her hands. I don't say that chopping your husband up is perhaps the best solution, but sometimes I wonder."

David Leveaux also consented to talk to Zinman. He regularly directed works at the Royal Shakespeare Company and the National Theatre. Since 1993 he had acquired another position, having been appointed artistic director of Theatre Project in Japan, where he had put on plays by Ibsen and Mishima. On a previous visit to New York he had won a Tony for his impassioned staging of the season's best revival, Eugene O'Neill's long-overlooked *Anna Christie* (1993). His lead actors were English.

Leveaux saw sexual desire – illicit, warped, repressed – as a dominant theme in *Electra*. That was why, to stress the erotic aspect of the tragedy, he had Clytemnestra first enter in a "glamorous red cocktail dress" that stamps her as a brazen seductress, or at least to make her seem to be one in the eyes of her daughter. Electra believes that her mother killed Agamemnon because she was infatuated with Aegisthus, a charge that Clytemnestra denies. Electra is bedraggled in appearance, starkly unlike Clytemnestra. The chorus consists of women "in peasant head scarves and mourning black", a community who now make up Electra's environment. Leveaux intended that the setting – a collapsed, tilted white marble column, a dirt floor, a few "broken, once elegant chairs" – should represent a lost splendour, the shattered aftermath of a bombing raid. Like so many other directors of the Greek tragedies already cited, he was convinced that they were strikingly topical, closely relevant to the contemporary world situation. Though the last two decades of the twentieth century and the millennium were considered to be peaceful, really there were small wars far and wide – in Northern Ireland, in Lebanon, in the Balkans, in Afghanistan, throughout Africa – from Algeria and the Sudan to Somalia, Angola, Congo, Rwanda – at a far outpost of Russia, on the islands of East Timor and Sri Lanka. Tribal feuds, ethnic cleansing, riotous slaughter accompanying fighting between Christians and Muslims, Jews and Arabs, Hindus and Sikhs. No, this was not peace. Leveaux recited for Zinman the words of Aegisthus, who beholds the corpse of the slain Clytemnestra and knows he is soon to die: "Shall there be killing after killing forever?" Leveaux, a pacifist, hoped that *Electra* would send a message. "Maybe there is a feeling that these plays actually address in an absolutely direct and compressed and necessary way the big issues we are facing now. It may be that we have less patience for moral nuance. And that we are hungry for something more substantial."

Leveaux revealed to Matt Wolf that this *Electra* had first been put on by him in Japan (1995) – an experiment, with the help of an interpreter. Sato Orie was her mother's bitter enemy there. In England he had perceived in Wanamaker a fury that could be unleashed that was "both adult in its expressiveness and childlike in its primal, unfettered force". As summarized by Wolf, the director believed that Ms Wanamaker's qualities "as a child-woman – enhanced by that notable pug nose and her sad, wounded gaze – had emerged even more essentially in New York. . . . 'It's this almost childlike presence in Zoë which opened up the possibility of Electra to me. You must see someone who in a sense has remained in the captivity of childhood because that's literally what Electra is: she has arrived in womanhood without having mediated that. . . . She suffers like a child; that's what makes her dangerous.'"

The "limited engagement" of *Electra* was twice extended, and it ended its run with a profit of $100,000, an unheard-of sum for the revival of a Greek tragedy. Frank McGuinness doubtless shared in the royalties, but naturally Sophocles got none – still, he might have had cause to be grateful.

To his fellow countrymen the twentieth-century Greek composer Mikis Theodorakis has been something of a "cultural icon", best known for his popular songs, many of them tinctured with a folk quality, and for his haunting scores, enhancing the widely distributed and admired films *Zorba the Greek*, *Z* and *Serpico*. These spread his reputation far beyond the borders of his native land, not only throughout Europe but also in America. Further adding lustre to his image is his personal history as a patriot who courageously resisted the dictatorship that ruled Greece during two-thirds of a harsh decade, a stand which earned him a nomination for a Nobel Peace Prize, though he did not come out a winner. What is less appreciated abroad, however, is that he is classically trained – he was a student of Messiaen's in Paris – and that his subsequent output comprises a lengthy roster of choral works, symphonies, ballets – one based on *Antigone* – and operas. For a time he put aside these serious endeavours, feeling that the world of classical music had become too limited, a conviction that inspired him to try to combine "high and low art", prompting his folkloric songs, written to be accompanied by the bouzouki and gaining very wide acceptance. In the 1980s he chose the classical realm again. Among his strivings in this later period have been three operas, all having as their subject-matter the stirring Greek tragedies.

The middle piece of this trilogy is an *Elektra* (1955), signalling that Theodorakis did not fear competition with the masterly Richard Strauss. The first performance of this work took place in Luxembourg (1995) when its begetter was about seventy. It was heard in New York in a concert version at Carnegie Hall (2000), the orchestra under the baton of Peter Tiboris. This event was sponsored by MidAmerica Productions, in collaboration with the American Hellenic Educational Progressive Association and other local Greek-American organizations eager to promote an interest in their countrymen's contemporary artistic achievements. The forces brought together were fully adequate: the Manhattan Philharmonic, the Nyack College Chorale and the Russian Chamber Chorus of New York, together with masked dancers borrowed from the Aquila Theatre Company.

The New York critics were disappointed. Leighton Kerner wrote in *Opera News*:

> The composer's other achievements notwithstanding, this enterprise was not a success. It should have been, considering the opera's source, which is nothing less than the *Electra* of Sophocles, the structure of which Spyros A. Evangelatos's libretto (as translated by Gail Holst-Warhaft, with projected titles by Cori Ellison) follows reasonably well. I fondly remember a New York performance of the play by the touring Greek National Theatre, when the tragedy ran its course with almost painful swiftness, and the choral chanting (with music by famed conductor Dimitri Mitropoulos) grew in intensity right to the final curtain. Nothing like that happens in Theodorakis's opera. Why? One reason is the old story of how much slower song is compared with speech. Not enough of Sophocles was cut, so what is a taut, 100-minute spoken drama becomes a flagging, nearly three-hour opera. Yes, powerfully compelling music might have sustained those three hours, but, on the evidence of his *Elektra*, Theodorakis is not a powerfully compelling opera composer. He can move the listener for a few moments when the hero-

ine, sister Chrysothemis, or mother Clytemnestra (even she!), expresses her emotions with music derived from touching examples of folksong. And he can heat up a scene superficially with a burst of polyrhythmic percussion. Toward the gory conclusion, the composer sets up a more sustained dithyrambic propulsion, but it seems merely too late to help, because so much dully harmonized and muddily orchestrated flab has preceded it.

Conductor Peter Tiboris, who organized the US première, may have contributed to the textural mud; although his Manhattan Philharmonic has a lot of fine musicians in its ranks, he didn't seem very interested in varying the prevailingly loud dynamics or refining timbres. His Electra was Reveka Evangelia Mavrovitis, a sometime Met mezzo who displayed a more vivid dramatic and vocal personality than could be expected from a perusal of the score. The other soloists were imported mostly from the Greek National Opera. Ioanna Firti's Clytemnestra (another mezzo, but misidentified in the program as a contralto) boasted an attractive, if rather slender sound. Soprano Medea Iassonidi's Chrysothemis sang prettily whenever Tiboris didn't drown her out, which was often. Baritone Tassis Christoyannis's Orestes, tenor Yannis Christopoulos's Aegisthus and tenor Angelo Simos's Pylades were acceptable. Bass Pavlos Maropoulos's Tutor definitely was not.

Kerner also found fault with how the dancers were used, "scrunched ineffectively between the orchestra and the singers".

Allan Kozinn, of the *New York Times*, was quite as unkind, his review appearing under the rude headline "Oracular and Talky, an 'Elektra' by a Greek". He spelled out his objections:

The story, based on the Sophocles version, is familiar from the more venerable Strauss opera, although here Orestes makes short work of slaughtering Clytemnestra and Aegisthus, to the general celebration of the Mycenaeans. Electra does not have an ecstatic dance and does not die, and Orestes is not tormented by the Furies.

A more telling musical difference between Strauss's *Elektra* and Mr Theodorakis's opera, though, is that where Strauss used the story as a canvas on which to paint a thoroughly Straussian opera, Mr Theodorakis's score seeks to evoke the spirit of Greek antiquity – or at least a cinematic version of that spirit. The vocal writing is generally slow and stately, with melodies that convey the character of grand pronouncements. The orchestration is large and lush, with percussion writing that often gives the music a ritualistic solemnity. And a chorus comments on what has been said, or on what the character who has just finished singing actually feels, adding a slightly oracular touch to the proceedings.

All told, this talky opera is a succession of monumental gestures: a listener was tempted to envision the action being performed in slow motion by eyeless bronze statues.

At distant removes, the play *Electra* was one of three tragedies scheduled for enactment during the summer of 2000 at Epidaurus: while the Strauss–Hofmannsthal musical version was listed for staging by the Santa Fe Opera Company in New Mexico (also in 2000) and by the Berlin State Opera in Sydney, Australia (again 2000), where it was a special feature of that city's three-week annual festival, an affair of lengthy, exuberant parades, free concerts and exhibitions. Offering what was characterized as a "high-energy" interpretation, the company from Berlin drew a sell-out audience, filling the modern opera house at premium ticket prices. Here a dramatic work written in archaic Greek, translated and sung in German, excited two thousand English-speaking listeners.

His agonized cry at discovering the horrible truth – an utterance unforgettable to those who heard it – made Laurence Olivier's Oedipus (1945) the one against which to be measured. Not many of his fellow actors in England and America were willing to risk it. Nor at any time soon afterwards were producers willing to finance productions of this most effective of tragedies. As has been remarked, a broad share of the public knew the grave personal history of Oedipus – Sigmund Freud's much talked-about theory of deep-rooted incestuous feelings accounted for that – but not all were eager to see a drama enacting the immortal legend. It resonates with echoes of the most forbidden of all sexual desires and arrives at a climax whereat the once proud and arrogant hero, having gouged out his eyes, staggers and gropes on to the stage, blood streaming from the empty sockets. Now he faces rejection and exile, his future destined to be only beggary and blind wandering. No, it is not an "entertainment" to which one is likely to take the children. (True, *Electra*, concerned with matricide, is not ideal fare for the young either.) Since *Oedipus* is short, the Old Vic had shrewdly coupled it with a prankish eighteenth-century afterpiece, Sheridan's satirical *The Critic*, in which Olivier portrayed the foppish Mr Puff, a comic character, allowing the actor to change his aspect altogether and exhibit his dazzling virtuosity.

Still, the role of Oedipus is refulgent if chilly. As has been seen, at cautious intervals some players did enter the lists, but not head-on. The most conspicuous was James Mason, under the aegis of Tyrone Guthrie (1954), but that was after a lapse of nine years and at Stratford in Canada, far from London and New York and from the most influential critics, though some did drop by. Because of many film appearances, Mason was fully as well known as Olivier and hardly lacking self-confidence.

At twenty-seven in 1968, the Canadian actor Christopher Plummer was not considered to be a serious rival to either of his two immediate predecessors, though his talents seemed to assure him a bright career. When Heath and Stattel and others came along in the 1970s, twenty-five years had already passed. Language barriers also muted comparisons: in Budapest, of course, the Oedipus, directed by Marton, spoke Magyar. Minotis, in Athens and on tours about Europe and the United States, used modern Greek, and Pasolini's crushed hero lamented in Italian – none had to fear matching Olivier's long-ago, commanding performance. (He was still active on stage and in films but essayed no other Greek tragedies.) By the late 1980s and 1990s, a half-century on, almost all who had experienced the *Oedipus* as conceived by the Old Vic and Olivier were gone (and the excelling Olivier, too); a wholly new generation of theatregoers and critics filled the stalls – orchestra seats – and lesser-priced balconies.

Even during the decades when stagings of Sophocles' great drama were sparse, the Oedipus story was being told in frequently repeated offerings of Igor Stravinsky's opera-cantata and Martha Graham's *Night Journey*; they became favourites on programmes by chamber orchestras and by Graham's own modern-dance company, which travelled widely. The Medieval Church Latin libretto for Stravinsky's piece, by Jean Cocteau, calls for a narrator speaking the local language, a part that was eventually taken by Cocteau's protégé, the "dashingly handsome" Jean Marais, who also served as director. In France, as well, Gide's translation of *Oedipus* and Cocteau's chic *The Infernal Machine* – Oedipus' confrontation with the Sphinx – were available for revivals at intervals.

To some degree – hard to determine – the Oedipus myth had a shadowy life in Nigeria due to *The Gods Are Not to Blame* (1969) by Ola Rotimi (b. 1938). This play was a variation on the undying legend, instilled with folkloric elements and indigenous tribal values; though in English. Rotimi had been educated abroad, his studies leading to his becoming a Master of Fine Arts at Yale (1965). An early work, *To Stir the God of Iron*, was produced at Boston University (1963), and a second offering, *Our Husband Has Gone Mad Again* (1965), was cited as "major Yale play of the year" during the same term in which he achieved his advanced rank. Granted a research fellowship at the University of Ife, he returned in 1966 to Nigeria, where *The Gods Are Not to Blame* had its first staging at the On-Olokun Centre. It was so successful that it has had many repetitions in Ife and throughout the country; it was also seen at the Drum Arts Centre in London in 1977, on that occasion directed by Rotimi himself. It has been taken up by the Yoruba travelling theatre companies that carry dramas to people everywhere in Nigeria. Ironically, Rotimi has confessed that as a consequence of having been out of touch with his native land so long during his formative years, the result for him has been "a certain disassociation from his Nigerian background and lack of fluency in the vernacular".

Beginning in 1977, he has held a post as head of the Creative Arts Center and art director at the University of Port Harcourt. Two of his subsequent scripts, *Kurunmi* (1969) and *Ovonramwen Nogbais* (1971), have historical subjects, dealing on an epic scale with past wars, the Ijaiye conflict and the hostilities that destroyed the kingdom of Benin. A later work, *If,* is more topical, depicting life in a building housing many families and their struggle to survive in the harsh conditions prevailing in the Nigeria of the day.

Rotimi acknowledges the influence of Shakespeare and O'Neill, with whose works he became acquainted in his boyhood owing to his family's taking pleasure in amateur productions. A stronger sway over him was exerted by John Pepper Clark and Wole Soyinka, the latter Nigeria's Nobel Prize winner, an openly defiant foe of the military dictatorship. George Axworthy (the source here) summarizes: "Rotimi's style is characteristically bold, theatrical, and emotional. Some critics accuse him of melodramatic triteness and superficiality on political and cultural matters. But no one challenges his ability to hold and move an audience or denies the great contribution he has made to the Nigerian theatre through his robust productions and extensive touring. He alone of the Nigerian dramatists writing in English has achieved the kind of rapport with Nigerian audiences enjoyed by the vernacular touring companies."

A recording of the Stravinsky *Oedipus Rex*, conducted by the composer himself and performed by the Cologne Radio Symphony and Chorus, was released in 1976. An earlier version led by Stravinsky existed, but this reissue was deemed technically far superior in nearly all respects; besides, who could question the authenticity of the interpretation? The appearance of this pressing allowed John Rockwell of the *New York Times* to discuss this unusual, indeed unique, music drama.

> Stravinsky's brief but monumental opera-oratorio is one of his most moving works. Composed in 1926 and 1927, it has never really entered into the international operatic repertory. Aside from its awkward length, it has its own intense static seriousness to blame. And yet this is a piece that for all its epic distancing and more deliberately stylized ritual can be powerfully affecting indeed, almost as if a more conventional rhetoric would cheapen the intensity of the tragedy.
>
> . . . Stravinsky's music may be outwardly in his frozen, stark, neoclassical vein. But there is a good deal of contained Russian expression here, too, and the balance between the heat of the drama and of the composer's temperament, and the coolness of the form makes this a masterpiece.
>
> Chief among its many virtues is Cocteau's unsurpassed French narration. In live performances, English may be the preferred language in the English-speaking world, but not on records, and in any

case both the English versions in print sound hopelessly fustian next to Cocteau's dry passion. The soloists are all excellent, from Peter Pears's anguished Oedipus to Heinz Rehfuss's vigorous Creon and Messenger to a surprisingly fresh-voiced Martha Mödl's eloquent Jocasta. The Cologne forces sound adept, the composer is an authoritative conductor and the mono-only sound is perfectly satisfactory.

Another treatment of *Oedipus Rex* had also been just reissued and was noticed by Rockwell:

Leonard Bernstein's recording was first released in 1973 as part of his Norton Lectures package; this is the first time it has been made available on a single disk. It is in modern sound, of course, the soloists are very good, particularly Tatiana Troyanos, and Mr Bernstein captures the spirit of Stravinsky's own conducting without slavishly subsuming his own personality. But in so doing he blurs the edges a bit, and in any event the Harvard Glee Club isn't the match of a professional chorus.

A second opportunity for John Rockwell to discourse on this piece – a fully live staged enactment – came about in 1982; as he reported them, the circumstances were somewhat confounding. The event took place in Lenox, Massachusetts, the site of Tanglewood, where are held the Boston Symphony's annual summer outdoor performances. Wrote Rockwell:

In Jean Cocteau's version of Sophocles's *Oedipus Rex* that serves as the text for Stravinsky's opera-oratorio, "Supernatural powers that watch us from a world beyond death" set "a trap" for Oedipus from "the moment of his birth."

These same powers might have seemed to have similarly cursed the Boston Symphony's centennial-season production of the work. Originally announced for April in Boston and New York, the production was to have been staged by Peter Sellars, the *enfant terrible* of Boston opera and theater direction, with Vanessa Redgrave as the narrator. But Miss Redgrave's support of the Palestine Liber ation Organization led to the cancellation of her appearance. That prompted Mr Sellars to withdraw, and the orchestra abandoned the whole program, which was also to have included Stravinsky's *Symphony of Psalms*, substituting Berlioz's Requiem.

Eventually it was decided to resurrect the Stravinsky bill for one performance only at Tanglewood, Friday night. This is the centennial year of Stravinsky's birth as well, after all, and the Boston Symphony had commissioned the *Symphony of Psalms* and presented the American premières of both works.

Sam Wanamaker, the American actor and director, agreed to replace Miss Redgrave and Mr

Sellars. But then Jessye Norman, scheduled for Jocasta, had to withdraw because of a back injury, and last Tuesday Kenneth Riegel, the Oedipus, nearly suffered a back injury of his own when he fell off the stage during a rehearsal.

After all this, the show went on, and everything turned out pretty well. Mr Wanamaker's narration was dry and matter of fact – preferable any time to mannered, actorish rhetoric – and his dramatic conception, while it certainly lacked whatever eccentric brilliance Mr Sellars might have brought to it, was at least functional.

Diaghilev's original staging emphasized the work's monumental formality by clothing the principals in evening dress, a device echoed at the Metropolitan Opera last season. The exigencies of the Tanglewood Shed, with the orchestra in black but still on stage and the dramatic action on platforms at the rear, imposed its own formality.

The soloists were dressed in full, vaguely Mediterranean costumes by Sarah G. Conly, and the action was focused on a raised stage in the center; it and the three stone portals and the other props, as well as the lighting, were designed by John Michael Deegan. The central stage was flanked by the chorus, in two-sided shawls that were deployed in various ways.

The acting was mostly stiff and restrained, but lapsed a bit too readily into melodrama at the climaxes, with the Messenger scurrying about in grief and Oedipus lurching off stage with a shiny red plastic bib to depict his bleeding eye sockets.

More effective were the Expressionistic choral movements by Pearl Lang, full of massed swaying and arm extensions that recalled Fritz Lang's *Metropolis*.

Seji Ozawa's musical conception suggested, at its worst, some asymmetrical Mendelssohn oratorio, disconcertingly sweet and lyrical for a score normally heard as great, jagged blocks of sound.

But as it progressed, Mr Ozawa's interpretation made its own, if still wrong-headed, kind of sense. The focus was on the singing – both the lyricism of the vocal lines and the opportunities for vocal acting. The orchestra responded well, and the singing was mostly first-rate.

Mr Riegel was especially convincing, dry but sensitive and impassioned, with a beautifully pure rendition of his final *Lux facta est*.

John Cheek made a sonorous Creon, and Glenda Maurice was probably better suited as a mezzo to the tessitura than the soprano Miss Norman would have been. Aage Haugland made a firm Tiresias, and Joseph McKee and John Gilmore handled the Messenger and Shepherd with unusual vocal allure, although Mr McKee sharped persistently at his repeated proclamatory line of "Divum Jocastae caput mortuum."

The Stravinsky opera-cantata reached Japan, the when, where, and how eluding present knowledge.

A rhymed-verse play, *The Darker Face of the Earth* (1995), a variation of the Oedipus theme, came from the pen – or word processor – of Rita Dove, while she was filling a two-year term as Poet Laureate of the United States. She chose to have it set on a pre-Civil War Southern plantation. A staged reading took place at the Unterberg Poetry Center, the participants directed by Derek Walcott, the Nobel Prize-winning poet. The leading role was assigned to Barbara Feldon. Ms Dove, her term as Laureate having expired, joined the cast. It was her stage debut. She explained to Nadine Brozan of the *New York Times*: "I had to shorten the play for this reading, and I decided to write in an ancient version of my own real role, that of poet troubadour. I'm not exactly the narrator but an all-seeing chorus who comments on the action." She added: "Doing this is exciting. For poetry you are in a room by yourself. This involves other people and other voices. I love the transformative nature of the way things change when you hear someone else's voice." The presentation was not reviewed.

Dissatisfied with his highly personal exploration of the Oedipus tale – with musical instruments of his own invention, as described on earlier pages – Harry Partch revised his work; after that, still not satisfied, he effected yet another re-editing of the score and text. This third and "final" version was performed in concert format at the Metropolitan Museum (1997) by Newband, a group of which Dean Drummond and Stefan Starin were co-directors. Also involved were the Purchase Contemporary Players; the staging was entrusted to Tom Horgan, well established in the realm of the avant-garde. As had happened before, not much attention was paid to Partch's very original creative output. But Paul Griffiths – an appreciative *New York Times* music critic as well as himself a librettist – had this to say:

> Harry Partch's vision of total musical theater surely did not include singer-actors reading from the book and decorous wafts of ritual. He wanted vividness. He wanted intoxication. His one-man dispute with Western culture was rooted in a dismissal of anything learned or abstract. He looked to the musical cultures of ancient China and Greece, in which sound, display, word and gesture were welded and magically potent. He spoke of the "emotional saturation, or transcendence, that it is the particular province of dramatic music to achieve." He was a hobo Antonin Artaud.
>
> But if Thursday night's performance of his *Oedipus* failed to live up to his ideas, the faults were at least as much in the piece as in the mildness and rehearsal quality of the theatrical presentation at the Metropolitan Museum. Quite simply, there isn't much music in this score. Partch insisted on one

thing at a time (this was another quarrel he had with the Western musical tradition) and he largely avoided having his singer-actors accompanied by instrumental music of any great elaboration.

Much of his *Oedipus* consists of declamation, whether spoken or chanted, with chimes, stationary backgrounds and cadences. Only toward the end, when we come to Jocasta's suicide and Oedipus's self-blinding, does the array of specially built instruments begin to wake up. At this point on Thursday one could begin to feel the heartbeat Partch was looking for, as an embracing percussion ostinato was joined by a shrill, trilling clarinet in mounting exhilaration.

Partch was obliged to make his own instruments because he needed a new tuning system, more on course with natural vibration. But he turned necessity into opportunity and created things as beautiful as their names: cloud chamber bowls, made from Pyrex carboys, or marimba eroica, with huge wooden slabs and resonators. He wanted his shows to look good, with his instruments set around the stage, though unfortunately in the cramped space at the museum they all had to be bunched together.

Still, opportunities to experience the Partch instrumentarium are rare, and it was excellent to be hearing live the authentic sonorities of the composer's aged recording: the reed-organ wheezes, the deep-bass thumps, the arpeggios from the zitherlike harmonic canon that sound like cast jewels. Dean Drummond, whose ensemble, Newband, has the care of the Partch instruments, was conducting a group of professional and student musicians.

Among the vocal performers, Joe Garcia commandingly brought before us an Oedipus speaking out of a snarl of contempt. Gregory Sims, a vital actor, made Creon's part passionately important, and Robert Osborne, as Tiresias, was able to convey the special qualities of Partchian incantation, which often seems to imitate the sick drone of someone on illicit substances.

The Classics Stage Company, which – as its name connotes – has devoted itself to reviving great plays from the past, yielded its premises to the Blue Light Theater for a more up-to-date *Oedipus* (1998) written and directed by Dare Clubb. Both Ben Brantley and his colleague Vincent Canby were interested and occupied their designated down-front seats. Brantley was only half won over by the evening's revelations. He began his critique by quoting a line from the stage: "You simpleton! You missed the point." After which came Brantley's own sentences:

That's telling him. The man at whom these words are yelled, in the latest play from the Blue Light Theater Company, is named Oedipus, and no one, of course, is more famous for missing the point until it's way too late to do anything about it.

Misreading auguries, refusing to look for answers inside himself, delegating blame like the paranoid head of a Fortune 500 company: the unfortunate habits that characterized Sophocles' mother-loving monarch are to some degree shared by the title character of Dare Clubb's . . . serio-comic meditation on destiny and its discontents.

But this younger, callower variation on the man whose name has been immortalized as a Freudian complex gets things wrong in ways that would make his classical prototype blush. Unlike the Sophocles character, who worked overtime to escape his predicted fate, this Oedipus is so eager to embrace his that he rushes to commit crimes that could be classified under the rubric "Sorry, wrong mother." Yes, the poor doofus kills the wrong man and beds the wrong woman: they're his adoptive parents, not his biological ones.

There's a certain collegiate glee in this antic scrambling of mythic literature, and the company of actors in *Oedipus*, which features the seriously talented movie stars Frances McDormand and Billy Crudup and is directed by Mr Clubb, brings undeniable zest to the interpretation of it. But don't go to the Classic Stage Company, where the work is being performed, expecting just fractured theogony tales. Mr Clubb's play is as earnest as it is irreverent.

Oedipus's road to self-knowledge has never been so long and winding, an itinerary that takes more than four hours and includes many detours through a world that is bleak, brutal and uncontrollably talky. In tone and structure, the play aspires more to Voltaire than to Sophocles. Indeed, Mr Crudup's Oedipus is first cousin to Candide: innocent, literal-minded and disastrously harnessed to a philosophy that the world around him keeps refuting. Or, as one character says late in the third and final act: "The gods don't frighten me. Men frighten me. Men with concepts."

Actually, another character says much the same thing in the first act. Despite its narrative sprawl, *Oedipus* is essentially a one-idea play, a series of riffs on a single moralizing theme. Mr Clubb creates a lineup of terminally self-involved creatures, out of touch with natural human feelings and paralyzed by a mindless devotion to theology and ideology.

They range from Oedipus's adoptive mother, Merope (Ms McDormand), whose more than maternal emotions inspire her to Byzantine Phaedra-like speeches of self-disgust, to a manic-depressive woodsman (Jon De Vries), eternally brooding over an oracle's pronouncement that he has no fate of his own. The play's central metaphor for all this circular, sterile thought is found in a scene in which the wandering Oedipus and his best friend, Teiresias (Jeffrey Donovan), find only saltwater to quench their thirst but drink it anyway.

Mr Clubb has come up with some appealingly goofy, deadpan jokes that play off the work's tragic antecedents. ("We'll suffer for this, probably," says Merope, after making love to young Oedipus, "but so what?") The script also reaches dangerously for real poetry, to an eloquence that tries to rival classical eloquence even as it parodies it, a little in the manner of T.S. Eliot, whose *Prufrock* poem is alluded to here. So we get high-flown lines like "Even the afternoon silences in your light-filled rooms have the shape of music," and "If there's no single truth, only a million versions of the truth, then what is beauty?" Now imagine lines like this multiplied to fill four hours.

The actors have been directed to pace the stage as they voice their characters' convoluted thoughts, which may be symbolically appropriate but is wearying to watch. There are some isolated, ingeniously staged touches, as when two anonymous figures in raincoats point out a raving madman with voyeuristic hisses and when a troop of bloodthirsty mercenary soldiers emerges from beneath the stage, but the production needs many more.

It is daunting to imagine what sitting through *Oedipus* would be like without the exceptional cast with which Mr Clubb has been blessed. Ms McDormand, the Oscar-winning star of *Fargo*, brings a hypnotic intensity to Merope, even if the monologues finally get the better of her, and her brief, incisive appearance as the riddling Sphinx, in the show's wittiest scene, is delicious. And while passive, Candide-like figures are seldom rewarding to actors, Mr Crudup, the fine-featured star of the movie *Without Limits*, winningly walks the line between spoof and solemnity, finding astonishingly varied line readings in his one-note character.

All the actors, including such gifted young New York stage regulars as Camilia Sanes, Johanna Day and Alan Tudyk, give off a charming air of being glad to be doing what they're doing here, shifting through multiple roles and giving diverse life to an elaborate story. They certainly provide the best argument for staying awake during this epic-length *Oedipus*. They even, from time to time, make you forget that although their characters cover many miles, the play in which they appear remains firmly lodged in one place.

Canby was in a thoroughly bad mood:

A nonstarter is Dare Clubb's *Oedipus*, a deconstructed adaptation of the Oedipus saga, which takes four hours to work wan, anachronistic variations on the story we mainly know from Sophocles' *Oedipus Rex* and *Oedipus at Colonus*. Presented by the usually astute Blue Light Theater Company, the exhausting, often ineptly croaked production is at the CSC Theater, staged by the author with unwarranted love and admiration.

Mr Clubb's main conceit is that Oedipus (Billy Crudup) goes to the oracle at Delphi as a young man, still living in Corinth with his (unknown to him) foster parents, King Polybus and Queen Merope. Told that his fate is to murder his father and marry his mother, the impressionable teenager, eager to honor the gods, rushes home and slays Polybus, only to learn that he, Oedipus, is a foundling. The poor kid has to start all over.

This much could be a rather funny revue sketch, suitable for presentation at year-end faculty revels. It is, unfortunately, no more than the first hour of Mr Clubb's *Oedipus*, which unravels like a slow-motion *Odyssey* as Oedipus tries to go home again to the natural parents he doesn't remember. Adventures of mounting inconsequence accumulate and, by the end of the fourth hour, confusion reigns, leaving the audience more exhausted than even the actors.

Mr Clubb is no wordsmith, or maybe he is and that's the problem. Writing in a poetic vein, he produces intentionally overstuffed lines that sound as if they had been decorated by Laura Ashley. Put in a reference to a babbling brook here, hang a simile associating something to a starry night there. His blunt anachronisms are even sillier.

There is his peculiar fondness for the word copulate, as something done by kings, queens and common people. The word stands out, for a purpose maybe, but without point in dialogue that otherwise makes free use of other contemporary vulgarisms. You might think he was writing about meerkats.

The cast also includes the Oscar-winner Frances McDormand, who plays both Merope and the Sphinx to no great advantage. Like everyone else in the cast, she spends much of the time rolling around on the stage floor or walking on her knees, like José Ferrer in *Moulin Rouge*.

The play ends with a crucifixion. If, like me, you had seen *Corpus Christi* the night before, that's at least one crucifixion too many in a single week.

(*Moulin Rouge* is a reference to a film about Henri-Marie Toulouse-Lautrec. *Corpus Christi* was a controversial play by Terrence McNally.)

In London, at the Barbican theatre complex, the Royal Shakespeare Company added *The Thebans* (1992) to the *ex post facto* improvised trilogy by Sophocles about Oedipus and his quarrelsome family. During previews, patrons could buy tickets for a single play rather than having to attend all three: *Oedipus Rex, Oedipus at Colonus, Antigone.* The man from the *Guardian* declared it: "Greek tragedy at its most compelling . . . music, movement and speech are deftly integrated." The members of the chorus were masked and clad in ankle-length, flowing white gowns, affording them ease in carrying out the director's choreography, though not all had the requisite grace.

For the salient year 2000, the theatre at Epidaurus – which is much more than a mere two millennia old – signalled the calendrical change with programmes including Euripides' *Herakles* and Sophocles' *Ajax* and *Oedipus Rex.*

From the UK, also in the year 2000, the Aquila Theatre Company brought its *Oedipus the King* to the new and resplendent Performing Arts Center in Newark, New Jersey, as well as to Lincoln Center in New York City. The small troupe headed by Peter Meineck – mentioned earlier – consisted at that point of only nine players; they were its permanent members; some British, some American. This mingling of nationalities prompted Actors Equity to recognize Aquila as duly unionized, the first company from overseas ever to be allowed to work in the United States without the usual complications and negotiations about casting.

Travelling assiduously, eight months a year, from north to south, east to west, occupying stages in regional and university theatres, the Aquila's mission is to revive great plays of the past, sometimes Shakespeare's works – *Julius Caesar, King Lear, The Comedy of Errors* – but chiefly the Greek tragedies and farces – *Philoctetes, The Birds, Lysistrata.* Some of its presentations are designed for audiences of children; the company has an arrangement with the Lincoln Center Institute to appear in forty New York City high schools with one-hour condensations of classic works. Said Professor Helene Foley of Barnard College: "The productions are clever and serious. They fill an incredibly valuable niche." Obviously the purpose is to instil in the young an interest in the best theatre literature.

The actors have to double in roles. As in ancient Athens, when the offering is a Greek piece, they are helped in doing this by wearing masks, somewhat over-sized, topped with hair. These are faithful copies of those shown encaustically on vases of the fifth century BC, and often grotesque, preserved in museums.

Of necessity, characters, lines and episodes have been cut from the scripts. What are not omitted, however are the "ribald asides and bawdy slapstick" that accelerate the farces; that is especially true of the half-dozen plays translated by Meineck himself. Such passages, replete with "crude and sexually explicit" speech, are emphasized and accepted with overt relish. The earthy – and "street" – aspects of Greek comedy testify to their enduring humanity, bridging thousands of years to engage modern tastes and as always amuse. (The Meineck translations have been published.)

Discussing the masks, Meineck remarked to a *New York Times* reporter, "The plays were prepared for a 17,000-seat open-air theatre with very long entrances. Characters had to be invested as soon as they walked on, especially since there were only two or three actors playing. You are not in a naturalistic, kitchen-sink theatre at all. You are in the land of mythos, mythology and legend."

In the Greek theatre, too, such disguise was imperative: elderly actors might be playing youths, and only men could take women's roles. Almost certainly the character portrayed would be very different from the performer himself. The mask was his very welcome shield and automatically bore much of the burden of impersonation.

Meineck had come to theatre by an indirect route, his compulsive interest in Greek drama certainly an unpredictable one considering his unliterary background. Born to a builder, he was raised in a working-class area of London. Expelled from school at fifteen for misconduct – a fight – at sixteen he joined the Royal Marines, possibly as a way to appease his natural combativeness. Though without a formal education or degree, he became a commissioned officer. Eventually leaving the service, he enrolled in the University of London and was fascinated by the "passionate energy" of the Athenian tragedies. As he put it to the reporter from the *New York Times*: "What I love about the Greek playwrights is that they were so well rounded. They were soldiers, politicians and playwrights. There was a time in my life where I was not the traditional person who would go into the theater. I immediately found a connection with these people. Aeschylus was at the battle of Marathon. He was regarded as one of the greatest playwrights the Greeks ever had, and yet when he was buried in Sicily, all it said on his grave was, 'Here lies Aeschylus who fought at the battle of Marathon.' And that is what his tomb should have said: In that battle the Greeks were freed from the tyranny of the Persians and went on to create the great democracy that was Athens."

In some of the plays, Meineck has warriors attired in modern Army uniforms. His justification for doing this: "In the Fifth Century the Greeks portrayed Homeric warriors in contemporary battle dress. What they wore as Hoplites at the battle of Marathon was what Achilles wore. These people were soldiers, the Greeks wanted to say, just like you."

To herald the arrival of the gods, the noise of bombers is heard. Electronic music, composed by Anthony Cochrane, one of the actors, accompanies much of the action, and there is considerable dependence on innovative lighting effects to compensate for the scanty settings. A large blue silk sheet serves in different places and plays to suggest "the sea, a tent, a cave, various landscapes and the interior of Julius Caesar's mind". When travelling, the company fits its scenery into a few large trunks.

The ensemble's movements and gestures are carefully stylized and well rehearsed, in some instances lending the action "a dreamy, dancelike quality", the robed, masked figures moving in choreographed patterns, at once near and remote.

There may be chanting as well as danced interludes. The dialogue is properly lofty, or it may be colloquial and "off the streets and out of the barracks", as determined by the dramatic situation. The chief goal is the utmost communication with the spectators.

As a component of a higher religious ceremony, awaited with keen anticipation each year by the citizenry, the plays could wield a strong political and moral influence; the playwrights were able to bring about significant betterment by questioning the rightness of civic leaders and events. As has been seen, some dramatists preached against war, tyranny, and corruption in their tragedies and comedies. Meineck believes this would still be true today.

It could have personal meaning for the spectator, too. "The audience can watch Agamemnon and enjoy the basic myth, but can also compare the myth to life and contemporary politics. This is why you see Greek drama set in Bosnia, although this is not necessarily what I would do. People turn to Greek tragedy when they are trying to express great stress, guilt or emotion. Sometimes it is how you feel about your wife, your kids, your brother, or your fears about survival. The *Oresteia,* after all, is about your son overthrowing you and your wife knowing your darkest secrets. Greek tragedy is a great leveler."

In collaboration with Paul Woodruff, Meineck has translated and adapted *Oedipus the King.* Besides guiding Aquila, he teaches at New York University's Tisch School of the Arts.

In Rome, as a capstone of the year 2000, reconstruction of the Colosseum was finally completed, making it once more a practical venue for theatrical events. The inaugural programme: the National Theatre of Greece, bringing *The Theban Plays*, the first of the three being *Oedipus Rex* followed by the other two on successive nights.

Anyone desiring to see *Antigone* more or less as Sophocles wrote it could do so by going to Britain's National Theatre where it was being enacted, jointly directed by John Burgess and Peter Gill, using a translation by C.A. Trypanis (1984). The title role was entrusted to Jane Lopotaire, regarded as one of the company's – and England's – foremost actresses.

Eight years later *Antigone* was on view again in London (1992) as a component of *The Thebans,* the Royal Shakespeare Company's venture alluded to a few pages earlier. Adrian Noble directed this, and a fresh translation was by Timberlake Wertenbaker.

Elsewhere the play was being offered somewhere in Greece almost every season, at Epidaurus, at mountain-high, fabled Delphi – where the air was clean, the vista magnificent – on the island of Rhodes or wherever a state-subsidized theatre was meeting its obligation to keep alive the nation's great heritage of classical scripts.

Finally, in Rome (2000) as has just been stated, *Antigone* was the second play given by the

National Theatre of Greece to celebrate the completion of the Colosseum's restoration as a site for dramatic spectacles.

Beyond those sites, a staging of the play in its original form was not readily found. Instead of staying with Sophocles' conception, his clear, taut delivery of the story, producers and directors were inclined to follow the example of Jean Anouilh, whose version, laid in Nazi-occupied Paris, had reaped a huge worldwide success. The trick is to alter the ancient script, update it, attempt extreme and daring variations of it on the pretext of making it more relevant, though the elements in it are already eternal universals: the struggle for freedom of religion, the maintenance of the rights of the individual when threatened by the state, the limits on how much force to use in order to seize and retain power. Anouilh's adaptation was a courageous act of defiance; he had put himself in physical danger, making him fully deserving of his reward. Fortunately, the majority of modern playwrights have only to fear the scorn of critics and unappreciative spectators.

The Living Theatre, the "pacifist and anarchist group" inspired and led by the fervent Judith Malina and her tall, balding husband Julian Beck, kept their Brechtian *Antigone* in the company's repertoire as they toured throughout Europe and the United States, their cast often parading in the nude to shock middle-class onlookers, the notoriety drawing people to the plays. The troupe's communal lifestyle and deliberate encounters with the police, as well as their endless court battles over unpaid taxes, theatre leases and landlord's claims, further contributed to the publicity they constantly garnered. At no time, however, was their sincerity, seriousness or idealism to be doubted. They were, like Oedipus' adamant daughter, ready to be martyred if need be. Appropriately their *Antigone* was offered for more than two decades; it was staged by them in New York as late as 1984.

Not as far from Off-Broadway as the Living Theatre might have strayed, the Pearl River Company, as has been observed, has had a predilection for experimenting with the Greek tragedies. Its selection in 1995 was *Antigone* at its theatre on St Mark's Place in the gentrifying East Village. D.J.R. Bruckner, of the *New York Times*, pronounced the story's dramatic force somewhat less than wholly realized.

> In a new production of *Antigone*, Shepard Sobel, the director, tries to take the audience inside the circle of the doomed family of Oedipus, making Sophocles' play more a domestic tragedy than the bloody public conflict it is in standard performances.
>
> He substitutes Queen Eurydice for the chorus, making her in effect the narrator. The device may give the story more coherence, but it is gravely distracting.

Thus, in early episodes, since there is no chorus for Creon to argue with about his ideas of strong kingly government, he can only address the audience directly, and the running commentary of Eurydice-as-chorus begins to sound like a string of asides, not a warning that his confidence and stubbornness will bring disaster.

And near the end, when Eurydice as Creon's wife emerges from the palace to learn how Creon's intransigence has led to the deaths of her son and Antigone, one has to wonder when she lost her memory.

The director also subdues the anger, the public posturing if you will, in the arguments between Antigone and her sister, Ismene, and later in those between Creon and his son, Haimon. The sense of intimacy – the Antigone-Ismene exchanges sound like quiet conversation – gives some emotional bite to the lines, but it makes it difficult for the audience to hear them as challenges to the established order of the world that will bring down the implacable judgment of heaven.

One leaves feeling that the destruction of all these people was dreadful, but not the cosmic event Sophocles supposed it was.

In the Living Theatre's production the body of Polynices was visible on stage throughout most of the play's unfolding, no easy task for the actor who was portraying the slain Polynices: he had to remain immobile and apparently not breathing for an extended time. The Malina–Beck intent was to have people face the ugly reality of death – it is a fact in warfare that should not be consigned to happening off-stage, out of sight, to spare the spectator's sensibilities. In *Antigone in New York* (1996) by Janusz Glowacki, a Polish playwright, a corpse appeared and disappeared and was on hand again, to evoke laughter. Glowacki, a political dissident in his homeland and in exile in New York for several years, was an established playwright, well known in Europe with a flair for the macabre and the ridiculous, an odd pairing. In New York he achieved a moderate commercial success with another comedy about the problems of foreigners like himself in finding and affording a decent place to live when with little or no funds. The same subject was addressed in his Off-Broadway *Antigone*, the half-title of which was most of what he appropriated from Sophocles. The play, first seen in New York in 1993, was given a second chance by the Vineyard Theater, a long-standing enterprise that boasted a stabilizing number of subscribers. D.J.R. Bruckner, sent by the *New York Times*, approved of changes that had been effected:

> Michael Mayer, the director, explores what "homeless" really means as the word applies to the characters, and with this direct approach he – and actors who know the value of restraint – give the play a unity that has eluded previous productions.

> All the crazy escapades of Flea, Sasha and Anita, denizens of a Lower East Side park, are still there, including the theft and burial of a body from a morgue. So are all the ethnic, political and literary jokes that have distracted actors and audiences. But here they are clearly seen as masks hiding memories, fears and longings. Home is an impossible place to these people; they cannot bear to inhabit their own lives.
>
> The changes made by Mr Mayer and this cast are not obvious in the first hour, which is filled with the usual comic capers. But then Flea (Ned Eisenberg) is made to acknowledge that his boasts about his girlfriend in his native Poland are pipe dreams. When he replies that he will stay with his companions only if all his lies are taken as truth, Mr Eisenberg turns Flea into a kind of revealing sibyl and one begins to see that Mr Glowacki's transformation of a Greek tragedy may be more than an act of blind *hubris.*
>
> Steven Skybell's Sasha is a ruin, but a great one. If he seems to be Flea's inarticulate dupe at first, once he begins to let Anita know how he has destroyed himself, his silence seems tragic in retrospect. And Priscilla Lopez gradually lets one see that the crazed Anita is more profoundly mad than one might suspect, and very like most of us at certain times of our lives.
>
> Even the policeman, who talks only to the audience and has seemed such a stick figure until now, suddenly fits in. Monti Sharp gives his easy patter the punctuating effect of a Greek chorus as he watches these people disintegrate, and his final announcement of their doom, which seemed just a clumsy ending to clumsy play, has the kind of punch this glib cop says he likes to throw. Finally, although he is not in the program's cast list, Michael Ringler is one of the funniest corpses imaginable, very real and very dead. It takes a confident director to make this figure so prominent right up the moment when the play turns dark. The confidence is justified.

(The frenzied and clumsy shifting about of a corpse – one that would not stay buried – was not a unique comic theme: a hilarious *faux-gangster* caper, *The Trouble with Harry* (1936), was one of Alfred Hitchcock's most popular films.)

At the Connelly Theater, also in Manhattan's East Village, a far more serious application of the provocative legend dramatized by Sophocles was a part of the New York International Fringe Festival (1998): *Antigone Through Time*, developed from an idea that had been cherished by Gloria Madden. It was further adapted, in the three months after her death, by the company she had headed, the fancifully named Madwoman of the Woods Productions. Anita Gates, of the *New York Times*'s staff, described rather than judged the work, perhaps out of respect for the recently deceased Miss Madden, whose unfinished concept might seem to some to have been naïve and sentimental, and in many aspects unoriginal. Still, the staging won praise.

There are moments in this piece that could have come straight from one of those movies about the travails of a struggling young New York actress. You know, the scene of her suffering through some pretentious, self-consciously avant-garde Off-Off Broadway production heavy on metaphor. But there are also moments in *Antigone Through Time*, which is visually striking from beginning to end, that shimmer with the beauty of dignity.

Action starts with wailing in the dark. Then, moving as one, a cluster of men and women appears, some with raised fists, some defensively shielding themselves. The play begins, not in ancient Greece, as the title might suggest, but in the 1940s on a Greek island, where some 3,000 women have been placed in an internment camp. They have been part of the Resistance to the German occupation of Greece and to the Fascist regime and have refused to sign a declaration of repentance.

A dozen actresses represent all the prisoners, their unity symbolized by identical, simultaneous postures and not-quite-dance movements. Two men with rifles walk among them. Early in the play, the women are lined up and one says: "I'm nineteen. I don't want to die." They are all shot dead by a firing squad. In the next scene they rise up, presumably now to represent the surviving prisoners. At times they sing in a kind of coarse folk harmony. At one point, they join in a single long-held note that calls to mind the chants of Tibetan monks. Near the end, the women put on long white veils and walk slowly and stiffly. Whether they are meant to resemble ghosts, brides or a less specific concept is hard to say.

Periodically during the play, the performers put on white masks and are transformed into characters in Sophocles' original *Antigone*. [Here a synopsis of the ancient tragedy is inserted. It ends with Tiresias persuading Creon to relent and free his niece, otherwise he will be hated by all. But it is too late.] Before dying, Antigone declares that she has "gone by the immortal unrecorded laws of God," rather than the edict of the current government. "As men's hearts go, I have done no wrong," she says. "I should have praise and honor for what I have done." This is, of course, exactly the position of Antigone's twentieth-century counterparts in the internment camp.

Richard S. Bach's direction is disciplined and sharp, and the original music, by Nana Simopoulos, is haunting.

Rounding out its scheduled presentation of three works derived from the Greek legends, the Unterberg Poetry Center in New York offered the première of Tom Paulin's *Riot Act* (2000) which was said to be based on *Antigone*, though the public announcement added nothing more, nary a clue to what was implied by the title. As before, the event was not reviewed.

Pour Antigone (*For Antigone*), a dance work, was a feature of the Lincoln Center Festival (2000). Ten years earlier a French choreographer, Mathilde Monnier, was stirred by the prospect of mixing the dynamics of Greek tragedy and the motivations of stage artists in modern Africa, especially those interested in dance in Mali and Burkina-Faso. As summed up in *Libération*, she hoped to combine "the ecstatic loose-limbed power of contemporary African dance and the austere sensuality of European postmodern performance". Choosing the weighty trials of Antigone as a vehicle to exploit "the coiled energy, frenetic struts, and gravity-defying pairings in which two dancers seem to inhabit the same being", she contrived a dance-story that brought the tragedy to pulsing life. The earthy, strident *Pour Antigone* was cheered at Lincoln Center.

The other classic plays, less favoured and even long neglected, were resurrected here and there, lifted from the browning pages of dusty library books, imbued with amazing new vitality by imaginative directors who sensed the persuasive illusion latent within them and waiting there to be released once more. Often the actors involved in such ventures were surprised by how strong and compelling the tragedies still are and how witty and entertaining are the few farces.

At Williamstown, in a *Hecuba* (1998), through the uncertain magic of revival, the Queen of Troy, once proud consort of Priam, exacted stern retribution for the slaughter of her sons and grandchild. Seldom seen, this drama regained its theatrical force.

A work with a close affinity to it, *The Trojan Women,* about the captive princesses weeping at the loss of heroic mates and helpless offspring, was brought back at the Old Globe Theater in San Diego (2000) and the Western Stage, Hartnell College, Salinas (2000), both in California. The Serban–Swados version of the play, separated from their much-vaunted *Fragments of a Greek Trilogy,* was revived for a second time by the Great Jones Repertory Company at La MaMa in New York (1996). Peter Marks, in the *New York Times,* wrote that the re-engagement was triumphant.

> Mr Serban has done more than faithfully reassemble the stunning sights and guttural sounds of his original. He appears to have uncorked all the play's rawness and vitality, as if they had been kept in bottles in the cellar of La MaMa all these years. For those who never got to see it the first time (or even the second: it was performed at La MaMa in 1987), the current restaging is an excursion back to the future of the theater, a return to the time when a new kind of environmental drama was emerging .... The action happens all around the audience.... Bare-chested men reciting what sound like ancient mantras and toga-clad women bearing torches push the audience aside to make room for a wagon that carries Helen (Joanna Peled) to her rendezvous with public defilement; later, the audience is herded to

> the sidelines to witness the murder of a virgin (Julia Martin). The chants to which Ms Swados sets her music are at once indecipherable and wildly evocative; by the end of the piece, they seem a clear expression of the Trojan women's terrible struggle to survive with some semblance of dignity.

At Epidaurus (2000) Ajax, gripped by madness, slew the innocent sheep kept as provision for his comrades-at-arms, and Herakles strode the sunlit platform before a throng in the vast, stony, multi-tiered arena.

The howls of the anguished Philoctetes, abandoned and solitary on an island, after being poisoned by a snake-bite, were heard again in *The Cure at Troy* (1990), an adaptation of Sophocles' script by the Irish poet Seamus Heaney – soon to be awarded a Nobel Prize. Heaney was moved to compose his first and only stage piece after the Berlin wall was suddenly razed. The democratic Václav Havel came to power in Prague, and the corrupt dictator of Romania was abruptly disposed of – an extraordinary surge of hope began to rise in the long-troubled world. Perhaps there was now a chance that the civil war in Northern Ireland, too, would end, a peace and firm reconciliation achieved, as happens after Philoctetes' fabled mighty bow is stolen from him and he comes to terms with his anxious fellow-warriors. Without him, a prophet has declared, the conquest of Troy is not possible; his assistance must be recruited. Heaney's play is a plea for the long killing to cease in Ireland. "Believe in miracles . . ." Leaders from both sides of the historic dispute, Republicans and Unionists, attended the première of *The Cure at Troy* given by the Field Day Company in Derry. Heaney's message was directed to them. In the words of an observer there, "In the theatre that night, all were addressed, all were implicated." In 1998 the play reached New York, enacted by the Jean Cocteau Repertory Company, and it was produced again a bare two months later by the Yale Repertory Theater in New Haven.

These are only a few of the scattered offerings – a full census is impossible, the world is so large, its cities so far apart.

In mid-career the poet and critic T.S. Eliot – another Nobel laureate – began to write "verse plays", his stated purpose to bring back a more elevated form of drama, the dialogue not in iambic rhymed couplets but rather embellished and at times epigrammatic, essentially a poetic prose. He began with *The Rock* (1934), a pageant about building a church, and had a major initial success with *Murder in the Cathedral* (1935), about the death of Thomas à Becket – it was later adopted as a libretto for an opera by Ildebrando Pizetti (1958). He made other sorties to the West End and Broadway with *The Cocktail Party* (1949), *The Confidential Clerk* (1954) and *The Elder Statesman* (1958) that were lighter – though somewhat laden with pieties – and commercially more profitable. All were supposedly modelled on familiar ancient Greek works: in the same order, Euripides' *Alcestis* and *Ion*, and Sophocles' *Oedipus at Colonus*. That is, he updated and transformed them into conventional drawing-room comedies with didactic passages, a rather unique mixture. Ironically, what Eliot did not foresee, and it only happened posthumously, was that a small collection of his whimsical poems would serve as the almost plotless "book" for the fantastical musical *Cats*, with a score by (Sir) Andrew Lloyd Webber, which set an unmatched record by prospering for eighteen years on Broadway, as well as having long stays in London and widely elsewhere, earning its sponsors over a billion dollars, a share of which vastly enriched Eliot's widow (his second wife) and estate.

The most studied and debated of Eliot's plays is *The Family Reunion*, which he conceived in 1935 and saw enacted in 1939. In advance, word was bruited about that it incorporated elements of the *Oresteia*, whereupon an aura of importance was automatically attached to it. Eliot blended with Aeschylus! As a highly esteemed critic, though he went counter to the mainstream, and as the editor of the literary journal *The Criterion* – none more lofty – he had become the most eminent figure in the narrow realm of English letters; no one's opinions were more respected and repeated in academic circles. He had firmly declared himself to be a royalist in politics – howbeit American-born – a convert to the Anglican creed, and a classicist in matters concerning the arts; so it was logical enough that Aeschylus' epic trilogy should have invaded and held captive his imagination. The rumour about *The Family Reunion*'s link to Aeschylus' mighty primordial tragedies has lingered in commentaries on it to the present day.

Are there significant parallels? The action takes place in the twentieth century. Harry, Lord Monchensey, has invited his kinfolk, mostly uncles and aunts, to his home in the North of England to celebrate his mother's birthday. The audience is invited to liken the ancestral Monchensey manor house to the House of Atreus. Harry is possessed by secret guilt feelings. On an ocean cruise his wife has vanished; it is assumed that she fell overboard and under cover of night was lost at sea. He is nagged by the possibility that he actually pushed her over the railing or that he saw her peril or intent to leap and did nothing to stop her. He cannot remember just what happened and does not know how to measure the depth of his responsibility – if there is any. His hidden doubts are the Furies that relentlessly and cruelly pursue him. They materialize in his drawing-room as white-cowled ghosts. The guests around him – the Elders – some of whom offer him advice, stand by as the equivalent of a Greek chorus. Finally one of them, who was his father's mistress, gives him sage counsel and helps him move towards recovery of his emotional balance. He must not try to elude the Furies; he must seek them out and come to terms with them to expiate the family's curse.

Here one ought to learn about Eliot's private life – his first wife suffered from manic-depression and paranoia. She had frequent fainting fits, hysterical outbursts, tirades aimed at him, jealous rages and other manifestations of mental illness that made their fifteen-year marriage a continuing source of misery for him. A communicant of the Church of England, he could not seek a divorce. He finally accepted a position to lecture at Harvard for a year, and while away from England he obtained a legal separation and never saw her again. She was subsequently committed for the rest of her life to an asylum for the insane.

Those who knew all this about him – his resentment of his wife for the lengthy unhappiness she visited on him, his possible repressed wish to be rid of her by whatever means – equate Harry's guilt feelings to what might have lurked unwelcomed in Eliot's mind. Since his death his problems have been well publicized by biographers, and an effective play has been written about him, *Tom and Viv* (1984) by Michael Hastings, seen in London and New York and eventually put on film (1994). The possible connection between Harry and Eliot having reached general knowledge adds to the spectator's interest in *The Family Reunion.*

At first Eliot's play did not live up to expectations. The senior critics complained that it was dull, bleak, slow, talky, even preachy. Eliot was intelligent enough finally to agree with them. He revised the script, and went on revising it. It was staged at the tiny Off-Broadway Cherry Lane Theater (1947) and again in London (1955), directed by the acclaimed Peter Brook; both times it failed. It got to Broadway (1958), where Brooks Atkinson of the *New York Times* dismissed it as "a wordy drama about uninteresting people engaged in a struggle they are not eager to explain". Again it failed. But Eliot's name is magic; a good many of the cognoscenti refuse to believe that a man of his genius could write a bad play – and, with all his revisions, it *had* become a perceptibly better script. In 1979 a London revival elicited surprising praise from the heretofore hostile critics. Eliot's enhanced language, and his introduction of the "chilling" Furies, were to their liking. Benedict Nightingale – to whom much is owed here – was captured by the poetry's "wintry music".

In 1999 the Royal Shakespeare Company offered the drama once more; Adrian Noble guided the actors, winning even more approval. John Gross described it in the *Sunday Times* as "a tense, gaunt, uncluttered production of Eliot's greatest play". Theatregoers in New York had another chance to see and hear it (2000) when the company on tour brought it for a brief stay at the Brooklyn Academy of Music.

Has Aeschylus influenced Eliot? Harry has not callously sacrificed his virginal youngest daughter to satisfy his vanity, and to let him pose as a leader of men. He does not absent himself for ten years wastefully besieging Troy, nor does he return boastfully with a concubine at his side. His vengeful wife does not greet him with deceptive speeches and entrap and kill him, brazenly and exultantly, and she is not slain by his son at the instigation of his implacable, brooding, almost deranged eldest daughter. Harry's crime may or may not be real; he is incapable of determining the answer. What Eliot endured is all too factual. Despite the *frisson* it adds to the play, it is hard to find that the oft talked about tie of *The Family Reunion* to the *Oresteia* is truly substantial.

In contrast to the Eliot play, Eugene O'Neill's *Mourning Becomes Electra* (1931) adheres closely to Aeschylus, his plot and characters. The American playwright calls his work a "trilogy", and takes thirteen acts to tell his story. That description and a roughly comparable length apply to the Aeschylus *Oresteia* too. The scene is transposed to New England, in the 1860s, at the very close of the Civil War. The action mostly proceeds in front of a large white dwelling; it boasts a neo-classical façade, adorned with portico and pillars, much like a Greek edifice (the fated House of Atreus). The people's names half-sound like those in Aeschylus' tragedy. Ezra Mannon (Agamemnon), proud, wealthy landowner, returns from his participation in the strife, where he has been a general. He is weary, spent. His wife, Christine (Clytemnestra), has been unfaithful to him in his absence. A foreigner, a somewhat exotic figure in puritan New England, she is passionate and bold. She is looked upon as "different" by her neighbours and therefore distrusted. They constitute the chorus, narrow-minded, watchful, gossiping, ready to spread defamatory rumours and quick to condemn what they do not like or understand. Christine, easily seduced, has fallen in love with Adam Brant, a sea captain with a mysterious past. She does not know that his pursuit of her is a carefully planned move by him to exact retribution from the arrogant Mannons; he is the illegitimate son of Ezra Mannon's father – hence, Ezra's half-brother – and has a deep grievance: when his mother, abandoned, desperately needed help, the Mannons had treated her badly. (Atreus, offended, had slain some of his brother's children, and Aegisthus' role in Argos – his liaison with Clytemnestra, and his usurpation of the throne – was impelled by a desire to avenge the wrong done *his* family.) Ezra and Christine have a son, Orin (Orestes), and a daughter, Lavinia (Electra); the young man, somewhat of a weakling, dotes overly on his mother; the young woman, who has an iron will, has an excessively strong bond with her father. Eugene O'Neill's time was the heyday of Freudianism, then just gathering in the American intellectuals.

Though Ezra Mannon has a reputation as having been harsh and abrasive – Christine fears him – O'Neill portrays him with surprising sympathy: the war has not wholly spared him – it has taken a nervous toll. The playwright adds two characters not in Aeschylus' *Oresteia*: Hazel and Peter Niles, who live nearby and are romantically interested in the young Mannons – a rather geometrical design, but they are bland characters and have only a small part in the plot.

Lavinia hates her mother – is jealous of her – and grows suspicious of Brant. She extracts the truth from him about his relationship with Christine. Brant warns Christine that Lavinia will certainly inform her father of what has occurred while he was away at the front. In a panic, to ward off his wrath, she poisons Ezra and takes flight, seeking refuge with Brant on his ship.

Discovering the poison tablets, Lavinia realizes what has happened. With difficulty, she convinces Orin that his compulsively adored mother has committed a murder. They follow Christine to the harbour, and confront the pair in the cabin of the ship. When Orin is completely persuaded of the lovers' guilt, his fury overwhelms him; he draws out a concealed weapon and shoots Brant, wounding him fatally. Lavinia is horrified by this unexpected denouement. What follows is Christine's suicide – she has brought about the deaths of both her husband and her truly beloved. The plot might seem overly melodramatic, but it is shielded by having the *Oresteia* as its precedent.

For the play's ending O'Neill breaks away from Aeschylus. Undetected as the agents of Brant's and Christine's demise, Orin and Lavinia go to recuperate on a tropical isle, a paradise. They are not beset by Furies. The warmth and lush beauty of the environment, the frank sensuality of the natives, bring about a gradual change in Lavinia; responding to the new world about her, she grows to be more and more like her mother, loving and passionate. She resolves to return to her home and marry Peter Niles. But as she has grown to resemble her mother, even physically, Orin has become attached to her. He fixes on her the repressed feelings he had for Christine, the object of an incestuous dream. He strongly opposes Lavinia's plan to wed Peter. To stop her, he threatens to accuse her of having shot Adam Brant. Finally, emotionally confused, realizing the hopelessness of what he is seeking in life, he emulates his mother and kills himself.

Lavinia retreats from the world, into the House of Mannon, shutting its massive door behind her, cutting off all contact with other people.

(After a brief experience with Freudian analysis, O'Neill himself was not persuaded of its efficacy, but he exploited what his audience was apt to believe. He tended to subscribe to Jungianism – *vide* his *The Emperor Jones.* Alice Brady was Lavinia, the acclaimed Russian-American actress Alla Nazimova Christine.)

Apart from flaws in their dialogue, O'Neill wrote powerful plays – he was yet another Nobel Prize recipient (1936) – and one American critic claimed on his behalf that, as of that moment, he was the world's foremost dramatist. Certainly he was the most innovative and imaginative writer at work in the theatre, without an equal since Strindberg, a formative influence on him at the start. In 1931

Mourning Becomes Electra, with its Freudian trappings and classical antecedents, became a major event on Broadway. Thirteen acts! Ticket-holders had to leave offices or workplaces in the late afternoon to catch the first play, there was a ninety-minute intermission when they could have supper at a nearby restaurant and then return as the drama resumed and continued late into the night (as spectators has also done for *Strange Interlude*, the lengthy O'Neill offering immediately preceding *Mourning Becomes Electra*). After its Broadway run the play was made into a film, with some changes in the cast. In 1967 David Marvin Levy chose to add music to it, a venture that was produced at the Metropolitan Opera House and well received – it was one of the very few American works ever put on there and even fewer considered successful.

In the seventy years since the play's staging, and especially since O'Neill's death (1953), no decade has passed without the revival of several of his plays, some more than once: *Anna Christie, Hughie, Moon for the Misbegotten, Long Day's Journey into Night, Marco Millions, Ah Wilderness, The Iceman Cometh* and others – but *Mourning Becomes Electra* has not been among them. Perhaps its excessive length and grim subject have been deterrents. Nor in thirty-one years since its première was the opera heard again. At last, in the season of 1998–9, it was on view once more, this time at the Lyric Theater of Chicago. The composer, long silent, explained that he had inserted several more melodious passages, to keep up with changing public taste.

Like André Gide, Jean Cocteau and Jean Anouilh, the diplomat, novelist and dramatist Jean Giraudoux (1882–1944) was interested in revisiting the Greek plays and employing them to create fanciful new perspectives on contemporary problems. To use the ancient dramas in this way was something of a vogue in Paris in the 1930s and 1940s. Giraudoux wrote three pieces that fit into this category, *Amphitryon 38* (1929), *La Guerre de Troie n'aura pas lieu* (1935; in Christopher Fry's inexact translation, *Tiger at the Gates*), and *Electre* (1937). The "*38*" attached to "*Amphitryon*" is Giraudoux's acknowledgement that a great many other playwrights before him had toyed with the legend of Jupiter's unfair seduction of Amphitryon's virtuous wife; the lecherous god does this by assuming the physical guise of her husband, a soldier gone to battle his country's foes. Giraudoux's deft, light-hearted treatment of the tale, dramatization of which had even been undertaken by Molière, delighted audiences everywhere and was a lucrative hit on Broadway when staged by the Theater Guild with charming Lynn Fontaine and skilful Alfred Lunt in the leading roles.

Appropriating Greek themes for modern French farces and comedies dated back sixty-five years to such pieces as the Offenbach–Halévy–Meilac tuneful and buoyant operettas *Orphée aux enfers* (1861) and *La Belle Hélène* (1864). Further evidence of that generation's fascination with classical antiquity, but in a decidedly more serious vein, is Hector Berlioz's *The Trojans* (1856–8), not derived from Homer's epic but from Virgil's *Aeneid.* Berlioz dedicated his four-hour work to the Roman poet, whose verses he had cherished from childhood. However, too grandiose and sweeping, the work was rejected by the Paris Opéra; only fragments of it were enacted in the composer's lifetime.

Not long after *Amphytrion 38* brought Giraudoux a reputation for being adept at fashioning high comedy, the political outlook in France changed markedly with the rise of Adolf Hitler and his Nazi legions, a threat on the country's eastern border that Giraudoux – a diplomat – and many fellow writers could readily perceive. His deep concern and darkening mood are reflected in his other two "Greek" plays. Both are pleas for peace, even if that entailed moral compromises. In *Tiger at the Gates,* which was staged in London and New York as well as Paris, Helen has just eloped with Paris. If the Trojans do not send her back to Menelaus, a combined Greek force will attack the city. The ultra-valiant Hector, knowing the horrors of war all too well, urges her return without delay. The Trojans, feeling their honour is at stake, are not willing to listen to him; they experience a patriotic frenzy, excitedly ready to take up arms. Hector tries to persuade Helen to leave of her own volition but does not succeed. She feels that it is her fate to stay in Troy. The Greeks send envoys, one of them the sly, cynical Ulysses, to negotiate with the Trojans. Ulysses demands that Helen be handed back "intact", an assurance that she and Paris have not engaged in love-making. Hector is willing to concede this, but his fellow Trojans view it as an insult, an implication that the noble Paris, son of King Priam, is impotent. The crowd in the street again responds with bounding fury. All of Hector's desperate efforts are in vain.

Intervention by the gods is also futile; they send a message, but it is so ambiguous that it defies interpretation.

Further parleys between the opposing forces reveal that Helen is really not the true issue: the Greeks seek economic prizes; Troy is rich, has warehouses filled with fine merchandise and piled with food from abundant harvests, and even stores of gold. They should pay reparations by sending shiploads of goods at regular intervals, since Greece is narrow and rocky, hence comparatively poor.

Faced by the Trojans' adamant stand, however, Ulysses offers to take back Helen regardless of whether she is repentant and her virtue "intact". A deal seems to have been reached and peace secured. But Ojax, a vulgar, drunken member of the Greek delegation, makes a coarse, insulting remark to Andromache, and popular anger erupts again. A demagogue accuses Hector of instilling cowardice in the Trojans. To silence him, Hector, his restraint no longer sufficient, stabs the man to death. The Trojans, in turn, kill the offensive Ojax. So the war will take place, and the city's destruction will follow.

Georges Lemaître, in his book *Jean Giraudoux, The Writer and His Work*, says that the play makes three major points: the first is that the diplomats – Hector and Ulysses – could have averted the war if left alone. (Giraudoux, himself a diplomat, may have been somewhat over-generous in citing the usefulness of his profession. He also asserts that it is permissible for them to be devious and to lie in reaching a pragmatic arrangement.) But the work of the negotiators is annulled by "the rantings of a handful of fanatics or ideologists. The latter are indeed capable of rousing to a pitch the stupid herd passions of the crowd and of bringing about catastrophic conflagrations." The third point is a concession by the playwright: Fate is another factor. "These troublemakers also appear as simply the instruments of an inexorable Fate. For the first time, Giraudoux introduces Fate as the hidden cause of all human actions and all world disasters. . . . The irresistible sway of Fate dominates all the developments of the Trojan tragedy. . . . The tragic poets of ancient Greece had already made of the vain struggle of man against destiny the essential element of their dramatic works. In his play Giraudoux succeeds in re-creating the heavy, oppressive atmosphere of unavoidable doom found in the masterpieces of Aeschylus and Sophocles. . . . Fate's invisible presence manifests itself through the prophetic sayings of Hector's sister Cassandra, the somber forebodings of Andromache, the colorful intuitions of Helen, and Ulysses' ironical skepticism. All those repeated warnings of an impending disaster conjure up a general feeling of dread that confers on the whole play an intense tragic power."

The women in the play are very well individualized and delineated, either representing passion and instinct – Helen – or prompted by reason and logic in discerning the distinction between good and evil – Andromache – who, when she realizes that the conflict cannot be averted, beseeches Helen "to love Paris, so that the war may have at least a legitimate cause". Elsewhere in the script, Hector asks the gods to advise him about what disposition should be made of the erring Helen but again gets contradictory replies, depending on which deity speaks to him, Aphrodite or Athena. One cannot look to Heaven for clear guidance.

Electre carries many of the same ideas. It differs from virtually all other treatments of the legend by being kinder to Clytemnestra and Aegisthus. At opening, Electra is to be wed to a peasant by Aegisthus' contriving, to reduce her rank; she will no longer have her royal status and be able to work mischief. Orestes arrives and intervenes, claiming her for himself – he does not reveal that he is her brother. He is not fully aware of why she is so vehemently opposed to their mother. When a Corinthian army lays siege to Argos, Aegisthus, a brilliant soldier, is willing and eager to take charge of the city's defence. During the rule of Clytemnestra the army has seriously declined in morale and effectiveness; the soldiers resent being commanded by a woman. Aegisthus seeks to marry her so that he can be the Argives' legitimate military leader. He is certain that he can hurl back the enemy. Electra is stirred to new heights of hostility by the prospect that he will be seen as a hero. It is not known in the city that Aegisthus and Clytemnestra are lovers.

Orestes finally reveals his identity to Electra, who is overjoyed that he is back in Argos: now her plan to avenge Agamemnon can be carried out. For a time she evades telling Orestes why she hates her mother but at last reveals that Clytemnestra is responsible for Agamemnon's death. Her deed calls for "full justice" and nothing less – Orestes, as his slain father's son, must take on the task of punishing her and the man – as yet unknown – with whom she committed adultery and conspired to remove the ruler of Argos.

Orestes is weak and wavering, unwilling to fulfil this dread filial obligation. He and Clytemnestra meet and find that they are "strangers" to each other, their relationship quite unreal, almost a "mirage". In an "atrocious" scene – the adjectives are Lemaître's – he and Electra try to force Clytemnestra to identify her lover. Alone with Electra, Clytemnestra admits that she fears her son and begs her daughter to protect her from him, an ironic touch that Athenian spectators would have liked.

Aegisthus, evil in the past, has been very changed by the crisis awaiting Argos; he has become devoted to the city and is eager to save it from disaster. He speaks of Argos lyrically. The dialogue throughout is in highly poeticized prose. Clytemnestra, possessed by her love for Aegisthus, has also been metamorphosed into a different, much better person. Electra refuses to acknowledge this.

This exchange takes place between mother and daughter, as Clytemnestra tells of her contentment, her new feeling of inward peace, her embrace of the world about her.

> CLYTEMNESTRA: I'm in love.
>
> ELECTRA: So everything's all right with you now?
>
> CLYTEMNESTRA: Yes, everything is.
>
> ELECTRA: And are the flowers obeying you? Are the birds speaking to you?
>
> CLYTEMNESTRA: Yes, they do. And the linden trees send signs to me.

Pathetically she reaches out, asking Electra to share this happiness with her, but her daughter voices only contempt.

Aegisthus pleads for Electra's approval of the marriage to Clytemnestra which will enable him to head the city's forces. His urgent request convinces her that he is the object of Clytemnestra's love and abetted the killing of Agamemnon. The thought of his becoming a hero in the eyes of the Argives is ever more abhorrent to her, not to be borne. She will act to prevent it; she and Orestes can do it by naming him as one of the killers of Agamemnon and the unrecognized usurper of rule over the city.

> Aegisthus: You admit that, if I marry Clytemnestra, the city will remain quiet and the family of the Atrides will be safe. Otherwise, there will be rioting and arson.
>
> Electra: It is very possible.
>
> Aegisthus: You admit that I alone can defend Argos against the Corinthians who are already at the gates of the city. Otherwise, there will be plunder and massacre.
>
> Electra: Yes, you would be victorious.
>
> Aegisthus: And you remain obstinate! You ruin my chances to accomplish my task. You sacrifice your family and your country to I don't know what dream.

She is unforgiving, rigid, inflexible. She is gripped by a vision of her having imposed "perfect justice", an absolute sentence that allows no exceptions. She is one of the ideologues of whom Giraudoux despaired in *Tiger at the Gates* who will die for a principle – and let others die as well.

At her bidding, the subservient Orestes kills Aegisthus and Clytemnestra; the execution takes place offstage and is reported by a messenger, an old beggar who has watched it. Justice is done, and Argos is doomed to chaos and annihilation.

Giraudoux's argument is that abstract ideas, an obsession to hold to the utmost consistency – as embodied by the unswerving, single-minded Electra – should not dominate human beings with their weaknesses and faults – Clytemnestra and Aegisthus – when the stakes are too high.

He added a comic subplot and new characters, wholly his invention, to which the action switches at moments to relieve the ever-increasing tension. Three Eumenides also intrude from time to time; their role is somewhat ambiguous, but their shrill cries contribute to the mood of foreboding that envelopes the drama.

Giraudoux's last years were unhappy, though not always so. At home, in Paris, his marriage was blighted by futile quarrels, partly due to his ceaseless philandering. He was glad to be away on official missions that had him almost circling the globe – alone; his travels allowed him a stay in New York. He served for a time as the Secretary of the French embassy in Berlin. Prolific, he kept busy writing plays – in all, nineteen, short and long – along with novels and books of essays. He had repeated success, especially with his fantastic *The Madwoman of Chaillot* (1945), a stinging satirical slap at corrupt financiers and promoters. His rising literary fame enhanced his career in diplomatic circles, though he could not avoid becoming involved in the endless political intrigues that went on in the Ministry of Foreign Affairs. At the outbreak of the Second World War, which he had feared was inevitable, he was named Minister of Propaganda. He proved to be an incompetent administrator, and his broadcasts – witty and learned – were over the heads of average citizens and of soldiers huddled in trenches on the Maginot Line. When there was a change in the heads of the government, he was removed from his post and assigned to lesser duties. With the collapse of the French army and the German occupation he joined the Vichy regime in the south, where General Pétain was supposedly allowed to operate freely. Giraudoux saw that Vichy was in reality a puppet regime and soon quit it. He returned to Paris, where he occupied himself with collecting and compiling evidence of Nazi atrocities. For some while it had been obvious that his health was failing. Suddenly he was seized by a violent illness and, after a few days of intense pain, he died. He was sixty-one. The cause of his death has never been clearly diagnosed; this led to rumours – never proved or disproved – that he had been poisoned by the Gestapo.

When the war ended victoriously, and the insurrections in Indochina and Algeria were finally settled, while the United States and NATO buttressed Western Europe from the threat of Russia and Communism, Giraudoux's "Greek plays" ceased to be topical. He is better remembered for other works – they are more often revived. This is not to say, however, that the threat of war will never again impinge on the minds of people and worry them, and Giraudoux's advice will once more be well worth heeding and pressingly relevant.

Two Off-Broadway offerings made use of characters from Homer's epics without being variations of the scripts of the three great Athenian dramatists but simply starting out on their own. One was *The Iliad: Book I* (1999), created and produced by the Aquila Theatre Company at the Clark Studio in Lincoln Center and next at the Performing Arts Center in Newark. The dialogue given the actors by Stanley Lombardo, who prepared a new translation of Homer's poetry, was in twentieth-century vernacular, rough and salty, but its rhythm preserving "much of the feeling of the Greek verse, its rumbles and melodies and silences, the beat of its pulse" – noted by D.J.R. Bruckner of the *New York Times*, who had equal praise for the company's effective choreographed movement, moody chants and interpolated dances, all of which were features of the staging. The use of these resources was consistent with how the Aquila troupe put on most of its projects.

The point of the dramatization is to equate the assault and siege of Troy and the counter-invasion of Nazi-held Europe by Allied forces in the Second World War and, above all, to illustrate the timeless horror of war, whether it occurs in ancient Greece or on a Normandy beach. Though the action takes place in Homer's time – or earlier – the troops wear modern battle-dress and display present-day weapons.

Bruckner was deeply moved by what he saw.

> War is hideous glory in Homer, elevating combatants to achievements that astound them, terrifying them with death and abandonment among the shades below and debasing them with runaway lusts. And the performance of *The Iliad* by the Aquila Company draws an audience so deep inside the great poem that one seems to experience what Homer's heroes did.
>
> . . . With no props but combat gear and four metal boxes the size of steamer trunks, seven actors and director Robert Richmond create Olympus, a storm-tossed armada, altars in temple sanctuaries and the beaches before Troy strewn with corpses and wrecked ships.
>
> . . . The Normandy metaphor is thrillingly embodied. Of course, the Greeks and the Allies came ashore in much the same way: here under the roar of aircraft suggested by Anthony Cochrane's musical arrangements. Later, enthralled by an argument between Achilles and Agamemnon over rejecting a ransom offered by a priest of Apollo for his daughter, we might forget Normandy. But Apollo in vengeance flings his whole quiver of arrows at the Greeks, and they soar over us into the soldiers' hearts with the same sound.
>
> Further on, as Odysseus and his men row a fleet of penitential offerings out to Apollo's priest in the harbor, we see they are manning the LST's of 1944.

What resonates here, as it does with so many other modern adaptations of Greek myths and dramas, is the impassioned advocacy of pacificism that motivates the writers, directors and actors who produce them. Keeping the peace at all costs has been a message common to most of the plays covered in this survey of twentieth-century redactions of the rich works – the inexhaustible legacy – of Aeschylus, Sophocles and Euripides. (To that short list the name of Aristophanes, the author of *Lysistrata,* certainly should be added.)

Mythos (1999) is the second play derived straight from Homer – or perhaps it should be described as not a play but a theatrical spectacle – to startle New York in this final year of the millennium. It had a sharp impact on the critics, if not on the general public, which had scant chance to see it, its engagement at La MaMa was so brief. Alisa Solomon reviewed the production for the *Village Voice*:

> First, a large banquet table stretches the entire length of the stage. Soon it splits in two, the halves sliding away from each other to outline a tomb. Moments later, those half-tables are upended and pulled

to the edges of the playing space. On the gravel ground in between, a snake slithers noisily in the dark, leaping up toward the platforms. Suddenly, the snake straightens out over the stage, each end pulled taut from the platforms. The lights come up to reveal that it is a sparkling string of seashells. An actor strikes it with a stick and water gushes out onto the floor.

These stunning scenic shifts unfold in the opening moments of Odin Teatret's *Mythos*, introducing a ninety-minute spectacle of visual and musical transformation. Eight actors work these miracles before our eyes with graceful ensemble precision. Meanwhile, they bring physical virtuosity and resonant singing – and a range of other-worldly sounds – to their portrayal of half a dozen ancient mythic figures.

These feats, and especially the fact that they belong to the theater and nowhere else, provide reason enough to celebrate Odin Teatret's first visit to New York since 1984. Based in the small Danish town of Holstebro, for nearly thirty-five years the company has meticulously developed what director Eugenio Barba calls Third Theater – neither the commodified and trendy avant-garde, nor the staid mainstream, but a sustained investigation of human form and feeling in the temporal frame of live performance. Carrying forward the legacy of Grotowski, with whom Barba studied, Odin develops pieces through actor improvisations, with Barba shaping a whole.

In *Mythos*, Odin juxtaposes a twentieth-century revolutionary against figures from Greek mythology, who welcome him into their underworld pantheon. Oedipus, Cassandra, Daedalus, Medea, Orpheus, Odysseus, and Sisyphus cavort on the narrow, gravel-filled playing space, which runs like the river Styx between two banks of spectators. They draw patterns in the pebbles, whether the deliberate labyrinthian lines etched by Daedalus, or the traces of sorrow left by a lamenting Medea, who buries the bones of her children among the stones. A terrified Odysseus exhorts them, again and again, to clean up their tracks. A man dutifully rakes them away.

Amid this cycle of remembered violence, the revolutionary – program notes identify him as the Brazilian soldier Guilhermino Barbosa – trudges purposefully around the perimeter, a candle flickering on the brim of his hat. He plays a tiny accordion and sings revolutionary songs from Germany, Russia, and Latin America. His repeated refrain is the *International.* Orpheus kills him by thrusting a sword through his accordion. The instrument is resurrected in an arresting moment, when it appears on one of the high platforms, played by two disembodied hands. Soon the stage is covered with disembodied hands, a reference to the practice of ancient soldiers cutting off the hands of their captives, and a wider, mushy evocation of the boneyards of Europe. Communism is laid to rest here, but its bloody deeds are as impossible to bury as those of the mythic Greeks.

Enraptured by its theatrical display, Solomon still felt that intellectually *Mythos* was too one-dimensional.

> For all its welcome, simple splendor, Odin's performances here also cast doubt on the abiding power of an aesthetic developed in a particular cultural moment. Though not nearly as slick or vacuous as Robert Wilson's *The Days Before: Death, Destruction & Detroit III* (which played at the Lincoln Center Festival this Summer), Odin's work also raises questions about the capacity of a theater of images to speak to an audience that is awash in images already. In this information age of visual bombardment, when everything from Shakespeare texts to Aryan Nation rants exist on a single, undifferentiated cyber-plane, and a Nike swoosh is stamped on Psalms and sneakers alike, the sneering Sixties rejection of discursive meaning feels like a luxury we can no longer afford. In this context, the philosophical and political naïveté of *Mythos* seems quaint and stultifying, inadequate to the work's own visual delights and demands.

D.J.R. Bruckner was again the *New York Times*'s representative. He had no quarrel with what the company had accomplished.

> Rhythm is the soul of Odin Teatret's sumptuous *Mythos*; music is a frayed thread barely holding the limbs of the actors together as the rhythm threatens to shake them to pieces, and language is a murmur of anger and wonder.
>
> "All dies, all is born again" are among the few intelligible words in this stunning performance, and they suffice. Eugenio Barba, the Italian founder and director of Odin Teatret, Denmark's most celebrated theater company, has sought for thirty years to escape from narrative and its nagging companions, calendars and clocks. In this work – the centerpiece of a program of seven Danish plays at La MaMa through the end of the month – the escape is complete.
>
> So perfect, in fact, that the performance can hardly be said to have an audience, only individual viewers or participants. Some look puzzled, restless; occasionally one will laugh, startling others. A young woman sitting next to me on opening night got it right: after a while one of her feet was unconsciously tapping; rhythm is understanding.
>
> Mr Barba carries the group theater idea further than his teacher, Jerzy Grotowski, did in Poland or the Living Theater did here. He presents a notion for a play and lets each actor develop a role, drawing on song, verse, dance, chants, acrobatics, whatever; only at the end does he try to draw a common progress (nothing so definite as a plot) from the cast's sounds and movements.

Mythos rests on an image of Guilhermino Barbosa, one of thousands of Brazilian soldiers who from 1925 to 1927 marched 15,500 miles through their country protesting Government corruption. Barbosa later barricaded himself in a jungle shack, remaining until his death faithful to his revolution. Myths that control civilizations also die, Mr Barba says, and in *Mythos* Greek mythical figures, who might, themselves, have just emerged from graves, struggle with the question of whether Barbosa and his ideal or we and our myths can be reborn.

Viewers sit on two sides of an oblong stage paved with loose black stones that are raked into labyrinths, oceans, graveyards or gardens by the tireless stone-pusher Sisyphus and others. Orpheus, the great seeker, little more than an animal skull above an empty cloak, drives fellow heroes into action. Cassandra, all fire and seduction, finds giddy freedom in her incredibility, and Medea's murdered children become countless legions in their mother's laments. Fear alone impels Daedalus to fly lest he fall; Oedipus survives, indeed thrives, on scorn for anyone with hope; and that primal shape-shifter, Odysseus, is so enthralled with human folly he never notices his own.

Amid these gods Barbosa's endless march gives tragedy itself a distinct gait until, in a surprisingly poignant moment, Orpheus stabs the soldier right through his accordion and he is reborn in an unforgettable vision of the accordion's playing itself somewhere above the earth.

Some vocal effects produced in songs and chants are wildly beautiful or terrifying, and one cannot quite imagine how they are made. The words are by the Danish poet Henrik Nordbrandt. La MaMa announces that all plays but one in Odin Teatret's presentations here are in English. Not quite. Most of the lines in *Mythos* are not translated, but in ways it is hard to put a finger on, the actors make the meaning transparent. One bit of translation might have helped: in talks Mr Barba has mentioned the ancient practice of military victors' cutting one hand off each prisoner no matter how many they captured. People seeing *Mythos* should know that, since hundreds of carved wooden hands have lives of their own in the play.

Odin Teatret, which has a big following in Europe and Latin America, has been seen here only once before, at La MaMa fifteen years ago. Since the very idea of group theater seems to have died out in this country, experiencing the almost religious intensity of *Mythos* leaves one feeling that this surprisingly effective meditation on death and resurrection is a fitting emblem for the company.

An interesting footnote: in 1962 technicians unwrapping an Egyptian mummy in the Louvre – an exceedingly delicate task – recovered strips of papyrus on which were 120 lines from a lost play by Euripides. Earlier 125 lines had been found elsewhere. By combining the two discoveries, scholars gained a fairly good idea of the script's content. Dating from about 453 BC, it concerned Erechtheus, a mythical king of Athens, who forfeited his life in a battle against Eumolplos, son of Poseidon, but saved the city. Athena appeared to his widow, Praxithes, and gave instructions for the courageous warrior's proper burial. His five daughters should be sacrificed and interred with him on the Acropolis; afterwards there must be further annual sacrifices in their memory: bulls slain, holy choruses sung by maidens. The bereaved Praxithes would be a priestess singled out to conduct higher ceremonies and place burnt offerings at the altar of Athena herself, who was the city's patron deity. A grim legend but one that, with its sentimental lures, might have appealed to Euripides and prefigured his *Iphigneia at Aulis.* Dr Joan B. Connelly, an archaeologist at New York University, closely studying Euripides' fragmented text in 1995, was convinced that the 524-foot frieze ornamented with bas-reliefs beneath the cornice on all sides of the Parthenon is a sculptured pictorial representation of the persons and events used by the poet in his dramatization of the myth. It is a memorial to the five innocent girls supposedly buried nearby on the Acropolis. The symbolism and even identity of the low-relief figures on the frieze have always puzzled scholars. Dr Connelly's conjecture is a persuasive clarification; stone panel by panel, the episodes superbly portrayed on the entablature match incidents contained in extant parts of the play.

6

GREEK LAUGHTER

The origins of Hellenic comedy are, like tragedy, also thought to have been in imitative magic and religious beliefs, the first forms arising from priapic revels associated with rites honouring Dionysus. Totemism was largely admixed with them, as with the beginnings of tragedy: the worshippers dressed in animal-skins or costumes that made them look like huge birds, and, prancing about huge phallic carvings, are said to have indulged in uninhibited sexual play, invocatory tribute to the fertility god. If tragedy evolved from festivals of mourning at the mutilation of Dionysus, comedy sprang from joy, his followers voicing their trust in his resurrection, symbolized by fields finally greening in the new hot light of noon. Accordingly, comedy was linked to the burgeoning that accompanies spring, the human spirit exuberant in rays of bright sun after long months of cloudy grey skies, the morning wind having a vernal freshness, the loam nurturing the strewn seed. Dionysus, as patron of fecundity, was the god of the grapevine, hence of wine and drunkenness. Sexual acts might be performed openly in the valleys and on the hillsides, where small village festivals occurred; such acts were flagrant imitative magic: so that the warming earth would propagate, the worshippers too went through the motions of propagation. The inspired sexual frankness of the Bacchae is rumoured in Euripides' drama about the frenzied, even delirious participants in such rites.

Gradually, in Athens, as the festivals took on a more disciplined shape, comic works assumed their place in the annual dramatic contests. (Professor F.H. Sandbach, of the University of Cambridge, points out in *The Comic Theatre of Greece and Rome*: "Competition was dear to the Greeks. The athletic contests at the court of Alcinous in the *Odyssey* appear to be purely secular, but the four great religious panhellenic festivals at Olympia, Delphi, Nemea and the Isthmus of Corinth, centred on a variety of races and other contests; at Delphi athletic events were an addition to original music competitions for pipers, lyre-players and singers who accompanied themselves on the lyre. At Athens a torch-race was held at more than one festival, and after Pisistratus' expansion of the Panathenaia in the sixth century prizes were offered there for the recital of Homer and for performances with pipe and lyre as well as for athletics and horse-racing. Consequently it is not surprising that when drama became part of the Dionysiac festivals, it too was made the occasion for competition.")

Comedies were first included in the Greater Dionysia, in the afternoon – after the tragic trilogy had been presented in the morning – in 486 BC, establishing a tradition to be continued for the next 350 years or more. This annual event occurred at the end of March and the beginning of April. The Lenaea, the lesser festival held at the close of January or the start of February, was largely dedicated to comedy from 442 BC on. Three comic writers were pitted against one another, each permitted to enter one work for enactment in the afternoon, while the morning was allotted to staging two tragedies. (Lenaea is derived from *lenai*, a term applied to women whose ecstatic behaviour affirmed that they were possessed by the potent, seductive Dionysus.)

Lionel Casson, in *Masters of Ancient Comedy*, informs us that the comic scripts were in verse too: "Most of the scenes were written in iambic lines of six feet each which the actors delivered in ordinary speech; some were in more complex meters, and for these the actors used a sort of recitative to flute accompaniment; then there were a considerable number of lyric passages that were sung to the accompaniment of flute or lyre."

Any description of how these light plays were done is mostly guesswork and guided by artefacts. A considerable number of comic masks have survived and there are amusing scenes deftly sketched on vases.

At the Greater Dionysia the morning's three tragedies offered by a competitor would be followed in the afternoon by a satyr play composed by the same poet. Satyrs were the mythical troupe of bearded, half-human, half-bestial, horse-tailed creatures who danced attendance on Dionysus, and the actors performing in these works were dressed to resemble them. (From such farces come our words "satire" and "satirical".) Very often, as remarked earlier, the satyr play was a vulgar burlesque of the heroic stories unfolded in the forenoon, with the identical characters, now grotesquely drawn and mocked. At a later time the satyr play might be given, instead, at the opening of a day's programme. It was incumbent upon Aeschylus, Sophocles and Euripides to provide satyr plays, and one – Euripides' *Cyclops* (*c.* 440 BC) – remains intact, but all the rest are lost except for fragmentary passages. This type of work is thought to have been created by Pratinas some time between 534 and 500 BC.

Ferguson quotes from the Latin poet Horace (with an infelicitous translation by Martin):

The bard who strove of yore in tragic strains
To win the goat, poor guerdon of his pains,
Anon brought woodland satyrs in, and tried,
If gay with grave might somehow be allied.
For only by the lure of things like these,
That by their novelty were sure to please
Could audiences be kept, who were, no doubt,
By the religious service half tired-out,
And, being flushed with wine, could scarce restrain
The lawless humor of their madcap vein.

To which Ferguson appends the comment: "It is important to remember that the authors of these plays were tragedians, not comedians. The plays are in fact a part of the picture of man that the tragedians seek to convey – 'the glory, jest and riddle of the world.'"

Aeschylus was renowned for his satyr plays, but all that remain of them are some scattered lines from *The Fishermen*, based on the legend of Danäe and Perseus. His Oedipus trilogy is said to have been capped by *The Sphinx*. To the same epoch, and ranked next to Aeschylus, by the philosopher Menedemus, was Achaeus, not otherwise a figure of note and possibly over-rated by Menedemus because they were fellow townsmen. Of Sophocles' output in this genre there are 400 lines of *The Trackers*, the story of which is borrowed from the Homeric *Hymn to Hermes*. A trickster, his doings celebrated in much ancient Greek folklore, is bold enough to steal Apollo's herd of cattle, covering his deed by ingeniously reversing and confusing their hoof marks and his own footprints. Exposed at last, he recompenses Apollo for the purloined cattle by giving the angry god a lyre, the first such musical instrument, fashioned by him in childhood from the shell of a tortoise that he had killed. Sophocles made changes in the story, among other details having Hermes kill the tortoise after he steals the herd and slicing and using the hide of the oxen for the lyre's strings. He is pursued by the pot-bellied, short-legged Silenus, the leader of the troupe of satyrs, who has been promised his freedom as a reward for catching the elusive culprit. Behaving like sniffing hounds, the satyrs are the "trackers"; then, hearing the sound of Hermes' lyre, Silenus panics and tries to take flight, but is held back by his followers. From a cave appears Cyllene, a mountain deity, a gigantic female figure, who is the baby Hermes' nurse. She relates how the precocious infant crept out of the cave, killed the tortoise and invented the lyre from its carapace, over which the fast-growing, six-day-old child stretched strands of ox hide and plucked them, evoking strange tones. The coherent remnants of *The Trackers* end there. Adapted from fragments found in 1907, it was given a revival, a rare event (1987), perhaps its first ever, by the Sidewalks Theater in New York at the Nat Horne Theater.

Ferguson finds the range of characters in satyr plays to be narrowly limited: besides the wily Hermes, the "god of thieves", they mostly include Odysseus, also a trickster; Autolycus, "the snapper-up of unconsidered trifles"; Sisyphus, who cheated death, and all the Coyotes and Ananses of East European myth; and, of course, the pimply Silenus and his band of "lewd ithyphallic" rioters, the noisy constituents in Dionysus' train. Since fantasy and whimsy are hard to sustain, the satyr plays tended to be short, and also because – as suggested by M. Croiset – an audience subjected to three harrowing tragedies in a single day would be too wrenched and wearied to enjoy a long prelude or postlude to them, for three days running. As Gassner puts it, "curtain raisers" and "after-pieces" served as relating bits of fluff.

Euripides' *Cyclops*, the sole complete satyr play still accessible, owes much to Homer, who has the war-veterans Odysseus and his companions putting ashore on an island during their voyage home from ravaged Troy; they are not aware that their haven is inhabited by a race of one-eyed monsters, the Cyclops, giants who gluttonously feast on human beings. Trapped, the unhappy travellers are forced into a cave and imprisoned in a sheep-pen, while their huge captor gorges himself on them two by two. Odysseus, identifying himself as Nobody, plies the giant with wine, something he has never tasted before and that utterly delights him; in return, he promises Nobody that he will be the last one eaten. Finally, overcome, the drunken Cyclops falls asleep; as the monster lies snoring, Odysseus heats a pointed stake in the fire and puts out his foe's only eye. Other giants hear his screams and ask, "Who's hurting you?" His reply: "Nobody." Deceived, his neighbours go away. The Cyclops' sheep need to be let out to pasture; he carefully runs his hands over their backs to make sure that none of his captives is astride them, but Odysseus and his companions are clinging to the underside of the creatures and make their escape.

The motifs in this folk tale are found in the legends of many other peoples; Ferguson says that over 100 versions of it have been traced in works such as the *Arabian Nights* – the adventures of Sinbad – and a host of stories of Beauty and the Beast.

Euripides rearranges elements of it; he sets the scene outside the giant's cave. He adds the sottish Silenus as a character. In search of Dionysus, who has been kidnapped by pirates, he and his prancing band of satyrs have been shipwrecked on this island and kept captive. They spot a Greek ship approaching – manned by Odysseus and his friends, who unwarily land and venture on to the beach.

They are greeted by Silenus and his satyrs and warned of their danger: the cannibal Polyphemus rules here, rounding up strangers and consuming them. There is much palaver about wine – Odysseus has stopped at the island because he and his shipmates are desperately in need of food and drink permitting them to continue their voyage. As the sailors and satyrs swallow the wine, they engage in drunken dancing and raucous singing. There is also boastful, bawdy talk about the rape of Troy and the beauty of Helen.

Polyphemus, who has been away, suddenly arrives. He chides the satyrs, whom he has left to care for his sheep. Suddenly he notices the Greek strangers and demands to know who they are; Silenus, intoxicated and unsteady, quickly changes sides, claiming that he has been beaten while trying to protect the Cyclops' possessions and accusing Odysseus of plotting to seize the giant, tie him up, flay him, disembowel him and sell him as a slave. Polyphemus, hearing this, says only "Really?" and adds: "Sharpen the axe and light the fire. I'm tired of venison and lion's meat. I've not had a good man for ages." Odysseus protests, vainly, that Silenus is lying, and the satyrs also accuse their leader of telling falsehoods, but Polyphemus is not convinced.

In a colloquy between the Cyclops and Odysseus with some remarks addressed to Silenus, Euripides seems to be parodying himself and in particular his "best professional debating style": and at the same time he enunciates once again his steadfast anti-religious and treasonable political convictions. "Look, Shorty," he says, "sensible men have one god – Wealth. All the rest is hot air. I'm not afraid of Zeus' thunderbolts. I'm as strong a god as he is. I don't care, because when it rains I go into my cave, and when I've had a good meal my noises rival his. My belly's my god. What more does anyone want than food and drink and no troubles? This is Zeus. It's legislation that causes all the trouble." (Translation: Ferguson) He also cannot see the sense of a war having been fought over a woman, especially one as fickle as Helen.

Odysseus has opportunities to escape, but he cannot leave without his companions whose aid he needs to man their ship. Two of the men have already been roasted and eaten. In a speech to the curious satyrs, who want to know what is happening in the cave, he gives an account in a speech that roughly parodies Aeschylus' diction. Now he conceives a plan: Polyphemus is wildly intoxicated. He must be encouraged to drink until he passes out. Odysseus reveals his intention of then blinding him by driving in a pointed whittled and painted olive stake; the satyrs, pleased with the idea, offer to help. There is another drunken dance; the Cyclops comes staggering from his cave and, hiccupping, joins the singing while clumsily stamping about in time to it. Finally, before falling asleep, he drowsily vows that "Nobody" – Odysseus – shall be his very last victim.

The "Nobody" incident ensues, as Odysseus carries out his attack on the somnolent giant, getting no help from the satyrs who are almost paralysed with fright. Left sightless, the cursing Polyphemus rouses and stumbles about, while Odysseus and his men, as well as Silenus and the satyrs, hasten away to the moored ship, at which Polyphemus tries to throw great rocks. The sheep are not used in the get-away – Euripides realized that such a departure would be too difficult to stage.

Much of the dialogue abounds with puns and obscenities, and doubtless the play had a topical context – social and political – endowing acidic nuances to fleeting phrases and allusions, which gave extra meaning to the action and speech. Some of these are hard to pinpoint, since the date of the play's production is uncertain.

The literary worth of *The Cyclops* is questioned. Ferguson cites several adverse opinions:

> Norwood writes, "Considered in itself it is of small value, though it must have formed an agreeable light entertainment." Grube assigns to it half a page in a book of 450 pages on *The Drama of Euripides*: "It is a competent piece of fooling, neither tragedy nor comedy but rather burlesque, with the wine-bibbing Silenus, the cowardly satyrs, the coarse, boastful, drunken Cyclops, as the butts. Tragic emotions are nowhere aroused, there is no subtlety, tragic or comic. It is all good, though not clean fun, and contains little or no trace of Euripidean techniques and skills. It therefore has no real place in a study of Euripides's dramatic art, beyond being a further proof of his versatility." Murray more fairly calls it "gay and grotesque" and speaks of its "farcical and fantastic note;" but he too says that it is without any *arrière pensée*.

For his part, Ferguson has a very different view; he is enthusiastic about *The Cyclops*:

> In the first place it is very funny. It wins laughs more readily from a modern audience than even Aristophanes. Its humor is obvious, knockabout, and none the worse for that. It is good theater. Silenus pretending to work is good theater. The satyrs' Sicinnis dance and their mime of folding flocks is good theater. The Cyclops's entry to a wedding song is good theater; so is the visible, physical contrast between the colossal giant and puny Odysseus. The fooling as Silenus drinks behind the Cyclops's back is good theater. The scene with the Cyclops drunk is good theater. The satyrs' spell-dance is good theater. The final scene and the blinded Cyclops blundering over the stage is good theater. . . . Drama means action; theater means spectacle. It is not the function of theater to express thoughts except

> through action. If the action has thought behind it, a play is more likely to have lasting qualities. But action comes first, and this is a play of action.
>
> Second, there *is* thought behind the action. The play is compact of the New Learning and the new rationalism. Patterson is right when he says, "The tragic characters of Polyphemus and of Odysseus appear sometimes to be used to give occasion to Euripides to launch, mostly for veiled purposes of humor, scoffing sentiments without absolute conviction of blasphemy, to make innuendo as at heroes and hero-worship, to emphasize for amusement the knavery and the semi-bestial nature of the satyrs and the satyr-chief Silenus. The play seems also occasionally intended to appeal to that restrained element of human nature which loves sometimes to relax and find almost barbaric amusement in moral revolt." This is true and well said. The whole of the Cyclops's speech – "Wealth is god for men of sense. . . . What do I care for Zeus's thunderbolt . . . ? My god's my belly. . . . As for those who have complicated life by making laws they can go to hell. . . ." – is designed to provide an intellectual shock, and there are many comparable passages.

Odysseus is portrayed as overly talkative and utterly unscrupulous. Is he being cast as a typical Athenian? Ferguson argues that Polyphemus is the underdog, and Odysseus hardly a sympathetic character, albeit puny and comic. "Is not Euripides fonder of the Cyclops in this conflict? Does he not side with him? Some spectators might leave the theater feeling uncomfortable about that."

Euripides was always experimenting. It is believed that on at least two occasions in the Greater Dionysia he replaced a satyr play with a work that was more serious, though substantially less than tragic. His *Alcestis* and *Orestes* are such pieces, and some scholars elect to categorize them as "pro-satyr plays". Later, Sophocles did the same with his *Electra*; he was ever ready to borrow the innovations of his younger competitor. What was the response of spectators who expected comic relief but were instead given these semi-serious plays? Ferguson speculates that Euripides and Sophocles found "irksome" the demand that they couple a satyr play with each tragic trilogy, incongruously rounding out a morning of sublime and moving poetry by shortly afterwards attaching a work descending into broad, coarse, slapdash humour. In any event, it later became the custom to place the satyr play first on the programme each day rather than at the festival's climax.

In his *Symposium* Plato has Socrates – probably his half-fictional surrogate – beg for combining tragedy and comedy into a single art-form and try to convince Aristophanes and Agathon that "the same man should be capable of writing comedy and tragedy" and that the talents of "a true tragic poet" and a "comic poet" could coexist in one person. The hour grows late, Socrates' two antagonists become inattentive, and first Aristophanes and then – at daybreak – Agathon drift into sleep with the argument unresolved. That Socrates was right was later to be proved by Shakespeare, Ibsen, Pirandello, O'Neill and a good many others.

The satyr play was not the only Greek comic form. A parallel evolution that superseded it has come to be known as Old Comedy, a genre not linked to tragedy and not turned out by serious writers but instead fashioned by a quite independent group of poets. Theirs were the noisy works that flourished at the Lenaea, offerings that were the robust equivalent of today's musical revue, replete with rowdy sketches, witty songs and energetic dances. These became a formal part of the Lenaea in 442 BC, a decade before the introduction of tragedies at that winter-time festival. As remarked, such comedies had been included in the Greater Dionysia forty-four years earlier (486 BC) but were a less prominent aspect of it.

The history of this kind of comedy is conjectural. The Dorians took credit for its invention, a claim matching the one they put forth of having originated tragedy. Crude slapstick can be traced back to early rustic festivals, arising spontaneously from their peasant participants, especially those who were largely extroverted and intoxicated. Aristotle suggests that the first author of somewhat composed, loosely structured comic works was Epicharmus of Megara (530–440 BC), a Sicilian poet residing in the then Dorian colony of Syracuse. About his life not much is recorded except that he was active at his new craft some time between 486 and 467 BC (or some say a bit earlier, *c.* 500 BC). There is even a question as to which Megara is intended: Megara Hyblaia in Sicily; or another Megara, a Doric town situated between Corinth and Athens, noted for producing many jesters and as the birthplace of many jokes. Aristotle equivocates concerning this, merely stating: "Comedy is claimed by the Megarians, both by those of the mainland who contend that it took its rise in their democracy, and by those of Sicily, because this is where Epicharmus came from, long before Chionides and Magnes." Some lines of Epicharmus' works remain: they evidence that he employed three actors, but as yet there is no sign of a chorus. He did inject word-play, patter songs, broad parody and farcical plot premises, all of which are to be enduring characteristics of the musical revue form. He mocked the gods, especially Poseidon, and the myths, Margot Berthold tells us, portraying "Hercules as a gourmand, attracted no longer by heroic deeds but only by the smell of roasting meat; Ares and Hephaestus, haggling with spite and malice over the release of Hera from the throne from which she cannot rise; or the seven Muses, appearing as the 'buxom, well-fed daughters of Father Pot-belly and

Mother Fat-paunch.'" He brought in or established the stock characters – the braggarts, cunning hangers-on and parasites, pimps, incoherent tipplers, foolishly deceived husbands – who were to populate burlesque and farce through the ages, from ancient Greece to the Renaissance in Italy, Spain, France and Elizabethan England, on to Molière, Gilbert and Sullivan, and the very present day.

Living to the age of ninety, Epicharmus is credited with some thirty-five or forty farces, not in the Athenian but the Doric literary tongue. His scripts also had a serious side and offered his hearers ethical advice, while also dispensing herbal recipes for illnesses: and he posed as something of a political scientist. A much-quoted line of his goes: "Still be sober, still be doubting – such the muscles of the mind." In his earnest moments he preached the doctrines of Pythagoras and Heraclitus.

Actually, some Athenians asserted that Old Comedy had antecedents going back far before 500 BC, but Epicharmus' literary career might have started in advance of that date, or his success might have had a decisive influence on what comic playwrights entering the Greater Dionysia and the Lenaea subsequently fashioned. His priority in shaping the form cannot be firmly disputed.

The names of many of those Greek comic poets survive, though again not their works. Pherecrates' *The Wild Men* japed at a group of Athenians who disdained "civilization" and talked of a "return to nature". There is mention of Sophron; Chionides, also cited by Aristotle, who is believed to have been the first to have carried off the prize for comedy (486 BC); and Magnes, mentioned too by Aristotle, won it no less than eleven times, beginning in 472 BC, most often at the Lenaea. His scripts bore titles such as *Birds*, *Fig-flies* and *Frogs*, but the texts are completely gone. More refined is said to have been the work of Ecphantides. In all, there are thought to have been at least 250 comic poets busy and thriving over a long historical span.

Contemporaries and rivals of Aristophanes in the fifth century BC were three major figures: Eupolis (*fl.* 429 BC) was acclaimed for his sharp wit and rich invention and garnered the first prize on seven occasions. He was a close friend of Aristophanes – they were the same age (born *c.* 445 BC) – and they often worked together on a script, but afterwards venomously hurled charges of plagiarism at each other.

Cratinus, an actor as well as a playwright, used his devotion to Dionysus as a handy excuse for satisfying his copious thirst. In *The Bottle* (423 BC) – written when he was ninety-nine – his wife, Madame Muse, and his inamorata, Mademoiselle Flask, compete for his sexual attention. He resolves his dilemma by quoting the motto of those artists truly devoted to the cult of Dionysus: "He who drinks water, gets nowhere." With *The Bottle* the aged Cratinus got first prize, outvying the twenty-one-year-old Aristophanes, whose entry *The Knights* finished an humiliating third.

In his plays, as in those by his compeers, Cratinus was unsparing when attacking public officials, exempting not even Pericles and making fun of the splendid buildings with which the tyrant had adorned the city, and dubbing that benign ruler the "Zeus of Athens!" and a "squill-head".

Crates began his stage career as a leading player in works by Cratinus, then undertook to create his own theatrical vehicles after 449 BC. The nonagenarian Cratinus, from whom Crates learned much, far outlived his talented pupil, however.

Using a tried-and-true stage device, these four playwrights incessantly abused one another, trading malicious gibes and flinging derisive taunts. As Berthold phrases it, "It was a crossing of swords, and each author sharpened his blade on the whetstone of the other's success." The best source of laughter at this period in Greece was largely the humour of insult. The rivals exchanged personal calumnies, often outrageous ones, which unfailingly elicited guffaws from most of the huge audience, though the imputed failings or misdeeds might have no basis in fact. Eupolis mocked at Aristophanes for his naked, bald pate, and Aristophanes dismissed Cratinus as quite senile, while accusations of stealing jokes and ideas were furiously tossed back and forth between all four. Other playwrights engaged in the raucous practice, too.

Almost from the start, Old Comedy openly and boldly voiced social criticism. Following the lead and example of Epicharmus and Cratinus, the fifth-century comic poets took advantage of the permissiveness allowed on a semi-religious, semi-magical occasion. The tyrants, councillors, big-wigs of the community, as well as fellow-artists, were belittled, deflated. The ritualistic circumstances provided a welcome licence for this.

Since a major segment of the audience was primitive and unlettered, the jokes tended to be physical, earthy, having to do with excremental and other bodily functions. A sure way to degrade a man was to poke fun at his sexual capability; either he was over-amorous, or impotent; or he was a notorious glutton, or had a weak-kneed timidity, or an excessive tendency to belch or break wind, or was cadaverous or paunchy. Such gibes at the prominent grew to be traditional and had to be borne with aplomb by the victims, much as by modern political leaders, the objects of newspaper cartoons and caricatures, who are supposed to join good-naturedly in the laughter directed at them.

This raillery also expressed a degree of wish-fulfilment similar to that of Henry Fielding, who centuries later stated that his purpose in writing comedy was "to laugh mankind out of its follies". True, such ridicule does not really avail very much: the wicked and foolish are most often too thick-skinned to be affected by simple mockery; but people do feel better after an attempt to prick the proud and arrogant foe, however slightly.

The sexual element in comedy, externalized at first in ribald hymns and overly graphic pantomime, has remained a constant ever since; and also from farce's origin in unbridled revelry comes the component of wild fantasy, in more recent decades refined to mere whimsy, that has also been a persistent facet of such pieces. Here let it be grasped that most farce has an erotic motif, as well as a touch of deliberate lunacy. Indeed, as Charles Lamb was later to discern, the vulgarity of comedy offers an outlet from long-held repressions, a *katharsis* of another kind, a highly necessary "safety valve" for both the community and the individual. To be shocked at the risqué nature of light plays, whether they be burlesques, frantic French bedroom farces or wry, witty, teasingly immoral English drawing-room comedies, is to misunderstand their function in civilized society. The stage is a social institution that serves, among other purposes, to proffer a vicarious – second-hand, it might be – sexual experience, a voyeuristic one, to the spectator. It is an outlet similar to that exampled by the Roman Saturnalia and its derivatives, the wild springtime carnival and pre-Lenten *mardi-gras*, and by latter-day artists' balls as well as by Christmas office parties and New Year's Eve and Halloween festivities, at which presumably respectable and conventional people suddenly break loose from social restraints and misbehave in ways that would astonish their neighbours and co-workers, were not their neighbours and colleagues noisily behaving in the same way.

In erotic comedies, sexual fantasies are enacted in a socially acceptable manner. Though only briefly, for an hour or two infused with healthy laughter, and with much harmless and safe titillation, the clamp of religious and familial prohibitions is released. Pent-up impulses are allowed some moments of freedom, however illusory.

Greek comic actors had talents and skills that naturally differentiated them from the tragedians. In the *Poetics* Aristotle refers again to the Dorians' claim to having originated the genre of comedy, an assertion that they supported "by pointing to the words 'comedy' and 'drama'. Their word for the outlying hamlets, they say, is *comae*, whereas Athenians call them *demes* – thus assuming that comedians got the name not from their *comoe* or revels, but from their strolling from hamlet to hamlet, lack of appreciation keeping them out of the city." Some further quotations from Aristotle about the development of comedy: "Its early stages passed unnoticed, because it was not yet taken up in a serious way. It was only at a late point in its progress that a chorus of comedians was officially granted by the archon; they used to be mere volunteers. It had also already definite forms at the time when the record of those termed comic begins. Who it was who supplied it with masks, or prologues, or a plurality of actors and the like has remained unknown." Here he singles out Epicharmus, as has already been noted. "The invented fable, or plot, however, originated with Epicharmus and Phormis; of Athenian poets Crates was the first to drop the Comedy of invective and frame stories of a general and non-personal nature, in other words, fables or plots."

By the time Aristotle wrote the *Poetics*, facts about the sixth century BC were already hazy and remote, even to him. Some scholars believe he composed a treatise on comedy along the lines of his essay on tragedy but that it is lost; or that his intention was to attempt an examen like it, but that he never got around to doing so, which is to be profoundly regretted.

In 486 BC, as has been said, somewhat structured comedies were officially admitted for performance at the Greater Dionysia and granted the right to a professional chorus, its members supplanting the amateurs and vagabond players heretofore improving such works while touring and entertaining in the provinces outside Athens. The chorus was larger than that designated for tragedy and had a more active part; it was composed of twenty-four actors – two groups of twelve each – enabling confrontations on roughly equal terms, to toss back and forth snide appellations, lampooning dignitaries, in farcical debates about a topical issue that provided a pretext for the play. From approximately 442 BC cash prizes were given for the best comedy. Five contesting groups (but later only three) competed for lucrative awards.

An opening procession marched to the Greater Dionysia. In it were comic actors attired in horns, tails, hip-fur, and particularly goat-skins stripped from beasts that had already been sacrificed to the deity. The marchers wore padded false male genitalia, puffed up to exaggerated size, to evoke laughter and also to remind onlookers of the progenitive nature of the god being honoured. Such phallic displays had long been part of the fertility rites from which comedy descended. In the plays themselves, male characters but not chorus members still exposed their enlarged, red-leather phalluses, and the striped *chitons* (tunics) were skin-tight and excessively short to suggest extra nudity, though in reality the actors were modestly covered by flesh-coloured tights. Bellies and buttocks were wrapped about and built up to look extended and grossly disproportionate. The costumes did not resemble ordinary Greek attire but tended to be humorous adaptations of the ornate robes and *chitons* worn by tragic actors; however, this varied from play to play. In some instances, young male and supposedly female characters might appear in costumes that were almost conventional.

For comedy, the limitation of three actors was gradually eased. The scripts show that four and even five were sometimes needed. The rules governing the Greater Dionysia and the Lenaea were not always the same. As was true with tragedians, comic actors got their payment from the state. In addition to the prize for the best tragic portrayal, a purse was given for an outstanding interpretation by a comedian. Only the lead performer in a work was eligible to win such an award.

Free-wheeling, loose, episodic, an offering in this genre elaborated some slight theme serving to connect slap-dash, satirical skits, the whole work barely hanging together. Any crazy, fantastic idea lent the piece a title and provided a simulacrum of a plot. A flow of indecent abuse, obscene jokes and burlesque sketches let the author heap his criticism on government officials, rival playwrights and other members of the "establishment". Perhaps no theatre in history has ever been as outspoken, especially in attacking living persons. In 440 BC censorship was imposed, but after three years it was rescinded, and the torrent of comic derision was resumed. This was a truly democratic stage with complete freedom of speech. What is more, the attacks were concerted – often all the playwrights chose the same subject or object for ridicule – which afforded them a palpable influence. Such assaults, giving voice to the feelings of the *poloi*, were feared and heeded – and resented – by the upper class.

The madcap premise of the play might be that the hero, anxious to stop the war, ascends to Heaven on a beetle's back; or else Bdelycleon tries to prevent his senile father, Philocleon, a compulsive jury-server, from yielding to his obsession by locking him up in his home. The jury enters, and the divided halves take opposite sides, joining the principals in debating the merits of the scheme. This was the *agon*. Now all comes to a halt and the audience is addressed directly by the lead actor and the chorus, and this phase of the performance, unique to Old Comedy, constitutes the *parabasis*. In it the playwright has an opportunity to harangue the spectators and express his impious views on any number of subjects. Next follow a series of farcical episodes in which the basic idea is put to the test of action: the result, invariably, is a pile-up of amusing if not hilarious misadventures. At the climax comes a revel, a feast or some other sort of merry-making occasion, with a turn in the plot that rescues or absolves the hero and brings a happy wind-up. The actors, the chorus members trained and agile, may dance wildly off.

In these nonsensical sketches are many reminders in spirit and detail of the primitive Dionysian improvisations, and this is especially true of the *parabasis*, which may have derived from a response by the leader to insults flung at the phallic masqueraders by onlookers – a rebuke, a lecture – and also true of the concluding revel, which seems to have reflected the original, once licentious Dionysian *comus*. That the chorus might be attired and masked as wasps, birds or frogs, in a tradition previously embraced by Magnes, not only hearkened back to the Athenian theatre's pervasive affinity to totemism, but also enforced the element of fantasy inherent in the story-concept, and lent the stage an extra dimension of spectacle from the weird and costly costumes of the actors representing huge insects and other spindling non-human living species.

About the dances, Brockett writes: "[They] were less dignified than those of tragedy. Many were intentionally ridiculous. . . . Comic choral dances were derived from many sources: animal movements, religious ceremonies, victory celebrations, and various other activities and rites. The individual actors performed dances which involved kicking the buttocks, slapping the chest or thighs, leaping, performing high kicks, spinning like a top, or beating other actors. The most common term for the comic dances is *kordax.*"

(O.G. Brockett also offers a brief description of the *sikinnis,* a feature of satyr plays and specifically called for in Euripides' *Cyclops*: "[It] probably involved vigorous leaping, horseplay and lewd pantomime. Often it burlesqued the tragic dances, the *emmeleia.*" Again, bas-reliefs on steles and outlined sketches on vases offer the clearest hints about this.)

Winning first prize assured the comic poet of a place in the following year's contest. This tradition was of major service to Aristophanes (*c.* 450–*c.* 387 BC), the best-remembered practitioner of Old Comedy, and the only one whose works are still alive – eleven complete scripts of the forty he is believed to have written. That they have been preserved is testimony to the high esteem in which they were held by his contemporaries; after 2,000 years they are still performed, still amuse, so that he is ranked as one of the world's great masters of comedy.

Of his life, too little is known. He is thought to have been born in Cydathene, a suburb or *deme* of Athens. The span of his active period as a poet coincides with that of Euripides and Socrates, both of whom were unfortunate targets of his hostile wit. He is one of the ornaments of the Golden Age of Greek theatre – Aeschylus, Sophocles and Euripides being the others – and his name is inevitably linked with theirs; but he should also be seen in a context that includes the three other prominent writers of Old Comedy in his day – Eupolis, Cratinus and Crates – the rivals whom he obviously surpassed; on the evidence, none was his equal then, and few since.

Though he excelled at comedy, Aristophanes had a serious purpose, a trait he shared with his rivals and important comic dramatists of much later epochs – Molière, Ben Jonson, Wilde, Shaw. The purveyors of Old Comedy found fault with and sought to reform the government of Athens. Most of them seem to have been conservatives, decrying the excessive radicalism of the party in power.

The early stretch of Aristophanes' career unfolded during the flourishing Periclean epoch, but also while the Peloponnesian War was going on, taking an endless toll of lives and treasure and ending with Sparta's devastating victory in 404 BC. Like Euripides, whom he so unsparingly calumniated, he was anti-militarist. Four of his plays express his fierce disapproval of the struggle.

By some accounts he was the son of a wealthy family, landowners, which might explain his seemingly innate political conservatism. His name itself means "the best made manifest" and is a token of noble birth. An intelligent observer, it hurt him to see Greek slaying Greek, but perhaps there were other reasons for his bias: most satirists tend to be against the "Establishment", or whoever is responsible for governing. The exercise of such power usually entails setting up a bureaucracy, which in train means inefficiency and, in time, corruption. Athens was a democracy, but many of its civic leaders were dishonest, and the aristocratic Aristophanes was gravely offended by much that he saw first hand in his cherished city-state.

He also had the conservative's natural yearning for a return to the "good old days", Athens's golden past, an age of simplicities and certainly a more austere virtue. He blamed the incessant demands of the war for much of the demoralization of his city, but also held the sceptical intellectuals and writers – including Socrates, Euripides and Agathon – at fault for Athens's peril and growing decadence. And, finally, the long war had forced him to abandon his country home and move within the city's walls for personal safety, and he disliked urban life.

His opposition to Pericles was strong, but even more virulent was his disapprobation of Cleon, the rich tanner, who assumed power after Pericles' death in 429 BC, and who led the militarists demanding an escalation of the hated war, to remove for all time Sparta's rivalry for economic and political leadership of Greece. To Aristophanes, Cleon was a brutal manipulator on behalf of grasping commercial interests, a heartless imperialist and a populist. In an Old Comedy there would be scant doubt as to who was being satirized, as the actors' masks, though ugly and distorted, often bore sharp likenesses to the intended victim, with even Pericles and Cleon being no exceptions.

Aristophanes' first produced play, *The Banqueters*, was staged at the Lenaea in 427 BC; he was about twenty. He submitted it under an assumed name, that of a prominent actor, Callistratus, and was awarded honourable mention; the text has vanished, as has that of his second entry, *The Babylonians* (426 BC), done at the Greater Dionysia, and for which he again borrowed the name of his friend Callistratus. His aim in *The Banqueters* was to satirize theories of "modern education" currently being much talked about and practised in Athens; he was, life-long, a deadly enemy of all artistic cults and intellectual fads. In *The Babylonians*, which had a political message, he was critical of the course of Athens's domestic and foreign affairs. Cleon, taking offence at a proliferation of nasty snipes at his person and official policies, had the young author brought before the Senate on a charge of slander, but at the session that heard the complaint the zestful playwright prevailed, merely having to pay a fine.

Aristophanes became even bolder in *The Acharnians* (425 BC), presented at the Lenaea the next year; it brought him the first prize. By now the unwelcome war had lasted six years, Pericles was dead four years, the hated Cleon was firmly in charge and militarism was riding high. But food was short; farms outside the city had been devastated; supplies had to be imported. Athens was trying to coax support from possible allies, the semi-barbaric Thracians and the rich but reluctant Persians.

For his hero, the poet chose Dicaeopolis ("Honest Citizen"), a tough, profane, independent farmer who has grown weary of the prolonged hostilities and deprivations. To protest, he goes to an assembly in the Pynx, an open space on a hillside adjacent to the market. Three times a month meetings are held here to discuss major civic problems. As usual, he is the first to arrive, as he wants a good spot to be heard and seen. This is Dicaeopolis ruminating aloud as he waits for the meeting to start:

> Here it is assembly day, we're supposed to meet at dawn – and the place is deserted. Everybody's jabbering at the market-place, and running every which way. . . . Even the chairman and his committee aren't here yet. They'll come hours late and spill into the place in a mob, shoving each other to get the front row seats. Wait'll you see. [*Shaking his head ruefully*] But how to get peace – that they don't care about one bit. [*Heaving a sigh*] Oh, Athens, Athens! [*Falls silent; then, more calmly*] I'm always the first to get to these meetings. I take a seat and, since I'm all by myself, I gripe, I yawn, I fart, fidget, stretch, scratch, scribble, figure my bills – and look out over the fields, yearning for peace to come back. I hate the city. I want my own village where you never hear things like [*imitating an Athenian street-hawker*] "Charcoal for sale! Oil, vinegar for sale!" We made everything there for ourselves; we never had to be sold on the place. [Translation: Lionel Casson]

Suddenly the chairman, the committee and a mob rush in, jostling for good seats, as Dicaeopolis has anticipated. The meeting proves to be highly unsatisfactory; his objections hooted down. Among those addressing the assembly is Amphitheus, an "immortal" – a messenger of the gods – whose diction parodies that of an Euripidean tragic character:

> The first of my name was child of Ceres and
> Triptolemus. Of him was Celeus born,
> Who wed Phaenarete, my grandmother.
> From her sprung Lycinus, and I from him –
> [Translation: Lionel Casson]

The gods have appointed him to arrange a peace with Sparta, but he needs money for travel expenses, and the committee refuses to vote him any. Dicaeopolis intervenes on his behalf but is overruled. But next a delegation of Athenians who have been sent to the Court of Persia appears, dressed in gorgeous Oriental costumes; they give far-fetched reasons for their four-year absence and receive a huge payment for their trouble. A bearded one-eyed Persian secret service agent has entered with them and delivers a message from his monarch: "*Iartaman exarx anapissonai satra*," which no one can understand. It is finally rendered to mean that the Persian king is sending gold, but the agent quickly corrects this. "You fat-ass Greeks. No get money." This contradicts the envoy's report. Dicaeopolis grasps the point: "He says the Greeks are a bunch of fatheads if they expect any money from Persia." An argument ensues as to just what the agent has said, but Dicaeopolis has it right. More parody of Euripides' poetic language is inserted here, sprinkled with scatological jokes and explicit allusions to bodily functions and sexual inadequacies.

Frustrated, Dicaeopolis hires Amphitheus to negotiate a private peace for him with the Spartans. The semi-divine messenger comes back with a choice of treaties, and Dicaeopolis accepts one that will maintain the peace for thirty years.

In his home, Dicaeopolis and his family – wife and children – celebrate the prospect of relief from the war. The rites are enacted with considerable mockery. But now the family is besieged by twenty-four angry Acharnians (the chorus), old veterans of Marathon, who are now vendors of charcoal – they are from Acharnia, a village quite near Athens. What Dicaeopolis has done is treasonable in their eyes, and they rain stones on him. He finally buys a truce by offering to stand trial for his act with his head on a chopping block.

While awaiting a decision on his fate, Dicaeopolis goes to the house of Euripides and asks to see him. "Is he in?" he asks the servant at the door, who replies, in the paradoxical style of his master: "He's in – and he isn't. If you can follow me." After some resistance, Dicaeopolis begins to shout and is heard by the great poet, who finally appears in a cart of the sort in which slain bodies are displayed in tragic dramas; he is resting on a couch and is attired in a flowing robe, of the type used by tragic actors, though his is somewhat the worse for wear. Dicaeopolis exclaims: "Look at those clothes! What do you do, wear rags from your tragedies? No wonder you write about beggars. (*Pleadingly*) Euripides! I beg you, on my knees, give me some rags from that old play of yours. I've got to make a speech to the chorus, (*pointedly, since lengthy addresses were a Euripidean speciality*) a long one. I've got to be good. If not, it means my life."

Euripides pokes around in a pile of discards, enumerating the many plays in which his actors have worn tattered garb. At Euripides' instruction, his servant brings a bundle of torn clothes for his visitor. Donning them, Dicaeopolis is inspired, his spirits lifted. He continues to make impertinent demands until Euripides is annoyed and orders him to leave. What is implied here is that Aristophanes is scornful of Euripides' sentimentality and his use of such devices for blatant tear-jerking.

At this point the action halts while the actor turns to the spectators and assumes the identity of the author, recounting how Cleon had summoned him before the Senate a year ago for uttering some unwelcome truths; he is about to do so again. He cannot be accused of slandering the state before strangers, for he is at the Lenaea – "We're by ourselves. There are no strangers in town yet." (The Lenaea, held during the winter months, was little attended by spectators from elsewhere in Attica, who did flood into Athens for the Greater Dionysia.) Proceeding, and reiterating emphatically that his role is that of a truth-teller, above all, he insists that the war had arisen from trivial causes and puts much of the blame for it on the Athenians themselves, including Pericles and Cleon, for having harshly mistreated the Megarians, who, blockaded and starving, had finally asked Sparta to aid them. The strife could have been avoided, and the Spartans were not without justification in coming to the assistance of their small ally.

Half the chorus is infuriated and condemns Dicaeopolis' unpatriotic stand, while the other half defends him; the argument escalates to a scuffle, with the anti-Dicaeopolites near defeat. They call frantically for the help of Lamachus, an Athenian general chosen by Aristophanes as typical of those with a pro-war mind-set. Coming forth from his house, sword in hand and dressed in shining breastplate and plumed helmet, Lamachus responds, speechifying in the Euripidean style. In return for the general's rebuke for his treasonable behaviour, Dicaeopolis vilifies him as a coward and cheat, a pocket-liner, one who has steadily robbed the state's coffers. (In reality Lamachus was an honest, courageous soldier, and after he was killed in combat Aristophanes belatedly sought to make amends.) The names of many prominent Athenian families, only slightly disguised, erupt throughout this scalding denunciation. Then both Lamachus and Dicaeopolis retreat into their dwellings.

The chorus, preparing for the *parabasis*, declare Dicaeopolis to have been the winner. In their song they pay further tribute to the playwright (Dicaeopolis as Aristophanes' surrogate) for his remarkable candour and his fearlessness in opposition to the wicked, scheming Cleon. His reputation for frankness has spread everywhere throughout Greece and Asia Minor, and, indeed, one reason that Sparta is warring with Athens is the hope of claiming the dauntless playwright for its own.

Another subject is abruptly introduced: the plight of aged, penniless Athenian veterans of former wars, especially the forgotten heroes who fought at Marathon.

Next comes a sketch, a strange bit of dark comedy, in which an impoverished Megarian farmer is so hungry and reduced in fortune that in desperation he sells Dicaeopolis his two little daughters hidden in a sack and passed off as piglets, with false snouts and hooves protruding through holes in the bag as part of the deception. The dialogue in this passage is laced throughout with sexual *double entendres* and is in Megarian dialect.

In a marketplace Dicaeopolis engages in barter with a Boeotian from whom he purchases mint leaves, thrushes and eels – precious delicacies – in exchange for handing over a trussed-up little man, Niarchus, an informer, one of the irritating army of spies who serve Cleon by infiltrating the city and reporting on so-called "subversive activities" by honest citizens. The Boeotian intends to take Niarchus to his native town and exhibit him, charging a fee to any who wish to view the miserable creature.

Lamachus dispatches a servant to buy some of Dicaeopolis' birds and eels, but the man is sent back empty-handed, with word that his master too should eat the spare rations that are doled out to his soldiers. The chorus sings Dicaeopolis' praises and deplores the hardships brought on by war. The advantages of peace are embodied by Dicaeopolis, who has made his separate peace and now lives high and bountifully.

A farmer enters, weeping: his oxen have been stolen by the Boeotians and he has been left destitute. He begs for a few drops from Dicaeopolis' flagon of peace, but is denied any. He is succeeded by the best man from a wedding party who bears a gift of meat for Dicaeopolis and pleads for a "cupful of peace" and is told that it is not to be shared at any price. A bridesmaid is more persuasive: she wants some "peace" to spare her husband-to-be from having to do military service, and Dicaeopolis grants her plea.

A messenger runs in, knocks on Lamachus' door, summons him to battle. A second messenger hurries in, informing Dicaeopolis that the priests of Dionysus await him at the Festival. While Lamachus dons his combat garb and Dicaeopolis packs his basket of rare treats, they exchange gibes, the warrior readying himself for a gritty time, the honest farmer for a wild, rich feast.

In the subsequent episode a groaning Lamachus is carried in, wounded, bedraggled and sore; Dicaeopolis staggers in, intoxicated, supported by two beautiful blonde flute-girls with whom he intends to disport through the night. He has won the drinking competition; his triumph is cheered by the chorus, until the entire cast leaves the stage singing and dancing uninhibitedly.

Sandbach comments:

> The praises of peace are sung by Aristophanes in several of his plays, but to praise peace and to be a pacifist are different things. "War is for the sake of peace," wrote Aristotle. Most people always want

> peace, but not peace at any price. They want peace with victory, or at least with safety. The route to peace may lie through war. Men can regret that, but they recognize it.
>
> To see *The Acharnians* as a manifesto in favour of peace is too simple. Most Athenians wanted peace, but they wanted it on their own terms. There was at this time no hope of a compromise, as had been made plain when in 430 they had tried to open negotiations. The coalition opposing them wished and hoped to destroy the Athenian Empire: the Athenians were determined to maintain it. For anything we know, Aristophanes shared this ambition. . . . He had no suggestion of how to make peace a practical policy. All he does is play with a fantasy of peace. His Dicaeopolis has no care for national interests, or indeed for any interests but his own. How delightful to imagine oneself for a moment enjoying the pleasures of selfishness! But this is no more than a holiday escape from reality. It is impossible for an individual to contract out of his country's war and, even if it were possible, peace cannot be made, as Dicaeopolis made it, without any terms except that it is to last for thirty years.
>
> Yet in a way *The Acharnians* had a political purpose. The Athenians were not agreed about the terms on which they would be ready to make peace. Aristophanes seems to have been one of those who believed the Peloponnesian War ought to have been avoided and ought to be brought to an end. He suggested therefore that its origins had been trivial, that the blame did not rest entirely with Sparta, and that if the two great powers cooperated, they could rule the world. If his play could exert any influence, it would be in favour of moderates who were ready to accept some compromise if the opportunity offered. At the same time he tried to discredit those who favoured fighting on for decisive victory by accusing them of making personal gains from the war.

Others hold that this reading of the play is scarcely borne out by the language and incidents Aristophanes inserted in it, that his purpose was clearly, defiantly political, that he was advocating peace with no reservations, while harshly flailing at the war-supporters as openly as anyone dared, castigating the ruling party as crowded with selfish opportunists, chicane opportunists, plunderers, true enemies of the state, all headed by the demagogic Cleon. Lamachus, the typical general, could hardly be portrayed more scathingly, if – as it turned out – unfairly.

John Gassner writes: "Dicaeopolis is an excellent comic hero; his unsentimental character is the illusionless Comic Spirit incarnate. Peppered with allusions to the rapacity of the people's leaders (Cleon is accused of having accepted a bribe of five talents) and with a parody of Euripides' lost *Telephus*, the play is humorously topical." (The encounter with the Acharnian charcoal-burners is said to be an off-beat parallel of one in Euripides' vanished work, produced thirteen years earlier, in which the hostage, not a bag of charcoal but a hapless child, fends off an assault.)

A first prize at the Lenaea came Aristophanes' way the next year with *The Knights* (424 BC), another onslaught against Cleon, who after a naval victory in the Bay of Pylos had just been granted, among other privileges and honours, the right to sit in the front row at the theatre, where if he so desired he could more closely watch this savage charade pointed at him. The "Knights" was the term used for the party of wealthy, elite Athenians to whom Aristophanes belonged who opposed the war. Cleon drew his strength from the farmers, their numbers far larger, who had been driven from their arable lands by the Spartan invasion; taking refuge in the city, they urgently wished the war to continue until they recovered their lost fields. With their support Cleon had been re-elected a general, to Aristophanes' intense chagrin and in spite of his vicious attacks. The tyrant had a violent streak and did not enjoy hearing a character in *The Acharnians* propose that the "tanner-turned-ruler be sliced into shoe-leather".

In *The Knights*, however, Aristophanes pushes on to take his personal revenge on the dictator who had impeached him. He can no longer use actual names, so he calls the slave-villain of the piece Paphlagon, connoting "blusterer" and "barbarian": he is further identified as a tanner. The rascal has got his grouchy old master, Demos (The People), completely under his thumb. His chief rival is a Sausage Seller, easily recognized by the audience as Hyperbolus, destined to be Cleon's successor but in no way superior in virtue. Two more slaves, representing the admiral of the Athenian navy, Nicias, and his vice-admiral, Demosthenes, try vainly to free the gullible Demos from the evil sway of the cunning pair whose schemes they oppose. They succeed only when the fleet mutinies against the Sausage Seller, who has outdone Paphlagon in dishonesty. Muses the tanner, taking stock of the Sausage Seller and somewhat taken aback by his earlier defeats by him. "He cannot be a greater thief than I am, but he may be a luckier one."

The Sausage Seller explains how he has prospered, though he lacks a formal education:

> I learned to take a false oath without a smile, when I had
> stolen something.

And Demosthenes says to him:

> In this very thing your greatness lies –
> In being a rogue, and impudent, and vulgar.

When the Sausage Seller confesses that his forebears were "Scum of the Earth!", Demosthenes replies:

Ah, I congratulate you!
That's a good start indeed for public life.

The Sausage Seller protests again:

But, sir, I haven't any education –
Just know my alphabet – and *that* damned badly.

Demosthenes is ready for this, too:

That's your one drawback – knowing it even badly!
Not educated men, not honest men,
Are qualified for Leaders of the Masses,
But ignorant scoundrels.
[Translation: F.L. Lucas]

Paphlagon, ignominiously reduced, becomes a peddler and is condemned to drink bath water.

Elsewhere in the play much fun is directed at oracles and the superstition that breeds them. Food plays a good part in the action: it is offered as a copious bribe, stolen, used as a weapon – the tanner is beaten with tripe by the Sausage Seller, who taints his own breath with garlic to help him score telling points in a debate. *The Knights* delighted its audience by its ferocity but is probably too topical – footnotes and a glossary are necessary to appreciate it – for it to thrive on a modern stage, and its humour is far too partisan and scurrilous for today's spectator to embrace.

The legend is that no actor dared to undertake the role of Paphlagon, fearing the vindictive Cleon. Thereupon Aristophanes, forswearing a caricature-mask, essayed the part himself, smearing his features with wine-lees as another silent comment, reminding everybody that the tyrant had an alcoholic's red, swollen visage.

A mere third prize went to Aristophanes' *The Clouds* (423 BC) which takes a different tack. Here the keen-eyed and merciless young playwright trained his sights on no less a person than Socrates. Old Strepsiades faces financial ruin and is being reduced to misery by his wastrel son's gambling debts and misconduct. Seeking to reform him and recoup his fortunes, the father urges the youth to enter Socrates' apocryphal school, the Phrontisterion or "Thinking Shop". There he might learn a glib illlogic, the new craft of argumentation called Sophistry. When the youth refuses, speaking contemptuously of Socrates and his fellow-philosophers, the father himself decides to enrol as a student. Soon he finds the artful thinkers pondering such questions as whether gnats hum through their mouths or backwards through their hindquarters. When the astonished Strepsiades meets Socrates himself, the ceaselessly interrogative meditator is suspended in a basket halfway between heaven and earth, the better to be near the Clouds and the ethereal source of his enigmatic conclusions. (It is these Clouds, who later comprise the chorus, that befog men's minds and supply them with vaporous phrases. Socrates asserts that they are the supreme deities.) Below him, his pupils, rumps upward, gaze steadfastly at the ground, contemplating more mundane matters: "Plumbing the depths that lie as deep as Tartarus . . ." A brief stay in this "Thinking Shop" is too much for the addle-pated Strepsiades; he withdraws from the school and finally persuades his son to go instead. After an initiation ceremony, during which he is garlanded with leaves, then sprinkled with flour, the youth gradually becomes wan, impudent, devious of speech, effeminate and debauched, all a result of the new permissive methods of teaching.

The play is yet another sharp thrust at "progressive education". It is filled with nostalgia for the older Athenian virtues of austerity, of past days when boys acquired physical fortitude by bathing in cold water, not warm, and took plenty of outdoor exercise, while learning respect for their elders, honesty of speech and forthright, manly behaviour. In the new day injustice rules everywhere, and all successful men, whether lawyers, public orators or poets, are blackguards. Even in the audience, such outright scoundrels comprise the majority.

Blasphemous ideas are put in Socrates' mouth: there is no Zeus, he declares; the Clouds rule the universe. Can Zeus make it rain (with his sieved chamber-pot in Heaven) when the sky is blue and cloudless? The Clouds alone make rain . . . *ergo* Zeus does not exist. What does account for everything is Vortex, or Rotation, a new scientific concept.

At the end, the son resorts to the Socratic question-and-answer formula for analysing a problem and "proves" to Strepsiades that it is perfectly proper for children to beat their parents; he does not spare the befuddled old man, who repents that he ever sent his offspring to hearken to Socrates. Hurting and aroused to anger, Strepsiades runs off to burn down the obnoxious "Thinking Shop".

Aelian relates that Socrates himself was at the performance, and hearing some strangers ask one another who he was, stood up that all present might behold him, his moon-face beaming and nodding to the throng of spectators as he acknowledged his identity, the gracious, amused victim of Aristophanes' sharp jests. Aristophanes' portrait of him, of course, is greatly distorted: in truth, Socrates had no school, and took no fees from his worshipful disciples for his disquisitions. It might be said that his role in the city was so well known that the audience could easily detect and correct for themselves the errors in the report of the philosopher's new teachings. Then again, it was not a Greek custom ever to be fair to an opponent. It has often been asserted, however, that this unjust and inaccurate picture of Socrates contributed to the climate of hostility that subsequently led to his trial and sentence of death on the ground that he was leading Athenian youth astray. If it is so, Aristophanes bears a heavy share of guilt for that great crime against humanity and genius, which, however, occurred two dozen years later. Both Socrates and Plato seem to have stayed on friendly terms with the exasperatingly critical playwright. Lucas argues, on Aristophanes' behalf, that Socrates "may well have educated some of his young men beyond their intellectual means", so that they spouted pseudo-ideas, adding din and confusion at a troubled moment, and hence he *was* undermining the morale of Athens and hastening its decline.

In any event, *The Clouds* was judged inferior to Cratinas' *The Wine Flagon* and Ameipias' *Connos*, and ended in last place. Subsequently Aristophanes revised the whole play, and it is the final draft – never staged in his lifetime – that has come down to us.

Many of the choral passages in *The Clouds*, as in the previous scripts, have a lyric beauty that sets Aristophanes' bawdy and raffish comedies apart from all others: he was a poet of surprising distinction, having a unique combination of talents that is manifest throughout the body of his work.

Unlike *The Clouds*, his next work, *The Wasps* (422 BC), has proved to be a truly viable comedy, one that is still staged. With it he is believed to have gained another first prize, in competition with *The Rehearsal*, which took second prize – and which was also his work, written under a pseudonym, "Philonides". (In this instance, the record of who won the awards is not quite clear.) As alluded to earlier, Philocleon ("Lover of Cleon") is obsessed by a desire to serve as a jury-man. He loves to hear legal arguments and is fascinated by courtroom histrionics and believes that by being on hand he is helping the cause of justice. His son Bdelycleon ("Enemy of Cleon") seeks to restrain the old man by locking him in the house. When a group of doddering fellow-jurors (the chorus attired as Wasps) comes to call for Philocleon, he tries all sorts of fanciful ways to escape from his detention; if inventively acted, this provides much visual humour: an attempt to exit up the chimney as if he were smoke; or taking flight from the roof, as if he were a swallow. Says Xanthias, in the Prologue:

Ours is a little tale, with meaning in it,
Not too refined and exquisite for you,
Yet wittier far than vulgar comedy.
[Translation: Benjamin E. Rogers]

As he persistently risks his life to get out, dangling from a rope and about to fall, the fanatical Philocleon begs to be buried "under the courthouse floor". When Bdelycleon frustrates him again and again, he is attacked by the "stinging" Wasps, who also charge him with "treason" (i.e., of being a monarchist), to which Bdelycleon rejoins that far too many loose charges like that are being hurled about in the city, where the moral climate has deteriorated. Furthermore, Athens is infested with false public informers, who are mere opportunists. As many as 500 jurors may sit on a case, mostly to collect fees. Father and son debate about the judicial system of Athens, which of course Aristophanes stigmatizes as vilely corrupt and unscrupulously manipulated by the thieving Cleon. The supposedly free citizens have actually become exploited slaves, in bondage to a flattering demagogue whose smooth tongue invariably misleads them. But Philocleon persists in his senile folly, until Bdelycleon arranges a mock trial in their household; a dog is arraigned for having stolen Sicilian cheese. The "Sicilian cheese" is a reference to the "Sicilian spoils" that an Athenian general, Laches, was accused of having taken as bribes from the city's foes; the indicted house dog, Labes, obviously represents him. By mistake, dropping his vote in the wrong urn, Philocleon for the first time in his life casts it for an acquittal. The case has been prosecuted by another dog, Cur, intended to be recognized as Cleon.

Cur's only utterance at the trial is "Bow". At a feast, Philocleon gets very drunk, does damage, tries to abduct a pretty girl and is threatened with several lawsuits.

In the *parabasis* Aristophanes chides his audience for not having voted first prize to *The Clouds* the year before. He boasts that the object of his derision had been no petty figure but a person of considerable power and menace, as they well know.

Over two thousand years later Jean Racine plucked a number of ideas from *The Wasps* for his own effective comedy *Les Plaideurs* (1668, *The Litigants*); though initially unsuccessful, it has held its place since in the French classical repertory as Racine's only sally into this genre.

Peace (421 BC; *Pax*) came at a moment when a treaty calling for the cessation of hostilities with Sparta was about to be ratified, after ten years of battles; hence the play is not as critical of Athens but rather somewhat celebratory. An exchange of hostages was under way, and the outlook was bright. The truce proved to be fragile and short-lived, but Aristophanes did not foresee the unhappy outcome. In a pure fantasy, he has the hero, Trygaios, fly up to Olympus astride a giant dung-beetle (doubtless with the help of a crane) to ask assistance in stopping the fighting; only to learn that Zeus and most of his divine court have taken leave, having moved on to much further heights. In the opening scene the journeyer's two slaves prepare the large-winged insect much as present-day mechanics might overhaul and make ready a jet plane or rocket for a flight into outer space. In the absence of Zeus, who has departed because he was revolted by the Greeks' predilection for mutual destruction, Hermes and the War God have stayed on and assumed control; while the unhappy goddess Peace has been brushed aside and shut away in a cave. Hermes informs Trygaios that the War God is planning to have the Greeks pounded to pieces and annihilated. What is required is a Pan-Hellenic effort, a display of unity, to rescue the goddess from her forcible detention. Trygaios, failing to get adequate cooperation from his fellow-Greeks – the Boeotians, the Argives, the Spartan militarists, the Megarians and the Athenian hard-liners – finally recruits a chorus of Attic farmers, as war-exhausted as himself, and, hauling on ropes, they finally succour the long-pent Peace. Descending to earth, Trygaios marries Oporo (Harvest) and presides over several antic scenes at this wedding-feast, where fun is gained at the expense of an oracle and a munitions-maker. The play abounds in buffoonery, but its principal feature is its pastoral lyrics, evocative of the lovely Attic countryside and rustic life. Aristophanes reveals here, as elsewhere, his deep attachment to his native landscape.

The Birds (414 BC) comes from a period seven years later; his output during the intervening span is no longer extant. This comic work is one of his finest and exhibits a salient advance in artistry, a magnificent expansion of his imagination. The imagery is delicate and fresh; it offers an odd and even paradoxical contrast to the Billingsgate that marks so much of his humour elsewhere. Aristophanes is frequently likened to Shelley as a romantic poet, and this play bears out the coupling. It won second prize at the Greater Dionysia.

Two disenchanted Athenians, Peisthetaerus ("Persuasive", and in the Greek given a variety of spellings) and Euelpides ("Hopeful"), guided by a crow and a jackdaw, take leave of *terra firma* and enter into a bird-realm; the chorus, welcoming them, consists of twenty-four different species of feathered and beaked creatures. There the two voyagers conceive a plot to take over the universe by building and defending a city with a high wall in mid-air. So situated, they can starve out the gods in Olympus by seizing all sacrifices sent up by the pious on earth. By artful flattery they persuade the birds to assist them. Quickly established, the new city, with its 600-foot-high wall, is called Cloud-Cuckoo-Land. The play becomes an obvious commentary on the Utopianism rampant in Athens at that time, when the Peace of Nicias had temporarily suspended the war with Sparta – a fifty-year truce was signed – and a new expedition against Sicily, just launched, was going well. In a surge of optimism, all sorts of aspiring proposals for reform, a better society, were being put forth by the Athenian intelligentsia. Aristophanes aimed his feathered barbs at the unrealistic afflatus of these windy talkers. In no time his founders of Cloud-Cuckoo-Land are bothered and overrun by the same poetasters, oracle-mongers, sycophants, public informers, parasites, tax commissioners, summons-servers, law-hatchers and other persistent nuisances that had plagued them before. Nor are the two elderly refugees from Athens any less conniving than the miscreants from whom they fled. This brave new world, alas, is no happier or more virtuous than the old one. Next, concealed from Zeus by a large umbrella, Prometheus appears to announce that the hungry gods are coming to sue for peace: deprived of humankind's offerings, they are famished. Peisthetaerus, advised by Prometheus, sets as his terms that he not only be given sovereignty over the cosmos but also one of Zeus' daughters, Basileia, as a bride. After some disputations amongst themselves, the Olympian envoys, sniffing succulent food that is cooking, yield to his every demand. The play ends with a hymeneal revel.

Once again, the author does not spare Socrates, though the jibes at him are comparatively mild. Another target is one Kleonymos, an ill-famed fat man who in the midst of a battle shamelessly dropped his shield and took to his heels. Aristophanes mentions him in several other plays, and here he is the inspiration of verses sung by the avian chorus (translation by William Arrowsmith):

Many the marvels I have seen,
the wonders on land and sea;
but the strangest sight I ever saw
was the weird KLEONYMOS-tree.

It grows in faraway places;
its lumber looks quite stout,
but the wood is good for nothing,
for the heart is rotten out.

In Spring it grows gigantic
with sycophantic green,
and bitter buds of slander
on every bough are seen.

But when, like war, cold winter comes,
this strange KLEONYMOS yields,

Instead of leaves like other trees,
a crop of coward's shields.

The erection of Cloud-Cuckoo-Land is a notable passage (again in Arrowsmith's rendition):

PEISTHETAERUS: The first thing to do is build one single bird-city;
Next, surround the atmosphere and the middle air
With a wall of huge, baked bricks – like Babylon.

Peisthetaerus, who by now has acquired wings, gives Euelpides specific instructions:

Hop it, man!
Quick, up the rigging of the air!
Hurry! Done? Now supervise the workers on the wall.
Run the rubble up!
Quick, mix the mortar, man!
Up the ladder with your hod – and then fall down!
Don't stop!
Post the sentries!
Bank the furnace!
Now the watchman's round.
All right, catch two winks.
Rise and shine!
Now, send your heralds off,
one to the gods above, one to the mortals below.
Then scurry back.

The swift pace, the appeal to the spectator's imagination, are magical.

The reluctant Euelpides dissents:

As for you, just stay right here –
    and I hope you choke.

Peisthetaerus retorts: "Obey your orders, friend. Unless you do your share we shan't get done."

A messenger brings word that the wall's "all up!" Peisthetaerus: "Splendid!" The messenger reports:

What a wonderful, whopping, well-built wall! Whew!
Why, that wall's so wide that if you hitched up
four Trojan Horses to two huge chariots
with those braggarts Proxenides in one and Theagenes in the other,

They could pass head-on. *That's* the width of your wall!

After exclamations of gratitude, Peisthetaerus asks: "Who in the world could have built a wall like that?"

Replies the messenger:

The birds.
        Nobody but Birds.
        Not one Egyptian,
No bricklayers. No carpenters. Or masons.
Only the birds. I couldn't credit my eyes.
What a sight it was:
        Thirty thousand Cranes
Whose crops were all loaded with boulders and stones,
While the Rails with the beaks blocked out the rocks
and thousands of Storks came bringing up bricks
and Plovers and Terns and seabirds by billions
transported the water right up to the sky!

PEISTHETAERUS: Heavens! But which birds hauled the mortar up?"

MESSENGER: Herons, in hods.

PEISTHETAERUS: But how was the mortar heaped in the hods?

MESSENGER: Gods, now that was a triumph of engineering skill!
Geese burrowed their feet like shovels beneath
and heaved it over their heads to the hods.

All this, which becomes very real, is accomplished verbally. We see nothing, yet we see it all. In his *The Theatre of Aristophanes*, a keen and thorough study, Kenneth McLeish remarks: "His (Aristophanes') interest is in the precise moments of vision, the points of balance themselves. Watching each of his plays, we first share with the hero his blinding instant of vision, then (with him) settle back to enjoy its consequences. In plays where the hero's vision, the informing metaphor, is pin-sharp, the crucial factor is fantasy. With Trygaios' decision to fly to heaven and argue with Zeus, or Peisthetaerus' plan to build Cloud-Cuckoo-Land, there is no arguing. Their schemes need no justifying, because they are self-evidently *right* – and what makes them so is the liberation from everyday restraint which fantasy gives them."

McLeish observes that Peisthetaerus is priggish and sober, very serious about what he is doing; Euelpides, a secondary character, is a clown, for whom Peisthetaerus is the "straight man" off whom he bounces the laugh-lines. Such a pairing of opposite characters is a part of Aristophanes' formula; it appears in most of his plays.

Of the language, McLeish has this to say: "[His] kind of fast, witty verse gives way to real poetry in two plays above all, *Peace* and *Birds*. In them, the literary language is not an addition, a decoration: it is used to articulate the major message of the play. There is a yearning in this poetry; the words, the metaphors reach out and express emotion and atmosphere conveyable in no other form." He points out, too, that the language of Aristophanes is always terse and clear.

The spectacular costumes of the chorus of birds and their many different kinds of plumage would provide the offering with another kind of poetry and enhance its whimsy and strangeness.

Aristophanes is able to take liberties in depicting actual persons because the element of fantasy in his work is ruling and omnipresent. "Once illusion has completely swallowed up reality," McLeish suggests, "truth to life becomes a matter of no importance. Obviously there would be no point to the joke unless Socrates, Euripides and the rest retained some part of their real-life characters. But equally obviously, once they become characters in the illusion, they move within the bounds and conventions of the illusion and not those of real life. . . . What truth to reality the characters ever had is as much swallowed up in illusion as that of Freud or Einstein in a comedian's patter today." Hence, one will find few clues in these plays as to what the freely maligned Socrates and Euripides were like, even though Aristophanes was personally acquainted with them.

Some stanzas of the *parabasis* were later singled out for translation by Charles Algernon Swinburne, among them lines describing the creation of the world from an egg laid "by black-winged Night", and a passage conveying, in imagery worthy of Aeschylus or Euripides, the care-worn lot of man.

Most of Aristophanes' comedies include sudden reversions, with the values held by the characters at the end quite the opposite of what they were at the start. There is a return from fantasy to reality. In *The Birds* Aristophanes laughs at the Utopians, yet permits them to triumph, so that possibly he may not have been wholly out of sympathy with them, however acerbic his view of them might have been; or else he merely realized, as a practising dramatist, that a farce should have a cheerful ending.

All too soon the war with Sparta was resumed. Aristophanes' nagging preoccupation with peace erupts again in his *Lysistrata* (411 BC); it is not known how it was received. By now, after twenty-one years of struggle, the odds had turned against Athens: the over-ambitious expedition against Sicily was a disaster; the city lost much of its reserve of manpower; several of its most powerful allies broke away, foreseeing further losses; and the Spartans won Persian support, the two forces joining with the aim of dominating the Aegean. In Athens itself an uprising impended. Aristophanes, disgusted with this gross and bloody misconduct of affairs, had abandoned all hope that Athenian men would ever govern themselves intelligently: the only alternative was that women might exhibit more common sense than ever had their husbands.

Accordingly, while their men are asleep, the women of Athens and neighbouring cities assemble for a discussion at dawn near a gateway to the Acropolis. Lysistrata, a strong-willed wife (her name means "Dissolver of Armies"), proposes a "sex-strike" to bring the errant, headstrong men to their senses. All those present take an oath to deny their physical favours to their spouses until a permanent peace is arranged. They also resolve to ask the women of Sparta to join them in their campaign to end the idiotic fighting.

When the old men learn of this odd stratagem, they besiege and attack the citadel in which their wives and daughters have shut themselves up and attempt to smoke them out, but are driven back with pots of boiling water and even hotter floods of verbal abuse. Some of the more amorous women weaken and try to steal away for a few hours of dalliance with their lovers, offering transparent pretexts, but are prevented from doing so. For the most part, the strikers are adamant in defending their self-imposed chastity. The high-point of the action is the teasing seduction of Cinesias, husband of Myrrhina, who at the conclusion of the scene leaves her frantic husband still unsatisfied. (Their names have sexual connotations.)

At last, almost maddened by frustrated passion, the men of both camps, Athenian and Spartan, capitulate and halt the ugly combat. The farce ends with a festive reconciliation, capped by singing and the usual energetic dancing.

The humour of the play is explicitly sexual, its fun unabashedly erotic – the men, with their bared, erect, exaggerated phalluses, bellowing for the physical pleasure and nervous relief now forbidden them, and the young, newly-wed women yearning for their husbands' kisses and embraces, but the laughter inspired by all this is healthy and natural. It is further redeemed by the author's essential sincerity, the despair and desperation that shine through his jests. *Lysistrata* is a timeless triumph for Aristophanes.

At the time of its production Athens could hardly have sued for peace: its outlook was too dark, and the terms exacted from the city would have been too Draconian. No record is left to tell where *Lysistrata* was given, at the Lenaea or the Greater Dionysia, and whether at that historic moment the audience was amused. That Aristophanes dared to write it shows again his courage and his enduring pacificism.

The play has interesting overtones of feminism: the women revolt against their accustomed role as mere sexual objects and inferior persons, the status they have too long held in Athenian society. When the men protest that women know nothing about politics and economics, they are reminded by Lysistrata that women, who must live within family budgets, are actually domestic treasurers. It should be kept in mind that the roles of the women, at least all speaking parts, were played by men.

The script abounds with an abundance of other felicitous touches. An instance: when the athletic Spartan women are glimpsed coming to announce their eagerness to cooperate in the strike, they are so muscular that they are initially mistaken for men. Another instance: a group of old commission merchants, profiting from the war, reveal in their senile debate how much they are moved by their cupidity; their arguments sound uncomfortably modern.

Though it is filled with illogicalities – the Spartan women would not so easily cross the Athenian lines, the horny soldiers of Athens could readily find sexual release without relying on their wives – *Lysistrata* differs from Aristophanes' earlier surviving plays in having a surprisingly tight, well-integrated story, presided over by a strong, unifying figure, the priggish, morally earnest Lysistrata who takes charge of everyone. Almost all its incidents and characters – especially the nicely delineated minor figures, each of whom has his or her own speech pattern and personality trait – are closely related: the story has structure. The play still belongs to the category of Old Comedy, since its premise is fantastic – a peace between states cannot be brought about by the stratagem employed by these naïve women – but overall it creates an impression of being unprecedentedly realistic; for these reasons it is a transitional work, anticipating the later genres now known as Middle Comedy and New Comedy.

Thesmophoriazusae (*Women at the Festival of Demeter*) was also produced in 411 BC, or perhaps in 410; if in 411, when *Lysistrata* appeared, it would be an unusual honour for Aristophanes to have been allotted two choruses in the same year. In this script he continued his harsh assaults on the Athenian intellectuals, particularly Euripides, about whom he had made a few sideswiping allusions in *Lysistrata*, together with once more parodying passages from that tragic poet's works; indeed, some of the speeches against war in *Lysistrata* are simply lifted from Euripides. It should be made clear that Aristophanes was not alone in choosing Socrates and Euripides as victims of his sharp jokes. Sandbach quotes lines from a fragment by Eupolis: "I hate Socrates, too, that beggarly chatterer, who has thought of everything except where his next meal is coming from." And, too, the Roman satirist Horace, who explained: "The poets Eupolis and Cratinus and Aristophanes and the other great men who created antique comedy felt no restraint against branding anyone who deserved to be noticed because he was a bad character and a thief, or an adulterer or assassin or of ill-repute in any other way."

Disheartened, Aristophanes seems to have left the political fray, having nothing more to say about the folly of war and the bane of corruption. Instead, he elects to write what is in large part a free travesty of Euripides' *The Bacchae*, which gives him an excuse to call the great and radical poet to account for his numerous unkind remarks about women. As the reactionary Aristophanes saw it, Euripides' influence over the Athenian mind was as harmful as that of Socrates. He proposes that Euripides and a kinsman (perhaps his admiring father-in-law Mnesilochos) pay a visit to another tragic playwright, Agathon.

At the moment, the women of Athens are gathering to observe the October festival of the Thesmophoria, in tribute to the Earth-goddesses Demeter and Persephone. Euripides hears rumours that this is to be an opportune occasion for them to plot his murder for having so brazenly defamed them. Euripides beseeches the androgynous Agathon to disguise himself in woman's clothes, which he can easily do, and overhear the plan, as well as to offer a defence of him there. Agathon refuses to undertake the risky enterprise, but Mnesilochos lets himself be persuaded to do it. In a scene that parallels the robing of Pentheus in *The Bacchae*, the willing father-in-law is closely shaved, attired as a woman, and slips off to attend the forbidden rite.

He listens to a babble of complaints against the tragic dramatist as the angry celebrants list all of the playwright's libellous portraits of them. When Mnesilochos tries to reply on Euripides' behalf, even daring to argue that many of the poet's observations are true, and declaring that women are worse than their detractor has ever shown them to be, his hearers grow suspicious. He is exposed as a female impersonator by Cleisthenes, who is allowed to be present because of his flagrant effeminacy, which virtually qualifies him as one of them. The furious women strip off Mnesilochos' disguise; in grave peril at their hands, he resorts to delaying tactics, until Euripides arrives to rescue him. Here ensues a series of burlesque episodes, each of them parodistic of devices in Euripides' tragedies, by which the two beleaguered men attempt to escape the avenging chorus. At one point Mnesilochos avoids dismemberment only by grabbing an infant from a woman's arms, warning that he will slay the innocent child if he himself is hurt, an action reminiscent of the seizing of a hostage by Clytemnestra's slayers in *Orestes*. But for a good reason the women are not deterred by his threat; in response to their surprising indifference, he unwraps the swaddled babe and discovers it is a wine-flask.

The women have smuggled it from the city not to have to pay tax on it. Mnesilochos, beset, swears he will "cut its throat" even so, whereupon its indignant owner bawls out: "Spare my darling! Or at least bring a bowl, and if it must die, let us catch its blood!" Mnesilochos' answer to this is to gulp down the entire contents of the flask.

Of course, Euripides, like his belittler Aristophanes, was a feminist, though many of his portraits of women – Medea, Phaedra, Electra, Helen – are far from flattering. Yet most are also viewed compassionately, as witness Alcestis, Hecuba, Iphigeneia, Andromache. Aristophanes seems to have been quite blind to Euripides' virtues. This is all the more baffling since Euripides also shared Aristophanes' passionate opposition to the war and openly expressed his opinion on the subject, which required courage.

What Aristophanes had brought to the stage with *Women at the Festival of Demeter* was a new theme: literary satire, a subject that had been partially foreshadowed by his mockery of philosophers in *The Clouds*. By modern criteria, *Women at the Festival of Demeter* is only moderately successful; it does not lend itself well to revival because a close knowledge of Euripides' lesser works is required. Sandbach, however, finds some of its episodes remarkably entertaining, especially those in which the actor playing Mnesilochos must pass himself off as a woman, a commonplace in Greek theatre, except that here he must do it in such a manner that he is discerned as actually a man. For this to be truly amusing calls for great skill on the actor's part; the unwitting clues to his gender should not be too obvious or broad. Also, in Sandbach's view, for Mnesilochos to seek deliverance by invoking devices from Euripides' melodramas is "in terms of dramaturgy, one of Aristophanes' finest inventions. The character of Mnesilochos and the direction in which the plot is moving fuse together and produce a magnificently comic and superbly generative idea, that of using Euripidean methods to escape from a situation brought about by Euripides in the first place. The triumph consists in the fact that for this character to have this idea at this point in the play is not the logical outcome of the action so far, but seems instead an inspiration of the moment, a flash of comic insight wholly appropriate to the character of Mnesilochos as we have seen it unfold before us. These moments of fusion between plot and character are rare in drama: this one, for sheer ludicrous rightness, for self-conscious generative *poneria* (cunning, or wiliness) is hardly matched until the Gadshill sequence in *Henry IV Part I* or the plot against Malvolio in *Twelfth Night*. This is to place Mnesilochos, as a comic character, in the highest company – and the fact that he seems as much at home there as Dikaiopolis, Agorakritos or Peisthetaerus do not, showing something of the character and quality of the play." A particularly sharp thrust, too, is that near the action's end Euripides himself has to don woman's garb and impersonate an old bawd and, after a crazy ride on the swinging crane, make a hasty, undignified exit pursued by a Scythian, all this yielding a climax of fast slapstick.

Another literary satire, a far more effective one, *The Frogs*, won Aristophanes the first prize at the Lenaea in 405 BC. Four months earlier Euripides had died in far-off Macedon, followed two months afterwards by Sophocles. But Aristophanes' feelings towards Euripides had not softened. In this play Dionysus, in his aspect of god of the theatre, but also assuming a humanized form, laments that tragedy has irretrievably declined, a consequence of the demise of its three great practitioners. Listing all the surviving playwrights, he dismisses them as mostly minor and inept – the only possible exception is Iophon, Sophocles' son; but no one can be sure how much of his work had been written by his father! So Dionysus resolves to seek out the recently departed Euripides in Hades.

To Xanthos, a comic servant, is given the first line of the play (as translated here by Benjamin Rogers): "Shall I crack any of those old jokes, Master, at which the audience never fails to laugh?" Dionysus replies: "Don't make them; no!" He complains that when he attends the works of Aristophanes' rivals – specifically, Ameipsias, Lycis and Phrynichus – they use such hoary jests it ages him a year. (Subsequently, Aristophanes inserts into the script practically the whole repertory of standard comic lines and tricks, cliché but of course surefire.)

Dionysus goes to call on Herakles, who had once ventured to the Underworld, and asks him what to expect from a visit to the nether realm. That great hero gives him helpful advice, much of it on various ways to kill himself, which Dionysus scarcely welcomes. Accompanied by the prattling Xanthos, the very human god begins his journey to the dark world. He encounters a corpse being borne to his grave and seeks guidance of him, but the corpse wants a fee, and Dionysus will not pay two drachmas; thereupon the corpse refuses to give him any instructions – greed, apparently, lives on beyond death. On his own, Dionysus meets Charon, rows with him across horrible Lake Acherusian, surrounded by a chorus of Frogs, whose creaking "*Brekeke-kex, ko-ax, ko-ax*" is one of the memorable refrains of this extravagant farce, and destined to become a favourite chant of Yale University students today.

In the Underworld, Dionysus finds that the recently arrived and pretentious Euripides has deposed Aeschylus from his throne as King of Tragedy, and the thundering, older writer furious at the usurpation. Euripides has garnered a following by appealing to the worst elements in Hell, which is well populated with pick-purses, house-breakers, parricides and their ilk. Harsh epithets are being exchanged, and this evolves into a debate between the two playwrights as to which is the better poet and craftsman. In the ensuing *agon* there now evolves a brilliant parodistic appraisal of the styles and accomplishments of the pair. The combatants are vividly characterized. This is how Aeschylus is seen:

> There will his shaggy-born crest upbristle for anger and woe,
> Horribly frowning and growling, his fury will launch at the foe
> Huge-clamped masses of words, with exertion Titanic up-tearing
> Great ship-timber planks for the fray.

And the cleverer Euripides:

> Here will the tongue be at work, uncoiling, word-testing, refining,
> Sophist-creator of phrases, dissecting, detracting, maligning,
> Shaking the envious bits, and with subtle analysis paring
> The lung's large labor away.
> [Translation: Benjamin Rogers]

Euripides refuses to offer prayers at the start of the trial. "My vows are paid to other gods than these." "What, a new coinage of your own?" "Precisely," replies Euripides, who then pays tribute to intelligence, instead, whose god seems to be an abstract, ethereal force.

Aeschylus accuses Euripides of having put depraved characters in his dramas, of having dressed them in tatters to evoke pathos, and of letting the once lofty and sublime stage degenerate to realistic squalor. He exclaims:

> No! no harlotry business deformed my plays.
> And none can say that ever I drew a love-sick woman all my days.

His goal has been to elevate his audience: "We, the poets, are teachers of men." And of his challenger: "Just consider what style of men he received from me, great six-foot-high heroical souls . . ." Nor does the austere playwright disdain to sneer at Euripides' personal life, his reputedly unhappy marriages. Euripides retorts that his predecessor is careless in his use of imagery and habitually repetitive, yet often obscure in thought. Dionysus sighs, momentarily undecided: "One is so clever, one delights me so."

In a final match between the two, the question as to which poet has written the "weightier words" is measured on a scale on to which quoted lines are tossed. Aeschylus asserts that he is at a disadvantage in such a contest:

> My poetry survived me: his died with him:
> He's got it here, all handy to recite.

Yet Aeschylus easily triumphs. While Euripides' lines are "light and wingèd", those of Aeschylus are far more substantial, if not leaden. "Chariot on chariot, corpse on corpse was hurled" is obviously a heavier image than any to be found in Euripides' lyric verse, which is far outbalanced. Euripides is deposed, Aeschylus enthroned again, with the suggestion that during his absence while on a revisit to earth he shall appoint as his successor the more modest Sophocles, not the rascally Euripides ever. It is clear throughout, of course, that Aristophanes is on the side of Aeschylus, the grand moralist, the traditionalist.

Critics have called this literary satire the "greatest of its kind in any language", though today perhaps much of its wit is accessible only to classical scholars or assiduous readers of footnotes. On

Aristophanes' part it is a brilliant feat of verbal memory and proof of his close acquaintance with the works of the tragic poets – he quotes so widely – and shows his uncanny skill in taking off the styles of both men. It should be appreciated that many spectators at its first mounting shared with him some degree of familiarity with the scripts under discussion. It so pleased its audience that it was accorded the very rare honour – possibly a unique one – of being repeated a few days later "by popular demand", and the author was crowned not with ivy but sacred olive leaves, a mark of high distinction accorded only citizens of Athens who had done it important service.

Much of its initial popularity, however, was owing to the urgent patriotism that it exhaled. Six months earlier, Athens had gained a major naval victory at Arginusae; the city's mood was still euphoric. Catching that spirit in many political allusions embedded in choric passages, Aristophanes exhorted his fellow citizens to declare an end to divisive party rivalries; to issue an amnesty to all political dissidents, especially the sponsors of the Council of Four Hundred the year before; and to enfranchise a broader segment of men living in Athens, to make the city-state even more democratic and representative. He had been in doubt as to how his bold advice would be received by the audience, and now was happily rewarded by its widespread approval.

Characterization in *The Frogs* is not as stereotyped as in the earlier works; Dionysus and Xanthos are complex and change as the play goes forward. This is another foreshadowing of Middle Comedy, of which Aristophanes' last two remaining works are to be examples.

This pair are lesser comedic accomplishments, possibly owing to the poet's age and the exhaustion of his inventiveness. He must also have been depressed by Athens's mounting ill-fortunes. *The Assemblywomen* (*Ecclesiazusae*, *c.* 392 or 389 BC) comes first. Not only is its date uncertain, but also at which festival it was presented and how the judges ranked it; it is a broad jape in which Athenian women impersonate male legislators, gain a majority in the Assembly, and by a clever tactic elect themselves to headship of the state. Praxagora, their leader, proclaims that women are too intelligent to let themselves be governed from now on by men who have proved to be utterly stupid. She proposes a kind of Socialism, the division of all wealth to all national residents except slaves. The play is a slap at radicalism and Utopianism, though milder and less sustained than *The Birds*. It has been suggested that Aristophanes had an inkling of the ideas set forth in Plato's forthcoming *The Republic* and hastened to deride them even before their appearance; doubtless they were already in the air of Athens, wherever emancipated philosophers gathered to talk and debate. In the "new order" established by Praxagora, wives too are communized, and old women – the veriest crones – have first choice in picking men as mates or lovers. A high point is the rather self-contained episode in which a trio of these grotesque ladies seeks to entice a handsome youth, who must select one of them. A special theatrical touch in this play is that male actors take the roles of women who resort to disguising themselves as men, a twist that Shakespeare is to adopt in several of his romantic farces, where the boy actors in his troupe play being girls who for self-protection, after being stranded by shipwreck, pretend to be boys.

F.L. Lucas says of *The Assemblywomen*: "The opening is passable . . . but the later scenes, with their amorous hags, show a grossness that seems to me merely revolting." John Gassner, however, has a different opinion of it: "The passion for ideal commonwealths receives in this comedy its most amusing and incisive treatment until the appearance of Aldous Huxley's *Brave New World* in the present century. . . . The risible consequences of this revolution comprise the bulk of the entertainment. And again as in *Lysistrata*, Aristophanes creates a well realized female character in a form of drama which ordinarily dispensed with rounded characterization; she is Praxagora, the leader of the women who tire of the dismal way in which men are running the world."

Athens lost its war with Sparta (404 BC), and as a consequence its empire, events which led to economic suffering and diminished political freedom. During this final period Aristophanes was mostly silent. In 388 BC he brought out the last of his extant works, *Plutus* (or *Wealth)*, which in form and content is the first pure example of Middle Comedy now accessible. It was no longer safe to attack the leaders of the state and other prominent public figures. In comic works the open expression of opinion in the *parabasis* was either truncated, softened or eliminated altogether, political controversy was sidestepped or avoided, and increasingly the subject-matter was apt to be the problems caused by romantic love, or a simple travesty of old familiar myths, parodies of them. Most likely there is no chorus; it was too costly to keep one, or its size is smaller. *Plutus* conforms to these rules; it is loose, episodic, gentle and generalized, rather than tart and specific, as Aristophanes' work had usually been. It makes fun of human foibles, of types, but has no lash, and spares individuals.

Plutus is the god of wealth (hence, the latter-day "plutocrats"); he is blind. Captured by an Athenian, he is healed of his affliction when taken to the temple of Asklepios; now he can distribute his bounty more evenly, at long last rewarding those who truly merit it. The leading character, Karion, a slave, depicted as "most faithful and most thieving", is an archetype of the cunning, amoral, intriguing servant who is to be a focal, dynamic figure in farce for centuries to follow – he is replicated in the plays of Terence and Plautus, as Mosca in Ben Jonson's *Volpone*, as the household barber Figaro in Beaumarchais' sprightly comedies, in the offerings of Goldoni – where he has feminine counterparts

– and hundreds more. This rascal also helps to unify *Plutus* to some degree, binding together some of the scattered incidents, a task which he shares with the more sober Chremylos, the foolish old master. The pair are shown together only once.

The villain of the piece, here, is Poverty, who is decisively put to rout. Her contention is that if everyone were rich, no one would do any work. Another of the villains is Hermes, portrayed as a deceitful rogue. To modern readers it might seem that in these pictures of the gods Aristophanes is overtly anti-religious, but this assumption may be mistaken. The Greeks saw no harm in mocking gods, attributing human traits and failings to them, freely belittling them, for in another phase of their lives they had a worshipful respect for the often fearsome forces they represented or symbolized. In Aristophanes and his plays there is nearly always a strain of deep religious emotion. McLeish says: "His sympathy is with the gods as natural powers, part of the ordered natural world with which the machinations of men are so often in conflict." The ceremonies at the climax of his comedies are celebrations of "a return to order, and god-in-order; the sacrifices in *Peace, Birds, Lysistra, The Women at the Festival, Frogs* and *Plutus*, like the religious endings of any of the other plays, restore religion to its proper place: the hearts and homes of ordinary people". In *Plutus* the deities Poverty and Hermes are treated cavalierly, but Athene and Apollo are addressed with reverence and honour; and at the end Hermes is converted to mending his ways. Towards oracles and the flocks of priests who mulcted the gullible citizenry, however, Aristophanes is invariably less than kind.

That Poverty is rudely belaboured is doubtless a reflection of the harsh conditions in which many Athenians were existing after the city's catastrophic defeat, though it gradually regained some of its former intellectual brilliance and affluence.

Most critics regard this play even less favourably than *The Assemblywomen*. Lucas puts it succinctly: "*Plutus*, since Byzantine days, has been dear to schoolmasters, as being, like *The Clouds*, comparatively decent. But its idea of establishing a welfare state by restoring the sight of the blind God of Wealth is wearisomely fumbled. '*It is idle to be assiduous in the perusal of inferior poetry.*'" (The play *does* contain some scatological passages.)

Yet it has its advocates, some full-voiced, some admitting to reservations. Among the latter commentators is McLeish, who on one page speaks of "the magnificent scene between Karion, the Just Man and the Informer", but on another refers to the script as, on first sight, "pallid and dramatically half-hearted". Then much later he observes: "The reader of *Plutus* may feel that there are too many similar characters, and in particular that the main generators of humour, Chremylos and Karion, are not sharply enough differentiated from each other. In the theatre, where we can *see* the difference, this 'problem' disappears. The plot moves like a Swiss weather-house: there are two kinds of action, each with its own protagonist, and they appear in alternation. But a single line of logic binds them together; the play is articulated not for reading but for performance, and its line is a performing line. Again there is a parallel in fine art: this time a series of panels illustrating different aspects of a single progressing theme."

McLeish suggests that the scene between Poverty and the Old Woman is too cruel, more so than any other in any of Aristophanes' plays, if enacted realistically. The behaviour of both characters should be exaggerated; they should be presented as cartoon figures, with Poverty's diction pretentiously grand, which it might be easy to do, since both are being portrayed by males in travesty, with the result that "the tone of the mockery becomes ironical instead of bitter, and the Old Woman's complaints and self-conceit hilarious rather than pathetic".

Actually, Aristophanes wrote at least two more scripts, now lost, that were staged after his death by his son: *Aiolosikon* and *Kokalos*, both of which were quite representative of Middle Comedy. In the first, the King of the Winds, Aeolus, appears as a cook; in the second, the poet gives a burlesque account of how Minos of Crete pursues Daedalus to a town in Sicily, where at the court of its ruler, Cocalus, he loses his life in a hot bath. For these two works, the late author used a pseudonym once more, as he had done with his initial entries in the festivals. Some believe he did this now so that his son might more readily launch a career of his own by having people assume that the younger man was in truth the source of the posthumous scripts.

Aristophanes, the great satirist, was an arch-conservative, a political and social reactionary, with a bias towards an agrarian way of life that belonged to a past that had already vanished. His answers to the problems of his day tended to be simplistic, overly idealistic. Yet he was shrewd, too, and worldly: he hoped and doubted at the same time. His work is everlastingly vital, refined and gross, funny and tedious. His comedy is both highly topical and universal; it is of his day and all time. He shared many of the beliefs of the radicals whom he flayed and was himself "advanced" in many ways. Athens would have done well to have heeded his impassioned warnings. He assailed impiety, yet himself travestied the gods. He was a moralist, whose comedies are still decried as decidedly immoral. He gives a marvellously detailed and intimate picture of many spheres of Athenian daily life, something not found in the works of the tragic poets, who set their scenes in a remote and mythical age. One comes upon contradictions, paradoxes, in almost every phase of his genius; he is almost impossible to classify or sum up in a few enlightening phrases. It is rare, indeed, for a sharp-tongued satirist to be a pastoral poet deeply in love with the music of words; for a classicist to be so romantic, for a romantic to be so hard-headed, for a lyric poet to write mostly about scabrous clowns. He was highly intelligent, yet had many blind-spots; he was intellectually honest, yet most dishonest in an argument. He is – Aristophanes.

Most revivals of the comedies offer drastically expurgated texts, the broad jokes about physical deformities, flatulence and excremental functions that evoked laughter from fifth-century Greeks no longer amusing to later generations of spectators. In addition, many topical allusions to politics or individuals are now either incomprehensible or confusing; hence they too are cut. So much is for ever lost. Yet much that is left is still healthily ribald, even daring, especially in academe, where the plays are most often staged. College students welcome them because of their frank sexuality, for ever appealing to the young; Aristophanes' is a candour that is acceptable because his plays are "classics", not safe to criticize as immoral or indecorous. Such stagings by undergraduate actors occur with considerable regularity, but notices of them are hard to gather because the majority of them are not covered by professional reviewers. That is also true of productions by regional and fringe groups, even those put on Off-Off-Broadway and beyond London's West End or scattered about the Continent. Any record of them is hopelessly incomplete. It is assumed that most frequently performed are *Lysistrata* and *The Frogs*, the one on commercial stages, the other in university settings.

Lysistrata was a full-fledged Times Square hit during the season of 1930, with Brooks Atkinson writing in the *New York Times*:

> On second thought, the *Lysistrata*, which was put on at the Forty-fourth Street Theater last evening, does not come direct from Athens. Between Aristophanes and us stands Norman Bel Geddes, scene designer extraordinary, who produced this version for the Philadelphia Theater Association several weeks ago, and whose bountiful scenery now sweeps up toward the flies in a Broadway playhouse. He has designed a magnificent production, imaginative, free, sculptural and colorful, and the concluding bacchanal, when viewed from the rear of the auditorium, is a memorable flow of color and motion.
>
> If *Lysistrata* were *Antigone* or *Electra*, this spacious edifice would be a masterful scene conception for the groupings and the declamation of Greek tragedy. But *Lysistrata* is horseplay, broader than a Second Avenue burlesque, full of rough-and-tumble, full of bawdry. The comic spirit could dance more freely if Mr Geddes had spared the picture somewhat and tightened the performance. When he has experienced actors at his command – Violet Kemble Cooper, Ernest Truex, Sydney Greenstreet –

Aristophanes triumphs over magnificence of scenery, for good actors know the craft of expression. But the pictorial quality of this *Lysistrata* is no unmixed dispensation for the younger actors. When the performance begins to sprawl, as it still does despite considerable cutting, you suspect that Mr Geddes's setting is more on the side of the tragedians than the mountebanks.

But that is a counsel of perfection, and *Lysistrata* is too hearty a comedy to be stared out of countenance by a promethean artist. Gilbert Seldes has written an English adaptation colloquial enough to be relished, and the sheer artlessness of the slapstick episodes makes them palatable and enjoyable even for the sciolists of Broadway. As every one must know by this time, *Lysistrata* is the story of the women of Greece who plot to conclude a tedious and ruinous interstate war by abstaining from love until their menfolk have made peace. Soldiers denied the consolations of domesticity grew less Martian and more reasonable politically.

So they do. As the most impetuous of the returned soldiers, Ernest Truex shows how shrewd Lysistrata has been, not only for Greece but for the craft of acting. For Mr Truex is a capital actor, and the crowning episode of the story becomes enormously funny in his harum-scarum playing. Miriam Hopkins and Hortense Alden, as young women whose high resolves are foreign to their instincts, have a mischievous sense of humor that is likewise entertaining. Members of the constabulary were present last evening to safeguard the morals of Broadway art patrons. Although the police listened to some of the raciest conversation to be heard outside the marts of commerce, they will be relieved to know that is tamer than what members of the Philadelphia Theater Association heard when *Lysistrata* opened in that well-bred metropolis.

. . . Violet Kemble Cooper appears here as Lysistrata. It is one of her best performances. Her voice has strength enough to dominate so vast a scene; her diction is excellent. She gives the part authority and stature. Sydney Greenstreet, as the President of the Senate of the City of Athens, gives it amplitude. Although *Lysistrata* is a robust comedy, it is not sophisticated. Instead of cracking jokes, it pummels and grimaces, or splashes jars of water on a parcel of feeble old men. And, although the pace of the performance is slow and uneven, and lacking rhythm, it is a tempo not unsuited to the festival quality of the humors.

Those who expected a neat, brisk show will be disappointed. But those who still like to snort over the earthy japery of elementary comedy will find the congenial version of *Lysistrata* has laughing matter of rare quality. Despite the fact that Mr Geddes has not found the style best suited to the Aristophanes spirit, he has mounted an unusual production. From several different points of view, including that of enjoyment, it is one of the most interesting ventures of the season.

(The "amplitude" of Mr Greenstreet's portrayal of the Senate President alludes to his physical girth.)

Some years later, an Off-Broadway production of the comedy with an all-black cast had only a short run. The ancient Greek caper was also sponsored by the Federal Theater Project during the Depression era, the late 1930s, when the Roosevelt administration sought to provide work for actors. Next, in the 1950s, another Off-Broadway revival was undertaken by the Phoenix Theater, an earnest group headed by T. Edward Hambleton and Norris Houghton. Dedicated to bringing back the classics, it held forth with spurts of brilliance in a large playhouse – formerly Maurice Schwartz's Yiddish Art Theater – on lower Second Avenue, where its financial and artistic history was one of hits and misses.

The New York critic Stanley Kauffmann visited Hamburg, Germany where he saw a "fascinating" production of *Lysistrata* at the Schauspielhaus (1971). He notes:

> Here the original scenery and costumes, by Erwin W. Zimmer, help the concept enormously. We see a huge curtain of unbleached muslin that drapes forward over the apron, completely hiding the stage. When it rises, we see wide steps leading up to a sort of low rectangular tunnel, all covered with leopard skin. The general effect is rough, strong, primal, an environment that blends perfectly the necessary sophistication and rudeness. This is further borne out by the costumes, which are like weathered ritual garments, and the half-masks that all the actors wear. Dieter Dorn's direction is particularly fine with the two choruses, the old men and old women. I could have done without some cuteness supplied by two non-speaking *compères*, but generally this was a vigorous, unified performance.

Once more in New York (1982), the Equity Library Theater – a group established by Actors Equity to showcase young performers – ventured another *Lysistrata* in its Master Building Theater located on Riverside Drive. John Corry, of the *New York Times*, gave this appraisal:

> *Lysistrata* is a satisfying play, not because it is a farce (there are funnier farces), not because it is an early plea for the emancipation of women.
>
> *Lysistrata*, of course, is supposed to have anticipated feminist movements from the bloomer girls to the Women's Strike for Peace to the proposed Equal-rights Amendment. As much as Ibsen's *A Doll House*, a more somber work, it argues for women's rights in the polity. But that scarcely explains why *Lysistrata* has stayed a part of the dramatic literature for two thousand years, or why it remains a satisfying play. Mostly it is satisfying because it is so civilized.

Aristophanes' women live in a traditional society. Permanent values stay in place. It is true that the women's husbands are forever going off and fighting in the Peloponnesian War; it is equally true that they are scared to death of their wives. "No man is ever happy unless he can really please his woman," Lysistrata tells the women. In fact, this is the antithesis of feminist political rhetoric. The rhetoric says that men couldn't care less. In 411 BC, Aristophanes knew better.

And yes, *Lysistrata* is a farce and a fantasy, but the assumption is that the men, denied conjugal rights by their wives, would not go off and seek their pleasures elsewhere. In a time of high divorce, open marriages and new freedoms, the assumption is rather sweet, not to mention civilized. The Spartan and Athenian husbands aren't repressed, only frustrated, and they want their wives so badly that they will end a war to regain them.

The wives, meanwhile, are equally desperate in wanting their husbands. So what if they have stormed the Acropolis and barricaded themselves in? Lysistrata must constantly rally the women to keep them there. They need their husbands. This doesn't have much to do with the shriller feminist rhetoric, either.

The Equity Library Theater is doing *Lysistrata* in two acts, and there seems to be a certain amount of padding, presumably so that we can see more of the young actors. This *Lysistrata*, for instance, concludes with Athenians and Spartans dancing to some pleasant music by Richard Weinstock. They seem to be doing a lengthy *hora.*

In the large cast, Madelon Thomas is a persuasive Lysistrata, and Deborah Allison is a lovely young matron. She and Scott Campbell, as her estranged and frustrated husband, play a wonderfully comic scene of *coitus interruptus.* Alan Fox's direction is sometimes too forceful – there is too much onstage shouting – but does uphold the old civilized verities.

Public television, in 1986, broadcast a foreign adaptation of the comedy. Of it, John O'Connor, watching it for the *New York Times*, offered his opinion:

A publicity release describes this effort as "a modern language version." That may be, but its import will be lost on most American viewers because the language is Swedish. This *Lysistrata* was made for television in Sweden and has English subtitles. The translation is indeed "modern" in the sense that it is peppered with a kind of earthy sexual slang, especially in describing various parts of the male and female anatomy. This is apparently close to the bawdiness of the original Greek, which we all heard about in school but seldom found in most approved translations.

> Produced by Inger Aby and directed by Goran Jarvefelt, this *Lysistrata* uses classical columns and spaces, occasionally dotted with barnyard animals, to suggest the play's locations. The actors are draped in appropriate fabrics, pastel soft and feminine for the Athenians, stark white and utilitarian for the Spartans. As in other Aristophanes works, much of the tough humor is employed against warmaking.
>
> But *Lysistrata*, of course, is also extraordinary as a feminist tract, which is the aspect emphasized in this production. Here is a play, written in 411 BC, urging women to leave their kitchens and conjugal beds until their husbands and sons agree to stop waging wars. Lysistrata, leader of the revolt, reminds her sometimes wavering followers of how they spend so much time longing for husbands away at the front. And back home, she adds, there's not a spare lover to be found.
>
> There is nothing genteel about these women as they set about making their very practical demands, including control of the treasury. After all, they argue, "you trust us with household budgets." At first the men are patronizing, assuring the rebels that "war is a man's affair." But gradually they lose their sense of humor, petulantly asking what the women have ever done for the wars. The answer: "We pay our taxes in baby boys."
>
> Aristophanes lets the women win the battle, but this well-played and intelligent version of the play leaves Lysistrata looking decidedly pensive and sad. She clearly knows that wars are hardly a thing of the past.

Hollywood discovered *Lysistrata* and transposed it to nineteenth-century Western America, retitling it *Seven Brides for Seven Brothers* (1954); it did exceedingly well at the box-office. The film, a musical directed by Stanley Donen, won applause for the remarkably athletic dancing of the men.

Peter Hall, having left the Royal Shakespeare Company, set as his goal the presentation of classic works on commercial stages where they would gather a good profit. One of his early ventures was *Lysistrata*, which opened at the Old Vic (1983), where it did so well that it was shortly transferred to the West End for an extended engagement.

William A. Henry III, of *Time*, was in London and judged the offering:

> The title role is played by Geraldine James, who starred in the television series *The Jewel in the Crown* and onstage as Portia to Dustin Hoffman's Shylock. But most of the time she and the rest of the cast wear masks, as the Greeks would have done. This helps ensure that the real star of the play is the play, which may be the most cunning blend ever of high moral purpose and low humor. Its premise is that war-weary women of Greece convene and vow to give up sex until their men give up battle. That is no

small sacrifice: the women are just as lusty as the men, and their triumph is of will over self, not of puritanical virtue over vice.

The language is explicit, the staging more so – the costumes display bulging breasts and buttocks and inflatable dildos, all apparently in keeping with the bawdry of the original style. In a further attempt to evoke antique comedy, or at least its descendants in vaudeville and burlesque, Hall interpolates music, dance and choral antics. The most modern moment has James remove her mask to confront the audience about global tolerance of violence. Translator Ranji Bolt, who also worked with Hall in *Tartuffe*, displays equal sensitivity to Aristophanes' world and to contemporary parallels in, say, Bosnia.

The sense of immediacy begins before the first word is spoken: the set suggests a much bombed city, its walls daubed with hate slogans. The women are identified chiefly by ethnic origin, and their delegate conclave thus calls to mind a peace conference, both for its noble intent and for the frequent ignoble assertions of personal privilege over public necessity. The most striking relevance comes at the end. In the midst of jubilation, the women acknowledge that the peace will be fleeting while the impulse to war is eternal. Aristophanes would recognize his world in this production. We chillingly recognize ours.

The Frogs was presented in a highly unusual manner at Yale University (1974) as reconceived by Burt Shevelove, the director, and Stephen Sondheim, the composer, both of whom were very well-established figures in the Broadway theatre. As an undergraduate at Yale some three or four decades earlier, Shevelove had made use of the campus swimming pool as the *mise en scène* for Aristophanes' farce and had enjoyed a modest, youthful triumph with it. Robert Brustein, the always controversial drama critic and theorist, who was now head of the Yale Repertory Theater, had a chance meeting with Shevelove and persuaded him to re-stage the piece; he thought it would earn badly needed funds for the Repertory Company and bring it attention, which would attract new students to the Yale Drama School. He was also impressed by Shevelove's production on Broadway, in collaboration with Larry Gelbart, the playwright, and Sondheim, of *A Funny Thing Happened on the Way to the Forum*, based on the Roman farces of Plautus, an offering which had been very profitable and had gone on to reap further success in Hollywood and become a film classic. Shevelove agreed to revive his original concept, but his ideas were now large-scaled, though the run was to be limited to one week and there was no thought of moving the production elsewhere, as most theatres were not likely to contain swimming pools. Yale's new, "palatial" Payne-Whitney Gymnasium had seats that could accommodate 1,700 spectators. The entire week's engagement was sold out well in advance of the first night.

During the planning and rehearsal periods, the scope of the presentation grew larger and larger. Shevelove, not satisfied with casting only members of the Repertory Company, insisted on bringing in several Broadway actors, including Larry Blyden, a star, as Dionysus. Sondheim steadily added new songs and demanded a large orchestra, all of which drove up costs; while the presence of strangers from the commercial theatre caused strains and inspired tensions among the actors regularly under contract to the company. (All this is related by Robert Brustein in his book *Making Scenes.*) Before long Brustein was pretty much left out of it. By the time the work reached opening night it had a cast and crew of over 100. The public notice was far greater than Brustein had anticipated. The second performance drew a covey of New York critics, as well as batches of Broadway celebrities, many of them leading producers, directors, players and artisans.

Among those there was Mel Gussow of the *New York Times* who sent back this description:

> As a theatrical event, the Yale Repertory Theater production of *The Frogs* is spectacular. It opened last night, in, of all places, the Yale swimming pool (inside the Payne-Whitney Gymnasium), which looks like an Olympic ocean next to Yale Rep's usual church-mouse home.
>
> On and off the pool, there is a cast of sixty-eight, including a twenty-one-frogman chorus. In some of the steeply inclined seats – one thousand six hundred of them are reserved for the audience – sit members of the Yale University Band. In ambition, this cross-century collaboration between Aristophanes and Burt Shevelove is breathtaking. Not satisfied merely to do to the Greeks what he did to the Romans (in *A Funny Thing Happened on the Way to the Forum*), Mr Shevelove has created an extravaganza that might stir the shades of Billy Rose and Mike Todd.
>
> Mr Shevelove's adaptation – he is also the director – is faithful to the spirit of Aristophanes while taking outrageous liberties with his text. Dionysus still journeys to Hades to bring back a poet from the dead to stimulate the living. But the key to Mr Shevelove's healthy disrespect is the statement inserted in the program: "The time is the present. The place is ancient Greece."
>
> The jokes, funny and ribald, are by Mr Shevelove, the music by his *Forum* partner, Stephen Sondheim. There are six "musical numbers," stretches of songs between the words, ranging from the effervescent *Parados*, the score for a sensational water ballet, to *Parabasis*, which simply marks time. Another week of effort from Mr Sondheim and the show might have the full score it deserves.
>
> The major shift in the play is that the verbal battle between Euripides and Aeschylus now takes place between Shaw and Shakespeare. This gives Mr Shevelove a chance to mock a gallery of dead authors from Beaumont and Fletcher ("Are they always together?") to Brecht ("A big troublemaker").

When Shakespeare beats Shaw and is about to leave Hades with Dionysus, Pluto bargains, "Take Shaw, and I'll throw in Ibsen."

That literary sparring match was a comic apex in the original. For this *Frogs*, Michael Feingold has culled quotes from Shaw and Shakespeare, and the result is, unfortunately, a dead spot in the show, proving that at least in this case Shaw and Shakespeare cannot compete with Shevelove.

But most of *Frogs* – ninety minutes, without an intermission – is good adulterated fun. Larry Blyden is a splendid, mock-confident Dionysus. He crosses the Styx as if it were the Delaware (and he, a toga-ed Washington) while frogs dip and flip like extras in a splashy M-G-M epic.

There are also antic contributions from Michael Vale as Dionysus's sausage-shaped slave (about an orgiastic feast in Hades, he reports, "The dead certainly know how to live."), Jerome Dempsey as a plain-spoken Pluto (he greets Dionysus warmly as "Zeus's boy!") and Alvin Epstein as an incredibly ancient and shortsighted keeper of the keys.

Though it is often inspired nonsense, *The Frogs* still needs more exercise of the author-director's imagination. Most of it is staged on a narrow edge of the pool. Too much of the time the pool itself remains an idle shimmering forestage. Carmen de Lavallade's choreography is too much confined.

After thirty-three years of contemplating another *Frogs* – Mr Shevelove first did it in the pool as a drama student – he rushed this one into production. On the opening night there were moments when the show seemed in danger of collapsing. When one actor forgot his lines, I half expected to see Mr Shevelove shove him into the pool.

Yale's *Frogs* runs only through Sunday, but a tour of out-of-town pools is very much in order before a Broadway theater is flooded.

T.E. Kalem, in *Time* magazine, was a yea-sayer.

Brekekekex ko-äx ko-äx! As the famed croaking chant, the croaking chorus of the frogs in Aristophanes' comedy, sounds over Yale's Payne-Whitney Gym pool, it signified that twenty-one young Yalies and New Haven townies skimpily clad in green fishnet tights are hitting the water. They fan out to the center of the pool and in a Busby Berkeley pinwheel formation circle the battered dinghy in which a wizened, whiskered Charon (Charles Levin) is poling across this Ivy League Styx. It is a moment of splashing good humor in this aquatic spoof of a spoof.

Adapter-Director Burt Shevelove and Composer-Lyricist Stephen Sondheim have teamed up to employ Aristophanes as a springboard for the sort of romping farce that they achieved together with a

Plautus original in *A Funny Thing Happened on the Way to the Forum.* The result this time, while thoroughly amiable, is more tentative and less hilarious, chiefly because the Aristophanic model does not offer as robust comic material as the Plautine.

The Frogs, as Aristophanes wrote it, is a kind of ironically motivated slapdash quest to restore a major dead dramatist to the ranks of the living. It might wryly be regarded as one of those periodic efforts to save the ailing theater. The god Dionysus (Larry Blyden) resolves to go down to Hades and bring back Euripides. In the Shevelove version, Bernard Shaw substitutes. As his companion, Dionysus takes along his obese, grumbling Sancho Panza-like servant Xanthias (Michael Vale). They have their slapstick encounters not only with the cranky Charon, who speaks like a movie gold prospector, but with enticing houris, underworld strong-arm men, termagants, drunks, and, finally, the haughty, unamused Pluto (Jerome Dempsey), god of the underworld. It seems that Shakespeare sits on the throne of honor as the No. 1 dramatist in Hades. (In Aristophanes' original it is Aeschylus.) A battle royal of quotations ensues between Shakespeare (Jeremy Geidt) and Shaw (Anthony Holland). The chorus of jurors votes against Shaw on the grounds that he is a dry, cerebral rationalist while Shakespeare is the archpoet of the human soul.

Shevelove has peppered the script with contemporary theatrical in-jokes and quizzical one-liners. As the god of wine and drama, Dionysus quips: "A little wine will get you through a lot of drama." One knows by past performance that the Sondheim lyrics are contrapuntally clever and that his music is astringently bittersweet, but the acoustics around the pool do not permit absolute proof. If Yale should opt for participatory theater, the show could close with a gorgeously refreshing swim-in.

Walter Kerr, in the Sunday edition of the *New York Times,* published a second critique of the production.

You must never again believe the canard that all critics are frustrated playwrights. It's the other way around. All playwrights are frustrated critics. Think about it for a moment, as I have had to do for some four or five hours recently. From Aristophanes onward, passing Greene and Beaumont and Sheridan along the way, right up to Tom Stoppard and just now Ira Levin, playwrights have been enormously happy to get their teeth into their fellows – or, failing that, into the fellows who are paid to sink teeth into their fellows. It scarcely matters whether it is reviewers or rival dramatists who are to be the object of a bloodletting. Give a playwright a chance to write a notice in a play and he turns into a cad from Transylvania on the spot.

Aristophanes, whose *Frogs* has completed a week's engagement on the slippery rim of a swimming pool at Yale, liked reviewing his judges and his competitors both. It so happened that Greek comic form allowed for a wide open choral passage smack in the middle of the play: the author could forget about his plot, if he had one, and concentrate on his real passions. Aristophanes was a man to seize opportunities: read his *Parabasis* and you'll find him telling his critics why they were wrong about his last play and warning them, in the case of *The Birds*, that they'll suffer a rain of droppings from the heavens if they don't like this one. He doesn't really do that in *The Frogs*, contenting himself with suggesting that honest men be put at the head of the Athenian government. But then he really doesn't have to. For the entire play is an act of criticism, give or take a gag or two.

The god Dionysus, father of both drama and wine ("A little wine will get you through a lot of drama," Dionysus Larry Blyden suggested in Burt Shevelove's adaptation at Yale), has decided that recent seasons in the Athenian theater have been desolate indeed. (Nice to be reminded of that.) His solution to the problem is not to build more municipal playhouses but to go to Hades and bring back the best dead dramatist he can pry loose. In the original, Aristotle opted for Aeschylus over Euripides, being a conservative at heart. In the Shevelove redaction, it's a choice between Shakespeare and Shaw. Shakespeare wins, which probably makes Mr Shevelove a bit of conservative, too.

Now Mr Shevelove had to make some such substitution as that: contemporary audiences just haven't seen or heard enough Aeschylus, or probably even enough Euripides. And, on the surface of things, this particular switch would seem a good one: Shaw loved baiting both Shakespeare and blank verse. It doesn't work out very well, though, for a most peculiar reason. Mr Shevelove has quite forgotten that Aristophanes was playing critic. In *his* version, Aristophanes took great glee – and spent quite a bit of time – in putting fast jabs to the ribs of both men, mocking their metrics, castigating the little tricks they used to get out of their plots, holding up their bad habits for all of the world to see. He was eating his playwright and having him, too.

Not Mr Shevelove. After an opening barb or so from a youthfully bearded Shaw (in knickers), he let the main event degenerate into a quoting contest, permitting each writer to declaim some of his handsomest lines. The whole point of the exercise thus went flat by evening's end: we were heading for a scalping and barely got fingers into hair or beard.

There were some nice things about the production: the adroit Mr Blyden cautioning the audience to be quiet in the cavernous gymnasium ("And though we welcome trays/ The echoes sometimes last for days"); Carmen de Lavallade wrapping herself sinuously about Dionysus's lavender tunic; com-

> poser-lyricist Stephen Sondheim turning occasionally sassy ("The author's reputation isn't based/ On taste"); the ride to Hades, across the vast pool, with flippered frog-folk half-clad in lily pads back-stroking Charon to his roost. This last effect was stunning enough to remind one and all that a *real* critic, name of Aristotle, pronounced spectacle an absolutely legitimate part of what was coming to be called drama.
>
> I think, though, that Aristophanes – as critic – might have questioned the wisdom of playing nine-tenths of the evening on a shallow, slippery ledge at great remove from the audience just to work in the one big splash. (The splash had consequences; several dancers on that rim went crashing to their knees.) And, though Aristophanes would have noticed a mild dig or two at dramatists (in Hades Bertolt Brecht is a "trouble-maker," Eugene O'Neill "a million laughs"), I don't think he'd have settled for that. He, dyspeptic fellow, was out for a savaging before bestowing his final praise.

Brustein himself was not really pleased with the enterprise. Because it was so costly it earned the Repertory Company only a small sum, $7,000, a disappointment. Nor did he think much of it as an artistic achievement.

> The critical response to *The Frogs* was wildly enthusiastic, which only helped to reinforce my lack of respect for New York critical standards. The show had some fine moments, to be sure, especially the thrilling first appearance of the swimming chorus of frogs, diving into the pool to the accompaniment of Sondheim's rousing music; but it failed to capture the anarchic spirit of Aristophanes the way I thought *A Funny Thing* had caught the spirit of Plautus. It was successful primarily as a stunt. Nevertheless, the critical ecstasy was unabated, and Martin Gottfried, then with *Women's Wear Daily*, used the occasion as an excuse for hectoring our theater about its insufferable superior airs. Writing that Shevelove's "theater intellect and know-how" was "a combination that every academic theater in the country ought to observe attentively. It is especially good that an institution such as the Yale Repertory Theater makes peace with the Broadway that it and theaters like it always met with an odd mixture of contempt, defensiveness, envy and insecurity." He also claimed that we were hypocrites, after charging us (wrongly) with having invited the opening-night crowd. "Even sorrier," he wrote, "was the Yale company's palpable reveling in the publicity and flash. This only betrayed the sham and hypocrisy that lies beneath our institutional theaters, crying for artistic purity and their decrying of the commercial theater's pressure."
>
> Gottfried had no way of knowing how bad I was feeling about having brought Broadway to Yale, or how bad our company was feeling about having been used for this purpose.

Subsequently, Brustein sent off a sharp letter to Gottfried, suggesting that he confine his reviewing to offerings more congenial to his own tastes such as he might find in frankly commercial playhouses. "Nobody can bar you from a public theater, but I was hoping, at least, that you might have the decency to recognize your prejudices and voluntarily stay away." Gottfried replied that Brustein himself had always been a tough critic when attending Broadway works. Brustein concluded once more from this experience that any attempt to conjoin Broadway and resident drama groups only resulted in a "misalliance".

He was in receipt of other complaints in the form of letters from subscribers to the Yale Repertory. A neurologist in the Medical School was outraged by the "scanty" costumes of the young male chorus, which exposed a "portion of their buttocks". The writer asked, in dudgeon, "Since when has Yale become so accustomed to public nudity that a production of this kind can be staged at commencement time without comment or caveat for the proud parents of graduates, alumni, faculty, children of faculty and the public at large?"

Brustein duly responded: "In your outrage and embarrassment over the bare buttocks of the swimmers, you apparently failed to notice that the show also featured an exposed breast on one of the actresses. Whatever your preference for male behinds as opposed to female mammaries, I hope you will agree that, in this time of equal rights for women, your failure to take note of this fact is an insult to the opposite sex. I promise not to report you to the women's movement if you promise not to report me to the Watch and Ward Society. Please feel free to be disgusted over all future productions of our theater."

Brustein meant to be facetious, but shortly he was in fact the butt of a protest from the Yale Women's Liberation Center who characterized *The Frogs* as "sexist" because it limited "the roles of women to sex objects and an ugly old hag. . . . The issues are too destructive of millions of people's lives to be treated as a joke." As might be expected, Brustein replied in kind: "I think your satire on the humorlessness of the extremist element in our society is priceless." He thanked the indignant young women for giving him a good laugh.

Yale's production of *The Frogs* became legendary. Sixteen years later it was replicated by John Gardyne in West London (1990) in a swimming pool at Brentford. (Shevelove had died by then.) In an interview Gardyne declared that he was seeking actors "who can sing, dance and act without drowning". He added: "Rehearsals raised a number of challenges I hadn't encountered before. Actors in a swimming pool lose all self-consciousness, become liberated with increased energy levels. But after twenty minutes of any rehearsal, mild hysteria usually sets in among the cast." He cited as his inspiration the pool itself, "a Victorian bathing house with a balcony". Among the show's backers was Cameron Mackintosh, concurrently the phenomenally successful producer of the *Phantom of the Opera* and *Cats*.

The Merton Floats, an amateur thespian group appearing in the gardens of Merton College, Oxford, put on *The Birds* in the spring of 1955. The word "floats" here is used as a synonym for "footlights", hence by application the acting profession, an echo of Dickensian English. Some twenty such student groups were then active at the various Oxonian colleges. Brock Brower, in a reminiscence in the *New York Times*, recalls how it was and still is:

> The best theater at Oxford is performed every Spring, not in theaters, but out in the university's lovely college gardens. Come the approaching solstice, drama societies rouse their mummers from Winter's footlight torpor and send them out into the natural *mise en scène* of an English garden, usually to perform some Elizabethan romance or Greek comedy. It is almost part of the curriculum during this Spring Trinity Term – when the weather is kinder and daylight lingers late in the evening.
>
> Visitors can brush up on their Shakespeare, or catch up on the classics, by drifting like wandering scholars from hedgerow to flower bed. Each college puts on one play, giving several performances in the latter part of the term, in late May or early June. The performances are open to both visitors and students, who pay a small admission charge at the gate of each college. The casts are made up of enthusiastic students, and the level of performance ranges from brilliant to indifferent, sometimes memorable but always amiable.
>
> This is far more than open-air theater. The blowing gardens and the ancient Oxford architecture *are* the Forest of Arden, Illyria, or Cloud-cuckoo-land. Buildings and grounds put the college theatricals into startling context.

An unhappy possibility, in England, is rain. Brower narrates, ruefully:

> We had a lot of it during Aristophanes' *Birds*. I was playing Herakles, in a white toga with a large "H." I got the part on the basis of accent – American, therefore suitable to the hyperborean caricature. Pure type-casting. But what I recall – as I entered brutishly down from the old Merton wall through Saturday's downpour – was the prim audience, placidly sitting there. Some had brought umbrellas, others held their programs stiffly over their heads. English patience, it makes the flowers grow.
>
> My friend Ken Cavander had done a new translation for our *Birds*. Ken was the kind of undergraduate you only find at Oxford – a stage-struck classicist. Reading the classics course called greats at

> Balliol, he had, during the Winter, done a new version of *Hippolytus* for the One Hundredth anniversary of the Oxford University Dramatic Society. Eventually, he translated the whole canon, concluding with an epic, mythic history of *The Greeks* for the Royal Shakespeare Company.
>
> For *Birds*, we had his Balliol friend Professor Bernard Williams as our director. It also helped to have Professor Williams's wife working on the costumes. He was married at that time to Shirley Williams, later Minister of Education in a Labor Government, and one of the three founders of Britain's Social Democratic Party. Those are the sort of "amateurs" – an honorific in English intellectual life – who mount these garden performances. The best known of these garden impresarios was the late Nevil Coghill, a professor of English at New College, who tutored both W.H. Auden and Richard Burton. In fact, he kept on tutoring Burton all that actor's life, constantly on call to disentangle some *Hamlet* quibble.

After discussing other classic works presented in these gardens, Brower took note that in the spring of 1990, following a lapse of thirty-five years, *The Birds* had once more been chosen as a vehicle.

Karolos Koun (1909–87), founder of the experimental Art Theatre of Athens and soon famed throughout Europe for his lively stagings of the Greek classics, especially Aristophanes' rowdy political farces, brought his presentation of *The Birds* to Paris (1962), where it won first prize in an international drama contest.

At Ypsilanti, Michigan, in the initial season – unfortunately fated to be the last season – the much-promoted, new-born Greek Theatre Festival followed its *Oedipus* with a mounting of *The Birds* (1966). It featured Bert Lahr, a much-admired Broadway clown. The staging was reviewed by Robert Kotlowitz in *Harper's Magazine*, who had found the presentation of the *Oedipus* worthy of respect.

> The company comes nowhere near this standard in its production of Aristophanes' *The Birds.* Using the William Arrowsmith translation, which often captures precisely the right skittery tone, only to lose it by throwing in arbitrary contemporary allusions, it moves raggedly around the Pisthetairos of Bert Lahr, who is on-stage almost the entire evening, raising more memories of *The Wizard of Oz* and *DuBarry Was a Lady* than creating a poor, bewildered Greek lost in Cloud-cuckoo-land. But Philip Piro's Poet catches the right lisping note amidst the fussy, preening bird-chorus, and Ruby Dee provides a moment of high good humor when she flies in on a Peter Pan wire as Iris, daughter of Zeus, down for a noisy visit from Olympus. There is also something happy in itself in the sight of Bert Lahr whacking a few pompous political and artistic types over the head with an inflated bladder, but the

> Aristophanic jokes are generally simpleminded and often incoherent, as is the entire "satiric" approach. Maybe the Athenians roared; in Ypsilanti there were only a couple of mild laughs.

Another critic at the Ypsilanti Festival was Stanley Kauffman of the *New York Times.* His summary of the event was brief, indeed. "*The Birds,* with the beloved Bert Lahr, was an under-rehearsed disaster."

New York's City Center was host to *The Knights* enacted by the National Theatre of Greece in a version directed by Alexis Solomos (1976). The usually obliging Clive Barnes, then drama critic of the *New York Times,* came from it in a fault-finding mood. The reason for his irritation:

> When a distinguished national theater – indeed one of Europe's major companies – comes here visiting on a Bicentennial goodwill mission, one longs to be courteous. But unfortunately, with its presentation of Aristophanes' *Knights,* the National Theatre of Greece is giving a quite dismally brilliant object lesson in how not to offer a foreign-language production for an English-speaking audience.
>
> In fairness, there is a large Greek-speaking population in New York City, and for this one is certain that this Aristophanes will be splendid. For one thing, the play is given in a translation and adaptation – according to the company's custom – from ancient Greek into the contemporary language. And certainly the performance is boisterous and attractive enough.
>
> Yet the English presentation is simply ludicrous. They are renting the usual electronic headsets, which usually carry a simultaneous translation of the text in English. The management is charging a two-dollar rental for the service, which seems a little excessive on top of, say, a twelve-dollar ticket. Yet this could be forgiven and forgotten had one been offered a decent clear translation.
>
> Instead of a simultaneous translation we are offered a pompously banal commentary by some professor of literature – he says – from New York University. This includes such gems of wisdom as these: "As opposed to *Oedipus at Colonus,* which is considered a tragedy, Aristophanes' *Knights* is a comedy." All helpful stuff. Or how about this? "This play might very well be a stripping away of Greek masks and of revealing the naked truth about the Greek character." This kind of thing is more distracting and humorless than Howard Cosell discussing a ball game.
>
> *Knights,* which is twenty-four hundred years old, is a strong political satire, a plea for political freedom in Athens in an attack on the reigning demagogue, Cleon, characterized in the play as Paphlagon. As in most of Aristophanes – *Peace,* for example – there is continual use of symbolism, and – presumably without a translation one could not tell – a great deal of sexual and scatological imagery. The politics of the play explain how two servants of Demos (symbolic of the democratic city state)

chafe under the rule of a new master (the Paphlagon-Cleon character) and install a democratically inclined sausage seller in his place.

The staging by Alexis Solomos is modern and stylized. The Knights themselves, representative of the Athenian middle-class, are given hobbyhorse steeds (shades of Jean Arouilh's *Beckett*) and the setting by Giorgos Vakalo is modishly pretty. The performances are vigorous.

Theodore Sarris and Kostas Kokkakis are the two drunken but sensible servants, Ghikas Biniaris is the conniving dictator. Stellos Vokovits makes a richly comic sausage seller, and the veteran Pandelis Zervos is the fine old man Demos, who represents the spirit of Athens.

Whether *Knights* was a wise choice for New York – political satire tends to lose its immediacy after the first thousand years or so – it is difficult to say. What is certain is that the efforts of this fine company could have been better served by a proper translation service.

(Barnes's quarrel seems not to have been with Aristophanes, the play or the acting, but with the New York University professor of literature. The Bicentennial celebration, in which the Greek company was joining, marked the 200th anniversary of the founding of the United States as a republic. Howard Cosell was a widely broadcasted sports commentator on television who had both fans and angry detractors.)

A like dilemma arose when *The Wasps*, performed by the King's College Classical Society of the University of London, was given at the Horace Mann Theater in New York under the sponsorship of the Columbia University's Classics Department (1981). "The only hitch," said the unsigned author of a *New York Times* notice, "is that the actors will speak in Greek. No matter. You can bone up on the play beforehand or read a synopsis in the program. *The Wasps* focuses on a father–son relationship and deals with problems familiar to our times – the generation gap and the uses and abuses of law in a democracy. The performance is broadly vaudevillian and understandable to non-classicists."

Passing mention might be made here of the overture and incidental music by the English composer Ralph Vaughan Williams for a staging of *The Wasps* (1909); a suite derived from that score, though a very youthful work, has held its place in the standard orchestral repertoire.

Peace was partially updated and converted to a musical comedy by Al Carmines, who saw it come to life at the Astor Place Theater for a modest run (1969). Marilyn Stasic, in the magazine *Cue,* ranked it as "the best Off-Broadway musical of the season". A clergyman, who turned out an endless flow of musicals and put on many of them in his church, Carmines was hailed by a *New York Post* critic as "the best living American composer". In his double role, religious leader and showman, he was for decades a prominent figure in the Off-Broadway theatre and remarkably prolific. He finally quit the pulpit to concentrate more faithfully on his heretofore avocation. In Carmine's version of *Peace*, Trygaios journeys upwards to avert a "heedless monster who is about to push a panic button and explode the world". One reviewer appended to his notice a warning that the work, though written by a man of the cloth, was "best suited to adults".

A vigorous enactment of Aristophanes' play was on view at the Edinburgh Festival (1970), earning this critique from John Barber in the *Daily Telegraph*:

> Pacifist leaflets were thrust upon Edinburgh theatregoers to underline the topicality of the Lyceum Theatre's Festival Production of the *Peace* of Aristophanes. There was no need. Especially, cynics might say, since the actors come from the Deutsches Theatre of East Berlin.
>
> This is not Brecht's Berliner Ensemble but sometimes you would hardly know the difference. The play is performed on a glaringly lit stage, the actors wearing masks, their costumes mostly of colourless sacking, and with musical interruptions in the abrasive style of Kurt Weill. It suits extraordinarily well the impudent and boisterous earnestness of the first ever black comedy, written during an uneasy lull in the Peloponnesian War which the Hellenes had already endured for ten ruinous years. If it is relevant today it must have been lacerating then.
>
> The performance is in German, of course, but batons are provided which whisper a simultaneous translation into your ear. It is hardly necessary. The actors mime the tale like huge droll puppets, pointing up the jokes with naïve grotesqueries and often breaking into song and dance to close harmony from trumpet, clarinet and trombone. Fred Duren plays the Attic farmer Trygaios, who flies to heaven on a dung-beetle – subject of many broad jests about animal functions – in order to expostulate with Zeus for allowing the war to go on. Here he finds the goddess Peace imprisoned in a pit. With the help of fellow Athenians she is released and the war ends – spelling trouble for Trygaios back on earth from war profiteers. But all ends with joyful wedding celebrations.
>
> The brutal simplicity of the production and the superbly drilled clowning of both actors and chorus give bite to the harsh messages: the Greeks are hacking themselves to pieces and are turning the fertile earth into a desert. The stark treatment did not for me, however, sound Aristophanes' tremulous optimism, or quite touch the lyrical praise of the blessings of peace – the olive groves, the fat geese and the marriage bed about which the poet is so eloquent. But there was wit amid the hurly-burly. Klaus Piontak's sinister Hermes is full of it. And much is made of the *parabasis* when the actors turn on the critics and invite the audience to praise as well they might the author's courage.

Benno Besson is the director of this rollicking and hugely Teutonic entertainment with music supplied on stage by Papa Binnes's jazz band.

Students of Fordham University in New York City discovered the inherent fun of *The Assemblywomen* when it was performed in Pope Auditorium on the Lincoln Center campus. In *The Ram*, the college newspaper, Jim Nedalka described the enactment as triumphant.

> What makes this revival outstanding is the way it's presented. . . . The whole of the theater is used. The company plays on stage as well as in and around the house, making the experience one of being in an arena; if you saw *Candide* on Broadway, you have some idea of the excitement of the production as the audience, to a degree, is involved in the show.
>
> The plot revolves around the women of Athens who unite to overthrow the inept men who comprise the government. Their leader is Praxagora, blithely portrayed by Margarita St Paul. But the burden of the show does not fall solely on her shoulders, for she is more than ably assisted by the rest of the company, which includes the chorus. True to Greek tradition, the chorus is strong, led by Diane Hammarth and Mary Jane Lauria, who set the pace for their followers as they sweetly sing and gracefully dance throughout the playing area. Nor is Praxagora the lone leader of the female revolutionists. Therese Renbecky, Meaghan O'Connell, Melody Sigut are three of the forward women of Athens in the year 392 BC. But the men are not to be left in the starting gate, especially since their masculinity is challenged. Praxagora's husband, Blepyros, her next-door neighbor, Pheidolos, and their mutual friend, Chremes, decide to fight back the best way they know how, but never quite get as far as they desire.
>
> The entire production of *The Assemblywomen* is under the imaginative direction of E.E. Young, faculty member in the theater arts division. Combining the total elements of the theater, he has incorporated the fine choreography of Silvia Shay Orensteine and Rayes's inspired score: he has placed them in, around, and against a strikingly graphic, and quite wondrous Michael Massee setting, which brings Aristophanes a worthwhile new life. Massee is also responsible for the design of the authentic period costumes, and Ms Lauria deserves praise for her creative make-up artistry. *The Assemblywomen* is a highly enjoyable musical evening (a little bit on the salty side) which runs through Saturday night at 8:00 p.m.

This critic adds a high note: "There is a matinée this afternoon at 2:00 p.m. and is well worth cutting class to see."

Sidewalks Theater, a professional, non-profit New York troupe formed in 1976 to focus on classical comedy and community service, also chose *The Assemblywomen.* They essayed a free performance outdoors, in Bryant Park, behind the main branch of the Public Library, in mid-Manhattan. The worthy cause to which the company was dedicating itself was a drive to clean up the park, which then was much neglected and abused. An announcement in the *New York Times* was to the effect that "a battle of the sexes will take place this afternoon, August 18, 1981; the battle is part of the plot, but it could spill over to spectators, who will be invited to participate in part of the presentation".

The *New York Times* gave this account of what ensued: "The men who rule Athens are ruining the nation, so a group of women decide to take charge. They don false beards and their husbands' clothes, proceed to the assembly and vote to give themselves power. The performance, in masks and period costume, included music, mime and improvisation." Whether any spectators joined in, and whether Bryant Park was cleaner thereafter, is not reported.

The Clouds was selected as a curtain-raiser by the London Small Theatre Company, a "fringe" troupe visiting New York and appearing at the Judith Anderson Theater, under the sponsorship of the Manhattan Punch Line Theater (1990). On the programme it preceded *Beyond Belief,* "a delightfully zany fantasy" written, directed and with music arranged by Fiona Laird, who also had adapted *The Clouds,* "one of Aristophanes' sendups of Socratic philosophy". Wilbur Hampton was the *New York Times*'s critic: "Ms Laird has wisely done little updating of the text but has employed Julie Speechley's outrageous costumes – the women in flower-pot hats or curlers and rubber gloves, and Socrates in a glitter-covered Elton John hat with purple glasses and elevator shoes – to help coax the laughter. The result is more of a college lampoon than a satire, but it sets the mood for what follows."

What Aristophanes would have thought of this, and other, *outré* adaptations of his works, it would be interesting to know. In any event, he still holds the stage, which would doubtless please him.

Most surely, too, it would have delighted him that, 2,500 years after his death, *Lysistrata* could still start an uproar in Athens. With the replacement of the military junta that had ruled Greece from 1967 to 1974, the theatre was at last set free and responded with sharp satire and overt criticism aimed at past and newly established notables. The *politiki ephitheorisi,* or political revue, which had been revived at the twentieth century's beginning, became exceedingly popular. Just as celebrities from Pericles to Socrates had been mocked and reviled centuries before, now many contemporary authority figures were subjected to similar ridicule and slander. Actors wore make-up to help them look like the celebrities they were caricaturing. The revues were mostly new works, in the undying Aristophanic tradition, but plays by the master himself had been brought back as early as 1957 to the theatre at Epidaurus, the arena hallowed by arching ages. A production there of *Lysistrata* (1986) had an immensely popular film actress, Aliki Vouyouklaki, in the role of Peace, scantily clad in a transparent body suit. Wrote a correspondent for the *New York Times*, Paul Anastasi: "Audiences roared as Athenians and Spartans vied to make her their most coveted trophy." However, some conservative members of the local theatre world were aghast that, in an attempt to draw larger audiences, film stars were being cast in the revered classics and allowed to appear on a once-sacred stage. "Reaction to the play was explosive even before its opening. George Armenis, one of the best known and respected actors in classical theatre, described the production as an insult to ancient Greek drama and to the ancient sites in which they were being performed. 'Aristophanes would turn in his grave,' Mr Armenis said. 'The theatres of Epidaurus and Herod Atticus are being irretrievably polluted.'" For the acting skills of such popular performers, Armenis had only contempt.

A like view was held by Karolos Koun, another well-known actor and director of classic drama, head of the prestigious Art Theatre, who protested: "Popularizing ancient plays does not raise them to the level of Aristophanes and Sophocles, but instead lowers them to ordinary needs." He told Anastasi: "The 'sanctity' of the ancient theatres should be safeguarded and their standards maintained, as they are at the Royal Shakespeare Company in Stratford-upon-Avon, England." Among other players who voiced outrage was a film actress, Anna Fonsou, who saw the venture as "an exercise in profit-making and opportunism, a Trojan horse in the arts, littering the holiest areas of our country and covering with filth whatever qualities remain in our theatre".

However, the box office was overwhelmed. Reported Anastasi: "Police had to keep order as thousands of Vouyouklaki admirers drove the country roads and packed the twelve-thousand-seat open-air theatre. Crowds returned *en masse* for Euripides' tragedy *Medea*, performed by the popular Greek acting team of Jenny Karezi and her husband Kostas Kazakos. The event made front-page news in Greek newspapers and, as is not unusual in Greece, became a political issue. The conservative opposition New Democracy Party accused the Socialist Government of exploiting movie stars for political gain, by creating a controversy that deflected public attention from more pressing domestic problems. And while the cabinet of the ruling Socialist Government was well represented at Epidaurus, New Democracy politicians stayed away."

Middle Comedy took over throughout the first seventy-five years of the fourth century BC, and, as has been stated, Aristophanes' *Pluto* is the only remaining intact example of it. The names of between forty and fifty playwrights who devoted themselves to this genre are listed in scattered sources, and some eight hundred plays are ascribed to this transitional period, stretching from 400 to 325 BC. From 338 BC on, Athens, defeated, was ever more subjected to Macedonian domination, its kings, Philip and his ambitious son Alexander, having increasing political and military influence and power. The intellectual climate was unhappily changed.

Fragments of scripts on faded, stiffened, yellowed, tattered parchments have been found, but for the most part what they preserve is not impressive as literature. Among the most acclaimed of the authors was Antiphanes (*c.* 388–*c.* 311 BC), credited variously with between 245 and 280 – or by another count, 365 – comedies. A foreigner, he obtained Athenian citizenship through the generous intervention of Demosthenes, the orator. Alexis of Thurii purportedly turned out 245 works.

By comparison, Anaxandrides of Rhodes, who penned a mere sixty-five scripts, might not have been deemed prolific. He captured first prize at the Greater Dionysia; in consequence, he was summoned to Macedonia by King Philip to furnish a comedy as part of the festivities honouring victory at Olynthus and to stay at court. Berthold remarks: "His departure from Athens is a straw indicating which way the political wind was blowing: Macedonia was aspiring to hegemony in Greece, and the glory of Athens was dimming."

It is assumed, though not positively known, that a censorship of some sort forbade satiric thrusts at and mockery of those in high office; in any event, such material seems to have disappeared from Middle Comedy. Perhaps when the state was no longer democratic and free but authoritarian, people lost interest in politics, the personalities of rulers, the ongoing rivalries and intrigues. The ordinary man had less responsibility for civic affairs. He no longer met in assemblies to hear debates on issues but instead stayed home and occupied himself with domesticity, absorbed by everyday matters.

The plays reflect this. As political satire evaporated, so did obscenity, which gradually diminished, though it never entirely disappeared. The *parabasis*, where the author was outspoken, was cut. The chorus grew ever smaller in number, as its role shrank, and sometimes it was not used at all. One reason for this is that Athens had fewer rich men to foot the cost of large, spectacular productions. Realism manifested itself in the acting and the plotting. Actors, though still masked, very seldom sported false paunches and exaggerated phalluses. But the plays continued to have elements of music and dance.

The plots of these comedies, and those that followed in the next genre that arose, New Comedy, are very often secularized versions of the old myths. As described in earlier chapters, the myths had taken shape through a process in which tribal culture heroes had gradually been enhallowed by antiquity and enskyed, gaining divine or semi-divine attributes, as ever more intricate legends were woven about them: now, in a far more rational age, inclining towards monotheism – Aristotle was reducing God to a rather abstract First Mover – a reverse process of decaelization was taking place: the stories about the fickle, promiscuous minor gods were retold in terms of mortals and their daily adventures and misadventures. In the theatre, the plots were age-old by now; possibly there were no new plots at all.

Other playwrights of the day included Alexis, Eubulus and Timocles. Some of the few lines surviving from these writers are epigrammatic and chucklesome. F.L. Lucas has translated samples. Here is a fragment from Antiphanes:

> "He has got married." "*What* is that you say!
> Got *married!* Why, I left him alive and walking."

A judgement:

> For one thing only will I trust a woman –
> Once she is dead, not to come back again;
> But trust her in nothing else, till dead indeed.

And this warning:

> Anyone that, born a mortal, fondly calculates that he
> Can in life have sure possessions, trusts an utter fallacy.
> One has all his coffers emptied by some public contribution;
> One, involved in litigation, comes to total destitution;
> Chosen general, one goes bankrupt; one, providing cloaks of gold
> For his chorus, as choragus, shivers ragged in the cold;
> Or, as triërarch, you're broken; or, as trader, in the waves
> Lose your all; you may be murdered, sleeping, walking, by your slaves.
> There's no wealth you can be sure of – only what you chance to pay
> In the purchase of enjoyment, as there passes day by day.
> Even *that* is none too certain. Spread although your table lies,
> Someone may, when least you think it, snatch it all before your eyes.

Out of all you own each moment, you can count as surely won
Not a thing except the mouthful that your teeth have closed upon.

Alexis of Thurii (*c.* 372–*c.* 270 BC) reached the age of ninety-eight or more and was the uncle of Menander, his illustrious younger peer. A character in one of his plays complains:

We married men alone
Must face an audit of our lives, not yearly,
But every mortal day.

A citizen voices anger at a corrupt official:

A new law, now, he's bringing in – pure gold!
That fishmongers henceforth must sell their wares,
Not seated, but all standing; and he says
Next year he'll make it "hanging"!

A servant has little patience with philosophical discussions:

Why do you chatter, tossing stupid phrases
From Academe, Lyceum, or Odeum –
Mere Sophists' gabble? There's no good in that.
Oh Sicon, Sicon, let us drink – drink deep –
Be merry while we have a soul to cosset!
Come, Manes, roister! Belly's best of all;
That's your real father, and your mother too.
Your lofty actions, embassies, commands
Are a bluster of empty boasts, as good as dreams.
Once your hour comes, then God'll strike you cold,
And leave you nothing but what you've drunk and eaten.
The rest is dust – your Codrus and your Cimon,
Your Pericles.

Like Antiphanes, his contemporary, Alexis was a naturalized Athenian. Italy was his birthplace.

Somewhat contemptuous of women, as apparently were so many of the Middle Comedy poets, was Xenarchus:

> What happy creatures, then, are grasshoppers,
> Whose females haven't even the tiniest voices.

Amphis had this to say of the revered philosopher:

> O Plato,
> How little you know except of looking gloomy
> With lofty-lifted eyebrows like a snail!

He preferred the rustic scene:

> Then is not solitude a thing of gold?
> The countryside is like a father, helping
> (As none else will) to veil life's neediness;
> But the city is a theatre where misfortunes
> Crowd before all men's view.

Eubulus (*fl.* 375 BC) was another of the misogynists:

> Curse on the cursed fool that was the second
> To marry a wife! For I can't blame the first.
> I suppose he hadn't learnt the curse they are;
> But the second knew all right! . . .
> Most hallowed Zeus, should I speak ill of women!
> Good God, let me perish sooner! There's no treasure
> That can compare with them. And if Medea
> Was a bad woman, still Penelope
> Was just a marvel! Say you, Clytemnestra

Was also wicked? But how good, Alcestis!
Someone may censure Phaedra. But by Heaven
There was that noble . . .
Dear, dear me,
How quickly my worthy women have run out! –
While still I have a whole long list of bad ones.

In much the same rueful vein:

Who was the first of men that drew or moulded
Eros with wings?
The man was only fit for drawing swallows;
Little he knew about the ways of Love!
For *he's* not light, nor easy to be quit of,
When once a man has caught the malady,
But desperate heavy. How should such a thing
Have wings! If any said so – utter nonsense!

In one of Anaxilas' comedies a character declares:

Why you are more distrustful than a snail,
That, when he travels, takes his house as well.

In a serious moment Mnesimachus muses on:

Our sleeps, that are Death's Lesser Mysteries.

Most likely these chips from the plays were saved because they were sharply meaningful to those who memorized or in some other way kept them. Though brief, they yield rewarding insights into the consciousness and everyday life of a fourth-century BC Athenian, who does not seem very different from a harried citizen of the twentieth century.

*

A half-century after Aristophanes' death a trio of writers of outstanding talent, if not genius, gave a fresh impetus to the lighter side of theatre, Diphilus, Philemon and Menander, perfecting the form of farce now called New Comedy, one that has more definite characteristics than the amorphous and largely unknown Middle Comedy was ever to achieve. Somewhat prominent, too, in this epoch, was Apollodorus of Gela, though he was not their equal.

New Comedy began to flourish shortly after the accession of Alexander the Great to the Macedonian throne (336 BC). The names of at least sixty-four playwrights of this period are known, and the titles of well over 1,000 scripts. Most of these, as must be obvious, were staged not in Athens but in other Greek cities that by now had built their own theatres and also held annual festivals. Of all these plays, only a tiny fraction remain, and all by a single dramatist, Menander. He is believed to have authored 105 comedies, of which only five have been found in various states of wholeness, along with many interesting fragments. The works of his highest-ranked contemporaries and competitors, Diphilus, Philemon and Apollodorus, together with lost pieces by Menander, are known derivatively; that is, Roman farce writers of a later date – in particular, Plautus and Terence – freely borrowed plots, characters and even metaphors, epigrams and witticisms from them, giving subsequent generations of classical scholars substantial clues to what the Greek New Comedies were like.

Fantasy and wild burlesque were replaced by stories having an ever closer resemblance to daily life, insisting on logic and consistent action. A special aspect of these scripts was the discovery and development of the love-theme, putting emphasis on the vicissitudes of the "eternal triangle", a subject which has preoccupied the craftsmen of comedy ever since.

Diphilus, a native of Sinope on the Black Sea, wielded broad strokes, more so than his rival Menander. Two of his plays, *Drawers of Lots* and *The Rope*, inspired Plautus to appropriate their plots and characters, and another had an exciting scene about the abduction of a slave-girl deftly lifted by Terence, who inserted it into a script of his own, *Adelphi*, frankly acknowledging his borrowing. He blended it with scenes from Menander, to form a new farce, which the Roman playwrights often did. Diphilus took first prize three times at the Lenaea. In a succeeding century, about the middle of the third, a contest was held for old comedies; it was won by Diphilus, with Menander coming in second. So Diphilus' appeal to the masses had not much lessened.

During his lifetime, Philemon's popularity considerably exceeded that of Menander. He is believed to have come from Syracuse before settling in Athens, where he won citizenship. Plautus got ideas for two farces from him, *The Merchant* and *Three Pieces of Silver*, and possibly also for a third, *The Ghost*, affording partial knowledge of Philemon's plot-making and story-telling. He too preferred broader efforts than did Menander. He garnered three first prizes at the Lenaea, and on one such occasion Menander is said to have asked him: "Tell me, Philemon, do you not blush each time you have defeated me?" What Philemon replied is not told, but it is claimed that he was skilful at organizing and generously paying for a claque, which may have inspired Menander's ironic query.

Of his plays, only a handful of snippets have been collected. In one is an indication that he admired Euripides – at least, he has a character exclaim:

> If, as some say, my friends,
> In every deed the dead had consciousness,
> I had hanged myself to see Euripides.

This departs from Aristophanes' scornful attitude, and testifies to the esteem in which this new age held the romantic tragic poet. Philemon seems also to have had sophisticated views on religion, inclined to conceive of an elusive, possibly abstract Deity:

> God wills not you should know Him – what He is;
> Then impious you,
> Seeking to know Him, that would *not* be known!
> [Translation: F.L. Lucas]

His dates are *c.* 361–*c.* 262 BC – a long life!

In the vast number of centuries since, however, the palm has been given not to Diphilus or Philemon but to Menander, though he won first prize on only eight occasions, and sometimes finished last. Nephew of Alexis of Thurii, he may have inherited his uncle's keen dramatic talent, though not his longevity. Born in *c.* 342, forty years after the death of Aristophanes, thirty years after that of Aristotle, he dwelt in a greatly changed world. He himself died in *c.* 290 BC, in a post-Alexandrine age.

Something of a dandy, with a flirtatious eye, he was depicted by a poet, Phaedrus, some four centuries later, in these phrases:

> Drenched with perfume, in a long-trailing robe,
> With delicate and languid pace he came.

Thus he might have been likened to an Oscar Wilde. He was handsome (though he had a squint), and rich, and urbane, with a refined wit and genuine culture, along with a streak of melancholy. He shared the bohemian morality prevalent in the Athenian world to which he belonged by birth and vocation, and his was a time that alternated between anarchy and decadence, Athens having become a mere colony, ruled first by Macedonia, then by Rome.

Menander's many love affairs, among them one with the courtesan Glycera, were notorious; and when Ptolemy I offered him a haven in Alexandria, now one of the Hellenistic age's centres of culture, he suggested that his rival Philemon be granted the refuge instead, explaining, "Philemon has no Glycera." (A mere *copy* of a portrait of this besought lady, painted by Pausias of Sicyon, afterwards sold for a small fortune.) Though most inconstant to her hitherto, Menander spent his final years as her faithful companion. Yet his tirades against marriage are endless, though now and then his characters put in a kindly word for the wedded state.

For a long time he was the personal friend of Demetrius of Phalerum, the Macedonian governor of Athens; it was the unpopular Demetrius' fall in 307 BC that brought Menander the invitation from the Egyptian ruler. He received a similar bid from the Macedonian court, where he was equally admired, but also turned it down, though one of his plays had just been denied staging in now censorious Athens. He stayed in his city, close to the two theatres, or else in his luxurious seaside villa in nearby Piraeus, in the company of his mistress Glycera, and never travelled abroad.

In refusing the Egyptian king's offer he wrote that he was flattered and tempted, yet had to admit that he was even more drawn to gaining the wreath of "Dionysus and his Bacchic ivy leaves, with which I would sooner be crowned than with the diadems of Ptolemy, in full view of my Glycera as she sits in the theatre".

In Rome's Museo Laterano is a celebrated relief portraying the playwright seated on a stool, holding in his hand the mask of a youth that might have been worn by a character in a farce, while on a table before him lie the masks of a courtesan and an angry old man; on the far side, facing him, is a statuesque female figure, perhaps his Glycera or a mythological personification of a *skene*.

What Diphilus, Philemon and Menander wrote are usually "comedies of errors": their chief plot springs from mistaken identity once again – as in Middle Comedy – sometimes because the heroes are twins, but also for a variety of other ingeniously contrived causes. All have happy endings, almost invariably betokened by a wedding or several of them. Stories are now well defined, the craftsmanship neat, however stereotyped; Euripidean tragicomedy had probably influenced the authors. The scenes are likely to be laid outdoors, in a bustling street. This lends them greater realism, enabling them to reflect vignettes of everyday life. The lasting formula of not-very-bright boy meets girl, boy loses girl, boy gets girl again, is now established, and the audience is persistently teased – then as today – as to how the affrighted and beset heroine is to retain her highly regarded but imperilled virginity. She might be a slave-girl; at the very last moment she is discovered to be the long-lost daughter of a rich or possibly noble family – she believes that her parents have perished during a storm at sea, and they think that the same fate has befallen her – whereas all have been safely tossed ashore, though somehow in widely separate climes. This leads to a joyful recognition scene, most often by means of a token, and to a satisfactory reunion at the denouement. Sometimes it is the poor young hero, deeply in love and distraught but unable to marry a girl of wealth or aristocratic lineage, who turns out to be the strayed scion of an equally affluent family. Very often he himself is unaware, until the last moment, of his distinguished antecedents. Fathers find alive a son or daughter presumably long dead, and supposed orphans are claimed by rich and fond parents, and slaves learn that they are actually freemen, or are liberated as a reward, and so on.

In these farces, authors frequently exploited a swollen vein of sentimentality and pathos. They are an inexplicit plea for sympathy for the seeming base-born and homeless. (The moral might be, to paraphrase a modern saw, "Be kind to your slave – who knows, he might turn out to be an heir to wealth and truly more patrician than you.")

To a degree, social criticism had not wholly vanished from the plays but instead is not overt but inherent in the subject-matter. There is also the paradox that the male slaves are invariably more cunning than their masters, whom they regularly outwit. If spectators were ready to accept this seemingly illogical premise, that too was an unflattering judgement on the ruling class, those who held high positions by virtue of their birth rather than their own talents.

The recognition scenes at the climax became an enduring device in farce, frequently utilized by Shakespeare, for instance when Viola and Rosalind reveal their true sex; by Molière in *Tartuffe*; as well as by Beaumarchais, in *The Barber of Seville* and *The Marriage of Figaro*; by Goldoni, in *A Servant of Two Masters*; by Goldsmith, in *She Stoops to Conquer*; until, after a thousand repetitions, by innumerable lesser playwrights, it was charmingly mocked by Oscar Wilde in *The Importance of Being Earnest* and by Gilbert and Sullivan in *Pinafore*, *Ruddigore*, *The Mikado* and *The Gondoliers*, where the humour of the "unmasking" arises from its long-since over-use and deadening over-familiarity. In some plays, as in *Tartuffe*, the recognition is not one of the character's actual identity but of his true nature, the hypocrite exposed, the villain finally seen barefaced.

The roles of the leading characters in New Comedy, as well as the minor ones, are largely limited to generalized types, or "stock" figures: in all, some twenty-seven distinct stock characters developed, distinguished by that many different traditional masks. These masks, which have survived, are astonishingly expressive. Furthermore, Menander excelled at individualizing these stereotyped characters, which he accomplished by adding to each man's conventional persona a unique obsession or habit, a striking mannerism, so that in at least one small facet of his nature he stands apart from all others.

The stock figures in New Comedy are also created by ascribing to each one a dominant trait commonly associated with his trade or profession: the swaggering hot-tempered soldier; the gluttonous cook; the resourceful servant, always scheming; the equally conniving lawyer; the voracious court parasite; a busy panderer; the quack doctor; the vulgar, good-natured courtesan; the sordid pimp; the evil procuress; the poor, honest young man, not too intelligent but brave; the beset yet still virtuous young woman; the rich, miserly old man (sometimes the uncle or guardian of the hero or heroine, and with his eye on marrying a hapless girl); the indulgent old man (most likely a parent); and a score more, all well known by now. Though shallow, such portrait-sketches are not unlifelike, and they represent a great advance over the fantastic, cartoon figures of Old Comedy. This cast of fixed characters is to populate farce, and be immediately but delightedly recognized by audiences, from Menander's time to the present day.

How else Menander contrived to individualize his people is well explained by Sandbach:

> [He] was not slow to make use of the traditional figures caricatured in Middle Comedy, soldiers, courtesans, cooks, and so on. But he was not content simply to repeat their traditional qualities; when he used old themes he made them a part only of an individual character, or he modified them; sometimes he even contradicted tradition, to create an effect by the unexpectedness of his treatment.
>
> The cook had been inquisitive, talkative and self-important. Sikon in *Dyskolos* shows curiosity as he questions Geta on his mistress's dream; he is not long-winded, but he talks to himself, using a vocabulary rich in oaths and in metaphors; he boasts, not of his cuisine, but of his large clientele and his technique in borrowing utensils; his conceit is shown by his reaction to Knemon's falling into the well:
>
> "Now the Nymphs have given him the punishment he deserves
> on my account. No one who wrongs a cook ever gets off
> unscathed. Our art has something sacred about it."
>
> By contrast the cook in *Aspis*, who is seen leaving, not as usual entering, his place of employment, com-

plains that things always go wrong for him. The cook in *Samia* enters in full flow of talk and questions, but is cut short. Later he tries with officious benevolence to interfere as Demeas turns Chrysis out of his house. All these cooks display or contradict traditional characters, but they do it briefly and in sentences woven into the texture of plot and dialogue.

The stupidity, arrogance and vulgarity of the professional soldier, together with his habit of romancing about his exploits, were certainly all exhibited by Bias in *Kolax* (*The Flatterer*) . . . But the three soldiers who appear in the partially surviving plays are sympathetically drawn. Thrasonides of *Misumenos* (*Hated*), wild with love with the captive girl in his power, not laying a hand on her when she shows her repulsion, and generously freeing her without ransom when her father appears, is the hero of the play. Yet he had talked of his exploits, a traditional motif, but it may be guessed, one made essential to the play, for it will have been one of these tales which made the girl suspect him of having killed her brother. Nor is there any reason to think that he exaggerated, for the prologue told that he had served with distinction.

There is no sign of any of the traditional defects in Stratophanes in *Sikyonios* (*The Man from Sikyon*). On the contrary, his actions are practical and decisive, nor does he forget, at the moment when he seems about to secure the girl he loves, to issue orders for the quartering of the men for whom he is responsible. One can believe that he was a good officer. Polemon, on the other hand, in *Perikeiromene* has neither the traditional qualities of the caricatured soldier nor those that are required in the field. He is hasty, uncertain of himself and impulsive, but he attracts sympathy by his bewilderment at the situation he has created by the outrage on the mistress he loves, his despair at the prospect of her leaving him, and his pleasure at her discovery of her father.

Similarly the selfish, acquisitive, lying and faithless courtesan, although no doubt a common figure in real life, was not according to Menander the sole type to be found in her profession.

Here Sandbach goes through the fragmented texts and Latin borrowings to show how the poet differentiates between a broad spectrum of such women, the *hetairai.* Some are still slaves, young, clever and good-natured, but ready to deceive, not unwilling to help others but also trying to win their own freedom by trickery. Such a one is Chrysis in *Samia*, who palms off another's child as her own, though it means that she is misleading the man who is keeping her. Thais, in *Eunuchus*, has a share of innate dignity and seeks to act generously, but is not blind to her self-interest. On the other hand, some of these women are portrayed as outcasts, depraved, sly, thoroughly unscrupulous.

In his depiction of slaves, Menander displays the same approach. Often they are empathetically drawn.

> He thought of them neither as mere instruments of their masters' wishes nor as vehicles for comic interludes; they act with their own motivation within a framework provided by the actions, characters, and intentions of their owners; they affect what happens, but do not direct it. This, it may be supposed, does not misrepresent the situation in many Athenian households.
>
> This method of writing, which gives large parts to slaves and develops their personalities on much the same scale as those of their masters, is a testimonial to the author's range of interest and sympathy.

Sandbach argues that in portraying household servants not as mere subsidiary characters, and certainly not as inferior persons, Menander was far in advance of later playwrights down to the present time, with a few exceptions – Jonson, Beaumarchais, Barrie, the creators of Mosca, Figaro and the quietly efficient, admirable butler Crichton.

It is thought that besides having had a special opportunity to learn stagecraft from his successful uncle Alexis, Menander was benignly influenced by his contemporary and mentor Theophrastus (370–287 BC?), the philosopher and author of *Characters*, the immortal collection of quick, sharp sketches of people encountered in a cross-section of his society and most likely of any community since then. Theophrastus was the inheritor of Aristotle's library, which also made him a particularly worthy teacher.

In later eras, other stock figures based on supposed ethnic and national traits have been added to the roster: the stage Irishman, pugnacious, loquacious; the canny, tight-fisted Scot; the phlegmatic Englishman, a bit slow to catch a joke; the garrulous, excitable Italian; the effete Frenchman; and – today – the camera-clicking Japanese tourist; along with the brash but shrewd Yankee.

To emphasize their universality, such characters from Greek days until the very recent past have borne generic and descriptive names: this is already seen in the Old Comedy of Aristophanes, and the practice is brought back in English farces from the Restoration onwards to the seventeenth and eighteenth centuries, where figures are named Morose, Manly, Fidelia – the hypocrite is Sir Joseph Surface; the gossip, Lady Teazel; the effeminate dandy, Sir Fopling Flutter. Sheridan's dame, who habitually mispronounces the polysyllabic words of which she is overly fond, is the buxom Mrs Malaprop. Today the naming is more oblique – the downtrodden hero of Arthur Miller's *Death of a Salesman* is Willie Loman (Low-man); the pure-in-soul young man in Tennessee Williams's *Orpheus Descending* is Val Xavier, suggesting his share of saint-like qualities; the essentially innocent but cruelly despoiled heroine of *A Streetcar Named Desire* is Blanche Dubois (White [Flower] of the Woods). The simpler device of earlier times has been relegated to the magazine and newspaper comic strip, where a timid character is called Casper Milquetoast, which suffices to explain him.

Concerning the characters that had begun to take shape in Middle Comedy and more gradually to become more rounded in New Comedy, Aristotle remarked in his *Poetics*: "Comedy would make its personages worse than the men of the present day." He meant that human shortcomings are exaggerated in comic portraits. He elaborated on this, if only briefly: "Comedy is an imitation of men worse than the average; worse, however, not as regards any and every sort of fault, but only as regards one particular kind, the Ridiculous, which is a species of the Ugly. The Ridiculous may be defined as a mistake or deformity not productive of pain or harm to others; the mask, for instance, that excites laughter, is something ugly and distorted without causing pain." Comedy exposes man's faults: his petty chicanery, his social hypocrisy and fawning, his vanity, his boastfulness and pomposity, his illicit longing to commit adultery – it is assumed that the "deformity" to which Aristotle refers is not a physical one but a psychological one, a character defect, perhaps a silly quirk.

If the Aristotelian definition holds true, it is understandable why others have said that comedy is more pessimistic than tragedy, for it regards human nature cynically, whereas the premise of tragedy is that man is capable of idealism and courage and has a potential for splendid gestures and deeds, though he may fail to achieve them, perhaps just missing his goal.

New Comedy plots, as already mentioned, revolve mostly about situations arising from mistaken identity. Superficially this is caused by a similarity of names, or from the characters being brothers or even twins, or from a self-assertive servant passing himself off as his master, all of which can be manipulated to yield hilarious complications. On this superficial level the motif is still much used even in sophisticated modern comedy, from *The Inspector General* and *Charley's Aunt* to *The Guardsman*, *Dear Ruth* and *The Cactus Flower*, to cite a few examples chosen at random.

It has a deeper historical and psychological significance, however: it is innately linked to the "changeling theme", the story of the foundling whose birth and identity are a mystery to him and others. This theme appears in tragedy as well, for instance in *Oedipus* and *Iphigeneia in Tauris*, and in Euripidean tragicomedy, in *Ion*; and it is still effective at the heart of a great work of fiction, centuries later, *Tom Jones*, by Henry Fielding, a novelist who began his career and first learned his craft as an actor and deft playwright.

Many theories about how the theme originated, and dramatic literature's long preoccupation with it, have been postulated. One is that mistaken identity and the possibility of one's being a "changeling" were highly plausible when few if any birth-and-death records were kept. This was especially true in times of chaos, such as existed during Athens's many years of warfare, capped by its subjugation. Throughout the ancient world it was not unusual for besieged towns to be overrun and sacked, families scattered, children orphaned, often too young to know who their parents might be. Even the wealthy and high-born might suffer this unhappy fate. Such confusion was augmented by the common practice of exposing unwanted children, as befell the infant Oedipus, put out to die on a barren mountain slope. The abandoned child was most likely to be female. Found, she might be brought up and sold to become a slave or courtesan.

Also, during certain orgiastic revels – the wild, primitive Dionysian ceremonies and, later, the Roman Saturnalia – many children were begotten by the intoxicated participants; afterwards the fathers might be forgetful, or simply unknown by the mothers – as, again, is suggested in Euripides' *Ion.* In both the sacking of towns and the revels, the children might be the consequence of casual unbridled rape.

The "changeling" theme might also have a psychological prompting. Otto Rank, in his *Myth of the Birth of the Hero*, traces an impulse in folk lore to deny a simple or natural birth to those intensely admired and revered and who are elevated to a semi-divine status; until ultimately a superior and even supernatural origin is attributed to such heroes – there could have been nothing ordinary about these extraordinary figures from their very beginning.

Some anthropologists, again, see the recurrent "changeling" motif as a secularized version of the myth of the resurrected Year-God, his appearance in another guise.

Psychoanalysts, too, point out that children often daydream that they are not truly the offspring of their all-too-dull, everyday parents; in their fantasies they are of royal or lofty birth. Angry children, especially if they have been richly fed on fairytales, will often cry out at offending parents: "You're not really my mother and father!" Some of this occurs, it is suggested, after the shock experienced when the child first learns of the details of the sexual act by which he was conceived; he retreats from images of that into a world of illusion in which he is the offspring of quite different, far less actual parents.

In the very familiar, oft-repeated motif of mistaken identity in comedy, some or all these many impulses may be united, and it illustrates again how closely theatre springs from and touches on deeply hidden impulses in human nature.

In New Comedy the play was structured to have an expository prologue and five sections or "acts"; and intermissions filled by incursions of the chorus, with songs and dances. By now the chorus was reduced to providing little more than these between-acts diversions, taking no significant part in the action, but at the intervals introducing a touch of brightness and joyousness. The *entr'actes* were often mere improvisations, inserted by the director or producer, rather than conceived by the author. Since the actors wore masks and the chorus sang and danced, the style of presentation was hardly realistic; New Comedy merely represented an advance towards a greater degree of naturalism but never fully arrived at it. The dialogue was mostly in "easy-flowing iambics". These light works were prototypes of what are much later called operettas.

The theatres in which they were staged were likely to be smaller, more intimate than those in Athens. As has been remarked, even lesser towns now had them, for theatre-going had grown to be a much-demanded entertainment. Actors earned substantial fees and enjoyed wide followings; the players' guilds were also well organized and in a commanding position to obtain privileges – they called themselves the "Artists of Dionysus". A compulsion to escape from the dire conditions and pressures of the day drew people to the theatres.

Though Menander was overshadowed by Philemon during their active careers, his reputation started to burgeon throughout the ensuing five or six centuries, with swelling tributes to his skill, his supremacy in handling this formalized sort of farce. His triumph, like that of Euripides, was posthumous. Some critics ranked him next to Homer! What created and kept his fame ever growing was not the scripts – after a while they were nearly all unknown – but rather a stock of delightful and treasured epigrams that are believed to be his, though even his ownership is not entirely certain. In any event, he provided the ancient – and modern – world with a host of aphorisms, memorable lines, through which run a pulse of melancholy. He is not profound, but practical and intelligent. For instance:

> Evil communications corrupt good manners.

(Menander is not the only pagan dramatist quoted by St Paul.)

> Whom the gods love, die young.
> Conscience makes cowards of the bravest men.
> I am a man, and consider nothing human to be alien to me.

(Possibly this was said by Terence.)

> Fight not with God, nor to the storm without
> Add your own storms.

We live not as we will, but as we can.
The man who does no evil needs no law.
Fortune is no real thing.
    But men who cannot bear what comes to them,
In Nature's way, give their own characters
    The name of Fortune.

Of Menander's writings only some four thousand lines exist, most of them scattered; the assumption is that they could be a 5 per cent remnant of his output. From them it is easy to believe that he was the friend of Epicurus, the philosopher who preached self-discipline and tranquillity, and whom Menander emulated with an outer serenity, earning him the high esteem of his contemporaries.

As if prescient of his own early death – most accounts say that he drowned while swimming and suffering a cramp in the sea of Piraeus, when he was fifty-two – he wrote reiteratively of his wish to avoid senescence:

Then take thy sojourn here as though
Thou wert some playgoer or wedding guest,
The sooner sped, the safelier to thy rest. . . .
  While he who tarries late
Faints on the road out-worn, with age oppressed,
Harassed by foes whom life's dull tumults breed;
Thus ill he dies for whom death long doth wait.
[Translation: Arthur Symonds]

And, again:

Him I call happiest
. . . that quickly gets him back
From whence he came, once he has gazed, untroubled,
Upon life's solemn pageants – stars and clouds,
Water and flame, and the sun that lights us all.

Whether you live but few years, or a hundred,
These will not change – and to the end of time
You will not look on sights of greater glory.
Consider, then, our span of days on earth
As it might be some fair – some foreign city –
With crowds and stalls, fun, dicing, pickpockets.
Leave early – and you'll slumber in your inn
Better provided for the road before you,
And free of enemies.
But he that lingers, loses and grows weary,
Till, bowed with years and burdened with his needs,
Bewildered, fleeced, among malignant faces,
He takes that last long road in bitterness.
[Translation: F.L. Lucas]

As well as:

Old age, our human body's enemy, you thief
Of beauty's moulded treasures, who re-draw the clean
Contour of manly limbs to make it ugliness,
And change swiftness of foot to endless faltering.
[Translation: Philip Vellacott]

He doubted that the gods watched over individual mortals. Man is the creature of his own impulses, and flourishes or fails in accordance with his attainment of self-mastery.

Do the Gods then take no heed
Of all our lives?" Yes; for in each of us
They have implanted our true character
As captain of our soul, who never leaves
His post. One man saves, and ruins another,
Who serves him ill. *This* god guides each of us

To prosper or to fall. And, would you prosper,
Be neither fool nor clown.
Do you imagine . . . the Gods
So leisured that they daily can dispense
To each man good and evil?
. . . In the whole world, say
There are a thousand cities – in each one
Dwell thirty thousand citizens. Think you
The Gods assign to every single one
His ruin or salvation?
[Translation: F.L. Lucas]

In his *Thrasyleon* he offers pragmatic counsel:

This "Know Yourself" is a silly proverb in some ways.
To know the man next door's a much more useful rule.
[Translation: Philip Vellacott]

He ceaselessly preaches the need for forgiveness, and shows a live concern for justice and other more elusive ethical values. By contrast, a homely picture is given in his *The Doorkeeper*:

It's no joke, to plunge into a family dinner-party, where
First papa leads off the speeches, cup in hand, and gives them all
Pointed good advice; mama comes second, then a grandmother
Rambles on a little; then great-uncle in a growling bass;
Then comes some old lady who alludes to you as "dearest boy".
All the time you nod your head and beam at them.
[Translation: Philip Vellacott]

So impressive was his "realism" that an enthusiastic Byzantine scholar somewhat breathlessly exclaimed: "O Menander, O Life, which of you imitated the other?"

In 1905 a team of French archaeologists, led by Lefebvre, exploring in Egypt, discovered strips of parchment wrapped around a papyrus on which was inscribed an ancient legal codex. On the strips were tattered pages of three of Menander's comedies, the first to be recovered. The fragments, though very badly damaged, were carefully fitted together and yielded substantial portions of his scripts, about half of *The Arbitration*, 700 lines; and about a third each of *The Woman of Samos* and *She Who Was Shorn*. At last a first-hand look at his work was accessible, but the results somewhat baffled scholars and critics.

Of *The Woman of Samos* (*Samia*), a youthful work, only two lengthy segments – actually less than a third of the original script – have been reconstructed; they are from the last three acts, but it is possible to hypothesize what went before. Though using familiar devices and characters, the plot is exceedingly complex and not easy to synopsize. The scene is Athens, in front of two houses, and so the action takes place in the street, as was the convention. Elderly, kindly, rich Demeas has rescued Chrysis, a lone, homeless young woman from the island of Samos, and installed her as his common-law wife. As he is about to depart on a journey, he learns that she is pregnant and orders her to get rid of the child, by leaving it exposed: otherwise, under Athenian law, it would grow up with the onus of illegitimacy. Chrysis dutifully consents to obey him. But unknown to them both, another child is on the way: Moschion, a young man-about-town, lives in the same house, having been adopted by Demeas years earlier, and has been having a secret affair with Plangon, daughter of Niceratus, who occupies the adjacent dwelling. Now Plangon, too, is awaiting imminent motherhood. Though Demeas and Niceratus are friends, and indeed are setting off on their journey together, they are not of equal status: Niceratus lacks wealth, and Demeas would hardly approve of Moschion, on whom he dotes, marrying a girl with no dowry, despite this young man's sincere love for her. He is also, by nature, somewhat irresolute.

Before the elders return to Athens, Plangon's baby is born. A bold scheme is concocted by Chrysis and Plangon's mother, whose help is solicited by the harried Moschion: the child's life will be saved by smuggling it into Demeas' house to be passed off as his, with Chrysis claiming that she had not disposed of it as he has prescribed. The servants, aware of what is going on, are sworn to silence. As Chrysis has anticipated, Demeas, on his arrival, is disgruntled to find "his" baby alive but soon yields to Chrysis' strong entreaties and accepts it. He then sets off a whole new train of complications by announcing that while on their journey he has arranged with Niceratus that Moschion and Plangon shall wed and without delay. What has led to this? Perhaps, while on their travels, Niceratus has done Demeas a substantial favour of some kind and is being rewarded, or else Demeas has finally heard rumours of Moschion's playing about and thinks marrying him off will put a stop to such irresponsible behaviour. The wedding is to occur that very day. Naturally, Moschion is euphoric.

Amid the bustle created by the servants as they prepare for the ceremony, Demeas, who has been seeing to all the details, enters the pantry and overhears a nurse, who is quieting the wailing infant, refer to it as Moschion's offspring, with a comment to another servant that Demeas should not be allowed to suspect anything of its true parentage. He almost instantly concludes that Moschion, his "son", has begotten the child by Chrysis, who has been wantonly faithless in her protector's absence. Though shocked, he keeps silent and walks about, observing everything closely. He thinks he will surely go out of his mind.

At this point, the extant script starts in the midst of Act Three. A growing heap of misunderstandings have followed from Demeas' mistaken idea of what has happened. Once more, half-concealed, he listens to an amusing exchange between a loquacious, self-important hired cook and his own valet, the sharp-witted Parmeno, who quarrel over trivial matters. "For god's sake, cook," says Parmeno, maliciously, "I don't know why you bother carrying a knife around. You can kill anything you want with that tongue of yours." Demeas interrupts them and, getting Parmeno alone, cross-examines him about the identity of the child's parents. In fear of a beating, Parmeno finally admits that Moschion is the father, but does not add that Plangon is the mother, and this further convinces Demeas that he has been betrayed.

Even more enraged, he confronts Chrysis, fiercely upbraids her, reminds her of all his kindnesses to her, and orders her to quit his house. In his thoughts, however, he soon forgives Moschion, transferring all the blame to Chrysis. The cook, an onlooker at the quarrel, tries to interfere but is sent packing and scuttles off. The tearful Chrysis, distraught and clutching the child, takes refuge in the house of Niceratus.

Some 140 lines are missing here. The text resumes where Chrysis, Plangon and her mother confer and decide to hold fast to their story. Meanwhile, finding himself in inextricable trouble, Moschion has confessed to Demeas, revealing his relationship to Plangon and the child. The old man delightedly declares that the wedding shall proceed at once. Then Demeas tells Niceratus that the baby is Plangon's, without acknowledging Moschion's complicity. Taken aback, Niceratus assumes that Demeas is cancelling the match, a prize in which he has exulted. His disappointment is acute, and his anger at his daughter seizes hold of him. He will kill the baby. To mollify the howling Niceratus and spare Plangon from paternal wrath, Demeas concocts a far-fetched explanation: Plangon has been impregnated by Zeus, through a hole in a leaky roof, much as the god had descended on Danaë in the time-old myth of the golden shower. Niceratus is not wholly deceived, but relents when he hears that in any event Moschion is ready to marry the errant Plangon.

In Act Four, Moschion is fuming that Demeas accused him of having an affair with Chrysis. A reflection on his character! How to respond to the insult? He will immediately leave Demeas' house, and even Athens, and enlist in the army – or, better, he will vehemently threaten to do so, and then yield to his "father's" repeated pleas that he stay. But what if the fond Demeas does not make an effort to restrain him? Parmeno tells Moschion that his conduct is foolish. Annoyed by Parmeno's intervention, Moschion strikes him, cutting his lip. . . . At this point the fragile script breaks off, but one supposes that the ending is happy, with lively singing and dancing at the wedding feast.

Demeas is an endearing character, benevolent, tolerant, genial, at moments whimsical, with a somewhat puckish sense of humour. He dominates the play; though the title is *Woman of Samos*, Chrysis is seldom on stage. She is sympathetic, well-meaning, if not consistently loyal to her generous patron. Moschion, weak-willed, is quite dimensional, prompted by conflicting impulses. The servants, especially Parmeno, the nurse and the cook, are lifelike. The dialogue has economy and vivacity. Even so, Sandbach remarks that it loses much in an English version: ". . . passages of translation can do no more than give the basic sense of the words. Even if a rendering in verse had been attempted, it must have been inadequate. Blank verse is the only possible form to represent the Greek iambic trimeter but, in comparison, it has few rules." The action is shrewdly paced, accelerating as the story progresses, with ever shorter scenes leading to a rapid wind-up, and a logically motivated celebration to top it off. Though many of the play's ingredients are unoriginal, they are handled with professional competence.

A more mature work, and one that sounds more serious notes, is *The Arbitration.* Again the scene is Athens, but on the outskirts; two houses fronting on a street that runs to left towards the city's centre, to right to open country. Less than a quarter of Act One has survived, but the situation is well known by way of Plautus. At the Tauropolia, a women's night-time festival, a young girl, Pamphila, is raped by the drunken Charisius. He does not know who his victim is, nor she who was her violator. In the struggle, however, she has seized a ring from his finger. Four months later they are married, and still do not recognize each other as having been participants in the revel. While he is on an extended journey she gives birth to her child and secretly exposes it on a nearby hillside, leaving around its neck a token trinket. Charisius, a hypocritical prig, learns from his servant, Onesimus, that his wife has borne an infant. Aroused, he wants to end the marriage, but fears to submit himself to open ridicule and his wife to scandal – the fact is, he still loves her. He decides to give her cause for divorce while consoling himself for her "infidelity" by taking up with Habrotenon, a harp-girl. His publicly rumoured carousals take place in the next-door house of his friend, Chaerestratus. The role he has assumed does not come easily, for spending liberally and roistering are not in his nature. Pamphila, alone and miserable, lingers on in her house, hoping to win him back. Her father, the ill-tempered, stingy Smicrines, getting word of his son-in-law's conspicuous misconduct, sets out to visit her. He intends to separate the couple and is much concerned about recouping for himself Pamphila's large dowry. What particularly shocks him is that Charisius is said to be downing drink after drink at a dollar a glass and paying his mistress at the extravagant rate of sixty dollars a day. Arriving at his destination, he does not find his erring son-in-law, and his daughter opposes her father's plan.

In Act Two he meets three peasants, one of them a woman holding an infant. The two men are loudly disputing over a division of the golden trinkets left with the baby, which Davus, a shepherd, had found abandoned to die on a brush-covered slope. The appearance of Smicrines, irritable but venerable and to be respected by virtue of his advanced age, is most opportune; he is drawn into arbitrating the quarrel. Davus wishes to keep the trinkets as his reward: he has rescued the child. Syriscus, a wood-chopper and charcoal-burner, who with his wife has adopted the infant, seeks to reclaim the baubles on the babe's behalf.

Each man states his case, often with violent gestures and language – a highly effective scene. The wood-chopper argues with lawyer-like logic:

> [*To his wife*] Hand me the baby. [*Turning to Davus*] Davus, my client is here for his necklace and birth tokens. He claims that they were intended for his neck, not your pocket. And I'm representing him, since he's my ward. You made him so yourself, when you gave him to me. [*Hands the baby back to his wife and again addresses Smicrines*] Your Honor, as I see it, what you have to decide is whether this jewelry, gold or whatever it is, should be kept in escrow for the child until he grows up, in accordance with the will of the mother, whoever she was, or whether this crook is to cheat him out of it, just because he was the first to find something that didn't belong to him. . . . Don't talk of "finding" something when a party's been wronged. That isn't finding, it's stealing! [*Turning back from Davus to Smicrines*] And there's this to think about; for all we know this child is above our station. [*Gazing off*] Even though he's been brought up among working people, the time may come when he'll show the stuff he's made of and go in for the sort of things gentlemen do – lion hunting, or an army career, or sports. [*Facing Smicrines again*] I'm sure you've been to the theater and remember lots of situations like this. There's the one where an old goatherd, fellow who wore clothes the same as mine, found those

> heroes Neleus and Pelias. When he realized they were above his station, he told them the whole story, how he found them and brought them up, and gave them a little bag full of their birth tokens, and this was the way they found out everything about themselves. They started out as goatherds and ended up as kings. But if a Davus had taken these tokens and sold them off to make himself fifty dollars, they would have gone through the rest of their days without ever knowing how high their station in life really was. [*Carried away by his own eloquence*] Why, once birth tokens saved a man from marrying his sister. Another time they helped a man find his mother and rescue her. Once they saved a brother. Life is full of pitfalls for every one of us. We've got to have foresight, we've got to be on the alert, we've got to look far ahead, as best we can. [Translation: Lionel Casson]

To be noted is how Menander wards off criticism for using an overworked plot-device, including one that Aristotle had already downgraded, a dependence on tokens for the inevitable recognition scene.

Smicrines promptly decides in the wood-chopper's favour, saying that the trinkets still belong to the child. The old man is unaware that he is presiding over a case that concerns his own grandson.

It turns out that Syriscus, the wood-chopper, is in service to Chaerestratus, which is why he and his wife have met Davus in front of the house where Chaerestratus and Charisius are now living. Davus stamps off. While Syriscus and his wife are examining the valuables they have recovered, Onesimus, Charisius' valet, comes from the house and observes them. Syriscus holds up a ring, trying to decipher its seal, and Onesimus spots it at once as belonging to his master, who had lost it while drunk at the Tauropolia. He demands that Syriscus hand it over. After some threats and debate, the wood-chopper reluctantly does so, fearful that otherwise he might offend Charisius. He departs, promising to seek arbitration once more and muttering, "Looks like I'll have to stop everything else and start practicing law. Only way a man can keep anything nowadays."

Act Three reveals Onesimus facing a dilemma: he had told Charisius about Pamphila's illegitimate child and had been treated harshly for informing his master of it; now, if he returns the ring, he might invite trouble. He has ventured to do so five times, but then held back. Habrotenon comes from the house, trying to escape the unwanted attentions of one of its drunken occupants. She wrenches loose from the grasp of this unseen brawler. Then, musing aloud, she complains that Charisius, having hired her to entertain him, actually shuns her company, never touching her, not even allowing her to sit next to him at table, so that she remains "as chaste as a bride in white".

Syriscus, rushing from the house, seeks Onesimus to demand back the ring. Onesimus admits that he is hesitant to pass it on to Charisius, for that would point to his master as the probable father of the child, by an unidentified woman – a possibility that Charisius would hardly welcome. Syriscus, hastily leaving on an errand in the city, replies: "That's your problem." Habrotenon, who has overheard this exchange, asks Onesimus if the infant in question is the one now being nursed by the woodchopper's wife in the house. "Poor little baby. It's so cute." When Onesimus tells her of the ring's likely link to Charisius, and his reluctance to hint at it, she exclaims: "Oh, how *could* you! When there's a chance this child may actually be your master's son, are you going to stand by and see him brought up in slavery? I could murder you! And I'd have every right." Habrotenon herself had been at the Tauropolia and, though she did not know the name of the girl who had been raped, had friends who had also been there and could probably tell her more. But then she spontaneously concocts a scheme: she will show the ring to Charisius and state that she was his victim that night, as well as claim that until that fateful moment she had been a virgin. She effectively rehearses the fictional account she will offer about how he had brutally attacked her. She will present him with the child as hers and his. "If it works, and he does turn out to be the baby's father, then we'll have lots of time to look for the mother later." Onesimus, enthusiastic about the deception, wants to know how he will profit from it. She makes vague promises; her own hope is that if Charisius believes her to be the mother, he will obtain her freedom from the slavery that she deeply resents and from the sordid way of life it imposes on her.

Gathering speed, Act Four – with many lines missing – relates how Habrotenon's ruse is successful. Charisius is convinced that she is the woman he, when drunk, violated at the festival and that the child is undoubtedly his. He acknowledges paternity of it, and installs Habrotenon in Chaerestratus' house as his mistress, shooing away all the hangers-on.

Smicrines returns to get his daughter, end the marriage, and especially to recoup her dowry from the spendthrift Charisius. Pamphila still resists his efforts; her heedlessness exasperates him. He demands to know how Charisius can afford to support two households in proper style, without running through his money. Besides, "A respectable girl is no match for a whore, Pamphila. She's been around; she knows all the tricks; she won't stop at anything; she knows how to get around a man."

At a crucial moment, however, Pamphila leaves her house and for the first time encounters Habrotenon and the baby, who is being carried out for an airing. Instantly the two women identify each other, Pamphila beholding the harp-girl as her rival, and Habrotenon recognizing her neighbour as the girl who had been attacked at the festival. In a few moments more, after awkward but necessary and helpful questions, Pamphila, even more astonished, observes the necklace on the baby. The two young women retreat into Charisius' dwelling to settle all matters.

At the same time, watched by Onesimus, his master Charisius has been seized by pangs of conscience, feeling that he has misjudged and mistreated his wife: if the child she bore was the consequence of rape, as he has discovered by eavesdropping on a conversation between Smicrines and Pamphila, she is blameless. He babbles words of self-recrimination – what a wonderful wife was his, and how wrongly and hypocritically he has behaved towards her. He will debase himself publicly, and he will definitely block any attempt by Smicrines to effect a separation. A little later, Habrotenon comes to him with word that the baby is not hers. She unburdens herself of her plan and her compelling reasons for it. At last he learns for certain that the child is his, and by his cherished Pamphila.

Much of Act Five is missing. Most of what remains has to do with the cantankerous Smicrines and his quarrel with Pamphila's old nurse, Sophrona, who is firmly opposed to his breaking up the young couple's marriage. He also has a rough battle of words with Onesimus, who is now back in favour with his master and, as always, too ready to intervene in household affairs. Onesimus apprises him that the once-exposed infant is his grandson, a suggestion that enrages the snarling old man, who threatens to have the valet whipped for daring to utter it. Sophrona vigorously affirms it. Smicrines: "This is terrible!" Sophrona: "It's the best thing that ever happened!" And here, the script dangles, unfinished . . . but one hardly doubts that Charisius and the faithful Pamphila are happily reconciled, the mercenary Smicrines forced to consent, and most likely the cunning Onesimus and good-hearted Habrotenon granted their long-sought freedom.

Once more the characters are stereotypes – the unfailingly virtuous Pamphila; the calculating Onesimus; the querulous, flaxy old father (or guardian); the golden-hearted but worldly courtesan – yet they are never "flat" but even more "rounded", quite plausible and recognizable, and each is consistently motivated and acts in accordance with his desires and predominant aims. What is more, the plot is developed in a way that attests to Menander's sophistication and considerable accomplishment as a playwright. The dialogue is natural, rapid, with that of the peasants having an appropriately rustic flavour.

To what is thought to have been Menander's best period, too, belongs *She Who Was Shorn.* The text is in broken segments from which the story-line can be deduced, especially since New Comedy scripts more or less adhere to a by now familiar formula. A brother and sister, twins, have been exposed as infants. Found by an old woman, she relinquished the boy to Myrrhina, who was rich and childless but kept the girl for her own. As a result of continuous wars, affairs in Corinth – where the play occurs – grew worse; the old woman could no longer support the girl, now of age. She maintained the fiction that the girl, Glycera, was her daughter, and gave her to a handsome, wealthy young professional army officer, Polemon, who was much smitten with her and made her his common-law wife. She could not hope for more, since – though free-born – she had no dowry. Successful in his career, Polemon bought a new house, which – of course – is next to that of Myrrhina, whose "son", Moschion, is now a pampered, reckless playboy. Passing his neighbour's house, Moschion's eye frequently alights on the attractive Glycera, nurturing in him a desire to possess her.

The old woman, weary and ill, nearing death, resolves to keep Glycera's secret no longer, imparts to her that she is a foundling, and hands over her long-hidden birth-clothes. Lest Glycera some day need help, the old woman tells her of the existence of her brother, whose name she also reveals. When Polemon buys his new house, Glycera appreciates that her brother lives close by but decides it best to be discreet and say nothing of it. She is unsure of how Polemon would welcome her relationship.

The street, with three houses fronting it, is where the story transpires. The third house belongs to Pataecus, an elderly friend of Polemon. The precipitating action occurs one evening as her maid departs and Glycera is standing at the doorway; Moschion passes by, observes her and impulsively rushes up, grasps and kisses her. Glycera, knowing he is her brother, does not break away but lingers in his embrace; this is seen by Polemon, who just chances to return. He misinterprets Glycera's conduct. In a jealous rage he charges her with infidelity, and to punish her he cruelly cuts off her hair. The deed is hardly consonant with his usual kindly nature. (It will be recalled that a similar retaliation was inflicted on young French women after the Second World War by their patriotic neighbours who had watched them brazenly consort with Nazi soldiers during the years of Occupation.)

Frightened, Glycera begs and receives shelter with her neighbour Myrrhina. Polemon has left his house and moved in with his friend and neighbour Pataecus. The servants – Glycera's maid, Doris; Polemon's adjutant, Sosia; Moschion's valet, Davus – become involved, being sent out to spy on what is happening. Polemon, grief-stricken, believes Glycera has gone to Myrrhina's to be with her new lover, a belief that the delighted Moschion mistakenly shares, as he eagerly schemes to lay suit to the refugee, only to be thwarted by his mother and Doris. The servants, at cross-purposes, do a good deal of bickering among themselves, trading insults. Polemon, who has been drinking copiously, is persuaded that he should storm Myrrhina's house with an "army" of friends and recapture Glycera, but the prudent, compassionate Pataecus warns him against the rash deed and offers to meet and talk with Myrrhina on his behalf.

As Act Three opens, the ragtag "troops" are milling about in front of Myrrhina's dwelling.

Pataecus comes out, having finished his parley with her. He instructs Polemon, who is now somewhat sober, to demobilize his "army". He emphasizes to the young officer that Glycera, not his legal wife, has a right to alter her feeling about him. Grossly mistreated, she has decided on a separation. "That girl is her own mistress." Moschion can be sued for his aggression, but Polemon would be on the wrong side of the law in a physical attack on him. His distraction wilder than ever, Polemon beseeches his friend to continue as an intermediary with Glycera. "My life depends on it." Pataecus agrees to carry on the delicate mission.

A lengthy gap in the text occurs here. But it is clear that Moschion has gone within and, instead of meeting and conquering Glycera, has simply been ignored and shut off from both her and his mother. Filled with vanity, he is fully convinced of his irresistible appeal in looks and attire and is baffled and disappointed at encountering any obstacles. But now he learns the true reason Glycera has fled to Myrrhina's house, and that he too is a foundling; he is even shown his "birth-tokens". In her conversation with Pataecus, Glycera offers her side of the story, why she is greatly aggrieved at Polemon. Bitterly, she says: "Let him insult some other girl from now on."

Her "birth-tokens" are still in a chest in Polemon's house; she asks Pataecus to help her retrieve them. He finds her firmly resolved to leave Polemon and reluctantly quits his errand. The chest is brought out and opened; Pataecus gradually recognizes the embroideries as his late wife's handiwork; for the moment he does not inform Glycera of this. It so happens that Moschion appears on the scene, glimpses the "birth-tokens" and notes their close match to his own, which he has just been shown by Myrrhina. He grasps at once that Glycera is his sister; yet he too keeps silent and, at a distance, listens to the exchange between Pataecus and Glycera, who has been asked about the source of the tokens. She does not reply readily, having been sworn to discretion by Myrrhina. The truth, of course, is that Glycera and Moschion are the children who had been unwanted by Pataecus and whom he had ordered to be exposed. Glycera's reaction at this discovery is a mixture of surprise, joy and deep hurt that he had abandoned them. He explains that he had been ruined, suddenly left a pauper by the loss of cargo on a ship that sank; he had felt unable to raise a family. As he says this, he is overcome by shame and despair. Moschion makes his presence known. Again, the text is interrupted, with 100 lines or more devoted to the dramatic confrontation now unavailable but easy to imagine.

In the final act, Polemon has been dispossessed from Pataecus' house and replaced there by Glycera, abruptly a person of high station. Polemon, apprised of the change in her fortunes, is more unhappy than ever, sure that his act of punishment is seen as more outrageous than before, and his hopes of recovering her affections even more unrealistic. Haggard and in disarray, he informs Doris,

Glycera's maid, that he means to hang himself. Doris promises that Glycera will forgive him, if he will vow to behave more calmly and trustingly from now on, a demand to which Polemon eagerly accedes. The maid returns with word that Glycera, in her fanciest new attire, is coming forth to rejoin him, with Pataecus beside her. Polemon agrees to a legal marriage and her father grants her a large dowry; he also announces that he is arranging a good match for Moschion. Preparations are begun for a joint celebration.

She Who Was Shorn proves to be more of a romantic melodrama than a comedy. To be noted is Menander's habit of using the same names for different characters in his plays. (For example, he has "Moschions" in at least four of his scripts, none of the four possessed of similar traits. His slaves, in particular, have a limited number of names; there is really no telling why.) In plotting, he is a fore-runner in cleverly employing another theatrical device: for the most part, the spectators know more about the characters than the characters know about themselves; here, that Glycera and Moschion are twins, of which they are only belatedly aware. This allows the spectators to watch them with a certain superior, amused detachment, the errors they make, the foolish things they do. Engendering suspense; how will they find out the facts, and what will they do when that happens?

Fragments of other plays – as, for instance, 400 lines of *The Sicyonian* – have been most frequently found in the cemetery of Ghoran, a village in Upper Egypt. The papyri on which they were inscribed had been later utilized, as an economy measure, for the mummy wrappings of minor Egyptian officials. When the tombs were opened, and the mummies bared, the patches of papyri were carefully separated from the corpses and, if of interest, painstakingly re-assembled – the mummy having first been sprayed with hot diluted hydrochloric acid. A Geneva bibliophile, Dr Martin Bodmer, purchased the papyri of *The Arbitration* in Cairo or Alexandria. Scientific tests suggest that the manuscript, a copy, dates from the first half of the third century AD. At that period, Greek was the language most widely read and spoken by educated Egyptians.

In *The Sicyonian*, set in Eleusis, a young girl is kidnapped by pirates and sold to a kindly old man who rears her like a daughter. She loves his handsome son. Her benefactor seeks to learn her origin and discovers, as might be expected, that he himself is her father, and that his son – whom she wishes to marry – is, alas, her brother. How Menander straightened out this daunting complication is not easily perceived, but the formula that supplied his hundred plots is once again apparent, as he exploits it inventively.

Other fairly extensive fragments, of a hundred lines or more, also discovered on papyri, are of plays titled *The Shield* (*Aspis*), *The Farmer* (*Georgos*), *A Double Deceit* (*Dis Exapaton*), *The Flatterer*

(*Kolax*), *Hated* (*Misumenos*), *The Man* (or *The Men*) *from Sikyon* (*Sikyonios* or *Sikyonioi*). As has been said, the best sources of Menander's comedies are the intact Latin adaptations of them.

In 1955, somewhat mysteriously, there appeared in Geneva the *complete* text of another play by Menander, *The Curmudgeon* (or *The Grouch*; *Dyskolos*), which has been dated to 316 BC, the only script for which the time of production can be placed with any exactitude. Who owned it, and how it reached him, was not at first made clear. The event caused a major stir, arousing a great deal of excitement and curiosity in the world of classical scholars and manuscript collectors.

The literary quality and the characterizations of *The Curmudgeon* are judged by many to be superior to Menander's later scripts: its plot is simple and neat. Short, it consists of only a thousand lines in six-beat iambics. An irascible, rich old farmer, Cnemon, falls into a well and is trapped. Despite his bellowing, his servants, happy at his discomfiture, refuse to help him. Finally, he is rescued with the aid of Sostratus, a rich young Athenian, and is cajoled by his stepson, Gorgias, into giving his daughter to the young Athenian in marriage. The play, written when the author himself was young, just twenty-five, is a lively, racy little farce, again with strong peasant colour, and contains some sharp satire on "animal sacrifices" at religious rites – the offerings have a way of being eaten by the celebrants.

The setting is Phyle, a country district beyond Athens. Between the usual two houses is an entrance to a grotto in which is a shrine dedicated to the god Pan. It is in this grotto or cave that the rites and feasts are held, and from which pour forth the dancers who entertain during the *entr' actes.* To be near the girl at whom he gazes, Sostratus dresses himself as a peasant, conceals his identity and goes to the fields with his hoe. The experience proves to be an ordeal. It is while reaching down and trying to retrieve a hoe that has fallen down the well that the irate Cnemon himself topples in.

(To intrude a personal note: long before 1955 I wrote a short farce, *Mario's Well*, set in an Italian village, in which a peasant falls into a well and cries for help; his neighbours, hostile because he is an atheist, will not drop a rope to let him climb out; instead, over-pious, they wish to exact a price – his conversion – for his rescue. In a one-act play by Luigi Pirandello, *The Olive Jar*, humour arises from a rather similar situation: the owner of an olive orchard is trapped in a huge jar from which his fellow-peasants hesitate to free him; to do so, they must break the jar, and it is much too valuable. Such coincidences support the belief that few if any new comic plots have manifested themselves during two thousand years.)

The Curmudgeon has a secondary theme: Gorgias, the stepson, marries Sostratus' sister, overcoming her father's objections. Others in the cast include a cook, farm workers and slaves, among them one more named Davus – incidentally, there are characters called Gorgias in two other works by

Menander. The slaves, arguing among themselves, contribute much of the noise and bustle – and zany confusion – required by farce.

The cook, Sicon, as always conceited and loquacious, holds a grudge against Cnemon because the dour old man does not appreciate fine cuisine. His falling in the well is a due punishment. "No one who wrongs a cook ever gets off unscathed. Our art has something sacred about it." It is the cook who is responsible for losing the hoe down the well; the rope snaps when he uses it to raise a heavy bucket.

Cnemon's misanthropy is summarized in a snarling speech: "It's that fellow Perseus in the story who's the really lucky one. For two reasons. First, he had wings so he never had to meet anyone walking around on the ground. Second, he had some sort of gadget to turn anyone who bothered him into stone. I wish I had it right now – I'd fill the place with statues. God almighty, the way things are these days, life isn't worth living." After his accident, and severely injured by it, he has a great change of heart, generously transfers half his estate to his stepson and consents to his daughter's marriage to Sostratus with a good dowry. In the last act he has a garland clapped on his head and, despite his protestations, is forced to join in the dancing.

There is a good deal of moralizing in the play, pleas for a return to solid old virtues, such as are embodied in Cnemon, apart from his sour nature. He believes in prudence, hard work, simplicity, honesty. He demands these qualities from others and, overall, has found them lacking in this new age.

The text of *The Curmudgeon* was found on eleven papyrus leaves; they reached Switzerland by way of Egyptian dealers in antiquities, then were purchased by Martin Bodmer. On the first leaf was inscribed the number 19, which has led some to think that copies of eighteen other plays may have also been discovered, but are being withheld to keep the price high by assuring that a Menander script is a true rarity; however, four decades have passed without any further announcement.

Though "complete", the text is far from perfect; a number of lines are gone, others have lost their punctuation, and many stage-instructions are missing, making for a formidable task of reconstruction. Bodmer passed along the script to Victor Martin, a widely respected Swiss scholar, to be edited. In 1959 the Greek "script" was published; soon after, an English version – a translation by Gilbert Highet – was printed in *Horizon*, a magazine, followed by inclusions in anthologies, among them Lionel Casson's – his offering a somewhat modern adaptation, so that the work could be more readily grasped by present-day spectators. *The Curmudgeon* was quickly given productions by college troupes and proved itself quite stageworthy.

Yet not everyone liked it, and among those not amused or impressed was Casson. In a preface to his adaptation, he wrote:

> There is a question that troubles a good many critics of today when they consider Menander: How could he have achieved such a towering reputation when his plots and characters were so limited? More particularly, how could ancient critics have singled out trueness to life as his forte when his stock in trade was basically the same romantic stuff that made up much of Greek New Comedy? *The Curmudgeon* unfortunately does nothing to answer these questions – or enhance Menander's reputation: it is pretty bad. We can guess why from a notice prefixed to the play that gives some details about its production: it was put on, and won first prize, at the Lenaea in 317 BC. In other words, it must be one of his earliest efforts. (It's interesting that the Athenians thought it good enough for first prize; either their taste had degenerated since the days of Aristophanes, or the plays pitted against *The Curmudgeon* were even worse, or both.) But what of mature plays like *The Arbitration* or *She Who Was Shorn*? In the battered remnants that have come down to us can we detect some trace of what had so captivated ancient critics, some gleam of that trueness to life they praised so highly? Each reader will have to judge for himself.

The plots and their outcome soon become predictable – that must be admitted. But the Greek spectator placed scant emphasis on suspense; the audience was not bothered if the premise or story outline was all too familiar; what counted was the author's treatment of it, as was also true of the earlier tragedies that dealt with the universally shared myths. Comedy, with a witty sprinkle of "Attic salt", a touch of poetry, a grace-note of pathos, a group of stock figures with recognizable and highly expressive masks, was soon an affair of infinite variation on small changes of fortune in the lives of very confused persons. Endless mix-ups were caused by attractive rascals for some amorous or mercenary purpose; their antics provoked hilarity and, mostly, sympathetic laughter. Thus New Comedy is a form that has scarcely altered since its long-ago inception, and its modern descendants – consciously or unconsciously ever borrowing the same plots, the same characters, by now old friends to us – still scamper about on Broadway and West End stages, to say nothing of the bright-lit stages of Paris, Berlin, Vienna, Rome and Budapest. As already remarked, very long is the list of major writers in this light genre who conform to the rules laid down by innovative predecessors like Menander and his rivals.

When Casson published his adaptations of the five longest surviving segments of Menander's works, Erich Segal, then lecturing in the classics department at Yale, reviewed them for the *New York Times*:

> Voltaire claimed that Dante would be a classic forever because nobody read him. Until recently, this was literally true of Menander. Ancient scholars revered him, but through the years his plays vanished, and all that remained were snippets quoted by grammarians. Thus, when Goethe apostrophized the

"unattainable charm" of Menander, it was solely on the basis of a collection of aphorisms. In the Nineteenth Century, George Moore had no more on which to justify admitting only Menander and Molière to the empyrean of comic writers. Of course, there were the Roman adaptations of Plautus and Terence, but this was hardly the same as having a real play or even a complete scene by Menander himself. He seemed destined to remain an "unattainable classic." Then, suddenly in 1905, the sands of Egypt yielded a manuscript with three large fragments, and next in 1955 an entire play. The discovery of *The Curmudgeon* was one of the most important papyrus finds of this century. It is the only complete Greek drama to come to us from antiquity – the late Third Century BC. In but fifty years, Menander has grown from a mere name to a full-fledged Oxford Text which will appear shortly, edited by F.H. Sandbach. This remarkable development has been a mixed blessing. Scholars are naturally pleased to have Menander's *ipsissima verba* at last, and yet are somewhat hard-pressed to explain its "greatness." His plots are repetitive. He lacks the vitality of Plautus and the song of Aristophanes.

But he is more important than both of them. For Menander canonized the comic form. It is Menandrian comedy that we still see throughout the Western world. His themes have had Molièresque and Shakespearean variation, but they remain his themes. In the best sense of the word, Menander is a classic.

But ironically, he was not popular in his own day, perhaps because he was too intellectual. It is no coincidence that his plots sparkle with Aristotelian precision; his teacher was Theophrastus who succeeded Aristotle as head of the Lyceum. Menander reflects not so much the actual life of his times as its philosophical climate. If he engages in Theophrastean character analysis, it is to express an ethical view: that the gods do not bother with individual men, that character is fate – although on special occasions Fate personified may appear unannounced to reward the just, discover lost children or revive dead soldiers. No specific mention is made of the constant warfare which plagued the Hellenistic world – we are curiously remote from it all. Though praised in antiquity for his "realism," Menander is infinitely less related to the world about him than Aristophanes.

His people are the familiar types of comedy: irate fathers, moaning lovers, clever slaves, nubile women. Ovid rightly hailed Menander as the father of romantic drama, but it is hardly a fine romance by modern standards. Menander's women rarely get to talk, rarely even have names – except for the courtesans. "Nice" girls are those who get raped at religious festivals, get pregnant and – it turns out – get married to the very man who raped them. In the end, everyone forgives everyone, a salient Menandrian theme. The real wonder of his universe is man's capacity for goodness. Says the playwright, "How glorious is a human being when he acts like a human being." If Menander is less than Aristophanes in vivacity, he is much more in humanity.

Segal took issue with Casson on how properly to translate certain words and phrases, such as giving a precise rendering of *hetairai* – he prefers "whore" to "common law wife" or "entertainer" – and regretting the substitution of "dollars" for "drachmae", but designates these as relatively minor quibbles. In his conclusion, he expresses gratitude to Casson "for the fascinating opportunity to discover that comedy has hardly changed in two thousand years".

With the unhappy drowning of Menander, and after him the death of Philemon (262 BC), the creative era of Greek comedy came to an end. Theatres were still crowded, new plays put on, but increasingly producers depended on revivals of older works to attract audiences. Attempts were made to transplant both tragic and comic theatre to Alexandria, but this was never fully realized. Increasingly, the spirit of the Hellenistic world, as it grew more serious, was antagonistic to comedy, and patriotism was no longer an invigorating spur. But more important, perhaps, what was lacking was the genius of an Aristophanes or the superior talent of a Menander; for a blaze of greatness in an era arises mostly from the contribution of an impassioned artist, whose spirit is committed and whose spark is incendiary.

The physical structure of the theatre had changed somewhat during the Hellenistic era. Only in Menander's time – about 325 BC – was the Theatre of Dionysus, hitherto considered temporary, finally given its permanent shape in stone. By then, it was viewed by some to be rather old-fashioned. Indeed, after 300 BC Athens was no longer looked upon as being, as Brockett puts it, "in the forefront of development". The historic stone arena was remodelled on several occasions during the next two centuries, and most markedly in the first century AD, when the stage was enlarged by extending it over a section of the orchestra, to have it resemble theatres then being erected in Rome. In what was left of the orchestra, a space surrounded by a stone barricade, gladiatorial combats – another importation from Rome – were sometimes held. In the fourth century, again emulating Roman models, the orchestra was sealed to allow for costly water-spectacles then much in vogue.

The auditorium was terraced, rising in three tiers, and capable of accommodating the entire population of Athens, 15,000–20,000 persons. At the direction of Lycurgus – in his role as the city's comptroller of finances (338–327 BC) – likenesses in polished marble of the tragic poets were placed in a colonnade along the open-air foyer, which was the rear wall of the *skene*.

This work was done at about the same time as the erection of a handsome new theatre in Epidaurus (*c.* 350 BC), designed by the architect Polycleites the Younger, which remains as the best preserved of its kind from Greek antiquity. As Berthold describes it: "Its auditorium resembles a giant shell set into a hillside. From the height of the sixtieth row one has an unimpeded view of the remnants of the *skene* building and the wooded plain beyond. Epidaurus conveys the experience of the ancient theatre; even without a performance, Aeschylus, Sophocles, and Euripides come to life; none of them lived to make use of the great theatres in Epidaurus, Athens, Delos, Priene, Pergamon, or Ephesus."

In any event, this was now an era when actors counted for more than dramatists. Aristotle speaks of it in the *Poetics*, lamenting that the players had too much influence, and that their virtuosity was more admired than the works in which they appeared. They could insist on changes in the scripts and were often heeded when they did so, if only to appease their vanity. Their organization, the Artists of Dionysus, maintained its strength and even gained further by including poets, musicians, chorus members, costumers, vocal coaches, recitalists who gave public readings of plays and lyric and epic verse, along with every sort of craftsman associated in stagings. Opportunities to offer plays now occurred more frequently, since new festivals were added, and there were also presentations that had no connection with Dionysian rites and celebrations. Traditionally, though not always, the actors' guild was headed by a priest of the cult of Dionysus. As theatrical activity spread across Greece, the players' union was finally divided into several branches, the Athenian, the Nemean and the Isthmian, and the Ionian and Hellespontine, each with its own centre serving as a local headquarters, and the groups were further subdivided into smaller guilds in ever more cities, until the rule of the Artists of Dionysus held sway over dispersed regions from Alexandria in Egypt to Teos in Asia Minor.

In New Comedy the number of actors in a play was still restricted, which may account for the restless coming and going of characters in Menander's works: a lesser member of the cast would hurry off, enabling him to change his mask and costume and return as someone else, even if it might be as a person of a different gender.

The stage was higher than before, elevated from eight to thirteen feet above what had formerly been a flat playing space or ring. It was also widened to as much as 120 feet, though still rather shallow, about a mere eight to thirteen feet in depth. The side wings, the *paraskenia*, were not kept; instead, both ends of the platform were left open. In some theatres the stage could be approached by ramps; in others, steps led to the enlarged area over the partly covered orchestra, which could be used by the chorus; in other theatres the only access to the stage was through doors in the *skene*. All these changes took place gradually, with no fixed date for them. By 150 BC, however, the basic shape of the Hellenistic theatre had fully evolved.

Scholars speculate that the raised portion of the stage was where the gods might appear, and perhaps where more recent works with small casts and no chorus were performed, and where dazzling effects might be displayed. The *proskenion* featured a row of pillars that were notched, possibly to hold painted panels; after the second century BC, however, the pillars are not notched, suggesting that the scenic panels (*pinakes*) were no longer used; later in the century, sizeable openings (*thyromata*) were made in the front of the *skene*, replacing one to three doors; through these apertures it is possible that graphic backdrops, individual settings, could be glimpsed – but this is conjecture.

The Greater Dionysia is believed to have continued until about the first century AD, the Lenaea not as long, perhaps to 150 BC. Of the many fifth-century tragic dramas revived, Euripides' works were the most in demand. The previous fare of the theatres was now partly supplanted; as has been said, they became available for gladiatorial contests, simulated sea battles, as well as the baiting and slaughter of captive wild animals, such gory spectacles due to crude Roman influence.

Productions were no longer paid for by the *choregoi*, socially ambitious rich patrons – their numbers were now too few and presentations too costly to be met by the contents of individual purses. Instead, the stagings were subsidized by the state. The official whose responsibility it was would negotiate with the nearest guild; contracts would be signed that specified in detail most of the services the actors and craftsmen were obliged to provide. After Alexander's demise his empire began to break up into small principalities, some of them hostile to one another and soon at war among themselves. Even so, guild members retained the almost unique travel privileges that allowed them freely to cross borders, at no risk of arrest and exempt from being detained anywhere for military service. Such freedom of movement led to a few of them being appointed as envoys between the feuding parties. But this did not imply that they were highly admired for qualities other than their theatrical gifts. Then as now, stage people tended to be morally suspect.

Costuming in New Comedy was also conventionalized. A male character would be attired more or less as he might be in ordinary life, wearing an *exomis*, a simple white tunic without a seam at the left. An old man would have a lengthy white cloak, a *himation*; a young man of high station, one of red or purple; a parasite or sycophant, one of black or grey; a slave, a short white one over his tunic. An old woman's garb would be green or pale blue, that of a priestess pure white, as would be that of a young woman. (All this is well detailed in books by Nicall, Brockett and Berthold.)

The players still used masks, as has been said. Brockett quotes from Pollux, who lists forty-four types belonging to New Comedy: "nine for old men, four for young men, seven for slaves, three for old women, five for young women, seven for courtesans, two for maid-servants, one for rustics, two for soldiers, one for flatterers, and three for parasites," an indication of a wide range of characters, however stereotypical they might be. Some of the masks were naturalistic, perhaps handsome; but others – for slaves, crotchety old men or broadly preposterous, interfering persons – were presented as grotesque caricatures. Another means of suggesting psychological traits and station in life was by the colour of the hair: a slave was usually portrayed as a redhead, a courtesan was artificially yellow-tressed, to make herself more flagrantly alluring.

Among the other forms of entertainment during the prolonged Hellenistic era were huge spectacles, pageants as large in scale as those of the Egyptians of an earlier epoch. Such a one, to celebrate a victory, was ordered by Alexander the Great; it was enacted by a throng of several thousands and put on with ostentatious appurtenances. But smaller kinds of theatre might consist merely of touring groups of jugglers and acrobats, dancers, a lone flute-player, who performed in streets and squares and solicited tossed coins from passers-by who halted briefly to watch or lingered to hearken to a professional storyteller as he heightened his dramatic tale with effective gestures.

Wordless drama – today, mime – also evolved, from a probable beginning in Megara in the sixth century BC. It doubtless arose from the same impulses as comedy and tragedy, a natural delight in imitation, coupled with a belief that magical control over events could be acquired by physically reproducing the movements and gestures that occurred in them. In some circumstances, exaggeration and caricature, as well as sharp if silent observation, played a part in this. What is more, the mime need not be a poet or a singer, but merely agile and expressive, hence another sort of artist joined the ranks of performers, if he had a shrewd eye and a flair for the dramatic. Homeric tales of gods, heroes and tragic heroines were apt to be beyond the scope of pantomime; the mime did best by representing the traits, and especially the foibles, of ordinary folk as seen and encountered in everyday situations, problems and responses mostly depicted mockingly.

At the very first a strain of totemism is apparent, an emphasis on copying the amusingly clumsy behaviour of animals; then, they are "anthropomorphized", given human traits. Often singled out for a role was the donkey, the farm people's sensible if plodding close daily companion. When bits of verbal wit were finally introduced, the donkey was allowed to speak; an example of this is found in a fragment by Sophron (*c.* 430 BC), who is thought to have been a precursor in lending mime plays primitive elements of literary shape; he had the actor costumed to represent a donkey complain of "munching thistles". ("Donkey plays" and dances are to persist in folk farces for centuries, even through the Middle Ages.)

In the fifth century BC mimes were to be met in the streets of cities throughout the regions of the Eastern Mediterranean, in Greek colonies from Southern Italy to Sicily, and north to the entire Attic Peninsula. Adaptive, they appealed to local concerns and scenes. In Sparta, for instance, a lone performer was apt to appear to be drunk, typifying a tipsy celebrant at a rustic Dionysiac revel; hence, in that city a mime came to be identified as *deikelos* (a souse) and his skits called *deikelon.* Elsewhere, in Thebes, where the Boeotian Kabeiric cult flourished and was frequently travestied, mimes were known as "volunteers".

With the decline of formal drama, the popularity of mime continued to grow. Wandering players displayed their skills in private homes at parties given by the very rich. Berthold tells of an Athenian writer, agriculturalist and sportsman, Xenophon (fourth century BC), who in his *Symposium* recollects how a mime and his troupe from Syracuse performed at a banquet held by another Athenian citizen, the affluent Callas, a festive affair at which a young girl played a flute and a boy and another girl danced to the music. And Berthold relates, too, that Socrates, a guest at the gathering, asked the entertainers to offer a version of the story of Dionysus and Ariadne. "That Socrates' request could be so easily fulfilled, without special preparations, demonstrates that the Greek mimes were as familiar with the heritage of mythical themes as their earlier counterparts had been on the banks of the Euphrates and the Nile, and as their successors were to be far in the future on the banks of the Tiber and the Bosphoros."

Further, from Berthold: "Numerous Attic vase paintings show a variety of young female entertainers. . . . On a fourth-century *hydria* from Nola (now at the Museo Nazionale in Naples) we see four groups training for various acrobatic feats. A naked young girl has arched her body into a bridge and supports herself on her elbows, at the same time pushing a *kylix* with her foot toward her mouth (around her calf she has tied a ribbon, the customary *apotropeion* of girl mimes); another girl is shown dancing between swords planted vertically in the ground, while a third one practices the *pyrrhic*, a mythological war dance, wearing a helmet and holding a shield and a lance."

It is of interest that mimes were the earliest performers in ancient times to admit women to their hitherto closed ranks.

By 300 BC mimes were finally allowed to participate in the official festivals, though membership in the powerful Artists of Dionysus was never opened to them. From 300 BC to 250 BC they were sufficiently recognized and favoured in Alexandria, the Egyptian centre of Hellenistic art and culture, to attract a school of "literary mime" poets who provided them with sketches to enact, short scenarios of a hundred lines or less, that were nuanced and even more realistic vignettes or snapshots of daily life. Eight playlets of this sort, by Herodas, living in Alexandria during the early decades of the third century BC, are still extant.

For the most part, sketches for mimes were in prose, but some – designated *mimeidoi* – were composed for singing and have been likened to latter-day musical-hall ballads and ditties. Those by Herodas (or Herondas?) are in iambics and deal with romantic intrigues, as confessed by lovelorn maidens; the chastisement of wayward pupils; the craft and wiles of matchmakers; and a range of intimate affairs of a not entirely proper sort. Berthold postulates that the lines written by Herodas were "most probably meant to be read or recited by an individual mime with a great range of voice".

To today's scholars, the best known of the mimes are those of Southern Italy, who came to be called *phylakes*. For a long time they too were studied on a collection of decorated vases, where episodes from their skits are illustrated; however, this is not a fully supported guess, as the vases are now dated a century older than they were previously. In some respects the scenes seem to be derived from Old or Middle Comedies, instead: the figures are dressed in the thickly padded tights and brief *chitons*, and boast the erect phalluses, characteristic of stage attire in those eras. The incidents portrayed are taken from mythology and again vulgarly burlesqued (the feats of Herakles much favoured), or from daily occurrences, showing average people quarrelling and fighting, committing devious thefts, engaged in pranks and more serious tricks, gorging themselves at feasts, making exuberant physical love.

Some thirty-eight skits by Rhinthon of Tarentum who supplied a variety of these subjects to the mimes of his day are accessible; he, too, belongs to the first half of the third century BC and is credited with having "formalized" works in this genre.

Stock characters – medical quacks, fortune-tellers, beggars, easily gulled country bumpkins – had now gained their long-lived place in the farces.

Having grown bolder, the mimes parodied excerpts from the hallowed tragedies of Aeschylus, Sophocles and Euripides, reducing the familiar plots and portentous violence to slapstick and raw buffoonery, the sublime poetry to rant, extending a category of humour that is never to disappear over twenty-odd centuries.

Experts in this field are fascinated by fourth-century vase-paintings that show how the mime plays were staged. Reproductions of drawings in Brockett outline a raised platform, supported by posts or decorative panels, affixed to which were draperies or additional painted panels. A rather steep flight of steps led to the platform and doubtless was ingeniously employed by the actors. At the back of the stage were a portico and door, or else columns and a façade covered with various decorative motifs;

on an upper level there might also be a window or balcony, or both. The properties consisted of whatever was called for: an altar, a throne, a chest, a table or – to suggest the outdoors – a scattering of simulated trees. In dispute is whether this set-up was merely temporary, erected wherever a travelling troupe elected to perform, or was permanent; also to be taken into consideration is whether the depiction is complete or over-simplified, since the vase painter had but little space for his picture; nor, most likely, was it ever to preserve for much later historians all the details of the scene on such a frail vessel.

The third century BC saw an important confluence of cultures between Greece and Rome, in which the superior philosophies and far more refined and sophisticated traditions of the Athenians quickly dominated. Transplanted and taking hold in the ruder, more masculine and extraverted world of imperial Rome, the conventions of tragedy and comedy had to undergo major changes.

7

ROME: SOCK AND BUSKIN

Quite as in Egypt and Greece, theatre on the Italian peninsula began with uninhibited folk celebrations: spring sowing rites, invocations to fertility, harvest festivals when the wheat was tall and tasselled and the purple grape clusters were warmed by sun and ready for plucking. Such ceremonies were apparently observed in Southern regions first by the Etruscans, the mysterious neighbours of the Romans, who later conquered and absorbed them, only to have their own culture pervasively influenced time and again by those they subjugated.

Tantalizingly little is known about the Etruscans, who for a time dominated the other peoples inhabiting the mountainous, boot-shaped peninsula. Possibly they had come as raiders from Asia Minor about 800 BC and settled beyond the river Tiber, in what is now historic, green-hilled Tuscany. To the south were flourishing Greek colonies, in Sicily and Apulia, whose principal cities – some of them independent but Greek-speaking and generally sharing Greek customs – were Syracuse and Taras (or Tarentum). From them, the Etruscans steadily and even avidly borrowed much. Their language still baffles scholars, though it is set down in Greek characters. Obviously they were familiar with Hellenic lore and mythology, in some measure imparted to them by illustrations on the well-chosen Greek pottery and metalwork they bought from sea-borne traders.

The chief source of knowledge about them is the paintings covering the inner walls of their tombs, together with a host of scattered and disinterred artefacts; the dusty, cluttered museums of today's Italy contain about 8,000 examples of Etruscan handiwork, relics such as vases crafted in the Greek style, embellished silver bowls, urns, cauldrons, ornate combs, helmets – dome-shaped – and swords, bronze warrior statuettes, animal figurines and some remarkable full-scale sculpture "discovered" and raptly doted on by a coterie of alert, sensitive twentieth century aesthetes. Most of these objects date from the eighth century BC and perhaps a bit earlier. The sinuous profiles of the portrait heads bear out the suggestions that these people belonged to a race that originated in Phoenicia, Anatolia or far-off Armenia or Western Iran.

The Etruscans were gifted. Their art-work is expressive, realistic. Even more than that of the Greeks, their productions were models for Renaissance craftsmen, when these relics, vigorous and self-confident, emotional, were first unearthed in the fifteenth century AD, stirring great surprise, admiration and emulation. The look on many of the faces is introspective or searching. In a later phase, starting in the fourth century BC, the sculpture has an archaic Greek quality, marking a turn away from Eastern styles, the ubiquitous hint of the semi-Oriental.

From such dispersed but graphic and revealing materials, Will Durant, in his *Caesar and Christ*, compiled this colourful sketch of life among the intelligent, upper-class Etruscans:

> The people are pictured on their tombs as short and stocky, with large heads, features almost Anatolian, complexion ruddy, especially in women, but rouge is as old as civilization. The ladies were famous for their beauty, and some of the men had faces of refinement and nobility. Civilization had already advanced to a precarious height, for specimens of dental bridgework have been found in the graves; dentistry, like medicine and surgery, had been imported from Egypt and Greece. Both sexes wore the hair long, and the men fondled beards. Garments followed the Ionian style: an inner shirt like a *chiton*, and an outer robe that became the Roman toga. Men as well as women loved ornament, and their tombs abounded in jewelry.
>
> If we may judge from the gay pictures of the sepulchres, the life of the Etruscans, like that of the Cretans, was hardened with combat, softened with luxury, and brightened with feasts and games. The men waged war lustily, and practiced a variety of virile sports. They hunted, fought bulls in the arena, and drove their chariots sometimes four horses abreast, around a dangerous course. They threw the discus and the javelin, pole-vaulted, raced, wrestled, boxed, and fought in gladiatorial bouts. Cruelty marked these games, for the Etruscans, like the Romans, thought it dangerous to let civilization get too far from the brute. Less heroic persons brandished dumbbells, threw dice, played the flute, or danced. Scenes of bibulous merriment relieve the paintings in the tombs. Sometimes they are symposia for men only, with vinous conversation; now and then they show both sexes, richly dressed, reclining in pairs on elegant couches, eating and drinking, waited on by slaves, and entertained by dancers and musicians. Occasionally the meal is adorned with an amorous embrace.

Upper-class women were educated. "Religion provided every incentive to a negative morality." Tinia, who commanded thunder and lightning, was abetted by Twelve Great Gods who were pitiless and feared. The future was read by studying the livers of sheep and observing the flight of birds. Animal sacrifice was a regular part of sacred rites, and the funeral of an important person might entail human slaughter and the burial alive of hapless victims.

Expanding their sway by force, the Etruscans pushed northwards to the foothills of the Alps and ever southwards to Campania, establishing colonies and finally taking over Rome, where their kings – the Tarquins – reigned from the middle of the seventh to almost the end of the sixth century BC, until the oppressive last of the royal line was deposed and Rome became an oligarchical republic. (My very brief account of this obscure race, who more or less vanished after 300 years as "a temporary civilizing force" in Italy, is borrowed from chapters in books by the already credited Nicoll, Gassner, Roberts, Brockett, Berthold, Sandbach, Casson and Gary Wills, in addition to Durant.)

Etruscan literature is wholly lost. In any event, the folk dances and farces were at first so crude that they were probably never scripted – they are known only by hearsay. Gradually they developed into two forms of popular entertainment. One was the so-called Fescennine Verses, the name taken from the Etruscan border town of Fescennium where they might have had their earliest utterance; or from the Latin word "fascinum", or "phallus", from which derives "fascinate". These were the recital and enactment with gestures of raucous poems, usually on the occasion by "actors" – or masked clowns – at birth celebrations or marriages, and appropriately erotic in content. Largely improvisations, they resembled the communal Greek revels that evolved into the mocking satyr-plays. Or, at the harvest season, they might be obscene and abusive exchanges in a light vein – the everlasting, primitive "humour of insult" – between amateur performers.

Horace (65–8 BC) alludes to Fescennine Verses as likely predecessors of Roman farce. Slightly later, the all-important historian Livy (59 BC–AD 17), as quoted by Sandbach, described an event in 364 BC when a festival – featuring a procession, a chariot race and a display of daring horsemanship – was put on to mollify the gods who had been punishing the city with a plague. On this occasion, according to Livy, "players were introduced from Etruria who, dancing to the music of a piper, but not singing themselves or miming any representation of song, moved not ungracefully in the Etruscan manner. Young men began to imitate them, bandying jokes in rough verses, and their movements did not discord with their voices. Native Roman professional performers were given the name of *histriones* because a player was in Etruscan called *ister*; they did not follow the earlier practice which alternated irregular unpolished improvised lines similar to the Fescennine Verses, but presented medleys in music, with song fitted to the strains of the pipe and suitable movement to go with it." Sandbach adds: "all these entertainments are thought of as preceding true drama. Some support for the belief that they had an origin in Etruria is given by the probability that the Latin words for stage, *scaina*, and mask, *persona*, are Etruscan deformations of the Greek *skene* and *prosopon*." Livy, however, does not specifically link Roman theatre to the earlier Etruscan.

In time, the Fescennine Verses were formalized, gaining a sort of traditional shape, their speakers professional, skilled performers hired for each occasion. When the Romans later adopted the recitals and exchanges, their subject-matter grew so licentious that they were finally proscribed, though they kept on being a favourite form of entertainment until imperial times, giving them a life of many centuries.

The other early genre of ancient Etruscan folk-farce was the less well-defined *saturae*: possibly descended from the Fescennine Verses, these were skits with embryonic plots but even more music and dancing; they were mostly prose medleys of obscene jests with indecent illustrative gestures. Some scholars argue that they were in verse. It is hazarded that they resembled modern variety shows and that they bore a kinship to Greek Old Comedy, though they were hardly of the stature of Aristophanes' fantasies and diatribes. Very likely they were associated with vintage festivities: "*saturae*" is related to "saturated", suggesting a full cask or overflowing jug, at hand and available after a rich reaping. As already cited by Livy, the performers in these skits and similar enactments were called *istri* (or *ister*), because many of them came from the town of Istria – which by way of the Latin "*istriones*" has led to the present-day adjective "histrionic".

A slightly more defined and cohesive form of early Roman play is the Atellan farce of Compagnia (or Compania), once more the name having been borrowed from the place in that province where these skits had their birth, Atella – today Aversa, later chosen to be one of the first cities in Rome to have a permanent stone theatre. Partly impromptu, and perhaps an outgrowth of a combination of elements of the Fescennine Verses and the *saturae*, the Atellan farces also show signs of Greek influence, the techniques of the mime Trantus who was based nearby in Hellenic colonies just to the south, below Naples and in Sicily. Atellan farces, dating to the fourth century BC in the provincial city and next reaching Rome during the first half of the third century BC, boasted stock characters that resembled those in Greek Middle and New Comedy: the stern or befuddled father; the sterling youth in love; the maiden whose virtue is in ceaseless jeopardy; the knavish servant far cleverer and more resourceful than his infatuated master; the swaggering warrior; the sly, self-serving parasite. From these are to descend the Commedia dell'Arte figures, the most surely immortal of all theatrical characters, who are to attain their apogee epochs later in the Italian Renaissance. A fresco in Pompeii includes an exact image of a humped-backed, beak-nosed Punchinello, attesting to his remarkable antiquity. Other characters of equally ancient lineage are the ebullient Harlequin, the simple-minded Bucco, the doltish but quick-witted Maccus, the senile Pappus. True, some of these amusing caricatures seem to have been purely Italian creations. Again, so obscure are the beginnings of Roman comedy, some historians believe that the Atellan works preceded rather than grew out of the *saturae.* Regardless of their exact chronology, the Atellan farces, like their Greek forerunners, incorporated parody and political comment, along with domestic intrigue and burlesqued mythology, and the actors were masked. With masks, the members of the Commedia dell'Arte family were even more enabled to acquire their everlasting personalities. Though the plots changed, the characters remained the same, their temperamental responses always predictable. Throughout all following centuries the dialogue was largely improvised from a very scanty scenario, and if ever a player found himself without an adequate reply to an insult or jest he had only to answer with a blow or kick, or any other kind of slapstick, as do Punch and Judy to the shrieking delight of children even now.

The occasion of the introduction of the *saturae* to Rome – to appease the gods who had inflicted a pestilence – saw this new kind of entertainment quickly made welcome. (To orient the reader: Aristophanes was now dead a decade and a half, and Menander still to be born.) A stage – perhaps Rome's first makeshift theatre – was put up for them in the Circus Maximus, where ordinarily chariot races were run. Evoking laughter, the comedians shortly became a regular feature of the city games or *ludi* (to continue with linguistic affiliations, "ludicrous", alluding to the buffoonish antics of actors at these frequent events). First introduced by the elder Tarquin in the sixth century BC to honour Jupiter, the holy day gradually became secularized into a holiday boasting every sort of entertainment for the restless, rowdy urban crowds: juggling, acrobatics, boxing matches. (The atmosphere was indeed circus-like.)

After the Punic Wars, Rome had no fewer than fifty-five holidays annually to which there were added these theatrical offerings, with the connection between religion and the rambunctious stage ever more tenuous. The festivals, solemn or light-hearted, might mark martial victories, dedication of monuments, funerals of eminent persons, testimonials that honoured laurel-wreathed heroes of the moment.

The Etruscan tomb paintings show that the platforms erected for plays at these festivals – no longer presented in the Circus Maximus – were surrounded by grandstands for the spectators, much as in that vast sports stadium, which was reserved for gladiatorial combats, animal baitings, chariot competitions and other diverse large-scaled presentations. The stages and onlookers' benches were temporary structures. Supposedly new accommodations were set up for each occasion. The sites chosen would often depend on which god was being propitiated, before the temple dedicated to him and in the precinct sacred to him, at an angle that would let the deity's statue view the performance. The proportions and other physical characteristics of these structures, how large or small, how flimsy or sturdy they were, are conjectural and often subjects of academic dispute.

Berthold suggests that in an early period the wooden platform occupied by the actors was rectangular, about three feet above the ground and approached by six or seven steps at one side. A plain curtain (*siparium*) closed off the back, a quite primitive arrangement. Sandbach says that the platform was supported by square posts or narrow columns, perhaps concealed by curtains. In many instances the players were not masked but were distinguished by wigs, especially the young men assigned to female roles. This sort of rough staging continued for about two centuries of the pre-Christian era.

In yet later decades it was customary for nearly all the spectators to stand in a semi-circle about the platform, with the exception of notables, such as senators and other state officials, who were seated in a few front rows. This was true until 150 BC; in 155 BC Cassius Longinus, a censor, built a stage with visibly decorated columns making the *scaenae frons* (equivalent to the Greek *skene*) more handsome, but once the *ludi* ended the Senate ordered the columns taken down. Soon after, in 145 BC, Lucius Mummius, wishing to celebrate his victory over Corinth, raised a costly wooden theatre to house some plays put on for the triumphal event; it set a precedent by having seats for all the spectators, but met a similar fate. Tacitus records that the ambitious structure was demolished at the termination of the games.

Overseeing the *ludi* and dramatic activities in Rome were two high-ranking officials, *curule aediles*, at first selected from the patrician class, but later appointments open to plebeians. This pair was responsible for keeping order at the festivals, monitoring the games, licensing and supervising all construction, approving the design of the temporary buildings.

Expenditures for costumes, the wages of actors and the director, were doled out by the *aediles*. All costs were subsidized by the state; it was part of the Roman policy of "bread and circuses", by which the always restive lower classes were held in check and regularly appeased.

Another feature of the *ludi* was the more indigenous Roman *mimi* and *pantomimi,* each a kind of vaudeville with acrobatics, sketches, music, with some Sicilian colouring. Greek Old Comedy, New Comedy and mime had long since greatly flourished in the Sicilian colonies and the regions of southernmost Italy, where they flaunted every kind of broad travesty. In Rome, too, the *mimi* and *pantomimi* were to prove more lastingly popular than the subsequent, more literary theatre.

The *pantomimi* was a solo performance. Legend credits its beginning to Livius Andronicus (270–204 BC), a freed slave, actor and poet, who became so hoarse during a recitation, from giving encores, that he called upon a boy to sing the lines for him while he concentrated just on conveying their meaning through gesture and facial expression. His substitution being very well received, it was often repeated and became a new genre. Instead of a mere boy singing and speaking, a chorus gradually took over the musical and vocal parts. The solo role might be a serious one, but just as often it was vulgarly comic, for Roman audiences were not too refined. The soloist was masked – unlike the knockabout performers in the *mimus* – and wore a "clapper" on his boot to stress the beat of words and the accompaniment of the "orchestra". He might impersonate several characters in turn, with changes of costume and mask, creating new moods. The true art of acting, dance and pantomime divorced from words is said to have reached an intense apotheosis in such performances. In much later, imperial times the soloists and chorus were lavishly attired and the stage richly set, and this kind of entertainment was much preferred by several emperors. One reason for the long-lasting popularity of the pantomimes was that the population of the vast Roman empire was polyglot, but expressive physical gesture could be understood everywhere.

In general, the Roman mimes did not use masks. The public called them *Sanniones*, "face-makers", a designation that was to survive in the Commedia dell'Arte clown Zanni, hence "zany". Berthold quotes Cicero's denigrating reference to him: "Can there be anything more ridiculous than Sannio, who laughs with his mouth, face, mocking gesture, with his voice, and indeed with his whole body?"

Between the acts at some plays, during the Ludi Romani, the *siparium* – white curtain – would be drawn open; the pantomimist stepped forward to project his humour, the inevitable coarse jests and flagrantly obscene gestures that constituted his stock-in-trade. Starting in 175 BC the spring festival, Ludi Florales, extended for several days, was given over entirely to mime, a display of that special, intimate art. The *mimi*, too, was the only form of entertainment in which women participated, exhibiting their talents as dancers and acrobats. In tribute to the goddess Flora, a female performer might climax her dance with a touch of nudity, casting aside her flowing gown, signifying the arrival of the season of flowering and leaping abandon.

The costumes varied. The early mimes who wandered the roads of Sicily and southern Italy might be garbed in rags. Later, in their first days in Rome, they wore the clothes of ordinary citizens. Incrementally, as they competed with the Atellan players, they borrowed characters and the identifying attire that had evolved and become affixed to them. Berthold describes a typical instance: "The fool wore a motley dress of patchwork (*centunculus*), such as Harlequin still wears today, and a pointed hat (*apex*; hence the later expression *apiciosus*). The mime wore only a light sole for footwear, and his sandal, which differed from the *cothurnus* of the tragic actor and the *soccus* of the comedian, earned him the nickname *planipedes* in Rome. The grammarian Donatus, however, has a less charitable explanation; the *mimus*, according to him, was called *planipedia* because its subjects were so flat and its players so low that it pleased only libertines and adulterers."

Besides proving his resourcefulness at pantomime when he had suddenly lost his voice, Livius Andronicus was a seminal figure in the growth of Roman drama. Born in the prosperous Greek city of Tarentum, which in 272 BC, shortly before his birth, had fallen to the Romans, he was brought to the capital city; enslaved to the wealthy house of Livius in which he served as a private tutor, he demonstrated a remarkable gift for language and shortly was given more responsibilities as an adviser on educational and cultural affairs. One of his tasks, skilfully accomplished, was to translate Homer's *Odyssey* into Latin Saturnian verse, providing an accessible text used by pupils in schools. The Senate also bade him compose Latin hymns, which he did successfully.

At the end of the Punic Wars (240 BC) he was asked (or ordered) to translate both a Greek tragedy and comedy for presentation at the Ludi Romani, for which he would also be the producer. He participated in them not only as the adaptor but equally as actor and singer. His offerings were staged in true Athenian fashion, for the Dionysian festivals had been observed in Tarentum, and he was familiar with the ritual and tradition. Encouraged, he translated many more Greek scripts, adhering to orthodox metrical patterns. The intelligentsia was completely won over by the masterly works, and henceforth the Roman literary stage slavishly aped Grecian models. Overawed by the lofty Athenian originals, the Roman theatre poets never surpassed them – indeed, they never came within distant reach of them. But again, at least in comedy, certain qualities were injected that were native to the Italian spirit: robustness, noise, a wantonness that passed over into scatology. It is easy to grasp why, when Christianity finally came, its bishops were anti-theatre.

The accomplishment of Livius Andronicus was emulated five years later by the Roman-born Gnaeus Naevius, a loyal son of Campania, considered to be his country's first true poet and dramatist. A veteran of the First Punic War, a fervid patriot, he fought abroad in Rome's legions and observed the costly mistakes and failures of its military leaders. Dedicated to the austere egalitarian principles of the Republic, he was deeply angered by the corrupt practices he saw being exercised on every side by many in power. His writing career, stretching from 235 BC to 204 BC (or 201 BC, the year of his death), began with an epic poem about the First Punic War, which he vividly recalled. After this came several tragic plays on Greek themes, together with a few dramas glorifying Roman history, the most successful of them his *Romulus*, which brought him prizes and honours. In contrast to Livius Andronicus, who did best with serious subjects, Gnaeus Naevius excelled at farces in a semi-Aristophanic vein. Titles of thirty of these survive but not the scripts, save for scattered quotable lines. Some of the plays may have been mere translations; if so, it is not known what proportion of his output they represent, but many of their titles are Greek and echo those of New Comedies. Caustic and wittily polemical, his criticism of high public figures offended the censor and Senate, who harshly retaliated by having him imprisoned and exiled; shut off from Rome, he died in the Phoenician city of Utica. An excerpt from one of his works, *Ariolus* or *The Soothsayer*, has its story taking place in a small Italian town, which argues that it might have been an original effort.

As was a custom, he left behind his self-authored epitaph:

> Were lady deities allowed to weep
> for men, the Latin Muses would
> for Naevius. For Orcus has him
> and, that large speech lost,
> all men are Latinless.
> [Translation: Garry Wills]

What ensued was a burgeoning of playwrights in Rome; their names still exist, together with fragments of scripts, but that is all. Among such almost forgotten writers are Titanius, Atta, Lucius Afranius, Marcus Pacuvius (220–*c.* 130 BC), Lucius Accius (170–*c.* 82 BC) and Status Caecillius, of whose highly esteemed comedies some 400 lines – largely out of sequence – have been discovered. Classic scholars have compiled the titles of about seventy farces and tragedies by minor dramatists belonging to this transitional era.

Better remembered is Quintus Ennius (239–169 BC), who similarly wrote in the epic form and for the theatre, though none of his plays is available; but he is recognized as having had a direct influence on his young successor Terence. The Romans distinguished two types of scripts; those adapted from the Greek were designated *fabula crepidata*, and those – much fewer in number – that exploited Roman subjects were spoken of as *fabula praetexta*. Being Italian, tragedies of the latter sort tended to reach for more striking effects than did the Greek, with extremes of emotion, engendered by dilemmas, the hero maintaining virtue, confronting vice, cherishing honour, displaying fortitude, accepting self-sacrifice. There was more emphasis on rhetoric and fantastic spectacle.

Ennius, too, left his own epitaph:

> No tears for me, no pomp of funeral hearse
> escort my spirit to eternal night;
> for every lip that flutters out my verse
> breathes what was me alive again, in flight.
> [Translation: Garry Wills]

The comic style adopted by the lighter writers was that of New Comedy, but for the most part the "chaste elegance" of Menander was replaced by Billingsgate and rampant obscenity in a frantic effort to get laughs. Jokes and jeers aimed at important bureaucrats grew ever louder. In response, censorship became so strict that an author who was deemed to have perpetrated libel could pay with his life. To be a comic writer was not without peril.

The most successful of all the Roman adapters of Greek New Comedies is Titus Maccius Plautus (254–184 BC), born in Sarsinia in the province of Umbria, directly north of Rome. He had a varied life, heightened by adventure. He served as a soldier, and at an early point in his career was an actor in the crude native works of the day, probably with a troupe of Atellan players, so that he was well acquainted with that genre. Faring poorly, he gave up the stage for a venture as a merchant, but failed at commerce, losing what little he had. He was reduced to grinding flour and peddling it in the street, trundling a small hand-mill, a menial occupation at which he prudently continued even after he wrote his first two plays, *Addictus* and *Saturio*; he proved wise, for both of them were badly received and promised him no succour. He was now past forty, a late starter.

With Plautus' third effort, some time around 204 BC, came triumph; for now he was borrowing his material from Menander, Philemon, Diphilus and other Greek authors, but skilfully refashioning their scripts for the rowdy local audiences. (The exact chronology of his works is not determined.) He added his own exuberance and earthiness to the refined verses and characters of the Greek originals. His travels, his years in military camps and as a merchant and street peddler, had taught him what tickled the average Roman. He himself had the common touch and was prepared to do anything to amuse unruly spectators, and his sole object was to make money. Coupled with these motivations, he had a hard-headed sense of practical theatre, learned during his years as an actor. In his very person he was a clown; he had red hair, a big stomach, very large feet. Prolix, he ground out perhaps 130 plays, though many of these attributions are most likely spurious. Of his works, twenty-one scripts survive, the largest number of any Classic dramatist, testimony to his zest and skill, and to posterity's anxiety to preserve and revive them.

Working quickly, he was careless. Most often he Romanized the Greek characters and situations, giving them Latin names and local settings, but not always, so that incongruities abound; but apparently this did not really bother anyone save a few rather effete and demanding critics. He changed the simple meters used by the Greek poets, employing a wide, more complicated variety of them in his lines to indicate changes of mood, inserted new and bawdier jokes, sometimes combined scenes from two or more Greek originals into a single new work, omitted the chorus completely, and took all the liberties a truly effective adapter should be bold enough to attempt. Horace, in his critical essay, found fault with him for his boisterous, slapdash methods, saying that he "ran around the stage in loose socks", referring to the low-heeled shoes that comedians wore (in contrast to the high-heeled buskins that lent dignity to the stride of tragic actors). All that Plautus sought was applause. Though his writing is wildly uneven, his talent is everywhere manifest. What he lacked in taste, he made up for in zest – he is rowdy and often hilarious. That was amply demonstrated in AD 1962 when a Broadway musical, in turn compounded of snippets of Plautus' themes and titled *A Funny Thing Happened on the Way to the Forum*, had a more than two-year run to full houses, and was subsequently a highly lucrative film, and then revived in New York to repeated applause (1998). Another Broadway hit, *The Boys from Syracuse* (1938), via Shakespeare's *The Comedy of Errors*, descends from a Plautine farce, as does Giraudoux's prankish transatlantic success, *Amphytrion 38* (1929). Two thousand years have not blunted the edge of Plautus' zany jokes, and especially not of the gamier ones. He grew so popular in his own time that though he was an actor–manager and playwright and an Umbrian as well, honorary citizenship was conferred on him. (The Senate, taking a jaundiced view of the depraved theatre of the day, had deprived those associated with it of the right to call themselves "Romans", a designation reserved for native-born inhabitants only, but occasionally an exception was made.) Soon afterwards he was granted the privilege, also reserved for Roman citizens only, of bearing three names, and promptly, proudly dubbed himself Titus Maccus Plautus – the "Plautus" having been his nickname and meaning that he was "Flat-footed", with a toed-out walk after the fashion of Charlie Chaplin, and "Maccus" identifying him as a "Clown", as was the stock figure so tagged in the Atellan farces.

Of the twenty-one scripts still extant, a half-dozen have been the most durable. *The Braggart Warrior* (*Miles Gloriosus*) gives new life and dimension to the Greek stock character of the fraudulently proud soldier and anticipates no less a figure than Shakespeare's boastful, paunchy Falstaff. So vain is this military "hero" that he complains, "'Tis a great nuisance being so very handsome," and so complacent that he is easily gulled by a wily servant. Led to the conviction that his neighbour's wife is enamoured of him, the warrior makes a fool of himself, a plot reminiscent of the greatly later *Merry Wives of Windsor.* Shakespeare's debt to Plautus is much wider than this and is ineluctably pointed out by college lecturers and writers of textbooks.

As has already been remarked, another plot refurbished by the busy Plautus is the Greek myth of how Zeus (here Jove) seduces Alcmena, the wife of Amphytrion, by assuming the mortal guise of that unlucky husband, who has unscrupulously been sent off to war. Giraudoux named his version of the comedy *Amphytrion 38* because the story had been used by at least thirty-seven other playwrights before him, the most notable of them being Molière. It is one of Plautus' gentler works, the human couple depicted with untypical delicacy at times, and he himself termed it a "tragicomedy", in the Euripidean manner of *Ion* and *Helen*, because he recognized that the characters and situation might have been treated more seriously.

Aularia, or *The Crock of Gold*, inspired Molière, who drew his *The Miser* from it, which in turn prompted an English version by Henry Fielding. The title figure, Euclio Senex, embodies the stock character of the skinflint curmudgeon: he even begrudges wasting his breath while snoring at night, so he sleeps with a bellows attached to his nose and tied around his neck. He collects the parings from his fingernails and rues the loss of water in tears shed by his rheumy eyes. He has found a pot of gold and trembles lest anyone else learn of it (a situation repeated in *The Rope*). He is unintentionally an obstacle to the marriage of a pair of young lovers. When the stolen gold is restored to him, the match finally takes place. In some instances, here and elsewhere, the allegorical names assigned to the characters are somewhat too bawdy for proper translation.

The Rope (*Rudens*) is another romantic, rollicking piece, this time taken from a play by Diphilus. Palaestra, the daughter of Daemones, an Athenian, has been abducted when a child. She grows up and comes into the possession of a procurer, Labrax, who has brought her to Cyrene, where the impoverished Daemones now lives. Labrax sells her to a young man, also an Athenian, named Plesidippus; but instead of delivering her to the youthful purchaser, makes off with her and his covey of other girls to Sicily. *En route*, they are shipwrecked by the intervention of a god. The mishap occurs close to shore. The girl and a pretty friend, Ampelisca, save themselves in a little boat and take haven near the simple cottage of her father who is impoverished and even now is a stranger to her. After a good deal of melodrama, many complications and a series of recognition scenes, the story attains a happy conclusion, with Daemones reclaiming his daughter, after he sees the requisite tokens, lost in the ship-sinking but adventitiously fished up from the sea-bottom. The familiar devices of mistaken identity and the ubiquitous changeling motif are very evident.

The Rope carries a message, a few spates of tart moralizing. When Deamones declares, "The wise man will always find it best to have no part in another's wrong. I don't care for wealth gained by deception," his slave Gripus replies: "I've often gone to the play and heard talk like that, with the audience applauding the words of wisdom. But when we went back home, no one acted on the advice he had heard." And harsh observations on human nature: Charmides, a malicious collaborator of Labrax, speaks directly to the audience, "I'm a believer in the theory that men get turned into different kinds of animals. If you ask me, that pimp is being turned into a bird – a jailbird. He's going to build a nest in the town lockup right now." (Translation: Lionel Casson)

The play's title alludes to a loose rope trailing from a satchel in which are the jewelled "birth tokens" that by lucky chance have been retrieved from the sea in a fisherman's net. The rope is pulled on in an angry tug-of-war between claimants disputing their rightful ownership of the procurer's wet satchel before its important contents are known.

The Rope had a later incarnation, in Elizabethan England, as *The Captives* of Thomas Heywood, and many other dramatists have happily borrowed story-ideas from its over-worked, complicated plot.

In fact, Plautus himself wrote a lively piece, *The Captives* (*Captiviti*), about a father who loses a pair of sons, one having been taken prisoner in war, the other having vanished much earlier. It is more sentimental, less ribald, than most Plautine works; yet also less romantic, for it has no love story. The narrative is intricate and repeatedly strains credulity, but that did not bother the author. The humour revolves mostly about who is deceiving whom, and who is related to whom, and at the close, of course, are the usual joyful reunions, with a slave discovering he is actually of good birth, the son of the man on whom he has been playing tricks, and who has severely mistreated him. This work was excessively admired by the eminent German critic and playwright Lessing, who thought no better comedy had ever reached the stage. In his prologue Plautus himself touts its virtues, pointing out how proper and original it is:

> It is not hackneyed or just like the rest;
> It has no filthy lines one must not quote.
> No perjured pander, and no wicked wench.

A particular favourite in this ingeniously contrived lark is Ergasilus, the hungry parasite, who confesses:

Grace is the name the boys have given me,
Because I'm always found before the meat!

That the play is more decorous than most of this period has made it more acceptable – in the recent past – for classroom study.

The Persian Stranger (or *Persa*) takes the spectator into a salacious *demi-monde* of pimps, courtesans and cozeners and in consequence has added value as a starkly emblazoned leaf of social history, which is true of most of Plautus' farces. They expose graphically the street-life, the daily doings of common folk, in the turbulent Greek and Roman worlds, with a realism that reminds one of the seventeenth- and eighteenth-century writings of English novelists and playwrights such as Defoe and Nashe, and the slashing caricatures of Hogarth.

The Trickster (*Pseudolus*) depicts the stratagems of a pander, Ballio, and of a cunning slave, Pseudolus, who outwits Ballio by stealing a slave-girl from him, on behalf of a young man to whom he volunteers his apt services. Ballio has intended her for a more lucrative market, an officer ready to pay well. If slave-girls are practically always the heroines of these farces, it is partly because girls high-born or even the daughters of solid Greek and Roman citizens seldom went abroad or fell into these daunting dilemmas; they were too sheltered, kept safely at home until they were married – though Roman folk ways did grant girls more freedom than they had in Greek society. Courtship, as now practised, did not exist in those times.

Plautus, like Menander before him, and even more Terence after him, was thus subtly propagandizing for such slave-girls, who might well be trained in many social arts, including flute playing and skill with the lyre, and educated in literature and philosophy to make them better conversationalists and altogether more intelligent and more congenial companions. These graces, however, did not really improve their essentially hard lot, adrift as they were, without suitable protectors, and for purchase by the highest bidder. One of the peripheral achievements of New Comedy, both in Greece and as paraphrased in Rome, was to earn sympathy for these unhappy courtesans, blameless outcasts.

Though *The Twin Menaechmi* is a lesser Plautine work, it has long been his best known and most widely read and acted, since it is the source (along with his *Amphytrion*) of Shakespeare's *The Comedy of Errors*, also a lesser work but the one most frequently studied in today's schools. In it are summed up most of the typical but never outgrown devices of New Comedy: it deals with identical twins, whose likeness to each other results in a bewildering succession of credible misunderstandings, offers spirited vignettes of everyday life, and presents a collection of stock figures, with a somewhat improbable climax and "happy" ending. At least eight Greek comedies treated with the theme of strikingly look-alike twins, but none remains. Here the pair, Menaechmus I and Menaechmus II (also called Sosicles), have become separated when one, at the age of seven and just losing his teeth, is kidnapped while at a fair with his father, a Sicilian merchant. Soon afterwards his father dies of despair. One boy is brought up by his paternal grandfather and begins to search everywhere for his twin. To assure more future confusion, his grandfather has renamed him after his lost brother, since it is the grandfather's name too, and he wishes to perpetuate it. After six years the young man's quest brings him to Epidamnus, where his twin has been reared by a rich merchant who is now dead. Since both twins boast the same name and indistinguishably resemble each other, chaos logically follows. Everyone in the city thinks Menaechmus II (Sosicles) is Menaechmus I, his wealthy foster-father's fortunate heir – even his mistress, wife and father-in-law fall into the natural error – and much of the mix-up is irresistibly mirthful. The play lacks the sharp characterizations that mark the best Plautine pieces, but plot-wise is one of the author's best scripts, since it moves at an exceptionally rapid pace. On hand is a comic doctor, a quack, prescribing his costly and preposterous nostrums. The grouchy, but commonsensical father-in-law is better realized than most. The names of the characters, again, serve admirably to describe them: the courtesan is Erotium (Lovey), her cook is Cylindrus (Roller), the mischievous parasite is Peniculous. He explains, "My nickname's Sponge, because when I eat I wipe the table clean." ("Sponge" for the Romans had a somewhat indecent connotation as well.) He does indeed have an inordinate appetite, but pauses to issue an eloquent plea for kindness in caring for slaves: if they attempt to run away, they should not be put in chains:

> You see, if you add insult to injury, a poor fellow will want all the more to escape and go wrong. He'll get out of his chains somewhat, you can be sure – file away a link, or knock out a name with a stone. That way's no good.
>
> If you really want to keep somebody so he won't get away, you'd better tie him with food and drink: hitch his beak to a full dinnerpail. Give him all he wants to drink every day, and he'll never try to run away, not even if he's committed murder. The bonds of food and drink are very elastic, you know: the more you stretch them, the tighter they hold you. [Translation: Richard W. Hyde and Edward C. Weist]

The language has this pithiness throughout. Having trouble with his wife, to whom he is unfaithful, Menaechmus I compares her to a customs officer:

I can't get out anywhere
But you want me to declare
All I've done and all I do.

Cynicism colours this work; both young men are unscrupulous, with no perceptible virtues; and with one exception, the decent slave Messino, they are surrounded by grasping, mercenary hangers-on.

It is notable with what apparent ease Plautus contrives to have the full action take place outdoors, in the busy street, where most intimate details of married life and the courtesan's bed are discussed frankly, with no strain on plausibility. This is why it has been said that the door is one of the characters of a Roman comedy, because the cast makes its entrances and exits through one or another so very often.

When Shakespeare borrowed this typical story, he cleaned up its more improper details, even though the Elizabethan audience was far from priggish. His chief addition, which he takes from *Amphytrion*, is to have the twin heroes attended by twin slaves, which cleverly augments the confusion. Shakespeare's handling is more sentimental, and his ending far happier – in Plautus' version Menaechmus I cruelly suggests that he would like to auction off his wife, and coldly grants Messino the privilege of conducting the sale. The slave, who has been freed, expresses doubt that anyone will take a fancy to the shrill-voiced lady.

Among Plautus' other works are *The Churl* (*Truculentus*), again whirling about the bewildering consequences of mistaken identity; *The Comedy of Asses* (*Assinaria*), in which a father tries to sell some of his wife's jackasses so that his son can purchase a girl, and is trapped while fondling the young man's light-of-love; and *Bacchides*, a sprightly account of the cavortings of two courtesans.

The dialogue, besides being sharp and racy, is dotted and heightened by puns, word-plays and alliteration. But Plautus has lyrical gifts as well. Speeches are interrupted by arias, often long plaints of love and similar expressions of longing by the troubled slave-girls and frustrated suitors. There are also patter-songs, with humorous content, not unlike those of Gilbert and Sullivan, to music by Plautus himself. The "orchestral" accompaniment was provided by flutes to which might be added harps, lyres, cymbals, trumpets or pipes, as were those of Greek New Comedy, all somewhat equivalent to operettas.

Modern readers are apt to find the exposition in the dialogue both too explicit and repetitive, with every detail of the plot clarified. But faced with an illiterate, unsophisticated audience – one that was far less alert than the Greek spectators for whom Menander and Philemon wrote – Plautus could do no less. Further, it was to assure that his listeners could follow the complicated plots that he prefixed the play with a prologue, a short synopsis of the story, so that the situation could be grasped more quickly once the action got under way. Plautus handles these prologues deftly and disarmingly. In *The Rope*, as if parodying a Greek tragedy, he has the god Arcturus, "Warder of the Bear", supply the background needed for comprehension, while himself taking credit for having intervened – *deus ex machina* – in the events. (A good deal of "mock-tragedy" tinges this play.) In the *Menaechmi* he has his actor say, tongue-in-cheek:

> I'm bringing you Plautus – by mouth, of course, not in person,
> And therefore I pray you receive him with kindliest ears.
> To the argument gird up your minds, as I babble my verse,
> And I shall explain it – in briefest of terms, have no fears.
> And this is the thing that poets do in their plays:
> The action has all taken place in Athens, they say,
> That the setting will seem to be Greek to you all the more.
> But from me you'll hear the truth – where it actually happened.
> The plot of the play, to be sure, is Greek, but not
> Of the Attic variety; Sicilian, rather.
> I've given you now of the argument merely the preface;
> But next the plot I'll generously pour out
> Not merely by peck or bushel, but by the whole barn,
> So kindly a nature I have for telling the plot.

Political commentary was risky, but social criticism is not entirely absent in Plautus. Scarcely as acidulous as Aristophanes, he none the less offers hints of what he might have been willing and capable of saying about Roman life and rule, were candour on those subjects permissible. Some of his views are found in *Truculentus*, and they crop up too in the *Miles Gloriosus*, where there is a reference to Cnaeus Naevius, who had suffered imprisonment and exile for having dared to deride the "Establishment"; the *Menaechmi* offers in passing a scathing picture of the judicial system, and two other plays, *Aularia* and *Epidicius*, allude to the repressive Oppian Laws that forbade women to wear gold ornaments and vari-hued garments – edicts revoked in 195 BC, when finally the women, aroused, swept into the Forum to demand the repeal of all such penitential symbolic gestures. *Bacchides, Cistellaria* and *Captivi* have references to Rome's endless foreign wars: the times through which Plautus lived and worked were turbulent, for it was then that Rome destroyed Carthage; echoes of the costly conflicts in North Africa, Greece and Magnesia are heard in almost all his works, however faintly. His talents in this respect were partly aborted. Yet by keeping most of his scenes in Greece, he was able to speak a bit more frankly, if obliquely.

In *The Haunted House*, a work of "unabashed tomfoolery", Theopropides, a wealthy Athenian, is away on a lengthy ship journey. In his father's absence, Philolaches, once a sober, well-behaved youth, has become a profligate, carousing with a drunken friend, Callidamates, and Delphinium, a courtesan. He purchases and sets free a very beautiful slave-girl, Philematium, after obtaining 15,000 drachmas from a professional money-lender. The young man is infatuated with the lovely girl, and she responds to him in kind, though her cynical maid, the crone Scapha, urges her not to rebuff the attentions of other men, since Philolaches' feelings for her will not last too long – no man's passion ever does.

The sudden, unexpected return of Theopropides instigates panic in Philolaches and his debauched friends, who after partying in the house are still too intoxicated to depart; now the self-confident ingenious slave Tranio takes charge. He locks up the house from the outside, with the still inert guests within. The father, arriving, is told that he cannot enter his home because it is haunted by the ghost of someone murdered far in the past, before Theopropides became its owner. The slain man is supposedly buried in a pit beneath the floor. For seven months, according to Tranio, no one has dared to enter the place. Hearing ungodly noises from within, the voices of the drunken Callidamates and Delphinium, the affrighted Theopropides takes to his heels.

The money-lender arrives to collect the interest on his 15,000 drachmas. Tranio tries to stave him off with a variety of pretexts. By now Theopropides has returned, having encountered the previous proprietor of the house who indignantly denies Tranio's tale of a murder in it. Overhearing the money-lender's insistence on payment, Theopropides wants to know what the fuss is all about. Tranio, beset, improvises an explanation: Philolaches has bought their neighbour's well-designed dwelling at a bargain price, to replace the accursed one. Theopropides is pleased at this sign of his son's sagacity and promises the money-lender full recompense no later than the next day. Quick-thinking, as always, Tranio contrives to have the delighted Theopropides taken on a tour of the neighbour's sumptuous home. Buying it was obviously a shrewd move.

However, the elaborate deception is soon exposed. Callidamates, restored to his normal self, acts successfully as mediator between the remorseful son and his father, whose anger at Tranio is not as readily appeased. To escape it, the slave takes sanctuary at an altar where he cannot be whipped or attacked. At the end, all is forgiven – perhaps a bit too easily for a convincing resolution of the otherwise neatly plotted play.

Plautus' fondness for puns and the earthiness of his dialogue are amply on display, as when Tranio retorts to another slave, who accuses him of plundering his absent master's bounty, "Stupid, how can I eat him out of house and home when he's not *in* the house?"

Scapha advises her mistress to avoid the use of costly scents:

> Because the right smell for a woman is no smell. You know those patched-up, toothless old crones who drench themselves with perfume and cover up their ugly spots with makeup? Well, once sweat starts mixing up with all that, they begin to smell like some sauce a cook's concocted: you don't know what the smell is from, but you do know it's pretty bad.

And:

> A lover just used jewels and clothes to buy himself a bedmate; he's not interested in those things himself. So why go to the trouble of parading them before him? Anyway, jewelry's for an ugly woman and gowns are for an old one to hide her age. A good-looking girl is better-looking in the nude than in a gorgeous gown. Good looks are ornament enough. [Translation: Lionel Casson]

An oddity is that many of the characters – Philolaches, Philematium, Scapha, Grumio, Delphinium – are on stage only in the opening scenes and are not seen again. Callidamates speaks for Philolaches at the climax; the errant son himself does not reappear, nor does his light-of-love. This may be because some of the actors were doubling in various roles. Songs are interspersed throughout the action; but never where they slow its forward propulsion.

Yet other plays by Plautus are *Stichus, Curculio, Epidicus, Casina, The Carthanian, Vidularia* and *The Casket.* All are believed to have been written between 205 BC and 184 BC, but that remains uncertain; in AD 1429 twelve complete scripts by Plautus were found in Mainz, Germany, by a youthful graduate law student, Nicholas of Cusa, an event which was to lead to renewed interest in the author, though it took a while longer for an appreciation of the lasting theatrical vitality of his contribution. Besides influencing Shakespeare and Molière, Fielding, Giraudoux, George Abbott, and

Rodgers and Hart, the works of Plautus have been a rich source of ribald incidents, effective plots and active characters for Goldoni, Udall, Jonson, Ariosto, Shadwell, Dryden and a great many more, almost every craftsman of commercial farce.

In early Republican times actors were outcasts; as already noted, they had to forfeit citizenship – Plautus being an exception. The theatre was looked at somewhat askance or down upon for its blatant immorality. Marriage between a senator and anyone linked to the profession of thespian was interdicted, whether to the child of a performer or even to a grandchild or great-grandchild of a player. A soldier daring to venture on to a stage faced execution. The performers' status as social pariahs was to burden them for centuries. Yet gradually certain actors won respect and fame, their names becoming immortal. Quintus Roscius (126?–62 BC), a tragedian but outstandingly a comedian, born a slave, earned a stupendous following. Pliny guesses that his annual income amounted to 50,000 sesterces (equivalent to $2 million).

His daily take – in modern terms – was about $175; he not only bought his freedom but grew so wealthy that for several seasons he performed without being paid. He added a third name, Gallus, a privilege reserved for Roman citizens, and sported an emblem designating him as having reached equestrian rank, a knighthood. Idolized by the masses, he received a gold ring from Sulla, Rome's happy dictator, who cultivated all the arts. Roscius was admired by Cicero, who took instruction from him and eventually served as his lawyer. In contrast to other *histriones*, whose style was over-stressed and bombastic, his was said to be restrained and far more natural; yet he moved spectators to tears or excited them to gales of laughter. He founded a school to train others in the same tradition of moderation. For centuries after, the highest tribute to an actor was to speak of him as a "new Roscius". This was particularly so as late as the nineteenth century when posters would announce the appearance of some travelling player in the hinterland or provinces as "the Young American Roscius", "the Scottish Roscius", "the Ohio Roscius", *et al.* (Vera Roberts cites a long list of actors of the Victorian age who sought to be described in that fashion.)

Almost equally acclaimed was Aesopus, who also established a school, and who too essayed both comic and tragic roles, but was at his best in serious works, winning explosive applause for his Agamemnon in Ennius' *Iphigenia* and as Atreus in Accius' *Clytemnestra*, and especially when he assumed the female lead in another Ennius drama, *Andromacha*. Despite his personal extravagance, he accumulated a vast fortune, disposing of 20 million sesterces in his will.

Lacking the versatility of this most renowned pair, the majority of the day limited themselves to either comic or tragic parts, or specialized as "gods, young men, good fathers, slaves, matrons, and respectable old women", the latter list being the range, according to Quintillian, of the beloved comedian Demetrius; whereas Stratocles, also a comic actor, was ranked high for his portrayals of "sharp-tempered old men, cunning slaves, parasites, pimps, and other such lively figures". (These quotations, too, are taken from Vera Roberts's *On Stage.*)

At first, the acting companies were small, four or six players, who could double in roles; but the number soon grew, since to hire a cast was not costly; most actors were drawn from the slave-class. Eventually a troupe might comprise fifty or sixty performers, more than might actually be needed, but this added to the possibilities for swarming spectacle. Selected for the profession, the slaves were given appropriate training. They had to have at least an elementary ability to sing and dance, though one of them might silently mouth the words while another, better equipped, vocalized for him, as in mime theatre.

Some actors "belonged" to the producer; they were slaves whom he had purchased and over whom he retained absolute control. Their daily lot was not always pleasant. Other slave-actors could be the property of a wealthy nobleman who basked in the prestige of owning a company of talented performers – as was the situation very much later in nineteenth-century Tsarist Russia – and who might rent or contract his entire private troupe to the state or a producer on a particular festive occasion.

The *aediles* acquired a script and the actors as a unit, a package, much as is done in Hollywood today. The producers or actor–managers (*domini*), such as Plautus, competed to sell their offerings. Plautus did not succeed in having all his works accepted and enacted. Not all producers were lead actors or wrote their own plays; some bought them from freelance poets; then the scenery, properties, costumes and musical arrangements had to be assembled. If the price was too high, the *aediles* – it was an honour to have been appointed one – might draw the needed extra funds from their own resources. It is not clear whether the script was merely read, and judged, before the contract was signed or was tried out in advance to determine if it played well or if any censorable content ought to be excised.

If a work was unusually well received, the producer might get a prize or bonus. Several plays, presented by rival troupes, would be mounted sequentially during the *ludi.* Bribery was known to be attempted, and claques might be a decisive factor, hired by the producer not only to attest by loud applause to the superiority of his play but also to boo and jeer at the entries of competitors. The aim of this frantic business was to win and hold popularity.

The actors had to compel attention and make themselves heard by an unruly, largely unschooled, jostling and elbowing crowd, against the simultaneous din and distraction of other entertainments: the juggling, acrobatics, animal baiting, athletic contest, wrestling and other combats surrounding the improvised stage.

As said before, it was to make sure that Plautus' listeners could follow the complicated plots that he prefixed every play with a prologue, a very short synopsis. He tells just enough to whet anticipation, yet does not give away too much of his story and thereby dilute suspense. Prologues of this sort become a fixed feature of comedies throughout the centuries, almost to the present day. Something like the introductory Plautine synopsis is still used for afternoon serial dramas on radio and television.

Roman comic writers added an epilogue, as well – this was a frank bid for clapping, as in *The Rope*, where Daemones bids Labrax to dine with him, then turns to the spectators:

> I should invite you in the audience, also, except that we're going to have nothing worth eating, and if I didn't think you all had dinner invitations anyway. But if you are willing to applaud heartily, come and make a night of it with me – sixteen years from now.

The epilogue was also a way of letting the untutored audience know that the play was over and it was time to disperse.

At first, the actors wore heavy make-up, rather than masks, because audiences were small. Wigs helped to designate the roles portrayed: a white wig for an old man, a black or brown for a young man, a red wig for a clownish slave, a blonde for a courtesan. Tragedians wore high-heeled shoes (buskins), comedians low-heeled slippers (socks), that enabled them to scamper about the stage, as mentioned before. When the size of the theatre was increased, masks came into use again. They were of a wide variety, as with the Greeks. It is said that Roscius was the first to insist on their re-adoption, partly to hide his squint. Fashioned of linen (mostly) or terracotta, attached to the wig and fully concealing the face, some were horrible, broadly grotesque or amusing, according to the role: sex, age, class, temperament and other characteristics were conventionally represented; they would be kept on a shelf off-stage, in the order in which the player would seek one for a very quick change; a fascinating collection of them is now on display in the British Museum. If the actors were masked, they could more easily double if need be, and plausibly pass as identical twins.

The shape of the nose – snub or sharp – the colour of the hair, the lines of the eyebrows, lips, the complexion's hue, allowed the audience to perceive at a glance what sort of person the actor was meant to be. As has been indicated, men took women's roles until the last phase of Roman theatre. (The word for mask was *persona*, and *dramatis personae* was a list of the "masks" to be used.)

Tragic actors were attired in long, sweeping robes (*syrmata*), as had been the Greeks; comedians donned short tunics, covered by a *toga*, though this is uncertain. The colour of garments, too, signalled the age, class and frequently the occupation of the character: young men wore purple, old men were garbed in white, parasites in grey, courtesans flaunted themselves in garish yellow. *Scabilla* (taps) might be affixed to wooden soles to add resonance to the dancers' rhythmic steps.

The shape of the stage for which Plautus wrote, and after him Terence, discernibly influenced the structure and performance of their plays, apart from there always being "street scenes". Shallow in depth, the platform grew disproportionately wide, stretching to as much as 100 feet, or even 120 or 180. Often a character comments on the approach of another who is glimpsed at a distance – "I see old Publius coming" – to "cover" smoothly the newcomer's entrance, the time it takes him to reach mid-stage. Sometimes, too, the comedian resorted to a "treadmill" effect, a running in place, to enliven his arrival or departure. At the back, replacing the plain curtain (*siparium*) was a wooden shed, providing a dressing-room, and by Plautus' day the platform (*scaenae frons*) had angled side walls and a roof, also of wood. The back wall had three doors – later, two more were added at the side – through which the players could ceaselessly enter and exit. The busy, emphatically slammed doors were virtually extra characters of the play. Each of the three or five doors might represent a different house, the row of them creating the requisite street. Extending the image, windows were sometimes inserted in the back wall, through which the occupants of each dwelling could look down and loudly comment on the action or participate in it.

Livy relates that in 99 BC naturalistic scenes were painted on movable panels that were easily shifted about, and two decades later (79 BC), according to Vitruvius, the Roman historian of theatre architecture, the side walls too were embellished with relevant paintings, introduced by Lucius and Marcus Lucullus, brothers. The stage-setting was finally more flexible and realistic. A subsequent development – to quote from Berthold – was "a system of *periaktoi*, three-sided devices arranged in perspective sequence and revolving around a pivot, so that any one-third turn adapted them to the changeable background. . . . Virgil describes how on one occasion the *scaena* walls divided and at the same moment the *periaktoi* turned." Also: "In early days, an altar was erected on the left side of the stage with the statue of the god in whose honor the play was performed; at funeral games, there stood a statue of the departed instead." (This is the altar to which the guilty Tranio retreats for sanctuary from his master's fury in *The Haunted House* . . . an ingenious ploy by Plautus to resolve the confrontation.)

For a long time, all seating was forbidden: it was a resort looked on as more suitable to the effete Greeks. But many in the audience brought their own stools or squatted on the bare earth. Then, in a measure of relaxation of the law, the noble, the rich and the highest public officials were permitted to avail themselves of a semi-circle of benches. Entrance to the play was free; slaves could attend, but had to stand; women were relegated to the rear. Much theatrical skill and a constant reliance on on-stage physical action – all kinds of buffoonery – were needed to hold the crowd's interest. The music and dancing helped, though the dancing was not integrated into the plot. In prologues, and even in the dialogue, the author might include an appeal for silence, begging that babies and rambunctious older children be hushed or in the future left at home, or that the women cease their shrill gossip.

Acting styles for tragedians followed the most stately Greek traditions. Speech was slow, declamatory. Schools taught vocal projection, stance, dignified movement and significant gesture. For comedians, singing and dancing must be well mastered. In farces, talking had to be rapid, facial expressions – for those unmasked – and gestures exaggerated. A considerable vocabulary of such effects had to be learned, the right intonation for each emotion or dramatic situation, the most graphic use of hands or appropriate body attitude in response to a shock, threat, challenge or whatever.

A North African slave of obscure origin, Publius Terentius Afer, was Plautus' only notable successor. Born in Carthage about 184 BC – if so, the very year that Plautus died – Terence, as he is now designated, was somehow brought to Rome where his enlightened master, Terentius Lucanus, a senator, recognized "his beauty and his genius" – the phrase is Philip Whaley Harah's – educated him, and set him free. Like Ennius, the young slave had unusual verbal gifts, coupled with clear intelligence, rare sensitivity, a lively and creative imagination. To manifest his gratitude he took his generous patron's name for his own. Little else that is factual about him is available. Some put the date of his birth as early as 195 BC, which would add a decade to his short life.

In what way had he been enslaved – had he been a prisoner of war? But Rome and Carthage were not embattled at that period. Also in question is his race; coming from Carthage, he is assumed to have been a Phoenician. Was he black? Or had he at least some Negroid strain? His last name, Afer, means "African". Some suggest that he was a Berber, belonging to the Arabic-speaking Kabyle tribe that inhabits the Riff. He is often described as having been "dark" or "swarthy", but that is hardly definitive; it merely implies that his complexion's hue was a cause of comment. (The chief source about him is Suetonius [AD 70–121?], the historian, whose biography of Terence is in turn quoted by Donatus, who in the fourth century assayed the playwright's accomplishments.)

Overcoming the social stigma and practical handicaps of his rumoured lowly birth and initial slave status, the young man's personal charm and literary talent quickly won him wider friendships in a circle of Roman patricians, including Scipio Africanus the Younger, rich and scholarly, and the much-respected Gaius Laelius, both very influential, who encouraged their protégé to write, and perhaps even assisted him in the composition of his works. Of him it is said that one day he attended, "poor and meanly clad", a banquet at the house of Caecilius Status, the most successful comedy author of the day. He went there because the *aediles* wished to have the older, established writer pass judgement on work submitted by the young man. As was appropriate, the would-be dramatist was assigned a humble bench at the table's end. But once he rose and began to read aloud the first scene of his play-in-progress, *Andria*, he was invited to a place next to his host and asked to remain after the dinner, so that Caecilius, delighted, might hear the rest. They became good friends.

Gossip, perhaps nothing more than envious slander invented and spread by his older competitor Lucius Lanuvinus, persisted in asserting that Terence's doting patrons, the wealthy and aristocratic littérateurs, rather than the young man himself, actually wrote the half-dozen extant plays that bear his name, as well as those that have disappeared. Possibly his tact, the risk of offending important friends, kept the ex-slave long silent about this rumour; if they were the authors, he would not expose and embarrass them; nor would he imply that they were incapable of creating the stage-works. However, in the prologue to *The Brothers* he openly acknowledged the gossip, lightly turning aside the whispers, his evasion neat:

> A number of people who wish our author none too well are claiming that certain gentlemen of distinction have been helping him with his plays – in fact, writing line for line with him. They think that this is a serious accusation, but our author considers it the greatest compliment to be counted a friend of men who are much beloved by all of you and by all our nation. Every one of us has had occasion to accept their help, and without reserve, in time of war, and in affairs of business or state. [Translation: Frank O. Copley]

How to read that? The dates of Scipio – he was between eighteen and his early twenties, hence somewhat younger than Terence – make it unlikely that he was the ex-slave's literary helper, though he and Laelius assuredly each lent a hand in getting the plays brought to the stage. A few recommendations from them and others for improvements of the texts, what has come to be called "constructive criticism", would not be unlikely; most playwrights, at all times, feeling a need for a more objective appraisal, seek and obtain relevant opinions from close associates.

The climate of the circle in which he lived, the artistic refinement that its members prized, explains the patrician bias of his plays: Terence did not write for everybody but rather for the approval of a select few, the high-placed, sophisticated, powerful and cultivated, who aspired to raise the level of Roman taste, which certainly was never to be the equal of that of subjugated Greece. He wrote a polished Latin, a chaste, competent style which these littérateurs wished to promote. (His mastery of what was for him a second language has justly been likened to the novelist Joseph Conrad's remarkable facility with English, despite his being Polish-born and his reaching Great Britain only after the onset of his mid-maturity.) He disdained making concessions to plebeian appetites for vulgar fun; he avoids indecencies: as has been said by others, his is high comedy that seeks to evoke the appreciative smile rather than the loud belly laugh. He was adept at epigrams, some of the best of which are translated from the Greek rather than truly his own, but he chose perceptively. He does not mix Greek words and phrases with Latin ones, as did the always impatient, careless Plautus. But if much of his elegance reflects the demands of those around him – they were gripped by a passion for all forms of Greek art and a compulsive wish to emulate them – doubtless it is also an expression of his own temperament, qualities that had led those dedicated Roman aesthetes to single out and value him.

With experience, he grew highly skilled at dramatic structure, clarifying story-lines, keeping firm control of the plot, at times simplifying it and making it more compact; or else adding sub-plots – some of his own invention – to enlarge the elemental conflict, thereby also increasing complications and suspense, and shortening the prologue, since now he had less need for one. Menander was his chief inspiration – four of the surviving six scripts are borrowed from that poet's canon; the remaining two are appropriated from Apollodorus of Carystus, one of Menander's minor disciples. He followed his Athenian sources very carefully, keeping the Greek titles of the New Comedy works he adapted, making sure, as Plautus did not, that all the characters bore their original Greek names, and always placing his settings in Athens or at least a Greek town. He transposed nothing into a Roman milieu. In consequence, he termed himself – with undue modesty – a mere translator, but in fact his adherence to his Greek models was by no means slavish; his own contributions are far more than stylistic. (He had another reason for consistently hewing to Greek locales and characters; to have Romans behaving so knavishly, guilty of such gross misconduct, would have been dangerous for him, especially since he was alien-born.)

One of his tricks is to heighten characterization by contrast, and he develops his people far beyond the bare requirements of the plot, making them more rounded. He does away with intervention by the gods, a too easy resolution. He replaces Menander's long monologues with the give-and-take of dialogue, gradually minimizing asides and direct speech to the spectators, and often substitutes physical action for narrative passages. All speeches are relevant, and jokes are not inserted just to get laughs – everything is intended to have the story move speedily forward. Exits and entrances are well motivated. All these technical improvements have served as precedents and transitions to today's faster-paced comedies, which is why Terence's works are easier to revive now than those of Plautus, paradoxically since the earlier author, often colloquial and genuinely fond of horse-play, shrewdly elected to write in a manner of "lusty exuberance" far more suited to the stage.

But actual production, in the hurly-burly of the crude Roman theatre, was not really Terence's goal, except of course that it might abet his income. One of his works, *The Mother-in-Law* (*Hecyra*), failed when spectators were drawn off by a bear-fight near by – or, some say, the feats of a tightrope walker. A revival of the play soon afterwards lost out again, this time to a gladiatorial combat. He hated the noise, the inattention, the stupidity that typified the bulk of his audience. He much preferred to have his plays given private readings at the homes of discriminating patrons, where the grace of his metrically correct verse, his whimsical humour, his tender portraits of young girls, might be more sympathetically adjudged. Intimate theatres, for such readings, were being built in the villas of the rich, and in them Terence's works were to have devoted re-hearings.

Though well connected, Terence had much difficulty finding productions at the *ludi* for his too-quiet plays. All were put on by the same actor–manager, Ambivius Turpio; and the music for all six is believed to have been composed by a talented slave, which is what the more fortunate Terence himself had once been.

His first staged work – at least of those surviving – *The Woman of Andros* (*c.* 166 BC, *Andria*), initially won him neither fame nor fortune. He may have been only nineteen when he submitted it and had it accepted. He borrowed the plot from Menander's script of the same title and combined it with a scene from another of the Greek poet's pieces, *The Woman of Perinthia.* Criticized by a rival for doing this, he retorted in a very brief prologue that the precedent for it had been set by no less masters than Naevius and Ennius, as well as by Plautus. Besides, he states, Menander's *Woman of Andros* and *The Woman of Perinthia* have almost identical plots, differing only in "dialogue and in manner of treatment". So why should he be castigated for having inserted a scene from one into the other? He warns the fault-finder that in turn he himself might be charged with far greater errors.

Though it is only mildly and intermittently amusing, *The Woman of Andros* unfolds an interesting tale. The kindly, affectionate Simo is disturbed by the prospect that his hitherto dutiful son, Pamphilus, wishes to acknowledge parentage of an illegitimate child about to be born to Glycerium, a girl from Andros, and sister to the recently deceased courtesan Chrysis. Indeed, the enamoured Pamphilus considers himself "married" to Glycerium, even though she is not Roman but foreign-born. Simo intends that his son shall wed, instead, Philumena, the only daughter of his affluent neighbour, Chremes. Another young man, Charinus, a friend of Pamphilus, considers himself in love with Philumena. This secondary theme is Terence's addition. Davus, Simo's slave, is the unwitting mischief-maker who acts to help his young master, Pamphilus, extricate himself from his dilemma. The resulting confusions follow mostly from Davus' busy contrivances, all of which miscarry. A minor figure is the addle-pated midwife, Lesbia. The new-born baby is soon another factor in the mix-up. At the end Glycerium is revealed to be not the sister of the generous dead courtesan, but instead Chremes' long-lost daughter, Pasibula, presumed drowned at sea (again), so all the strands are tied up satisfactorily.

What is exceptional is not the plot, which is handled none too well – Terence had much to learn this early in his career – but the people, father and son, husband and wife, master and slave, friend and friend, all portrayed as good, tactful, with divided loyalties; in the instance of Simo and Pamphilus, an anxiety not to go beyond certain self-imposed limits in exerting paternal authority and expressing filial rebellion. Apparent here are a subtlety and dimensionality never evident in Plautus' farces. Father and son genuinely respect each other and are mutually fond. But lacking is the physical energy that possesses most Plautine characters, that prompts them to rush about obsessively, with ruthless aggression. This, and the absence of colloquial speech, may account for the play's pervasive blandness.

The young author is all too aware of the over-familiarity of his New Comedy plot and slyly makes a point of it. Davus, the clumsy but well-intentioned slave, reveals at the very beginning that the hero and heroine, frantic to enhance Glycerium's image and status, are trying to concoct some far-fetched story about her to pass her off as an Attic citizen. " 'Once upon a time there was an old man, a trader. He suffered shipwreck on the island of Andros; he died there.' Thereupon, they say, this girl was thrown up on the beach, and Chrysis' father took her in, poor little orphan! What a yarn! It doesn't ring true to me, but they like the story." At the climax, of course, this account proves to be factual in every detail, though neither Pamphilus nor Glycerium wholly realized it. The resolution is brought about by Crito, a kinsman of the late Chrysis; most opportunely he arrives from Andros to tell Glycerium that he is ready to settle any claim she might have to the estate left by Chrysis, which he believes is legally his – but he hopes to avoid litigation. He proves to be a long-time friend of Chremes and hence a highly creditable witness.

Oddly, the *women* of Andros never appear but are only referred to; Chrysis is no longer among the living, and Glycerium is suffering labour pains off-stage, whence her anguished cries are heard; nor is Charinus' beloved Philumena ever seen. Also, in this somewhat immature script, Terence is still employing frequent asides and soliloquies.

The Mother-in-Law (*Hecyra*), Terence's second play, had three productions until it was enacted in full and accounted a success. The first, in 165 BC, lost out, as has been mentioned above, when the competition of a bear-fight or tightrope walker proved too much for it. He alludes to this "unheard-of bad luck" in a prologue – of which only a fragment survives – to another attempt to put on the work in 160 BC, which also was disastrous and for almost the same reason: the audience left *en masse* in order to watch a match between teams of gladiators. But Terence and his producer were commendably persistent; a third try later in the same season prevailed at last. In the prologue, on this occasion, Terence begs: "Today there's no disturbance; everything is peaceful and quiet. I have the chance to stage this play: you have the opportunity to do honour to the theatre. Don't you be responsible for causing the near-disappearance of the art of the playwright; no, add your voice to mine in its encouragement and support." Speaking through the actor who delivers the prologue, he adds: "If I have never been greedy in setting a price on my talents, but have always firmly believed that my main job was to entertain you to the best of my ability, then grant me this favour." He tells the spectators that he has entrusted his life's interest to their sense of fair play. They should not let "captious critics irresponsibly hold him up to ridicule". The audience's courteous attention will encourage him and other poets to write plays, and actor–managers will find it worthwhile to buy and stage them. He speaks as might a playwright in any age.

The Mother-in-Law is taken from Apollodorus (300–260 BC) and there are also traces of Menander's *The Arbitration*, after whom Apollodorus often modelled his work. The usual ingredients are here, and specific details of the plot will be recognized by the reader of the earlier synopsis: a girl, Philumena, has been violated by a young man, Pamphilus, who later marries her, unaware that she is his victim. While he is on a journey, she bears a child; on his return, Pamphilus suspects her of infidelity, not knowing that he himself is the father; in consequence, a divorce impends. A novel feature here is a kindly courtesan, Bacchis, a former, long-time and serious partner in dalliance with the young man, who helps the hapless Philumena prove her guiltlessness, though doing so is hardly to the elder woman's own interest. The innocent butt of all the play's intrigue is Sostrata, the wife's mother-in-law, with whom the girl pretends to have squabbled as a pretext for returning next door to her parent's home, denying herself to visitors, while bearing her child in secret. Blamed by her husband, Laches, for breaking up their son's marriage, and caught in a dilemma by the divided loyalties of her son, the unlucky mother-in-law must suffer the reproaches of one and the protestations of the other until the end of the plot, when the truth comes out. In an off-stage recognition scene, the identity of Pamphilus' rape victim is finally proved by a token, a ring.

The picture of family life is remarkably warm and tender, and surprisingly modern. All the people are generous-spirited and discreet, and prompted by affection and a desire to have the young couple happily reunited. This is sentimental comedy, and the psychology in it grows ever more subtle. Actually there is little in the play to evoke outright laughter; humour would not seem to have been its principal aim. At best it is chucklesome. Once again, as in *The Woman of Andros*, a pivotal female character is never seen on stage, and for the same good reason: Philumena is busy having a child.

The Self-Tormentor (163 or 162 BC, *Heauton Timoroumenos*), derived from Menander, once again studies the father–son bond and the many difficulties of the relationship. In a witty prologue, Terence asserts that his adaptation is "completely faithful" to the Greek original. He had been accused by Lucius Lanuvinus of not having written the plays attributed to him and also of "contaminating" Menander's scripts, making changes in them, inserting scenes from his other plays. This is the prologue in which he couched his cogent response, not denying the charge but citing "excellent" precedents for what he has done. He adds that he will continue doing it. The speaker, the actor–manager Ambivius Turpio, also begs the spectators not to be noisy, as he is growing old and tired of having to shout loudly to be heard. He is also weary of forever being called upon for the most taxing roles: "the bustling slave, the bad-tempered old man, the greedy parasite, the shameless sycophant or the money-grabbing pimp". In brief, like actors everywhere, he objects to being type-cast. And: "If a play requires a lot of energy, they come rushing to me; if it's easy, they offer it to some other company."

Menedemus forbids his son Clinia to wed the girl he loves. After a bitter quarrel, the son is cast off, penniless; he becomes a soldier with Rome's legions in Asia. Remorseful, the elderly Menedemus withdraws to a farm to punish himself for having excessively chastised his son and virtually seeks to work himself to death. He spurns help, wanting to save his money to requite the absent Clinia. A neighbour, Chremes, also elderly, observes his friend's self-destructive toil and ventures words of warning. He is told to mind his own affairs. Chremes replies: "I am a man; I consider nothing human alien to me." (It is said that this line, ever since very widely quoted, was immediately hailed with appreciation and applause by its first Roman audience.) Menedemus, pressed, blurts out why he is obsessed by guilt. "I have an only son – just a boy, he is. What did I say? I *have* a son? I should say, I *had* one, Chremes. I don't know whether I *have* one or not." He spells out the nature of the quarrel. Chremes says Menedemus' fault was a lack of trust in his son and obviously no openness between parent and child. Menedemus sadly concurs.

At the Feast of Dionysus, held in Chremes' house, *his* son, Clitipho, brings a guest, Clinia, a chum from childhood, home from his travels and met by chance. Chremes is not aware that Clitipho, his own son, is full of rebellion against *him.* Chremes' belief is that parents have a duty to rein in their young to teach them decent conduct: not to drink, waste money, chase after women. Clitipho complains: "Fathers are so unjust! They don't understand young people at all! They think we ought to start being old men the minute we stop being boys. . . . They set up the rules by the way they feel now, not by the way they used to feel when they were our age." He stresses, too, the importance of frankness between father and son, and exclaims how rare it is. Chremes, overly stern, is not practising what he preaches. And Clitipho vows that if ever he has a son of his own, he'll treat him more wisely.

The complications get under way when Clinia and Clitipho, guided by the latter's scheming slave Syrus, seek to marry young ladies of their choice. Clinia pretends to woo the frivolous, mercenary Bacchis, the courtesan of whom Clitipho is enamoured. The plan goes awry. The wary fathers combine to outwit the sons; the sons are in collusion to deceive their fathers; all with the best intentions. The "generation gap" in ancient Greece and Rome is beautifully illustrated. At moments the plot becomes so involved that it is hard to keep up with it. Antiphila, beloved of Clinia, turns out to be Clitipho's sister, believed dead (an unwanted daughter, as an infant she was given away to an old lady from Corinth who died and foolishly left her in the care of the business-minded Bacchis, to whom the old lady was in debt for 1,000 drachmas – the girl was being held as "security"; none the less, she has preserved her virtue. As the story progresses the fathers reverse their roles: Menedemus lectures and helps Chremes, much as his elderly neighbour had earlier harangued and assisted him.

Eventually, a reconciliation is arrived at all around; Clinia marries his Antiphila with everybody's blessing, and the irresponsible Clitipho gives up the idea of keeping the courtesan of Bacchis and dutifully consents to a match with a respectable girl, from a wealthy family, chosen for him by his much concerned mother and father.

Once more the humour is gentle, rather than uproarious, and the outstanding aspect of the play is the author's nice feeling for character, the rounded portraits; its people have many shifting moods and are ambivalent at times, yet are truly appealing. With this work Terence won himself a success at the *ludi* and now a measure of popularity.

More boisterous by far is *The Eunuch* (161 BC), the most purely farcical of Terence's half-dozen known works; its source is Menander's *The Parasite*. Terence was not aware, or so he asserts in his very short prologue, that both Naevius and Plautus had previously done Latin versions of the same play, each of them retaining the title used by Menander. Accused by his spiteful rival Lucius Lanuvinus of outright theft, Terence retorted in a phrase destined to echo through the ages: "Nothing is said today that hasn't been said before." The unflattering truth is, however, that Terence "lifted" two of his principal characters from the earlier adaptations by Naevius and Plautus; the pair are Thraso, a braggart warrior, and Gnatho, an ingratiating fawner. In his defence, he states that the play is wholly filled with stock characters from Greek New Comedy, as are other contemporary works in which are usually found – in his own words – "the hustling slave, the worthy matron, the wily courtesan, the suppositious child, the master tricked by his slave"; and what is the harm in his borrowing two more of them? After that, he pleads for silence from the audience, as had become his habit, so that *The Eunuch* might be "understood and enjoyed".

A bold young lad of good family, Chaerea, falls in love at first sight with Pamphila, a pretty slave-girl. Though only sixteen, the precocious youth disguises himself as a eunuch, and is set to guard her, but instead while she is asleep falls upon her and rapes her. This is done at the suggestion of Parmeno, his elder brother's unscrupulous, manipulative slave. A real eunuch is charged with the deed, to his bewilderment, but after a beating is finally exculpated. The defiled girl turns out to be free-born, which means that the delighted Chaerea might marry her. His father is quickly persuaded to give consent when a slave-woman, Pythias, tricks him into fearing that Chaerea is about to be castrated for his crime. It has been emphasized that marriage is the most frequent conclusion to a Terentian play; such "moral rectitude" is a mark of his work.

But the youngsters are minor figures in the noisy, fast-moving action which circles around the tangled schemes of Thais, a courtesan who is seeking to protect and restore to her rightful estate the virginal younger girl; the plans of Parmeno, the familiar intriguer; and those of Thraso, the cowardly and slow-witted boaster who is wooing Thais with bounteous gifts; and the hopes of Phaedria, Chaerea's elder brother, who is also madly enamoured of the well-meaning but artful courtesan. (By now it is salient how favourably and sympathetically Terence tends to depict courtesans and slave-girls – having himself belonged to the slave class, he both appreciated their plight and seems to have dedicated himself to propagandize on their behalf.) To win Thais, Thraso has purchased Pamphila from her avaricious uncle, after she has been kidnapped and orphaned by pirates; and with the same aim the infatuated Phaedria has obtained the old eunuch Dorus to serve in Thais' establishment. Which of her two lovers shall Thais choose? She elects to keep both, with their mutual consent, sleeping with Phaedria while Thraso, living in the same house, foots the bills. This ending might seem overly cynical, hardly an example of "moral rectitude" unless it is seen in its social context, belonging to a day in which the impetuous sexual adventures of young men before marriage might well be viewed with amused tolerance.

The play is rowdy, and far more outspoken than most of Terence's work, yet one imagines that in the earlier version by the lusty Plautus its treatment was decidedly more gross. It has inspired a host of imitations, including William Wycherly's *The Country Wife*, one of England's best-known comedies, which borrows the basic idea (though little more) of this Latin adaptation of a third-century Greek farce. Good jokes, like this one, are told over and over; they are never exhausted.

The superiority of Terence – and, of course, the play's originator Menander – shows itself in several astute speeches about the nature of infatuation; the psychology of unhappy and jealous lovers is exactly described, with Thraso and Phaedria as instances, and the realist Parmeno serving as shrewd diagnostician.

The most liked of Terence's works, *Phormio* (161 BC), owes its plot to another of Apollodorus' scripts, *The Litigant*. Copley, whose clear and lively English translations are used throughout this passage, remarks: "It contains all the elements that we regard as characteristic of Roman comedy: love intrigue; mild social satire; rapid, witty dialogue; and restrained but still delightful humour. The stock characters are all there." He might have added that it also brings together and employs all the most-used situations and effective turns of story. Yet it is marked by a surprising freshness which accretes from its always deft verbal shafts, its well-paced development – incident following incident plausibly, and the construction always lucid. Terence changes the title of the play and names it after a devilishly clever parasite, Phormio, who is the mainspring not only of this farce but the model of a vital line of resourceful parasites and intrigues that culminates in Jonson's Mosca, Molière's Scapin, Beaumarchais' Figaro, and their many quick-thinking, sharp-dealing successors.

While rich, old Demipho is away on a business journey, his impulsive son Antipho falls in love with Phanium, a poor but respectable Athenian girl who has lost her parents and has no dowry. Indeed, she does not even know who her father was. A man-about-town, Phormio, concocts a scheme: he goes to court on Antipho's behalf, presenting himself as a witness, claiming that since Phanium is a cousin and a penniless orphan, Antipho, her next of kin, is obliged by law to marry her. The eager

Antipho, questioned, assents: the marriage is consummated. But now the young man begins to fear the consequence when his father comes back. Demipho, returned, is enraged to discover what has happened. He sends for Phormio, and loudly denounces him, for Phanium is most certainly not a relative. He offers Phormio a bribe to get rid of her. Finally agreeing to help, after feigning reluctance, Phormio perceives how he can extract a good-sized sum from the old man. He proposes to have Antipho's marriage annulled; then he himself will wed Phanium, with Demipho providing the dowry. He does not really intend to do any of this; it is just a way of fleecing the old man.

The subplot concerns Phaedria, Demipho's nephew, who wishes to purchase a lute-girl, but he must raise 3,000 drachmas, as she is about to be sold to another. He has only a short time in which to find the money.

Phaedria's father, Chremes, brother of Demipho, is a bigamist, heading two families, the second on the island of Lemnos, neither one knowing about the other. He, too, has been away from Athens on an errand, to sell a piece of property belonging to Nausistrata, his first wife, the lawful one; but while pursuing this task he revisits Lemnos and learns that his long-abandoned second wife is dead and has left a daughter for whom he begins a search. An old nurse, Sophrona, gives him a clue to the girl's whereabouts. Of course she is none other than the supposedly parentless Phanium, and he is naturally pleased to be apprised, in his re-arrival in Athens, that she is married to Antipho, his nephew; the two young people actually *are* cousins. He is anxious, however, to conceal this fact from the sharp-tongued Nausistrata, who in general makes his days at home ceaselessly miserable. He does confide in his brother, Demipho, and is told of the bribe paid to Phormio, who has stated that in order to marry Phanium he must pay reparations to another young woman to whom he has pledged his hand – a fiction created by the greedy parasite. With Demipho's knowledge of Phanium's true identity, the situation is greatly changed; Phormio's intervention is no longer needed. He is in no hurry to return the 6,000 drachmas that he has extorted from the two conniving old men; Chremes has contributed a share of the payment. When they insist on recouping the money, he threatens to expose Chremes' guilty secret to the termagant Nausistrata. Intimidated, they yield; then appalled at being blackmailed, they retract and again resist him. Annoyed and impatient, Phormio does tell Nausistrata about her husband's having had an extra family on Lemnos. She takes the news with surprising calm, partly because Demipho offers an explanation of his brother's misconduct:

> It wasn't, you know, because he'd lost interest in you or didn't love you any more. He had too much to drink once, about fifteen years ago, and forced some poor young woman, and the girl here was the

result. He never had anything to do with her after that. The woman is dead; she's passed away, and she was the one thing that would have caused difficulties here. So please be reasonable – just as you always are.

Her response:

Be reasonable? Well! I'd like to be sure that this will be the end of it! But why should I think so? Am I supposed to believe that as he gets older he'll behave himself better? Look at me, Demipho. Am I getting any prettier or any younger? What reason can you give me for expecting, or even hoping, that he will ever be any different?

She is not deceived by Demipho's gloss of Chremes' shameful deeds.

Have you ever heard anything worse? You men! But when it comes to your wives, you're "too tired"! Demipho, I appeal to you; I'm sick of talking to him. Was this why he had to make all those trips to Lemnos and stay there so long? Are these those "poor business conditions" that kept my income down?

Demipho continues to seek forgiveness for the errant Chremes. Phormio informs them that he has given Phaedria the 3,000 drachmas to buy the flute-girl whom he so ardently desires. Chremes, whose money it was, strongly objects. But Nausistrata concurs:

Well! Does that seem so awful to you, Chremes, if your son, who's a young man, has one mistress, while you have had two wives? Completely shameless, that's what you are! How will you have the audacity to say anything to him about it? Just answer me that.

Nor will she forgive Chremes.

Phormio asks a favour: Will she invite him to dinner? As a further rebuke to her husband and her brother-in-law, she promptly does so.

This is only a simple outline of an intricate play which has many other strands, some of them woven by Geta and Davus, slaves of Chremes and Demipho, who also serve as expositors of much of the complicated action while passing moral judgements on the characters.

Once more a feminine participant is unseen, Phanium. Perhaps Terence sought to have some of his people talked about but not appear in order to keep his cast small, as a measure of economy; or else he was not keen on having many young women's roles: they are usually described as irresistibly beautiful and would have to be enacted by boys and young men of whom a satisfactory number might not be available.

As said before, the best portrait is that of the high-living, urbane Phormio who pays tribute to his fine life as a "parasite": "Just think, you don't have to have a penny, but here you come all fresh and clean from the baths, not a worry in the world, while he (your host) fumes and frets over expenses. Just to see that you have a good time, he pays the bill. You're supposed to get first choice of the food and drinks. They put a wonder-dinner in front of you." He explains to Geta what a "wonder-dinner" is. "Why, a dinner where you wonder what to take first."

Presumably *The Brothers* (160 BC) is Terence's last script. Largely derived from Menander's *Adelphoi*, it also includes one scene from Diphilus' *Companions in Death* (*Synapotheskontes*), a train of action omitted by Plautus in an earlier version of Diphilus' work. Terence comments in his prologue that he has translated this incident "word for word", though Plautus had found it uninteresting. He asks the spectators to judge for themselves whether he has been guilty of plagiarism in doing so. The restored episode describes how a young man forcibly rescues a slave-girl who is being mistreated by a pimp. As usual, in his prologue Terence discusses matters other than the plot, which he allows to develop without clarification in advance.

The brothers in this play are Demea, a farmer, and his wealthy sibling, the unmarried Micio, who laments being childless, while Demea has two sons, Ctesipho and Aeschinus, the younger, second brace of brothers. Micio, who has money and much affection to offer, is permitted to adopt and raise Aeschinus. Demea and Micio have very different beliefs about how the young should be trained. Demea is austere, rigid. He forces Ctesipho to toe the mark at every moment and is greatly pleased with the tractable youth, who works hard, saves his wages and does not drink. Micio, on the other hand, is highly indulgent and grants the adopted Aeschinus a totally free rein. Explains Micio:

> He's my pride and joy – the only thing in life I really care about. And I do everything I can, too, to make him feel the same way about me. I give and forgive; I don't feel that I have to exert my full authority over him. Then, too, there are things that most young fellows try to keep from their fathers – the "boys-will-be-boys" kind of thing – but I've taught my son to tell me everything. Because if a boy gets in the habit of lying or deceiving his father, he'll be all the more likely to try it with other people. I think it's better to discipline children by developing their sense of decency and their gentlemanly

instincts, than by making them fear authority. My brother doesn't agree with me in this; in fact, he doesn't like it at all. He keeps coming to me and scolding at me: "What are you doing, Micio? What do you mean by ruining our young man? Why is he getting involved with these women and these drinking parties? Why do you give him money for things like that? Why do you buy him those expensive clothes? You must be out of your mind!" Well, now, Demea himself is much too strict, quite unreasonably so. In my opinion he's completely wrong in thinking that paternal authority based on force will carry more weight than authority that grows out of love. Here's what I think, and I'm convinced that I'm right. The man who behaves well because he's afraid of being punished does so only as long as he thinks he may be caught. If he thinks he can go undiscovered, he reverts to his natural tendencies. The man whose devotion you've won out of kindness acts out of conviction. He's anxious to give as much as he's received, and he's always the same, whether or not you're there. A father's job is to train his son to do the right things as a matter of course rather than through fear – in fact, that's the difference between a father and a master. A man who can't do this had better admit he doesn't know how to handle children.

The play opens with a report of scandalous behaviour by Aeschinus: he has broken into the house of Sannio, a procurer, and carried off a slave-girl, Bacchis, now returned, whom he is very anxious to purchase. Actually, he is guiltless of the break-in; he is covering up for his roistering brother Ctesipho, who is finally rebelling against the long restraints laid on him by his father, and is in town on a protracted spree. What is more, Aeschinus is going to great lengths to help his brother assemble the 4,000 drachmas required to buy Bacchis. He is assisted in his ruses and money-raising schemes by a trio of busy slaves, Syrus, Parmeno and Geta.

For his own part, Aeschinus has made pregnant a respectable young free-woman, Pamphila. When this unhappy young lady hears of Aeschinus' purported housebreaking and pursuit of the slave-girl, she believes herself abandoned by him and, with her mother, bewails her sorry plight.

Demea, learning that his "model" son is on the loose in the city, leaves behind the farm and frantically sets out in search of him, while the two young men try to conceal their joint enterprise from him and the more tolerant Micio. Demea is misled by Syrus, Micio's ranking slave, who sustains the fiction that Aeschinus is no longer interested in Pamphila, the unhappy girl experiencing the pains of childbirth, but has instead turned his energies to obtaining Bacchis, the flute-girl. The father is told that Ctesipho has gone back to the farm and to his chores there. Demea discovers that this is untrue; his runaway son is still engaged in pleasure-seeking.

Micio hears what is happening. Encountering Aeschinus, he teases him, pretending to believe the account of his misconduct, and beholds him utterly contrite. Hesitantly, he grants Aeschinus permission to wed Pamphila and offers to keep Bacchis under the protection of his house. When Demea is told of this, he is appalled and declares that his brother is "raving mad". Micio admits that he is not happy about Aeschinus' choice of a wife. "If I could change it, I would; but since I can't, I'm simply taking it in my stride. The life of human beings is just like shooting dice. If you don't get the throw you'd like best, then you've got to use your brains and make good on what *does* come your way." Demea simply cannot understand this. To him, his brother's attitude is utter lunacy.

Micio's responses to the behaviour of others are governed by his peculiar theory about human nature.

> In any individual, Demea, there are lots of signs that tell us what he's really like. As a result, when two people perform the same act, it's often quite possible to say that one of them can be permitted to do it and the other can't, not because the act is different but because the people are. Now, in our two boys I see lots of reasons for being confident that they'll turn out as we want them to. I see common sense, intelligence, a sense of propriety, mutual affection – anybody would know that they are fine, well-educated boys. Any time you want to tighten the reins on them, you can.

Yes, he admits, they are careless with money. What of it? "Demea, old fellow – in all other respects we get wiser as we get older; there's just one bad trait old age brings to us; we worry entirely too much about money. Time will make the boys quite sharp enough about that." Micio proposes that he will lay out whatever is necessary to indulge the young men, while Demea should continue to pile up a fortune to provide them legacies. Persuaded, Demea acquiesces to Ctesipho's keeping the flute-girl, but predicts that her life on the farm will not match what she is accustomed to: "She'll be covered with soot and smoke and flour, because I'm going to set her to cooking and grinding grain. On top of that, I'll send her out to gather straw; I'll make her as hard and dry and black as a piece of charcoal." Micio is amused: "Good. Now you're showing sense. And I have one further suggestion: Make the boy go to bed with her even when he doesn't feel like it."

However, Demea is now determined to win his sons' affections: he is aware that both of them resent him and are exceedingly fond of the easy-going Micio. Thereupon the old farmer sets out to change his ways, greeting everybody in a friendly manner, spending whatever is needed. He begins by speaking courteously to his slaves. He discovers that he can quickly gain favour by proposing a costly wedding for Aeschinus and Pamphila, to be paid for by Micio. Somewhat taken aback, Micio is forced to assent.

Demea also suggests that Micio marry Pamphila's husbandless mother. Aeschinus endorses this idea. After much pressure and cajoling, Micio meekly capitulates, even though he does not know the lady.

Then Demea gets Micio to give away some land and even free two of his slaves, reminding him of "what you were saying a while ago, so wisely and so well: 'It's a very common failing among men to become too interested in money when we get old.'" In an aside, he adds: "I'm cutting his throat with his own knife."

Demea closes the play with a little sermon of the fault of self-indulgence and the virtue of thrift. Aeschinus is brought to agree, promising to submit to Demea's wisdom in the future.

(A noticeable feature of these six plays is the repetitious use of names for the characters, among them Chremes, Sostrata, Bacchis, Davus, Geta, Phaedria, Pamphila. In doing this Terence was carrying out a Greek tradition.)

Philip Whaley Harsh writes:

> *The Brothers* is a brilliant exposition of one of life's most perplexing problems. "Every father is a fool," says a fragment of Menander, and a German proverb runs: *Vater werden ist nicht schwer, Vater sein aber sehr.* ("To become a father is no weighty task, but to be one is – very.") The urbane and spineless Micio at the opening of the play is a firm believer in modern education with no fear and no discipline; love and trust are sufficient. The boorish Demea is equally convinced of the need of old-fashioned severity and suppression. These ideas are dramatically illustrated by their results: the resourceful young Aeschinus, who loves Micio but is deplorably inconsiderate of him and of others, and the profligate Ctesipho, whose feelings for Demea are hardly more than respectful hatred, born of fear and frustration. Portrayal of character by contrast is extended even to the slaves: the clever Syrian and the plodding Nordic (Geta). Here, especially, character is elaborated for its own appeal and beyond the requirements of the plot. But throughout, not the external action – though the two plots are skillfully maneuvered – but the characters are the main concern. This is high comedy at its best. Incidentally, this play gives a charming view of the cultured sophistication of Athens.
>
> True, soliloquies are repeatedly used to expand the portrayal of the main characters. From these and from Micio's overconfidence and Demea's futile busyness it is clear that both fathers have blundered and must in the end abandon their prejudices and compromise. Demea is the first to recognize

his error, and he changes with a vengeance – a vengeance on Micio, who cannot say "no" to anything, even marriage in old age.

Somewhat different is Sandbach's appraisal of the play's ambiguous ending. Synopsizing the plot, he concludes:

> In the last act this martinet (Demea) declares in a monologue that he sees that indulgence is the way to win popularity and that he will adopt that course for the brief spell of life that is left him. He proceeds in some amusing scenes to practise a new-found affability and generosity, not at his own expense but at that of his brother, whom he provides with a widow as his wife. In Terence's play the permissive parent feebly resists, but is so accustomed to letting people have their way that he has to accept this bride. Donatus remarks that in Menander he raised an objection to the marriage, and if he did not resist this, the heaviest of all the demands made on him, it is unlikely that he made difficulties about any of the others, none of which are unreasonable. In Terence, his ineffective objections are designed to show a lack of will.
>
> Finally his brother says that the object of his apparent change of character was to show that the other's popularity did not depend on what was right and good and a true way of life, but on complaisance and indulgence. He offers himself as one with the knowledge to reprehend, correct, and where suitable to support the young; thereupon the permissively educated son declares that he will accept his guidance. Although Molière, Lessing and Goethe all felt that this ending was wrong, orthodoxy interprets it as supporting the view that the right form of education is a mean between the strict and the permissive. However much this may appeal to those who subscribe to that view, I do not believe that this was the play's intended message. The reason for the martinet's change of front must be given by the monologue; it was to win popularity. It is a dramatic necessity that the speaker of the monologue utters what he believes to be the truth. What he here says is quite inconsistent with putting on an act for a short time with the intention of exposing the weakness of his brother's way of life. It follows that Terence has altered the balance at the end of the play, to bring down the scales on the side of the man whose stern hard-working parsimonious austerity accorded more with Roman ideals than did his easy-going life-enjoying brother.

The thoughtful tone of Terence's comedies, which anticipate Molière's best works, is well evidenced by the long semi-philosophical speeches and arguments in *The Brothers.* Though at moments a farce, overall it is a rather sober work. Subsequent plays inspired by it are Molière's *School for Husbands* and Fielding's *The Fathers.*

In his many sketches of well-to-do young men like the heirs of Demea, who seem to be mostly hedonistic drinkers and wenchers, Terence usually portrays them as weak cadgers, and not very bright, though physically able and attractive, with many pleasant traits. Even though he borrows them from the Greek authors whom he faithfully "translated", it is significant that he selects only those plays in which the young men are presented in this fashion. Whether this represents a shrewd and critical appraisal of the young men-about-town he observed in the aristocratic Roman society he was lucky enough to have penetrated, or whether it betrays a touch of natural envy and resentment on the part of an impoverished former slave, is open to conjecture.

The facts about Terence's early death are as uncertain as those about the date and place of his birth and about his racial strain. In 159 BC, stung by his rival's repeated charge against him of plagiarism, he set sail for Athens, wishing to acquaint himself further with the works of Menander and other Greek playwrights and also to prepare some original scripts, at a distance where he could not be suspected in the least of having been helped in their composition by his two high-ranked patrons and friends. On the voyage home to Italy the vessel was storm-tossed and sank, its passengers sharing the fate of the many journeyers often alluded to in his plays. Some legends have him drowned then, others have it that his manuscripts, of which there were a large number, were lost in the angry sea, the mishap causing his health to decline until he died of heartbreak. By most accounts he was only thirty, by others thirty-five or thirty-six.

Writing about him later, Julius Caesar paid tribute to his considerable achievement but estimated him as only a "half-Menander". Since we lack more of the Greek poet's work, the fairness of this comment cannot be judged; but the extant texts of Terence are far superior to the fragments that remain of Menander's writings. Cicero and Horace held him in the highest esteem. The beauty of his Latin style had a lasting influence on subsequent Roman writers. He kept his comedies free of cheapness and coarse appeal, a fastidiousness of taste that may explain why in the Middle Ages even cloistered nuns had very little hesitance about translating and adapting them, one of the most venturesome being Hrosvitha, Abbess of Gandersheim, who in the tenth century AD let the members of her community act in works somewhat modelled on his. (The good lady did deplore the "lasciviousness" of his heroines, most of whom – as has been remarked – are ceaselessly talked about but remain unseen. Terence was able to give them more imputed freedom of action, because of the altered role of Roman young women, who were not kept shut in as had been Greek girls of good family. Here he introduces a new kind of "love interest" that will appear in comedy ever after. His heroines are reckless, impulsive, have pre-marital affairs and bear illegitimate children, some as the unwanted consequence of their walking out alone or going by themselves to parties and being raped.) Later, in Elizabethan England, he was much read, admired and copied. He excels in irony and ever fresh psychological insight. Even more important is that his craftsmanship, which steadily improved, was to set enduring standards for farce.

The Romans' greatest artistic talent was for architecture. Eventually the stages were roofed, and the theatres built of stone; they were comparatively small but soon grew in size, and in time became immense. The first of these, at the direction of Pompey, the general and triumvir, was erected in 55–22 BC and was copied throughout the vast domain. The Greek theatre in Lesbos inspired him. The Roman prototype rose at the southern flank of the Campus Martius, where remnants of it are to be seen. The law against such edifices still prevailed, so Pompey concealed his purpose: avowing that he wished to celebrate a military victory, he incorporated a high-gabled shrine in the building and boldly designated it a Temple of Venus. It consisted of rows of semi-circular benches or seats – the *cavea* – with all seats affording a full view. The stage was low, seldom elevated more than 5 feet; it had also been deepened considerably, its dimensions about 20 by 100 feet. Pompey explained that the tiers of benches, divided by two broad aisles, were steps leading to the goddess's image, but no one took this description seriously. The orchestra, semi-circular, too, was paved but reduced in size and on occasion was adapted to permit extra seating. The back wall was pierced by large centre doors and there were doors at either side of the playing area, and steps led from the stage to the floor of the viewing space. A significant change was that stage and auditorium were now more closely integrated. Overhead was a colonnaded gallery lined with sculptures. A great deal of money was lavished on the outer structure which was adorned with reliefs; and the *frons scaenae*, or back wall of the stage, was similarly ornate. The audience was dispersed through arched tunnels appropriately called *vomitorii.*

Several of the temporary theatres that shortly preceded or followed the permanent one put up by Pompey were also elaborate. Writes Brockett:

> In 99 BC Claudius Pulcher is said to have erected a theatre with such realistically painted details that birds tried to perch on them. Pliny (AD 23–79) states that Marcus Aemilius Scaurus built a theatre in 58 BC with a stage of three stories, the first of marble, the second of glass, and the third of gilded wood, the whole being decorated with 360 columns and 3,000 bronze statues; the auditorium supposedly accommodated 80,000 persons. Pliny also states that in 50 BC, Gaius Sribonius Curio built two theatres back

to back, each on a pivot; while the audience remained seated, the two parts supposedly revolved to form an amphitheatre. Although modern historians seriously question his reliability, Pliny's accounts are indicative of structures sufficiently unusual and sumptuous to have become legendary by Pliny's time.

(Various explanations are given for the long-lived official edict against permanent theatres. Brockett summarizes a pair of possibilities: "Unlike the early Greeks, the Romans presented plays in honor of many gods, each of whom had his own sacred precinct in which it was considered unsuitable to dedicate offerings to any other god." To erect a theatre celebrating only one god might give offence to all others in the thronging pantheon, and therefore too many such edifices would be required if each precinct paying tribute to and watched over by its special deity had one, all of which would be very costly. Brockett says this interpretation may be correct, but adds: "On the other hand, there was always a group in Rome who objected to theatrical performances. Some historians believe that it was a concession to this group that no permanent theatres were erected prior to 55 BC.")

Pompey's motivation may have been a desire to enhance his prestige over that of the Senate and that of the *curule aediles*. He was successful at that, but soon grandiose theatres began to proliferate. One of Julius Caesar's acts, after coming to power and superseding Pompey, was to send his "friend" Brutus to Naples to hire "Dionysiac artists" for appearances on Rome's expanding stages. The dictator also ordered the construction of a new and larger stone theatre to outrival Pompey's. Situated below the Capitoline Hill, near the Tiber, it was incomplete when the ruler was struck down by conspirators, to die at the very foot of Pompey's statue.

This edifice was rounded off in 13 BC by Caesar's nephew, Augustus, founder of the dynasty that was to reign in the Roman Empire for many generations. Just two years earlier, the consul and inordinately rich capitalist Lucius Cornelius Balbus had initiated a second stone theatre bearing his name; a few fragmentary remains of it are preserved along the Via del Fianto, not far from the Palazzo Cenci.

Sited on the foundations laid by command of the murdered Caesar, the Theatre of Marcellus – so called by Augustus in memory of a young nephew – was larger than those of Pompey and Balbus and could hold 20,000 spectators; its outer walls, still vertical, suggest what must have been its original monumentality and splendour.

In AD 80, during the reign of Vespasian, and eight years abuilding, the Colosseum – which also functioned as a theatre – provided an arena for games and huge spectacles, selected by the Roman populace as its most satisfying forms of entertainment, with most performances customarily presided over the Emperor himself.

The basic pattern was established by these four great theatres and lent itself to borrowing by others on a smaller scale, mostly in the second century AD; a host of replicas arose in cities throughout the Empire: in Italy at Herculaneum, Pompeii, Ostia, Aosta, Falerii and Ferentum; and also along the North African coast, as in Sabratha in Libya; across the Mediterranean in Spain and southern France; and further off in Asia Minor, in places like Jerash and Petra (in what is now Jordan). In many instances they were first built to entertain Roman occupation troops. The first century structures in Libya seated 5,000. It is said that no fewer than 125 such permanent theatres were erected, some retaining the basic Greek style, some in the architecturally new Roman idiom. In addition, the still standing Greek theatres everywhere were rehabilitated, their façades often flamboyantly embellished with statues in niches, enriched columns, architraves, cornices and friezes with bas reliefs. Even the hallowed Theatre of Dionysus at Athens was remodelled by Nero. An impressive number of these open-air theatres, enduring though in partial ruin, are even now utilized for special occasions: operas, ballets and the like, as at Arles and Orange, in France; and Syracuse, in Sicily.

Lacking the beautiful simplicity of Greek architecture, the Roman theatre was nevertheless impressive, partly because marble, gilded wood and glass were the building materials, as in earlier efforts. Many were on level sites rather than hillsides. To spare the spectators from the sun, bright-tinted awnings (vela) with paintings on them were spread over the whole *cavea*, and the stale humid air was cooled by slaves who moved along the aisles spraying rosewater over the perspiring crowd. A degree of "air-conditioning" was also achieved by conduits through which flowed small streams of cold water.

The stage machinery was ingenious, and for the first time in theatrical history a front curtain (*auleum*) makes its appearance, but it did not fall from above, or draw apart, but instead sank in a recess near the edge of the forestage, from which it later rose again; it was fancifully embroidered. At first, when theatres were roofless, productions were given by daylight; but it is believed that torches and lamps lit the stages of the subsequent, fully enclosed playhouses, at least for special events, as a novelty.

Much information about these vast, splendid structures has been preserved in a ten-volume book by Marcus Vitruvius Pollio (first century BC), *De Architecture*, which contains detailed designs for the theatre he envisioned as the ideal one. The ruins themselves, especially a small one at Pompeii, seating 1,500 spectators, give other clues to the typical layout of the interior and the look of the exterior.

It is not clear to what extent scenery was simply painted on the back curtain – a street of houses, for a comedy – or on a revolving *periaktoi*, which differentiated locales, or whether there were added solid pieces, three-dimensional representations that could be shifted about as required. The action in a tragedy usually took place before a handsome palace or stately temple, and a permanent set depicting one or the other could suffice for any number of dramas. The same might be true for comedies. Brockett suggests: "There was probably little attempt to change the visual appearance of the stage from one play to another. As the Prologue of *The Menaechmi* says: 'This city is Epidammus during the performance of this play; when another play is performed it will become another city.' The audience probably depended primarily upon the dramatists' words to locate the action." That would apply to works by Plautus and Terence. Later Brockett quotes from Vitruvius, writing about 15 BC, about how a tragedy might be presented: "The *scaena* itself displays the following scheme. In the center are double doors, decorated like those of a royal palace. At the right and left are doors to the guest chambers." On the *periaktoi*, he says, are three decorated faces. "There are three kinds of scenes, one called the tragic, second, the comic, third, the satyric. Their decorations are different and unlike each other in scheme. Tragic scenes are delineated with columns, pediments, statues and other objects suited to kings; comic scenes exhibit private dwellings, with balconies and views representing rows of windows, after the manner of ordinary dwellings; satyric scenes are decorated with trees, caverns, mountains, and other rustic objects, delineated in landscape style." The exact meaning of this last phrase has caused much academic debate, with no precise determination of what Vitruvius might be describing. Roman painting is traditionally schematic and delicate, and it would seem that the scenery was similarly impressionistic, highly conventionalized, with scant attempt at realism.

When spectacle became more important than the story and verse, the stage set became a larger element. Usually the front curtain was lowered out of sight beneath the platform before the spectators arrived, so that the actors had to take their places in full view; but after the second century AD the curtain, now suspended from overhead, concealed the scene and was raised by pulleys only when the action of the play began; this allowed the audience to be surprised by the abrupt revelation of striking effects, which increasingly Roman theatregoers demanded.

The effects throughout the play might be compelling, even overwhelming; the emphasis was on pageantry. Cicero comments disparagingly on a production of Accius' *Clytemnestra*, given during the inaugural season of the Theatre of Pompey, where no less than six hundred mules were herded across the stage. He also objected to the display of three thousand bowls in a vanished drama titled *The Trojan Horse*. (Much of this stress on spectacle came from the plays being performed to celebrate an important military triumph, when it was customary for the victor to parade boastfully in view of the audience with his booty, including files of captive monarchs and clusters of defeated, chained enemy soldiers, all now destined to become slaves. Since most of the plays were not good or sturdy enough to stand on their own, these visual adornments were helpful additions to them.)

In Corinth, for one especially elaborate and grandiose ballet, the climactic scene had a fountain atop "Mount Ida" spurting not volcanic flames and ashes but a strong perfume, over a stage populated with animals, live trees, a stream, plants and shrubs, until at the end the mountain itself sank beneath the horizon – the subject of the ballet was the *Judgment of Paris*, danced by beautiful, scantily clad young men and young women, their costumes diaphanous. Exploding mountains that spewed lava, earthquakes and other cataclysms resulting in collapsing palaces were more commonplace. In Lucius Afranius' *House on Fire* a dwelling was totally burned on the stage, an incident said to have been watched with intense fascination by the Emperor Nero.

The stages had trapdoors, through which supernatural apparitions could emanate. At the huge Colosseum a crane lifted and transported the heavy wild animals that were to be baited and slaughtered, as many as 5,000 on a single occasion. But men and women perished there, too, in the gladiatorial combats between war captives, slaves and condemned criminals; or Christians were victimized and tortured. Human combatants might be dressed in animal skins. Chariots raced in swirls of dust, at peril to their drivers.

Sea battles were a favourite kind of spectacle. In artificial lakes, specially constructed in watertight amphitheatres, two fleets of triremes and quadriremes met head on. As many as fifty vessels engaged in such mock encounters, or *Naumachiai*, on "seas" as much as 2,000 feet long, 1,800 feet wide, with up to 1,900 sword-wielding participants. Though the actors were instructed to spare one another, the "plays" often got out of hand and were bloody; afterwards the bodies of the more luckless were dragged off to lairs occupied by ferocious beasts that were destined for fatal confrontation with unfortunate prisoners. This was often dangerous theatrical fare. So real were the enactments at these "Roman holidays" that barriers separated onlookers from the arena to spare them the risk of injury and death, when what had been mimic became cruelly actual.

Though Romans preferred comedy to tragedy, neither Plautus nor Terence enjoyed much popularity in post-Augustan years. They were honoured, but their works were infrequently produced, nor did new comic writers of note appear to replace them. For a time, farces based on Greek models gave way to more original offerings on Roman subjects, but this material was soon exhausted. Because of the purity and elevation of his style, Terence's plays continued to be read – very often pupils were required to study them. But the true apotheosis of both Plautus and Terence was to occur after many centuries in the late Middle Ages and early Renaissance, often far from Italy. As Lionel Casson puts it, "Ancient comedy did not so much die as get elbowed off the stage. The villains of the piece were the mime and pantomime." In a new epoch, Plautus and Terence were rediscovered with delight and recognized as exemplars without peer from whom writers in subsequent generations borrowed characters and plots, much as they themselves had pilfered subject-matter from the Greeks. They were also to teach the Elizabethans and others a great deal about the craft of fashioning a comedy.

Tragedy never truly prospered on the Roman stage. After a promising beginning, its attraction steadily declined. As has been detailed, Livius Andronicus introduced the genre with his translations from the Greek. Out of respect to him, the Senate permitted Roman poets to incorporate; they were allowed to hold gatherings for literary discussions in the Temple of Minerva on the Aventine. Gnaeus Naevius, though driven from the capital and dying in exile because his opinions were controversial, had the high regard of Plautus and Terence, who mention him frequently in their writings, as did later poets, which suggests that he was viewed as a figure of considerable accomplishment.

Even more fulsomely praised was Ennius, though no belated plaudits equalled those that were self-bestowed; he had proclaimed that the soul of Homer, which had temporarily resided in Pythagoras, and afterwards in a strutting peacock, inhabited his body, which accounted for his rare poetic skill. His plays were admired, none the less, for showing a marked Euripidean influence, reflecting much of Euripides' impiety and radicalism, and he was responsible for changing the style of Latin verse on the stage.

Among the successors of these three were Pacuvius and Accius, who pleased the patricians, but failed to win lasting audiences. In their works, the distinction between *fabula crepidatae* – in which the actors wore Greek garb – and *fabula praetextae* – in which they appeared in the Roman toga, the purple-edged mantle of magistrates – still persisted; it was a way of signalling the locale of the drama and its subject. But the plays of all these men are lost, after having been only sporadically revived; it would seem that they were not prized enough to have extra care and effort taken to preserve them. With the passage of time, those who went to watch the performance of a tragedy were more likely to choose one that was not an adaptation but a Greek original – by Aeschylus, Sophocles, Euripides – for these were already deemed to be "classics".

The one Roman writer of tragedy whose work has come down, and who exerted a powerful sway over the drama's future shape, is Lucius Annaeus Seneca (4 BC–AD 65). Born in Córdoba, Spain, he was a small boy when brought to Rome. His father, a Roman citizen, was enthusiastic about rhetoric, and obviously transmitted some of his passion for it to his son, a talented pupil who absorbed all the education available in the capital. Reaching young manhood, he practised law, gaining attention for his oratorical skills. He also excelled in amatory exploits, even winning the favour of women in the imperial family. This nearly led to his untimely end; in AD 41 he narrowly escaped from a death sentence passed on him by the Senate when a spiteful royal lady accused him of adultery with a rival. He was exiled to Corsica, where at least he could indulge in his other major interest, philosophy, a discipline in which he had early distinguished himself: from Attalus he had learned about Stoicism, from Sotion about Pythagoreanism, and from an uncle-by-marriage, the Roman governor of Egypt, the art of politics; and after inheriting his father's sizeable fortune he could spare more time to write on metaphysical subjects.

It is also possible that during this spell of banishment he vented his bitterness in the pessimistic dramas that were his great literary achievement. This is not certain: some scholars date all of them later. He had a melancholy side, by his own account having once youthfully contemplated suicide, staying his hand only because he did not wish to inflict the burdens of shock and sorrow on his father. He suffered from asthma and weak lungs, which may also have affected his moods, darkening his outlook.

He was summoned back to Rome in AD 49 by Agrippina, the new empress, who chose him to tutor Nero, her son. In AD 54, at seventeen, Nero succeeded his stepfather Claudius as emperor, perhaps with the assistance of Agrippina, who is thought to have hastened her consort's death by feeding him poisoned mushrooms; he was her third husband, she his fifth wife. With the youthful Nero enthroned, Agrippina attained the apex for which she had long fought. Seneca was promoted to be virtually co-regent with the prefect Burrus. For five years these two gave the Roman Empire superior government, with Seneca also contriving to grow immensely rich, partly by money-lending at usurious rates.

The psychotically vicious Nero reached his majority in AD 59; he shortly marked it by the murder of his ruthless mother. Seneca had to help the new emperor justify this matricidal deed. But he gradually fell in imperial esteem. In AD 65 Seneca was charged with taking part in a conspiracy and told by the ruler to commit suicide, as he promptly did with Stoic dignity, drinking hemlock and reclining in his bath. Slitting his wrists he slowly bled to death. His wife sought to emulate him, contrary to his wish; she was prevented from doing so by Nero's physician, who applied a tourniquet above her cuts. Seneca's marriage to this noble lady, Pompeia Paulina, had been remarkably long and constant, unlike others in the wanton world in which they lived. Shortly after this dire event, Seneca's two brothers were ordered to kill themselves and hopelessly obeyed the command. Presumably the goal of the conspiracy was to supplant Nero.

During his years of highest prosperity Seneca was popularly faulted for his extraordinary ostentation. But he contributed a good part of his fortune to help rebuild Rome after the devastating conflagration attributed to the mad Nero. His personal habits were ascetic, and he fasted strenuously, to the point of emaciation. A good reason for this was that he too feared poisoning by his antagonists. He tried to withdraw from court intrigue, to dwell quietly and safely at his country villa, but was never fully able to do so. He had too many political enemies.

He is best known for his gloomy, even apocalyptic philosophical essays, supposedly written for the edification of his royal student: *On Anger*, *On the Brevity of Life* and the like. But though they are still read, while his plays are very rarely revived, his work in play-form has influenced a legion of later major dramatists, especially the Elizabethan and Jacobean masters, not least among them Shakespeare, and the French Baroque writers, a roster culminating with Racine. Of his ten tragedies, nine are on subjects implanted in his imagination by a close reading of Euripides: *Medea*, *Agamemnon*, *Oedipus*, *Phaedra*, *Thyestes*, *Hercules Mad*, *Hercules on Oeta*, *The Phoenicians* and *The Trojans*. The exception, *Octavia*, is a *fabula praetexta*, a history of Nero's first wife and her death; a touch of special interest is that Seneca himself is a leading figure in it. But the script's authenticity has been questioned; many think it is not from his hand.

Seneca's handling of Euripidean themes is very different from that of his model. Poetry is replaced by a passionate rhetoric that has high moments, but too often descends to bombast that today is often tedious to read. The action is far more violent, excessively so; the characters have grossly inflated emotions, which in turn prompt the exaggeratedly stressed speech. Overall, his plays lack taste and "classical restraint". But he lived and wrote during one of the most crazedly violent eras in history, under the aegis of a depraved empress and her insane son, with the author's seemingly lofty existence hedged about every day by terror, ugly decadence, his life always in jeopardy. It was hardly a background that would fit him for the composition of any kind of serene art.

His perspective was quite unlike that of his Athenian predecessors: he was a statesman, an essayist and primarily concerned with philosophical ideas; hence his plays tend to be overwhelmingly verbal, the ceaseless flow of words impeding the narrative's forward thrust. So marked is this fault, it is usually suggested that he never intended to have his plays staged; he hoped only to have them read, discreetly passed about from hand to hand, or else recited at select private gatherings, as the fastidious Terence had also preferred.

His characters are primarily concerned with the political aspects of their dilemmas; there is an emphasis on dynastic struggles, as one might expect from a writer who was an active governor of men. The dramas might be construed as warnings to Nero and his mother to avoid the extremes they practised.

The overriding philosophical tone of the plays is Stoic, though Seneca also claimed to be a disciple of Epicurus. Their gloomy view of life and the world, their preoccupation with suffering and death, with gory detail, makes them repellent to many today. His characters learn that their ill-fortune is compounded when their passions overcome their reason. Passion and ignorance are man's besetting sins. Reason is the spark of the divine in him. But the forces of evil predominate in the Senecan vision of the world, and here – for the first time – the absolute villain, that essential and haunting figure of melodrama, makes an appearance. Living uneasily at the degenerate court of Agrippina and the deranged Nero, Seneca believed with good cause that some men are totally wicked, menacing servants of darkness. He is quite without Aeschylus' faith in an ultimate Heavenly Justice, and he does not portray the nearly even balance of good and bad traits found in the more human characters of Sophocles and Euripides, men mostly good but each with a tragic flaw, as Aristotle put it. Here, instead, is inhuman baseness unalloyed.

Of his plays, *Medea* and *Phaedra* are considered to be the best. In both, a compulsive need for vengeance is given full voice in florid declamation by hurt, desperate, offended women. Seneca had suffered at the hands of a jealous woman who felt herself rejected by him; her charges against him had brought about his eight-year exile in Corsica, so it must have been easy for him to write such speeches with great feeling. Medea's dread resolve to punish Jason and his second bride is immediately announced, heightening a suspenseful revulsion with which the spectator awaits its fulfilment. The outraged princess vows: "If Grecian or barbarian cities know crime that this hand knows not, that crime be done!" Seneca might have been thinking, too, of Agrippina and some other rapacious women at Nero's court; however, everywhere is verbal excess, and what might be a work of fury and fiery intensity is drowned in a tidal wave of words:

> Not the swift rivers, nor the storm-tossed sea,
> Nor wind-blown ocean, nor the force of flame
> By storm-wind fanned, can imitate my wrath.
> I will o'erthrow and bring to naught the world! . . .
> I will attack
> The very gods and shake the universe!
> [Translation: Ella Isabel Harris]

And so on. Her rant is endless. Such hyperbolic rhetoric soon palls. Medea loses humanity and becomes a mere monster, her own hands already stained by past crimes against her father and brother. Jason, however, comes off better. He has a sound excuse for his dereliction; he must marry Creon's daughter to save his own life and that of his sons. It must be granted, too, that some lines shine with searing imagery. Invoking the help of the gods, as she prepares the fatal robe for Creusa, Medea pleads:

Now, Hecate, add
The sting to poison, keep the seeds of flame
Hid in my gift; let them deceive the sight
Nor burn the touch; but let them penetrate
Her very heart and veins, melt all her limbs,
Consume her bones in smoke. Her burning hair
Shall glow more brightly than the nuptial torch.

It is hard to believe that a gentle philosopher composed phrases as sadistic as these. At the end, she slays both her little children, one before the appalled Jason's very eyes, thus going far beyond the hideous scene conceived by Euripides. In vain the father begs that the remaining son be spared. "Let one suffice for vengeance." She replies:

Had it been
That one could satisfy my hands with blood,
I had slain none. Although I should slay two,
The number is too small for my revenge.

She draws out the agonizing moment: "It is my day; haste not, let me enjoy." As she departs exultantly in her chariot, she casts down the bodies of her dead children to the arms of the stricken man. Was there ever a mother such as this?

In *Phaedra* the drama no longer centres on the priggish, virtuous Hippolytus (hence the change of title from Euripides' version), but on the ill-starred Cretan princess. Unhappy, left behind and alone by the journeying king, Phaedra's grief is fed and grows, heated within her "as the vapor glows in Etna's depths". In her forced chastity she lusts for her handsome stepson, of an age scarcely less than her own. She blames her desire on her tainted heritage.

No daughter of unfaithful Minos' house
Is free from love – love ever joined with crime.
[Translation: Ella Isabel Harris]

The nurse tells her this is only an evasion of her own responsibility for her feelings. Here, then, Phaedra's motivation differs from that given her in Euripides' play, where the blame is put on heartless Aphrodite. Phaedra herself is fully accountable for her illicit love. The nurse does not abet her mistress, but seeks to hinder her adulterous passion, until she is moved to intervene, seeking to soften Hippolytus' harsh rejection, lest the humiliated Phaedra kill herself. He, fearful of women, is not persuaded.

Phaedra's lust is inflamed further because she beholds in the son his father as a young man again:

The face that Theseus in his boyhood bore,
When first his cheeks were darkened by a beard. . . .
How glorious he was then!

She confesses to the youth that, for her,

In thee
Shines forth his manly beauty unadorned
But greater . . .

When she throws herself at his mercy, avowing her love, he is amazed and angry at her "baseness". This scene parallels the one that Euripides was forced to excise from his first version of the legend. Whether Seneca had access to that earlier script, or whether he composed this episode entirely on his own, is not known. Hippolytus, aghast, almost slays Phaedra with his sword, but then drops it, turns, and rushes away.

Theseus returns from his involuntary sojourn in the Underworld. At the nurse's prompting, Phaedra hastens to fend off possible charges by her stepson. She asserts, while holding up the sword, that he has sought to ravish her, otherwise threatening her life. This is another change from the Euripidean play where, before her husband's homecoming, the guilty Phaedra hangs herself but leaves a note accusing Hippolytus of attempting a rape. The enraged Theseus calls down a curse upon his son, demanding his death at the hands of Neptune, who as payment for past favours has pledged help to the king.

The chorus invokes Heaven for pity but expects only deafness. It demands to know how these things happen:

> Since by thy power alone the balance weight
> Of the vast universe revolves, why, then
> No longer careful of the race of men,
> Careless to punish evil or reward
> The good, doest thou desert Hippolytus?
> Fortune by ways unordered rules man's life;
> The worse she cherishes, and blindly flings
> Her gifts, and base desire conquers law,
> And fraud is king within the palace walls.
> The populace rejoice to give the base
> High office and to hate the very man
> Whom they should honor. Rigid virtue finds
> The recompense of evil, poverty
> Follows the pure in heart, and strong in crime
> The adulterer reigns.

This bitter chant is doubtless Seneca speaking for himself.

A messenger brings word of the dreadful fate that has overtaken the righteous prince: a monster, rising from the ocean's depth and frightening the horses to overturn Hippolytus' chariot, has caused the rider's mutilation, pictured most horribly. His once indescribably handsome body has been torn asunder. At the news, Phaedra grasps the same sword to impale herself. She confesses her lie, but dies still unrepentant of her incestuous love. Theseus is left to mourn his son and berate himself for his hasty deed of vengeance, and to heap infamy on his self-slain wife. He too pleads for death, and prays it may be a painful one, well deserved. He tries to reassemble for burial the scattered parts of the youth's body, but it is impossible. For Phaedra he has absolutely no forgiveness.

In *Thyestes*, which is about the woes of Atreus' brother, the reader is almost literally asked "to sup on horrors", for in one scene the messenger relates in minute detail how this drunken, singing kinsman, a guest in the Mycenae palace, unwittingly eats the stewed limbs and spitted and roasted members of his slaughtered children. A Fury, in an early speech, has proclaimed, "Blood mixed with wine shall in thy sight be drunk." In this dark work, not only are the sufferings of Thyestes and his mad brother Atreus spelled out, but also – in the prologue – the eternal torments of their dead father Tantalus. Boasts Atreus: "Death is a longed-for favor in my realm."

This preoccupation with pain and gory deeds might indicate that Seneca had a neurotic fixation on such experiences, but nothing else in his biography bears out that assumption: he is portrayed as quietly meditative. Or it might be a reflection of what he knew his listeners or readers most enjoyed. (Of all subjects, the *Thyestes* theme was said to have been the most attractive to Roman authors and chosen by them for their tragic dramas.) Yet it is more logical to suppose that, while an official at the most depraved imperial court in human history, watching an almost measureless empire ruled by an irresponsible poltroon, he wrote all too precisely about the great world of powerful men as he personally saw and shared in it. Atreus declares:

> Integrity,
> Truth, loyalty, are private virtues; kings
> Do as they will.

And, again:

> Here is the greatest good of royal power:
> The populace not only must endure
> Their master's deeds, but praise them.

Was he not holding up a frightful mirror in the hope that at least a few other influential dignitaries might gaze at it and share his treasonable moral judgement? It is significant that in this play he also offers a prescription for true kingship: it is self-knowledge.

> Death seemeth hard to him
> Who dies but too well known to all the world –
> Yet knowing not himself.

And it lies in having modest desires:

He has a kingdom who can be content
Without a kingdom.

As for young princes:

If they learned
The way of treachery and crime from none,
Possession of the throne would teach it them.

In *Phaedra* he had held out a contrasting picture, a tribute to nature and the redemptive life of those who dwell close to it, as does Hippolytus, the eager, devout huntsman, far from a corrupt career in city and court:

The proud man drinks from golden cup, the cause
Of anxious care; how sweet it is to drink
From hollowed hand the water of the spring!

Seneca's *Oedipus* is very different from Sophocles' exemplary tragedy, and is considered to be quite inferior. In lengthy opening speeches, the curse that has gripped Thebes is described for pages by Oedipus, Jocasta and the chorus, in obsessive detail that again betrays what seems to have been the author's perverse interest in the pain, sickness and death imposed by the gods on man and animals, the herdsmen's stricken flocks. Even the once green fields around Thebes have dried and grown barren, the stark forests despoiled of leaves and branches. By comparison, Albert Camus' *The Plague* is a pallid account of pestilence. Particularly bloody is a sacrifice performed by Tiresias; and when the ghost of Oedipus' slain father, Laius, appears, it too is gory.

In the twentieth century, this barbaric script commended itself to the director Peter Brook, an English disciple of Antonin Artaud, proponent of the Theatre of Cruelty. The determinedly adventurous Brook staged it in London, where it provoked a scandal. It might also have been chosen for production by Paris's Grand Guignol, the French capital's long-time stage devoted to bloodcurdling thrillers intended to excite and shock by showing every sort of act of torture and physical mutilation, sometimes carried to such excess as to elicit gasps and nervous laughter. Grand Guignol is to comprise yet another dramatic genre, with its special audience hoping to be frightened, avid for *frissons.*

In Seneca's version the sharp dispute between Oedipus and the blind Tiresias, a high point of the Greek original, is omitted, but the quarrel between the angry king and his brother-in-law Creon is retained and ends with Creon's arrest as a traitor for having named Oedipus as the seed of the pestilence. Throughout the work, a comparatively short one, the irony and urgency that Sophocles gives the story are lacking. The piling up of horrors becomes overly grotesque and the final effect – as critics have declared – operatic.

Much of Seneca's script, also, is taken up with necromantic rites. In sum, the extraordinary length of the speeches, with their many mythological and historical allusions and digressions, lends credence to the argument that Seneca meant them to be read in private, not spoken aloud. They can be looked upon as "closet dramas", the first example of works in that bloodless category of plays known to theatre historians.

It is paradoxical, however, that owing to the violence exploited in them, these unstaged works are to inspire in later generations the "revenge tragedy", the most active form of serious drama ever conceived. Especially is this true of *Thyestes*, which became a model eagerly accepted by the leading Renaissance poet–playwrights, notably in England, extolled and adopted there by such towering figures as Kyd, Marlowe, Ford, Middleton, Shakespeare, Beaumont and Fletcher, Webster, as well as by men of impressive talent elsewhere; it did have a very marked appeal to the Elizabethans and Jacobeans. Is that because theirs was a period of extraordinary peril and cruelty on every side? Theirs was also an age when poetic – even florid – diction and intellectual pretensions were in vogue, and a familiarity with classical imagery was deemed a sign of high cultivation. So Roman literary formulas were to be embraced.

Beyond question, Seneca's heavily allusive choric passages, the endless recital of mythological lore, cause him to seem pedantic. They are so digressive that they rob many scenes of inherent power: interest is aroused by the plot, then dissipated by the static chants. Nor is Seneca a true poet; he is a master of strong prose. By now the chorus had almost disappeared from Greek drama. Seneca restored its role, providing ever longer odes, often extraneous to the action; they fulfil no purpose other than as a display of rhetorical virtuosity, exposing his pleasure in studding his lines with erudite references, his considerable knowledge of Greek legends. His is a prime exhibition of pan-Hellenism, all too typical among Roman intellectuals then. If, as may be supposed, his readers or listeners enjoyed such shows of rhetoric, didacticism and sermonizing, philosophizing and decorative pedantry, his indulgence in them is justified. He should be judged by the taste of his time, not of a later day.

An important innovation is Seneca's division of his plays into five acts, marked by four choral songs. The first act is given to exposition, though Seneca assumes substantial previous knowledge on the reader's part. The characters also tell, in emotionally charged outbursts, what their fate is to be; they are inexplicably prescient of their future. This reduces the suspense to an interest in how well the story will be told, with what motives the characters will be endowed, in what eloquent phrases they will express themselves. The outcome and what leads to it are almost wholly known in advance. In the second act, a friend or companion tries to persuade the protagonist to hold back from a contemplated deed, but the plea for restraint is futile: the passion-swayed Medea or Phaedra, the evil Atreus, cannot be deterred; thus the depth and strength of his or her misguided impulse is exposed. In the third and fourth acts, the rash crime is committed and appraised by others.

In the fifth, the bloody consequence is shown, and almost starkly the story ends. Something like this five-act structure was foreshadowed though not as clearly and firmly demarcated, in the slightly earlier comedies of Terence, as well as in the Athenian tragedies; and it sets a form that will be copied in the Renaissance and Baroque Age and become the fixed one for serious drama until almost the end of the nineteenth century.

With their many deficiencies as effective theatre, Seneca's plays are not without virtues. Certainly they contain strong passages, for at his best Seneca exhibits language that stirs the hearer, as in *Hercules Mad*, and the lengthy recitations are often offset by brief, sharp exchanges between the characters, bouts of give-and-take with stinging impact, a forensic or debating style that probably descends from the Greek *stichomythia*.

Apparently denied to the stage during Seneca's lifetime, and long after, one of his tragedies, *Phaedra* (retitled *Hippolytus*) was finally enacted in the Forum at Rome (1486) under the guidance of the eminent humanist and teacher of rhetoric Pomponius Laetus (Giulio Pomponia Leto), the same year that a Plautine farce, *Menaechmi*, was resurrected at the court of the Duke of Ferrara, and Vitruvius' encyclopaedic treatise on classic theatre architecture was published. The production of the *Hippolytus*, somewhat adapted, was commissioned and subsidized by the Spanish cardinal Riario; Pomponius Laetus himself directed it and had a role in it. The Phaedra was a youth, a pupil at Pomponius' Academy, Tommaso Inghirami, later a papal favourite. The offering made such a strong impression that Pope Innocence VII requested a repetition of it at his Castello Sant'Angelo, and it was done again in the Palazzo Riario. One reason Seneca was so influential in the Renaissance is that his works were known and accessible in Northern Europe long before those of Aeschylus, Sophocles or Euripides.

Could Seneca's plays survive twentieth-century and perhaps later stagings? T.S. Eliot urged that they be broadcast by radio, simply as readings, and predicted success for them in the purely aural medium. Unexpectedly, as was mentioned above, the *Oedipus* was indeed put on by the National Theatre in London (1968) and created a sensation, but this was largely because of the unusual fashion in which Peter Brook elected to present it, utilizing avant-garde devices, such as outlandish humming and clashing electronic music, together with a banal jazz score; Oriental ritual borrowed from Japanese Noh drama; the actors in modern dress, their costumes sometimes made only of paper; all this combined with unprecedentedly bold symbolism, the cast parading and dancing around a huge golden phallus while singing *God Save the Queen* with the audience invited to join them. Brook was assuredly correct in thinking that Artaud's theories lent themselves all too well to Seneca's flaring melodrama. The leading roles on this occasion were taken by the renowned John Gielgud as Oedipus, and the equally acclaimed Irene Worth as Jocasta, who at the end dies not by hanging but by thrusting a sword into her womb. Whether any of the notoriety instantly reaped by this production was owing to some intrinsic merit of the script was a question that divided the critics and the public as well. The language of the play, in describing Oedipus' blinding, is said to have turned many queasy stomachs. Laurence Olivier, at that time artistic director of the National Theatre, was embarrassed by the project yet hesitated to reject it, fearing that Brook would complain of being handicapped by English prudery and unofficial censorship. According to Donald Spoto's biography of him, Olivier considered the offering to be "adolescent indulgence . . . not merely in bad taste but anti-theatrical", and subsequently his status as head of the National suffered for his having permitted this *Oedipus*, helping to shorten his tenure in that post. Despite the director's shock tactics and the wide publicity, the play had only a modest run.

Martin Esslin, the English theatre historian and critic, provided the *New York Times* with this account.

> A Peter Brook production is an experience. It must therefore be recorded and described. As the members of the audience enter the theater, they are startled by a strange, haunting noise that fills the air, half hum, half chant. They then discover that, standing motionless and leaning against the pillars that support the dress circle and galleries, there are statuesque figures, like caryatids, men and women, members of the chorus, all dressed alike in dark brown slacks and sweaters. It is this chorus that emits the strange humming and wailing sounds. On the stage are other members of the chorus, grouped around a vast golden cube that revolves slowly in the center ("looks like the gold reserve at Fort Knox" said a voice next to me in the stalls). The back and sides of the stage are paneled in sheets of gold-colored

metal. Gradually, the hum increases; then the chorus on the stage and in the auditorium begins a rhythmic drumming, African, primitive, ritualistic. The play has started.

Sir John Gielgud, Oedipus, delivers his opening speech. And again and again the action is interrupted by strange hisses and shouts, groans and wails from the chorus, and weird electronic music from backstage.

The protagonists (Gielgud, Worth . . . Colin Blakeley as Creon, Frank Wylie as Tiresias) are dressed almost as simply as the members of the chorus. They emerge from the chorus and do not wholly impersonate their characters. For example, while Ronald Pickup, as the messenger, describes the horrifying scene of how Oedipus ripped out his own eyes in a frenzy of self-punishment, Gielgud sits onstage quietly, his face averted. Yet at other times the protagonists act with the utmost intensity, as when Creon tells the grisly tale of how the murdered King Laius, Oedipus's father, was summoned from the underworld and accused his son. As Creon nears the climax of his report, he becomes possessed and begins to turn round and round like a whirling dervish, only at the end to collapse in total exhaustion.

The great golden cube can be opened to serve as the interior of a chamber, or, when all four side panels are lowered, as an open platform. And, as the haunting cries of the chorus resound throughout the theater, from the highest galleries down to the stalls, the audience is literally surrounded, *trapped* in the net of archetypal tragedy.

The acting is magnificent: Gielgud, regal, mild and mellifluous as long as he feels free of guilt, turns at the end into a pitiful wreck of a man. Irene Worth displays a strength which seems new even in this always powerful actress, and Colin Blakeley's rough voice and squat figure provide a splendid contrast to Gielgud's elegance.

As Esslin sees it, Jocasta's self-destruction by thrusting the weapon into her womb is appropriate, since that is the source of the tragedy, whence her son Oedipus emerged.

In Brook's terrifyingly real and yet symbolical staging of the scene, she crouches onto a sword which sticks out from the ground.

There could hardly be a more nerve-wracking ending to a play. But Brook, not content with this degree of blinding frankness, has another – and to my mind mistaken – image up his sleeve. After Oedipus has groped his way off-stage, and Jocasta's body has been taken from the sword on which it was impaled, and the stage is empty, a strange object, covered by a gold and velvet cloth, is carried on to the accompaniment of obsessive drumming. It is placed in the middle of the stage, the men who brought it leave and, as the last one departs, he pulls the cover away . . . [Here is revealed the enormous gilded phallus] soaring up like the column of a Greek temple. The drumming becomes more and more intense until it is deafening, and the houselights go on. And the audience begins to titter and to laugh.

Admittedly, such a giggling, embarrassed reaction might be the one which Brook intended; but even so, I doubt whether this final shock effect is rightly judged – not because it is in bad taste, but because the symbol is misapplied. After all, the impulse that drove Oedipus to his doom was, strictly speaking, anything but phallic. He did not marry his mother because he wanted to commit incest, or because he was lustful, but simply because he had been offered the throne of Thebes and the hand of the Queen. The Oedipus complex – that is, the audience's unconscious desires as they identify with Oedipus and think of their own mothers – might be described as phallic, but not the story of Oedipus himself.

The problem of this final symbol highlights, also, the main problem of this kind of theater: Brook has undertaken to revitalize ritual, to make the theater the source of emotional experiences that can no longer be provided by a church which has become respectable and no more than a mild social occasion. But the efficacy of ritual depends on the vitality of the beliefs from which it emerges. It is the desperate search for *contents that are still alive*, which still have the power to stir an audience, that drives directors of genius like Brook or Grotowski into the world of sexual symbols – and even in plays where these symbols are not strictly applicable. What one would have needed at the end of *Oedipus* would have been the mask or statue of one of the gods – Apollo, or Zeus, or Dionysus – who presided over the hero's tragic fate. But they would not have had any impact on a contemporary audience. So Brook chose Priapus, a minor deity who had nothing to do with the case, just because *his* image is the only one that still has an immediate meaning to us. True enough, but it is the wrong meaning, and produces, as the audience reaction at the first night showed, the wrong reaction. The men in the audience look at their lady companions to see if they will blush, and the ladies, to show that they are not disconcerted, giggle. That is not the emotion ritual should evoke.

Nevertheless, apart from this final phallic fallacy, Brook's production is a triumph. In directing a classical tragedy, true to its spirit, without distortion, he has succeeded in making use of the techniques of Artaud, Brecht and the Happening, and has fused all these elements into a coherent artistic whole, a creation of tremendous and unforgettable impact.

Clive Barnes, the English-born drama critic of the *New York Times*, visited London for a survey of its current stages and made a point of taking in the much-publicized *Oedipus*:

It was natural, I think, that an age that could adopt so firmly Antonin Artaud's phrase, "the theater of cruelty," should find itself more attuned to the Roman tragedies of Seneca than to the Greek tragedies of Sophocles.

. . . Seneca was a Roman and Stoic. His view of tragedy was a man caught up in a predestined web of chance, and it was a view that had considerable influence on Elizabethan and Jacobean drama. His version of *Oedipus* is less concise, even less vigorously dramatic than that of Sophocles, but undoubtedly its emphasis upon blood and upon human suffering gives it a modern ring. Here is the squalid pain of tragedy, rather than nobility – tragedy must be borne, because it is man's lot. But the messy details are never glossed over.

Mr Brook, it seems, feels our modern lives lack a sense, an appreciation, of ritual and that the theater should move toward meeting this deficiency. As a result, this *Oedipus* is seen solely in terms of ritual: it is like a masque followed by an anti-masque, or a minuet contrasted with a jig.

The chorus members are spread around the theater – some on stage, others strategically placed in the auditorium. At times they speak, but more often their comments are sibilant hisses and rhythmic gasps.

Mr Brook's scenery, designed by himself, consists of a huge cube, the sides of which can be let down to provide a raised platform for the principal actors. The chorus and most of the actors and actresses are dressed in brown turtleneck sweaters and brown pants. Oedipus and Jocasta wear black.

The ritualistic staging is extraordinarily effective in providing the right emotional counterpoint of stoicism to Seneca's flamboyant, bloodstained and yet grimly effective poetry.

In the translation by David Anthony Turner, adapted by Ted Hughes, little is left to the imagination. The description of Oedipus tearing out his own eyes might prove too graphic for the comfort of the squeamish, and Oedipus's measured progress to the hell of absolute truth is made to suggest almost the ritual cruelty of the bullring.

At the end, with Jocasta self-impaled on Oedipus's sword and the blind king himself setting out to banishment, Mr Brook unexpectedly embarks on a wild anti-masque. The chorus puts on gaudy gold paper costumes and dances up and down the theater aisles and around an enormous golden phallic symbol on the stage (why the phallic symbol? Is Mr Brook trying to shock or is he, less convincingly, suggesting that sex was the root cause of Oedipus's fate?) to the accompaniment of a jazz band marching and playing *Yes, We Have No Bananas*!

The result is electrifying. The artificiality of the theater is flashed home with lightning speed and the audience, shattered by the gory saga, is forced to see its function in what Mr Brook insists is a

> ritualistic event of cleansing. To say that this is a thrilling evening in the theater is to miss its purpose, because much more it is one of those rare evenings that force you to reassess what the theater is all about.
>
> The acting, stylized and superbly disciplined, is worthy of the concept. John Gielgud's Oedipus, agonized and baffled, is perfect, as are Irene Worth's deep-voiced, dark-toned Jocasta and the impassioned Messenger of Ronald Pickup.

In Rome, dramatic criticism was ably practised. Julius Caesar, the military genius, and Cicero, the stirring orator and capable man of letters, expressed their views on Plautus and Terence, as has been noted. But far more important were the commentaries of the poet Horace (Quintus Horatius Flaccus, 65–8 BC), who emulated Aristotle in a verse essay, *Epistle to the Pisos* – that is, a letter to the Piso family – now better known as *The Art of Poetry*. It offers epigrammatic advice, of a practical sort, to other writers. Though many of his insights are borrowed from Aristotle, Horace restates very well the ancient Greek critic's shrewd precepts, some of which had undergone a good deal of modification after a lapse of centuries.

Horace draws a clear distinction between tragedy and comedy; he insists that the two genres are wholly separate and ought always to be so. Firmly embraced, too, is Aristotle's dictum that in a stage-work action, not words, should embody the story and characterize the participants, who are to be judged by what they do, not what they say or what is said about them. The virtues of brevity and clarity in constructing the plot are to be recognized, and this applies as well to the dialogue, which should be plain. For the best effect, fancy writing – "purple patches" – should be avoided. The playwright has to revise his work ceaselessly, rearranging the story to give it a more logical order. Opening *in medias res*, he should get to the point of it immediately.

He should not aim beyond his powers, but choose a subject within the compass of his talent. He must first feel what he describes. But form is as important as feelings. His characters, too, should try to control their strong and often overpowering emotions. A study of the Greek dramas shows that their authors eschew the portrayal of horrible events in full view of the audience; that is the classic way of treating such anguishing acts.

The poet–playwright should not listen to the praise of friends, but hearken only to qualified critics. After a script is completed, it is best to set it aside for at least eight years, then reinspect it to determine if it still commends itself to him. Only then should he make ready to offer it to public gaze.

Most influential was Horace's emphasis on religiously observing the three unities of time, place and action. A play should have a single plot or principal incident, occur in one setting, within a brief compass of time – Aristotle had somewhat tentatively suggested a mere twenty-four hours; that results in the most compact and successful handling of the narrative. This rule, prompted by Aristotle's passing comment but stressed by Horace, is to be overly honoured during the seventeenth and eighteenth centuries, the Neoclassical Age in Western Europe, and fasten upon Baroque drama a straitjacket of form that almost squeezed the life and breath from it.

The decline of Roman drama continued, but the mimes and pantomimes more than held their own. Many languages resounded in the empire, and the silent performances were communicable to all, which assured them widening popularity, a literal universality. They were increasingly more lavish and more indecent. Fortunes were expended on their settings and costumes. Since these ballets competed with and were preferred to plays, they were a factor in the rapid extinction of the spoken drama.

Though the mimes had little status under the law, some were held in high personal regard by the imperial family and the nobility. Paris the Younger became the favourite and lover of the wife of the Emperor Domitian, which cost him his life. Meeting him in the street, after learning of the liaison, the Emperor grabbed hold of him and stabbed him to death. His father, the senior Paris, had earlier gained considerable influence at Domitian's court where, taking offence at some verses by the satirist Juvenal that libelled dancers, irately intervened and had the hapless poet exiled to Egypt.

Seneca, whose attitude towards the vulgar theater of his day was usually one of contempt, on a special occasion had some unruly spectators flogged for interrupting a performance by the mime Mnester, though he also dismissed with scorn all the young aristocrats of Rome who were infatuated with the pantomimes. Often the mimes entertained in the villas of the wealthy, sharing the debauchery there. Even more prominently now, women played feminine roles in the sketches, contributing to the further debasement of this form of theater, the actresses too frequently being wantons whose company could be purchased for an evening off-stage. But in equal measure the pantomimes reflected the corruption and decadence of the regimes. Heliogabalus, reportedly, had sexual acts performed openly by his acting troupe.

It was while attending a theatrical performance of this sort that the mad, tyrannous Emperor Caligula was assassinated, and it is said that the whole audience, taking flight, narrowly escaped slaughter by his guards.

Bold mimes sometimes attempted political satire, too, though it was highly risky. Caligula decreed an actor be buried alive in the amphitheater for having dared too far in a would-be sly allusion. When Emperor Vespasian died, the mimes staged a mock funeral. In a reference to Vespasian's notorious penury they had his "corpse" suddenly sit up and inquire how much his ostentatious funeral cost. "Ten million sesterces," he was told. "Give me one hundred thousand and throw my body into the Tiber," cried the "dead" Vespasian, to the delight of the hooting mob.

Nero took part in public performances, revelling in the applause he evoked from the amused spectators, whose true emotions it would be hard to gauge. Jealous of the growing popularity of Paris the Elder, he summarily had that talented interpreter beheaded.

Many renowned poets wrote scenarios for the pantomimists and enriched themselves. They also provided the verses sung by the background chorus. In the opinion of commentators of the day, such libretti were of little merit. The mimes still offered mostly acrobatics, juggling, snake-charming, bell ringing and the same raucous sketches and improvisations that had always comprised their programmes. But they kept alive the stock figures who were to outlast even the Dark Ages and reappear long afterwards.

Some mimes, like the unlucky Paris the Elder, were lastingly famed. The Emperor Augustus, offended, banished the actor Pylades from Rome; the edict caused such an outcry that it was quickly rescinded. Pylades was a Greek, born in Cilicia in Asia Minor, whose *métier* was tragic pantomime, roles in which he was "sublime, moving, and a man of many parts". His greatest portrayal was that of Agamemnon. He was able to convince his sponsors of the need for substantial musical accompaniment, the addition and use of many instruments. Founding an academy, he oversaw the training of young dancers and mimes. He was also the author of a treatise on the underlying theories of his specialized art, a text unfortunately lost.

Bathyllus, a contemporary of Pylades, was equally popular and had as his patron the fabulously rich Maecenas, to whose house he had come as a slave. A Greek youth, born in Alexander, he entranced Roman matrons who adored him for his feminine grace and sensitivity, and most effusively when in a solo he enacted the myth of *Leda with the Swan.* The director and leading player of a troupe was called an *archimimus.*

Quintilian (*c.* AD 40–118) wrote of the best mimes of his day, during the reign of Domitian, that they could convey every emotion by gesture alone. "They can speak, entreat, promise, call, dismiss, threaten, and implore; they express revulsion, fear, question, refusal, joy, grief, hesitation, confession, remorse, moderation and excess, number and time. Are they not capable of exciting, calming, beseeching, approving, admiring, showing shame? Do they not, like adverbs and pronouns, serve to designate places and persons?"

With the Byzantine era, in both halves of the now split empire, water ballets and aquatic games had a growing vogue; for these, performed in well-caulked pools, many Greek theatres had to be redesigned, allowing mimes and nereids to disport themselves while re-enacting cherished mythological tales and allegories. The poet and acrid epigrammatist Martial (*c.* AD 40–101), a friend of Seneca and Lucan, describes such a ballet in which a lovesick Leander desperately sought to swim across a simulated Hellespont to reclaim a lost, languishing Hero, only to perish, the visual effect almost too realistic.

The obscenity that ran riot in the offerings of the mimes and pantomimes soon won them the deep opprobrium of the Christians, now a steadily rising movement, at first deemed subversive. In turn, the players did not hesitate to deride the fanatical, self-sacrificing adherents of the new religion, burlesquing what was known of the baptism ceremony, mocking the Crucifixion, travesties not forgotten by the Faithful after their eventful triumph. In AD 275, in Asia Minor, the esteemed mime Porphyrius accepted the persuasive, radical creed, as did his fellow artist Ardalio a year later. Then, in AD 303, in Rome during the reign of Diocletian, when persecution of the followers of the messianic Jesus was at its fiercest, the player Genesius joined his cult and became a martyr on its behalf; he was later to be named the patron saint of actors.

Constantine, ruling the Eastern Empire, decreed that all foreigners engaged in the arts were to be banished, but mimes were exempted, and their number then was no less than six thousand. His Empress, Theodora, had herself once been a mime: she was a stepdaughter of Emperor Maximian.

Of all enemies of the theatre, none was more scathingly outspoken than the "Latin Father of the Church", Tertullian (AD 160?–230?), who inveighed against it and foresaw the retribution that lay ahead for it. "Other spectacles will come that last eternal Day of Judgment . . . when all this old world and its generations shall be consumed in one fire. How vast the spectacle will be on that day! How I shall marvel, laugh, rejoice, and exult, seeing so many kings – supposedly received into heaven – groaning in the depths of darkness! – and the magistrates who persecuted the name of Jesus melting in fiercer flames than they ever kindled . . . against the Christians! – sages and philosophers blushing before their disciples as they blaze together! . . . and tragic actors now more than ever vocal in their own tragedy, and players lither of limb by far in the fire, and charioteers burning red on the wheel of flame."

Readying for battle against a rival contender to the throne, Maxentius, at Saxa Rubra (AD 312), on the afternoon before the fray, Constantine claimed to behold a flaming cross in the sky, and the Greek words "*en toutoi nika*" – "in this sign conquer" – and had Christ's initials inscribed on his standard. Encouraged to advance against his foe, he prevailed over Maxentius, who together with thousands of his loyal troops died in the Tiber. Constantine, convinced that from now on he should cast his lot with the Christians, issued an edict assuring them of toleration and finally asserted that he embraced their teachings. Historians are not sure whether the conversion was sincere or merely politic – the Emperor was not much interested in theological matters, but having the Christians on his side, gaining the support of the ever more influential bishops, was much to his advantage. All religions were now permitted, but during the rest of Constantine's reign Christianity steadily become dominant, the official faith.

With this change of climate, all forms of drama were gradually proscribed. In the fifth century AD stage activity was curtailed; no good Christian could attend a performance, let alone take part in one. In the sixth, the theatres were closed for ever. Most crumbled or were razed, their rich marbles carried off for building materials; others were transformed into medieval fortresses, castles, even shoddy slum tenements. The great amphitheatres also fell into ruins, many of them despoiled during the barbarian invasions that overthrew the Roman Empire. For the next fifteen centuries the Church denied actors the right to receive the sacraments, nor could they be buried in consecrated ground. During the Dark Ages that ensued, extending five hundred years, actors were mere wandering, hardy groups of mountebanks or earnest, fugitive players, in good part social outcasts.

GENERAL INDEX

Notes: Titles of plays and other works which receive frequent mention or detailed analysis have independent main headings; works receiving only passing reference appear as subheadings under the author's name. Detailed analysis is indicated by **bold** type.

INDEX OF PRODUCING COMPANIES/VENUES

INDEX OF CITED AUTHORS

Notes: Books are indexed under the author's name, followed by the title where this is mentioned in the text. Reviews are indexed by the title of the periodical, followed by the reviewer's name where given. This index lists only modern authors; classical commentators such as Aristotle are to be found in the General Index.